KU-166-341

Rhett Butler's People

Also by Donald McCaig

Canaan

Jacob's Ladder: A Story of Virginia During the War

An American Homeplace

Nop's Trial

Nop's Hope

Eminent Dogs, Dangerous Men

The Butte Polka

Rhett Butler's People

Donald McCaig

MACMILLAN

First published 2007 by St Martin's Press, New York

First published in Great Britain 2007 by Macmillan
an imprint of Pan Macmillan Ltd
Pan Macmillan, 20 New Wharf Road, London N1 9RR
Basingstoke and Oxford
Associated companies throughout the world
www.panmacmillan.com

ISBN 978-0-230-70395-7

5 7 9 8 6 4

A CIP catalogue record for this book is available from the British Library.

Printed and bound in Great Britain by
Mackays of Chatham plc, Chatham, Kent

This is a work of fiction and is the product of the author's imagination. Any relationship with real events, places or people is entirely coincidental.

Endpaper pen and ink drawing of Charleston Harbor by William Hill, ca. 1851, is courtesy of the collections of the South Carolina Historical Society.

For Paul H. Anderson

Faithful Fiduciary

Above all, love each other deeply,
Because love covers over a multitude of sins.

—1 Peter 4:8

Part One

Antebellum

Chapter One

Affairs of Honor

One hour before sunrise, twelve years before the war, a closed carriage hurried through the Carolina Low Country. The Ashley River road was pitch-black except for the coach's sidelights, and fog swirled through the open windows, moistening the passengers' cheeks and the backs of their hands.

"Rhett Butler, damn your cross-grained soul." John Haynes sagged in his seat.

"As you like, John." Butler popped the overhead hatch to ask, "Are we near? I wouldn't wish to keep the gentlemen waiting."

"We comin' down the main trunk now, Master Rhett." Although Hercules was Rhett's father's racehorse trainer and Broughton's highest-ranking servant, he'd insisted on driving the young men.

Rhett had warned, "When he learns you've helped, Langston will be angry."

Hercules had stiffened. "Master Rhett, I knowed you when you was just a child. Was me, Hercules, put you up on your first horse. You and Mr. Haynes tie your horses behind. I'll be drivin' the rig tonight."

John Haynes's plump cheeks belied his uncommonly determined chin. His mouth was set in an unhappy line.

Rhett said, "I love these marshes. Hell, I never wanted to be a rice planter. Langston would go on about rice varieties or negro management and I'd not hear a word for dreaming about the river." Eyes sparkling, he leaned toward his friend, "I'd drift through the fog, steering with an oar.

One morning, I surprised a loggerhead sliding down an otter slide—sliding for the pure joy of it. John, have you ever seen a loggerhead turtle smile?

"I don't know how many times I tried to slip past a sleeping anhinga without waking her. But that snaky head would pop from beneath her wing, sharp-eyed, not groggy in the least, and quick as that"—Rhett snapped his fingers—"she'd dive. Marsh hens weren't near as wary. Many's a time I'd drift 'round a bend and hundreds of 'em would explode into flight. Can you imagine flying through fog like this?"

"You have too much imagination," Rhett's friend said.

"And I've often wondered, John, why you are so cautious. For what great purpose are you reserving yourself?"

When John Haynes rubbed his spectacles with a damp handkerchief, he smeared them. "On some other day, I'd be flattered by your concern."

"Oh hell, John, I'm sorry. Fast nerves. Is our powder dry?"

Haynes touched the glossy mahogany box cradled in his lap. "I stoppered it myself."

"Hear the whippoorwill?"

The rapid pounding of the horse's hooves, the squeak of harness leather, Hercules crying, "Pick 'em up, you rascals, pick 'em up," the three-note song of the whippoorwill. Whippoorwill—hadn't John heard something about Shad Watling and a whippoorwill?

"I've had a good life," Rhett Butler said.

Since John Haynes believed his friend's life had been a desperate shambles, he bit his tongue.

"Some good times, some good friends, my beloved little sister, Rosemary . . ."

"What of Rosemary, Rhett? Without you, what will become of her?"

"You must not ask me that!" Rhett turned to the blank black window. "For God's sake. If you were in my place, what would you do?"

The words in sturdy John Haynes's mind were, I would not be in your place, but he couldn't utter them, although they were as true as words have ever been.

Rhett's thick black hair was swept back off his forehead; his frock coat was lined with red silk jacquard, and the hat on the seat beside him was beaver fur. John's friend was as vital as any man John had ever known, as alive as wild creatures can be. Shot dead, Rhett Butler would be as emptied out as a swamp-lion pelt hung up on the fence of the Charleston market.

Rhett said, "I am disgraced already. Whatever happens, I can't be worse disgraced." His sudden grin flashed. "Won't this give the biddies something to gossip about?"

"You've managed that a time or two."

"I have. By God, I've given respectable folk a satisfying tut-tut. Who has served Charleston's finger pointers better than I? Why, John, I have become the Bogeyman." He intoned solemnly, " 'Child, if you persist in your wicked ways, you'll end up just like Rhett Butler!' "

"I wish you'd stop joking," John said quietly.

"John, John, John . . ."

"May I speak candidly?"

Rhett raised a dark eyebrow. "I can't prevent you."

"You needn't go through with this. Have Hercules turn 'round—we'll enjoy a morning ride into town and a good breakfast. Shad Watling is no gentleman and you needn't fight him. Watling couldn't find one Charleston gentleman to second him. He pressed some hapless Yankee tourist into service."

"Belle Watling's brother has a right to satisfaction."

"Rhett, for God's sake, Shad's your father's overseer's son. His employee!" John Haynes waved dismissively. "Offer some monetary compensation. . . ." He paused, dismayed. "Surely you're not doing this . . . this *thing* . . . for the girl?"

"Belle Watling is a better woman than many who condemn her. Forgive me, John, but you mustn't impugn my motives. Honor must be satisfied: Shad Watling told lies about me and I have called him out."

John had so much to say, he could hardly talk. "Rhett, if it hadn't been for West Point . . ."

"My expulsion, you mean? That's merely my latest, most flamboyant disgrace." Rhett clamped his friend's arm. "Must I enumerate my disgraces? More disgraces and failures than . . ." He shook his head wearily. "I am sick of disgraces. John, should I have asked another to second me?"

"Damn it!" John Haynes cried. "Damn it to hell!"

John Haynes and Rhett Butler had become acquainted at Cathecarte Puryear's Charleston school. By the time Rhett left for West Point, John Haynes was established in his father's shipping business. After Rhett's expulsion and return, Haynes saw his old friend occasionally on the streets of town. Sometimes Rhett was sober, more often not. It troubled John to see a man with Rhett's natural grace reeking and slovenly.

John Haynes was one of those young Southerners from good families who take up the traces of civic virtue as if born to them. John was a St. Michaels vestryman and the St. Cecilia Society's youngest ball manager. Though John envied Rhett's spirit, he never accompanied Rhett and his friends—"Colonel Ravanel's Sports"—on their nightly routs through Charleston's brothels, gambling hells, and saloons.

Consequently, John had been astonished when Butler came to the wharfside offices of Haynes & Son seeking John's assistance in an affair of honor.

"But Rhett, your friends? Andrew Ravanel? Henry Kershaw? Edgar Puryear?"

"Ah, but John, you'll be sober."

Few men or women could resist Rhett Butler's what-the-hell grin, and John Haynes didn't.

Perhaps John *was* dull. He never heard about amusing scandals until Charleston society was tiring of them. When John repeated a clever man's witticism, he invariably misspoke. If Charleston's mothers thought John Haynes a "good catch," maidens giggled about him behind their fans. But John Haynes had twice seconded affairs of honor. When duty came knocking, it found John Haynes at home.

Broughton Plantation's main trunk was a broad earthen dike separating its rice fields from the Ashley River. The carriage lurched when it quit the trunk to turn inland.

John Haynes had never felt so helpless. This thing—this ugly, deadly *thing*—would go forward whatever he might do. Honor must be satisfied. It wasn't Hercules driving the team; it was Honor's bony hands on the lines. It wasn't .40-caliber Happoldt pistols in the mahogany box; it was Honor—ready to spit reproaches. A tune sang in John's head: "I could not love thee Cecilia, loved I not honor more"—what a stupid, stupid song! Shad Watling was the best shot in the Low Country.

They turned into a brushy lane so infrequently traveled that Spanish moss whisked the carriage roof. Sometimes, Hercules lifted low-hanging branches so the rig could pass beneath.

With a start, John Haynes recalled the story of Shad Watling and a whippoorwill.

"Ah," Rhett mused. "Can you smell it? Marsh perfume: cattails, myrtle, sea aster, marsh gas, mud. When I was a boy, I'd get in my skiff and disappear for days, living like a red indian." Rhett's smile faded with his reverie. "Let me beg one last favor. You know Tunis Bonneau?"

"The free colored seaman?"

"If you see him, ask him if he remembers the day we sailed to Beaufort. Ask him to pray for my soul."

"A free colored?"

"We were boys on the river together."

Indeterminate gray light was filtering into the carriage. Rhett looked out. "Ah, we have arrived."

John consulted his pocket hunter. "Sunrise in twenty minutes."

The field of honor was a three-acre pasture edged with gloomy cypresses and moss-bedecked live oaks. The pasture vanished in the fog, inside which a voice was crying hoarsely, "Sooey! Soo cow! Soo cow!"

Rhett stepped down from the carriage, chafing his hands. "So. This is my destination. When I was a boy dreaming of glories awaiting me, I never dreamed of this."

Cattle bawled inside the fog. "We wouldn't want to shoot a cow." Rhett stretched. "My father would be furious if we shot one of his cows."

"Rhett . . ."

Rhett Butler laid a hand on John Haynes's shoulder. "I need you this morning, John, and I trust you to arrange matters properly. Please spare me your sound, kindly meant advice."

John swallowed his advice, wishing he hadn't remembered about Shad Watling and the whippoorwill: After Langston Butler built Broughton's grand manor house, his overseer, Isaiah Watling, moved his family into the original Butler home, which was convenient to the rice fields and negro quarters. Huge live oaks, which had been saplings when the Butlers first arrived in the Low Country, shaded the small, plain farmhouse.

Nesting in a live oak, that whippoorwill welcomed them from twilight until dawn.

Apparently, Belle, the Watling girl, thought the bird was seeking a mate. Her mother, Sarah, said the bird was grieving.

The question of whether the bird was flirting or weeping was mooted at daybreak, not long after they moved in, when a shot blasted through the house. When his mother rushed into his bedroom, Shad Watling's smoking pistol lay on the windowsill. "Fool bird won't rise me up no more," Shad Watling grunted.

In poor light at sixty paces, Shad Watling had shot the tiny whippoorwill's head off its body.

John Haynes asked Rhett, "You've heard about that whippoorwill?"

"Just a yarn, John." Rhett scratched a match on his boot sole.

"Shad Watling has killed before, Rhett."

The match sputtered and flared as Rhett lit his cigar. "But only negroes and men of his class."

"Do you believe your gentle birth will turn a bullet?"

"Why, yes," Rhett said solemnly. "Hell yes! Gentle birth's got to be good for something!"

"Comes somebody," Hercules spoke from his elevated seat.

Breathing hard, a young man emerged from the fog. His frock coat was folded over his arm and his trouser knees were wet where he'd stumbled. "Darn cows," he confided. He shifted his jacket and offered his hand to John Haynes, then thought better of it and made an awkward bow instead. "Tom Jaffery. Amity, Massachusetts. At your service, gentlemen."

"Well, Tom." Rhett smiled. "It seems your Charleston visit will be a memorable one."

Jaffery was two or three years younger than Rhett and John. "They'll never believe this in Amity."

"Lurid tales, Tom. Lurid tales are the South's principal export. When you describe us to your friends, remark the devilishly handsome, gallant Rhett Butler." Rhett's brow furrowed thoughtfully. "If I were telling the tale, I wouldn't mention the cows."

"Has your principal arrived?" John asked the young Yankee.

Tom Jaffery gestured at the fog bank. "Watling and that Dr. Ward, too. They don't care for each other."

John Haynes took the younger man's arm, walking him out of Rhett's earshot. "Mr. Jaffery, have you seconded these affairs before?"

"No, sir. We don't hardly do this kind of thing in Amity. I mean, my grandfather might have done it, but nowadays we don't. I'm a novice, so to speak. My aunt Patience passed to her Heavenly Reward and she bequeathed me a sum, so I set out to see the country. Tom, I says to myself, if not now, for goodness' sake, when? So there I was, admiring your Charleston harbor, which is, if I might say so, every bit the equal of our famous Boston harbor. Anyway, there I was when Mr. Watling approached me and asked was I a gentleman, and I said I certainly hoped so. When Mr. Watling asked if I would second him, I thought, Tom, you've come to see the country, and see the country you shall. I'll never get a chance like this in Amity."

John Haynes didn't tell the younger man that Shad Watling's choosing a Yankee stranger to second him was a calculated insult.

"Are you familiar with your duties?"

"We seconds make sure everything happens regular."

John Haynes eyed the young Yankee thoughtfully. "Seeking reconciliation between the principals is our primary duty," he said with the regret of the man who has failed that duty.

"Oh, my principal isn't contemplatin' reconciliation. My principal says he anticipates shootin' Mr. Butler in the heart. He and Mr. Butler are old acquaintances."

"It will be light soon. We generally let sunrise be our signal."

"Sunrise suits you, suits us."

"When the sun comes over the horizon, the gentlemen choose their pistols. As the challenged party, your man chooses first. Shall we load now?"

John Haynes braced the mahogany box on the carriage fender, unlatched it, and removed a pistol. The sleek knurled butt felt alive in his hand, as if he'd clutched a water moccasin. "As you see, the pistols are identical. While you observe, I'll charge one pistol. You will charge the second."

John poured powder, set a round lead ball into an oiled cloth patch, and rammed it home. He placed a cap under the hammer and eased the hammer to half cock.

"They'll never believe this back home," Thomas Jaffery said.

The morning gathered light, the fog tore into streamers, and two ghostly vehicles swam into sight across the meadow: a one-horse chaise and a mule-drawn farm wagon.

Rhett Butler untied his horse from behind the carriage and pressed his face against the beast's powerful neck. "You're not frightened, are you, Tecumseh? Don't be. Nothing's going to hurt you."

"This meadow, John—they grew indigo here in my grandfather's day. There's a pond in the woods where pintails hatch their young. Muskrats are fond of young pintails, and sometimes a brood will be paddling along, until one is pulled under—so swiftly, they don't make a flurry. Our trunk master, Will, trapped muskrats here."

"Rhett, we seconds will speak with Watling. What apology will you accept?"

Rhett squeezed his eyes shut obstinately. "Shad Watling claims I am father of his sister's child. I have said Watling is a liar. If Watling admits his lie, I will withdraw my challenge."

"Will you offer compensation? Money so the girl can go somewhere to have her baby?"

"If Belle needs money, I will give her money. Money has nothing to do with this."

"As your friend, Rhett . . ."

"John, John . . ." Rhett muffled his face in Tecumseh's neck. "A friend would help me finish this thing."

Shadrach Watling's farm wagon was heaped with broken wheels, hubs, and rims. "Morning, Mr. Jaffery, Mr. Haynes. I see you brung Butler."

"Shad . . ."

"It'll be 'Mr. Watling' today."

"Mr. Watling, I trust we can reach an accommodation."

"B'lieve Butler 'commodated my sister. B'lieve I'll 'commodate him."

"When Rhett Butler treated you as a gentlemen, he complimented you."

Shad spat. "I'm thinkin' of westering. Goddamn, I'm sick of the Low Country. Rich bastards and niggers. Niggers and rich bastards. I got cousins in Missouri."

"Wherever you go, you'll want money. If your sister, Belle, were to go with you, the scandal would die."

Watling chuckled. "Butler offering me money?"

"No, sir. I am."

"All comes down to money, don't it?" Watling spat again.

Shadrach Watling was a beardless, thickset man. "Naw, not this time. I got a grudge against Butler. Even though Pa whipped Belle good, she never would say 'twas Rhett topped her. Ain't no nevermind. I'm craving to put a bullet in Butler. He weren't no 'count as the Young Master and I hear he weren't no 'count as a soldier boy, neither. Butler ain't worth a bootful of warm piss."

Shad Watling eyed the river. "Gonna be light directly. I got four busted wheels for the wheelwright, and he starts his day early. Bein's I'm the challenged man, I'll be namin' the distance. Figure fifty paces'll be far enough for me to hit and him to miss. I wouldn't want be nicked by no stray ball." His stubby, stained teeth glistened in silent laughter.

Swaddled in thick woolen robes, the surgeon was snoring in his buggy. When John Haynes tapped his boot toe, Franklin Ward opened his eyes and yawned. "Ah. Our business . . ." He unbundled, stepped down, and faced away; the stink of his urine made John Haynes's nose twitch. The doctor wiped his fingers on his coattails.

Dr. Ward offered his hand to Rhett, "Ah, the patient, I presume!"

Rhett grinned. "You have appliances for extracting the bullet, Doctor? Probes? Bandages?"

"Sir, I studied in Philadelphia."

"Doubtless, Philadelphia is an excellent city to have studied in."

Shad Watling ambled behind, grinning absently and scratching his thigh.

"Mr. Butler," Tom Jaffery asked, "why are you removing your shirt?"

"Hold it for me, John? I take off my shirt, my Yankee friend, so the bullet won't push cloth into the wound."

"Maybe you jest like goin' naked." Shad Watling eyed the slighter man disdainfully. "Me, I generally don't take off more clothes'n I got to."

"Gentlemen," John Haynes interrupted, "this is a terrible, deadly business and I must ask again if honor wouldn't be served by Mr. Watling's retraction, an apology and recompense from Mr. Butler."

Gooseflesh pimpled Rhett's arms in the chilly air.

"Fifty paces," Shad said, "oughta serve. Butler, you remember your nigger pal, Will? How Will cried for mercy? If'n you cry for mercy, maybe I'll let you off." Watling showed his teeth again. "Let me see them pistols. Yank, did you watch Mr. Haynes load? Didn't double-charge one of them pistols, did he? Might have had one charge already in the barrel 'fore he poured the second charge atop?"

The Yankee was shocked, "Mr. Haynes is a gentleman!"

"He score his bullet? Little ring cut into the bullet so it gobs when it hits. Inspected his bullet, did you, Yank?"

Young Jaffery repeated, "Mr. Haynes is a gentleman."

"Sure as hell. Sure as hell. Gentleman don't score no bullet, no sir. Gentlemen won't double-charge no pistol. Now, which of these here pistols did Mr. Haynes load?"

"I loaded the near pistol," John said.

A horn sounded in the woods, a long exuberant note, like fox hunters sighting their quarry. Seconds later, moisture streaming off its wheels, an open landau clattered onto the field. Two young sports stood between its seats, one with a coach horn at his lips, which he dropped to grab a seat back, else the stop would have pitched him headlong. "Hallooo! Hallooo! Have we missed the fun?"

Their elderly driver cackled. "Told you I'd get us here in time," he said. "Didn't Colonel Jack find these scamps?"

Colonel Ravanel had been a respectable rice planter until his wife, Frances, was killed. Whether Jack's subsequent dissipation was from grief or the absence of marital inhibitions was not known. In Charleston, where gentlemanly drunkenness was only forbidden clergy, Colonel Jack Ravanel was a drunk. In a city where every gentleman gambled, Jack was banned from respectable gambling clubs. Jack was a genius with horseflesh, and horse-mad Charleston forgave him much for that.

John Haynes stepped to the landau. "Gentlemen, this is an affair of honor. Decorum . . ."

The young men wore short brocade jackets, bright ascots, and pants so tight, a codpiece was unnecessary. Although Jack Ravanel was old enough to be the young men's father, he was similarly garbed.

"Country wench gets one in the oven and that's an affair of honor?" The horn blower sounded a blast. "Whooooa, Johnny Haynes. It's one of Rhett's damn jokes, that's what it is."

John Haynes bristled. "Henry Kershaw, this is an affront. You are unwelcome here."

Big Henry Kershaw was reeling. "You mean Cousin Rhett is going through with this? Damn me, Edgar, I'll settle tomorrow. Rhett, that you? Ain't you cold? We been drivin' through this damn swamp for hours. Colonel Jack says he used to own this ground, but he must have been sober at the time. Edgar Puryear, don't you hog that whiskey!"

Tom Jaffery asked, "Mr. Haynes. Is this regular?"

"You the Yankee we heard about?" Henry Kershaw asked.

"Yes, sir. From Amity, Massachusetts."

"Man can't help where he's born. Say, you ain't one of them damned abolitionists, are you?"

Rhett Butler silenced John Haynes with a touch and asked in the quietest voice, "Edgar, Henry, Jack—have you come to see me die?"

Edgar Puryear pasted an apologetic expression on his face. "Jack promised this was a lark, Rhett; a lark! He said you'd never fight a man over . . . over . . ."

"A 'lark,' Jack? If my father discovers your part in this, he'll see you in the workhouse."

"Dear Rhett! Do not speak cruelly to Old Jack!"

"Henry Kershaw is drunk—Henry will do anything when he is drunk. Edgar Allan has come to watch. Edgar is a great watcher. But what dragged the aged reprobate out of his whore's warm bed on a cold morning?"

Jack Ravanel's smile was ingratiating. "Why, Rhett, old Jack's come to help you. I've come to talk sense! We'll all have a friendly drink and recall happier times. Rhett, have I told you how I admire Tecumseh? By God, there's a horse!"

For an instant, Rhett was stunned. Then his mouth twitched into a chuckle, which became a laugh, which became so hearty Rhett bent over laughing. This laughter infected the sports, who wore smiles on their faces, and the young Yankee chuckled.

Rhett wiped his eyes. "No, Jack, you shan't have Tecumseh. John, if I am killed, my horse is yours. Now, Watling. Choose your pistol."

"God Almighty!" Henry Kershaw gaped. "Rhett means to go through with it!"

Colonel Jack's eyes narrowed. He lashed his team off the field.

Deep in the woods, a grouse drummed on a hollow log. The huge sun rose steaming out of the river, restoring yellows, blues, and pale greens to the land from which fog had exiled them.

John Haynes shut his eyes briefly in a wordless prayer. Then he said, "Gentlemen."

Shad Watling had lost something to Rhett's great laughter. Something had got away from him. His prey had tripped the trigger but left the trap empty. Shad snatched a pistol, examining it as if it might be faulty. " 'Young Marster' Butler. Christ, how the niggers fawned over you!"

The other long-barreled pistol hung loose in Rhett's hand; his smile was so big, it traveled down his naked arm to the muzzle, as if the pistol, too, were smiling.

In the river morning, a thick, angry man stood back-to-back with a half-naked, smiling man.

Each would step off twenty-five paces. When the sun cleared the horizon, John Haynes would give the command to turn and fire.

The duelists stepped off twenty-three, twenty-four, twenty-five paces. . . . The sun clung to the horizon.

"They'll never believe this in Amity," Tom Jaffery whispered.

The sun strained upward until a white space opened between its rim and the riverbank. In a clear voice, John Haynes called, "Gentlemen! Turn! Fire!"

Rhett Butler's hair lifted to a wind gust off the river. Butler pivoted, presenting a fencer's profile as his pistol rose.

Shad Watling fired first, an explosion of white smoke at the muzzle when the hammer struck home.

Nine years earlier.

At his father's impatient gesture, Langston Butler's elder son prepared for his caning. He removed his shirt and folded it over a straight-backed chair.

The boy turned and set his palms flat on his father's desk. The fine leather surface gave infinitesimally under his weight. He fixed his eyes on his father's cut-glass inkwell. There can be a world of pain in a cut-glass inkwell. The first searing blow caught him by surprise. The inkwell was half-full of blue-black ink. Rhett wondered if this time his father might not be able to stop. When the boy's sight blurred, the inkwell seemed to float in a mist of tears.

This time, too, his father did stop.

Hands curled in frustration, Langston Butler hurled his cane to the floor and shouted, "By God, boy, if you weren't my son, you'd feel the bullwhip."

At twelve years of age, Rhett was already tall. His skin was darker than his father's and his thick jet black hair hinted at Indian blood.

Although the boy's back was a mosaic of livid stripes, he hadn't begged.

"May I dress, sir?"

"Your brother, Julian, is dutiful. Why must my elder son defy me?"

"I cannot say, sir."

Langston's office was as spare as Broughton's family quarters were opulent. The broad desk, a straight-backed chair, inkwell, blotter, and pens were its entire furnishings. No engravings or paintings hung from the picture rail. Ten-foot-tall undraped windows offered an unimpeded panorama of the plantation's endless rice fields.

The boy took his white chambray shirt from the chair and with a just perceptible wince draped it over his shoulders.

"You refuse to accompany me when the legislature is in session. When prominent men meet at Broughton, you vanish. Wade Hampton himself asked why he never sees my elder son."

The boy was mute.

"You will not drive our negroes. You refuse to learn to drive negroes!"

The boy said nothing.

"Indeed, it is safe to say you reject every proper duty of a Carolina gentleman's son. Sir, you are a renegade." With his handkerchief, Langston wiped sweat from his pale forehead. "Do you think I relish these punishments?"

"I cannot say, sir."

"Your brother, Julian, is dutiful. Julian obeys me. Why won't you obey?"

"I cannot say, sir."

"You cannot say! You will not! Nor will you accompany your family to Charleston. Instead, you swear you'll run away."

"Yes, sir, I will."

The angry father stared into the boy's eyes for a long time. "Then, by God, let the fevers have you!"

Next morning, the Butler family departed for their Charleston town house without their elder son. That night, Dollie, the colored midwife, rubbed salve into the welts on the boy's arm. "Master Langston, he a hard man," she said.

"I hate Charleston," Rhett said.

On the river plantations, the rice seed was clayed and planted in April and trunk gates were opened for the sprout flow. The rice would be flooded three more times before harvest in September. Maintenance and operation of the great and lesser trunk gates were so vital to the crop that Will, Broughton Plantation's trunk master, ranked in the slave hierarchy second only to Hercules.

Although Will obeyed Master Langston and Isaiah Watling, he obeyed no other man, including Shad Watling, the overseer's twenty-year-old son.

Will had a cabin to himself. He owned a table, two chairs, a rope bed, and three cracked Spanish bowls that Louis Valentine Butler had taken from the *Mercato.* A decent year after Will's first wife died, Will jumped the broomstick with Mistletoe, a comely girl of fifteen.

Fearing the deadly fevers, Low Country planters shunned their plantations during the hot months. When Langston came out from the city to inspect his crop, he arrived after daybreak and departed before dark.

Barefoot and shirtless, his son hunted, fished, and explored the tidal marshes along the Ashley River. Young Rhett Butler was educated by alligators, egrets, osprey, rice birds, loggerheads, and wild hogs. The boy knew where the negro conjure man found his herbs and where the catfish nested. Sometimes Rhett stayed away from Broughton for days on end, and if his father visited during one of Rhett's absences, the elder Butler never asked after his son.

Overseer Watling supervised the floodings and hoeings of the tender rice plants. Watling determined when dike-burrowing muskrats must be poisoned and the rice birds shot.

Although they were more resistant to fever than their white masters, rice negroes worked knee-deep in a subtropical swamp, and inevitably some sickened. In Broughton's dispensary, Overseer Watling's wife, Sarah, and young Belle dosed victims with chinchona bark and slippery elm tea. The white woman and her child helped Dollie deliver babies and salved the backs of the men and women their husband and father had whipped.

Some negroes said Master Langston was less likely to pick up the bullwhip than Boss Watling. "Master Langston ain't gonna get no work out of a man laid up in the dispensary."

Others preferred Isaiah Watling. "Boss Watling, he hard all right. But he don't lay no whip on you less'n he got to."

Young Master Rhett pestered his father's servants with practical questions: Why were the trunk gates made of cypress? Why wasn't the rice hoed after the harvest flow? Why was the seed rice winnowed by hand? The negroes ate the fish and game Rhett brought and the white boy spent Sundays, the negroes' day of rest, in the quarters. Rhett accompanied Will on trunk inspections, and often at noontime the two shared a meal on the riverbank.

When he felt the urge, Shadrach Watling visited the quarters after dark. Usually, Watling sent the girl's family away: "Might be you could take a meander down by the woods." Sometimes Shad gave the husband or father a demijohn of popskull to while away the hour.

But Mistletoe, the trunk master's new wife, didn't want to fool with the overseer's son, and when Shad Watling wouldn't leave his cabin, Will tossed him into the street, a circumstance that delighted the other negroes.

When Langston Butler heard what Will had done, he explained to Overseer Watling that negroes must not laugh at the Overseer's son, lest they laugh at the Overseer next and ultimately at the Master himself.

Three hundred negroes lived on Broughton with a handful of whites, some of them women. What prevented those negroes from rising up and murdering those whites? Langston Butler told Isaiah Watling that revolt could not be suppressed after negroes have begun muttering and sharpening their hoes, their rice knives. Rebellion is quelled by crushing the first defiant glance, the insolent whisper, the first disrespectful snicker.

"Will's a good nigger," Watling said.

"Your boy will do the punishing."

"Shadrach?" Watling's eyes were anthracite. "Have you been satisfied with my work?"

"It has been satisfactory."

Watling bowed his head and muttered, "I got to tell you, Master Langston. Will had just cause. My Shadrach . . . Shadrach ain't no account."

"But he's white," Master Langston replied.

The sky was unseasonably clear that August morning; the air was dead and heavy.

Broughton Plantation's rice mill was brick; its winnowing house was whitewashed clapboard. The dairy, negro houses, and infirmary were tabby—cement of crushed oyster shells and lime. Tall and windowless, with its thick iron-banded door, Broughton's meat house was as forbidding as a medieval keep. Every Sunday morning, standing before this vault of plentitude, Overseer Watling distributed the week's rations to the servants shuffling past. "Thank you, Boss Watling." "We sure does thank you, Boss."

Isaiah Watling was the giver of all good things, as well as the source of all punishment.

Broughton's whipping post was a blunt black cypress stub five feet six inches high and eighteen inches in diameter. An iron ring was placed where a man's wrists might be fastened.

Will had asked the young Master to intercede, and Rhett confronted the overseer. "Watling, I am giving you an order!"

Isaiah Watling studied the boy as if he were something curious washed in on the tide. "Young Butler, when you defied Master Butler to stay, I asked him who was Master when he was off in town. Master Butler said I was to follow his orders, that you weren't to give no orders. Now, young Butler, the niggers is here to see justice done and to learn respect. Will's insolence bought him two hundred."

"It'll kill Will. Damn it, Watling, it's murder."

Isaiah Watling cocked his head as if listening for something faint and far away. "The nigger's your father's property. Very few of us, young Butler, get to be our own men."

His son Shad's bullwhip coiled lazily before he popped a trumpet-vine blossom off the well house. The negroes stood silently, men to the fore, women and children behind. Tiny children clung to their mothers' shifts.

When Isaiah Watling led Will out of the meat house, the trunk master blinked in the brightness. When the overseer tied Will's wrists, Will didn't resist.

Rhett Butler had not yet come into his adult courage and could not watch his friend be killed. When Watling bared Will's back, Mistletoe fainted and Rhett bolted for the river, deaf to the whip crack and Will's grunts, which became screams.

Rhett jumped into his skiff, loosed the mooring line, and let the river take him away. A rainsquall descended and he got soaked through. His boat went where the current willed. Rain drummed in the boy's ears and he blinked rain from his eyelids.

Rhett Butler swore that when he was a man, he would never be helpless again.

Rain fell on the boy. Rain fell harder. Rhett couldn't see the bow of his boat. Water lapped at its thwarts.

His sail exploded into tatters. He lost an oar. When a drifting cypress trunk threatened to roll the skiff, he broke his other oar fending it off. He inspected the stub as if, had he the wit, he might yet row with it. He bailed until his arms ached. When he shouted to ease the pressure in his ears, the wind snatched his shout away.

The river broached the trunks and flooded rice fields, and sometimes Rhett's skiff was in the channel and sometimes scudding above what had been acres of Carolina's finest golden rice.

Suddenly, as if he'd been washed into a different universe, the wind and rain stopped. In the calm, Rhett's skiff drifted gently through brightness at the tip of a whirling funnel that rose up, up into a heaven, which was so dark blue, Rhett imagined he saw stars. He had heard about the hurricano's eye. He never thought he'd see one.

The current bumped the waterlogged skiff against a jumbled shoreline of uprooted, broken trees. Rhett tied his skiff to a branch before clambering inland toward the sound of hammering.

As a young man, Thomas Bonneau had been freed by the master who had fathered him. Thomas Bonneau's white father deeded his son five acres of land on a low rise beside the river, where Thomas built a modest tabby house, whose thick, homely walls had resisted previous hurricanoes. Bonneau and a boy about Rhett's age were on the roof, nailing shingles.

"Look, Papa, yon's a white boy," the boy, Tunis, said.

The two slid to the ground and Thomas greeted the half-drowned

Rhett. "Come with us now, Young Master. These walls has sustained us thus far. God grant they sustain us a mite longer."

Inside his one-room house, Thomas Bonneau's wife, Pearl, and two younger children were piling trunks, fish traps, a chopping block, and chicken coops onto a rickety mound to clamber onto the ceiling joists.

"It ain't hurricano's rain nor wind kills you," Bonneau explained as he took his joist. "Ol' hurricano raises up a mighty tide what drowns you."

Tunis passed the youngest children to his father, who set them next to him under his strong arm. When they all were astride a joist, Bonneau spoke in a singsong: "And God said to Noah, 'The peoples is corrupt and so I will raise a mighty flood. But you and your family gonna swim above the flood. . . . ' " Whatever more he said was snatched away by the wind.

When it came, the storm surge crashed against the little tabby house and forced the door. Water foamed beneath Rhett's dangling feet and the joist he straddled vibrated between his thighs. Thomas Bonneau leaned his head back and shut his eyes and the cords of his neck were taut with praising God.

That was the worst of it.

As all storms must, this storm ended, the waters receded, and as ever after such storms, the sun illuminated a brilliant new world.

Thomas Bonneau said, "If I ain't mistook, that's a macaw in yon tree." A bedraggled blue-and-yellow bird clung weakly to a leafless branch. "Lord knows where he been blowed from."

They dragged the muddy trunks and broken fish traps outside and Pearl Bonneau stretched a line to dry their clothes. Pearl wore her wet petticoat while her dress dried; the others went naked.

Tunis and Rhett collected storm-beached fish while Thomas Bonneau started a fire with the dry inner bark of a cedar tree.

When they were seated around the fire, turning fish on sticks, Thomas Bonneau offered thanks to God for sparing his family and the Young Master.

"I'm not the Young Master," the white boy said. "I'm Rhett."

Ten days later, when Rhett returned to Broughton, Will had been buried in the slave cemetery and Mistletoe had been sold South. Broughton Plantation was miles of drowned, stinking rice plants.

Langston Butler was personally supervising a gang repairing breaks in the main trunk while Watling's gang restored the interior trunks. Men trundled wheelbarrels of fill; women and children emptied pails and buckets in the breaches.

Rhett's father's boots were filthy and he hadn't shaved in days. His soft hands were cracked and his fingernails were broken. Langston Butler greeted his son, "We accounted you dead. Your mother is grieving."

"My mother has a tender heart, sir."

"Where have you been?"

"The free colored Thomas Bonneau saved me from the hurricano. I have been helping his family restore their homestead."

"Your duty was with your people."

Rhett said nothing.

His father ran his forearm across his sweaty forehead. "The crop is lost," he said distantly. "A year's work destroyed. Wade Hampton asked me to run for Governor, but now, of course . . ." Langston Butler looked into his son's unforgiving eyes. "Sir, have you learned anything from the trunk master's fate?"

"Yes, sir."

"Humility? Obedience? A proper deference to authority?"

"I have often heard you say, Father, that knowledge is power. I accept that conclusion."

Despite his obligations at Broughton, that same week Langston Butler took his son to Charleston to begin acquiring the education that distinguishes a Low Country gentleman.

Cathecarte Puryear was Charleston's most visible intellectual, and the city took pride in him, as they might in any curiosity—a two-headed calf or a talking duck. In Cathecarte's student years, he'd boarded beside Edgar Poe at the University of Virginia, and, as everyone knows, poetry is contagious.

Cathecarte Puryear's contentious essays in the *Southern Literary Messenger* had twice produced challenges, which he had accepted, but on both occasions, after declaiming his belief that affairs of honor were "designed by the mentally unfit, for the mentally unfit," Cathecarte discharged his pistol into the air. He was never challenged again. There is no honor—and may be dishonor—calling out a man who will not return fire.

Cathecarte was president of the St. Cecilia Society, which sponsored uplifting concerts and Charleston's most popular balls. Most of Charleston's intellectuals were clergymen or, like the Unionist Louis Petigru, lawyers by profession, but thanks to his deceased wife's considerable fortune, Cathecarte Puryear never had to earn his bread. He tutored a few well-bred young gentlemen because, as Cathecarte often explained, "noblesse oblige."

Eleanor Baldwin Puryear (d. 1836) was Cathecarte's sole poetic subject. Philistines said exchanging Eleanor's handsome dowry for literary immortality was a fool's bargain.

A weary, preoccupied Langston Butler assessed his son for the prospective tutor: "My eldest son is intelligent but defiant. The boy disregards my orders and flouts those distinctions of rank and race that undergird our society. Though Rhett reads, writes, and does sums, gentlemen would not recognize my son as one of them."

Cathecarte beamed encouragement. "Every young man's mind is a 'tabula rasa,' sir. We may impress upon that blank slate whatever we desire."

Langston smiled wearily. "We shall see, shan't we?"

After Langston left, the tutor said, "Sit down, young man. Do sit down. You prowl like a caged beast."

In rapid succession, Cathecarte asked: "Aristotle taught which famous general, young man? Please decline *amare.* Which British king succeeded Charles the First? Explain the doctrine of separation of powers. Recite Mr. Poe's 'The Raven,' Mr. Keats's 'La Belle Dame sans Merci.' "

After the silence became oppressive, Cathecarte smiled. "Young man, apparently I know many things which you do not. Just what do you know?"

Rhett leaned forward. "I know why trunk gates are made of cypress.

Everybody says the mother alligator eats her own babies, but she doesn't; she totes 'em in her mouth. Conjure men take four different cures from the jimsonweed. Muskrat dens always have one entrance below the water."

Cathecarte Puryear blinked. "You are a natural philosopher?"

The boy dismissed that possibility. "No, sir. I'm a renegade."

After that interview with Cathecarte Puryear, Rhett Butler climbed steep stairs into the heat of an angular room whose window overlooked Charleston harbor.

Dirty clothes were strewn on one unmade bed and highly polished riding boots rested on the pillow of the other.

Rhett unpacked his carpetbag, tossed the boots on the floor, and sat by the window, watching the harbor. So many ships. What a vast place the world was. He wondered if he would ever succeed at anything.

A half hour later, his roommate came clattering up the stairs. He was a slight lad, whose long fingers nervously flicked pale hair off his forehead. He lifted his boots and examined them suspiciously. "You're Butler, I suppose," he said.

"And you are?"

The lad drew himself up. "I am Andrew Ravanel. What do you make of that?"

"I don't make anything of that. Should I?"

"Well, I guess you'd better!"

When Andrew cocked his fists, Rhett hit him in the stomach. The other boy slumped onto his bed, trying to catch his breath. "You shouldn't have done that," he gasped, "You had no right. . . ."

"You were going to hit me."

"Well," Andrew Ravanel's smile was innocent as an angel's. "Well, maybe I would. But maybe I wouldn't have."

In the next few months, Rhett understood how lonely he had been.

Andrew Ravanel was a city boy; Rhett had never lived where gaslights flickered. Rhett looked at the practical side of things; Andrew was a dreamer. Andrew was shocked by Rhett's indifference to rank: "Rhett, you don't thank a servant for serving you; serving you is his reason for being."

Rhett excelled at mathematics and Andrew liked to show his friend off by asking Rhett to add complex figures in his head. Rhett didn't know how he could do it; he just could.

Andrew was an indifferent scholar so Rhett tutored him.

Cathecarte's other pupils were Henry Kershaw, a hulking seventeen-year-old who spent his evenings on the town; Cathecarte's own son, Edgar Allan, who was Henry Kershaw's acolyte; and John Haynes, heir to the Haynes Shipping Company. John's father, Congress Haynes, approved Cathecarte Puryear's pedagogy but not his good sense. Consequently, Congress's son lived at home.

As night cooled the great port city, Rhett and Andrew would perch in their dormer window, discussing duty, honor, and love—those great questions every boy puzzles over.

Rhett didn't understand the bleak moods that sometimes overwhelmed Andrew. Although Andrew was almost recklessly brave, trifles could prostrate him.

"But Cathecarte condescends to everybody," Rhett explained patiently. "That's what he does. You must not pay him any mind."

Rhett could neither reason nor jolly Andrew out of his despair, but since it seemed to help, Rhett sat quietly with Andrew through the darkest hours.

Though Cathecarte Puryear railed against "planter philistines," he never questioned Charleston's tradition that young gentlemen should raise hell until they were safely married. Andrew's father, Colonel Jack Ravanel, acquainted Rhett with spirits and escorted the boy on his fifteenth birthday to Miss Polly's brothel.

When Rhett came downstairs, Old Jack grinned. "Well, young sir. What do you think about love?"

"Love? Is that what it's called?"

After three years studying with Cathecarte Puryear, Rhett could do calculus, read Latin (with a dictionary), knew the names of every English monarch since Alfred, the fancies of Charleston's prettiest whores, and that a straight never, never beats a flush.

In the same year Texas annexation was debated in the United States Senate, Cathecarte Puryear published his notorious letter. Why Cathecarte was impelled to advance his opinions wasn't clear. Some thought he envied poet Henry Timrod's growing fame; others said it was the rejection of Cathecarte's poems by the selfsame *Charleston Mercury* that published his scurrilous letter (bracketed with its editor's disclaimers).

"Nullification," Cathecarte Puryear wrote, "is stupendous folly; and nullification's adherents are reckless fools. Can any sane man believe the Federal government will permit a cabal of Carolina 'gentlemen' to determine which Federal laws they might choose to obey and which they will not? Some of these gentlemen are whispering the dread word 'secession.' I trust that when Mr. Langston Butler and his friends finally commit suicide, they will do so privately, without involving the rest of us in their folly."

Although Rhett's father couldn't challenge Cathecarte Puryear—"the villain has made a mockery of the code of honor"—Langston could and did remove his son from Puryear's influence.

As their carriage rolled down King Street, Langston told Rhett, "Senator Wade Hampton has engaged a tutor for his children. Henceforth, Hampton's tutor will instruct you too." He examined his son skeptically. "I pray you are not already infected by Puryear's treasonous beliefs."

Rhett studied his father's sour, angry face and thought, He wants me to be the man he is. Rhett jumped out of the carriage, darted behind a brewer's dray, and disappeared down the street.

Thomas Bonneau laid down the net he'd been mending. "What you doin' here, young man?"

Rhett's smile was tentative. "I had hoped I might be welcome."

"Well, you ain't. You's trouble."

Glasses dangling from one hand, Tunis came outdoors. He held *The Seaman's Friend* in the other.

Desperately, Rhett pronounced, "That book has ketch rigging wrong."

Tunis rolled his eyes. "Daddy, I b'lieve young Master Butler sayin' he a sailor. You reckon?"

Rhett wore a short blue jacket over a broadcloth shirt. His trousers were so tight, he dared not touch his toes.

The Bonneaus were barefoot and Tunis's dirty canvas trousers were belted with a rope.

Quietly, Rhett said, "I've nowhere else to go."

Tunis examined Rhett for a long time before he laughed, "Eight bushel of oysters that book cost me and Young Master here says it's mistook."

Thomas Bonneau's cheeks filled and expelled a puff of air. "I expect I gonna regret this. Sit yourself down and I'll show you how to mend a net."

The Bonneaus raked oyster banks below Morris Island and fished off Sullivan's Island. Rhett rose with them hours before dawn, worked with them, laughed with them, and one memorable Sunday when Thomas, his wife, and the younger children were at church, Rhett and Tunis sailed Thomas Bonneau's skiff down the coast all the way to Beaufort.

Young Rhett Butler had never imagined he could be so happy.

Every negro on the Ashley River knew about Thomas Bonneau's white "son," but it was thirteen weeks before Langston Butler discovered Rhett's whereabouts and Broughton's launch tied up at the Bonneaus' rickety dock.

Langston Butler towered over Thomas Bonneau, "Many legislators wish to exile Carolina's free coloreds or return them to slavery. That is my view, as well. Should you interfere with my family again, I vow that you, your wife, and your children will toil under Mr. Watling's lash."

On the long pull upstream to Broughton, Langston Butler didn't speak to his son, and when they landed, he turned Rhett over to Isaiah Watling. "He's a rice hand like any other. If he runs or disobeys, introduce him to the bullwhip."

Watling assigned Rhett a cabin in the negro quarters. Its straw pallet danced with fleas.

The stretch flow had been drained two weeks previously and the rice was thriving. His first morning in the fields, the mosquitoes and gnats were so thick, Rhett swallowed mouthfuls. Twenty minutes after sunrise, the overheated air sucked his breath away.

Thigh-deep in mud, he hoed as far as his arms could reach before, extracting one leg at a time, he shifted to a new stance.

A big man on a big horse, Shadrach Watling watched from the levee.

At noon, the work gang paused for beans and cornmeal ladled from a common pot. Since Rhett didn't have a bowl or spoon, he waited until another man finished to borrow his.

It was ninety-five degrees that first afternoon and red and purple flashes played across Rhett's eyes.

By custom, after a worker finished his allotted task, his time was his own. By three o'clock some of the stronger men left the field and by five o'clock only two middle-aged women and Rhett were still working. At 8:30, when Rhett was done, he and Shad Watling remained.

"Best watch for snakes." Shad grinned. "We lost a nigger in this patch last week."

Rhett's delirium of working, eating, and working again was relieved by fitful snatches of sleep. When Rhett did meet a water moccasin, he watched indifferently as the snake slithered past his bare legs.

On his tall, bony mule, Overseer Watling visited each of his gangs. The handle of the bullwhip hanging from his saddle bow was bleached from the sweat of his hand.

Despite the heat, the overseer wore a black frock coat and his shirt was buttoned to his chin. His wide-brimmed straw hat clasped his close-cropped skull.

At dinnertime on Saturday, he beckoned to Rhett.

Watling had big ears, a big nose, long arms, big hands; his face was lined with hard work and bitterness.

Watling laid his pale, empty gaze on Rhett. "When I was bankrupted and come to Broughton, many stretch flows past, you was an ornery child, but I believed there was hope for you. It is writ that by tribulations we shall one day rise. Young Butler"—the overseer started his mule—"our day will come."

By the second week, Rhett worked as well as an old woman, and by the end of the third he could keep up with a negro boy of ten.

In the evenings, Rhett slumped on a chopping block in the dooryard.

Although Broughton's negroes had been told to shun him, they slipped him food from their own meager stores.

By September, young Rhett Butler was a full-task rice hand on Broughton Plantation.

As Carolina's delegates were boarding the schooner for Baltimore and the Democratic party's convention, Senator Wade Hampton took Langston Butler aside to ask about a rumor that Langston's son was working beside negroes in the rice fields.

"My son wants discipline."

Wade Hampton was a physical giant who owned 3,500 slaves. Now, he frowned.

Hampton explained the Democratic party could not afford a scandal.

"Sir, my son must have discipline."

So Senator Wade Hampton arranged Rhett Butler's appointment to West Point.

When Isaiah Watling rode into the quarters that evening, Rhett Butler was sitting cross-legged in the doorway of his cabin, watching rice birds wheel over the river.

Isaiah Watling dismounted. "Master Butler wants you in town," he said. "Boat's waitin' at the landing." After a pause, Watling added, "For a white boy, you was a pretty fair nigger."

In Charleston, Rhett was bathed and barbered. His clothing was altered for his new musculature. Before all his insect bites had healed, Rhett boarded a northbound schooner.

Young Rhett Butler stood at the rail as the schooner cleared Charleston harbor. He should have been excited about his prospects, but he wasn't. His body didn't feel right in gentleman's clothing. Fort Sumter grew smaller and smaller, until it was a dot on the gray ocean.

Chapter Two

Rosemary Penelope Butler

Rhett's sister, Rosemary, was four years old when Rhett left the Low Country, and afterward, when the child tried to remember her brother, no matter where she tried to force her thoughts, an image crept into her mind: the wolf on the front of her fairy-tale book. The wolf was long-snouted and scraggly, but how sly and what big teeth!

Those weeks Rhett was hidden by the Bonneaus, Langston Butler's anger filled every nook and cranny of the Charleston town house. Servants tiptoed, little Rosemary hid in the nursery, and Elizabeth Butler retired to her bedroom with a sick headache. Rosemary thought Rhett must be powerful and very wicked, since her father hated him so.

Rashes erupted on Rosemary's arms and legs. She woke at the least sound and couldn't get back to sleep. If she just didn't think about that scraggly wolf, if she could picture dolls or dancers or pretty dresses, that wolf wasn't lurking in the dark shadows beneath her bedroom window and couldn't be hiding under her bed.

Rosemary's mother, Elizabeth, had been the beloved only daughter of the very wealthy Ezra Ball Kershaw. A dutiful, pious wife, Elizabeth trusted the Bible to answer her questions and provide eventual justice. She prayed for her children and, without mentioning it to him, she prayed for her husband. Now, Elizabeth Butler took uncharacteristically bold action and asked her friend Constance Fisher—nobody in Charleston was more respectable, or richer, than Grandmother Fisher—if Rosemary might visit the Fishers for a time.

Grandmother promptly agreed. "Rosemary and my granddaughter Charlotte will keep each other occupied."

That afternoon, Rosemary's clothes and favorite dolls were packed and loaded in Grandmother Fisher's carriage. Afterward, Rosemary slept more nights in the Fishers' East Bay mansion than in her own home. Her rashes disappeared.

Little Charlotte Fisher was a serene, uncomplaining child who thought the best of everyone. Charlotte believed Rosemary's brother couldn't be that bad. Nobody was *that* bad. Charlotte never complained when her older brother, Jamie, teased her. One afternoon when Rosemary was out of sorts, she snatched Charlotte's favorite doll. Charlotte wouldn't take it back when Rosemary repented. Weeping, Rosemary threw her arms around her friend's neck. "Charlotte, I'm sorry, but when I want something, I want it *now.*"

Three years after Rhett left for West Point, Charlotte's brother, Jamie, burst into the family room.

Charlotte closed her book on her finger and sighed. "Yes, brother . . ."

"*Yes,* yourself." Arms folded, Jamie leaned against a sofa arm so he wouldn't crease his trousers.

"Jamie . . ."

"Rhett Butler's been expelled," Jamie blurted. "He's back in Charleston, though heaven knows why." Jamie raised his eyebrows theatrically. "I mean, nobody—absolutely nobody—will receive him. He's living with Old Jack Ravanel. He and Andrew always were thick as thieves."

Rosemary frowned. "What's 'expelled'?"

"Thrown out of West Point. Exiled. Entirely and totally disgraced!"

Rosemary felt sad. How can a wolf not be a wolf? she wondered.

Hastily, Jamie added, "You mustn't worry, Rosemary. Your brother has lots of friends. Andrew and there's Henry Kershaw, Edgar Puryear—the, uh . . . that crowd."

Which was not reassuring. Jamie had previously regaled the Fishers' supper table with tales about "the Flash Sports." Everything Rosemary had heard about these young men was wicked or alarming.

That evening, Grandmother Fisher scolded Jamie for upsetting the child.

"But Rhett is disgraced. It's true," Jamie insisted.

"The truth, Jamie, isn't always kind."

Rhett Butler's reappearance inspired the Flash Sports to new outrages. Somehow, Rhett slipped two of Miss Polly's pretty, overdressed young Cyprians past the ball managers into the Jockey Club Ball. Before they were escorted out, the giggling girls recognized a St. Michael's vestryman of previously impeccable reputation.

One midnight outside a waterfront gambling hell, two ruffians accosted Rhett.

Rhett said mildly, "I've only one bullet in my pistol. Who wants the bullet and who wants his neck broken?"

The thieves backed down.

Rhett and Andrew brought a dozen horses from Tennessee to Charleston in four days, changing horses on the fly. Rumor persisted they'd barely outrun the horses' legitimate owners.

And all Charleston buzzed when on a two-dollar bet, the blindfolded Rhett Butler jumped his gelding, Tecumseh, over the five-foot spiked iron fence into St. Michael's churchyard. Sunday morning, curious parishioners and an angry vicar inspected the deep holes Tecumseh's hooves had left in the turf. Knowledgeable horsemen shuddered.

Jamie Fisher had a better heart than he liked to admit and he censored that news. "Rhett plays poker," Jamie stated. He lowered his voice to a whisper. "He plays for money!"

"Of course he does," sensible Charlotte retorted. "He has to get money somehow, doesn't he?"

Although the girls didn't know all Rhett's sins, they knew his sins were very numerous. One morning, when the sympathetic Charlotte called her friend "poor, dear Rosemary" once too often, Rosemary smacked her friend in the eye. The startled child burst into tears and Rosemary fell into her arms and, as little girls will, they solaced one another.

One special morning, when Grandmother Fisher entered the family room, Charlotte forgot the toast she had been slathering with red currant jelly and Rosemary set her teacup down.

Grandmother Fisher was not quite wringing her hands. She studied Rosemary as if the child's demeanor might answer some question.

"Grandmother," Charlotte asked, "is anything wrong?"

Constance Fisher shook her head—a little shake—and straightened. "Rosemary, you've a caller in the withdrawing room."

"A caller, Grandmother? For me?"

"Your brother Rhett has come for you."

That story-book wolf flashed into Rosemary's mind and she glanced at Charlotte in alarm.

Grandmother said, "You are not obliged to see him, child. If you prefer, I'll turn him away."

"Rosemary, he's disgraced," Charlotte fretted.

Rosemary set her lips in a determined line. She was old enough now to face a story-book wolf. Besides, Rosemary was curious: Would her brother's sins show in his person? Would he be hunchbacked, or hairy, with long fingernails? Would he smell bad?

As they passed down the hall, Grandmother murmured, "Rosemary, you mustn't mention this visit to your father."

Rhett Butler wasn't a scraggly old wolf. He was young and tall and his black hair glittered like a raven's wing. His coat was the russet of a newborn fawn and his black planter's hat rested in his big hands like an old friend.

"Who have we here?" her brother asked. "You needn't be afraid of me, little one."

When Rosemary looked into Rhett's smiling eyes, the wolf went away forever. "I'm not afraid," she said stoutly.

"Grandmother Fisher told me you're a spark," Rhett told her. "I believe you are. I've come this morning to take you for a drive."

"Young Butler, I may live to regret this. How in the world you managed to get expelled from West Point, I don't know"—Grandmother raised a preemptory hand—"and do not wish to know. But John Haynes speaks well of you, and John has a level head. If your father hears you've been here, he'll be . . ."

Rhett grinned. "Outraged? Outrage is my father's dearest companion." Rhett's bow was deferential. "I am indebted to you, Grandmother Fisher. I'll have Rosemary home for supper." He knelt then so he was no taller than she. "Sister Rosemary, I've a spirited horse and the lightest sulky in the Low Country. Wouldn't you like to fly?"

That afternoon, Rosemary met Tecumseh, Rhett's three-year-old Morgan gelding. The sulky was not much more than a woven cane seat on tall wheels whose spokes were thinner than Rhett's thumbs. Tecumseh floated along at a trot, and when Rhett Butler asked for the gallop, their sulky left the ground.

When Rosemary'd flown about as long as a little girl should fly, Rhett returned her to Grandmother Fisher's and carried her into the house. Rosemary had never felt as safe as she felt in her brother's arms.

On his second visit, Rhett took Rosemary boating. Everyone in the harbor seemed to know him. The sloop they boarded belonged to a free colored man who called her brother by his Christian name. Rosemary was surprised when her brother clasped a negro's hand.

Charleston harbor was busy that afternoon with fishing boats, coastal ketches, and oceangoing schooners. With Old Glory snapping from its parapet, Fort Sumter guarded the harbor mouth. The waves were higher outside the harbor, and Rosemary got thoroughly wetted with spray.

When they returned to Grandmother Fisher's, Rosemary was sunburned, tired, and thoughtful.

"What is it, little one?"

"Rhett, do you love me?"

Her brother touched her cheek. "As my life."

Inevitably, Langston learned his son had visited the Fishers, and he removed Rosemary to Broughton.

A month later, Rosemary was roused after midnight by a carriage in the drive—Grandmother Fisher's carriage—and before she was fully awake,

Charlotte was in her bedroom and in her arms. "Oh, Rosemary," she said. "I'm so sorry this is happening."

Which is when Rosemary Butler learned that her brother Rhett was to fight at daybreak, a duel with Shadrach Watling, who once shot a whip-poorwill's head from its body.

Daybreak came and went. At the sound of distant shots, Rhett's mother rushed to the withdrawing room window, peering with myopic, blinking intensity.

"Probably market hunters," Rhett's brother, Julian, announced. "Shooting passenger pigeons." Dr. Ward's wife, Eulalie, nodded in agreement.

Charlotte Fisher's warm hand found Rosemary's cold one and squeezed it hard.

Color flushing her ashen cheeks, Elizabeth Butler rang for a servant. "We will take refreshment."

Rosemary closed her eyes so tightly, red spots flashed behind her eyelids as she prayed silently, Please God, keep my brother safe. Please God. Make Rhett safe!

Quiet as church mice, concealed behind a love seat's curving arm, Rosemary and Charlotte were in the farthest corner of the big, chilly room.

Constance Venable Fisher cleared her throat to issue an opinion. "Langston has chosen a singularly unfortunate time to do his accounts!" Mrs. Fisher's judgmental nod bored through the withdrawing room door, marched down the hall, down the grand staircase, through the public parlor into Langston Butler's office.

Julian replied, "Father is a man of regular habits. Saturday mornings, he does accounts."

Seated on the hard upright chair she had taken as the spinster's due, Miss Juliet Ravanel said, "Sometimes men conceal their fears by punctiliousness. Perhaps Mr. Butler—"

"Nonsense!" Constance Fisher pronounced. "Langston Butler is stubborn as a root hog."

Uncle Solomon, Broughton's houseman, brought tea and a platter heaped with the ginger cookies Cook usually baked only during Race

Week. When Mrs. Butler asked for sherry Uncle Solomon replied, "But Missus, it ain't hardly day. Sun just comin' up."

"We will take sherry," Mrs. Butler insisted. After Solomon shut the door too noisily, she said, "As Mr. Butler says, 'Negroes take advantage of their masters' kindness.' "

"Everyone recalls how the Butlers kept slavery in the United States Constitution." Miss Ravanel refreshed a boast with which everyone present was all too familiar. Mrs. Butler took her bait. "Why, yes. My husband's beloved uncle Middleton headed the South Carolina delegation. . . ."

"Yes, dear," Constance Fisher said, not unkindly. "We know all that. Rhett is nothing like Middleton. Rhett favors his grandfather Louis Valentine."

Elizabeth Butler put a hand to her mouth. "We mustn't speak of *him.* Langston never mentions his father's name."

"Dear me, why ever not?" Constance Fisher said cheerfully, "America is a new nation. Blood money is scrubbed clean in a generation."

Broughton had been an unprofitable indigo plantation that couldn't provide for the brothers who'd inherited it. Louis Valentine Butler took himself off to New Orleans and a lifelong association with buccaneer Jean Lafitte, while Middleton Butler entered the slave trade. Fortunes were being made importing Africans, but Middleton's captains paid too much for sickly specimens and his negroes who survived the Middle Passage were discounted at the sales. Middleton quit the business when Charleston's council ordered him to dump dead negroes farther out to sea. Corpses were washing ashore at White Point, where Charleston's gentry took Sabbath promenades.

Since Middleton Butler didn't choose sides until the American Revolution was safely won, he acquired three hundred Loyalist acres forfeited to patriots. As a delegate to the Philadelphia convention, Middleton Butler did keep slavery in the newly minted Constitution.

In 1810, Louis Valentine Butler captured the *Mercato,* a Spanish silver ship, off Tampico and bought a thousand acres of prime rice land for Broughton. Langston Butler, Louis Valentine's son, quarreled fiercely with his father and moved in with his bachelor uncle, Middleton. Louis Valentine bought two thousand more acres. The purchase money came from prizes taken off the Texas coast. (Although Louis Valentine swore they'd been Spanish and Mexican ships, rumor persisted they'd been flying the American flag.)

Successive Broughton overseers were hard-pressed to support Middleton's extravagant Charleston establishment.

One bright morning in 1825, Louis Valentine Butler sailed from Galveston in *The Pride of Charleston,* and was never seen again. Later that year, Middleton Butler's creditors attended that gentleman's funeral, paying homage to an American patriot while seeking their due from Langston Butler, the Butler heir. Langston Butler sold two hundred slaves to satisfy creditors' claims and married fifteen-year-old Elizabeth Kershaw. Miss Elizabeth was notable for her piety and plain features.

When Elizabeth Butler's firstborn, Rhett Kershaw Butler, emerged into the world, the infant had his caul clenched in his fist, a circumstance Broughton's conjure men said was an unusual, powerful omen. Whether for good or ill, they wouldn't say.

Although the African slave trade had been outlawed two decades before, slave ships sometimes slipped into Charleston harbor, and Langston Butler was a willing buyer of Angolans, Coromantees, Gambians, and Ebos: coastal Africans resistant to fevers and familiar with rice production. He completed Broughton Plantation with two thousand acres from Colonel Ravanel (who was too despondent after his wife's death to drive a hard bargain).

Rhett's father founded the Ashley River Agricultural Society. After experimenting with rice varieties, Langston selected Soonchurcher Puddy, an African variety that winnowed well and produced a plump grain. When Wade Hampton invited Langston to run for the Carolina legislature, Langston entered the Low Country's richest, most exclusive men's club.

The morning of Rhett's duel, Langston's younger son, Julian, drank tea while the ladies took sherry. When Solomon failed to brim her glass, Constance Fisher tapped it impatiently.

From behind the sheltering love seat, Charlotte Fisher smelled ginger cookies—a warm tingling in the back of her nose. With a sigh, Charlotte set her wants aside. How could she be thinking of ginger cookies when

Rosemary's brother might be wounded or dead? Charlotte Fisher had a thoroughgoing respect for grown-up wisdom—grown-ups were *grown-ups*, after all—but Charlotte had concluded they were wrong about Rhett Butler.

"Belle Watling *is* pretty," the unpretty Miss Ravanel remarked, "for a rustic."

Elizabeth Butler shook her head, "That girl has sorely tried her father's patience." When Langston was away, Elizabeth Butler joined the overseer's family for Sunday prayers. Elizabeth was vaguely comforted by the simple farmhouse where she'd once had her hopes—giddy newlywed hopes—for a happy life. Isaiah Watling's fierce, unbending Christianity consoled her.

"The field of honor—it's a lovely meadow beside the river. The oaks are dripping with Spanish moss. When I married, I dreamed Langston and I might picnic there one day. We would have such *fine* picnics." Mrs. Butler dropped her eyes. "How I ramble on; pray forgive me." She glanced at the tall clock, upon whose serene face a gilt quarter moon was slowly plunging into an enameled sea. She rang Uncle Solomon again. Had he wound the clock recently, and if so, had he changed the hands?

"No, missus." Solomon licked his lips. "I winds the clock Sundays. You want it winded now?"

She dismissed him with a dispirited wave. "An apology . . ." Mrs. Butler said. "No one expects Rhett to *marry* the girl."

"Excellent notion! An apology!" Miss Ravanel applauded.

"My brother would never apologize!" Rosemary's protest startled her elders, who had forgotten the little girls. "Shad Watling is a bully and a liar! Rhett would never apologize to Shad Watling." Though Rosemary's cheeks flushed, she wouldn't recant—not one word! When sensible Charlotte squeezed her friend's ankle, Rosemary shoved her hand away.

"Rhett never liked Charleston." Mrs. Butler's eyes roved. "Rhett said the only difference between alligators and Charlestonians was that alligators showed their teeth before they bit."

"Rhett favors his grandfather," Constance Fisher repeated. "That raven hair, those laughing black eyes." Her voice traveled back in time. "Mercy, how Louis Valentine could dance."

"Why couldn't that girl have gone away!" Elizabeth Butler cried. "She has connections in Missouri."

Miss Ravanel averred there were many bastards in Missouri. Perhaps there were even more bastards in Missouri than in Texas.

Julian Butler compared his watch with the tall clock and retarded the clock. "We won't hear the shots. Too distant."

His mother gasped.

"Julian," Constance Fisher said, "your brother may be a rogue, but you are a dunce."

Julian shrugged. "Rhett's latest escapade has upset our household. All the servants wear long faces. Thinking Cook had prepared these cookies for honored guests"—Julian afforded them a nod—"I complimented her. 'Oh no, Master Julian. I bakes 'em for Master Rhett. After he done fightin'."

Charlotte whispered, "Rosemary, please don't say any more. We must be perfect possums." Charlotte added wistfully, "I would so like a ginger cookie."

The big clock ticked.

Julian cleared his throat, "Mrs. Ward, I'm less familiar with Savannah's first families than I should be. You were a Robillard, I believe?"

Miss Ravanel remembered some gossip. "Wasn't some Robillard on the brink of consummating an unfortunate alliance—with a cousin, was it?"

"Dear Cousin Philippe. My sister Ellen thought Philippe was magnificent." Eulalie giggled (by now she'd had her third glass of sherry). "I suppose a lion *is* magnificent—until he *eats* you."

Miss Ravanel recalled details. "Didn't the Robillards exile Cousin Philippe and marry the girl off to an Irish storekeeper?"

Eulalie tried to bolster family dignity. "My sister Ellen married a successful businessman. She and Mr. Gerald O'Hara have a cotton plantation near Jonesboro. Tara it is called." She sniffed. "After his family estate in Ireland, I presume."

"Jonesboro would be in . . . Georgia?" Miss Ravanel stifled her yawn.

"Indeed. Ellen writes that her daughter Scarlett is 'a Robillard through and through.' "

"Scarlett? What a curious name. Scarlett O'Hara—those Irish, dear me."

Hands clasped behind his back, Julian said, "It'll be over now."

Elizabeth Butler's voice chimed with false hope. "Rhett and Shad will have made amends and galloped off to Mr. Turner's tavern."

Constance Fisher said, "Julian: If your father has finished his accounts, might he condescend to join us?"

"Langston Butler's work is never done," Julian intoned. "Fourteen thousand acres, three hundred and fifty negroes, sixty horses, including five of the finest Thoroughbreds . . ."

"But only two sons," Constance Fisher snapped. "One of whom may be dying of a bullet wound."

Elizabeth Butler put her hand to her mouth. "Rhett is at Mr. Turner's tavern," she whispered. "He must be."

When Rosemary heard the hoofbeats, she ran to the window, flinging it open wide, so damp air rushed into the house. On tiptoes, the child pushed her torso outside. "It's Tecumseh!" she cried. "I'd know his gallop anywhere. Oh, listen, Mama! Can't you hear? Rhett's in the lane. It *is* him! It's Tecumseh!"

The child bolted from the room, hurtled pell-mell down the broad staircase, past her father's office, and outside onto the oyster-shell drive, where her brother was reining in his lathered horse. A grinning Uncle Solomon took Tecumseh's bridle, "I gratified you home, Master Rhett," Uncle Solomon said. "All us coloreds gratified."

The young man slid off his horse and scooped his sister into the air, squeezing her so fiercely, it took her breath. "I'm sorry I frightened you, little one. I wouldn't have you frightened for the world."

"Rhett, you're hurt!"

His left sleeve was empty. His arm hung inside his black frock coat.

"The ball didn't touch bone. It's gusty beside the river at sunrise. Watling didn't allow for gusts."

"Oh, Rhett, I was so afraid. What would I do if I lost you?"

"You haven't lost me, child. Only the good die young." He set his sister at arm's length, as if stamping her forever on his memory. His black eyes were so sad. "Come with me, Rosemary," he said, and for one exalted instant the child misunderstood. For a few seconds, Rosemary thought she and Rhett would flee this joyless house, that she'd wave farewell from Tecumseh's back as brother and sister flew away.

She followed her brother onto the long, empty piazza in front of the house. Rhett put his good arm around his sister's thin shoulder and turned her so they overlooked their family's world. On the patchwork of sunlit rectangular rice fields, gangs were spreading marl, chanting as they worked. Though the words were inaudible, the tone was sweet and sorrowing. The Ashley River's tidal arc outlined Broughton's main trunk. On that trunk, a horseman galloped toward the east field and Isaiah Watling.

"Bad news rides the swiftest horse," Rhett said quietly. After a pause, he added, "I shan't ever forget how beautiful this is."

"Is he . . . Is Shad Watling . . ."

"Yes," Rhett said.

"Are you sad?" Rosemary asked. "He was a bully. You needn't be sad."

Rhett smiled. "What a wonder you are."

Mrs. Butler and her guests were waiting in the public parlor.

When she saw her son's empty sleeve, Elizabeth Butler gasped and her eyes rolled back until the whites showed. Julian helped her to a bench, murmuring, "Dear Mother. Mother, please."

Eulalie Ward's eyes were enormous. "Franklin?" she squeaked.

"Madam, your Franklin is unscathed except by his own flask. The good doctor has no stomach for this business."

Ledger in hand, Langston Butler erupted from his office and strode to the shelves, where he slotted the ledger among its fellows.

Turning, he glanced at his elder son. "Ah yes, the bad penny." Langston Butler went to the family Bible and opened it to those pages where Butler births, marriages, and deaths had been recorded since the Bible had been printed in 1607. He extracted a silver penknife from his waistcoat to whittle quick curls from his goose-quill pen. He laid the quill against the glossy walnut stand and when he tipped his nib, he cut so deep, he marred the wood.

With trembling hands, Langston Butler inspected the Bible record.

"The Butlers have boasted patriots, faithful wives, dutiful children, and respectable citizens. But there is a wicked strain in Butler blood and some herein this Book, my own father among them, have been hangman's bait." Langston's glare at Grandmother Fisher dared her disagreement.

Langston continued. "Today, we concern ourselves with a disobedient scion, a rebellious and impertinent youth. When his parent sought acceptable conduct, that youth defied him."

Elizabeth Butler wept silently. Julian Butler stifled a cough.

"When, at wit's end, that parent enrolled the boy in West Point, even their famous disciplinarians could not subdue him. Cadet Butler was expelled and returned to the Low Country, where he proved a dissolute rakehell and impregnated a girl of the lower classes. Did you offer Watling money?"

"You are the rich planter, sir, not I."

"Why did you challenge Watling?"

"Watling lied about me, sir."

Langston brushed it away. "Watling is dead?"

"He is emptied of mischief."

With deliberate strokes, Langston Butler struck his son's name from the Bible. He capped the inkwell, wiped the nib, and laid the pen down.

Wordlessly, Langston Butler herded his family and friends back through the broad doors into the family quarters. Julian took Rosemary's hand before she could elude him.

Langston Butler closed the walnut doors and set his back against them. The air shimmered between father and son. "As you have no further business with the Butler family, sir, you may depart."

Chapter Three

"Beloved Brother Rhett . . ."

In the years to come, little Rosemary wrote her brother faithfully. She told him about her piebald pony, Jack, who had the pleasantest manners. Rosemary rode Jack everywhere. "Mother says I am becoming a Wild Indian. Have you met any Wild Indians?

"When I ask him to jump," Rosemary wrote, "Jack swivels his head and rolls his eyes and lays his ears flat. I believe Jack is insulted!"

When a water moccasin struck Jack, Rosemary wrote how she and Hercules sat up through the night with her dying pony. Though Rosemary's hand was steady, this letter was spotted with tearstains.

Rosemary had returned to the Fishers and wrote about that household.

Charlotte doesn't think ill of anyone. I don't think her brother, Jamie, intends to be cruel, but his friends are so clever and reckless, Jamie must act as they do. One morning, he came home while Charlotte and I were at breakfast. Jamie's clothes were filthy! He stumbled and he smelled very bad! When Charlotte reproved him, Jamie called Charlotte "an interfering hussy." Charlotte set her lip and refused to speak to Jamie. For days and days, Jamie pretended nothing was wrong, but in the end he apologized! Charlotte is exactly like Grandmother Fisher—the best of friends but stubborn to a fault!

Jamie is gentler than he wants us to think! When he isn't with his friends, he tells us amusing stories. Some are not true! Jamie loves horses and is the best rider I have ever seen! Hercules lets Jamie ride Gero, though

Father would be furious if he knew! Have I told you about Gero? Hercules says Gero is the fastest Thoroughbred in the Low Country.

Jamie's friends are Andrew Ravanel, Henry Kershaw, and Edgar Puryear. Weren't they your friends, too? Jamie says John Haynes is a "young stick," but he daren't criticize John Haynes in Grandmother Fisher's hearing! John Haynes asks if I've heard from you and I am sorry I must tell him I haven't!

If I were older I would join you and we could travel even to Egypt. I should very much like to see the pyramids. Have you seen the pyramids?

In much the same way that Rosemary knew Jesus loved little children, she knew Abolitionists were wicked and Yankees hated and feared Southerners, even children like herself. From more personal experience, Rosemary knew grown-ups argued fiercely about politics and that friendships were made or discarded depending on what other grown-ups were doing far away in the United States Congress.

When Rosemary was ten, Congress passed the Compromise of 1850 and Nullifiers and Unionists became friendly for a time. Langston Butler, who hadn't spoken to Cathecarte Puryear since he removed Rhett from Cathecarte's tutelage, nodded to Puryear on Queen Street.

When Mrs. Stowe's novel, *Uncle Tom's Cabin,* was published, all Charleston deplored the wicked book. Grandmother Fisher said it was too simple for Rosemary and Charlotte.

"How can it be too simple for children?" Rosemary asked, desperate to read the book everybody was talking about.

"Simple in the sense of being simpleminded," Grandmother Fisher grumbled.

In her next letter, Rosemary asked if Rhett had read *Uncle Tom's Cabin.*

This brief political tranquillity ended when Rosemary was fourteen and Congress passed the Kansas-Nebraska Act. In the West, slave owners and abolitionists were murdering one another.

At about this time, Rosemary began paying rather more attention to Charleston's eligible bachelors. "Edgar Allan Puryear claimed Andrew Ravanel cheated at cards, so Andrew challenged him," Rosemary wrote.

"Everybody thought they'd fight, but Edgar apologized, so now people suspect Edgar is a coward. Jamie Fisher calls Andrew a 'beautiful' horseman. Do you think a man can be beautiful?

"Henry Kershaw caned a free colored tailor in front of his shop after the tailor asked payment of an overdue bill. The man died of his injuries. (Father joked that the tailor got his due!)"

Rosemary described Congress Haynes's funeral, when mourners blocked Meeting Street from Queen Street to White Point. "John Haynes asked about you again. How I wish I had some news of you, dear brother!

"Do you remember visiting me when you first came back from West Point? I was such a child and you seemed so very tall! Do you remember going sailing?

"Last Saturday, Gero beat Mr. Canby's Planet, and Colonel Ravanel's Chapultapec. Hercules took credit and tried to order a basket of champagne to celebrate *his* victory. Hercules said he wanted to 'treat all the white gentlemen.' What a notion! Father sent Hercules back to Broughton to 'refresh his manners.' "

Rosemary assured Rhett: "Mother loves you, Rhett! I know she does!" This was conjecture; after her elder son was banished, Elizabeth Butler burst into tears on the rare occasions Rhett's name was mentioned.

Abolitionist murders in distant Kansas disrupted long-standing Charleston connections. Cousins quit speaking to cousins. Charlestonians once deemed extreme were lauded as visionaries. Grandmother Fisher kept Langston Butler's friends from expelling the Unionist Cathecarte Puryear from the St. Cecilia Society. In response, Langston Butler withdrew his fifteen-year-old daughter from the Fisher home again.

Thereafter, Rosemary saw Charlotte and Jamie Fisher only at social gatherings. To Rhett, she wrote, "Jamie and Andrew Ravanel's sister, Juliet, have become bosom friends. She and Jamie hone their tongues on one another, sharpening them for their victims."

Rosemary told her brother that Andrew Ravanel had swept Mary Loring off her feet. All Charleston expected Andrew and Mary to be affianced, but, attended by salacious rumors, Mary Loring left suddenly for Split Rock, North Carolina. Andrew was now courting Cynthia Peterson.

"My maid Cleo means well but is upset by trifles. Cleo is a flibbertigibbet!

"You remember pert little Sudie? Well, Sudie has jumped the broomstick with Hercules and has her firstborn! Hercules couldn't be prouder. He sends his regards!"

She concluded this letter, "Please do write. I miss you awfully and yearn to hear all your news. Your loving sister, Rosemary."

Hercules told Rosemary where to send her letters.

When Rosemary asked how Hercules knew Rhett's whereabouts, he laughed. "Miss Rosemary, don't you reckon horses talk to each other? Everywhere they goes, horses is talkin'. I sneaks into the stalls at night and listens."

So Rosemary addressed letters to "Rhett Butler, San Francisco, California Territory" and "Rhett Butler, General Delivery, New Orleans, Louisiana." She sealed them carefully and doubled the postage. "Be sure and mail this today, Uncle."

"Yes, Miss," Uncle Solomon replied, although for some reason, her letters made the old houseman uneasy.

Rosemary never heard from her brother, and as the years passed, her weekly letters became fortnightly and then monthly.

Rosemary's final letter was written on the eve of her debut to Charleston society at the Jockey Club Ball. In that letter, sixteen-year-old Rosemary confided her fears that no young man would sign her dance card and that her white satin gown was more girlish than womanly.

Cleo fussed at her: "We ain't gonna get ready less'n you quit scribblin' and get to dressin', Missy." Rosemary ignored her maid and went out to the yard, where Hercules was grooming Gero.

Without preliminary, Rosemary said, "Writing to my brother is useless. My brother is dead."

"No'm, Master Rhett ain't dead."

Rosemary put her hands firmly on her hips. "How do you know?"

"The horses, they—"

She stamped her foot, "Hercules! I am no longer a child."

"Yes, Miss." He sighed. "I can see you ain't." As Rosemary stormed back to the house, he returned to grooming. "Be easy now, Gero. Miss Rosemary distress 'count of she goin' to the Jockey Club and she feared the young gentlemen won't favor her."

Rosemary concluded her letter: "Although some of my letters may have gone astray, you must have received others. Your silence is too cruel. How I wish I knew your whereabouts and circumstances. I will always love you, brother, but in the face of your obstinate silence, I will not write again."

Rosemary was as good as her word. She didn't write Rhett that her debut had been notable, that Andrew Ravanel had flirted outrageously and taken four waltzes. Nor did she tell him that during the intermission, Grandmother Fisher had said, "John Haynes is thoroughly besotted with you. A girl could do worse than John Haynes."

Nor that she had replied, tossing her head, "John Haynes can't sit a horse. It's a wonder he doesn't injure himself."

"But Andrew Ravanel can sit a horse?"

"He is the handsomest man in Charleston. Every belle has set her cap for Andrew."

"I believe what you call a 'cap,' dear, Mr. Ravanel's sporting friends call a 'scalp,'" Constance Fisher replied.

Chapter Four

Race Week

Three years before the War, a full nine years after Rhett Butler left the Low Country, on a February afternoon Rosemary Butler stood before her pier glass, dissatisfied. She thought herself too tall and her torso was unfashionably long. Her entirely ordinary auburn hair was parted in the center and curled in ringlets. Her features were, Rosemary believed, too strong, and her mouth too generous. Her candid gray eyes, she thought, were her only good feature. Rosemary stuck her tongue out at the mirror. "You are no friend!" she announced.

Rosemary's dress, a textured print in green polished cotton, was new for Race Week.

Race Week was the pinnacle of Charleston's social season. The rice had been harvested, dried, winnowed, hulled, sold, and shipped; the negroes had been given their annual clothing issue and enjoyed their Christmas holiday. The planter families were in town and their mornings hummed with gossip about the rare doings of the night before and anticipations for the evening ahead. Smart new carriages and refurbished, highly polished older ones promenaded in the great loop down East Bay, up Meeting Street, and down East Bay again. The latest Paris fashions (as adapted by London pattern makers and sewed by Charleston's free colored seamstresses) were admired at the Jockey Club and St. Cecilia Society balls. Yankee excursionists gawked at grand town houses, throngs of negroes, splendid racehorses, and the most beautiful belles in the South.

Cleo burst into Rosemary's bedroom, wringing her hands. "Missy, they's somebody here to see you."

"I'll be down directly. Show the gentleman into the drawing room."

"He ain't . . . Missy, he waitin' in the yard. He . . . he ain't no gentleman!" Cleo's lips clamped tight. She would say no more.

The public rooms of Langston Butler's Greek Revival town house had carved marble mantels and varnished cherry wainscoting. A shaded piazza encircled the entire second story.

The servants' staircase at the back of the house was narrow, steep, and unpainted. Up these stairs, servants carried plates and tureens for Langston Butler's political dinners. Armloads of fresh linens came up these steps. Down came dirty sheets, pillowcases, underclothing, and tablecloths. Down, carefully, came the family's chamber pots.

During this season, just fifteen Broughton servants attended the Butlers. Uncle Solomon, Cleo, Hercules and Sudie, and Cook had a room each above the kitchen/laundry house. Lesser servants slept in cramped quarters above the stable.

Usually, the yard was a beehive of washing, laundering, mucking out stables, and grooming horses, but Gero was running in today's noon race and everybody was at the racecourse.

"Hello?" Rosemary called.

The stable smelled of axle grease, neat's-foot oil, and manure. Curious horses lifted their heads above their stall doors.

Rosemary's visitor clutched his parcel so hard, he'd indented it.

"Why, is it Tunis? Tunis Bonneau?"

Like his father, Tunis Bonneau had been a fisherman and market hunter, but these days Tunis was a pilot for Haynes & Son. Rosemary knew the man by sight, although they had never spoken.

"Tunis Bonneau . . . didn't someone tell me you'd married?"

"Yes'm. Last September. My Ruthie, she's Reverend Prescott's eldest."

Tunis's wire-rimmed spectacles and solemn expression made him seem a dark edition of a Puritan schoolmaster. His clothing was spotless, pressed, and he smelled faintly of lye soap.

"I was asked to bring you this." Bonneau pushed his parcel at Rosemary and turned to leave.

"Wait, Tunis. Please. There is no card. Who sent it?" Untied, the parcel revealed an oversized yellow silk scarf fringed with exquisite black knots. "My goodness! What a gorgeous shawl."

"Yes, Miss."

When the virginal girl settled the silk on her shoulders, it caressed and made her feel vaguely uneasy. "Tunis, who sent this to me?"

"Miss Rosemary. I don't need trouble with Master Langston."

"Was it . . . was it Andrew Ravanel?"

"It weren't Andrew Ravanel gifted you. No, Miss."

Rosemary said determinedly, "You will not leave until you tell me."

Tunis Bonneau took off his glasses and rubbed the mark they'd left on his nose. "He reckoned his letters weren't getting to you, so he asked me to bring you this. I seen him in Freeport. He ain't changed none." Tunis turned the glasses in his hand as if they were an unfamiliar object. "I sailed as pilot on the *John B. Elliot,* carryin' rice and cotton, bringin' back locomotive wheels for the Georgia railroad. Soon as I seen him, I knowed who he was. Rhett Butler ain't changed none."

Rosemary felt a catch at her throat and she gripped a stall rail to steady herself.

"Rhett been with them freebooters in Nicaragua, but he quit that business."

"But he's . . . Rhett's dead!"

"Oh no, Miss. Mr. Rhett ain't dead. Why, he's right lively. That man always sees the amusin' side of things."

"But . . . but . . . not a single word to me in nine years."

Tunis Bonneau breathed on his glasses and wiped them with his handkerchief. "Miss Rosemary, your brother did write to you. He wrote plenty."

Chapter Five

Notes in Bottles

Occidental Hotel,
San Francisco, California Territory
May 17, 1849

Dear Little Sister,

Although I disembarked from The Glory of the Seas *six long hours ago, the earth still wobbles beneath my feet.*

Our captain and his son rowed we passengers ashore fearing The Glory *might join the hundred ships deserted by sailors who became gold seekers. Their masts are a dismal forest beside Long Wharf.*

The wharf itself was a hubbub of runners for restaurants and hotels, brothels and gambling houses. Sharpers offered to buy and sell gold. One well-dressed man diffidently begged a meal.

I played cards on the voyage around the Horn. Because they were going to be rich soon, the aspirant gold seekers were contemptuous of the cash money already in their possession and played as if prudence showed no faith in their glorious future. Consequently I arrived in this city with a considerable "grubstake" (the money the argonaut uses to finance his prospecting).

During our tedious voyage around the Horn, the argonauts explained why they had uprooted themselves from occupations, friends, and family for a dangerous voyage and uncertain future. To a man, and earnestly, they insisted they were not doing it for themselves. No indeed! They were adventuring for those selfsame wives and children they'd left behind. They'd left their families for the sake of their families! Apparently, American wives and children cannot be satisfied until an argonaut showers them with gold!

This is not Charleston. San Francisco boardwalks flank mud streets, which suck the shoes off my feet. Tents and wooden shacks coexist side by side with brick buildings so new, they glisten.

Three years ago, before gold was discovered, San Francisco had eight hundred citizens. Today it boasts thirty-six thousand. From the wharf to the sheltering hills, the city echoes with the banging and clattering of new construction. In this town, Sister, even loafers with nowhere to go hurry to get there.

Chinese, Irish, Italians, Connecticut Yankees, and Mexicans: The new city hums with new people and newfangled notions.

Although I miss you and my Low Country friends, I am no exile. I feel the exultation of a prisoner released into the sunlight of a new morning. There are cities besides Charleston and they are good places to be!

Please do write me here at the hotel. They will hold my mail for me. Tell me about Charlotte and Grandmother Fisher and especially about your doings. Of all my old life, Dear Sister, I miss you most.

Your Loving Brother, Rhett

March 12, 1850
Goodyear's Bar, California Territory

Dear Little Sister,

Goodyear's Bar is a surpassing ugly gold camp: a high-country mudflat spotted with dugouts, tents, and windowless log huts where lucky miners occasionally earn two thousand dollars from a wheelbarrel of pay dirt.

Even rich argonauts must eat, and their picks and shovels have a way of wearing out, and common decency (and below-zero nights) demand trousers and shoes.

Sister, I have become a merchant—one of those tedious fellows whose ef-

forts underpin every aristocracy. With my grubstake, I purchased a heavy freight wagon and four sturdy mules. I paid twice as much as I would have in Carolina for brined beef, whiskey, flour, shovels, picks, and rolls of canvas.

I loaded my rig and goods on a steamship, which puffed up the river to Sacramento, where I chaffed until the trails into the high gold country were almost passable. Sister, your merchant brother shoveled through three-foot snowdrifts to deliver his goods to Goodyear's Bar.

I have never had such a glorious welcome. No provisions had reached the camp since October; the miners were famished and fell on your brother with hosannas.

They had gold but nothing to spend it on! Within an hour of my arrival, I sold everything except my revolvers and a mule.

I returned through the snowbanks, keeping a wary eye on my back trail. I had much to protect.

When I delivered this booty to Lucas and Turner's bank vault, even the impassive Mr. Sherman, the managing partner, raised his eyebrows.

I've had no reply to my letters. I pray you are well and yearn to hear your news.

Now it is time for a warm bath and bed.

Your Loving Brother, Rhett

September 17, 1850
St. Francis Hotel
San Francisco, California

Dear Little Sister,

Don't tell Father that I've become respectable. Butler General Merchandise has a second-floor office on Union Square and warehouses in Stockton and Sacramento.

Would you recognize your brother in his dark business suit, neat gaiters, and inoffensive foulard? I feel like an actor in a very strange play.

I do have a knack for it—making and getting money. Perhaps because I see money as a commodity with no religious significance.

I no longer play cards. Getting wagons to gold camps like Goodyear's Bar, Bogus Thunder, and Mugfuzzle (though no metropolis, Mugfuzzle exists) makes poker seem a puny gamble. Why should I sit, midnight after midnight, in a room rank with tobacco smoke just to separate drunken fools from their money?

The argonauts are crazed with greed. No insurance company will insure their lives. Cholera kills them, drink kills them, and accidents kill them. Since there is no law in the camps, disputes are routinely settled with pickaxes, fists, or guns. If all else fails, often they kill themselves.

The argonauts are as ready to fight as our Low Country aristocrats, but their reasons are more transparent. There is no prattle about "honor" here.

We Californians say "back in America" to refer to our former home. Mr. Clay's clever compromise and Mr. Calhoun's death were hardly noticed here.

Men move faster out here, but are no wiser.

I have not received one letter from you and no longer expect one. You cannot be deceased—I would feel it if you were. I assume Father has forbidden you to write.

Things may improve, even at Broughton, and writing to you refreshes you in my mind and heart. I feel your love as I write and return it to you tenfold.

Your faithful correspondent,
Rhett

June 19, 1851
St. Francis Hotel
San Francisco, California

Dearest Rosemary,

"The Sydney Ducks are cackling tonight." That's what this city's wits say when some honest man is robbed, beaten, or shot. While San Francisco has always had rough elements, a recent immigration of freed Australian convicts has made it far more dangerous.

I am not worried for myself, my business, or my drivers. I have a (entirely undeserved) reputation for ferocity.

As Mr. Newton taught us, for every reaction, there's an equal and opposite reaction, and when I was invited to dine with three upstanding citizens, I suspected their motives.

The banker W. T. Sherman is older than I, with the triangular face of a praying mantis, a short beard, and phenomenally large eyes. Brown eyes are supposed to be soft and revealing of character. Sherman's are as revealing as two lumps of coal. He is asthmatic, one of the palest men I've ever seen. Neither he nor anyone else anticipates a long life for him.

He is a practical man, one who does not flinch at necessity.

Collis Huntington is one of those men who believe their own rectitude gives them the right to make other men cower. He is a competitor of Butler General Merchandise and we've crossed swords a time or two.

Dr. Wright, the least of this triumvirate, is nervous, dressed like Beau Brummell, and claims to have invented the phrase "the Paris of the Pacific" to describe this city. He has, so far as I can make out, no other accomplishments of which to boast.

We dined in a private dining room at the St. Francis, where, after the usual hemming and hawing, they proposed I join their nucleus of a vigilante society, which would, as Huntington elegantly put it, "hang every thief and miscreant on this shore of the Bay."

Mr. Sherman said civic disorder threatened business interests. He spoke of the "necessity" of action.

I reminded Sherman that necessity is not always just or worthy.

Huntington and Wright were genuinely offended—they'd assumed I was their natural ally: a man who could kill with clean hands.

I told them neither yea nor nay.

Sister, I am not a reflective man, but that night I wondered who I had become. What distinguishes the merchant who hangs a thief to preserve his fortune from the planter who whips a negro to death for insolence?

I determined I would not be that man. As I would not be hanged, I would not be a hangman.

I have determined to try my fortunes elsewhere. Volunteers are combining to overthrow Cuba's Spanish overlords, and perhaps I'll lend them a hand. If you can write, I will pick up my mail c/o General Delivery, New Orleans.

Your puzzled brother,
Rhett

March 14, 1853
Hotel St. Louis
New Orleans

Dear Little Sister,

Proper Charlestonians would be shocked by this city. It is so French. New Orleans' citizens—all good Catholics—are preoccupied with food, drink, and love—though not necessarily in that order. In the old quarter, the Vieux Carré, the fragrance of sin drifts through the orange and lemon blossoms. I can attend a ball every night: formal, informal, masked, or the sort of affair I attend with a pistol in my pocket. I play cards at Mcgarth's, Perritts, or the Boston Club. I enjoy four racetracks, three theaters, and the French Opera House.

The city is the freebooters' home port. These young Americans have taken Manifest Destiny as a personal creed. Their destiny, manifestly, is to conquer and loot any Caribbean or South American nation too weak to defend itself. Most believe Cuba would make a first-class American state once we run off the Spanish.

I have invested in several freebooting expeditions—if demand increases profits, patriotism swells the trickle into a flood. Until now, I haven't been tempted to enlist myself.

New Orleans is a city of beautiful women and its Creole ladies are cultured, cosmopolitan, and wise. They have taught me much about love—a pursuit which is second only to the longing for God.

Doubtless my Creole mistress, Didi Gayerre, loves me. She loves me to distraction. After six months together, she is eager to marry, bear my children, and share my uncertain fortunes. She is everything a man could want.

I do not want her.

My initial fascination has turned to boredom and a mild contempt for myself and Didi for pretending to believe what we know is not so.

Love, Dear Sister, can be terribly cruel.

I will not stay with her from pity. Pity is even crueler than love.

The less I love her, the more desperate Didi becomes, and only physical separation will cure our problem.

We were supping with Narciso López, a Cuban General who is organizing an expedition. He already has three or four hundred volunteers—enough, he assured me, to defeat any Spanish army. Once we land, Cuban patriots will swell our ranks. He told me with a wink that there is conquistador gold in the Spanish treasury. Havana, he added, is a beautiful city.

Didi ignored his barrage of reasons. She was wearing a high-bodiced brocade gown and an astonishingly red hat. She ate nothing. She was pouting. Our omelettes were perfectly prepared and our champagne chilled, but Didi was grumpy and objected to everything the General said. No, the Cubans wouldn't rise up. The Spanish army was more formidable than a few hundred American adventurers.

López, who is a pompous man, explained how conquering Cuba would make us rich. "It's the white man's duty, Butler," he advised.

"To become rich?" I teased him.

"Our duty to transform a primitive, superstitious, authoritarian country into a modern democracy."

That theory prompted a torrent of Didi's angry French, whose precise meaning López may not have understood, but he certainly got the gist.

He leaned forward and with a condescending smile said, "Butler, are you one of those fellows whose wench tells him what to do?"

Didi stood so abruptly she knocked over the champagne bucket. She stabbed pins into her bright red hat. "Rhett?" she insisted. "Please . . ."

"You must excuse us, General," I said.

Didi was rigid on my arm. The St. Louis's doorman summoned our cab.

A filthy woman beggar limped toward us, mumbling her feeble entreaty.

López followed us onto the sidewalk, apologizing, "Señor Butler, I did not intend to insult you, nor your lovely companion.

"Madre de Dios!" The beggar had come close enough to offend his nos-

trils. She was one of those desperate creatures that service Irish stevedores behind the levees. Her hand trembled with entreaty.

"Leave us!" The General raised his cane.

"Don't, General." As I went into my pocket for a dime, I recognized a familiar face beneath her grime. "Dear God, are you . . . are you Belle Watling?"

It was she, Dear Sister, a woman I had never thought to see again. John Haynes had financed Belle's escape from the Low Country. I hadn't known she'd come to New Orleans.

Some weeks later Belle told me, "I always loved the sea. I thought things would be different here." Apparently, Belle fell in with a cardsharp who used her as collateral when the pasteboards failed him. Belle's son is in the Asylum for Orphan Boys.

I will try to improve her circumstances before General López and I embark for Cuba.

Belle begs you not say anything to her father, Isaiah. She is as thoroughly disowned as I am.

All my love, Rhett

July 1853
Cuba

Beloved Sister Rosemary,

The beach at Bahia Hondo is the most beautiful I have ever seen. Silver sand and cerulean sea seem as endless as eternity—a destination certain Spanish officers are hastening me toward.

The Spanish forces were not defeated. The Cubans did not welcome us as liberators. Ah well.

Fleeing Didi's arms into a Spanish firing squad was not my cleverest maneuver.

I've set a gamble into motion and may yet escape my fate, but the odds are long and time is short.

A corporal promises to post this letter. As with the bottle the marooned sailor tosses into the sea, I pray it will find some reader.

How dear is soft, warm sand. How tender the sandpipers wading in the shallows. Though their lives are only a few seasons, they are no less God's creatures than we.

Sister, if I leave you with one piece of advice, it is: Live your life. Let no other live it for you.

The Spaniards ordered us to dig our graves for the afternoon entertainment. As American gentlemen, naturally we refused. Ha, ha. Let the peasants dirty their *hands!*

Rosemary, of all those I have known on this gracious earth, I regret only leaving you. . . .

Think of me sometimes,

Rhett

Chapter Six

A Negro Sale

Rosemary's head was spinning. "My father burned my brother's letters? My letters, too?"

"I sees Solomon in the fish market one day—your houseman Solomon—and we gets to talkin'. Ol' Solomon, he hates to hand over them letters to Master Langston, but he got to do what he been told."

Rosemary felt sick. She asked the question that, as Langston's dutiful daughter, she had never dared. "Tunis, why does my father hate his son?"

Tunis Bonneau was a free colored—free to walk the streets without a pass; free to gather for worship services at the First African Baptist (provided one white man was present at the service); free to marry another free colored or a slave he bought out of servitude. He could not vote nor hold office, but he could keep his own money and own property. He could legally learn to read.

Because they were neither property nor white men, free coloreds made the Masters nervous.

Hence, Tunis Bonneau didn't see what he saw, didn't speak of what he knew, and pretended an ignorance so profound that it defied penetration. When white men questioned him, Tunis would reply, "Mr. Haynes, he tells me to do it." Or "You have to ask Mr. Haynes 'bout that."

Although she knew this perfectly well, Rosemary was too upset to think clearly, and she grasped Tunis's sleeve as if to shake the answers out of him. "Why does Langston hate Rhett?"

Tunis sighed and told Rosemary everything she had never before wanted to know.

While Tunis was informing Rosemary about Will, the trunk master, the hurricano, and that summer, long ago, when her brother became a full-task rice hand, her father, Langston Butler, was losing a horse race.

The Washington Racecourse was a four-mile flattened oval bordered by Charleston's oldest live oaks. Its white stucco clubhouse was reserved for Jockey Club members, but its clapboard grandstand and the great meadow were free to all. White and black, free and slave alike, witnessed Langston Butler's defeat.

Virginia and Tennessee horses came to Charleston for the fastest track and richest purses in the South. Horses, grooms, and trainers boarded in great wooden stables whose wide center aisles accommodated horse and negro sales.

The noon race had been a rematch between Langston Butler's Gero and Colonel Jack Ravanel's Chapultapec. The horses were evenly matched, betting was brisk, and the pair started to a roar from the stands. Although Chapultapec was behind at the far turn, he passed the tiring Gero in the straight and won by two lengths. In the winner's circle, Colonel Jack jigged with pleasure.

At the clubhouse rail, three young sports and Colonel Jack's spinster daughter relished the Colonel's extravagant self-satisfaction.

"Jackie, Jackie." Jamie Fisher chuckled. "Mustn't tweak the tiger's tail. Juliet, your father makes a wonderfully smug bow."

Edgar Puryear was an assiduous student of powerful men and noted Langston Butler's overseer conferring with his master. "Hmm, what might those two be up to?"

"Who gives a damn," Henry Kershaw growled. "Lend me a double eagle!" Henry Kershaw was big as a prime young bear and had a similar temper.

"Henry, it was my double eagle you wagered on Gero. I haven't another." Edgar Puryear turned his pocket inside out. "So, Gentlemen—and Lady—how will Langston even the score?"

"Perhaps he'll welsh on his bets," Juliet Ravanel suggested.

"No, no, sweet Juliet," Jamie Fisher said. "You've confused one

Charleston gentleman with another. Rosemary's father, Langston, is the bully; your father, Jack, is the welsher."

Miss Ravanel sniffed. "Why I tolerate you, I do not know."

"Because you are so easily bored," Jamie Fisher replied.

Although the acerbic spinster and the tiny youth were inseparable, no scandal touched them. Whatever the nature of their attachment, everyone understood that it was not romantic.

The next race was at two o'clock. Whites and coloreds promenaded the racecourse and meadow, while in the Jockey clubhouse, servants unpacked picnic hampers and popped corks.

On the racecourse, auctioneer's men were crying the negro sale: "John Huger's negroes. Rice hands, sawyers, cotton hands, mechanics, house niggers, and children! One hundred prime specimens!"

Edgar Puryear relieved an auctioneer's man of a sale catalog and ran his finger down the list. "Andrew means to bid on Lot sixty-one. 'Cassius, eighteen years. Musician.' "

"Cassius will fetch a thousand," Henry Kershaw said.

"Eleven hundred at least," Jamie Fisher corrected.

"A double eagle?" Henry wagered.

"You haven't a double eagle," Jamie Fisher replied.

Though he outweighed Jamie Fisher by eighty pounds and was used to getting his way, Henry Kershaw smiled. Whatever their inclination, given Fisher's wealth, even prime young bears smiled.

"Juliet, what does Andrew want with a banjo player?" Edgar Puryear asked.

"When Andrew is melancholy, music uplifts him."

Henry Kershaw drank and offered Juliet his flask, which she refused, shuddering. Henry remarked, "You can't guess what horse I saw last week pulling a nigger's fish wagon."

"Tecumseh?" Jamie Fisher said. "Didn't Rhett Butler leave his horse with the Bonneaus?"

"The best Morgan in the Low Country hauling fish," Henry Kershaw continued. "I offered two hundred, but the nigger said the horse wasn't his to sell."

"Tecumseh is worth a thousand," Edgar Puryear said. "Why didn't you force the nigger to sell?"

Henry Kershaw grinned. "Maybe you'd try that trick, Edgar, but I'll be damned if I would. Rhett might return one day."

"Where is Butler anyway?" Jamie asked.

"Nicaragua, Santa Domingue?" Henry Kershaw shrugged.

Edgar said, "I hear he's in New Orleans. Belle Watling, Rhett Butler, Rhett's bastard . . . isn't that a brew?"

Juliet Ravanel raised her eyebrows. "Edgar, you hear the most fascinating gossip. Didn't the Watling girl go to kin in Kansas?"

"Missouri. And no, she didn't," Edgar replied. "The Missouri Watlings are death on abolitionists. Don't you read the papers?"

"Now Edgar," Juliet said coquettishly, "why should we frivolous ladies read the papers when we have our gentlemen to explain *everything*?"

Jamie Fisher coughed to hide his grin.

"I think," Miss Ravanel said, "it is far more interesting to ask what Langston's daughter will do with my dear brother. Rosemary is positively throwing herself at Andrew."

"Some hussy is always throwing herself at Andrew. I don't know why he puts up with it." Jamie sniffed.

"For the same reason he tolerates you, dear Jamie." Juliet smiled sweetly. "My brother needs his admirers."

"How long will it take Andrew to catch Miss Rosemary?" Edgar mused.

"Before the end of Race Week." Juliet Ravanel wagered five dollars on it.

Shaded by live oaks across the racecourse, Grandmother Fisher, her granddaughter, Charlotte, and John Haynes were picnicking. Haynes & Son placed advertisements in Philadelphia and New York City papers: "CHARLESTON RACE WEEK: ROUND-TRIP PASSAGE, LODGING, MEALS—ALL INCLUDED!" John booked his tourists into the Mills Hotel on Queen Street, where Mr. Mills set Charleston's finest table.

One New York tourist made no secret of his abolitionist sympathies and offended Southerners who boarded the excursion schooner in Baltimore.

When the Abolitionist learned Mr. Mills was a free colored, he rejected his accommodations and demanded his money back. Since there were no other rooms to be had in Charleston during Race Week, he finally accepted his, but he still wanted a refund. "Yankee principles are wonderfully flexible," John Haynes said. "Charlotte, you aren't yourself this afternoon. Where is our Charlotte's sunny smile?"

"Charlotte's mooning over Andrew Ravanel," Grandmother Fisher said, tapping the picnic hamper peremptorily. "Cook does the finest chicken in the Carolinas."

"Grandmother! I am not mooning!"

"Of course you are, dear. Andrew Ravanel is gallant, daring, handsome, charming, and bankrupt. What young lady could ask for a better suitor?"

After praising Cook's chicken, John continued: "I hoped I'd see Rosemary this afternoon. I begged for a waltz last night, but her dance card was full."

Despite the efforts of Charleston's cleverest dressmakers, Charlotte Fisher was not attractive. Her hair was mouse-colored, her complexion unfortunate, and her waist more resembled the bee's than the wasp's. Charlotte set her lip. "I'm not certain Rosemary and I are friends anymore."

"Charlotte, don't be a goose. You and Rosemary have been friends since you were five years old," her grandmother objected.

John Haynes sighed. "Why must Charleston's most charming belles vie for the same gentleman? An ordinary fellow like myself doesn't stand a chance. Though I've no grudge against Andrew, if he stumbled and broke his aristocratic nose—a slight disfigurement, I'd wish him no worse—I'd not grieve."

Grandmother Fisher said, "John, you do go on."

Haynes smiled. "I suppose I do. I must ask you ladies: Don't you think I would make an excellent husband? . . . Thank you, Grandmother Fisher, I will try a drumstick."

Spectators and buyers drifted toward the long barn that housed the negro sale. Inside, buyers mixed freely with the merchandise. The negro women wore modest cotton dresses and handkerchief turbans, the men linsey-woolsey jackets, their trousers belted with rope. At each wearer's whim, the men's slouch hats had been shaped into dashing or practical or disreputable configurations. The negro children wore cleaner, newer clothing than their parents.

Novice slave buyers had that nonchalant, knowing expression men assume when out of their depth.

Cassius, the musician Andrew Ravanel coveted, leaned against a stall door, arms crossed and banjo slung over his shoulder. He was a smooth-faced, fattish, very black young negro, with a complacent air some whites thought disrespectful.

"Let me hear you pluck that thing, boy."

Cassius tapped his banjo respectfully, as if it had powers of its own. "Can't do it, Master. No sir. Auctioneer say I'm zactly like a fancy wench: I can't give nothin' away for nothin'! Who buys me, buys my music. . . . Master," he said solemnly, "I can make a Presbyterian kick up his heels!"

Most negroes made themselves agreeable, seeking kindly buyers and those who might buy a family intact. "Yes, Master, I a full-task rice hand. Been in them rice fields since I was a tad. Got most my teeth, yes sir. My nose broke account of a horse kick me. I ain't no hand with horses. My wife, she a laundress, and my son, he a quarter-task hand and he ain't got all his growth."

Field hands were commanded to bend this way and that so any ruptures would be apparent. Some were asked to pace rapidly to and fro or prance in place as shrewd buyers evaluated their stamina and wind.

"How often you get to the dispensary, boy?"

"You say you bore three live children? Hips like yours?"

The auctioneer was florid, jolly, and on the best of terms with the buyers. "Say, Mr. Cavanaugh, you needn't bid on this lot. Lot fifty-two's what you want: light-skinned wench, fourteen years old, Lot fifty-two. Don't I keep you in mind? Don't I now?

"Mr. Johnston, if you don't bid more than seven hundred dollars for this prime buck, you ain't as shrewd as I make you to be! Seven, seven, I say seven. Won't you help me out, boys? Seven, going once, going twice. Sold for seven hundred dollars to Drayton Plantation!" The auctioneer took a quick sip of water.

"I remind you, gentlemen, of our terms. The successful bidder pays one half the winning bid in cash and signs surety for the balance to be remitted no later than thirty days, secured by a mortgage on the purchased negro."

He smiled broadly. "Now, let's get on with the sale. Lot fifty-one: Joe's a prime boy, twelve or thirteen years. Step up on the platform, Joe, so folks can see you. Now, Joe ain't one of your spindle-shanked boys; he's already putting on frame, and in a year or so he'll be a full-task hand. A sharp fellow"—the auctioneer put his finger to his nose and winked—"could buy Joe cheap, feed him up, and by next planting he'd own a man, having paid a boy's price! Joe, turn 'round and pull off that shirt. Anyone see a mark on that back? Mr. Huger, he was a fine gentleman, but he weren't scared of the bullwhip, no sir. Joe never needed no whip because Joe's a respectful nigger, ain't you, Joe? Do I hear two hundred, two hundred dollars? Two, two, five, I have five. Do I hear five fifty, five fifty, five fifty? . . . Sold to Mr. Owen Ball of Magnolia Plantation."

Andrew Ravanel leaned indolently against an empty stall. His horseman's sinewy legs were cased in fawn-colored trousers, his frilled shirt was framed by the lapels of a short yellow jacket, his broad-brimmed hat was beaver felt, and his boots had the deep transparent gleam of frequent polishing. Andrew raised one indolent finger to Puryear and Kershaw as they came near. Andrew had a nighthawk's complexion, his pale skin so transparent, one could almost see his moods. There was tension under his fashionable languor, as if the fop were a coiled spring.

Edgar Puryear struck a match to light Andrew's cigar and nodded at the high yellow on the block. "Fine wench."

Henry Kershaw craned to identify the bidder. "That's old Cavanaugh. I wonder if Cavanaugh's wife knows she wants a housemaid."

"Maid she may be . . ." Andrew drawled. Henry Kershaw guffawed.

Edgar Puryear said, "Isn't that Butler's man? Isaiah Watling? There, behind the stanchion."

Andrew Ravanel said, "One wonders how he could remain at Broughton after Rhett killed his son."

"Man's cracker trash," Henry Kershaw snorted. "Overseer's jobs ain't as easy to find as sons. If Watling wants more sons, he can go to the quarters and make 'em."

Andrew Ravanel said, "But Watling is said to be pious?"

"Supposed to be. Him and Elizabeth Butler pray together every time ol' Langston's out of town. Course, there's prayin' and prayin'."

"Henry, you are a vulgar fellow," Andrew said without animosity. "Lot sixty-one. That's my Cassius."

Kershaw scratched himself where a vulgar man scratches and said, "My flask's dry. I'm off to the clubhouse. Edgar?"

"I'll stay."

Andrew opened the bidding for Cassius at four hundred dollars.

"I have four hundred. . . . Six? Sir, are you sure? Yes, sir. I have six hundred for this fine young negro. Banjo throwed in with the man—one price takes both of 'em."

"Why's Watling bidding?" Edgar Puryear asked. "Langston has no need of a banjo player."

At eight hundred, everyone had dropped out except Isaiah Watling and Andrew Ravanel.

Isaiah Watling bid nine fifty.

When Andrew Ravanel bid one thousand dollars, Watling lifted his hand until he had everyone's attention. He climbed onto a tack box, head and shoulders above the crowd. "Mr. Ravanel, sir. I have my instructions from Master Langston Butler. I'm to ask how, if you win this nigger, you will pay for him. Where's the cash to be paid today? Where's your five hundred dollars?"

Andrew Ravanel stiffened as if struck. Surprise, outrage, and embarrassment chased across his face. When Andrew turned to Edgar Allan, his friend was gone. Those closest to Andrew pretended they weren't looking at him. Those farther away concealed grins.

"Good sirs, good sirs!" the auctioneer cried.

"You gave us the rules," Watling reminded the auctioneer. "I suppose you'll stick to 'em."

Someone cried, "Yes, yes."

Another: "Rules are rules."

"Stick to the damn rules."

Andrew shouted, "Watling, by God, I'll—"

"Mr. Ravanel, I ain't actin' for Isaiah Watling. I ain't my own man no more. I'm actin' for Master Langston Butler. It's Master Butler askin' Mr. Ravanel: 'Where's your five hundred?' "

"Are you saying, my word, the sworn word of Andrew Ravanel—"

"His *word*?" an anonymous voice.

"A Ravanel's *word*?" an anonymous guffaw.

"If Mr. Ravanel ain't got it, Mr. Auctioneer, my nine hundred fifty dollars buys the nigger. I'll pay cash in full."

The news of Andrew Ravanel's humiliation (some called it his "comeuppance") flashed through the clubhouse. Jamie Fisher felt like someone had punched him under the heart.

When Jamie found his friend Andrew Ravanel was clutching the grandstand rail, white-knuckled.

"My friend Edgar saw it coming. Edgar Puryear can spot these plays a mile off. But when I turned to Edgar, Edgar wasn't there. I've seen Henry Kershaw lose a thousand on the turn of a card. But where was friend Henry?" Andrew's wounded eyes passed over the crowd, which was more indifferent to Andrew Ravanel than that young man imagined. "My little friend, Jamie Fisher. They tell me Jamie is the richest gent in the Carolinas. Five hundred dollars is pocket change to young Fisher!"

"I'm sorry, Andrew. If I'd been there . . ."

"Christ, Jamie. How can I bear it! In front of everyone—everyone! Christ! You should have heard them laughing at me. Andrew Ravanel, Andrew'll bid when he can't pay! Oh my God, Jamie, I wish I were dead!"

"Should you challenge Watling, I will second—"

"Jamie, Jamie. I cannot challenge Watling." Andrew's voice was weak as a ragpicker's horse. "Isaiah Watling is no more a gentleman than his son was. If I challenge Watling, I confess Andrew Ravanel is no gentleman."

"But Rhett fought Shad Watling."

"I don't want to talk about Rhett Butler! Jamie. I have never wished to talk about Rhett Butler! Surely I have made myself clear!" When he tried to light a cigar, his hands shook and he flung the match down. "Damn Langston Butler! I know that auctioneer; he would have taken my IOU."

"It's only a banjo player, Andrew."

" 'Only a banjo player'?" Andrew's tight laugh condescended to Jamie's naïveté. "Is Langston Butler planning a musicale? Perhaps Langston Butler wants instruction in banjo picking? Do you think so, Jamie? I think Langston Butler has purchased an unusually expensive rice hand." Andrew continued as if explaining to a child. "Langston Butler revenged himself on Jack Ravanel by humiliating his son. All Charleston has the measure of Andrew Ravanel now. Andrew Ravanel is a sham!"

Jamie Fisher's throat constricted. "Andrew, I . . . I don't know . . . Andrew. You are so fine and rare. I'd—"

Andrew cut him off with a gesture.

Negroes with Jockey Club armbands were clearing people off the track.

"Andrew?"

"For God's sake, Jamie. Won't you be silent!"

As the track emptied, a horsewoman trotted through the officials, ignoring their gestures to leave the track.

Andrew froze: a hawk who sees its future. He breathed, "Why, there's Rosemary."

"Looking for you, surely." Relief at the distraction lifted Jamie's voice an octave. "Andrew, I must tell you about Juliet's amusing wager. . . ."

"Oh dear, Jamie. Something's wrong. Rosemary's upset. Look how she saws the bit, asks her horse to trot, then curbs it."

Jockey Club functionaries cried, "Miss!" and "The race, miss!" but jumped out of her way. Rosemary searched faces along the rail, her yellow silk scarf streaming behind her, a defiant banner.

"My," Andrew Ravanel said thoughtfully, "Rosemary *is* angry, isn't she?"

Rosemary's horse reared when she jerked its reins. "Goddamn you, horse, settle! Andrew! Where is my father? Have you seen my father?"

Andrew Ravanel fell into a deep, cool stillness. Time had slowed to this simple moment. "Beautiful Rosemary," Andrew said almost wistfully, "your esteemed parent has left the racecourse."

A Jockey Club steward, a white man with a his green sash of office, hurried toward them. "Madam! Madam!"

"Damn you, horse! Damn you! *Will* you stand still!" Rosemary used her quirt. "I must find my father." Rosemary's face twisted. "I have news. This day I have learned why my father is truly damned."

With an imperious gesture, Andrew Ravanel stopped the steward in his tracks, stepped onto the track, caught Rosemary's bridle, and brought her agitated horse to a standstill.

One steward, one horsewoman, one gentleman holding her horse—otherwise, the racecourse was empty.

The rage at the core of their tableau drew every eye.

On the clubhouse veranda, a Yankee visitor turned to his Charleston host, "What the devil?"

His host replied, "You're in Charleston now, Sam. Enjoy the fireworks."

If Rosemary hadn't been adrift in helpless, inarticulate fury, she would have been alerted by Andrew's too-sweet tone. "Stay a moment, dear Rosemary. We'll sort things out. Here, let me help." Andrew formed a stirrup with his hands.

Hastily, Rosemary dismounted. "Must I still call Langston Butler 'father,' Andrew? He has lied to me. He has destroyed my brother. He . . ."

"Langston Butler has so much to answer for."

Andrew Ravanel took Rosemary into his arms and, in the full view of all Charleston, kissed her fiercely and lingeringly on the lips.

Chapter Seven

Matrimony Is an Honorable Estate . . .

I believe Rosemary rather enjoyed it," Andrew Ravanel said carelessly.

Andrew, his father, Jack, and Langston Butler stood in the foyer of Colonel Jack's King Street town house. The room had been hard used—the broad plank floor scarred by spurs, the benches scuffed from serving as bootjacks.

Butler had neither removed his hat nor relinquished his cane to the stand. He gripped that cane as if it might become a weapon. "My daughter's romantic impulses are not at issue."

Langston Butler emptied a pouch onto the hall table. His disdainful index finger stirred the due bills, notes, and promises to pay. "Twenty cents on the dollar is the fair market value of Ravanel honor."

"Perhaps, sir, you intend my son to be affianced to your daughter?" Colonel Jack hoped.

"A Ravanel for a son-in-law?" Red spots blossomed on Langston Butler's pale cheeks. "A Ravanel for *my* son-in-law?"

Andrew Ravanel took a step forward, but his father caught his arm.

"I have come to advise I have purchased your notes and mortgages and they are of this date due and payable. This house and your remaining properties will be sold to satisfy your debts. Henceforth, Chapultapec will race under Butler colors."

"Now Langston." Colonel Jack chuckled. "You didn't come to our humble home to possess it. Butlers grabbed Jack's good lands already, and an agriculturalist like yourself doesn't covet the poor ground I still hold.

I know you, Langston. I've known you since you were a grasping, flint-hearted, arrogant boy. You've a proposition for Old Jack, some little *arrangement* to quell gossip and, may I suggest, improve the Ravanel fortunes to a modest degree? Have I the right of it, sir?"

Langston smiled a singularly unpleasant smile. "Your wife, Frances, was widely admired, Jack. There was no more gracious gentlewoman in the Low Country."

Jack Ravanel went white. "You will not speak of my wife, Langston. You will not sully her precious name."

Langston tapped the heaped notes. "Do I have your undivided attention? Tonight at the Jockey Club Ball, I shall announce my daughter's engagement to Mr. John Haynes. After my announcement, your son will make a public apology for any misunderstanding caused by his unseemly behavior at the racetrack this afternoon." Langston turned a cold eye on Andrew. "Perhaps you were inebriated, sir. Perhaps you were so overcome with joy on learning of my daughter's betrothal you forgot yourself." Langston shrugged. "I leave the details to you. If you cannot tell a plausible lie, I daresay your father can coach you. After I accept your apology, you will announce your engagement to Miss Charlotte Fisher."

"Sir, I would not marry that girl if every blemish on her face were worth ten thousand dollars."

"As you wish." Langston Butler waited silently while the Ravanels, father and son, uttered all the hot, helpless words they had to utter before accepting the inevitable.

In the face of her granddaughter's joy, Constance Fisher reluctantly acceded to her engagement to Andrew Ravanel.

To escape her father's house, Rosemary agreed to marry John Haynes; what Tunis had told her made living there intolerable. When she said as much, Langston replied, "I do not ask why you obey, merely that you do."

When the betrothed couple met privately in Langston Butler's drawing room, John Haynes said, "Rosemary, this is more than I ever had dared to hope." He knelt before her. "Although I fear your answer, dearest, I must know. Is our marriage *your* decision?"

Rosemary hesitated before saying, "John, I shall try."

Stolid, respectable John Haynes became a happy, grinning boy. "Well then. Dear me. Well then. Nothing fairer. Dearest Rosemary. My dearest Rosemary . . ."

Charlotte and Andrew were married in April, and Charlotte was, if not a beautiful bride, a radiant one. Charleston matrons clicked their tongues and hoped marriage would steady Andrew Ravanel.

Langston Butler gave a certain negro banjo player to Mr. and Mrs. Ravanel. Even Isaiah Watling hadn't been able to turn Cassius into a rice hand.

Two weeks later, when Rosemary and John Haynes stood before St. Michael's altar, John glowed with happiness. Rosemary was wan, and uttered her vows so quietly, few behind the front pews heard them.

As the couple emerged from the church, Tunis Bonneau waited at the curb, holding a roan horse by its bridle.

"My God," Rosemary said. "Tecumseh!"

"Your brother Rhett gives him to you and Mr. Haynes, Miss Rosemary," Tunis said. "He writes that he is wishin' you happiness on your wedding day."

Langston Butler turned to his new son-in-law. "Sir, I will take that animal and dispose of it."

John Haynes squeezed his bride's hand. "Thank you sir, but no. The horse is a gift from my friend and Mrs. Haynes's brother which she, and I, accept with pleasure."

Chapter Eight

A Patriotic Ball

Few Charlestonians believed Andrew Ravanel's racecourse kiss had been as innocent as that gentleman afterward claimed, but the compromised parties were safely married. On the strength of Andrew's new Fisher connections, Langston Butler quietly unloaded Colonel Jack's notes at fifty cents on the dollar.

Mr. and Mrs. John Haynes were seen about Charleston in a handsome blue sulky with Tecumseh in the shafts. John Haynes had paid three hundred for the rig—on his bride's whim, it was reported.

Some said Rhett Butler had been seen in New York. An English ship captain told John Haynes his brother-in-law was speculating on the London bourse. Tunis Bonneau, who was now Haynes & Son's chief pilot, said Rhett was in New Orleans.

Although the Hayneses showed proper deference to Rosemary's parents and exchanged pleasantries after Sunday services, the younger couple retained their separate pew and Rosemary visited her mother only when her father was out of town. Mr. and Mrs. Haynes resided quietly at 46 Church Street and in due course were blessed with a daughter they christened Margaret Ann.

Mr. and Mrs. Andrew Ravanel took up housekeeping in the Fishers' East Bay establishment. Charleston's moneylenders were dismayed to learn Constance Fisher would not be responsible for Ravanel debts.

Andrew Ravanel's new manservant, Cassius, accompanied Andrew everywhere, waiting outside gambling hells or saloons until all hours. Often,

Cassius led his master's horse home at daybreak, with Andrew nodding in the saddle. When Andrew, Jamie Fisher, Henry Kershaw, and Edgar Allan Puryear went hunting, Cassius cooked their simple meals, blacked their boots, and picked lively tunes. Henry Kershaw insisted that Cassius's sojourn in Langston Butler's rice fields had improved the negro's picking. Cassius's music had become more, Henry vowed, "heartfelt."

After Grandmother Fisher deplored Andrew's habits once too often, Mr. and Mrs. Ravanel quit Charlotte's childhood home for Colonel Jack's shabby town house, where the couple abided with that gentleman and his daughter, Juliet.

In happier times, these matters might have excited greater curiosity, but these were not happy times. "Secession"—for thirty years the firebrands' whisper—had become a full-throated shout.

On October 16, 1859, John Brown murdered the peace. John Brown discredited peacemakers, sundered families into Unionists and Secessionists, and divided Presbyterians, Episcopalians, and Baptists into Northern and Southern congregations. With a handful of men, vague plans, and a willingness to murder for principle, John Brown descended on Harpers Ferry, Virginia, intending to spark a slave insurrection. Brown brought a thousand sharp steel pikes for the slaves to use on their masters.

Low Country planters had a blood fear of insurrections. French refugees from the Santa Domingue insurrection (Eulalie Ward's parents, the Robillards, among them) had arrived with dreadful stories of innocents murdered in their beds, ravished women, infants' brains dashed out against doorsills. Nat Turner's and Denmark Vesey's slave insurrections had failed, but John Brown was a white man backed and financed by white men. Some Yankees claimed the murderer was a saint.

After Brown's raid, moderates were discredited, firebrands like Langston Butler controlled the legislature, and ordinarily prudent men hung on their every word. Cathecarte Puryear was voted out of the St. Cecilia Society.

Although John Brown was captured, tried, and hanged, Low Country militias were forming before his body cooled: the Palmetto Brigade, the Charleston Rifles, the Charleston Light Horse, Hampton's Legion. British ships delivered rifles, cannons, and military uniforms to Charleston's wharves. Young men swore off drinking, and gambling hells fell on hard times. Cassius mastered new patriotic tunes as they were written.

The year between Brown's raid and Abraham Lincoln's election was rife with omens. Seven pilot whales stranded themselves on the sands of Sullivan's Island. Geese flew south two months earlier than usual. The rice crop was the most bountiful in living memory. Negro conjure men muttered and prophesied Armageddon. Jamie Fisher told his sister, Charlotte, he felt like a bird hypnotized by a snake.

Andrew Ravanel was elected captain of the Charleston Light Horse. When a subscription was begun to provide uniforms for the elite militia company, differences were set aside and Langston Butler made a generous contribution.

One Saturday morning in early November, Colonel Jack Ravanel was found dead on the breakwater behind Adger's Wharf. Although Tunis Bonneau's father-in-law, the Reverend William Prescott, mentioned the old sinner's demise in his Sunday sermon, Old Jack's passing went otherwise unremarked. Charleston's attention was fixed on the presidential election to be held the following Tuesday.

Of the four presidential candidates that year, only one was thought to be an outright abolitionist, and though that man received almost three million fewer votes than his rivals and not a single vote in ten Southern states, that man was elected President. Many white Southerners believed the only distinction between President Abraham Lincoln and John Brown was that John Brown was dead.

Just six weeks after Lincoln's election, the Convention of the People of South Carolina met to briefly debate, then unanimously adopt an Ordinance of Secession. Church bells pealed, militiamen marched, and bonfires roared in the streets.

The new militias drilled on the Washington Racecourse. The Charleston Light Horse wore gray pantaloons, high cordovan boots, and a short green jacket crisscrossed with gold braid. Enlisted men had gray kepis; officers wore a black planter's hat embellished with an egret's plume.

Edgar Puryear and Henry Kershaw were elected lieutenants and Jamie Fisher was enrolled as Chief of Scouts.

Charleston's ladies turned out to admire the Light Horse's agreeably frightening drills: left hand on the reins, right on the saber, each bold rider drawing his blade in a flashing silver arc before crashing through the ranks of straw dummies. The dummies carried broomstick rifles and were dressed in Federal blue.

The ladies admired these young men who had spurned the dishonored red, white, and blue for the brave new palmetto banner.

Rosemary Haynes cheered until she was hoarse.

Andrew Ravanel was transformed. The melancholic roisterer became cheerful; the man who'd been oblivious of other's sensitivities became solicitous. As a servant of the new republic, Andrew Ravanel became a king.

Like thieves in the night, Charleston's Federal garrison withdrew itself into Fort Sumter, the powerful island fortress in the heart of Charleston harbor. Indignant Charlestonians protested this seizure of Carolina property and Mr. Lincoln was informed that any attempt to relieve or supply Fort Sumter would be severely rebuked.

When she came home to her own doorstep after a morning applauding cavalry drills, Rosemary's heart sank. She took a deep breath and comforted herself: Meg is waiting for me. Those mornings the Light Horse didn't drill, Rosemary woke with a headache and stayed in bed until noon.

Rosemary Butler Haynes knew she mustn't give in to disaffection. John Haynes was a good man. Had John Haynes ever claimed to be a horseman? On the contrary, he joked about his poor seat. If John Haynes's fingers were ink-stained, John was in trade: how could they not be stained?

Yet some mornings after her husband left for work, sitting alone, the memory of Andrew Ravanel's kiss overwhelmed her. A chasm had opened between her and Charlotte. When her old friend called at 46 Church Street, "Miss Rosemary, she ain't at home"; "Miss Rosemary, she indisposed." How could Rosemary chat with the old friend who shared Andrew's home, his life, his bright hopes, his bed?

Rosemary tried very hard to banish regrets for what her life might have been.

Rosemary's husband brought small gifts; a silver bud vase, a rose-gold filigree brooch. Was it John's fault the vase was too fussy and the brooch didn't match anything Rosemary wore?

John never talked politics and never watched the Light Horse drills. He even defended Charleston's few remaining Unionists: "Can't we differ without impugning honest men?" Every morning excepting the Sabbath, John walked from Church Street to his office on the Haynes & Son wharf. All day, he negotiated with ship captains, shippers, consignors, and insurers. One spring evening, Rosemary happened to be at the front windows as her husband hurried up the steps of his home, a glad smile flickering on his lips. Thereafter, she avoided the front windows when John was due. Rosemary stayed in her room while John played with Meg for an hour before supper.

After supper, they heard Meg say her simple prayers and put her to bed. Then John Haynes read aloud to Rosemary from Bulwer-Lytton or some other improving novelist. "Of course, my dear, if you'd prefer something lighter? One of Mr. Scott's works?"

John concluded every evening with prayers for Charleston and the South. He prayed its leaders would be wise. He prayed for the health and happiness of friends and kinfolk, one at a time, naming each. At the top of the stairs, as they turned to their separate bedrooms, John Haynes sometimes inquired hopefully how his wife was feeling.

"No dear," Rosemary would murmur. "Not tonight."

Sometimes, Rosemary felt so guilty that she'd say too brightly, "Oh, I feel fine, John." Her husband would spend the night with her and depart the house next morning whistling. Rosemary desperately wished John wouldn't whistle. Whistling gave her a headache.

Their little daughter was Rosemary and John's shared joy.

The father said, "When I drove little Meg to White Point Park, she stood up in her yellow shawl and saluted the soldiers. When a cavalryman drew his saber to return her little salute, the blade's scrape against its scabbard frightened Meg and our poor darling burst into tears."

The mother said, "Did you see what our scamp did with her blue shoes? She never liked them, so she told Cleo to give them to some poorer child. 'I gots too many shoes.' "

Mississippi, Florida, Alabama, Georgia, Louisiana, and Texas followed South Carolina out of the Union.

Although that January was exceptionally cold—there'd been snow in the Piedmont—Charlestonians ignored the discomfort to attend the first Race Week ever held in an independent South Carolina.

John Haynes had canceled his New York and Philadelphia excursion boats but filled vacancies with Richmond and Baltimore tourists.

Judges of horseflesh said Langston Butler's Gero's matchup with John Cantey's Albine was the most thrilling race in a hundred years; it was rumored Butler had turned down $25,000 for Gero.

Hibernian Hall had been decorated in patriotic motifs for the St. Cecilia Society ball. The gay banners of Charleston's militia companies adorned the walls and a ferocious (if somewhat cockeyed) eagle had been painted upon the dance floor.

As a ball manager, John Haynes wore a white boutonniere.

The society's orchestra was composed of house servants spared from their usual duties. It was a standing Charleston joke that Horace, the orchestra master, could not read a note of the music he arranged so fussily before him. Nevertheless, his versatile orchestra performed stately French quadrilles as well as the exuberant reels the young people preferred—reels driven by Cassius's flashing banjo.

This evening on the brink of war, Charleston's belles had never been more beautiful. These young virgins were every grace and prayer for which brave men have ever fought and died. No one in the ballroom that night ever forgot their heartbreaking beauty.

Their squires were solemn and proud under the grave responsibilities thrust upon them. Not far beneath their visible bravado was each young man's desperate hope that he might prove worthy when the test came.

War fever pushed gaiety toward hysteria. Would the Federals abandon

Fort Sumter, or must it be shelled into submission? Would Virginia and North Carolina secede? Langston Butler and Wade Hampton were in Montgomery, Alabama, to help choose a provisional president for the new Confederate States of America. Toombs, Yancey, Davis—who would be the man of the hour?

Why, Jamie," Rosemary said, "why aren't you in uniform?"

"I look like a jumped-up monkey in my uniform," the slender youth admitted.

Rosemary's face was flushed with excitement. "Will we go to war, Jamie? It's awful of me, but I hope we will."

"Andrew is bloodthirsty, too." Jamie shuddered. "Look at him. Wearing spurs at the St. Cecilia Ball! Dear me."

Andrew Ravanel smiled at her.

Rosemary wouldn't meet his eye. "And you, Jamie? How is it with you?"

Jamie Fisher shrugged. "I am not warlike. Oh, I'll fight if I must, but war will be so darned uncomfortable." His ironic smile dropped from his lips. "What will war do to our horses? What do horses care about politics?"

Juliet Ravanel tapped Jamie's elbow with her fan. Miss Ravanel was much in demand as a regimental flag embroiderer, and her new prominence had mellowed her. Her taffeta ball gown was perfectly cut and sewed but, alas, purple was just not Juliet's color. "Mrs. Haynes." She mock-curtsied. "Isn't this a gala? Is your card filled?"

"What dances John didn't take, elderly Haynes cousins have. Balding men with wooden teeth and execrable breath are eager to squire their captivating kinswoman."

Miss Ravanel examined her card, "Jamie, I have two waltzes and the promenade open."

"Do you promise not to lead?"

Juliet's smile could have frozen salt water.

Provided his partner was careful of her toes during intricate figures, John Haynes could manage a quadrille. Rosemary smiled fixedly during the deux temps. "Sorry, dear," her husband whispered. "Mercy. What a clodhopper I am." John's hand on her back was flat as a meat platter, and his hand at her waist was thick and possessive. Bowing afterward, John said earnestly, "Rosemary, you are the most beautiful woman in the hall. I am the happiest husband in South Carolina."

Rosemary fought the urge to reclaim her hand. "Only South Carolina?" she managed to say.

"In the world. On every blessed continent of the blessed world." His plump, warm lips kissed her hand.

Another deux temps, a promenade. As they were forming for the quadrille, there was a stir at the door and a manager hurried up to them. John bent his head to the man's whisper.

John Haynes turned to his wife. "Dearest, I must go to the wharf. Someone has landed munitions that may have been intended for the Yankees. Give others my dances. Please don't let me spoil your evening."

Rosemary promised.

Ten minutes after John Haynes left, Andrew Ravanel was at Rosemary's side. He smelled strongly of bay rum and slightly of perspiration. His bow was lavish. "Rosemary . . ."

"Captain Ravanel, are we speaking?"

Andrew's smile was wistful. "You have every right to be angry. I am the worst scoundrel in the Low Country."

"The last time we were on familiar terms, sir, you compromised me. I believe I owe you my matrimonial status."

"Are you the worse off? Surely John Haynes is an . . . adequate husband."

Rosemary narrowed her eyes. "Take care, sir."

Andrew's eyebrows raised in mock surprise. "If I have given fresh offense . . ."

"I haven't forgiven you for your earlier offense," Rosemary said.

"I haven't forgiven myself! I lie awake wondering if my mad kiss was worth the reckoning. But Rosemary, wasn't that a transporting moment? God! I will never forget how . . . Rosemary, I despise irony. Don't you hate it, too? How *ironic* that my declaration of love should drive us apart—each into another's arms."

"Declaration of love? Captain, am I an idiot? Do you think I might mistake what you did for a declaration of love?"

Andrew put a hand over his heart. "When I am mortally wounded, on some distant battlefield, my last thoughts will be of that kiss. Would you let me go to war without a waltz?"

"In that extremis, sir, one's last thoughts are of one's beloved. As you pass to your eternal reward, it will be Charlotte's face you will recall, not mine. Unless, of course, a more recent conquest pushes Charlotte aside."

Andrew flushed, then laughed so infectiously nearby couples smiled. Andrew laid his hand upon his heart. "Rosemary, I cannot promise fidelity, but I guarantee your exclusive possession of my last thoughts."

"There won't be a war anyway."

"Dear Rosemary, of course there'll be a war. Our uniforms are pressed, swords honed, and pistols primed. Rosemary, the orchestra is tuning. I haven't forgotten what a marvelous dancer you are."

Dancing with Andrew Ravanel was a dangerous, brilliant conversation. Andrew anticipated her nuances and enhanced them; his rhythms reflected Rosemary's and commented upon them.

The music—one of Mr. Strauss's waltzes in three-quarter time—ended too soon. As other dancers were honoring their partners, Rosemary fluttered her fan.

"Another?"

Andrew Ravanel danced all John Haynes's dances. During the first intermission, Grandmother Fisher took Rosemary aside. "Charlotte has left in tears! Rosemary, think what you are doing!"

But Rosemary couldn't think about it. She had denied herself too long.

At midnight, after the quadrille, couples promenaded into the dining room for the cold collation. Men stepped out onto the piazza to smoke and the scent of tobacco wafted into the too-hot high-ceilinged dining room. Men and women Rosemary had known all her life wouldn't meet her eye. She might have been invisible.

"As well be hung for a sheep . . ." Andrew murmured in her ear, and then called, "Henry Kershaw, you rogue. Will you take supper with us?"

Us? *Us?* Rosemary hadn't thought to become an *us.* "No," she blurted, jerking her arm from Andrew Ravanel's.

Gentlemen moved aside when Rosemary fled onto the piazza. Across the street, in the circle of gaslight outside Garrity's saloon, drunken militiamen were singing.

Damn, damn, damn!

Constance Fisher joined her, pulling her shawl close. "Child, where is your cloak?"

Rosemary shook her head.

"I must say, my dear . . ."

Tears flooded Rosemary's cheeks, "Oh, Grandmother Fisher, I am a fool, such a fool. Whatever have I done?"

The old woman relaxed slightly. "Child, you have been extremely unwise."

"What must John think? What will Charlotte?"

"Were she I . . ." The older woman warned.

"Oh, Grandmother Fisher! What shall I do?" Rosemary grasped the balustrade to steady herself.

Grandmother Fisher gripped her shoulders. "You will do what Charleston ladies do. Presented with mulatto children who resemble their husbands like peas in a pod; awakened by their husbands' drunken footfalls approaching their bed you will do what Charleston ladies have always done: you will fix a smile on your face and pretend that God's in His heavens and nothing—absolutely nothing—is wrong in His world."

For the rest of that evening, Rosemary sat with Constance Fisher. When Andrew Ravanel sought to approach, his wife's grandmother's glare repelled him.

Andrew whirled by with the youngest, loveliest maiden at the ball. The girl never took her adoring eyes off the chevalier.

He is a magnet, Rosemary thought. What does a magnet think of consequences?

Very late in the evening, there was a flurry at the doorway. John Haynes bustled toward his wife, beaming with pleasure. He shrugged off Juliet Ravanel's importuning hand with, "Another time, Juliet, please."

The dark-haired gentleman who'd followed John Haynes into Hibernian Hall gave his cloak to a footman. Horace, the orchestra leader, lost the beat, and the musicians faltered. Gradually, dancers stopped, turned, stared.

Rosemary gasped.

A red carnation adorned Rhett Butler's wide velvet lapels. His shirtfront was resplendent with ruffles; his studs were gold nuggets the size of peas. He held a wide-brimmed planter's hat at his side. Her brother's hands were so much bigger than Rosemary remembered.

"Evening, Cap'n Butler," Horace said. "We ain't seen you in such a spell."

"Evening, Horace. And you—you must be Cassius, the banjo man? You're known, son. They've heard about your picking as far away as New Orleans."

Cassius struck three high lonesome chords. "Sir, thank you, sir. I reckon everybody's heard of Cap'n Butler."

Rhett raised his hands. "Please don't stop the dancing on my account. Don't let me interrupt your festivities. There's far much too much to celebrate. Who would have predicted brave Charleston would goad the sleeping Federal giant?" When Rhett Butler bowed, his black hair gleamed.

"Edgar Puryear. So you're an officer now. Is that Henry Kershaw? My God, it's *Lieutenant* Henry Kershaw? And my old friend Andrew . . ."

Andrew Ravanel was speechless, transfixed.

The laugh lines at the corners of Rosemary's brother's eyes were familiar and dear. How could she have forgotten how graceful he was? Rosemary walked to him as if in a dream.

Rhett's eyes stopped laughing.

Cassius struck the first gentle notes of Stephen Foster's "Slumber My Darling" and paused.

"Little Rosemary, my beloved sister." Her brother's eyes were moist as he took her hands. "May I have the honor of this dance?"

Chapter Nine

A Barbecue at a Georgia Plantation

Rhett Butler hadn't felt so helpless since that night twelve years ago, when he drank whiskey on Colonel Jack's porch and found nothing worth living for.

Fort Sumter fired upon! What did the fools think they were playing at!

Rhett said, "I'll take delivery at the railhead, Mr. Kennedy, my Atlanta bank will honor the draft."

Frank Kennedy stroked his skimpy gingerish beard and turned Rhett's check over, as if there might be more information on the blank side. "Yes, of course," he said. "Of course . . ."

"If you are worried . . ."

"Oh no, Mr. Butler. No sir." Frank Kennedy shook his head too vigorously.

The two men stood in the main room of Kennedy's Jonesboro store. Hay cradles, smoked hams, and pitchforks hung from the rafters. Aisles were crammed with dry goods and farm supplies. The store stank of liniment, molasses, and pine tar.

The respectable citizens of Charleston, Langston Butler among them, had ignited a war! The smug, virtuous, hymn-singing, damnable fools!

A negro clerk was cautiously ladling turpentine into an earthenware crock, another swept the floor. Despite his unprepossessing appearance, Kennedy was a man of consequence who owned fifty slaves, a second store in Atlanta, and thousands of acres in prime Georgia cotton.

Rhett had bought Kennedy's stored crop and stood to make a fortune. He should have felt good about that.

He felt like hell.

"Your business reputation is excellent." Kennedy blinked and backtracked. "I mean . . ."

Rhett was expressionless. "Some say I'm a renegade."

Kennedy ran a hand through his hair. "No offense, sir. I meant no offense." He folded Rhett's check and inserted it into his wallet. Having pocketed the wallet, he patted his pocket.

Rhett Butler didn't voice his opinion that renegades might rob you or call you out but they wouldn't fuss you to death.

A thought struck the embarrassed merchant. "Say, Butler." Unconsciously, Kennedy patted his pocket again. "Have you anything on this afternoon? Wouldn't you like a day in the country? John Wilkes's son is getting engaged and John is hosting a barbecue. Everyone's invited. Twelve Oaks' hospitality . . . why, I can't praise it too much." His face went blank as he sought an encomium. "Twelve Oaks' hospitality is famous!" He pointed more or less northward. "All the way to Atlanta. Please join me. I'll bring you back in time for your train."

Since Rhett's train wouldn't leave until ten that evening and, in his dismal state of mind, an afternoon in the Jonesboro Hotel would be an eternity, Rhett Kershaw Butler accepted Frank Kennedy's invitation. More often than we care to admit, inconsequential decisions change our lives.

Kennedy's buggy rolled past thickets of tender glowing redbuds. Spice bushes perfumed the air. Dogwoods shimmered like ghosts in the woods beside the road.

This display, north Georgia at its most beautiful, plucked at Rhett's heart. He'd wintered in Manhattan, where war talk dominated every dining room and gentleman's club. Rhett had heard Abraham Lincoln speak at Cooper Union and thought the gangling, long-faced westerner would make a formidable enemy. A hundred thousand Yankees were forming into regiments. He'd traveled to New Haven, where a gun maker told the affable

Mr. Butler he couldn't find the machinery he needed. "I have more contracts than I can fill," the man complained. "Butler, can you help me buy barrel lathes?"

One Sunday afternoon, Rhett toured the Brooklyn Navy Yard, where a hundred warships were being fitted. Hammering and forging and coppering hulls and painters on scaffolds and hundreds of women sewing in the sail lofts. On a Sunday.

As the South prepared to fight Goliath with gallantry.

Damn the fools!

Rhett Butler loved the Southland's gentle courtesies and hospitality, the fiery tempers just beneath languid drawls. But if a fact was disagreeable, Southerners disbelieved that fact. For how could fact outfight gallantry?

Frank Kennedy misinterpreted Rhett's silence as a stranger's unease crashing a party whose host he'd never met. Frank provided reassurances. Their host, John Wilkes, was "a Georgia gentleman of the old school" and Wilkes's son, Ashley, although younger, of course, was of the old school, too. Ashley's bride-to-be was "a little slip of a thing," but Melanie Hamilton was, Frank assured Rhett, "a Spark."

Getting no response from his guest, Frank went on to name the young bloods who'd be there: the Tarletons, the Calverts, the Munroes, and the Fontaines. "When Tony Fontaine shot Brent Tarleton in the leg—both of them were drunk as lords!—they made a joke of it! A joke!" He shook his head: deploring men he half wished to be.

Rhett Butler wasn't too sentimental to profit from Southern blunders. The South grew two-thirds of the world's cotton and Rhett knew Lincoln's navy would blockade the Southern ports. After the ports were closed, cotton prices would skyrocket. Rhett's cotton would be safe in the Bahamas before Federal blockaders came on station.

The money was nothing: ashes in his mouth. Rhett felt like a grown-up watching children playing games. They yelled, they gestured, they pretended to be Indians or Redcoats or Yankee soldiers. They strutted and played at war. It made Rhett Butler want to weep. He was helpless to prevent it. Utterly helpless.

His guest's silence made Frank Kennedy uncomfortable. He babbled, "John Wilkes is no rustic, Mr. Butler. No indeed. The Wilkeses' library has so many books; why, I expect John has hundreds of books! John Wilkes has read everything a gentleman should read and his son, Ashley, takes after John. As they say, 'The apple never falls far from the tree.' You'll meet Gerald O'Hara, too. Fine fellow! Gerald's from Savannah. Not originally, of course, originally, Gerald's from Ireland. Not that I have anything against the Irish. I'm keeping company with his daughter Suellen, so I couldn't have anything against the Irish, ha, ha."

When he looked for Rhett's reply, Rhett's eyes were remote. "At any rate," Frank filled the silence, "Gerald bought Tara Plantation and that's how Gerald came to Clayton County." Frank gave his horse a stern look. "Suellen is a peach." Frank slapped his knee. "A Georgia peach."

They continued in silence.

Rhett was picturing Charleston, where men who'd been Rhett's schoolmates were manning guns hammering Fort Sumter while their elders made speeches each more belligerent than the last.

Might Rhett persuade Rosemary and John to leave? "Just until this shakes out, John. California has opportunities for a man like you. Or London, John. Wouldn't your Meg love to visit London? And Rosemary . . ."

Andrew Ravanel and Rosemary had created a scandal at that patriotic ball. John and Rosemary weren't speaking.

"My Suellen can be 'sharpish,' " Frank Kennedy was saying. "But she soon repents. You're a man of the world, Butler. You know what I mean."

Rhett held his sharpish tongue.

They forded the Flint River and trotted briskly up a rise. The flat-roofed, many-chimneyed plantation house was smaller than Broughton but grand enough for all that. Broad Corinthian columns supported a roof that shaded broad verandas on three sides of the house.

"You'll see for yourself," Frank Kennedy insisted. "Twelve Oaks' hospitality—why, it's legendary!"

There was a bustle at the turnaround, where riders dismounted and carriages disgorged their occupants. Negro grooms removed horses and rigs while guests exchanged enthusiastic greetings with neighbors they hadn't seen since last week.

The tang of barbecued pork flavored the hickory smoke.

On the veranda, maidens in their prettiest outfits flirted with beaux in tight gray trousers and ruffled linen shirts. Older folks solemnly considered symptoms and remedies while children darted like barn swallows across the lawn.

Was this the last glorious, graceful Southern afternoon? Or was it the Southland's funeral?

Frank and Rhett were greeted by a white-haired patrician with a young woman at his side. "John Wilkes, John's daughter, Miss Honey Wilkes: Mr. Rhett Butler. Mr. Butler and I had business today and I thought we'd flee our cares for a while. John, I hope you don't mind."

"My home is open to any gentleman," John Wilkes said simply. "Welcome, sir, to Twelve Oaks."

"You are too kind."

"Your accent, sir?"

"The Low Country, sir, born and reared."

Wilkes frowned, "Butler . . . Rhett Butler . . . Wasn't there . . . Don't I recall . . . ?"

The flicker in the older man's eyes told Rhett that Wilkes had indeed 'recalled' . . . but Wilkes's smile never faltered. "No matter, I suppose. Tom! Bring the salver. Mr. Kennedy and Mr. Butler have had a dusty journey."

Honey Wilkes was waving eagerly. "Oh look, Daddy. It's the O'Haras. Frank Kennedy! Shame on you! Aren't you going to help Suellen down?"

Frank hastened to his duty. With a polite nod to his host, Rhett withdrew to a quiet corner of the veranda. He wished he hadn't come.

Twelve Oaks buzzed like a honeybee swarm on its mating flight. There'd be marriages made today and doubtless a scandal or two. Swirling through the floral and Parisian perfumes, amid the gaiety, flirting, and jests was romance, as fresh as if no man or maid had experienced romance before.

Rhett's eyes fell on a very young woman in a green dancing frock and his heart surged. "Dear God," he whispered.

She wasn't a great beauty: her chin was pointed and her jaw had too much strength. She was fashionably pale—ladies never exposed their skin to the brutal sun—and unusually animated. As Rhett watched, she touched a young buck's arm both intimately and carelessly.

When the girl felt Rhett's gaze she looked up. For one scorching second, her puzzled green eyes met his black eyes before she tossed her head dismissively and resumed her flirtation.

Forgotten the looming War. Forgotten the devastation he expected. Hope welled up in Rhett Butler like a healing spring. "My God." Rhett moistened dry lips. "She's just like me!"

His heart slowed. He looked away, smiling at himself. It had been a long time since he'd made a fool of himself over a woman.

Rhett followed his nose around the plantation house to the barbecue where, scattered under shade trees, picnic tables were draped with Belgian linen and laid with English silver and French china. He took a seat at a half-empty table and a servant delivered Rhett's plate and glass of wine. When his thoughts circled back to that girl he shook his head and drank a second glass of wine.

Although the pork had a deep, smoky flavor and the potato salad was a perfect admixture of tart and sweet, two drunk young bucks at the foot of the table were glowering at the stranger, and before long they'd make a remark that couldn't be overlooked. Rhett refused dessert and decamped to the shade of a venerable black walnut tree to light a cigar. When John Wilkes joined him, Rhett complimented his host. "Hospitality like yours, sir, stops at the Mason-Dixon line. Hospitality cannot survive Yankee winters."

"You are too kind. Mr. Kennedy tells me you've been up north recently."

"Yes, sir."

"Will they fight?"

"They will. Abraham Lincoln won't show a white flag."

"But surely, our brave young men . . ."

"Mr. Wilkes, I am a stranger and you welcomed me to your home. I believe that defines the Good Samaritan. I am grateful, sir."

"Too grateful to tell your host what you think of Confederate prospects?"

"Mr. Kennedy says you have a fine library. Perhaps, later, you can show it to me."

That girl—the green-eyed girl in the dancing frock—had seated herself among her beaux, and her rosewood ottoman might have been a throne. She was a princess; no, a young queen among favored cavaliers. The girl was responding too eagerly to compliments and jests, almost as if she were an ingenue overplaying her first big part.

"Fiddle-dee-dee!" she derided an admirer's inept sally.

Despite Suellen O'Hara's obvious dismay, Frank Kennedy was fetching this girl dainties—although any of Wilkes's servants could have performed that humble chore. Rhett half expected the man to kneel.

Wilkes followed Rhett's eyes. "Scarlett O'Hara. Beautiful, isn't she?"

"Scarlett," Rhett savored the name. "Yes, she is."

"I'm afraid our Scarlett's a heartbreaker."

"She's never met a man who understood her."

Wilkes misread Rhett's intensity and frowned, "Aren't beaux and balls what a young lady should concern herself with? Would you rather Scarlett trouble her pretty head with war and armies and politics?"

"I hope to God she'll never need to," Rhett replied. "There are worse things than beauty and innocence."

"My son, Ashley, has enlisted." Wilkes indicated a slender young man seated cross-legged beside the girl who must be his fiancée. Ashley Wilkes was his father's son: tall, gray-eyed, and blond with an aristocrat's confident grace. His fiancée laughed prettily at some private jest.

Wilkes unburdened himself with this stranger precisely because Rhett *was* a stranger. "Some of my acquaintances—influential, far-seeing men—are exiling their sons to Europe."

"Mr. Wilkes, there are no good decisions left to us, only painful ones."

Wilkes sighed heavily, "I suppose you're right." He became the host again with "Excuse me. I believe the Tarleton twins have lingered too long at the brandy cask."

Scarlett flirted, demurely accepted each compliment, flattered outrageously and, from time to time, beneath lowered eyelids Miss O'Hara cast glances at . . . young Wilkes? Oh yes, she did. And Rhett caught her doing it.

Whispering confidences to an admirer, Scarlett looked past the man's shoulder to Wilkes. When she caught Rhett's eye again Rhett laughed. Because he understood. Oh yes, he did. The heartbreaker was using the besotted males to make Ashley Wilkes jealous. For Wilkes's sake, she'd bewitched every available male—as well as some, like Frank Kennedy, who weren't as available as they might have wished.

Apparently the heartbreaker was heartsick for another woman's prize. Poor, lovely, unhappy child!

At Rhett's laughter, Scarlett O'Hara flushed to her roots before refuging among her admirers.

It was inevitable. Some fool would mention the unmentionable, what every person here was trying to ignore. The fatal words "Fort Sumter" were uttered and the romantic languor of a spring afternoon vanished like a dream.

"We'll whip the Yanks in a month," one gallant promised.

"Three weeks," another supposed.

"Hell—excuse me, ladies—they haven't the guts to fight."

"Any Southerner can whip four Yankees."

"If they want a fight, by God, we'll give them one."

One aged dodderer shouted incoherently and brandished his cane. Faces were red with drink, passion, or both.

Pressed for an opinion, young Wilkes said that he'd fight if he had to, of course he would, but war would be terrible.

That incomparable girl adored her hero with her eyes.

"And you, sir," Wilkes turned to Rhett. "My father says you have spent time among our former countrymen."

Which is how Rhett Butler came to say everything he had promised himself he must not say; knowing even as he spoke that his words were futile and he was speaking to men deaf to them.

"I answer only to my conscience. I will not fight a war that will destroy what I hold dear."

"You ain't gonna fight for your country?" one boy brayed disbelief.

Other young men formed a circle around the stranger. The queen's cavaliers rose to their feet, alert for apostasy.

In for a penny, in for a pound . . .

Like a schoolmaster instructing dull students, Rhett described Yankeedom and its tremendous mills and humming factories. He evaluated its wealth—the California gold and Nevada silver—the Confederacy did not possess. He explained in detail why England and France would never recognize the Confederacy.

"This isn't General Washington's war, gentlemen. France won't bail us out this time."

The young bucks pressed nearer. None smiled. The air was still like it gets before a thunderstorm.

"I have seen what you all have not: Tens of thousands of immigrants who'll fight for the Yankees, the factories, the foundries, the shipyards, the iron and coal mines—everything we lack. Why, all we have is cotton and slaves and arrogance. The Yankees'll lick us sure."

With a monogrammed linen handkerchief, Rhett brushed a speck of dust from his sleeve.

Insects buzzed. Somewhere, a servant dropped a plate and was instantly shushed.

Beneath his imperturbable manner, Rhett Butler was laughing at himself. Despite his intent to remain silent, he'd offended everybody. That girl had loosed his tongue and he'd acted like a too-bright schoolboy. Rhett turned to John Wilkes. "Your library, sir. I'd be obliged if I could see it now."

Wilkes entreated his guests. "Ladies and gentlemen, you'll excuse us. Earlier, I begged Mr. Butler for his candid opinion of Confederate prospects and he has accommodated me." Wilkes smiled tersely. "Too candidly, perhaps. If anyone has objections, raise them with me. . . ." Their host raised an admonitory finger. "Privately." Turning to Rhett, Wilkes said, "Our library? Sir, I don't believe Clayton County has a finer."

It was a handsome high-ceilinged room, thirty feet on a side, whose walls were covered with books, even above the windows and door.

Wilkes gestured perfunctorily, "These are biography and history. These are novels on the shelves beside that chair; Dickens, Thackeray, Scott. Most of my guests will be resting soon, repairing for this evening's dancing. Our fiddler is famous here in the countryside. Perhaps you'll stay."

"My regrets, sir. My train departs at ten."

"Ah." Wilkes touched the side of his nose and looked at Rhett for a long moment. If he may have wished to say more, he contented himself with, "If there are virtues worse than beauty and innocence, sir, overmuch candor is among them. Now sir, I must return to my guests. I've feathers to unruffle."

The library walls were thick and high ceilings kept the room cool and Rhett Butler was suddenly very tired. He stretched out on the long high-backed couch and closed his eyes.

Women. All those women. Rhett remembered how Didi always took one forkful from his plate and went through his wallet when she thought he was asleep. He smiled. He hadn't thought of that in years. Scarlett O'Hara . . .

Rhett dozed. One restless dream became another, then another. And then, through the fog of sleep, he heard voices.

"What is it? A secret to tell me?"

She took courage, "Yes—a secret—I love you."

He said, "Isn't it enough that you've collected every other man's heart here today? Do you want to make it unanimous? Well, you've always had my heart, you know. You cut your teeth on it."

Puzzled, Rhett swam upward through the layers of sleep. When his eyes snapped open, his cheek was pressed against a leather bolster and his mouth was dust dry. The voices he'd been dreaming continued remorselessly.

"Ashley—Ashley—tell me—you must—oh, don't tease me now! Have I your heart? Oh, my dear, I lo—"

Ashley? Now who the hell was Ashley? Exactly where was he, anyway? Rhett's mind cast for a mooring. Fort Sumter. Frank Kennedy's cotton. A backwoods plantation with pretensions. The library. Scarlett? Scarlett who? Rhett frowned. His cheek was stuck to the leather bolster.

Somebody—Ashley?—said, "You must not say these things, Scarlett!"

That Scarlett. Rhett came suddenly and entirely awake.

An earnest voice droned on earnestly, "You mustn't. You don't mean them. You'll hate yourself for saying them, and you'll hate me for hearing them."

Rhett thought, So much for your adoring glances, Miss Scarlett. He'd slept on his right side and his pocket watch was pressing into his hip and his feet were numb. He should have removed his riding boots. A better man than I, Rhett thought, would leap up, apologize, and assure the lovers he'd heard nothing as he hurried from the room. Fortunately, I am not a better man.

She said, "I couldn't ever hate you. I tell you I love you and I know you must care about me because . . . Ashley, do you care—you do, don't you?"

"Yes. I care."

Tepid response, young man, Rhett thought, grimacing as he unstuck his cheek from the leather.

"Scarlett, can't we go away and forget that we have ever said these things?" Young Wilkes dithered for a few minutes more before he reached the crux of the matter, "Love isn't enough to make a successful marriage when two people are as different as we are. . . ."

Rhett thought: Aha, Irish immigrant's daughter and the aristocrat. She's good enough to toy with but not good enough to marry.

Wilkes went on: "You would want all of a man, Scarlett, his body, his heart, his soul, his thoughts. And if you did not have them, you would be miserable. And I would not want all of your mind and soul and you would be hurt . . ."

Rhett thought: That's a *real* gentleman: Nothing ventured and absolutely nothing lost.

They wrangled toward the traditional finale: She slapped his face and he elevated his aristocratic chin and, with honor, if not dignity, intact, marched from the room.

Rhett meant to stay hidden until Scarlett left, too, but his heart was alight with laughter and when Scarlett hurled crockery at the fireplace and fragments landed on his couch, he raised up, ran a hand through his sleep-rumpled hair and said, "It is bad enough to have an afternoon nap disturbed by such a passage as I've been forced to hear, but why should my life be endangered?"

She gasped, "Sir, you should have made known your presence."

"Indeed. But you were the intruder." He smiled at her and, because he wanted to see her eyes flash, he chuckled.

"Eavesdroppers . . ." she began a denunciation.

He grinned. "Eavesdroppers often hear highly entertaining and instructive things."

"Sir," she said decisively, "you are no gentleman."

"An apt observation. And you, Miss, are no lady." He loved how her green eyes flashed. Might she slap him too? He laughed again because life is so surprising. "No one can remain a lady after saying or doing what I have just overheard. However, Ladies have seldom held any charms for me. I know what they are thinking, but they never have the courage or lack of breeding to say what they think. But you, my dear Miss O'Hara, are a girl of rare spirit, very admirable spirit, and I take my hat off to you."

His laughter chased her out of the room.

Chapter Ten

The Merry Widow

A full year later, the blockade runner *Merry Widow* tied up at the Haynes & Son wharf: three days from Nassau and six hours of moonless silence slipping through the Federal blockade. Rhett Butler stepped off the boat into flaring gaslights and stevedores' bustle.

John Haynes shook his partner's hand. "You shaved it close this time, Rhett. It'll be light in fifteen minutes."

"Tunis can see our cargo into the warehouse. Join me for breakfast?"

"Give me a few minutes with Tunis. The market café?"

In that first light, Rhett walked the East Battery, enjoying a beautiful city. The briny air was overlaid with the scent of mimosa. Here and there, a gray-clad sentry stood on the parapet, his glass fixed on the Federal fleet.

In the market, fishmongers cried their wares while housemen, cooks, and mammies haggled over produce and freshly baked bread. Many stall holders wore the brass free colored badges the city council had recently issued.

Looking as fresh as if he hadn't been up all night, Rhett Butler threaded through the market, leaning inside a stall to shake a hand or share a joke. Every free colored knew Rhett had hired Tunis Bonneau as his pilot, even though white men wanted the job.

John Haynes was at a corner table with a cup of coffee.

"Ah, John. It's good to be home. Lord, I'm famished. Yankee warships whet my appetite. Only coffee?"

"An uneventful voyage, Rhett?"

"There are more blockaders and they're getting smarter." Rhett rapped the table. "Knock wood."

"Rhett, if they ever corner you, for God's sake, don't try to escape. Run the *Widow* aground or surrender. The *Widow*'s paid for and we've made a decent profit."

"But John," Rhett said solemnly, "it's an adventure! Heart in the throat, hair bristling on your neck; don't you want to trade places?"

John smiled. "Rhett, I'm a stodgy young businessman who intends to become a stodgy old businessman. I'll leave the adventuring to you."

When Rhett ordered sausage, eggs, grits, and coffee, the waiter apologized, "Captain Rhett, we got to charge more. Everything's got so high!"

"Damn profiteering blockade runners," Rhett intoned. The waiter laughed.

"So tell me, John. How is my beautiful niece, Meg? Has she been asking for her uncle Rhett?"

John happily reported his daughter's doings. "Rhett, being a father is like being a child again. Meg makes the familiar world new."

"I envy you your daughter, John."

"You'll be a father one day."

"Will I? I'm told a woman is needed for that project."

John laughed. "Rhett, you're handsome, bold, and rich—you have your pick of women."

When Rhett last visited 46 Church Street after his previous run, the tension between Rosemary and John was so palpable, their attempts at civility so strained, that Rhett didn't stay an hour. It was that damned Patriotic Ball. Andrew Ravanel had driven a scandal between Rosemary and her husband.

Rhett asked lightly, "What good woman would marry a brigand, John? The brigand's life is apt to be short and his finances irregular. Maritally, he is a dreadful prospect."

When the waiter brought Rhett's breakfast, he dug in with a will. "I did meet a Georgia girl last spring. . . ." Rhett chuckled. "Alas, she was immune to my charms."

"Poor, poor Rhett. Tell me honestly, friend. Can we win this war?"

"John, one hundred revolvers leave Colonel Colt's New Haven factory each day. Each takes a standard bullet and the cylinder from one revolver fits any other. Yankees are engineers and Southerners are romantics. In war, engineers whip romantics every time."

"But don't you think—"

Rhett forestalled this evasion. "John, I wish nothing more than your and Rosemary's happiness. Old friend, can I do anything to reconcile you and my sister? If you wish, I'll speak to her. Sometimes a kinsman . . ."

John Haynes picked at a gouge in the wooden tabletop. Despising himself, John Haynes read every newspaper account of Andrew Ravanel's military exploits: "Daring Raid"; "Ravanel's Brigade Strikes Tennessee!"; "Colonel Ravanel Takes a Thousand Prisoners!": "Behind enemy lines, with Federal cavalry in hot pursuit, the audacious Colonel Ravanel paused to telegraph the Federal War Department to complain about their horses he was capturing."

John's eyes were so pained, Rhett fought an urge to look away.

John said quietly, "My Rosemary . . . says she did not marry me of her free will. She married me to escape her father's house." He kneaded his left hand with his right. "I have not upbraided her about the Patriotic Ball, but Rosemary hasn't forgiven me for not being . . . Andrew. My dear wife believes as she had been her father's chattel, she is now mine. No better than a slave. Rhett, Rosemary has called me 'Master John.' "

Rhett winced. After a moment, he said, "Why don't I rent a rig and we'll go—you and I, Meg and Rosemary—for a jaunt in the country."

John shook his head, "I cannot. I must see the *Widow*'s cotton properly stowed." John took a sip of cold coffee and said too brightly, "Tell me about this Georgia girl?"

"Ah yes, Miss Scarlett O'Hara." Rhett was happy to drop the painful subject. "Last spring, while you Charlestonians were busy starting this war, I was in Georgia buying cotton. I was invited to a barbecue at the local mugwump's plantation. Said mugwump's son was to marry an Atlanta cousin. These country aristocrats don't bring new blood into the family if they can help it. I liked John Wilkes, but Ashley, the son, was so genteel, he squeaked. The prettiest girl there was Miss Scarlett O'Hara, and Miss Scarlett had it in her head that Ashley Wilkes ought to marry her instead of his fiancée! John, a love tragedy was on the boil!

"Unfortunately for my dishonorable intentions, since the young lady couldn't marry Wilkes, she married the nearest boy at hand: the fiancée's brother, Charles Hamilton." Rhett shook his head ruefully. "What a waste."

"Hamilton? O'Hara? A Georgia family? Near Jonesboro?"

"The same. Lord, I envy Charles Hamilton his nights of love with that incomparable girl before going off for war. So many tender adieus. So many, many tender adieus."

"Charles Hamilton is dead."

"What?"

"And the Widow Hamilton is in Charleston, visiting her aunt Eulalie Ward. What do you say to that?"

Rhett Butler grinned like a schoolboy. "Why, John, what excellent news! On my last run, I brought Eulalie Ward's daughters some Paris brocade. Perhaps I'll call on them this afternoon and see what they made of it."

Civilians and newly minted Confederate soldiers promenaded past the great black guns emplaced on Charleston's White Point Park.

"What if they shoot they guns, Miss Scarlett?" Prissy stepped back from the second-floor window. "They big guns all 'round and Federal blockaders swimmin' in the sea and I afeared." Her brow furrowed until her thought meandered to its destination: "I afeared for Baby Wade."

Who was, Scarlett O'Hara Hamilton noted gratefully, nodding off to sleep in Prissy's arms.

"What if Wade 'n me takin' the air when they start shootin'? What if they sail into the harbor shootin' they guns? Little Master Wade be scared out of his skin!"

Charleston, the Cradle of Secession, was acutely sensitive to Federal victories. Some Federals boasted, "Charleston *is* where the revolt began and the revolt will end where Charleston *was*." Last December, a fire in the city's heart had destroyed eight blocks of churches, homes, and Secession

Hall itself. Some whispered that "the burnt district" portended Charleston's future.

"I wish the Federal fleet *would* come in," Scarlett said more to herself than to Prissy. "Anything to break this monotony."

Scarlett O'Hara Hamilton loathed widowhood. She despised her drab mourning clothes, her dutiful sackcloth and ashes.

At least in Charleston, she could wear lavender sleeve piping! At Tara, any outfit that wasn't utterly drear brought her mother Ellen's swift reproach: "Dear Scarlett, people might misconstrue your true feelings."

Her true feelings . . .

Solemnity was crushing her. Who was this morbid creature in black veil and flat widow's cap? Was this caricature really Scarlett O'Hara, the gayest, most fetching young woman in Clayton County? Must Scarlett repel every admirer for her dead husband's sake—whose passing Scarlett regretted less than the loss of a favorite pony? Charles Hamilton had been such a boy; his lovemaking so earnest and tedious!

Life was terribly unfair! Scarlett must pretend to the world that her heart was buried with Charles while she dreamt of Ashley Wilkes, the man she should have married. Ashley Wilkes. Ashley's smile. Ashley's drowsy gray eyes. In her cold widow's bed, Scarlett relived every moment she and Ashley had spent together—strolling through Twelve Oaks' scented rose garden, Ashley's quiet kindnesses, the books he'd mentioned, the great paintings he'd seen on his European tour, their happy rides through the Georgia countryside. Their love had been too precious and tender to need voicing, until that fatal afternoon in the library at Twelve Oaks when Scarlett had spoken her love and Ashley had rejected her to marry another.

Very well, then. If Ashley would marry mousy Melanie Hamilton, Scarlett could bewitch Melanie's naïve brother, Charles, and marry him!

Six months afterward, Charles had succumbed to some silly camp disease and Scarlett was pregnant, widowed, and fitted out in black.

Scarlett had tried to grieve for Charles. She had *tried.*

Concerned about her daughter's health, and hoping a change of scenery might improve Scarlett's spirits, Ellen O'Hara had sent Scarlett to Charleston to visit her aunt, Eulalie Robillard Ward.

Scarlett had had hopes for Charleston; Charleston had a *reputation.* But it was more tedious than Tara had been.

Every afternoon, Eulalie's friends gathered to reconsider Charleston's petty scandals and compare genealogies.

Scarlett's mother was infrequently mentioned in her sister's home, and when someone did speak of Ellen Robillard O'Hara, they spoke in tones reserved for the gentlewoman who is rather more ill than she admits.

Young Prissy tended Baby Wade as earnestly as a child cares for her favorite doll. "Hear Baby Wade? I believe he snorin'. Now ain't he a wonder!"

"Don't all babies snore?" Scarlett sighed, and went downstairs for another long afternoon pulling lint with Aunt Eulalie Robillard Ward and her friends.

Since the Confederacy had no linen bandages, gentlewomen rummaged their attics for chemises and camisoles that could be reduced to lint for stanching wounds.

Eulalie's fastidious brother-in-law, Frederick Ward, had abandoned his customary wing chair for a settee at farthest remove from the undergarments the ladies were disassembling; Frederick Ward thought novels immoral and had been known to leave the room rather than subject himself to "bohemian" opinions.

He rose at Scarlett's entry. "Good afternoon, Mrs. Hamilton."

In Frederick's considered opinion, lavender sleeve piping was inappropriate for a widow whose husband had not been in his grave twelve months. Young Mrs. Hamilton seemed unaffected by Frederick's disapproval, and rarely showed the deference one expected from an upcountry Georgia girl among her betters.

The widow Eulalie Ward had worn black for years, but Charlotte Fisher Ravanel had donned her mourning garb last month when Grandmother Fisher died.

Charlotte Ravanel and Rosemary Haynes made up their differences at the funeral, where Charlotte completely forgot the Patriotic Ball. Juliet's cleverest innuendoes were blunted on Charlotte's forgetfulness. "I do wish

I knew what you were talking about, dear, but I had a headache and left the ball early."

Lifting her eyes from the chemise she was pulling apart, Juliet Ravanel said proudly, "This morning's *Mercury* compared Andrew with Stonewall Jackson."

Scarlett Hamilton yawned. "General Jackson is the homeliest man alive."

Aunt Eulalie's lapdog, Empress, barked.

Rosemary Haynes grinned. "Ah-ha! That's why the Federals run from Jackson. They are repelled by his visage! Here's a plan! We'll rout the Federals with likenesses! Our generals can use special batteries to bombard our foes"—Rosemary tugged an imaginary lanyard—"with daguerreotypes of homely Confederates. The Federals will run like rabbits! The South may lack flour, shoes, fabric, sugar, coffee, and tea, but we've plenty of flat-faced, scraggly-bearded, wall-eyed, leering, two-toothed males."

Her conceit was greeted by chilly silence. Scarlett muffled a coughing fit in her handkerchief.

Eulalie's tiny spaniel barked again and Eulalie said, "Empress does not appreciate your joking, dear. Who would have imagined that my sweet little dog would be patriotic?"

Scarlett couldn't resist: "She has a patriot's brains."

Another silence. Scarlett shut her eyes. Lord! She was enmired in dullness. Dullness smothered her so, she could not breathe. Scarlett's great fear was that one morning she'd be unable to remember—as the Wards could no longer remember—what joy was.

Juliet Ravanel broke the silence, "Rosemary, I hear your brother is back in Charleston."

"Yes, he spoils Meg terribly."

"Didn't I hear his son is in New Orleans?"

"Dear Juliet"—Rosemary smiled, tight-lipped—"I wouldn't expect you, of all people, to repeat scurrilous gossip."

Juliet Ravanel smiled right back at her.

Meanwhile, bored Scarlett was populating an imaginary bestiary: Frederick Ward was an overfed yellow tabby cat, the high-colored Juliet Ravanel a cardinal. Eulalie's daughters, Patience and Priscilla, in identical green brocade, had lizards' features and reptilian attitudes. In her mourning habit, poor Aunt Eulalie was a perfect crow.

While Scarlett daydreamed, conversation turned to a Robillard connection killed at Shiloh.

Frederick set his index finger to his chin. "Pauline's daughter's husband, hmm. Wasn't his first wife a Menninger? Hmm. If memory serves, Menninger senior's son, James, had that plantation on the Ashley, below Grafton, hmm. Didn't he marry that girl—dear me, I can't recall her name—that Richmond belle?"

At that instant, had the Devil himself appeared shrouded in smoke, Scarlett would have taken his bargain gladly for one more barbecue, one more night of waltzes and music and fun.

But the moment passed and Scarlett's immortal soul shrank from the brink. "I believe I'll take the air," she said, not troubling to conceal her yawn behind her black silk fan.

Outdoors, Charleston's heat struck Scarlett like a wet woolen glove. Shading her eyes, she squinted against the glare. How she wished she were at shady Tara.

The garden separated the Ward house from dependencies concealed behind a thick boxwood hedge. Louisiana iris bloomed beneath flame-colored azaleas whose scent was overwhelmed by lavender.

Frederick Ward's son Willy and his friends were gathered beneath an ancient eucalyptus. Willy Ward's friends wore the elaborate uniforms of the Palmetto Brigade, the Moultrie Guards, and the Washington Light Infantry. Oh dear! Scarlett knew they *would* prate on about the War, and she must pretend to be fascinated by their gallantry. Scarlett Hamilton was so sick of boys!

Inhaling Charleston's moist, heavily scented air, Scarlett recalled Tara's subtly aromatic roses. The memory was so poignant that, hundreds of miles from home, Scarlett closed her eyes and swayed.

"Cousin Scarlett! Cousin! Are you unwell? Let me help you into the shade. You aren't accustomed to our sun." His face solemn with concern, Willy Ward guided her to a chair.

"Why, thank you, Willy." Scarlett's smile was wistful.

Although Willy had been quickest off the mark, other young men rushed to attend the lovely young widow. One suggested a cold cloth; another offered lemonade. Did she wish a parasol?

"Oh, thank you all. You are too kind!"

Across the garden, a middle-aged man in civilian clothes was leaning against the gate. His arms were crossed and a smile flickered across his lips. Scarlett's heart started thumping so fast, she put her hand to her chest.

"Cousin Scarlett, you are so pale!"

"Yes, Willy," Scarlett gasped, "I am pale. Ladies are *supposed* to be pale. Don't fuss!"

That Man touched a forefinger to the brim of his gleaming panama hat.

Willy knelt beside Scarlett's chair. "Your face is turning red! This dreadful heat! Let me help you indoors."

At Twelve Oaks, *That Man* had overheard her pleading to Ashley, begging Ashley to love her as she loved him, her plea rejected by the finest, noblest . . .

Now *That Man* dared to put a finger to his lips, as if he knew her intimate thoughts but vowed to keep her secret.

"He . . . the man in civilian clothes?" Scarlett choked out.

"The notorious Captain Butler," a blond youth in a Zouave uniform replied. "I do not know why Mrs. Ward admits him."

"Butler's bold enough," Willy Ward conceded. "On his last run, he steamed through the blockade in broad daylight. Butler convinced the blockaders he was a Federal mail boat, and they escorted him into the harbor!"

Butler approached Scarlett as a big cat might: with a deliberate, lazy confidence. Swarthy, tall, and unusually muscular for a Southern gentleman, his frock coat was black broadcloth, his shirt was ruffled at the cuffs, and his foulard was the delicate blue of a robin's egg. Though he swept his panama from his head, his gesture seemed less chivalrous than it might have.

"My dear Mrs. Hamilton, I was devastated to hear of your husband

Charles's death. '*Dulce et decorum est pro patria mori.*' " He paused, smiling. "Perhaps you were not cursed with a classical education. ''Tis sweet and honorable to die for one's country.' A sentiment that, doubtless, these gallant officers share."

"And you, sir—you do not serve?" Scarlett inquired innocently.

"Some of us are not heroic, ma'am." Although his hat swept low again, his gesture reeked of mockery. "How proud you must be." He smiled at the young men. "How proud you all must be."

The young officers bristled, although they weren't exactly sure why.

Willy Ward thought Butler presumptuous to approach the finest girl Willy had ever seen, right here in the family garden. Willy was concocting a rebuke when Scarlett dumbfounded him. "Gentlemen, please do excuse us. Captain Butler and I have something to discuss."

Reluctantly, the young men withdrew out of earshot, although Willy kept a sharp eye on the couple, as if, piratically, Captain Butler might seize the young widow and escape with his prize.

Rhett Butler appraised Scarlett impertinently. "Black isn't your color, my dear. Paris fabrics are subtler this season. They have a taffeta the color of your eyes."

Scarlett looked at him straight. "Captain Butler, at Twelve Oaks, matters were not as they may have seemed. I indulged a lighthearted flirtation on the eve of my old friend's wedding. Neither Ashley Wilkes nor I actually *meant* what we said. I'm sure any gentleman"—Scarlett almost choked on the word—"must understand."

Rhett placed a hand over his heart. "How well I do! Doubtless the gallant Wilkes took your pretty entreaty as whimsy; of no more consequence than the butterfly's flirtation with the flower." Butler's eyes were laughing at her. Laughing! "For my own part, should I ever have the pleasure of meeting you again, I'll pretend your meaningless flirtation never occurred. Why, we can pretend we've never met." The man beamed in the most aggravating manner.

Scarlett had never met anyone so hateful. She stamped her foot. "Oh, fiddle-dee-dee!" Her dramatic exit was marred by a slight stumble on the doorstep.

As Scarlett burst into her aunt's withdrawing room, Frederick Ward's eyes widened as one of his habitual opinions rolled toward its inevitable, unstoppable conclusion, no longer Frederick's creature, but its own: "Perhaps Philippe Robillard was too breakneck for sister Ellen, hmm? But to marry a coarse, striving Irish immigrant like Gerald O'Hara . . ."

Frederick's opinion was trampled under Scarlett's impatient query. "Aunt Eulalie, why *do* you admit Captain Butler? He is no gentleman."

Flustered, Aunt Eulalie wagged her several chins. "Why, he, he . . ."

Having dispatched her aunt, Scarlett turned on Frederick. "Did I hear you correctly? Did I hear you say my mother married beneath her? God's nightgown, sir!" Scarlett erupted, in a passable replication of her father Gerald's earthy brogue. "Faith! If it's thin blood my father was wantin' to marry, look no further than the Robillards! Begorrah, they've no blood at all!"

Chapter Eleven

Some Lovers

The Ashley River rolled brown and dirty in spate. The rice fields had been planted and flooded and plantation houses stood above glistening water like islands. Rice birds exploded from the roadside as a bright blue phaeton sped past. Drays and farm wagons pulled to the verge to let the gentlefolk by.

"Oh look, Rhett," Rosemary said. "They're repairing the old Ravanel place."

Rhett reined in Tecumseh.

Workmen swarmed over the farmhouse roof, pulling up broken cedar shingles and letting them fall into the head-high weeds around the foundations. On a scaffold, three workmen were extracting a rotted window, casement and all.

Rhett said, "William Bee bought it for his son. Bee has made so much money running the blockade, he can afford whimsey." Tecumseh champed at the bit. "Easy, boy. I wonder how much paint it will take to cover that house's sins?"

"Were you there often?" Rosemary asked.

Rhett shrugged. "When I was young and filled with despair. The last time . . ."

"Rhett?"

A warm September rain glistened the cobblestones as young Rhett Butler rode Tecumseh toward Grandmother Fisher's. Rain dimpled the Charleston harbor where distant Fort Sumter floated in and out of the mist.

Rhett was in a black humor. Last night, Henry, Edgar, and Old Jack Ravanel had helped him celebrate a poker win until his winnings were a memory. Rhett had drunk too much, and at daybreak, when he stepped out of Miss Polly's, he'd flinched and squinted against the scorching sunlight. He'd thought, For you, Little Rosemary. I must change my life.

Last night, Henry Kershaw had been coarser than usual, Edgar Puryear's sycophancy more irritating, and Rhett had noticed Old Jack Ravanel eyeing him with the affection a bobcat reserves for a plump hare.

Why had he come back to Charleston? To flaunt his West Point disgrace before his father's political cronies? There were so many places he'd rather be, so many things he'd rather be doing. Rhett Butler was weary of annoying, stupid people, tired of shocked dismay on dull, utterly predictable faces. After a bad night, young Rhett Butler took a deep breath of salt air. He'd go to Rosemary. Perhaps her child's love could save him.

When Grandmother Fisher answered the door herself, Rhett's hopes crumpled. "Rhett, I'm sorry. I don't know how your father learned you'd been visiting! I've never seen Langston so furious. If I'd been a man, I believe he would have called me out." Grandmother set her lips. "Rosemary is Langston's daughter. There wasn't one thing in the world I could do."

"Where is she?" Rhett demanded.

"At Broughton. Langston said . . ."

Rhett jerked his head, as if pulling words out of her.

"Your father told me she'd stay until you were dead or gone from the Low Country. Damn the man! Come inside, Rhett, and we'll talk. I am not without influence and . . ."

The clatter of Tecumseh's hooves obliterated what more she might have said.

On rain-slick cobblestones. Rhett galloped Tecumseh through the city. Cabbies cursed, riders drew up sharply, and servants leaped from his path. The great horse hammered along, tireless as a steam engine.

After an hour, he slowed Tecumseh to a canter, then an easy walk. When the horse shook his head, hot horse spittle spattered Rhett's cheeks. They were well out of the city on the River Road.

Young Rhett Butler believed the years to come wouldn't be different from the years he'd already lived. He was disgraced; he would be always be disgraced.

He was alone; he would always be alone. Rhett could endure being unloved. He could not live without loving.

It was twilight when Rhett turned into Colonel Jack Ravanel's lane. Jack had been involved in a particularly dubious financial scheme and was eluding the bailiffs.

Jack's lane was unkempt and overgrown. Outside the dooryard, Rhett unsaddled Tecumseh and rubbed him down. The horse's legs trembled with fatigue.

Old Jack didn't stir from the piazza. "You drive that horse too hard, boy," he said. "I admire that horse. If you're going to kill him, might be you could sell him to me instead."

"Hay in the shed, Jack?"

"Where it always is. There's a bucket next the well."

As Rhett watered his exhausted animal, he whispered, "Don't you, by God, founder on me, Tecumseh. I couldn't stand it if you foundered!"

The horse pushed his nose into the bucket.

The Ravanel farmhouse ("plantation house" was too grand a name) had been built by Jack's grandfather and ill maintained for years. Rhett climbed its moss green cypress risers.

The porch smelled dank, as if decades of river mists had congealed in the rotten wood and peeling paint.

Without rising, Old Jack waved a languid welcome. "We have Jack's plantation to ourselves, young Butler. All the sports are in town. Hell, I wish I was in town."

The prospect of another debauched evening made Rhett faintly ill.

"You're not looking pert, son. Woman trouble, I wager." Jack slid a nearly full whiskey bottle toward the younger man. "This'll cure her. This'll cure love pains, failures, and guilt. It'll help you grieve and help you forget."

Although the old reprobate rarely bought a round, Rhett was too low to be suspicious. He drank deeply from the bottle.

"She must have been a pretty wench," Jack observed. "Love, my boy—"

"Don't say anything about love, Jack. This is Rhett, remember? I know you, Jack."

"Ah? Do you?" After a hot glance, Jack reverted to his familiar jokey self. "Why, of course you do. Who knows Old Jack better than his friends. Carpe diem, eh, Rhett?"

Rhett should have been warier, but despair had blinded him to everything but grim prophecies.

Jack left the bottle and disappeared indoors.

As the moon slunk across the sky, young Rhett Butler drank whiskey and felt like dying. The evening star was low on the horizon when Jack came outside, yawning. "Man is born to troubles, eh, Rhett?"

Rhett had drunk his way through drunkenness into a weary, irritable sobriety. "Anything you say, Jack."

"I say that I hate to see a clever boy so downhearted. Why, if Jesus Christ himself stepped onto this piazza with the keys to Paradise, I reckon you'd turn Him down."

Rhett turned bloodshot eyes on the old scoundrel. "You want something, Jack. Spit it out."

Years afterward, Rhett stared at the old house.

"Rhett? Where did you go?" Rosemary asked.

"Sorry, Sister. I was woolgathering. Edgar Puryear loved to come to Jack's. Edgar enjoys other men's weaknesses. Andrew hated it. Andrew was more fastidious than his father."

"And you?"

Rhett shrugged. "I thought hell was where I belonged."

A skid of old shingles slid down the mossy roof and landed with a crash. Tecumseh flattened his ears. "Easy, boy. Easy." Rhett's strong hands spoke through the reins.

Meg and Cleo were in the groom's seat behind. Rhett felt Meg's sweet breath on his neck, "Mommy, how far are we?"

"Not far, dear," Rosemary said. "Look there! That snag in the river. See the eagle?"

Rhett flicked the reins and Tecumseh danced before settling into a brisk trot.

The buggy coming toward them was as solemn black as the smallish mare drawing it. When Tunis Bonneau drew up, he tipped his hat to Rosemary. Rhett tipped his to Mrs. Bonneau.

Ruthie Prescott Bonneau was a light-skinned, plump young woman, corseted and stayed within an inch of her life. "Good afternoon, Captain Butler. Isn't this a fine afternoon?"

" 'No spring or summer beauty hath such grace . . .' "

Mrs. Bonneau's smile was reserved. "My father, Reverend Prescott, taught me my letters. I am more familiar with Dr. Donne's sermons than his poetry."

Rhett stretched, "But it is a day for poetry, isn't it?"

Tunis said, "Hello, Tecumseh. Miss Rosemary, I see you're takin' good care of that horse." Tunis nodded to the groom's seat. "Little Miss Meg. How you today?"

Meg put her thumb in her mouth.

Ruthie said, "Captain Butler, every Sunday at the First African, we pray you and Tunis have a safe voyage."

"Well," Rhett grinned. "That's my prayer, too."

"Got a letter from Daddy Thomas," Tunis said.

Rhett explained to Rosemary, "Tunis's parents immigrated to Canada."

Ruthie said, "My husband's father has a home in Kingston, Ontario, Mrs. Haynes. Thomas Bonneau says things are better there."

Tunis said, "Papa says Canada is cold as the dickens."

Rhett steadied Tecumseh. "Tunis, I swear this horse wasn't skittish when I left him with you."

"Might be negro horses got more cause be skittish than white men's horses," Tunis deadpanned.

"Maybe they do at that," Rhett said. "Good to see you again, Mrs. Bonneau. Please thank the First African for their prayers."

Tunis nodded and clucked to his mare.

As the respectable black carriage went around the bend, Cleo muttered, "Them free coloreds think too high of themselfs."

They trotted past Hopeton and Darien Plantation. Gangs were still planting at Champney.

"We never planted so late at Broughton," Cleo disapproved. "Overseer don't 'low it."

"You're not at Broughton now, Cleo," Rosemary reminded her maid.

"Don't I thank Jesus for that!"

Rhett said, "I hear Wade Hampton bought the old Puryear place."

"Cathecarte Puryear lives in London now. Apparently war frightened his muse."

Rhett shook his head. "Poor Cathecarte. Lord, how he envied men with talent. Edgar's a provost in Atlanta—that's Edgar's kind of work, you know. In his whole life, Edgar has learned one trick: how not to be his father." He flicked the reins. "Maybe that's all any man learns."

Rosemary touched her brother's sleeve. "There's our lane—beyond that big cypress."

The carriage wound through oaks dripping with Spanish moss into a clearing where Congress Haynes's fishing camp perched on pilings like a wading bird.

Rosemary inhaled deeply. "I love it out here," she said. "We don't come enough. If business doesn't keep John in town, civic duties do. Isn't this a lovely day?" She basked her face in the sun. "Isn't it?"

As Rhett and Rosemary stepped onto the porch, Meg ran toward the river. Skirts lifted, hat clapped to her head, Cleo hurried after, crying, "Now don't you go gettin' in that mud! Watch out for snakes! Don't you fall in that ol' river!"

Congress Haynes had built this simple camp on a breezy mosquitoless point: a railed roofless porch outside one big room with a soot-blackened fireplace, crude benches, and a table with men's initials carved into the wood.

As a boy, Rhett'd sailed by here, mosquito hawks whupping as they swooped and bats twittering while Congress Haynes's friends—too far away for Rhett to make out their faces—sat in the lamplight drinking and laughing. Drifting down the dark river, the invisible boy had wondered if he might ever be one of them.

Now Rhett set a foot on the railing and lit a cigar while Rosemary unpacked their hamper and placed silver stirrup cups on the rail. "When I was a little girl, I'd dream of all the exotic places you were visiting. Tell me, Brother, are the pyramids as grand as they say?"

Rhett uncorked the wine. "Never got to Egypt. Maybe after the War."

Lost in thought, Rosemary watched the river. "I'm worried about Mother. She never comes to town, her friends don't visit, and Father makes excuses why his dear, devoted wife can't accompany him to Governor Brown's fêtes." Her brother poured wine. "Mother says Isaiah Watling believes the War was prophesied."

"Watling?"

"He and Mother pray together. They meet in his house and pray. Isaiah's wife died sometime last year." Rosemary raised a hand to forestall objections. "It's only praying; that's all. Langston knows about it. There's nothing between them." Rosemary's wry grin. "Except, perhaps, the Book of Revelations."

"Prayers can be a powerful bond. Sit beside me. We'll have our picnic in a little while."

While Rosemary rested her elbows on the rail. Absent her marital tensions, Rhett's sister seemed years younger.

A dark-haired white child and an angular black girl ambled hand in hand beside the river. The child's babble rose and fell with the breeze. Sandpipers patrolled the riverside, dabbing the mud with sharp pointed beaks. Clouds as fat as cotton bolls drifted lazily overhead. Pistons harrumphing, a riverboat tugged a string of empty rice flats upstream. When the helmsman waved, little Meg waved back enthusiastically.

Rosemary asked, "Do you think Father ever loved Mother?"

"On at least three occasions, Langston Butler loved his wife. Men can't rise from a woman's bed indifferent to the authoress of their pleasure. Belle Watling's Cyprians joke about the marriage proposals they get."

"Belle Watling?"

"Belle's left New Orleans for Atlanta." Rhett laughed. "Belle claims she's a Confederate patriot. In fact, she's a businesswoman and New Orleans's Federal conquerors are partial to negro sporting houses."

Chin in her hand, Rosemary examined her brother. "Rhett, what is Belle Watling to you?"

Rhett's smile stretched into a mocking grin. "Has the Scapegrace

Brother taken up with the Soiled Dove? Will Butler bastards be born in a sporting house?"

Rosemary flushed. "Rhett, I didn't mean . . ."

"Dear Sister, of course you did. Women can never be kind to a woman who sells her favors. Favors are to be bestowed only after elaborate ceremony and payment in full."

"Rhett, please . . ."

"Some years ago in New Orleans, Belle and I went into business together. I keep an office in Belle Watling's sporting house; it amuses me when respectable businessmen sneak up her back stairs."

Meg was collecting mussel shells on the riverbank.

"And who is Scarlett Hamilton to you? After you stirred her up yesterday, she marched into Eulalie's drawing room and reduced Frederick Ward to stuttering. Poor Frederick couldn't exit in a huff—he was in his own home! Rhett, what on earth did you say to that young woman?"

Rhett's face was rueful. "I seem to have a knack for annoying her." He grinned. "But damned if I can resist."

"Scarlett would be very beautiful, I think, if she weren't so unhappy."

"You see, Sister, little Miss Scarlett has no idea who she is. Her charming tricks attract men who are unworthy of her." Rhett's voice dropped to a whisper. "Hindoos believe we have had lives before this. Is it true?" He raised a mocking eyebrow. Perhaps Scarlett and I were star-crossed lovers; perhaps we died in each other's arms. . . ."

"Why, Rhett," Rosemary teased, "you, a romantic?"

Rhett spoke so softly, Rosemary had to lean nearer to hear him. "I want that woman more than I've ever wanted a woman in my life."

Rosemary squeezed his hand. "There's the brother I know!"

On the riverbank, Meg was singing, "Lou, Lou, skip to my Lou . . ."

Rosemary stared at the muddy water. "I do not think I can ever love John Haynes. Not like that."

Rhett let the power drain from her words before replying. "John's a good man."

"Do you think I don't know that?" she said. "Do you think that makes a whit of difference?"

"Perhaps—in time . . ."

"Don't worry, Brother, I won't create a second scandal." Rosemary's voice faded to a whisper. "I see my life ahead as an unbroken stretch of days, each day exactly like the last, each as empty as the last."

Her smile was so pained, her brother couldn't look at her.

"I am my mother's daughter and I will cut my cloth to reality. But by God, I will not pray. I will not pray!"

Cleo's squeak was an imprisoned scream. She scooped Meg up and ran toward the camp. "Oh, Captain Rhett," she cried, "Captain Rhett. Get you gun."

"Pass Meg to me, Cleo," Rosemary knelt and reached down. "I'll take her."

As she lifted the frightened child to her mother, Cleo shook with impatience. "You gots to shoot him!"

"Who must I shoot, Cleo?"

"That fox. I see'd him!"

"You saw a fox?"

"In the broad daylight!" Impatiently, Cleo recited the country truism: "See a fox in daylight, fox he mad. Fox bite you, you go mad, too." Cleo raised her arms and Rhett plucked her onto the porch.

Below, a young vixen slid over a log on the riverbank.

Rhett squinted into the sunlight. "She's not mad, Cleo. Her fur is glossy and she moves normally. She's no threat." Rhett peered closely. "She's lost her cubs, or maybe never had cubs. She wouldn't be so sleek with cubs pulling her down."

"What she doin' out in broad daylight scarin' folks?"

Cleo had her answer when a dog fox crossed the log and marked. The vixen pretended to find something and pounced, her tail flouncing marvelously. She rolled on a tussock of marsh grass, all languorousness and pleasure. Her tail was so bushy, she seemed more tail than fox.

"Look at her! She's flaunting herself!" Rosemary said.

"Indeed she is," Rhett said.

The old dog fox's muzzle was scarred and he favored a forefoot, as if he'd lost toes in a trap.

Little Meg cried out, "She's so pretty!"

"She is, sweetheart," her uncle said. "That fellow thinks she's pretty, too."

"Is he her husband, Uncle Rhett?"

"He wants to be," her mother said. "See, Meg, he's courting."

The child knelt below the rail to see better. "Does she like him, too?"

"She's pretending she doesn't know he's alive," her uncle Rhett said.

A skinny, half-immersed driftwood log next attracted the vixen. One end was ashore and the river plucked at the other. She trotted gaily down its length. The dog fox hesitated. The vixen turned at the end of the log and sat grinning at him.

Reluctantly, the dog fox stepped onto the driftwood and tiptoed toward her.

His added weight was too much for the log's hold on the bank and it launched, turning in the swift current. The purely disgusted expression on the dog fox's face made Meg laugh.

Peals of childish laughter pursued the star-crossed lovers down the river to the sea.

Chapter Twelve

A Bastard

Tazewell Watling pressed his forefinger under his nose so he wouldn't sneeze. Swirling yellow-brown smoke drooped over the earth, draining livelier colors from the sunset. The light penetrating this pall was the color of dirty linen and the sun was a pale silver disk on the horizon. Burning coke, sulfur, white-hot iron, ammonia, and less identifiable stinks cluttered the air.

Through Alabama and western Georgia, the train had traveled a single track. Now that track divided and divided again and the train overtook a freight on the left, then a string of flatcars. A self-important yard engine huffed at them, squealing, veering, passing so close, Taz might have reached out his window and touched it.

"First time to Atlanta, boy?" The Confederate corporal beside Taz hawked on the floor.

"I am from New Orleans," Taz said with a boy's flimsy hauteur.

"Over there, that's the rolling mill where they make plate for our ironclads. I got a brother works there. Lucky bastard's exempted from the army. Over there's J. W. Dance revolvers and them brick smokestacks—no, those un's over there—that's the naval gun factory. Four railroads roll into this town, son—four altogether different railroads!" He jabbed an elbow into the boy's side. "What you think about that!"

How could Taz find his mother in this smoky cauldron?

Factories fronted the tracks; houses faced away from it. A few dwellings were brick, but most were dingy clapboard. Cows, pigs, and chickens grazed in half-acre pastures. The houses huddled closer together as the train rolled into the city. Broad streets seemed to snap open and shut. Taz saw three- and four-story brick and stone businesses and warehouses, and countless carriages and wagons.

Was that woman on the corner Belle Watling? That face in the landau, was she his mother?

Tazewell Watling's oldest memory was night in the cavernous dormitory of New Orleans' Asylum for Orphan Boys: children coughing and whimpering for their mothers. Taz lay on a rush pallet with other children pressed against him, and the dampness on his thigh was where one of the younger boys had wet himself.

Taz was hungry and afraid but would not cry. Boys who cried disappeared into the infirmary, where they died, and were buried in the asylum's verdant, lovingly tended cemetery. Most of the orphans were Irish and the nuns were French Sisters of Charity who took their vows of poverty so seriously, they starved themselves. Embracing hunger as a virtue, the Good Sisters were imperfectly sympathetic to hungry children.

Yet, when the Mardi Gras Krewes paraded down Royal Street, these same self-abasing sisters waved gaily from their balcony to catch the strings of bright, worthless beads drunken mummers tossed to them.

The Sisters of Charity said Taz's mother was a fallen woman condemned to the fires of hell. A good Catholic boy like Taz would never see his mother in heaven.

Taz believed them—and he did not believe them. In his child's heart, night fears gave way to mornings when miracles might happen.

Four years ago, Rhett Butler had been such a miracle. Scrubbed until his skin glowed, the boy had been summoned to the Mother Superior's office to meet a big smiling stranger. A cup of the Mother Superior's weak tea stood untouched at the man's elbow. In a place that reeked of carbolic and lye soap, the stranger smelled of good cigars, bourbon, and pomade. "I am your guardian, Tazewell Watling," Rhett Butler told him. "A guardian's not as good as a father, perhaps, but I'll have to do."

The next day, in his new suit, Tazewell Watling was delivered to the

Jesuit School of the Catholic Society for Religious and Literary Education, attached to the enormous Jesuit church. There, Taz was enrolled, shown his bed (which he was forbidden to lie upon in the daytime) and the peg where he was to hang his coat.

His mother, whose visits to the asylum had been sporadic, now visited regularly. Belle wore prettier dresses and seemed happier. Tazewell believed Mr. Butler was his mother's miracle, too.

When Taz started at the Jesuit School, his reading was poor, his spelling impossible, and he had no mathematics. The Jesuits would remedy these deficiencies.

At the Asylum for Orphan Boys, only a few boys knew their fathers, and none of these elusive creatures ever visited. Tazewell Watling loved and needed his mother; he hadn't even imagined a father.

But at the Jesuit school, Tazewell Watling learned fathers were necessities. As an older boy, Jules Nore, patiently explained, "We boys are educated to become gentlemen. You, Watling, cannot be a gentleman." Jules Nore frowned and corrected his overgenerous appraisal: "You can't be *anything* without a father. Bastards like you, Tazewell Watling, are meant to serve gentlemen, open our carriage doors, clean the mud from our boots. . . ."

For this appraisal, Taz bloodied Jules's nose. When Jules's friends piled on, Taz gave a good account of himself.

A bastard can't ever be anything!

As they rolled into the Atlanta railyard, another train drew alongside. Like theirs, it overflowed with Confederate soldiers, some standing between cars, others on the tops of the cars. Cheers volleyed from one train to the other. In Taz's car, one soldier struck up a banjo and another tootled a mouth organ, though they weren't playing the same tune.

Side by side, the trains raced toward the huge open-ended brick Car Shed, which they penetrated with bells clanging and brakes shrieking. The sun vanished and cinders, unable to escape through the Car Shed's roof, clattered like buckshot onto the tops of the cars.

"This is it, boy." The corporal hefted his haversack. "The bustlingest town in the Confederacy. You can find anything you want in Atlanta." He winked. "Might find some things you'd be better off without."

Across the filthy brick platform, a hospital train was disgorging soldiers wounded at the Fredricksburg fight. Men supported one another or hobbled along on crutches. Negro litter bearers carried the severely wounded.

Behind the cluster of ambulances at the end of the platform, Peachtree Street was stalled carriages, angry teamsters and riders taking to the sidewalks as pedestrians cursed them.

Taz intercepted a well-dressed civilian, "Sir, can you direct me to Belle Watling's establishment?"

The gentleman eyed Taz up and down. "I will not. You look to be a decent young lad who cannot possibly have business at"—he twisted his mouth around the name—"Chapeau Rouge."

"You're acquainted with Chapeau Rouge, sir?" Taz asked pertly.

"Insolent whelp!"

Atlanta was colder than New Orleans and Taz could see his breath.

The soldier Taz accosted was more helpful. "Boy, just walk on down Decatur Street. When it gets right lively, you's 'bout where you want to be."

Brick sidewalks gave way to boardwalks, which gave way to dirt paths beside rutted streets. The gaslights quit with the business district. The overcast sky was a glowing ceiling through which neither stars nor moon penetrated.

After twenty minutes or so, Tazewell Watling came to a cluster of saloons and cribs, tinkling pianos, hoots, and braying laughter. "Please, sir. Which is Chapeau Rouge?"

The soldier was too drunk for words. His finger slewed up and down the street before settling on a two-story frame house with drawn curtains and a demure red lantern in its parlor window. This house had known better days and loomed over its shabby neighbors like a disapproving aunt. Behind a picket fence, the front yard was neat; its rosebushes were pruned for winter. The negro on the porch was smoking a cigar. His dark suit looked scratchy. A pale scar divided the man's face from chin to forehead. "Boy," he growled, "you got no business here. Git!"

Taz set his bag down and massaged his cramped hand. He said, "Abraham Lincoln emancipated the negroes. Why don't *you* git?"

Belle Watling's bully, MacBeth, said, "I'm a 'Lanta nigger. Them 'mancipators don't scare me none."

Tuesday after the battle of Fredricksburg, Chapeau Rouge was quiet. Last Saturday, the telegraph had brought news of the great Confederate victory, so Sunday morning, Belle Watling's top Cyprian, Minette, had sought out the soldiers' widows who filled in when Belle expected an overflow crowd. The Chapeau Rouge was usually closed on the Sabbath, but the Federal losses at Fredricksburg had been so huge, their mighty army so thoroughly humbled, that Belle ran out of champagne by six Sunday evening, dispatched MacBeth twice to replenish the brandy, and a score of exuberant patriots were still waiting on her doorstep at eleven that night.

Monday, Belle's Cyprians had moped around the establishment, sore, weary, and hungover, but by Tuesday evening the house had recovered its equilibrium and Minette had almost been glad to welcome the provost officer they'd nicknamed "Captain Busy."

The Chapeau Rouge was the most expensive sporting house in Atlanta. Its callers were high-ranking Confederate officers, speculators, and profiteers. It had been unexceptional in New Orleans's Vieux Carré but was considered highfalutin in earthier Atlanta.

In its parlor, hand-tinted lithographs of Parisian street scenes hung on flocked red-and-green-striped wallpaper. The ormolu mantel clock was flanked by tall marble Venuses in coy poses. Belle's spittoons were stored in cupboards unless requested. Her "Frenchy" furniture encouraged tough men to sit straight with their hands in their laps. To these men, Belle's Cyprians were as exotic as egrets. At the slightest provocation, the girls would burst into giggles or swift incomprehensible Creole.

Rhett Butler owned a share in the Chapeau Rouge and kept an office upstairs. Would-be troublemakers departed quietly when MacBeth told them, "Sir, I reckon you best be goin' home now. Wouldn't want to fetch Captain Butler."

Minette was a courtesan, and a shrewd one. To provide for her old age,

Minette bought house lots in New Orleans' Garden District and she tithed to the Good Fathers for the future of her soul. When Madame Belle invited Minette to work at the Chapeau Rouge, Minette nearly turned her down because Madame Belle was decidedly *not* a courtesan.

Although Madame Belle was older than Minette, she was a child as only American women can be children—infuriating children! A courtesan understands the nature of the transaction; the American is likely to confuse it with love—a confusion from which, Minette believed, only her sound Creole advice had kept Belle Watling.

Tonight, Minette smiled her courtesan's smile and told Captain Busy how dapper he looked.

"Ah, Minny. Have you changed your hair? It seems much redder than it was. Did I hear Rhett is back in town?"

What questions this man asked! He'd sit in the parlor on a slow rainy afternoon and ask question after question. Minette once heard Eloise describing her first lover—a neighbor boy—while Captain Busy chuckled as she recounted the poor boy's fumblings. Captain Busy advised Hélène on constipation, suggesting remedies when everyone knew Hélène's laudanum was the culprit! Once Captain Busy had asked Minette how she avoided pregnancy!

Captain Busy was extremely curious about Captain Butler: where he was, what he was doing, what he thought about this or that. How was Minette to know what Rhett Butler thought—and what business was it of Captain Busy's?

When Minette complained about the meddlesome provost, Rhett was amused. "Edgar is still trying to solve the mystery of life, Minette. Let him stew."

Edgar Puryear was a slender fellow, whom men remembered, after he had left the room, as shorter than he was. He had a bony long face, big ears, and a wide, expressive mouth; his fine eyelashes protected eyes as bright as a curious sparrow's.

Something about Captain Busy made ordinary Confederate soldiers want to knock him down, and when the liquor flowed on payday nights, his sergeant, Jack Johnson, accompanied him.

Tonight, the provost asked Minette for brandy. "Just a tot, dear Minny," putting his fingers two inches apart.

Power fascinated Edgar Allan Puryear. Rhett's father, Langston Butler, was powerful because he was rich and ruthless—rich *because* he was ruthless. Charlotte Fisher Ravanel was powerful because she was rich, and Andrew Ravanel was powerful because war rewards courage.

Edgar Puryear didn't understand Rhett Butler's power.

When young Rhett first arrived at Cathecarte Puryear's school, Edgar had gone upstairs to assess his father's new pupil. Rhett looked at Edgar, looked *through* him, and disregarded him in a single instant. Wait a minute, young Edgar wanted to protest. I am not merely what you see. I am more than that! But thereafter, Edgar only earned Rhett's half-amused smile. When Edgar flattered Rhett, Rhett mocked his flattery. When Edgar bought an expensive foulard for Rhett, Rhett never wore it. One evening, Edgar spotted it around the neck of Miss Polly's negro doorman. The only time Edgar summoned up courage to explain himself, Rhett interrupted before he'd finished three sentences—"Not now, Edgar"—and left the room.

Rhett Butler was never cruel to Edgar—not as Henry Kershaw and Andrew Ravanel could be cruel—but Rhett's indifference was worse than cruelty. Was that Rhett's secret? Might Rhett's indifference be his power?

When Rhett Butler was expelled from West Point (and no Charlestonian would have been surprised had young Butler put a bullet in his head), Only Edgar Puryear had greeted him at the dock. "Damn, it's good to see you, Rhett. Been too long! Come along with me. Polly's got a new girl with the most amazing appetites. . . ."

Rhett had smiled the half smile Edgar hated and said, "Not now, Edgar," and walked into town.

Coal scuttle in hand, the Chapeau Rouge's housemaid hesitated in the parlor doorway.

"Ah, come in, child."

"Sorry, sir. I didn't know anyone—"

"No matter. No matter. Do your work. Afraid I'll bite you?"

"No, sir."

"I'd never bite anyone as pretty as you."

The girl blushed.

"Tell me, child, when is Captain Butler expected?"

"Don't know, sir."

When she knelt to scoop coals into the stove, her dress stretched across her back and every knob on her long spine was visible. When Minette brought the captain's brandy, she snapped, "Lisa! You are not to come into the parlor in the evening!"

The startled housemaid tipped her scuttle and coal skittered underneath Captain Puryear's wing chair. He opened his knees so she could reach between them.

"Clumsy child," Minette hissed. "Leave them. You can pick up after the captain departs."

"Minny, do you think Lisa might care for me?"

"Lisa is a child, Captain," Minette said coolly. "She does not entertain callers."

When MacBeth came in, clutching a strange boy's arm, Lisa took the chance to flee.

MacBeth told Minette, "Boy says he's Miss Belle's sprout."

Brown hair combed to the side; the boy's narrow face was older than his years. Minette compared him with the daguerreotype enshrined on Madame's dressing table. "But *mon petit,* you are with the Good Fathers! You are in New Orleans!"

Taz spread his hands as if he had no idea how he found himself in Atlanta. He smiled a charming smile.

"Says he's Miz Belle's," MacBeth repeated.

Edgar Puryear's attention fixed on Taz. "Boy, who are you? How are you called?"

"I am Tazewell Watling, sir."

"Watling, by God! And you were born?"

"In New Orleans, sir."

"Not where! *When?* Why should I care *where* you were born? Let me calculate. Twelve—no, it'd be thirteen years ago!"

"I have thirteen years, yes, sir."

"Captain, *cher*. There will be time for questions later, no? The boy has come to see his dear Mama."

Captain Puryear stood and studied Taz like a buyer inspecting a colt. "Yes, there is a resemblance, a definite resemblance—those ears, that nose!" He toasted the boy. "Tazewell Watling! By God, you're Rhett Butler's bastard!" He drained his brandy and set the glass on the mantel.

"You are mistaken, sir. Captain Butler is my guardian."

"Why, of course he is. No doubt about that. He's whatever the old tomcat says he is."

The mantel clock ticked; the fire hissed in the parlor stove.

Taz had traveled far and he was tired. "I will inform Captain Butler of your interest in my parentage, sir."

Captain Puryear's eyes went flat. "We'll discuss this another time, boy. Minny, you can bring me another brandy? The French brandy this time, eh, *chère*?"

Minette hustled Taz down the hall into what had been a family dining room but was now Belle Watling's boudoir, the sanctuary of an uneducated woman with money. Dark silk moiré drapes covered the windows and muffled the street noises. Her lamp globes were painted with plump, garish flowers. Belle's coverlet was rose brocade and numerous large and small fringed pillows were arranged at the head of her bed. Warm, perfumed air enveloped Taz. This overwhelming femininity made him uneasy.

His mother peered over her reading glasses. "Taz," she said, stunned, "But I was just writin' you!"

"Madam, *le bon fils*!" Minette nudged the boy toward his mother.

Taz tried to forestall Belle's protest. "Please, Maman, I am so happy to be here. Can I stay with you?"

"But Taz . . ."

"I crawled through the Federal lines, right past their sentries. One of 'em near stepped on me! If he had, I don't know what I'd have done! I hadn't brought any food and hadn't had anything to eat and, Maman, I was *hungry*. Anyway, then I met up with some drovers taking cattle to Montgomery and they gave me corn cakes to eat. When I got to the railroad, the provosts wouldn't let me on the train. The soldiers snuck me on."

Her son flew into Belle's arms. "Lord knows, I've missed you, darling boy."

Minette opened the liquor chest, muttering, "'Minny'! 'Minny' he calls me! If Minette is good enough for the baptismal record, it is good enough for Captain Busy!"

Belle gently brushed her son's hair off his forehead. "Minette, not now, please."

"Eloise won't come downstairs when that man's in the house."

"Yes, Minette. Later, please."

"Captain, here is your *French* brandy!" Minette spat in the tumbler before she filled it and left.

Mother and son embraced and talked and embraced again. A little later, Lisa brought a tray with soup and bread. Taz ate at his mother's dressing table, among her pomades and potions. "Lisa is pretty, isn't she, Maman?" he said between bites.

"The poor child's husband's killed in the War. They had only one day together. Only one day! When she come to our doorstep, I took her in."

Belle laid comforters on the floor beside her bed, and after the boy fell asleep, Tazewell Watling's mother watched him for some time before she kissed him on the forehead and extinguished the lamp.

The next morning, when Taz returned from the necessary, smoke was rising from the kitchen chimney. Lisa jumped back from the stove she'd been feeding. "You scared me. Ain't used to no early risers."

"I don't need much sleep," Taz said. "In New Orleans, we don't sleep hardly at all."

She cocked an eyebrow. "That so?"

"Day or night. Something's always doing in New Orleans." He rubbed his nose. "Atlanta's so smoky. How do you stand it?"

"Ain't bad once you're used to it."

"Maman says you are a widow."

"My Billy's kilt."

"I've never been married," Taz said.

"Course you ain't been married. You're just a baby."

Taz drew himself up. "In New Orleans, we say, '*L'heure coq cante, li bon pour marie!*'" He translated politely, "'When the cock crows, he's ready to marry!'"

"You talk funny," she said. "Talk some more."

In French, Taz told Lisa she had pretty eyes. Lisa colored, for the French language cannot disguise sentiment. Taz added, "I suppose you heard I'm a bastard."

"I don't know I ever met a bastard."

"Well, now you've met one, what do you think?"

"I think I was cookin' oatmeal and might be you'd want some."

Later, Taz met the Cyprians: Eloise, who had the longest black hair he'd ever seen, and Hélène, whose eyes were sleepy from laudanum.

MacBeth's knuckles were broken and flattened from fighting. MacBeth had been reared in Atlanta. "I'm a city nigger," MacBeth said. "I don't wear no kerchief. There's a hat on *my* head."

Taz asked MacBeth about Captain Butler.

"Captain Butler comes and goes," MacBeth said.

"Does Butler sleep here? In the house, I mean."

"You mean do he lie up with your mama?" MacBeth asked with a straight face.

Taz balled his fists, but MacBeth glowered until the boy relaxed. Taz looked off and whistled tunelessly. "Did you ever kill anyone?" Taz asked.

"Only niggers," MacBeth said.

Taz clicked Rhett's door closed behind himself and sniffed. Stale cigar smoke and dust. So this was his father's office. Until the provost captain had spoken, Taz hadn't suspected. When he'd asked Belle about his father, she'd always said, "There'll be time for that when you're grown."

Well, he was grown now.

His father's office was nothing special: a desk, a ponderous iron safe, a walnut daybed, two sturdy chairs, and an oak chifforobe. The front windows overlooked the walk, where MacBeth was raking cigar butts from the flower beds. The rear windows framed Belle's stable and, behind it, a weedy pasture ending at a vividly green margin of swamp grass beside a murky creek.

Taz spun the dial and tried the brass lever, but Rhett's safe was locked. He leaned back in his father's chair.

Several times, Belle had told Taz how she and Rhett had been reacquainted: "If I hadn't passed the St. Louis Hotel that day, Taz, honey, I reckon things would have been bad for me. I didn't have nothin', nary a dime. I'd give you up to the orphanage and I was too shamed to even come visit you. Honey, I saw these fancy folks outside the St. Louis and thought they might just spare me somethin'. I didn't have no pride, honey. You got no pride when you're down-and-out. Anyway, I didn't recognize him at first, but he knew me right off. Rhett Butler took care of me. Took care of me and took care of my darling boy, too."

Rhett's suits and starched shirts hung in the chifforobe above two pairs of riding boots in stretchers. There was nothing in the desk except pens, ink, writing paper, and Charles Dickens's *American Notes.*

Taz swiveled the chair. Scuffs on the chair rail showed where Rhett Butler had rested his boot heels. Even scooted down as far as he could get, Taz's feet couldn't reach them.

Taz ate breakfast with Lisa and supper with the Cyprians at four o'clock. Before sundown, he went upstairs and sat on Rhett's daybed, reading Mr. Dickens until after midnight. He heard laughter, unsteady footsteps outside the office door, and Cyprians giggling.

After MacBeth had seen their last guest out, Belle locked the front door, snuffed the red lamp and the parlor lamps, and went upstairs to fetch her son.

Belle Watling was not a beautiful woman, but she was lively and appealing. One year for her birthday, Rhett bought her a gray silk Paris gown. Belle folded it and laid it in its original paper wrapping deep in her bureau drawer. She wouldn't wear it. "Nobody would know me," she said.

Another time, Rhett suggested Belle wear less face powder. He sat her before a dressing mirror, washed her face with warm water, and cleansed it with cotton. "You don't need rouge, my dear. Your cheeks glow like pippins."

The Belle in the mirror seemed ten years younger, innocent and shy. The country girl looking at her made Belle cry.

On Saturday night, army payday, three days before Christmas, a wreath hung on Chapeau Rouge's front door. Sergeant Johnson grinned at his boss. "Merry Christmas, Captain."

After Edgar Allan Puryear went inside, Sergeant Johnson put his boot on the porch railing and lit his pipe.

From the green velvet love seat in the parlor, a one-armed major asked Edgar, "Aren't there enlisted men's brothels where you might better spend your time, Provost Captain? Or are they a little . . . rough for you?"

When Edgar Puryear pursed his lips, the major rose, drawing Hélène after him. "Let us continue upstairs, my dear." Hélène covered her mouth and giggled.

A trio of artillery lieutenants came in laughing but made faces at the provost's back and took their custom elsewhere.

Paydays were Chapeau Rouge's busiest nights, and Minette smiled through her teeth. "Captain Puryear, I am so glad you are here tonight."

"Because?"

Minette went on. "You are so curious to learn about our young Tazewell. Captain Butler is expected this night. Miss Belle and MacBeth are at the Car Shed awaiting his train. You will satisfy all your questions from—how you say?—the horse's mouth."

To Minette's satisfaction, Edgar flinched. "Will you take a brandy while you wait, Captain?"

Edgar Puryear went to the mantel clock and stared unseeing at its elaborate gilt hands. He took a sharp breath and turned. "Fetch the boy."

"Captain?"

"Fetch the boy, Minny, or I'll have my sergeant fetch him."

When Minette brought Taz downstairs, she warned him about Captain Busy. "He is like the alligator," Minette said. "He is most dangerous when he smiles."

The provost captain indicated a chair, but Taz remained standing. "Sir?"

"When your father and I were your age, boy, we were great friends." Edgar smiled. "Some of the things we got up to." Edgar chuckled reminiscently.

"Sir?"

"You know, boy. As close as we were in those days, Rhett never told me he was courting Belle Watling. Rhett was a gentleman, you see, and Belle—" Frowning, Edgar turned at the interruption. "Ah, Lisa. Come in, my dear. I was hoping I'd see you again."

The girl stood in the doorway with a telegram in her hand. "Please, sir . . ."

"Come in. Do come in. What have you there?"

She approached with downcast eyes.

"Bring it to me, Lisa."

"Sir, this ain't for you. It's from Captain Rhett for Miss Belle."

His snapping fingers were a magnet. Edgar read the flimsy, crumpled and dropped it on the floor. "No great matter, child. My friend Rhett's train is delayed." The Captain stretched out his legs and crossed his ankles. "No, Lisa, you mustn't go. It's rude to leave your guests before the party ends." He cocked his head. "I'll bet you didn't know that Tazewell is Captain Butler's son? No? Friend Rhett plays his cards so close to the vest."

Minette said, "You may go now, child. You have duties in the kitchen."

"I haven't said she could go." Captain Puryear smiled, as if Minette had made a forgivable blunder.

Minette shrugged. She was a courtesan after all, not the girl's mother.

Taz stepped between Lisa and the Captain's wing chair.

"Fond of her, are you, boy? Do you like money, girl?"

Lisa tucked her hands under her apron. "Everybody likes money," she announced scornfully.

Edgar whispered, "Pretty little trifle, isn't she, boy?" With the air of a man with all the time in the world, he opened his purse and extracted a twenty-dollar gold piece, which he turned in the light before he laid the coin on the mantelpiece. "Ever seen one of these before, girl?"

Lisa was drawn to it. "That's right smart of money."

The silver dollar Captain Puryear set beside the gold piece seemed its poor relation. "The act doesn't last thirty minutes and it's not as if you haven't done it before." He stroked the girl's arm like a man pets a strange cat and murmured, "That bedroom at the top of the stairs, Minny, is it available?"

"Captain!" Minette protested. "Lisa is a child. I am the courtesan!"

"Minny," Puryear said, "if I'd wanted your favors, I'd have had them." To Lisa: "Go ahead, girl. Touch the money."

To Taz's shame, his voice broke when he said, "Leave her be!"

"Do you fancy her, boy? Look at her, Tazewell Butler. Lisa's so greedy. Such pretty trash and so, so greedy." Edgar dipped into his wallet for a second silver dollar. He slid the coin atop its mate so slowly, it hissed.

Mesmerized, Lisa took a step toward the money.

"The hell you say! The hell!" Tazewell Watling swept Puryear's coins onto the floor.

Lisa dropped to her knees chasing the gold piece, which had rolled underneath the love seat. Grinning from ear to ear, Edgar rocked back on his heels, laughing.

Taz hurled the mantel clock, but the provost ducked. The missile exploded into springs, cogwheels, and broken glass.

"Dear me! Dear, dear me!" Edgar Puryear chuckled.

His eyes changed when Taz picked up a Venus statuette.

"Boy, you wait one minute! You wait! Strike a Confederate officer, and by God . . ." Edgar blocked Taz's blow with his right arm. He yelped, "Goddamn you, boy! You hurt me! That's enough!"

Taz's lips were drawn over his teeth. "You bastard!" Taz feinted, and when the provost tried to grab the statue, Taz backhanded him across the nose. Edgar's eyes teared.

"Jesus Christ, Busy!" Sergeant Johnson spoke from behind Taz. "He's just a goddamned kid!"

Despite which, the sergeant knocked the kid unconscious with his shot-loaded sap.

When Taz woke, his left foot was warm because someone was vomiting on it. Taz retracted his foot. His head pulsed so bad he opened his mouth to let the pain escape. In a corner, a soldier rested his forehead against the wall he was pissing on. Taz touched the knot on his head. He'd lost a shoe and his pockets were turned inside out. When he shut his eyes, he saw blue-and-orange pinwheels. Moonlight trickled through a high barred window. The Judas hole in the cell door was a perfect circle of unblinking yellow light.

Hours went by before an aged negro called softly through that hole, "Lookin' for Watling. Tazewell Watling? Watling with us tonight?"

Taz followed the negro down the corridor into a guardroom with a bench along one wall and a table behind which a Confederate colonel sat, thumbing through papers. He didn't look up at Taz.

At six in the morning, Rhett Butler's shirt was fresh and he was clean-shaven. Taz could smell his pomade. "Taz, you broke poor Edgar's nose. He can't show his face in public."

Pain jolted behind Tazewell's eyes. "Captain Puryear is a blackguard."

"Edgar hasn't the guts to be a blackguard, Taz. Edgar just dirties what he touches." Rhett's big gentle fingers explored the boy's skull and he peered into his eyes. "Your noggin's fine, boy. In his line of work, Sergeant Johnson is a virtuoso."

"Sir, Captain Puryear was taking liberties."

"Edgar has unusual tastes. I'll take you back to the Jesuits. You can't learn to be a gentleman in jail."

Taz was tired. He hurt and he smelled bad. Had his father ever been tired or sick or hurt or afraid? Were his clothes always immaculate? Did he always smell of pomade?

Taz summoned up his boy's dignity. "Sir, in the orphan asylum we boys said that the sun rises in the east and sets in the west for the finest gentleman and for that gentleman's bastard alike."

Chapter Thirteen

A Legendary Rebel Commander

From childhood, Melanie Hamilton had known that she would marry Ashley Wilkes because "The Wilkeses always marry cousins."

Every summer, Melanie and her brother, Charles, rode the train from Atlanta to Jonesboro, where John Wilkes's body servant, Mose, met them at the depot. Mose always had molasses candy in his pocket and always pretended that this time he'd forgotten it.

The Twelve Oaks Wilkeses were the Hamiltons' grandest relations and Charles and Melanie arrived in their stiffest, starchiest clothing. They'd been scrubbed to a fare-thee-well. Aunt Pittypat's injunctions ("If you let your napkin fall, don't pick it up." "Don't ask to ride Cousin India's pony. Wait until India offers.") were unnecessary: the Hamilton orphans were overawed.

Charles enjoyed these visits; Melanie didn't. Atlanta was a city, and despite the Wilkeses' fine library and finer manners, Twelve Oaks was the country. All those impersonal trees amid which a child might so easily become lost, that dark muddy river in which that child might drown. And so many dreadful bugs! Honeybees and newsbees and bumblebees and yellow jackets and mud daubers and sweat bees and paper wasps and the nasty bugs that tangled themselves in Melanie's hair, and the whining bloodsuckers trapped inside her bed netting that kept her awake half the night. Charles said that if you let them drink their fill, the spot wouldn't itch afterward. It was horrible to watch Charles let some mosquito fill its pendulous bright red abdomen on his thin outstretched arm.

Charles started calling Twelve Oaks "the Kingdom of Bugs," swooping and buzzing at Melanie until she didn't know whether to giggle or cry.

Since Melanie would one day marry Ashley Wilkes, she wanted to love Twelve Oaks as Ashley loved it, but the prospect of becoming the next Mrs. Wilkes, managing that enormous house, servants, and household economy, daunted her. When Ashley's mother died, Ashley's sisters, India and Honey, worked awfully hard. One day, Ashley's wife would be expected to manage everything by herself.

Melanie and Ashley would take their place at Twelve Oaks as Ashley's parents had, and Twelve Oaks would sustain them until they made their final journey to the graveyard atop the hill behind the house.

The courting couple climbed the stone steps to that graveyard to sit beneath its canopy of aged chestnuts and elms. There they exchanged those solemn sentiments young people utter in such a place.

Melanie did love Twelve Oaks' gardens: the magnolias, azaleas, rhododendrons, and Bourbon roses. Her happiest memories were of sitting beside Ashley beneath the wisteria, whose thick vines were as old as the manor house itself.

The couple talked about books and beauty. They discussed Mr. Scott's *Ivanhoe* and Mr. Dickens's *The Old Curiosity Shop*.

Ashley and Melanie's courtship was so muted, others could be excused for not noticing it. They were spared those painful doubts, hesitations, half commitments, bold advances, and wounded retreats of those unfortunate lovers who do not marry cousins. One spring afternoon, Ashley asked Melanie to marry him and Melanie said yes. Ashley wore, Melanie later recalled, a rose in his buttonhole. Melanie was surprised by how thoroughly she enjoyed Ashley's kiss.

After a year of service with his Georgia regiment, Ashley had volunteered for Ravanel's brigade because, as Ashley wrote Melanie, "I thought it my duty."

Melanie could not criticize her husband's decision, but his transfer to Ravanel's dangerous brigade gave her sleepless nights.

Not long after he joined Ravanel, Ashley regretted that decision.

"Charleston gentlemen aren't Georgia gentlemen. That the Low Country is the known universe and that Charleston is the center of the universe, they have no doubts. When I describe Twelve Oaks' gardens, the rare roses great-grandmother brought from Virginia's Tidewater—those same roses *her* great-grandmother brought from Surrey!—they tell me the roses beside the Jockey Club are the 'prettiest in the South,' though they can't name the variety!"

In a postscript, Ashley added, "Colonel Ravanel is an inspiring commander, but I'd never leave him alone with my sisters!"

In the hectic, thrilling days as the South went to war, Miss Melanie Hamilton had married Mr. Ashley Wilkes, and Miss Scarlett O'Hara had married Mr. Charles Hamilton. Neither couple had time to take a breath. At first when tradesmen called Melanie "Mrs. Wilkes," she didn't know whom they were talking to.

Six months later, Melanie was devastated when her brother, Charles, died. Melanie had been a toddler when she and Charles were put in Aunt Pittypat's care. Christened Sarah Jane Hamilton, the plump, childlike woman had been "Pittypat" as long as anyone could remember. Her household had been so happily disordered that "Pittypat's" was where all the neighborhood children came to play. Melanie couldn't remember her dead father and mother. She loved her brother, Charles, as only an orphan can love.

Melanie had been such a sickly child, she knew Atlanta's doctors by their unique tread on the stairs. Melanie had expected to die young, but Charles was supposed to live forever!

When Charles died, the Hamiltons' shared childhood died with him: Mose's molasses candy, the closet under Pittypat's stairs, which had been their secret hiding place, the silly childhood jokes, which could still fetch an adult's reminiscent smile. "The Kingdom of Bugs" died with Charles Hamilton.

In the first year of the war, with Ashley in the army and Charles in his grave, Melanie Wilkes was desperately alone.

Getting through each long, long day, smiling at those who needed her smile, commiserating with the kind souls who'd come to commiserate with her: Melanie's duty was her refuge.

Melanie diluted her own grief worrying about her brother's widow, Scarlett. Melanie entirely approved when Scarlett's mother sent the young widow to visit kinfolk in Charleston. At the station, Melanie told her sister-in-law what Melanie didn't believe herself: that grief for Charles would one day end.

When Scarlett's Charleston visit didn't improve the young widow's spirits, Melanie suggested Pittypat invite Scarlett and Baby Wade to live with them in Atlanta. Pittypat hemmed and hawed. Finally, she said, "I'm afraid Scarlett is not a quiet person, dear."

Melanie said they had responsibilities to the woman Charles had chosen and to Charles's infant son, Wade Hampton Hamilton. Pittypat, as she always did, gave way.

Melanie's sister-in-law was as vibrant as Melanie was demure. Scarlett feared nothing, Melanie's courage had never been tested. Scarlett had had a dozen eager suitors, Melanie had only been courted, and very quietly, by her cousin. Perhaps Melanie hoped some of Scarlett's vitality would rub off on her. She very much wanted her sister-in-law to be her friend.

Not long after Scarlett arrived at her home, Pittypat's fears were realized. Scarlett rubbed Pittypat's dearest friends, Mrs. Merriwether and Mrs. Elsing, crossways. Melanie made excuses for Scarlett and kept the peace. And Melanie loved Baby Wade. Baby Wade had Charles's sweet, trusting eyes.

When Captain Butler started calling on the Widow Hamilton, Pittypat's friends, who could be so kind to sick children and elderly servants, were horrified—and made their disapproval felt.

Melanie'd heard awful things about Captain Butler, and, as luck would have it, neither Pittypat nor Scarlett was home the third time Captain Butler paid a call.

Melanie thought Rhett Butler was handsome in the way a big cat is handsome. He was more muscular than most gentleman, though his tailors had done their best to disguise that.

Captain Butler was devastated Mrs. Hamilton wasn't at home. He was leaving Atlanta tomorrow and his visit had been a spur-of-the-moment impulse.

"Captain Butler," Melanie said, "you are said to be a scoundrel."

"Why, yes." He smiled. "I suppose I am."

"Yet you are well-spoken and have a gentleman's bearing."

"Appearances, Mrs. Wilkes, are famously deceiving."

"Today, you bring Paris shoes for Pittypat and an English toy for Baby Wade."

"Mrs. Wilkes, any housebreaker worth his salt disarms the guard dogs before he rifles the family silver."

"Men say you are a sharp trader, but honest."

He brushed off her mild praise as if brushing crumbs off his lapel. "Businessmen flatter a thief rather than confess he outwitted them."

"Mr. Butler?"

"Yes, Mrs. Wilkes?" His broad smile was heedless of consequence.

"I am told, Captain Butler, you believe this war is a fool's enterprise."

His amusement vanished. "Dear lady, this war is already terrible. I fear it will become more terrible. It will destroy the South."

She offered her small hand. "It is a pleasure to welcome you, Captain Butler. Do come in. Might I brew you a cup of tea?"

From that moment, no one but Scarlett could speak ill of Rhett Butler in Melanie's presence.

Melanie was glad when Rhett's sparkling gig pulled up outside Pittypat's picket fence. In their topsy-turvy world, Rhett Butler was normalcy. His brushed-felt hat refuted the fact that fine hats were not to be had at any price; Rhett's polished shoes denied that good shoes were unobtainable; the delicacies he brought were evidence that somewhere the world was not at war.

Sitting comfortably in their parlor, Rhett indulged Pittypat's curiosity about the latest Paris fashions and what was worn at the Court of St. James.

Melanie had always yearned to travel and delighted to hear Rhett's tales of New Orleans' raucous funeral bands and the wild California gold camps. (Mugfuzzle indeed!)

Rhett and Scarlett clashed like flint and steel. It was none of Melly's affair, but there was something so magnificent about Scarlett and Rhett separately, Melanie couldn't help hoping they would combine. Melanie couldn't understand why Scarlett was cold to Rhett—unless her heart was still pledged to Charles. Rhett would mock Scarlett's coldness and leave angrily, and Scarlett would march through Pittypat's house, opening and slamming every door.

This particular morning, Captain Butler was out of town and the three ladies of Pittypat's household were driving to the National Hotel for the reception Dolly Merriwether had organized for Andrew Ravanel. The ladies hoped that Colonel Ravanel's adjutant, Ashley Wilkes, might accompany him.

It was a glorious, clear, cold winter day. The ambulances creaking through the city were so commonplace, people no longer noticed them.

"Melanie! You mustn't return those soldiers' waves," Aunt Pittypat said. "They may not be gentlemen."

"They are our dear boys," Melanie Wilkes replied, and then cried out, "Boys, we are so proud of you!"

At her impropriety, Pittypat's aged houseman, Uncle Peter, grumbled and popped the reins. The mare picked up her pace for a moment before resuming her habitual amble.

Carriages, horsemen, and pedestrians were converging downtown. Blue bunting draped the gaslights, and Confederate flags fluttered from every window.

Pittypat said, "They say Colonel Ravanel's banjo player accompanies him everywhere. I'm told Colonel Ravanel's officers are jolly."

When their carriage could get no nearer the hotel, the ladies descended and Pittypat instructed Uncle Peter to collect them no later than five o'clock.

"Yes, Miss Pitty. I be doin' my best."

The crowd at the Car Shed was so thick, the ladies couldn't get through. At Scarlett's suggestion, they crossed behind the freight depot and, ignoring Pitty's complaints, picked their way across the tracks into the small park facing the National Hotel. From this vantage point, they couldn't see Colonel Ravanel's train puff into town, but they heard the welcoming shouts. A rolling barrage of huzzahs attended the hero's progress down Pryor Street and, pulled by citizens, his carriage hove into sight while boys ran ahead shouting importantly, "Make way for Colonel Ravanel! Make way!"

"Oh dear," Aunt Pittypat said. "I feel faint."

Scarlett was hopping with impatience. "Do you see him? Melanie, do you see Ashley?"

"You mustn't faint, Aunty. Scarlett, I can't make out who is in the carriage. Please, Scarlett, you are taller than I!"

On tiptoe, Scarlett couldn't see through the forest of men's stovepipe hats.

"We won't get into the reception," Aunt Pittypat wailed. "We won't see Ashley, and Uncle Peter will forget to fetch us and we shall have to walk home. The shoes Captain Butler brought are pinching my feet!"

"If you'd given Captain Butler your correct size, your shoes might fit," Scarlett snapped.

"My dear! Everybody knows I have the smallest feet in the family!"

Scarlett bit her tongue and said, "Melly, aren't there stairs around back? Can we get in that way?"

"But dear," Pittypat protested, "those are servants' stairs."

Melanie said, "Take my arm, Aunt Pitty. Please, gentlemen, let three ladies pass! Thank you, sir. Sir, thank you. You are so kind."

They hadn't invitations, but Dolly Merriwether couldn't welcome her friends Pittypat and Melanie while turning Scarlett away. "Why, Scarlett," Mrs. Merriwether said with a tight smile. "I am so glad you've come to honor our Colonel."

Scarlett curtsied. "Dear Mrs. Merriwether, you know how I adore our brave soldier boys."

Mrs. Merriwether blinked like an owl.

"We hoped Ashley would be with Colonel Ravanel. Have you seen him, Dolly?" Melanie asked.

"Dear, I haven't been able to get near the Colonel. Half Atlanta has pushed itself into our fête. What good are invitations when no one respects them?"

Scarlett pushed through the crowd. A rail-thin, whitish blond Confederate officer had his ear bent to Dr. Meade, a bearded physician who shared his community's good opinion of himself. Andrew Ravanel turned to Scarlett with a bow. "Had I known Atlanta possessed such beautiful belles, I should have visited before."

Searching for Ashley, Scarlett's eyes roved beyond the guest of honor. Offhandedly, she said, "It is just as well you don't come often, Colonel Ravanel. You've turned our city into Bedlam."

"Isn't it terrible?" His grin was innocent, a boy's grin. "Dr. Meade, won't you introduce us?"

Scarlett couldn't see Ashley anywhere.

"Colonel Ravanel, Mrs. Charles Hamilton. Mrs. Hamilton's husband gave his life for the Cause."

Melanie came to Scarlett's side.

"So very many sacrifices . . ." The Colonel bent to kiss Scarlett's hand. "And this other lovely lady is . . ."

"Mrs. Ashley Wilkes, Colonel. My husband, Major Wilkes, is on your staff."

The Colonel's smile froze in place. "Major Wilkes has returned to his regiment."

Melanie frowned. "But he just joined you."

"Wilkes asked to return to his Georgia regiment and I honored his request."

"But . . . I knew nothing. . . . Colonel, the mail is so unreliable! Please, tell me: How is my husband? Is Ashley in good health? Good spirits? Has he warm clothing?"

"Wilkes was healthy enough when I last saw him."

Melanie's brow furrowed. "But Colonel Ravanel . . ."

Dr. Meade rescued the Colonel from further awkward questions. "While our soldiers suffer dreadful hardships, speculators make fortunes. I have composed a strong letter to the *Gate City Guardian* denouncing those who convert public shortages to private gain." Dr. Meade paused for effect. "Colonel Ravanel, aren't you Charlestonian by birth? You must know Rhett Butler."

"Why, yes. His father, Langston, is in the Carolina legislature. Rhett's the black sheep, I'm afraid."

Melanie Wilkes said, "Captain Butler is my friend."

Dr. Meade bowed stiffly. "Mrs. Wilkes, I do not dispute Butler's charm. Tell me, Colonel, do you know what army 'Captain' Butler is a 'captain' in?"

Scarlett barely heard these trivialities. She was so disappointed she could scream! She'd so hoped to see Ashley. Just a moment, one precious moment! What nonsense was Dr. Meade speaking now? Was he condescending to Rhett Butler? "Doubtless, Dr. Meade, you'll be glad when Captain Butler returns, so you can state your patriotic views to his face." Scarlett's smile was deliberately insincere. "Come, Melanie, we must share the Colonel with his admirers."

Colonel Ravanel said, "My dear Mrs. Hamilton. You mustn't." He placed a hand on his breast and declaimed, "If you go, the light will leave the room."

"Colonel, it's winter and gets dark early. If you need light, purchase a lantern."

Melanie's worried eyes hadn't left the Colonel, "When I write my husband, Colonel Ravanel, might I convey your regards?"

"You needn't trouble yourself, madam. Captain Wilkes is well aware of my regard."

On their ride home, Aunt Pittypat prattled about how handsome the Colonel was. "What did he say to you? Melly? Scarlett? Every word! Oh dear, Melly, are those tears I see?"

That evening, Melanie was so worried about Ashley, she took a sleeping draft. Pittypat was in the kitchen soaking her blistered feet while Scarlett took sassafras tea in the parlor. Daguerreotypes elbowed one another across Aunt Pitty's crowded mantel, prints from *Godey's Lady's Book* hung beside painted miniatures, silhouettes, and indifferent watercolors.

Every precious object held a memory. "That china press belonged to Melly's mother—it would feel so *unwanted* in the attic."

Scarlett shifted seashells (collected on a Savannah beach twenty years ago) to make room for her cup. Scarlett didn't care for sassafras tea, but she cherished her moments alone.

She closed her eyes to thank God that Ashley had left Colonel Ravanel's brigade! The newspapers' "legendary Confederate" was reckless with his men's precious lives. What if she lost Ashley?

Ashley killed! How could she have thought it! Quickly, she prayed, asking God to forgive her. She hadn't meant it!

A terrific jangling erupted on Aunt Pitty's front porch and a tenor voice sang, "If you want to have a good time, if you want to have a good time, jine the cavalry!"

When the bewildered Uncle Peter opened the door, Colonel Ravanel swept his plumed hat almost to the floor. "Good evening, Mrs. Hamilton. I have come to offer innocent diversion to Atlanta's loveliest lady!" The negro with the Colonel tapped his banjo significantly. His face was solemn as, one slow note at a time, he plunked the familiar "Lorena."

The Colonel recited the lyrics. " 'The years creep slowly by, Lorena. The snow is on the grass again. . . .' "

"Sir . . ." Uncle Peter protested.

"Go to bed, Uncle. Old boy like you needs his rest."

"You may leave, Uncle Peter." Scarlett rose from her chair. "Sir, I do not recall inviting you here."

" 'The sun's low down the sky, Lorena. The frost gleams where the flowers have been. . . .' "

"Your memory has failed you, Colonel. I am not called Lorena."

He sighed profoundly. "Such a melancholy tune. We lonely soldiers sing it 'round our watch fires while dreaming of home and loving hearts we have left behind." His sad eyes invited her tenderest understanding. "Duty, dear Mrs. Hamilton—may I call you Scarlett?—duty is a harsh taskmaster."

"Sir, are you drunk?"

Aunt Pittypat hobbled into the parlor, "Why, Colonel Ravanel . . ."

"You may return to the kitchen, Aunt Pitty. Colonel Ravanel is just leaving."

"But Scarlett . . ."

"Please!"

Shaking her head, Pitty withdrew.

The banjo player was so brilliant, he nearly blunted Scarlett's wrath. With soft notes, the banjo player mimed his master's disappointment. His chords were silent sobs. He sought memories of happier times, changed keys, and struck up the lively "Ye Cavaliers of Dixie."

Colonel Ravanel confided proudly, "Cassius's repertoire is endless."

"Doubtless your repertoire is equally extensive, as I'm sure Mrs. Ravanel can attest. I thought your wife, Charlotte, a pleasant woman. Certainly she is more tolerant of fools than I. Good night, Colonel Ravanel. Take your orchestra with you."

His amused eyes froze. "I am not accustomed to mockery."

"I am not accustomed to impromptu musicales in my parlor."

"Cassius!"

When the negro's flying fingers stilled, his final notes hung in the air like dust motes. For the second time that evening, Andrew Ravanel swept his plumed hat so low, its feather ticked the floor. "Madam, I so admire a patriotic gentlewoman."

"'Patriotic'? Dear, dear me!" Scarlett covered her mouth in mock astonishment. "I didn't know *that* was 'patriotism.' I believe what you intended has ruder names, though no well-bred Georgia lady would admit to knowing them."

Chapter Fourteen

Wedded

Rosemary Haynes strove to overrule her own heart. If she pretended with enough determination, her lie might become true and she would love her husband. She swallowed her yawns at John's nightly reading and even suggested a book or two. Some evenings, when her husband turned to her at the top of the stairs, Rosemary found a smile.

"Am I hurting you?"

Her fists clenched at her sides. "John, dear. Please, take your own satisfaction."

Though conversations as husband and wife lurched like a wagon with a bent wheel, as Meg's father and mother they had no end of things to say to each other.

Rosemary was endlessly bemused by this wonderfully different edition of herself. Meg never dissembled. Sunny one moment, weeping the next: Meg had no natural reserve.

One evening when the parents came downstairs after hearing the child's prayers, John asked, "Why was she praying for horses? Meg was commending every horse in creation."

"When Cleo and Meg went to White Point today, apparently they came upon a cabbie beating his horse. Cleo told me the horse was old—too old to pull anymore. Some adults were remonstrating ineffectually but Meg ran at the cabbie and pummeled his legs." Rosemary smiled fondly. "I suppose Meg's assault must have shamed the spectators, because an officer bought the poor beast on the spot."

"Our dear daughter despises cruelty. The horse—"

"Yes," Rosemary said, "I imagine our Good Samaritan shot the beast soon afterward, but Meg imagines him whole and well in green pastures. I had a pony when I was a child. Jack, my Jack. Perhaps Meg—"

"Meg is too young for a pony."

John Haynes was invited to the legislature to discuss strategies for defeating the Yankee blockade.

Waiting for the Columbia train to depart, Rosemary's husband ventured, "I hate to leave Meg," adding quickly, "I'll miss you, my dear, of course." John Haynes longed for better words, magic words that could make things different between them. His voice faded. "Oh yes, I will miss you."

Despite a headache coming on, Rosemary advised, "John, please remember to dress warmly. You know how easily you take cold. Do remember to eat breakfast."

"Yes," he said. "Well . . ." They embraced stiffly. She patted his hand.

He said, "Good-bye, my dearest."

Rosemary smiled and waved as John's train left the depot. But once his car was out of sight, Rosemary slumped on the nearest bench. Her temples throbbed. She shut her eyes and made herself breathe deeply.

She heard a train: its bell, the hiss of escaping steam, the rumble of porters' wagons and passengers' greetings. Brisk footfalls paused before her, and when Rosemary opened her eyes, Andrew Ravanel was smiling down.

Her headache was gone in an instant. Rosemary felt lighter—so much lighter that, like thistledown, she might just float away.

"Well, hello there, Rosemary. Funny place to nap."

"Good heavens, Andrew! I hadn't known you were due. Where's your welcoming committee?"

The Colonel laughed. "General Bragg says it does Southerners good to see me now and again." Andrew pressed a hand to his breast melodramatically. "Dear Rosemary, I am a cheap utensil, like a bullet mold or mess kit, to be used until worn out and discarded."

Rosemary smiled brilliantly. "Then all this 'gallantry' is a sham?"

"Why, of course it is! But can you keep a secret? War is grand fun!"

The negro carrying Ravanel's carpetbag had a banjo over his shoulder.

"Cassius, find us a cab. I'll slip into Charleston like a thief in the night. Come, Rosemary, I will take you home."

As their cab was trotting down Meeting Street, Andrew described his Atlanta reception. "As I climbed into the carriage, men were unhitching the horses. Had I fallen among horse thieves? But no! These citizens had it in their heads they must pull my carriage. They took up the shafts, trotting along so vigorously I wondered why such robust specimens weren't in the army.

"Next, I was bundled from my carriage, hoisted onto their shoulders, and deafened by cheers. I was rushed up the hotel stairs, worried my brains might be dashed out against the ceiling. At last I was set down, grateful to be on my own pegs. There, I met two of the grandest curmudgeons who ever curmudged. The good Dr. Meade delivered a denunciation of your brother, Rhett, that blistered my eyelashes, until I told Meade if Rhett were present, he wouldn't dare speak so boldly." Andrew took Rosemary's hand. "The other curmudgeon, Mrs. Merriwether, is so formidable, we should clad her in iron plate and sail her down Charleston harbor. Spouting commonplaces to port and starboard, she would wreak havoc in the Federal fleet. And those other Atlanta ladies . . ."

"Swooning at your feet?"

"A sad lot. One poor soul was the wife of the worst officer I've ever commanded. I lied shamelessly. By the time I finished singing Major Wilkes's praises, he was more vital to the Cause than Lee himself."

Andrew caressed the soft skin on the back of Rosemary's hand: an exquisite touch on the boundary between pleasure and pain. "But Rosemary, here I am describing tiresome people with the loveliest woman in Charleston at my side."

Rosemary recaptured her hand and sat up straight. "You forget I am a wife and mother, Andrew."

"Why, so you are. That is as it should be. Happy mother, satisfied wife."

As they rolled past the burnt district's ruined homes and churches, Andrew recaptured her hand. "Remember how it feels when you take a good horse over the jump, that instant when you trust the horse, give it its head, and it sails up and up, as if you are sailing into the blue, and you know in the next second, you are immortal. Do you remember, Rosemary, how it feels to be immortal?"

Rosemary spoke ever so softly. "No . . ."

"We soldiers scurry and wait and suffer saddle sores and weather and awful food, and some days if it weren't for Cassius's banjo, I swear we'd all desert to the enemy. But one morning, we meet our foe in all his awful glory, and in that moment time stands still. Rosemary, isn't this your house? May I come in?"

"Yes," Rosemary said.

Servants know everything. Servants change rumpled bedclothes, and scrub undergarments; they hear ecstatic cries behind closed doors.

Next morning, Cleo told Cook, "That Colonel fellow, he get to the withdrawing room, but he never got past it, and when it looked like he was a-goin' to, Miss Rosemary, she ask me bring Miss Meg down so the colonel could admire her. Little Meg don't take to him. No she don't. The child starts a-carryin' on and a-kickin' her feet, so Miss Rosemary takes her off, and though the Colonel, he waits in the withdrawing room for near an hour, Miss Rosemary never come back."

Disappointed, Cook said, "They didn't do nothin'?"

"Oh that Colonel, he surely wanted to do somethin'. He was like a stallion prancin' 'round a mare, snufflin' and showin' his teeth, and might be Miss Rosemary wanted to, too, but God tell her, 'Don't you dare! Keep yourself for your husband!' Good thing that Colonel din't look at me the way he look at Miss Rosemary, 'cause I swear I never seen no handsomer man."

Cook shook her head, "Nothin'?" She brightened, "I'd wager the white folks will think they did."

Andrew strode rapidly down the Battery, taking no notice of those who recognized him. Cassius trotted beside him.

Although Andrew banged the door knocker of the Fisher mansion, it was some time before his wife, Charlotte, came to the door. "Andrew!" she gasped. "You're home. I've prayed—"

Andrew brushed by her, waved Cassius inside, and slammed the door on all the world. "Where's the damned houseman? I was knocking forever!"

Charlotte's smile flickered. "I had no idea you were coming. . . . Oh God . . . so very glad . . ." Charlotte hurled herself into his arms and kissed him full and hungrily on the lips. Charlotte pushed him to arm's length, the better to drink him in. "Are you home, then, dear husband? Are you truly home?"

The hall was dim, the tables and chairs shrouded. Overhead, the unlit chandelier glittered like icicles. Andrew shivered.

"Juliet and I don't heat the front of the house anymore," Charlotte explained. "We're living in the family room."

"But, the servants . . . surely . . ."

"Dear me, Andrew. They're gone. Jolly and Ben and Martha ran away. When our negroes reach Yankee lines, the Yankees emancipate them." She glared at Cassius. "You won't run away, will you?"

"Oh no, Missus. I'ze a good nigger."

Andrew sent him away.

Charlotte said, "Juliet will be so glad to see you. She's gone to the market. There is still food to be had, but it is frightfully dear."

The family room's windows looked out on the winter garden. Formerly, this had been where children did their lessons and Fisher women could undo their stays and drink a cup of tea. Grandmother Fisher had always taken breakfast here.

Now, Charlotte's and Juliet's pallets flanked a four-plate cookstove, and the long table had been pushed against the window wall to serve as pantry, bearing enameled canisters, graduated from largest to smallest, and a five-gallon cask beside the Portland clock from Grandmother Fisher's office.

Charlotte stuffed wood into the stove. "We'll have a nice cup of tea, Andrew. Unless . . . if you'd rather—we've so much brandy and wine. Juliet and I haven't made a *dent* in Grandmother's wine cellar."

"Tea will be fine."

As if Andrew were a luxury she couldn't get enough of, Charlotte didn't take her eyes off her husband. She filled her kettle from the cask, chattering all the while. "We draw water from the cistern every morning, so we have water all day. Juliet and I take turns carrying it in. Oh Andrew, I am so glad you're home!"

Wisps of smoke squirted from the stove grates.

"Charlotte, dear Charlotte . . . I have something to tell you. . . ."

"Yes dear?" Charlotte splashed water on the stove. Smoke poured from the grates as water beaded and popped. "Oh dear, what have I done?"

Andrew opened the damper. "I'm afraid you smothered your fire."

Coughing, Charlotte opened windows to let the smoke escape. "Oh Andrew, I'm sorry I'm useless. I'm the worst domestic on earth. We ladies were never expected to know how to start a fire or cook our supper or make our own beds. I'm sorry to be so helpless!"

Andrew took the kettle from her and set it on the quieted stove.

"Sit down, Charlotte. Please, just for a minute. You don't need to do anything now. Tomorrow, I'll buy new servants."

"But Andrew . . . Just as I start to get to know them, they'll run away."

He straddled a bench. "Please, Charlotte. Do sit down. We'll talk about servants later. I have a confession."

Charlotte's happiness became alarm. She sat slowly.

"When Juliet comes home today, she will have news of . . . of . . . a new scandal."

"Scandal? Dear Andrew; you just got here. You haven't had time for a scandal!"

"Rosemary and I . . ."

Charlotte's lips firmed. "No, Andrew. Not Rosemary. Rosemary's marriage—well, it isn't everything she wanted, but Rosemary wouldn't hurt me! Not . . . not . . . Not again!"

Andrew touched his heart. "I was rash, Charlotte. I was alone with Rosemary in her home. I was careless of her—of *your* reputation. But I swear before God that nothing happened."

Charlotte sagged. She moistened her lips. "Rosemary was always prettier than I. Everybody loved Rosemary even when we were little girls. Andrew,

I know you have not always been faithful to me. Don't lie to me now. Please . . ."

Andrew's eyes tried to reassure her.

"I would particularly hate it if you betrayed me with Rosemary. I don't know if I could live on if you betrayed me with Rosemary."

He took his wife's unresisting hand. "Charlotte, dearest. On my honor, I did not."

Charlotte considered her husband while a minute ticked by before she rose and slid the kettle to the back of the stove. "Then that's settled."

"Rosemary . . ."

She tapped his lips "Hush," she said, "I believe you, Andrew. I have always believed you. Please go down to the cellar and fetch a bottle of champagne. It's been so long since we had occasion to celebrate."

As Andrew had predicted, Juliet Ravanel learned Rosemary Haynes and her brother had spent two hours alone together. Her informant's eyes gleamed with malicious pleasure. Inadvertently, Juliet fanned the very fires she intended to damp when she snapped, "Dear, what could Andrew and Rosemary have possibly done in that short time?"

You may imagine what Charleston's wits made of that.

Chapter Fifteen

A Child's Refuge

Fruiting wood glistened pink and bluebirds fluttered in Pittypat's garden. After the springtime roads were firm, the mighty Federal juggernaut would head south to crush the Confederate nation, and Major Ashley Wilkes was with the ragtag army that would confront it.

Without mentioning their prayers to one another, Pittypat, Melanie, and Scarlett prayed separately for Ashley first thing on waking and last thing before sleep.

On April 29, 77,000 Federal infantry and 3,000 cavalry crossed Virginia's Rappahannock River on the five pontoon bridges General Joseph ("Fighting Joe") Hooker had constructed.

General Lee's forty thousand met them in a scrub forest near Chancellorsville.

Fighting Joe boasted, "I've got Lee just where I want him."

Six bloody days later, an ashen-faced Abraham Lincoln learned of Hooker's army's destruction. "My God, my God," the President whispered, "what will the country say? What will the country say?"

In mid-May, Melanie was in the kitchen placing crab-apple cuttings in a vase when Uncle Peter answered the front door.

Scarlett was at the breakfast table, stirring oatmeal she claimed "wasn't fit for horses."

Uncle Peter popped in to announce, "Mr. Tarleton in the parlor, Misses."

Scarlett gasped, "Tarleton? Which Tarleton?"

The grinning soldier wore a Federal officer's coat, dyed butternut and reenlisted in Confederate service.

"Why, Brent Tarleton." Scarlett smiled at the young man who had been one of her most ardent suitors. "Lordy, it's good to see you."

"Miss Scarlett!" Spontaneously, the young man dropped to one knee. "Marry me!"

Scarlett picked up her cue and fluttered girlishly. "But sir," she cried dramatically, "aren't you plighted to my own dear sister Careen?"

"Hang Careen!" Brent's gesture consigned Scarlett's sister to the rubbish heap. His bright eyes were wide and happy. "You cannot refuse me this time, Miss Scarlett!" The young soldier's too-serious mien faltered. His mouth twitched and he burst into laughter, which the delighted Scarlett joined in. Brent brushed his trouser knee. "Dear Scarlett! Were we ever so young as all that?"

She shook her head. "I'm not sure I remember." Scarlett took the soldier's hands fondly. "Brent, you are a dear boy and it's wonderful seeing you again. Tell me, how are your brothers?"

"Well, Boyd's a captain now and my feckless twin, Stuart, *was* a sergeant until he punched our lieutenant. Somebody had to punch him, and Stuart won the toss." Brent patted his breast pocket, "I have here a letter from Private Stuart Tarleton to Miss India Wilkes. It is a rare curiosity—the first letter Stuart ever wrote to anyone! Brother Boyd's in the infirmary with soldier's disease and brother Tom is lazing about on General Ewell's staff; we tease him unmercifully."

"Ashley?" Melanie put in eagerly.

"Your husband's fit as a fiddle, ma'am." Brent dove into his pocket for a thick packet. "Major Wilkes is more accustomed to letter writing than brother Stuart."

When Melanie took Ashley's precious letters, she shivered as at her husband's touch.

Brent Tarleton had been furloughed for the spring planting.

Melanie breathed, "Might Ashley be coming home, too?"

"Reckon not, ma'am. I reckon the army don't need Brent Tarleton bad as it needs Major Wilkes."

"Then I must be so grateful for his letters." Melanie swallowed her disappointment. "Won't you take breakfast with us? It's only oatmeal, but we have maple syrup yet."

"If you don't eat, Pitty's horse gets it," Scarlett said.

"Ma'am, I'm obliged to you, but I got to get on home. I've been thinking on Miss Careen." He fingered his officer's coat. "Do you think Careen'd want a Yankee's sword for a souvenir? I could've brought one, but I thought maybe she wouldn't care for it."

At the front gate, Brent said he'd carry Melanie's letters on his return to the army. "Everybody says we'll be going north. We got the Federals on the run now and figure to hit 'em in their own country." He paused. "Everybody says we can whip 'em."

"If you can't?" Melanie asked quietly.

Brent Tarleton took off his hat and scratched his head. His smile was the flashing smile of the boy he'd been: the ardent suitor, the rakehell rider, the lad who feared nothing. "If we can't whip 'em, I expect they'll know we tried."

As Brent Tarleton predicted, in June, General Lee crossed the Potomac into Pennsylvania. One Atlanta paper trumpeted, "The fox is among the chickens!"

In the National Hotel casino, Rhett Butler observed publicly, "General Lee can't fight Chancellorsville twice." These days, no decent Atlanta home except Pittypat's was open to Captain Butler, and Pittypat's friends berated her for admitting "that unpatriotic profiteer"!

When Pittypat's resolution faltered, Melanie reminded, "Aunt Pitty, hasn't Captain Butler always been good to us?"

"Why yes, he has, but . . ."

"Then it is our Christian duty to return his kindnesses. Dear Aunt, if people had listened to Captain Butler, this war would never have started and our dear Charles would be alive."

Melanie had lost track of her brother's sword. Charles's commanding officer had sent back her brother's sword and diary, with his letter of condolence. Charles's diary contained only two entries: "Arrived at Camp Foster. Introduced to Wade Hampton. He's a giant!" and, dated two months later, "Feeling a little under the weather. So to the infirmary. I hope I'm not sick long." Melanie had bundled these treasures with a daguerreotype of Charles taken the day he left for war. Melanie believed she'd given them to Scarlett, but Scarlett said no, Melly was mistaken. When Melly wrote Twelve Oaks, John Wilkes answered Charles's things were at Pittypat's, when were Melanie, Scarlett, and little Wade coming out for a visit. Scarlett said John Wilkes must be mistaken. She distinctly remembered seeing Charles's sword at Twelve Oaks.

In the best-ordered life, there is at least one instance when a distracted foolishness combines with a second foolishness to swell into calamity. When the unhappy person realizes the course to which he or she is by now fully committed, the only hope is to look neither to left nor right, but press straight ahead.

Which is how sensible Melanie Wilkes found herself in a closet, overhearing words she desperately regretted hearing.

Alone in the house one warm afternoon, on sudden inspiration, Melanie opened the closet under the stairs where she and Charles had played as children, guessing (correctly, as it turned out) that's where Charles's things had gotten to.

The closet was narrow, with a sharply slanted ceiling, and as deep as the stairway was wide. Originally used to store table leaves, lamp chimneys, winter drapes, and linens, Pittypat hadn't objected when Melanie and Charles turned the odd-shaped closet into a playroom. Door louvers shed faint illumination inside, and it became a favorite refuge in games of hide-and-seek. By the neighborhood children's common consent, any child in that hideyhole was invisible.

With a wisdom one mightn't have expected of her, Pittypat accepted that magic principle, and many a child-size tragedy—an unearned reproach, a best friend's snub, an excruciating embarrassment—was solaced in that small room. Many a child's tear had been shed there, many a child's direst vengeance contemplated; its mellow walls had absorbed so many frustrated sobs.

Invariably, Pittypat and Uncle Peter were astounded when a child burst out with tearstained cheeks but laughing, all good nature restored.

Like other childish things, the closet was gradually abandoned, but it had been so sacrosanct that it stayed empty for years, until someone—Pittypat, Uncle Peter, Cook—unthinkingly stored Charles's things in the place where the boy Charles had been invisible, and where one afternoon his grown sister opened the refuge and stepped inside, stooping for a parcel which had the unmistakable silhouette of a scabbarded sword.

The door swung shut and Melanie sat on the floor. Charles's presence was so strong in this place, she could almost hear him, outside the louvered door, hide-and-seeking through Pittypat's parlor. "Is dear Melly behind the love seat? No. Under the table? No. Behind Aunt Pittypat's drapes? Not here, either. Oh, where has sister Melanie gone?"

But it was Charles who was gone, and Mrs. Ashley Wilkes held her brother's things on her lap and stroked them, thinking how little, how very little, remains of us when we're gone. She wept herself into an unhappy slumber.

Melanie was startled into wakefulness when she heard Scarlett calling for her in the parlor.

Good Lord! How must it seem—asleep on a closet floor with her brother's sword in her lap?

"Melly! Pittypat is taking supper with Mrs. Meade tonight! Are you home, Melly?"

Mrs. Ashley Wilkes's mind spun. She'd wait until Scarlett left the room! Then she'd emerge and compose herself!

"Ah, Scarlett, I find you at home."

That familiar deep voice. Oh dear, Captain Butler was here, too!

Melanie knew she was acting the fool. Enough! She'd struggle to her feet with all those clunks and clatters—for the closet was very narrow—come out with her brother's sword, and say . . . Oh dear, what could she say? Melanie Wilkes could not submit herself to that ludicrous humiliation. They'd be leaving in a moment. On pleasant afternoons, Rhett and Scarlett always visited on the front porch.

Outside the door, Melanie heard thumping sounds and the scrape of heavy furniture being shifted.

"What the devil are you doing?" Captain Butler inquired.

"Nothing."

"On hands and knees behind the love seat? You're doing nothing?"

"You might help me, Rhett Butler, instead of standing there like a bump on a log! If you must know, I'm looking for Charles's sword. I put it somewhere, and now Melanie wants the darn thing and I told her I didn't have it."

"So. If you find it, the sword will just 'turn up'? Scarlett, have I ever accused you of being an honest woman?"

"Rhett, help me! It's just a stupid sword."

"Scarlett, why don't you put away those widow's weeds and we'll run away to New Orleans. You never cared for Charles anyway."

"Don't be ridiculous."

"Honey, I'm the only man in the world who understands you—and admires you despite."

"You forget, New Orleans is in Federal hands."

"Scarlett, Scarlett. Money can go anywhere."

In her closet refuge, Melanie pressed her hand to her mouth. Didn't care for Charles? How could she not? Why, Charles was the most lovable boy in creation. When Charles laughed every bit of him laughed. Charles sang—off-key perhaps—but with all his heart. Charles ran to the river faster than Melly's little girl's legs could follow. "Wait for me, Charles! Wait for me!"

"New Orleans is the most cosmopolitan city in America. It'll suit you fine."

"Captain Butler, you flatter me. I am no cosmopolitan."

He laughed. "You're as green as grass, my dear, but you'd give your eyeteeth to be cosmopolitan. If Charles's sword was undistinguished, why not just buy another one?"

"Of course it wasn't distinguished. Nothing about Charles was distinguished. But it was his grandfather's sword!"

A tear trickled down Melanie's cheek. She heard cloth rustle as Rhett embraced Scarlett, murmuring, "I hope one day you won't speak so harshly of me."

"Why should I say *anything* about you? Aren't you a war profiteer? Shall I name the Atlanta homes that welcome you, the respectable families 'at home' when you call?"

He chuckled. "Should I give a damn about those biddies?"

"Why, of course you shouldn't, Captain Butler. You are beyond such mundane concerns. But we mere mortals have friends, and most of us are well regarded by decent society. I believe most of us are even welcome in our parents' homes!"

Cloth rustled again. "Ah, thank you for releasing me," Scarlett said. "I was beginning to fear for my chastity."

"Mrs. Hamilton, you flatter yourself."

Rhett's angry departing footfalls were accompanied by Scarlett's triumphant humming. When Scarlett finally left the parlor, Melanie Wilkes was able to release her anguished, lonely sobs.

Chapter Sixteen

The Burnt District

The first time the Federal fleet attacked Fort Sumter, Charleston citizens had enjoyed a picturesque victory. The hearty roar of patriotic cannon produced waterspouts, which drowned the Federal ironclads as if they were water beetles. When the *Keokuk* sank off Morris Island, Dahlgren guns were salvaged from the wreck and Charlestonians rejoiced that the enemy's own weapons would be turned against him. The *Mercury* concluded that the city's defenses were impregnable: "Battery Wagner commands the western shore, Fort Moultrie the eastern; and in the harbor mouth, Fort Sumter defies everything the Federal Invaders hurl against her!"

Charleston's military commander, General Pierre Beauregard, was less sanguine and urged civilians to evacuate the city. Some wealthy citizens closed their homes and moved their households inland. Although the Langston Butlers made no new arrangements, the Wards decamped to Macon, Georgia, where Frederick's cousin had a plantation.

Haynes's kin in Hanging Rock, North Carolina, invited the Charleston Hayneses to bide with them "until this unpleasantness is finished."

"I will stay here," Rosemary told John.

Thus far, every Federal attack had been repulsed. Sleek blockade runners—the *Bat,* the *Condor,* the *Venus,* the *Advance,* the *Let 'er Rip,* the *Annie,* the *Banshee*—lined Charleston's waterfront from Adger's Wharf to Government Wharf.

Then everything changed. In the third July of the War, proud Southern heads began to bow.

On a hot, rainy afternoon, anguished Charleston citizens collected outside the King Street telegraph office for the casualty lists from a Pennsylvania town no one had previously heard of. The news from Gettysburg could not have been worse: 17 Confederate generals and 28,000 soldiers killed or wounded.

That wasn't the end of it. The very next day, Charleston learned that Vicksburg's besieged garrison had surrendered. The Mississippi was in Federal hands and the Confederacy cut in two. That afternoon, people prayed in the streets outside Charleston's overflowing churches.

On July 10, a Federal division landed on Morris Island, and by nightfall, they'd driven the Confederate defenders to Battery Wagner's outer defenses.

Guns thumping, Federal ironclads prowled the island's shoreline. At 46 Church Street, little Meg stayed in her room with her hands clamped over her ears.

When her father came in that evening, Meg saw his face and burst into tears. John told Rosemary, "William Stock Bee's son was killed today. When William came to my office, the good old soul could scarcely speak."

"His only son. The poor, poor man."

"Frederick Ward's son was killed, too. I understand Willy Ward died gallantly. 'Gallantly'!" John choked on the word. "Excepting Battery Wagner, Morris Island is in Federal hands and attacks on Wagner are sure to come. I've train tickets to Hanging Rock for you and Meg."

"I will not go."

"Wife!"

"This is the first time since January you have called me by that honorable name."

"My God, Rosemary!"

Husband and wife looked at each other helplessly. Neither reached out and the moment passed.

When John Haynes was told that his Rosemary had spent hours with the seducer Andrew Ravanel, in John's own home, John had been heartsick. John had never accused Rosemary. He didn't need to.

For her part, Rosemary knew she hadn't compromised her husband's honor. But Rosemary had been tempted, and the temptation lay almost as heavily as an actual betrayal.

Innocent but ashamed, Rosemary Haynes answered her husband's silent accusations with silence. Since January, they'd not had one easy, trusting moment.

A week after the landing, Federal gunfire swelled. Overlapping concussions made a breeze that ruffled window curtains as far inland as 46 Church Street. Very late that afternoon, despite a throbbing headache, Rosemary walked to the White Point promenade.

Exploded sand drifted in silver-gray plumes over Morris Island. Fort Sumter was obscured by smoke.

Dusk turned to dark. Guns flared like fireflies. Confederate gunboats shuttled wounded men and replacements across the harbor.

Citizens on White Point prayed or chattered or drank. After midnight, the guns stopped winking and Sumter became a black silent hulk. A half-moon poked through the yellow overcast.

A Confederate gunboat steamed past and a sailor yelled, "We busted 'em. Our boys busted 'em. The Federals . . . some of them Federals was niggers."

The attack on Battery Wagner had failed. In the morning, when Federal prisoners were brought into the city, that sailor's report was confirmed. The soldiers who'd assaulted Battery Wagner had been negroes from the Fifty-fourth Massachusetts U.S. Colored Troops.

Rosemary half-expected Cleo or Joshua to mention what they surely knew: that negro soldiers had attacked Southern white soldiers and nearly defeated them. Cleo acted as if nothing untoward had happened. Joshua said he was glad the Federals had been repulsed. "I don't want no Yankees comin' in Charleston."

"Really, Joshua?"

"You know I doesn't. I been Master Haynes's body servant since he was a boy."

The negro prisoners were kept in the city jail while politicians debated their fate. Some legislators, Langston Butler among them, wanted the negroes "returned to that servitude for which they are best suited." General Beauregard wanted them treated as ordinary prisoners of war.

Federal ironclads and shore batteries continued pounding Confederate defenses.

At Church Street, neither husband nor wife said one word more than necessary. Meg pretended nothing was wrong and chattered while her parents moved silently through the house. One especially grim evening, Meg screwed up her courage to suggest all three play a game. When that idea died a-borning, Meg said, "If we can't play a game, we can sing together!" and she marched around the room singing "The Bonny Blue Flag," accompanying her performance with nervous giggles. When Rosemary picked her daughter up, the child burst into tears.

That night, Cleo put Meg to bed. "It's all right, honey. It's all right. It's the darn ol' war, that's all."

Downstairs, Rosemary said, "John, I'm not sure how much more of this I can stand."

At 5 A.M on August 17, the Federals opened fire on Fort Sumter. Their gunners worked in shifts, four hours off, eight on. Each volley flung one and a half tons of iron at Sumter's brick walls. Federal ironclads paraded before the fort, adding their guns to the tumult. One by one, the fort's guns were blown off their trunnions and silenced, and by noon Sumter was a heap of broken bricks.

Charleston citizens who ventured from their homes moved hurriedly, furtively.

Most Federal batteries quit at dark, but a single gun fired every five minutes throughout the night.

When Rosemary came downstairs in the morning, her eyes were red-rimmed. "John . . ."

"Do not say it, I beg you."

"John, I must leave you. Just for a while."

"Rosemary, please . . ."

"Meg and I are moving into the Mills Hotel for a few days."

John covered his face with his hands.

Rosemary Haynes took a deep breath. "I did not betray you with Andrew Ravanel."

Her husband didn't seem to hear. "Andrew is in the newspaper again. The worse things get, the harder Andrew fights."

"I did nothing. . . ."

"Rosemary, I understand how a woman would be attracted to Andrew. . . ."

Rosemary quit trying. "I hate those damn guns," she said.

That afternoon, Cleo packed their things and they drove uptown through the burnt district to the Mills Hotel.

The speculators in the hotel dining room that evening flaunted new riches. Every watch fob and chain was large and bright shiny gold.

"Ma'am." One man removed the stovepipe hat he'd worn during his meal. "Henry Harris. Glad to make your acquaintance. Your brother, ma'am. I can't say too much about your brother! Hard to pull the wool over Captain Butler's eyes!" The speculator set a finger beside his nose and winked. "Him and that nigger Bonneau—they're deep ones! Ma'am, I got to be frank. Frankness is my weak point. I got to have ten cases of Frenchie champagne, and Cap'n Butler always brings in the best. Ma'am, if you see your brother afore I do, tell him Harris will meet any offer and better it by ten percent. Tell him that."

"Mama, is he talking about Uncle Rhett?"

"I'm afraid he is, dear."

"Uncle Rhett is my friend!" the child declared.

"Yes, dear, he is," her mother said. "Sir, you must excuse us."

In their second-floor suite, Rosemary pulled the drapes closed. The Federal guns were not firing tonight and peace blessed the city. Cleo took Meg into the smaller bedroom to undress her, while Rosemary wondered what she was doing here. What was wrong with her? Why couldn't she love a good man?

At her bedside, Meg prayed for her uncle Rhett and Joshua and Cleo and her grandfather and grandmother Butler and all the soldiers in the War. She prayed the shelling wouldn't start again, because it scared Tecumseh.

Meg prayed, "Please, dear God, let Mama and Papa and me be happy again. Amen."

Sometime later, a porter's knock was attended by a note slid under the door.

In John Haynes's hand it said, "On any terms, Rosemary. I need you."

Might it be? Might John's love alone be enough to sustain them? Surely not! Surely no woman's heart could be transformed by a husband's devotion! Rosemary clamped her eyes so tight, she saw shooting stars. "Oh, please, God . . ." she prayed.

Briskly, she said, "Cleo, I must go home."

"Yes, Miss. I have Tecumseh brought 'round."

"No. I can't wait. Keep Meg, Cleo. . . ." Rosemary took her servant's brown face between her pale hands, "I may not return tonight."

"Yes, Miss." The servant looked her mistress in the eye. "I hopes you doesn't."

On Meeting Street, a startled gentleman gave up his cab. "Forty-six Church Street! Please!" Rosemary urged the driver, "Please hurry!"

When her husband answered the door, Rosemary searched his face, as if his familiar lines and furrows might tell a new and different story.

When John said, "Dearest . . ." Rosemary touched her finger to his lips, led him up the stairs into her bedroom, and that was the last word they spoke to each other.

Meg cried so piteously after her mother left that Cleo took her into her pallet at the foot of Rosemary's empty bed. "S'all right, honey-child. You Mama with you Daddy. They come get us tomorrow."

"Cleo, I'm afraid."

"Nothin' be 'fraid of. Time we go to sleep."

Little Meg was restless, and each time Cleo almost drifted off, the child would murmur or rutch around. Finally, the child put an arm around Cleo's neck and her sweet breath tickled Cleo's cheek and they slept.

A terrific flash and bang brought Cleo bolt upright. "S'all right, honey," she said reflexively.

The room's windows glowed as if white-hot and Cleo shielded her eyes. Meg wailed. "Hush, now. T'ain't nothin', nothin' t'all." Cleo disentangled from the bedclothes and, with Meg clinging to her, padded barefoot to the window.

A stream of fire like molten lava cascaded down the building across the street. Cleo put a hand to her mouth.

Footsteps thudded past her door. "Fire! Fire!"

Men ran down the hallway. "The damn Yanks are shelling the city!"

Meg cried, "Cleo, I don't like it here."

"Don't neither," Cleo said. "We goin' home now. I gonna need your help, honey. Turn loose my neck and get on your own two feet and we get you dressed."

Thunderous footfalls outside their door, like cattle stampeding. Cleo dropped Meg's dress over the child's upstretched arms and groped for her shoes—one beside the bed, another under the bureau. A fresh explosion was not so near.

"Please . . ." Meg whispered.

Cleo draped a blanket over her shift and set the child on her hip. "Put your arms 'round me and hang on, baby!"

Cleo hurried down the stairs. In the hotel lobby, half-dressed men were in a panic. Some ran into the dining room, others into the lobby. When a near miss shook the building, speculators dove onto a floor awash in cigar butts and overturned spittoons.

Meg wailed, "Mama."

Cleo said, "Honey, I gettin' you to your Mama."

They sped through the hotel kitchen.

The hotel's stable boys had run off and terrified horses reared, whinnied, and kicked in their stalls. Tecumseh's eyes were white and rolling. Cleo threw a bridle on him, set the bit, and led the quivering animal into the alley. She boosted Meg onto his neck and scrambled up behind. "Grab Tecumseh's mane, child."

"Cleo, I'm scared!"

"Darlin', don't you be scared! I needs you not be scared!"

Above the burnt district, a slice of moon scudded between clouds. The shells of burned buildings were almost homes or almost churches: eerie mockeries of human hopes. The ruins thrust shadow fingers across the street, snatching at the woman and child.

A shell burst directly overhead and bright fire streamered to earth. Meg screamed and Tecumseh clamped the bit between his teeth and bolted. "Tecumseh, whoa! You whoa now!" Cleo hauled at the reins with all her strength. The wailing child lost her grip on the mane and slid down the horse's neck. "Tecumseh!" Cleo shrieked.

As Cleo loosed the reins to snatch at the child, Tecumseh swerved and servant and child thudded onto the cobblestones.

With her breath knocked out of her, Cleo frantically patted Meg's small body. Cleo struggled to one knee. She'd bitten her tongue through and swallowed hot thick blood. "You a'right, honey? Is you hurt?"

Meg whimpered, "Cleo, can't we please go home?"

"We go home soon as they stop shootin'. Directly, we go home."

Cleo sought the familiar among the ruined spires and walls. "Look, child. There's the ol' churchyard. There's that Round Church. Look, that's its churchyard. We hidin' in the churchyard until we go home."

John and Rosemary found them among the shattered tombstones. Meg's body lay half underneath Cleo, who, with her last breath, had tried to shield the child from the bombardment.

"Oh my God," Rosemary Haynes sobbed. "I should never have left her."

John Haynes took his only child in his arms.

Chapter Seventeen

Love Tokens

The sleek gray blockade runner eased through the shallows north of Rattlesnake Shoal. In this second dark night of the moon, starlight reflecting off the ocean provided enough light for sharp eyes to see twenty yards. Behind its surf fringe, the Carolina beach was paler than the ocean.

A barefoot leadsman ran to the *Merry Widow*'s wheel and flicked his fingers twice: "two fathoms." Tunis Bonneau touched the lead to his tongue and murmured, "This oyster beds. We comin' up on Drunken Dick."

Rhett squeezed Tunis's shoulder for reply.

The *Widow*'s oversized engines burbled through underwater exhausts. Her hinged stacks lay flat, offering no silhouette against the pale beach. A hundred feet away, the runner might have been mist above the swell.

Bringing a runner through the Charleston blockade was more dangerous after the Federals took Battery Wagner. With Federal guns commanding the deepwater ship channel, no runner dared sail west of Fort Sumter. The eastern passage, Maffitt's Channel, was narrow and crooked. Before the War, buoys had marked Rattlesnake and Drunken Dick shoals, but the blockaders had removed them. At low tide, stretches of Maffitt's Channel were four feet, four inches deep. Loaded, the *Widow* drew four feet.

Just beyond Drunken Dick, the runner must veer to starboard and run for Charleston harbor's remaining entrance.

To keep Federal ironclads out of the harbor, Confederate defenders had floated a log boom studded with contact torpedoes across the channel from Sumter to Fort Moultrie on the eastern shore. The hundred-yard gap in that boom, directly under Moultrie's guns, was the passage into the harbor.

The Federals knew runners must come in during the dark moon. They knew the channel the runners must take. They knew the tiny entrance they must pass through. Sharp-eyed young Federal lookouts rubbed their eyes, straining to penetrate the night. They listened past the wheeze of their own breathing, the thudding of their hearts.

After Battery Wagner fell, most blockade runners had quit Charleston for Wilmington, North Carolina, where runners had two coastlines to sneak along and two inlets to slip through—both protected by Fort Fisher, a colossal sand fort astride the narrow peninsula between the Cape Fear River and the Atlantic.

Approaching Charleston, Tunis Bonneau kept his 180-foot side-wheeler inshore in that shifting watery hollow where ocean swell became surf. Though Federal warships kept well offshore, picket boats patrolled the shallows. Twenty-foot dories couldn't sink or board the *Merry Widow*, but their flares could direct the warships' guns onto the unarmed, unarmored runner.

Five knots. Tunis Bonneau stood on tiptoes, squinting. Breakers boomed and surf whumped onto the beach, hissing as it ebbed.

The *Widow*'s bow lookout raised his left arm, meaning, "picket boat on the port bow." Tunis bent to the speaking tube and asked the engine room for more steam.

The coxswain of the Federal picket boat saw something—a shape that might or might not be a ship, might or might not be a runner. He fumbled a signal flare from its tin chest and shouted, "Ahoy! What is the countersign?"

Engines quivering its deck planking, the *Widow* was making nine knots. "The Union Forever!" Rhett Butler sang out.

Tonight's countersign was "Gettysburg," but last night's had been "Preserve the Union." The coxswain had flare and match in hand but hesitated. Might this be a Federal vessel whose captain was on the wrong page of the signal book? There'd been no runners in weeks, and the overzealous coxswain who called fire onto a Federal gunboat faced certain court-martial. "Countersign!" the coxswain demanded again.

"Dishonest Abe!" Rhett shouted.

The coxswain had lit the flare when the *Widow* sliced into the dory, dragging eight Federal sailors into her slashing paddle wheels.

"Brave fellows," Tunis Bonneau said.

"But indecisive," Rhett replied.

"Slow ahead," Tunis murmured into the speaking tube.

Tunis steered by dimly seen land shapes and familiar currents tugging at the wheel. He trusted the memories in his hands.

The *Merry Widow* proceeded without further difficulty until she'd weathered Drunken Dick. Fort Sumter was off her port bow when the first Federal flare streaked into the sky.

Tunis called for full steam, the deck crew hove her hinged stacks upright, and the *Widow* lunged forward like a racehorse at the starter's gun.

Picket boats and warships sent up red, green, and blue signals, "Who are you? Are you ours?"

Rhett fired the *Widow*'s own red and green flares: nonsense signals.

Tunis Bonneau panted, as if faster breathing could make the *Widow*'s side wheels turn faster. The deck shuddered beneath his feet.

The first Federal shells fell short by twenty feet. Spume drenched the *Widow*'s deck crew.

"Their marksmanship has improved," Rhett said. He climbed a paddle wheel housing and put his glass to his eye, as if the bellowing Federal guns were harmless fireworks on a pleasant summer evening.

The bow lookout strained to spot that narrow gap in the torpedo boom.

Since the Federal guns couldn't track a racing runner, they had zeroed on the boom opening, and the *Widow* wallowed and bucked through near misses, as thoroughly drenched as if beneath Niagara Falls.

In full daylight, the lethal boom lay low in the water; by the dark of the moon, it was invisible. Tunis steered for the thickest concentration of waterspouts, praying the Federal guns were well pointed. The *Widow* shuddered: hit. Hit again, she shook like a wet dog. Tunis almost lost his grip when the wheel kicked in his hands. Another near miss slapped him into its spokes.

They were through. The boom's pale cypress logs and greening, barnacled iron torpedoes passed six inches to port.

Fragments from a final burst rattled onto the deck.

After the Federal guns quit, Tunis bent sideways to shake water out of his ears.

Rhett stepped down from the housing, folded his telescope, and lit a cigar. His match's flare was so bright, it hurt Tunis's eyes. In a hoarse voice, Tunis ordered Mr. MacLeod, the *Widow*'s engineer, to check for damage.

"We come through again," Tunis told Rhett.

"That was the easy part," Rhett said. "Lord, I dread our arrival. Poor, poor Rosemary."

News of Meg's death had reached Rhett in Nassau.

"I hate this war," Tunis said.

"Some say it will set your people free."

"Yes, sir. That's what some people say."

The city was dark. Charleston's church steeples—mariners' beacons for generations—had been painted black so Federal gunners couldn't aim by them.

Marked by the streak of its fuse, a shell arced from Federal guns into the city. A brief flash was followed seconds later by a dull rumble.

Tunis felt river currents in his wheel. The land breeze stank of brick dust and fires. "Slow ahead."

Rhett tried a joke. "Now I've sold you the *Widow,* Tunis, you must be more careful with her."

"Ha-ha."

Charleston's waterfront was wrecked. The *Widow* thrummed upriver past burned wharves, clipper ships moldering at their moorings, and steamers, decks awash, settled on the river bottom.

Engineer MacLeod reported shell damage was minor but that the *Widow*'s oversized steam engines had torqued their steel mounts and twisted the ship's starboard knees.

Most of Charleston's speculators had left for Wilmington, but, alerted by the Federal welcome, men at the Haynes & Son wharf were eager to do business.

Tunis reversed his engines as the *Widow* eased into her mooring and crewmen fended her off the bumpers.

Flickering lanterns illuminated the wharf. Someone cried, "Rhett, I got to have me some silk and perfumes."

"Buttons and epaulets," another voice called.

"I'll take twenty of champagne!"

The *Widow* was snubbed fore and aft, and with loud whooshes, the boilers vented steam. In the silence, Rhett could hear the river lapping at her hull. "Can't help you tonight, gentlemen. I've got no luxury goods. I've got thirty cases of cotton-carding combs, fourteen cases of Wentworth rifles, army shoes, uniform cloth, and minié balls. Perhaps you'll join me in a cheer for the Bonny Blue Flag That Bears a Single Star?"

"Christ!" someone said. "You pick a hell of a time to get patriotic."

A heavy hammer was banging in the engine room: Mr. MacLeod repairing engine mounts.

Disappointed speculators abandoned the wharf to a blue sulky and a black buggy.

"I reckon that's Ruthie and Rosemary," Tunis said.

"Tunis, why do we give our hearts to be broken?"

"Reckon we'd be better off if we didn't?"

Rhett's sister waited beside the sulky. She seemed smaller than Rhett remembered her.

"Dear Rosemary." He enfolded her in his arms.

For a moment, she resisted; then she gave a racking sob and convulsed. "Why, Rhett? Why do they murder our children? Have they no children of their own?"

In punctuation, a shell exploded in the city. Rhett held her until she stopped quaking and some tension leaked out of her. "Thank you," she said very softly. He released her and she wiped her eyes and tried to smile. She blew her nose.

In a calm, flat voice, she said, "Meg was so tiny. Almost as if she were an infant again. When John picked her up, one of her shoes fell off. You know, we never did find her other shoe. My baby's face was filthy, so I took my handkerchief to wipe her face, but John jerked her away. Rhett . . . Margaret Haynes was my own baby, but I had to beg before my husband let me clean her dear forehead. Her lip was cut—here—but it was not bleeding. She was cold as clay. With these fingers, Rhett, I closed my baby's eyes."

Rhett held her again. Absent the tension that had animated her, Rosemary was a rag doll. Rhett asked, "John? . . ."

"He walks the streets every night, utterly indifferent to the bombardment. Why, Rhett"—she offered a ghastly smile—"our free colored firemen see more of my husband than I do. Isn't that peculiar?"

"I will go to him. . . ."

Rosemary clutched Rhett's arm. "You cannot! He will not see you! John begs that as his friend you will not go to him."

"If an old friend can't—"

"Rhett, please believe me. John Haynes will not admit you to our house."

At the other buggy, Ruthie Bonneau was whispering fiercely, "Go on, now, Tunis Bonneau. You go on!"

Tunis crumpled his hat in his hands, "Miss Rosemary, me and Ruthie, we're right sorry 'bout your trouble. We always thought high of you Hayneses."

Rosemary looked past him. Absently, she stroked her horse's muzzle. "I wonder if Tecumseh remembers Meg," she said softly. "I look into his large mild eyes and . . ." She put her hand over her face to muffle a sob.

"Every night, me 'n' Ruthie, we prays for you, Miss Rosemary," Tunis said desperately. He helped his pregnant wife into their buggy and drove off.

Rosemary searched her brother's face. "Rhett, I have been so blind, so terribly blind! I wanted what I ought not and lost all the precious hours I might have had with my child and my husband. . . ." She paused and took a breath. "Brother, you must not make my mistake. Promise me . . . promise you'll do something for me?"

"Anything."

"You love Scarlett O'Hara." She stopped Rhett's lips with a soft fingertip. "Rhett, please, for a change, don't say something cynical or amusing. You love the woman and we both know you do. Brother Rhett, you cannot be superior to love. Go to Scarlett now. Be as straightforward with her as you've always been with me." Turning to her sulky, Rosemary retrieved a parcel wrapped in butcher's paper and unfolded one corner to reveal bright yellow silk. It was the scarf Rhett had given her so many years ago. "This was Meg's favorite thing. She'd wrap it around herself and pretend she was a bird or a butterfly. It'd float behind her when she ran, like . . . angel . . . wings."

"Rosemary, I can't take this."

"Yes, you can, Brother. We Butlers have never been good at loving. We've loved too late, or wrongly, or not loved at all. Give Scarlett this scarf. Years ago, it proved your love to me. Now my poor Meg has added her child's love, too. Please, Rhett, give it to the woman you love."

"Rosemary, you and John . . ."

"You can do nothing for us now."

"I would—"

"I know you would, dear. Hush. Go. There's a five A.M. train."

The brother kissed his sister and walked uptown.

Twenty minutes later, at the depot, the provost wouldn't let Rhett board the Georgia train until Rhett showed him Rufus Bullock's pass. "Sir, there's room in the officers' car."

Since Rhett had studied artillery at the Point, he appreciated the artillery major's account of the Chickamauga victory, and when Rhett brought a bottle of rum from his carpetbag, the major decided this civilian wasn't a bad fellow after all. As their train raced the sun into the west, Rhett, the major, and two junior officers settled into a game of stud poker.

By nightfall, Rhett had cleaned them out, but it was only Confederate money, and there were no hard feelings.

The next day, as the train crossed into Georgia, a nineteen-year-old lieutenant—"Biloxi, Mississippi, born and reared, Mr. Butler"—said, "We're hittin' Billy Yank hard; whippin' him most every scrap. Federals surely can't take more losses bad as Chickamauga. One or two more whippin's, ol' Lincoln will sue for peace."

Looking into the lieutenant's hopeful face, Rhett felt a thousand years old.

Their train was sidetracked in Augusta.

Inured to delays, the officers headed for the nearest saloon, but Rhett found Rufus Bullock at the Southern Express office.

Bullock had come south before the War to superintend the Adams Railway Express Company. An affable, even-tempered man; when Rufus Bullock strolled down Main Street, respectable Georgians felt he was just the sort of man they liked to see strolling down Main Street, even if Bullock *was* a Yankee. When the War began, the Southern Express seceded from its northern parent and Rufus Bullock became the new company's president.

Soon, Bullock was coordinating Confederate telegraphy and shipping army payrolls. As his responsibilities increased, Bullock became acting chief of the Confederate railroads and was commissioned as a lieutenant colonel. Bullock never wore a uniform; for Rufus Bullock, war was business as usual.

With the confidence of old familiarity, Rhett plunked down a bottle on Bullock's desk.

"My Lord, Rhett, where did you find this?"

"Bahamian rum. Twenty years old, aged in wood. Without your pass, Rufus, I'd never have gotten out of Charleston."

The bottle vanished into a drawer. "Rufus Bullock understands you brought military stores this run, Rhett. Rufus asked himself, How can Rhett Butler profit from military stores?" Bullock chuckled comfortably. He was a comfortable man.

"I am reformed, Rufus. No more blockade running. When John Haynes is able to think about business again, I hope John will quit the business, too."

"I heard his daughter was killed. Tragic."

"Yes. Rufus, put me on an Atlanta train."

"Even Rufus Bullock can't help you there. Every car we have is packed to overflowing with supplies."

"Rufus, I know you. There is nothing you can't do."

Rhett rode in the locomotive with Mr. Bates, the dour engineer, and a huge, silent negro fireman.

The sun was setting as they rolled out of Augusta. Rhett took refuge atop the tender. Sprawled across cordwood in the wood car, hands laced behind his head, Rhett tried to recall exactly what Tunis Bonneau had told him about love—what was it, six years ago?

They'd met on the Freeport docks and the friends who hadn't seen each other since Rhett left the Low Country had repaired to the nearest skibberdeen and proceeded to drink it dry.

Tunis caught Rhett up on Charleston doings. "Your sister, she growed into a mighty handsome young woman."

"If I give you a Cuban shawl, will you take it to her?"

"Surely will." Tunis wasn't as drunk as Rhett. "Something troubling you?"

"A woman. Nothing at all."

"You ain't actin' like she's nothin'. You love her?"

He'd snorted, "Love?" Rhett drank straight from the bottle. "I have been in love too many times. Then I climb out of bed and put my trousers on. There is something about the humble act of donning trousers that trivializes love."

"Now you joshin' me."

"Am I?"

Tunis had told Rhett shyly that he was courting Ruthie Prescott, Reverend Prescott's oldest daughter. "Ruthie's high-headed and it's a chore, sometimes, gettin' next to her, but she's the one for me. Rhett, you ever been in love?"

"Friend, why these questions?"

"Was you ever with a gal that you felt like you would never be right or full or good if you wasn't with her no more?"

"I've felt flattered and sometimes thrilled. But, no, that's not how love was."

"Then you never been in love," Tunis Bonneau said firmly. "Not really. 'Cause that's what love be."

Now, every stroke of the pistons, every turn of the driving wheels brought Scarlett closer. The engine's rumble echoed in Rhett's heartbeat. Faster! Faster!

Every other woman, every previous passion was lifeless by comparison; yet Rhett had never told Scarlett what she meant to him. He'd jibed. He'd hidden behind a false indifference.

"Damn coward," he whispered.

Armed with Rosemary's precious gift, Rhett could tell her how he felt. By God, he would!

A euphoric Rhett Butler stepped down into the cab and gave cigars to Mr. Bates and his fireman.

The open firebox roared. Sparks and cinders burned tiny holes in Rhett's black broadcloth suit.

Enlivened by the excellent cigar, Mr. Bates volunteered, "This drivin' at night is nervy business and I don't care for it. I can't see nothin', and if the Federals were to jerk up the rails, I wouldn't know it until this here engine was flyin' through the air! Mister, it is troublesome gettin' out of her onct she commences tumblin'. There's the steam, you see. Steam'll pluck the flesh off a man to bare bones." Mr. Bates puffed his cigar with entire satisfaction.

They paused every two hours while Mr. Bates filled the boiler. Rhett and the fireman heaved four cords of wood into the tender.

Come daybreak, the train was transversing the Georgia piedmont.

"Cap'n Butler," Mr. Bates said, "Yonder's Stone Mountain. We'll be in Atlanta within the hour."

"Unless the Federals have torn up the tracks."

"No sir," Bates snorted. "Federals'll never come within a hundred miles of Atlanta."

As the train was pulling into the Car Shed and the wheel brakes were still squealing, Rhett shook Mr. Bates's free hand, slipped the fireman two bits, and swung down. One hand holding his hat, he dashed down the platform to the cab rank.

Rhett climbed up beside the driver and gave Pittypat's address.

The driver eyed his grubby passenger disapprovingly. "You sure you can pay?"

"I'm sure if you don't set off immediately, I'll strangle you," Rhett replied.

The cabbie lashed his horse into a trot.

The fastest wasn't fast enough.

At Pittypat's, Rhett hammered on the door.

"Wait a minute! Just a blamed minute! I'm a-comin'!" After Uncle Peter opened the door, he drew back. "Cap'n Butler?" Uncle Peter was aghast. "My goodness, what you been gettin' up to?"

In the parlor, Pittypat put down her mending. "Oh dear, Captain Butler! Have you been in a fire? Your clothes . . . And you always wear such beautiful clothes. Is that your hat? Bless your heart! Wouldn't you like to wash your hands? Peter, fetch a basin and pitcher!"

"Miss Pittypat, you are too kind." Rhett set his carpetbag down and opened it. "Please, you'll have to take it out. Yes, the small parcel. That's it. My hands . . ."

As Pittypat unwrapped a rectangle of exquisite Belgian lace, Rhett said, "The instant I saw it, I said, 'Won't this make Miss Pittypat a lovely collar.' "

"Oh, Captain Butler. How can I ever thank you?"

"I deserve no thanks, Miss Pitty, for adorning a lady who needs no adornment at all."

"You're talking blarney." Scarlett sniffed as she came into the room. "Captain Butler, have you quit bathing?"

Pittypat fled with her gift.

Rhett had cinders in his hair and his face was streaked with soot. His clothes had been drenched with seawater, dried into shapelessness, and scorched with hot cinders. His shirt cuffs were ripped, his fingernails broken, and the hat in his hands was a felt rag. Scarlett stalked around him like an offended cat.

"I was so eager to see you, my dear," Rhett said, "I didn't tarry. . . ."

"Eager to see me? Why on earth would you be eager to see me? Dear me, I certainly hope I haven't *encouraged* you. Captain Butler, mightn't you have washed before calling on a lady?"

Uncle Peter brought in pitcher, basin, lye soap, and a threadbare towel. As Rhett bent to wash his face, Scarlett continued mercilessly: "How long have you neglected us? Did we see you in May? July?" Her laugh was light and careless. "No matter, I suppose. How time flies."

Rhett toweled his face. "I was trying to resist your fatal charms."

"Lord love us," Scarlett snorted. "What a creature is the smooth-talkin' man. Do go on, Captain Butler. That nonsense about my 'fatal charms,' I rather liked that."

When Rhett handed Uncle Peter the soot-blackened towel, Peter took it out at arm's length.

Rhett had sought a new beginning. He'd wanted to tell Scarlett about little Meg, about Will, the trunk master, about the yellow scarf. He'd wanted to tell Scarlett he loved her.

He couldn't talk. In Pittypat's parlor, unable to sit down lest he soil the furniture, unable to touch lest he smudge something, silently Rhett Butler gave Scarlett O'Hara his lover's gift—a dirty parcel wrapped in filthy butcher's paper.

"What's this?" Scarlett unwrapped it. She gave the yellow silk scarf a cursory glance before draping it carelessly over a chair. "Thank you so much, Captain Butler. You are too kind."

Suddenly, Rhett Butler was choking with rage. He swallowed the knot in his throat and said coldly, "Oh, it's nothing—a gewgaw, the smallest token of my admiration for a lady who is as beautiful as she is kind."

After Rhett left Pittypat's, he walked the streets until his temper cooled and he found himself outside Belmont's, Atlanta's finest jeweler.

In this third year of the war, Mr. Belmont had repurchased so much jewelry and sold so little, he'd considered closing his doors. When Rhett Butler asked to see Mr. Belmont's finest cameo brooch, Mr. Belmont practically skipped to his vault.

As always, Belle's Cyprians made over Rhett. "But you are so filthy, *cher.*" Minette giggled. "Let me scrub your back, no?"

Hélène laid a horse blanket over the settee so Rhett could sit while Minette poured his champagne. Minette told Eloise to fetch hot water upstairs for Rhett's bath.

"Why can't Hélène do it?"

"Because you have strong, fat arms."

When Rhett inquired about Lisa, Minette dismissed the girl with a shrug. "Lisa took Captain Busy's advice and left our Chapeau Rouge for a . . . a *sporting house.* Lisa is no courtesan!" Minette leaned forward conspiratorially. "Captain Busy is gone from Atlanta. Captain Busy was distressed at his transfer. He blames you." She winked.

Rhett had a second glass before he went upstairs to bathe and shave.

That evening, Rhett took Belle Watling to dine at the Atlanta Hotel and over brandy afterward, he gave her the cameo.

"Oh Rhett! It's too fine! It's . . . You've always been good to me! You know I—"

He silenced Belle with a "Hush" and a smile.

"Rhett, why are you givin' me this? It's too grand for a woman like me."

He reached across the table to tilt her chin. "Because, dear Belle, I cannot give you a yellow silk scarf."

Chapter Eighteen

Fox on the Run

In the first year of the War, the Light Horse became Ravanel's Brigade in General Bragg's Army of Tennessee. The brigade raided behind Federal lines in Kentucky and Tennessee, ambushing Federal contingents, smashing supply trains, burning railroad bridges, and blowing railroad tunnels.

Loyalties in Border States were divided, and if some ladies spat at the Rebels when they rode by, others were eager to prove their devotion to the Cause in person, to the dashing young Colonel who embodied that cause.

Andrew Ravanel loved these ladies but never could remember their names.

While their Colonel was being entertained, Andrew's scout and his banjo picker would sleep in the stable, on the front porch, once in a broken-down carriage, and once, shivering, in a corncrib with lattice walls.

"She do squall," Cassius had remarked.

"Like a cat in heat," Jamie Fisher replied. "I wish I had another blanket."

"Don't believe I'll ever be warm again," Cassius said. "Damn! What the Colonel doin' to that gal?"

"I hate to imagine." Jamie lay curled, warming his hands between his thighs.

"How come you never get yourself a gal, Master Jamie? I mean, I seen some of them ladies lookin' at you." Cassius raised his head from his pallet. "Might be you could find yourself a gal wasn't so noisy."

"Listen! Do you hear horses approaching?" Jamie took his revolver and strode into the moonlight.

In the glory days, their Federal foes were conscripts on their first horses and many of those horses had recently pulled plows. Federal commanders quarreled and postured like fighting cocks and the Confederate's awful rebel yells terrified many an incompetent federal commander to surrender without firing a shot.

Jamie Fisher was a tireless horseman with a keen eye for topography; he knew instinctively where the brigade should bivouac, which roads could be impassable in wet weather, when and where pickets should be stationed, when a ford was good and when, despite unriffled water and what seemed a hard gravel bottom, a crossing should not be attempted.

One night, as the scout and banjo picker lay in the loft of another patriotic lady's horse barn, Cassius confided that he'd once jumped the broomstick with a girl, Desdemona, just a slip of a thing. Cassius told Jamie, "When Master Huger sold my wife away, I bawl just like a baby."

At the Cynthiania skirmish, Federal cavalry killed Captain Henry Kershaw and very nearly captured Colonel Ravanel. Major Wilkes, the brigade's Georgia adjutant, criticized Colonel Ravanel for his failure to post pickets and for ill treatment of Federal prisoners captured after the brigade retook the town.

Ravanel's men took Major Wilkes's criticisms badly and the brigade's officers sneered that Wilkes was an "overly sentimental rustic aristocrat." When Wilkes left the brigade, Jamie Fisher accompanied him to the depot. Although Jamie hadn't spoken out as Wilkes had, Andrew's actions had distressed him, too. "The war has cost the Colonel too many friends," Jamie told Wilkes.

Ashley Wilkes shook his head no. Inadequate justification.

"Andrew is a good man," Jamie said. "Everybody loves him."

"Sometimes those who are easiest to love," Wilkes replied, "are hardest to respect."

Reputation often lags behind deeds, and Andrew Ravanel's fame grew even as his veterans wore out horses trying to replicate early, easier triumphs. They took risks they wouldn't have a year before.

The Army of Tennessee's commander, Major General Braxton Bragg, was a crook-backed, bearded martinet whose dark eyebrows collided over his nose. Bragg had a bad stomach, bad nerves, and such painful boils, he could not sit his saddle. General Bragg was evidence for the theory that bad luck finds those who deserve it.

Bragg decided to send Colonel Ravanel to Atlanta and Charleston, where patriotic citizens were eager to applaud the Confederate hero. Bragg cautioned Andrew, "Sir, you must never forget you are my personal emissary; you are representing Braxton Bragg!"

As they left headquarters, Jamie said, "Dear God, Andrew. Bragg's *personal* emissary—ain't you proud?" When Jamie broke up laughing, Andrew swatted him.

Jamie helped Andrew pack and gave him a new hat to replace the one the Federals had ruined at Cynthiania. "You'll want a feather," Jamie said. "For the ladies."

Andrew clasped his brother-in-law's shoulders. "I need no feather, Jamie. You are the feather in my cap."

"Give my love to dear Sister Charlotte," Jamie said happily.

Colonel Ravanel's men followed their leader's progress with great interest.

An Atlanta corporal's sister wrote, "Colonel Ravanel and his nigger banjo player came courting Charles Hamilton's widow, but she run him off. Everybody's laughing about it." His troopers were pleased their Colonel was up to his old tricks but were glad he'd been rebuffed. Some hadn't seen their wives or sweethearts since the previous spring.

The Colonel's assignation with Mrs. Haynes prompted rough jokes.

The color sergeant guffawed. "Two hours together not enough? Don't take me ten minutes."

To his troopers' surprise, Andrew came back from Charleston much subdued. Officers who joked about their Colonel's liaisons—as had been their custom—were brought up short and Andrew shunned his favorite drinking companions. Cassius took to playing slow, sentimental ballads.

When Jamie asked about the Atlanta widow, Colonel Andrew Ravanel had a rueful smile: "I'd rather face a Yankee division than Scarlett O'Hara

Hamilton. 'Colonel Ravanel. Get out of here and take your orchestra with you.' "

Which is how Cassius was renamed "Andrew's Orchestra."

Andrew asked Charlotte's brother about his wife: what had Charlotte been like as a child? Was Charlotte present when he kissed Rosemary Butler at the Washington Racecourse? "I was so angry at Langston Butler, so humiliated, I would have done anything—so long as it was rash!"

Jamie thought Andrew as faithful husband would take some getting used to, but was amused when ladies hoping to entertain "the celebrated Colonel Ravanel" were turned away with a smile and, "Madam, were I not a married man, your virtue would be imperiled."

Then came the Gettysburg, Vicksburg summer and newspapers that once lauded Colonel Ravanel changed their tune. *The Charleston Mercury* recalled the Cynthiania fight and how a Federal officer had strutted down a public street wearing Colonel Ravanel's hat.

General Bragg, who would soon lose his command to General Johnston, forbade raids and used Ravanel's Brigade as regular cavalry. That fall, Andrew took a second furlough in Charleston.

Mr. and Mrs. Ravanel were never at home to callers and they ignored all invitations. Juliet Ravanel was uncharacteristically reticent when friends asked about the couple.

On this occasion there was no scandal, and soon after Andrew returned to the army, Jamie got a letter from Charlotte. "Please don't let Andrew do anything rash. I fear my beloved husband does not think himself worthy of me. I fear Andrew will do something foolhardy to burnish a reputation which is already bright as the noonday sun! Please, Jamie, keep Andrew safe for my sake and for our son!"

Five weeks later, on a drizzly December afternoon, on a ridge overlooking Pommery, Ohio, Jamie Fisher was musing about church bells. "How could I ever have thought church bells were lovely? Didn't church bells mean families promenading Meeting Street on Sunday morning?"

Through his glass, Colonel Andrew Ravanel studied the village, whose church bells clamored like terrified geese: "The rebels are coming! Alarm! Alarm!"

The interludes between Pommery's bells were filled with fainter bells from the countryside.

"They are God's bells, Jamie. Shame on you." Andrew snapped his glass shut. "Shall we ride through or around? Should we give the citizens of Pommery something to tell their grandchildren?"

"No, Andrew. There's bound to be some graybeard hugging his musket and dreaming of potting a Confederate."

Andrew Ravanel shifted in the saddle. "How close are the Federals?"

"Three battalions two hours behind."

"They won't get away this time."

"Ha-ha," Jamie said.

Andrew asked Jamie about their route home.

"Cobb's Ford was passable two weeks ago, but it's rained enough to float the Ark."

Absently, Andrew stroked his horse's neck. "Cassius can't swim."

Jamie leaned to him. "If we ride hard, we'll strike the Ohio River tomorrow night."

Andrew Ravanel stood in his stirrups to wave his men around this Yankee town. They were going home.

Two weeks earlier, Andrew Ravanel had crossed the Ohio into Yankeedom with two thousand fresh, well-armed Confederate cavalrymen intending to wreck railroads, torch army storehouses, steal horses, and enlist sympathetic recruits to the Cause.

The raid had gone badly. Alerted by telegram, Federal brigades pursued relentlessly. Only hard riding and Jamie Fisher's cleverness avoided the fixed battle they could not hope to win.

They'd run and ducked and fought through when they couldn't avoid it. Their dead had been left unburied, their wounded abandoned at crossroads. Exhausted men simply sat down and waited for the Yankees to take them. Of their four field guns, they had one left.

The three hundred survivors of Ravanel's Brigade were bearded, dirty, and festooned with guns; they looked more like bandits than soldiers. The horses they'd bought from Ohio farmers (paying with Confederate currency) hadn't the speed or endurance of the mounts they'd started with.

That evening it rained, a cold rain that plucked dead leaves off the trees and mashed them on the road. To spare their horses, the troopers walked, clinging to stirrups. As the blood slowed in Andrew Ravanel's veins, an all too familiar despair burdened Andrew's heart and he shouted to Cassius, "Pick us a tune, boy!"

Cross-legged on the gun's limber box, a tattered umbrella protecting his banjo, Cassius tried to please, but his tunes were off-key or tunes Andrew had tired of long ago.

Icy rain trickled off Andrew's hat brim and down his neck.

Cassius wrapped his precious instrument in his jacket and hunched over it, miserable and still.

There was just enough moonlight for a man to see the man in front of him. Sometimes the color sergeant had trouble keeping to the road. Men gnawed biscuits while they walked. They stepped out of the column to relieve themselves and then ran to catch up. The rain worked through their collars and shoulder seams and boot soles. Their slouch hats collapsed. Their souls retracted. Sometimes when a trooper remounted, his horse protested. Sometimes an exhausted horse crumpled and sent its rider sprawling before weary men dragged the horse back onto its feet.

When Andrew had left Charlotte at the Charleston depot, Charlotte had told him, "Dearest, I know you better than anyone on earth and do not doubt you have done things of which you are ashamed. Your shame proves you are a very good man."

Andrew had loved many women. Only Charlotte had kept him safe.

On the fifteenth morning after they'd invaded Federal territory, the rain let up and a chill wind brushed the clouds away. As the sun rose, the earth sparkled. After scouting their back trail, Jamie Fisher reported they'd slipped their pursuers. "But they must have guessed where we're bound."

"Yes, Jamie."

"They'll block the fords."

"Jamie, you worry too damned much."

They crossed a broken plateau. From time to time, the road dipped into a ravine, where they forded tumbling, muddy streams with water up to their horses' bellies. White-tailed deer went crashing away through the underbrush. They rode by deserted hardscrabble farms. As the day warmed, the plateau opened into flat pastureland and at midday they turned up a lane toward a two-story clapboard farmhouse. They heard the back door slam, then rapid, fading hoofbeats. The kitchen stove was still hot and side meat sizzled in a skillet. Jamie Fisher ate a piece, licked his fingers, and poured Andrew a cup of coffee. "We can reach Cobb's Ford by dark," Jamie said.

Andrew sat at the kitchen table with the cup between his hands. The chipped cup was everyday crockery; Grandmother's china would be in the china press in the parlor.

Outside the house, the color sergeant was shouting, "Unsaddle your horses and rub them down! If you're tired, they're tireder. Murphy, wake up, man. Damn it, you ain't dead yet!" Boots stamped through the bedrooms overhead and Andrew could hear drawers being pulled out. Had his men always been thieves? He remembered a Federal running down Cynthiania's main street with a tall clock in his arms. Poor fool wouldn't need to know the time where Andrew's saber had sent him.

There'd been so many poor fools.

Jamie was going on and on about Cobb's Ford.

Andrew was so tired, so terribly tired. He lifted his coffee cup with two hands, brought it to his lips, and swallowed.

Jamie said, "Andrew, they must not beat us to the river."

Where on earth did Jamie find his strength? "Jamie," Andrew said. "For God's sake, Jamie."

Andrew managed to put the cup down without dropping it. His hands lay open and unresisting on the table.

"Andrew, it's five hours to Cobb's Ford. Only five hours. Rest the horses for an hour if we must. We can cross before dark."

Andrew wished Charlotte were here. Charlotte always knew what to do. He'd resented that when they were first married. How badly he'd treated her then.

When Jamie rapped the table Andrew raised his head. Jamie said, "Andrew, you cannot funk now."

Andrew said thickly, "I'll be damned if I let some nancy boy tell me what to do!"

Andrew Ravanel put his head down on his arms and closed his eyes.

The men unsaddled and rubbed their horses down. They stripped and laid their clothing in the sun to dry. They crawled into stalls and haymows and slept.

Two turkey buzzards circled overhead, studying the garment blossoms below them.

Toward sundown that evening, the men woke and put on dry clothing and reprimed their pistols. In a hog scalder in the farmyard, they boiled a half dozen of the farmer's hams and three bushels of potatoes. They fished their dinners out of the kettle with pitchforks.

Men belched and lit pipes. The color sergeant said, "I never thought we was ever gonna get here."

"Might be we'll stay and take up farmin'," someone replied.

Andrew never came out of the house. Jamie Fisher was off scouting or something.

The sky was clear and washed with stars and once a meteor flashed into the earth.

Cassius played "The Arkansas Traveler" and "Soldier's Joy" and the young men danced hornpipes and jigs or whirled one another across the barnyard under brilliant watchful stars.

At dawn, they mounted up, and a few hours later, the plateau ended at the edge of a fog sea. Across that a rumpled fog coverlet, just two miles ahead, the plateau resumed in the Confederate States of America.

"If we could walk across fog," Andrew Ravanel said.

Jamie muttered, "Since you can walk across water, why not fog?"

"Jamie, I'm sorry. I shouldn't have said what I did."

"You are such a bastard, Andrew."

"Old Jack left his mark on me. But you can't doubt that I need you, Jamie. Just a little while longer. A few more hours and we'll be home."

Jamie Fisher didn't reply.

The road angled down the face of the plateau onto cropland alongside the Ohio River. The husks of unpicked field corn were wreathed in fog.

The Ohio was a mile across at Cobb's Ford: a broad reach of shallow water to Macklin's Island and a deeper channel beyond. The low island was two hundred yards of jumbled driftwood and brush. At low water, wagons could cross to the far shore, the Confederate shore, without wetting the wagon box. At high water, the Ohio River was navigable from Pittsburgh to New Orleans and shallow-draft stern-wheelers pushed barges through the deep channel.

This morning, the island was invisible in fog.

Jamie Fisher reined up at a mire of horse and wheel tracks. He heard the whuff and clink of shovels on Macklin's Island.

"They beat us here," Andrew said. "A regiment?"

"A full brigade." Jamie pointed at some deeper ruts. "Those'll be gun carriages."

Andrew Ravanel got off his horse and walked to the river's edge, where the roots of a toppled sycamore fingered over the water like an unanswered prayer.

Behind the island, on the Confederate shore, treetops emerged serenely from the fog.

The remnants of Ravanel's Brigade arrived behind Andrew and his scout. "I could sleep for a month," Andrew said.

Jamie said. "There's a ferry at Parkersburg, but that's thirty miles upriver."

Some men led their horses to water; others crossed a leg over their saddles and took a dip of snuff. They could read tracks, too.

A trooper galloped in from the rear guard. "Colonel, there's a Yankee brigade comin' off the plateau behind us."

Jamie said, "They won't get away this time."

Andrew said, "Jamie, I . . . I don't know. . . ."

Jamie Fisher said, "Andrew, you must lead. There's no one else."

Andrew hesitated before he straightened into Colonel Ravanel, the legendary rebel commander. "Thank you, Jamie," he said.

The Federals on Macklin's Island had ridden all night and had been digging since arriving at the island. They were tired and cross, and the soldier who carelessly threw a clot of dirt on another's boots was cursed. They hadn't had breakfast.

That shriek, that ululating rebel yell, made Federal gunners jump for their guns. Cavalrymen dropped their shovels to snatch up carbines. They laid cool stocks against their sweaty cheeks and drew back the iron hammers.

A squall of swirling Confederate horsemen appeared out of the fog, galloping, wheeling through the shallows, screeching their hair-raising screech, firing revolvers in the air. One hundred, two hundred, a thousand—God, how many were there?

As suddenly as they'd appeared, before one Federal fired, the terrible host retired into the fog as two Confederate officers galloped toward the island under a flag of truce.

A middle-aged Yankee major met them on the shore. As the horsemen reined up, the major adjusted his hat so it sat squarely on his head. Above the freshly turned dirt of new trenches, carbine muzzles tracked the Confederates.

Ravanel eased into his saddle. "Major, do you remember when real soldiers didn't burrow in the ground like moles?"

The major sat his horse nearly as well as Andrew did. The major's gear—like the man himself—was worn but well kept. "I had friends who wouldn't burrow like moles. I remember them in my prayers."

Andrew Ravanel had known and despised men like this major all his life. These respectable, boring, sturdy, everyday men had disapproved of Jack Ravanel and they disapproved of Jack's son, too. As the Ravanel fortunes leaked away, men like this had prospered because they lacked imagination to do anything daring or brilliant or amusing or something just for the hell of it.

Looking into the major's stolid face, Andrew knew before he spoke that his bluff would fail. "You know who I am. You know I've two thousand men and six field guns, and if I have to roust you off this island, I'll roust you. Surrender, and I'll parole you and your men. We'll pass over and go our own way and you'll be no worse off than you were yesterday. Resist, and your lives are forfeit."

The major nodded as if he'd expected Andrew's threat and judged Andrew's performance acceptable. "Colonel Ravanel, it is a pleasure to make your acquaintance. Me and my boys have been hopin' to learn if you are as all-fired terrible as the newspapers make you out. Sometimes, sir, newspapers don't get things exactly right."

"Surrender, sir, and let us pass."

"Oh," the Federal major said easily, "I reckon I won't." He smiled. "But you're welcome to give us a try."

Andrew could see the channel on the far side of the island. Reach that channel and they could swim to the Confederate shore. "Glad to make your acquaintance, Major," Andrew managed, and threw off a brisk salute before he and Jamie wheeled and splashed back into the fog.

His men looked to Andrew expectantly.

"They'll slaughter us," Jamie said. "I counted eight guns. Andrew?"

Andrew turned toward the island. The fog had settled and he couldn't see anything but spindly treetops. The far shore was more visible: the steep riverbank, then a belt of fog, then trees.

Jamie was saying something.

The fog was lovely, swirling, and blown to wisps. He fancied he saw Charlotte's face and Charlotte's loving eyes.

"Andrew!" Jamie hissed. "For God's sake, Andrew!"

He would never see Charlotte again. He would never see his son. There'd be a generation of Southern sons who'd never know their fathers. Andrew supposed that wouldn't be all bad.

Jamie was suggesting some other place they might cross, someplace he'd discovered when he scouted Cobb's Ford. A few miles up the river. They'd have to swim.

Why had he left Charlotte? He could no longer remember.

Comforting darkness descended on him.

"Andrew!" Jamie whispered urgently. "You mustn't, Andrew!"

Andrew Ravanel was accounted a brave man in a nation of brave men, but perhaps the bravest thing he ever did was throwing off that darkness, and shouting in a brigade colonel's voice, "Follow me upriver, boys! It's Rock Island Prison or home!"

Filling the road shoulder-to-shoulder, Ravanel's Brigade cantered up the river road through tendrils of fog. When an exhausted horse collapsed, the nearest man snatched its rider and swung him behind. More horses fell. In the cornfields beside the road, fog rose like smoke from ghost campfires.

"Here!" Jamie shouted, and the Confederates quit the road for the riverbank. They reined blown horses beside a floating dock where a half-sunk rowboat was tied.

The river was narrower here, half a mile maybe. Across roiled, muddy water, the Confederate shore was featureless.

Jamie sang out, "If you want to have a good time, if you want to have a good time, if you want to have a good time, jine the cavalry!"

A messenger from the rear guard: "They's a-comin'. Federal brigade's a-comin'."

Colonel Ravanel mounted the bank, where everybody could see him. "Boys, we've had our fun and it's time to pay the piper. Across the river is freedom. This side is a Yankee prison camp. Men who can't swim or won't can stay here with me. We'll hold 'em off while the rest of you get across."

Troopers lashed their boots to their saddles and kneed their horses into the turbulent brown river. Some clung to their horses' necks, some swam, hanging to the stirrups. They angled downstream in the current.

The gun crew unlimbered their solitary gun, unstoppered its muzzle, and pointed it down the foggy road where the Federals must come. Others dragged the rowboat out of the water to shield the gun crew.

"Andrew, your horse can swim it," Jamie said. "I'll command the rear guard."

Although it was hard getting the words through his constricted throat, Andrew said, "What, Jamie—and let you have all the fun?" Colonel Ravanel smiled like his old self and tucked his hands under his coat, where nobody could see them shaking.

A whistle screamed, and with its bow chasers blazing, a Federal gunboat charged out of the fog into the swimming Confederates.

Waterspouts lifted from the river, wide and white at the top, darker at the base.

It was a turkey shoot.

The bow chasers fired as fast as they were reloaded. Horses screamed. Men and horses died. Debris floated down the river: That rolling lump had been a horse; the speck beside it may have been its rider's hat.

Despite the industrious gunboat, a handful of Andrew's men gained the far shore, scrabbled up the bank, and disappeared into the fog. Cassius had lost his banjo.

"There goes your orchestra," Jamie whispered.

When the gunboat turned downstream, it was killing men and horses that were already dead. Blood sparkled over its stern wheel and formed a slick in its wake.

The Federals' swallowtail pennants snapped smartly as they came up and their officers were grinning until they saw the carnage in the river. The gunboat paraded up and down, whistling proudly, like the clever device it was.

Andrew Ravanel saluted his captors. "Good morning, gentlemen. I believe you've been looking for us."

Chapter Nineteen

The Yellow Silk Sash

Christmas furlough ended and thousands of Georgia soldiers were returning to their regiments. They were townsmen and farm boys, lawyers, blacksmiths, doctors, schoolmasters, farriers, wheelwrights, and planters departing their families for Virginia, where the Federals would attack again as soon as the roads were firm enough to support their mighty guns, endless supply trains, and their rank upon rank of well-fed, well-armed blue-clad soldiers. For three years, these ordinary Southerners had met and blunted Goliath's attacks—and paid a bitter price.

At the Atlanta depot, Major Wilkes's new uniform coat and bright yellow sash stood out. Not every soldier had an entire uniform—most wore homespun or captured Federal uniforms dyed with butternut hulls. The officers' horses' ribs poked through drum-taut skins like ladder rungs.

Wives hid their tears and their soldier husbands smiled. Older children knew how to keep silent, but children too young to accept Poppa's brave lies were inconsolable. The soldiers' leave-taking was accompanied by the wails of heartbroken children.

Ashley Wilkes could distinguish a Rubens from a Velásquez and knew if a Mozart concerto was early or late. He'd visited the Tower of London and the confluence of the Rhine. He had toured European gardens, from Blenheim to Versailles, and understood which fine roses grew best in Georgia clay. Despite his doubts about the war, he was a good officer. Although Ashley wasn't a man his fellows clapped on the back, he was liked and trusted. Major Wilkes was a thoughtful, erudite man. Nothing in his thirty-three years had prepared him for being in love with two women.

He loved his wife, Melanie, and he loved . . . "Her," although he could not bear to name Her. She'd been the neighbor girl, an amusing companion, the youngster for whom he had high hopes, the delightful friend, the virginal daughter of an Irish immigrant planter; she'd been Ashley's Galatea until the day he returned from his European tour and, in his absence, the girl had become: "Her."

Ashley Wilkes had read about women. Medea, Lady Macbeth, Juliet, Isolde, Desdemona, even the scandalous Madame Bovary—Ashley understood them all. But he did not understand Scarlett, nor did he understand his longing for her. He'd spent his life denying ungentlemanly appetites. Ashley Wilkes was shocked how much he wanted her.

And Ashley did love his wife; she was everything he'd hoped for. He'd spent every hour of his leave with Melanie and in her arms. They'd closed their bedroom door on the world's sorrows and fears.

Somewhere, somehow, Melanie had found the fabric to sew a uniform coat for her beloved husband. The warmth cosseting Ashley's slender body was Melanie's warmth.

But moments before he'd left for the depot, Scarlett caught Ashley alone and gifted him with a beautiful silk sash she'd sewn herself. And, alas, Scarlett had confessed her love.

Ashley hadn't answered. What could his answer be? Without any reply, promise, or excuse, he'd left Scarlett on the doorstep. What else might a gentleman have done?

At the depot, in his fine new uniform and fine new sash, Major Ashley Wilkes was a man tormented.

Mornin', Major." Cade Calvert coughed into his handkerchief. It would have been bad manners to notice that Cade's white handkerchief was spotted red. Cade's brother Raiford lay with the Confederate dead at Gettysburg.

"Train ain't goin' nowhere." Tony Fontaine lifted his bottle in greeting.

His brother Alex was passed out, head on his haversack, unmindful of men stepping over him.

"There's no locomotive." Among these ragged men, the exquisitely tailored civilian stood out like an exclamation point.

"Prolly some damn speculator needed it!" Tony said pointedly. Tony's brother Joe had been killed at Gettysburg, too.

Ashley turned. "Ah, Captain Butler . . ."

"My compliments, Major Wilkes. Your sash is exceptionally fine."

This rich man with the hot black eyes had been courting Scarlett. Everybody knew he had. "My sash is a gift from someone dear," Ashley replied.

"I haven't seen such silk since Havana. Tied in a lover's knot? Mrs. Wilkes is an excellent seamstress."

"Melanie?" Ashley blushed. "Why, yes. Yes, she is. Apparently, our departure is delayed; our train—"

Tony Fontaine stumbled closer to wash Ashley with whiskey breath. "Major, did I ever say how much I admire you? I mean, you're a . . . you're a real *gentleman*. By God, if you ain't!"

"They're bringing a locomotive from Jonesboro." Rhett shrugged. "An hour, perhaps two. Major, might I buy you a drink while you wait?"

Ashley Wilkes felt rubbed raw. The prospect of Tony Fontaine's drunken encomiums while Cade Calvert spat blood into his handkerchief was more than he could bear. At least Butler was a gentleman. "I could use a drink, sir."

As they passed down Decatur Street, Butler made conversation, "So many hotels have been converted into hospitals, there aren't many decent saloons left." He rubbed his hands. "War or peace, vice must be served. Here we are, Major."

The lobby and saloon of the National Hotel was wall-to-wall officers drinking the dregs of their Christmas furlough. The door to the hotel casino was guarded by bouncers, who uncrossed thick arms to let Captain Butler and his companion pass.

In this spacious room, one negro was polishing the roulette wheel while another washed glasses behind the bar. At a green baize table, a croupier played solitaire. In the silence, Ashley heard him turn each card. The mulatto who greeted them wore formal trousers and a fresh ruffled shirt but no jacket. "Afternoon, Captain Butler. Major. I'm afraid play won't begin until seven . . ."

"We're not here to play, Jack. You don't mind if we take a quiet table? Perhaps some champagne?"

"We've no Sillery, Captain. Haven't had any Sillery since the last cases you brought."

"I've quit the blockade-running, Jack. We'll drink the best you have."

When the bottle came, Butler filled Ashley's glass, which Ashley promptly drained. Rhett refilled it. "That is an *unusually* fine sash," he persisted. "I swear that's Havana silk."

"Were you in Cuba long?"

"I'm wondering where your wife found that silk."

"Melanie is resourceful. I'm told Cuba is lovely."

"It is an island blessed with expansive beaches and ineffectual firing squads. I admire your wife, sir. If I may say so, Mrs. Wilkes is the finest lady in Atlanta."

"I shall miss her terribly."

Rhett Butler's eyes bored into Ashley's. "How lucky you are to have a wife as able"—he indicated the sash—"as she is virtuous."

The croupier spun his wheel. The ivory ball whirred and clicked.

Ashley hadn't been in a room like this, a room managed solely for men's pleasure, since the War began. It recalled the graces for which he'd been born. Ashley leaned forward, smiling, "Butler, you were at Twelve Oaks' last barbecue. Remember the French lilacs and dogwoods? Did you tour our rose garden?

"Every planter in Clayton County envied us Mamaluke, our fiddler." Ashley chuckled. "That negro never did a lick of honest work. I believe our servants had more fun at our parties than we did." Ashley shook his head wonderingly. "They were like happy children."

The tension in Captain Butler's body warned Ashley he was on dangerous ground. "As a Charleston gentleman, doubtless you have similar recollections. Barbecues, balls, race meets . . ."

Rhett overfilled Ashley's glass and swept the spill off the table with the edge of his hand. "My father's horses were so splendid, they made my heart ache. We Butlers ate with English silver off French porcelain. In the spring, Broughton Plantation's azaleas could dazzle a man's senses." Rhett raised his glass in a toast. "Wilkes, did you ever whip a servant? I mean personally. Did you ever whip a man yourself?"

Ashley felt ambushed. "Whip a servant? Why, we never needed to. Why would we? I don't recall my father whipping any negro. I recall naught but kindness."

"What did you do with . . . 'impertinent' negroes? Sell them?"

A suppressed childhood memory returned: a weeping negress clutching Ashley's father's knees as the slave speculator's cart took her husband away.

For a moment, Ashley was speechless. Bottles clinked as the bartender restocked the bar.

Ashley coughed and dabbed his lips. "They say Grant will lead the Federals against us this spring. My company is reduced to ten men, my regiment to sixty." Why did some men hate beauty? What had gentle beauty done to earn Rhett Butler's contempt? "I fear for our Confederacy," Ashley concluded.

Rhett eyed his guest as if prey. "Tell me, Major Wilkes. You're a man of cultivated sensibilities. Have you ever had a divided heart? Have you ever tossed and turned, wondering, Does she love me? Do I love her? I sometimes wonder, sir, how the grown man's yearnings differ from the schoolboy's sweaty torments."

"I have not had a wide experience with women."

"I have. In my experience, they are as different from one another as a rose from a petunia, a Morgan from a Standardbred. Each woman is totally unique."

"Is each worthy of love?"

"I do not believe we have choice in that matter. We do not choose whom we love; love chooses us."

Ashley frowned. "Surely, sir—so many fortunate marriages have been arranged. Don't you think we can learn to love?"

Rhett bit the tip of his cigar, spat, and lit his match. "No, Major Wilkes, I do not. I think most men and women live their whole lives without knowing love. They accept a simulacrum for the real thing. They confuse cold gray embers for a raging fire."

Ashley Wilkes opened his watch. "Our locomotive will be here soon."

"Tarry awhile, Major Wilkes. You've time and it is quieter here. I understand you quarreled with Andrew Ravanel."

Ashley asked, "Isn't it awful what the Federals are doing with Colonel Ravanel?"

Rhett snorted. "Proud Colonel Ravanel jailed as an ordinary horse thief? I tell you, sir. Andrew's lucky to be a convict in the penitentiary. The Federals treat criminals better than their rebel prisoners. I'm told you complained to General Bragg about Andrew."

"Bragg is a punctilious fool."

Rhett drawled, "Why, of course he is. Your complaint was . . ."

Ashley touched his glass for a refill. "I volunteered for his brigade."

"Bugles blowing, gallant deeds, that sort of thing?"

"Look here, Butler. I find your manner very nearly offensive."

"My apologies. You were Andrew's adjutant. . . ."

"You knew Andrew Ravanel in Charleston?"

"We were school chums. There was a time I would have done anything for Andrew. Your complaint?"

Ashley said, "Colonel Ravanel is no gentleman."

"Andrew had his own doubts about that."

Ashley looked down at his hands. "Very well, then. If you must know. We'd been raiding and it hadn't gone well. Our brigade crossed the Licking River into Cynthiania, Kentucky, which was safely Confederate. Children ran beside us, shouting, 'Ravanel! It's Colonel Ravanel.' Women waved, but even Andrew was too tired to respond. He was in one of his moods, so Henry Kershaw took charge. Captain Kershaw billeted us officers in town. The color sergeant bivouacked the brigade west of town.

"Henry didn't set out pickets and we were abed when Federal cavalry struck at dawn. Andrew and I fled in our nightshirts. Did you know Henry Kershaw? That loudmouthed, drunken bully?"

"You are too kind to Henry."

"Henry didn't run. Henry Kershaw snatched up Ravanel's plumed hat and strode onto the street, pistol in hand, buck naked except for the hat, screaming that he was, by God, Colonel Ravanel and damned if he'd run from damn Yankees! Henry got off a shot before they killed him. A company of green Federal cavalry, just a foraging party who'd stumbled on us by chance."

Ashley Wilkes continued: "The brigade heard the shooting and were already mounted when we reached them. Colonel Ravanel was livid.

"The Federals never dreamed we'd counterattack. They were looting the town. One unlucky corporal was dragging a hall clock taller than he was. They didn't put up much fight.

"Their captain was wearing Andrew's hat. He hadn't had the wit to discard it. When he tried to give it back to Andrew, Andrew refused. 'Why sir, the hat's yours. A trophy of your gallant action.'

"We dressed Henry Kershaw and laid him in a mule cart. Andrew commanded our prisoners to follow and he adjusted the traces so the Federal captain could pull the cart. 'Henry would have wanted it. Surely you wouldn't deny the man you murdered this final courtesy . . .'

"When the Federal faltered, Colonel Ravanel lashed him as he might have lashed a mule, and when we reached the graveyard, the man crumpled to his knees. Again, Andrew refused to accept his hat. 'No, sir. You killed a man for that hat and it's yours. It'll be something your grandchildren can boast about. Now, you wouldn't leave Henry unburied, would you?' "

Ashley continued, "After he dug the grave, the man collapsed beside it while Andrew Ravanel read the burial service. Then Andrew turned to the captain, 'You dug the grave big enough for two.' "

Ashley said, "Before our men and his, the officer got down on his knees, clutching at Andrew's legs and begging for his life."

Rhett Butler pursed his lips. "Andrew never did know what he was doing until it was mostly done."

Ashley's eyes were haunted. "Andrew laughed at the man. 'Give me back my hat,' he said, 'It doesn't look right on a coward.'

"We left that officer with the soldiers he had commanded." Ashley paused. "In the past, I have admired wit as an ornament. I had not dreamed it could be so ugly."

"Truth beauty, beauty truth, eh, Major?" Rhett Butler said. He rose to go. "I do admire your yellow silk sash. I can sense the love in it. My best compliments to your wife."

Chapter Twenty

A River of Blood

Nominated for a second term, Abraham Lincoln said, "I do not allow myself to suppose that the delegates have decided that I am either the greatest or best man in America, but rather that it is not best to swap horses while crossing the river. . . ."

It was a river of blood. On May 8, in the fourth year of the War, Ulysses S. Grant began his spring offensive. By June, Grant had lost sixty thousand men. At Cold Harbor, he lost seven thousand in eight minutes.

In the west, General Sherman was moving on Atlanta. General Johnston's outnumbered Confederates beat off Sherman's attacks at Dalton, Resaca, and Pickett's Mill, but after each victory, the Confederates were outflanked and forced to abandon their positions because the Federals threatened their supply lines. Reacting to jibes that he wasn't a fighting general, Sherman fought a stand-up battle at Kennesaw Mountain. Three thousand dead Federals later, Sherman knew War is Hell.

When she learned that Ashley was missing in action, the very pregnant Melanie Wilkes fainted dead away. She begged Rhett to learn what he could. Some who'd been West Point cadets with Rhett Butler were now Federal generals, and from one of these, Rhett learned that Major Wilkes was alive, a prisoner in the Rock Island Prison Camp.

On July 12, 1864, surrounded by his cheering officers, William T. Sherman stood on a hilltop six miles north of Atlanta.

After months of Federal bombardment, Charleston was no longer a beautiful city. Streets perpendicular to the Federal guns had been hit hardest when shells penetrated roofs and exploded inside, collapsing house walls into the street. Fennel grew waist-high in abandoned gardens and loose cows grazed on Meeting Street. Broken glass glistened between cobblestones, dusted fence railings, and sheeted the walkways like frozen rain.

Although the next house was a ruin, thus far 46 Church Street had been spared. John Haynes refused to leave. He told Rosemary, "Go if you must. You will be safer in the north of town." Talking to John was like trying to drag a ghost back into the world of the living.

By July, the Federal blockade of Charleston harbor was complete and the last die-hard blockade runner was forced aground on Rattlesnake Shoal. The speculators vanished. Haynes & Sons ships rotted at the wharf and spiders spun webs in the windows of its empty warehouse.

Through the long daylight hours, John Haynes sat on his daughter's bed, staring at nothing. At night, he walked the city amid the incendiaries, the toppling walls, and Charleston's beleaguered fire companies..

Rosemary spent her days at the newly established Free Market, distributing food to Charleston's soldiers' families. Monday: yams. Tuesday: cornmeal. Okra on Wednesday. Shy children clung to their mothers' skirts. From time to time, some child would do or say or stand or smile as Meg might have, and Rosemary's heart broke afresh.

On Sunday, the Free Market was closed. Although John no longer attended services, Rosemary went faithfully, praying God would tell her why He had taken her child. After the service, she walked uptown—the Fishers' East Bay mansion had been shelled and Charlotte and Juliet were renting a small house north of the Shell District.

Their forced intimacy and Charlotte's difficult confinement had challenged Juliet's domestic skills and Charlotte's natural cheerfulness.

Charlotte wrote daily to her imprisoned husband. She entrusted some letters to the mail, some to private couriers. Charlotte Fisher Ravanel had important connections, and some letters had been hand-carried by prisoner-exchange commissioners. She wrote Andrew about their move, describing their cottage as "snug as a doll's house" and "surpassingly comfortable." She reported her unshakable certainty that Andrew Ravanel was to have a son. Charlotte never mentioned the doctor's unease, nor the agonizing pains that shot through her abdomen. Charlotte signed her letters "Your dear little wife, your loving spouse, I miss you so much! Praying for your return, I am . . ."

Charlotte had yet to receive a reply.

Juliet said, "Andrew? A letter writer? Lord no. I don't recall Andrew ever writing a letter."

"But dear Sister, he must know how precious his words would be?"

"Perhaps Andrew's letters are confiscated," Juliet suggested.

"Jamie's letters get through."

Jamie Fisher wrote detailed accounts of their bored jailers and the prisoners' pranks. When he warned of Andrew's deepening melancholy, Charlotte wrote, "Dearest husband, Your forced inactivity invites despondency. Please take regular exercise! Men of passionate dispositions (like yourself, dear) must exercise every day. When you are outdoors, turn your face to the sun. Sunlight strengthens the pineal gland!"

Although her letters to her husband were uniformly cheerful, Charlotte let herself complain to Juliet. "We were happier than we'd ever been. Why did Andrew raid into Ohio?" Charlotte pressed her hands into her back. "Sometimes I think I am carrying a pachyderm instead of a son. Juliet, why are men so cruel to those who love them?"

"I am sure I don't know," Juliet said with her old asperity. "Were we spinsters better at gauging men's hearts, we would not be spinsters."

On a steaming hot August morning, after Charlotte Ravanel had been in unsuccessful labor for forty-eight hours, Rosemary Haynes laid her ear against her friend's distended abdomen. Straightening, she gave Juliet the tiniest nod: no, no heartbeat.

Juliet said, "The doctor is dozing in the kitchen. I'll fetch him."

"Oh dear friend, please don't bother the poor man," Charlotte whispered. "Tarry awhile. Haven't we had such pleasant times? Who has ever had better friends than you?" Charlotte Fisher Ravanel's smile was reminiscent.

"How lucky I was to marry Andrew! All the girls had their caps set for Andrew." She closed her eyes. "I am sleepy now. I believe I will rest beside my baby. Tell me, Rosemary. Doesn't Andrew's son have his father's eyes?"

A bleary sun hung over the deserted harbor as Rosemary made her way home. The Federals were attacking the few harbor forts still in Confederate hands. So far away, their musketry sounded like a baby's rattle.

Outside 46 Church Street, Joshua was saddling Tecumseh.

"Joshua, what are you doing?"

John's servant adjusted the stirrups. "Master Haynes goin' for a soldier, Missus."

Saddlebags in hand, John came out, moving more briskly than he had in months. "Ah, Rosemary. How are Charlotte and the baby?"

"Dead. Charlotte and the baby, too. Oh, John, she so wanted that child. She . . ."

As if his wife were too fragile to embrace, John gently touched Rosemary's hair. Tears trickled down his good open face. "My dear, I am so sorry. Charlotte was too fine for this sinful world."

Rosemary indicated Tecumseh. "John, what is this?"

"I left a note on your bedside table. You couldn't have missed it."

"John!"

"General Johnston has asked for volunteers. Haynes and Son is ruined; our ships might as well be moored on dry land. Rosemary, can you forgive me? I cannot grieve any longer." Her husband's tiny smile was the first Rosemary had seen in months. "Who knows, perhaps they'll give me a commission. Lieutenant Haynes—wouldn't that be grand? You mustn't worry, dear. John Haynes will be the carefulest old soldier in the army."

He passed the saddlebags to Joshua. "You needn't fear for yourself—Rhett invested our profits in British bonds. There'll be money to sustain you, whatever may happen."

"John, wait! You cannot go! You cannot! Why . . . Tecumseh is gun-shy!"

He patted the horse's flank. "As I am. I suppose we both must overcome terrors."

"But why are you doing this? You cannot bring our Darling back!"

He gripped his wife's shoulders so tightly, he hurt her. "Rosemary, my life is ashes. I had thought myself protected by the modesty of my ambitions: I would be nothing more than an honest businessman, loving husband, and father. That is everything I ever wanted." He shook his head sadly. "What a very great distance we Southerners have come."

Although the words *Stay with me* trembled on Rosemary's lips, she could not utter them.

John Haynes nodded as if to himself. "So I am away. Though it is hard to credit, apparently our country needs its portly, middle-aged businessmen. President Davis says we can win. If we hold Atlanta, hold Petersburg, and hold Charleston, Abraham Lincoln won't be reelected. If Lincoln loses the election, the Federals will quit this struggle. They have suffered terribly; their losses have been even greater than ours. Surely they are as weary of the ghastly business as we are."

"John, would you lie to me? Now?"

His eyes soft with affection, he touched his lips to her hand. "Rosemary, Rosemary. Yes, I would lie to you." John Haynes turned her palm upright, as if memorizing each precious line. "I would lie to Jesus Christ Himself to save you hurt."

Chapter Twenty-one

Atlanta Burns

Rhett Butler was outside the National Hotel when the first Federal shell hit Atlanta. Fire bells jangled. "There, over there!" A sharp-eyed boy pointed at a column of smoke above the rooftops.

Rhett pushed through gawkers into the hotel saloon. Since the bartender was outside, Rhett stepped behind the bar and drew his own beer, which he carried with the bartender's newspaper to his usual table in the back. When another shell loosed dirt and paint flakes from the pressed-tin ceiling, Rhett covered his beer with his hand.

Everyone hoped John Hood, the western army's new commander, would whip Sherman and save the city. If the hotel cellar was turned into a bombproof, there'd be no more cold beer.

One paper praised General Hood, who had previously lost an arm and leg defending the Confederacy. "Indisputable proof," the paper claimed, "of the General's fighting spirit."

Yesterday morning at Confederate headquarters, Rhett had watched in disbelief while two strong men hoisted the General onto his horse and tied him to it.

That first shell flattened Mr. Warner's house on the corner of Rhoades and Elliot streets, killing Warner and his six-year-old daughter. Subsequent shells killed a woman who was ironing shirts. Another was fatally wounded waiting to board a train. Sol Luckie, a free colored barber, died when a shell glanced off a lamppost and exploded at his feet.

Two of Atlanta's four railroads were already in Federal hands. Frightened businessmen crept up the back stairs of the Chapeau Rouge to offer Rhett businesses for a song.

After Hood's army confiscated Atlanta's civilian horses and rigs, Rhett walked from the Chapeau Rouge to the hotel. When a street was blocked by fire equipment, Rhett detoured.

When the morning sun flared through the front windows of the hotel saloon, Rhett folded his cards and walked back to the Chapeau Rouge. If he lost a thousand one night, he won a thousand the next. It was all the same to him.

What a fool he was. What a goddamned fool! In this city, besieged on three sides by an enormous army that was closing the last bolt-hole, Rhett should have left weeks ago. There was absolutely nothing to keep him in Atlanta.

Except Scarlett O'Hara.

Pittypat and Peter had evacuated, but Scarlett stayed behind with Melanie Wilkes, who had been terribly weakened by the birth of her son.

Rhett should leave for London.

Or New Orleans. He hadn't been there since he returned Tazewell Watling to the Jesuits.

In March, in May, and twice in July, he'd packed his bags.

Then he'd remember her long neck—so proud but so vulnerable. Or he'd recall her scent—*her* scent beneath her perfume. Once, he'd turned back because of how bravely she tossed her head.

Rhett'd unpacked his bags and got thoroughly drunk.

The last time Rhett Kershaw Butler had felt this helpless, he'd been a field hand in his father's rice fields.

Outside the city, at Peachtree Creek and Ezra Church, General Hood hurled weary, outnumbered Confederates at well-fed, rested Federals who mowed them down like wheat. The Federals quit bombarding Atlanta and shifted to Hood's left flank, where they broke the Atlanta and West Point Railroad and advanced on Jonesboro and the Macon and Western. Jonesboro was the key to the city. If Jonesboro fell, the last railroad into Atlanta, Hood's sole supply line, would be cut.

Ambulances with side curtains lifted for air streamed down Marietta Street. Small boys ran alongside, fanning flies off the wounded.

Fresh rumors arrived at the saloon on the half hour: "Cleburne's flank attack has failed!" "My cousin's on Brown's staff. He says Brown can't hold out."

By midafternoon gamblers were offering four to one against Hood.

Rhett Butler sat alone at his table.

Believing Sherman's Jonesboro attack a feint and that the Federals intended to attack Atlanta itself, General Hood withdrew his army into the city. Thirty thousand soldiers stumbled down Decatur Street. Their dust whitened the saloon's front windows.

That night, the saloon was feverishly gay. Normally humorless men told one joke after another; Baptists who had never touched whiskey staggered. Sometime after midnight, a tall woman in mourning garb sat beside a dusty, opaque window, loosed her long hair, and wept.

Though the tables were full and men stood three-deep at the bar, Rhett Butler sat alone playing solitaire: black jack on red queen, black queen on red king. Rhett poured himself a drink. What the hell was he doing in this town?

In time, Rhett Butler walked out into a crystal-clear dawn. Small songbirds sang. The buzzards rested on their roosts. They had a busy day ahead.

Hood's dirty, exhausted soldiers slept in doorways and sprawled, snoring, on the boardwalks. Rhett rubbed his face. He needed a shave.

The Chapeau Rouge's parlor was a jumble of empty glasses and bottles. A love seat was overturned and both marble Venuses were gone.

"Mornin', MacBeth."

MacBeth had bags under his red-rimmed eyes and a bruise on his cheek.

"Rough night?" Rhett supposed.

The bouncer touched his bruise. "Everybody crazy! Actin' like they don't give a damn."

The kitchen stove was still warm and Rhett drew water to shave.

Rhett went upstairs to his office. His desk was bare; his safe was open and empty. He'd already burned what should be burned and buried what should be buried. Rhett Butler was free as a bird.

He sat at his desk and opened the drawer: pens, paper, ink, a blotter. They might have belonged to anyone.

What was he doing here?

Jesus Christ! What had love done to him?

At four that afternoon, Federal guns roared at Jonesboro. Hood had been tricked. The Confederate army was in the wrong place.

Accompanied by the distant rumble of guns, Rhett Butler walked back to the saloon, took his customary seat, and cracked a fresh deck.

The Federals outnumbered Jonesboro's defenders five to one. The Macon and Western, Atlanta's last railroad, fell into Sherman's hands.

"Hood's pullin' out! The army's skedaddling!"

"Anybody who don't want to live under Yankee rule, better get the hell out of 'Lanta." Some men scurried into the saloon; others scurried out. Rhett laid a black nine on a red ten.

Belle Watling came in. She'd been drinking. "Oh Rhett. What should I do? The Federals . . ."

"You needn't do a thing." Rhett poured Belle a drink. "The Yankees won't eat you, you know. Just keep your Cyprians indoors for a day or two. Then double your prices."

"Rhett, after all you've done for me, I hate to ask, but—can I come with you?"

Rhett's long fingers riffled his cards. "What makes you think I'm going anywhere?"

"Oh, I don't know, Rhett, I don't know!" Belle wept. "For God's sake, take me with you!"

He gave her his handkerchief. Belle Watling blew her nose and said she was sorry to be a burden.

A bartender came to the table, "Captain Butler, there's a nigger wench outside yellin' for you. Says it's important."

In the street, marching soldiers broke around Scarlett's bawling maid,

Prissy. "Cap'n Butler, Cap'n Butler. Miss Scarlett want you. She and Miss Melly, they needs you bad. You got to come."

"Come in off the street, Prissy, and tell me what you want."

She shook her head vigorously. "No, sir. I ain't comin' no nearer that saloon. Devil, he got long arms. Miss Scarlett, she evacuatin' and she need your horse 'n' carriage."

"My horse and carriage have been confiscated. I doubt there's a rig left in the city."

"Oh Lord, Cap'n Butler. If you has been confiscated, what we goin' to do? Miss Melly, she so sick. Her 'n' her baby. And there's Miss Scarlett 'n' little Wade. What we gonna do?"

Rhett's soul woke like a cat stretching in the sun. New blood coursed through his body. A grin found his face but he forced it into hiding. Scarlett needed him.

"Please, Cap'n Butler!"

"You go back to Miss Scarlett. Tell her I'm coming, Prissy. Don't dawdle now."

When Rhett went back inside, Belle Watling was peering into her empty glass. "I s'pose I don't need to ask who's askin' for you. I s'pose I know who you're goin' to."

"Dear Belle," Rhett said gently. "Go on home now. Your girls need you."

The rig Rhett stole was a sorry one: a spavined old nag pulling a wagon that looked to fall apart momentarily.

Anyway, it was a rig.

The evacuating Confederates were burning their supplies and the air smelled of burning hams: hams Confederate commissary men had confiscated from poor farmers who'd hoped to feed their families. Those tremendous explosions were munitions Rhett himself might have run through the blockade. Uniforms, saddles, whiskey, bacon, boots, blankets, tons and tons of cornmeal—all burning. The flames made Atlanta's night as bright as day.

Prissy was pacing outside Pittypat's front gate when Rhett turned into the street. She ran into the house, shouting, "Cap'n Butler, he come. Cap'n Butler here, Miss Scarlett!"

As Rhett drew up to the front gate, a tremendous blast rang in his ears. One hand shading her eyes, Scarlett stepped onto the front walk. The shock wave streamered her black hair and molded her dress to the soft curves of her body.

As fragments pattered the road and flame tongues licked the sky, Rhett Butler tipped his hat to Scarlett O'Hara. "Good evening. Fine weather we're having. I hear you're going to take a trip."

"Rhett Butler, if you make jokes, I shall never speak to you again."

Despite fire, blasts, and Yankee invasion Rhett was happy as a schoolboy. How her green eyes flashed!

He told her the hard truths: If they tried to flee south, Confederate soldiers would confiscate the horse and wagon, and every other road was in Federal hands. "Just where do you think you are going?"

"I'm going home," she said.

"Home? You mean to Tara?"

"Yes, yes! To Tara! Oh Rhett, we must hurry!"

Impossible: A burning city lay between them and the Jonesboro road.

She broke down, wailing and pummeling Rhett's chest. "I will go home! I will! If I have to walk every step of the way."

She would, too. Rhett knew she would. She'd do anything. She was capable of anything to get what she wanted.

Gently, he touched her hair. "There, there, darling," he said softly. "Don't cry. You shall go home, my brave little girl. You shall go home. Don't cry."

Prissy padded the wagon with quilts while Scarlett and Rhett went upstairs. The aroma of camphor and rubbing alcohol in Melly's room made Rhett's eyes water. The new mother was as colorless as her cotton sheets. Beside her, her baby was asleep. His mouth made tiny suckling motions. "I'll try not to hurt you, Mrs. Wilkes. See if you can put your arms around my neck."

"Baby Beau!" Melanie whispered.

"We'll let Prissy bring your baby. He'll be fine." Rhett slipped one arm under Melanie's shoulders and the other beneath her knees and lifted her. She didn't weigh eighty pounds.

"Please . . . Charles's things. We mustn't leave them." Melanie gestured weakly toward Charles's sword and the daguerreotype.

A hint of a smile found Rhett's lips. "I can't think Mrs. Hamilton would let me forget Charles's things."

Scarlett stowed Charles's mementos in the wagon. Gently, Rhett placed Melanie on the quilts beside her baby.

Thank you for helping us, Captain Butler." Melanie's voice was like paper rustling.

Although every nerve in his body was tingling, a deep calm had settled into Rhett's core. This was why he'd stayed in Atlanta. This was what he'd always meant to be. She needed him. Only him.

When little Wade hesitated, Rhett said, "Get in the wagon, son. Wouldn't you like an adventure?"

"No!" the boy said, and hiccuped. Rhett laughed as he scooped Wade aboard. Prissy scrambled into the back as Rhett lifted Scarlett onto the seat beside him.

"Wade, honey," Melanie murmured to her frightened nephew, "please slip that pillow behind me."

When she leaned forward so the boy could place the pillow, Melanie Hamilton Wilkes bit her lip so she wouldn't cry out. She mustn't faint. She mustn't!

Little Wade's hot breath was in her ear. "Aunty Melly, I'm scared."

"Sweet boy, there's much to be scared about," Melanie whispered. "But you are a brave young soldier, Wade, aren't you?"

"I suppose, Aunt Melly."

As they creaked off, Scarlett wailed. "I forgot to lock the front door!"

Rhett's roar of laughter cured Wade Hamilton's hiccups.

The rickety old horse and wagon headed toward Atlanta's burning heart.

Inside dark, seemingly abandoned houses, householders were hiding the family silver or burying Grandfather's Mexican War pistol.

Near the city center, the night was loud with creaks, cries, and hoofbeats—the tumult of a great army in retreat. Rhett turned into a side street. A tremendous explosion sucked the air from their lungs and Wade began hiccuping again. "That will be Hood's ammunition cars." Rhett reached behind him to give Wade's knee a reassuring squeeze.

Rhett had hoped they could slip around the fire, but this night every road led to hell. He lashed the old horse into a shambling run and curled his fingers around his revolver. His woman was pressed against his side and heaven help the fool who tried to stop them!

On both sides of Marietta Street, warehouses were ablaze. Looters scurried off with their prizes. Drunks reeled around a shattered whiskey barrel.

Suddenly, Rhett pulled the wagon over the boardwalk and stopped, concealed under an outdoor stairwell.

"Hurry," Scarlett said. "Why are you stopping?"

"Soldiers."

They might have been a thousand-man regiment once, but they weren't a hundred tonight. A lifetime ago, wives and sweethearts had sewn fine uniforms and embroidered their flag and they'd had a name—they'd been the Grays or the Zouaves or the Troop or the Legion. They'd come from no place special, a town or a county where everybody knew everybody, and they'd enlisted with their brothers, cousins, and neighbors and elected the Master of the biggest plantation as their Colonel because they sure as hell wouldn't take orders from just anybody.

Their friends had died at their sides, and their cousins and their brothers and their Colonel—oh, he was long dead—and the Colonel who'd replaced him—what was his name?—dead, too. How many Colonels had there been anyway?

They walked as if their springs were broken, as if they had walked so many miles, one mile was no different from the next, one battle no different from the last. They held their rifles like old friends. Their sweetheart-sewn uniforms were long gone. They wore homespun and scraps of Federal uniforms, and some had short jackets and some long ones, and a few walked bare-chested through the flickering glare.

They scarcely lifted their feet, but their sliding strides would carry them onward until at last they fell. For some, that would come as a blessing.

A boy soldier trailed behind. Perhaps he'd been a drummer boy when they'd had drums, but rifles were easier to come by than drums. The boy dragged his rifle in the dust.

He stopped in his tracks, wobbled, and fell on his face. Wordlessly, two men fell out. One, whose black beard was the only substantial thing about him, gave his and the boy's rifle to the second man, slung the boy across his shoulders and walked on.

Rhett Butler removed his hat.

After the last soldier turned the corner, Rhett lashed the horse forward.

The burning city sucked air into its great lungs. Windows popped and blackened the street with burned glass.

Scarlett cried, "Name of God, Rhett! Are you crazy? Hurry! Hurry!"

Prissy screamed.

Flames shot from eaves; oily smoke rolled from roof caps. Heat scorched their faces and they squinted against the glare. Rhett urged the horse into a shuffling trot, terror motivating the beast more than the lash. Fire to the left and right; only a narrow tunnel between. Wade shrieked again and again as heat waves crashed over them and bricks and timbers thudded into the street.

The railroad tracks they bumped across were clear proof that this conflagration had once been a city where ordinary men went to work every morning and newspapers were published. Preachers preached, bankers banked, and grocers had produce to sell.

When they finally emerged on a side street, it was immediately cooler. The fire was behind them. Little Wade's wails diminished to muffled sobs and hiccups.

Nobody else on the road. On the outskirts of the city, houses were farther apart and the road was bordered by elm trees. The fire wind rustled leaves. The city glowed at their back.

Rhett drew rein.

"Hurry, Rhett. Don't stop."

"Let the poor brute catch his breath."

Their sweat dried in the cool air.

Rhett Butler was immensely weary. He had done what he had promised her. She wouldn't need him now. She'd never wanted him. Never. He asked if she knew where they were.

"Oh yes. I know a wagon trace that winds off from the main Jonesboro road and wanders around for miles. Pa and I used to ride it. It comes out right near the MacIntosh place, and that's only a mile from Tara."

He glanced at her face. She was yearning for Tara. Scarlett O'Hara was pure yearning. She and he were two of a kind, but she didn't know it, and she never would.

Some men could love without being loved. Rhett envied them.

Her body was warm against his. He could feel her heartbeat.

It was as if something inside him had snapped. All tension drained out of him. He was as tired as if they'd made love for hours.

That drummer boy couldn't have been more than twelve years old. He should be drifting down a river in the fog, watching for loggerhead turtles on otter slides.

He told her to go on to Tara without him. She had her horse and wagon and she knew the way. He was going to join the army.

"Oh, I could choke you for scaring me so! Let's go on."

"I am not joking, my dear. Where is your patriotism, your love for Our Glorious Cause?"

"Oh Rhett," she said, "how can you do this to me? Why are you leaving me?"

Too little, too late.

Rhett Kershaw Butler put his arms around Scarlett O'Hara Hamilton and pressed his lips to hers. He felt her lips melt and awaken to his kiss.

He would never get over her.

He stepped down from the buggy into the darkness beside the road.

Chapter Twenty-two

After Franklin

That fall, after unavailing appeals to less devastated regions of the Confederacy, the Charleston Free Market ran out of food and closed. Rosemary walked home through the rubble-strewn streets, entered her home through the front door she no longer bothered to lock, and sat across the room from John's favorite chair. After a time, she retrieved the mantel's sole ornament, a silver bud vase, and polished it.

The very next morning, a furloughed convalescent delivered her husband's letter: John was managing "pretty well for an old fellow" and had been promoted. Henceforth, all the world might address him as Captain Haynes—a promotion General Stahl made "only because there were no worthy men seeking it."

General Forrest took a liking to Rhett," John wrote, "and wanted to commission him an officer. When your brother declined the honor, the ferocious Forrest was greatly amused. I see Rhett whenever our cavalry is in camp. He is in excellent spirits and has acquired a follower, one Archie Flytte, who attends upon Rhett faithfully as a dog. Flytte is a penitentiary bird pardoned to join the army. Although the man is devoted to Rhett, his affection is not reciprocated.

"After Atlanta fell, we marched north. General Hood believed if the Confederate army stood between General Sherman and his Knoxville supply base, it'd bring Sherman boiling out of Atlanta. Once again, Hood misjudged General Sherman, who burned what was left of Atlanta and marched off vigorously in the opposite direction.

"As Sherman proceeds through Georgia, he is wrecking the east-west railroads as thoroughly as he previously wrecked our north-south lines. After those railroads are destroyed, dear heart, you and I will be marooned separately for God knows how long. Rosemary, will you come to me? In anticipation of your favorable decision, Rhett's friend Rufus Bullock has telegraphed you a railroad pass.

"I will understand perfectly if you don't wish to hazard such an arduous, perhaps dangerous journey, but it would make me so glad to see you. We have so much to make up for, so much to talk about. Our Darling Meg lives in both our hearts. Dear Rosemary, I miss you more than I ever dreamed. My baseless jealousy kept us apart. All the fault is mine. I reproach you for nothing. Please come to me.

"Your loving husband, John."

Rosemary rushed from room to room, pulling clothing from drawers and chifforobes. She had packed three portmanteaus and a steamer trunk before plumping down on the trunk, covering her face, and giggling. What a ninny!

She stuffed what she absolutely had to have into a carpetbag. Her only ornament was a filigree rose-gold brooch. Why she had ever disliked it, she could not recall.

Rosemary picked up her railroad pass at the depot, where she boarded the train to Savannah.

Next morning in Savannah, Rosemary changed to the Georgia Central, which by noon the following day was huffing cautiously into Macon.

Sherman's cavalry was nearing the city and Macon's depot was clogged with refugees.

Before he burned Atlanta, General William T. Sherman had proposed, "War is cruel and you cannot refine it," a proposition he'd further tested on the undefended farms and towns along his line of march.

Even before Rosemary's train reached the platform, refugees were swarming aboard, hoping to assure a place for themselves when the train departed. When told the locomotive needed fuel, men, children, clergymen—even respectable matrons—passed balks hand over hand up to the wood car.

Militia guarded the Southwestern train Rosemary wanted to board. Their captain had lost an arm at Chancellorsville, and said he didn't know Rufus Bullock from "Gee Crackey." He hadn't known the Confederacy *had* a "Railroad Bureau." He touched Rosemary too familiarly. Since the captain chose who rode the train, he said, he picked the prettiest.

Rosemary thanked him and brushed his hand aside as if she hadn't noticed it. She had seated herself in the car when a familiar voice hailed her from the platform. "Rosemary Haynes! Dear Rosemary! Please, please speak to these men!"

The Wards had evacuated Charleston to refuge at a cousin's plantation near Macon. A scant year later, Sherman's bummers torched that plantation and the Wards fled again. Eulalie Ward and her brother-in-law, Frederick, hadn't changed clothes in days. Eulalie's shoes were broken-soled; Frederick, who had always worn a hat out of doors, was bareheaded and his pate was painfully sunburned.

"Rosemary, they let you on the train! Please help us get on, too. We must flee Macon. We have nothing left. Nothing!"

Before the war, Frederick Ward had been a rich man with a rich man's comfortable opinions. Now his sister-in-law led him by the hand. "Stand straight, Frederick. You mustn't be mistaken for a man of no consequence."

"But Eulalie, I *am* a man of no consequence."

Many years ago, when Eulalie's husband died, she thought she had lost everything. She'd never dreamed she had so much more to lose. Willy was dead and her daughters had run off with Sherman's soldiers. Eulalie and Frederick got so hungry, they'd killed Eulalie's little dog, Empress—and then been unable to eat her.

From the rear platform (Rosemary didn't consider getting off the train), Rosemary begged the militia captain to let the Wards board. "Ma'am," he said, "ain't no place for 'em. Less'n you hop off and make room."

As the overloaded train pulled out of the depot, Rosemary looked anywhere but at the refugees on the platform.

Where the tracks had been torn up by Sherman's cavalry and hastily relaid, the ramshackle train crept no faster than its passengers, who got off and walked alongside. That night, male passengers held lanterns for the trainmen bracing long bars under the sagging rails to level them as the cars tottered over.

Twelve hours and ninety miles later, the train reached Albany, Georgia. Rosemary paid five dollars for three corn pones and, with other weary, unwashed refugees, slept on the depot floor until daybreak.

The Selma and Meridian train was a miracle. Untouched by the war, its cars weren't shot up, and its locomotive's bulbous smokestack didn't have a single bullet hole—not one! Although the paint was faded, every car was dark green, with black trim.

The train click-clacked over level rails at a breathtaking thirty miles an hour. The tubercular veteran beside Rosemary had traveled extensively in New England before the war and announced, "By golly, ma'am, we might as well be in Massachusetts!"

This paragon train ended at Demopolis, where the passengers were ferried across the Tombigbee River. From there, they hiked four miles to a log platform, where a wheezing locomotive and familiar mismatched, bullet-pocked cars awaited them. In Meridian, Mississippi, Rosemary took a hotel room and slept like the dead. The Mobile and Ohio train she boarded next morning delivered her to Corinth, Mississippi, at dusk. That night, she slept in the depot. At two o'clock the following afternoon, the Memphis and Charleston train brought supplies, conscripts, and Rosemary Haynes into Decatur, Alabama, the end of the line.

The train disgorged barrels of gunpowder and brined beef, boxes of minié balls, and conscripts onto the platform. The youngest conscript was three days past seventeen, the eldest forty-nine. Most of the conscripts hadn't anything to say, but one fellow in a beaver-collared frock coat confided to Rosemary Haynes that he was too valuable to the war effort to be expended in battle, and a bucktoothed boy chewed his thumbnail and said he'd desert first chance he got. When they stepped down in Decatur, provost's men formed the conscripts into ranks and told them that aspiring deserters should be able to outrun a bullet.

After five hard days' travel, Rosemary was grateful for the unvibrating, untrembling platform beneath her feet. She relinquished her carpetbag to old Joshua. "Have you been waiting long?"

"I reckon."

She almost didn't recognize the horse tied to the hitching rail. The knacker man would make no profit on him.

"What have you done to Tecumseh?" Rosemary cried. "Oh my poor boy!"

"He old, Miss Rosemary," Joshua replied. "He born in them olden times."

"He was sound until he went into the army. You were a good boy, weren't you, Tecumseh?"

The gelding lifted his head and nickered a welcome, and Rosemary thought that was the saddest thing of all. "Joshua, Tecumseh wants an apple."

"Miss Rosemary, whatever oats or apples or corn we gets, we eats. When horse dead, I reckon we eat him, too."

Since the railroad bridges north of Decatur had been burned, Hood's supplies and conscripts were off-loaded and freighted by ox, mule wagon, or shank's mare to Columbia, Tennessee. Sometimes, Rosemary rode Tecumseh. From pity, she usually walked. Army supply wagons spilled off the narrow road, cutting ruts through adjacent fields. There were no fences: their rails had fed soldiers' campfires, and if any livestock survived, they were hidden deep in the woods. That night, Rosemary slept beneath a supply wagon.

In the morning, rain plucked the last leaves off the trees and overflowed the ruts. Tecumseh couldn't carry a rider anymore. A little after dark, they entered Pulaski, Tennessee, where Rosemary bought some oats, which the gelding picked at. Joshua slept in a stall with the horse.

Rosemary's hotel room was unheated, but by doubling her threadbare blanket, she was warm enough. She dreamed of John and Rhett on a June day when the sun was so bright and Rhett had brought picnic baskets with more food than they could eat and Tecumseh grazed in timothy so tall, it tickled his belly.

Although there were trains running out of Pulaski, the pale-faced young provost wouldn't let Rosemary board. "Ma'am, I couldn't let you on this train were your pass signed by President Jefferson Davis himself."

"I have traveled from South Carolina to see my husband in the army."

"So far as that?" The young provost quoted, " 'Who can find a virtuous woman? For her price is far above rubies. The heart of her husband trusts in her. . . . Her children arise up, and call her blessed.' "

"The Federals killed my daughter. Meg would have been six next March."

"Ma'am, I'm sorry to carry on. I was a seminarian before the war."

"Do you still believe in God?"

The young man looked away. "I guess I've gotten used to it."

Rosemary, Joshua, and the stumbling Tecumseh passed haphazard piles of discarded Federal equipment: artillery horses shot in their traces, overturned wagons. Files of Federal prisoners were marched south. The prisoners wore Confederate rags, their guards sported warm blue Federal uniforms.

In Columbia, Tennessee, Rosemary bought corn pones and brown beans for herself and Joshua.

That evening, as they walked toward Franklin, Tennessee, Rosemary heard distant thunder as if a thousand wagons were rumbling across a wooden bridge.

"They's fightin'," Joshua said.

"They can't be fighting. The Federals are running away. Why would they be fighting?"

"They's fightin'."

As light faded from the sky, the rumble grew louder and Rosemary could distinguish individual explosions. Muleteers pulled off the road to let fleeing Confederates by.

Rosemary and Joshua bucked a tide of ambulances, blank-faced deserters, and walking wounded. Provost officers cursed and flailed at the men with the flats of their swords. The deserters ducked or left the road and kept moving south.

The frosty Milky Way stretched across the heavens to the horizon, where it drowned in the ruddy penumbra of guns.

"I am Captain John Haynes's wife. He's with General Stahl's command. Sir, do you know my husband?"

"Sorry, ma'am."

The firing stopped.

"Rhett Butler, my brother, he's with General Forrest. Do you know Rhett Butler?"

"Ma'am, I served with General Bates."

Joshua stopped on the roadside and took off his hat. "Miss Rosemary, this here horse ain't goin' no farther."

Tecumseh stood with legs splayed, head down.

"Me and horse come a far piece with you and Mister John," Joshua said. "But we ain't comin' no more."

Rosemary walked into the starry night alone.

Dim yellow lanterns bobbed where two great armies had fought. Here and there on the gentle rolling landscape, a campfire flared. The air tasted like burned pepper and Rosemary smelled blood: rich and sour and salty.

The faces of the men tending the wounded were black from powder and some were as bloody as the men they were ministering to. "My husband is with General Stahl's brigade," Rosemary appealed.

The boy's eyes shone like a minstrel's in blackface. "Ma'am, I believe General Stahl's been kilt. They was in the center of the line, twixt the house and the cotton gin."

"Where are his men now?"

"Ma'am," the boy said cautiously, "I believe most of General Stahl's men are layin' twixt the house and the cotton gin."

Dawn washed out the lanterns and dimmed the campfires. Wounded men begged for water. The earth bristled with frost.

Rosemary tried to staunch a wounded officer's bleeding, tying his belt above the mangled hole in his thigh. Frost glistened white on the blood he'd spilled. He convulsed and gasped and was astonished by death.

The sun rose. Civilians came from Franklin to help and marvel.

What was John Haynes wearing? Was he still stout? Had he grown a beard? Rosemary would have recognized her husband instantly by his walk or the angle at which he carried his head, but in the jumble of dead men, she couldn't distinguish one from another.

There were more dead on the gentle rise before the abandoned Federal breastworks.

A wounded boy lifted himself onto one elbow.

"I've no water," Rosemary said. "I'm so sorry."

Some of the dead wore grim expressions, some were determined, others were savoring a joke. Three weeping solders knelt beside a dead comrade.

To another boy, she said,"There'll be someone to help you soon. I'm sorry. I've no water. I'm sorry."

Rosemary intercepted litter bearers. "I seek my husband. May I lift the cloth from his face?"

The Federal breastworks were fronted by a spiked abatis where dead men were impaled, frozen in final attitudes. An elderly woman asked if Rosemary had seen her grandson, Dan Alan Rush. "We call him Dan Alan, account of his daddy was Dan, too."

"Mother, I'm sorry. I haven't seen your grandson. I am seeking my husband, Captain John Haynes."

"My grandson was a bright spark." The woman smiled. "They said he lies hereabouts."

Two riders came along the face of the breastworks.

Rosemary waved frantically."Oh dear God! Rhett! Rhett!" she shouted.

The horsemen galloped and her brother jumped down and took her in his arms. "Rosemary! Oh Rosemary, I wish you had not seen this."

"Oh Rhett! Thank God! Dear Brother, you are alive!" Rhett's uniform was torn and filthy, but he wasn't wounded. Merciful heaven!

"I haven't found John. Rhett, do you know where he is?" Rosemary pushed hair off her eyes. "John may be hurt. . . ."

"Yes, he may be hurt."

"Likely he's kilt." Rhett's companion spat tobacco juice.

"Shut up, Archie," Rhett said.

The leather-faced man beside her brother had the tip of his wooden leg in a makeshift scabbard. He had a poor man's teeth and the lips of a hard one.

Rhett said, "Rosemary, this was the worst thing I've ever seen."

"Then you ain't never been to the penitentiary," his companion said.

"Archie"—Rhett pointed—"go through the Federal position and collect any repeating rifles you find."

As Archie left, Rhett said, "The Chinese believe if you save a man's life, you are obligated to that man forever." He took his sister's icy hands and rubbed them. "Dear Rosemary, do you have nerve for this?"

At her nod, Rhett boosted her onto his horse.

The ditch before the Federal breastworks brimmed with dead men, packed so tightly that some were upright, unable to fall. Soldiers and civilians were dismantling the tableau to get at wounded men underneath.

Rosemary asked, "Does John have a beard now?"

"He is clean-shaven."

Rosemary had never thought she'd see an exposed human brain or an adolescent boy with a neat scorch mark around the bullet hole in the center of his forehead. Dizzy, she clasped the horse's neck and pressed her face into its coarse mane. "I despair, Rhett. Dear Brother, John and I were so far apart."

"Rosemary, John often spoke of you. He never stopped loving you."

Rosemary wiped her eyes as they entered a farmyard where so many horses and men lay in death. It had been a prosperous small farm, but every outbuilding—the corncrib, cotton gin, woodshed, chicken coop—and the farmhouse itself had been perforated by hundreds of bullets. A dead Federal was pinned to the woodshed by a bayonet through his neck.

When Rhett jerked the bayonet out, the dead soldier crumpled, groaning with expelling gas. "I knew it would come to this. I knew it! What sentimental urge brought me to fight for this 'Glorious Cause'?" Tears streaked Rhett's powder-blackened cheeks.

"General Hood was out of temper. The Federals had slipped his net and he'd be damned if they'd get away. 'Attack!' " Rhett whispered. " 'Prove you are brave enough to face fortifications!' " Her brother was honestly bewildered. "Twenty thousand men marching straight into the Federal guns, flags flying and officers waving swords, and, Rosemary"—Rhett's eyes brimmed again—"the bands were playing 'Dixie.' 'In Dixieland I'll take my stand. To live and die in Dixie.' Oh Rosemary. I've never, never . . ." Rhett dropped the bayonet beside the soldier it had slain. "More bad news, Sister. Belle Watling's son, Tazewell, has enlisted. That boy followed my stupid, stupid example."

Archie Flytte rode up and said. "Ain't no repeating rifles. Federals took 'em." He stuffed his lip and, having settled his chew, said, "Your husband's shot, ma'am. I met up with a feller from Captain Haynes's regiment. They carried your husband into town." He pointed toward Franklin.

"Oh thank you. How can I thank you?"

"Let me 'n' your brother get about our business. Genr'l Forrest's musterin'. We 'uns movin' out."

Rosemary kissed her brother's cheek. "Take every care, Rhett. You have custody of my heart."

Bounded by a gentle arc of the Harpeth River, Franklin, Tennessee, had nine hundred citizens, a fine new courthouse, and three academies, which along with the First Baptist and the First Presbyterian Church were now hospitals. Rosemary Haynes stepped around the blood, ignored the moans of the wounded, and inspected the ranks of dead men laid out-of-doors.

She was directed to a private home on Market Street. The tidy frame house was marred by bloody drag marks across the porch and an amputated forearm in the coal scuttle beside the door.

The elderly woman who answered Rosemary's knock was dressed as primly as a schoolteacher.

"I was told my husband . . . Captain Haynes . . . might be here."

"I'm afraid I don't know them by name, dear, but do, please, come in."

John wasn't with the four men lying in the front parlor, nor the three in the bed, nor the two on the bedroom floor.

A surgeon, the elderly woman explained, visited every few hours, and in the meantime she and her sister saw to the men's needs. "We've potato soup. We bring them water. They complain of the cold, though we've burned so much coal already. I hope for a mild winter."

Her younger sister tugged Rosemary's sleeve. "My dear, there is one poor fellow out back in our garden. We put him there for the others' sake."

A bullet had shattered John Haynes's right elbow and that arm was turned backward at an impossible angle. Another bullet had bloodied the breast of his broadcloth coat, the same coat John wore when he left home. His trousers were rough homespun and too big for him. His feet were bare.

When Rosemary knelt and kissed her husband's brow, his flesh was warm, and for an exhilarating instant, Rosemary believed John was still alive. "Oh John, oh John," she said. "I'm here. It's your Rosemary, your own wife. Oh John, please . . ."

The small garden had been neatly put away for the winter. The beanpoles were lashed together, the strawberry bed covered with straw. Wooden buckets were overturned under a light dusting of snow. Even as Rosemary kissed his cheeks, John Haynes's flesh cooled.

Behind Rosemary, the old woman said, "I am sorry, child. Your husband did not suffer and was conscious until the end. He believed you were coming to him and yearned to live long enough to see you one last time. When he understood that was not to be his fate, he begged me: 'Tell my Rosemary to trust her good heart.' He spoke of a daughter he would meet in Paradise." The old woman touched Rosemary's trembling shoulder. "Near the end, he became delirious. Child, your husband's final words were, 'Take me to my wife.' "

Chapter Twenty-three

The Last Runner

Just after midnight some six weeks later, Rhett Butler threaded his way through gin poles, drays, and stevedores on the Wilmington wharves, where the *Banshee,* the *Let 'er Rip,* and the *Merry Widow* were moored bow-to-stern. Sweating workers hove, skidded, suspended, and stowed cotton bales aboard the blockade runners. In the southwest, the night sky pulsed where the Federal guns were hammering Fort Fisher. Light off the wharves sparkled the black river.

In his dark suit and captain's cap, Tunis Bonneau was checking his manifest when Rhett said, "Captain Bonneau."

Turning at the interruption, Tunis's frown became a grin. "Rhett Butler—I'll be darned to tarnation!" His glasses gleaming in the torchlight, Tunis clasped his friend's hand.

The stacks of the adjacent runner puffed heavy black smoke. Tunis gave his manifest to a crewman. "Tell Mr. MacLeod get up steam."

"You believe Fisher will fall?" Rhett asked.

"The Federals got a mighty landing party and a mighty fleet. Maybe Fisher beat 'em off, maybe she won't. If she falls while we're still in Wilmington, they'll capture my boat."

"You heard about John Haynes?"

Tunis removed his cap. "Ruthie wrote me. Mr. Haynes, he was a good man. All the time I knew him, I never heard him do nothin' to hurt nobody."

"At Franklin . . ." Rhett cleared his throat. "At Franklin, John wanted to be certain the men in his rear rank saw their officer. . . ." Rhett swallowed.

"So he stuck his sword through his hat and waved it over his head." Rhett cleared his throat.

When a burly crewman approached, Captain Bonneau stayed him with a gesture.

"Tunis, what in God's name was John Haynes doing charging Federal breastworks with his hat on the tip of his sword? *John Haynes?* John was the most pacific man on earth."

Stevedores skidded five-hundred-pound cotton bales onto slings and eased them onto the *Widow*'s deck. The smoke that rolled from her stacks settled as a noxious fog on sweating men and cotton.

"Did Miss Rosemary . . . did she bring Mr. Haynes home?"

"Ah, Tunis . . . John's buried in Franklin. Things as they are, Rosemary couldn't get him back to Charleston."

Tunis's crewman said, "Mr. MacLeod's compliments, Captain. He'll have steam up in a quarter hour."

Tunis dismissed the man with a nod. Rhett wiped his eyes. "Damn smoke," he said.

Tunis looked away from his friend. "My boy Nat's startin' to talk. First thing he said was 'boat.' Ruthie says he calls every blessed thing 'boat.' He'll be a sailor, like his daddy."

"Good news, friend. Calls for a celebration."

"Some other night, Brother Rhett. I got to be in open water before sunup."

"Tunis, I've a favor to beg."

"Sure, Rhett. Anything."

Tunis's smile vanished when Rhett told him what he wanted. He set his lips and jammed his captain's cap down on his head. "Can't do it, Rhett. Can't chance waitin' another day. If you had that boy here now, course I'd take him, but I can't wait. The Federals're corkin' the bottle. What wants to be drunk wants to be drunk tonight."

Rhett breathed a tuneless whistle. "That's that, then. Seems a shame a fifteen-year-old boy won't get a chance to grow up, but I guess boys aren't worth as much as they once were." Rhett opened his cigar case but closed it and put it away. "Taz won't surrender, Tunis. He'll get himself killed."

Beside them, the *Banshee*'s lines were loosed. Her great paddle wheels revolved as stevedores leapt for the wharf. As she churned into the current, her helmsman saluted Captain Bonneau.

Tunis clicked open his gold hunter. "*Banshee* will be in Nassau Monday. If I cast off now, I'd beat her there. Rhett, I . . . Tarnation!"

Tunis closed his eyes and his lips moved in prayer. When he opened his eyes again, he smiled; not a big smile. "Rhett, what's say you and me celebrate my Nat's first word? I'll wait on your boy. Might be Fort Fisher will keep 'em off one day longer. Can't know what them crazy Johnny Rebs might get up to."

Near noon the next day, Major Edgar Puryear climbed to the second floor of the Commercial Hotel. At his knock, a barefoot, barechested, unshaven Rhett Butler let him in. "Good morning, Edgar, if it *is* still morning." At the sink, Rhett emptied the water jug over his head. "Edgar, never drink rum with a sailorman." He yawned. "I trust Fort Fisher remains in Confederate hands?"

Edgar Puryear tossed an envelope onto the bureau.

Rhett opened the window, leaned outside, and listened to the distant guns. "Don't sulk, Edgar. I won't forget you for this."

Edgar Puryear touched a scar on his nose. "Isn't he the boy who struck me? Your son."

"My 'ward,' Edgar. '*Ward.*'" Rhett chuckled. "You're not the first man ever laid low by Venus."

Edgar didn't share Rhett's amusement.

Rhett took the paper from the envelope and examined it. "Taz's orders, signed by the General himself. Good, excellent. By the way, how do you get on with Bragg?"

"Braxton Bragg enjoys flattery."

"Ah. You've a gift for that." Rhett took a fresh shirt from his carpetbag.

Puryear cleared his throat. "After the War, you'll be the richest man in the South."

"And this might be a good time for the farsighted soldier to explore postwar employment?"

"It'll be a new shuffle after the War. There'll be opportunities for the right sort of man."

Rhett said, "Umm."

"You were celebrating with Captain Bonneau? The nigger captain? Rhett, you have some strange friends."

Despite the raw January air, Rhett stood at the open window, hands clasped behind his back. He spoke as though Edgar Puryear weren't in the room. "When I woke this morning, I was remembering a time Tunis and I took a notion to sail his father's skiff down the coast to Beaufort. Damn fool idea—fifty miles in open water—but we set sail without a care. That sky—I do believe the sky was bluer in those days. I remember the sun on my back, the hard seat of the skiff, the snap of the sail. So many years have passed, but I cannot remember a happier day."

That afternoon, the wharves were quiet. Smoke wisping from her stacks, the *Merry Widow* was the only runner left in Wilmington.

Rhett shook hands with the crew he'd once commanded. Mismatched paint mottled the *Widow*'s hull where shell holes had been patched, and the starboard paddle-wheel housing was new. In the engine room, new iron braces clamped oversized engines to their frames. Mr. MacLeod, the engineer, greeted Rhett with a reproach. "Your last Charleston run, Captain Butler! My vessel still suffers from it!"

Just at dusk this 14th of January 1865, the last Confederate blockade runner slipped her moorings and eased into the Cape Fear River. The long gray ship was one of the fastest vessels afloat; some said she was *the* fastest.

The *Widow* hugged the western shore, making just enough speed to maintain steerageway.

The Federals had landed above Fort Fisher and severed the fort's land connection to Wilmington. Federal campfires dotted the narrow peninsula between the Atlantic and the river.

When their pickets spotted the *Widow,* the Federals gathered on the bank to see the legendary runner. The river was too wide here for their field artillery, and as the graceful boat slipped downstream, these Yankee soldiers threw their hats in the air and cheered her.

Tunis anchored below Fort Fisher, just above the bar where the river emerged into open ocean.

The Federal fleet was pounding the great sand fort, and from the *Widow*'s deck, Fort Fisher was a colossal sandstorm: sand plumes and dirty sand clouds tossed aloft by artillery concussions. Tunis shouted to Rhett over the pandemonium. "Ten o'clock, Rhett! You hear?" Tunis tapped his watch. "You ain't here by ten o'clock, with or without your boy, I'm pullin' out."

Rhett bowed. "I am obliged to you, Captain Bonneau."

"And don't you *ever* tell Ruthie I done it!"

Rowing himself to shore in the *Widow*'s dinghy, Rhett tasted sand in his teeth.

Since he'd received no reinforcements from Braxton Bragg, General Whiting, Fort Fisher's commander, had stripped other river forts of men, and as Rhett tied up, a gunboat was disgorging soldiers onto the wharf. These artillerymen were like no Confederates Rhett had seen in years: well fed, their uniforms entire and recently laundered. Until today, these men had had a good war. Perched in gun batteries above the river, they'd lobbed an occasional shell at Federal blockaders venturing too close, but they'd never been under fire themselves. Grateful runner captains had kept them supplied with victuals and whiskey.

Formed into ragged ranks, these comfortable soldiers peered unhappily at the maelstrom ahead.

Rhett turned to a corpulent captain whose uniform had fit less snugly four years ago. "Nice day," Rhett observed.

The ocean was a mirror except where short rounds fell and spouted. White streamers marked projectiles' arcs into the battered fort. Each Federal vessel was visible, as if under slight magnification. The breeze their firing created was strong enough to whip the smoke from their gun muzzles. The ironclads *Pawtuxet, Brooklyn, Mahopac, Canonicus, Huron, Saugus, Kansas, Pontoosuc, Yantic, Mohican, Monadnock, New Ironsides, Pequot, Senaca, Tacony, Unadilla,* and *Maumee* stood a thousand yards offshore, fronting wooden warships *Minnesota, Colorado, Tuscarora, Mackinaw, Powhatan, Wabash, Susquehanna, Ticonderoga, Juniata, Vanderbilt,* and

Shenendoah. A dozen smaller warships were farther out, attended by eighteen gunboats and twenty-two troop transports.

Fort Fisher was contiguous sand dunes in an upside down L. The long leg of the L faced the Federal fleet, and the short leg crossed the peninsula, facing the Federal landing party. Fisher's sand dunes were fifty feet wide and thirty feet high, linked by gun platforms in the saddles between.

Before the Federal bombardment, Fort Fisher had had barracks, corrals, and a parade ground. These had been pounded so thoroughly, not a scrap remained.

The corpulent captain raised his hand and ordered his men to the double-quick. Rhett took a deep breath, lowered his head, and ran like a hare. He pounded along the road until it disappeared in shell holes. Rhett's legs ached from running through soft sand and he stumbled and fell. Exploding sand erupted around him and concussions slapped his eardrums. The sand deluge filled his shirt, pants, and boots and thickened every strand of his sweaty hair.

Fort Fisher's flag was a torn rag on a spliced flagpole. Some risers on the Headquarters Battery staircase were shattered; others, two and three in a row, were missing. Rhett clambered up rails, risers—whatever he could grab hold of. The battery's guns had been dismounted and one gunbarrel flung partway down the sea face. Across the saddle between the dunes, sandbags were piled waist-high. Behind them, an officer had his glass trained on the Federal fleet. At his feet, his orderly kept his back against the sandbags.

"General Whiting?"

The General snapped his glass closed. "If you are a journalist, sir, inform your readers we will hold this fort."

"I have come from General Bragg."

The General's face flamed with eagerness. "Is Bragg sending reinforcements?"

"I am not privy to General Bragg's plans, sir." Rhett wiped his envelope clean of sand before giving it to the General.

Braxton Bragg's orders transferred Private Tazewell Watling from the

18th North Carolina Junior Reserves to Colonel Rufus Bullock's Department of Railroads. Rhett Butler, of that department, would escort Private Watling.

General Whiting said, "I ask Bragg for reinforcements and he takes the men I have."

"Watling's just a boy, sir. He's fifteen."

"The Federals outnumber us four to one."

The winter night was closing down and each minute was darker than the last. When the Federal fleet abruptly stopped firing, silence rang like a carillon. Whiting's orderly stood up, stretched, and took out his pipe.

"Don't light that pipe, Sergeant," Whiting said. "They may not be finished with us."

One by one, the anchored fleet's portholes illuminated. Bugles, some discordant, some sweet, sounded the dinner call.

"I don't suppose you'd take Private Watling's place, sir? You're no boy of fifteen." The General waited, head cocked for Rhett's reply. "I thought not." General Whiting endorsed Bragg's orders with a pencil stub. "Are you sure Bragg said nothing of a counterattack? Did you see signs he might come to our relief?"

Rhett spoke carefully: "Yesterday, General, there were wagons at Bragg's headquarters. I believe General Bragg was evacuating."

General Whiting smacked his fist into his palm. "He cannot abandon us. Not even that goddamned Bragg. . . . I will write him myself. Bragg must understand!" The General scrambled down the broken staircase.

When the orderly lit his pipe, the match flare was blinding. "Might as well get kilt tonight as tomorrow," he opined.

Like ants from an anthill, Fort Fisher's defenders emerged from bombproofs deep under the dunes. The full moon brightened the fort. While quartermasters rolled barrels and relayed boxes of hardtack, hungry soldiers formed ragged lines.

The wiry corporal finished his side meat and licked his fingers clean before he'd touch Rhett's document. The corporal ran his forefinger over each word and refolded the paper into the envelope. "Watling know 'bout this?"

"No."

"Watling's a good boy. Most of these Junior Reserves are plumb petrified. Some of 'em won't come out of the bombproofs even when the Federals ain't shootin'." The corporal was missing a front tooth. "Watling was our powder boy long as we still had us a gun to shoot. Us gunners think high of that boy, mister."

"You don't mind my taking him out?"

The corporal grinned a gap-toothed grin. "Take me, too?"

Chewing on a biscuit, Taz Watling sat on the trunnion of a dismounted Columbiad. His uniform hung loose on his skinny frame. "Be damned," Taz said. "I thought you were in the army."

"Rode with Forrest for a spell."

"They say Forrest's had twenty horses killed under him."

"That's what they say."

Out on the ocean, an ironclad fired. The streak of the burning fuse arced across dark water, dropped into the fort, and exploded.

"They'll hit us tomorrow," Taz said matter-of-factly.

"They only outnumber you four to one."

"Don't joke. You're always joking."

"You mean this isn't funny? Eighteen hundred brave men waiting to die while Braxton Bragg is skedaddling? Got to hand it to ol' Brax."

"I was proud when you joined the army," Taz said. "What are you doing here? Why are you in civilian clothes?"

"My uniform hatched lice." Rhett perched on an empty powder keg and lit a cigar. "The Army of Tennessee's finished, so I got reassigned. I thought I'd look you up."

The interior of the fort was moonlit sand except for sparks from cigars and pipes. Out on the ocean, the Federal fleet was a floating metropolis ablaze with light. On the peninsula, Federal campfires flamed from shore to shore.

"I understand you're a hero. I had hoped your expensive education would prevent that."

Taz shrugged. "The Creoles say, *'Capon vive longtemps.'* Probably my Butler blood. Wasn't Great-Grandfather a pirate?"

" 'The coward lives a long time,' " Rhett translated. "Creoles are feisty bastards. I don't know if Louis Valentine Butler would have called himself a 'pirate.' Louis would have preferred 'Gentleman of Fortune.' "

The boy sighed. "Anyway, I'm glad to see you."

Rhett wiped sand from his silver flask and unscrewed two nesting cups. Rhett filled his before filling one for the boy.

A fiery streak passed overhead and its concussion pressed Rhett's jacket against his back.

The boy took a mouthful, gagged and coughed.

"Don't waste it, son. That brandy's older than you are."

Taz took another swallow. "I haven't heard anything from my mother. We get no mail."

"Belle was fine when I passed through Atlanta. She's safe there. The Federals won't come back."

Taz drank his brandy in brave gulps and passed his cup for a refill. "Might as well get drunk once in my life."

"Might as well." Rhett brimmed the cup.

They drank for a time.

Taz said, "Being a powder boy isn't easy as you'd think. I run to the bombproof magazine—that tunnel is six hundred steps, by my count—for a twenty-five-pound powder bag, which I tote back to the gun. Federal shells flyin' around like . . . like"—he gestured—"like damn sand fleas. If you get buried in sand, you better claw out, or you'll suffocate. I'll take another drink, thank you. I'm thirstier'n I thought.

"I'd rather be a powder boy, anyway, than hid in the bombproofs, breathing twice-breathed air and stinkin' buckets to do your business in. Damn! If this is how brandy tastes, it's a wonder anyone drinks it!"

The unfamiliar taste didn't deter him from drinking too much too fast. Taz rambled on about Fort Fisher, how proud he was to have the gunners' respect, until his speech began to slur. When the cup dropped from his nerveless hand, the boy murmured, "Why won't you be my father?" and slid down onto the sand.

With the wiry corporal on one end of the litter and Rhett on the other, they carried the boy to the dock.

"What's your name, Corporal?"

"Why'd you be wanting to know?"

"Might meet up after the war."

"Small chance of that." The corporal added, "If you keep this young'un alive, he'll make a man one day."

Fifteen minutes before Tunis's deadline, Rhett's dinghy bumped against the *Merry Widow* and her crewmen plucked the unconscious boy aboard.

When Rhett returned to the fort, the corporal said, "Didn't expect to see you again. Federals'll be hittin' us tomorrow."

"Did you ever love a woman?"

Startled: "My wife, Ella, died three years past."

"You lost everything."

"I reckon."

After a time, Rhett said, "Anyway, it's a fine moon."

The corporal nodded. "You got the boy away?"

"Tazewell Watling's going to England."

"I'll be! I've heard tell England is a green sort of place. I heard folks is happy there."

"In any event, they're not shooting each other."

"My," the corporal said, "wouldn't that be pleasant?"

The next morning when Taz Watling woke, his headache woke, too. He was lying on a hard deck, surrounded by cotton bales, whose woody, oily smell passed through his nose straight to his stomach, and he crawled backward out of his cotton cave to a ship's rail (where in hell *was* he?) to vomit. His head thumped with each spasm and he opened his eyes wide to relieve the pressure on his skull. He got up. He brushed sand off his knees. He was in a boat on a flat sea. They weren't going fast. A stream of water shot from the bow into the sea. The sun was not quite high noon. Goddamn Rhett Butler. Taz's headache settled into a throb. His stomach was empty, thank God. What boat *was* this? Men climbed from the hold to rig a windlass. After it was rigged, a cotton bale emerged into sunlight. They swung it out and dropped it over the side.

Taz asked a sailor where they were.

"Day and a half day from Nassau if she floats. Lend a hand. Heave on that rope when I say 'Heave.' "

When Taz pulled the thick hemp rope, his head expanded like one of the pig bladders children inflate and pop at Christmastime. The sailors wore clean singletons, clean duck trousers. Taz was dirty and he smelled bad.

When her belowdecks cargo had been jettisoned, the *Widow*'s crew breathed easier and the helmsman lit his pipe.

Tazewell Watling felt light as a feather. As he mined the bitterness of Rhett Butler's betrayal, Taz discovered he hadn't wanted to die after all. This expanse of milky green sea was so flat, at the horizons he could see the earth curve. Sandy, dangerous, noisy, doomed Fort Fisher seemed very far away. His head stopped hurting and he was hungry.

He went belowdecks to the galley, where he found a half-carved roast of beef and some bread.

Four men labored at the hand pump in the cavernous hold. Water ran in through bulkhead seams. In the engine room, one of the two engines was cold. Exhausted men sprawled on pallets inches above the water-slick deck.

Nobody questioned Taz; nobody seemed to care who he was.

About three o'clock, the crew started jettisoning deck cargo. Cotton bales splashed over the side and bobbed in the *Widow*'s wake.

A weary negro captain issued the orders.

Taz cleared his throat politely and said, "I am Tazewell Watling. I am not aboard of my own will."

"I know who you is." Another cotton bale splashed into the sea and scraped along the hull. "This was to be the *Widow*'s last run. Me and Ruthie and Nat was goin' to Canada. My father's in Kingston. He says there's no such thing as a nigger in Canada."

The Federal gunboats that tried to stop the *Merry Widow*'s flight hadn't hurt her; she'd hurt herself. Her overpowered engines had torqued plates apart, popped rows of rivets, and sprung the vessel's knees. Although

Mr. MacLeod had caulked and plugged every hole he could, he couldn't reach all of them, and water was within six inches of the fireboxes when they started heaving cargo over the side.

"Are we sinking, sir?"

Another bale hit the water and thumped and bumped along the hull. "Rhett's made arrangements for you, boy. We get to Nassau, I'll put you on a ship. They expectin' you in England."

"Sir, I am a Confederate soldier."

"You a *what*?" The negro captain's mouth worked furiously. "Mercy," he said. He turned to his crew. "That's enough overboard, Mr. MacLeod! Let's see if we can keep a couple to sell." More to himself than to the boy, he added, "One thousand dollars for one bale of cotton. One thousand dollars."

It was a bright day. Taz had been a powder boy in the greatest Confederate fort ever known. He'd done dangerous duty and through no fault of his own his life had been spared. He'd been prepared to die, but he hadn't, and the sun had never shone so bright as it shone on him today. Tazewell Watling was a young man on his way to a new life. The hair on his arms tingled.

Her engine strained as the *Merry Widow* wallowed across the glassy green sea. She had been sleek and beautiful and fast, but she was beautiful no more. If she got to Nassau, the ship breakers would take her.

Captain Tunis Bonneau turned his bloodshot eyes on his passenger. "Boy," he said, "there ain't no Confederates no more."

Part Two

Reconstruction

Chapter Twenty-four

A Georgia Plantation After the War

Charleston surrendered, Columbia burned, Petersburg fell, Richmond burned; the Confederate armies surrendered. It was finished. After four bitter years, the war was over. From the Potomac to the Rio Brazos, grass softened the abandoned earthworks, skeletons of men and horses vanished beneath new growth, and by June's end, when the grass slumped in the heat, only burned plantation houses, shattered cities, and broken hearts testified to what had happened to the South. That spring, the songbirds' bright chittering fell on ears still tensed for the thunder of guns. Gaunt survivors of once-feared armies laid down their weapons and started their weary walk home.

With her moistened fingertip, Scarlett O'Hara Hamilton captured the last crumb of corn bread on her plate. "Mammy, we must give smaller portions to the vagrants."

Plates clattering angrily as the old servant carried them to the kitchen, Mammy grumbled, "Tara ain't never turned folks away hungry, and these boys ain't no vagrants; they's soldier boys!"

Though Tara was off the beaten track, those soldier boys arrived daily. "Jest passing through, ma'am. I'm a-goin' home. Got young'uns I ain't seed since '63. Hope they remember their old pappy." Last night, an Alabama boy had slept on Tara's parlor floor and breakfasted on corn bread before leaving. Tara's remaining cornmeal—seven precious pounds—was locked up in Gerald O'Hara's liquor cabinet.

Tara's dining room wallpaper had been jerked away in strips by Sherman's bummers searching for valuables. Some of the mismatched chairs around the dining room table were wired together. "I'ze no cabinetmaker, Miss Scarlett," Pork had explained. "I'ze Master Gerald's valet."

Melanie rose from her chair. "I'm a little tired. If you don't mind terribly, I'll lie down until we hill the potatoes. Scarlett, dear, you will wake me?"

At Scarlett's terse nod, Melanie produced her sweetest smile. "If you won't call me, dear, I won't be able to rest. You can't do it all by yourself."

"Why, of course I'll wake you," Scarlett lied, kissing her sister-in-law's cheek.

The Yankees wouldn't steal anything more. Tara had nothing left to steal. Of its hundred beef and milk cows, two hundred hogs, forty horses and mules, fifty sheep, and countless chickens and turkeys; one horse, one milk cow, one cranky elusive sow, and two elderly hens survived. What the Yankees hadn't killed, they'd stolen.

Tara's field workers—even dependable negroes like Big Sam—had run off. Only the house servants—Pork, Mammy, Dilcey, and Prissy—were still at Tara, and sometimes Scarlett wished they'd run too. Four more mouths to feed.

In her dawn-to-dark fight to keep Tara alive, even Ashley Wilkes had faded from Scarlett's mind. She didn't know whether Ashley had died in the Federal prison camp, as so many had, or would be coming home one day. Most nights, Scarlett managed a brief prayer for Ashley before her exhausted mind succumbed to sleep. Some nights she forgot.

A year ago when Rhett Butler abandoned her outside burning Atlanta, Scarlett had been running to her childhood Tara, where her Mammy would warm some milk and her mother, Ellen, would lay cool cloths on her brow. War's terrors would be banished as Scarlett fell into her mother's loving arms.

Her dream had been short-lived.

One day before Scarlett got home—one irrecoverable day—Scarlett's mother, Ellen, had died of fever. Ellen died with a man's name on her lips: Philippe—a French name.

Now there was nobody left on earth who could teach Scarlett how to live. "Philippe"? She didn't know any Philippe and she had more important things to worry about.

Sometimes, Scarlett believed Gerald O'Hara should have died with his wife. Scarlett's father was a shell of the shrewd, impetuous, sturdy man he'd been. Though Gerald still sat at the head of the table and ate his meager portion without complaint, her father's mind was broken.

Now he rose. "I think I'll rest now, my dear. This afternoon, your mother and I are riding to Twelve Oaks."

"That will be nice," Scarlett said, though John Wilkes was long dead and Twelve Oaks burned to the ground.

Scarlett kept up the pretense because pretense was better than Gerald O'Hara's lucid moments, when he remembered everything he had lost and crumpled in paroxysms of weeping.

Little Wade drummed his heels against his chair rungs, whining he was still hungry. "Wade, you'll just have to wait. When Mammy bakes corn bread, you can have the bowl."

Scarlett tied her bonnet before going outdoors, where Pork waited, wearing the cast-off Sunday coat Gerald had given him years ago. Tight-lipped with determination, Pork began, "Miss Scarlett!"

Pork's too-familiar complaint rolled over her: "Miss Scarlett, when my old master tried to buy me back from Master Gerald, he offered eight hundred dollars, which was right smart of money in them days. Yes, Miss, it were! Master Gerald wouldn't take no money for me account of I'ze Master Gerald's personal valet. I ain't one to brag on myself, but some folks say I is the best valet in Clayton County. And I ain't gonna hill no potatoes!"

"Pork," Scarlett restrained her temper, "if a strong man like you won't help, how can we women do the work?"

Out of the corner of her eye Scarlett spotted her sister leading their only horse to the mounting block. "Suellen! Suellen! Wait!"

Suellen was wearing her good dress and had a plump white peony in her thin, lifeless hair. "Suellen, where are you going?"

"Why, I'm going to Jonesboro, Sister dear. It's Tuesday."

Frank Kennedy had been Suellen's "intended" for years. Although his

Jonesboro store had been destroyed, every Tuesday Frank brought dry goods and groceries from Atlanta to swap for eggs, butter, honey, and whatever small family treasures the Federals had overlooked.

"Suellen, I'm sorry, but we need the horse today. Dilcey knows where the Yankees threw away a barrel of weevily flour. Think how good biscuits would taste!"

Suellen threw her peony in the dirt as she stalked indoors.

Scarlett held her tongue.

The Yankees had burned $200,000 of Gerald O'Hara's stored cotton. A few months later, they returned to burn the tiny crop Scarlett had gleaned: perhaps $2,000. A month before the Confederate surrender, Scarlett had replanted. If this year's scant crop survived weevils and bindweed, come fall it might fetch $200: A fortune.

Before the War, Scarlett believed only imprudent people ate their seed corn. Now she understood the bitter truth that people ate their seed corn and their seed potatoes and made bread of their wheat seed when they were hungry enough. Scarlett was thankful Tara's people couldn't eat cotton seed!

Scarlett grieved each time they had to butcher one of their sow's thirty-pound shoats—a shoat who in time would have become a three-hundred-pound hog!

Pretty Scarlett was stark-featured with fatigue; gay Scarlett was always cross. Proud Scarlett would do anything—literally anything—for Tara and its people. Gerald O'Hara's daughter did work she'd never dreamed of. Scarlett had hoed until blisters came and weeded until pigweed tore her blisters open. She'd worked until her back and shoulders ached. Scarlett had lost so much weight, she fit into dresses she'd last worn when she was thirteen. The woman who'd come home to Tara to be a child again had become its mistress, distributing food, disarming squabbles, tending the sick, encouraging the weary.

She tied the horse and turned to Pork. "Pork, if you can't hill potatoes, perhaps you'd grease the windlass."

As if explaining to a child, Pork said, "Miss Scarlett, I'ze Master Gerald's valet. . . ."

Scarlett felt heat at the roots of her hair. She smiled sweetly and said, "I wonder if some other Clayton County family might need a valet."

Pork shook his head sadly. "Miss Scarlett, why you so hard?"

Why? *Why?* If Scarlett hesitated, if she lost heart, if she once—as she sometimes wished to—broke down and wept, everything would be lost.

Pork ambled off on a vague search for some kind of grease for the windlass.

Gerald O'Hara's thousand-acre plantation had shrunk to a hundred-foot kitchen garden and one five-acre cotton patch. Scarlett squinted so she wouldn't see the brambles and blackberry bushes encroaching.

Scarlett did servant's work and she ate servant's food: chickweed, dry land cress, dandelion greens, and wild mustard. Scarlett stooped in the shade of a live oak where the poke hadn't bolted yet. They'd have poke greens for supper.

A stranger was riding up their lane on a donkey so small, the rider's boot tips brushed the ground. His ill-fitting green civilian coat was new, his beard was short, and his whitish blond hair a stubble. He had more flesh on him than the paroled soldiers who came to Tara. At the foot of the final rise, his donkey stopped, stretched its neck, pointed its muzzle to the skies, and brayed. The rider waited, slack-reined, until the donkey exhausted its complaints.

Judging by his new coat, the man was a Carpetbagger; though not a prosperous one.

Though the rider might have made quicker progress leading his donkey, he rode the disgruntled beast to Scarlett's feet. "Nice morning," he observed.

"If you're a Carpetbagger, sir, you are not welcome."

This jerked a startled laugh from him. "Carpetbagger, ma'am? Madam, I have sinned grievously, but that particular sin has eluded me. Might I water my steed?"

Scarlett pointed to the well.

The ungreased windlass squealed when the man turned the crank. "Then you must be a Scalawag," Scarlett decided. "Nobody else wears new clothes."

He poured water into a bucket for his donkey. "Your windlass needs lard," he said.

He peeled off his new coat and hung it on the windlass handle. With a quick jerk, he ripped a sleeve off. Broken threads fringed an empty armhole. He stuffed the sleeve into his pocket before redonning his coat. "A 'Scalawag,' ma'am? One of those Southerners who were secret Union sympathizers—keeping their opinions to themselves until the Yankees were victorious? No, ma'am, I'm a convict released from the Ohio Penitentiary, issued these clothes and ten dollars, with which I bought this noble steed, Chapultapec." He patted the animal's haunch.

"That's a mighty fancy name for a donkey."

His face was transfigured by his grin. "I am an incurable romantic. You don't recognize me?"

Scarlett frowned. "No . . . I'm afraid I don't."

"Perhaps if I wore a cavalry officer's hat with an egret plume? If I had a banjo player accompanying me? Surely, Miss Scarlett, you didn't have many callers who brought their own orchestra."

Scarlett blinked. "*Colonel Ravanel?*"

He bowed deeply. "I had hoped you'd find me unforgettable."

"You were that." Something tugged at Scarlett's memory. "Didn't I hear you'd lost your wife?"

"My Charlotte is with the angels."

Scarlett's mind raced. When she'd met Charlotte Ravanel at Aunt Eulalie's, she'd thought her a worthy, uninteresting gentlewoman: a woman other women confide in. But Charlotte had been a Fisher: heir to one of the South's great fortunes. Doubtless, Charlotte Fisher's attic had its trunks of worthless Confederate currency, as Tara's did. But so much money couldn't *all* be gone. Scarlett smiled sadly, "Colonel, my condolences for your loss."

Didn't Charlotte have a brother? "And Jamie Fisher?" Scarlett asked.

"Jamie and I shared a cell. 'Eat your oatmeal, Andrew! Do take some fresh air! Andrew, you must not be bitter.' " Andrew Ravanel said, "Jamie couldn't understand how bitterness solaces a man."

For her own part, Scarlett thought bitterness was like nostalgia: It got in the way of what needed doing. Feeding Tara's hungry people, restoring its house and outbuildings, hiring workers, buying livestock, and planting a thousand acres in cotton would leave no time for bitterness.

"Colonel Ravanel, you'll take supper with us?"

"Thank you, no. I couldn't."

"My goodness, surely you're hungry?"

"I cannot pay."

"Gracious!" Scarlett said. "If you must pay, sir, your supper will cost you one Confederate dollar!"

Pork was snipping roses in the dooryard. Every morning, fragrant bouquets appeared in the parlor, the dining room, and Gerald's bedroom. "Pork, didn't I tell you to grease the windlass?"

"Yes, Miss Scarlett. I pick these flowers first."

"The flowers are pretty, but every bucket is heavier because the windlass needs grease. When you're finished with that, start hilling the potatoes."

Pork's lips were a rebellious pout.

"I hear the Yankees have banned the bullwhip," Andrew Ravanel observed mildly. "But your plantation is so far off the main roads . . ."

Pork drew himself to his full height. "I ain't never been whipped! Master Gerald don't 'low no whippin' at Tara."

The Colonel pulled the torn sleeve from his pocket and popped it against his pant leg.

Pork's mouth fell open and his roses dropped from his hand. In a dead voice, he said, "Yes, Miss Scarlett. I go grease the windlass."

As she and the Colonel entered the front hall, Scarlett apologized. "I'm afraid Sherman's soldiers visited us."

"My recent quarters, Miss Scarlett, were nothing to boast about."

Scarlett showed the colonel into the dining room. "Excuse me, Colonel. I'll see about your supper."

She found Mammy kneeling on a stool, washing kitchen windows. "Mammy, we'll want that corn bread, and there're poke greens under the live oak behind the well."

"Miss Scarlett, this corn bread's for supper."

"Mammy, the gentleman is our guest."

"I seen that fellow through these windows." Mammy snorted. "What gentleman only got one sleeve to his coat?"

"He ruined his coat so he wouldn't be mistaken for a Scalawag."

"He did what?" Mammy shook her head. "Lord have mercy!" She climbed down and went for the greens.

Scarlett raced up the servants' stairway to her bedroom. Her cracked mirror revealed a too-brown, unladylike face, but her hair was clean. She undid her bun and rearranged her hair to frame her face. She dabbed a drop of precious cologne behind each ear.

In nightshirt and riding boots, Gerald emerged from his bedroom. "Have you seen Ellen?" he inquired anxiously. "We should be at Twelve Oaks by four. John will want to have a drink before we dine."

"I'll remind her, Father. Please excuse me. I'm attending to a guest."

"Shouldn't I greet him?"

"I shouldn't think so, Father. You don't want to tire yourself before your ride to Twelve Oaks."

Gerald O'Hara waggled his finger, "Don't forget to remind your mother," and closed his door behind him.

When Scarlett returned to the dining room, Mammy was laying out food previously intended for everyone's supper.

Colonel Ravanel indicated his plate. "You are generous."

"Goodness, Colonel. It's just a snack. Before the War, Tara's hospitality was legendary."

So she wouldn't stare at his overfull plate, Scarlett asked if the Colonel had passed through Atlanta.

"From Whitehall and Broad, I could not see a building standing." The Colonel's fork conveyed a stack of glistening greens to his mouth and he munched with a ruminant's mindless satisfaction. "The city center is destroyed."

"The train station? The Car Shed?"

"The Yankees dragged straw inside and fired it. Whatever survived the fire was treated to explosives and battering rams." Ravanel's smile was hard.

"Only a Yankee General could make his reputation by burning an undefended city."

Atlanta destroyed? Scarlett couldn't bear to think of it. Atlanta had energy and ingenuity by the bucketful. If Atlanta was destroyed, what hope was there for the South?

The Colonel guessed Scarlett's thoughts. "They won't let us up. The Carpetbaggers and Scalawags are backed by Union bayonets. They mean whites to be ruled by niggers."

Scarlett tried not to watch his fork scoop, wrap, and lift. It entered his mouth; his mouth closed. "If brave men like you are so discouraged, what can the rest of us do?"

"Men like me?" An ugly laugh. "Romantic fools tilting at windmills." He pushed his empty platter aside and wiped his mouth on that torn sleeve. "I don't suppose you'd have brandy. . . ."

"Only white liquor, I'm afraid."

"Yes?"

"We use it medicinally."

"I'm not as particular as I was."

Scarlett went to the kitchen for the corn whiskey she kept hidden from Gerald. Mammy inquired, "Is the gentleman feeling poorly?"

The Fisher heir contentedly sipped corn liquor and smiled on Scarlett. "It has been so long since I've been in any lady's company, let alone a handsome lady like yourself."

Demurely, Scarlett lowered her eyes.

"Two long years . . . I had nearly forgotten . . ."

Scarlett couldn't remember when she'd had enough to eat.

"I regret our encounter . . . that night in Atlanta. My unsought advice, dear Mrs. Hamilton: Never be an honoree. While fools are honoring you, you cannot escape them. When I came to your home, I was tired of fools, tired of myself, and I'd had too much to drink. Scarlett—I may call you Scarlett? You were the one bright moment that day, and for thanks, I insulted you. Please accept my apology." Ravanel chuckled reminiscently. " 'And take your orchestra with you!' "

Scarlett issued the invitation she'd issued to so many ragged, hungry strangers, but this time, she blushed. None of those strangers had been a Fisher heir. "Sir, you are welcome to stay at Tara tonight. Melanie Wilkes will be delighted to have your news. We've not heard from her husband."

"He'll be alive," the Colonel said carelessly. "Men like Wilkes live forever."

Scarlett hid her wince. "If you've finished, I'd like to show you Tara."

Tara had been Gerald O'Hara's dream.

Tara's whitewashed brick walls and broad roof would shelter the children, kinfolks, and guests enjoying Gerald's hospitality. "No foofaraw" Gerald had told his wife, Ellen. "Just a big comfortable farmhouse. I cannot abide drawing rooms and withdrawing rooms and private family rooms—for what is my house if not for my family?" When Ellen wanted a ballroom, Gerald snorted. "Won't we be dancing in our parlor, Mrs. O'Hara, anytime we have a mind to?"

Tara had no basement, because if Gerald O'Hara feared anything, it was snakes, and Gerald was certain basements harbored snakes.

Gerald wanted porches front and back—"where we can sit of a summer evening." Off the front bedroom would be Gerald's balcony, where Tara's proprietor could stand in the morning brightness, overlooking a lane bordered by chestnut saplings and red clay fields verdant with flowering cotton.

The leaded lights and semicircular fanlight framing the front door were Gerald's concession to his wife's notions.

If Gerald's house had been battered by the War, his plantation had been destroyed. "Our pecan trees bore the fattest nuts in Clayton County. The children's swing was here. The Yankees burned the pecans. They burned the swing, too," Scarlett said.

"This is where the cotton press stood. My father always bought the most up-to-date machinery. 'Why should men do work dumb machines can do?'—that's what my father said.

"This was our dairy. See! That's the spring box beside that collapsed wall.

"As you see, they didn't burn the negro cabins."

The Colonel kicked a charred board. "You'll need them when the niggers come to their senses. Thousands and thousands are sleeping in the streets of Atlanta. If the Yanks didn't feed them, they'd starve."

What did Scarlett care about negro refugees? "With a thousand dollars, Tara could get back on its feet. Just a thousand. There's nothing wrong with the land; they can burn our buildings and kill our livestock, but, by God, they can't kill our land!"

"Aren't you the pretty Amazon." When Andrew Ravanel took Scarlett's hand, his convict's hand felt unpleasantly soft. "I dislike traveling alone," he said. "Can I convince you to accompany me to Charleston?"

Though Scarlett had expected an invitation, she'd not expected such a bold one. "An unmarried man and woman traveling together? Sir, what will people think?"

Ravanel's contemptuous laughter shocked her. "My dear Scarlett, they're dead. Everyone whose opinion mattered is dead. Only cowards, traitors, and . . . convicts survived the war. Jeb Stuart—the lilies of the field bowed in homage when General Stuart rode by. Pious General Polk has taken his sermons to heaven, where he and Stonewall Jackson can preach to each other. Cleburne, Turner Ashby, brave little Pegram—my friend Henry Kershaw—that brave, dumb bastard—even Rhett Butler is dead."

Scarlett felt as if she'd been shot through the heart. She whispered, "Who?"

Colonel Ravanel picked up a crockery shard and flipped it into the ruined springhouse. "Rhett was in Fort Fisher when the Federals assaulted. It was a butcher's shambles." His voice lost its bitter edge. "Rhett and I were friends once. He was the best friend I ever had."

"But Rhett . . . Rhett never believed in the Great Cause. . . ."

"No, but he loved a gallant gesture." He eyed Scarlett curiously. "I'm surprised you knew him."

Knew him? *Knew* him? Had she known him at all? Rhett Butler dead? He couldn't be dead!

"Now I've distressed you. I am sorry. I didn't know you knew Rhett."

Scarlett's mind whirled. What had she thought? Certainly that she'd see him again, that Rhett's knowing, mocking smile would infuriate her again. She bit the inside of her lip so she wouldn't cry. Gone? Those rare moments when she and Rhett had *understood* each other—gone forever? "Where . . . where is Rhett buried?"

"The Federals marked their soldiers' graves. They dumped ours in the ocean."

It was as if she'd lost a part of herself: an arm, her hand, her heart. Rhett Butler dead! Hopelessness washed over her and she sat heavily on the stump of what had been Tara's grandest chestnut tree How could she go on? Numbly, she repeated, "Rhett Butler . . . dead?"

Andrew Ravanel offered useless male consolations: Perhaps Rhett hadn't been killed with the others. Rhett was a cat. Rhett had nine lives. . . .

Scarlett couldn't bear this man one moment longer. "Sir, please recall that I am Mrs. Charles Hamilton, a respectable widow. I decline your improper invitation. I cannot imagine what you were thinking of. Now, sir, you must go. You've made your intentions all too clear. You cannot remain at Tara."

Softly he said, "Years ago, I loved him, too."

"Love Rhett Butler? That arrogant, insulting, self-satisfied . . . Why would anyone love Rhett Butler?"

"As you prefer."

The tall man mounted his small mule and rode away.

The sun went behind a cloud.

Scarlett wanted to go upstairs and lie down. She felt so weak and helpless. Lord, how she wanted to lie down.

Instead, she straightened and started for the potato patch. She and Pork would hill the potatoes. Then she would look for more poke greens.

Later, she would tell Melanie about Rhett. Melly had always favored him.

Chapter Twenty-five

A Low Country Plantation After the War

Six months later, a horse and rider trotted down the Ashley River Road. The horse was a coal black stallion, eleven hands high, of the breeding for which the Low Country had once been famous. The rider had the careless grace of a grandee. During the War, countless graves had been filled with men like him and the bones of their beautiful horses bleached in cornfields and peach orchards across the reunited nation.

One year ago, General Sherman's army had swarmed down this road. Burned chimneys emerged like cautionary fingers out of the roadside brambles. This toppled gatepost led to the ruin that had been Henry Kershaw's boyhood home. From a swing suspended from that fire-blackened oak, little Charlotte Fisher had kicked her legs, shrieking, "Higher! Higher! Oh, push me higher." This overgrown lane curved up to the burned mansion where Edgar Puryear's mother had died.

As the rider approached, two rail-thin pariah dogs slipped into the brush.

Across the river from Broughton Plantation, Rhett Butler pulled off his riding boots, socks, and trousers. He tied his boots to his saddle and wrapped his trouser legs over his stallion's eyes for a blindfold before he clucked the animal into the muddy river.

The horse forged across and clambered up Broughton's main trunk, where Rhett dressed.

The main trunk was covered with blackberry brambles and the rice fields were shallow tidal pools where squawking mud hens swam away from the intruder.

Deer and feral hogs had made trails through the untrimmed boxwood hedging Broughton's lane.

The carriage turnaround fronted a fire-streaked brick facade and window holes as empty as a skull's eye sockets. The front door yawned wide. Among the furniture dragged outdoors and burned, Rhett recognized the walnut podium that had held the Butler family Bible.

Hummingbirds buzzed the trumpet vine invading the broken piazza.

Rhett stepped across the thick vines to the overlook where he'd stood twenty-five years ago. Rhett's memory of Broughton's symmetrical, productive rice fields overlay ruptured trunks and shimmering saline pools that no planter could ever crop again. "Yes, it was beautiful," Rhett murmured.

A voice quavered at his elbow. "Yes, sir. It t'were. Master 'n' Mistress Butler ain't receivin' callers no more."

The aged negro supported himself on a gnarled driftwood cane. His eyes were filmed white.

"Good morning, Uncle Solomon," Rhett said.

"Young Master Rhett? That be you?" The old negro's fingers fluttered over Rhett's face. "We heard you was killed. Lord be praised! How do you fare, Young Master? You ain't been home in such a time!"

Rhett wished to see his parents if they still lived.

"Oh, yes. Master and Mistress still livin'." He lowered his voice. "Master Langston, he's got White Plague. He shrunk to a nubbin.

"All our niggers run off 'ceptin' me." Uncle Solomon tut-tutted. "Hercules and Sudie, they gone to town. Hercules say he won't work for no Butlers no more." The old man's lower lip quivered with indignation. "That nigger gettin' above hisself! I born on Broughton, lived all my days on Broughton, and Broughton Plantation be where I lie down."

"Yes, Uncle. Then my parents are in town?"

"Town house blowed to bits! Nicest house on Meeting Street. None nicer! Market niggers used to call me 'Mr. Solomon' account of I come from that house. The Master and Mistress bidin' with Overseer Watling now."

"Watling?"

"You been gone such a time, Master Rhett! Such a time! Master Langston said he wasn't leavin' Broughton no more. Your sister and her husband comes out sometimes. Miss Rosemary wants Master Langston and Mistress 'Lizabeth come stay with them. But you know how Master Langston be."

"John Haynes is dead, Uncle. John died in the war."

"Not Mr. Haynes. Colonel Ravanel, your sister's second husband."

"Andrew Ravanel?"

"Yes, sir. Old Jack's boy. They say he was a hero in the War, but I don't know about that."

"Andrew Ravanel? . . ."

"All the womens gettin' married. One day they widow, next day they wife, next day they carryin' a child. . . ."

Isaiah Watling's home stood at the tip of a peninsula bounded by shallow tidal flats. Game chickens pecked in the yard. The ribby milk cow had a turpentine-soaked rag wrapped around her head to protect her from mosquitoes.

A young man was whittling, leaning back in a chair beside the front door. When Rhett tied his horse to the fence, the young man let his chair down with a thump. His pale blond hair was balding off his sloping forehead. His nose was sharp and his eyes were so light, the pupils were almost invisible. An oiled revolver was stuck in his belt.

"Nice horse," he observed. The young man cut a long peel from his whittling stick. "Yankees got all the good horses these days." His grin lacked upper teeth and his right cheek was puckered by a scar. He answered Rhett's gaze. "I was yelling to Frank when I got shot. Spect you heard of Frank. Frank James's a heller." He tapped his scar. "Bill Quantrill said a man should keep his mouth shut, but sometimes it pays to have it open, don't it?"

He elaborated. "I mean, if I hadn't had my mouth open, that bullet would have took out my bottom teeth, too. I expect I'll get back with Frank and Jesse one day."

"I am Rhett Butler. Are the Butlers here?"

"I reckon."

"Suppose you could tell them I've come?"

The young man stood. "I'm Isaiah's nephew, Josie. I rode with Bill

Quantrill until the Federals cut him down. They was figurin' to do me too, so I come east to renew family acquaintances." He winked. "Rhett Butler, Uncle Isaiah hates you like poison. I expect one day he'll take revenge on you. Waitin' on revenge is a hopeful thing, don't you think?"

Josie approached him as a pit dog approaches. "I known better men'n you killed for worse horses than that one."

"Four years of war; aren't you tired of killing?"

Josie shrugged. "I been doin' folks since I was a sprout. Spect I got a taste for it."

"If you're going to use that revolver, do. If not, tell the Butlers I'm here."

"Ain't you the feisty son of a bitch." Without taking his eyes off Rhett, he shouted, "Uncle Isaiah! Feller's come!"

When he opened the door, Isaiah Watling shaded his eyes against the sun. "Young Butler. You are not welcome here."

Josie Watling set a boot on a fence rail, crossed his arms, and grinned like a man who wasn't nearly as bored as he'd thought he'd be.

"Your home, Watling? Isn't this Broughton Plantation? Isn't this the Overseer's house? I'm here to see the Butlers."

"You've no kin here."

"Suppose you let us decide that."

Isaiah Watling's hot eyes bored into Rhett's for a long moment before he wheeled and went inside.

"Nice day," Josie said. "Me, I always did like the fall of the year. You can see folks creepin' up better onct the leaves are gone." After a time, he added, "You ain't no talker, are you?" Josie Watling scratched his ear with the front sight of his revolver.

Isaiah Watling reappeared and jerked his head. Rhett followed him up the dimly remembered stairs of the house the Butlers had inhabited until their grand house was built. He entered the modest bedroom his parents had shared when he was a child. The room was neat. The floor had been swept. Medicine vials and a bowl of yellow sputum threaded with blood crowded the table beside the bed where Rhett Butler's father lay.

Langston Butler had been a big man and his bones still were. His skin was yellowish except for bright red spots on his cheeks. His curly brown hair was still without a streak of gray.

"You have the consumption," Rhett said.

"Have you come to tell me what I already know?"

"I've come to help. I can provide for you and Mother."

Langston Butler wheezed and choked. His eyes bulged with outrage at his helplessness. He spat into the bowl beside the bed. "You will not disturb Elizabeth. My wife has Jesus Christ and the devoted Isaiah Watling. Why would Elizabeth Butler need you?"

"Sir, you agreed to see me. You must have had some reason."

"You were said to be dead and I am more interested in resurrections than I was." The old man's smile was a ghastly slash. "Julian will inherit. You will not attend my funeral."

"Do you believe you can be Broughton's Master beyond the grave? Father . . ."

Langston Butler turned his face to the wall.

"I reckon you oughta git now," Josie Watling leaned against the door frame. "Uncle says I can shoot you if you don't do like the old rooster says. I guess I could shoot you. I admire your horse."

Isaiah Watling was in the yard.

"Watling, your daughter Belle is safe in Atlanta. Your grandson, Tazewell Watling, is in an English school. I have good reports of him."

"Belle may yet repent," Isaiah said. "Thanks to you, my son Shadrach will never repent. Rhett Butler, you consigned Shadrach Watling to eternal damnation."

Josie Watling hid his smile behind his hand. "Ain't he a heller?" he asked. "You ever see such a one?"

When Rhett rode down the lane between the flooded rice fields, he felt a spot burning between his shoulder blades—the same feeling he'd had when some Federal sharpshooter was drawing a bead.

A meandering path had been cleared down Charleston's Meeting Street, where whites combed through rubble for something to sell and negro gangs under Federal noncoms pulled down ruined walls. When

Rhett went by, the men stopped working. A young negro called, "Bottom rail on top now, mister."

Here and there, a house had been spared; here and there, an entire block. Forty-six Church Street's window glass was so new, the putty hadn't cured. The raw pine front door swung easily on new hinges when Rhett's sister, Rosemary, answered his knock.

Her face drained of color and she braced herself against the door frame. "Rhett . . . you, you're not dead. . . . Oh Rhett! My God, Brother!" Her smile was bright, but she was weeping. Rhett took her in his arms, murmuring into her hair until she pushed him away, dabbing her eyes. Rosemary asked, "Is it ungrateful to be astonished when prayers are answered?"

"I came nearer to shaking hands with Saint Peter than I liked. You didn't get my telegram?"

She shook her head.

"Then," Rhett grinned, "I'll have to be the answer to your prayers."

"Oh Rhett! You haven't changed."

"Little Sister, I understand congratulations are in order."

"Congratulations? . . ." When Rosemary put her hand to her mouth, it was her mother's gesture.

"Congratulations, Mrs. Ravanel. May you be as happy as . . . as happy can be."

Rosemary led her brother inside. Some of the parlor furniture dated from her first marriage, but the love seat and sofa were new. "Sit, dear Brother, and I'll bring you something. Brandy?"

"Nothing now, thanks."

"Please, Rhett. Don't be angry with me."

"Angry? Why should I be angry?"

"Rhett, I . . . I thought you were dead! Not one word!"

"I'm sorry. I telegraphed before I left for London. The Federals are after my money. Thus far, my banker, Rob Campbell, has fended them off, but meantime, Sister, I am in reduced circumstances."

"John left me well provided for. If you need . . ."

"I've enough cash for a time. And"—he fingered his lapels—"my credit is good with my tailor. Money is"—he shrugged—"merely money. I am sorry I worried you."

She considered for a time before speaking plainly. "After John was killed, I didn't think I wanted to live. My child, my husband, and—I thought—I'd lost you, too." She touched Rhett's cheek. "You are real, aren't you?"

"Too real sometimes."

"Then Andrew came back to Charleston. Two orphans in a storm."

"Andrew always had a curious effect on women." Rhett raised one finger. "Don't mistake me, Sister. Andrew was my friend, and for your sake, we will be friends again." Rhett smiled at the slight swelling of her belly. "I see I am to be an uncle again. I rather like that role. Uncles get to buy toys and accept the child's kisses, but when the child is fractious, uncles can ride away."

"We need a child. Andrew . . . Sometimes Andrew gets lost. Our child will bring him home." Rosemary cocked her head, "And you, Rhett? What of Miss Scarlett?"

"Who?"

"Rhett, this is Rosemary you're talking to!"

"That's finished. It ended one evening on the Jonesboro road. Love overwhelms us like a squall on the ocean and departs as swiftly as it came."

"Um."

"No more remorse or confusion."

"Um."

He frowned. "Why the smile, Sister? That oh-so-slightly condescending smirk?"

Rosemary laughed. "Because my big brother knows everything about everything but won't confess his own heart."

Beneath his black hood, a Yankee daguerreotypist was immortalizing East Bay's dramatic ruins.

The Federal fleet lay at anchor inside the harbor. Captured blockade runners seemed embarrassed to be flying the Stars and Stripes.

Rhett was heading for the Haynes & Son offices when a shout intercepted him. "Hullo there, Rhett. Aren't you the bad penny?"

"Jamie Fisher, I'll be damned. The war didn't grow you taller."

"'Fraid not. Lord, it's good to see you." Jamie shook Rhett's hand. "Come see what we've done to Grandmother's house. I've patched the roof myself. Aren't I the worker bee?"

The Fisher mansion's gray slate roof was spotted with black tarry repairs.

Jamie stuck his head inside the front door. "Juliet, Juliet—come see who's risen from the dead."

Juliet Ravanel removed a dusty kerchief. "Why, Rhett Butler. Bless your black heart!" Juliet calculated the price of Rhett's suit. "Thank God the War didn't leave everyone a pauper!"

Jamie sighed. "My poor sister, Charlotte, put every penny of our money into Confederate bonds. To show faith in Andrew, I suppose." He paused. "There was so much money. You'd think she'd have overlooked *something*." Jamie spread his arms. "Rhett, standing before you is Charleston's most popular equestrian instructor. I teach the children of Yankee officers how not to fall off their ponies."

"The Confederates' daring scout is in great demand," Juliet observed, smiling.

"I am strict with the parents because they expect strictness from a Daring Confederate Scout, but their children see right through me. They recognize another spoiled child when they see one!" With a flourish, Jamie ushered Rhett into the house. "Mind the top step, Rhett."

They'd papered and painted the front hall and the circular staircase was polished to a soft cherry glow.

Jamie opened the drawing room door on a jumble of broken bricks, laths, and plaster, explaining, "We haven't begun on the downstairs. But three bedrooms are finished and rented to Carpetbaggers."

"Gold," Juliet said with real feeling. "They pay in gold."

"Your new brother-in-law says only traitors rent to Carpetbaggers." Jamie's face hardened, "By God, when Andrew finds solvent Confederates for our rooms, we'll put the Yankees into the street. Rhett, I fought beside Andrew. We shared a cell in that damned penitentiary. Rhett, it is difficult, so *very* difficult, to keep someone alive who does not wish to live."

"Andrew has always been melancholy."

"Andrew snubs me—and his sister, Juliet—in favor of the worst gang of 'patriots' who ever sharpened a bowie knife."

"Ah," Rhett said. " 'Patriots.' I had hoped we were done with patriots."

Juliet interrupted. "Enough about my silly brother. You remember Hercules; he and Sudie live above our kitchen house."

Jamie's habitual cheerfulness returned. "Hercules mounted new wheels on a wrecked ambulance, painted his rig yellow and black, and Juliet stenciled 'For Hire' on the panels."

"An excellent stencil it is, too," Juliet preened.

"In my grandfather's old beaver hat, Hercules is the perfect image of the antebellum Charleston cabbie. The Yankees ask Hercules where we hid our racehorses. When Hercules told one fellow that Chapultapec was last seen pulling a gun carriage, the man burst into tears. Rhett, surely you'll take tea with us?"

"I'd love to, but I'm off to congratulate my new brother-in-law."

Juliet sniffed.

Rhett was mounting his horse when a carriage drove up and Jamie advised, "Here's Hercules now. Rhett, you really must admire his cab."

Hercules helped a heavyset black woman to the sidewalk. "Mr. Rhett, we been searchin' everywhere for you. We heard you was back in the city."

Ruthie Bonneau's dress was buttoned to the neck and her hair was confined by a dark hair net.

"Mr. Rhett," Hercules said. "I spect you know Mrs. Bonneau."

"We are old friends." Rhett doffed his hat.

"Captain Butler," Ruthie Bonneau said, "I need your help. Tunis is in jail. They're going to murder my husband."

Chapter Twenty-six

Bottom Rail on Top

Southerners who had detested and vilified Abraham Lincoln, even those who had greeted Lincoln's first election with secession, were appalled by his assassination. Whatever else Abraham Lincoln might have been, Southerners knew he was a forgiving man. Touring Richmond after the Confederate capital fell, Lincoln was asked what should be done with the defeated rebels. Lincoln had replied, "Let 'em up easy, boys. Let 'em up easy."

Radical Republicans in Congress were not so inclined. Some had lost sons and brothers to rebel bullets; the influential Senator Charles Sumner had been beaten nearly to death by a Secessionist and Confederate raiders had burned Congressman Thaddeus Stevens's iron foundry to the ground. When Lincoln was murdered, these radicals took control of the United States government. They overrode President Andrew Johnson's vetoes, and when Johnson opposed them, they nearly had him impeached. The Congress dismissed elected Southern governors and appointed Republicans. Many of the men thus installed were hacks, zealots, or both.

Congressman Thaddeus Stevens believed the victors should "Strip a proud nobility of their bloated estates, reduce them to a level with plain republicans; send them forth to labor, and teach their children to enter the workshops or handle the plough, and you will thus humble the proud traitors."

Hordes of newly freed slaves flooded Southern cities. Northern missionaries flocked to a South that considered itself sufficiently Christian already, thank you. The Freedmen's Bureau fed ex-slaves, began educating them, and oversaw their labor contracts. Blue uniforms were everywhere.

Before the War, many Southern slave owners had honestly believed that their negroes were (never mind they might be sold in lean times) a part of their white Masters' families. Consequently, when negroes located buried family treasures for Sherman's bummers and abandoned their plantations en masse, these whites felt as if their beloved (though devious and slow-witted) children had betrayed them.

Carpetbaggers—some from Northern cities where hundreds of negroes had been lynched in wartime riots—rode in on moral high horses to teach Southerners how to treat the negro.

Southern Scalawags with no war record or prewar stature welcomed the Carpetbaggers with open arms.

Anyway, that's how Southern whites saw it.

Southern negroes were more apt to call this turn of events "bottom rail on top."

Tunis Bonneau had stayed in Freeport until the blockade was lifted. Three months after Abraham Lincoln died, the British steamer *Garrick* passed Fort Sumter—a rubble heap flying the largest Stars and Stripes Tunis Bonneau had ever seen.

The *Garrick* tied up at Government Wharf beside a troopship unloading discharged colored soldiers. These unafraid, skylarking negroes in blue uniforms stirred Tunis's hopes. In mortal combat, negroes had proved they were the white man's equal in courage and love of country. If negroes could be soldiers, why not citizens?

Ruthie was working an oyster skiff. "Tunis, I couldn't just move back in with Mama and Papa. I'm Mrs. Bonneau!"

"The *Merry Widow* . . ." Tunis began his confession.

"You hush up about that old boat." Ruthie kissed him.

From Ontario, Thomas Bonneau wrote, "Queen Victoria love her colored children same like she love her white children."

Tunis thought they should go to Canada and start over.

Ruthie said Canada was too cold and too far. Her kinfolk were in the

Low Country. And things *were* changing. Throughout the South, negroes were allying with sympathetic whites to agitate for negro rights.

"Why fight for rights from men who hate us when Canada got rights already?" Tunis said.

"This is my home, Tunis Bonneau," Ruthie replied. "I'd be sorrowful if we left."

And that was that.

After Tunis delivered his oysters to the market, he washed up and walked to his father-in-law's church, where every evening negroes were shaping the new world a-borning.

Tunis and Reverend Prescott traveled to Atlanta where white Republicans like Rufus Bullock and negroes—most who'd been free coloreds before the war—were petitioning the United States Congress. Freedom elixir was in the air. Negroes stood at the gates of the Promised Land.

"Petitioning the United States Congress," Tunis said. "My, my."

The *Atlanta Journal* described this meeting as "Cannibals and Carpetbaggers."

Reverend Prescott was to preach in the city, so Tunis boarded the train home alone.

Twenty miles south, wheel bearings in the wood car went dry, and their train screeched and smoked into Jonesboro for repairs.

White passengers disembarked and went into the railroad hotel. Tunis found shade on the platform, sat beside his bag, and closed his eyes.

Two hundred miles from Charleston's wetlands, Tunis was dreaming about swamp grass parting for the bow as he poled through the shallows. It was such a pleasant dream, he didn't notice the white woman until she kicked his foot. Tunis opened his eyes and scrambled to his feet. "Ma'am?" He removed his hat.

She was white and young. She'd had a few drinks. "Whew," she said, "you're a good-lookin' buck."

"Thank you, Miss. I'm waitin' on the train be fixed."

She shaded her eyes to inspect the station clock. "Won't be for a while."

Tunis extracted his watch and consulted it. "Train be rollin' soon as they hitch up a wood car."

"We got time," she said. "You want to have fun?"

"Ma'am?"

"You ain't stupid, are you?"

Tunis scratched his head, "Yes, ma'am. Reckon I is."

When she stamped her foot, her bootlace came undone.

"Why don't you kneel and tie up my lace?"

"Ma'am, nigger like me get in trouble touchin' a fine white lady like yourself."

"Well, ain't we par-tic-u-lar? What if I said you could touch any part of me for a dollar?"

"Ma'am, I'ze a married man."

"But all you niggers—all you niggers want to get a white woman alone and take off her clothes and do things to her. Don't you?"

"No'm."

"Jesus Christ," the young woman said to nobody in particular. To Tunis, she said, "You think I never been with a nigger before?"

"Excuse me, ma'am. I mighty thirsty. B'lieve I'll go down the street and find me a drink of water."

"Boy, you ain't goin' nowhere, till I'm finished with you."

Tunis replaced his hat. He said, "Miss, my wife's name is Ruthie; my son is Nathaniel Bonneau. I'm waitin' for a train to take me home. I got nothin' to do with you and I don't want nothin' to do with you. If you need a dollar, I'll give you a dollar, but leave me in peace." Tunis reached in his pocket.

"Why you hinckty son of a bitch," the girl said. Her eyes wandered over the empty platform. "Help," she said conversationally. After this rehearsal, she said "Help" several times, louder, until the white men came.

Chapter Twenty-seven

The Fastest Ever Was

Although the settees in the lobby of the Jonesboro Hotel had memorized the shapes of old men's bony buttocks and spittoons testified to old men's tobacco habits, there were no old men loafing here this afternoon. Jefferson Davis peered from a picture frame above the stairwell as if Jonesboro, Georgia, were still a Confederate town and Davis still president of a nation.

Despite the keys in the cubbyholes behind him, the hotel keeper looked Rhett Butler straight in the eye. "I'm full up. I ain't got no rooms." The bone buttons on the man's butternut shirt had replaced buttons stamped "C.S.A." and an unfaded patch on his sleeve showed where sergeant's stripes had been. He pulled a tin can from under his counter and spat.

Rhett set his carpetbag down, walked back to the front door, and lit a cigar. The old men were holding down benches in Courthouse Square. Younger men gathered on the yellowed lawn. Every hitching post on the square had a horse tied to it; some had two.

Cattycorner from the courthouse, the bank's new wooden sign declared it was the First National Bank of Jonesboro and possessed Capital—$75,000. The bank's previous identity, Planters Bank, was carved in enduring stone over the lintel. The bank's new name and new money would be Yankee.

Rhett returned to the hotel keeper. "What regiment, Sergeant?"

The man snapped to defiant attention. "Goddamned Fifty-second Georgia."

"Stovall's Brigade? Weren't you boys at Nashville?"

"What if we was?"

"Well," Rhett said, "if you'uns had come up a little faster, maybe we'uns wouldn't have skedaddled."

"The hell you say. You rode with Forrest?"

"Rhett Butler, C.S.A., at your service, sir."

"Well, I'll be skinned. Mr. Butler, you sure as hell ain't dressed like one of us. You dressed zactly like one of them."

Rhett smiled. "My tailor is a pacifist. I'll want a clean room with fresh linen."

The hotel keeper piled keys into a metal jumble on his counter. "You can have number three, four, five, or six. I won't rent no room to no Carpetbagger." He cocked his head. "You sure you ain't no Carpetbagger?"

Rhett raised his right hand, "On my father's honor."

The man considered. "That'll be all right, then. Room's two bits. Rooms're all the same, except six has a balcony."

"Uh-huh."

"Room six's over the square, so you can see the fun tonight. Mr. Butler, I thought you was a Freedmen's Bureau spy—though Freedmen's Bureau don't hardly come into Clayton County without a company of Bluebellies to safekeep 'em."

The second-floor hall was narrow, the necessary was downstairs out back, and the transom wouldn't open, but number six was clean, and when Rhett lifted the coverlet, no bedbugs scurried for cover.

Rhett pulled off his boots, hung his jacket over the chair, and laid back on the bed with his hands behind his head. He'd give the hotel keeper time to let everybody in Jonesboro know the stranger was "one of us."

Rhett hadn't seen a single black face since he got off the train: a bad sign.

His eyes wide open, Rhett remembered Thomas Bonneau shouting psalms into the hurricano. He remembered Tunis explaining how he loved Ruthie: truly and for a lifetime. After an hour, he washed and shaved. He checked the cartridges in his .32 rimfire revolver and dropped the gun in his coat pocket.

The courthouse's thick cement columns would have supported a structure twice as big. Rust streaked from clock hands seized up at 2 and 4. Wizened hulls hung from chestnut trees. Some of the men had crutches or were missing an arm or leg. Most wore reworked Confederate uniforms. When Rhett turned onto the walk, a one-legged young man on crutches planted himself in his path. "Hear tell you fought with General Forrest."

"I did."

"Mister"—the cripple rocked back onto one crutch to point with the other—"that fella wants to have a word with you."

"Goddamn it, Captain Butler!" Archie Flytte stood on the courthouse steps. "I heard you was residin' in hell."

Rhett lifted his arms: alive, alive-o. He shouted, "Flytte, you as ornery as you were?"

After Rhett Butler saved Archie Flytte's life, the ex-convict had attached himself to Rhett. He'd bragged on Rhett: "Cap'n Butler, he's educated." "Captain Butler, he's seen a bit of the world." "Captain Butler, he can speak the Latin. I've heard him with my own ears."

When Archie's adulation became intolerable, Rhett told him if he didn't shut up, he'd shoot him; after which, Flytte bragged that "Captain Butler would put a bullet in you for doin' him a kindness!"

"Well Archie," Rhett now said, "what do we have here?"

"Got us an uppity nigger."

"What's he done?"

"Oh hell, he'll tell you hisself. Boy loves to talk. He'll talk your ear off."

The sheriff's office was four steps down in the courthouse basement. "Mister, you tell 'em in Atlanta I had nothin' to do with this. I'm tryin' to do my duty, but what can one man do?" Evidently, the sheriff thought Rhett was from the Freedmen's Bureau. "My deputies have made themselves scarce. Bill Riley, my jailer? He never come back from supper. What can one man do?"

"Mind if I talk to the nigger?" Rhett asked. "You wait here, Archie!" He winked. "You'll scare the boy dumb."

The sheriff said, "Sure, mister. Sure, talk to him. It's too damn bad he got himself in a fix like this."

The jail corridor smelled of lye soap, chamber pots, and soured lives. One cell was occupied.

Tunis sat with his back to the whitewashed stone wall. An eyeglass lens was gone and the other was cracked. His Sunday suit was ruined. He glanced up but didn't stand. " 'Lo, Captain."

Rhett whistled soundlessly. "They beat hell out of you."

"The sheriff's not all bad. He sent Ruthie my telegram."

"Why you?"

When Tunis shifted, he held his breath until his sore body accepted its new position. "My good luck I spect. Your boy—I got your boy on the English steamer. Boy didn't seem altogether fond of you."

"He's not. The *Widow* sank?"

"Not two miles off Freeport. What possessed you to put such big engines in that boat?"

"Seemed like a good idea at the time."

Half an hour later, when Rhett emerged from the cells, the sheriff asked, "Where'd you run across him?" For a second, Rhett thought he meant Tunis. "That Archie fella . . ." Through the low basement window, Rhett could see men's boots and trouser legs. "Only three families up in Mundy Hollow. I reckon I'm kin to all of 'em. Archie was in the penitentiary, you know."

"He killed his wife."

"Hattie was foolin' around. She was my mother's aunt's cousin: The Flyttes never was any account. The Watlings, seems like they couldn't make a go no matter how they tried. And the Talbots—any Talbot with get-up-and-go got up and got. I'm Oliver Talbot," the sheriff introduced himself. "Next you'll ask my regiment. Sooner or later, everybody does." He revealed his left arm: a stub with a wizened hand. "Born that way," Talbot said. "I got to be sheriff when all the able-bodied men was in the army. Now the Federals want to replace me with somebody who didn't ever hold no office nor fought for the Confederacy, either. Ain't many men around here can say that."

"Sheriff . . ."

The man wouldn't be sidetracked. "Course, there's Bill McCracken. When the provosts come to conscript Bill, Bill run into the woods. Bill can't read nor write, but might be that won't matter. And he's never spent a day sober, but might be that won't matter, neither. Some sheriff. Where'd you know Archie Flytte?"

"Forrest's division."

"Uh-huh. Archie and his bunch been terrorizin' our coloreds. Freedmen's Bureau come out twict account of Archie Flytte. Course no white man would testify and no coloreds dared to." He scratched his head. "Last boy they killed, first thing they did was cut off that boy's member. You tell me, mister, why they'd do such a thing. Then they laid him on a heap of chestnut rails and burned him to death. Boy was already dead when they hung him." The sheriff jabbed a thumb toward the cells. "Nigger probably told you he didn't do nothin'."

"Would it make any difference?"

"Prolly not."

"What are you going to do?"

"I telegraphed Atlanta. Maybe they'll send some Bluebellies, maybe not. It gets dark about six; that's when I go home for dinner. I b'lieve I'll stay home afterward."

"The woman who complained? Where can I find her?"

"Little Lisa? Oh, she's a shame. She's a cryin' shame."

Bert's Saloon was across the tracks in Darktown. Bert, a fat man with greasy black hair, said Rhett would find Lisa out back. "Second door from the left." He opened his mouth in a soundless laugh. "No accountin' for tastes."

The whores' cribs were in a long, low clapboard building. Crude doors cut in the walls didn't disguise its origin as a chicken house. When Rhett knocked, a muffled voice told him to go away.

"Miss?"

"Goddamn it, go away."

The smell was worse inside. Where walls met the ceiling, latticework provided light and air. A spindly washstand held a milk-glass pitcher. Mended, neatly folded cotton stockings were stacked in a wooden crate turned on its side. Long-dead flowers protruded from a liniment bottle. An empty bottle lay beside the bed. The lump under the bedcovers moaned and a woman's hand emerged to wave him away. "Get out," she said without believing any man would ever do what she wanted.

Rhett poured brandy from his flask into its cup and folded the woman's fingers around the cup. Her head emerged from the covers. She brought the cup to her mouth, chattered it against her teeth, and swallowed. She waited to see if it would stay down. The moment passed and she tapped the cup, and Rhett refilled it and she swallowed again. She sat up and cuffed hair out of her eyes. She was naked. "Thanks, mister. You're a pal."

She fingered her cheeks and jaw to see if she'd suffered injuries she couldn't remember. Her eyes slipped in and out of focus. "My God," she said, "I know you."

"Lisa?"

"Captain Butler? I sure as hell never thought to see you no more." When she smiled, she was young again. "You got any more brandy?"

Rhett emptied his flask and she drained it like medicine."You want to turn around while I get my clothes on?" She giggled. "Listen to me, little Miss Touch-Me-Not." Frowning, she added, "It's because I knew you before, don't you see."

Rhett went to the open door and lit a cigar. The cigar smelled good.

Behind him Lisa said, "How's that boy of yours? What's his name? Tuck?"

"Tazewell is safe. He's in school now."

"He was a good boy. I liked him. You can turn around now. You got another flask? My stomach's rilin' me."

Rhett shook his head.

She put her hands on her hips. "Look at me, Captain! Ain't I the goddamnedest mess?"

Her dress was a plain yellow cotton shift. She was barefoot. Rhett said, "Come with me. I'll buy you supper."

The girl snickered. "Me in the Railroad Hotel dining room? Wouldn't that be something? Naw, Captain. Bert has an understanding with Sheriff Talbot. Bert's girls don't cross the tracks and Sheriff don't come down here."

"Weren't you on the depot platform?"

"I can pick up fellows on the platform." Her brow furrowed. "That why you come? The nigger?"

"He claims you accused him falsely, that he did nothing disrespectful."

"Well, he would say that, wouldn't he? Captain, Bert'd be glad to sell you a bottle and you and me could get better acquainted. Your son and me were gettin' right friendly. Might be you'd enjoy havin' a girl your boy wanted? I ain't but eighteen."

Rhett couldn't hide his wince.

"Little rough for you, Captain? Ain't you a man of the world? Whores can't be no big surprise to Captain Rhett Butler."

"Why did you lie?"

She balled her fists. "What makes you think I lied?"

"I've known Tunis Bonneau all my life."

"Well, I reckon you're gonna have to find yourself a new nigger."

Rhett opened his wallet and took out greenbacks. "Sometimes we Southerners talk about the North as if none of it was worth a damn. There are small towns on the Maine seacoast where a Confederate widow with a little cash might make a new life for herself. Or maybe she'd go west—young women are scarce out west. A pretty woman could pick and choose."

"Why don't you go buy that bottle," Lisa said flatly.

"Don't you want more than this?" Rhett gestured at her crib.

Her features closed up tight. "You bastard. You want me to tell folks I lied? Tell everybody in town Lisa has got herself lower than a low-down, dirty nigger?"

As a gray-faced Rhett Butler came up the courthouse walk, Sheriff Talbot was leaving. Men looked at the clouds or anywhere but at the sheriff, who didn't say a word as he brushed past.

"Where you been, Captain Butler?" Archie asked.

"With a whore."

Archie's smile shrank. "I don't hold with whores."

As the sun dropped behind the courthouse roof, bottles appeared.

Archie said, "I b'lieve Sheriff Talbot was hoping the Bluebellies would get here before dark."

Rhett asked, "Why wait for dark?"

"Some things ain't fittin' for women and children to see."

"You always were fastidious."

"And you always liked to use two-bit words. I guess you figured they'd make me mad. Captain, you can't make me mad. No way in hell you can make me mad. You saved my life, and maybe my life ain't worth much, but you're the only one ever saved it."

"What if I told you that boy didn't do anything?"

Archie was genuinely puzzled. "He's a nigger, ain't he?"

As Rhett went inside, one fellow flung a rope over a stout limb and others tore down the rail fence around a free colored's house. The free colored had left for the North and the poor whites who'd rented his house didn't object.

The sheriff had locked his file cabinets and desk. His wastebasket was set neatly on the desktop for the negro sweeper. Rhett suspected it'd sit there for a good while.

In the dim cell, Tunis was on his knees, praying.

"Lisa won't change her story."

"Don't reckon it'd make much difference if she did."

"She wouldn't take money."

"Might be you could get some of it to Ruthie and my boy?"

"I'll take care of Ruthie and the boy."

"You don't owe me. Wasn't Captain Butler tied down the steam-escape valves. Captain Bonneau done that." A faint smile flickered over Tunis's face. "That night, I knew the Federals would be waiting for us to come out. Over the Cape Fear bar, we was doing twenty-two knots. My boat was the fastest ever was."

"You'd still have the *Widow,* hadn't been for me."

"You never did like nobody to do nothing for you, do you, Rhett? Always got to be Captain Butler's hands on the wheel. Well, Rhett, my boat's sunk and I'm gonna die. Ain't nothing you can do to change that."

"You always were a hardheaded son of a bitch."

"The negro who ain't hardheaded'll be a nigger all his life. I ain't scared of dyin'. But I fear what they're gonna do to me before I die. When you see Ruthie, tell her I love her. Nathaniel Turner Bonneau—darned if that boy's name don't have a ring to it."

Rhett said, "It surely does."

Outside the jail, men's voices rose like surf building before a storm.

Tunis smiled. "Ain't it funny what a man thinks about? I'm scared, so dam—darned—scared. And all I can think about is happy times. I'm remembering first time I laid eyes on Ruthie. It was a Baptist picnic and I bought Ruthie's cake. It was an apple cake. I remember how I felt when little Nat was born and how it was that last time we run the Charleston blockade. I never said, Rhett, how you was: Captain Rhett Butler standin' on his wheel housing and all the Federal shots and shells on this earth couldn't make him step down."

"Some things stick in the mind," Rhett said quietly. "Did you know Will, the trunk master?"

"Daddy Thomas spoke high of Will."

"Will was a better father to me than my own father. I couldn't save him, either."

The two men were silent until Tunis swallowed and said, "There's one thing you can do for me, Rhett. I don't want them to do to me what they're goin' to. I need you . . . I need for you to shoot me." Tunis rubbed his lips, as if cleansing the words he'd spoken. His smile was sudden, nervous, luminous and his words tumbled over one another, as if he might not have time to finish. "Remember when we was kids and took my daddy's skiff all the way down to Beaufort? Darned if Daddy didn't tan my hide! Worth it, though—just the two of us and a following wind. I never saw a sky so blue. Rhett, it's worth living a man's whole life if just once, just one time, he gets to see a sky that blue."

The men who became beasts that night at the Clayton County courthouse had been soldiers who killed and had friends killed at their sides. Death was no stranger. Tonight was the nigger's turn; tomorrow might be theirs. Though some in that mob were crazy or simple or drunk, others were respectable men acting from what they saw as duty.

If before the War these respectable men hadn't "slipped down to the quarters" to enjoy a black girl, they knew men who had. Unmanned by defeat and afraid of the future, these men could not imagine that black men would not do to white women what white men had done to their women.

Archie Flytte told them, "You and you and you, go get the nigger. Any more, we'll be getting in each other's way. Somebody splash lamp oil on the bonfire."

When they heard the shot—more like a popgun than a pistol—Archie understood right away. "Now wait a damn minute," he said. "Just wait one goddamned minute."

Archie ran through the jail to the cell where Tunis Bonneau lay dead on the stone floor.

When Rhett Butler popped a match to light his cigar, the flame shook.

"Damn you, Butler." Archie kicked the cell door. "Goddamn you, Rhett Butler. Why the hell did you do that for?"

Rhett Butler said, "The nigger was disrespectful to a white woman."

Chapter Twenty-eight

In Federal Custody

The mob swarmed down the corridor into the cell: a fug of unwashed bodies, whiskey fumes, and rage. A balding middle-aged man kicked Tunis's head again and again. "Damn you, nigger! Damn you!"

An indignant graybeard pronounced, "Dead ain't no zample to nobody! Dead nigger ain't no zample."

They eyed Rhett Butler from the corners of their eyes like wolves circling a campfire. Rhett kept his hand on the revolver in his coat pocket.

Archie Flytte's hard voice slashed through their mutterings. "Captain Butler, he didn't mean nothin' by it! Captain Butler's a gentleman. You know ary gentleman with a lick of sense?"

"He should take the nigger's place," a disappointed boy spluttered.

"What's that you say, boy? You sayin' we should string up one of General Forrest's troopers? Hang a man fought b'side Archie Flytte? Well, you son of a bitch." Archie grabbed the boy's shirtfront and flung him into the crowd.

The graybeard said, "We got to make a zample!"

Another old man said disgustedly, "Aw, the hell with this. I'm late for dinner."

"Leave Butler be. There's niggers to burn." A cackle at his own wit, "You hear that? 'There's niggers to burn'!"

As they passed Tunis's corpse down the corridor, men punched and clutched at Tunis's groin and spat. One mad-eyed man dabbed blood from the bullet hole in Tunis's forehead and stuck his finger in his mouth.

After the mob followed the corpse outside, Rhett and Archie were alone in the sheriff's office.

Archie brought a lint-covered plug of tobacco from his pocket, bit off a chaw, and settled it under his lip. "All those months we was ridin' together, I done like you said. I fetched firewood and watered the horses and 'twas me foraged our grub. Was there a rocky place to lie down and a smooth place, you spread your slicker on the smooth. I pretended I never know'd you was lookin' down on me. I guess you figured I was dirt-stupid. Captain Butler, you saved my life. Account of that, I was beholden to you. Well, Captain Butler, I ain't beholden no more. You and me are quits."

After Archie left, Rhett slumped against the rough stone wall and released his revolver. His hand ached from gripping it. He looked at his trembling hand, opened and closed his fingers. It was a hand, only a hand—whatever it had done.

He heard the *whump* when lamp oil ignited their bonfire. The basement windows glowed red. They darkened when they tossed Tunis onto the blaze.

Rhett snuffed the lantern and sat in the dark behind the sheriff's desk while the mob screeched and hollered and an off-key voice wailed, "I'll live and die in Dixie! I'll live and die in Dixie!"

When the stink of burning meat seeped into the basement, Rhett lit another cigar and puffed until the tip glowed. He coughed and gagged and his stomach heaved. He puffed until the cigar scorched his fingers.

Sometime later, they dragged Tunis out of the fire to hang him. They started shooting. They yelled and shot for a time.

About four that morning, the moon set and men went home to their warm beds, their beloved wives and children.

It was getting light when Rhett came out. Three men sat by the bonfire, passing a bottle. What had been Captain Tunis Bonneau—Ruthie's husband, Nat's father, Rhett's friend—dangled from the limb of a chestnut tree. It looked more like last year's Yule log than a man.

Something glittered at Rhett's boot tip. He bent for the metal frames of Tunis's lensless glasses.

One of the drunks tottered to his feet, wobbled toward the fire, saved himself by throwing his arms in the air, got turned properly, and zigged and zagged down the street.

Cooing and clucking, pigeons fluttered onto the courthouse lawn. Two ravens settled in the chestnut tree. One opened its wings and cawed. The other dropped onto the burned thing and pecked at it.

Sheriff Talbot arrived. "Mornin', Butler." The sheriff's glance never wandered to the torso. "I b'lieve you killed my prisoner."

"Yes."

"Well, I ain't sayin' if I'd been the nigger I wouldn't have wanted you to do what you done, but that don't change the facts."

"Facts don't change."

"No sir, they don't. You killed the nigger what was in my custody and I got to arrest you and hold you until the Bluebellies get here. I'll have your pistol, sir. I hope you don't mind, but I've got a job to do."

They sat on the courthouse steps until a vedette of Federal cavalry trotted up Jonesboro's main street. Their captain swung down, shook out stiff legs, and rubbed his buttocks. He glanced at the charred thing that had been a man. His men loosened saddle girths and turned their horses onto the lawn to graze. Ignoring the sleeping drunks, a trooper kicked the fire into flame. The captain wore the aggravated expression of a veteran who'd drawn unpleasant duty. He nodded to the sheriff.

"This here's Rhett Butler," Sheriff Talbot said. "Was him killed the nigger."

"Butler? . . . Butler? . . . Sir, we've been looking for you. You'll come with us to army headquarters."

"That nigger was in my custody and Butler shot him dead. This is his pistol what done it."

The captain stuck the gun in his belt. "Sheriff, cut that *thing* down and get it buried."

"I don't know if I can, Captain. The boys hung it up and they'll cut it down. They won't want anyone foolin' with it."

"Sergeant!"

When the sergeant approached, the ravens flew, cawing angrily. The sergeant cut the rope with his saber. The thud of Tunis Bonneau hitting the ground settled in Rhett's soul forever.

That afternoon, Rhett Butler rode with the Federal patrol along the Macon and Western Railroad into Atlanta. Burned and exploded railcars had been dragged aside and shiny new rails snaked along the old roadbed.

Central Atlanta was a moonscape of broken walls, toppled chimneys, brick piles, and broken melted machines whose original purposes were unguessable. The Georgia Railroad Bank had been reduced to a broken wall. The Car Shed's great roof was crumpled like a blanket over its ruins. An open-air locomotive round table had been hastily constructed within the roofless circular walls of what had been a roundhouse.

Federal soldiers were everywhere; their tent city overflowed the public square.

While blue-clad soldiers drilled and ex-slaves explored their freedom, Atlantans were rebuilding. Here, men laid reclaimed bricks atop a fire-scorched wall; there, a rickety scaffold held workers setting a keystone in place.

Before Rhett and his escort reached Federal headquarters, the news was out: "Captain Butler's back and he's been arrested." "Rhett Butler's with a Federal patrol."

The patrol crossed the devastated rail yard into a neighborhood that had escaped the fire.

Rhett had been inside Judge Lyon's house—now army headquarters—before the War. The house's Corinthian columns needed paint and the balustrade was gap-toothed where balusters had been ripped out for kindling.

Rhett was escorted past a brace of saluting sentries into what had been the judge's office. Three officers warmed themselves at the fire and a pan-faced first sergeant was writing in the daybook.

He set down his pen. "Who do we have here, Captain?"

"Picked him up in Jonesboro. Rhett Butler. He killed a negro."

An officer came over. "Rhett Butler, Rhett Butler. I'll be. . . . I'll wager you don't remember me."

Rhett blinked and shook his head.

"Tom Jaffery. Remember? The field of honor? Charleston? Lord, I was green."

"You're a captain now," Rhett observed.

"Never was good at anything but soldiering." Jaffery paused. "We've been looking for you. Orders straight from the top. 'Bring in Rhett Kershaw Butler.' "

Rhett said. "You've brought me in."

The sergeant inscribed Rhett's name in the daybook and barked, "Hopkins, telegraph the War Department, we've got Butler." He accepted Rhett's wallet and watch, which he absently pocketed.

Tom Jaffery escorted Rhett down the street. "Butler, what have you got yourself into now?"

Firehouse Number Two overlooked the fire scene it had been powerless to prevent. It was still very much a firehouse. Sentries didn't conceal the original purpose of the wide arched doors through which fire engines had come at the gallop while alarm bells were ringing from the squat cupola on the roof.

The engine floor held petty malefactors.

Along the second-floor hallway, a sentry stood before each door. A leather fire helmet hung beside the window of Rhett's small room. An iron bed and deal table completed the furnishings. It was bitter cold.

Jaffery hesitated before saying, "I'm sorry to see you in this fix. Is there anything I can do? Anyone you want told?"

"I'd like writing materials." Rhett paused. "Jaffery, that foggy morning beside the Ashley—what did you think of us?"

Tom Jaffery said, "I thought you were lunatics. Every one of you."

After the captain departed, the sentry outside Rhett's door settled in his chair, which squeaked when he shifted his weight. From time to time, he coughed.

Rhett laid Tunis's smashed glasses on the table. They might have been some small harmless creature's skeleton. He could see his breath and he clenched his jacket lapels together. Rhett heard the rasp and pop of the match when his sentry lit his pipe. He smelled burning tobacco.

He heard a thump from the adjoining room when that room's occupant came off his bed. The other prisoner paced back and forth.

Below his high barred window, the moon rose over miles of shadowy ruins. Scavengers scuttled through the razed city, seeking shingles for kindling and scrap iron and brass to sell. Before dawn, Rhett knew several scavengers by their size, their speed, and how they moved from shadow to shadow, but he couldn't tell whether they were black men or white.

A young private with jug ears and a blotchy complexion brought him a bowl of cold oatmeal and the writing materials he'd asked for. When Rhett asked for a second blanket, the boy apologized. "I can't, sir. Orders from the War Department. What did you do to make 'em so mad?"

Rhett jotted a quick note to a Connecticut Senator with whom he had done wartime business. He spent the rest of his morning penning a long letter to Ruthie Bonneau.

Rufus Bullock's luxurious sideburns had been barber-trimmed, and when he sat on Rhett's bed and crossed his legs, his shoes were so new the soles weren't scratched. Bullock's wool overcoat was thick as a horse blanket.

Bullock shook his head heavily. "Rhett, what have you done? Rufus Bullock is a man of consequence in Georgia's Republican party, but Rufus had to beg General Thomas himself for a visit. I came as soon as I could."

"Tunis Bonneau . . ." Rhett began.

"They don't care about the negro. They'll only hang you if you force their hand."

"The negro's name was Tunis Bonneau. He was a free black. His family home was on the river below Broughton."

"I've met him. His father-in-law, William Prescott, is prominent. Rhett, the murder charge is a pretext." Rufus peered around the room suspiciously before whispering, "They say you've got the Confederate treasury."

Rhett closed his eyes. "Ah, yes. *That* treasury."

Rufus frowned. "Rhett, this is no laughing matter!"

"Rufus, my friend, it certainly is. The Confederacy never had a treasury.

All the Confederacy had was a printing press." With some effort, Rhett stayed polite. "You're looking prosperous, Rufus."

"The Republicans want Rufus Bullock to run for governor."

"Ex-Confederates can't hold office."

"I wasn't a Confederate."

"That colonel's commission you held?"

"Honorary, Rhett. Purely honorary. Rufus Bullock never took the Confederate oath. During the war, he represented the Southern Express Company, overseeing freight shipments. If the Confederate government hired the company, how could Rufus refuse? Business is business, is it not?"

"So Rufus, you are a Scalawag."

He puffed out his chest and wagged his finger. "Rufus Bullock is Northern-born!" Rufus chafed his hands. "Cold in here."

"It is."

"Rhett, my friend, please listen. The congressional Republicans Sumner, Blaine, Thad Stevens—they won't be put off. If you don't want to be hanged for murdering Tunis Bonneau, you'd best be *flexible* about your money."

"Thank you, Rufus. I'm sure you mean it kindly."

Rufus Bullock talked until he tired of his own arguments. When he rose to go, Rhett gave him his letters to mail. Bullock inspected the addresses. "Rhett, how did you know the Senator?"

"I know a good many people, some less honorable than you, my friend."

"I've a courier going to Washington tomorrow. He'll hand-carry this."

Rhett shrugged. "As you like. The letter to Mrs. Bonneau is more important."

Rufus Bullock left without his new wool overcoat, but that evening, when the private brought Rhett's supper of cold beets and potatoes, he took it away.

Chapter Twenty-Nine

The Gallows in the Garden

Despite a starvation diet and temperatures only slightly above freezing, Rhett was neither cold nor hungry. He was not angry or afraid.

The prisoner in the next room coughed and moaned in his sleep. Although Rhett never communicated with him, his presence was a vague comfort.

Rhett thought about Tunis Bonneau. He wondered what became of trunk master Will's wife, Mistletoe.

Except the hours during the warmest part of the day, when he was able to sleep, Rhett sat bolt upright on his iron bed, watching the desolation beneath his window. It was an opera without music. From dark to dawn, scavengers roamed and scurried and fought over prizes. From sunrise to sunset, in this blasted heath, new buildings went up. All the scavengers' ferocious energy changed nothing, but the builders were altering the ruined city's skyline.

Rhett did not count the days and weeks he'd been a prisoner.

One morning, it snowed. Fat, slow flakes softened the wounded landscape. Loud-booted soldiers came for the prisoner in the next room. "Private Armstrong, it's time." The man's fight shook the connecting wall. When the thumping and gasping and cursing ended and the man was restrained, he shouted, "No! No! No!" His denials diminished as the soldiers bore him down the stairs and away still crying, "Noooooo."

That same afternoon, two negroes wrestled a hip bath into Rhett's room and the splotchy-faced young private brought buckets of steaming water. "It's going to be all right now, sir," the boy said. "Mr. Puryear's here from Washington. Everything will be all right now."

When Rhett was naked and wrapped in a fresh woolen blanket, the private gave him a bar of French milled soap. "It was in your bag, sir. I hope you don't mind."

As Rhett eased into the hot water, he murmured, "Get thee behind me, Satan."

Peanut, the National Hotel's barber, came to shave Rhett. When the private stepped out of the room, the negro whispered urgently, "Miss Belle says to take heart. Mr. Bullock workin' on gettin' you out. He workin' on it!" What more the barber might have said was cut short by the private's return with the carpetbag Rhett had last seen in the Jonesboro Hotel.

"I'm sorry, Peanut. I've no money."

"That's all right, Captain Rhett. Miss Belle done took care of me."

After Rhett was dressed in his own clean clothes, Captain Jaffery came for him. He winced at Rhett's emaciation. "I'm sorry," he said. "I couldn't prevent this."

Rhett clasped the man's shoulder and followed him down the stairs.

In the street, drovers lashed horses through part-frozen mud. Thick red clay coated their wagon spokes and broke off in chunks from the turning wheels.

A skim of snow frosted the headquarters balustrade.

Captain Jaffery escorted Rhett into the guardroom. "Wait here. I'll let Mr. Puryear know you're here."

The small tree in the guardroom was adorned with red and green paper streamers, apples, and harness bells. Rhett warmed himself at the fire. A red-faced, mustachioed captain smacked his fist into his palm. "The Klan is undoing everything we fought for."

But a lieutenant was grinning as he aimed an imaginary rifle and made cocking sounds: "Ku. Klux. Klan."

Jaffery led Rhett up the spur-scarred black walnut staircase. Before tall double doors, Jaffery offered his hand. "Whatever happens," he said, "good luck to you."

The former drawing room's sixteen-foot ceilings were framed by elaborate plaster cornices. Undraped floor-to-ceiling windows overlooked what had once been a rose garden.

The gateleg table beside the windows was set for two. The starched linen tablecloth had *L*'s embroidered in the corners; the heavy silver was London-made. A bottle of Sillery chilled in an ice bucket.

A gallows had been erected in the garden and footprints, half-filled with snow, crossed the yard and up thirteen steps to the platform. The trap hung open, a dark square hole in the snowy platform. Two sets of fresher footprints dipped under the platform and an outline in snow was where the coffin had waited for its burden: that coffin now propped upright beside the garden gate. The snow that fell on the coffin was melted by fading body heat inside. Its planks glistened.

"Good-bye, Private Armstrong," Rhett said softly. "May you find the next world more to your liking."

The drawing room door clicked open. Without turning, he said, "Hello, Edgar. So you are to be my Tempter."

"Ah, Rhett, I came as soon as I heard." Edgar Allan Puryear's stiff tweed suit was set off by a new vest and a braided-hair watch chain. His smile was supremely confident. "I trust you weren't too uncomfortable. I came straightaway."

"I must thank you, Edgar. I don't believe I ever owed a man a bath."

Edgar pulled back a chair. "Do sit down, Rhett. Please. We'll eat and talk and see if we can't get you out of this mess. Socrates!"

A gray-haired negro houseman answered Puryear's shout. "You may serve us, Socrates." Before the servant was out of earshot, Edgar confided to Rhett, "Judge Lyon's man. I don't know what we'll do when his kind are gone."

"Serve ourselves? So, Edgar. I see you've landed on your feet."

Edgar Puryear rested his elbows on the table. "You and I could see this coming, couldn't we, Rhett? Fools may have clung to chivalric fantasies, but not us businessmen, eh?"

Rhett nodded at the coffin in the garden. "Private Armstrong—was he a businessman?"

"Armstrong? Oh my, no. Common murderer. Shot his sergeant while drunk." Edgar frowned thoughtfully. "A little less whiskey and he wouldn't have done it, a little more and he couldn't. Of such slight miscalculations are fortunes lost and men hanged."

Rhett sat with his hands folded while Edgar Puryear shook out his napkin and tucked it into his vest. Socrates opened the champagne, filled their glasses, and stood impassively against the wall.

"So you're a hangman now, Edgar?"

Edgar Puryear choked on his champagne. "Oh, no, no. I had nothing to do with *that,*" he said, gesturing vaguely at the windows. "Routine military court-martial, customary sentence. No, Rhett, I'd rather men *not* hang! A toast, Rhett, to the future, *your* future."

"I won't drink with you, Edgar," Rhett said.

Puryear's glass was extended in his toast. After the slightest pause, he drank and Socrates refilled his glass. Puryear wiped his mouth. "As you wish," he said. When Edgar snapped his fingers, the houseman rolled the serving cart to their table.

"Will you try the quail, sir?" The houseman uncovered a chafing dish. His serving fork and spoon hovered above aromatic delicacies.

"Nothing, thanks, Socrates," Rhett said politely.

"Captain Butler, we got the fricasseed sweetbreads, the fresh mountain trout, and the Virginia ham General Thomas favors. We got the yams, the fried greens, the wild rice, the beaten biscuits. . . ."

"Please serve Mr. Puryear. He seems . . . puny."

Edgar asked tightly, "So Uncle, you know Mr. Butler?"

"Oh yes, sir. All us coloreds know Cap'n Butler. From during the War, sir."

"Then you know he shot a negro."

Socrates shook his gray head. "Yes, sir. We heard all 'bout that. Sure is pitiful when the United States Army can't protect decent coloreds."

Edgar made his choices with a quick jabbing finger. When his plate was brimming, he said, "Wait outside, Uncle. I'll call you if I need you."

Edgar picked at his food. "Rhett, do you really think you can defy the United States Congress by refusing to eat supper?"

"Edgar, thank you for your concern, but I'm not hungry. I have feasted in Federal custody. Delmonico's could not have fed me better."

The champagne he gulped didn't improve Edgar Puryear's humor. He wiped his hands on his napkin, blew air past his lips, straightened his tie, and started afresh. "Rhett, the United States Congress is very angry. They hanged Mrs. Surratt—whose worst crime was keeping the boardinghouse where John Wilkes Booth plotted. Dr. Mudd, who innocently set the assassin's broken leg, languishes in prison. The Yankees are in a hanging frame of mind, Rhett. In times like this, it doesn't do to stand out from the crowd. Rhett, you stand out."

Rhett said nothing.

"The sweetbreads are delicious," Puryear said.

Rhett's grin flashed.

Edgar Puryear pushed his plate back. "Rhett, they don't give a damn about that negro you killed."

"I believe I'm the only white man in Georgia who did give a damn about him," Rhett said evenly.

"That girl, that Lisa? I've been to Jonesboro. . . ." Edgar smirked. "I've sported with little Lisa."

Rhett shrugged. "No accounting for tastes."

Puryear extended an accusatory finger. "Rhett Kershaw Butler, did you or did you not hold the blockade runner the *Merry Widow* in Wilmington harbor on the night of January 14, 1865, in order to take on a special cargo?"

"You know I did, Edgar. You know why I did."

"Did you or did you not load the Confederate treasury on that vessel?"

Rhett leaned back in his chair, laced his hands behind his head, and stretched. "Oh, Edgar. You are such a . . . such a *painful* person! Is that the best scheme you and your Yankee friends can concoct to steal my money?"

"Do you think we'll let you keep the fortune you made violating the United States blockade?"

"Edgar, I am thoroughly busted. You see before you living proof of imprudence. Though my dear mother preached a penny saved, a penny earned and so on, I was deaf to her entreaties. I am broke, busted, flat as a johnnycake."

Edgar waggled his finger. "Don't underestimate us, Rhett. Our agents have interviewed your banker—what's his name . . . Campbell? We don't want all of your money. We'd be satisfied with a . . . reasonable portion."

Rhett got to his feet. "Thank you for the best dinner I've had in weeks, Edgar. I think I'll skip the coffee tonight. Coffee disturbs my sleep."

Chapter Thirty

Deception

After this interview, Rhett was given three blankets, ordinary soldier's rations, even the occasional newspaper. Edgar Puryear visited twice but hosted no more gallows-side suppers. Although he insisted Rhett must turn over his blockade-running profits to Federal authorities, Edgar's most persuasive argument—that Rhett would be hanged if he didn't—weakened every day. To Rufus Bullock's amazement, powerful senators were acting on Rhett's behalf. By the New Year, nobody, excepting Captain Butler himself, recalled that Rhett Butler had shot and killed Tunis Bonneau.

One brisk January afternoon, Captain Jaffery knocked. "You've a visitor, Captain Butler. Your 'sister' Scarlett is here to see you." Jaffery grinned like a schoolboy.

"Dear, dear Scarlett. How good of Sister to come," Rhett replied, his mind in a turmoil.

"Handsome woman, your sister." Jaffery handed him his jacket.

"Why, yes, I suppose she is." Scarlett. Sunshine and hope and everything he had ever wanted. Grimness and sorrow receded into the past.

The two men clattered down the firehouse stairs, past the sentries into the cold. Exuberance rushed in where Rhett's resistance to Scarlett had once lodged, and he couldn't stop smiling. He called out, "Good morning, sir. Isn't this a grand morning?" to a mud-spattered teamster whose overloaded wagon was mired to its hubs. The teamster gave him a look.

Rhett tipped his hat to a pair of Atlanta ladies who were not too busy snubbing the hated Yankee soldiers to snub the notorious Captain Butler.

Up the familiar steps, into Federal headquarters, a right turn, then into a roomful of anonymous Yankee soldiers and Scarlett.

When he saw her, Rhett Kershaw Butler forgot who he was and every hurtful lesson he'd learned. They'd been such a long time apart; it seemed a lifetime.

Scarlett wore a moss green velvet gown and a gaily feathered bonnet.

She was in the room with him. She'd come to him. Her smile. Herself. He fought back tears. "Scarlett!" He kissed her cheek. "My darling little sister."

A Yankee captain protested: "Most irregular. He should be in the firehouse. You know the orders."

"Oh for God's sake, Henry," Captain Jaffery replied, "The lady would freeze in that barn."

That the brother and sister might have privacy, Tom Jaffery evicted two clerks from an orderly room that had once been a butler's pantry. Lit by a single window, lighter-colored plaster showed where the plate racks had hung. Sheaves of military orders dangled from nails driven into the wainscoting.

When Rhett bent to kiss Scarlet, she turned her face away.

"Can't I really kiss you now?"

"On the forehead, like a good brother."

"Thank you, no. I prefer to wait and hope for better things."

Rhett Butler felt like a young man again. As if everything were possible, as if the world were brand-new.

Scarlett told him Tara had escaped the War unscathed. She said her son, Wade, and Melly's little Beau were fine, that Tara had an able farm manager in Will Benteen.

"And Mr. Ashley Wilkes?"

Carelessly, Scarlett said that Mrs. Wilkes was glad to have Ashley home again. Will Benteen was courting her sister Carreen. Suellen was still chasing that old maid Frank Kennedy.

Rhett chuckled, "Old Frank may be a bore, but he's got money."

Scarlett made a face.

She paused and then spoke so softly, Rhett had to lean forward to hear. "Mother passed away. Of the fever. She was . . . dead when I came home to Tara." Her eyes brimmed.

"I am so sorry, my dear. Your father, Gerald?"

Scarlett looked away. "Gerald keeps himself busy."

Was that a false note in her voice? Perhaps her father wasn't as well as she claimed. Gerald must be getting on in years.

It didn't matter. Scarlett had come to see him. She who'd spurned him when he was rich and free had come to see an impoverished prisoner the Yankees were threatening to hang.

He told her she looked lovely. He asked her to turn around.

As she spun, her lovely green dress wafted, exposing lace-trimmed pantalets. He clasped his hands behind his back to keep himself from devouring her then and there.

Scarlett told him that Tara's faithful negroes had hidden the plantation's livestock in the woods, where Sherman's bummers couldn't find them, and Tara'd cleared twenty bales of cotton last year and things would be even better this year—but (she sighed) it was so terribly dull in the country. She'd become accustomed to city life.

Rhett wondered how Scarlett could be bored, unless she'd gone through all the country boys.

"Oh Rhett, I didn't come all the way out here to hear you talk foolishness about me. I came because I'm terribly distressed about you. When will they let you out of this terrible place?"

"And when they do?" he asked softly, leaning closer.

Scarlett blushed like a maiden. As he leaned toward her, she raised her hand tenderly to his cheek. It was scratchy. Puzzled, he lowered her hand and turned it over. Scarlett's palm was raw and cracked and her fingernails were broken. He stared, uncomprehending. She didn't resist when he took her other hand and turned it over, too. Just as his hands had been when he labored in Broughton's rice fields.

Rhett licked his lips. As he had soared, he plummeted. His heart shriveled into something hard and mean. Dully, he asked, "So you have been doing very nicely at Tara, have you? Cleared so much money on the cotton, you can go visiting. Why did you lie to me?"

Deep in her astonishing eyes he saw a flare—like a hunted vixen's in the lamplight. "They can hang me higher than Haman for all you care." Rhett let her hands drop. What a tawdry room this was. What had been generous as hope became a dirty little closet inhabited by Tunis Bonneau's murderer and a female cheat.

Money. She wanted money. Sure, she wanted money. She talked fast, her words tumbling over one another. Tara, her beloved Tara, was to be sold for unpaid taxes, and Scarlett didn't have a cent. She'd fashioned her velvet dress from Tara's window curtains. "You said you never wanted a woman as much as you wanted me. If you still want me, you can have me. Rhett, I'll do anything you say, but for God's sake, write me a draft for the money."

What a wonder she was! Scarlett O'Hara had priced his love. Three hundred dollars—he could enjoy his faithless darling for the price of a London suit or a pretty good horse. When you thought about it, three hundred was a bargain. Some Paris courtesans charged more than that. "I haven't any money," Rhett said wearily.

She attacked him. She sprang to her feet with a cry that quenched the hum of soldiers' voices in the next room. Rhett clamped a hand over her mouth and lifted her off her feet. She kicked, tried to bite. She tried to scream.

It took all his strength to hold her. Rhett thought, She would do anything. She is just like me.

Scarlett's eyes rolled back in her head as she fainted.

Yankee officers rushed in to revive the young lady. Captain Jaffery fetched a glass of brandy.

When Scarlett O'Hara left that place, she was a defeated child, lost in her fake finery and a bonnet whose gay feathers—Rhett now knew—had been plucked from the tail of a barnyard rooster.

That night, Rhett dreamed he murdered a little girl. Put his rimfire pistol against her forehead and pulled the trigger.

Two weeks later, when Captain Jaffery brought news of Scarlett's elopement, he was puzzled. "But didn't your sister tell you she planned to marry?"

For a moment, Rhett didn't trust himself to speak.

The captain clapped Rhett's shoulder. "Perhaps Miss Scarlett thought her big brother might not approve of her new husband! Nothing to worry about: Frank Kennedy is thoroughly respectable." Captain Jaffery scratched his ear. "I'm a little surprised a woman like your sister would fall for fussy old Frank—and wasn't Frank engaged to marry another?" He smiled ruefully. "A woman's heart"—Jaffery put his hand over his own—"who can understand it?"

"If Kennedy's got three hundred dollars, I can."

The forsythias were blossoming when Rufus Bullock brought Rhett's pardon. It bore the signature of a Connecticut Senator who was not known as a forgiving man. Rufus asked, "Rhett, that letter you wrote him—in heaven's name, what did you say?"

Rhett smacked dust from the hat he hadn't worn in months and set it at a rakish angle. "Rufus, the Senator made a fortune during the War manufacturing the cotton linings of Federal officers' coats. Did you ever wonder where the Senator found that contraband cotton?" Rhett Butler grinned broadly. "Rufus, let us leave this place. It is spring."

Chapter Thirty-one

A Southern Belle

The summer was droughty. The corn crop was poor, the cotton hardly worth ginning. White preachers couldn't explain to their flocks why God had abandoned the Confederate republic. Some preachers contemplated suicide; others quit the pulpit. Negro preachers and parishioners penned eloquent petitions to the United States Congress seeking their promised rights. Some prominent ex-Confederates—General Wade Hampton in South Carolina and Virginia's General William Mahone among them—said negroes must have voting rights, arguing that the South must be rebuilt by blacks and whites together. But Georgia's General John B. Gordon and Tennessee's General Nathan Bedford Forrest used their wartime prestige to restore the prewar order.

Yankee idealists bought tickets South to promote negro education and citizenship. Republican congressmen who'd lost friends and kin to Confederate bullets sought revenge. Opportunists wanted to roll the Southern corpse over to see if there was anything underneath worth stealing.

The U.S. Army turned over railcars and locomotives to the same railroad companies they'd recently wrecked. Although Southern railroads had to pay their workers with sides of bacon and bags of flour, track was furiously relaid, bridges and tunnels were rebuilt, and if passengers sometimes had to transfer to wagons for a stretch, the trains were running.

With the profits of Frank Kennedy's store, Scarlett O'Hara Kennedy bought a sawmill. Financed by torrents of Yankee money, Atlanta was rebuilding at a breakneck pace. Brick, Portland cement, and lime fetched premium prices, and wagonloads of north Georgia pine rolled down Marietta Road to the Kennedys' sawmill. Proper Atlantans sniffed that Mrs. Kennedy "wore the pants in *that* family." But Scarlett was too busy to care. She bought a second sawmill and persuaded Ashley Wilkes to run it.

When Scarlett and Frank Kennedy's daughter, Ella, was born, Scarlett's daughter strongly resembled her homely husband.

When Gerald O'Hara died, Scarlett's money and her farm manager, Will Benteen, were already rebuilding Tara.

One morning, as Belle Watling dug deeper than usual in her bureau drawer, she was struck by a possibility that made her gasp.

Belle's laundry woman had run off with Dr. Jewett's Scientific Remedy Medicine Show, which Belle didn't learn until MacBeth returned her laundry unlaundered. At the bottom of her bureau Belle found a garment wrapped in parchment paper. She pulled back a corner to reveal the rich gray fabric of the dress Rhett had given her long ago. Belle sat down, breathless with calculation: *Scarlett O'Hara was Scarlett Kennedy now. They had a daughter. The Kennedy marriage should last until Scarlett was an old woman.*

The rest of that day, Belle went about the house humming and singing nonsense songs until Minette complained that she, Minette, had been a habitué of New Orleans's Opera St. Louis and Belle's "omp-pah-pahs" and "oh doodah days" were hopelessly unmusical.

"Oh Minette," Belle replied happily. "Can't expect a soiled dove to sing like a dove, now can you?"

To the dismay of several older customers who had favored a comfortable (less demanding) paramour, Belle quit receiving gentlemen callers. On a diet of greens, bread, and water, her waistline shrank.

One afternoon, MacBeth drove her to the Wilkeses' home.

"Go 'round back," Belle said nervously. "Through the alleyway."

Outside the gate of the Wilkeses' kitchen garden, Belle hesitated. Who was she to ask anything of anybody?

Why, she thought, I am Ruth Belle Watling; that's me. Her courage plucked up, she brushed past Melanie's fall greens and baskets of just-dug potatoes.

When she knocked at the back door, a curtain pulled back and a solemn little boy peered at her. He stuck his thumb in his mouth. In response to Belle's reassuring smile, the child let the curtain fall and ran to the front of the house. "Mama, Mama!"

"What is it, Beau honey? Is something wrong?"

Belle heard a woman's footsteps. "Is someone here, Beau? How good you are to tell me."

The woman who opened the back door was thin—too thin—and her dark eyes were enormous. "Why . . . Miss Watling. What a pleasant surprise!"

"Mrs. Wilkes, I didn't want to shame you, so I come 'round back."

"How could you shame me, dear? Please, come in."

Belle eased into the kitchen. When Melanie suggested they proceed to the parlor, Belle demurred. "Thank you, ma'am, but the kitchen's fine."

Staring at the stranger, Beau wrapped around his mother's legs.

Melanie pulled out a stool. "Won't you sit? Will you take a cup of tea?"

Belle's mouth was dry from nervousness. "I wouldn't mind a glass of water."

Melanie worked the pitcher pump until cool water splashed. Like all Atlanta well water, it tasted of iron.

"Mrs. Wilkes, I thank you for seein' me and I won't pester you much. You ain't so snooty as them other ladies and I thought I might ask you . . ."

Melanie's gentle smile invited Belle's confidence.

There were fresh daisies in a vase beside the sink and bright windows overlooked a lovingly tended garden.

"Right nice garden," Belle said. "Right nice greens."

"Thank you. You shall take some with you."

"Oh, no Mrs. Wilkes. I didn't mean I wanted none." Belle dropped her eyes. "I was just sayin' they was nice."

"Well," Melanie said, "I always have a cup of tea this time of day. Won't you join me?" She stooped to shake the stove grate and add wood to the firebox.

It was a newfangled stove with a water tank perched beside the hood. When Belle admired it, Melanie said ready hot water was convenient. Belle asked if Mr. Wilkes liked managing a sawmill, and after a slight hesitation, Melanie told her, "Mr. Wilkes was reared as a gentleman."

Belle asked if Miss Pittypat Hamilton still owned the house behind the garden and Melanie said yes, that she and her brother, Charles, had been raised by Miss Pittypat and when the Wilkeses returned to Atlanta after the war, they'd been fortunate to rent the house that backed up on Melanie's childhood home. So many memories.

"Mr. and Mrs. Kennedy livin' with Miss Pittypat now?"

"Why yes, they are. We're doubly blessed. My son and I spent the last year of the War on Mrs. Kennedy's family plantation, Tara." Melanie added, "Of course Scarlett wasn't Mrs. Kennedy at that time. Scarlett is my brother Charles's widow."

Belle yearned to ask if the Kennedys' marriage was happy, but she couldn't think how to phrase that question. She set her teacup down so quickly, it clicked against the saucer. "Mrs. Wilkes, a gentleman has took my heart."

"Why Belle, what good news! My own marriage has been so fortunate, I pity women who've never wed."

"Things ain't gone so far as that. The thing is, Mrs. Wilkes"—Belle's face glowed with earnestness—"my gentleman's a Gentleman and I ain't no Lady."

Melanie thought before replying. "I'm not sure, Miss Watling, how important that distinction is. Doesn't God love all his children?"

"Maybe He does, but all His children surely don't love all His other children. Generally, Gentlemen, they love Ladies, and the Other Sort loves the Other Sort."

Belle wished she could be as serene as Mrs. Wilkes. She wished she didn't feel sweat starting. What if a drop ran down her arm, where Mrs. Wilkes could see it? She gulped tea and pressed on. "I came to ask you, Mrs. Wilkes. How can I turn myself into a lady?"

The tiny flicker at the back of Melanie's eyes almost killed Belle's hopes then and there, but Melanie's smile was kind. She said, "I've never thought about it. To be a lady doesn't one act and seem like a lady?"

"I don't know, Mrs. Wilkes. That's why I come."

"But your . . . occupation . . ."

"I don't see no more callers. I just own the place."

"I see."

"I mean, how can I *seem* like a lady? I dunno know how to act and I dunno how to dress. Mrs. Wilkes, I dunno know how to think like a lady thinks!" When Belle opened her hands helplessly, a cold drop of sweat trickled down her rib cage. "Mrs. Wilkes, where can I get clothes like yours?"

"Dear me, Miss Watling. Being a lady is more than—"

"I got money."

"I'm afraid money—"

"But right clothes and money are a start, aren't they?"

"Well, I suppose they might be. . . ."

So later that week, without telling a soul, Melanie Wilkes escorted Belle Watling to Atlanta's best dressmaker. Miss Smithers was an octoroon who had been free colored before the War, and no white women had higher standards of propriety.

Nowadays, most of Miss Smithers's business came from Carpetbaggers' or Yankee officers' wives. Her establishment was a shotgun house on Mitchell Street. In her front room, one dressmaker's dummy wore a delicate high-necked blouse, while another was naked brown muslin stretched over a wire frame. Bolts of cloth—piqués, lawns, worsteds, failles, velvets, and brocades—draped Miss Smithers's counters and pattern books were stacked higher than the diminutive dressmaker's head.

She touched the pattern books. "What style do you fancy, Miss Watling? Paris, London, New York, Boston?"

"You make Mrs. Kennedy's clothes?"

"Why yes, I do."

"I want to be somewheres between her and"—Belle pointed at her companion—"Mrs. Wilkes here."

Unwrapped, the parcel Belle held so tenderly contained the gray dress Rhett had given her. "Oh dear, I'm afraid I cannot alter this garment." Miss Smithers held the dress up. "The neckline and bodice . . . I'm afraid not. And we don't wear hoops these days."

"Can't you find the same fabric? My dearest friend give me this."

Miss Smithers thought to explain that no two fabrics were exactly alike, that this weave was French, that . . . the seamstress relented at the hope in Belle's eyes. "I will see what I can do," she said.

After they had arranged for dresses, blouses, and jackets, Melanie took Belle to the German shoemaker, where Belle was fitted for three pairs, one in patent leather.

Before they parted, Melanie said, "I'm afraid, Belle, that being a lady is more than proper clothes. It is an attitude. From your . . . experience, you may know more of business and politics than ladies are supposed to know. Gentlemen are pleased to think ladies are ornamental, and it is an ill-advised ornament who contradicts her gentleman."

"Thank you."

"You'll want to read books—novels, because ladies are frivolous; poetry because ladies are sentimental; and sermons, because we are pious. If you must read essays, Mr. Emerson might be best. Your gentleman may have a nodding acquaintance with his works." Melanie paused. "Your diction, Belle . . ."

"The way I talk, you mean?"

"Imitate the heroines of novels. Ladies talk as they do."

Although Mr. Belmont's jewelry store had burned and his safe hadn't proved as fireproof as its maker had promised, Belmont had set up again not far from his prewar location. Belle wanted ear bobs to match the cameo she showed him. "They got to match this brooch. It is my prized possession."

Fine jewelers are as discreet as undertakers and priests. Belmont admired the cameo extravagantly, as if he'd never seen it before, and sold Belle the most expensive cameo ear bobs he had.

Belle's new gowns were prints in muted shades. Her blouses were lawn and silk, with lace at the neckline. When Belle stood before Miss Smithers's pier glass, she didn't recognize the lady looking back at her.

"Mercy me," Belle gasped.

"Yes, Miss Watling." The dressmaker smiled, satisfied. "Yes indeed!"

Emboldened, Belle promenaded into the Kimball House, Atlanta's newest hotel. Glittering crystal chandeliers hung over a lobby whose black-and-white checkerboard floor was scattered with Oriental rugs. A porter waited, poised, beside Atlanta's first steam "elevator." Although Belle saw a few gentlemen she'd known in a business way, none recognized her. Over tea—"So refreshing, don't you think?" Belle told the waiter—Belle studied real ladies covertly, how they held their teacups, where they set their spoons, and how they folded their napkins.

Tuesdays and Thursdays, Belle took tea at the Kimball House, and one fine Sunday she attended church—not St. Philip's Episcopal, where the Wilkeses worshiped, but the Second Presbyterian, which Belle figured wouldn't be so hoity-toity.

After the service, Belle introduced herself to the preacher as Mrs. Butler—the Savannah Butlers—visiting Atlanta kin.

"I hope you'll worship with us again, Mrs. Butler," the clergyman said.

Tazewell Watling wrote his mother about his friends at his English school, their sports, and his successes on the rugby team. Not long after he arrived at Shrewsbury School, he'd concluded a letter with "When Captain Butler visited London after the Confederate surrender, he telegraphed the Headmaster his intent to visit me. I asked the Head to tell Captain Butler that I would not see him."

When she began her transformation, Belle wrote:

Dear Taz,

Do you see many lords and ladies in England? Have you ever seen Queen Victoria? I would love to see the Queen and all those fancy castles.

Minette is running the house while I try on fancy dresses and drink tea at the Kimball House. Atlanta is so up-to-date! They've even got an elevator!

Say, what do you think of Sir Walter Scott's Ivanhoe? ***It's a funny old book, but I'm partial to it.***

Dear son, there have been some mighty changes in your old Ma's life. I ain't going to let anybody tell me who I am!

Who knows, I might even marry somebody!

I miss you, dear Taz!
Your loving Ma, Ruth Belle Watling

Rhett was out of town two weeks in three and Belle forwarded his mail to the St. Nicholas Hotel in New York City, the Spotswood in Richmond, or the St. Louis in New Orleans.

When Rhett was in Atlanta, Belle lingered in his office, knitting while he did accounts, answered correspondence, and signed documents she didn't pretend to understand. Having learned from *Godey's Lady's Book* about British tea customs, every afternoon at three, she brought a tray with biscuits, cups, and her new china teapot.

Her Cyprians exchanged knowing looks.

Lisa, the country girl who'd been Belle's housemaid during the war, returned to the Chapeau Rouge looking for work. Lisa confessed she'd fallen on hard times, become nothing better than "a slut" and "a common drunk." She confessed, "Miz Watling, I can't half tell you the wickedness I got up to." Lisa hadn't touched a drop in six months, and Belle had always had a soft spot for the girl.

Two days later, Rhett came downstairs and met her.

Lisa licked her lips, "Please, Captain Butler, I ain't that girl no more."

"Get out," Rhett said.

For fear he'd murder her, Lisa departed so precipitously that she left her belongings, which MacBeth bundled and took to the sporting house where she'd found work. Belle didn't dare ask Rhett why he'd banished the girl. Some months later, Belle heard Lisa had been taken up by a rich Scalawag and Belle figured things had turned out as well for little Lisa as they were going to.

Three days after the Georgia legislature unanimously refused to ratify the Fourteenth Amendment, a telegram came for Rhett: "Father died today. Burial Friday. Please come. Rosemary."

"Oh Rhett, I'm sorry," Belle said.

"Funnily," Rhett said, "I am, too."

Chapter Thirty-Two

Miss Elizabeth Kneels

Langston Butler's anger had defied the undertaker's art: The poor man's attempts to pad and pinch the corpse's features into a pleasant expression had been defeated by the resolutely down-turned mouth, puckered lips, and frown lines no embalmer's wax could disguise.

Langston Butler had sought deference, obedience, and power. He'd never pleasured in the inconsequential: a heron's awkward flight, the evanescence of riffles on a sandy beach, the astonishing softness of the underside of a woman's arm. In his entire lifetime, Langston Butler had never once chanced being a fool.

Tennyson's poem echoed in Rhett's mind: " 'Tis better to have loved and lost than never to have loved at all."

St. Michael's stained-glass windows had been taken out during Charleston's bombardment and hadn't been returned. Langston's bier was in the shadows of lantern light.

When the church doors were opened for the coffin to pass out, a lance of afternoon sunlight thrust into the sanctuary and haloed the pallbearers' heads. These were men of Langston's generation: Secessionists, Nullifiers, men whose abstract political theories had been refuted in blood.

The churchyard was bounded by the high iron fence Rhett and Tecumseh had jumped; how many years ago?

How easily he could have impaled the horse or himself on those brutal spikes. How easily he might have been thrown, maimed, or killed. Life hadn't been worth much: a gewgaw, a trifle to be carelessly thrown away.

Lord, Rhett thought, was I so miserable then?

His gaze found poor troubled Rosemary. Thank God she had her baby. For a time at least, little Louis Valentine Ravanel would be all the world to her.

Rhett had heard reports of Andrew Ravanel's Klan activities. His sister's husband was becoming notorious. Andrew was so angry about "betrayals," "Southern rights," "niggers," "Carpetbaggers," Rhett couldn't talk to him.

What had happened to the boy Andrew had been? Where had that decent, brave, romantic, melancholy boy gone to?

After the burial, Langston's negro mourners, Hercules and Solomon, made themselves scarce. Julian Butler stayed just long enough to relate some statehouse gossip and assure Rhett that if he ever needed anything from the legislature, anything at all . . . Julian had lost all his hair. His skull gleamed like a newly laid egg.

Isaiah Watling was helping Elizabeth Butler into his wagon when Rosemary interrupted. "Mother, you'll be staying with us now. We've plenty of room. You can help with the baby."

"May I?" Elizabeth's eyes widened as her old lips formed a smile. "May I? Why, I'd never considered I might. Rosemary," she beseeched, "Might I? I would so like to stay. I would! I'd attend vespers at St. Michael's. Vespers is such a *gentle* service."

"Miss 'Lizabeth," Isaiah intoned. "Ain't we been prayin'? Ain't we been Bible readin' and prayin' mornin' and night?"

"I suppose so," Elizabeth said. "But God wants things to be *nice.* Remember what Jesus said about the lilies of the fields! St. Michael's kneeling stools are kinder to old knees than your bare wooden floor."

"I'll fashion you a kneeling stool, soon as we get home to Broughton, Miss 'Lizabeth."

"My mother will stay with Rosemary," Rhett said.

Isaiah Watling's merciless eyes found Rhett's.

Elizabeth babbled happily, "Oh dear Rhett, may I stay? I've always loved Charleston. Do you remember when you told your father that the only difference between Charlestonians and alligators is that alligators show their teeth before they bite? Oh Rhett, you were *such* a renegade!" She covered her mouth to hide her giggle.

Isaiah Watling ran his tongue around his teeth and the inside of his mouth. "I'll be goin', then. Miss 'Lizabeth, I'll pray for you long as I am able."

"Why, Isaiah," Elizabeth Butler spoke as if to a remote kinsman, "bless your heart."

The old man set his hat squarely on his head. "Miss Rosemary," he said, "I expect you'll take good care of Miss 'Lizabeth. I'd be obliged to you." Isaiah Watling's smile was unexpectedly kind. "Mr. Rhett Butler," he prophesied, "my day will come."

Chapter Thirty-three

The Wednesday-Night Democrats

Three days later, just before ten in the morning, Rhett entered Chapeau Rouge's kitchen. "Good morning, dear Belle." He kissed her cheek and cocked his head quizzically. "What a lovely dress. It flatters your complexion. And that ribboned hair net! Even Charleston ladies aren't so fashionable. Don't tell me, Belle. You have a beau!"

Belle flushed. "Don't be a silly. Who'd want an old cow like me?"

He took her hands and smiled the smile Belle loved. "I would, for one." He released her. "Now, Belle, let's have your news. What are Rufus Bullock and the Republicans up to? Have the Carpetbaggers looted the Georgia Railroad? Is Edgar Puryear lobbying for the Pennsylvania? What will the Yankees do about the Klan?"

Belle brewed coffee and brought Rhett up-to-date. Out back, MacBeth was whistling as he curried the horses.

Belle asked, "Was Papa at the burying?"

"He was. With your delightful cousin Josie."

"Uncle Abraham's boy."

"Josie Watling is a dangerous young man."

Belle refilled Rhett's cup. "I haven't seen Uncle Abraham since we was back at Mundy Hollow. Our homeplace ain't—I mean *isn't*—five miles out of Jonesboro, but I never wanted to go back. I b'lieve Cousin Josie did some awful things in the War."

"I hear Josie's in the Klan."

Belle shrugged, "So's Archie Flytte, 'n' Frank Kennedy 'n' Mr. Ashley

Wilkes. Nowadays, half Atlanta's gentlefolk got a white robe in their closet. How's your sister farin'?"

"Drawn. Distracted." Rhett stretched luxuriously. "What's this about the Klan?"

"MacBeth won't drive Yankee officers home no more—no matter how drunk they is. It ain't safe for negroes to be out at night. And t'other night, Rhett, after we closed up, I thought I heard somethin', so I stuck my head out back, and there was riders beside the creek. Fifteen, twenty of 'em in white robes and pointy caps. They wasn't comin' for us, but they scared hell out of me."

"The Yankees won't let armed night riders terrorize the countryside."

Belle went to her icebox for a bowl of eggs. "Well, Rhett honey. Despite the world's troubles, the sun's shining and it's gonna be a fine day, and I'm of a mind to cook you breakfast. There's country ham, and it won't take five minutes to fry a mess of eggs."

Rhett pushed his chair back. "Sorry, Belle, I've business downtown. I've bought stock in the Farmer's and Merchants' Bank. I've got to look in on my investment."

"The hell you will!" Belle said, surprising both of them. "Captain Rhett Butler, you sit down at that kitchen table! Your darned business isn't near as important as tellin' me about your Daddy's buryin' 'n' Miss Rosemary 'n' all the rest."

Ruefully, Rhett settled back. "Well, Belle, I guess I could eat something."

Over breakfast, they conversed as companionably as an old married couple.

"How was Papa, then?"

Rhett shrugged. "Unchanged. I vetoed his plan to keep Mother at Broughton. If he were a different man, I'd say he's sweet on her." He drank coffee. "Andrew won't have free negroes in his home—not that volunteers would be easily found. Andrew's 'principles' mean Rosemary must care for an infant, plus a senile old woman."

Belle softened, remembering. "Andrew was gentle, Rhett."

"Well, he's a Grand Wizard now. Charleston's grandees flatter Andrew shamelessly but never invite him to their homes."

"Poor Andrew."

Rhett crumpled his napkin beside his plate. "You care for him still?"

"I care for the girl I was." Belle blinked. "I hope that girl's still inside of me some'eres. Tell me, Rhett; can you ever forgive your father for what he done?"

"Forgive him? Dear Belle, I forgave him years ago. Only a fool doesn't forgive. The worse fool forgets." Rhett gave her his flashing grin. "Now, let me tell you about my nephew. Master Louis Valentine Ravanel. What a set of lungs that boy has. . . ."

That night in her lonely bed, Belle Watling went to sleep smiling, her pillow Rhett's compliment: "I would, for one."

As per their custom, on New Year's Eve, over a glass of champagne, Belle paid Rhett his share of the profits from the sporting house. As she did every year, she reminded him why she'd named it as she had.

When she pressed him to check her figures, Rhett said, "Belle, if I had to check your books, I'd find another partner."

That night, they both got a little tipsy.

When Rhett was in town, the Chapeau Rouge was calmer and friendlier. Rhett worked at his desk until late afternoon; then he went out to dinner and played cards at the Girl of the Period saloon until midnight.

As Taz's letters came, Belle laid them on Rhett's desk, and he returned them the next day without comment—even those where Taz complained about his bastardy.

In the privacy of her boudoir, Belle read her novels. She didn't care for Mr. Thackeray but enjoyed Mr. Dickens's *Oliver Twist.* Belle's eyes were wet when she closed that book. She read Mr. Hawthorne's novels, and one bitter February afternoon after Mrs. Elsing snubbed her in the Georgia Bank, Belle told Rhett, "Now I know how poor Hester Prynne felt."

Rhett raised an eyebrow. "'Hester Prynne,' Belle?"

March came in like a lion. The United States Congress disbanded Georgia's legislature and the state became "Military District Number Three." White Georgians vilified Rufus Bullock and his Republicans as traitors.

Atlanta was restless that cold spring night. Federal sentries heard hoofbeats where no horsemen could possibly be; dogs set to howling across the city and quit as suddenly as they had begun. Small clouds scudded across the sky and smoke whipped sideways from the chimneys.

Chapeau Rouge's gentlemen callers were as jittery as the elm branches scratching the house. Yankee officers who usually talked too much were secretive, and normally reticent men spouted information. Minette could hardly keep them in brandy. Officers arrived, sat for a moment, then departed. Whenever someone new came in, officers surrounded him, whispering questions.

That afternoon, a white woman had been attacked outside Shantytown, where many freed negroes lived. When she heard the dreadful news, Eloise swooned and had to be revived with smelling salts. The Cyprians were desperate for details: Had the white woman been raped? Beaten? Killed?

In her bedroom, Belle was reading Mr. Dicken's *Bleak House* while her parlor stove glowed red and the wind rattled the stovepipe against its tin collar.

Belle was snug and happy when a ruckus erupted in the front of the house. Hastily, Belle threw on her pink robe and came into the parlor just as her callers were exiting onto the front porch and dooryard. A patrol was dismounting outside her gate.

"Did you arrest 'em, Bob?"

"Naw, but we kilt several. Huzzah!"

Belle pushed onto the porch. "What on earth is going on? Think of the neighbors! Come back inside! All of you!"

The officers ignored her. "How many'd you kill?"

"Dunno. They dragged 'em off."

"How many of our boys got hit?"

"Callahan and Schmidt. Schmidt was gut-shot."

"Captain Jaffery knows who they are and he's layin' for 'em. Captain Bateson's got patrols out. The bastards ain't slippin' away this time!"

Hot breath at Belle's ear. "Miss Belle, you got to come. You got to come right now." MacBeth's scar was pale against his dark skin.

Belle followed MacBeth through the house into the stableyard. The pungency of hard-ridden horses and the coppery stink of fresh blood made her ill.

"I got their horses in the stable," MacBeth whispered hoarsely. "I rub 'em down now."

"Wait, MacBeth!" Belle said, but MacBeth kept walking.

The stair rail to Rhett's office was blood-smeared, and Belle hiked her robe over spattered risers. When she pushed the office door open, frightened eyes turned to her.

Pittypat's brother, Henry Hamilton, dropped his head back into his hands. Hugh Elsing resumed whispering to old man Merriwether.

Dr. Meade was probing a wound in Ashley Wilkes's shoulder. White-lipped with pain, Melanie Wilkes's husband lay on the daybed while, kneeling beside him, Rhett dropped one bloody cloth into a bucket and patted the wound with a clean one.

Hugh Elsing hissed, "We wanted to teach the niggers to keep their black hands off our womenfolk."

Dr. Meade scrabbled through his bag for forceps. "Wilkes," the doctor said, "this will hurt like blazes. Do you want leather to bite? You mustn't cry out."

With a terse nod, Ashley refused.

The big elm tree's branches whisked the clapboard like a broom. Rhett looked up. "Sorry, Belle. I didn't know where else to bring them. The Yankees were on our heels."

"And you?" Belle asked. "Was you with 'em, Rhett?"

"Me? A Klansman?" He snorted. "I was playing stud tonight with two captains too drunk to keep their mouths shut. Seems they were keeping an eye on these gentlemen. Our brave Klansmen meant to ride through Shantytown shooting any negro too slow to get out of their way. The Yankees set a trap.

"I rode to warn them, but they were in the trap already." Rhett shrugged. "So I sprang it before the Yankees could. Mr. Colt's revolvers make a lovely racket. The Yankees thought I was a brigade!"

Ashley bucked under Dr. Meade's probe and Rhett used his whole strength to hold him down.

Hugh Elsing persisted, "The Fourteenth Amendment gives the vote to negroes and takes it from every man who saw Confederate service. We are beneath the conqueror's boot. . . ."

Rhett flared. "If it wasn't for your womenfolk, I'd let you all hang. What in pluperfect hell did you think you were doing?"

Belle's front door slammed and officers careened into the yard below the window, serenading. "Just before the battle, Mother . . ."

The room got so deathly still, the *plunk* of the bullet into the bucket made everyone jump. Rhett stifled Ashley's moan. Below, a Yankee stepped around the corner to pee and hummed as his water splashed the ground.

Belle touched Rhett's arm. "Mr. Wilkes . . . will he—"

"He'll live. Christ, what a mess! There are two dead men in the basement of the old Sullivan house. I stuffed their robes up the chimney. They called themselves 'The Wednesday-Night Democrats.' Clever, yes? Under that guise, they met to decide which uppity negro needed their attentions." His face was grim. "The fools could hang for this night's work."

Grandpa Merriwether's face was so red, Belle feared he'd burst a blood vessel. "Get us horses, Butler! We can pay. We'll run tonight. We'll run to Texas."

Belle couldn't forget how kind Mrs. Wilkes had been. She asked, "Couldn't you just say they were here?"

Rhett snorted. "Atlanta's fanciest gentlemen in a sporting house?"

"My girls . . . my Cyprians will swear they were here all night. They come upstairs—every Wednesday night, you said?—just a few girls. The Wednesday-Night Democrats are extremely discreet."

Rhett mulled her idea before breaking into the biggest grin Belle had ever seen on his face. He chuckled. "My, my, Miss Belle. What *will* people say?"

Dr. Meade peeked outside and drew the curtain.

Rhett gestured to the frightened, thoroughly subdued Wednesday-Night Democrats. "Atlanta's most respectable citizens, dear me. Dear, dear me. Belle, you're as clever as you are good." He cleared his throat. "Boys, I sure as hell hope you're good at charades."

After Dr. Meade bandaged Ashley's shoulder, Rhett fashioned a sling and draped the man in his cloak. Rhett patted raw whiskey on Ashley's pale cheeks.

Calm as General Lee issuing battle orders, Rhett spelled out everyone's roles in the performance. "Wilkes," Rhett said, "if we can't convince them, you're hung. The Yankees will be waiting at your house, so we must be very drunk, falling-down drunk. Elsing, can you play the drunken fool? I know you can play the sober one."

When Rhett splashed Ashley's shirt with whiskey, the reek overpowered the blood smell.

"Dr. Meade? Mr. Merriwether? You'll have starring roles!"

"What about me?" Henry Hamilton demanded.

Rhett thought for a minute before shaking his head. "Sorry, Henry, all our speaking parts are cast. You'll have to be stage manager."

Rhett and Hugh Elsing supported Ashley down the back stairs and out where MacBeth saddled their horses. The cold air revived Ashley and he mounted without assistance. In the saddle, he swayed for a perilous instant before he straightened to say, "Do or die trying."

After they rode away, Belle pressed a double eagle into her bouncer's hand. "MacBeth, you don't know nothin'."

MacBeth's eyes were old with understanding. "No, ma'am, I never knew that Miz Kennedy was skeered this afternoon and I never heard no Klansmen was gonna shoot up Shantytown and I never heard no Yankees was goin' to bushwhack 'em. Never heard nothin' about Captain Butler savin' the Kluxers. No, ma'am. I'ze just a dumb nigger. I don't know nothin'."

"You said . . . Mrs. Kennedy?"

"Miz Kennedy what owns the sawmills."

"Was she . . . hurt?"

"Naw, Miss Belle. Two thiefs grabbed at her, but that Tara nigger, Big Sam, he kilt one 'n' chased the other'n off. Skeered Miz Kennedy plumb to death."

"Just 'skeered'?"

"In Shantytown, one skeered white lady is a world of trouble."

Listening for Federal patrols, the three riders slipped through Atlanta's dark streets and alleyways. As they neared Ashley Wilkes's home, the night air seemed to thicken. Wind swirled dust at their horse's hooves.

"Sing, my thespians, sing! Make a joyful noise unto the Yankees!" Rhett leaned back and bellowed Sherman's hated marching song:

"How the darkies shouted when they heard the joyful sound,
How the turkeys gobbled which our commissary found,
How the sweet potatoes even started from the ground,
While we were marching through Georgia.

"Elsing! Damn it! Sing!"

Shouting and weeping Sherman's anthem, three drunks rollicked up to the house where Captain Tom Jaffery and his men were waiting to arrest Klansmen with blood on their hands.

At the Chateau Rouge, Belle directed Act Two.

Dr. Meade tried to refuse his role. "I'm to brawl in a . . . a sporting house? I've never *been* in a sporting house!"

"More's the pity. You're in one now. Might be you'd druther hang?"

When Meade patted too little whiskey on himself, Henry Hamilton doused him so thoroughly, Grandpa Merriwether pocketed his pipe. The thoroughly respectable Henry yanked their shirts out of their trousers, popped Grandpa Merriwether's top vest button, and tugged Dr. Meade's collar askew.

Hands on hips, Belle surveyed them. "Gents, you sure look the part. I spect you got hidden talents."

Shortly afterward, two of Atlanta's first citizens, apparently drunk as lords, tumbled into Belle's parlor, punching each other ineffectually. Belle yelled for MacBeth to fetch the provosts. Since some officers in the parlor were supposed to be searching for Klansman, this occasioned a general exodus as, getting into the spirit of things, Meade and Merriwether punched and slapped each other, shouting invective rarely heard in the Chapeau Rouge.

The provosts found two gentlemen rolling in Belle's flower bed. Their muffled threats and curses were indistinguishable from muffled laughter.

Protesting that hers was an orderly house, Belle wrung her hands as the provosts separated the combatants and arrested them. From the corner of her mouth, Belle told MacBeth, "You don't know nothin'."

"I'ze an ignorant nigger," MacBeth assured her.

Two hours after the provosts left, Archie Flytte brought a buggy around the back of the Chapeau Rouge with the bodies he'd collected from the Sullivan house.

"Rhett fooled the Yankees?" Belle asked anxiously.

Archie spat.

Belle was weak-kneed with relief. "Mrs. Wilkes's husband . . . he's safe?"

"I reckon."

Belle eyed him curiously. "You don't like Captain Butler, do you?"

"Used to be beholden to Butler. I work for Mrs. Wilkes now."

MacBeth and Archie laid out two dead men in the vacant lot behind the Chapeau Rouge. Archie placed a recently fired pistol beside each man's cold right hand and doused their uncaring faces with whiskey. He asked MacBeth, "Nigger, you scared of the Klan?"

"Oh yes, sir," MacBeth replied. "I mighty scared."

"Don't got to be scared of these two." Archie nudged a corpse with his foot. "They's 'gentlemen.' "

He tucked the empty bottle into a dead man's armpit.

The *Atlanta Journal* reported that two Atlanta gentlemen had gotten drunk, quarreled, and shot each other. The city was shocked and fascinated.

Belle and her Cyprians were summoned to Federal headquarters, where they swore on the holy Bible that the suspected Klansmen, Ashley Wilkes, Hugh Elsing, Henry Hamilton, Dr. Meade, and Grandfather Merriwether, had been in the Chapeau Rouge on the night in question, carousing with the notorious Captain Butler, as was their Wednesday-night custom. The group called themselves the Wednesday-Night Democrats to deceive their wives. "They raise hell at my joint, and they're cheapskates to boot," Belle wailed.

The Yankee officers couldn't keep grins off their faces. The Atlantans who'd snubbed them and their wives had been dramatically and publicly brought low.

Afterward, when the Yankee officers' wives smiled condescendingly to the wives of the Wednesday-Night Democrats, those proud Southern women would gladly have seen Rhett Butler hung.

Rhett Butler had rewritten the story. He'd transformed Frank Kennedy from a Klansman killed during a Shantytown raid to a quarrelsome drunk who died in a stupid fight in a vacant lot behind a brothel. For Frank's funeral, Rhett Butler dressed in a dark blue London suit and carried a rakish malacca cane.

"Do you got to go?" Belle asked listlessly.

"Not go? Not go, my dear? Aren't I the scoundrel who foiled the wicked Yankees while making Atlanta's best citizens look like hypocrites? Of course I'm going. I intend to crow."

"Miss Scarlett will be there?"

"Where else would you expect Frank's grieving widow to be?"

Rhett had a red rose in his lapel. Belle wondered where he'd gotten it. Her roses were still in bud.

"Rhett, you're not going to . . . Not . . . again?"

He kissed her forehead. As a brother might.

The funeral was at three that afternoon and Rhett didn't come back to Chapeau Rouge afterward. That evening, Belle sat at her dressing table, staring at the silly, vulgar woman looking back at her. A lady? What the hell had she been thinking?

Minette stuck her head in. "Miss Belle, *chère*. It is payday. . . ."

"Yeah," Belle said. She unfastened her blue faille dress and let it fall to the floor. She plucked the cameo ear bobs from her ears and dropped them in a little velvet bag. She pinched color into her cheeks, and with her carmine lip rouge, she slashed a whore's mouth over her own.

Chapter Thirty-Four

Some Damn Mistake

Rhett was in England when MacBeth asked Belle if he could store some old furniture in Rhett's office.

Belle frowned. "No, you can't. Captain Butler will want his office when he comes back."

MacBeth said, "No'm. Captain Butler ain't comin' back here. He be with Miz Kennedy when he come back."

"You're a damn fool. He gave up on her years ago."

MacBeth said, "Uh-huh."

Belle got a strange note from Taz.

Dear Maman,

I am so happy for you—and for myself, of course. Captain Butler has invited me to celebrate at the Brooks Club with his English friends!

Your loving son, Tazewell

This puzzling message was followed by silence: no explanation and no further letters.

"Must be some damn mistake." Belle was whistling in the dark.

Yankees, Carpetbaggers, and ex-Confederates kept a polite truce within the Chapeau Rouge, but those same gentlemen who used one another's Christian names in Belle's parlor led Yankee patrols or rode with the Klansmen those patrols were pursuing.

In December, Rufus Bullock gave the keynote address at the "Black and Tan" constitutional convention. The convention, which included thirty-seven negro delegates, rewrote Georgia's constitution. For the first time, women could own property in their own name and negro males could vote. Georgia's newspapers mocked the delegates, their abilities, speech, and manners.

"Uppity" negroes and white Republicans felt the lash of the Klan's displeasure. Only Klansman and Yankee patrols rode by night.

The day after Christmas, Belle received a letter from Rhett—the first he'd ever written her. She took it into her bedroom, sat, and poured a large brandy before opening it.

Dear Belle,

I can't say I'm easy or comfortable writing, but it's best you get the news from me. Taz is in New Orleans. The boy is well—so far as I know—but he's mad as a wet hen. I guess I can't blame him.

The letter rattled in Belle's hands. Taz, in New Orleans?

Rob Campbell, my banker, is a Scot who was a junior partner when we met but now heads his firm. I trust him, and when I decided to curtail Taz's military career, I wrote Rob for help.

When Taz landed in England, he was taken to Rob's London office. Taz was still wearing his Confederate uniform. Rob asked, "Whatever shall we do with you, young man?"

"Why, sir, should you do anything?"

"Because my friend Rhett Butler has asked me to look after you."

"I thank you for your concern, sir, but I would not be more obligated to Mr. Butler than I already am."

Rob's tailor measured the boy for new clothes, but instead of waiting for them, he sent Taz off to Shrewsbury. Rob's a Shrewsbury "Old Boy."

Did I say Rob was clever? Taz arrived at that school in his tattered gray uniform, which did more for his acceptance than a peerage might have.

Hell, sons of peers were a dime a dozen at Shrewsbury. But no other boy had soldiered in a war.

About this time, Federal officials appeared at Rob's bank with impudent questions about my accounts. I'd forewarned Rob and he was ready for them.

I came to London, where Rob was stonewalling the Federals. Though there was smoke aplenty, Rob convinced me there wasn't too much fire.

When I telegraphed his Headmaster, that gentleman said Taz didn't wish to see me. I might have forced the issue but didn't want to upset the boy more than he already was. The Headmaster assured me Taz had made a promising start, particularly in mathematics and French. He speaks Creole, but the mathematics surprised me.

Fortunately, Rob Campbell had taken a liking to your son.

Belle whispered, "Course he did. Who wouldn't love my Taz?"

At the end of that first term, Rob invited Tazewell to spend his holidays with the Campbells.

Rob's got a fine plump wife and two daughters, shy Claire and Amanda, who will be a real head turner when she grows up. Anyway, the Campbells' home became Taz's. I suspect Rob hoped he and Claire might form an attachment one day. I know Rob intended to offer your son a place at his firm after he completed school.

I got regular reports from Rob but heard nothing from Tazewell himself. Although I would have preferred a friendlier relationship, I am not unaccustomed to the villain's role so long as your son needed me in it.

Taz is in New Orleans because of me. It's my doing, my mistake, and I wish it hadn't happened, but I can't hold the boy's hand until he grows up. I had business with Rob Campbell, and afterward, we strolled over to Burlington Arcade to visit London's fancy jewelers. Since Sutliff's makes tiaras for the Queen, I figured they'd be good enough for Scarlett. Poor Rob was aghast when I bought the biggest, gaudiest engagement ring he'd ever seen. He swallowed his sense of proprieties, offered congratulations, and suggested a celebration at his club three days hence.

I telegraphed Shrewsbury to invite Taz down to London for the party, and that's where I slipped up. Either my telegram was ambiguous or the Headmaster misinformed him. Anyway, dear Belle, somehow Taz got it in his head I was going to marry you!

Belle put the letter down, downed her drink, and said to nobody in particular, "Rhett Butler and Belle Watling? Married? Jesus Loving Christ!"

Brooks is a stuffy London Club and Rob's guests were dusty financial types, but Belle, you would have been proud of your son. I was glad to see him, presumed he'd forgiven me, and we spun yarns about Fort Fisher, playing off each other like Tambo and Mr. Bones. When I said, "Your corporal said you made a better soldier than I did," everyone laughed.

Once we were seated, with waiters standing by, Rob rose to offer his toast, but Tazewell interrupted. "Excuse me, sirs. Mr. Campbell, Mr. Butler, honored guests . . . before festivities begin, I have a confession to make."

Belle, your boy nearly broke my heart. He made a heartfelt speech about all I'd done for him, his eternal gratitude. He mentioned my kindness, generosity, and—Lord help us—my wisdom.

These fathers and grandfathers were all for filial gratitude and heartily applauded Taz's sentiments.

Then Rob lifted his glass, "To my friend Captain Rhett Butler and his betrothed, Mrs. Scarlett Kennedy."

The color left Taz's face and I thought he was going to faint. Too late, I understood that Taz had thought I was marrying you, and now felt like the greatest fool on the face of the earth.

If grown men dread humiliation, young men die rather than endure it. I've known young fools who jumped horses over five-foot spiked fences for a two-dollar wager.

Tazewell set his glass down untouched and ran from Brooks.

I followed but lost him in the damn fog.

When Tazewell didn't return to Shrewsbury, I hired a detective, who learned that your son had booked passage for New Orleans.

So Taz is back where he started from, sadder, I am sure. I pray he is wiser.

I'm sorry, Belle. I wouldn't have had this happen for the world.

Yours always, Rhett

On New Year's Eve, Belle Watling put on her prettiest dress and took a bottle of champagne and her account books to Rhett Butler's office. That year, Belle drank alone.

Chapter Thirty-five

The Quadroon Ball

That spring, Republican Rufus Bullock defeated ex-Confederate General George Gordon for Governor. For the first time in history, there would be negroes in the Georgia legislature.

Atlanta's grande dames saw the betrothal of the Widow Kennedy to Rhett Butler—Dark Prince of War Profiteers—as one more sign of moral decay. The grande dames vowed they would *never* forgive Butler for his shoddy trick. The Wednesday-Night Democrats' wives had received the Yankee ladies' *understanding* smiles: "Boys will be boys, won't they, dear?" Each smile had felt like a blow.

Mrs. Merriwether admired Scarlett's ring too extravagantly: "My dear! I don't think I've ever seen such an enormous stone!" Mrs. Meade recalled Frank Kennedy too fondly. "Why, it's so *hard* to believe poor dear Frank is gone."

Aunt Eulalie penned "the most difficult letter of my life," begging Scarlett to cancel her nuptials. "Please don't disgrace the Robillards again," she pleaded.

Scarlett wanted a lavish wedding, but Rhett thought better of it. "Why give the old biddies the satisfaction of spurning our invitations?" he said.

In a small ceremony, Rhett and Scarlett became Mr. and Mrs. Butler and afterward took sherry with a few guests in the rectory. Melanie Wilkes admired Rosemary Ravanel's toddler. "Cherish these years," Melanie advised. "They fly away too soon."

The kindness in Melanie's face touched Rosemary's heart. "My daughter, Meg, was killed in the war, but I pray for her every single night. How silly I am! Praying for a child already in heaven."

"You're not silly at all," Melanie replied. "Your Meg knows you love her. Can't you feel her watching over you? Here, take my handkerchief. Your Louis is such a *sweet* little boy."

Thus, Rosemary Ravanel and Melanie Wilkes became friends.

Rhett had leased one of Mr. Pullman's newfangled sleeping cars to convey the newlyweds to New Orleans. When the wedding party arrived at the train station, half of Atlanta was gawking at the marvel: a private parlor car that transformed itself into a rolling bedroom. What was the world coming to?

Rhett pretended they'd come to honor the bride and groom. "Good afternoon, Mrs. Merriwether. So good of you to come. I regret we couldn't invite our friends to our wedding, but Scarlett—you know how shy she is—Scarlett insisted on a private affair. Ah, Mrs. Elsing! How kind you are to see us off. How is my good friend Hugh?" He winked. "Haven't Hugh and I had ourselves some wild times!"

As offended ladies withdrew, Scarlett suppressed her giggles.

On that triumphant note, on a beautiful May afternoon, Rhett and Scarlett Butler boarded a railroad car paneled in Philippine mahogany and green velvet. The rose petals in the crystal sconces glistened with moisture, the tablecloth was damask, the Sillery perfectly chilled.

When Rhett raised his glass to his bride, Scarlett announced, "I never said I loved you, you know."

Rhett's glass hesitated. "You pick this moment to remind me? Scarlett, what incredible timing!"

"I'm the only woman you know who'll tell you the truth. You've often told me I am."

Rhett shook his head ruefully. "Yes, honey, I suppose I did. Sometimes I say the goddamnedest things."

As dusk settled on the piedmont, their porter lit lanterns, drew the curtains, turned down their bed, and closed the door behind him.

"Tara is just beyond those hills," Scarlett mused. "When I was a young girl, how could I have imagined . . ."

The backs of Rhett Butler's hands were furred with the softest curly hair. Except for the creases across his knuckles where the flesh was as white as hers, Rhett's fingers were tanned. His strong fingers could untie a bow or unhook a stay as delicately as if a cat had brushed Scarlett's shivering skin.

In the morning, as their train rushed through the Alabama countryside at a breathtaking clip, the porter brought steaming-hot water for Scarlett's hip bath.

Rhett Butler sat in an armchair, smoking a cigar.

"What are you looking at?" Scarlett tried to cover her breasts with a washcloth.

Rhett laughed until Scarlett started laughing, too, and the washcloth fell away.

They had their first quarrel soon after they got to New Orleans. "Why can't we move to the St. Charles?" Scarlett demanded. "This"—she dismissed their luxurious suite—"is the *Creole* hotel."

"Yes, dearest." Rhett pressed studs into his cuffs. "Which is why we are here. The St. Charles caters to Americans. Americans are great engineers, moneymakers, and moralizers, but they don't know how to eat. If you don't know how to eat, you cannot know how to make love."

"Rhett!"

He grinned at his bride. "I've rather enjoyed our marital relations."

"That doesn't mean we need to talk about them."

"When food and love are forbidden topics, conversation descends to politics." As an orator might, Rhett set his left hand in the small of his back. "Tell me, Mrs. Butler, will Georgia ever be free of Carpetbagger rule? Is Governor Bullock's concern for the negro a ruse to get their votes?"

When he ducked, Scarlett's shoe clattered against the shutters behind him.

That night, the lobby was thronged with well-dressed European travelers and wealthy Creoles. When Rhett asked the doorman to summon a cab, Scarlett said, "Rhett, I didn't know you spoke French."

"Creole isn't exactly *French,* honey. Parisians can't make head or tails of it."

The doorman drew himself up to his full five foot two. "Monsieur, that is because our French is ancient and pure. The Parisian French have bastardized a beautiful language."

Rhett's inclined his head. *"Sans doute, monsieur."*

Every morning, disdaining the hotel waiters, Rhett went to the kitchen to fetch Scarlett's breakfast tray. Scarlett's day began with caresses and beignets and the bitterest, blackest coffee she'd ever tasted.

"My dear, you have jam at the corner of your mouth."

"Lick it off."

They never left the hotel before noon.

Rhett knew every shop in the city and fashionable dressmakers greeted him with a kiss on the cheek and news of old acquaintances. "English, please." Rhett smiled. "My wife is a Georgia lady."

The new high waistlines flattered Scarlett's neck and bodice and she bought so many gowns, Rhett had them packed in steamer trunks and shipped home. They bought a Saint Bernard puppy for Wade and a coral bracelet for little Ella. Though Scarlett said she'd never wear it, Rhett bought a shimmering red petticoat for Mammy.

One languorous, sensual day blurred into another. Scarlett hadn't been flattered so shamelessly since she was a maiden. Despite her wedded state, more than one Creole gentlemen made it clear he would gladly have taken matters beyond admiration. Rhett took no offense at the flirtations but never left her alone with another man.

New Orleans winked at behavior that would have set Atlanta tongues wagging. Scarlett could get tipsy. She could play chemin de fer. She could flirt so outrageously, Atlanta biddies would have thought it adulterous.

At Sunday Mass in St. Louis cathedral, Rhett leaned over to whisper a joke so crude, it set her choking and coughing. Rhett joked when he should have been solemn, was solemn when he should have jeered. He was delighted by Louisiana's Carpetbagger legislature, praising its every folly, reveling in its corruption, as if madness were the natural state of affairs.

Scarlett adored Creole cooking. Lunching at Antoine's one afternoon, when Scarlett speared the last mussel from Rhett's plate he grinned. "If you grow round and fat, I shall take a Creole mistress."

Scarlett looked for the waiter. "Let's order more crawfish."

Rhett reached across the table, took her left hand, and with his thumb caressed the tender web between Scarlett's thumb and forefinger.

Hoarsely, Scarlett said, "I don't want any more. Quick, Rhett. Let's go back to the hotel."

One afternoon, Rhett hired a vis-à-vis to drive them along the levee, where Mississippi River paddle wheelers were exchanging cargoes with deep-water ships. Since the Federals captured New Orleans early in the War, the city hadn't been bombarded and became the South's busiest port. The stevedores were immigrant Irish, glad to have twelve hours' work for fifty cents. They lived in shantytowns behind the levee with worn-out wives and too many squalling, dirty children. Startled to hear her father Gerald's familiar accent, Scarlett gripped Rhett's arm.

"What is it, sweetheart?"

"Promise me, Rhett. Oh, promise me I'll never be poor again."

Per New Orleans custom, they dined late and afterward attended balls—public and private, costume and masked. Or they gambled at the Boston Club (named from the popular card game, not the Yankee city). After Scarlett understood bezique, she won more than she lost.

One night during a memorable run of luck, Rhett insisted they leave immediately.

Scarlett nursed her anger until they were in their cab. "I was having fun! I was winning! You don't want me to have my own money!"

"My dear, money means much more to you than it does to me."

"You want to own me!"

"Money means even more to the gentlemen whose pockets you were emptying. I know those particular gentlemen. I've known them for years."

Scarlett tossed her head. "Why should I give a darn about them?"

"You needn't, but I must. Since they cannot possibly seek satisfaction from a lady, they must challenge her escort. The levee is damp at daybreak, and I'd hate to catch a chill."

Several evenings, Rhett went out on business, leaving Scarlett in the hotel to try on her purchases.

One tiny cloud drifted across Scarlett's happiness. The young man was dressed soberly, more like senior clerk than a man about town. He was usually in the lobby when they passed through, leaning against a pillar with his arms crossed or sitting in a club chair reading a newspaper. He chatted familiarly with the doorman.

He watched them come into the St. Louis and watched them go out. He frequented the same restaurants.

"Who is that boy?" Scarlett whispered. "He was at the Boston Club last night. Why is he interested in us?"

"You needn't worry yourself, dear," Rhett replied. "He fancies he has a grievance with me."

"What grievance? Who is he?"

"How kind you are to worry about me," Rhett said. "Really, you needn't."

"Worry about you?" Scarlett sniffed. "Don't be silly. You can take care of yourself."

Still, the young man was a cloud.

Those profiting under the Reconstruction government were building homes in what, not long ago, had been truck gardens outside the city. This "Garden District" was growing so rapidly that fine new mansions were fronted by streets where municipal horsecars sank to their hubs in mud. Unfinished mansions were surrounded by stacks of raw lumber (which Scarlett thought compared poorly with Georgia pine). Evenings were punctuated by carpenters' hammers tapping away like woodpeckers until it was too dark to see.

Captain Butler and his beautiful bride were invited to fêtes where cotton factors and riverboat owners mingled with hard-faced men whose easy laughter never reached their eyes. Although they were expensively dressed, their lapels were too wide and their trousers too tight. They favored bright parrot colors. These men spoke of Cuba and Nicaragua as casually as if they'd just come from there and might go back tomorrow. Their women were too young, too pretty, too fashionably dressed, and didn't try to conceal their boredom.

The hard men were more courteous to Rhett than to one another.

"How do they know you?"

"From time to time, I've put a little business their way."

In a Touro Street mansion, a house so new Scarlett could smell the wallpaper paste, an old woman introduced herself. "I am Toinette Sevier." Her smile was charmingly insincere. "Sevier is my maiden name. I prefer to forget my husbands. You are a Robillard, I believe. You favor your mother."

Scarlett felt like someone had stepped on her grave.

Toinette Sevier's skin was age-spotted and her pink scalp gleamed through thinning white hair. Her jeweled rings, bracelets, and necklace proved she'd once been a desirable woman.

"Ellen and I were Savannah belles too many years ago. I did know Ellen's beau, Philippe, rather better than I knew your mother."

Philippe! A name Scarlett had banished to the furthest corner of her memory. On her deathbed, Scarlett's mother's final plea had been for "Philippe!"

A servant replaced Toinette's glass with another. Her smile was reminiscent. "Philippe was a flame that grows hotter and brighter, until it consumes everything—or should I say everyone—it touches."

Scarlett didn't want to hear another word. Ellen O'Hara had been the finest lady, the most perfect mother. . . . Scarlett drew herself up to reply, "My mother never spoke of the man."

"She wouldn't." The woman's old eyes had seen everything. "There are Catholics and Catholics, my dear, and Ellen Robillard was a penitential one."

In New Orleans, Scarlett was happy—almost too happy. She did miss her sawmills: the buying and selling, the satisfaction of besting shrewd businessmen. And she missed Ashley. She missed his face, the now-too-rare spark in his tired, dear brown eyes. Ashley Wilkes was Tara and Twelve Oaks and everything Scarlett had ever desired! In this mood, with Ashley on her mind, she couldn't remember why she'd married Rhett Butler.

Scarlett resented Rhett's power. His embrace overwhelmed her resistance; his kisses won his way with her. Scarlett just *knew* Rhett wanted her to become someone less than she was: a devoted wife who was as good as she was stupid. In this half-bored, half-resentful mood, Scarlett went through Rhett's portfolio one morning while he was fetching her breakfast.

Some of Rhett's papers were in Spanish and bore elaborate wax seals. She found bills of lading—one for "two trunks, by rail to the National Hotel, Atlanta. HANDLE WITH CARE!"; one for Wade's Saint Bernard puppy: "Special Handling! Express car!" She found a bill from Peake and Bennett, London tailors, a letter of credit from the Banque de New Orleans in an amount that pleasantly surprised her, and a ticket for a ball, two nights hence, at the Honeysuckle Ballroom.

One ticket. Not two.

Of course Rhett had been with other women. He'd made no secret of that. But Scarlett had assumed that now they were married, she would satisfy him. The "business" Rhett went out for at night—what sort of "business" was transacted between midnight and dawn? Scarlett's ears burned. She'd been a fool!

When Rhett brought her breakfast, Scarlett was in her petticoat before the pier glass. "Look how fat I am," she announced.

When he put his arms around her, she stiffened. "I won't eat anything, ever again, no matter how hungry I get. Oh Rhett, I remember when a man could put both hands around my waist and touch his fingertips." When Rhett's fingertips failed to meet by three inches, Scarlett burst into tears.

That afternoon, Rhett went out again on his mysterious "business." Scarlett went to the lobby, where the watchful young man nodded politely. The doorman was loading a Yankee family into a cab when their little boy kicked his shin. "The young monsieur is certainly a lively boy! Yes, madame, he is certainly lively."

The doorman pocketed his five-cent tip, massaged his ankle, and turned to Scarlett. "Yes, madame? Artaud is at your service."

"I wish a ticket for the Honeysuckle Ballroom."

The doorman smiled like someone who hears a joke he doesn't understand. "Madame?"

"The Honeysuckle Ballroom? Surely you've heard of it."

Artaud cautiously admitted he might have heard of that establishment. It was on Bourbon Street, or was it Beaubein?

Scarlett offered a banknote. "The ticket is ten dollars, I believe."

The doorman put his hands behind his back, "*Je suis désolé, madame. Désolé!* I cannot help you."

The watchful young man paused in the doorway, "*Pardon, madame.* White ladies are not welcome at the Quadroon Ball." The young man strolled away, whistling.

"What, pray, is a 'Quadroon Ball'?"

The doorman produced a pained smile. "I cannot know, madame, and if I could know, I could not say. Forgive me, madame. . . ." He turned to an elderly French lady who wished to know which church had an eleven o'clock Mass.

In the Boston Club that evening, Toinette Sevier was accompanied by a good-looking Creole half her age.

"Excuse me, madame . . ."

"Ah, Mrs. Butler. I understand you fancy bezique?"

Scarlett didn't want chitchat, "Madame Sevier," she asked, "are you respectable?"

The old woman chuckled, "My dear, old age makes all of us respectable. I am far more respectable than I ever wished to be. Henri, be a dear and fetch me some champagne."

"Then you don't know about the Quadroon Ball."

She clapped her wrinkled hands in glee. "On the contrary, Mrs. Butler. Every lady knows about the Quadroon Ball, but she'd risk her reputation admitting it."

"Will you risk your reputation?"

"My dear. My reputation has been blacked more thoroughly than an old boot. What do you wish to know?"

"Why can't I buy a ticket?"

"Because Quadroon Balls are for white gentlemen and quadroon girls seeking connections with them. Neither negro men nor white ladies may attend. A few daring white women have slipped in—it is a masked ball—hoping to catch their husbands *en flagrante.* When they were discovered, the city buzzed about it for weeks. Delicious scandals. Absolutely delicious."

Rhett was out when the porter delivered an envelope to their room. The envelope was of good quality and on it, in a slanting hand, someone had written, "Compliments of a friend." Scarlett found a ticket for the Honeysuckle Ballroom inside.

When Rhett returned, he eyed Scarlett quizzically. "What are you up to, my little sparrow hawk? You were grouchy this morning. Now butter wouldn't melt in your mouth."

"Oh Rhett, I'm not feeling well. I can't go out tonight."

Rhett eyed her skeptically. "I wouldn't want you to waste away. I'll fetch something from Antoine's."

Scarlett was in bed with the shutters closed and a cold cloth on her forehead when Rhett returned with her favorite delicacies: clams swimming in butter, delicately crusted prawns, a langoustine opened like a pink-and-white flower.

"Oh," she said. "I couldn't eat a thing. Here." She patted the bed. "Sit beside me."

Men are such deceivers! Rhett seemed almost . . . concerned. He touched her forehead. "May's too early for the fevers. Shall I fetch a doctor?"

"No, my darling husband. You're the only medicine I need."

He shook his head. "Then I'm sorry to disappoint you. I must go out for a few hours."

"Where are you going, darling?" Her voice was light and unconcerned.

"Nowhere you need to worry about, my poor darling. Some business I must attend to." Rhett leaned closer, his eyes glowing. "What do you have on your mind, my dear? Are you thinking again? Your angelic countenance betrays you."

"Can't I go with you?"

He laughed. "No, my dear, you certainly cannot. Anyway, as I seem to recall, you aren't feeling well."

He donned the frock coat the tailor had delivered yesterday and the silk foulard he'd worn at their wedding. Rhett bent to kiss her forehead. "Try to eat something," he said, and closed the door softly behind him.

She plundered her wardrobe, dropping rejected gowns on the floor. Yes, her blue taffeta—Rhett'd never seen her in it. And that new black mantilla! She lay flat on the bed, cinching her corset until she gasped. She braided her hair into coils tucked under her blue velvet hat. Her sequined half mask concealed everything but her eyes.

Carriages deposited gentlemen outside the Honeysuckle Ballroom and slipped around the corner into Bienville Street. The negro doorman was dressed as a Zouave in baggy red pants, a short blue jacket, a broad red sash, and a Turkish fez, which perched atop his huge skull like the turret of an ironclad.

"Bonsoir, madame. Comment allez-vous?"

He hesitated before accepting Scarlett's ticket. *"Et la Maman de vous, mamselle?"* He peered closely at her. "Mamselle, are you lost? Have you perhaps arrived at the wrong address?"

The watchful young man appeared and took Scarlett's arm. "I see you got my ticket." Scarlett's escort made a joke in rapid-fire Creole and the doorman laughed and bowed them inside.

As they ascended a broad carpeted staircase, Scarlett asked, "What did you tell him?"

"A crude joke. At your expense, I'm afraid."

"How dare you!"

They paused on the mezzanine before white doors. "Mrs. Butler, you wish to attend the Quadroon Ball?"

"I do, but . . ."

"Well then, madame. . . ." The young man opened the doors for her.

The Honeysuckle Ballroom had high ceilings with intricate plaster cornices, white-and-gold wainscoting, and furniture in the Empire style. Tall windows opened onto a wrought-iron balcony where gentlemen could smoke. Refreshment tables lined one end of the hall.

Across the room, Rhett was deep in conversation with a middle-aged mulatto woman wearing a dark brown dress with a Baptist bodice and neckline.

Scarlett's escort disappeared.

Scarlett had expected something wicked, perhaps even *le cancan*. Alas, this ball was no different from respectable balls, except the ball managers were negro matrons.

White men and young women danced and exchanged pleasantries. The cushioned chairs on both sides of the balcony were reserved for the girls' watchful chaperones. The girls were light-skinned and well mannered.

The orchestra struck up "The Blue Danube," Mr. Strauss's popular new waltz.

"*Mamselle, si vous plais?*"

The gentleman bowing to Scarlett was younger than she and prematurely bald. "English, please," she said.

On the dance floor, Scarlett was whirled back into her carefree girlhood. Marriage could go hang, and Rhett Butler, too! She would enjoy herself tonight—if only her partner were a better dancer. He moved stiffly and was half a beat behind the measure, and he would keep apologizing! "*Pardon, mamselle.* You said English, did you not? I am so sorry!"

At last, the Blue Danube rolled to the sea; her partner bowed, wiped his forehead, and cleared his throat. With his eyes fixed somewhere over Scarlett's left shoulder, he enumerated assets: his new house on Canal Street, his half interest in a warehouse near the Morgan railroad depot, five percent of the Banque du New Orleans and 10 percent of a six-hundred-ton sidewheeler. "And"—he blushed furiously—"I am faithful!"

"Sir? Why are you telling me this?"

"Mamselle. I am considering you. I hope you will do me the honor of considering me." He wiped his sweaty face. "Please to do me the honor of introducing me to your mother?"

"Sir, my mother is with the angels."

"Your aunt, then, your cousin . . ."

"I cannot think Aunt Eulalie would approve of you, sir."

When the orchestra struck up again, Rhett swept her onto the floor. Awkwardness was banished. The air seemed to shimmer.

"Mamselle," he said, "how well you dance."

"As you, sir. Have you taken lessons?"

Rhett flashed a dazzling grin. "Forgive me if I interrupted delicate negotiations between you and that gentleman. . . ."

"Sir?"

"I will top any offer he has made."

"He owns ten percent of a steamboat, sir."

"I own fifty percent of six steamboats."

"The gentleman has five percent of a bank."

"I own two banks outright and am partner in a third."

"Ah, but sir. The young man says he is faithful."

"You believe I am not?"

"Sir, you mustn't read my mind."

Rhett whirled her. "In any marriage, at least one must be faithful. Are you faithful, madame?"

The mulatto woman in the brown dress interrupted their waltz. *"Qui êtes-vous?"* she snapped. "What is your name?"

Rhett answered for her. "Madame Gayerre, may I present my wife, Madame Butler."

"This is a respectable ball," the furious woman said. "Not a farce."

"We'll leave quietly, madame. There need be no scandal."

She huffed but withdrew.

Rhett's authority was as delicious as it was hateful. At the door, Scarlett paused. "Which young girl was the 'business' you spoke about?"

Rhett nodded to a girl sitting alone—as proud and resigned as an Aztec sacrifice. "Madame Gayerre needed my advice about her niece Solange's future. I've known the Gayerres for years."

From the balcony, the watchful young man raised a glass to Rhett and Scarlett.

"Ah," Rhett said, "so Tazewell was behind this nonsense."

The Zouave doorman summoned them a cab.

Rhett set his hat on the seat. "Quadroon girls come to be attached to white gentlemen: a *placege*. Their mothers negotiate the little house he must buy for her, the amount to be deposited in her account, the bonus for a child.

"Solange had two suitors, an elderly gentleman who is unlikely to make many demands and that fellow you were dancing with. I advised her to accept the elderly gentleman."

"So the disappointed suitor was pursuing me."

Rhett laughed, "My dear, you could do worse than ten percent of a steamboat."

In their suite, the fully dressed Rhett Butler watched as Scarlett slowly removed her blue hat, her ball dress, her stockings, and her chemise. She loosed her hair.

"My God," Rhett said hoarsely.

Savoring her power, tingling from the top of her head to her toes, Scarlett did not remove her mask.

Chapter Thirty-six

A House for Monsieur Watling

Three days after he landed in New Orleans, Tazewell Watling was employed by the cotton factor, J. Nicolet et Fils. Nicolet's sixteen-year-old-son, François, had died of yellow fever, and Nicolet was moving his wife and daughters to Baton Rouge's healthier climate. When Taz arrived in the city, Nicolet's wife and daughters were already installed in their new home, but Nicolet himself hadn't left New Orleans.

J. Nicolet had long needed an assistant, and since he would now be in Baton Rouge much of the time, this need had become acute, but the prospect of hiring someone for the position his son would naturally have assumed had depressed him into immobility.

The morning Nicolet's belated advertisement finally appeared in the *Picayune,* Nicolet climbed the stairs to his dusty office over the Gravier Street warehouse. Tazewell Watling was waiting for him.

Tazewell held Nicolet's newspaper and beignet while Nicolet fumbled for his keys. Inside the office, Nicolet waved Taz to his visitor's chair and settled himself behind a desk whose surface was buried beneath cargo manifests, shipping news, and cotton reports.

"I am responding to your advertisement, monsieur," the young man said.

Nicolet had placed his advertisement hurriedly, so he couldn't change his mind. "I did not expect anyone so soon."

"The *Picayune* can be got at its offices at six A.M.," the young man said.

"I see."

"Is something wrong, monsieur?" the young man asked.

Nicolet blinked rapidly. Of course there was something wrong. This young man was not beloved François. He said, "No, nothing. As I intend to be out of the city often, I require a reliable assistant. Reliable!" Nicolet grumbled. "Most young men are not reliable; they loaf and smoke cigars, play cards!"

"I do not play cards, monsieur."

"My business is not big enough to pay the excessive salary young men demand."

"My requirements are modest."

"Cotton factoring is a complex business that takes years to understand."

"I make no promises I may not be able to keep, monsieur. I promise that I will *try*."

Nicolet unfolded his newspaper and glanced at the dark lines of type without reading. He set his beignet on the newspaper. Every morning, he ate his beignet while reading the shipping news. "Diderot's Bakery makes the best beignets in the city."

"Oui, monsieur."

As they continued this disjointed interview, Nicolet was mollified by Taz's idiomatic Creole and Jesuit education. Like most Catholics, Nicolet overestimated the rigors and effect of Jesuit training. "Your family, young Watling? They live in New Orleans?"

"My parentage is . . . irregular," Taz said.

"I see." Nicolet removed his glasses, breathed on them, and wiped them, with his handkerchief. New Orleans' commerce was intensely personal and he wanted a young man with connections. His François had had connections. The same week he fell ill, François had been invited to join Comus, the prestigious Mardi Gras society. Everyone had loved François. Everyone!

"Monsieur, if I am distressing you . . ."

Nicolet waved that away. The cotton factor was wise enough—and in enough pain—to know that he could not bear to interview a second young man, who would no more be François than this one. "Watling, you are not the first bastard I have known. Because of the good Jesuit fathers"—Nicolet managed a smile—"I will employ you. I can afford seven dollars a week."

In the next hectic weeks, J. Nicolet taught Taz how to combine cotton shipments from the Creole planters into cargoes for the Liverpool commission men. Taz learned to distinguish between long and short staple, middling and lesser grades of cotton, and J. Nicolet showed him the tricks scoundrels used to pass off inferior, dirty, or ill-ginned cotton as better than it was.

Every morning, Taz was at J. Nicolet's office before his employer and he left after J. Nicolet quit for the day. In the warehouses and on the levees, he dogged J. Nicolet's heels with so many questions his amiable employer complained, "*Ca qui prend zasocie prend maite*" (the man who hires an employee, takes a master). J. Nicolet wondered if, despite Taz's Jesuit education, the young man wasn't too *American.*

Taz had a room in a boardinghouse whose hallways reeked of lye soap and boiled cabbage.

When Taz finally wrote Belle, he exaggerated his prospects. About his escape from England, Taz wrote only, "Maman, it was time I made my own way in the world."

Belle replied promptly:

Darling Boy,

I was so glad to get your letter! I was worried about you! I am happy you are in New Orleans with such a grand position.

The Chapeau Rouge is booming. Carpetbaggers and Yankee officers are rolling in money. Minette begs to be remembered to you. Taz, will you please send her three pounds of New Orleans coffee?

My Darling Boy, how could you have thought Rhett Butler would marry a woman like your old Ma?

Rhett has always loved Scarlett O'Hara. Rhett loved her when she was married to Frank Kennedy! I pray for Rhett's sake their marriage will be lucky.

Taz crumpled Belle's letter. How dare Rhett Butler not love his mother. How dare he!

Jules Nore, who'd explained Taz's bastardy at the Jesuit School and had his nose bloodied for his trouble, was now employed by the Olympic Steamship Company. Jules and Taz resumed their acquaintance.

The two young men happened to be in the Boston Club when the honeymooning Butlers made their appearance.

A hush fell. All eyes turned to the couple.

Nobody else existed for these lovers. Complex intimacies and private jokes flashed in his knowing glance, her lowered eyelids, the quiver of her lip. These two were so beautiful, unfaithful husbands remembered how lovely their wives had once been and roués recalled their innocent first loves.

His father's bride was the loveliest woman Taz had ever seen, and he hated her. He hated her for being graceful; he hated Scarlett for not being Belle.

Did his father's bride know he had a son? Had Rhett Butler bothered to mention his bastard?

Taz haunted them. He found reasons to while away hours in the St. Louis Hotel and the Boston Club. Taz neglected his work, abbreviating the lengthy courtesies Creole planters were accustomed to.

Tazewell Watling didn't know what he was doing, or what he wanted. Did he want Rhett to acknowledge him? Explain why he hadn't married Belle? Taz's mind swam with resentment.

And Rhett Butler strolled past with a nod and smile, as if he and Taz were distant acquaintances.

Although J. Nicolet had never done business with Captain Butler, he knew who he was. Everyone knew Captain Butler. "Butler is a serious man, young Watling. What is your interest in him?"

To Nicolet, Taz's vague reply was a confession of paternity. So J. Nicolet told him the stories about Captain Butler in Cuba and Central America. "I don't doubt he wished to see Cubans freed from the Spanish tyrants but"—Nicolet snorted—"Butler wasn't indifferent to Spanish gold. Of course he was a young man then. No older than you are today."

"Did he . . . Was he married?"

Nicolet shrugged. "Butler kept a Creole girl. From the Gayerre family. She was very beautiful."

"Called . . . Belle?"

"She was called Didi. While he was away, Didi died trying to lose Butler's baby. He hadn't known she was carrying his child. Butler was devastated. During their mourning, Butler and the Gayerres grew close."

"Even now," J. Nicolet said, "the Gayerres ask Butler to decide a delicate matter at the Quadroon Ball."

Resentment is a dish of mixed flavors. Angry, ashamed, woozy with excitement and the anticipation of how Butler might react, Tazewell Watling escorted Mrs. Butler to the Quadroon Ball.

The next morning, J. Nicolet was in the office when Taz arrived.

When Taz said, "Good morning, sir," Nicolet didn't stop scribbling in his ledger.

"Sir . . ."

J. Nicolet slammed the ledger shut. "You work hard and have learned my business. I planned to leave you in charge this summer. When I am in Baton Rouge, will you be arranging J. Nicolet's cotton shipments, or producing scandals?"

Tazewell Watling laid his order book on his employer's desk. "I was a fool, sir. I regret very much what I did last night and I have forfeited your confidence. My orders are complete as of yesterday." The young man put on his hat. "Sir, I am grateful for your many kindnesses."

Doubt clouded J. Nicolet's face. *"Merci pas coute arien."* (Thanks cost nothing.)

"Sir?"

"My family is content in Baton Rouge and I miss them very much." J. Nicolet waggled an admonitory finger. "Young Watling, without warning I will return from time to time to see if you are shipping cotton or making scandals. Because of my family I will give you this opportunity. One only!"

But J. Nicolet left New Orleans in June and didn't return until October.

New Orleans businessmen dreaded the word *epidemic* and deplored its appearance in the newspapers. On June 22, the *Crescent* reported that "yellow fever has become an obsolete idea in New Orleans." Although forty people died of yellow fever on July 4, the *Picayune* denied it was an epidemic. Only after wealthy Toinette Sevier vomited blood and collapsed in the Boston Club was an epidemic admitted, and those who could flee the city began doing so.

By the end of July, the Charity Hospital, Maison de Santé, and the Turo Infirmary overflowed. Victims were tended in the orphanage, insane asylum, and public ballrooms. Funeral processions jammed the streets and coffins were stacked head-high in the cemeteries because there weren't enough workers to inter them.

New Orleans stank of death.

Born and raised in the city, Tazewell Watling had more resistance to the disease than the poor Irish immigrants, who died by the hundreds.

Although the larger cotton factors had closed and British cargo ships anchored well out in the channel lest they be forced into "yellow jack" quarantine when they arrived home, men had cotton to sell and there were small craft to take it to the ships.

Tazewell Watling made up cargoes from dawn until the sun sank over the river. He penned terse responses to J. Nicolet's lengthy, worried telegrams. Nine hundred and sixty people died the first week of August. Twelve hundred and eighty-eight the second week.

As the only functioning cotton buyer, young Watling might have taken advantage of sellers desperate for cash to get their families out of town. Taz paid the regular price with a shrug. "We must help one another in these hard times, eh, monsieur?"

When cooler weather arrived and the epidemic wound down, those who'd lived through it felt like veterans of a war. When the big cotton houses reopened, many who'd done business with Monsieur Watling during the epidemic continued doing business with him. J. Nicolet's profits swelled dramatically.

Tazewell Watling had earned an honest man's reputation in a dishonest age. Tazewell did business with Democrats and Republicans and kept his political opinions to himself. He enjoyed a wide circle of acquaintances. Many New Orleanians had concluded that Captain Butler was Tazewell

Watling's father, but since Taz didn't discuss his parentage, the topic wasn't raised in his hearing.

He became a man about town. Tazewell was quick to buy a round, and Jules Nore's joke was asking for a cigar and passing Taz's case until it was empty. Taz frequented sporting houses but had no favorite. Despite hints from several mamas, he never again attended a Quadroon Ball. When Tazewell's gambling friends asked for a loan to tide them over, Taz excused himself by saying he sent his money to his mother.

Three years after Taz started at the firm, J. Nicolet made him a partner. "You will do all the work and I will receive half the profits, *oui*?"

Jules Nore was a lieutenant in the Mystick Krewe of Comus, the oldest of the Mardi Gras parade societies. Jules invited Taz to join.

"But Jules," Taz said, "I'm a bastard."

Jules was puzzled. "What difference does that make?"

Four years after Tazewell Watling returned to New Orleans, he bought a stone house on Royal Street in the Vieux Carré.

The evening he recorded his deed, Tazewell Watling returned to his unfurnished home and sat on the parlor floor, with the French doors open on his garden.

His L-shaped kitchen was awkward and his parlor was small, but there were two bedrooms on the second story—one with a separate entrance.

There were lime trees in his garden. There was a frangipani and a palm tree. The air was redolent with flowers.

Tazewell Watling sat listening to the faint clip-clop of horses on Royal Street. His moon rose over his lime trees.

The next morning, Tazewell Watling wrote, "Dear Maman, I hope you will consent to visit me in New Orleans. I have a grand surprise for you."

Chapter Thirty-seven

A Silly Joke

One brisk Atlanta morning, outside the Farmer's and Merchants' Bank, Rhett passed an elderly couple selling apples from a farm wagon. The man called in a singsong, "Keepers, I got keepers. I got ciders, dessert apples'll melt in your mouth. I got your pie apples and cobblers. I got yellows and reds and stripes! Apples, I got your apples!"

The man's Confederate coat had been neatly patched; his wife's coat had been sewn from a blanket. It was impossible to guess their age. Her teeth were gone and his few were tobacco-stained. His hat, which might have once been a soldier's, was a color somewhere between brown and green. She knelt in the back of the wagon, sorting apples from one cask to another, setting each gently to avoid bruising them.

"Here, mister," the man cried. "Can you afford a penny for an apple? Take some home to the wife and young'uns."

The woman looked at Rhett through clear blue eyes and said, "Jimmy, maybe the gentleman don't got nary wife nor young'uns. Maybe he got nobody to take an apple to."

The man's face fell. "Nobody to take an apple to? Mercy! What a world we're a-livin' in, Sarie June. What a world!"

Laughing, Rhett bought a peck of Esopus Spitzenbergs because he liked the name.

As she slipped apples into a sack, the woman asked Rhett if he had children.

"Three."

"How are they called?"

"Wade Hampton will be nine next month, Ella—let's see—she's four, and my Bonnie Blue is a year and eight months and four days."

"She's yer favrit? You lit up when you thought on her."

"She is my own. She is beautiful."

"Sure she is." The woman reached into a smaller cask for three large yellow apples. "These Smokehouses are too sweet for grown-ups. But young'uns can't get enough of them." As she wrapped each separately in newspaper, she said, "This 'un is for Wade Hampton, this is for Ella, and I reckon this big one will suit your little Miss Bonnie Blue. No, no charge for the children."

As she tied his sack with the children's apples on top, Rhett asked, "How long are you married?"

"How long's it been, Sarie June?" The man grinned. "Nigh on to forever."

He danced away from her swat.

The old man continued, "I reckon I can't remember a time when we wasn't married. Oh, it's been a sorrowful time. This woman has been a tribulation."

This time, her swat connected and they laughed merrily at his wit and her vigorous response.

When he stopped chuckling, he added, "My Sarie could have had anyone she wanted. Oh, the boys were clusterin' around her like bees at a cider press. But Sarie chanced on me. Lovin's a chancy thing. You chance it every day."

Rhett tied the sack behind the saddle, mounted his horse, and cantered down Mitchell Street. He and Scarlett lived in a showplace on Peachtree Street. They spent more for supper at the Kimball House than the old couple made in a week. Atlanta's important men, Governor Bullock himself, called on them.

But Rhett and Scarlett had never shared a silly joke. Never.

She had never said she loved him. Knowing what her answer would be, he never asked.

Sometimes, Rhett felt like a man falling from a precipice, powerless to direct his fall or undo the disaster. Although he and Scarlett hadn't been married three years, like the apple seller, Rhett couldn't remember a time when they weren't married. His and Scarlett's quarrels were more real than his memories of other women's embraces.

He loved her and couldn't leave her. Rhett's wife thought she loved Ashley Wilkes. Rhett bought her what she asked for. Her carriage was trimmed in cherry veneer. If she fancied a gown or a trinket, it was hers.

Sometimes he despised himself. Did he think he could buy her? Maybe after Scarlett was happy, after she finally owned everything she ever wanted, maybe then she would open her heart.

She loved her sawmills because she was a shrewd businesswoman. She loved her sawmills because she could be with her manager, Ashley Wilkes. She was at the mill with Ashley today. When she came home, she'd have that faraway look in her eyes.

Sometimes, Rhett regretted not letting the Yankees hang the man.

The Butler home was dark and opulent, with carved wood paneling, heavy furniture, and floor-to-ceiling drapes. The gaslights were on.

He gave the sack to Mammy, explaining that the children were to have the wrapped apples when Bonnie rose from her nap.

"Mr. Rhett, these Smokehouses—childrens gonna love 'em." Mammy confided, "They so sweet, they make my teeth ache."

He bounded up the stairs and turned into the nursery. He put his finger to his lips so the other children wouldn't wake Bonnie. Gently, he tugged her coverlet to her chin. Her eyelashes were gossamer, the tenderest things in the world. For some damn reason, a tear moistened his eye. Wade was tugging his sleeve as Ella silently urged him to sit down. When he did, she curled up on his lap. Why did children smell different than grown-ups?

Wade was showing him something—a dark gray stone that turned wonderfully red when he licked it.

When she came in, Scarlett took everything in at a glance. She had that look in her eyes. "I want to talk to you." She marched into their bedroom. Silently, Wade put his marvelous stone back into his pocket. As he dislodged Ella, Rhett ruffled her hair.

He closed her bedroom door behind him. "Rhett, I've decided that I don't want any more children. "I think three are enough."

Lord, she was beautiful. Beautiful and blind. If Ashley Wilkes would have her, if she ever got her dream, she wouldn't want it. Only the unattainable would satisfy her.

"Three seems an adequate number," he said.

She flushed. "You know what I mean. . . ."

Damn her for a fool! They could have been happy. No, something more than happy. Something . . .

"I shall lock my door every night."

"Why bother? If I wanted you, no lock would keep me out."

He left her then and returned to the nursery, where Wade and Ella greeted him with smiles. *Smiles.*

In a bit, his darling Bonnie would wake and they would all go down to the kitchen and eat apples and perhaps enjoy a silly joke.

Chapter Thirty-eight

A White Robe

Rosemary Haynes Ravanel stood trembling on her front steps. Angry fingers tucked the butcher paper parcel, as if rewrapping could make things right. Excepting the tic at the corner of her mouth, Rosemary's face was impassive. Someone might be watching. Someone might have seen her open the parcel. That gentleman strolling down the sidewalk tipped his hat. That horseman rode past without a glance. That curtain on the second-story window across the street—did it flutter? Damn them! Oh damn them all to hell!

The parcel she carried into her home—into her *home*—contained three yards of cheap white cotton fabric, a red ribbon for the breast cross, and a crudely printed note: "Dear Missy, please make this into a robe and mask for the Ku Klux. Make it big!"

It was Christmas day. The holly Rosemary had strung in the hall was cheerful green and red. The juniper wreath on the drawing room door had a wonderful clean smell.

Inside her *home!*

Rosemary flung the parcel down. "How dare they!" she whispered. Her breath came as fast as a trapped sparrow's. How dare they!

When had Southern Honor died? At Pickett's charge, at Franklin? Had all the honorable men died?

Rosemary thought she might be sick.

Southern Honor had come to this: a ruffian thinking to impress his comrades because his KKK robe, his murderer's garb, had been sewn by his commander's wife.

For that's how things were done these days, done so decent citizens could deny the terror that rode by night. "Oh no sir. I know nothing of the Ku Klux Klan. Yes, I sewed a robe similar to what you describe, but I don't know who provided the fabric nor who wore it. After I had sewn the robe, I left it on my doorstep, and it was gone by morning.

"I know nothing of murders, whippings, and beatings of negroes and white Republicans. You say negro women are raped? I know nothing of negro families hiding in the woods, or their shacks burned to the ground, of men and, yes, women dragged out of their homes, never to be seen again. My husband? Andrew is often away. He is sometimes absent for weeks. But surely it is not a wife's place to question her husband's whereabouts. You say my husband is prominent in the Ku Klux Klan? Andrew has never spoken to me about any Ku Klux Klan."

Charleston newspapers reported on the *alleged* Ku Klux Klan and chided Republicans for exaggerating its influence.

> *William Champion was paid a visit the other night by Certain Citizens who apparently objected to his inciting Negroes to Rebellion. Mr. Champion will be seen no more in the Carolinas.*

> *The body on the station platform was identified as that of Senator Arthur DeBose, the Radical Negro Legislator. Although passengers were waiting for the noon train, no one was able to identify DeBose's assailants, who rode away unhindered.*

When Andrew was in the Low Country, he usually stayed at Congress Haynes's old fishing camp. Sometimes, Rosemary only learned he'd been there after he'd gone again.

Occasionally, very early, she'd be startled awake by Andrew's footsteps passing her bedroom door.

Andrew was so gaunt, he seemed to have grown taller. His wrists were taut as braided rope. When Rosemary spoke to her husband, he flinched, as if surprised at her temerity. He answered her anxious questions about Haynes & Son as if that firm were owned by strangers.

One November morning, when Rosemary came downstairs, she'd found her husband's riding boots beside the bootjack, where he'd left them last night. The uppers were flecked with dark blood, the toes crusted with clotted gore. At arm's length, Rosemary had carried them upstairs and set them outside her husband's bedroom door.

Most of what Rosemary knew about her husband's activities, she learned at the Charleston market.

"I understand your husband has been in York County, Mrs. Ravanel. Please tell the Colonel every decent white woman thanks him!"

"Mrs. Ravanel, my up-country cousin is deathly afraid the niggers are going to murder her in her bed. Mrs. Joseph Randolph of Centreville. Please mention Mrs. Randolph to your husband."

"I saw your husband with Archie Flytte and Josie Watling on the River Road yesterday. I declare they had a stern look about them."

Negro fish and produce mongers Rosemary had known all her life wouldn't meet her eye.

When Andrew tried again to recruit Jamie Fisher, Jamie had replied to his former Colonel, "I have followed you to the gates of hell, but I will not follow you into the Klan."

Andrew had accused Jamie of being a moneygrubbing innkeeper.

"Really, Rosemary," Jamie told her later, "I couldn't think what to say. So, I tried to make a joke. I told Andrew the only men who could wear dresses without blushing were Scotsmen and priests. I thought Andrew was going to knock me down."

Now, Rosemary went to the kitchen to boil water for oatmeal. When it was ready, she set it on a silver tray to carry upstairs. Her son Louis Valentine's little bed was in his grandmother's bedroom. Sometimes, Elizabeth Butler cared for the boy, sometimes the boy cared for his Nana; they were playmates.

The child's sweet temper was hitched to a precocious adult knowingness. He'd sit and listen to Nana's Jesus stories all day, but when she turned to the harsh Old Testament prophets, Louis Valentine's little face would darken. He said, "I hate it when God is mean!"

In the bleak aftermath of the War, when Rosemary and Andrew married, Andrew Ravanel had wanted a son, and their lovemaking had been urgent, if not tender. After Louis Valentine was born, Andrew lost interest, as if a live birth were everything he required.

Andrew never asked after Louis Valentine. He seemed to have forgotten he had a son.

As Rosemary set the tray down, Elizabeth Butler was tasking her grandson to name the wise men.

"Melchior," Valentine said confidently. "Bal . . ." He shook his head, disgusted with his failure.

"Balthazar?" Elizabeth prompted.

"Yes, Nana. And Caspar, too!" Valentine ran to kiss his mother. "Good morning, Mama. Mama? Mama, are you sad?"

"It's all right, dear. Mama's sad this morning. Not sad about you. I couldn't be sad about you!"

Elizabeth said, "The wise men came from the East!" She confided, "Isaiah Watling believes they were Chinamen!"

Louis Valentine considered this theory gravely. "Chinamen are on the bottom of the world?"

"Yes, dear."

"Why don't they fall off?"

"Because God loves them, dear. God loves all his children."

Rosemary set two places at the table and bowed her head while Louis Valentine said grace. She took their chamber pot downstairs to the necessary, emptied and washed it.

Afterward, she carried her own tepid, half-solidified oatmeal into the family room, where, in the silver chest, she kept Melanie Wilkes's precious letters. Without those letters, Rosemary thought she would go mad.

Dearest Rosemary,

Please forgive my bleak indiscretions. I hope you understand that I confide to you what I cannot confide to another. If I didn't have you to unburden myself to, I don't know what I would do. Should I set dissembling aside and shout the truth?

My beloved husband, Ashley, has always been attracted to my dearest friend Scarlett. I had hoped that your brother would cure Scarlett of this infatuation, but she—the friend I love more than any on earth—yearns after my husband so openly, sometimes I must needs look away. Sometimes, when Scarlett is wearing that particular dreamy expression, I ask, "Dear Scarlett, what are you thinking?" She'll answer that she's thinking about the garden, the children, politics, or some other matter that never crosses her unhorticultural, unmotherly, unpolitical mind. I pretend to believe her because, dear Rosemary, I must pretend.

We are, all of us, imprisoned by Love.

When I was a girl, I thought Love attended one like a floral perfume. Now I think Love is more like a drunkard's craving for wine. The drunkard knows his desire destroys everything precious to him. He knows he will despise himself tomorrow, and yet he cannot forswear wine!

Dear Rosemary, Scarlett thinks it is merely ill fortune she and my husband are so rarely alone. I confess my design: I would as soon leave those two together as a drunkard with a case of brandy!

Whenever Scarlett visits Ashley's mill, that evening my husband comes home to me a different man. Even as he kisses me glad hello, poor Ashley's troubled eyes shout that he'd rather be with another.

Your brother is trying to persuade Scarlett to sell her sawmills to Ashley, so they'll have no excuse to be together!

I dare not conceive again. Dr. Meade has uttered the direst warnings. Consequently, Ashley and I cannot enjoy those intimate relations which bond a husband and wife. I miss Ashley so!

Since Rhett and Scarlett's happiness is so interwoven with my own, I wish I could write that their marriage was happy. Rhett is not unfaithful, nor is Scarlett, but they are as discontented as two philanderers. When differences arise, they are not resolved; misunderstandings are taken to heart; each one's privacies make no space for the other; and last month, Mammy, Scarlett's dear old nurse, confided (in her usual oblique fashion) that they no longer share a bed.

Scarlett has so identified herself with Atlanta's Carpetbaggers that respectable people snub her on the street. As if to goad Mrs. Meade and

Mrs. Elsing, Scarlett routinely entertains Governor Bullock and his cronies—Puryear, Kimball, and Blodgett. Rhett avoids these gatherings like the plague.

Oh Rosemary, Rhett and Scarlett are so dear to my heart! If your brother hadn't been driving that dreadful night we fled Atlanta . . . and afterward, when hard times stalked the land, if Scarlett had not been Mistress at Tara, I don't believe my son, Beau, or myself would have survived.

Scarlett and Rhett are not like you and me. Heads turn when they walk into a room. They expect duller folks' deference.

When the Queen of Sheba came to Solomon's court, she brought a powerful retinue: soldiers, viziers, and serving maids. Her horses were caparisoned with gold and precious rubies. At Jerusalem's gates, Solomon's guards stood aside to let them pass.

The Queen had come to Solomon to ask questions she had considered all her life, questions her most learned advisers could not answer.

I don't imagine she went to him that first day, nor even the second. Minor officials would scurry back and forth; perhaps there was a welcome feast, with Solomon at the head of an enormous table and Sheba at the foot.

But soon, for she was a mighty Queen, she would have had her audience. Solomon was robed as richly as she. He was handsome. He had a hundred concubines, many of them younger and lovelier than she.

When Sheba asked him a question, Solomon answered it. When she asked another, he answered that, too. He answered all her questions.

The Bible says, "The spirit went out of her." What use was her power and wealth when he could answer any question she put to him?

How she must have hated him.

Rhett and Scarlett's link, the only thing they agree on, is their daughter, Bonnie, whom they love to distraction. I'm afraid Rhett spoils Bonnie. He takes her with him everywhere. She's such a charming creature!

Little Bonnie has accomplished a miracle. She has made Rhett Butler—promise you won't laugh—respectable!

When Rhett learned the Butler children weren't being invited to children's parties because society disapproved of their parents, he mended fences. When he has a mind to, your brother can charm the pelt off a grizzly bear!

Did the Confederate Orphans and Widows need help? "Will a hundred be enough?"

Prominent Confederate officers—General Forrest in person!—trooped through Atlanta to establish Rhett's Confederate credentials. He has distanced himself from the Carpetbaggers, even Rufus Bullock, his old friend.

The same ladies who cut your brother dead six months ago fawn over him, and Wade, Ella, and little Bonnie Blue attend every children's soiree!

I pray that Rhett and Scarlett may yet be happy. I pray that A Little Child Shall Lead Them . . .

As I pray for you and little Louis Valentine.

Your friend, Melly

That afternoon, Rosemary shepherded her mother and son from 46 Church Street to the East Bay Inn.

Federal warships were still anchored in Charleston harbor and there were more blue-clad sailors than civilians on the promenade.

Coastal shipping was brisk and Haynes & Sons' deserted wharf was a bleak exception to the prosperous maritime scene.

EAST BAY INN

JAMIE FISHER, MISS JULIET RAVANEL, SOLE PROPS.

The modest black-on-green sign might easily be overlooked by the hasty or vulgar traveler. The inn itself looked as if dirt entered at its peril.

The door brass of the old Fisher town house was polished mirror-bright. The front hall was Christmassy with wreaths and holly. A sprig of mistletoe hung above the drawing room door.

"Dear Rosemary!" Juliet wiped her hands on a towel.

"Juliet, it is so good to see you. We've been too much strangers."

Juliet had aged into a ramrod-straight woman whose gray-flecked hair was contained in a tight bun. Her skillfully made dress was too youthful for her.

"Happy Christmas, Juliet," Rosemary said, kissing her cheek. "Our estrangement is not my desire."

Juliet's polite smile warmed a degree. "My brother is a reckless fool.

May I take your coat? Oh, here's Louis Valentine. Louis Valentine, you are so grown up."

Grown up or no, Louis Valentine tucked himself behind his grandmother's knee.

"Mrs. Butler, Merry Christmas. So good of you to come. Louis Valentine, there are children in the drawing room and the prettiest Christmas tree! Captain Jackson's daughter is June. Sally is the blond girl."

At this, Valentine shed all caution and marched into the other room, from whence a little girl cried, "Mustn't touch the tree! Miss Juliet says we mustn't touch the tree!"

Rosemary and Juliet lingered in the hall while Elizabeth Butler followed her grandson.

"Rhett's upstairs. His Bonnie and your Louis Valentine make our Christmas complete."

The inn's paneling gleamed. The hall chandelier glittered like icicles.

"What a magnificent piece, Juliet. What a miracle it survived the shelling."

"Don't be a ninny. When it came trundling down the street on a scavenger's cart, we bought it for five dollars. I live in fear that one day someone will ask, 'Where on earth did you find So-and-so's chandelier? Jamie washes it. It has one thousand and six crystals, and he never puts them back as they were."

"I was practically raised in this house," Rosemary said. "Grand, difficult Grandmother Fisher. Poor dear Charlotte . . ."

"I regret every unkind word I ever said to her."

"In the end, Charlotte loved you." Rosemary inspected a framed print. "Isn't this a blockade runner? Isn't it the *Bat*? And you with a houseful of Yankees? Juliet, what a subversive creature you are!"

Louis Valentine's squeal drew his mother's attention.

Some of the drawing room furniture was neatly repaired, but the love seat and two chairs wanted reupholstering. Elizabeth Butler and her grandson stood hand in hand before an ornament-bedecked Christmas tree.

When Louis Valentine reached for the candles, a girl warned him, "You'll burn yourself! Silly boy."

Juliet introduced Rosemary to the Yankee mothers, Mrs. Jackson and Mrs. Caldwell.

In this room, little Rosemary Butler and little Charlotte Fisher had tiptoed around Grandmother Fisher's precious Chippendale furniture! Rosemary shook her head to clear the cobwebs.

Louis Valentine left his grandmother to help the girls build a fortress of brightly colored wooden blocks. He announced, "It's Fort Sumter."

"It is not," a Yankee girl demurred. "For if it is Fort Sumter, we shall have to knock it down."

"Jesus Christ is returning," Mrs. Butler informed the mothers. "I expect Him any day."

Rosemary felt her brother's familiar hand on her shoulder. "Rosemary, Mother, say hello to my beautiful Bonnie Blue."

The toddler had Scarlett's dark hair and her father's captivating smile. Her blue velvet dress matched her hair bow. "Daddy says you 'good Butler.' Who the bad Butlers?"

"Bad Butlers?" Elizabeth frowned. "Why, there are no bad Butlers."

Rosemary laughed, "Your father flatters me, honey. Do you want to play with your cousin Louis Valentine?"

"Please." A child's clumsy curtsy.

Bonnie flopped down with the other children and began removing blocks from the fortress they were erecting.

Rhett watched her lovingly. He asked his sister, "Would you take some Christmas cheer? They've turned Grandmother Fisher's withdrawing room into a bar."

Two Yankee officers had the morris chairs in the bow window. The Butlers shared a couch before the crackling fire. Jamie Fisher bustled in. "Rhett, I was at the market when you checked in. Happy Christmas! Happy Christmas, Rosemary."

"You've done great things here, Jamie."

"We're planning to serve meals. Our dining room is enormous, and Lord knows, Charleston has enough unemployed cooks."

How odd, Rosemary thought, that after what he'd been through, Jamie

Fisher was still an innocent. His sister, Charlotte, had been an innocent, too. Who could think them worse off?

Jamie said, "Will you try our eggnog? I made it myself."

After pouring tall mugs of his foamy concoction, Jamie excused himself.

One of the Yankee mothers appeared. "Madam, if I may intrude. . . . Your companion . . . the old woman . . ."

"Our mother. Yes?"

"Doubtless the Book of Revelations is a commendable text, but . . ." The woman sighed, a noble sufferer.

"Madam," Rhett intoned, "Revelations is a sacred book. Many sinners have been saved from perdition thereby."

"Your mother . . ."

Rosemary smiled reassuringly. "Can be overwhelming, I know. Why don't you leave her with the children. Adults find Mother . . . difficult, but children see straight to her heart."

The woman snapped, "In Connecticut, madam, we don't nursemaid our children with the Book of Revelations." She marched out, and Rosemary heard the woman's daughter wail, "Mama, I was having fun!"

Rhett shook his head, "Poor Mother."

"She's happy, Rhett. Perhaps there's more to life than happiness, but at Mother's age, there can't be much more."

A log toppled in the fire and sparks rushed up the chimney.

"Perhaps," Rhett said. "Do you remember the first time I came here?"

"I'll never forget. How old was I, six or seven?" Rosemary took her brother's hand. "Do you still love me, brother?"

"As my life."

The Yankee officers finished their drinks and left.

Rhett was grave. "My Washington friends say President Grant has lost patience with the Klan. Rosemary, Andrew's activities are too well known."

"Andrew and I don't talk about that." She set her mug down. "We do not talk at all."

"Please warn your husband. The Yankees want to hang somebody."

"Andrew won't listen to me, Rhett. I doubt he hears me." She rubbed her hands. "I do not know what Andrew hears these days."

Across the hall, the children's noises were happy. "And your Scarlett? How is Scarlett?"

"My wife is in good health."

"And . . ."

"I'm afraid there is no 'and.' " When Rhett drank, eggnog frosted his mustache. For a moment, Rosemary's strong brother seemed a clown with dark, sad eyes. "She was everything I ever wanted. She is everything I want. Scarlett . . ." He wiped the foam with his handkerchief. "Funny how things turn out, isn't it?" He set his glass aside. "I've brought a rocking horse for Louis Valentine."

"He'll be delighted." Rosemary considered for a moment before saying, "Haynes and Son . . ."

"Is bankrupt. I know." He took her hand. "Andrew has squandered John Haynes's legacy on the Klan. You're lucky the house is in your name. You mustn't worry, Rosemary. I'll always take care of you, Louis Valentine, and Mother."

When Rosemary leaned back, the fire warmed her cheeks. She felt so tired. She might close her eyes and doze.

Her brother was talking about money. Rosemary didn't want to think about money. She opened her eyes and said, "Thank you for caring, dear brother, but some things I must do for myself."

It rained that night—an icy winter rain. When Rosemary heard Andrew at the door, she set down her mending basket and went into the front hall. Andrew stared at his wife. "Rosemary."

"Good evening, husband," Rosemary said calmly. "Where have you been?"

Andrew shut the door and shrugged out of his slicker. His shirt was soaked. "You don't want to know."

"Yes, husband, I do want to know."

He cocked his head as a man who spies a curiosity: a cat that dances, a dog reputed to speak.

"Business," Andrew said.

"What business do you have, husband? The bank is foreclosing on Haynes and Son."

He dismissed that enterprise with an angry head shake. "Don't you know, wife, that the South Carolina legislature is a snake pit of Scalawags, Carpetbaggers, and niggers. They are not our government!"

"Are *you* our government, husband? Doing under cover of darkness what honest men will not do in daylight?"

She gasped when he gripped her arm, "Which 'honest men'?" His voice frightened her. Her husband had used that voice beside fires where terrified men waited to be murdered. That voice had destroyed women's hopes and mocked children's pleas. "Andrew," Rosemary whispered, "where have you gone?"

"Wife, I haven't changed. Others may have changed, but I have not."

"Andrew, you're hurting me!"

As suddenly as he'd grabbed her, he let go. Rubbing her arm, she picked up the parcel from the hall table and thrust it at him. "This came this morning, husband. There's a note."

He glanced at the note. "Patriotic Southern women make our robes. What of it?"

"Patriotic?"

He said, "If we don't protect our women, who will?"

Rosemary frowned. "How do you protect us, Andrew? From what threat do you protect us?"

"Fellow wanted to boast about his 'special-made' robe." Andrew's laugh was three sharp barks. "Do you imagine I enjoy doing these things? Wife, do you think me heartless? Rosemary, I am doing my duty."

Though Andrew went on about corrupt Carpetbaggers, Southern rights, and insolent niggers, Rosemary didn't listen. She was tired of him.

When Andrew wound down, Rosemary said, "Andrew, I don't want you here."

Her husband paled. His eyes roamed. He licked his lips. Rosemary could smell the stench of Andrew's body and the corruption of his breath.

She said, "You can't ever come home again."

Chapter Thirty-nine

Natural Wonders

On a drizzly March morning, Scarlett O'Hara Butler dressed for Governor Bullock's celebration.

Mammy said, "Honey, only actresses bare their chests, and you ain't no actress. That gown ain't hidin' half what it s'posed to!"

"In Paris, it is the height of fashion."

"'Lanta ain't Paris nor anywhere's else, neither. You is a married woman!"

Married—how Scarlett loathed the word. *Married* meant *Don't* and *forbidden*! After she married Rhett, Scarlett gave her mourning clothes to the Confederate Widows and Orphans. She wished she could give her marriage to the widows and orphans too!

Between *married* and *mother,* Scarlett felt like a mule dragging logs through the tuckerbrush.

Rhett loved children—provided Prissy changed them and Scarlett nursed them and bore them in pain and sweat and blood. Why shouldn't Rhett love them?

Scarlett chose her memories as if picking scenes for the parlor stereograph. Tara was Gerald O'Hara's laughter and Ellen O'Hara's caring hands. Twelve Oaks was brilliant parties, doting admirers, helpful darkies, and Ashley Wilkes—*her* Ashley.

Scarlett never recalled her mother's self-martyrdom, her father Gerald's drunken blather, or Ashley's discomfort with the role he been cast in at birth.

In New Orleans, Toinette Sevier had hinted to Scarlett about Ellen's doomed love for Philippe Robillard. How like her love for Ashley! Scarlett never wondered if Ellen's love for Philippe was a sorrow at the heart of her parents' marriage.

Scarlett O'Hara Butler's sixteen-inch waist was no more and her flashing eyes had seen too much of life, but she could still turn men's heads.

Mammy tugged at her neckline. "Child, you're bound for mischief. Associatin' with Carpetbaggers and Scalawags. Think what your Mama would say!"

Trust Mammy to put a chill on things.

When she informed him he was a hypocrite, Rhett didn't deny it. The new Rhett Butler reveled in hypocrisy!

In public, Rhett never smiled when he ought to frown. He no longer confused simple souls or confounded cleverer ones. Whatever absurd notion Mrs. Meade or Mrs. Elsing advanced, Rhett solemnly agreed with it. Had one of the grande dames opined the moon was made of blue cheese, Rhett Butler would have wondered aloud if it just might be Stilton.

Sunday mornings found Rhett, Ella, Wade, and Bonnie settled in their pew at St. Philip's. Mr. Rhett Butler even had a desk at the Farmer's and Merchants' Bank.

Why was Rhett able to do anything he wished to do? A woman mustn't do this; a woman mustn't do that. Run her own business? Scarlett might as well have stripped off her clothes and ridden naked down Peachtree Street!

Lord, how she missed her sawmills. Somehow—afterward she was never quite sure how—Rhett had tricked her into selling them. He'd confused her and made her so angry, she'd sold her sawmills to Ashley.

Scarlett felt like she'd sold part of herself. Her sawmills were sound, profitable businesses, and if she'd wanted to sell, Lord knows, she'd had plenty of offers. She'd built them by herself! They were tangible evidence of who she was and what she could do.

She couldn't drive past them anymore without wanting to weep.

On this rainy Saturday, Rhett was in the library reading the newspaper while Wade, Ella, and Bonnie sat on the rug, playing a game that involved lining up the household spoons in ranks at their father's feet.

Without preamble, Scarlett said, "Children, please play somewhere else. Your father and I need to talk."

Wade and Ella obeyed, but Bonnie climbed onto her father's lap, stuck her thumb in her mouth, and examined her mother with her wide blue eyes.

"Bonnie should stay, dear wife. One day, Bonnie will marry. By observing our affectionate interchanges, Bonnie learns what she can expect from her own marriage."

"Certainly, dear husband. Bonnie should know everything there is to know about marriage. Has our daughter visited the Chapeau Rouge?"

Rhett grinned. "Ah, you still have ammunition in your pouch and do not hesitate to fire it. Scarlett, have I told you lately how much I admire you?"

Her face softened. "Why, no. . . ."

"My dear, I applaud you for being the most resolutely selfish woman I've ever met."

"Thank you, husband," Scarlett said, "for your candor."

Rhett sighed. "Bonnie, I'm afraid your Mama is right; you're too young for your parents' marriage. I don't know when you'll be old enough. I'm not sure I'm old enough."

With love in his eyes, Rhett watched the child scamper from the room, Scarlett felt a jealous flash and then confusion. How could she be jealous of her own child?

"So you're off to celebrate the Pennsylvania Railroad's capture of the Georgia Railroad. Why not celebrate with a masked ball? Aren't masks traditional in bandit society?"

"Aren't you the one to talk! Wasn't Rufus Bullock your friend?"

Rhett shrugged. "Rufus and I have done business from time to time."

"Now that it suits Captain Butler to be oh so respectable, his old friends fall by the wayside?"

He folded his newspaper. "Am I to have a sermon on loyalty from Miss Scarlett? Please continue."

Scarlett flushed. Why had she ever married this hateful man?

Rhett tapped his newspaper. "Better hurry, dear. If you hesitate, Rufus might not be Governor. His powerful friends are jumping ship and he's lost control of the legislature. Rufus's wife took their children north so they won't be insulted on the streets her husband governs. Edgar Puryear is Rufus's only friend. Poor Rufus."

Rhett opened the heavy drapes to watch his wife's carriage make the turn onto Peachtree Street.

When Prissy came in to say she was taking the children to play at the Wilkeses', Rhett waved an indifferent hand. The house—her house—was so big, he didn't hear them go. This miserable day mocked spring's promises. Pale yellow forsythia bent beneath raindrops and the lilacs were blue with cold.

How had he come to this?

Blinded by love. All his experience, his travels, the women he'd known—nothing had assuaged his insane yearning for the woman he married, whose heart he could not win.

For her and her children, he'd become respectable—a respectable hypocrite: "Neither hanged nor a hangman be." If Atlanta's leaders decided to raid Shantytown again, Rhett Butler would ride with them.

He'd do anything for her, he'd give her anything. . . .

His wife thought she loved another man, but he knew better. Her love was dreaming for a way of life she'd envied and never understood as a child. Daughter of an Irish immigrant who'd married above himself: poor covetous Scarlett.

She'd burn through Ashley Wilkes in six months. He was far too gentle a flower.

Rain slid down the windowpane. Rain dripped from the lead mullions.

Rhett Butler snorted, laughed at himself, and went to the fireplace to stir the fire.

He heard her carriage on the cobblestones. When she came into the parlor, he lowered his book. "You're home early."

She made a face and went to the cabinet for a brandy. She downed it with a shudder.

Rhett closed his book and laid it on the end table. "Bulwer-Lytton's new utopia. He imagines we can all be happy and good."

"We can't?"

"Perhaps if, like the creatures Bulwer-Lytton imagines, we live in a cave at the center of the earth. On earth's surface, goodness and happiness are in short supply."

"Rhett, why did you make me sell my mills?"

He got up to pour his own drink. "You know perfectly well why I *helped* you sell your mills. So you wouldn't be closeted with the little gentleman every day."

"You resent Ashley Wilkes because he is so fine."

"I pity Wilkes because he is too fine." He set down his glass. "Scarlett, need we do this?"

She searched his face and sighed. "We do have a talent for discord." Her smile was almost friendly. "You were right, Rhett. As usual. Governor Bullock is finished and his celebratory luncheon was a tedious sham. The Pennsylvania Railroad people were disappointed you didn't come."

"There is a limit even to my hypocrisy."

"And that is?"

Rhett chuckled.

"Your friend Captain Jaffery has been assigned to Custer's regiment."

"The Seventh's in Carolina locking up Klansmen."

"Jaffery hopes they'll go back out west. On . . ." She paused for effect. "The Northern Pacific."

"I trust you've not put money in that folly."

"Jay Cooke is the cleverest man alive and his Northern Pacific will be a bigger success than the Union Pacific. Everybody says so."

"Will it?"

She arched her eyebrows. "I suppose you've heard about the Natural Wonders?"

He stepped nearer and frowned. He asked, "How much have you had to drink?"

Defiantly, she poured herself another and smiled over the rim of the glass. "Near the Yellowstone River on the Northern Pacific route, there's an amazing realm of therapeutic hot springs and spectacular geysers."

"Geysers? Scarlett . . ."

"Geysers spout hot water, a hundred feet high, as regularly as clocks chime the hours. Don't give me that look, Rhett. Jay Cooke—"

"Hot water? Spouting? Why do you want to be rich, darling? You already have me."

She smiled confidently, "Why yes, I do."

When he touched her arm, the warmed silk of her dress thrilled his fingertips. Speaking very quickly, Scarlett added, "Jay Cooke had Congress name this region Yellowstone National Park. The Northern Pacific's cars will be filled with tourists visiting Yellowstone National Park. Wouldn't you?"

"Excuse me. Wouldn't I what?"

"Wouldn't you like to see steaming water erupting as regular as clockwork?"

Close to her, he inhaled the scent of her hair and murmured, "Doubtless the Sioux will welcome these tourists with open arms."

She backed away. Nervously, she patted her hair. "Tourists will take the train to see mineral pools and geysers! They will go to see the Natural Wonders!"

His grin was amused. "Scarlett, you are a Natural Wonder."

Her eyes softened. Her lower lip trembled. Then he saw a flare deep in her eyes. Fear? Was that fear? What was she afraid of? She turned for the door.

"I never said I loved you, you know," she said, as if she weren't quite sure.

The air in the small space between them hummed.

More firmly she said, "I don't, you know."

His muscles ached from holding still, from not reaching out and taking her. In a husky voice, he managed to say, "I admire your candor." Because his hands ached to touch her, to ravish her, to close around her throat and murder her, Rhett Butler bowed stiffly, brushed past his wife, and walked out of the house onto Peachtree Street, hatless in the cold rain.

Chapter Forty

A Murderer's Son

In November, President Ulysses S. Grant declared South Carolina in rebellion, suspended habeas corpus, and sent the Seventh Cavalry to smash the Klan. Former Confederate generals Gordon and Forrest were summoned before the United States Congress, where they reluctantly admitted they might have known people who might have been associated with the "so-called" Ku Klux Klan but they personally had had nothing to do with it.

A fortnight after Andrew Ravanel was arrested, Elizabeth Kershaw Butler sat bolt upright in her bed and emitted a faint unearthly cry, which woke her daughter dozing in the armchair at her side. When Rosemary held a mirror to her mother's mouth, the glass didn't fog.

Rosemary's son, Louis Valentine, was a sound sleeper and merely murmured when she carried him to her own bedroom and placed him in her bed. Rosemary went to the kitchen and made herself a pot of tea. She didn't weep for what she had lost. She wept for what her mother had never had.

It was early—before dawn. Though she had expected this death for some time, it still took her by surprise.

Later that day, Rosemary wrote her friend.

Dearest Melanie,

My mother, Elizabeth Butler, went to her Heavenly Reward early this morning. Mother did not suffer at the end.

As you must have heard, Andrew Ravanel has been arrested for his Klan activities. Last Saturday, I brought his clothing to a camp outside Columbia. The camp is run by Federal cavalry, and whether for his previous rank or because they secretly share his views, Andrew has his own tent in that overcrowded pigsty. I had not dreamed there were so many Klansmen!

Andrew says once the special courts are ready, he will be tried for several negro murders.

There. I have said it. My words change nothing Andrew has done, nor my confusion and heartbreak. Violence and bitterness sully the innocent with the guilty! Will my sweet Louis Valentine grow up as the son of a convicted murderer?

Rhett warned Andrew things would come to this, but Andrew was too proud to listen.

Louis Valentine knows something bad has happened to his father. I haven't found the words to explain.

My father once said there was bad blood in the Butlers, a Butler curse. I believe the curse was lovelessness.

I married my husband John to escape my father's tyranny and I devalued John's simple goodness until it was too late. Goodness works slowly, dear Melanie, and adds to our store in tiny increments. As a girl, I was enchanted by Andrew—the bravest rider, best dancer, the boldest fighter, the man who could commit himself utterly to whatever he did! Did I hope his desperate courage would rub off on me?

Whether the penitentiary or defeat destroyed him, I cannot say. But gallant Andrew has transformed himself into a terrifying grotesque.

What will I do now, dearest Melanie?

Unlike Scarlett, I have neither the inclination nor ability for business. I was reared to bear babies, love a man, and keep a home. I seem to have inherited my mother's reclusive nature and don't leave 46 Church Street for days at a time.

My brother Julian was ejected from the legislature with the Carpetbaggers he'd attached himself to. He has found work as a clerk.

Ladies I worked with at the Free Market have started a school for girls: the Charleston Female Seminary. They have invited me to teach. I can speak a little French and am exquisitely sensitive to proprieties (if only from flaunting them). I suppose I would be a good-enough teacher.

I will bury my mother, and when Rhett comes, I will not—I Will Not—ask him what to do!

I have married one good man and one rakehell. I do not think I will marry again, but if I did, I'd want someone who needed me.

I thank God for our friendship.

Always your,

Rosemary

Chapter Forty-One

The Bottle Trees

Andrew Ravanel thought he'd seen the bearded nigger before. He'd been sold at John Huger's sale, the sale where Andrew tried to buy Cassius. Wasn't he a wheelwright? A carpenter? The bearded nigger said, "Guilty."

The tall nigger said, "Guilty."

The nigger in the yellow vest said, "Guilty."

The bald nigger said, "Guilty."

Andrew scratched the back of his neck. It was hot for so early in the year. So many people crammed into the Charleston courtroom, it was bound to be hot.

The scrawny nigger said, "Guilty." There wasn't any meat on that boy. He wouldn't make a half-task hand.

The four-eyed nigger said, "Guilty." What did a nigger need glasses for? They couldn't read. It was ironic: twelve niggers pronouncing judgment on a Colonel of the Confederate States of America.

The wizened nigger said, "Guilty." Why did some of them shrivel up like dried-apple dolls?

"Guilty." Lord, that nigger was fat. How could anybody say they hadn't been treated right? If this nigger'd been a hog, he'd have been ripe for slaughter. Get some real hams off that boy.

"Guilty."

"Guilty."

Andrew turned to nod at a couple of good old boys, who pretended they didn't know him.

"Guilty."

Six months ago, you bet they would have known him. Andrew caught Rosemary's eye. She looked as fresh as if she'd just stepped out of the bath.

"Guilty."

Guilty of what? Guilty of resisting the oppressor's government?

The Federal judge rapped his gavel. "Mr. Ravanel. The jury has found you guilty of four counts of intentional manslaughter. Do you have anything to say to this court?"

They called Judge Boyd "Pit Bull" Boyd. He surely looked like one.

"*Colonel* Ravanel, Your Honor," Andrew said.

"*Colonel* Ravanel. This court is willing to entertain evidence of your repentance, some acknowledgment of your terrible deeds, before passing sentence. As your attorney will warn you, *Colonel* Ravanel, without repentance, it will go hard on you. Sentencing hearing will be in this courtroom tomorrow, ten o'clock. Do I have your word of honor as a gentleman you won't run?"

Andrew smiled, thinking, My word of honor, Pit Bull? But before he could speak, Andrew's lawyer, William Ellsworth, popped up. "You have my word, Judge Boyd. My client will be here."

"Then, Andrew Ravanel, you will remain free on bond to prepare an entreaty that will move our hearts. Tomorrow at ten." The judge's gavel fell.

Being convicted felt no different than unconvicted. He was no better or worse.

When Ellsworth tried to precede him, Andrew pushed ahead through a throng of glaring negroes, and whites' sly winks.

Rosemary was in the lobby, where Custer's soldiers kept the crowd at bay. "Andrew, I'm sorry."

Why was Rosemary sorry? No jury of black apes had convicted her of anything. She hadn't been insulted by a Yankee judge in front of all Charleston.

"Can I come home?" Andrew said.

Rosemary frowned. "No," she said.

Before the War, this courthouse lobby would have been scrubbed every day. Before the War, Low Country planters came here to settle boundary disputes and contracts. Andrew's shoulders drooped. He'd been fighting so long, so very long. There was nothing left. "Give my best to the boy."

"To your son."

"Yes, to Valentine."

Andrew's lawyer hustled him out a side door into a closed carriage. Ellsworth lit his pipe. It took him three tries to get it going. "You hadn't a chance," he said.

"Oh, I don't know," Andrew said lightly. "I was hoping some jurors remembered me from before the War."

The lawyer puffed furiously. "I did my best. I got the charges reduced from murder. I got you released on bond."

Andrew slid his window open.

Late-morning sun fluttered into the carriage as they turned onto King Street past the post office. They edged around a beer wagon. Two men rolled barrels down a ramp. Behind their iron fences, the city's gardens flourished. The scents of decay and rebirth made the air shimmer.

"You must prepare a plea. Convince Judge Boyd you've seen the error of your ways."

"What does it matter?"

His lawyer's face was sour as an unripe pippin. "Judge Boyd has considerable sentencing leeway. He's gone easy on Klansmen who repented. President Grant doesn't want martyrs."

Andrew's mind drifted on the lawyer's sea of *if*s, *but*s, and *maybe*s.

"We cannot contest what you did. . . ."

A Unionist nonentity before the war, Ellsworth had been a reluctant advocate, torn between his desire to be counted among the Old Gentry while never condoning nor *appearing* to condone the Klan. That same gentry had been glad when the Klan frightened Republicans out of the legislature, provided they didn't have to know how the frightening was done.

Andrew said, "Can't make a cake without breaking niggers."

"What? What's that you say?"

Andrew Ravanel hadn't been afraid to get his hands dirty. Josie Watling, Archie Flytte—maybe they didn't scrape off their boots before they walked into the drawing room, maybe they didn't care where they spat, but they weren't afraid to get their hands dirty. Andrew's palms itched. "What . . . ?" Ellsworth asked.

"I said," Andrew repeated, "here we are."

Ellsworth's office was three doors down from the Unionist lawyer Louis Petigru's. Petigru hadn't survived the war. While he was alive, everybody had reviled Petigru for his Unionist views. They praised him after the man was safely dead. That's how things were.

Andrew stepped down from the carriage.

"Come into my office. We have work to do."

"I thought I might see a minstrel show."

"You'd what?" Ellsworth gaped.

"The Rabbit Foot Minstrels are at Hibernian Hall. A matinee."

The lawyer removed his glasses and pinched his nose.

Andrew asked, "Is Rhett Butler paying you to defend me?"

"Why shouldn't I defend you?"

"You might get your hands dirty."

"Colonel Ravanel, I already have!" Ellsworth snapped. "Charleston's better homes are no longer open to me. I don't know when we can return to St. Michael's. My wife and I cannot hold our heads up in decent company."

"Sir," Andrew said, "you'd hold your head higher if you emptied the rocks out of it."

"Eh? What did you say?"

"I said there's a matinee."

"What are you talking about? We've got to work on your plea."

"What made you think I wanted to plead?"

"You'd rather face ten years at hard labor?"

Andrew snorted a harsh laugh. "Sir, I have faced worse."

"Be here, at the office, tomorrow by eight. We'll prepare your statement then." The lawyer spoke to Andrew's back.

Andrew rented a bay gelding at the Mills Hotel livery. He'd stayed at the Mills since the trial opened. He hadn't asked who was paying his bills or who'd put up his bond.

A decent horse under him, beautiful Charleston at his feet, and a fine day! What more could any man ask?

Andrew tipped his hat to white and black alike. The negresses turned away; some ducked into doorways. Ladies pretended they didn't see him. Poor whites and prostitutes waved or blew him a kiss. The comedy amused him.

Charleston's rice trade was finished—reduced to fading signs on boarded-up businesses: JAMES MULROONEY: RICE FACTOR; JENKINS COOPERAGE: RICE CASKS, A SPECIALTY.

The harbor was full of bustling steamers. Andrew dismounted, tied his horse, and leaned on the rail.

A negro boy, eight or nine years old, came along, pressed his skinny buttocks against the rail, and rutched. His shirt was out at the armpits, his trousers were belted with rope, and he was barefoot. "Plenty boats," he ventured.

When Andrew looked at him, the boy slid away.

"I won't hurt you," Andrew said. "You needn't be afraid of me."

"I ain't scared of you nohow," the boy said, but came no nearer.

"These ships go everywhere in the world."

"Naw, not them li'l things!"

"Some mighty little boats have crossed the ocean."

"I know 'bout boats," the boy said scornfully. "My Daddy works in the fish market."

"If we put you niggers in those ships, we could send you back to Africa. Would you like that?"

The boy shook his head vigorously. "I never been to no Africa." So not to disappoint the friendly white man, he added, "I been to Savannah onct."

As he mounted, Andrew flipped the boy a dime.

He rode down Anson Street, past Miss Polly's old sporting house. What a time they had had! Lord, Lord, what a time! Edgar Puryear, Rhett

Butler, Henry Kershaw—what a time! And Jack Ravanel. What would his father advise him? Andrew muttered in Old Jack's tones, "Ride like hell, boy! Don't waste time lookin' over your shoulder."

Miss Polly's was roofless and shell-pocked. A yellowed muslin curtain dangled from a second-story window. How eagerly they had sought life. They couldn't wait for life to come to them; they must meet it halfway.

Rhett Butler had been his particular friend. Andrew had gambled with Rhett Butler, drunk with him, and they'd galloped breakneck into the sunrise. Dear God, Andrew thought, I've lost everyone.

He drew up before the East Bay Inn and waited until Jamie Fisher came out, a white apron around his waist. "Ah," Andrew cried, "the boldest scout in the Confederacy."

Jamie's apron was spattered with what looked like tomato pulp.

"I didn't come to the trial. I thought you wouldn't want me there. Judge Boyd?"

"Pronounces sentence tomorrow. My lawyer thinks I'll get off light if I grovel, but"—Andrew grinned—"if the Pit Bull is out of sorts or Mrs. Pit Bull quarrels with the judge over the breakfast table, he might give me ten years. You know how I thrived in the penitentiary."

"Andrew!"

He shook his head. "Jamie, don't worry. It won't come to that."

"Andrew, won't you come inside? Juliet would love to see you."

"I bear my dear sister no animosity. I forgive everyone. I forgive the Yankees, the niggers, even that nigger-loving President Grant. But . . . some other time. Jamie, you and I have somewhere to go."

"Andrew, I'm preparing—"

"No buts, Jamie. We're attending a matinee at the Hibernian Hall—the Rabbit Foot Minstrels, direct from Phila-damn-delphia. The headliner is?" Andrew applauded. "Why, none other than my nigger, Cassius!"

"Andrew, my guests . . ."

"For old times' sake, Jamie."

Jamie had moisture in his eyes, "On the day before your sentencing, Andrew? Are you mad?"

Andrew Ravanel grinned. "Why yes, Jamie. You know I am."

The wooden-legged veteran selling tickets snapped to attention. "Colonel Ravanel, glad you come, sir. These boys put on a great show. You won't be disappointed."

"Where'd you lose the leg?"

The man smacked his wooden leg like a soldier slapping a rifle stock. "Sharpsburg, Colonel. Let me get the manager. You and Mr. . . ."

"My scout, Jamie Fisher."

When Andrew made to pay, the man wouldn't take his money. The manager arrived, apologizing that the audience wasn't so high-toned as Andrew was used to, and escorted Andrew and Jamie to the best seats in the house. The men they displaced were inclined to dispute until told for whom their seats were required. They doffed their caps and one man saluted, saying, "God bless you, sir" and "You taught those Yankees a thing or two" and "Ten more like you and, by God, we'd have won the war," at which sentiment, the house broke out in rebel yells.

The manager cordoned off their chairs with a rope. Men seated beyond the rope offered them flasks, cigars, and plugs of tobacco. Andrew's eyes fixed on the curtain, where painted nymphs and cherubs frolicked.

The audience was rough. The women were bawds and whores. A handful of Federal soldiers sat in the last rows.

That Patriotic Ball, so long ago, when he'd first tried to seduce Rosemary Butler—Lord, she'd been gangly and fresh as a newborn filly—that ball had been in this room. Andrew wondered if that Confederate eagle was still painted on the floor, entombed beneath layers of dirt and spit and trampled cigar butts.

Rosemary bore no resemblance to that leggy girl who had enchanted him. Andrew said, "Don't fidget, Jamie. Everybody loves us here."

There was rustling behind the painted curtain before a banjo clanged, frailing the notes. Andrew elbowed Jamie. That'd be Cassius.

The curtain opened on a stage and a semicircle of empty chairs. As the offstage banjo plunked "Old Dan Tucker," white men in blackface pranced in to stop before each chair, eyes front, still as statues. Tambo and

Mr. Bones had the end chairs, and the armchair center stage was the Interlocutor's.

Jangling his tambourine, Tambo took his seat. The Interlocutor marched in, bowed and froze halfway through his bow. In blackface like the white players, Cassius ambled across the stage, grinning and mugging, until he reached Mr. Bones's chair, where he, too, froze.

The Interlocutor revived from his frozen bow and strolled past his company, miming astonishment, as if he'd never seen any of the performers before. He prodded them as a child might if loosed in a wax museum.

INTERLOCUTOR: Gentlemen, be seated.

[*Tambo's tambourine and Cassius's banjo made a cross fire.*]

BONES: Music makes me feel so happy!

TAMBO: Well, you ain't goin' to be happy no more. You're going to be a 7th Cavalry soldier and I'm goin' to train you. I'm a first-class soldier trainer, I is. I'm a lion trainer, I is.

BONES: You is a lion trainer?

TAMBO: That's what I said. I'ze a hard-boiled lion trainer, I is.

BONES: You're a lion son of a gun.

TAMBO: Was your pappy a soldier?

BONES: Yessir, he was at the battle of Bull Run. He was one of the Yankees what run.

[*Rebel yells.*]

[*More jokes followed by banjo and tambourine duets and sentimental ballads. For forty minutes, the audience sang along with familiar tunes and shouted old jokes' punch lines.*]

BONES: I got a poem I can recite.

INTERLOCUTOR: Well, go ahead and recite it.

BONES:

Mary had a little lamb,
Her father killed it dead,
And now it goes to school with her
Between two hunks of bread.

INTERLOCUTOR: Mr. Bones, it's a good thing you can play that banjo better than you can write poetry.

At this invitation, Cassius played for twenty minutes without interruption. He moved his audience from patriotic fervor to sentimental tears. His dance tunes pulled them into the aisles.

After his final note, Cassius froze again, chairs scraped, and men coughed. The Interlocutor said, "Corporal Cassius: Pride of the Rabbit Foot Minstrels, finest banjo picker North or South. Boys, Cassius is a Confederate veteran."

When the rebel yell rose again, the Yankee soldiers slipped out of the hall.

Chuckling, Andrew said to Jamie, "A nigger pretending to be a white man pretending to be a nigger. Now, that's *unusual.*"

For their finale, the Rabbit Foot Minstrels promenaded, singing rousing tunes, until the manager jumped onto the stage, "Ladies and gentlemen, your attention! We are honored to have a hero among us this afternoon: Colonel Andrew Ravanel, the Tennessee Will of the Wisp, the Carolina Cougar, the Thunderbolt of the White Knights of the . . . of the . . ." He shook his head. "Can't say *that* name. It'd get me in deep!"

Laughter and cheers. Despite Jamie's protests, Jamie and Andrew were propelled onto the stage and the troupe resumed promenading while Cassius strummed "Dixie." Performers and audience sang until the manager drew the curtains.

When the curtains opened for bows, Andrew and Jamie stood at attention stage front. The troupe took four curtain calls before the Interlocutor called it quits and clapped Andrew on the back as if he were a fellow trouper. Some minstrel men left the stage, others shared a flask. Cassius rested his banjo on a chair and sat on the floor beside it, sticking out his legs. "Colonel, Captain. Been a long time."

Andrew chuckled, "The last time I saw you, boy, you were climbin' an Ohio riverbank like the hounds of hell were after you."

"Oh my, I was scared. Them Yankees was killin' everybody in sight!" He shook his head. "Them olden times, mercy! I lives in Philadelphia now. Got me a wife and two baby girls."

"Philadelphia? Don't you miss the Low Country?"

Cassius smiled faintly. "Rabbit Foot Minstrels, we been everywhere—Boston, Buffalo, all over the country." He cocked his head, "How you farin', Mister Jamie? You find yourself a wife?"

Jamie made a wry face. "Haven't found a woman who'll put up with me."

Andrew's eyes gleamed. "You're a headliner now, aren't you, boy? Bet you got plenty of money. All the money you need. You remember when I tried to buy you and Langston Butler's overseer shamed me?"

"I remember bein' sold, Colonel Andrew. Ain't the kind of thing a man forgets."

Jamie said, "Andrew, I've got to get back to the Inn. Maybe you'll join us for supper?"

"You gonna invite this boy here for supper, too? Not much difference twixt him and your damn Yankees. He's got money. He can pay."

"I believe"—Cassius started to rise—"I'll get this nigger makeup off me."

When Andrew shoved him, Cassius and the chair went over backward. Cassius's banjo skidded across the floor with a metallic ring. Cassius caught himself on his hands.

"I'm just a banjo picker!" he said to nobody in particular. Andrew lifted his boot and stamped it on Cassius's right hand like a man smashing a spider. He would have stamped again if Jamie hadn't grabbed him with surprisingly strong arms and dragged him off as the manager entreated, "Colonel Ravanel, consider what you are doing, sir."

Moaning, Cassius tucked his hand to his chest.

"Nothing's changed. You got that, boy!" Andrew was shouting as Jamie wrestled him outside. "Nothing has changed!"

Outside Hibernian Hall, Andrew rubbed his mouth.

His chest heaving for air, Jamie Fisher kept a short distance away. The short distance was a great distance. "Good-bye, Andrew. I wish you well. I have always wished you well."

Bottle trees lined the lane to Congress Haynes's old fishing camp. At first, there'd only been a few bottles and Andrew had knocked them down. But whenever he visited the camp, there were more bottles, until the niggers had blue, green, red, and clear glass bottles tied to the branches of every tree and bush strong enough to bear them. Colored light spots chased down the lane when the sun struck the glass and the faintest breeze was enough to set them jingling. One night, he and Archie Flytte had waited up, hoping to catch a nigger hanging a bottle, but Archie got jumpy after the moon set and the wind started. When Andrew asked if he was afraid, Archie was scornful. The bottles were supposed to scare off the spirits of the dead, and Archie wasn't dead by a long sight. But Archie left for Georgia before midnight and Andrew got drunk, and in the morning the cypress beside the porch, not ten feet from where he'd passed out, glistened with bottles that hadn't been there the night before.

The camp's broken front door had yawned open since Custer's cavalrymen booted it in.

Excepting rat droppings and leaves blown across the floor, the cabin was as he'd left it.

He'd been treated well in that overcrowded prison camp. Hard evidence against Klansmen was hard to find and many witnesses were afraid to testify. The Yankees turned Klansmen loose because they couldn't get enough evidence or didn't have enough room or simply lost patience. Josie Watling hadn't been caught and Archie Flytte hadn't come back after the night of the bottle trees.

When Andrew was in the prison camp, Rosemary had brought clean clothes.

She said, "I'm sorry. I'm sure this is hard for you."

"Not at all," Andrew had replied. "I'm used to being imprisoned."

He'd lied. The camp was a vise whose jaws screwed tighter and tighter, squeezing the life out of him.

When Lawyer Ellsworth announced he was released on bond, Andrew stepped out of the camp gate, newborn, like a boy in the exciting world with no school today. But when Andrew returned to 46 Church Street, his wife wouldn't let him in.

At dusk, the wind off the river set the bottle trees to jingling. It was a fine sound. Say what you would about niggers, they made music.

Andrew felt fine. Late on a gentle spring afternoon, the river rolling past as it had before he came and would after he was gone, and all the lawyers and judges gone, too, Rosemary, Jamie—all of them gone.

Poor dear Charlotte had loved him. She had known who he was and loved him anyway. Sometimes he heard Charlotte's sweet voice in the bottle trees.

Andrew dressed in his Confederate Colonel's uniform and sat outside in the dusk. He'd forgotten how stiff the military collar was.

Small boats sailed up and down the river. Swallows swooped after insects. A heron landed in the shallows and stalked fish, lifting one leg at a time. That'd be the last thing a fish would see, that motionless leg in the water, looking just like a weed or stick.

Andrew's revolver was as familiar to him as Charlotte had been. The long browned barrel was white at the muzzle from much firing; that chip on the grip was where he'd cracked some nigger's skull.

As the moon rose, a pregnant vixen came out of the bushes to fish for crayfish. Andrew considered shooting her but decided not to.

To the merciful shall mercy be given.

At first light, Andrew Ravanel, late Colonel, C.S.A., went inside to write a letter to his firstborn son and shot himself.

Chapter Forty-two

Legacies

The Chapeau Rouge had just closed when a heavy knock brought MacBeth to the door. He cracked it open and then slammed it shut. "Miss Belle . . . They's some mens, Miss Belle, wants talk to you."

"At this time of night? Who . . ."

"Miss Belle . . ." MacBeth was rigid with fear. "They ain't wearin' no hoods, but they's Kluxers."

Belle ran to her bedroom for her revolver, and when she returned, MacBeth had vanished.

Belle stood indecisively, listening to feet shuffle on the porch. She took a deep breath, cocked her revolver, and jerked the door open. "Jesus Christ," she gasped.

Isaiah Watling slapped his daughter's cheek so hard, she almost pulled the trigger. "Thou shalt not take the name of the Lord thy God in vain."

"Poppa! After twenty years you hit me. . . ."

"Why didn't you tell me, Daughter? Why didn't you say something?"

A younger man was with Isaiah and a third at the curb held their horses. Belle was trembling so violently, she used both hands to uncock her revolver.

"I trusted him, Daughter. I believed the man who dishonored you was a Christian gentleman."

The porch creaked when the younger man shifted his weight. He cleared his throat. " 'Lo, Cousin Belle."

At her father's impatient gesture, the young man withdrew into the shadows.

"We were young, Poppa," Belle said. "Was you ever young?"

"No," Isaiah said, "I had no time to be young."

His eyebrows were untrimmed. He had clumps of hair in his nostrils and ears. Belle smelled the bitter metallic stink of an outraged soul.

"You have your mother's eyes." Isaiah pursed his lips. "I'd forgotten that." His curt head shake buried that memory. "I trusted Colonel Ravanel. I trusted him."

"Andrew loved me, Poppa. I cried when I heard . . . what he done to himself."

Isaiah rubbed his hand across his face. "Colonel Ravanel left things for the boy—his pistol, watch, a note. . . ."

"My Tazewell is a gentleman, Poppa," Belle insisted. "He's got schooling and he's in the cotton business in New Orleans. He even bought himself a house!" Belle rubbed her cheek.

He said, "I should never have come to the Low Country. Your mother hated to leave Mundy Hollow, but I said we had to start over somewheres else. So we come to Broughton. I was Master Butler's man, body and soul, for thirty-two years. Thirty-two years, body and soul."

"This parcel . . . it's from Tazewell's father?"

"Only ones besides us at the Colonel's burying were Yankees lookin' for Klansmen."

"Uncle Isaiah never held with the Klan." Belle's cousin grinned at her. "Uncle Isaiah's . . . 'fussy.' Him 'n' me, we found the Colonel. We was going to spirit him away to Texas, but the Colonel got his own self away first. I reckon he would have done right good in Texas."

"This is Josie, Abraham's son."

Josie touched his hat. "Pleased to meet you, cuz. Nice place you got. That's Archie Flytte with the horses."

Belle's hands trembled. "Father, did you love Mama?"

"Your mother was devout."

"Did you love her?"

"Daughter, I love the Lord."

Belle had believed her father was a simple man; she'd never before guessed how much his simplicity cost him.

"Colonel Ravanel lied to me," Isaiah said. "And your brother, Shadrach, died for Colonel Ravanel's lie. Shadrach never had no days to repent of his sins."

An unkind thought flashed through Belle's mind: Shadrach died because he'd challenged a better shot.

Josie said, "Dead is dead."

"Rhett Butler lied."

"He never did. Rhett never said nothin'. He just let 'em believe whatever they wanted to believe."

"Butler murdered your brother and disgraced his parents. Honor thy father and thy mother that thy days may be long upon the land the Lord thy God has given you."

"Even now, after all this hurtfulness . . ." Belle's hands opened and closed helplessly. "You can't forgive?"

Belle's father handed her the parcel. "By my lights, I did my best."

The parcel was heavier than it looked. "I reckon we all do the best we can," Belle said. "Won't you come in? I've a picture of your grandson."

For one moment, she thought Isaiah was going to take off his hat and step inside. They'd go to the kitchen—they wouldn't need to be in the business part of the house. She'd make coffee for her father. She remembered he took sugar in his coffee—heaping tablespoons of sugar.

Isaiah Watling touched the package. "Give these to your son." He turned away.

"Uncle likes to say our day will come," Josie observed, "but it ain't come yet."

Chapter Forty-three

Ashley's Birthday Party

Melanie was preparing a surprise birthday party—Ashley's first since the barbecue at Twelve Oaks, eleven years ago, when he and she had announced their betrothal.

The Wilkeses' home was nearly ready. The mantelpiece had been scrubbed with Sapolio, the gilt mirror frame had been dusted, every grate and stove was freshly blacked, and the winter carpets had been taken up and brushed. Pork and Peter had sprinkled tobacco on them before carrying them to the attic.

As chairwoman of the Confederate Widows and Orphans Society, Melanie knew all Georgia's Confederate greats: General John Gordon, five times wounded at Sharpsburg; Robert Augustus Toombs, Confederate Senator and Secretary of State; even Alexander Stephens had accepted Melanie's invitation. Vice President Stephens's two-volume justification of secession, *A Constitutional View of the Late War Between the States,* had pride of place in many Southern households (where it was more honored than read). Ashley's spinster sister, India, wanted the book beside the family Bible in the parlor, but Melanie said no. "What if someone decides to raise a constitutional issue with Mr. Stephens? What will happen to Ashley's party then?" Mr. Stephens's volumes remained locked in the bookcase.

India was an efficient worker, but she upset the negroes. When set to a task, Aunt Pittypat managed—she'd polished all the glassware, including that borrowed for the occasion—but left to her own devices, Pitty flittered from one unfinished task to another. Only Scarlett worked without instructions. Scarlett was the best negro driver, too.

Since preparations were moving along nicely, Melanie took a cup of tea to the second-floor landing, her desk, and her interrupted letter to Rosemary.

Melanie entirely approved of Rosemary's decision to teach at the Female Seminary. "You have suffered a terrible grief, dear friend. The children will heal you as you instruct them."

She tapped the pen against her teeth, thinking.

As for myself . . . when I learned I could have no more children, I assumed I would be as satisfied with the warmth that attends lovemaking as by the lovemaking itself. Ashley is an affectionate husband, but absent the—if you will permit me—"tender violence" of the act—I am blushing, dear friend—our heart passion fades year by year, unvarying season by unvarying season. Oh, I know, a decent woman shouldn't desire her husband's ardent embraces, but . . .

Miss Melly! Miss Melly!" Scarlett's servant Pork stomped upstairs and loomed over her like a tree poised to fall. Although Pork couldn't read, Melly slipped her letter under the blotter. "Miss Melly! That Archie, he won't let me hang no more lanterns in the garden. He done told me to git. I'ze skeered of that old man!"

"Ask Scarlett what to do, Pork," Melanie replied. "I'm sure there's other work to do."

After the big negro grumbled back down the stairs, Melanie inked her pen.

Sometimes I happen across your old Overseer's daughter, Belle Watling. Dear Friend, I have only known my Ashley, whose touches were so lavish, his pleasure giving so much keener than his pleasure taking. I have fancied asking Belle (but of course could not), "How is it to have had so many men? Are all men the same?"

Oh, Rosemary, it has been eight years—eight long years—since Dr. Meade told Ashley I must not bear another child. I know I should put my

desires aside—but I cannot. Sometimes, Ashley does or says something; sometimes he catches the light in a certain way and I positively burn for my husband's embraces! Dear Friend, he is so beautiful! There are contrivances which would permit intimacies without the consequences we fear, but Ashley, dear Ashley, is too proper, and on the single occasion I dared to mention them, Ashley turned red as one of Pitty's azaleas and he stuttered (Ashley never stutters), saying, "Gentlemen do not employ such devices!" I'm sure Belle knows about them and would tell me if I dared to ask.

Scarlett peeked through the banisters at Melanie's ankles and said, "Melly, Pork is perfectly capable of hanging a few Japanese lanterns. Archie gave Pork one of his 'looks' and Pork will be quaking all afternoon. Why do you let that smelly old hillbilly in your house?"

"Archie is so good with the children," Melanie replied.

In the past, Archie had been given to mysterious disappearances and everybody knew he was in the Klan. But he was wonderful with the children.

After Governor Bullock fled, Scarlett stopped entertaining, and her Peachtree Street mansion became a mausoleum. The Butler children spent more time in the Wilkeses' home than their own. Sour, one-legged old Archie Flytte entertained them for hours.

"If Peter is done polishing the floors, Pork and he can lay the summer matting," Melanie said.

"Humph." Scarlett's head disappeared.

Melanie Wilkes tapped her pen against her teeth.

Dear Rosemary, I am loath to add to your burdens but must tell you that last Saturday, over luncheon at the Kimball House, Scarlett and Rhett lit into each other like cats and dogs. I heard about their quarrel from three different sources! Their only real bond is their shared love for little Bonnie—"Bonnie Blue." Your niece is a sunbeam who lights everywhere she goes. Mrs. Meade makes Bonnie her special pecan fudge and Mrs. Elsing sets the dear little thing on her lap and tells her how things were when she was a girl. Those who once deprecated your brother have taken him into their hearts. Not their least reason is the love Rhett lavishes on his daughter.

All she needs say is, "Daddy, pick me up!" Rhett picks her up, and when she tugs at his mustache or hair or when she is fretful, as all children sometimes are, Rhett never loses patience with his Bonnie Blue.

Scarlett was peeking through the banisters again, "Melanie, who are you writing to?"

"I am writing Rosemary. Two tired housewives complaining about their children. Sometimes, dear Scarlett"—Melanie slipped the letter into the drawer and turned the key—"I wish I had your gift for being in the world. I wish I had your will!"

"If will was as powerful as it's supposed to be, Melly, we'd presently be Confederate citizens. I'm going to Ashley's sawmill to see Hugh Elsing."

Melanie clapped her hands. "That's perfect. That's absolutely perfect. Could you possibly keep Ashley there until five? If Ashley comes home earlier, he'll catch us finishing up a cake or something and his surprise will be ruined."

Hastily, Melanie concluded her letter.

Dear Rosemary, jealousy is so corrosive that I'd almost rather be betrayed than live in fear of betrayal! If I could not put my trust in Ashley, if I did not believe he loves me, I would go mad.

I knew from childhood that Ashley and I were intended for each other. We are cousins, and "the Wilkeses always marry cousins." We were spared the tribulations of courtship—does he or doesn't he love me; do I or don't I truly care for him? I knew I was to marry Ashley and I loved him. Not love Ashley? I cannot imagine it!

Yet, sometimes, I wonder how it might have been. . . . Are Scarlett's passions richer and more profound than mine, or have I read too many novels?

Must love always be such a puzzle?

Melanie signed and sealed the letter. Downstairs, Pork and Uncle Peter were arguing how the summer floor mats should be laid. Melanie could smell furniture polish and baking pies.

How grateful she was! During the War, she'd been so afraid for Ashley. One alert sharpshooter, one of the myriad illnesses that killed soldiers weakened by hunger and privation—there were so many ways she might have lost her precious husband. Melanie Hamilton Wilkes bowed her head and gave thanks.

Chapter Forty-four

Desire

Desire too long denied makes the heart sick.

Sun pouring through the windows illuminated order books and a calendar whose dates were crossed off with *X*'s. Sawmill dust furred windowsills, shelves, Ashley Wilkes's rolltop desk, and his hat.

That hat was their mute chaperone.

A man and a woman alone together, after so many years.

Scarlett notices the gray in Ashley's hair and thinks, He will never be young again, and the thought makes her want to cry for him and for herself.

Scarlett has not been with a man since Bonnie Blue was conceived. Ashley has not been with a woman for eight years.

It is Saturday afternoon. The whining saws are shut down and oiled for the Sabbath; there's no lumber crashing onto ricks, no foreman shouting orders. The mill hands have been paid and gone home. Dust motes dance in the sunlight.

"The days are getting longer," Ashley says.

Scarlett says, "Yes, yes, they are."

A spring fly, one of the fat, lazy flies that appear as seasons change bats against the window glass, trying to reach the outdoors. It will die, as so many of God's creatures do, without ever fulfilling its desire.

Scarlett O'Hara is thinking how sad life is, how unutterably sad, as she steps into the embrace she has wanted for so long.

Ashley and Scarlett fit perfectly in each other's arms.

The office door bangs open. India Wilkes, Archie Flytte, and Mrs. Elsing are in the doorway. Gaping.

Scarlett is lost.

Chapter Forty-five

She

The cuckold Rhett Butler rode Atlanta's dark streets. He galloped his horse down Decatur until it was a country road, before wheeling back into the city.

When his great black horse slowed, Rhett used his spurs savagely. "Damn you, behave! You will behave!"

He could not trust himself. That was his worst realization—knowing he could not trust himself. Four years. For four years he'd slept alone while she mooned after Ashley Wilkes.

Earlier tonight, he'd forced her to attend Melanie's party. Thinking what? That Melly would denounce the adulterous pair? What a comedy! Ashley and Melanie playacting the happily married couple. Melanie welcoming Scarlett as a sister while vicious whispers took wings behind ladies' fans.

The cuckold Rhett Butler. Oh no, she hadn't given her body to Ashley. Just her goddamned, yearning, hopeful, scheming soul.

He emptied his flask. He emptied a second. He galloped by Chapeau Rouge without seeing. MacBeth, who'd raised a hand in greeting, let it fall to his side.

He couldn't go near his wife until he could trust himself. His wife! He couldn't go home until Scarlett was safe behind her locked bedroom door. "Home." Rhett spat the epithet between his horse's hooves.

When he came into the parlor, she was there. She was sneaking a glass of brandy. She paled when she saw him.

His resolutions vanished like smoke. His hands ached with the need to hurt her. He would have killed her on the spot. Killing would cure her of yearning for Ashley.

"You drunken fool. Take your hands off me."

"I've always admired your spirit, my dear. Never more than now, when you are cornered."

"You can't understand Ashley or me. You are jealous of something you can't understand." Regal as a queen, she tossed her head and straightened her wrap, rising to go.

He caught her. He pressed her shoulders against the wall.

"Jealous, am I? And why not? Oh yes, I'm jealous of Ashley Wilkes. I know Ashley Wilkes and his breed. I know he is honorable and a gentleman. And that, my dear, is more than I can say for you—or for me, for that matter. We are not gentlemen and we have no honor, have we? That's why we flourish like green bay trees."

When he turned to the decanter, she bolted.

Rhett caught her at the bottom of the stairs. His hands slipped under her dressing gown onto her sleek skin. He whispered hoarsely, "You turned me out on the town while you chased him. By God, this is going to be one night when there are only two in my bed!"

Rhett scooped and carried her up the broad staircase of the great house he'd built for his bride. She trembled in his arms, mesmerized by his rage. On the landing, when she took breath to scream, he stopped her mouth with his own. She was his creature; he had nurtured her and taught her and devoted himself to her. She was his and he would use her as he saw fit.

He carried her into the darkness at the head of the stairs, his mouth pressed to hers, their breath intermingling.

In her bed, in her dark room, she opened to him like a flower and he crushed that flower for its loveliness. Even when she let her love roll down, even that couldn't quench his hunger.

Hours later, Rhett rose from the bed where Scarlett slept, exhausted. He didn't know who had been the victor, who the victim. He pressed his aching head between his hands. His eyes were sore, his lips were sore, his tongue was swollen, his body was sticky with his sweat and hers. He smelled like the woman he had violated.

"My God," Rhett Butler whispered, "I am just like my father."

Chapter Forty-six

Eugenie Victoria Butler

When Bonnie Blue's parents were fighting—which they did an awful lot—the house swelled up with anger, until Bonnie put her hands over her ears so she wouldn't hear it pop. Yesterday had been 'specially bad. The grown-ups were going to a party at Aunt Melly's house, so Bonnie thought everybody would be happy, but that afternoon Big Sam came 'round to the back, and when Mammy heard what Big Sam had to say, she put on her sorrowful face, and pretty soon all the servants had sorrowful faces and they wouldn't tell Bonnie, but she knew it was something bad.

Her Mother came home and hid in her bedroom, but when Daddy Rhett came home, he made her go to Aunt Melly's party. Bonnie knew Mother didn't want to go to the party, but Daddy Rhett made her go.

That night, Bonnie couldn't sleep, and when she heard loud voices downstairs, she opened her door just a crack and she saw Daddy Rhett carrying Mother up the stairs just like she was a baby. They were kissing, so maybe they'd made up and weren't going to fight anymore.

Next day, Mother didn't come down until almost suppertime and she was happy as a cat with fresh cream, but Daddy Rhett was gone. When Bonnie asked when he'd be home, Mother smiled mysteriously and said, "When he's done feeling guilty, sweetheart." That evening, Mother went around humming, and after dinner she brought out the stereograph and Wade and Ella and Bonnie Blue sat with her on the sofa, taking turns looking at pictures of a big river in China and Chinamen wearing hats like upside-down bowls.

Mother expected Daddy Rhett to come home, but he didn't. Not that day nor the day after nor the day after that. Mother stopped humming and was short with everybody, and when Wade suggested they take out the stereograph and look at pictures, she snapped at him.

When Daddy Rhett did come home, they fought again—worse than ever!—and Daddy got so mad at her Mother, he threw his cigar down on the parlor carpet, which stunk up the whole house!

Later, Mammy pretended to be cheerful as she packed Bonnie's clothes, saying Bonnie was going away with Daddy Rhett for a while, but Mammy's old sad eyes knew better.

"Mammy," Bonnie asked, "what's a divorce?"

"No such a thing! They ain't doin' no such a thing!" When Mammy sighed, all of her sighed, not just her mouth. "They just considerin', that's all."

Belle Watling was waiting at the railway station.

When Bonnie was introduced to Belle—whose name Bonnie had heard a lot when Mother was angry—Bonnie drew herself up and asked, "Are you really a fallen woman?"

Belle's smile dimmed and then brightened again. "Well, honey, I reckon I am."

"Where'd you fall from?" the child asked.

"Not too high, honey. I reckon where I fell from wasn't too high." Belle took Bonnie's hand to help the child into their Pullman car.

Bonnie was delighted by the Pullman. She couldn't get over how couches became beds, and she made the porter transform them three times before she was satisfied.

Bonnie knew her mother was the most beautiful woman in the world, and when she saw pictures of queens in storybooks, she knew they were just like Mother. Daddy Rhett was the kindest, smartest, funniest man, and the best horseman, too. Why, his black stallion was almost as fast as her pony!

Bonnie knew they loved her and she knew they loved each other, too. So why couldn't they just say so and not fight anymore?

But that was before and this was now, and Bonnie raced up and down the Pullman car with Prissy chasing her. "Watch out for that table! Don't go out that door! We coming to a tunnel! Cover you eyes!"

The world flashed by the windows. Plowmen were turning the earth in glistening red furrows. In towns, people got on the train or got off the train and stood on the platform, greeting and gossiping, and luggage carts trundled and the bell clanged and the conductor shouted "All 'board!" and swung on the train. Bonnie wondered if he ever got left behind.

Sitting in Belle Watling's lap, Bonnie asked about water lilies in the swamp they were crossing and a blackened plantation house on a hill. "Are there ghosts?" Bonnie asked.

"Yes, honey, there are. But they won't hurt you."

When they sat down for dinner, Daddy Rhett complimented Belle on her gown and she blushed, "Miss Smithers helps me pretend I'm a lady."

Bonnie's father's smile was so sad. "Belle, dear Belle. You know we can't choose our heart's desire."

"You think I don't know that, Captain Smarty?" Belle retorted. "You think I don't know a thing or two about desires?"

He laughed then, his old laugh, and Bonnie's pealing laughter harmonized and Belle's mock-stern expression dissolved into giggles.

The next morning, Bonnie stood on the seat as their train rumbled into Charleston. When her father offered his hand to guide her through the big brick depot, Bonnie preferred to walk by herself, thank you, but she let him lift her into the cab.

Bonnie was glad to see her cousin Louis Valentine again. While her father and her aunt Rosemary talked about the things grown-ups talk about, Belle and Prissy took Bonnie and Louis Valentine to the promenade to see the boats. Prissy chattered with Belle just like Belle wasn't a fallen woman.

Bonnie wanted to stay longer in Charleston, but her father said they couldn't. Bonnie pouted until they were back in their dear familiar Pullman car. She ate her dinner and climbed into her little bed. Since Bonnie was afraid of the dark, her father left a light burning where she could see it through the bed curtains.

Bonnie woke to cypress swamps that gave way to shacks and shanties, then more substantial buildings, and then their track joined another as they sped past old stone houses Daddy Rhett called "the Vieux Carré. It's the old French Quarter, Bonnie." Their train rolled along the levees above the wharves and the ships in the big river. Bonnie was fascinated by the steamboats and she begged until Daddy Rhett gave his laughing promise that yes, yes, they would take a steamboat ride. Because as Bonnie Blue asserted, "I had to leave my pony behind and I miss him very much, but I shan't miss him so much when I'm taking a steamboat ride."

Chapter Forty-seven

A Catholic City

A spring morning in the Vieux Carré: Church bells echoed in the narrow streets, the birds-of-paradise were flowering, and behind wrought-iron gates overripe lemons and oranges were dropping from the trees.

Waiting beside Rhett for a cab, Belle Watling remembered the pregnant young girl she'd been in this city so many years ago.

"What did you say, Belle?" Rhett asked.

"I spect I was talkin' to myself. I was thinkin' how New Orleans seemed like the biggest city in the world." Belle added, "Lord a mercy, I was scared."

Rhett helped her into an open landaulet. "Do you remember when you and me met up outside the St. Louis Hotel? That Didi woman you was with? Mercy, what a beauty! She was wearin' the brightest red hat I'd ever seen. Sometimes I still dream about that hat. . . ." She touched Rhett's arm, "If you hadn't found me that day, Rhett, I . . ."

"But I did, Belle." He smiled. "Very occasionally, things turn out better than we expect."

Belle knew Rhett's marriage wasn't one of those things. That foolishness between Mr. Wilkes and Miss Scarlett had birthed something terrible. Belle'd never known Rhett so drawn and sorrowful.

When they stopped at number 12 Royal Street, Rhett said, "I think it best if you meet Taz alone. I don't want his dislike of me ruining things. I'll be back in an hour."

"But Rhett!"

He helped her down and gave her Andrew's bequest. "Go on, Belle. Go brave." The cab horse's iron shoes rang on the ancient cobblestones.

Belle had moved Andrew's things from Isaiah's rough paper parcel to a nice poplar box, which seemed more respectful. Now, with the box in her hands, she wondered if she couldn't have found a nicer one—maybe walnut. Belle told herself, Ruth Belle Watling! Don't be a ninny! and yanked the bellpull more vigorously than she'd intended.

On tenterhooks, she listened for his footsteps and the rasp of drawn bolts. The gate creaked, swinging open. "Maman!"

Belle dissolved in tears. "You've grown a beard!"

"I was just about to go out. . . . I am surprised, so happy you are here! Please, please come in."

Taz's little garden was the prettiest Belle had ever seen. Its lime tree was certainly the most fragrant. What a sweet little bench! What a cunning little fish pond! The house—was this her dear son's house? What a perfect little house! Belle sniffled into her handkerchief.

Taz threw his arms out to encompass it all. "Maman, it is yours!"

Belle froze like an animal sensing a trap. "But Taz, my home's in Atlanta."

"Come in, Maman," Taz adjusted. "Please. I'll make tea. English tea. Unless you'd rather have water or a glass of wine?"

"Taz, who would have dreamed . . ." Belle's gesture was a mother's delight. "Honey, you've done right well for yourself!"

"Maman, I have done it all for you." Taz flashed his familiar grin. "And I'm not always so pompous. I promise you I'm not. Why didn't you tell me you were coming? *Bon Dieu,* I am so very happy. Please, let me show you the house." Taz laid Belle's box on a window ledge and led her into the kitchen, which had just enough room for both of them. "Oh," Belle said, "it's so cozy and snug!"

The front bedroom's balcony overlooked the garden. When Taz said, "This will be your room," Belle pretended she hadn't heard. The bedroom in the back had a separate staircase, which would be ideal—as Belle understood—for the young man about town who might come home late.

Back in the parlor, Taz insisted Belle take his new chair, a Suffolk chair, which, he told her, "was made in New York City."

"I don't believe I ever sat in a more comfortable chair."

When Belle ran out of things to admire, silence filled the room. The birds twittered loudly in the garden.

"I've missed you, Taz," Belle said.

"I missed you, too." Impulsively, Taz knelt and pressed her hand. "I am a full partner of J. Nicolet. We do a very good business and employ four men."

Belle beamed at her boy.

Taz rubbed his palm across his forehead. To Belle, that familiar gesture recalled the little boy he'd been, and tears welled in her eyes. He said, "You know what I wish for. I never could fool you."

Belle went to the window and pushed the shutters open. She said, "I'd forgotten how well things grow in New Orleans."

"Will you come here and live with me?"

Belle turned to him with a tremulous smile. "Taz, I've a business to look after."

"Sell it. You won't want for anything. I can provide. . . ."

"Taz, my dear boy, I thank you from the bottom of my heart, but I can't."

"But Maman," Taz spoke as if to a child, "here in New Orleans, you would be a lady."

Belle restrained her laugh. Belle Watling, a lady! "No, my darling," she said. "I'd spoil everything. Think what J. Nicolet would say when he learned your mother is nothing but a common—"

The ringing bell saved Belle. She said, "Get the gate, Taz. Rhett and me'll tell you everything you want to know."

Outside that gate, with Bonnie Blue's tiny hand in his own, Rhett Butler had slipped into that mood where the deepest affections are colored by sorrow and love's losses seem the greater part of love.

How had the boy he'd brought from the Asylum for Orphan Boys become this young man standing before him? The young man's eyes were honest and calm. "Welcome to my home, sir. I owe you an apology."

"This is my Bonnie Blue," Rhett said.

"Hello," Bonnie piped up. "I'm four. I've had my birthday."

Taz smiled. "A fine thing it is to have a birthday. But are you sure you're four? You're so tall for four."

"I am very tall," Bonnie assured him. "I have a pony."

"A pony! My goodness!" Taz ushered them into his garden.

Poplar box in her lap, Belle waited on the circular stone bench beneath a lime tree. Bonnie dashed to the tiny pool, where goldfish flashed under a carpet of water lilies.

"I thought we'd talk better out-of-doors," Belle said quietly. "Ain't this place pretty, Rhett?"

Taz began, "Sir, I must apologize. I have been an ungrateful fool. I—"

Rhett put a finger to his lips. "Shh."

"Sir, I—"

"It was nothing, Taz." Rhett grinned. "On second thought, I'm glad it's over." He took Belle's hand. "Your mother and I . . . for a good many years we were custodians of another man's reputation. A man who had more to lose than we did. Andrew Ravanel was one of the bravest soldiers in the Confederacy. In his last moments, he thought of you."

"But . . ." Taz opened the box and stared, unseeing, at a revolver, a Confederate Colonel's epaulets, a heavy silver watch, and a folded piece of paper.

Since the goldfish wouldn't come out from beneath the lily pads, Bonnie ran to the grown-ups and stood on tiptoes to see what was in the young man's box. Maybe today was his birthday.

Rhett said, "The grateful citizens of Cynthiania, Tennessee, gave your father that watch, Taz. There's an inscription."

Tazewell turned the heavy watch in his hand. "*Merde!* You're saying Andrew Ravanel was my father? *Colonel* Andrew Ravanel? Why did you let me think I was your bastard. Why not tell me the truth?"

"Read the note, honey," Belle said softly.

To whom it may concern,

I acknowledge Tazewell Watling as my firstborn son and bequeath him these, my worldly goods. I pray he will do better with his life than I have done with mine.

Andrew Ravanel, Colonel, C.S.A.

Taz folded the note. Opened it a second time and stared.

"Taz," Rhett said quietly, "please, sit down."

When he did, his mother put her arm around him.

Rhett took a deep breath. "I've always loved New Orleans. It's a Catholic city, tolerant, sensual, and wise. The Low Country, where your mother and I grew up, Taz . . ."

Rhett stopped and began again. "Planters like my father, Langston Butler, had the power of life and death. Everything and everyone on Broughton Plantation belonged to the Master. Langston's slaves, Langston's overseer, Langston's horses, Langston's overseer's daughter, Langston's wife, Langston's daughter . . ." Rhett coughed. "Even Langston Butler's renegade elder son. To trifle with the least of Langston's possessions was to trifle with the Master himself."

Belle sighed. "Don't it seem so long ago?"

"Taz, it's a long story your mother and I have to tell. Do you think you could find a glass of wine?"

When Taz and Bonnie went in the house, Rhett strolled the garden, hands in pockets, whistling softly.

Taz returned and set the tray on the bench.

"I don't want any wine. I'm too little." Bonnie went back to the pool and lay down on the edge, where the goldfish couldn't see her.

Belle said, "Mama and me kept the Broughton dispensary, and sometimes I'd come into Charleston to the apothecary's for quinine bark, and one day Andrew was there. First time we set eyes on each other, we fell in love. Don't smile at me, Rhett Butler. You know it happens. Hell, you *know* it does. Anyway, that afternoon me and Andrew strolled around White Point Park, gabbin' and lookin' at each other. I reckon I wanted to eat him up.

Well, nothin' happened that day and I caught the ferry back to Broughton, but I wasn't really surprised when a negro woman delivered a note sayin' I should meet Andrew at Wilson's Roadhouse.

"Well, I snuck away that day, and a week later I snuck away again, and it wasn't long before we were doin' what the preachers say we shouldn't. It never troubled me none, and if Mama knew, she never said nothin'. I never met none of Andrew's kin nor his fancy friends—until the morning Rhett rode up to Wilson's, and then everybody thought Rhett and me . . .

"Andrew was so secretive about us. I always knew we wasn't meant to marry."

Rhett said, "Andrew's father, Jack, sold land when he had to and wrote as many IOUs as there were fools to accept them. He loved fast horses."

Bonnie sang, "Come out, little fishies. I won't hurt you."

"Somehow my father and Jack Ravanel were involved in a rice-factoring syndicate, and when the syndicate collapsed, my father ended up with Jack's IOUs—which pleased neither of them: my father because Jack hated to pay and Jack because if any man in Carolina could squeeze a dollar out of him, that man was Langston Butler.

"Langston let Jack know his patience was running thin. Langston could ruin Jack, and Jack knew it.

"When Jack learned about Andrew and your mother, he worried. If Langston discovered his debtor's son was trifling with his overseer's daughter, that'd be the last straw. Jack ordered Andrew to stop seeing Belle, but Andrew refused.

"Jack always liked to have an edge, and when he didn't have one, he introduced a wild card. I didn't understand until years afterward—but angry, confused Rhett Butler was Old Jack's wild card.

"It worked, too. My father was so busy disowning me, he never found out about Andrew and Belle."

When Rhett hitched himself into the window casing, his long legs just touched the ground. He offered his cigar case to Taz. When Taz declined, Rhett took his time lighting up.

"Andrew was touchy, proud, and melancholy, but he was my friend. When I came back from West Point disgraced, I lived with the Ravanels."

"Colonel Jack got you drunk," Belle said stoutly.

Rhett laughed. "Belle, nobody but me gets me drunk. I was desperately unhappy, and Jack merely provided the whiskey and a gloomy porch where I could drink it. After he'd let me stew in my own morose juices long enough, Jack told me his son was involved with a slattern—sorry, Belle—and that if I was Andrew's friend, I'd disentangle him. I have forgotten many things about those days, but I remember that morning. . . ."

"I'm to spoil Andrew's fun? Come now, Jack."

Colonel Jack's tongue whipped like a snake run over in the road. Jack had ten thousand reasons why Rhett should help Andrew. Rhett was weary, part drunk, and plain didn't give a damn. He'd have done anything just to shut Jack up.

"You'll talk to him, then?" Jack said. "Wilson's Roadhouse? Boy, you're a good'un. Don't anyone tell you you're not. If the slut's father finds out about this, there's no telling . . ."

Rhett was thoroughly sick of Jack and thoroughly sick of himself, and there are worse things than a ride into the breaking day. Tecumseh's trot was smooth as glass.

The river was changing from black to silver and work gangs' lanterns flickered in the fields before Rhett reached the Summerville crossroads. When he turned into Wilson's stableyard, Andrew was outside, smoking. "Thank God, Rhett. Thank God it's you."

A lamp glowed in the upstairs room where Belle waited for her lover. That same night, she'd told Andrew she was carrying his baby.

Andrew clutched Rhett's arm. "Rhett, she wants me to marry her. Rhett, I cannot; you know I must not." Andrew tried a ghastly joke. "I am my father's last negotiable asset!"

When Belle came down into the yard, she was in love and beautiful. "Andrew? Who's with you? Why, it's Young Master Butler." The young woman trusted that her love would see her through anything. "Andrew and I have been . . . keeping company. I got to go home now. Will you take me home, Young Master?"

Rhett would.

The sun rose as the two rode down the main trunk. Silent rice gangs watched them pass, shading their eyes against the sun.

Rhett's mind was clear as it had not been since he left West Point. He felt better than he had in months. Rhett Butler had absolutely nothing more to lose.

Belle's cheek was warm against his back.

"Do you love anyone, Young Master?"

"My sister, Rosemary. . . ."

"Ain't we lucky? Ain't it better lovin' than bein' loved?"

Twenty-four years after that morning ride, Rhett Butler laid his hands on Tazewell Watling's shoulders and said, "*Dites moi qui vous aimez, et je vous dirai qui vous etes:* Tell me who you love and I'll tell you who you are."

At Taz's suggestion, they dined at Antoine's, where the waiters fussed over Mr. Watling's mother and Captain Butler's little girl. Belle said it was the happiest day of her life.

The next day, they took a train to Baton Rouge to meet Tazewell's Watling's partner. While Rhett, Taz, and J. Nicolet discussed common acquaintances, Belle, Prissy, and Bonnie walked along the bayou, where Prissy was scared half out of her wits when a harmless-looking log turned into an alligator.

In Baton Rouge, they ate at a fisherman's café. Bonnie loved the *boudin* but shuddered at the langoustine. "It's a big spider!" Bonnie insisted.

Back in New Orleans, they attended the races and saw *The Marriage of Figaro* at the French Opera House. One entire morning, Rhett and Bonnie rode uptown and downtown on the street railway because that's what Bonnie wanted.

Bonnie lifted her little face to his and said, "I wish Mother was here."

Rhett's eyes were so sad. "Yes, sugar. I wish she was, too."

The rains that happy week were tropical rains, which cooled the earth and disappeared into mist as they fell.

Rhett forgot his promise to take his daughter on a steamboat ride. He would regret that unkept promise for the rest of his days.

Chapter Forty-eight

Miss Melly Asks for Help

A year and a month after Rhett and Bonnie visited New Orleans, Melanie Wilkes wrote her friend:

Dearest Rosemary,

I trust this finds you in good health and spirits. Do you like teaching at the Female Seminary?

Rosemary, how can two stick-in-the-muds like us have become such dear friends?

Dr. Meade is outside my door issuing instructions to Pittypat. The good doctor leaves me with admonitions and an array of varicolored potions and pills! When men can fix something, they fix it. When the repair is beyond them, they harrumph and dither!

Although Dr. Meade blames me for the fix I'm in—I can see reproach in his eyes—he cannot decently utter them. Would any man presume to tell a wife she should have refused her husband's embraces?

He is less forbearing with Ashley, and my guilty husband avoids him. When Dr. Meade manages to ambush Ashley, my husband comes to my room so contrite, I must lift his spirits. Falsely cheerful wife and contrite husband: What geese we are!

Dr. Meade blames Ashley for my pregnancy. Ashley is a gentleman and no gentleman could admit that his mousy, sickly wife has been a Salome whose allures the helpless male could not resist.

Yet, Dear Friend, I confess that unlikely tale is the Truth, that this plain girl can, when needs must, be a Salome of the first order!

A year ago in April, Scarlett and Ashley gave way—only for a moment—to the impulse that had smoldered in them for so many years. Ashley's sister India, Archie Flytte, and old Mrs. Elsing—Atlanta's prime busybody—caught them in an embrace. Naturally, India raced to me with their news—and on Ashley's birthday, too, with our house prepared to receive guests and Japanese lanterns glowing fetchingly in our garden.

Dear Rosemary, where it comes to my family, I am a mother tiger, and I understood perfectly, as India gleefully delivered her news, that I might undo two marriages, my own and your brother Rhett's. India's face positively glowed with malicious satisfaction. She has always hated Scarlett.

I thought to myself, India, you are Ashley's sister. Why can't you see this must destroy the brother you love as thoroughly as the woman you despise?

So I pronounced India a liar. I said that my husband, Ashley, and my dear friend Scarlett would never betray me. I ordered India from my house. When Archie Flytte corroborated India's tale, I expelled him, too. Subsequently, Archie has uttered the vilest threats—not against me—against Scarlett and Rhett! I fear they have a bad enemy there.

When my guilty Ashley returned home, I never gave the poor man a chance to make excuses, but met him with an embrace which I trust was more ardent and familiar than Scarlett's!

Ashley desperately wanted to confess. His lips trembled with yearning. I stayed his confession with a kiss.

Honesty is a blunt tool: pruning shears when sewing scissors are what's wanted! I could not let my husband confess because I could not grant him absolution!

Scarlett and Rhett arrived after Ashley's party was well under way. (I've no doubt your brother made Scarlett "face the music.") At our front door, I took my dear friend's faithless arm and smiled at her for all the world to see.

Our guests that night included prominent men, a few so prominent (and distracted), nobody'd told them about Ashley's fall from grace. Generous spirits accepted my faith in my husband and my friend. Cynics thought me a booby and snickered covertly.

But scandal was stopped dead at my reputation.

That night, after our guests went home, Ashley proved in the most primitive, convincing fashion that he was mine and mine alone.

Ashley and Melly Wilkes were like newlyweds. We conversed about books and art and music—never a word about politics or commerce—but our nights were so voluptuous, I blush to remember them! We never discussed what might come of our concupiscence. Perhaps we dreamed that after Beau's difficult delivery, I could not conceive again.

Since I cannot believe God can be heartless, I must believe He knows best, and so I am come to childbed.

If I survive, it is God's will. If I do not, I pray my baby will live. She is so clever and vigorous, and she so wants to live. I say "she" because I am already close to her, closer than I could be to any male child. I confide in her. I have told her how her father was shaped for a finer world than the rough-and-tumble one we inhabit. I urge my daughter to make her world one where gentle souls like Ashley may live in honor and peace.

Rosemary, it must be possible! We born in the nineteenth century stand at the gates of Paradise, where there will be no more wars and everyone will be happy and good!

What will my daughter know of our world? If life before the War seems remote to me, how will it seem to her?

Will we Confederates become sentimental ghosts? Our passions, confusions, and desires reduced to a distant idyll of faithful darkies, white-columned plantations, handsome Masters and Mistresses whose manners are as impeccable as their clothing?

Oh Rosemary, our lives have been severed into a "before" that grows more remote daily and a "now" that is so modern, the paint hasn't yet dried.

I am so ungrateful! The sun shines outside my window and I hear the shouts of children playing while I indulge these melancholy fantasies.

Dearest Rosemary, I have skirted the true purpose of my letter. You must come to Atlanta.

I am sensible of your responsibilities to your school but beg you to think of your brother. When Bonnie Blue was killed, I feared for Rhett's sanity.

It might so easily have been different. Little Bonnie mightn't have urged her reluctant pony to jump those hurdles. The pony might not have stumbled. Children fall from horses every day. Some of brother Charles's falls left Aunt Pittypat gasping. Most children do not die by falling from ponies.

Bonnie's death ripped her parents' hearts—as you surely understand.

For four days, Rhett stayed with his poor dead child in a room ablaze with lights. Rhett would not suffer Bonnie to be buried—laid forever into the dark she had always feared!

It is still hard to believe she is gone. Sometimes when I hear hoofbeats, I look to the street, expecting to see Bonnie on her fat pony beside her proud father, Rhett reining his great black horse in to accommodate his daughter's pace. . . .

Those who say Atlanta is heartless should have seen the mourning for this child. So many came to the funeral, a hundred stood outside.

If Bonnie's death dealt your brother a fearful blow, his disintegrating marriage has undone him.

Rosemary, in his heart your brother is a lover. The shrewd businessman, the adventurer, the dandy are but costumes the lover wears.

Bonnie Blue was the last linchpin in Rhett and Scarlett's marriage. Rhett saw Bonnie as Scarlett unspoiled, a Scarlett who loved him without reservation. And Scarlett loved Bonnie as a reborn self, as an image of what she might have become if only, if only. . . . Bonnie knew her needs, as Scarlett does not, and while Scarlett beguiles our admiration, Bonnie commanded it.

Rhett and Scarlett have always been combatative, but they were grandly, triumphantly combative—the clash of two unmastered souls. Now it is painful to be with them: such bitter, weary language; so many ancient slights reprised; hurts recollected over and over, as if the hurts were fresh and the wound still tingling.

Rosemary, your brother needs you.

I am not much traveled. Once, when I was very young, Pittypat,

Charles, and I traveled to Charleston. I thought it so much more sophisticated than Atlanta! We stayed in Mr. Mills's hotel (does it still exist?), and in its dining room, I was offered escargots accompanied by the device one holds them with while spearing meat from the shell. I thought the device was a nutcracker and was trying with Atlantan determination to crack a snail shell when our kind waiter rescued me. "Oh no, miss. No, miss! We does things different in Charleston!"

I suspected then, and believe now, there are many things Charleston does differently—things busy Atlanta neglects or doesn't do at all.

I cannot remember my father, and my mother is only a vague shape, a warmth, not unlike the warmth of baking bread. I recollect a mother's touch, so gentle, it might have been a butterfly's. When our parents died, Charles and I went to Aunt Pittypat's: two children whose guardian was little more than a child herself. Uncle Peter was the grown-up in our house! What a happy time we had! Pittypat's silliness (which irritates adults) charmed us, and among children, Pittypat's kind heart and silly airs flowered into something like wisdom. One day, she bet that we couldn't outrun Mr. Bowen's sulky. (Mr. Bowen, our neighbor, had famous trotters.) Charles and I hid in the shrubbery until Mr. Bowen turned into our street, and we darted in front of him, running as fast as our stubby legs could, while Mr. Bowen (forewarned by Aunt Pittypat) restrained his horse so we could win the race. As I recall, our prize was oatmeal cookies, two each, which were easily the best cookies I've ever had. I was a grown woman before I realized their deception—that two small children could outrun a fast trotter. Mercy!

Now, when we drive out on a Sunday afternoon, I am toted to the carriage like baggage and swaddled like an infant against the "fierce August cold."

In the country, Ashley sighs at the ruins of every familiar plantation, their gardens as reclaimed by wildness as if the land still belonged to the Cherokees. When I tug his sleeve, Ashley reluctantly returns to the present.

We "do things different" in Atlanta these days, too. Dear Rosemary, we are nearly recovered from the War and prosper stupendously. On market days, farmers' wagons fill Peachtree and Whitehall streets from boardwalk to boardwalk. The gaslights have extended almost to Pittypat's and all the central streets are macadamed. They're building a street railway! We are readmitted to the Union, the Federal troops are out west with General Custer, and Atlanta is doing very well, thank you.

When Louis Valentine comes of age, he would have a bright future here. Atlanta has wholeheartedly embraced the Modern Age and there will be opportunities for a young man with his Uncle Rhett's connections.

How practical I've become, when those times I recall most fondly were so impractical: Pittypat, Charles, and Melanie playing at life!

I miss Charles each and every day. In my heart, he is fixed as a young man of twenty-one, recently married to Scarlett O'Hara of Tara Plantation. It must have been War Fever, for certainly if any two human beings were unsuited to each other, it was my sweet Charles Hamilton and Scarlett O'Hara.

I solace myself with the thought that Charles died happily wed. Had he lived, they would have made each other miserable.

I suppose I shall be seeing Charles soon. It will be lovely to ask what he thinks of all our goings-on.

I send you my best love.

Your Devoted Friend,
Melanie Hamilton Wilkes

Chapter Forty-nine

A Deathwatch

As Melanie Wilkes was dying, Rhett Butler waited in the parlor of his mansion on Peachtree Street, listening to the clock.

It was October. A dark, drizzly afternoon.

His glass of cognac had been distilled from grapes Napoléon's armies might have passed. It tasted like ashes.

The Governor of Georgia, Senators, and United States Congressmen had been entertained in this room. The workman who'd fitted its chair rails had got more pleasure from this house than Rhett ever had.

The big house was quiet as a tomb. After Bonnie died, he'd shunned Ella and Wade. He was afraid he'd look at the living children and think, It might have been you instead of Bonnie. If only it had been you. . . .

Mammy and Prissy took the children out of the house to play. When it rained, Ella and Wade played in the carriage house.

He'd quit going to his desk at the Farmer's and Merchants' Bank. Yesterday—or was it the day before?—the bank's president had come, deeply worried. Although the Farmer's and Merchants' hadn't invested in the Northern Pacific, when Jay Cooke declared bankruptcy, the New York Stock Exchange collapsed. All over the country, depositors raced to their banks to withdraw their savings. Banks had failed in New York, Philadelphia, Savannah, Charleston, and Nashville. The Farmer's and Merchants' didn't have enough cash to meet the demand.

"Rhett," the president begged, "could you help?"

Rhett Butler pledged his fortune so Farmer's and Merchants' depositors could withdraw their savings in cash—every cent. Since they could, they didn't.

Rhett didn't care.

The clock chimed the hour: six funereal strokes.

A gust in the still room ruffled the hair on the nape of his neck and Rhett knew Miss Melly was dead.

Melanie Wilkes was one of the few creatures Rhett had ever known who would not be deceived.

As the brown autumnal light leaked out of the room, Rhett lit the gaslights.

Had he loved Scarlett, or had he loved what she might become? Had he deceived himself—loving the image more than the flesh and blood woman?

Rhett didn't care.

If she *had* betrayed him again and again with Ashley Wilkes, Rhett didn't care. Ashley was free now. If she still wanted the man, she could have him.

That evening, when Rhett's wife came home from Melanie Wilkes's deathbed, she told her husband she loved him. Scarlett had never said that before, and Rhett may have believed her. But he didn't care.

Rhett Butler looked into the pale green eyes that had mesmerized him for so many years and did not give a damn.

Chapter Fifty

The Hill Behind Twelve Oaks

Upon Rhett's terse telegram, Rosemary resigned from the Female Seminary, packed, and gave the keys of 46 Church Street to her brother, Julian.

Louis Valentine was entranced by his first train ride. They overnighted in the Augusta railroad hotel and Big Sam met them at Jonesboro the next afternoon.

Wealthy Yankees had leased what remained of Twelve Oaks Plantation for quail hunting. Excepting oat patches grubbed here and there for game birds, the plantation had reverted to brush.

"Keep your hands inside, Young Master," Big Sam advised Louis Valentine, "else you get 'em ripped." Brambles squeezed the lane. Blackberry canes scratched the panels of their carriage.

Brick chimneys rose from the rubble of what had been Twelve Oaks' manor house. Its toppled columns were half-buried under mats of Virginia creeper. The turnaround was newly opened. The stubble crackling under their wheels hadn't seen full sun since the War. Glossy Atlanta phaetons were parked beside rickety farm wagons. Horses, several still in work hames, were hobbled here and there. Negroes gathered beneath an ancient chestnut tree that had survived Sherman's fires.

"We cain't get no closer," Big Sam advised. "Got to walk to the buryin' ground."

"Where can I find my brother, Captain Butler?"

"Reckon he's with Mister Will. They cleared this turnaround yesterday."

As they walked past parked carriages, an amiable face poked out a window: "Lord a mercy, ain't that you, Miss Rosemary? And there's Louis Valentine, too. Honey, don't be shy."

"Why, Belle, hello. I didn't know you knew Melanie."

"I thought right high of Mrs. Wilkes. I wouldn't set myself up as Mrs. Wilkes's friend, but she was awful good to me. I couldn't go to St. Philip's for the funeral, but I thought I could come here, it bein' outdoors 'n' all."

"Melanie wouldn't have minded."

"What Mrs. Wilkes minded wasn't what other folks mind. Mrs. Wilkes, she was a Christian!"

"Yes, she was. How I wish . . ." Rosemary searched Belle's face. "Melly was very worried about my brother."

Belle's smile vanished. "Rightly so. I've never seen Rhett so poorly. First off, he loses that dear child, and now this! What's he gonna do? Him and Miss Scarlett . . . he moved out on her. Just up and left. He ain't stayin' at my place, neither. I don't know where he's at!" Belle dabbed her eyes with a handkerchief. "I can't ruin my face. I got to look decent for the buryin'."

Louis Valentine clung to Big Sam's hand. "I hates to see it like this," Sam told Rosemary. "I recall when Twelve Oaks was a *real* plantation. Good cotton growed in these bottoms—high-dollar cotton."

"Where can I find Captain Butler?"

"Prolly the graveyard. Day before yesterday, he come out. Been workin' since." Big Sam shook his head at this turn of events. "Cap'n Butler workin' like a nigger! You want I should carry you, Young Master?"

"I can walk by myself!" Louis Valentine asserted. "I'm seven!"

The Wilkeses' aesthetic sensibility had been expressed in every aspect of plantation life. Their parties had been famous for gaiety and the beauty of the attending belles. The wittiest bon mots had been uttered in the Wilkeses' drawing rooms, where Clayton County preoccupations with drinking, hunting, and horses got short shrift. From the veranda, beyond Twelve Oaks' lush gardens, one could just see the sparkling shallows of the Flint River.

Behind the main house, a shaded path climbed broad stones to the hilltop where, above Twelve Oaks' tall chimneys, a filigreed iron gate admitted mourners to the family graveyard. Within, huge oaks brooded over lichened headstones. Arrayed below this somber yard had been the plantation crops, manor house, gardens, and dependencies. On a clear day, everything one could see belonged to the Wilkeses; yet within these graveyard walls, all human desires, pride, wealth, and power came to their humble conclusion. For the Wilkeses, even death had an aesthetic dimension.

Now the stone treads were askew or broken and brambles plucked at Rosemary's sleeves. The oaks were stumps; they'd fed Sherman's campfires. Deer and feral hogs had browsed among the headstones, and the morally instructive vista had been swallowed by saplings, blackberry thickets, and strangler vines.

The two oldest graves (Robert Wilkes 1725–1809; Sarah Wilkes 1735–1829) were flanked by the inhabitants' descendants. Here were Melanie's parents, Colonel Stuart Hamilton (1798–1844), "Sorely missed," and his wife, Amy, "Loving Mother."

John A. Wilkes, Ashley's father, lay beside his wife. Charles Hamilton, C.S.A. (1840–1861), was against the wall with the cousins.

Tiny stones marked Wilkes infants' graves.

Rhett Butler slumped on a toppled headstone. When he looked up, Rosemary winced at the pain in his eyes.

"Oh Rhett, poor dear Melly."

Rhett Butler's collar was undone and his shirt was filthy. When he brushed hair from his eyes, he streaked his forehead with red Georgia clay. His voice was dull as a dirty stone. "All the sweet, kind souls are gone. Bonnie, Meg, John, and now Melly."

Men were chopping brush and crying instructions as the hearse lumbered up the back slope.

"Sister," Rhett said. "No, please, don't touch me. I don't think I could bear being touched." Almost as afterthought, he added, "I've left her. I'd thought . . . I'd hoped . . ." He straightened his slumped shoulders. "I believed we were two of a kind. All those goddamned years . . ."

"What will you do, Rhett? Where will you go?"

"Who the hell cares? There's always somewhere."

With a moistened handkerchief, Rosemary scrubbed dirt from her brother's forehead.

Louis Valentine was investigating tombstones. "Look, Mother," he called, "he was just a baby."

Because she couldn't bear her brother's pain, Rosemary went to her son. She read, "Turner Wilkes, August 14–September 10, 1828. Our Heart's Desire."

Rhett's hoarse voice intruded: "Turner was Ashley's older brother. If Turner Wilkes had had the decency to survive, Melanie would have married Turner and Ashley could have married Scarlett and I wouldn't have wasted my life."

"Rhett, can't you forgive her?"

Her brother shook his head wearily. "Of course I forgive her. She is who she is. I can't forgive myself."

Skidding hooves, rattling trace chains, and nervous advice announced the hearse. The glass-paneled conveyance had carried the deceased from St. Philip's in dignity but was in peril climbing the steep, partially cleared slope. Brambles scratched the glass and undertaker's boys held back thicker branches that might have shattered it. Behind the hearse, Will Benteen led the horses of the family carriage.

At the grave site, the strong helped children and the infirm. A white-faced Beau Wilkes clung to his father's hand. Wade Hamilton stepped around his father Charles's grave.

Little Ella clutched a bouquet of wilted chrysanthemums.

Scarlett's eyes were brimming with unshed tears.

Half Clayton County was here. The Wilkeses had been a grand family and country folk are proud of their grand families.

Faces Scarlett knew were worn with age and privation. Here was Tony Fontaine, back from Texas. And Alex Fontaine had married Sally Munroe, his brother Joe's widow. Beatrice Tarleton was whispering to Will Benteen—probably about horses. Beatrice Tarleton loved her horses more than her daughters. Randa and Camilla Tarleton had red clay on their Sunday shoes. They'd have to scrub them before they taught school tomorrow.

Betsy Tarleton hovered beside her mother to avoid her fat, ill-natured husband. Beatrice paid Betsy no mind.

Suellen O'Hara Benteen glared at Scarlett. Will had told his wife Scarlett would be staying at Tara after the funeral.

As her marriage disintegrated month by month, week by week—sometimes Scarlett believed, hour by hour—Scarlett had found refuge investing money. She'd always been shrewd. Hadn't she built the two most profitable sawmills in Atlanta? Rhett had insisted the railroads were overextended, that more track had been built than there were passengers, or freight.

She'd show him! She'd bought Northern Pacific bonds.

After Bonnie died, Rhett had vanished into another world—a world she could not enter. Nothing she said seemed to touch him. Her sincerest promises were as ineffective as her tantrums. Rhett had looked at his wife with tired, sad eyes and abandoned her to sit beside Melanie Wilkes's deathbed.

When Scarlett's regrets and self-recriminations were too much for her, she'd gone downtown to her broker. Jay Cooke's Northern Pacific Railroad had been the sole happiness in Scarlett's life. With no effort and no suffering on her part, Northern Pacific track marched inexorably west as its bonds rose buoyantly into the skies. Natural Wonders!

After Scarlett ran through the money she'd got for her sawmills, she mortgaged the Peachtree Street mansion. In Melanie Wilkes's final days, Scarlett had borrowed against Tara.

And now, Melanie was gone and Scarlett's Northern Pacific bonds were worth just as much as the trunks of Confederate currency in Tara's attic.

Scarlett would come home to Tara. Tara would provide for her.

"Dear Rosemary," she said mechanically, "so good of you to come."

"Melanie Wilkes was . . . I will miss her very much."

"I needed her," Scarlett said, ignoring the total stranger at his sister's side. The stranger wet his lips as if he might have something to say, but of course he didn't. Neither of them had anything more to say.

The pallbearers slid the ornate casket, which Melanie Wilkes would never have chosen, from the fragile glass hearse Melanie would have thought pretentious.

As the pallbearers marched to the grave, Will Benteen eased forward on the heavy coffin's handles to bear the weight Ashley couldn't.

The rector wrapped his surplice around his neck. He began the graveside service. Wild geese honked by. A raven cawed in the brambles. Beatrice Tarleton coughed.

Scarlett closed her ears and kept her eyes focused on nothing.

Will's negroes took hold of the ropes and on Will's "Together, boys," they walked the casket over the grave and lowered it.

Ashley clasped his son and wept. Beau stared at his shoes.

A balloon of grief rose in Scarlett's throat. It hurt to swallow.

She trickled her bit of red clay onto Melanie Hamilton Wilkes's coffin lid and wiped her hands on her skirt.

She heard a horse crashing down the slope, and when she turned, Rhett Butler was gone from her life.

The grave at her feet might have held Scarlett's heart.

Part Three

TARA

Chapter Fifty-one

Will Benteen

When Miss Scarlett moved back to Tara and Uncle Henry Hamilton put her fancy Atlanta house up for sale, Will Benteen smelled trouble.

Miss Scarlett and Captain Butler were split; everybody knew that.

When Captain Butler galloped off after Mrs. Wilkes's burying, Will had been glad to see him go. As Will told Boo, his farm dog, "Sometimes critters got to lick their wounds."

Tara's overseer was a mild-eyed Georgia Cracker with receding sun-bleached hair, wrists and neck red as fresh-cut beets. He was mostly head and chest, his real leg almost as spindly as the wooden leg he'd earned at Gettysburg. His fingers were as big around as his daughter Susie's wrists.

Once, in the hard years after the War, when Scarlett was sending every profit from her Atlanta sawmills to Tara, she'd complained, "Will, before the War Tara provided for the O'Haras, not the other way around."

Will had removed his shapeless hat and scratched his forehead. "Well, Miss Scarlett, I spect you might lease Tara to some Yankee."

That was the last time she complained.

Nowadays, Tara had to support everybody again. There were the negroes—Dilcey, Prissy, Pork, Big Sam, and Mammy—as well as Miss Scarlett, her children, and the Benteens.

Not long after the city folks came, seven-year-old Ella had a fit. At the supper table, she gave this unearthly cry and fell out of her chair. Although she was unconscious, her eyes were rolling, her legs were kicking, and Will

Benteen couldn't hold her still. Directly she came out of it, white-faced and a little shaky, but she'd scared the daylights out of Will.

Beau Wilkes was at Tara, too. Mr. Wilkes wasn't in any shape to care for his son. And after the funeral, Miss Scarlett had asked Miss Rosemary and her boy to stay.

Will had a notion why Miss Scarlett had invited Captain Butler's sister and son. It was one of those things Miss Scarlett did without thinking. Miss Scarlett took advantage before anyone else saw there was advantage to be had. It was her nature.

When Suellen figured it out, she told her husband, "It's a dirty trick, Will Benteen, using Rhett's sister as bait."

Will had shushed her with a kiss. Will could shush Suellen when nobody else could.

Suellen O'Hara hadn't been Will Benteen's first choice. Will had courted Carreen, the youngest O'Hara daughter, but Carreen made up her mind to join a Charleston convent.

By then, Tara had become Will's home, but despite the relaxed attitudes after the War, he couldn't share a house with the unmarried Suellen. And proud Suellen had no other suitors and nowhere else to go.

Despite its unsentimental start, Suellen and Will's marriage had been happy. Their six-year-old, Susie, was willful, but her parents loved her all the more for it. As Suellen liked to say (remembering how Scarlett had stolen her beau Frank Kennedy), "Nobody will ever pull the wool over Susie's eyes!" Robert Lee, the Benteen boy, was so shy and sweet, sometimes his father couldn't bear to look at him.

Will had come to Tara a wounded veteran. As Tara had healed him, Will'd healed Tara. With Miss Scarlett's money, Will had rebuilt Tara's cotton press, bought Cyrus McCormick's newfangled mowing machine, and replaced the dozens of small tools: the four- and six-tooth crosscut saws, the saddle clamps, the augers and awls Sherman's soldiers had stolen or ruined. Will's gangs had uprooted cedars and blackberry brambles, replaced split-rail fences, reroofed the icehouse and meat house, cleaned and pruned the orchard, doubled the kitchen garden, built a twelve-stall horse barn, fenced a hog lot, and erected a whitewashed board and batten cotton shed on the foundations of the old one.

To make room for Scarlett, the Benteens evacuated Gerald and Ellen's front bedroom. "There can only be one Mistress at Tara," Will had told his angry wife, "I reckon she'll be Miss Scarlett."

But Scarlett hadn't wanted her parents' bedroom with Gerald's balcony and the canopied bed where O'Haras had been begot, born, and died. Instead, Scarlett took her old room at the head of the stairs, beside the nursery.

After the War, Tara's field workers had left for the city they'd heard so much about. After several hungry years, most returned to Clayton County, living in the run-down Jonesboro neighborhood everybody called "Darktown."

Scarlett asked Will Benteen, "Why don't they live on Tara like Big Sam and the house negroes?"

"Miss Scarlett, they'd rather live in the worst broken-down shanty than back in Tara's 'Slave Quarters.' B'sides, what would we do with 'em in the wintertime?"

"Tara always found work for its people."

"Miss Scarlett," Will explained. "They ain't Tara's 'people' no more. I need field hands from March to September and I pay a fair wage. Full-task hands get fifty cents a day."

"The rest of the year, what do they live on?"

"They're free labor now, Miss Scarlett." Will had sighed. "Wasn't us set 'em free."

Miss Scarlett had rushed the cash from this year's cotton crop into the Atlanta bank—had taken it into town personally. When Will had told her they'd want new work harnesses for the spring planting, she'd replied, "Will, we'll have to make do with the old ones."

Love trouble and money trouble: Will didn't know which was worse.

Captain Butler was in Europe with Mr. Watling.

Evenings in the parlor, Miss Rosemary read her brother's letters aloud. Mr. Rhett described Paris racetracks and cathedrals and artists and joked about the cardinals' hats hanging high in the Cathedral of Notre Dame. "The French believe that when the hats fall down, the cardinal enters heaven. Some of those hats have been hanging for centuries!"

Will marveled with the children. He felt sorry for Miss Scarlett. She seemed so *neglected.*

Miss Rosemary was modest and helpful, and Tara accepted her and Louis Valentine without a ripple.

Miss Rosemary became the schoolmarm and the nursery was her schoolroom.

Suellen managed the house negroes, except Mammy, who managed herself.

Sundays, Big Sam drove the buggy into Jonesboro, where Rosemary and the children worshiped with the Methodists. The negroes walked across the tracks to Reverend Maxwell's First African Baptist.

Money or no money, they wouldn't go hungry. The summer's produce had been put up and stored in Tara's root cellar, where glistening rows of Mr. Mason's patented canning jars were filled with peaches, berries, tomatoes, and beans.

A three-year-old ox had been butchered and packed in brine. Fifteen hogs had been slaughtered, butchered, salted down, and hung in the meat house to take the cure. Will Benteen's hams were locally famous, and every Christmas, he hand-delivered a ham to favored neighbors as "a little something from Tara."

Although Will was a crop farmer, his first love was animals. Like Mrs. Tarleton, Will Benteen was mad about horses. He liked Tara's cattle and mules and he befriended his hogs: Tusker, Runt, Big Girl. He admired their pure *piggishness.* When Big Girl got sick, Will sat up half the night dosing her with turpentine.

The hog killing on the first chilly day in November was bittersweet. Yes, Will'd filled Tara's meat house, but tomorrow morning he'd not go to the hog lot. Big Girl wouldn't be there to grunt her greeting and snuffle his pant legs.

Saturday mornings, Ashley came out from Atlanta. He'd thank Scarlett for keeping Beau and often brought her a small gift: an embroidered lawn handkerchief or a tin of English toffees.

Ashley said nobody was building. His saws were idle and his lumber turned blue in the stacks. The Kimball House had closed its doors. "It's this depression," Ashley said, as if it didn't really concern him.

"Goodness, Ashley." Scarlett frowned. "Don't you care?"

"I care that Monday morning, I will be deciding which worker I will let go and how he'll feed his family."

Ashley took coffee with Scarlett, Beau, and Rosemary and he'd quiz his son about Beau's progress with McGuffey Readers, but Ashley never drank a second cup before he left for Twelve Oaks, where he'd climb to the hilltop graveyard and talk to Melanie.

Gentle Melanie didn't share Ashley's regrets. She assured her grieving husband they would be reunited one day. As they talked, Ashley cleaned the graveyard, tossing dead limbs and brush over the wall. On his third visit, he brought a poleax to open up the vista. Melanie had always loved the view from here.

He spent the night in Twelve Oaks' negro driver's house. As at Tara, Sherman's men had spared the negro quarters. This was the one night in the week when Ashley Wilkes's sleep was dreamless and untroubled.

Before Ashley left for Atlanta, he'd dally at Tara and reminisce about times gone by. Sometimes, Scarlett was bemused by Ashley's sonorous, gentle voice. When she was irritable, she'd remind him he had a train to catch.

One Saturday morning when Ashley arrived, his cheeks were ruddy and his eyes sparkled. Scarlett had been doing accounts at the table. Rosemary set aside her mending. "I've sold the sawmills," Ashley announced. "A Yankee from Rhode Island. Goodness! The man has no end of money."

Scarlett's mouth tightened. "Atlanta's most modern sawmills. Ashley, how much did he pay?"

His happiness deserted his eyes. "I won't need much," he said. "I'm coming home to Twelve Oaks. I'll live in the driver's house."

Rosemary took his hand. "I'm delighted you'll be our neighbor. But what will you do with yourself out there?"

"I won't be alone!" Ashley's words tumbled out. "I'm hiring Old Mose—you'll remember Mose—and Aunt Betsy to help me. It'll be good to have them back on the place. The formal gardens. Scarlett remembers them, don't you, Scarlett? Wilson, the Jonesboro liveryman—every summer, Yankee tourists hire Wilson to drive past our 'picturesque ruins.' I'm going to restore the gardens. We'll clear the brambles and wild grapes and get that old fountain flowing again. Do you remember the fountain, Scarlett? How beautiful it was? The gardens will be Melanie's memorial. Twelve Oaks—as it was, as it is supposed to be. Melanie loved it so."

"Mr. Wilkes," Rosemary smiled, "you have a gentle heart."

Scarlett frowned. "You'll charge the Yankee tourists to tour your gardens?"

"Why, I hadn't thought about charging. I suppose . . . I suppose I could."

Abruptly, it turned colder. The Flint River froze solid and Tara's stoves glowed red. Rosemary moved the schoolroom downstairs into the parlor. Fog hung above the horse troughs, where warmer springwater flowed.

Four days before Christmas, Tara's people were at the breakfast table when Mammy marched in from the meat house so angry, she could hardly speak. "They's ruint! They's sp'iled! Been some deviltry here!" Mammy propped her bulk against the dry sink and took deep breaths. "Ain't no colored folks done this, neither."

Scarlett was on her feet. "What is it, Mammy?"

Mammy pointed with a quivering arm.

When the children made to follow, Scarlett snapped, "Ella, Wade, Beau—all of you, stay in the house. Rosemary, Suellen, tend them, please!"

The meat house door had been crowbarred off its top hinge and hung slantwise across the opening. Will Benteen dragged the door aside and cautiously stepped into the building. "Lord have mercy!" he groaned.

Scarlett cried, "Oh Will!"

Every one of their cured, wrapped hams had been cut down. They lay on the dirt floor like so many slain babies. The casks of brined beef had been overturned and manure strewn over everything.

Mammy was behind them in the doorway. "Weren't no coloreds!"

"Mammy," Scarlett snapped, "I can see that!"

Tail between his legs, Boo poked his head inside the forbidden sanctuary and sniffed.

Meat and manure sloshed beneath their feet. The stink was overpowering.

"Can't we just wash them?"

Will picked up a ham, dropped it, and wiped his hands on his pant legs.

"No, ma'am. See how somebody cut 'em open? That meat's tainted, Miss Scarlett. Pure poison."

Will stepped out of the meat house, walked around the corner, and threw up.

The wide-eyed Mammy trembled. "Them bummers, they come back," she whispered. "I knew they comin' back one day."

"The War is over, Mammy," Scarlett snapped. "Sherman's bummers can't hurt us anymore!"

Although Boo had barked during the night, Will hadn't left his bed to see what the dog was bothering about. Now, growling importantly, Boo led Will and Scarlett to the spot outside the garden fence where horses had been tethered. Will knelt to inspect the tracks. "I reckon there was three of 'em." Will shook his head. "What crazy bastards would—Scuse my language, Miss Scarlett."

"Goddamn the bastards!" she said.

Will followed the tracks to the Jonesboro road, where they disappeared.

None of the negroes would set foot in the violated meat house—not even Big Sam, who'd been Tara's Driver under Will Benteen and Gerald O'Hara before. "I never thought you'd turn coward, Sam," Scarlett hissed, "Not *Big* Sam."

Her harsh words washed over Sam's bowed head. "Some things it don't do for coloreds to fool with," he said.

So Will, Scarlett, and Rosemary loaded the defiled meat into a wagon and drove it to the boneyard—that upland gully where Tara's dead animals were left to rot.

As the hams rolled and bounced down the slope, Will whispered, "Good-bye, Big Girl. I'm truly sorry what they done to you."

Chapter Fifty-two

Warming Soil

Their money might have become worthless overnight and their elected government might have fallen, but their cool, dark, solid meat houses reminded country people that true prosperity came from the work of one's hands, and God's providence.

Neighbors came to view the sacrilege. "What kind of minds would think to do *this?"* Men muttered threats and prowled the farmstead as if the violators might still lurk nearby. Will guided parties to where they'd tied their horses and men knelt to trace the tracks with their fingertips. Tony Fontaine and his brother Alex argued over the size of one horse's shoes.

Mrs. Tarleton slipped around to the paddock, where Will kept his new foals. Normally, she would have asked Will to join her so she could remark—for the umpteenth time—how her stallion's qualities were appearing in his foals. Not today.

As if at a funeral, women brought bread and casseroles; Mrs. Tarleton gave Suellen two hams. "So you'll have something for Christmas."

Suellen said they'd keep them indoors in the pantry, where they'd be safe.

Safe. How could they be safe?

Eventually, the neighbors went home. The house negroes were frightened, and by 5:30 winter dark, excepting Mammy who slept behind the kitchen, the negroes were in their cabins behind latched doors.

Boo was excited and too aware of his responsibilities, and that night he barked whenever a fox or polecat slipped through the farmstead. Will Benteen would wake up, pull overalls over his nightshirt, and shove his bare feet into cold leather brogans. He clumped down the back stairs and slipped outside with his shotgun.

When he came back to bed, Suellen grumbled sleepily and pulled away from his cold embrace.

In the late afternoon, Christmas Eve, a Railway Express wagon delivered a large wooden crate emblazoned with shipping labels. Will and Big Sam helped the driver unload the heavy crate and gave him a mug of Christmas cheer, which he downed with one eye cocked at the lowering clouds.

Will agreed yes, it did feel like snow.

Big Sam said, "Won't nobody be on the roads tonight."

"I won't be, that's certain." The driver left for Jonesboro at a brisk clip.

After supper, everyone gathered in the parlor to decorate the Christmas tree Big Sam had erected that afternoon. With whispered speculations and many side glances at the mysterious crate, the children hung the tree with apples, walnuts, and paper cutouts. Will stood on a kitchen chair to place Rosemary's newly sewn pink-and-white silk angel at the top. The grown-ups hung the candleholders higher than little hands could reach.

Boot scraping on the porch signaled Ashley Wilkes's arrival. His hat and coat were dusted with snowflakes, "I'm sorry I'm late. I was pruning crab apples and lost track of time. Happy Christmas, Beau!" He hugged his son. "Happy Christmas, everyone!"

As Rosemary poured Ashley Christmas punch, Will took a nail puller to the wooden crate. When the nails screeched, the children put their hands over their ears.

Rhett had sent Ella an exquisite French porcelain doll, Beau and Louis Valentine got ice skates and, to his delight and the younger boys' envy, Wade received a single-shot .22 rolling-block rifle with a note in the trigger guard. "Wade, I'm trusting Will to show you how to shoot this. If you are sensible and become a good shot, when I come home we'll go hunting together."

There was a gold locket for Rosemary, and for Scarlett a green velvet hat that matched her eyes. Although there was no note for her, Scarlett's heart leapt for joy. Even when Ella knocked over her punch glass, Scarlett didn't stop smiling.

More snow fell and Louis Valentine and Beau went onto the front porch to slide noisily from one end to the other. Ashley had brought small gifts for the children, and Will gave his Suellen a red wool nightcap. It was nearly midnight before Rosemary ushered protesting children upstairs to bed. Yawning, Will and his nightcapped wife retired.

Ashley sat by the fire. "What a wonderful evening." After a long silence, he said, "Scarlett, do you ever miss the old times, the warmth, the gaiety?"

Scarlett teased, "Like the Twelve Oaks barbecue when I confessed my love for you and you turned me down flat?"

Ashley took a poker, knelt, and stirred the fire. "I was promised to Melanie. . . ."

"Oh Ashley, fiddle-dee-dee," Scarlett said, not unkindly.

When Ashley raised his eyes to hers, they had a new light—a light Scarlett understood all too well. She sat bolt upright. "Goodness," Scarlett said. "I hadn't realized the time!"

Dear God, what was Ashley taking out of his pocket? Was it a ring box? Scarlett sprang from her chair. "Oh Ashley, I'm simply exhausted. All this excitement! Please see yourself out!"

"But Scarlett!"

Scarlett ran up the stairs and locked her door behind her.

Dear Lord, if Rhett got wind of this, if he thought she and Ashley . . . He'd *never* come home!

Although Wade had his new rifle, his mother had kept Rhett's note to the boy, and as she undressed, Mrs. Rhett Butler read it again. Her husband had written, "*when* I come home." Those were Rhett's exact words. As she let her hair down, Scarlett was a happy woman.

Brilliant stars illuminated snow as glossy as unskimmed cream. Ashley's horse trudged homeward. Deep in the woods, a frozen tree cracked like a rifle shot. Ashley snuggled into his buffalo coat.

He whispered to his Melanie, "Dear Heart, I told you it wouldn't work. You think I need someone to look after me, but Scarlett isn't the type to look after grown men. The look on her face when she realized I was going to propose . . . Oh Melly!" His laugh rang out. His horse's hooves crunched through frozen snow. "Our first Christmas apart, dear Melly. Ashley and Melanie Wilkes. Weren't we the luckiest couple on earth?"

The driver's log house fronted Twelve Oaks' neglected garden. Ashley had scrubbed the heart-pine floor with sand, whitewashed the logs, and hung Uncle Hamilton's Mexican War sword over the fireplace.

He knelt to light a blaze. He would sit up until the fire got going. He had so much to tell Melanie.

Boo didn't bark that night and Will Benteen slept spoon-fashion behind his wife. The tassel of Suellen's new nightcap tickled his nose.

It warmed in January and the snow retreated to the shade. The Flint River ran brown and so loud, they could hear it from the house. When it froze again, the snowmelt became a bright, hazardous glaze, which kept those without outdoor chores indoors next the fire. Every morning, Big Sam split the firewood young Wade carried in.

Will Benteen visited every farmhouse and poor-white shanty for twenty miles around. Who had a grievance against Tara? Had anybody boasted about vandalizing a meat house? Somebody at the Jonesboro market told Tony Fontaine the Klan was involved, but Will thought that unlikely. "The Klan's finished, Tony. Anyways, the KKK never pestered Democrats."

The hayloft of the horse barn was the highest vantage point in the steading, and when the ice melted and riders were traveling the road again, Will toted quilts and an old straw tick up the ladder to the loft.

Suellen told Will he was wasting his time, that whoever had wrecked their meat house had "had their fun."

"Honeypie," Will said, "when Boo barks at night, I plumb hate to keep wakin' you."

Suellen said if anything happened to Will, she'd never forgive him.

That evening, Big Sam stared up at the loft door and called, "I'm sorrowed 'bout this, Mr. Will. But this ain't no business for colored folks."

"See you in the mornin', Sam."

Uncertain about the change in routine, Boo lay in front of the horse barn for an hour before he got to his feet, stretched, and resumed his nocturnal patrol.

The moon illumined frozen earth. It was a windless night. Wrapped in quilts, Will slept deeply all night long.

The next night was as uneventful as the first.

His third night in the loft, Will startled awake to scuffling sounds. Somebody was climbing the ladder. Will's hand crept from the warm quilts to his shotgun's icy steel barrels. His finger found the triggers.

When Will felt a tremor in the loft floor, he cocked the hammers: *clack, clack*.

"It's me, Will," Wade Hamilton whispered.

Will let the hammers down. "Son," he said as the boy's head cleared the hatch, "you skeered the bejesus out of me."

"I came to help." Wade slid his new rifle into the loft. "It isn't right, you bein' out here by yourself."

A grin crossed Will's big face. "Is that gun loaded?"

"No, sir. I thought maybe you could show me."

"In the morning, Wade. I thank you for comin', but I reckon I'll handle this business my own self."

Will was still grinning when he dropped off to sleep.

In the morning, when Will came into the house for breakfast, Suellen pouted. "Oh, here's my husband now. I was wondering if I still had one."

Though she tried to pull away, Will kissed her. "Mornin', Sweet Pea. I got to tell you that sleepin' with a shotgun is a darn sight colder than sleepin' with you." He swatted her behind.

"Please, leave off, Will. The children . . ."

"Yes'm."

Will and Big Sam got ready for planting. They checked and trimmed the workhorses' hooves, polished and oiled the plow soles, and inventoried hames and work harnesses.

"Mr. Will," Big Sam complained. "We got to buy some new harness. These lines dried out and cracked."

"Put together harness from what's sound."

Big Sam cocked his head, "Mr. Will, is Tara broke?"

Will didn't answer.

On the second of February, a full moon sailed across a cloudless sky and Will slept restlessly in the too-bright night. He woke to Boo's furious barking, followed by shots that came so fast, Will didn't know how many had been fired. He backed so quickly down the ladder, he missed a rung and almost fell. In stocking feet, he jogged toward the barking.

That low dark shape speeding toward him was Boo. The dog's ears were flattened against his head.

"S'all right, Boo," Will said thickly.

At the paddock gate in the bright moonlight, Will saw it all. "Christ Jesus," he said. "Christ Jesus."

One foal was blindly racing the fence in a panic. The other stood trembling over her dead dam. The two mares seemed smaller than they'd been when they were alive. The second foal lowered her long neck to bump at her dead mother's flanks. Like all frightened babies, she wanted to nurse.

Tara's neighbors came. Men stood in groups in the paddock, speaking in low tones.The women stayed in the kitchen and said how frightened they were. They asked who would do such a wicked thing. Mammy insisted, "This ain't colored folks' work." Tony Fontaine hunted for tracks, but the ground was too hard.

Mrs. Tarleton took the foals to rear on goat's milk. She said there was a special place in hell for anybody who'd shoot a horse.

When they could stomach it, Sam and Will wrapped chains around the mares' hind legs and dragged them to the boneyard.

The weather warmed, the ground thawed, and though Will still slept in the hayloft, like other Clayton County planters he spent his days plowing and ridging the cotton fields.

Before daylight, Big Sam put hames and harnesses on the big, stolid workhorses. Sam might say, "Right nippy this mornin'," or "Look here, Dolly's got a gall."

Will might say, "Feels like weather coming in."

The two men rarely said much more. Big Sam always fitted the hames. Will always lit the tack room lantern and snuffed it when they went out.

As soon as it was light enough to keep to their furrows, they lowered their plowshares and plowed until noon, when they rested the horses and ate the dinner Suellen brought them. Will never tired of hearing about Tara before the War, and Sam obliged by describing Tara's barbecues and the time Gerald O'Hara organized a horse race down the Jonesboro road. "All the young bloods was bettin' and drinkin' and it's a wonder none of 'em fell off and got kilt.

"Miss Ellen, she was a good Christian woman. 'Deed she was. But sometimes her bein' so good made everybody else feel bad. Master Gerald, oh he had a temper." Sam shook his head. "Master Gerald jest like a summer rain—get you wet 'n' gone. Wet 'n' gone."

While Will smoked his pipe, Sam'd talked about Darktown doings. Sam didn't approve of Reverend Maxwell, the First African Baptist's new young preacher. "That boy don't know his place," Sam said. "He born up north. He never been bought nor sold."

After dinner, they'd hitch up and plow until dusk, when they returned to the barn, rubbed down and fed their horses. Will never went into the paddock where his mares had been killed.

One Sunday after church, Rosemary and Beau Wilkes rode to Twelve Oaks. It was a crisp February day and every branch tip glowed pink with new life.

Ashley's grandfather, Virginian Robert Wilkes, had built his plantation in a wilderness. His negroes felled the timber and burned or uprooted stubborn stumps from what became Twelve Oaks' cotton fields. As his plantation prospered, Robert Wilkes added outbuildings, servants' quarters, and, ultimately, his Georgian manor house. The gardens at Twelve Oaks were a project of Robert's old age and his lifelong urge to civilize wilderness.

Huge magnolias had marked the garden corners. Dogwood, redbud, sparkleberry, and crab apple were the backdrop for flowering perennials. Spirea bushes shaded garden paths and the formal rose garden—fragrant with Bourbon roses—had been framed with boxwood. An arched Chinese footbridge had crossed a tiny stream banked with camellias, and an iron trellis, covered with abelia, opened on a tiny park where a fountain splashed.

That was before Sherman came.

The carriage turnaround was black where Ashley had burned brush. More brush, piled higher than Rosemary's horse, awaited the match. She and Beau dismounted and Beau ran down a stubbly path toward the sound of singing.

They emerged into a clearing where a dry fountain was overseen by a rearing, life-size bronze horse. Ashley was stabbing a sword into the earth beside the fountain. Unaware of his audience, he sang, "De Master run, ha, ha." Ashley stabbed a new spot. "And de darkies stay, ho, ho." Ashley dropped to hands and knees and wiggled the sword. "Must be the Kingdom comin' and de day of Jubilo!"

"Daddy," Beau cried, "that's Grandpa's sword!"

Ashley looked up and grinned, "Hullo, Beau. I didn't hear you. Mrs. Ravanel, welcome to Twelve Oaks." Wiping red clay onto his trousers, he rose and gestured at the sword. "I'm probing for its valve box. I never thought to become a plumber."

When Rosemary eyed the rearing horse, Ashley said, "I bought it in Italy years and years ago. They *said* it was Etruscan." He raised a skeptical eyebrow.

Beau freed the sword and wiped it with dead grass.

"Beau, the saber is an excellent tool for splitting kindling or finding buried water valves."

" 'Ye shall beat your swords into plowshares?' " Rosemary suggested.

"Something like that. Here, Beau, try it on these blackberries. Keep the handle free at the base of your palm. Good." The father adjusted the son's stance.

Beau slashed a blackberry cane at the height of a man's heart.

"Excellent, Beau. My saber teacher would have approved. Mrs. Ravanel, how good of you to bring my son. Won't you come to the house? Beau, I'll carry the sword."

Smoke wisped a second, smaller cabin. "Mose is a better Christian than I. Won't find Mose workin' on the Lord's Day, no sir." Lithe as a boy, Ashley sprang onto his porch. "Won't you come in, Mrs. Ravanel? I can offer tea."

"If you'll call me Rosemary."

"Rosemary it is."

Ashley's cabin was a one-room log hut with a stone fireplace. Its windows sparkled, and the bed was neatly made. Horticultural books lined the table. Cattails stood in a jar on the dry sink.

Ashley said, "*Typha domingensis.* Our red-winged blackbirds nest among them."

Beau stirred the fire, took the wood basket, and went for firewood.

"He's a good boy," Rosemary said.

"Thankfully, Beau favors his mother." Ashley hung a kettle on the pot hook and swiveled it over the fire. "This'll only take a minute." With no special inflection, he said, "I found some letters in Melanie's desk. I didn't know my wife had a faithful correspondent. I'll return them if you wish."

"I think . . . at the time . . . Melanie's letters saved my sanity. My husband Andrew . . . It was . . . it was all so tawdry." Rosemary clasped her arms around herself. "Those awful memories. No, I shan't want my letters; please burn them."

Ashley stared into the fire. "I loved her so much. Melly . . . is with me always." He grinned suddenly. "She approves of all this, you know—selling the sawmills, becoming a gardener."

"Why, of course she does!"

Beau set the wood basket on the hearth. "Father, could I call on Uncle Mose and Aunt Betsy?"

"I'm sure they'd love a visit." When Beau was gone, Ashley explained, "Aunt Betsy is a prodigious baker of oatmeal cookies."

When the kettle was hissing, Ashley filled a stained Blue Willow teapot. "I found this half-buried beneath a garden bench. I suppose some Yankee looter set it down and forgot where. It was my mother's."

As she measured tea, Ashley said offhandedly, "Did Scarlett tell you I tried to propose to her?"

"Why, no, Ashley. She didn't."

Ashley's laugh was self-mockery, relief, and joy. "I'd half-persuaded myself Melanie would have wanted us married. I thank a watchful Providence and Scarlett's inherent good sense; she scorned my proposal." Ashley retrieved two mismatched cups.

"Ashley," Rosemary said softly, "why are you telling me this?"

"Because I am done with deception. I shan't conceal my true feelings ever again."

By the first week in March, Will Benteen and Big Sam had finished plowing the river fields and moved onto the uplands. Like most countrymen, they rarely remarked the beauty about them, but each savored the expansive vista, with Tara stretching at their feet.

At noon every day, Will visited the river fields to crumble soil in his hands and test its temperature.

When the rains came, they quit and put up the horses. The wet clay soil was too heavy to plow.

"We'll fix harness until this lets up," Will said. "We're ahead of ourselves anyways."

Rain turned the Jonesboro road into gumbo, and since they couldn't get to church that Sunday, Rosemary read psalms in the parlor, Big Sam and Dilcey adding vigorous Baptist amens. The children recited the prayers they offered every night at their bedsides, and Scarlett shut her eyes when Ella begged God to bring Daddy Rhett home.

Lord, how she missed him. Not his wit, nor his power, nor his physicality—she missed *Him*!

Sometimes in her lonely bed, Scarlett startled awake, listening for her husband's breathing. She'd reach across the quilt to pat where Rhett should be.

Her skin was too sensitive, her hearing painfully acute. She flinched at sudden noises and heard visitors in the lane long before anyone else. She would stand for long minutes staring out the window at nothing at all. "Dear God," she prayed, "please give me one more chance. . . ."

Uncle Henry Hamilton arrived after the dinner dishes had been washed and put away. The bad road had turned the hour's ride from Jonesboro into four. Uncle Henry was wet and cold and his rented horse was knackered. He couldn't possibly return to the depot for the last train.

"Sit by the fire and we'll find you something to eat, Uncle Henry," Scarlett said. "Prissy, please make up the front bedroom."

Mammy had an apple pie in the pie safe, corn bread and brown beans in the warming oven. Pork carried Uncle Henry's saddlebags upstairs.

Happy to do work he'd been trained to do, Pork laid out Uncle Henry's shaving things on the nightstand and fetched a pitcher of water.

Will came in blowing on his hands. The cold was stiffening the road, and if Uncle Henry left early tomorrow morning, he'd make a quick journey.

Mollified by a full belly and warm fire, Uncle Henry folded his napkin in precise folds. "Scarlett, if we could have a moment—privately?"

Suellen had been hoping for some Atlanta gossip and abandoned the dining room with ill grace.

Scarlett's heart sank. Oh my God, something's happened to Rhett! Henry has some awful news about Rhett! But he was saying something about a fire. "A what?" she asked. "What fire?"

Uncle Henry gave her a strange look. "Your Atlanta home, dear Scarlett," he explained a second time. "I'm terribly sorry. They couldn't save it. Captain Mulvaney arrived ten minutes after the alarm, but his men couldn't even get the furniture out."

"My house . . . burned?" Scarlett's mind raced ahead.

"I'm sorry to be the bearer of bad news," Uncle Henry said. "I fear, I very much fear it will be a long time before Atlanta sees so grand a home again."

"Gone?"

"Mulvaney's men saved the carriage house." Uncle Henry leaned forward confidentially. "Dear Scarlett, I don't wish to alarm you, but Captain Mulvaney believes . . ." Uncle Henry cleared his throat.

"Believes what?"

"There'll be nothing in the papers, my dear. I saw to that!"

"Uncle Henry! What are you trying to say?"

"Scarlett, the fire was set."

Bored housebound children were playing noisily on the front stairs.

Scarlett thought, Some child's going to fall and there'll be wailing. Scarlett let her annoyance smother the elation she felt. "The carved staircase, the Oriental rugs, the bureaus, Rhett's books—everything gone?" Despite her intentions, the corners of Scarlett's mouth twitched upward in a smile.

Uncle Henry frowned. "I'm sorry, Scarlett, I cannot share your amusement."

"Forgive me, Uncle Henry. But I owe so much money, and Tara sucks up every penny, and that house was fully insured."

Uncle Henry put on his glasses, removed papers from his jacket pocket, and unfolded them as one who already knew what they contained. "You were insured with the Southern Benefit Insurance Company? Edgar Puryear's firm? Were you insured with anyone else?"

"No. Southern Benefit covered everything."

Uncle Henry sighed, refolded, and pocketed her policies. "Then, my dear, I'm afraid there is no insurance. Edgar and the Southern Benefit Insurance Company are bankrupt. In this depression, your house wasn't Atlanta's first arson."

Scarlett frowned. She said, "Someone is trying to destroy me."

"What are you saying? Who . . ."

"I don't know who." Scarlett shook her head, clearing cobwebs. "Never mind. Henry, there's nothing you can do. Sell the lot. A double lot on Peachtree should be worth something!"

"I'll do what I can," Uncle Henry said.

It didn't rain the morning Uncle Henry left for Atlanta and didn't rain thereafter. The soil warmed to Will's satisfaction. Tara's horses were fit and eager to work.

The third Saturday in March, Will Benteen rode into Darktown to let Tara's field workers know there'd be work Monday. "Usual rate for full-task hands. Twenty plowmen, twenty sowers. Start at daybreak in our river fields."

Before daylight on Monday, Will and Sam loaded seed, shovel plows, and spare traces into the wagon. It was still dark when they led the workhorses down the winding path they knew by heart. It was chilly in the bottoms, Sam dozing while Will smoked his pipe.

The sky lightened, but fog clung to the lowlands. Songbirds woke and started chirruping. Will tapped dottle out of his pipe, got down from the wagon, stretched, and yawned. He'd eaten a big breakfast to prepare for this day's work.

At ten o'clock, when Will Benteen galloped into Darktown, he found only women and children. The wives told Will his field hands were sick in bed or working in Atlanta or off visiting kin. One wife looked him straight in the eye. "You know how it is, Mr. Will," she said.

"No, Sadie, I don't know," Will said. "I'm ready to plant cotton and I've got no workers. I know I pay good wages and I believe I've treated you fair. No, I don't know how it is."

Gently but firmly, she closed the door in Will's face.

The negroes wouldn't come to Tara and Tara's neighbors had their own cotton to plant. Ashley came, but Mose refused. "I'ze a Twelve Oaks nigger. I don't work nowheres but Twelve Oaks."

Ashley Wilkes had never steered a shovel plow, so Will walked alongside until Ashley got the hang of it. Dilcey had sown cotton, and though she claimed she'd never done "such a thing," so had Prissy. Although Pork complained, he hung the canvas seed bag around his neck and walked behind, sprinkling seed in the shallow trench the plowmen opened in the cotton ridges. Scarlett, Rosemary, and Suellen rode behind the sowers, their workhorses pulling drag boards to cover the seed.

It didn't rain.

Will quit sleeping in the hayloft. At day's end, Will was too weary to hear Boo's bark.

Mammy rose at four A.M. to light the stoves and cook breakfast. After they ate, they gathered at the horse barn. Pork muttered, "Praise the Lord old Master Gerald ain't alive to see what we has come to." Suellen reminded Will they'd never had trouble getting workers until "certain parties" returned to Tara. As their wagon rolled to the field, Rosemary sat bolt upright with her eyes closed, trying to snatch a few more minutes of sleep.

At noon, young Wade brought their dinner and stayed to fetch water for workers and horses. Mammy milked, gathered eggs, slopped the hogs, and tended the younger children. At dusk, when Tara's weary workers trudged back to the house, Mammy had supper waiting.

When Rosemary read her brother's letters, the children could hardly keep their eyes open. Rhett joked he'd almost been buried in the hold of a Scottish herring schooner under a ton of wriggling fish.

Louis Valentine made a face.

Ella asked, "Mama, when is Daddy coming home?"

The last Sunday in April dawned a warm, sweet morning. Honeysuckle and spicebush scented the air. Little Ella accompanied Mammy to the milk house. The child liked it when Mammy squirted milk into the mouths of the barn cats, who waited beside the milking stool in a comical expectant row.

"What's that, Mammy? Beside the gate?"

Mammy snatched Ella's hand. "Honey, you come away with me now. Don't get no nearer to that."

Ella fell to the ground, convulsing.

Long tongue covered with flies, white teeth bared in a defiant snarl, Boo's bloody head was perched on the gatepost.

At dusk, Will found Sam beside the river, where suckers were spawning. Although a shadowy flotilla of the big bony creatures darkened the pools, Sam's fishing pole lay beside him on the bank. Will's knees cracked as he sat. "Gettin' old," Will said.

An osprey hit the water and rose with a wriggling fish in his talons.

"Sorry about Boo," Sam said. "I thought high of that dog."

"Uh-huh." Will fumbled when he lit his pipe.

After awhile, Sam said, "I'm deacon there at the First African."

"Big job," Will said.

"You think lyin' is when you don't say what you know or just when you outright tell a lie?"

Will was saved from answering when his pipe went out. After a time, Big Sam added, "Niggers skeered. That's why they ain't comin'."

Will relit his pipe, made a face, and tapped the soggy dottle onto a rock. "Figured it was something like that. Who scared 'em?"

"Look at that scamp! I bet that fish three feet if he a inch."

"He's big all right."

The two men recalled the biggest suckers caught in the Flint River and agreed that Tarletons' Jim's forty-pounder, as weighed on Beatrice Tarleton's hog scales, was the "biggest hereabouts."

Sam said, "I knowed it all along, Mr. Will. You think it's a sin, my not tellin'?"

Will ran a twig through his pipe stem. "I reckon, you bein' a deacon and all."

"I knowed it was," Sam said unhappily. "Darned if I didn't."

Quietly, Will asked, "The same boys that spoiled our meat, killed our mares, and"—Will coughed—"Boo?"

Sam sighed. "I reckon. Little Willy what works at the Jonesboro market heard them jokin'."

"Who was joking?"

"That horse breaker fella. Willy heard him say, 'I like my hog meat without the horse shit.' Horse breaker's uncle—name of Isaiah, same as the prophet—no, sir, Isaiah didn't care for sech rough talk. Course, little Willy pretended he hadn't heard. They's three of 'em: the horse breaker 'n' Isaiah 'n' that Archie Flytte from up Mundy Hollow."

Will Benteen asked Sam what was the best bait for suckers or if it was true they'd bite on most anything. Then Will recalled how Mrs. Tarleton had admired Sam's favorite workhorse, Dolly, when Dolly was a foal.

In his own good time, Sam said, "The horse breaker and Archie Flytte was Kluxers. They got all 'round Clayton County after the War." Sam shivered. "I reckon Archie'd kill a colored man soon as look at him. 'Twas Archie kilt that negro Senator down by Macon. Strung him up like man weren't no account at all!"

Will rode to the Tarletons'.

Mrs. Tarleton snorted. "Horse breaker! Josie Watling *claims* to be a horse breaker! Says he's been out west where the tough horses are. Arrogant pip-squeak. You know Jim Boatwright, owns the cotton warehouses? Jim hasn't got the sense God gave a goose. Jim had a Thoroughbred filly that was a little wild, a spirited filly, just the kind of horse anybody'd want to have. When the filly bucked Josie Watling off, Watling took a barrel stave to her. Damn fool took out her eye."

Just past ten o'clock the following morning, Big Sam tied Scarlett's buggy to a hitching post outside the courthouse. Scarlett wore a high-waisted, severe dress and the hat Rhett had sent her for Christmas. Big Sam hurried to help her down.

"Sam, wait here for me."

"I be at the hardware, Miss Scarlett. Mr. Will need'n' plow points."

The sheriff's office was in the courthouse basement, and the air cooled as Scarlett went down the steps. Inside, the wall behind the sheriff's desk bore a Clayton County map, yellowed wanted posters, and the obligatory lithograph of Robert E. Lee on Traveller. Sheriff Oliver Talbot stood to greet her, and when Scarlett introduced herself, Talbot said he was so pleased, so pleased. He knew Mrs. Butler's husband.

"You served with Rhett?"

"No, ma'am." He pivoted to show her his withered arm. "Born that way, ma'am. Ugly, ain't it." Sheriff Talbot chuckled, "My wife says, 'Praise God, Olly. Your poor arm kept you from bein' kilt in the War.' "

Scarlett said, "My plantation has been vandalized and the negroes are too frightened to work for me."

"I knew your father, too. Gerald O'Hara was a grand gentleman. Mrs. Butler, who do you suspect?"

Scarlett described ruined hams rolling down the slope into the boneyard and a foal trying to nurse its dead mother.

"Twenty-eight hams, you say. Two mares. A dog?" Sheriff Talbot frowned. "Tell me what niggers done it and I'll show them the error of their ways."

"This wasn't negro work, Sheriff. Only white men could be so malicious—the same white men who set fire to my Atlanta home. The finest home in Atlanta, burned to the ground."

Sheriff Talbot's smile shrank. "Mrs. Butler, I can't do nothin' 'bout 'Lanta. J. P. Robertson, he's 'Lanta sheriff. Vandalizing isn't white man's work."

She named Isaiah and Josie Watling and Archie Flytte. "Flytte hates me. He was a convict, you know. Archie murdered his wife."

Talbot nodded. "Poor Hattie Flytte was kin to me, Mrs. Butler. I knowed Archie before he was sent up and I know him now. Ol' Archie's a rough customer. But wreckin' your meat house? That ain't like Archie.

These other fellows? Isaiah Watling is a pious, hardworkin' man. When he still had his farm in Mundy Hollow—oh, must have been 1840 or '41 . . ."

"Sheriff, please spare me your affecting reminiscences. My family is of some consequence in this county."

Sheriff Talbot's smile vanished as if it had never been. "Mrs. Butler, every white citizen is of consequence in Clayton County. I know those boys you're namin'. And they ain't no angels. But they wouldn't do somethin' like what you're sayin' they done. You got you some impudent niggers out your way and I certainly mean to look into it."

When Scarlett came into the bright sunshine, a leathery oldster was leaning against her buggy. He tapped his hat brim. "Mornin', Miz Butler. I'm Isaiah Watling and I knew your husband when he was Young Master at Broughton Plantation. I hear Butler's in Europe." He tut-tutted. "It's a caution how some people get around. When you write your husband, you'll tell him Isaiah Watling was asking after him."

"Mr. Watling, what are you doing? Why are you tormenting us?"

He cackled. "There's torments and torments, Miz Butler, but the worst is the torments of hell." He pointed a bony forefinger at her. "Archie says you are Jezebel, but you don't look like I imagine Jezebel to be."

"If I catch you sneaking around my property, I'll have you horsewhipped."

"Whipped, Miz Butler?" He considered. "Miz Butler, as much whipping as I've seen and done in my long, long life, I can't say it ever did a lick of good." Isaiah Watling's eyes crinkled with amusement, "I b'lieve I made a joke. 'A lick of good,' my, my."

When Scarlett looked around the empty square, she felt a chill. "Where's Sam? He was supposed to wait for me."

"Was that big nigger yours, Miz Butler? I believe he has done run off."

"Sam's a good negro. He wouldn't leave me."

"Well then, I'm right sorry he's run off, ma'am. But might be that boy won't quit runnin' until he's far away."

Chapter Fifty-three

A Telegram

The Georgia Railroad telegrapher reckoned he could send a telegram care of Rob Campbell in London, England—they had the transatlantic cable—yes ma'am. But it might take some time, account of he'd never sent a telegram to London, England, before. He checked his book and whistled. "Ma'am, it's gonna be a dollar a word."

Scarlett's pencil pressed deep into the message pad where she wrote. "Rosemary needs you." She handed the pad to the clerk but snatched it back to add, "I need you. Darling come home."

Chapter Fifty-four

Glasgow

Tazewell Watling wanted to tear the damn thing up, but he returned it to its envelope and gave the boy sixpence.

Who touched his cap anxiously. "Sir, you will deliver this to Mr. Butler?"

"When I find him."

Six months before, when Rhett Butler had walked into Nicolet and Watling's office, Tazewell had scarcely recognized him. Once-elegant clothes hung on his gaunt frame. He had the face of an old man.

Rhett rolled his hat in his hands. "I'm going abroad, Taz." His weary smile was sadder than no smile would have been. "The grand tour. Museums. Historic places. Fine art." He paused. "I wondered if you might join me."

It was on Taz's tongue to say October was the firm's busiest month. Ships were backed up at Nicolet's wharf and so much cotton was coming in, they'd rented a second warehouse. Taz looked into his guardian's blasted eyes and said, "Of course I'll come."

They caught the mail steamer that same day.

Belle had written Taz about Rhett. "Honey, I never seen him so bad. First Bonnie Blue and then Miss Melly. It'd be hard enough if Rhett and Miss Scarlett could console one another, but they can't. I'm fearing Rhett ain't got much to live for."

Rhett didn't speak about this, and they were in England's Bristol Channel before Rhett mentioned Melanie Wilkes. Seabirds whirled and dipped over white chalk cliffs. "Miss Melly couldn't be deceived," Rhett said. "Melanie Wilkes never doubted her heart."

Tazewell Watling looked away so he couldn't see the tears streaming down his guardian's face.

Taz didn't ask about Rhett's wife. That Scarlett's name never crossed Rhett's lips told Taz everything he needed to know.

The bellman at their London hotel unpacked their luggage while Rhett sat, hands between his knees. Taz wanted to call on the Campbells, but Rhett said he was too tired.

Taz spent a pleasant afternoon renewing his acquaintance with the Campbell family, but when he returned to the hotel, Rhett was gone. The doorman said Rhett hadn't taken a cab; he'd walked into Mayfair. "The gentleman seemed distracted like," the doorman said. "Like the gentleman had something on his mind."

Rhett's tailor hadn't seen him and he hadn't been to the gambling clubs. Of course they knew Mr. Butler. Was Mr. Butler back in London?

Three days later, wearing the clothes he'd worn when he disappeared, Rhett came back to the hotel. He was filthy and unshaven. Perhaps he'd slept in his clothes. "It's no use, Taz. I can't forget. Drink, laudanum, women—I never thought I'd curse my memory." He looked at his hands. "You may as well go back to New Orleans. I am grateful you interrupted your work to come, but . . ."

Taz said, "I'll draw your bath."

Rob Campbell provided the necessary letters of credit and would forward their mail. Taz bought tickets for the Dieppe steamer. Taz made sure Rhett had fresh shirts and tempted him to eat.

In December, Paris was bitter cold and its famous light was unforgiving. Rhett couldn't keep warm. Sometimes when they went outdoors, he wore two overcoats.

Like a dutiful son with his frail parent, Taz escorted Rhett to the Louvre, Notre Dame, and the Opéra Garnier. Taz chattered through the long silences. When Taz did ask a direct question, Taz's companion replied courteously, but Rhett made few observations and no suggestions. He initiated nothing.

One afternoon on the rue de la Paix, they strolled past excited young ballet dancers entering a *maison de couture.* Taz tipped his hat to the girls and observed, "There are other women, you know."

"How dare you say that to me!" Rhett's eyes flared so hot, Taz took a step backward.

Taz would wake in the middle of the night, to find Rhett sitting at the window. Winter moonlight bleached his face.

Every week, dutifully, Rhett wrote the children. He asked Taz to read his letters before he mailed them. "Just the musings of an utterly ordinary tourist," Rhett said. "I mustn't frighten them."

In his letters, Paris sights Rhett had apparently passed without noticing were described in engaging detail. All their days were sunny. Rhett was amused by Paris's famously truculent cabmen and waiters, who pretended they couldn't understand Creole French.

Taz's letters to Belle were cheerful, too.

Rosemary wrote, care of Rob Campbell, that she was staying at Tara "until I decide what to do with my life."

Belle wrote Taz, "Your Grandpa Watling's come by twice. Might be one day I can get him to take a cup of coffee."

Buying Christmas presents was an agony. Though the temperature was below freezing, Rhett sweated through a Harris tweed coat. After he bought the children's gifts, he bolted from the cab into a milliner's shop on the Place de la Concorde. He wasn't inside five minutes.

With a groan, Rhett collapsed in the seat. "There. That's done. Taz, I don't think I can do more. Would you see everything is shipped?"

That night, Rhett vanished from the hotel. He was gone a full week, and a gendarme and his captain brought him back. "No, monsieur," the captain told Taz, "Monsieur Butler has committed no outrages. But the gentleman takes his life in his hands. . . ." He paused. "In Montfaucon, where we found your friend, gendarmes travel in fours."

"Rhett?"

He coughed. He couldn't stop coughing, but he waved away Taz's help.

"Perhaps Monsieur is ill?" The captain of gendarmes wondered.

"He is," Taz said, and gave the man twenty francs.

If Paris was cold, Glasgow was colder. Taz and Rhett spent their first night at the Great Western Hotel opposite Gallowgate railway station. There weren't many people in the enormous dining room: a handful of commercial travelers reading as they ate alone, an elderly couple with their grandchild enjoying a celebratory evening out. The old couple consulted carefully before ordering a bottle of the cheapest champagne.

Rhett picked at his food and drank nothing. In the morning, he was gone.

Taz visited Glasgow's hospitals and the central jail, where he was directed to the Gartnavel Lunatic Asylum.

After Scarlett's telegram came, Taz placed an ad in the *Glasgow Herald*:

> ANYONE KNOWING THE WHEREABOUTS OF MR. RHETT BUTLER—A MIDDLE-AGED AMERICAN GENTLEMAN, TALL, WELL-DRESSED, APPARENTLY MENTALLY DISTURBED—CAN CLAIM A SUBSTANTIAL REWARD FROM MR. TAZEWELL WATLING AT THE GREAT WESTERN HOTEL.

Four days later, a nervous cabman drove Taz to an alehouse in the slums of Glasgow's East End. "It's a wee bit risk, man," he'd advised. "It'd be a wise man who took precautions."

Coal smoke was so thick it was dusk at 4:30. Tenements loomed over a narrow street lit on one corner by a gaslight's dirty circle of light. Taz said, "I'll pay after I see Mr. Butler."

The cabman snarled, "I'll have my dosh now. I'll not set foot in yon place."

"If you want your money, you'll wait."

The cabbie stood in his box to peer up and down the street. A cat squalled in an alleyway.

"I'll double your money if you wait."

The cabman subsided, "I canna say I will and I canna say I willnay. For God's sake, man, be quick."

The moment he passed through the unmarked front door, Taz's eyes watered. The low room was blue with smoke and reeked of unwashed bodies.

Old stinks had varnished the tin ceiling brown. Thick stools lined the bar; there were benches at the tables. The furniture was too heavy to use as weapons.

In the back of the dim room, wearing a mink-lined cape, gold nugget shirt studs, and thick gold watch chain, Rhett Butler was at a table with five of the worst ruffians Taz had ever seen.

"Hello, Taz. Come here and I'll introduce you. Remember my grandfather, Louis Valentine? Broughton Plantation was purchased by worthies just like these."

"God, don't he go on?" one worthy chuckled.

Rhett's clothes were rumpled and he hadn't shaved, but he was cold sober and the glass before him was untouched.

"I've a cab, Rhett."

"The night is young, Tazewell Watling, and I'm discussing love with Scottish philosophers. Mr. Smith, at my left, claims regular thrashings warm the marital bed. Mr. Jones—this sturdy, sandy-haired fellow—holds similar opinions."

"Can't have 'em puttin' on airs," Jones affirmed.

"Certainly not," Rhett agreed.

"Rhett, I've been looking everywhere for you." Taz handed the telegram to Rhett.

Kill or cure: Those were the words Tazewell Watling thought while his friend read Scarlett's brief message.

Staring at the missive, sweat beaded Rhett's forehead.

Then with his old litheness, he rose to his feet. "Well, gentlemen, regrettably, all good things must come to an end."

Smith objected: "Here, now; where're you going?"

Jones got up and tugged his cap over his eyes, "We was goin' to have us a rare old time."

"Somehow"—Rhett chuckled—"I suspected that was your intent."

Jones dropped his hand and came up with a thick wooden truncheon. Something sharp gleamed in Smith's hand. The bartender dropped his rag, hurried out the back, and let the door clunk shut behind him.

"You'll stay wi' us, sir. Just for a wee while."

Tazewell drew his revolver from his jacket pocket and pointed it casually at the ceiling. “I’m sorry to disappoint you, gentleman, but our cabman won’t wait.”

“Good Lord,” Rhett mocked him, “we might have to walk back to our hotel? Good night, friends. Perhaps we’ll meet again.”

Jones’s truncheon dangled in his hand. He grinned. “Aye, sir. Come back anytime, sir. We’ll be lookin’ for yer.”

Outside, their cabman was signaling urgently, but Rhett patted his pockets and frowned. “I left my gloves.”

“For God sakes, Rhett, are you mad?”

Rhett puzzled for a moment before smiling his once-familiar smile. “Loving is a chancy thing, Taz. You risk your immortal soul.”

Chapter Fifty-five

Drought

Clayton County was dry. Bindweed was strangling the tender cotton plants. With Big Sam gone and Ashley back at Twelve Oaks, Will Benteen started cultivating before light, trusting his horse to stay in the furrows. Instead of resting at noon, Will hitched a fresh horse and kept working, eating cheese and bread as he walked behind the plow.

But Will's plow couldn't weed the ridges and couldn't thin the cotton plants to eight inches apart. Hoeing wants human hands. Only Mammy, who was too old, and three-year-old Robert Benteen, who was too young, were spared stoop labor.

For the hundredth time that morning, Scarlett shook weeds off her hoe. "Wade Hampton Hamilton! Hoe the weeds, not the cotton."

"Yes, Mother." Though he'd severed the plant's roots, Wade heeled it carefully back into place.

Scarlett closed her eyes, seeking patience. Dilcey called, "You doin' all right, Miss Scarlett?"

Scarlett snapped, "If you'd spend less time gabbing and more time hoeing, we'd get through this field."

Wade muttered under his breath, "How can we do that?"

Which was, Scarlett thought but didn't say, a good question.

Spindly cotton plants languished behind the little band of cultivators. Ahead, there were so many weeds, it was hard to spot the cotton.

Yesterday, Will had told Scarlett they must abandon the upper tract.

"We won't get there before the cotton is strangled, Miss Scarlett. No sense me tillin' it. I can do more, hoein' alongside you all."

Louis Valentine Ravanel and Beau Wilkes shared a row. Like the grown-ups, Wade had a row to himself. Will Benteen worked two.

Clouds drifting lazily across the sky chased shadows across their tiny patch of the world.

Although they no longer went into Jonesboro for church, they quit work at noon on Sunday, and weary, silent children climbed into the wagon. In the heat haze, traces jingled. Will murmured, "Get up now, Molly," and the horse's big hooves clopped the dry ground.

At the horse barn, the children scrambled down, while Pork, Dilcey, and Prissy headed toward the quarters.

"Suellen, please get the children washed. I'll help Will with the horses."

"Don't reckon I need help, Miss Scarlett," Will said.

"I reckon you do," Scarlett said.

Rosemary was briefly puzzled by the black carriage in front of the house. Surely she knew it? "Why, Belle Watling. What a surprise."

In her modest brown check dress, Belle might have been any country woman come to call. "I'm sorry to be a bother, Miss Rosemary, but I just had to come."

"I'm always glad to see a friend of Rhett's, Belle. Is it dry in Atlanta? I swear we're burning up. Please, won't you come in the house?"

Belle hesitated at the threshold.

"Please, come in." Rosemary led Belle into the cool parlor. Dried sweat coated Rosemary's skin and made her sticky. "Won't you sit? Can I fetch some refreshment? We've fresh buttermilk. . . ."

"Oh, no. I don't need nothin'. I just come to . . . tell you, you and Miss Scarlett . . ." Belle laid her gloves across an arm of the love seat, then picked them up and fiddled with them. Belle took a breath. "Miss Rosemary, you and me, we've been friendly, but I believe Miss Scarlett hates me. What I got to say is important, and I'd 'preciate your fetchin' her."

Rosemary stepped into the hall to call upstairs. "Wade! Please fetch your mother. Tell her it's important."

Belle amended: "Say it's life or death."

The boy clattered down the back stairs. Rosemary asked Mammy to bring water to the parlor.

When Rosemary came back into the room, Belle was examining the portrait over the mantelpiece. Startled from her reverie, Belle said, "I guess she was a real lady."

"I believe Mrs. Butler's grandmother was married three times."

"I'm sorry to show up without no invitation." Belle bent to the roses Pork still picked every day. Belle said, "I got to water my roses with well water. Roses don't care for well water."

When Mammy brought the pitcher and glasses, her mouth was set in a tight line. Rosemary forestalled her vocal disapproval, "Thank you, Mammy. The children can take dinner in the kitchen."

Mammy mumbled, "Poor Miss Ellen be rollin' in her grave. . . ."

A dirty, sweat-streaked Scarlett untied her sunbonnet as she came into the parlor, " 'Life or death,' Rosemary? Ah, Miss Watling . . ."

"Missus Butler, I wouldn't have troubled you, but . . ."

"You certainly needn't trouble us anymore." Pointedly, Scarlett stood aside so Belle could leave.

"Scarlett . . ." Rosemary protested.

Scarlett's smile was steely. "Dear Rosemary, Louis Valentine is filthy as a chimney sweep. Shouldn't you see to his bath?"

"Scarlett, I don't imagine Belle drove out from Atlanta unless it was important."

Scarlett brushed dirty hair off her forehead, went to the hunt board, uncorked the decanter, and poured a brandy. She tossed it back and made a face. "Miss Watling, excuse my manners. You are . . . unexpected."

"This ain't easy for me," Belle began. She sipped from her glass. "You've got better water than in town."

"Belle," Rosemary said, "what . . ."

Belle rolled the cool glass on her forehead. "Miss Rosemary, I wouldn't be alive today hadn't been for Rhett Butler. Likely my boy, Tazewell, would be dead, too."

"Miss Watling," Scarlett interrupted. "I've been in the field since daybreak. I am filthy and irritable."

Belle Watling rested her head on the back of the love seat and shut her eyes. In a dull voice, she said, "Poppa blames Rhett for all his sorrows. Poppa says Rhett lured my brother, Shadrach Watling, into a duel and shot him dead, account of Shad killed that trunk master, Will."

"What on earth are you talking about?" Scarlett demanded.

"Poppa's been comin' by," Belle kept her eyes shut. "Every Sunday, ten o'clock sharp, Poppa comes by."

Isaiah Watling would come up Belle's walk without noticing how nice she'd kept the lawn, nor her roses, nor the cheery petunias in her window boxes. Belle always had a coffeepot and sweet rolls on the porch in case he'd take something, but he never did. "Mornin', Poppa."

He always came by himself. He left Archie and Josie back in Mundy Hollow.

He'd sit on the glider, feet flat on the floor so the glider wouldn't glide. He kept his hat on. "Daughter." He said the word as if he wasn't sure she was.

Isaiah never asked about his grandson, but he didn't seem to mind when Belle read Tazewell's letters; his descriptions of the Severn Bore, Notre Dame, and Longchamps Racecourse, where Taz and Rhett met Mr. Degas, a painter. "I think a painting should look like what is painted, don't you?" (Belle agreed with his commonsensical view.)

"Think of that, Poppa," she said. "They got racetracks in France just like we got here."

As Belle folded each precious letter, her father always asked, "Does the boy say when they're comin' home?"

"No, Poppa."

"Butler can't hide behind Miss Elizabeth no more."

They sat on that porch like any father and daughter on the porch of any house on a perfectly ordinary Sunday morning. Belle picked at a sweet roll.

Sometimes, Isaiah didn't say one word. Other times, he recalled the Watling farm in Mundy Hollow, naming every horse and even that old hound dog her brother, Shad, had loved. "Everybody said your mother's elderberry jam was the best they ever ate," Isaiah said. "I never cared for elderberry myself."

He, Josie, and Archie were living just down the road. "The home place is nothin' now," Isaiah said. "House 'n' barn's fallen in—like we was never there."

Isaiah had tried to beat the wickedness out of his son.

"Shad was hard-hearted," Belle said.

"That don't mean Rhett Butler should have shot him."

"I'm your daughter, Poppa."

"I been ponderin' on that." The glider squeaked. "You ever consider repentin'?"

"Miss Watling," Scarlett interrupted. "Your father and his gang have terrorized us and frightened our field hands away. I don't know what grievance he imagines he has with me."

"Oh, he doesn't! Archie Flytte hates you, but Poppa don't think nothin' about you."

"Miss Watling," Scarlett said, "you said you had a 'life or death' matter . . ."

Belle set her water glass down. She picked up her gloves and folded them. Softly, she said, "I never thought this'd be so damned hard."

"Belle . . ." Rosemary prompted gently.

"Miss Rosemary, you know how Poppa felt about your mother. He thought she was a saint on earth. You know Poppa—once he gets an idea in his head, there's no shakin' it. Miss Scarlett, Poppa ain't worried 'bout you, but he's wanted to kill Rhett for the longest time, and now Miss Elizabeth is passed away and Poppa's joined up with that Flytte fella and Cousin Josie . . . it's bad."

"But . . ." Scarlett said.

"So long's Rhett's across the sea, they can't do nothin', so they been botherin' you so you'll beg him back." Belle was anguished. "Whatever you do, Miss Scarlett, please don't ask Rhett to come home."

Chapter Fifty-six

Three Widows

Although the Jonesboro telegraph office was closed Sundays, Scarlett interrupted the telegrapher's supper and cajoled him until he agreed to accompany her to the railway station, where the telegrapher topped his instrument's batteries, rolled up his sleeves, tested his signal strength, and sent Scarlett's frantic warning rattling across the Atlantic.

Scarlett paced until the key clattered Rob Campbell's reply; "Rhett and Tazewell sailed for New York Thursday."

"Are you all right, ma'am?" the telegrapher asked. "Won't you sit down?"

"Send my message to the St. Nicholas, the Astor House, the Metropolitan, the Fifth Avenue . . . for God's sake, send it to all the New York hotels!"

"Ma'am," the telegrapher said. "I don't know the New York hotels. I never been to New York."

Scarlett wanted to slap the man into usefulness. She wanted to weep in frustration. "Send it to the hotels I named," Scarlett said through clenched teeth.

Riding back to Tara, Scarlett's mind whirled. What could she do? What could any woman do?

On the road between somewhere and somewhere else, she reined in her horse. The sky was blue. She could hear a warbler in the brush beside the road. As coldly and clearly as she'd ever known anything, Scarlett knew that if Rhett Butler were murdered, she'd want to die, too.

Curiously, her harsh self-sentence eased her soul. Her mind stopped spinning and she understood what she'd need to do.

As Scarlett dismounted, Rosemary ran to her. "Did you warn Rhett?"

Scarlett took off her bonnet and shook her hair loose. "They've already sailed. When Rhett comes to Tara, the Watlings will ambush him."

Rosemary clamped her eyes shut for a moment. "Damn them!"

"Yes, goddamn them all! Where are our preening male champions when we really need them?"

In the parlor, a subdued Mammy brought the two women hot tea. The house was quiet; the children were outside playing in the long twilight.

"Rosemary," Scarlett began, "we are unalike in many respects, but we love your brother."

Rosemary nodded.

"And we would do anything we had to do—anything necessary—to keep him from harm."

"Scarlett, what are you thinking of?"

"Two times, I've worn black for husbands who died protecting Southern womanhood. I loathe mourning. I will not wear black for Rhett Butler."

Scarlett poured their tea, added Rosemary's cream and her sugar. When she gave Rosemary her cup, it chattered against its saucer. "Rosemary Butler Haynes Ravanel, like myself, you are twice widowed. When your husbands went off to fight, were you glad to see them go?"

"What? Are you *mad*?"

"On the contrary. I may be, after many years, putting men's madness aside." Scarlett went to the decanter and poured a healthy tot of brandy into her tea. "Oh, I know, I know. Ladies don't drink brandy in their tea. Frankly, Rosemary, I no longer care what ladies do or don't do."

"Scarlett, I feel like a horse is running away with me. Tell me what you're planning. Please! I beg you!"

So Scarlett told her.

First thing Monday morning, Dilcey heated water and they bathed in the kitchen—Scarlett first, then Rosemary while Scarlett toweled herself and dried her hair. Field-work grime turned their bathwater gray. Mammy ironed petticoats as they sat side by side, wrapped in towels, while Dilcey braided and coiled their hair.

Mammy was torn between dismay at what Scarlett might be up to and delight in their transformation.

The men had been exiled from the house, and after their hair was done, in their shifts, the ladies searched Scarlett's trunks for clothing. When Scarlett unfolded a pink watered-silk dress, a receipt fluttered to the floor: "Mme. Frère, Bourbon Street."

"Dear me," Scarlett said. "Rhett bought this in New Orleans." She held the dress up to Rosemary. "It flatters your complexion."

"The bodice? Scarlett, I am not so well endowed. . . ."

"Dilcey will take a tuck in it." Scarlett chuckled. "Did Rhett ever tell you how he and I attended the *notorious* Quadroon Ball?"

As the ladies prepared, Pork bridled Tara's handsomest saddle horses. He rubbed them down, picked loose hair, and clipped their manes and tails before tying them to the hitch rack for Prissy's attentions. In the tack room, he found two dusty sidesaddles and patted the smaller one reverently. "Miz Ellen," Pork said. "Everything's changed at Tara. Not for the better, neither."

As she plaited manes and tails, Prissy chattered. "They sure gonna look nice, ain't they? Is Miss Scarlett 'n' Miss Rosemary goin' to a barbecue? Way they fixed up, I bet that's where they goin'. Reckon we goin', too?" She took a step back to admire her work. "I puttin' ribbons in the manes and tails. Pork, what color do you reckon?"

"Miss Scarlett's be green," Pork pronounced authoritatively.

The Jonesboro market shared its siding with the slaughterhouse and MacIver's cotton warehouse. During the harvest, cotton was auctioned here, and throughout the year, Clayton County farmers came to buy and sell livestock. The market's pens and rough shelters butted against the tracks. At the south end of the market, sale animals were delivered, weighed, numbered, and penned until they were driven down the market's wide aisles, gates slamming behind them, into a hundred-foot sale ring enclosed by a horse-high, bull-stout oak fence. On market days, negroes perched on this fence, while whites enjoyed the relative comfort of an open wooden grandstand. Under the grandstand, two dour women in the sales office accepted payments, deducted the market commission, and issued the ticket that let the successful bidder claim his beast. Beside the sales office, a colored woman had a wooden booth where she sold ham slices and corn bread. Out of respect for the Baptists, she kept her demijohn of white liquor beneath the counter.

The market was loud with the bawling, squealing, baaing, whinnying, clucking, and hee-hawing of mules, horses, hogs, geese, ducks, and chickens.

That particular Monday morning, parched grass crunched underfoot and red dust filmed cattle, corrals, and the grandstand. Men's hat brims were tinged red. The dust smelled of dried manure.

Order buyers making up consignments for Atlanta butchers wore linen suits and affixed their ties with gold stickpins. But most here today were poor men who'd brought in a hog or sought a milk cow with a few more seasons left in her. Some men were shoeless.

By one o'clock, the market was humming. Livestock came into the auction ring, the auctioneer cried his singsong, and the dust hung in the air like red fog.

When the two ladies appeared, startled farmers nudged one another. One simpleton rubbed his eyes and whistled. "Gol-ly!"

Fringed silk parasols protected the ladies' delicate complexions; elbow-length gloves protected their delicate hands.

Rosemary smiled graciously. "Why, thank you, sir." The young farmer who opened the gate had never heard a sweeter voice.

They were the perfection of Southern womanhood—the ladies their own wives, worn by toil and childbirth, could never be. Of course they weren't dusty—no fleck of dust would dare light on them. Their eyes passed over the man beating a sick cow to its feet, three-day-old veal calves bleating for their mothers, and a market worker lashing a reluctant bull into a pen. Ladies never noticed such things. They were too fine to notice such things. Men took off their hats and smiled as they passed.

A man who had been the Tarletons' overseer in happier days sang out, "Mornin', Miss Scarlett," and accepted her nod as from a monarch.

News of the ladies' arrival sped through the sprawling market and men started toward the auction ring as if some unusually valuable horse or bull was to be sold. Drovers who'd been inspecting a jenny's hooves turned her loose, and negroes slopping market hogs put their buckets down.

In the grandstand, the Atlanta buyers sat on cushions, at eye level with the auctioneer on the far side of the ring.

High above, in the top row, Isaiah Watling dozed in the sun while his nephew Josie read Ned Buntline's dime novel *The Scouts of the Plains* and thought the Plains were exactly where Josie Watling ought to be. In Buntline's book, Buffalo Bill dropped a hostile redskin a mile away with a single shot. Josie Watling scratched his head. He'd never shot anybody so far off.

Jesse and Frank James were robbing trains. Josie'd never robbed a train. Josie Watling worried he'd been Back East too long and maybe when he got West again, he wouldn't be able to kill a man a mile away, and maybe he'd be no account at train robbing. How did a man rob a train anyway? How did you get it to stop to be robbed?

His snoring uncle Isaiah had a spit bubble at the corner of his mouth. Most of the time, Isaiah was just another old coot. Only thing kept Isaiah going was Rhett Butler. Josie reckoned that after they planted Butler, Isaiah Watling could die in peace.

It had been Archie Flytte's notion to hound Mrs. Butler until she brought her husband home. Archie hated the Butlers like poison. Uncle Isaiah had been too damn holy for the meat house, too holy to scare niggers, and too holy for the damn yappy dog, but when they torched that big house in Atlanta, Josie'd had to drag the old fool away. He'd been staring into the flames like they was his destination.

Josie went back to his book. Buffalo Bill was strolling into the Comanche Saloon, where bad hombres were dividing loot from a holdup. "There was gunplay in the air," Ned Buntline wrote.

In the dusty sale ring, Archie Flytte was chivvying cattle while the auctioneer cried, "Hundred, hundred, one bid takes all. Mr. Benson's steers. Put a little fat on these boys and they'll make you money. Do I hear a hundred?"

Nervous steers swirled through the dust while Archie kept them moving, turning them this way and that for prospective buyers.

Dust hung in the air. Steers bawled. Their hooves thumped the dirt, Archie cried, "Soo cow! Soo cow! Huh! Huh!" and the auctioneer chanted his chant. Two ladies trotted their beribboned horses right into the sale ring.

"Archie Flytte," Scarlett sang out. "We would speak to you and your . . . accomplices."

Archie frowned, mistepped on his wooden leg, and just caught his balance. Absent Archie's attentions, the steers retreated to the far end of the ring.

"Ladies!" the auctioneer called. "Please, ladies. You're interrupting our sale."

Amused by the man's effrontery, Scarlett replied, "Don't distress yourself, sir. We shan't keep you long. Terrible wrongs have been done us, and I'm sure that you, as a Christian gentleman, would wish to see matters put right."

She searched the grandstand and ventured a wave to men she recognized. "Many of you know me by my maiden name, Scarlett O'Hara, others as Mrs. Rhett Butler. My sister-in-law"—her gloved hand indicated Rosemary—"Mrs. Ravanel, is the widow of Colonel Andrew Ravanel, whose name is familiar to every Southern patriot.

"Isaiah Watling, is that you lurking up there? And you, sir, you must be Josie Watling. I've heard rather too much about you."

Stepping from seat to seat, the Watlings descended the grandstand and climbed over the barrier into the ring. The auctioneer wanted to protest but held his tongue when an Atlanta buyer shook his head.

"Archie Flytte. I am glad you've finally found suitable employment. You were miscast as Melanie Wilkes's baby-sitter. I shudder to think of someone like you alone with innocent children. Isaiah Watling, how ever did you drive Big Sam off? What threats did you employ?"

"Isaiah!" Rosemary nudged her horse forward. "Shooting horses? Frightening negroes? Murdering a poor dog? You? What would . . . what would my mother, Elizabeth, have thought of this . . . this *wretchedness*?"

When the old man straightened, the years dropped away and his eyes flashed like a goshawk's. "Your brother murdered my only son. Rhett Butler condemned Shadrach Watling to eternal hellfire."

"You're a liar, Isaiah Watling," Rosemary declared. "Your son fought Rhett Butler on the field of honor. How does that justify tormenting innocent widows and children?"

Scarlett appealed to the crowd. "Sirs, these sorry creatures shot two nursing mares, drove off our field hands, vandalized our property, and—for a joke—murdered our faithful watchdog." Scarlett pointed a finger. "Tell us a lie, Watling. Before man and God, claim you are innocent!"

"Give 'em hell, Miss Scarlett," a man in the grandstand cried. When Josie turned to identify the speaker, many men met his eye. Some stood. Their muttering was a gathering storm.

Rosemary paced her horse in front of the grandstand, "Gentlemen, while I have been in Mrs. Butler's home, we have been besieged and terrified by night riders. What cowards stoop to frightening women, children, and negroes? What will they do next? Will they murder my child—Colonel Andrew Ravanel's son?"

Two young farmers dropped from the grandstand into the auction ring.

"My son, Shadrach, he—"

"Overseer Watling," Rosemary snapped, "you forget yourself! Shadrach Watling was a bully and a brute."

"Tell 'em, Mrs. Ravanel. Don't let 'em get away with nothin'!" A strongly built farmer clambered into the arena. Men reached for stock whips and stockmans' canes. Josie Watling fingered his holster.

"Oh!" Isaiah cried out. "Oh! You are so high-and-mighty! You Butlers stand so much prouder than anybody else! You bankrupt who you wish, shoot who you want, insult who you feel like insulting, and ride away without a care! You own everything." He aimed an accusing finger. "Eye for an eye, tooth for a tooth!"

In that frozen moment, with spittle glistening on Isaiah Watling's lips, Ashley Wilkes and Will Benteen strode into the auction ring.

Rosemary gasped.

Scarlett cried, "Go away! Please! We're managing! We are taking care of this!"

Ashley Wilkes marched across the hard red clay like the Confederate Major he'd been. His riding whip dangled from his right hand. "It's all right now, Scarlett," Ashley said. "We'll straighten things out!"

"Oh no, Ashley, we—"

Ashley slashed his whip across Flytte's face. "Scoundrel, you will stay away from Tara! You will! Or by God, I'll . . ."

Archie barely had time to raise his arm before the whip landed again.

"You damn rogue! You *will* keep away from us!"

The lash coiled around Archie's upraised arm. He clamped his arm to his chest, and when Ashley jerked to free the whip, Archie came with it, crashing into his assailant. "You will never trouble decent folks again!" Ashley gasped.

"Oh, trouble you!" Archie stomped his wooden peg on the arch of Ashley Wilkes's foot, and when Ashley tripped, the old rooster rode him down into the dirt.

The ladies' horses tried to not step on the men rolling under their hooves, but Rosemary's wheeling horse landed a hind hoof on Ashley's ankle. Panicked steers stampeded and farmers jumped for their lives.

Archie clenched his fingers around Ashley's throat.

Although Ashley pummeled Flytte's back, Archie's hard hands were tightening. When Ashley tried to buck, attempted to roll to his knees, the older man stayed with him. As Ashley pried at Archie's hard fingers, Will Benteen circled, shouting, "I'm gonna put a bullet in you, Flytte. Let go of him or, by God, I'll shoot you!"

At Will's pistol shot, Scarlett's horse reared and her hat flew off. She dragged the reins with both hands. Her horse backed frantically until its hindquarters crashed into the oak fence. Men were yelling; steers were bawling.

Josie drawled, "Well, I'll be a son of a bitch if you ain't kilt Archie Flytte. I swear to Christ, I never thought Archie could be kilt!"

Scarlett was looking down at Will, at Will's sweat-stained hat. Over the bellowing steers, she heard Will's voice clear as day, "For God's sake, don't! I've got two children."

"Well, don't you think ol' Archie mighta had some children? You ever think to ask him that?"

The second shot was louder than the first had been, and Scarlett's ears rang. Will groaned, but it wasn't a groan living men make.

Rosemary was steadying Scarlett's horse as Josie said, "Uncle Isaiah, I got to skedaddle. I ain't gettin' nowhere in this line of work. Leastways with Jesse and Frank, when you shoot somebody, you get paid for it."

Chapter Fifty-seven

Rain

Calloused hands tenderly laid Will and Ashley on feed sacks in the wagon bed. They covered Will's still form with a horse blanket. Rosemary knelt in the wagon, bathing the unconscious Ashley's face.

Some who escorted Scarlett and Rosemary home were farmers who had known Will Benteen or the O'Haras for years, but most were loafers with nothing better to do.

"After he kilt Will, that Josie came toward me with his gun still smokin'. You bet I got out of his way. Spect I'd have give him my horse if he'd asked."

"They had horses, Charlie. A roan gelding and a bay mare."

"Hank, I know they had horses. Weren't I there when Josie Watling bought the mare from Mr. Petersen? Weren't I?"

"Well, they wouldn't have wanted your horse, would they?"

Their inanities fell like dull blows on Scarlett's febrile mind. Why had Will and Ashley come? Scarlett hadn't told them about her plan; she'd claimed she and Rosemary were going into Atlanta. "Bankers," she'd lied. God knows how the men had discovered her true intention and come to their rescue.

When the entourage reached Tara's lane, Suellen and Dilcey came running, and Suellen screamed when she saw Will's riderless horse. "Will! Oh no! Not my Darling Will!" She dashed to the wagon, lifted the blanket from her husband's face, and fainted. If Dilcey hadn't caught her, Mrs. Benteen would have fallen to the ground.

Men quit jabbering to help the new widow into the house. Children and servants gathered helplessly on the porch. Prissy wailed.

A farrier—he'd shod Gerald's horses in the old days—advised Scarlett, "They ought to pay for this. Miss Scarlett, you just say the word!"

A rage at male idiocy blinded Scarlett for a moment. Tight-lipped, she managed, "Thank you. Thank you for your kindness. Mammy, take the children into the house. Prissy, stop your nonsense! Prissy!"

Mammy gathered the children like a mother hen gathers chicks.

"Gentlemen, if you'll take our horses to the barn, and could you four please . . . carry this gentleman—Mr. Wilkes—into the parlor."

"His ankle's smashed, Miss Scarlett," the farrier observed. "Reckon it hurts like the devil."

"I reckon," she snapped.

They carried Will to the springhouse and laid him out on the cool stones beside the milk cans. "No, gentlemen, no. We'll not be needing more help, thank you. You've done too much already."

Unwilling to see their adventure ended, they milled about for another twenty minutes before they departed.

Scarlett and Rosemary made up a bed for Ashley on the parlor floor. Rosemary said, "Prissy! Find an old sheet and tear it into strips, about"—Rosemary held her hands four inches apart—"so wide. Dilcey, fetch warm water and soap."

When she and Rosemary were alone, Scarlett said, "*What* did they think they were doing?"

Rosemary said, "Some of Ashley's ribs are cracked and his throat is swelled nearly closed. I believe his ankle is broken."

After Mammy got Suellen to take a dose of laudanum and put the widow to bed, she and Prissy washed Will's body and dressed him in his Sunday suit.

Young Dr. Bryan was establishing his practice, and he made a point of noting that, although a native Georgian, he'd studied medicine in Richmond. He set Ashley's ankle and made a wintergreen poultice for his throat. Diffident while doctoring, he was assertive with his reckoning.

"Ten dollars? My goodness, Doctor. Where did you serve in the War?"

"Mrs. Butler," the doctor replied, "I was thirteen when the War ended."

At twilight in Tara's little graveyard, Pork dug Will Benteen's grave.

Scarlett said, "It isn't deep enough. Pork, you're the only man left. Dig deeper."

When Scarlett returned to the house, Suellen Benteen was waiting for her. Scarlett's sister's face was raw from crying. "When my Will told me you were coming home to Tara, I told Will we should go away. 'Tara will be Scarlett's,' I said. 'It won't be our home anymore.' I begged my Will to leave. I told him, 'My sister Scarlett has never been anything but trouble.' You stole Frank Kennedy from me and you got Frank killed. Now you got my Will killed, too." She burst into anguished sobs. "What am I going to do without Will? Dear God, what will I do?"

Scarlett went upstairs, where, still dressed in rumpled finery, she fell on her bed and slept dreamlessly until her eyes snapped open in the stark light of morning and everything came flooding back.

In later years, Scarlett remembered only fragments of the next days: the coffin maker rattling up the drive with his toe pincher bouncing in the wagon; the children whispering past Suellen's closed bedroom door. Neighbor women brought food nobody wanted to eat and neighbor men did Will's chores.

Rosemary tended Ashley behind the parlor's closed door while mourners trooped through the dining room, where Will Benteen was laid out.

An expressionless Suellen O'Hara Benteen received those who would have consoled her. At her side, Scarlett understood vital bonds had been severed; henceforth, she and Suellen would be sisters in name only.

It was hot. The roses heaped on Will's coffin in such profusion didn't entirely disguise the smell.

Will Benteen had been a lapsed Baptist, but since Jonesboro's only Baptist church was the African Baptist, he was buried by the Methodist preacher, who afterward invited Scarlett to next Sunday's service.

"I'm a Catholic," Scarlett replied.

"That's all right," the preacher said cheerfully. "We welcome every sinner!"

After the burying, Suellen Benteen and her children left for Charleston, where'd they'd bide with Aunt Eulalie. As their wagon rattled down the lane, Scarlett went to the horse barn to feed the horses. With the leather feed bucket Will and Sam had used for so many years, she poured feed into the long trough.

Sleek dark heads bent and chewed as if nothing at all had happened. Scarlett whispered, "How can Tara live without Will?" One horse lifted its head, as if trying to understand. He twitched his tail and went back to eating. Silent, hot tears streamed down Scarlett's face until she could see nothing—nothing at all.

After Ashley's fever broke, he was too weak to go home. He spoke quietly when spoken to, volunteered nothing, and never asked about Will. Rosemary sat with him in the dim, quiet parlor and fed him broth and weak tea. For reasons Rosemary never fathomed, she told Ashley things. In her quiet, calm voice, meticulously identifying the year, month, and circumstances, Rosemary Butler Haynes Ravanel told Ashley Wilkes about walking out the back door of the little house in Franklin, Tennessee, knowing the body lying in the frozen garden was her husband John. "I only loved him after it was too late," Rosemary said. She spoke about her darling Meg; how Meg had loved horses and been betrayed by a horse. "Tecumseh was afraid. How can you blame a horse for being afraid?" Rosemary told Ashley about finding Andrew's bloody boots. They were English boots and Andrew had once been proud of them. She told the silent Ashley things she had never told anyone—not Melanie, not even her brother Rhett. She told him how lonely she'd been growing up at Broughton. She told him how much she'd missed her brother Rhett. She told Ashley about her pony, Jack.

Sheriff's Talbot's office was a cool underground den.

Scarlett demanded, "Why haven't you arrested them?"

"Who should I arrest, Mrs. Butler?"

Scarlett wanted to shake the blandness off the sheriff's face. She pushed words past her teeth. "The Watlings! Isaiah and Josie Watling murdered Will Benteen!"

The sheriff rolled his chair against the wall and leaned back to examine the fly-specked ceiling. He grunted, bent, and spat into the spittoon.

"Well?" Scarlett demanded. "When are you going to arrest them?"

"I reckon, Mrs. Butler, I reckon there's two ways of lookin' at this. You got your 'pinion and some folks got 'nother 'pinion."

Scarlett blinked. "Whatever are you talking about?"

"Some folks say Mr. Wilkes started that fight."

"They'd shot my horses, burned my Atlanta home, and frightened off my field workers. Sheriff, they intended to murder my husband!"

"Did they? I always figured Mr. Butler could take care of hisself. Didn't I hear your husband was in Europe somewheres? I don't know that the Watlings ever been to Europe—leastways they never said they had."

Sheriff Talbot went in his drawer for a leather sap. He got up, plucked his hat from the hat rack, and rolled it in his hands. "Mrs. Butler, some folks b'lieve—and I ain't sayin' I disagree—that Ashley Wilkes started that fight and Will Benteen murdered Archie Flytte once Flytte was getting the better of Wilkes."

"Ashley was defending Tara. Those Watlings—"

"B'lieve you mentioned that, Mrs. Butler. B'lieve you mentioned that several times. But you never showed me no proof." He set his hat on the back of his head so it framed his face like a picture frame. "Mrs. Butler, I don't mean to hurt your feelin's, but I am inclined to b'lieve that Mr. Wilkes attacked Archie Flytte unprovoked and when Archie resisted, Will Benteen shot Archie. Josie Watling killed Benteen trying to save Archie's life. Least that's how I see it. You might see things different." He slipped the sap into his trouser pocket "Now, ma'am, I got to get to Darktown. Another cuttin'. Ain't it peculiar? Niggers cut each other, where a white man'd use a gun. You reckon that's because they're more primitive?"

"The Watlings—"

"Won't bother you no more, Mrs. Butler. The Watlings done left Clayton

County. Josie and old Isaiah lit out after the fight and nobody's seen 'em since. Weren't no Flyttes willin' to bury Archie, so the County buried him." He shrugged. "Far as this sheriff's office is concerned, everything's square. Archie's dead, Will Benteen's dead, and the Watlings are gone. Josie Watling was always kiddin' about Jesse James. Said he rode with the James brothers during the War." Sheriff Talbot opened the door to show Scarlett out. "You reckon next time we hear about the Watlings, they'll be robbin' trains?" The sheriff locked the door behind them and peered at the cloudless sky. "Darned if it ain't dry." He added, "Watlings was a good family. Hard workers. I swear Isaiah Watling near worked himself half to death tryin' to make a go of that hardscrabble farm. Sorrowful, ain't it—how things turn out?"

When she got back to Tara, Scarlett rode into the river fields. Will's furrows between the cotton ridges had been smooth red clay. Now they were greened with weeds. Oat sedge tangled the ridges where her cotton plants, each set eight inches from its neighbor, turned hopefully toward the beckoning sun.

Before daybreak next morning, Scarlett was in the horse barn. The work harness was so heavy, she dragged it over the horse's rump, and the hames were an awkward nightmare. She guessed which straps to buckle and rebuckled what seemed too loose or tight.

When she came into the house, Tara's people were in the kitchen, the children poking sleepily at their breakfast. Scarlett took fried side meat off the counter and ate without sitting down. She said, "Now Will is gone, we'll have to do without him. Lord knows, there's enough work to go around. Mammy, you'll tend Ashley. Ella, honey, stay here and help Mammy. I don't want you taking one of your fits. Everyone else into the fields. Yes, Pork, I know what you're going to say: 'But Miss Scarlett, I'ze been a valet all my life!' " Scarlett's mimicry was so accurate, even Pork cracked a smile.

It was cool at first. Rosemary and the youngest children worked a row. Dilcey, Wade, Pork, and Prissy each had a row. Scarlett took Will's job: plowing up one long row, down another, steering a plow whose tall wooden handles were whitened from strong men's sweat. The horse knew its job and marched forward phlegmatically, but the plow handles jerked and bucked and whenever the plow hit a rock, the handles kicked against Scarlett's small hands until her palms ached.

Sun was the enemy.

Leather traces lay across Scarlett's shoulders as if she were in harness with the horse. She stumbled and turned her ankles on the rough ground. Sweat stung her eyes and half-blinded her. The dust the horse raised mixed with her sweat and caked her face.

At noon, they stopped under the shade trees beside the river. When Scarlett knelt and splashed cool water on her cheeks and neck, it ran over her breasts. Rosemary knelt beside her. "Y'all Georgia planters surely do live a life of ease."

In the long afternoon, Dilcey began a chant Scarlett had heard all her life.

"It's a long John," Dilcey sang.

Prissy answered, "It's a long John."

"He's long gone."

"He's long gone."

"Mister John John."

"Mister John John."

"Old big-eyed John. Oh, John John . . ."

Stumbling behind the horse, fighting the plow handles, Scarlett breathed in time with that ancient African measure.

They placed Ashley on folded blankets, with his plastered ankle propped on the tailboard of Twelve Oaks' wagon.

Ashley's fine gray eyes looked into Rosemary's. "Thank you for . . . talking to me."

"That day at the market," Rosemary said, "you did the best you could."

Ashley Wilkes closed up. "I got Will killed."

It clouded over the afternoon they finished hoeing. Big-bellied rain clouds rolled over the horizon.

Tara's dusty, sweaty field hands were on the porch drinking cool water when two riders appeared at the bottom of the lane.

Scarlett leapt to her feet as if she'd been stung, ran into the house, and pounded up the stairs like a schoolgirl.

In her bedroom, she kicked off her brogans, dropped her sweat-stained dress in a heap, dipped a washcloth into the water pitcher, and attended to her arms, face, and breasts. She snatched a fine green silk gown from the chifforobe, snapped and tied it. She hadn't time for corset or shoes.

Downstairs again, Scarlett emerged barefoot as a grinning Pork took her husband's reins.

There were new deep lines at the corners of his mouth and under his eyes. Scarlett yearned to hurl herself into his arms, but she wasn't *that* easy. "Pork, it isn't the Second Coming. It's only Mr. Butler come home."

Rhett's hungry eyes devoured her. "I thought you might need a Savior."

"You look like you've been through hell."

"There were one or two bad days." His smile was so warm, so *knowing.*

He swung down, scooped Ella up and set her on his hip. Scarlett took an involuntary step toward him but dug in her heels. How dare he be so confident, so *sure* of her. Scarlett tossed her head. "And how was Paris?"

Rhett's warm smile became his too-familiar infuriating grin and he laughed. The children—it had been so long since she'd heard the children laugh—the children laughed with him.

A raindrop. Another. Raindrops puffed the dry lane.

"This gent is Tazewell Watling. You might remember him."

"My escort at the Quadroon Ball," Scarlett said, even though her heart was rebelling: No. No! What's wrong with me? I should be in Rhett's arms!

Rain splashed her cheeks.

Tazewell Watling turned beet red. "I was a fool, Mrs. Butler. I pray you'll forgive me."

Fool, no fool—what did Scarlett care?

"You've been in the sun," Rhett noted.

Anxiously, Scarlett touched her tanned cheeks. "My complexion . . ."

"Dear brother . . ." Rosemary kissed her brother on both cheeks. "You are here and everything will be all right. I know it will." Rosemary turned to Rhett's companion, "Mr. Watling, I am Rosemary, Rhett's sister. I'm so glad . . . so very, very glad. Come with me and I'll show you where to unsaddle your horses."

Scarlett said, "Dilcey, tell Mammy the prodigal has returned. Take the children and give them a bath. They're filthy."

Louis Valentine was catching raindrops on his outstretched tongue. Wade was grinning like an idiot. When Rhett set Ella down, she clung to his legs until he said, "Go get cleaned up, sweetheart. Your mother and I want to talk."

Rain washed Scarlett's forehead and hair.

Rhett said, "Scarlett, honey, show me your hands."

Scarlett tucked them in her armpits.

"By God, Mrs. Butler. It's good to see you."

The earth was warm and wet under Scarlett's feet. Soaked through, her gown clung to her body like a nightdress. Scarlett was so happy, she thought she might faint. So she lifted her chin defiantly. "Is it now, Mr. Butler? Weren't you in such a tearing hurry to leave me?"

Chapter Fifty-eight

The Glorious Fourth

The next morning, Scarlett stepped onto Tara's veranda and shaded her eyes against the sunrise. Was that a horse in the river fields? Rhett was hunkered over a cotton ridge, examining plants. After some time, he remounted and proceeded up the rise to the steading, touching the broad brim of his planter's hat as he rode by. "Good morning, Mrs. Butler," he said. "I believe we can expect another fine day."

"I expect we can, Mr. Butler." Scarlett's smile was lazy and sly.

Later, with Wade Hampton's enthusiastic help, Rhett visited Tara's hog pens, the meat house, the cotton press, and the weedy upland fields. He checked every harness in the tack room. Wade showed Rhett the post by the milking barn where Ella had found Boo's head and they visited Will Benteen's grave.

After supper, Rhett perched on the top rail of the corral while Rosemary and Taz brought Tara's horses out of the barn one by one.

That evening, Rhett invited Wade Hamilton to join the grown-ups at dinner, which the beaming Pork served in the dining room. Wade was tongue-tied with good behavior. Tazewell Watling proved to be a funny, self-deprecating raconteur. His deadpan descriptions of how sophisticated Parisians reacted to "l'Américain's" Creole French had everyone laughing.

Over coffee and Mammy's pecan pie, Scarlett asked Taz what cotton would fetch in the fall.

"Sea Island middling: thirty cents. Piedmont: thirteen to eighteen."

"As little as that?" Rhett rose. "Scarlett, honey, perhaps you'll show me Tara's books."

The light glowed in Scarlett's office until very late.

Scarlett woke from a dreamless sleep when Rhett's footsteps hesitated at her bedroom door. His name swam toward the surface of her sleepy mind and she would have called him, but he passed on.

Next morning at breakfast, Rhett asked what everybody wanted from Atlanta.

"I'll accompany you," Tazewell said. "I've gifts for my mother."

Scarlett took a breath. "Mr. Watling, please convey my best regards to your mother. Without Belle's warning, my husband might have ridden into a fatal ambush."

Rhett chuckled. "My, my, Mrs. Butler. How very . . . *predictable* my life would have been without you."

When Wade wanted to go, too, Rhett said, "Be ready at the horse barn in ten minutes. We won't wait."

Wade clattered up the stairs.

Rhett turned to Scarlett. "Rosemary says the Watlings have fled the county."

"So Sheriff Talbot says. Rhett, Talbot said he knew you?"

When Bonnie Blue died and when Melanie died, Rhett had hugged his sorrow to himself, as if sorrow were all he had left. Now he said softly, "One day, I'll tell you about Tunis Bonneau."

Scarlett and Rosemary waved them off and Scarlett turned to her friend. "My God, has Rhett been here only two days?"

Rosemary said, "My brother can be rather . . . daunting."

"He's changed, Rosemary. He's the same Rhett he was, but he's different, too. I . . . I feel like a maiden again." She paused and in a soft voice added, "I pray life will be good to me!"

"Of course it will, dear."

"Do you really believe so? Oh, please say you do!"

Only Louis Valentine, who had mastered six of McGuffey's seven readers, was disappointed when Rosemary canceled school that day. Beau asked to accompany Rosemary to Twelve Oaks, but she said no, he could go after his father was feeling better.

Rosemary packed a hamper with corn bread, Mammy's greens and side meat, and the remnants of last night's pecan pie.

The rain had refreshed the red dirt countryside and birds were twittering. Rosemary smiled when she thought about her brother and Scarlett. As if by mutual consent, they played the long and happily married man and wife, toying with each other, building tension until the air between them crackled. Last night when Rhett escorted Scarlett into the dining room, the rustle of her crisp petticoats had been electric.

Ashley's modest home was disagreeable.

Unwashed clothing heaped a corner and dirty dishes cluttered the dry sink. Ashley's precious books were strewn here and there and his bedclothes were ropes of discontent.

Rosemary threw the door and windows open and hummed as she cleaned. When the room was to her satisfaction, she picked lilac-pink roses for a jar beside her picnic hamper.

She brought *The Gardens of England* onto the porch and sat listening to a newsbee, a swallow's chirrup, the distant tap of a woodpecker.

The sun warmed her face, and Rosemary turned pages slowly, pausing at each hand-tinted daguerreotype. Gardeners impose human values on disorderly nature, knowing full well that nature must win in the end. Gardening is gentle gallantry.

When Ashley arrived he flipped his reins over his horse's head, loosed the crutch tied behind his saddle, pulled his sound foot out of the stirrup, swung it over the horse's neck, and slid down the horse's flank onto his crutch and uninjured foot. "As you see," he said, "I'm not completely helpless." On foot and crutch, crabwise, he clumped up the steps into the cabin.

He hadn't shaved. His trousers were smeared with red clay.

He glanced at the roses, "Old Pink Daily makes a poor cut flower. The petals fall off."

Rosemary said, "Should I regret picking them?"

Ashley slumped in a chair and leaned his crutch against the dry sink. "I'm sorry, Rosemary. You don't find me at my best. Mose says Rhett is back. That must be a relief."

Rosemary retied her bonnet. "You'll find a pecan pie in the hamper. Perhaps it will sweeten your disposition."

"Oh Rosemary, please don't leave. I'm sorry. I don't mean to drive you away."

She hesitated, "There are greens, and Mammy's corn bread, too."

Ashley said, "I am partial to greens and corn bread. Thank you, Rosemary. Won't you bide for a while?" He massaged his underarm, which was sore from the crutch. "I never knew how . . . *convenient* two legs are."

"Ashley, you tried to help, and I am grateful. You risked your life. . . ."

"I got Will Benteen killed."

"Shut your mouth, Major Wilkes. You will not blame yourself."

Ashley grimaced. "Rosemary . . . dear, kind Rosemary, you've never been sick of yourself. You've never prayed for the courage to end—"

"Ashley Wilkes! Need I remind you my husband took his own life?"

He dropped his head in his hands and groaned.

Rosemary rapped a spoon against a bowl and said, more tenderly, "Eat, Ashley. It'll put iron in your blood."

He did and muttered, "It tastes like a rusty barrel hoop."

Rosemary smiled at Ashley's tiny joke and thought, It's a start anyway. Thank you, dear Lord.

Ashley wouldn't murder himself. Ashley Wilkes had no dreadful secrets to rise up and swallow him.

When Rhett and Wade returned from Atlanta, Wade was wearing his new hat at the same jaunty angle Rhett wore his.

Taz had stayed in town. "Belle and Taz have some catching up to do," Rhett told Scarlett, adding, "Belle hasn't seen hide nor hair of the Watlings. She thinks they've gone west. 'Poor Poppa ain't got no home.' "

"I hate that old fool," Scarlett said.

"A lifetime of disappointments can make a dangerous man."

That afternoon, after the children finished their lessons, Rhett asked, "Who wants to learn how to ride?"

The smaller children tried to outshriek each other. Rhett held up a hand and said, "We'll go to the horse barn and I'll teach you, provided you do exactly as I say."

Scarlett blanched.

Rhett touched her cheek. "Sweetheart, remember how much Bonnie Blue loved her pony? Bonnie would have wanted us to remember that."

Rhett set each child on a tame workhorse and led it around the corral on a longe line. "Ella, hang on to the horse's mane.

"Beau, you must look where you want your horse to go!"

Scarlett went into the house to her office. On the desktop, tied with the black silk ribbon befitting important documents, were the deeds to Tara and her Atlanta property. In appropriate places, her loans were declared "satisfied."

Scarlett dropped her head into her hands and cried.

In the morning, Rhett rode into Jonesboro, where he crossed the tracks into Darktown. He reined up at Reverend J. Robert Maxwell's modest home next to the First African Baptist Church. Rhett tied his horse to the picket fence and waited until a plump young man came onto the front porch. "Good morning, Reverend Maxwell," Rhett said. "Do you suppose we'll get rain today?"

The young man assessed the sky. "I don't believe we will. I believe it will be hot."

"It might at that. I'm Rhett Butler."

"Yes, sir. I heard you were at Tara Plantation. Won't you come in? My wife is just making coffee."

The Reverend's parlor boasted one reading chair, three straight chairs, and a New Haven clock on the mantel. The bare oak floor and front windows gleamed. The men took chairs facing each other and discussed weather and crops until Mrs. Maxwell (who seemed young to be married) set a tin tray on a third chair between them.

When Rhett thanked her, Mrs. Maxwell blushed and withdrew.

The men busied themselves with cream and sugar. "Mr. Benteen was a fair employer," the preacher said. "I wish there were more like him."

"Most planters don't understand free labor any better than free laborers do," Rhett said.

"That's true, sir. That's true." The young man nodded. "It's a new world for us all."

"A better one, I hope."

The young man cocked his head, listening for overtones. "Some white men don't hope so." He eyed Rhett over the rim of his coffee cup. "I've heard about you, Mr. Butler. The Reverend William Prescott preached in my church."

"Reverend Prescott is a powerful preacher."

"Praise the Lord. William told me you shot his son-in-law."

"Tunis Bonneau was my friend."

The young preacher set his cup down. "That's what William said." He ran his hand over his face as if brushing away cobwebs. "I pray those terrible days are over."

The mantel clock ticked.

Maxwell continued: "Reverend Prescott related a curious story. He said you bought a ship from his daughter—a sunken ship."

"The *Merry Widow* sank in my service." Rhett leaned forward. "What did William Prescott say about his daughter?"

"Mrs. Bonneau has moved to Philadelphia. She has her son, Nat, to think about." Maxwell put down his coffee cup and went to the window. When he turned, sunlight haloed his head and Rhett squinted to make out his expression. "Mr. Butler, you may know we are asking the legislature for negro normal schools so our children can be educated by negro teachers."

Rhett set his cup on the tray.

Maxwell continued. "You have many powerful friends. I'd take it kindly if you spoke to them."

After a moment, Rhett said, "I will."

The young minister steepled his fingers. "Just how can I help you, Mr. Butler?"

At daybreak Scarlett woke to chanting: "Long John. Long John. Be a long time gone." Tara's workers were filing across the sunrise. As they had done so many times before, in good years and bad, they went down into the bottoms, spread out, and started to work.

Scarlett hurried downstairs into the kitchen, where Rhett and Rosemary faced an enormous breakfast and the beaming Mammy. "Rhett," Scarlett cried, "they're back. Tara's people are back."

"Why, yes, my dear, they are."

"But how?"

Her husband shrugged. "We've work to be done and they have families to feed. They've no reason to be afraid anymore. I said we'd pay a little more."

Scarlett's stood up. "More? More? Why, they hardly earn what we're paying them now!" But even as she was speaking, her sore back reminded her of hoeing and plowing and stooping. She laughed at herself and said, "I suppose Tara can afford to pay a little more."

After Taz returned from Atlanta, he and Rhett called a meeting of cotton planters. Tony Fontaine and his brother Alex came, and Beatrice Tarleton arrived on the stallion that had sired Will's orphan foals. Mr. MacKenzie, a dour Yankee who'd bought ruined plantations for a dime on the dollar and suspected he'd paid five cents too much, was accompanied by the shy Mr. Schmidt, who asked Mrs. Tarleton if she knew who'd lost a roan gelding he'd seen running loose.

Scarlett and Rhett greeted them at the door, and when everyone was settled in the parlor, Rhett introduced Taz. "Mr. Watling is a partner in a New Orleans cotton-factoring firm."

"Well, I'll be dam—darned," Beatrice Tarleton said, "At long last, I get to meet Rhett's bastard. I've must say, young man, you don't favor your father!"

Accustomed to Beatrice's bluntness, her neighbors chuckled. The Yankee planters kept their expressions blank.

"I'm sorry to disappoint you, madam," Taz said pleasantly. "In fact, my father was Colonel Andrew Ravanel. You may know of him?"

"I'll be damned." Beatrice settled back in her chair.

"Only if the Lord dislikes rude old women," Rhett sang from the back of the room.

Taz explained their crops fetched poor prices because the British market was depressed and New England mills wanted well-packed, graded, carefully ginned cotton.

A planter's association was formed on the spot, with Rhett as president and Tony Fontaine as vice president. Tazewell Watling was asked to contract for ginning and warehousing in the association's name.

The field hands hoed the cotton bottoms and sowed the uplands in oats. Tara began to look like Tara again.

Rosemary spent most afternoons at Twelve Oaks.

Sunday, Belle Watling came to visit her son. After dinner, Taz drove Belle to the railroad station, leaving Rosemary and her brother on the porch. The children were playing at red indians on the lawn while fireflies blinked cryptic messages.

"It is so peaceful here," Rosemary said.

"On a summer evening, the countryside seems eternal."

The children's play dissolved into giggles.

"You're thinking about Bonnie Blue?"

Rhett was quiet for a time. "I just wish I knew who Bonnie would have become."

"Yes," his sister said. "My Meg would be a young woman today, worrying if she were pretty enough to catch a beau. Brother, life is too cruel."

Rhett took a cigar from his case. "I sometimes think if there's any purpose for our being on earth, it's to testify about those we've lost." He nipped the end of his cigar. "You're seeing Ashley?"

"Ashley is a good, gentle man."

When Rhett struck his match, his cheekbones were dramatic. "I suppose he is. But is the world good enough for Ashley Wilkes?"

Rosemary rested her chin on her hand. "Ashley is the man he is—as you are, Rhett."

"I suppose so." Rhett leaned over the railing to call, "Children, time to come in. Time for prayers and bed."

When she woke next morning, Scarlett stretched luxuriously. The linen sheets caressed her like a lover. Waiting for Rhett to come to her was excruciating but so delicious. One day, one day soon . . .

After breakfast, Scarlett carried her coffee onto the front porch, where Rhett was on the porch swing. "Your dahlias are lovely."

"My mother disliked them. Ellen said dahlias were 'all show.' "

He laughed, "Isn't 'show' a flower's duty?"

"Perhaps. Rhett . . . I . . ."

When he touched his finger to her lips, shivers ran down her spine. "Hush now. Don't spoil it."

In the river fields, the cotton blooms peeked like snowflakes amid the green.

Rhett said, "I want to host a barbecue. Just like old times. We'll invite everybody. Do you remember the barbecue where we met?"

"I am hardly likely to forget."

"There I was, innocently napping, and when I sat up, my eyes lit on the loveliest girl I'd ever seen. And she hurled crockery at me!"

Scarlett slipped her hand into his. "I've always been sorry I missed," she whispered. And they laughed at their silly joke.

Preparations began.

"But the Fourth of July is a Union holiday," Scarlett objected.

Rhett said. "Dear, we *are* the Union now." Rhett made plans as if no Southerner could possibly object to celebrating the anniversary of the day Vicksburg fell and Gettysburg was lost.

Apparently, Rhett had gauged sentiment correctly, because no one refused Tara's invitations, and Beatrice Tarleton asked if she could bring her visiting grand-niece with her.

Mammy and Dilcey went through the poultry yard like Grim Reapers. Rhett bought hams. Early tomatoes were commandeered from gardens near and far; lettuce and pole beans were picked, new potatoes dug.

Ashley asked the fiddler who had been Twelve Oaks' principal musical ornament to lead their orchestra. "Yes, sir, Mr. Wilkes. Be like it used to be."

Tara's stove roared until Mammy complained that the kitchen was "hotter than Tophet." She and Dilcey baked apple, chess, pecan, and rhubarb pies.

Rhett set the children to churning ice cream they stored in tall tin canisters in the icehouse.

Since they hadn't played together in years, Ashley's musicians practiced at Tara and barbecue preparations were accompanied by fiddle, two banjos, and a mandolin.

The Fourth of July dawned cool, with no rain clouds on the horizon.

Pork had the buggy at the Jonesboro station for the noon train. Listening to Pork and Peter argue over who should drive her, Miss Pittypat beamed. "My," Pitty said, "isn't this just like old times!"

Although the invitations stated 2:00 P.M., some guests arrived before noon. Of course they asked to help. Of course they got in the way.

Neighbors rolled up Tara's lane in battered farm wagons. Atlanta gentry rented every rig in the Jonesboro Livery.

Aunt Pittypat fretted, "Dear Rhett, do you think . . . well, do you think it's entirely proper? It is July Fourth and so many of us recall this date unhappily. . . ."

When Rhett kissed her cheek, Miss Pittypat forgot what else she meant to say.

If any Southerner objected to the Fourth, they didn't say so, and the Yankee planters Rhett had invited were too courteous to recall the past.

At a country barbecue on a hot afternoon in Clayton County, Georgia, the War finally and entirely ended.

At two on the dot, Reverend Maxwell and his wife drove up in their plain Baptist buggy. Rhett greeted them in the turnaround, tipping his hat to Mrs. Maxwell. "So glad you could join us today, Reverend. We are honored."

The Reverend said, "Thank you. I have heard so much about your beautiful plantation."

"You know Dilcey, of course. She'll show you around."

The Fourth of July and a little too much brandy tipped the balance for Tony Fontaine, who marched to Rhett with fire in his eyes. "Damn it, Rhett!"

Rhett clasped Tony's shoulder and said. "Tony, everybody's here for a good time. I'd take it unkindly if you spoiled our fun."

Tony looked past Rhett's smile to his cold, intelligent eyes. "Rhett! Damn it! I just can't. . . ."

"You'll be leaving, then. So sorry. It was good of you to come."

Tony Fontaine said, "But damn it, Rhett!"

"So good of you to come."

So Tony Fontaine and his protesting wife departed. Although everyone knew what had happened, nobody remarked about it. Polite Southerners don't notice what they oughtn't.

To his dismay, MacBeth was in livery, and when Pork said, " 'Bout time niggers dressin' like they should," MacBeth cursed him blue. Belle Watling's loose gown flattered her figure.

Ashley Wilkes and Rosemary described Twelve Oaks' gardens in more detail than Uncle Henry wanted to hear.

Hickory smoke from barbecue pits curled through the boxwoods and a breeze off the river kept mosquitoes at bay. Guests lined up at buffet tables.

"Won't you take a little ham, Reverend? An end piece?"

"Thank you, Dilcey."

These pleasures were enhanced by memories of prior occasions oh so long ago.

As dusk thickened, the men were drinking harder, so Rhett had Reverend Maxwell's buggy brought around.

"Mr. Butler," Maxwell said, "thank you for a memorable afternoon."

As the sun dipped behind the hills, women put on shawls and the orchestra tuned instruments. Rhett and Taz brought exotically labeled boxes onto the side lawn. "You stay on the porch," Rhett admonished the children. "Ella, Beau, Louis Valentine: If you step onto the lawn, you'll have to watch from indoors."

"Can I help?" Wade asked.

"If you do exactly as Taz and I say."

Chinese rockets soared into the night sky over Tara, streaking and exploding and showering streamers. At each explosion, the children cried, "Ohhhh." Ella covered her ears and adults applauded.

After the last rocket was fired, the children rushed onto the lawn to investigate their burned shells and marvel that anything so homely could have contained such beautiful stars.

The parlor, center hall, and dining room became the ballroom Ellen O'Hara had asked Gerald for. The orchestra set up on the stairs. Although Rosemary put the younger children in bed, within minutes they were peeking down through the balustrades.

In his Sunday suit and stiff celluloid collar, Wade dogged Tazewell Watling and hoped no grown-up would ruffle his hair. His great-aunt Pittypat said, "Wade, you are the very image of dear Charles!" A tear tracked down her old wrinkled cheek.

Beneath the portrait of Scarlett's grandmother, Beatrice Tarleton and Alex Fontaine were discussing a loose horse several men had seen. Mrs. Tarleton disbelieved. "I know every roan between here and Jonesboro."

Beatrice's daughters were somewhere about. Her sons, Brent and Stuart and Tom—Scarlett's ardent suitors before the War—were now just sad memories.

Scarlett sighed.

As if he'd read her thoughts, Rhett took her hand. "Darling, if there are ghosts here tonight, they want us to be happy."

The little orchestra interspersed waltzes with reels. To the older guests' dismay, the musicians refused to play "them old-timey" quadrilles.

After Taz danced with his mother, he partnered Beatrice's grand-niece Polly—a brown-haired, shy slip of a thing.

Belle Watling glowed with pleasure. "Look at my boy," she whispered to no one in particular. "Lord, will you just look at him."

Beatrice Tarleton inclined her head to the woman beside her, "Miss Watling," she said, hoarsely, "things are not as they were."

"I . . ."

"I believe it's for the best. I don't know what got into people. All that needless straitlaced respectability. Did we actually think God cared if a man got a peek at our legs? Tell me, Miss Watling"—Beatrice looked Belle square in the eye—"are all men the same?"

Belle coughed and patted her throat. "Gracious," she said. Then she leaned in confidentially, "There's men and men, don't you know."

Ashley and Rosemary sat on the porch swing, discussing nothing really—but enjoying their conversation immensely.

Desserts were served on tables on the lawn, but once the breeze died, the mosquito hordes descended and everyone carried their plates indoors.

In her high-backed wing chair, Miss Pittypat reflected happily and sadly how much dear Melanie would have enjoyed this evening.

When the fiddler struck up "Soldier's Joy," Rhett offered Scarlett his hand.

"Rhett, I've been so foolish."

"Yes, we both have been." Mr. Butler led Mrs. Butler onto the dance floor.

When we met, Scarlett thought, I was a child. Rhett helped me become who I am.

"My dear," Rhett murmured politely, "it's a reel, not a two-step."

Scarlett O'Hara Butler whirled. Whirled like the girl she had been, like the girl who dwelled in the depths of her heart. She whirled as a child whirls, as a young girl whirls, as a woman whirls, and her man was beside her, his hand quick to capture hers. So much love sparkled in her husband's eyes that for the first time in her life, Scarlett Butler wasn't afraid of growing old.

At midnight, despite many protests, the band put their instruments away.

Rhett had a special train waiting in Jonesboro for their Atlanta guests. Nearer neighbors lingered in the turnaround.

"Thank you so much for coming," Scarlett repeated. "Certainly we'll do it again."

As the last buggy lamp dwindled down the lane, Rhett closed up the house.

Scarlett found Belle Watling in the upstairs hall. She wore an astonishingly pink dressing gown.

"I don't think I've ever had a lovelier day," Belle said. "Thank you, Miss Scarlett, for having me to stay."

Scarlett kissed the pink creature on the cheek. "Good night, Belle."

In her bedroom, Scarlett luxuriated in her undressing. Rhett would come to her tonight—her tingling skin assured her he would. Humming, she dabbed cologne behind each ear and beneath the soft curves of her breasts.

Rhett had never seen the sheer nightgown she put on. Scarlett felt like a precious gift.

When she opened the curtains, cool blue moonlight flooded the room.

Scarlett knelt beside her bed and crossed herself. She thanked God for Tara and Ella and Wade and everybody who loved her. She thanked God for bringing Rhett home.

Then she smelled smoke.

Chapter Fifty-nine

My Day Is Come

Scarlett coughed and coughed. Shadows gathered at the base of her bedroom door and oily black smoke trickled, then surged inside and up the wainscoting.

Rosemary cried, "Fire! My God! Fire!"

When Scarlett touched the doorknob, she jerked back with a gasp. It was hot as a stovetop!

Shirtless and barefoot, Rhett burst in from the nursery. "The fire's in the stairwell," he said matter-of-factly. "Help me get the children out."

Everything was happening so quickly! When Rhett took her hand, Scarlett protested, "But I'm not dressed!"

In the nursery, smoke drifted lazily through the moonlight. Among scattered toys and books, the children sat around Rosemary, who held Louis Valentine in her lap. As icy calm as her brother, Rosemary said, "Tazewell's gone for his mother."

"Good man." Rhett knelt at child's eye level. "Ella, it's past your bedtime. What are you doing up so late?"

Ella put her hand over her mouth; her fear transmuted into giggles.

"Beau, are you my brave boy? I need you to be brave tonight."

Beau blew his nose hard.

Rhett said, "We're counting on you, Wade Hampton Hamilton."

Outside the nursery door, the fire sounded like a great beast crackling through the undergrowth. Hurry! Scarlett thought. We must hurry!

Rhett turned to the shivering Louis Valentine, "How old are you, Louis?"

"Seven, Uncle Rhett."

"You were named for a pirate. Did you know that?"

"Yes, sir."

"Rhett!" Scarlett protested.

Rhett squeezed Scarlett's hand but kept his eyes fixed on the child. "Then you'll have to be brave as a pirate. Right, Louis Valentine?"

Louis Valentine squeaked, "Yes, Uncle Rhett."

"Good. Because when we go through that door, it's going to be hot and black and frightening. We will hold hands so nobody gets lost or left behind. Scarlett will lead us, then Wade, then Louis Valentine, then Rosemary, then Ella. Beau, you'll take Ella's other hand—you mustn't let go of it—and I'll hold your hand and come last. Join hands now. Good. Hang on tighter than you've ever hung on to anything. Hang on hard!"

As Rhett was talking, the room filled with smoke and Ella started coughing. Scarlett prayed Ella wouldn't take one of her fits.

"We're going to crawl down the hall underneath the smoke to the servants' stairs and down those stairs to the kitchen and outside," Rhett continued. "You mustn't tarry and, even if you are scared, you must pretend you're brave. You cannot turn loose of the hands you are holding. Do you understand?"

A ragged chorus of yeses. Ella muffled a sob.

In the same even tone, Rhett said, "Scarlett, honey, take Wade's hand. Off we go."

Though her teeth were chattering, Scarlett said, "Mr. Butler, are you sure this is the way to the Honeysuckle Ballroom?"

Rhett snorted. Scarlett hitched her nightgown above her knees and knelt.

Rhett threw the hall door open on suffocating black smoke tongued by sullen yellow flames. Scarlett crawled into it. Each wooden floorboard was outlined by light from below; the ceiling had disappeared in swirling blackness. Scarlett's neck was so hot. What if her hair burst into flames? It was farther to the servants' stairs than Scarlett remembered. She crawled, with Wade's hand clamped behind her, and when her fine new nightgown slipped under her knees and hampered her crawl, she ripped it.

The fire roared like an angry bear. The floor scorched Scarlett's hands and knees and she gasped for air. Wade's hand in hers was slippery with sweat. Rhett's bellow cut through the roar: "Children. You must not let go. Hang on with all your might!"

Ella shrieked, "I want my mother!"

"I'm here, honey. Keep crawling." Scarlett hacked a painful cough.

Ahead in the smoke, a darker rectangle became the stairwell. With her free hand, Scarlett groped for the top stair, crying, "I'm at the stairs. I'm starting down." She coughed until it felt as if she were coughing up lung tissue. Clinging to Wade's sweat-slippery hand, Scarlett backed down—two, three steps. Cool air rushed up the stairs, lifting the smoke above her. Feeling with toes for each invisible riser, Scarlett backed down the narrow pitch-black stairs.

Far behind, Rhett shouted, "Hands tight! Hold tight!" When Wade misstepped, his hand was snatched from hers and she blocked his body so he wouldn't tumble down. Wade said, "Sorry, Mother," sounding just like Charles Hamilton.

In the tiny vestibule outside the kitchen, Scarlett tried to remember whether the latch was on the left or right. Somewhere above, Rhett cried, "We are nearly there! Louis Valentine! Pirates never snivel!"

The narrow door swung open on Mammy in nightdress and calico nightcap. The old negress said helplessly, "Scarlett, honey. We is on fire."

Scarlett pulled Wade into the cool kitchen.

"Yes, Mammy, we're on fire. Ring the farm bell and rouse everybody." Scarlett handed Louis Valentine into the kitchen, then Rosemary and Ella, then Beau, and finally Rhett Butler, who was tucking his scorched hands into his armpits.

"But it was such a fine barbecue," a dazed Mammy said. "We ain't had such a time in years!"

Scarlett cried, "Oh Rhett! Your hands, your poor, poor hands!"

"Left my gloves in Glasgow," he replied lightly.

Rosemary shepherded the children into the yard as Mammy's bell clamored the alarm. The steading was dark and quiet. When Ella collapsed, Rhett caught and carried her. Ella's chubby bare feet dangled from his arms. Rhett laid Ella in some grass beside the springhouse and said, "Poor child. She was as brave as she needed to be."

"I'll stay with Ella," Rosemary said. "Wade Hamilton, please heed the younger boys."

Taz leaned a ladder against Gerald O'Hara's balcony, where his unflustered mother was waiting. Flames flickered behind Tara's upstairs windows. Ellen O'Hara's fanlight and side lights glowed white. An empty fuel can lay next to the front door. Scarlett could smell kerosene in the wood smoke.

Tara's front stairs, where the orchestra had played Strauss waltzes just hours before, were burning.

Rhett braced the ladder as Taz climbed.

Grass beside the house was scorched. The boxwoods were burned sticks. As if ghosts were sitting in it, Tara's porch swing creaked back and forth.

Her pink dressing gown as intact as her dignity, Belle Watling backed down the ladder rung by cautious rung.

Negroes ran to the house. Dilcey shouted, "Tara! We got to save Tara!"

Scarlett woke from her stupor. "Rhett!" she cried. "My God! It's Tara." She darted for the door as the fanlight popped and flame blossomed on the underside of the porch roof.

Rhett caught her around the waist and lifted her off her feet. "No!" he said. "It's too far gone."

She kicked at his shins. "Not Tara. I won't lose Tara."

"By God! I won't lose you! Not ever again!" Rhett bore Scarlett away as flames burst through the soffits and over the roof peak.

The heat was blistering. Rhett, Scarlett, Tazewell, and Belle retreated to the turnaround.

Scarlett wept angrily. "We should have tried!" She flailed at Rhett's chest. "We should have done *something*!"

The fire roared and Tara's windows glowed like Satan's eyes. Hoofbeats in the lane: the neighbors. Too late. Altogether too late.

"Oh Rhett," Scarlett moaned, "it's Tara. It's Tara." She buried her face in his shoulder.

"Yes, honey. It was."

The voice wasn't as loud as the fire. "My day is come."

The ragged old man had twigs in his beard. His greasy hair was knotted into tangles. He'd got too near the fire and his shirtfront and sleeves were scorched here and there. He held a rusty single-shot dueling pistol.

"Rhett Butler," Isaiah Watling repeated dully, "my day is come."

Rhett pushed Scarlett aside. "Good evening, Watling. You didn't need to burn my wife's house. I'd have come out if you'd asked."

"Cleansing fire . . ." Isaiah mumbled.

"I don't recall needing a cleansing fire," Rhett said. "But I'm not particularly religious. Doubtless, you know a good deal more about cleansing fires than I do."

The old man found a residue of energy and straightened. "You murdered my son, Shadrach. Because of Rhett Butler, the Young Master of Broughton Plantation, my boy burns in hell."

Through chattering teeth, Scarlett yelled, "You! Leave Tara! Depart from us, you miserable creature!"

Rhett said, "Isaiah, if I hadn't killed your son, somebody else would have. You know that. Shad Watling wasn't going to die in bed."

"Nor will you, sinner!" With trembling hands, old Isaiah raised his pistol.

Rhett took a step toward him. "Give me the pistol, Isaiah."

Belle ran to her father, crying, "Poppa! Poppa! Please! You mustn't!"

The report wasn't loud: a crack, not much louder than a stick breaking. Belle Watling shuddered. Tucking her pink dressing gown neatly so no one could see her bare legs, Belle sat down on the mounting block.

Belle said, "Poor, poor Poppa," and died.

Chapter Sixty

Tomorrow Is Another Day

After years of wondering about the place, Mrs. Meade and Mrs. Elsing visited the Chapeau Rouge. It was their patriotic duty.

Nine years after the War, the Confederate story had flowered into a flamboyant, romantic myth. Certain lurid events that had once embarrassed these ladies had become prominent in their family legends. As Mrs. Elsing told her grandchildren, "When Georgia's Yankee occupiers were hanging brave men right and left, Belle Watling's ruse saved your father from the gallows. You simply cannot imagine!" Mrs. Elsing's astonishment at Yankee gullibility was renewed every time she repeated the familiar tale. "The Yankees actually believed Hugh Elsing would brawl in a sporting house! Imagine that!"

But a legend is one thing, a sporting house another, and when the ladies' coach stopped before the notorious place, the ladies almost told their coachman to drive on. They were greatly relieved to see others they knew, respectable citizens come to pay their respects to Atlanta's most notorious fallen woman.

Tell the truth, they were disappointed. Afterward, Mrs. Meade told her friends, "Why, Miss Watling's parlor seemed very nearly respectable!"

Mrs. Elsing, who detested French decor, disagreed. "Too ar-tis-tic, my dear. Far too ar-tis-tic."

The Chapeau Rouge hadn't changed since the days when Confederate officers rollicked there and veterans returned to honor the young men they had been. In uneasy association, reputable and disreputable Atlantans waited on a walk bordered by Belle's fragrant roses.

MacBeth greeted those he knew and those he didn't with the same impersonal "Mornin', sir, mornin', ma'am. Glad you could come out on such a sorrowful day."

Inside, curiosity seekers who expected gay cockatiels and exotic flamingos found wrens: Belle's black-clad Cyprians.

Several presently respectable matrons had worked here during the War. Mrs. Gerald D. had been the vivacious "Miss Susanna" and "L'il Flirt" was now Mrs. William P. By neither word nor gesture did the Cyprians recognize their former comrades.

The mortician's men had delivered fifty straight-backed chairs and shifted Belle's parlor furniture upstairs. They'd set the coffin on sawhorses and draped the bier in black crepe. They'd placed scores of wreaths and floral arrangements to best advantage.

Belle was laid out in a gray silk dress of distinctly old-fashioned cut. Her hair was loose on the white satin pillow and her hands were crossed devoutly. She looked like a child wearing her mother's ball gown. A broad red ribbon with *Beloved* in black letters was draped across her coffin.

An ashen-faced Rhett Butler accepted condolences. "Yes, she was a fine woman. Belle had a trusting heart. Yes, Belle meant a great deal to me. Thank you, Henry, for coming."

Mrs. Butler stood beside her husband. "So glad you could come, Grandfather Merriwether. I hope you'll partake of our refreshments. Kitchen's through that door."

Scarlett introduced the young man: "Belle's son, Tazewell Watling. Mr. Watling is a cotton factor from New Orleans. A Confederate veteran, yes."

Stunned by grief, Tazewell Watling accepted well-meant condolences from strangers. Though he thanked each politely, their kind words meant nothing. Tazewell's mind was regretting what so easily might have been: his mother in the sunshine in his little Vieux Carré garden, happy at last. How he wished he'd kept one, just one, of his mother's silly, precious letters!

Although respectable Atlantans eschewed Belle's lavish funeral feast, rougher citizens and their womenfolk gathered in the kitchen for roast beef, ham, and whiskey. They complained about the national depression and wondered when Atlanta would get up and get going again. They toasted Belle's memory. They recounted Belle's kindnesses when they'd been down on their luck.

The *Atlanta Journal* reporter wrote,

> *Wearing clanking leg irons, his wrists cuffed with bracelets of iron, the murdered woman's father was escorted to the wake by Clayton County sheriff Oliver Talbot. As mourners recoiled in horror, the bearded patriarch who had taken his daughter's life approached her bier. No fatherly tenderness softened his stony features; he uttered no grief-stricken cry. His finger had pressed the fatal trigger. His daughter had fallen at his feet, crying piteously. But if Isaiah Watling felt remorse, he showed none.*
>
> *What thoughts must have tormented his obstinate mind; what fevered emotions must have been quenched by his obdurate will. He bent for a moment over his daughter's coffin and was seen to place something therein.*
>
> *But his grandson, Mr. T. Watling of New Orleans, detected this movement, retrieved the old man's offering, and, as Watling was led away, the young man returned it to him. . . .*

"I believe sir, you forgot this." Taz placed the New Testament into his grandfather's shackled hands.

"I weren't . . ." With rheumy old eyes, Isaiah searched his grandson's face. He licked his lips. "I weren't never my own man. . . ." He dropped his gaze, and when Sheriff Talbot tugged, the old man followed, obedient as a dog.

Rhett had persuaded a reluctant St. Philip's rector that Belle Watling should rest in the city's oldest churchyard. The rector picked a site against the back wall, where Belle's presence wouldn't offend. Rhett tapped a bishop's prominent stone. "Belle never fancied old Charley anyway."

And so, on a beautiful Sunday morning, Ruth Belle Watling was laid to rest. Dew sparkled the grass. Churches tolled Christians to worship. Its bell chiming prettily, one of Atlanta's new streetcars rolled past.

Wade Hamilton and Ella Kennedy flanked Scarlett. Beau Wilkes and Louis Valentine Ravanel stood with Ashley and Rosemary. The rector read from the Book of Common Prayer. The children were awed. Louis Valentine shuffled his feet.

Tazewell Watling wept.

The rector got away as soon as he decently could. Negroes with shovels waited at a respectful distance.

Ashley Wilkes offered Rhett his hand. "I am sorry, Rhett. Belle was a fine woman. She saved my life."

Rhett took the slighter man's hand. "How many years have we known each other?"

Ashley considered, "We met in '61."

"Thirteen years. Strange, it's seems so much longer. How's your garden coming along?"

Ashley brightened. "Wonderfully well. I've got the fountain flowing. You must stop by some time and see it." Ashley took Rosemary's arm. "Your sister is becoming a horticulturalist."

Rosemary asked, "Have you ever wondered why it is, brother, that men pretend to take care of women, when it's generally t'other way 'round?"

Rhett kissed Rosemary's forehead.

Tazewell had been away from his business too long and he left for the railroad station.

When the Butlers reached Aunt Pittypat's, Rhett's strength abandoned him and he stumbled on the stairs. In what had been Melanie Wilkes's bedroom, Scarlett helped her husband undress. When she put Rhett into bed, his teeth chattered and he shivered so violently, Scarlett undressed, slipped under the covers, and held him until he slept.

As late-afternoon shadows passed through the room and wind rustled the elm tree outside the window, Scarlett woke in Rhett's arms.

Tara, Scarlett thought. She would have wept, but she'd wept herself dry.

She sat up and rubbed her eyes so hard, she saw stars. "Fiddle-dee-dee!" Scarlett O'Hara Butler informed the world.

Rhett muttered sleepily and she smoothed the hair off his forehead and kissed his lips. "I'd better see to the children," Scarlett said. "There'll be coffee when you come down."

Mammy and Ella were on the back stoop stringing beans. Pitty, Wade, and Uncle Peter were in the garden.

"We pickin' 'em 'fore they're by," Mammy said. Her old fingers flew. "Mr. Rhett all right?"

"I believe he is. I was trying to remember, Mammy; when did you come to Tara?"

"Goodness, child. I come with your Momma when she was married."

"Did you know Philippe Robillard?"

Mammy's lips set themselves in a familiar stubborn line.

"Mammy, they're all dead. The truth can't hurt anyone now."

"Honey, you ain't lived so long as I have. Truth can hurt whenever it's told." Grudgingly, Mammy admitted, "I never cared for Master Philippe. He was a reckless man."

"Like Rhett?"

"Mr. Rhett? Reckless?" Mammy's ample flesh shook with laughter. "Mr. Rhett never reckless with people he loves."

Everything had changed. Everything Scarlett had willed, everything she had once wished for—utterly changed.

Could she, like Ashley, re-create a version of what life had been before the War? Bountiful azaleas and wisteria artfully draped over ruins? Scarlett snorted.

She and Rhett might rebuild Tara. Or maybe they'd just travel for a time. There were a world of places Scarlett had never seen. Maybe she and Rhett would go to Yellowstone and see those Natural Wonders: hot water spouting out of the ground, regular as clockwork. Mercy!

In that mood, she greeted Rhett when he came down. "Good afternoon, darling!" she said.

He raised his eyebrows. "Am I your darling, then?"

"You know you are. Rhett, please don't mock me anymore."

His infuriating grin vanished. "Honey, never again. I promise."

Each looked into the other's soul. Her eyes were green; his were dark.

He said, "Life has hurt us again."

"A worse hurt than those hurts we have already endured?"

"No," he said. "I suppose not."

Then Rhett Butler laughed, laughed out loud, and he scooped Scarlett up and waltzed her around the kitchen, smothering her with kisses, to Ella's delight and Mammy's consternation. "Mr. Rhett! Mr. Rhett, you gettin' everything upset!"

Rhett Butler smiled that smile of his and said, "Wife, you are the most captivating woman in the world."

Scarlett said, "Mercy, Mr. Butler. Isn't life surprising?"

WHICH WASN'T NEARLY:
THE END

Acknowledgments

This unusual collaboration was driven by two very different storytellers' imaginations and the history of that thrilling and terrible period that made the United States what it is today. Like Margaret Mitchell, I have taken some liberties with history. Civil War historians will notice that I've attributed some of Confederate raider John Hunt Morgan's exploits to Colonel Andrew Ravanel. General Morgan was not Andrew Ravanel and did not survive the war. Likewise, Cuban historians will set the date of General Narciso López's assault several years earlier than I have here. Like the Bay of Pigs and the Iraq invasion, López's invasion used good motives to conceal venial ones and, like them, failed. López was garotted in Havana and his American freebooters—excepting one man—shot. That exception asked the Spanish commander to post a letter to the still powerful Senator Daniel Webster, which he signed "Your affectionate nephew." His successful ruse sounded like Rhett Butler to me.

I am grateful to those who helped *Rhett Butler's People:*

In Georgia:

Mr. Paul Anderson
Mr. Hal Clarke
The Special Collections at Emory and Henry University
The Atlanta History Center
Hofwyl-Broadfield Plantation State Historic Site

In New Orleans:

Ms. Penny Tose
Mr. Henri Schindler
Mr. Arthur Carpenter, Loyola University Special Collections and Archives
Louisiana State Museum and Historical Center
Howard Tilton Memorial Library at Tulane University
Historic New Orleans Collection, Williams Research Center

In Charleston:

Mr. Nick Butler
Dana and Peggy McBean
Dr. J. Tracy Power
Captain Randy Smith
Mr. Peter Wilkerson
Dr. Stephen Wise
The Charleston Museum
Charleston Library Society
South Carolina Historical Society
Charleston Preservation Foundation and
the staffs of the Nathaniel Russell, Aiken-Rhett, and Edmondston-Alston houses

Elsewhere:

Mr. Thomas Cartwright and
The Carter House Museum, Franklin, Tennessee
The International Museum of the Horse at the Kentucky Horse Park
The Alderman Library at the University of Virginia
The Leybum Library at Washington and Lee University
Ms. Jennifer Enderlin at St. Martin's Press

And especially my beloved Anne, whose courage never flagged.

BOOKS
THAT CHANGED
HISTORY

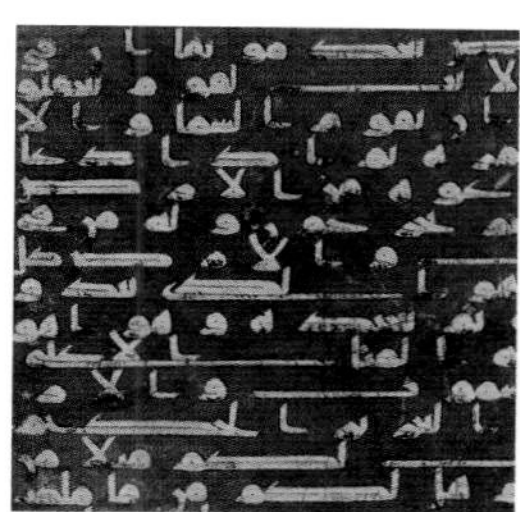

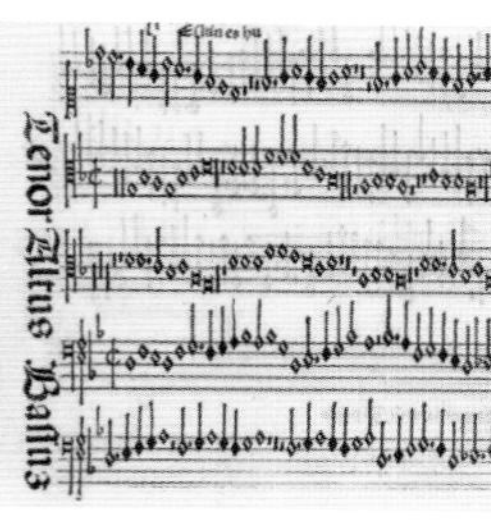

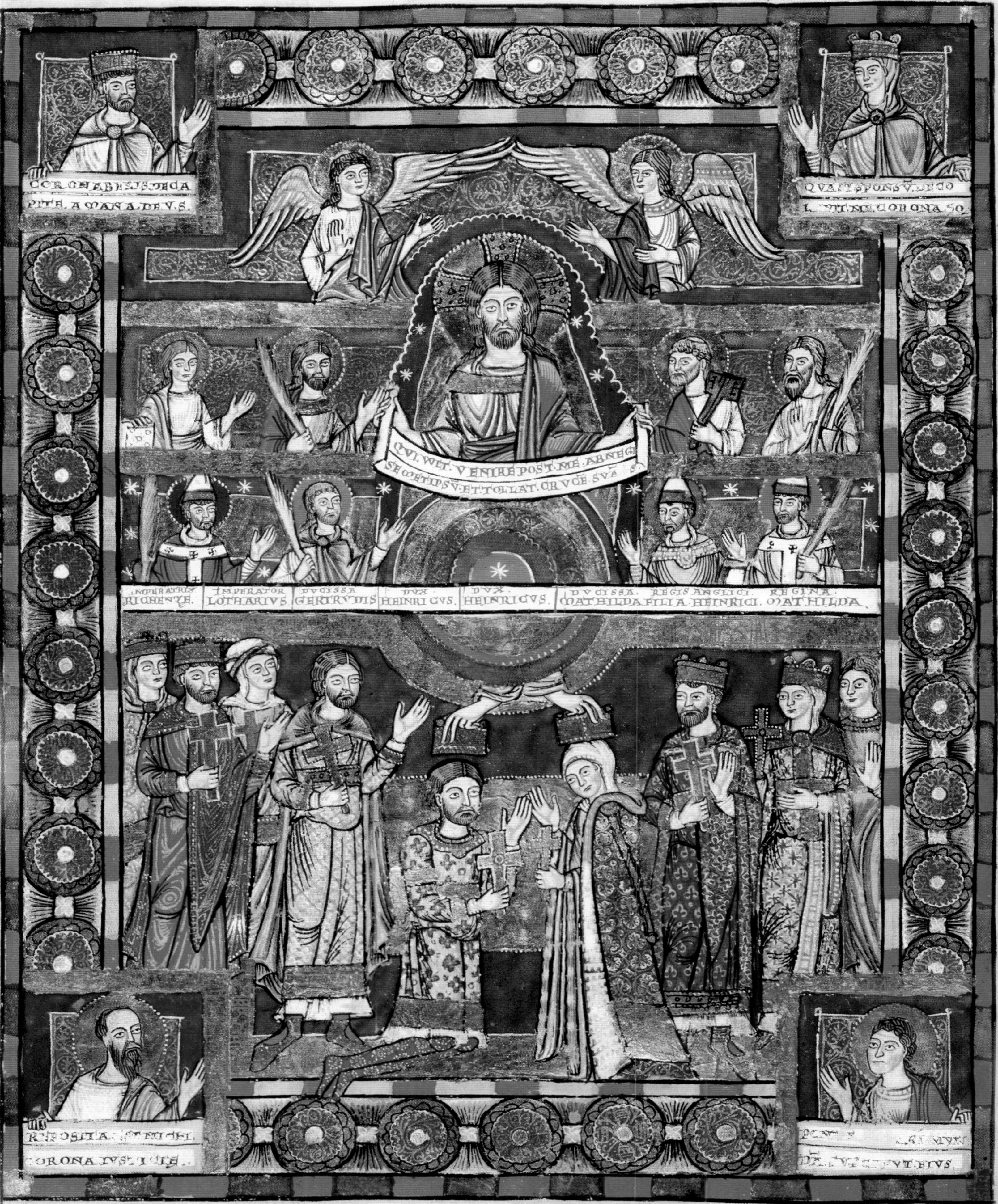
QVI. VVLT. VENIRE POST. ME. ABNEG
SEMETIPSV. ET. TOLLAT. CRVCE. SVA
IMPERATRIX RICHENZE.
IMPERATOR LOTHARIVS
DVCISSA GERTRVDIS
DVX HEINRICVS.
DVX. HEINRICVS.
DVCISSA. MATHILDA FILIA. HEINRICI.
REGIS ANGLICI
REGINA. MATHILDA.

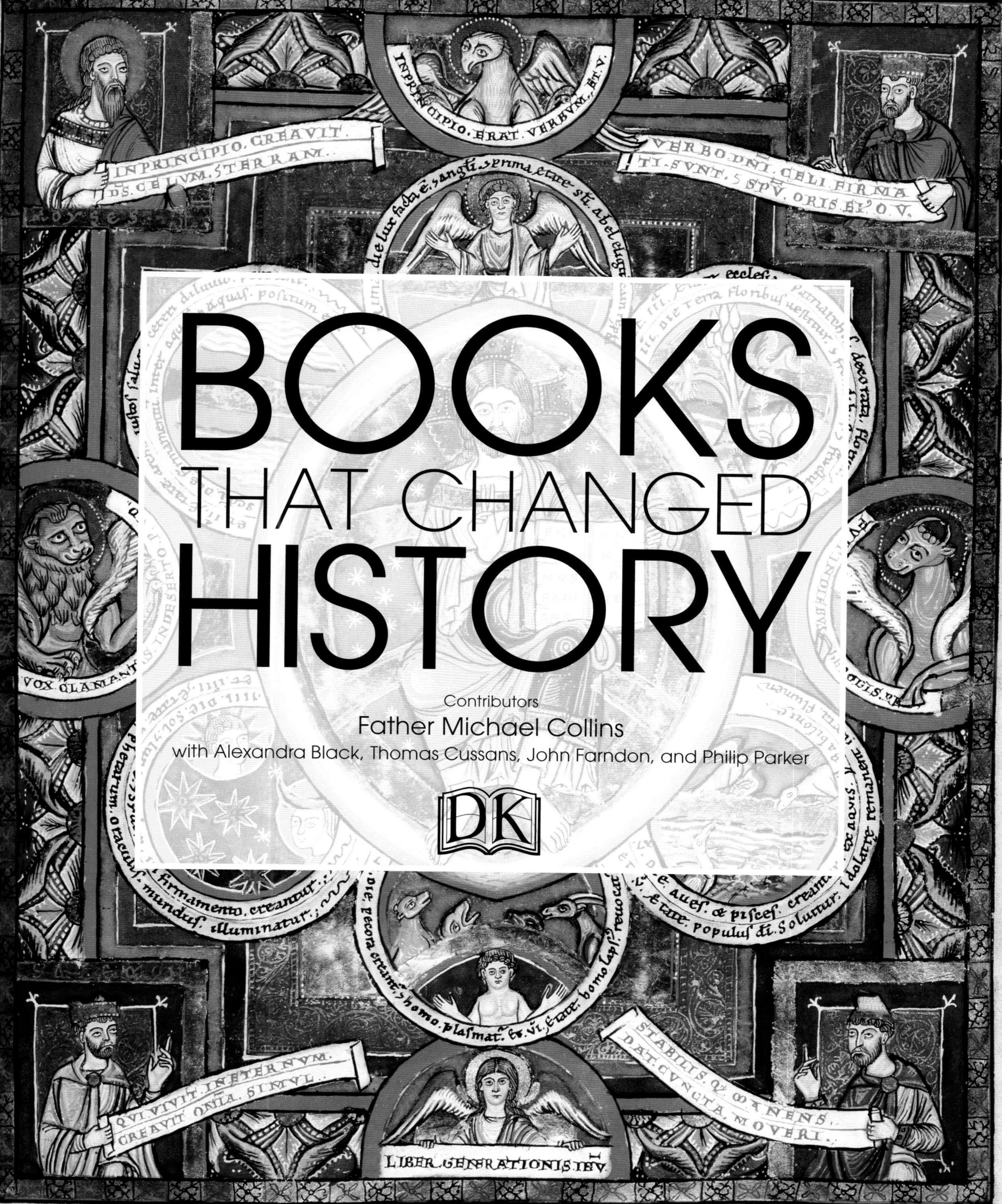

BOOKS THAT CHANGED HISTORY

Contributors
Father Michael Collins
with Alexandra Black, Thomas Cussans, John Farndon, and Philip Parker

DK

Senior Editor Kathryn Hennessy
Senior Art Editor Jane Ewart
Editors Jemima Dunne, Natasha Khan, Joanna Micklem, Ruth O'Rourke-Jones, Helen Ridge, Zoë Rutland, Alison Sturgeon, Debra Wolter
Designers Stephen Bere, Katie Cavanagh, Phil Gamble
Managing Editor Gareth Jones
Senior Managing Editor Lee Griffiths
Picture Researchers Roland Smithies, Sarah Smithies
Senior Jacket Designer Mark Cavanagh
Jacket Design Manager Sophia MTT
Jacket Editor Claire Gell
Pre-production Producer Gillian Reid
Producer Mandy Inness
Publisher Liz Wheeler
Art Director Karen Self
Publishing Director Jonathan Metcalf

DK INDIA

Senior Managing Art Editor Arunesh Talapatra
Senior Art Editor Chhaya Sajwan, Devika Khosla
Art Editor Meenal Goel
Assistant Art Edtior Anukriti Arora
Editor Nishtha Kapil
Pre-production Manager Balwant Singh
Production Manager Pankaj Sharma
DTP Designers Jaypal Chauhan, Nityanand Kumar, Mohammad Rizwan

First published in Great Britain in 2017 by Dorling Kindersley Limited
80 Strand, London WC2R 0RL

2 4 6 8 10 9 7 5 3 1
001-300185-September/2017

A CIP catalogue record for this book is available from the British Library

ISBN 978-0-2412-8933-4

Printed and bound in China

A WORLD OF IDEAS:
SEE ALL THERE IS TO KNOW

www.dk.com

Contents

Contributors

Lead Contributor
Father Michael Collins
Michael Collins is a graduate of the Pontifical Institute of Christian Archeology in Rome. His initial passion for books and writing stemmed from his interest in calligraphy. It was further fuelled when he discovered that the *Book of Kells* was once owned by an ancestor, Bishop Henry Jones, who donated it to Trinity College Dublin in 1663. Michael has published books in 12 languages.

Alexandra Black
A freelance author, Alexandra Black's writing career initially took her to Japan. She later worked for a publisher in Australia, before moving to Cambridge, UK. She writes on a range of subjects, from history to business and fashion.

Thomas Cussans
A freelance historian and author based in France, Thomas Cussans was for many years a publisher responsible for a series of bestselling history atlases. He has contributed to numerous DK titles, including *History: The Definitive Visual Guide.*

John Farndon
A Royal Literary Fellow at Anglia Ruskin University in Cambridge, John Farndon is an author, playwright, composer, and poet. He has written many international bestsellers and translated into English verse the plays of Lope de Vega and the poetry of Alexander Pushkin.

Philip Parker
A historian and former British diplomat and publisher, who studied History at Trinity College, Cambridge and International Relations at the John Hopkins School of Advanced International Studies, Philip Parker is a critically acclaimed author and award-winning editor.

Foreword
James Naughtie
An award-winning radio presenter and broadcaster, James Naughtie began his career as a journalist before moving to radio presenting in 1986. For over 20 years he co-presented on BBC Radio 4's *Today* programme, and he has chaired Radio 4's monthly bookclub since it began in 1997. James Naughtie has chaired both the Man Booker and Samuel Johnson judging panels and written a number of books including *The Rivals: The Intimate Story Of A Political Marriage*; *The Accidental American: Tony Blair And The Presidency*; *The Making Of Music*; *The New Elizabethans* and *The Madness of July.*

1450–1649

1650–1899

1900 ONWARDS

Foreword

The afternoon light fades in the scriptorium where a monk works patiently, in silence, at his long table. He has a line of pots for his colours – ultramarine and azurite, white lead and verdigris, cuttlefish ink and cochineal, madder and the rich red known as dragon's blood – and boxes for his precious gold and silver leaf. The single illuminated letter on the page in front of him has already been shaped in burnished gold. Over many hours the paints will turn it into a picture that will gleam for hundreds of years.

Polish the lens of memory a little more, and think of a group of men somewhere near the geographical heart of Europe in the middle of the fifteenth century, gathered in a workshop rather than a monastery, and standing around a simple wooden machine. One of them pulls on a long handle to turn a thick screw that lowers the flat platen so that it presses down on a sheet of dampened paper. After a few moments, when the screw is turned the other way to release the frame that holds the paper in place, they see before them, printed by perfectly ordered type, a page of Gutenberg's Bible.

These are scenes from a story that springs forward to the eighteenth-century libraries in great houses where men of means built high shelves for their leather-bound books – the first novels in English, travelogues and beautifully-illustrated descriptions of flora and fauna, perhaps a precious copy of Robert Hooke's *Micrographia* from the previous century, and certainly Dr Johnson's dictionary. The classical texts are all there, from Homer and the histories of Herodotus to Ovid and Virgil.

And then, within a hundred years, books were finding their way into ordinary homes. Perhaps they were borrowed from Mudie's travelling library, where people could get the new novel from Charles Dickens or Wilkie Collins, or maybe Darwin's *On the Origin of Species*. Mr Mudie had ordered five hundred copies before publication because Darwin was a customer. In the Victorian parlour, beside the piano, there were books. An idea had been born that would one day be called the mass market.

Science and politics, history and travel, natural exploration as well as literature would be available to everyone. When Allen Lane published his first Penguin editions, with the orange covers that became an emblem of literacy between the two world wars, he was a pioneer in the fight to set free the liberal imagination. In the paperback era, everyone could learn, explore the past, and revel in a fictional world that knew no boundaries, taking them from the nineteenth-century novel to Joyce and the poetry of Eliot, to stories and thrillers of all kinds and even, at the end of the century, to an unlikely boy touched by magic and destined to be an entertainer both for children, and their parents and grandparents, all around the world.

Yet this is only the story as it is told in Europe. The veneration of Greek and Roman art and literature in the Renaissance, and the power of the Christian tradition, obscured the written legacies of other civilisations. From India, the *Mahābhārata* – maybe the longest epic poem of them all – and philosophy from China, learned and beautifully crafted Persian books on medicine and astronomy, and mathematics in Arabic.

The artistry of these texts – like the luminous brilliance of a medieval Book of Hours in Europe – is the indestructible evidence of our collective desire to find permanent physical expression for the scope of our imaginations. A never-ending quest. Everyone who responds to the beauty of the calligraphy and illustration in these early books, and the sheer confidence and energy that flows from the pages, is reminded that every book is an act of creation, whether it is a novel, a history, a scientific theory, a religious text, or a piece of polemic.

Old or new, the books selected for this volume have changed lives, and remind us who we are. They are both mirror and lamp – reflecting us to ourselves with remorseless honesty and also shining light in dark places, the unknown, or the dangerous. We find our own fears in books, as surely as we find solace and escape.

To love a book is to get to know a friend whom you want to keep, despite everything. We all have books from childhood that fall open predictably at a favourite page, or a novel we have read so often that its spine needs running repairs. And in an age when the electronic book has opened another chapter in the long story, many readers have rediscovered the aesthetic power of a fine book that is also a beautiful object. Among the many joys of books, that is one that never fades. Enlightened publishers have realized at last that it is a contemporary challenge to them, and long may they remember it.

In these pages we find many of the books that have shaped our world. They are wise and revelatory, radical and even outrageous, some of them surprising in the impact they have made, and so many of them still inspiring. Some represent the best of us, and others do not, but collectively they remind us that the book is indeed the friend that will never let you go.

That is why we cherish it so much.

JAMES NAUGHTIE

Scrolls and Codices

Books are almost as old as writing itself, and their coming marks the watershed between prehistory, when mankind's story was passed on only by word of mouth, and history, when it was recorded for future generations to read.

The first books were written on a wide variety of materials, including clay tablets, silk, papyrus (made from reeds), parchment (animal skins), and paper (pulped rags). They were bound together in various ways, although sometimes they were not even bound at all. One of the world's oldest books is the Sumerian story of Gilgamesh, an ancient epic, which was written down on a collection of clay tablets nearly 4,000 years ago.

Until the development of the printed book in the 15th century, most books came in the form of scrolls or codices. Scrolls are sheets of papyrus, parchment, or paper stuck together end-to-end then rolled up. The Ancient Egyptians wrote on papyrus scrolls at least 4,600 years ago. Codices (or a codex, singular) are stacked sheets of papyrus, parchment, or paper joined down one side and bound between a stiff cover so they can hinge open – rather like a modern book, only handwritten. Codices date back at least 3,000 years, but are often associated with the spread of Christianity across Europe.

Every copy of a scroll or codex was compiled from manuscripts written out laboriously by hand. This made them extremely rare and precious objects. The investment of time and effort meant that only the most wealthy and powerful people could afford to have them made. But their rarity and the way they carried exact wordings into the future gave the earliest books an authority that seemed almost magical. For example, the Ancient Egyptian Books of the Dead were scrolls buried with a deceased person to enable them to carry words that had the power to guide them even in the afterlife (see pp.18–23).

Books became the foundation stones that the world's great religions were built upon. They were used to record ancient stories and beliefs. Some works even helped local beliefs to develop into major religions by spreading the definitive words of a great sage or prophet far and wide, and through time from generation to generation. Christians spread Christ's words through their Bible, Jews studied the Torah (see p.50), while Muslims followed the Qur'an, Hindus the *Mahābhārata* (see pp.28–29), and Taoists the *I Ching* (see pp.24–25). All of these books still have a profound impact on lives today, thousands of years after they were first written.

▲ **EGYPTIAN BOOKS OF THE DEAD** No two Books of the Dead are the same – each was tailored to the deceased and their needs in the afterlife. They consist of spells and illustrations on papyrus, and date from around 1991–50 BCE.

▲ **MAHĀBHĀRATA** Written in Sanskrit, this epic poem recounts tales of ancient India. The text reached its final form in around 400 BCE. The manuscript above depicts a battle between Ghatotkacha and Karna, and dates from around 1670.

> To preserve the memory of the past by putting on record the astonishing achievements of our own and of the Asiatic peoples
>
> **HERODOTUS**, GREEK HISTORIAN SETS OUT HIS AIM IN WRITING *THE HISTORIES*, C.450 BCE

▲ **DEAD SEA SCROLLS** Created between around 250 BCE and 68 CE, the Dead Sea Scrolls are a collection of 981 manuscripts discovered in the Qumran Caves on the shore of the Dead Sea. Most of the manuscripts contain Hebrew scriptures, others are non-canonical texts, while others are in such a poor condition that they cannot be identified.

Indeed, the painstaking process of writing a book out by hand was often an act of religious devotion in itself. Many monks laboured long to produce "illuminated manuscripts" of dazzling beauty such as the *Gospels of Henry the Lion* (see pp.60–63) or the *Book of Kells* (see pp.38–43).

However, it wasn't only religions that harnessed the power of books. Books stored ideas and information to be accumulated over time, so that each generation built on the learning of those who had gone before, gradually expanding the stock of human knowledge.

Writers such as Ibn Sīnā (see p.56), for instance, combined his own medical knowledge with that of previous generations to create a definitive textbook for physicians, *The Canon of Medicine* (see pp.56–57). There were very few copies of books, however, so the libraries that collected them, such as the great Greek library at Alexandria in modern-day Egypt, and the libraries of the Muslim world became the great engines of knowledge. During the Middle Ages, scholars would travel thousands of miles simply to read a rare copy of a key book.

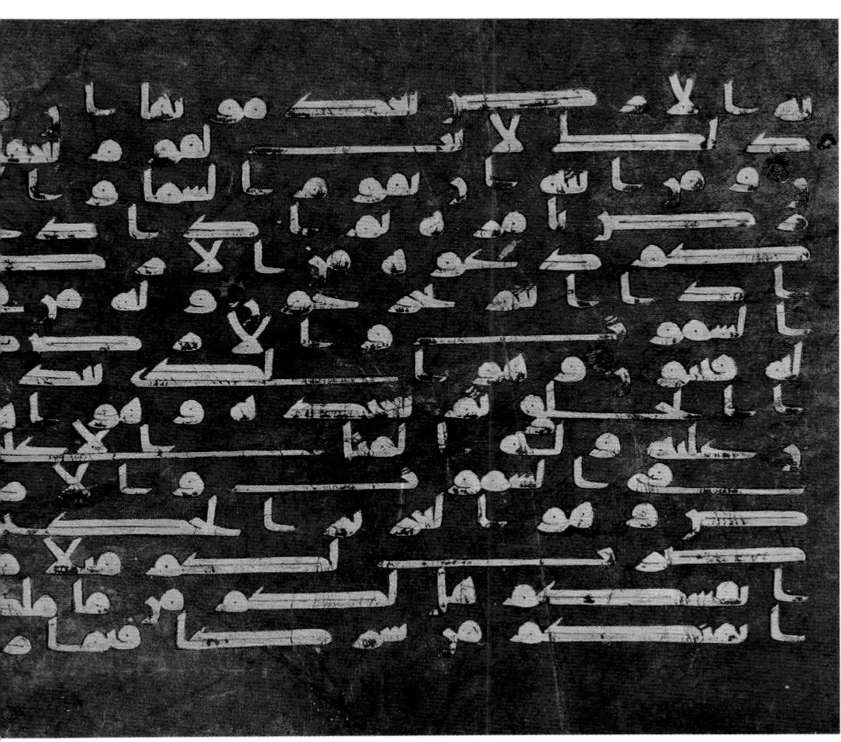

▲ **THE BLUE QUR'AN** Most likely produced in North Africa in around 850–950 CE, it is thought that the *Blue Qur'an* (see p.44–45) was compiled for the Great Mosque of Kairouan in Tunisia. The gold letters are written in Kufic calligraphy.

▲ **BOOK OF KELLS** Brilliantly illuminated with rich colours and gold leaf adorning the text, the *Book of Kells* was created in Ireland in around 800 CE. The manuscript contains the Gospels and the tables of the Eusebian Canons, shown above.

The Printed Book

Printing dates back over 1,800 years to carved wood blocks in China and Japan that were used to stamp religious images onto paper, silk, or walls. By the 9th century, the Chinese were printing entire books, including the *Diamond Sutra* (see pp.46–47) of 868 CE, the oldest surviving dated example. The Chinese even invented a form of movable type, which involved building up pages from ready-made collections of letters. But it was in 1455 in Mainz, Germany, when Johann Gutenberg used movable type to print the Bible, that the printed book really arrived.

The Gutenberg Bible (see pp.74–75) was a large luxury item, that only the rich could afford. But printers were soon making smaller, cheaper books. One of the pioneers of mass printing was Aldus Manutius (see pp.86–87), a Venetian scholar who set up the world's first great publishing house, the Aldine Press, in the 1490s. Manutius introduced the elegant, easy-to-read Italic (from Italy) typeface, and the handy octavo-size book – similar to a typical modern hardback. Books were no longer just kept in libraries but could be read anywhere. Within 50 years of the first printing of Gutenberg's Bible, there were 10 million printed books, and the Aldine Press was launching titles with initial print runs of 1,000 books or more.

The impact was both public, as ideas were shared quickly among numerous readers, and private, as books allowed people to explore their imaginations at home. Interestingly, many of the first ideas shared through print were ancient ones. The Aldine Press concentrated on publishing the classics, leading to a revival of interest in Virgil and Homer, Aristotle and Euclid. All the same, newer books such as Dante's *Divine Comedy* (see pp.84–85) and *Hypnerotomachia Poliphili* (see pp.86–87) soon became classics, and print ensured their style influenced writers across Europe, including William Shakespeare in England.

Printed books like Andreas Vesalius's revolutionary work on anatomy (see pp.98–101) and Galileo's watershed tome on the Earth's place in the universe (see pp.130–31) did not only help spread scientific ideas rapidly; they also consolidated knowledge, as many people could turn to exactly the same source. They created a sense that the understanding of the world was gradually increasing.

Also encouraged by the printed book was the expression of individual thought. Before print, a writer was generally an anonymous scribe, merely copying words rather than creating an original work. But printed books prompted individual authorship, and made living authors celebrities,

▲ **DIAMOND SUTRA** The earliest surviving complete printed book, which bears an actual date, is the *Diamond Sutra* of 868 from China. It was printed using woodblocks and predates the Gutenberg Bible by almost six centuries.

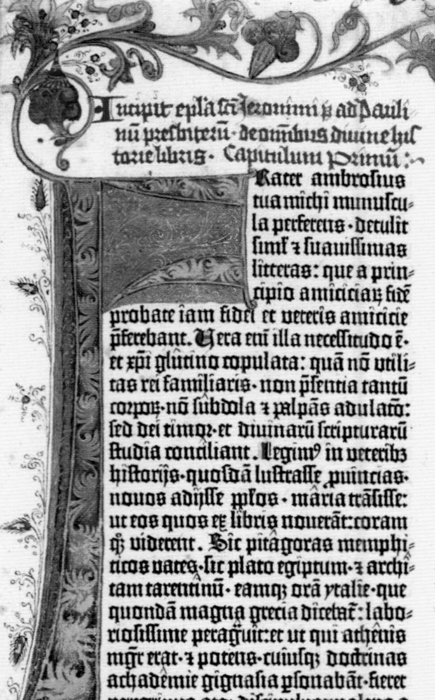

▲ **GUTENBERG BIBLE** Marking the arrival of the European printed the book in 1455, the Gutenburg Bible was the first printed using movable type. However, its richly illuminated pages were accessible to only an elite few due its high price.

> He who first shortened the labour of copyists by the device of movable types was… creating a whole new democratic world
>
> **THOMAS CARLYLE**, SCOTTISH HISTORIAN, 1795–1881

➤ **DIVINE COMEDY** Dante completed his narrative poem in 1320, but the first printed edition was not published until 1472. Its publication helped to standardize the Italian language and the work has influenced artists and writers across several centuries.

such as Miguel de Cervantes with his epic, *Don Quixote* (see pp.116–17). This elevation of individual expression may have been a factor in the great revolutions in European thought – the Protestant Reformation, the Renaissance, and the Age of Enlightenment.

One of the surprising impacts of printing, however, was the stimulation of a development in national languages, such as English, French, and German. In the Middle Ages people in Western Europe spoke such a mix of dialects that someone from Paris was virtually unintelligible to someone from Marseilles; scholars, however, often conversed in Latin. But printed books helped to standardize national languages. The King James Bible, the first authorized bible in English, played a huge part in setting the form of the English language as its words were read every week in churches across the land.

▲ **THE NUREMBERG CHRONICLE** Printed in 1493, the *Nuremberg Chronicle* (see pp.78–83) is a richly illustrated account of biblical and human history. It is one of the earliest examples of illustrations and text being fully integrated.

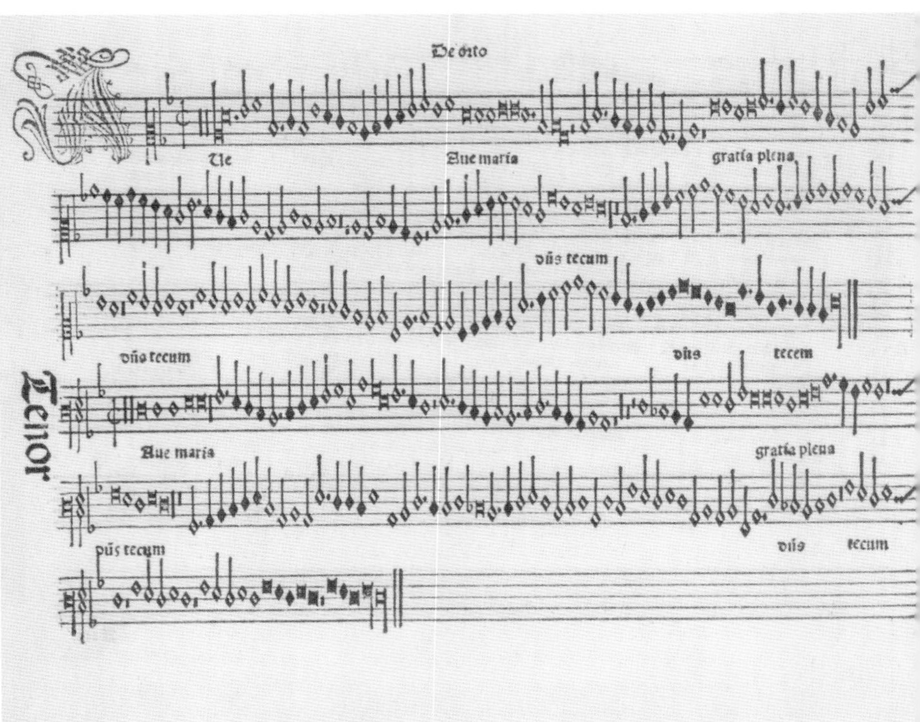

▲ **HARMONICE MUSICES ODHECATON** Published in 1501, Ottaviano Petrucci's *Odhecaton* (see pp.88–89) made sheet music more widely available. Each song has lines for a number of instruments, allowing musicians to read the same page.

Books for All

The 18th century saw an explosion of book publishing and printing in Europe. This period was called the Age of Enlightenment, and books helped to spread knowledge on an unprecedented scale. During the Middle Ages, fewer than 1,000 copies of manuscripts were made in an entire year across the whole of Europe; in the 18th century, 10 million books were printed every year – a staggering 10,000-fold increase in production.

Books became available everywhere, and at a relatively cheap price, and so increasing numbers of people learned to read. In western Europe fewer than one in four people were literate in the 17th century, but by the mid-18th century two thirds of men were literate and more than half of women. A massive new readership was born, which in turn fuelled the demand for books.

New kinds of books emerged, too, including popular information titles. Previously, factual books had been created mostly for specialists, but in the 18th century learning became more democratic, and books helped to ensure that knowledge wasn't only for the elite. Canny publishers realized that there was a huge market among the public for books that would help them understand what was known about the world around them.

At the same time, many writers earnestly wished to spread knowledge and enlightenment as far as possible. Writing books, in some ways, became a revolutionary act. When Denis Diderot (see pp.146–49) created his great encyclopaedia in the middle of the century, he was seeking not just to provide people with information; he was also striking a blow for democracy by showing that the world of knowledge was every man and woman's right, and not just the divine right of kings and aristocrats. Thomas Paine took up the call for the rights of every human being with his *Rights of Man* (see pp.164–65), which was widely read and studied, and underpinned the French and American Revolutions.

Books were also the medium by which scientists and philosophers introduced their ideas to the world. In some ways the Enlightenment had been prompted by Sir Isaac Newton's ground-breaking book *Philosophiae Naturalis Principia Mathematica* (see pp.142–43) in which he introduced his laws of motion. Newton's book showed that the entire universe was not a magical divine mystery, but that it ran on precise mechanical laws, which could be studied and understood by scientists. Meanwhile, Robert Hooke introduced a previously unsuspected microscopic

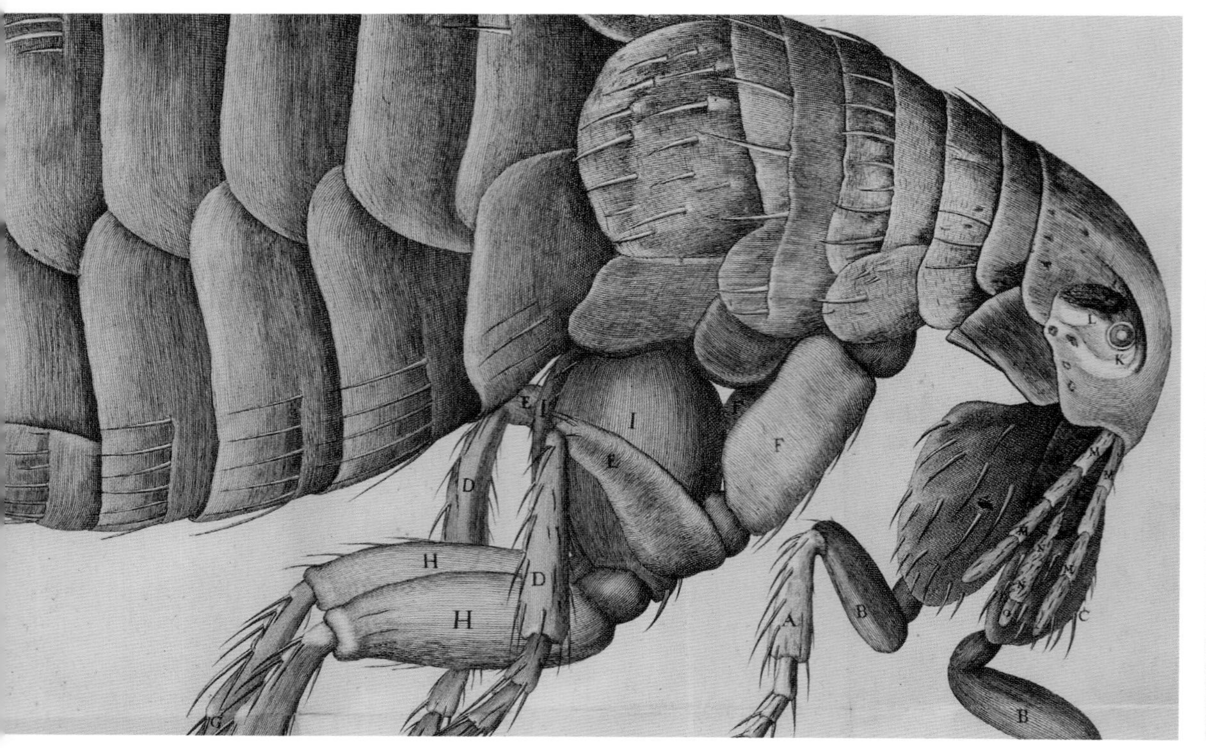

▲ **HOOKE'S MICROGRAPHIA** Published in 1665, Robert Hooke's ground-breaking *Micrographia* revealed a miniscule world that readers had never experienced before. Exquisitely intricate illustrations, such as this large fold-out drawing of a flea, depicted creatures and objects in monstrous yet beautiful detail.

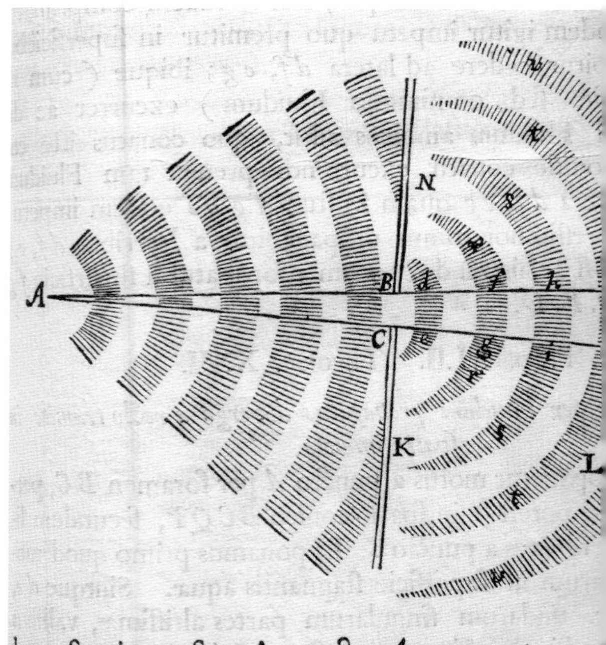

▲ **PRINCIPIA MATHEMATICA** Newton's 1687 work laid out his explanation for the orbit of the spheres. Despite the dense subject matter, it won him instant fame.

> ... bound together solely by their zeal for the best interests of the human race and a feeling of mutual good will
>
> **DENIS DIDEROT**, ON THE WRITERS OF *ENCYCLOPÉDIE*, 1751

world with his *Micrographia* (see pp.138–41); Carolus Linnaeus showed how nature could be pinned down and classified in his *Systema Naturae* (see pp.144–45); and Charles Darwin showed how life evolved in his *On the Origin of Species* (see pp.194–95). By the end of the 18th century there were also books showing how even human society could be analyzed and understood. Adam Smith's *Wealth of Nations* (see pp.162–63) provides the theoretical basis for capitalist economic systems, while Karl Marx's *Das Kapital* (see pp.200–201) created a powerful counterargument that started revolutions that are still in progress today.

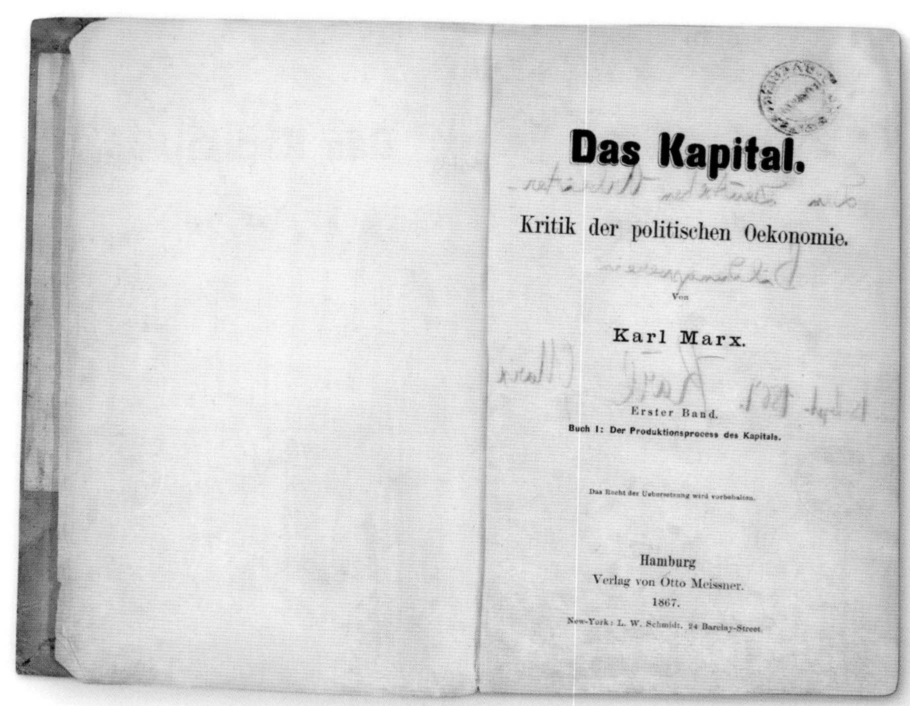
Das Kapital.
Kritik der politischen Oekonomie.
Von
Karl Marx.
Erster Band.
Buch I: Der Produktionsprocess des Kapitals.
Das Recht der Uebersetzung wird vorbehalten.
Hamburg
Verlag von Otto Meissner.
1867.
New-York: L. W. Schmidt. 24 Barclay-Street.

▲ **DAS KAPITAL** Published in 1867 at a time of immense social and industrial change, Marx's polemic was a timely account of the injustices suffered by many under the capitalist system. Though the book had a small readership at the time, Marx's influence lasts to the present day.

Besides the great theoretical works, fiction was developing as a genre, and novels such as *Tristram Shandy* (see pp.156–59) responded to the increasing consciousness and imaginative private life of individuals. Initially, novel-reading was the domain of wealthy ladies of leisure. However, Dickens's *The Pickwick Papers* (see pp.178–79) was serialized in cheap weekly instalments, each with a cliff-hanger ending to keep the reader hooked. This helped his novel reach vast numbers of ordinary people and, for the first time, the book was entertainment.

[152]

CHAP. XL.

I Am now beginning to get fairly into my work; and by the help of a vegitable diet, with a few of the cold ſeeds, I make no doubt but I ſhall be able to go on with my uncle *Toby*'s ſtory, and my own, in a tolerable ſtraight line. Now,

Inv. T.S   Sculp. T.S

Theſe

[153]

Theſe were the four lines I moved in through my firſt, ſecond, third, and fourth volumes.——In the fifth volume I have been very good,——the preciſe line I have deſcribed in it being this :

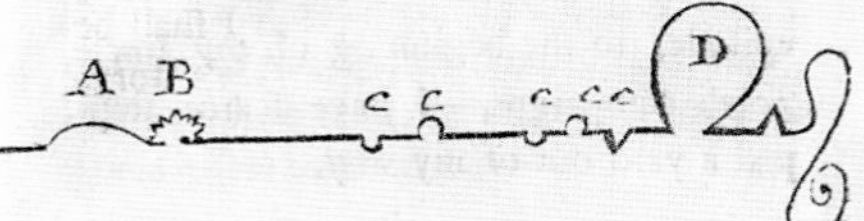

By which it appears, that except at the curve, marked A. where I took a trip to *Navarre*,—and the indented curve B. which is the ſhort airing when I was there with the Lady *Bauſſiere* and her page,—I have not taken the leaſt friſk of a digreſſion, till *John de la Caſſe*'s devils led me the round you ſee marked D.—for as for *c c c c c* they are nothing but parentheſes, and the common *ins* and *outs* incident to the lives of the greateſt miniſters of ſtate; and when compared

▲ **TRISTRAM SHANDY** Laurence Sterne's comic novel was published in 1759. It purports to be the biography of the title character, Tristam Shandy, and is characterized by frequent plot diversions and a playful use of language, drawing heavily on the poets and satirists of the 17th century.

▲ **PICKWICK PAPERS** The serialization of *The Pickwick Papers* in a magazine secured its popularity before being published in book form a year later.

The Modern Book

Throughout the 20th and 21st centuries, the book world has grown on a scale unimaginable even in the Victorian age, when the popular novel first appeared. The figures are extraordinary: more than a million new titles are now published every year in the US alone, and the number of copies printed around the world annually runs into trillions. The choice for the average reader is immense, with an estimated 13 million previously published books to choose from as well as the year's new titles.

Books are now incredibly cheap to buy, and are no longer thought of as luxury items. Penguin revolutionized the book industry in the 1930s by introducing inexpensive "paperback" books (see pp.230–31), and mass-marketing by giant retailers such as Amazon has pushed the price down even further. Even a new book can often be bought now for little more than the price of a cup of coffee. The coming of electronic e-books has meant that the content of books can also be accessed instantly anywhere.

Yet only a tiny proportion of the millions of published books is ever read by more than a handful of people. Although three-quarters of Americans read more than one book a year, most read no more than six. Very few books are read by a significant number of people. Nevertheless, some books of the last hundred years have left an indelible mark, not because they were widely read, but because they changed the way people thought. One of these is Einstein's *General Theory of Relativity* (see pp.226–27. In this book Einstein presented theories that overturned the view of the universe dating from the time of Newton, and led to a profound shift in our knowledge of time. Few people have actually read the work, and of those who have, fewer still understand it fully. And yet the impact of its ideas has rippled out far beyond the scientific world.

Throughout history, certain books have sparked controversy, whether for political, moral, or religious reasons. After World War II Hitler's manifesto *Mein Kampf* (see pp.242) was banned as extremist in many European countries – Poland only lifted the ban in 1992 and Germany in 2016. In 1928 D.H. Lawrence published *Lady Chatterley's Lover* (see pp.242) but it was banned in the US and the UK for breaking obscenity laws. The bans were lifted in 1959 and 1960 respectively.

A new kind of book, designed to draw public attention to specific issues, emerged in the 20th century: books became an effective way of voicing protest. Rachel Carson's *Silent Spring* (see pp.238–39), for instance,

▲ **LE PETIT PRINCE** Antoine de Saint-Exupéry published his novella for children in 1943. Illustrated with exquisite watercolours by the author, it became a classic of children's literature and has been translated into more than 250 languages.

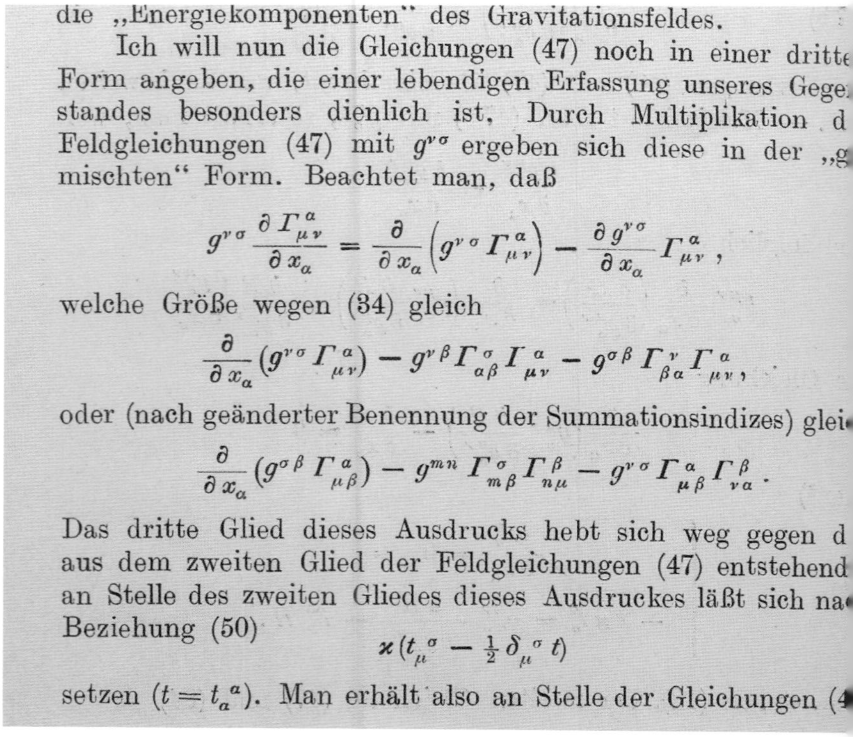

die „Energiekomponenten" des Gravitationsfeldes.
Ich will nun die Gleichungen (47) noch in einer dritt
Form angeben, die einer lebendigen Erfassung unseres Gege
standes besonders dienlich ist. Durch Multiplikation d
Feldgleichungen (47) mit $g^{\nu\sigma}$ ergeben sich diese in der „g
mischten" Form. Beachtet man, daß

$$g^{\nu\sigma}\frac{\partial \Gamma^{\alpha}_{\mu\nu}}{\partial x_{\alpha}} = \frac{\partial}{\partial x_{\alpha}}\left(g^{\nu\sigma}\Gamma^{\alpha}_{\mu\nu}\right) - \frac{\partial g^{\nu\sigma}}{\partial x_{\alpha}}\Gamma^{\alpha}_{\mu\nu},$$

welche Größe wegen (34) gleich

$$\frac{\partial}{\partial x_{\alpha}}(g^{\nu\sigma}\Gamma^{\alpha}_{\mu\nu}) - g^{\nu\beta}\Gamma^{\sigma}_{\alpha\beta}\Gamma^{\alpha}_{\mu\nu} - g^{\sigma\beta}\Gamma^{\nu}_{\beta\alpha}\Gamma^{\alpha}_{\mu\nu},$$

oder (nach geänderter Benennung der Summationsindizes) glei

$$\frac{\partial}{\partial x_{\alpha}}(g^{\sigma\beta}\Gamma^{\alpha}_{\mu\beta}) - g^{mn}\Gamma^{\sigma}_{m\beta}\Gamma^{\beta}_{n\mu} - g^{\nu\sigma}\Gamma^{\alpha}_{\mu\beta}\Gamma^{\beta}_{\nu\alpha}.$$

Das dritte Glied dieses Ausdrucks hebt sich weg gegen d
aus dem zweiten Glied der Feldgleichungen (47) entstehend
an Stelle des zweiten Gliedes dieses Ausdruckes läßt sich na
Beziehung (50)

$$\varkappa(t_{\mu}^{\sigma} - \tfrac{1}{2}\delta_{\mu}^{\sigma} t)$$

setzen ($t = t_{\alpha}^{\alpha}$). Man erhält also an Stelle der Gleichungen (4

▲ **RELATIVITY** In 1916 Albert Einstein published *General Theory of Relativity* with the specific aim of bringing his theories to a wider lay audience, who had no background in theoretical physics.

> … the average book fits into the **human hand** with a **seductive nestling**, a kiss of **texture**, whether of cover cloth, glazed jacket, or **flexible paperback**

JOHN UPDIKE, *DUE CONSIDERATIONS*, 2008

alerted people to the terrible damage farm pesticides were inflicting on wildlife, and it had a huge impact on the way people think of the environment.

Children's books first appeared in the 18th century, with titles like *Fables in Verse* (see pp.160–61), but it was in the 20th century that books became an integral part of childhood in the developed world, shaping the way readers in their formative years viewed life. Today children's literature is a sophisticated genre, with highlights such as Antoine de Saint-Exupéry's *Le Petit Prince* (see pp.234–35).

Now, 45 trillion pages are printed every day, accessible to billions of people. Books help us to share experiences, stories, and ideas in our hugely populated world in a way that would otherwise be impossible.

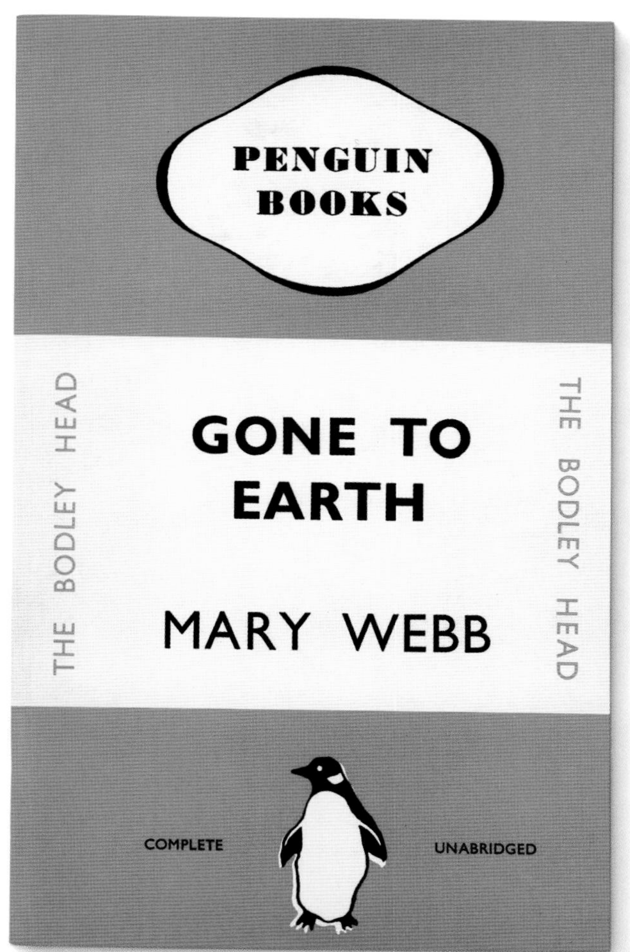

▲ **PENGUIN PAPERBACKS** With its simple, and now iconic, cover design, the Penguin paperback changed reading habits in the 20th century. Mass production made books affordable and opened up a world of literature to a wider readership.

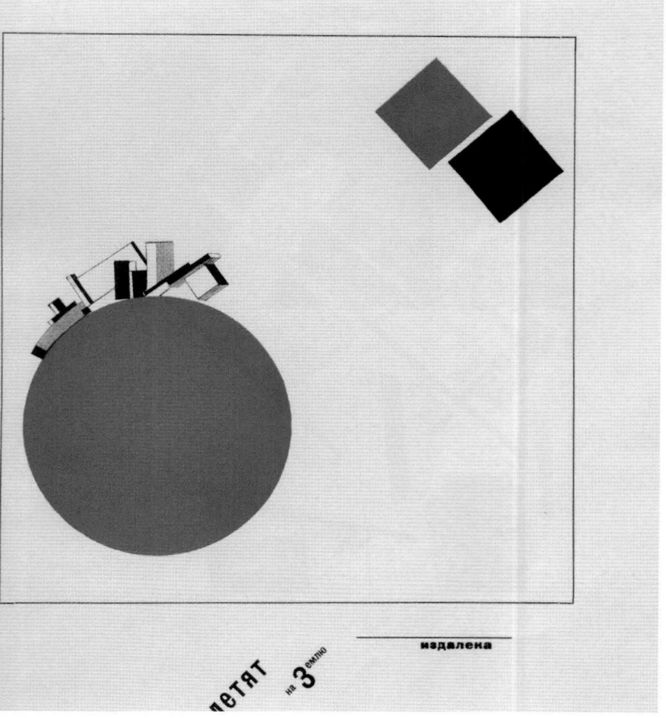

▲ **PRO DVA KVADRATA** El Lissitzky's *About Two Squares* (see pp.228–229) was published in 1922. This children's story acts as an allegory of the superiority of the new Soviet order.

▲ **SILENT SPRING** The book that triggered the start of the environmental movement, *Silent Spring* (see pp.238–39), was published by Rachel Carson in 1962. Her evocative language, accompanied by beautiful illustrations, drew public attention to the dangers of pesticide use.

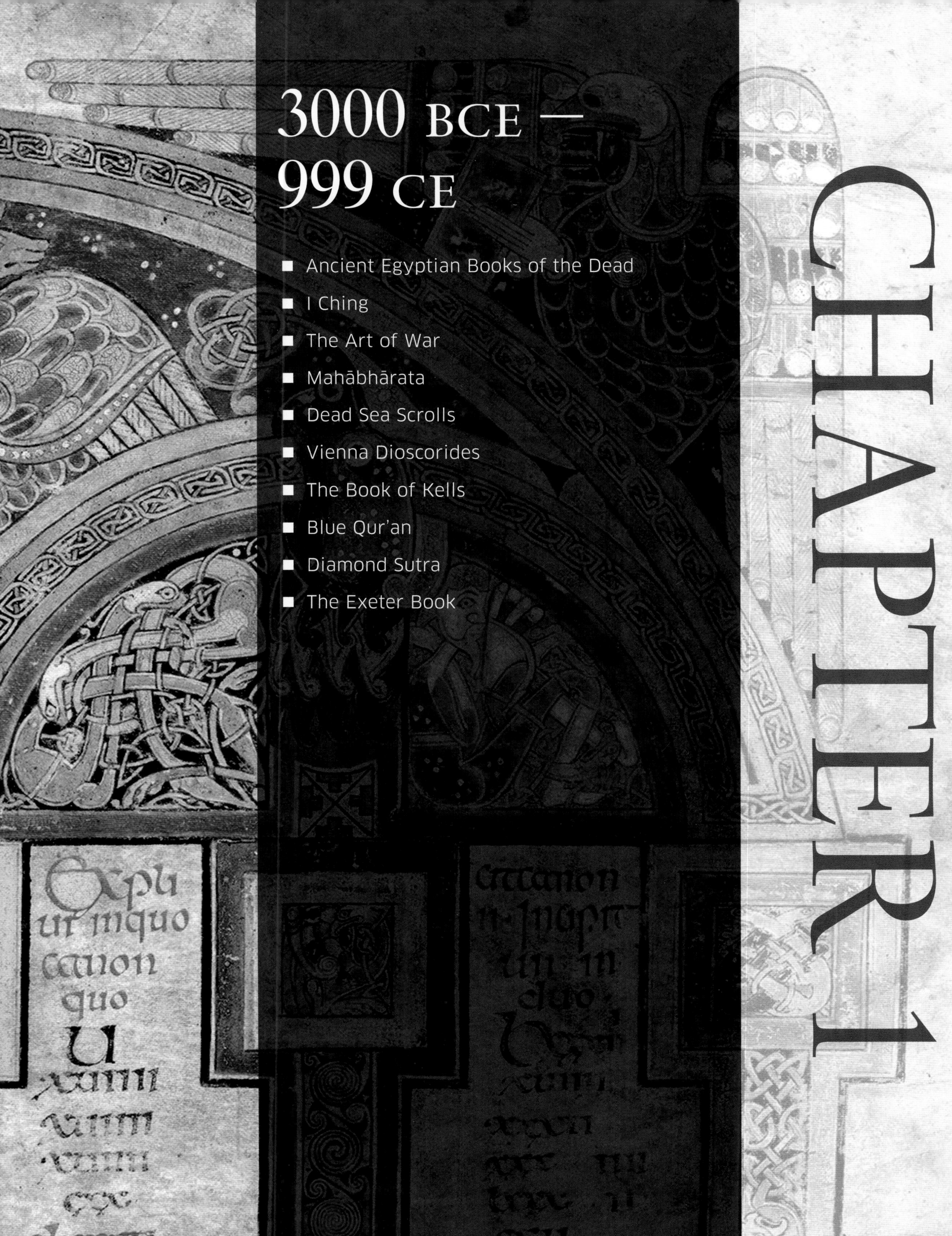

CHAPTER 1

3000 BCE — 999 CE

- Ancient Egyptian Books of the Dead
- I Ching
- The Art of War
- Mahābhārata
- Dead Sea Scrolls
- Vienna Dioscorides
- The Book of Kells
- Blue Qur'an
- Diamond Sutra
- The Exeter Book

Ancient Egyptian Books of the Dead

c.1991–50 BCE ▪ PAPYRUS SCROLLS ▪ c.1–40 m × 15–45 cm (3–130 ft × 6–18 in) ▪ EGYPT

VARIOUS AUTHORS

The Ancient Egyptian Books of the Dead were funerary texts that were used for nearly 1,500 years. They took the form of spells (both magical and religious) and illustrations inscribed onto a papyrus scroll that were buried in a tomb with the deceased. It was believed that these spells gave the souls of the dead the knowledge and power they needed to navigate the treacherous netherworld in safety, and to achieve a full afterlife.

Books of the Dead were created by highly skilled scribes and artists. Often more than one scribe would work on a single text, typically writing in cursive hieroglyphics (picture symbols) or hieratic script (a form of hieroglyphics used by priests), in black and red ink on papyrus scrolls. Illustrations depicted the journey through the netherworld, with vignettes accompanying the spells. The first Books of the Dead were prepared for elite figures, but by the New Kingdom era (c.1570–1069 BCE), the texts had become available to wider society – the most elaborate versions date from this time.

The books were organized into chapters, and scribes composed the contents according to the patron's request, incorporating a selection of the 192 prayers available that best reflected how the patron had lived their life. No two books are the same, although most include Spell 125, "Weighing of the Heart", which instructs the soul of the deceased on how to address Osiris, god of the afterlife, following successful judgement of their earthly life.

The term "Book of the Dead" was coined by Prussian Egyptologist Karl Richard Lepsius (1810–84), but a closer translation of its Egyptian name is the "Book of Coming Forth into Day". These pictorial guides for the dead provide vital insight into the Ancient Egyptian beliefs about the afterlife and a tantalizing glimpse into a vanished civilization.

IN CONTEXT

The tradition of providing the deceased with a text to help them on their journey in the afterlife dates back to the Old Kingdom (3rd millennium BCE), when funerary texts were written on the walls of burial chambers. At the start of the Middle Kingdom (c.2100 BCE), they were mostly written inside coffins. It was these so-called "Pyramid Texts" and "Coffin Texts" that evolved into the Books of the Dead. The papyrus scrolls were rolled up and typically inserted into a statue or encased within the wrappings of the body during mummification. Other objects considered necessary for the journey ahead, such as food and protective amulets, were included in the tomb, and the spells in the book guided the deceased in how to use these items to navigate the netherworld.

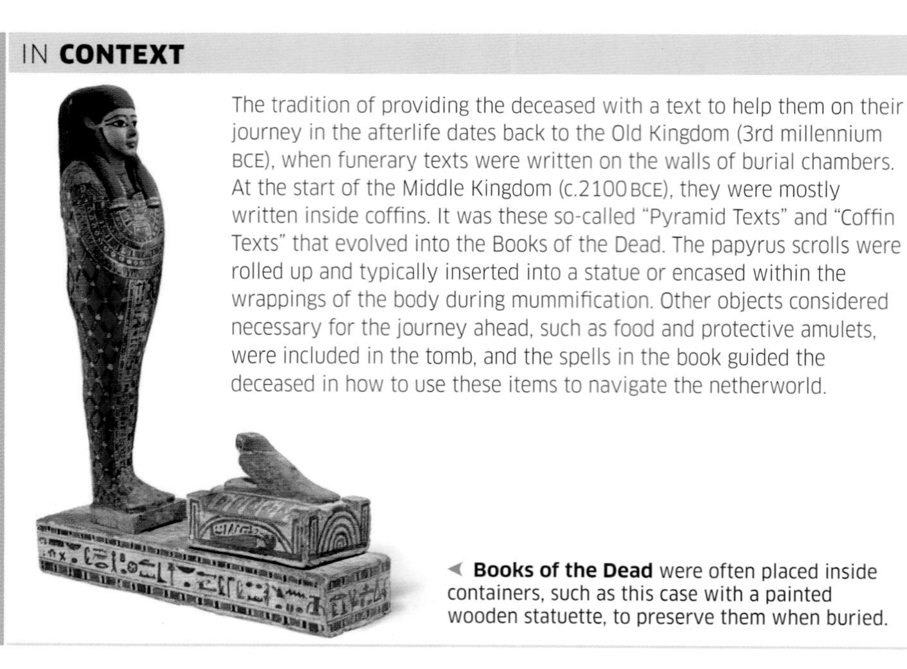

◄ **Books of the Dead** were often placed inside containers, such as this case with a painted wooden statuette, to preserve them when buried.

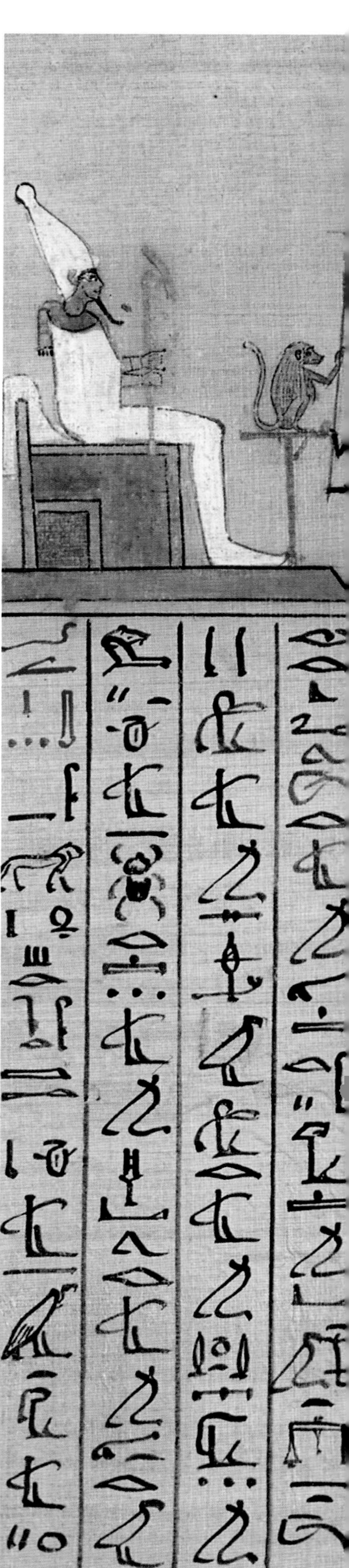

► **FINAL TEST** This section of scroll belongs to the Book of the Dead of Maiherpri, who lived during the 18th Dynasty. It illustrates his final test in the netherworld – the weighing of his heart, with Ammut, the winged devourer of souls, looking on. Ancient Egyptians believed that the heart was the seat of human intellect and emotions, and during the mummification process it was not removed.

Greenfield Papyrus – In detail

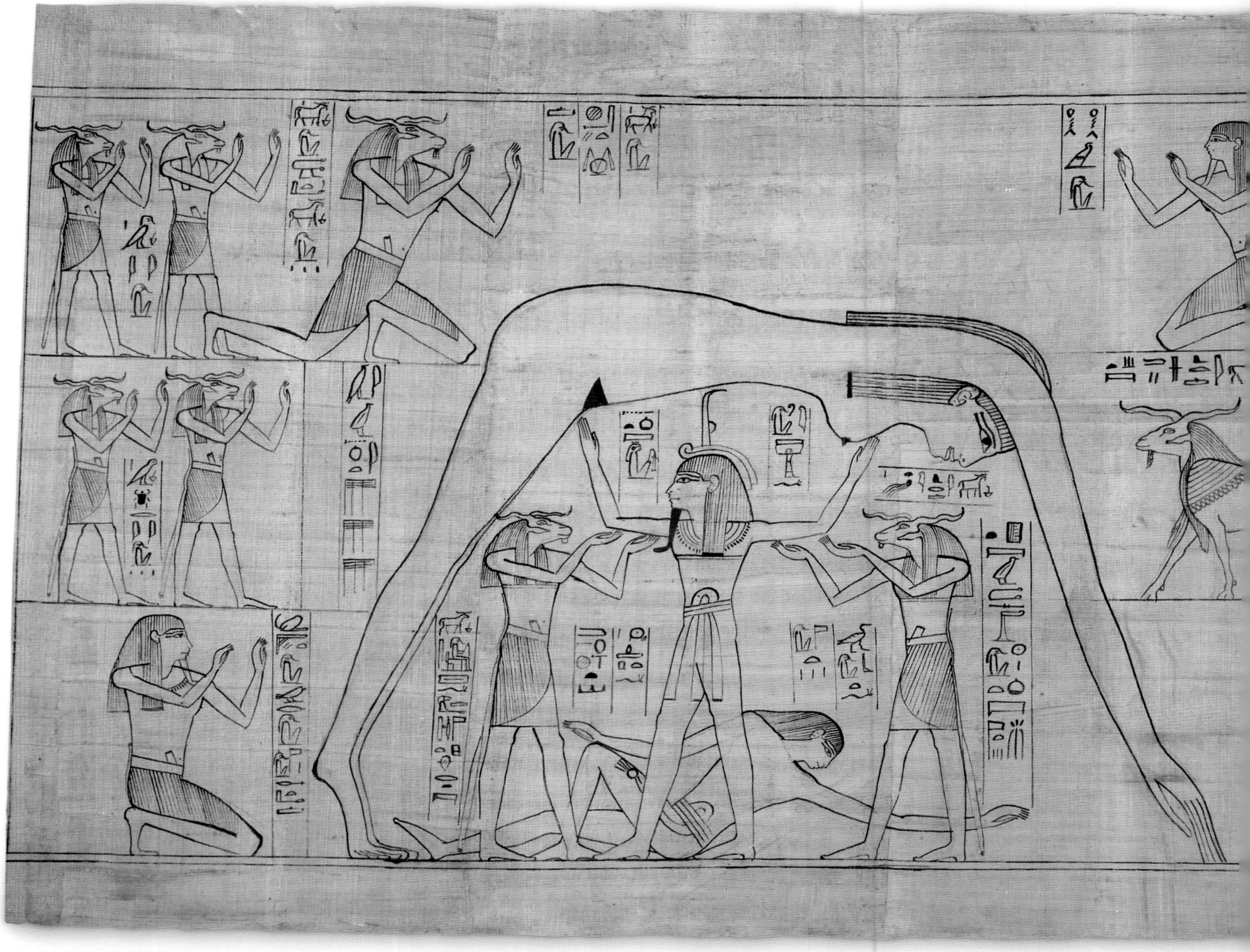

ON TECHNIQUE

The scrolls used for Books of the Dead were made from the papyrus plant, a type of reed that grew abundantly in Ancient Egypt, mostly on the banks of the River Nile. Its green bark was peeled back to reveal the white pith beneath, which was cut into long strips. These were then soaked in water for two to three days to release glue-like chemicals. To form the page, the strips were then laid out side by side, slightly overlapping, with a second layer of strips laid on top of them at a 90-degree angle. These were pressed between wooden boards to squeeze out water and bind the layers together. After being dried, the papyrus was polished with a stone to smooth out any ridges and imperfections, providing a better-looking finish. Individual pages were then either cut to measure, or sheets were glued together to the required length of a scroll.

➤ **The first known use** of papyrus, the world's oldest writing surface, dates back to the 1st Dynasty of Ancient Egypt (c.3150–2890 BCE). Egypt's dry climate is the reason that so many ancient documents have survived.

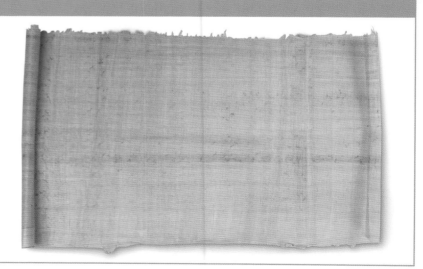

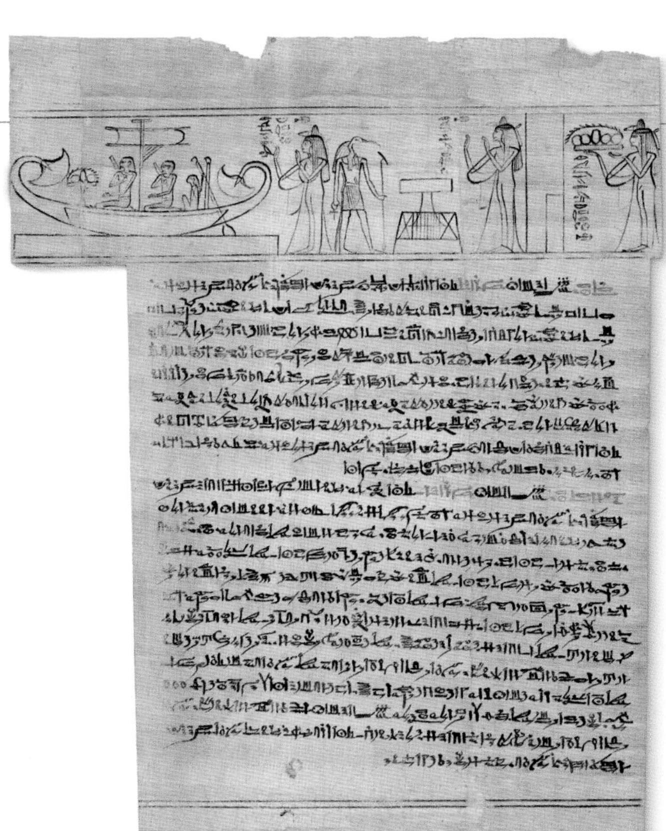

◄ **SEPARATE SHEET** Measuring almost 37 m (121 ft), Nestanebetisheru's papyrus is the longest known example of an Egyptian Book of the Dead. In the early 1900s this scroll was cut into 96 separate sheets to make it easier to study, display, and store. These are now mounted between protective layers of glass.

▲ **CREATION OF THE WORLD** Nestanebetisheru was the daughter of a high priest and a member of the ruling elite. Her Book of the Dead, dating from around 950–930 BCE, is one of the most beautiful and complete manuscripts to have survived from Ancient Egypt. It was donated to the British Museum by Edith Mary Greenfield in 1910, and is often known as the Greenfield Papyrus. Here black line drawings depict the creation of the world, with the goddess of the sky, Nut, arching over Geb, the reclining god of the earth.

◄ **MAGIC SPELLS** The deceased, Nestanebetisheru, is shown twice in this black line vignette. She kneels before three gatekeepers and also before a bull, a sparrow, and a falcon. Accompanying the illustration and written in hieratic text in black and red ink is a spell. This Book of the Dead includes a huge number of magical and religious texts, some of which are not found in any other manuscript, suggesting that they were added at Nestanebetisheru's request.

Book of the Dead of Hunefer – Visual tour

KEY

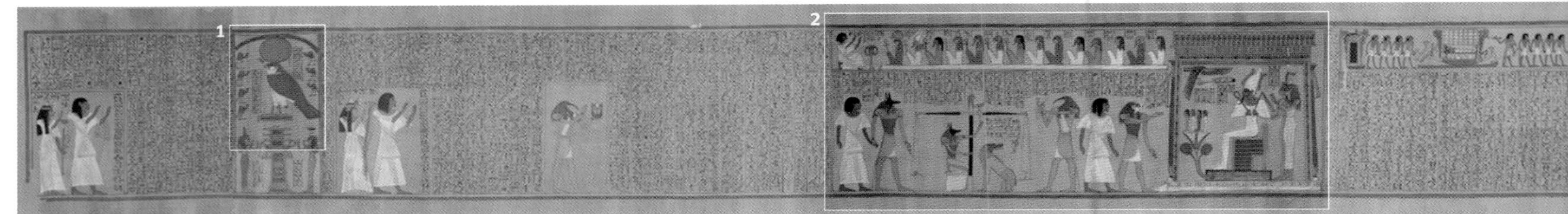

➤ **ILLUSTRATED HYMN** This detail from Spell 15 of the Book of the Dead of Hunefer, a royal Egyptian scribe (c.1280 BCE) illustrates the opening hymn to the rising sun. Horus, the god of the sky and one of the most significant Ancient Egyptian deities, was often represented as a falcon (as here) or as a falcon-headed man. The solar disc above his head signifies his connection to the sun, while the curved blue line is thought to represent the sky.

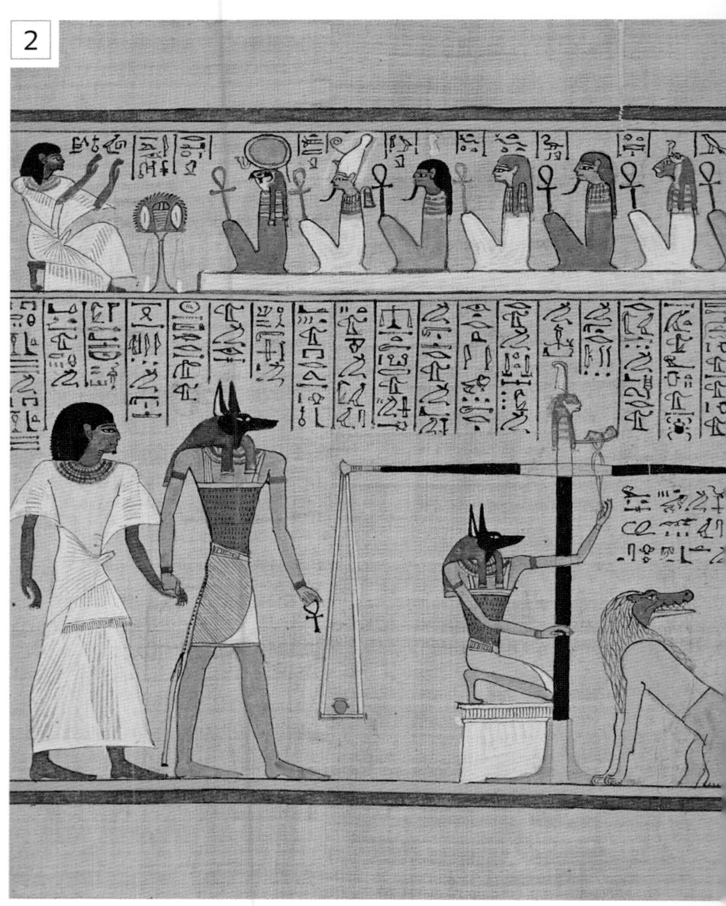

➤ **HUNEFER'S JUDGEMENT** The scribe, Hunefer, is shown being led by the jackel-headed Anubis towards the scales of judgement, where his heart is weighed. He passes the test and is then led by Horus to meet Osiris, god of the afterlife, seated on his throne.

▲ **HIEROGLYPHICS** The Book of the Dead of Hunefer is one of the finest ever discovered, and the handiwork of expert scribes, possibly Hunefer himself. The hieroglyphic text is inscribed in black and red ink with black dividing lines in between. Black ink was typically derived from carbon, and red ink from ochre.

➤ **BOARD GAME** Hunefer is shown here playing a board game. This may have been a favoured pastime during his life, but there could be a deeper significance that correlates victory in the board game with victory over obstacles encountered in the netherworld – thereby ensuring Hunefer's successful entry into the afterlife.

▲ **BURIAL CEREMONY** This vignette illustrates the mummified body of Hunefer being symbolically brought to life in the "Opening of the Mouth" ceremony, reuniting Hunefer's spirit with his corpse. His widow is shown in mourning, while a priest in a jackal mask, impersonating Anubis, the god of embalming, supports the mummy. The semi-cursive hieroglyphs above contain the ritual declarations.

▲ **SNAKE BEHEADING** Spell 17 in Hunefer's Book of the Dead includes an illustration of a cat killing a snake. This image comes at the end of a band that runs along the top of the sheet, which also features Hunefer worshipping five seated deities. These are named in the black cursive hieroglyphic captions.

I Ching

C.1050 BCE (WRITTEN) ▪ ORIGINAL MATERIAL AND DIMENSIONS UNKNOWN ▪ CHINA

AUTHOR UNKNOWN

The oldest of the Chinese classic texts, the *I Ching*, or *Book of Changes,* was originally used as a divination guide to help followers interpret the casting of yarrow stems or coins as a means to understand life, make decisions, and predict events. Its origins are obscure, but it evolved over 3,000 years during which "commentaries" were written incorporating Taoist, Confucian, and Buddhist beliefs, such as the 17th-century example shown far right.

The main body of the *I Ching* is divided into 64 sections, each one corresponding to a named and numbered symbol called a "hexagram". Each hexagram is made up of six horizontal lines, with a broken line denoting yin, and a solid one meaning yang. The order in which the stems or coins are cast determines which hexagram is referred to, for which the *I Ching* provides explanatory text, sometimes cryptic, or a "judgement", to interpret its meaning.

Although no parts of the original *I Ching* exist, its ideas are still used by millions of people worldwide to answer fundamental questions about human existence.

IN **CONTEXT**

The *I Ching* developed from the ancient Chinese belief that the world is the product of duality: of yin (negative/dark) and yang (positive/light), and that neither element can exist without the other. Central to the *I Ching*'s purpose as an oracle is the idea that every conceivable situation in human life is the result of yin-yang interplay, and can be encapsulated within and interpreted by its hexagrams.

The earliest known Chinese symbols for yin and yang, along with basic hexagrams, are found in inscriptions made on "oracle bones", the skeletal remains of turtles and oxen used in shamanistic divination practices during the Shang dynasty (1600–1046 BCE). The practice of using oracle bones in fortune-telling declined when the *I Ching* gained popularity during the Zhou dynasty (1046–256 BCE).

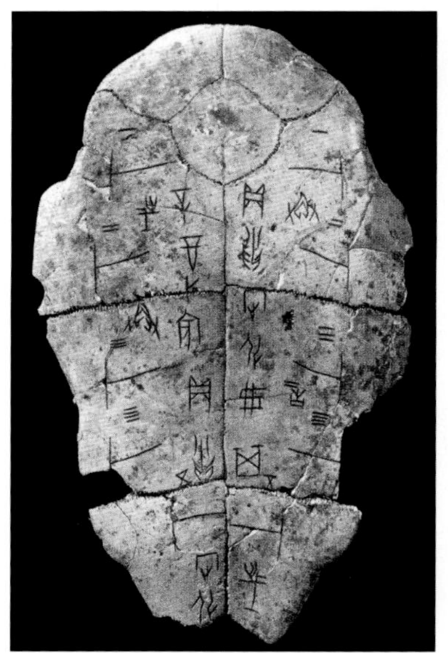

▲ **This turtle shell "oracle"** dates from c.1200 BCE. Fortune-tellers burned a shell or bone until it cracked, read the resulting lines, and sometimes carved an "answer".

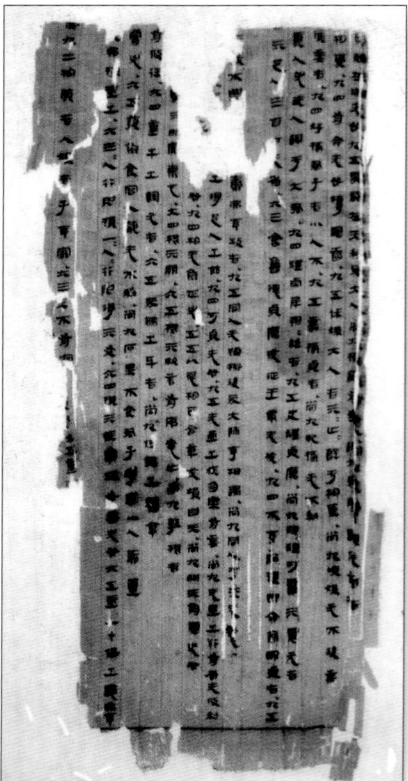

◄ **CONFUCIAN COMMENTARY** Unearthed in 1973 from Han Tomb 3 at the Mawangdui archaeological site, this fragmented length of silk is a Confucian commentary on the *I Ching*'s 64 hexagrams. Dating from early in the reign of Wendi (180–157 BCE), the fourth Han emperor, it is one of the detailed texts and essays made by Confucian scholars following the death of Confucius (551–479 BCE), the great Chinese philosopher (see p.50). Confucius studied the *I Ching* extensively, and viewed it as a manual by which to live in order to attain the highest level of virtue, rather than as a means of divination. The commentaries Confucius wrote were more detailed and extensive than any other at the time.

五經正義表
臣无忌等言臣聞混元初闢三極之道分焉醇德
既醨六籍之文著矣扵是龜書浮于溫洛爰演九
疇龍圖出扵榮河以彰八卦故能範圍天地埏埴
陰陽道濟四溟知周萬物所以七教八政垂炯戒
扵百王五始六虛貽徽範於千古詠歌明得失之
跡雅頌表興廢之由實刑政之紀綱乃人倫之隱
括昔雲官司契之后火紀建極之君雖步驟不同

▲ **COMMENTARIES** In 136 BCE the format of the *I Ching* was standardized, and remains unchanged today. The first part of the work, the hexagrams and their interpretation, are appended by the Ten Wings, or commentaries, as seen on this edition printed during the Southern Song dynasty (1127–1279).

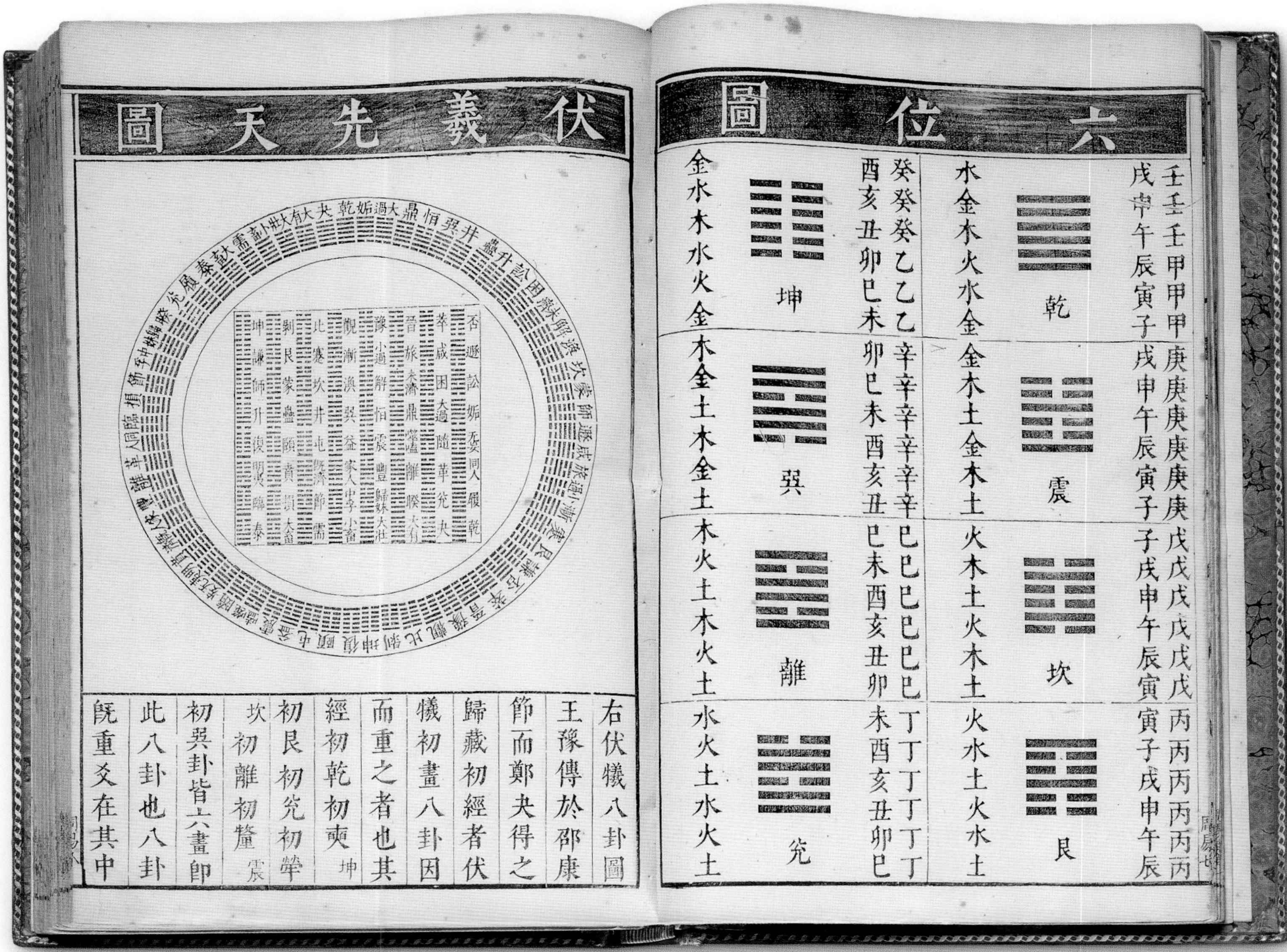

▲ **MING DYNASTY EDITION** Towards the end of the Ming dynasty (1368–1644), printed copies of the *I Ching* were becoming scarce. This edition was published in 1615 by Wu Jishi, and features a claim on the title page to be a faithful representation of the original.

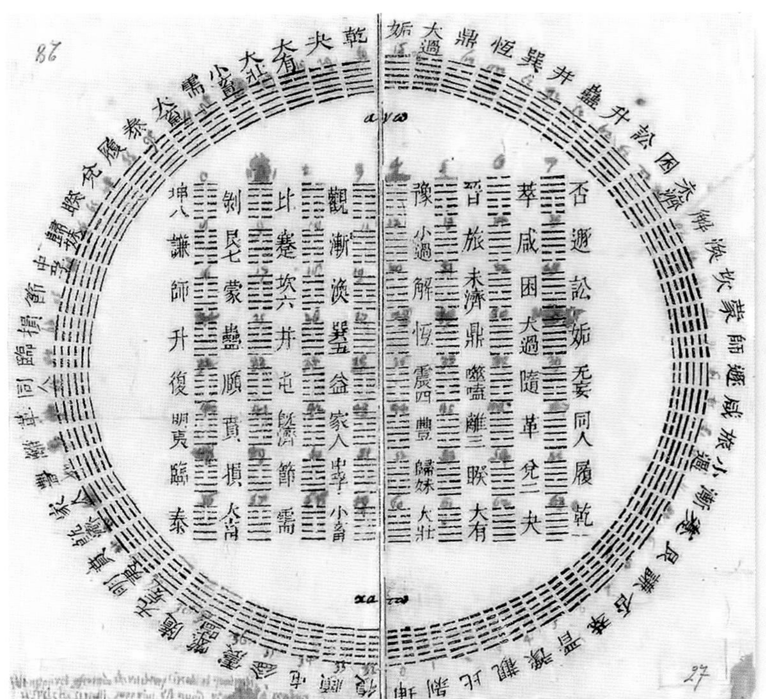

> If some years were added to my life I would devote fifty of them to the study of the Book of Changes and might then avoid committing great errors

CONFUCIUS, *ANALECTS VII*

◄ **CULTURAL TRANSFER** The *I Ching* was known about in the West in the 1600s, although was only first studied in detail in 1701 by German mathematician and philosopher, Gottfried Wilhelm Leibniz. The pages here show his own handwritten notes on the chart of hexagrams.

▲ **NATURAL MATERIAL** In China, about 2,000 years ago, a variety of materials were written on: shells, bones, occasionally silk, and, more commonly, readily available bamboo slips. Bamboo was cut and then its surface shaved and cured, before being dried and split into strips or "slips", as seen here, which were bound together to form what was, in effect, a book.

The Art of War

C.500 BCE (WRITTEN), C.1750 CE (VERSION SHOWN) ■ BAMBOO ■ 6,000 WORDS, 13 CHAPTERS ■ CHINA

SUN TZU

Whatever the uncertainties of its dating and authorship, *The Art of War* has proved one of the most enduring and influential texts from the ancient world. This military manual is divided into 13 chapters, shown here written on bound bamboo slips – typical of Chinese writings of the time. The book comprehensively covers every aspect of training, organizing, and leading armies. Given the endless conflicts of the times in which the text was written, the Spring and Autumn period (770–476 BCE), its practical application was clear. But it is a mark of its exceptional longevity that when, 1,500 years later, Emperor Shenzong (1048–85) decreed the creation of the *Seven Military Classics*, a collection of military textbooks, the first work to be cited was *The Art of War*. As such, it was required reading for all officers in the Imperial Chinese Army. Even today, 2,500 years later, it is widely read by military leaders across the world, inspiring those as diverse as Napoleon and Mao Tse-tung. Perhaps more strikingly still, it has also found a ready audience among business leaders.

The Art of War is a supremely practical work. Its prime concerns are preparedness, discipline, strong leadership, and the absolute importance of dictating the terms of battle, rather than responding to those of the enemy.

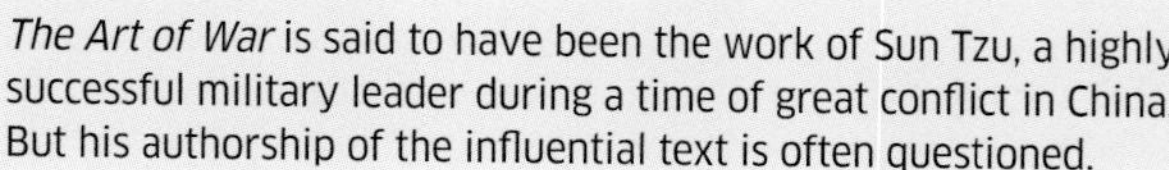

SUN **TZU**

544–496 BCE

The Art of War is said to have been the work of Sun Tzu, a highly successful military leader during a time of great conflict in China. But his authorship of the influential text is often questioned.

That Sun Tzu was a Chinese general and military strategist is widely agreed. But whether he was the sole author of *The Art of War*, or whether the work was a distillation of existing Chinese military theories brought together under his name remains uncertain. Similarly, there are arguments that the book may have been compiled in the later Warring States period (475–221 BCE). The uncertainty and intrigue surrounding the book's origins only add to its appeal.

In detail

▲ **BAMBOO SLIPS** With only one line of text per slip, the medium of bamboo books encouraged simple, pithy statements. A fine brush rather than a pen was used to paint the intricate ink characters onto the slips.

▲ **BOOK BINDING** The slips were bound together with silk cord or lengths of leather, which meant that they could be rolled up and transported easily. They also proved remarkably durable – much more so than European works on parchment from the same period.

> Appear weak when you are strong, and strong when you are weak

SUN TZU, *THE ART OF WAR*

IN **CONTEXT**

The oldest surviving copy of *The Art of War* was one of several works discovered in 1972 in two tombs, dating from the Han dynasty (202 BCE–9 CE). They were unearthed by workmen at the foot of the Yinqueshan, or Silver Sparrow, mountain in Shandong, eastern China, and this location gave the works their name: the Yinqueshan Han Slips. Among the 4,942 bamboo slips found was a copy of a later military manual *Art of War*, by Sun Bin, who is presumed to be a descendant of Sun Tzu. Both texts are believed to have been buried between 140 and 134 BCE. Their discovery was one of the most significant Chinese archeological finds of the 20th century.

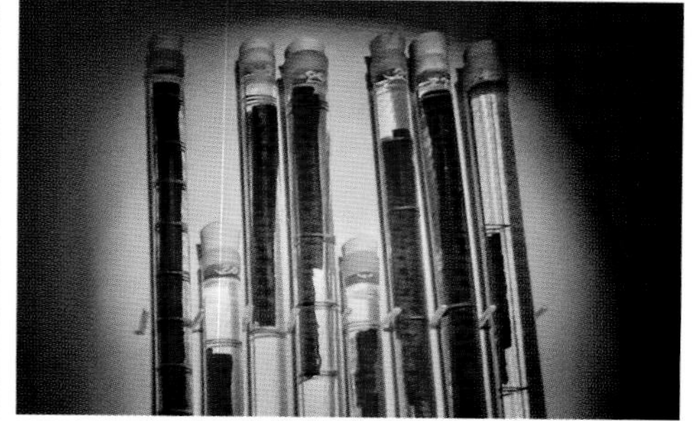

▲ **These bamboo slips** dating from the 2nd century BCE are the oldest copy of *The Art of War*.

Mahābhārata

400 BCE (WRITTEN), C.1670 (VERSION SHOWN) ■ PAPER ■ 18 × 41.7 cm (7 × 16 in) (SHOWN) ■ INDIA

SCALE

VYĀSA

Said to have been dictated by the sage Vyāsa in a cave in Uttarakhand, northern India, the *Mahābhārata* is the longest epic poem ever created, comprising over 100,000 couplets. According to the text, this epic was extended from a 24,000-couplet version called *Bhārata*. The oldest text fragments date back to 400 BCE, but there is no definitive original written version and many regional variations have developed over time. The piece of the *Mahābhārata* shown here dates from 1670 and is written in Devanāgarī script – characterized by the horizontal line that runs along the top of the letters.

At its heart is a tale of the struggle between two sets of cousins: the Kauravas and Pandavas. The Pandavas are the five sons of the deceased King Pandu, and by a trick of fate each of them marry the beautiful Princess Draupadi. After a game of dice, the brothers are forced into exile for 12 years and if found by the Kauravas will be forced into exile again. The story culminates in a cataclysmic battle, after which the Pandavas regain their kingdom.

The *Mahābhārata* is a fascinating source on the evolution of Hinduism. Its central story is just one of many folk tales, histories, and philosophical and moral debates within it. The *Mahābhārata* also includes the 700-verse Hindu scripture *Bhagavad Gita*, which presents the concept of *dharma* (or moral law), the bedrock of Hinduism.

▲ **THE FINAL BATTLE** This is a section from a version of the *Mahābhārata*, dating from around 1670. Originating from Mysore or Tanjore in southern India, the text is written in black and red ink on paper, and the illustrations are painted with opaque watercolour and gold leaf. The text is taken from the tale of the struggle between the Pandavas and the Kauravas. The central scene depicts the mighty battle between the coarse-featured Ghatotkacha (upper right, identified by a label in the margin above) and Karna, the best fighter on the Kaurava side. Karna suceeds in killing Ghatotkacha with a magic weapon given to him by the God Indra.

VYĀSA

C.1500 BCE

According to Hindu tradition Vyāsa is the legendary Indian sage, said to be the author of the *Mahābhārata*, as well as one of the compilers of the Vedas.

Legend has it that Vyāsa lived around 1500 BCE in Uttarkhand, northern India, and was the son of the Princess Satyavati and the scholar Parashara. His father had been promised by the God Vishnu that his son would be famous in return for the severe penance Parashara had done for Vishnu. Vyāsa grew up in the forests, living by the river Satyavati with hermits who taught him the ancient sacred texts of the Vedas that he developed to create the *Mahābhārata*. Tradition states that he composed his epic over two and a half years, dictating it in a cave to his scribe Ganesha, the elephant god, although the poem is more likely to have been the result of an oral tradition.

Whatever is here, is found elsewhere. But what is not here, is nowhere else

THE BOOK OF THE BEGINNING

IN CONTEXT

The earliest versions of the *Mahābhārata* were written on manuscripts made from dried palm leaves. One of the oldest writing materials, palm leaves were first used in southern Asia. The scribe cut letters into the leaf with a needle, then filled the marks with a soot and oil mixture.

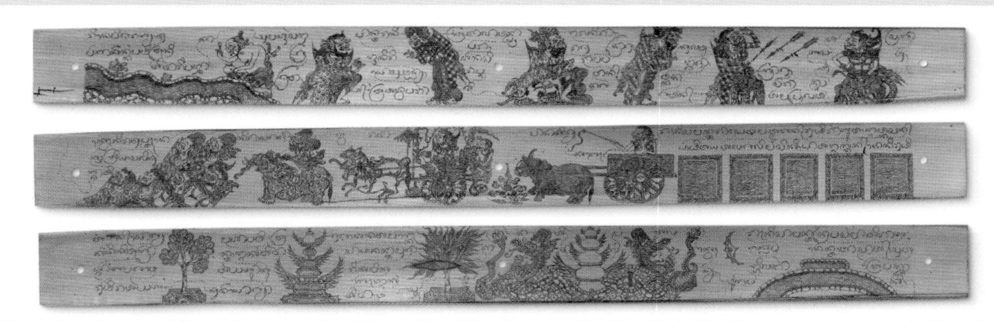

► **These 19th-century palm-leaf manuscripts** are from Bali. The *Mahābhārata* stories were recounted across Southeast Asia and are found in many forms, from scrolls to paintings and temple decorations.

Dead Sea Scrolls

250 BCE–68 CE ■ VELLUM, PAPYRUS, LEATHER, AND COPPER ■ VARIOUS SIZES ■ 981 SCROLLS ■ ISRAEL

VARIOUS AUTHORS

For more than 18 centuries, a collection of scrolls lay hidden in caves near the ancient settlement site of Qumran, on the north western shore of the Dead Sea in Israel. Known as the Dead Sea Scrolls, they are the oldest copies of Jewish texts in existence and have shed light upon Jewish and Christian understandings of the Bible. Their chance discovery in 1947, by a Bedouin boy searching for a lost goat, sparked one of the most exciting archaeological hunts of the 20th century. In total 11 caves containing pots with scrolls inside them were discovered and 981 scrolls collected, together with other artefacts, such as coins and inkwells. Only a few complete scrolls were found, but some 25,000 fragments were also unearthed. The majority of the Dead Sea Scrolls are made of animal skin, but others are made of papyrus or leather, and one of copper. While most of the scrolls have Hebrew text, some have text in Aramaic and Greek.

It is not known why the scrolls were hidden or by whom. One theory is that it might have been an act of protection against the Roman occupation of Jerusalem, and the people's property, around 60 CE. Today the collection is housed in a specially built museum, the Shrine of the Book, in the grounds of the Israel Museum in Jerusalem.

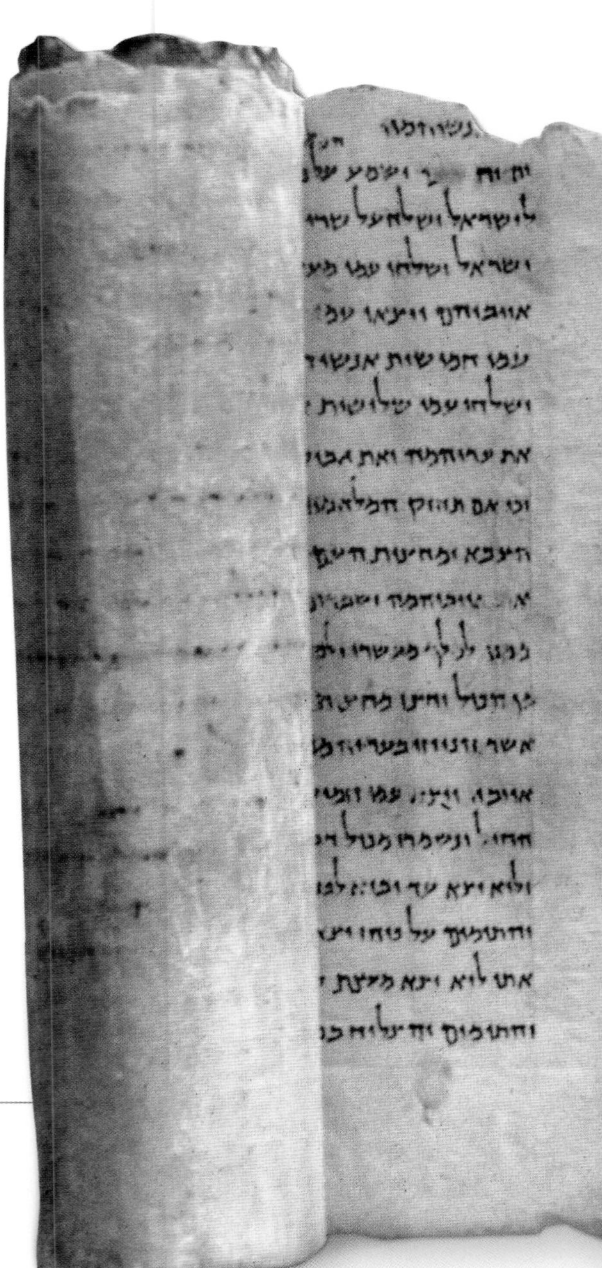

▲ **INNER PORTION** Measuring around 8.15 m (25 ft) this scroll, the longest of the Dead Sea Scrolls, was found in Cave 11 in 1956. It is made from 18 pieces of the thinnest vellum found in the caves, and the inner portion is its best-preserved section as it was not as exposed to the elements as the outer sheet was. The Hebrew text is written in the square Herodian script of the late Second Temple Period. As with many Hebrew texts written in this period – and all of the Dead Sea Scrolls – the scroll is read from right to left. This scroll takes its name from the text, which is written in the form of a revelation from God to Moses, and describes the building of a temple similar to those built in the Israelites' camps on their exodus from Egypt. The text suggests that Solomon should have followed these guidelines when he built the Temple in Jerusalem.

Temple Scroll

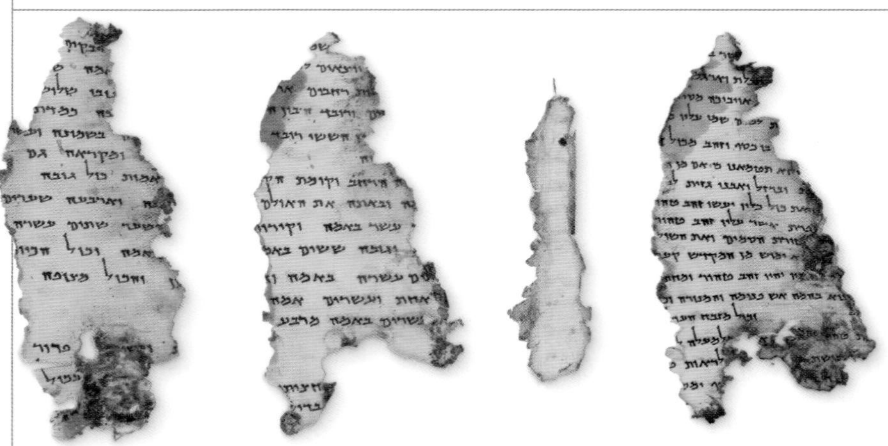

▲ **SCROLL FRAGMENTS** While the main part of the Temple Scroll is the most complete, there are many fragments like these from one end of the scroll. The Hebrew script, which reads from right to left in neat lines, is remarkably clear right up to the damaged edges, and so in spite of the damage, scholars have been able to translate the text. The content corresponds closely to the biblical Books of Exodus and Deuteronomy.

> ... I was privileged by destiny to gaze upon a Hebrew Scroll which had not been read for more than 2,000 years
>
> **PROFESSOR ELIEZER LIPA SUKENIK** OF HEBREW UNIVERSITY, IN HIS DIARY ENTRY, 1940s

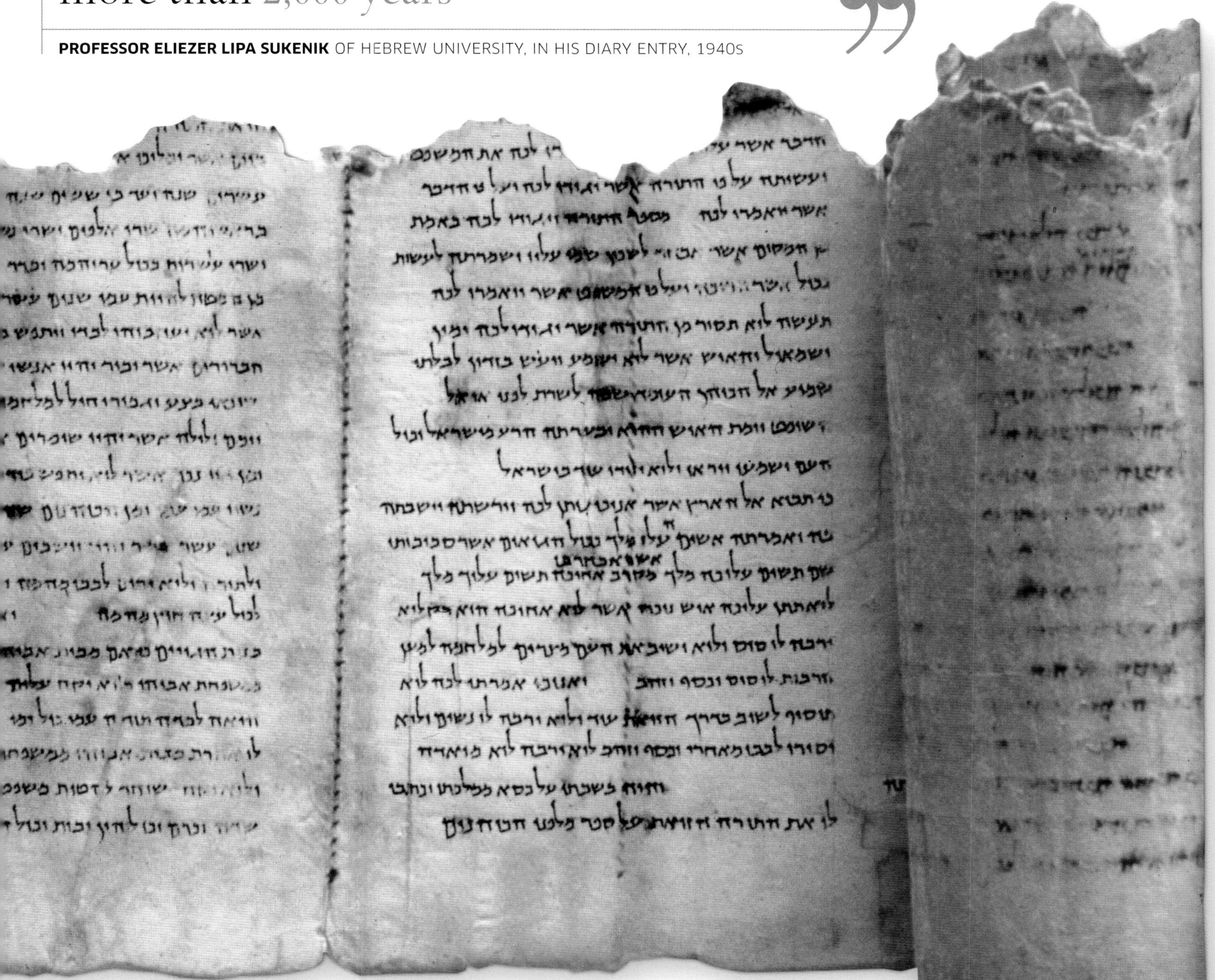

◄ **DAMAGED SHEETS** The three columns shown (columns 42, 43, and 44, from left to right) are from the central section of the scroll. The torn edges are a result of the way the scrolls were rolled tightly in the storage jars (see image, top left), and also due to careless handling since their discovery. However, with modern imaging techniques, experts have been able to decipher the writing even on damaged fragments.

The Great Isaiah Scroll

▲ **LAST SECTION** One of the first scrolls found in 1947, this scroll, which features all six chapters of the Book of Isaiah, is the only complete book from the Bible found among the scrolls. It is the best preserved of all the biblical scrolls, and this last section shows the edges of the sheets are only very slightly damaged. Dating from the 2nd century BCE, it is the oldest Old Testament manuscript known by more than 1,000 years.

Habakkuk commentary

◀ **HABAKKUK COMMENTARY, OR HEBREW PESHER** This text, written in the 1st century BCE, is written on two pieces of leather, sewn together with linen thread. It tells how the prophet Habakkuk sees Israel facing danger from a foreign enemy, just as the writer of the scroll sees danger from the Romans. This commentary is considered a crucial source of information regarding the people of Qumran's spiritual life.

▲ **FIRST SECTION** The Great Isaiah Scroll features 54 columns of text, and the first four are shown above (text was read from right to left). The scroll is written in Hebrew on 17 pieces of parchment (either goat or calf). The black ink used was made from soot from oil lamps, which was mixed into honey, oil, vinegar, and water. As can be seen here, no punctuation was used.

The War Scroll

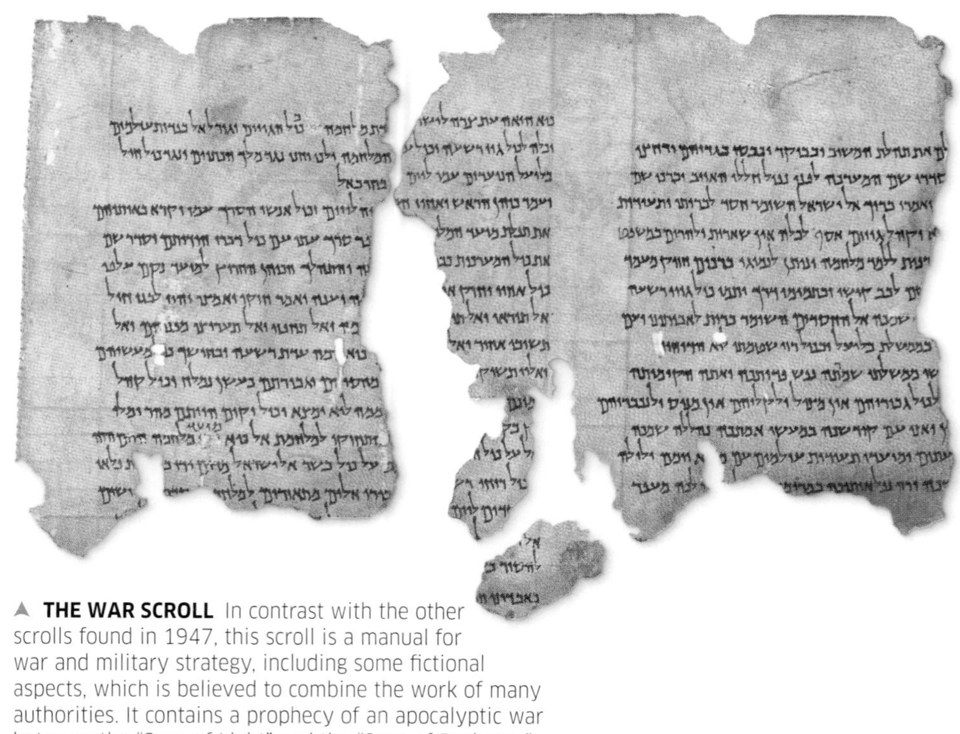

▲ **THE WAR SCROLL** In contrast with the other scrolls found in 1947, this scroll is a manual for war and military strategy, including some fictional aspects, which is believed to combine the work of many authorities. It contains a prophecy of an apocalyptic war between the "Sons of Light" and the "Sons of Darkness".

IN **CONTEXT**

The first seven of the Dead Sea scrolls were discovered in 1947, when local Bedouin shepherd Edh-Dhib happened to throw a stone into one of the caves, only to hear something smash – one of the clay pots containing the scrolls. Despite being told that the scrolls were worthless, Edh-Dhib took them to an antiques dealer, and they quickly came to the attention of American scholar John Trever. Two years later a full scale archaeological expedition was launched. In 1953 they found a copper scroll, which seemed to be a treasure map. By 1956 11 caves had been excavated and hundreds of scrolls and manuscripts unearthed. In February 2017 another cave was discovered, but while objects of interest have been found, it has yet to yield any manuscripts or scrolls.

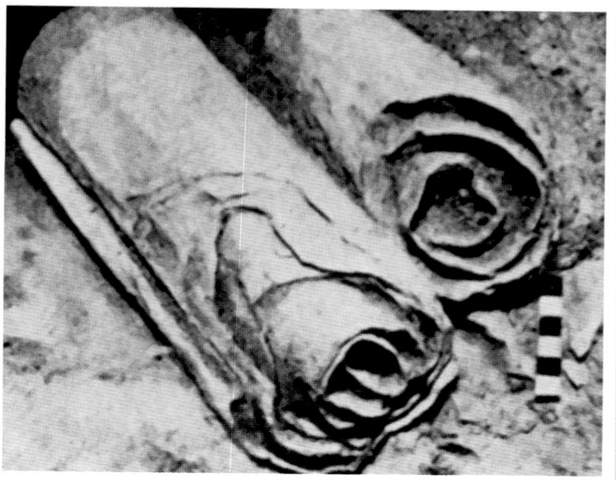

▲ **Many of the scrolls** found lying in the caves had been damaged, some so badly that it has not been possible for archaeologists to identify or translate them.

Vienna Dioscorides

C.512 CE ▪ VELLUM ▪ 37 × 30 cm (14 × 12 in) ▪ 982 FOLIOS ▪ BYZANTINE EMPIRE

SCALE

PEDANIUS DIOSCORIDES

Also known as the *Juliana Anicia Codex*, the *Vienna Dioscorides*, is the oldest surviving copy of Pedanius Dioscorides's classic work on herbal remedies, *De Materia Medica* (*On Medical Matters*). One of the most important medical works of the Greco-Roman world, the original text was written in about 70 CE by Pedanius Dioscorides. It exhaustively lists the medical properties of 383 herbs and 200 plants.

The *Vienna Dioscorides* is a copy of *De Materia Medica*, produced about 450 years later in Constantinople – then the capital of the Eastern Roman Empire. The work was dedicated to Princess Juliana Anicia, daughter of the Emperor Flavius Anicius Olybrius, and a patron of the early Church and healing. In 1569 the Holy Roman Emperor Maximilian II purchased the manuscript for his Imperial Library in Vienna, from where the book takes its name.

The combination of detailed information and visual richness in this codex (an ancient, handwritten text in book form) is unrivalled in early Byzantine art. It is unknown if Dioscorides's original manuscript was similarly illustrated, but the *Vienna* copy contains over 479 sumptuous images of plants. Whether these were drawn from nature or from existing depictions is also unclear. The book contains three further works besides Dioscorides's herbal remedies: a medical treatise believed to have been written by the 1st-century CE Greek physician, Rufus of Ephesus; a simplified version of a 2nd-century Greek treatise dealing with snakebites, thought to have been written by Nicander of Colophon; and an illustrated treatise on birds.

PEDANIUS **DIOSCORIDES**

C.40–C.90 CE

Pedanius Dioscorides was a Greek physician, pharmacist, and botanist, whose seminal work *De Materia Medica*, or the *Juliana Anicia Codex*, remains the single most important source of knowledge about Ancient Greek and Roman medical practices.

Dioscorides was born in Anazarbus, Cilicia, although few details of his life are known. He is believed to have practiced medicine in Rome during the reign of Emperor Nero (37–68 CE) before serving as a surgeon with the Roman armies. At this time he travelled widely across the Roman Empire, and was able to study the medicinal properties of many plants and minerals, which he used in the compilation of his major text, *De Materia Medica*. Dioscorides is believed to have taken 20 years to produce this text in which he divided plants according to their medicinal and botanical properties. Originally written in Greek, it was later translated into Latin. The work is a remarkable record of natural history and the enduring influence of ancient learning.

▼ **LIFELIKE ILLUSTRATIONS** Naturalistic images of the plants were intended to help the pharmacist easily identify herbs when making remedies. Full-page images were generally accompanied by descriptions of their properties on the facing page. The illustration here, from folio 174, is typical, with both root and plant shown. The Greek text is written in "uncial" characters (capital letters) which developed, in both Latin and Greek, in 3rd century.

▲ **TITLE PAGE** The codex's inscription describes the work's scope of "plants, roots, seeds, juice, leaves and remedies", and explains its alphabetical ordering.

> For almost two millennia Dioscorides was regarded as the ultimate authority on plants and medicine
>
> **TESS ANNE OSBALDESTON**, ON *DE MATERIA MEDICA*, 2000

◀ **PORTRAIT OF THE PATRON** The codex features the oldest painting of a patron with its image of Princess Juliana Anicia. She is flanked by the allegorical figures Magnanimity (left) and Wisdom (right). A putto (cherub) offers her the manuscript.

In detail

▲ **WIDE INFLUENCE** Following the fall of Byzantium to the Ottomans in 1453, Arabic plant names were added to the manuscript. The *Vienna Dioscorides* impacted as deeply on Arab learning as it did on later European learning.

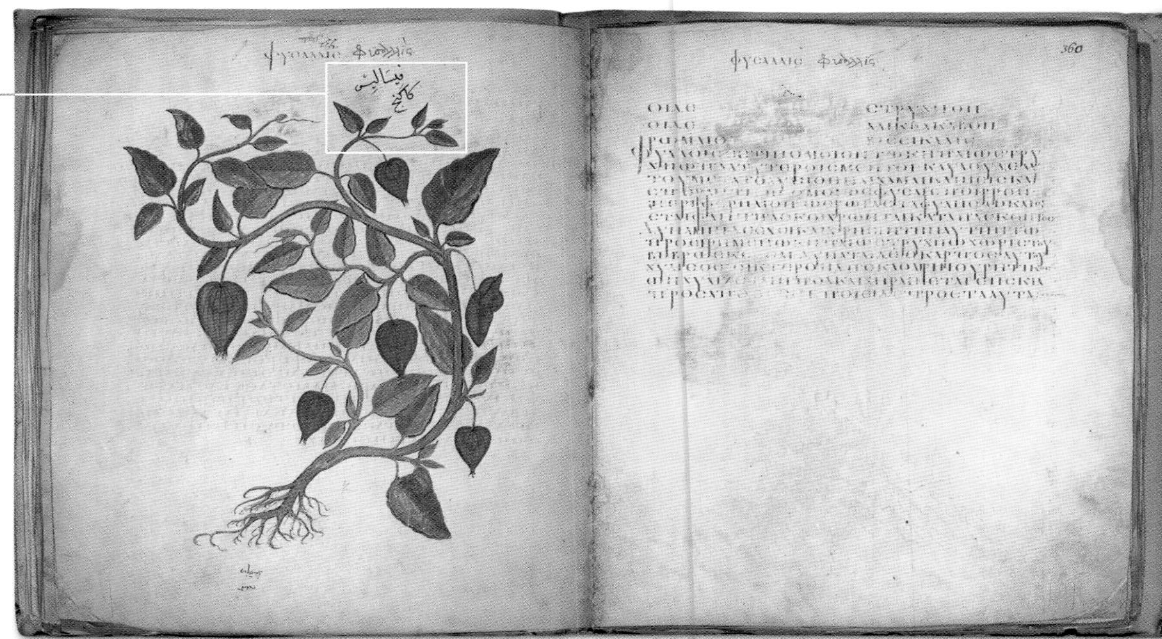

► **SUGGESTED REMEDIES** In the text facing this picture of a winter cherry, Dioscorides recommends the plant's stem as a sedative. Mixed with honey, it was claimed to improve vision; and with wine, to ease toothache.

▲ **DRAWING FROM LIFE** The illustrations in the *Vienna Discorides* were the product of exact observation, as shown in this depiction of a yellow horned poppy. Later Byzantine art would become progressively more religious and restrained by imperial priorities, projecting ever more elaborate visions of grandeur.

► **TIP TO ROOT** Dioscorides examined every part of the plant. Roots, leaves, flowers, and berries were all included in the drawings so that pharmacists could see all the relevant parts that could be used as ingredients. On this page, the artist decorated the vellum before the scribe added the text.

➤ **TREATISE ON BIRDS** Forty Mediterranean birds were described and illustrated with delicately painted line drawings. The inclusion of this work, thought to be by Dionysius (1st century CE), makes the *Vienna Dioscorides* the oldest known illustrated treatise on birds.

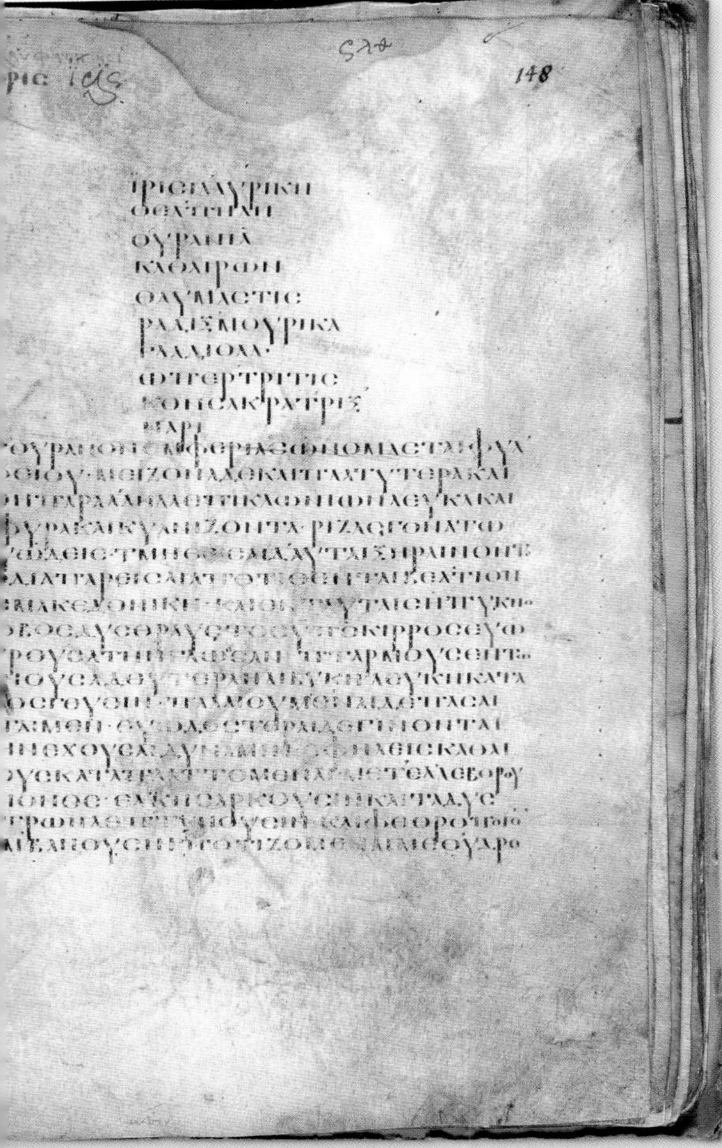

IN **CONTEXT**

De Materia Medica collated the wisdom and practice of generations. As late as the 1930s, an ageing Greek monk was observed treating patients according to the remedies laid down by Dioscorides. In fact, for at least 1,500 years after his death, Dioscorides's *De Materia Medica* remained the standard pharmacological work across the West and the Arab world, translated into Arabic and Persian, as well as – in the Middle Ages and the Renaissance – Italian, French, German, and English.

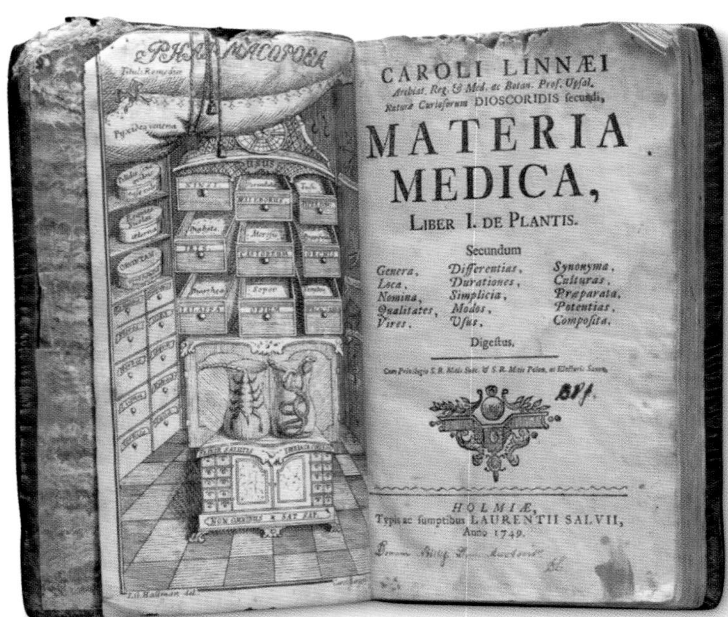

▲ **Swedish botanist Carl Linneaus** was deeply influenced by Dioscorides, and, in his 1749 *Materia Medica*, made the novel division of plants into genus and species, producing the first modern classification of plants. The frontispiece shows a cabinet with plants and herbs.

Book of Kells

C.800CE ▪ VELLUM ▪ 33 × 25.5 cm (13 × 10 in) ▪ 680 FOLIOS ▪ IRELAND

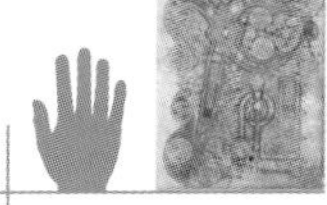
SCALE

IRISH COLUMBAN MONKS

Dating from around 800 CE the *Book of Kells* is the finest surviving illuminated manuscript from the Celtic medieval period, boasting a design of unsurpassed complexity and extravagance. The sumptuously illustrated text consists primarily of the four Gospels in Latin, based on St Jerome's 4th-century translation of the Bible. Believed to be the work of three artists and four scribes, it is written in the formal script known as Insular majuscule on vellum (prepared calfskin). Today the manuscript contains 680 folios – around 30 others have been lost over time. With its full-page illustrations, abstract decoration, and coloured lettering, it is the most lavishly decorated example of an Insular manuscript – a decorated manuscript produced in the British Isles between the 6th and 9th centuries. The transcription, however, was particularly careless, with letters and entire words missing or repeated, indicating that the book was intended for ceremonial use rather than for daily services.

Also known as the *Book of Columba*, the manuscript was composed by Irish monks, followers of the 6th-century Irish saint, St Columba. Their order had fled from their abbey on the Scottish island of Iona during Viking raids in the 9th century and taken refuge in the monastery at Kells, north of Dublin. The manuscript may have been produced either wholly in Iona or in Kells, or started in Iona and completed in Kells. A medieval source states that it was stolen in 1006 for its *cumdach* – the ornamental box in which it was stored. Although this was never recovered, most of folios of the manuscript were. The current binding by British book-binder, Roger Powell dates from 1953. Powell divided the manuscript into four volumes to help preserve it while on display in the Old Library at Trinity College, Dublin, where it has been kept since the 17th century. It remains a central symbol of Irish culture and identity.

ON **TECHNIQUE**

At least 185 calfskins were used in the production of the *Book of Kells*. The word vellum (prepared calfskin) on which the book was written comes from *vitulum*, the Latin for calf. All other animal skins are called parchment. Each skin was soaked in lime, dried, and scraped smooth with pumice before being cut into folios. From the Latin for "leaf" (*folium*), a folio is a two-sided page, with "recto" defining the front side, and "verso" the reverse. Before the scribe began to write, the page was scored with pinpricks, and horizontal lines were drawn with a blade to guide the scribe. Quills, made from feathers, were trimmed and cut diagonally to form a nib. Ink was made from soot or iron gall mixed with gum arabic, and seven pigments, derived from a wide range of sources, were used for the illustrations in the manuscript.

▲ **This folio** from the *Book of Kells* shows the use of red pigment, which came from lead, and green, from copper sulphide.

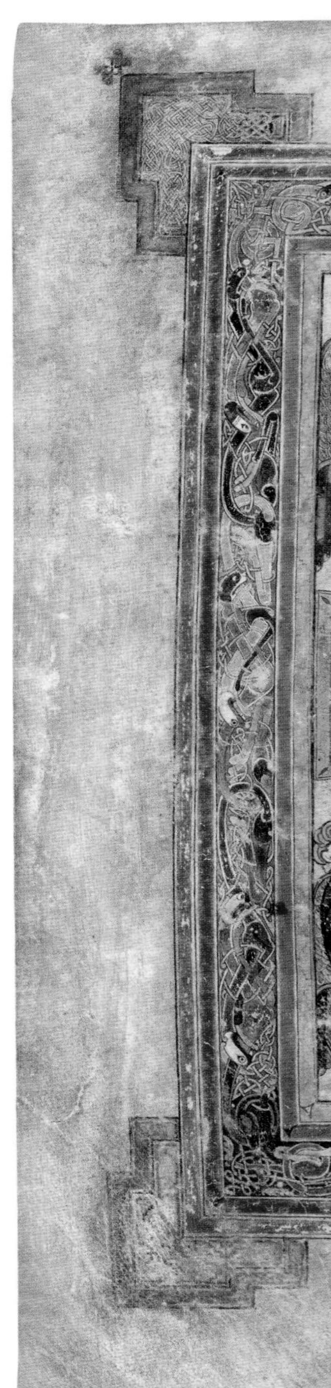

➤ **FACING PAGES** The *Book of Kells* exhibits the oldest existing depiction of the Virgin Mary in a Western manuscript. Wearing Byzantine robes, she sits on a throne with the young Jesus on her lap. The surrounding angels hold stylized fans, possibly inspired by Egyptian Coptic art. Notable features are the unusual representation of the Virgin's breasts, her apparently two right feet, and Jesus's elaborate blond hair. The page is an appropriate accompaniment to the *Breves causae* of Matthew (the summary of the Gospel) that begins opposite it. This is the most elaborately decorated page of text in the manuscript, starting with an elegant, elongated letter "N". The Latin reads: "*Nativitas XPI in Bethlem Judeae Magi munera offerunt et infantes interficiuntur Regressio*" ("The birth of Christ in Bethlehem of Judea; the wise men present gifts; the slaying of the children; the return").

> It is widely regarded as Ireland's greatest historical treasure… one of the most spectacular examples of medieval Christian art in the world
>
> **UNESCO'S MEMORY OF THE WORLD REGISTER**

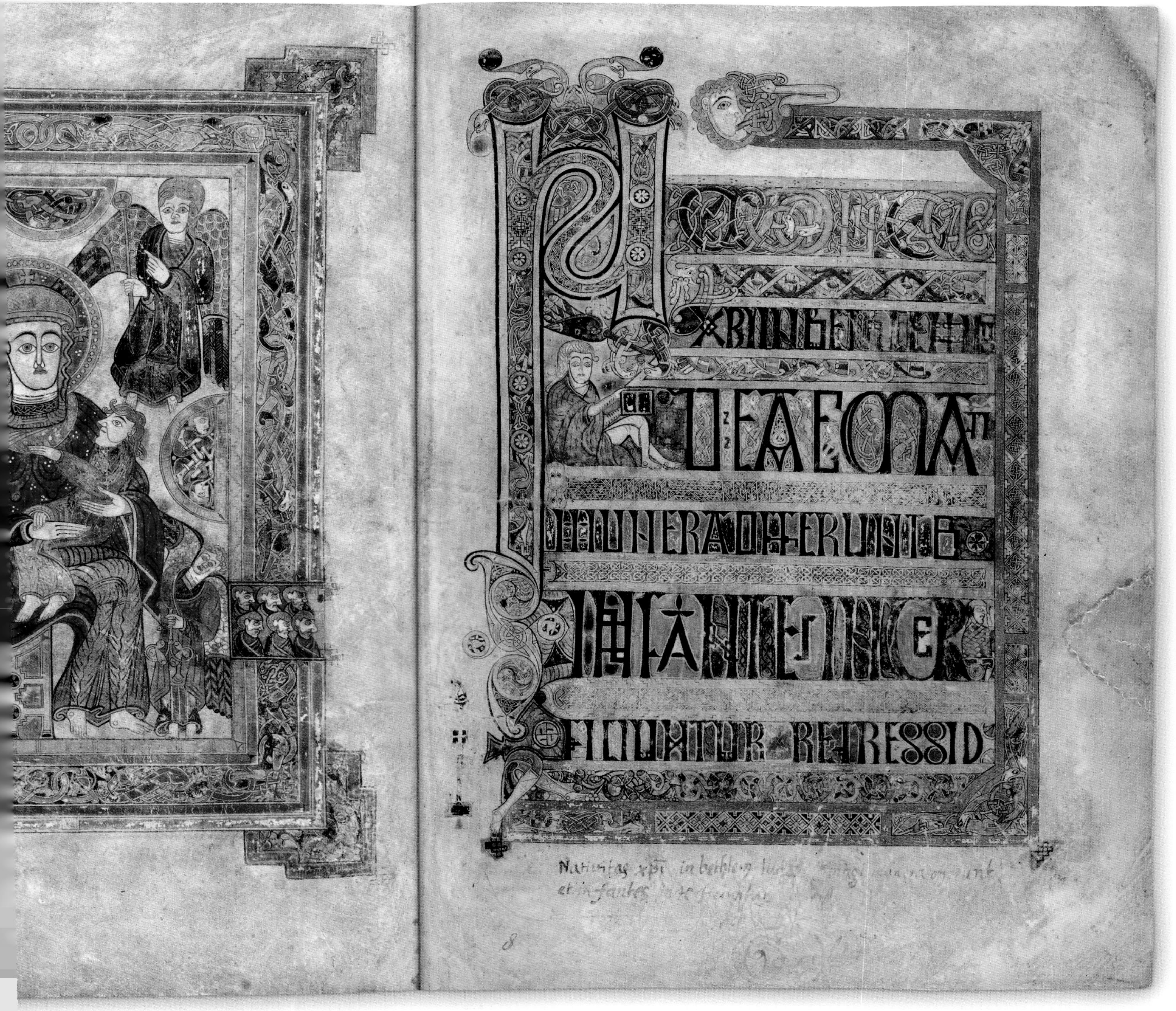

▲ **CHI RHO** The most famous page of the *Book of Kells* is known as the Chi Rho. These are the first two letters of the word "Christ" in Ancient Greek – *Chi* is written as "X" and *Rho* is written as "P". Heavily stylized, they are the focus of this page, which illuminates the Gospel of St Matthew, relating Christ's birth. The page also features the letter "I", for *Iota*, the third letter in the word Christ, and the word *generatio*. This is the opening of the verse that reads, "This is how Christ came to be born".

Visual tour

▼ **HIDDEN IMAGES** The Chi Rho page is renowned for its concealed illustrations of animals and people. Here, a blond man's head set on its side finishes the elaborate curve of the *Rho*, resembling the letter "P", while a third Greek letter, *Iota*, an "I", passes through its centre. It is thought by some academics that the head represents Christ.

▼ **INTRICATE DESIGN** Squeezed between the right-hand curls of the letter Chi, or "X", is this exquisite swirling motif. The artist's work shows such extraordinary detailing and delicacy that it has been compared to that of a goldsmith.

▲ **HEAVENLY ANGELS** Angels, drawn as male figures with wings and blond hair, appear to rise out of one of the cross arms of the Chi, or letter "X". Positioned just above, but not seen here, is a third angel. These divine messengers of God were sent to spread the word of the birth of Christ – the word "angel" comes from the Greek *angelos*, meaning "messenger".

➤ **ANIMAL MOTIFS** Towards the bottom of the page, two cats appear to be watching a pair of large mice holding a white disc in their mouths. The disc may represent a Holy Communion wafer but its precise symbolic significance, and that of the creatures, has been lost over the centuries.

In detail

▼ **GROUP EFFORT** The *Book of Kells* is thought to have been the combined work of three monks writing the Latin text, and four decorating the pages and colouring the initials. It is the first known Irish manuscript in which every single opening letter is illustrated, and the first medieval manuscript with spaces between the words to make reading easier.

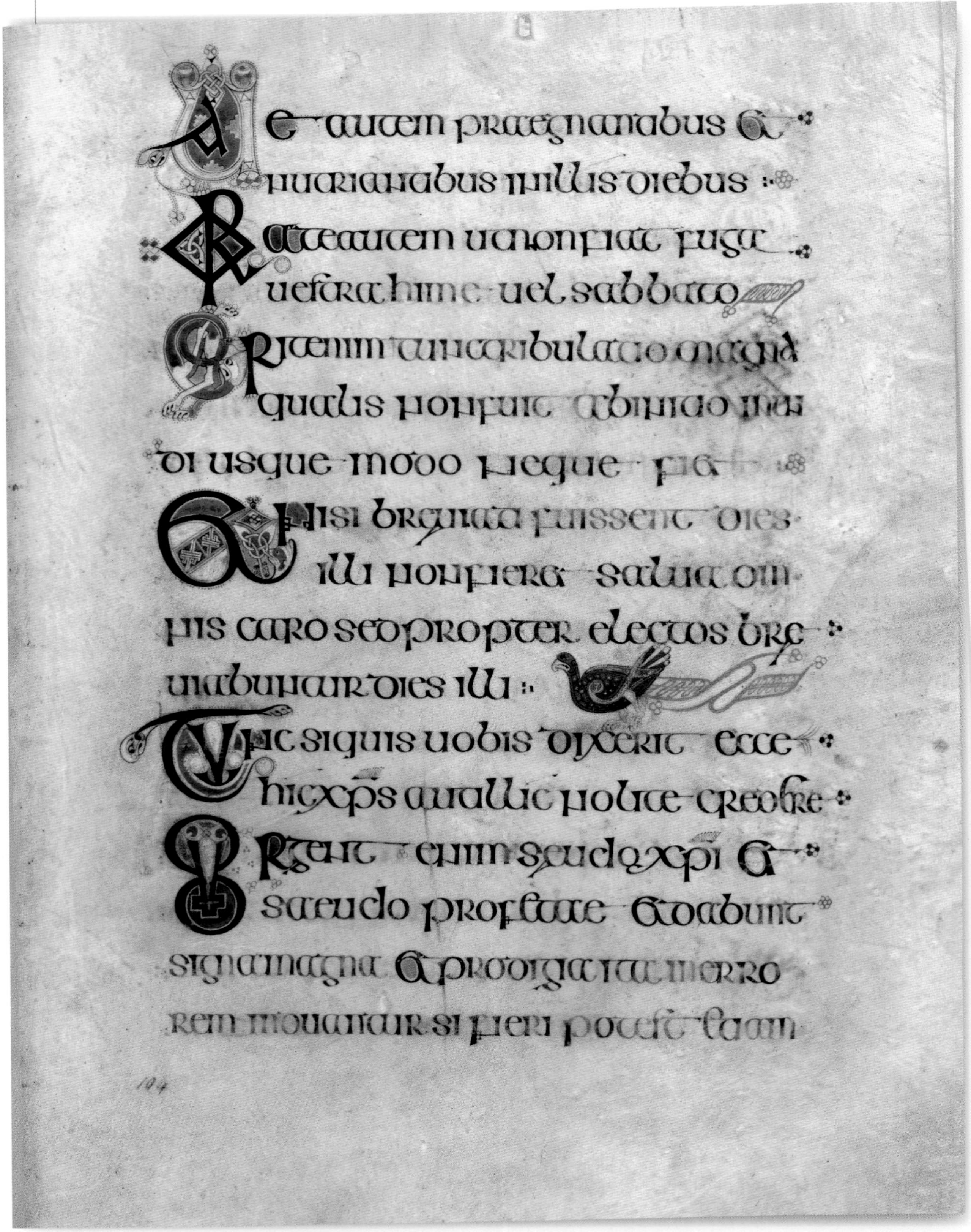

▲ **ILLUSTRATED LETTER** Folio 124r from the Gospel of St Matthew uses an elaborately illustrated initial letter "T" and a fierce fire-breathing lion to symbolize Christ's crucifixion.

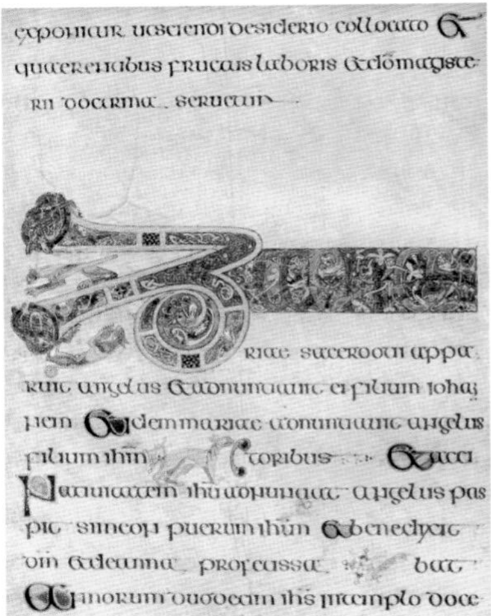

▲ **STYLIZED SCRIPT** This detail from Folio 19v features an ornate letter "Z", followed by *acha*, with the rest of the name *Zachariae* relegated to the next line, as the scribes prioritized decoration.

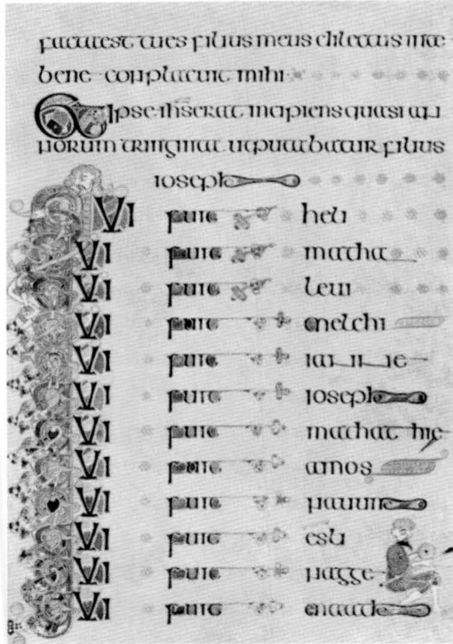

▲ **REPEATED WORDS** Folio 200r illustrates the genealogy of Christ. *Qui* ("Who") is repeated at the start of each line, and illustrations of intertwined serpents link the generations.

▲ **PORTRAIT PAGE** Among the purely decorative pages are a number of portrait pages. Above, the purple-robed Christ, flanked by four angels, is shown seated and holding a Book of the Gospels in his hands. The two peacocks are symbols of Christ's resurrection.

► **CANON TABLES** The eight canon tables at the start of the manuscript are an index to those passages that are shared between the four Gospels. Each table is illustrated. The patterned architectural columns are topped by a half dome enclosing fantastical creatures.

▼ **CARPET PAGE** Even though carpet pages – so named because they resemble oriental rugs – are characteristic of Insular manuscripts, there is only one in the *Book of Kells*. Geometrically precise and highly ornamental, it is dominated by roundels created with a pair of compasses. The circles are filled with over 400 discs and spirals of incredibly detailed workmanship.

RELATED **TEXTS**

The *Lindisfarne Gospels* is another beautiful example of Insular art, written and decorated in the early 8th century at the abbey of Lindisfarne, an island off the northeast English coast. Although smaller and far less elaborate than the *Book of Kells*, it boasts similar patterns and colours. It also features ornamental carpet pages, like the *Book of Kells* (see left), with one at the beginning of each of the Gospels. The text of the Gospels was translated from Latin into Old English and written between the lines of the manuscript in the 10th century. This makes it the oldest existing translation of the Gospels in the English language.

▲ **A cross-carpet page** from the *Lindisfarne Gospels* facing beautifully decorated initials and display capitals.

The Blue Qur'an

C.850–950 CE ▪ GOLD ON DYED VELLUM ▪ C.30.4 × 40.2 cm (12 × 16 in) ▪ 600 PAGES ▪ TUNISIA

SCALE

AUTHOR UNKNOWN

The Qur'an is the core Islamic text, which Muslims believe was revealed to Muhammad by God between 609 and 632 CE. This sacred work describes God, and humankind's relationship to Him, and gives directives in order for His followers to achieve peace in this life and thereafter – every Muslim is expected to be familiar with its teachings.

Dating from the late 9th to early 10th century, the sumptuous Blue Qur'an is one of the most beautiful copies of the book ever produced, and takes its name from the vivid indigo dye that colours its pages. The visually contrasting gold text is a rare feature in books of this period, although it does follow Islamic tradition, where many religious texts were written in gold or silver on dark surfaces. The scribe who wrote the Blue Qur'an used elongated strokes in order to make the script fill the pages in a manner pleasing to the eye. Clarity has been sacrificed for aesthetics, as there are no diacritical marks (such as accents) above or below letters to indicate vowels, and the calligrapher has also inserted spaces within words simply to make the columns of text align.

Little is known of when, where, and how the Blue Qur'an was produced, although it is speculated that it may have been produced in Baghdad, capital of the Abbasid caliphate, or Cordoba in Spain, capital of the Umayyad caliphate. The most widely accepted theory is that it was commissioned for the Great Mosque in Kairouan, Tunisia. It is possible that the unique colouring may have been used in an attempt to echo the imperial blue or purple used for similarly opulent documents of the contemporary and rival Byzantine empire. Certainly the use of indigo and gold was expensive, suggesting that it was commissioned by a very wealthy patron, possibly the caliph or one of his inner circle. Today, the folios have been divided and are kept in different museums around the world, although most are held at the Bardo National Museum in Tunis.

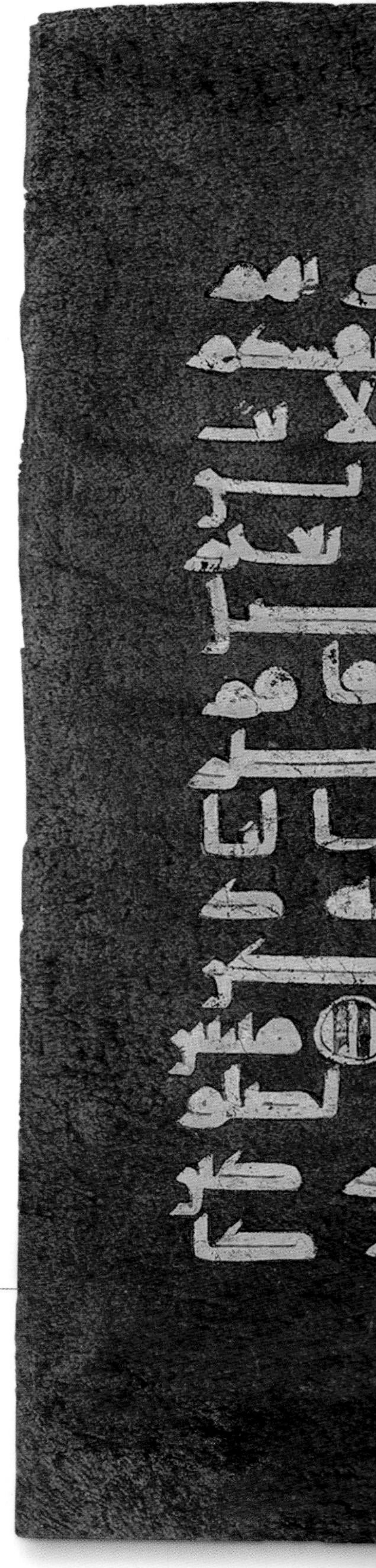

In detail

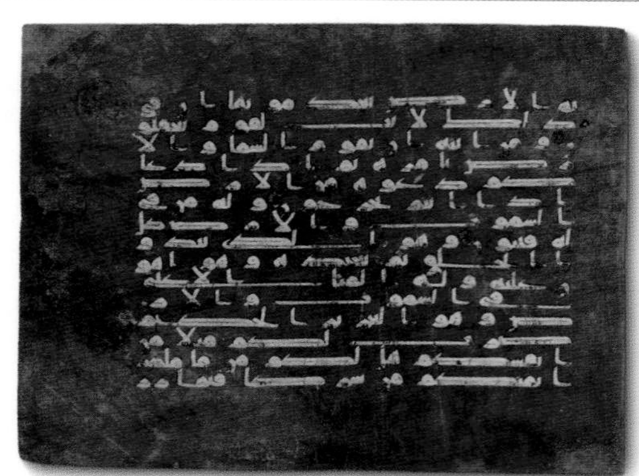

▲ **EVEN LINES** Part of the visual appeal of the pages is due to their 15 lines of equal length. Most contemporary copies contained only three lines per page. To achieve these equal lines, the scribe manipulated letters and omitted important grammatical marks.

▲ **GREATEST TO LEAST** The Qur'an consists of 114 chapters, or *surah*, each consisting of a series of verses, or *ayah*, of varying lengths. Perhaps confusingly, the chapters follow no chronological or thematic structure, but are arranged by length: the longest first, the shortest last. In the Blue Qur'an the chapters are separated by silver rosettes, all long since faded as a result of oxidization.

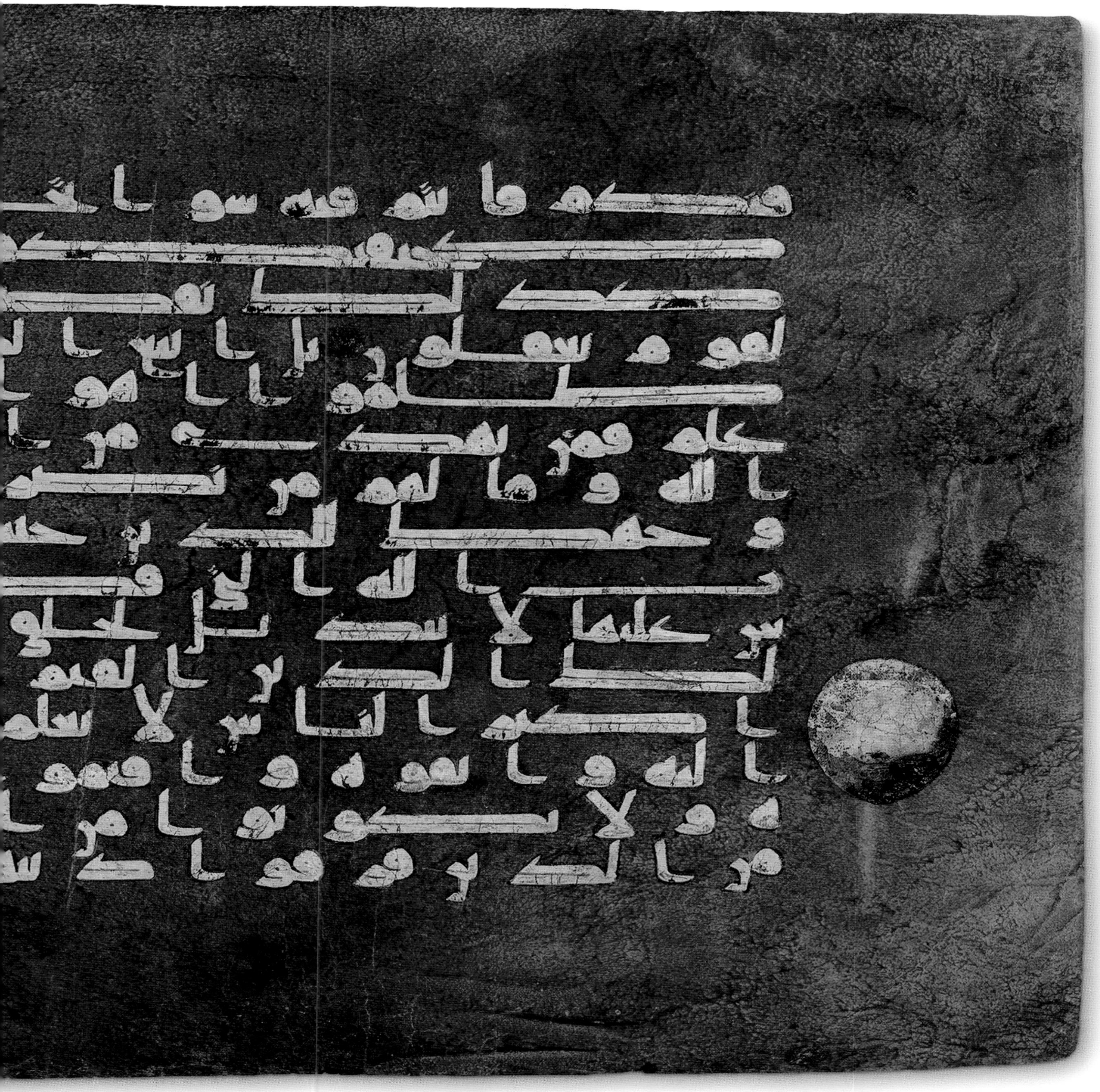

▲ **KUFIC SCRIPT** The Blue Qur'an is written in Kufic script. This is the earliest form of Arabic script, named for Kufa in Iraq, where it was developed during the late 7th century. Its horizontal format is typical of 8th–10th century copies of the Qur'an. As with all Arabic scripts, it is read from right to left.

This is the book about which there is no doubt...

THE QUR'AN, 2:2

Diamond Sutra

868 CE ▪ PRINTED ▪ 27 cm × 5 m (11 in × 16 ft) ▪ CHINA

SCALE

AUTHOR UNKNOWN

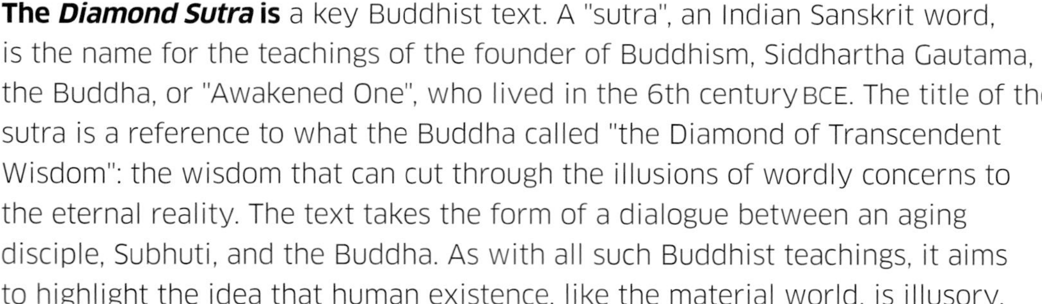

The *Diamond Sutra* is a key Buddhist text. A "sutra", an Indian Sanskrit word, is the name for the teachings of the founder of Buddhism, Siddhartha Gautama, the Buddha, or "Awakened One", who lived in the 6th century BCE. The title of the sutra is a reference to what the Buddha called "the Diamond of Transcendent Wisdom": the wisdom that can cut through the illusions of wordly concerns to the eternal reality. The text takes the form of a dialogue between an aging disciple, Subhuti, and the Buddha. As with all such Buddhist teachings, it aims to highlight the idea that human existence, like the material world, is illusory.

The added importance of the scroll, now in the British Library, is that it is the oldest complete printed document in the world whose date is exactly known. The scroll was discovered in 1900 by a Chinese Daoist monk, who found it in the Caves of the Thousand Buddhas, a warren of tunnels dug into a cliff outside the Silk Road settlement of Dunhuang, northwest China (see p.51). With it were 60,000 other paintings and documents, all apparently hidden for safe-keeping in around the year 1000 CE. In 1907 the scroll was acquired by a Hungarian-born explorer, Marc Auriel Stein, who sent it to the British Museum.

The *Diamond Sutra* is a precise example of the sophistication of Chinese printing, which developed in the 8th century, and of Chinese paper-making, which developed earlier still, perhaps in the 2nd century BCE. It is also a remarkable testimony to the spread of Buddhism from its Indian heartlands.

➤ **ILLUSTRATION** The opening of the *Diamond Sutra* reveals its only illustration, and the earliest surviving example of a woodcut illustration in a printed book. It shows the Buddha in the centre of the scene, clearly a figure of authority, as he dispenses the wisdom of the sutra to the crouching Subhuti at the lower left of the frame. The Buddha's disciples surround him.

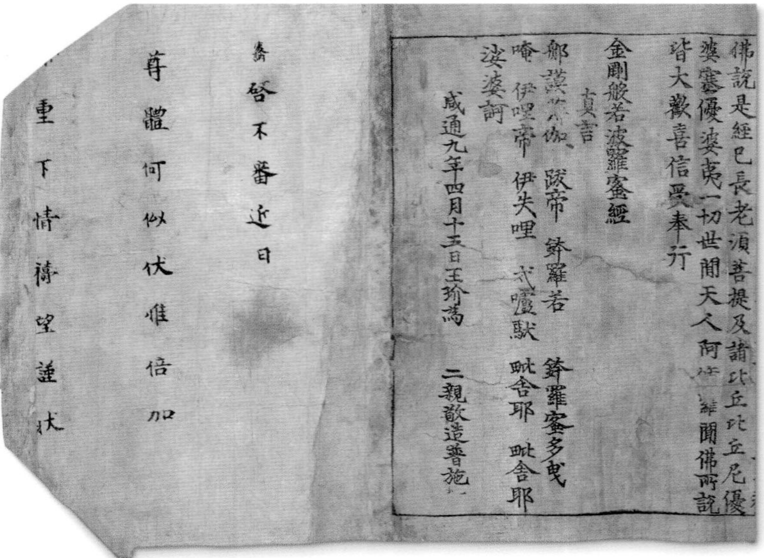

佛說是經已長老須菩提及諸比丘比丘尼優婆塞優婆夷一切世間天人阿修羅聞佛所說皆大歡喜信受奉行

金剛般若波羅蜜經

真言

咸通九年四月十五日王玠為 二親敬造普施

◄ **EXACT DATE** At the foot of the scroll is an inscription, or colophon, which reads: "Reverently made for universal free distribution by Wang Jie on behalf of his two parents, 11 May 868". Such precise dating of the time of commissioning makes this scroll unique.

▼ **LARGE SCALE** Due to the length of the text, it was created in seven sections that were then pasted together. The scroll was designed to be unrolled from a wooden pin, or stave, and to be read, top down, from left to right. Reciting the Sutra was intended to help bring happiness in rebirth.

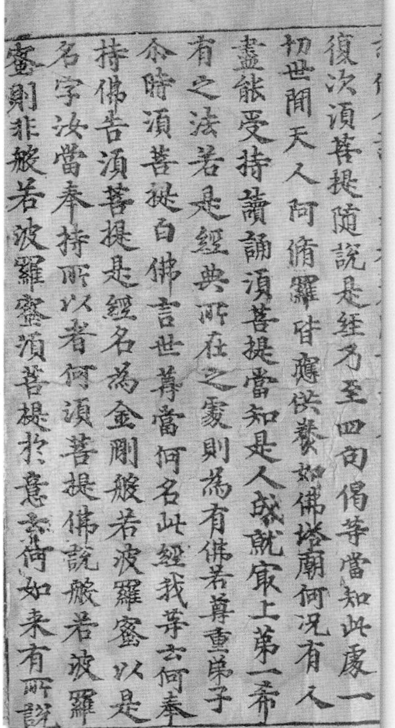

復次須菩提隨說是經乃至四句偈等當知此處一
切世間天人阿脩羅皆應供養如佛塔廟何況有人
盡能受持讀誦須菩提當知是人成就最上第一希
有之法若是經典所在之處則為有佛若尊重弟子
爾時須菩提白佛言世尊當何名此經我等云何奉
持佛告須菩提是經名為金剛般若波羅蜜以是
名字汝當奉持所以者何須菩提佛說般若波羅
蜜則非般若波羅蜜須菩提於意云何如來有所說

▲ **EARLY PRINTING** Following the printing methods used in 9th-century Tang China, wood blocks (painstakingly carved from painted originals) were used to print onto a paper dyed with a substance made from the bark of the Amur cork tree. Nothing comparable would be produced in Europe for another 600 years until the arrival of Gutenberg's Printing Press.

> All conditional phenomena are like a dream, an illusion, a bubble, a shadow
>
> **THE *DIAMOND SUTRA***

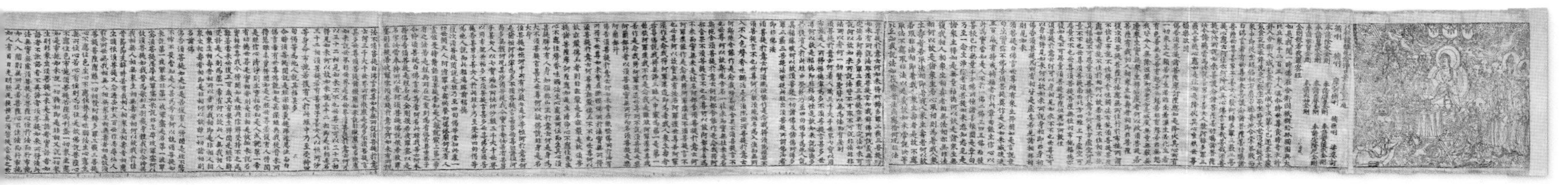

The Exeter Book

C.975 CE ■ VELLUM ■ 32 × 22 cm (12 × 9 in) ■ 131 PAGES ■ ENGLAND

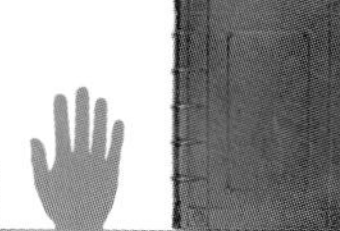

SCALE

AUTHOR UNKNOWN

The largest and most varied collection of medieval Anglo-Saxon poetry, *The Exeter Book* is one of only four Anglo-Saxon collections of poetry to survive. Most likely written around the end of the 10th century, it has been described by UNESCO as "the foundation volume of English literature, one of the world's principal cultural artefacts". The book takes its name from Exeter Cathedral, to whose library Bishop Leofric bequeathed the volume at his death in 1072. It was written in the scriptorium of an English Benedictine monastery and has no single theme, but contains poems and riddles. The poems cover a wide variety of subjects – religion, the natural world, and animals. There are also several "elegies" concerned with themes such as exile, loneliness, fate, the acquisition of wisdom, and loyalty. Famously, the book contains almost 100 riddles, possibly intended to be performed. Some are unclear in their meaning, but a handful are plainly intended as lewd double entendres. Scholars have identified many elements of the book's religious and secular poems as dating from centuries before their written form, some of which may originate in the 7th century CE.

Written on vellum in Old English, the book is testimony to the civilizing influence of the Church, specifically of the oldest monastic order in England, the Benedictines, and to the emerging Anglo-Saxon taste for literature and the power of the written word. As such, it is a glimpse into the Anglo-Saxon culture of post-Roman Britain, and sheds light on the monastic enclosure where it was scribed. As a literary work its impact can be seen in the work of writers, such as J.R.R Tolkien (1892–1973) and W.H. Auden (1907–73).

➤ **SINGLE SCRIBE** *The Exeter Book* is the work of one scribe. It is penned in a sombre brown ink, in what one expert has described as "the noblest of Anglo-Saxon hands". The calligraphy – regular, rhythmic, and rounded – is extraordinarily consistent throughout. While the book contains no illustrations, there are, however, a number of soberly restrained decorated capital letters, as shown here.

In detail

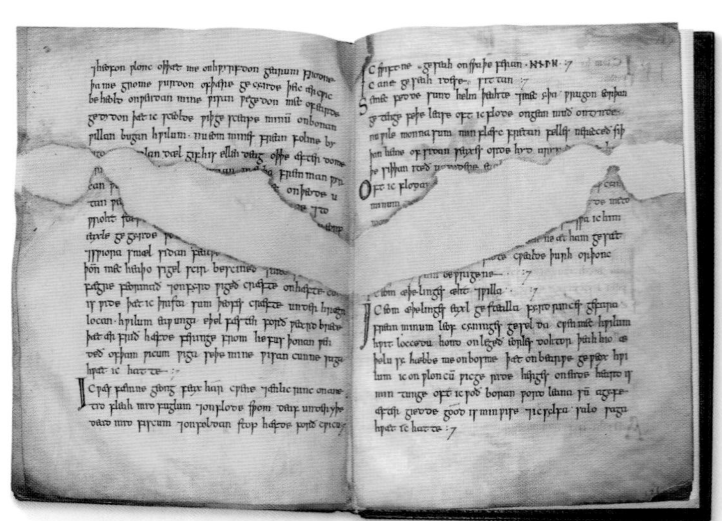

▲ **DAMAGED PAGES** *The Exeter Book* did not always receive the care it deserved. Its first eight pages are missing, while other pages have been damaged. Those shown here, for example, were burned when a firebrand was placed on it. The book has also been marked by spillages of glue and gold leaf, as well as a large gash and a sewn-up tear.

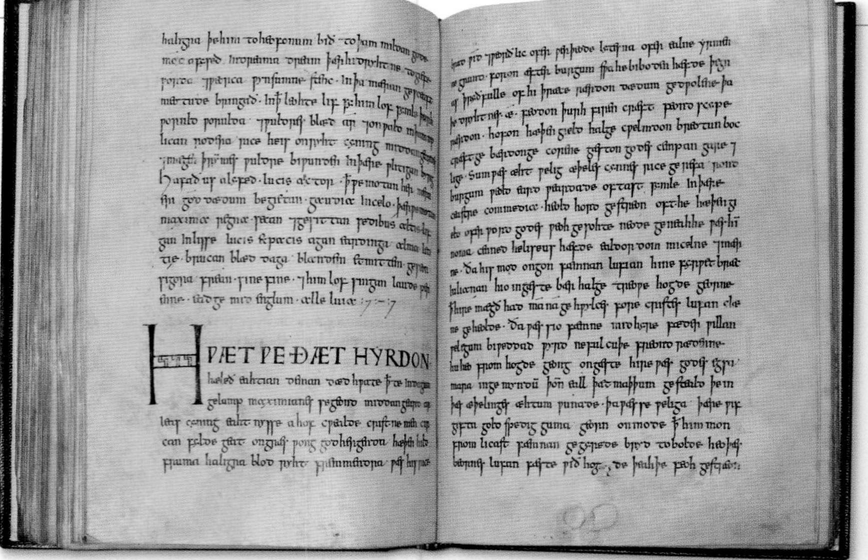

▲ **LATIN ALPHABET** The Old English script uses the Latin alphabet, with a number of letters, such as "G" and "D", written in a form principally found in manuscripts from the British Isles. A large "H" indicates the start of one of the longest poems in the book: an account of St Juliana of Nicomedia (in modern-day Turkey), an early Christian convert martyred in about 300 CE having refused to renounce her faith and marry a Roman senator. The poem is characteristic of the medieval world's veneration of early Christian martyrs.

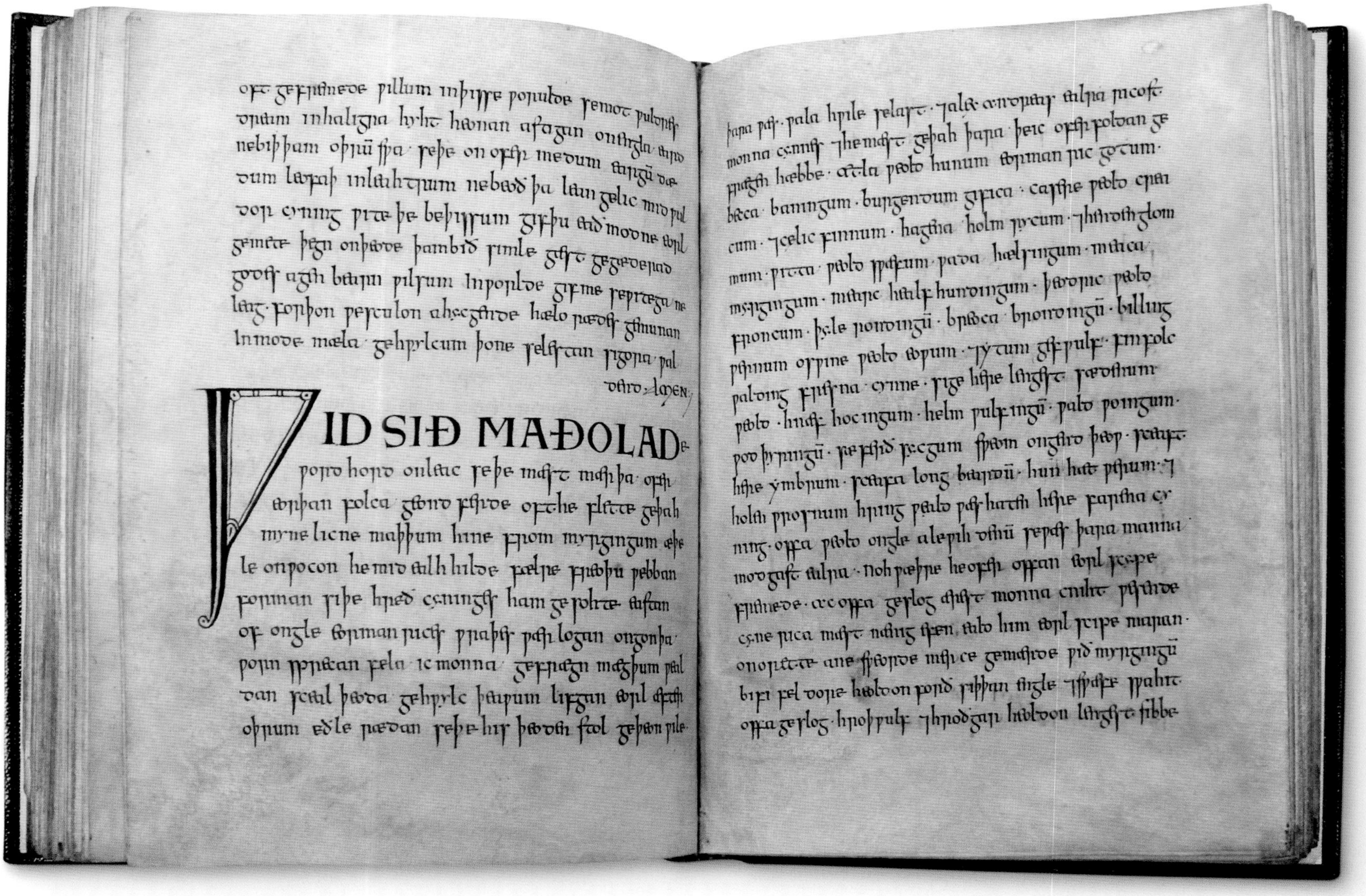

> The wonder is that any part of it should have survived
>
> **R.W. CHAMBERS**, FRIEND OF J.R.R. TOLKIEN

RELATED **TEXTS**

While *The Exeter Book* contains the largest and most important collection of Anglo-Saxon poetry, the best-known single Anglo-Saxon poem is the 3,000-line epic *Beowulf*. It seems likely that this poem was composed in the 8th century, although it clearly reflects an earlier, possibly 6th-century oral tradition. The single existing original Anglo-Saxon copy seems to have been written in about 1000 CE. This classic story, which tells how the great warrior Beowulf slew the terrible monster Grendel and his equally fearsome mother, accurately reflects the Anglo-Saxons' Germanic origins. It is a compellingly rich picture of honour and heroism poised between a pagan past and a Christian future. Translated into many languages, the story has also been adapted into films, operas, and computer games.

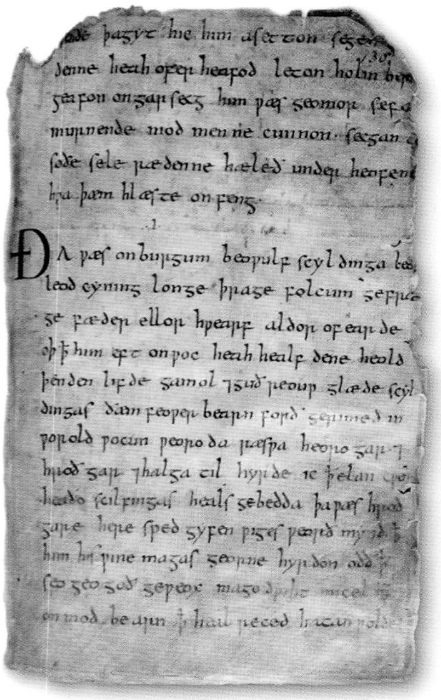

➤ **The sole, fragile copy** of *Beowulf* is held in the British Library. It is the work of two scribes, their handwriting clearly distinguishable. It is unknown where in England the manuscript was originally produced.

Directory: 3000 BCE–999 CE

RIGVEDA

INDIA (C.1500 BCE)

Originally passed down via oral tradition, The *Rigveda* is the oldest of the four ancient Hindu sacred texts, known collectively as the *Vedas*. The book is a collection of hymns dedicated to the Vedic deities. The longest and most important of the *Vedas*, it was probably composed in the northwestern region of the Indian subcontintent, and is written in an ancient form of Sanksrit. It comprises 1,028 hymns and 10,600 verses of varying lengths, which have been divided into 10 books known as *mandalas* (or "circles"). The *Vedas* are the basis of all Hindu sacred writings, and some hymns of the *Rigveda* are still used in Hindu ceremonies today, making it one of the world's oldest religious texts still in current usage.

THE ILIAD AND THE ODYSSEY

HOMER

GREECE (LATE 8TH–EARLY 7TH CENTURY BCE)

These two ancient Greek epic poems dating from the late 8th to the early 7th century BCE, are the oldest known works of Western literature. *The Iliad* is set during the Trojan War, while *The Odyssey* describes Odysseus's journey home following the Fall of Troy. Both poems are attributed to the poet Homer, although some scholars believe they are the work of multiple contributors but ascribed to a single identity: Homer. The poems were written in a dialect known as Homeric Greek and more copies exist than of any other ancient Western text. The most famous, *Venetus A*, dates to the 10th century and is the oldest complete text of *The Iliad*.

The science of the erotics from a *Kama Sutra* of the Pahari school, Northern India.

TORAH

ISRAEL (C.LATE 7TH CENTURY BCE)

The most important document of the Jewish faith, the Torah is said to have been dictated by God to Moses while on Mount Sinai. The text on a Torah scroll is taken from the first five books of the Hebrew Bible (the Old Testament) and is handwritten on parchment from a kosher animal. The writing of the scrolls is believed to date to the eighth century BCE but the oldest complete scroll in existence dates to 1155–1225 CE. Parts of the Torah text have also been found on fragments of a Hebrew Bible dating back to the late 7th century BCE.

THE ANALECTS

CONFUCIUS

CHINA (WRITTEN C.475–221 BCE; ADAPTED 206 BCE–220 CE)

This collection of the teachings of the Chinese philosopher Confucius (551–479 BCE) is one of the central texts of Confucianism. Written with brush and ink on strips of bamboo bound together with string, *The Analects* was complied by Confucius's followers after his death. While it is unlikely to be a record of the exact words of Confucius, it is considered to be a representation of his doctrine. *The Analects* is made up of a series of short passages divided into 20 books, and encompasses ethical concepts for the Confucian way of life. During the Song Dynasty (960–1279) *The Analects* was classified as one of the four texts that encapsulate the core beliefs of Confucianism.

THE HISTORIES

HERODOTUS

GREECE (C.440 BCE)

Written by the ancient Greek historian Herodotus (c.484–c.425 BCE), *The Histories* is widely acknowledged to be the earliest existing work of history in the West. It examines the growth of the Persian Empire, the events that lead to the Graeco-Persian Wars (499–449 BCE), and the eventual defeat of the Persians. Herodotus also describes the belief systems and spiritual practices of these ancient civilizations. The oldest existing complete manuscript of *The Histories* dates to the 10th century CE, but much older papyri fragments have been found, primarily in Egypt. This text is considered to have established the genre of history writing in Western culture.

TAO TE CHING

CHINA (C.4TH CENTURY BCE)

A classic text of Chinese philosophical literature, the *Tao Te Ching* (or *Dao De Jing*) is the basis for philosophical and religious Taoism. Most scholars attribute it to the Chinese sage and teacher Lao Tzu. However, little is known about him and some argue that he never even existed. The text was originally written in a form of calligraphy known as "zhuanshu", and comprised 81 short, poetic chapters divided into two sections: the *Tao Ching* and the *Te Ching*. Versions of the manuscript have been discovered written on bamboo, silk, and paper. The oldest fragments date to the 4th century BCE, yet some scholars believe the *Tao Te Ching* may have existed as far back as the 8th century BCE. It has been translated into western languages more than 250 times and is considered one of the most profound philosophical texts on the nature of human existence.

THE SYMPOSIUM AND THE REPUBLIC

PLATO

GREECE (C.385–370 BCE)

These are two of the 36 dialogues written by the Classical Greek philosopher Plato (c.428–c.348 BCE). Plato's dialogues were grouped into early, middle, and late periods, and both of these texts fall into the middle period. It is through his dialogues that Plato gives voice to Socrates, the founding father of Western philosophy and Plato's mentor, who was executed for his beliefs. Socrates is given a central role in Plato's philosophical works, and much of what is known about Socrates today comes from these dialogues.

The Symposium is a fundamental philosophical treatise on the nature of love, which it examines through a witty discussion between a group of men at a *symposium* (an ancient Greek "drinking party") with Socrates at the centre. This philosophical and literary masterpiece has influenced generations of writers and thinkers, and provides the basis of the concept of "platonic love" – a deep but non-sexual love between two people.

The Republic is by far the most famous and widely read of Plato's dialogues, and is considered to be one of the world's most influential works of philosophy. This dialogue discusses the meaning of justice – asking what it is and considering whether the just or the unjust man is happiest. Again Socrates is the central character. *The Republic* is a key document in the history of Western political philosophy.

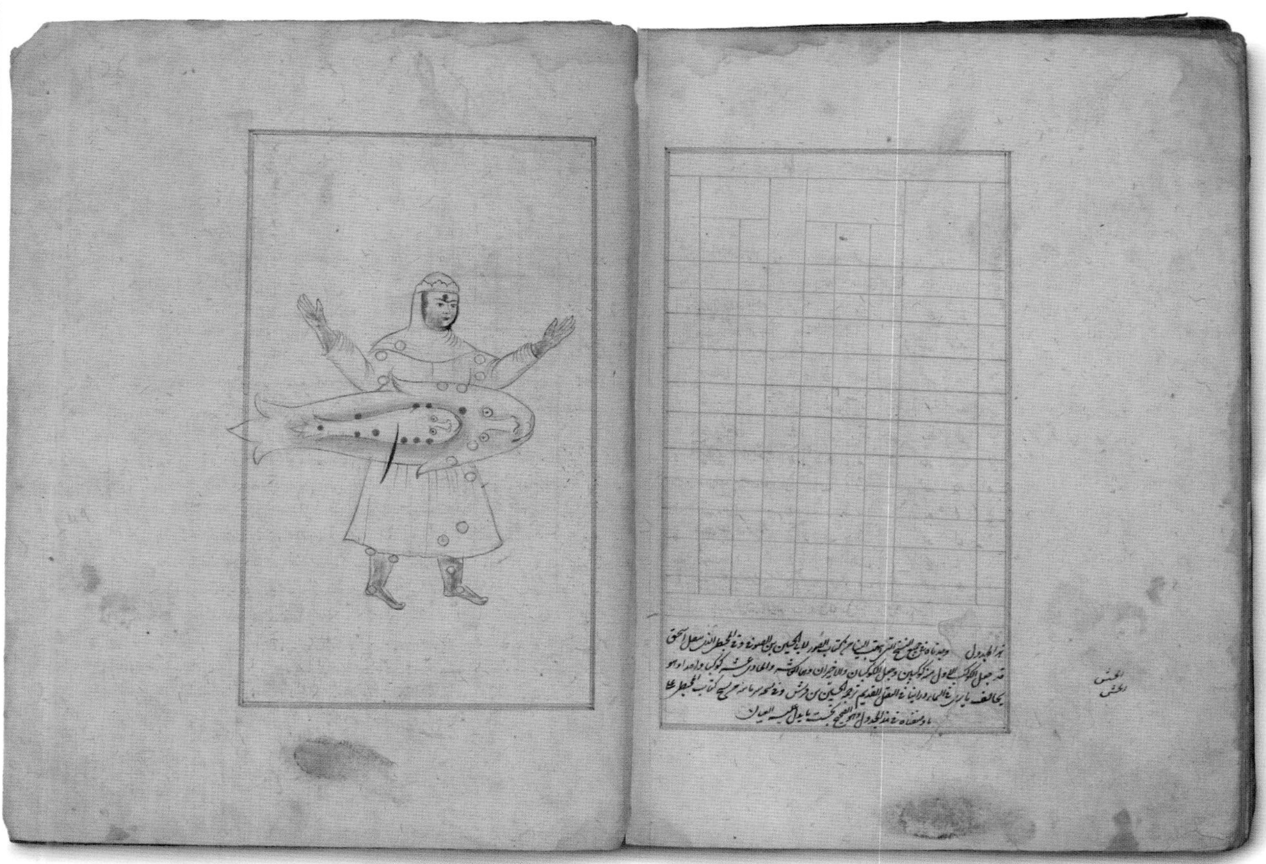

Andromeda with a fish across her waist representing the Andromeda Galaxy, from the *Book of the Constellations of Fixed Stars*.

◄ KAMA SUTRA
MALLANAGA VĀTSYĀYANA

INDIA (200–400 CE)

This ancient Sanskrit text was compiled by Hindu philosopher and sage Mallanaga Vātsyāyana and is considered the first comprehensive work on human sexuality. It comprises 36 chapters of 1,250 verses, which are then separated into seven parts. The text acts as a guide to good and fulfilled living, the nature of love, and how to create a happy marriage through a combination of physical and emotional love. In Western society *The Kama Sutra* has come to be a by-word for a sex manual, but in reality the original manuscript, written in a complex form of Sanskrit, was a treatise on love in which the 64 sexual positions described form only a small part. It was published with an English translation in 1883 by the British explorer Sir Richard Burton.

DUNHUANG MANUSCRIPTS

CHINA (5TH–11TH CENTURIES CE)

An important collection of around 60,000 sacred and secular documents, the *Dunhuang Manuscripts* were discovered in 1900 by the Chinese monk Wang Yuanlu in a cave in the town of Dunhuang, China. Believed to have been sealed up for 900 years, the manuscripts date to between the 5th and 11th centuries. They were primarily written in Chinese and Tibetan, but examples of 17 different languages are represented, some now extinct, such as Old Uyghur and Old Turkic. The sacred texts include Buddhist scriptures, as well as Taoist, Nestorian Christian, and Manichean writings. The secular manuscripts cover a wide range of academic disciplines, such as mathematics, astronomy, history, and literature, as well as wills, divorce papers, and census registers, so provide scholars with invaluable insight into the period. Perhaps the most important discovery was the world's earliest example of a printed book – the *Diamond Sutra* (see pp.46–47), a Buddhist text written in 868 CE.

THE KOJIKI
O NO YASUMARO

JAPAN (C.712 CE)

The oldest existing written record of Japanese history, *The Kojiki* (or *Record of Ancient Matters*) was compiled from an oral tradition. The author, O no Yasumaro, was commissioned to write it by the Empress Genmei. *The Kojiki* begins with the mythology of Japan's creation (supposedly from foam) and goes on to discuss gods and goddesses, historical legends, poems, and songs; it also provides a chronology of the Imperial line from its beginning up to the reign of Empress Suiko (628 CE). The book divides into three parts: the *Kamitsumaki* (the age of the gods), the *Nakatsumaki* (from Emperors Jimmu to Ojin, the 15th) and the *Shimontsumaki* (continuing up to Suioko, the 33rd Emperor). Shinto, the national religion of Japan, is believed to be largely based on the mythology outlined in *The Kojiki*. When the book was compiled there was no written Japanese language, so the text uses Chinese characters to interpret the Japanese sounds, a writing system known as *Man'yōgana*. *The Kojiki* was first translated into English in 1882.

▲ BOOK OF THE CONSTELLATIONS OF FIXED STARS
ABD AL-RAHMAN AL-SUFI

IRAN (964 CE)

This treatise, known in Arabic as *Kitāb suwar al-kawākib al-thābita*, was composed by Persian astronomer Abd al-Rahman al-Sufi (903–986). Earlier, the Greek astronomer Ptolemy (100–168 CE), had constructed an elegant mathematical model of the movement of the heavens as spheres rotating around the unmoving Earth. Al-Sufi's book was a brilliant attempt to combine the theories proposed in Ptolemy's *Almagest*, (one of the sources of al-Sufi's text), with his own astronomical observations. The book presents tables listing the names of hundreds of stars as well as descriptions of the 48 constellations, known as Fixed Stars, which, according to the medieval conception of the universe, inhabited the eighth of the nine spheres around the Earth. Each description is accompanied by two illustrations in mirror image, showing how the constellation appears in the sky and through astronomical instruments.

CHAPTER 2

1000 — 1449

- The Tale of Genji
- The Canon of Medicine
- The Domesday Book
- The Gospels of Henry the Lion
- Les Très Riches Heures du Duc de Berry

The Tale of Genji

1021 CE (WRITTEN), 1554 CE (VERSION SHOWN) ▪ SIX PAPER SCROLLS ▪ DIMENSIONS UNKNOWN, ORIGINAL SCROLL c.137 m (450 ft) LONG ▪ JAPAN

MURASAKI SHIKIBU

The crowning glory of Japanese literature, *The Tale of Genji* (*Genji monogatari*) by noblewoman Murasaki Shikibu is often considered to be the world's first full novel. Although the original manuscript has been lost, fragments of the text are preserved on a 12th-century illustrated hand scroll. Later depictions of the story such as the scrolls shown here, created in the 16th century by female *Genji* artist and scholar Keifukuin Gyokuei (1526–after 1602) – were based on edited versions of the manuscripts made by two Japanese poets in the 13th century.

The long and complex, two-part narrative is largely set in the imperial court of early 11th-century Heian-Kyō (now Kyōto), and features over 400 characters. However, 41 of the 54 chapters tell the adventures and romantic liaisons of Genji, the emperor's son. Murasaki wrote *Genji* while serving as an attendant at the Japanese court, and part of its appeal lies in her vivid portrayal of the rivalries and intrigues of this rarefied world; Heian courtiers were obsessed with rank and breeding, and were acutely attuned to the beauty of nature and the pleasures of music, poetry, and calligraphy. The book is also revered for its great psychological insights. The suffering endured by its major female characters – Genji's myriad lovers – is described with great sympathy; none more so than that of Murasaki, Genji's favourite wife, who dies of a broken heart. But the novel's main theme is the impermanence of life, its fleeting pleasures, and the inevitability of grief. Even in modern Japan, *Genji* remains a cultural icon.

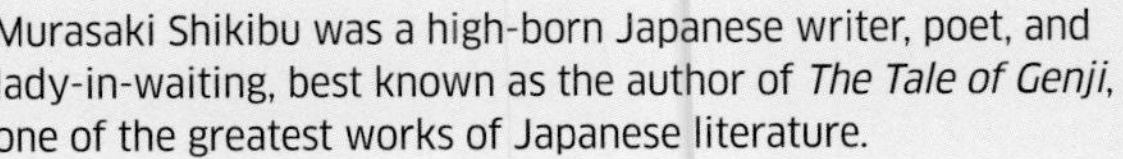

MURASAKI **SHIKIBU**

c.978–1014

Murasaki Shikibu was a high-born Japanese writer, poet, and lady-in-waiting, best known as the author of *The Tale of Genji*, one of the greatest works of Japanese literature.

Murasaki Shikibu, a descriptive name, was born in Kyōto into one of Japan's leading families (the Fujiwara clan) – her real name is not known. She received a good education before marrying one of her cousins, with whom she had a daughter. In 1001 Murasaki's husband died, and four years later she was summoned to serve at the court of the empress. Although the precise dates when she wrote her epic novel are not known, it is most likely that it was during her service at the imperial court. The first 33 chapters of *Genji* are written with extreme consistency, yet discrepancies in later chapters suggest that the latter half was written by another author.

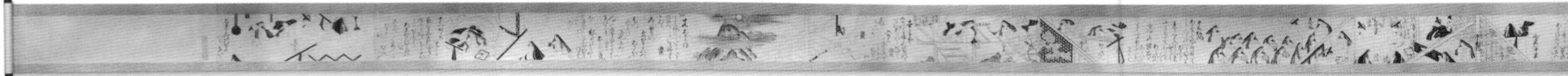

In detail

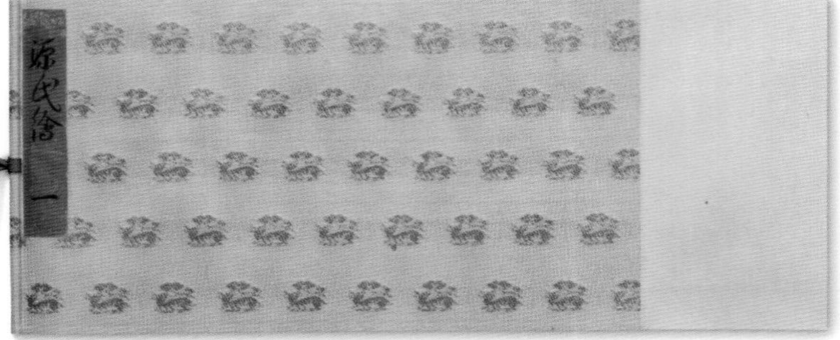

▲ ***HAKUBYO GENJI MONOGATARI EMAKI*** The hand scroll shown here, created in 1554 by aristocratic painter, Keifukuin Gyokuei, is thought to be the first version and commentary of the *Genji* prepared by a woman for female readers. Knowledge of the *Genji* was considered to be a sign of status in 16th-century Japan, and for women, it could help them to secure a favourable marriage.

▲ **SCROLL ENDS** A hand scroll is held in a reader's hands and read from right to left, as Japanese is written. The reader unfurls the left-hand portion of the scroll, which is bound around a dowel, while rolling up the right-hand portion. Typically, only an arms-length of the narrative is visible at a time. There are six scrolls in the *Hakubyo Genji Monogatari Emaki*; the ends of scroll two are shown above and left.

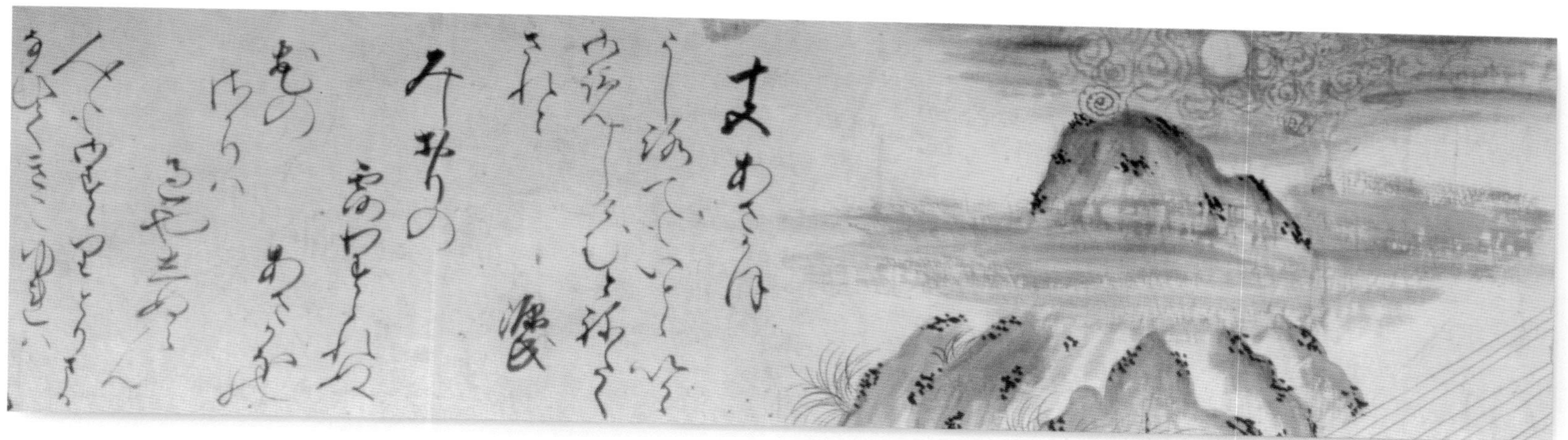

▲ **VISUAL NARRATIVE** The *Hakubyo Genji Monogatari Emaki* features a number of different, highly stylized forms of calligraphy that have long held a cult following in Japan. Designed for visual appeal rather than legibility, it renders the text almost impossible to read.

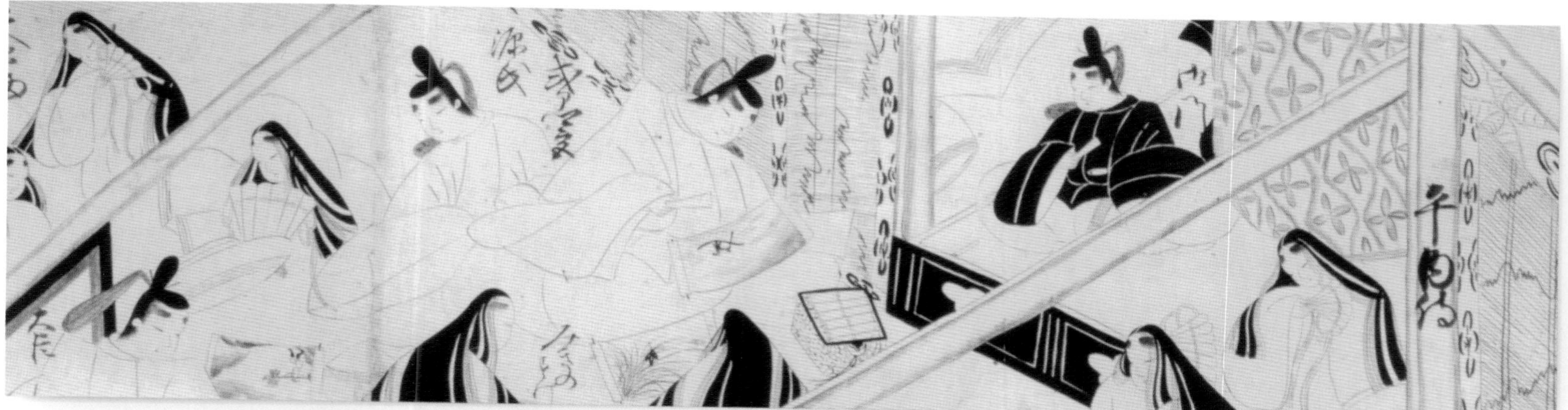

▲ **SCENE WITH COURTIERS** Many illustrations in the *Genji* depict scenes occurring inside buildings at the Heian court, seen from above, as if the roof has been removed (as shown here). It gives the reader a sense of watching events unfold as they happen, as described in the accompanying text.

▼ **WHOLE OF SCROLL TWO** Illustrated hand scrolls play an important role in the tradition of Japanese story telling. From the 12th century wealthy patrons commissioned them for their own pleasure, and *The Tale of Genji* was one of the most popular narratives.

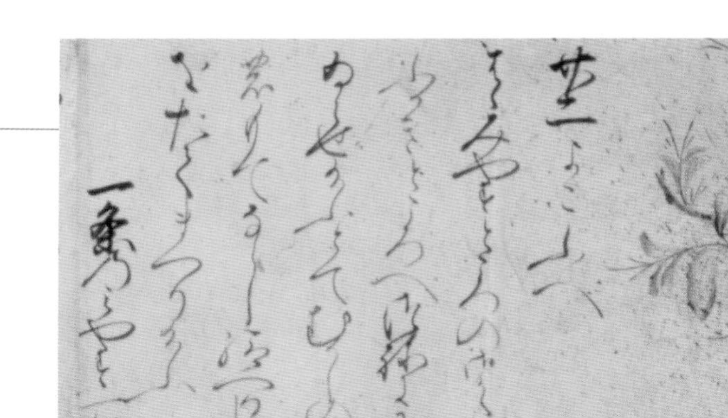

▲ ***HIRAGANA* SCRIPT** The phonetic script in which *Genji* was written, seen here on the scroll, was known as "women's hand". Almost colloquial, *hiragana* became the language of poetry. Highly nuanced, and rarely direct, it used imagery, such as the blooming of a flower, shown above, to convey emotions.

IN **CONTEXT**

The Tale of Genji is enduringly popular in Japan; over the past 1,000 years it has been presented with text-and-illustrations in various mediums, including scrolls, albums, books, fans, screens, and woodbock prints. The novel was revered during the Edo period (1615–1868), which saw a revival of classical Heian culture, particularly among Kyoto courtiers and merchants. More recently it has been the subject of paintings, films, operas, and animé, and modern translations have been published in Chinese, German, French, Italian, and English.

► **This vividly coloured** 17th-century painting depicts a scene in chapter five, "Young Murasaki".

Canon of Medicine

1025 CE (WRITTEN), 1600s (VERSION SHOWN) ▪ PAPER ▪ DIMENSIONS UNKNOWN ▪ 814 PAGES ▪ PERSIA

IBN SĪNĀ

Considered a landmark in the history of medicine, *Al-Qānūn fi al-Tibb*, or the *Canon of Medicine*, was written in 1025 by Persian polymath, Ibn Sīnā. It became a standard reference source for medical practitioners in both the Islamic world and the universities of Europe until the 18th century.

A vast work of over half a million words, the *Canon of Medicine* surveyed the entire field of known medical knowledge, including the work of Galen of Pergamum (129–216 CE), and ancient Arabian and Persian texts. It examined diseases of every part of the body, while also recommending herbal cures and surgical interventions. It was the first book to lay out principles for experimental and evidence-based medicine, and to spell out protocols for testing new drugs. Ibn Sīnā wrote it in five distinct volumes, each addressing a different aspect of medicine. Book I covers the theory of medicine; Book II looks at simple, medically active substances; Book III describes diseases of each organ; Book IV looks at whole body diseases; and Book V is a directory of 650 drugs.

As well as bringing together existing knowledge, the work also contained some of Ibn Sīnā's own highly perceptive insights. He was the first to recognize that tuberculosis is contagious; that diseases can spread through soil and water; that a person's emotions can affect their state of physical health; and that nerves transmit both pain and signals for muscle contraction.

The *Canon* was first translated into Latin in the 12th century and adopted by the faculty of medicine at the University of Bologna in the 13th century. Between 1500 and 1674 some 60 editions of part or all of the *Canon* were published. The pages shown here are from a 17th-century Arabic edition, thought to have been copied from Ibn Sīnā's original writings.

IBN **SINA**

c.980–1037

Known in the West by the Latin name Avicenna, Ibn Sīnā was a Persian polymath and physician, and one of most significant thinkers and prolific writers of Islamic Golden Age.

Abū 'Alī al-Husayn ibn 'Abd Allāh ibn Sīnā was born in Bukhara (modern-day Uzbekistan). He knew the Qur'an by heart by the age of 10, studied Greek and mathematics as a teenager, and by 16 was a qualified physician. He spent some years working in medicine before being appointed as a minister to a prince in Buyid (an area of modern-day Iran). He wrote about 450 books, of which 250 survive. His body of work includes *The Book of Healing*, a landmark book on philosophy, writings on astronomy, geography, mathematics, alchemy, and physics, as well as medicine. In the latter period of his life he was in service to a governor in Persia who sponsored much of his work.

In detail

▲ **ELABORATE DECORATION** Many pages of this edition are illuminated with coloured ink and gold leaf. Showing motifs from Islamic architecture, they may have been added at a later date.

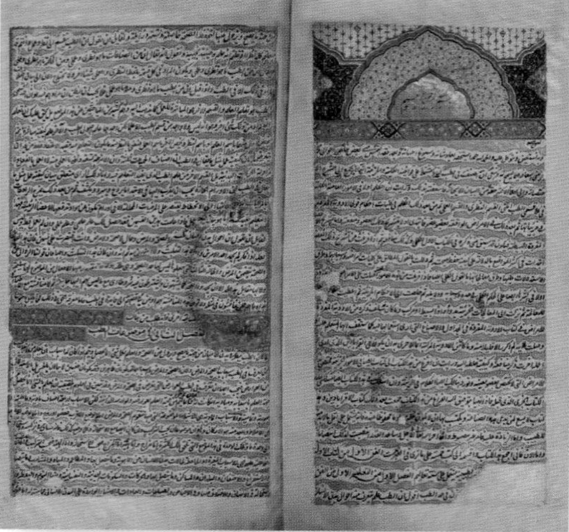

▲ **THE PREFACE** In this text Ibn Sina describes the task of the physician in preserving the well-being of his patient, and the art of restoring a person's health using the appropriate procedures and medications.

▲ **HANDWRITTEN PAGES** Printing was well established by the 17th century, but this edition written by hand was painstakingly copied directly from Ibn Sīnā's original work, indicating its importance.

▲ **COMPREHENSIVE DIRECTORY OF MEDICATIONS** These pages come from Book V, in which Ibn Sīnā described hundreds of drugs, attributing them to Arabic, Indian, and Greek sources. He included ingredients and recipes, and added his comments on the effectiveness of the remedies.

Therefore in medicine we ought to know the causes of sickness and health

IBN SĪNĀ, ON MEDICINE, C.1020

IN **CONTEXT**

Ibn Sīnā's original text was translated into Latin in around 1140 by Italian scholar, Gerard of Cremona (1114–87). Cremona travelled to Toledo in Spain, a seat of Islamic learning, specifically to learn Arabic in order to translate Ptolemy's *Almagest* – a study of astronomy. He was one of the most prolific translators of Arabic texts, completing around 80 works. In addition to the *Canon of Medicine*, Cremona also translated several works by Aristotle and significantly helped to spread the wealth of Arabic knowledge.

▶ **Medical miniatures** are used to illustrate a range of health problems in this 14th-century version of Gerard's Latin translation.

The Domesday Book

1086 ■ PARCHMENT ■ LITTLE DOMESDAY – c.28 × 20 cm (11 × 8 in), 475 PAGES ■ GREAT DOMESDAY – c.38 × 28 cm (15 × 11 in), 413 PAGES ■ ENGLAND

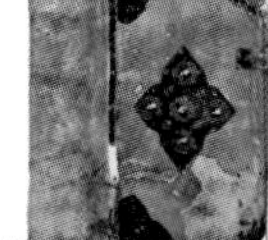

SCALE

VARIOUS SCRIBES

England's earliest surviving public record, compiled between 1085 and 1086, exists as two books known collectively as the Domesday Book. It was instigated in December 1085, when the Norman ruler William the Conqueror commissioned what was to be the largest land survey carried out in Europe until the 19th century. The king instructed his officials to prepare a land registry of all the shires, or counties, of England.

Representatives travelled across England and parts of Wales, and counted 13,418 places, or manors, within the realm. They recorded how much land, livestock, and resources each one owned, and what they were worth. By the following August, the officials began passing the information on large rolls (hence the survey's official title The Winchester Roll, or King's Roll) to the scribe to begin the compilation. There were two books: the Little Domesday Book, which is considered a first draft, includes details of three eastern counties; the Great Domesday Book, which was never fully completed, includes most counties apart from Northumberland and Durham. Both were written in Medieval Latin, a language that was used in government documents and by the Church, but that most of the population barely understood. Today both volumes are kept in a locked chest at the National Archives in Kew, London.

The reasons for commissioning the survey are unknown. William may have wanted to calculate tax due to the Crown from England's landowners, as in the 11th century English kings needed to raise money to pay a levy, known as the *Danegeld*, to protect the country from marauding Scandinavian armies. However, 1086 also marked the 20th anniversary of William's victory at the Battle of Hastings over Harold Godwinson, the last Anglo-Saxon monarch. As the Domesday Book records the land and holdings of King Edward the Confessor, who died in 1066 and those of King William, it may have been a means of legitimizing his reign – if so, it was in vain considering William died in 1087 before the project was completed. The survey was dubbed the Domesday Book because it was considered the final word on who owned what, and as such was compared with the Last Judgement, or domesday, in the Bible. Today it is valued as a key source for historians.

In detail

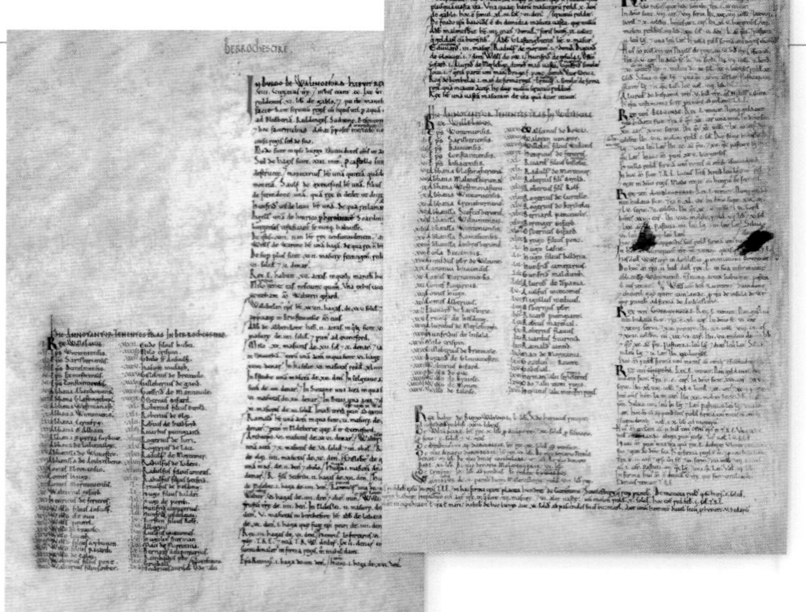

➤ **LANDOWNER LISTINGS** *(left)* Each county "chapter" begins with a list of landowners, starting with the king, followed by the bishops, abbots, and lastly those of the lay barons. Each of their lands are divided into "hundreds" (areas) and then into the manors held within it. This page for Berkshire lists 63 landowners.

➤ **MARGINAL NOTES** *(centre)* Historians believe that one scribe was responsible for compiling the Great Domesday Book, but the hand of a second scribe appears to have made some amendments. Here, the scribe was given new information after the entries were completed so it has been included as a footnote.

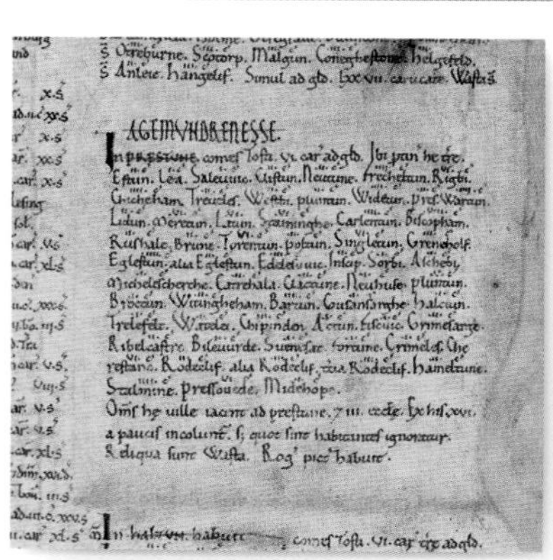

▲ **HIGHLIGHTING SUBJECTS** In order to draw the reader's attention to a word or place-name, the scribe would strike through it with a red line, as shown in this detail from the chapter on Yorkshire. This process is another form of rubrication (see right).

> ... there was no **single hide** nor a yard of **land,** nor indeed... **one ox** nor one **cow** nor one **pig** which was left out

ANGLO-SAXON CHRONICLE, 12-CENTURY ACCOUNT OF THE RECORDING OF THE DOMESDAY BOOK

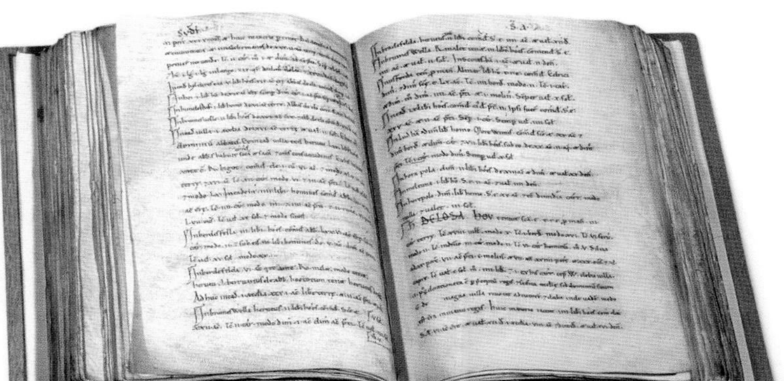

▲ **LITTLE DOMESDAY BOOK** This smaller, but longer, book covers only the counties of Essex, Norfolk, and Suffolk, and is more detailed than the Great Domesday Book, showing how much information was omitted from the latter. The text in it is also written across the page, differing from the columns used in the Great Domesday. It is thought that at least six scribes worked on it.

ON **TECHNIQUE**

Writing the Domesday Book began with the preparation of parchment from around 900 sheepskins. The skins were soaked in lime and scraped clean, then stretched over a frame and allowed to dry. Scribes prepared quills from the wing feathers of large birds, often geese. A right-handed scribe would take a feather from the left wing of the bird, as it curves to the right; a left-handed scribe would use a right wing. The plumes were cut back and the tip was placed in hot sand to strengthen it, then carved to shape. The resulting quills resembled a chisel. Scribes worked with a quill in one hand and a knife in the other to sharpen the quill and scrape away mistakes before the ink dried.

▲ **A scribe** used a small, sharp knife to shape the "nib" and cut a "slit" in the tip, like a fountain pen.

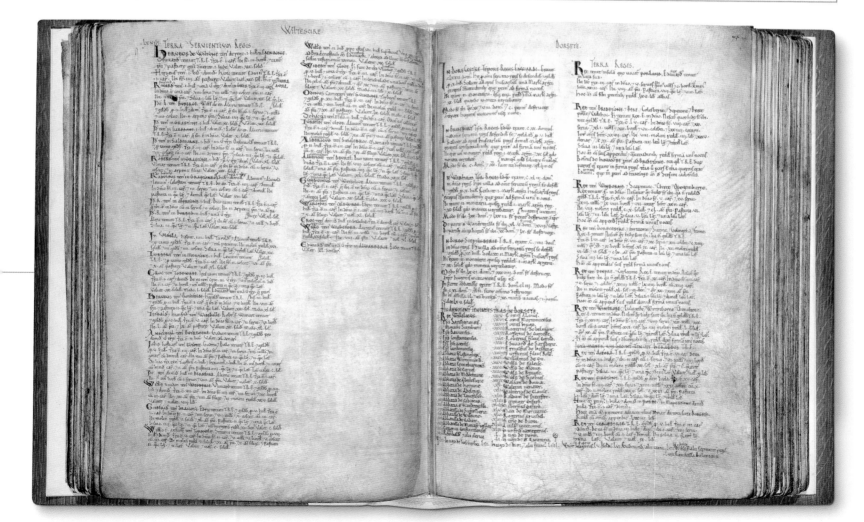

▲ **COLOUR CODING** The scribes wrote most of the Great Domesday Book, shown above, with black ink, which was made from oak galls – small fungal growths on oak bark. They used red ink, made from lead, for initial letters and numbers before a name, and for the most well-known method of rubrication, where the scribe added text in red for emphasis.

The Gospels of Henry the Lion

c.1188 ■ PARCHMENT ■ 34.2 × 25.5 cm (13 × 10 in) ■ 266 PAGES ■ GERMANY

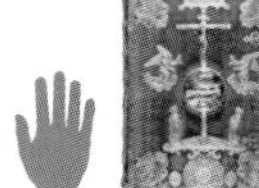

SCALE

MONKS OF HELMARSHAUSEN

One of the masterpieces of Romanesque German medieval art, *The Gospels of Henry the Lion* is an illuminated manuscript of the four biblical gospels by Matthew, Mark, Luke, and John. This work of extraordinary beauty was created by the Benedictine monks of the Helmarshausen Abbey in Germany, who were commissioned around 1188 by Henry the Lion, Duke of Saxony. It is so highly prized that when it was sold at auction by Sotheby's in 1983, a consortium paid €16 million to buy it for Germany – the highest price paid for such a book up to that time. It is now kept in the Herzog August Library in Lower Saxony, Germany, where, due to its fragile condition, it is only rarely exhibited.

The book consists of 266 parchment pages, brilliantly coloured in reds, blues, and greens. Expensive pigments and gold leaf feature extensively throughout. There are 50 full-page miniature illustrations, and every page is ornamented with either initials, decorative borders, or images. Both the exquisite calligraphy and illuminations are identified as the work of a single monk, Herimann, in the dedication, but it is possible that he led a team.

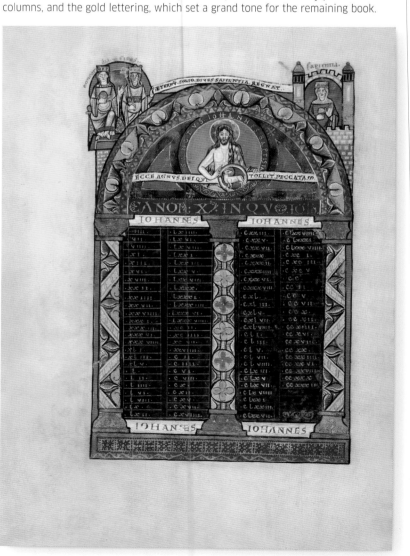

HENRY **THE LION**

c.1129–95

The Duke of Saxony and Bavaria, Henry was one of the Welf dynasty's most powerful princes. A patron of the arts, Henry founded several cities, the most notable being Munich in Bavaria.

When Henry was made Duke, first of Saxony (1142), then Bavaria (1156), he became one of the most powerful rulers in the Holy Roman Empire, second only to the Emperor Frederick Barbarossa, his cousin. His first marriage, to Clementia of Zähringen, was annulled under pressure from the Emperor who felt it made Henry too powerful; in 1168, he married 12-year-old English Princess Matilda. Henry and Matilda presided over a time of expansion and cultural enrichment for Saxony and Bavaria, including the founding of Munich and the building of Brunswick Cathedral. In later years, Henry's relationship with the Emperor soured and he was twice forced into exile and eventually deprived of his dukedoms. His nickname came from the bronze lion made for his castle in Brunswick. There is also a legend of a loyal lion that accompanied Henry on his pilgrimage to the Holy Land, and refused to eat after he died.

The *Gospels* was commissioned by Henry in honour of the recently completed Brunswick Cathedral, and was intended for the altar in the chapel of St Mary. Henry may have been inspired to commission the manuscript when he and his young wife Matilda, daughter of Henry II and Eleanor of Aquitaine, were in exile in England in the early 1180s, with time to strengthen their biblical appreciation.

▼ **DECORATIVE CANON TABLE** This canon table – the final of five at the beginning of the *Gospels* – depicts John the Baptist in the upper centre as he points to the Lamb of God. The detail, however, is in the intricately patterned columns, and the gold lettering, which set a grand tone for the remaining book.

Peter, this book is the work of thy monk Herimann 

THE MONK HERIMANN, AN INVOCATION TO ST PETER FROM THE PREFACE OF *THE GOSPELS OF HENRY THE LION*

◄ **ORNATE BINDING** The book was rebound with red silk velvet and elaborate brasswork in 1594, reflecting its perceived value in the 16th century. Beneath the silver gilt crucifix are figures of the Virgin Mary and St John. They stand on the hill of Golgotha, on which the skull of Adam is visible. Below this is the coat of arms of the Dean of St Vitus Cathedral in Prague. The crystal dome at its centre contains relics of St Mark and St Sigismund.

In detail

◄ **WORDS OF ST JEROME** The Latin translation used in the book was written in 383 CE by St Jerome. The preface by St Jerome dedicates the *Gospels* to his patron, the Blessed Pope Damasus, and opens with a beautiful illuminated "B" for *Beatus*, meaning "blessed" (above).

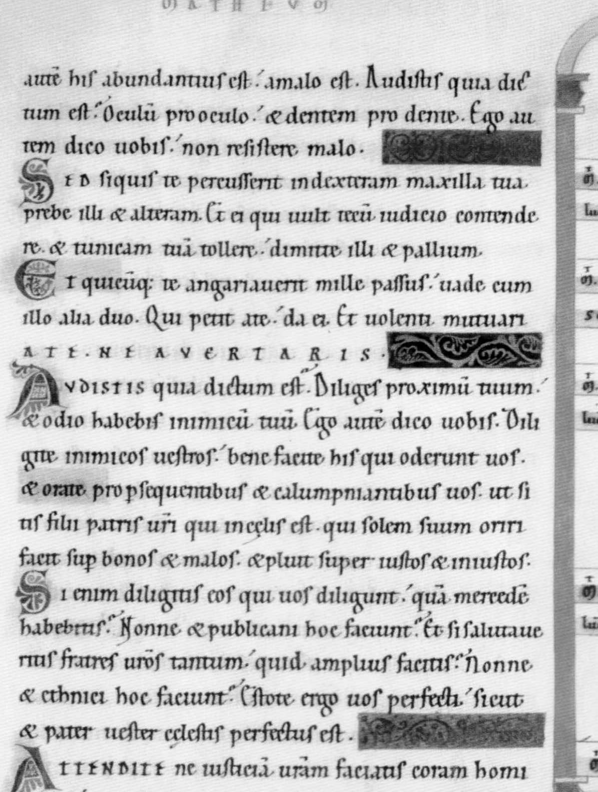

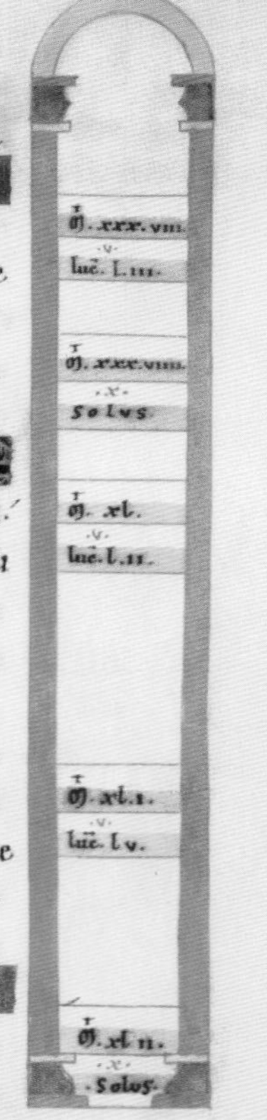

◄ **ATTENTION TO DETAIL** This page, though less lavish than most, is rich in coloured details, with five small illuminated capitals, three friezes, and a romanesque arch. Herimann would have written the black text first, leaving space for the illustration to be added afterwards. More complex illustrations would be sketched out on wax tablets, then traced onto the manuscript before being coloured in. The glorious pigments in illuminated manuscripts, such as in these *Gospels* – the vivid reds, blues, and greens – were intended to reflect God's glory.

▲ **SPIRITUAL CORONATION** The most famous illustration in the Gospels shows the coronation of Henry and Matilda (bottom left), with Christ placing the crown on Henry's head. As Henry was never crowned, the crown may be symbolic of eternal life, a reward for his part in commissioning the book. The upper frieze shows Christ with eight saints, and these include Thomas Becket, whose death Matilda's father, Henry II, was implicated in – a gesture of atonement. The right-hand page shows Christ with the four gospel writers and six roundels with images of the Creation.

… a national treasure that was witness to the emergence of the German nation

MR HERMANN ABS, THE PURCHASERS' SPOKESMAN AT THE SOTHEBY'S AUCTION, 1983

Les Très Riches Heures du Duc de Berry

c.1412–16 ▪ VELLUM ▪ 29 × 21 cm (11 × 8 in) ▪ 206 BOUND SHEETS ▪ FRANCE

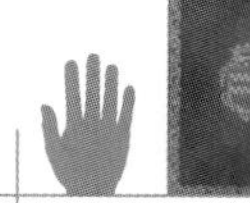

SCALE

LIMBOURG BROTHERS

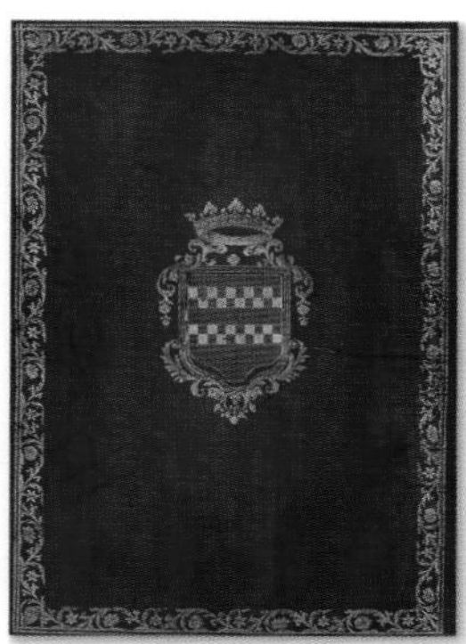

The crowning achievement of illuminated book illustration, *Les Très Riches Heures du Duc de Berry* is the finest surviving example of a medieval "book of hours": a compendium of prayers, Bible verses, psalms, and other Church texts designed for private use by lay people rather than clergy. These pocket-sized volumes became widely popular in the 14th century, and by the 1500s were being mass-produced by scribes and illuminators who hand-painted them with decorative letters, borders, and miniatures in glowing, vibrant colours. Many books of hours were modestly decorated, but others were luxurious status symbols that reflected both the piety and wealth of their owners.

The *Très Riches Heures*, commissioned by the French prince Jean, duc de Berry, was created between 1412 and 1416 by three Dutch illuminators known as the Limbourg brothers. The book is large and elaborate, with Latin text skillfully interwoven with naturalistic illustrations. Many of its 206 folios of vellum boast full-page paintings, as well as 132 exquisite miniatures. There are scenes from the Bible and the lives of the saints, but the best-known section is a beautiful liturgical calendar, illustrated with the "Labours of the Months", which, seen from the perspective of an aristocrat, offers an idealized view of social and economic life in early 15th-century feudal Europe. The calendar's 12 full-page miniatures show the seasonal activities performed by the duke and his court, and the peasants who worked on his land. In 1416 all three brothers and the duke died, and the book was left unfinished. It then passed through the hands of several owners before being completed by artist Jean Colombe (1430–93) in around 1485, although other painters may have worked on it. Held by France's Musée Condé, a facsimile is on display to prevent light damaging the original.

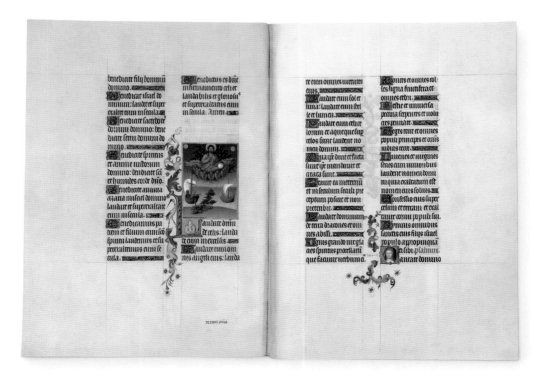

JEAN DE FRANCE, **DUC DE BERRY**

1340–1416

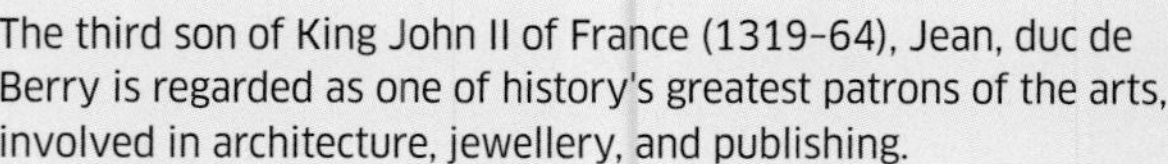

The third son of King John II of France (1319–64), Jean, duc de Berry is regarded as one of history's greatest patrons of the arts, involved in architecture, jewellery, and publishing.

Jean de France was a wealthy and powerful aristocrat, who was awarded the duchies of Berry and Auvergne, and later Poitou. Throughout his life, the duke was an active sponsor of the arts and invested a fortune in the acquisition of beautiful artefacts, including jewellery, fine fabrics, tapestries, paintings, and illuminated manuscripts. He commissioned many of the pieces in his collection of treasures, and was always highly involved in the artistic process. Yet the duke's lifestyle was extravagant and profligate, and the heavy taxes he imposed on his lands to support the war made him unpopular, leading to a peasants' revolt in 1381–84. By the time that he died, his estate was so impoverished that it was unable to pay for his funeral.

◄ **ILLUMINATED PSALMS** The vivid illustrations throughout *Les Très Riches Heures* serve to convey both God's power and his message. Here Jesus Christ is depicted holding a globe, hovering above the land and sea, demonstrating his dominion over Earth.

▼ **OPENING OF THE LITANIES** This large double-page miniature appears at the beginning of the book's litanies – a structured series of prayers or invocations used in church services and processions. Litanies were also used at a time of crisis, as shown in this illumination, which depicts the newly elected Pope Gregory (reigned 590–604) leading a vast procession through the city of Rome, during an outbreak of plague. The pontiff is shown begging God for mercy, while the presence of Archangel Michael with his sword sheathed symbolizes the end of the plague.

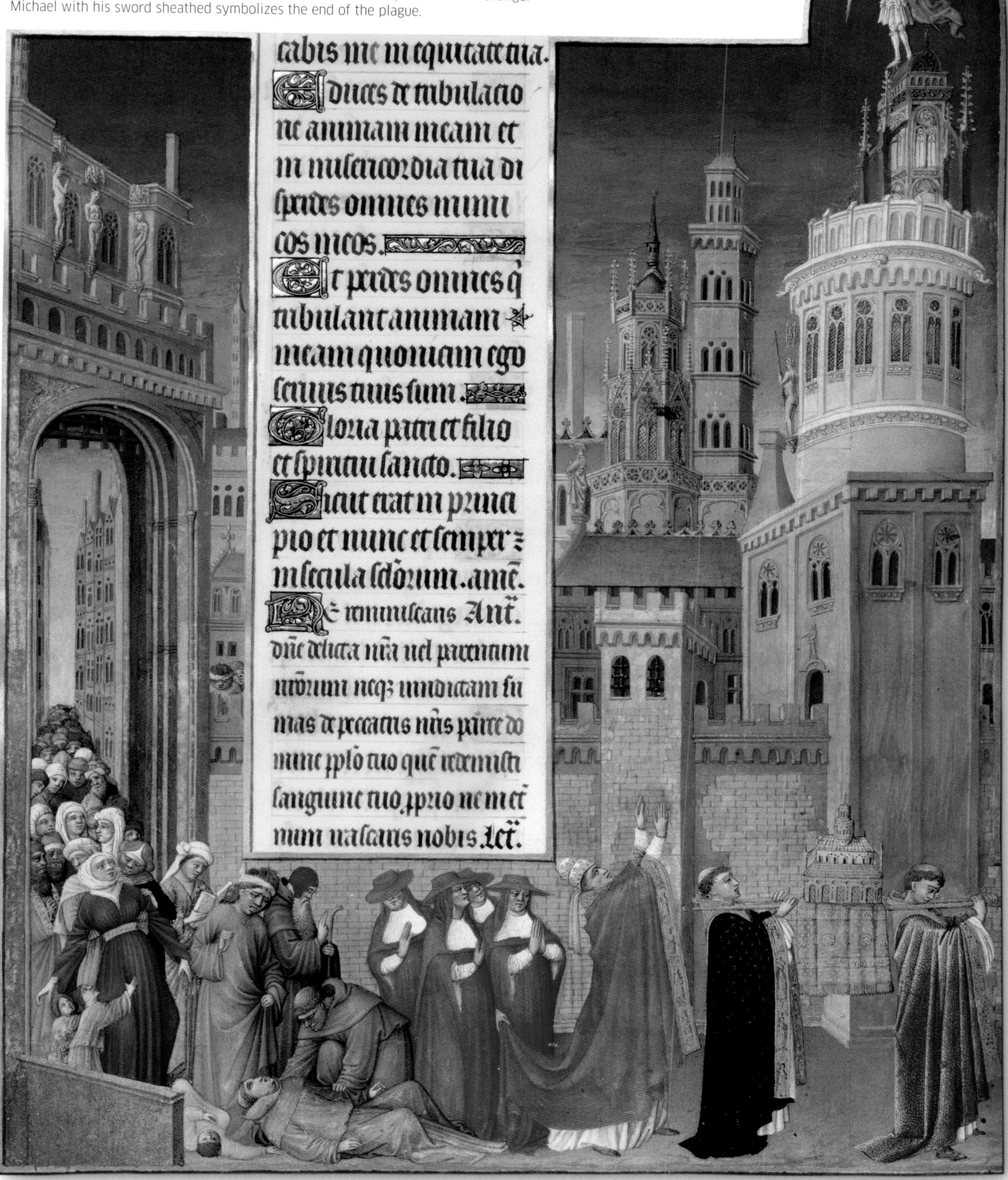

In detail

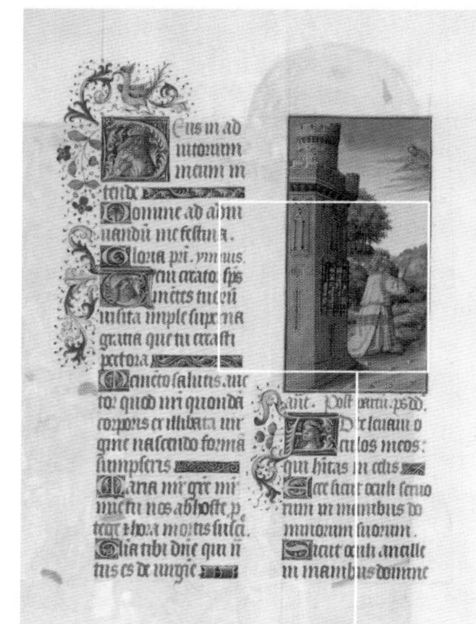

➤ **LATER ILLUSTRATORS** Following the death of the Limbourg brothers, numerous illuminations were needed to complete *Les Très Riches Heures*, including this miniature attributed to Jean Colombe. It is one of many by the artist that depicts David, King of Israel, kneeling before God in various settings.

▲ **DETAIL FROM PRAYER OF DAVID** The figures peering out from the barred window in the tower are probably the servants and handmaid referred to in Psalm 122 – "Behold as the eyes of servants are on the hands of their masters".

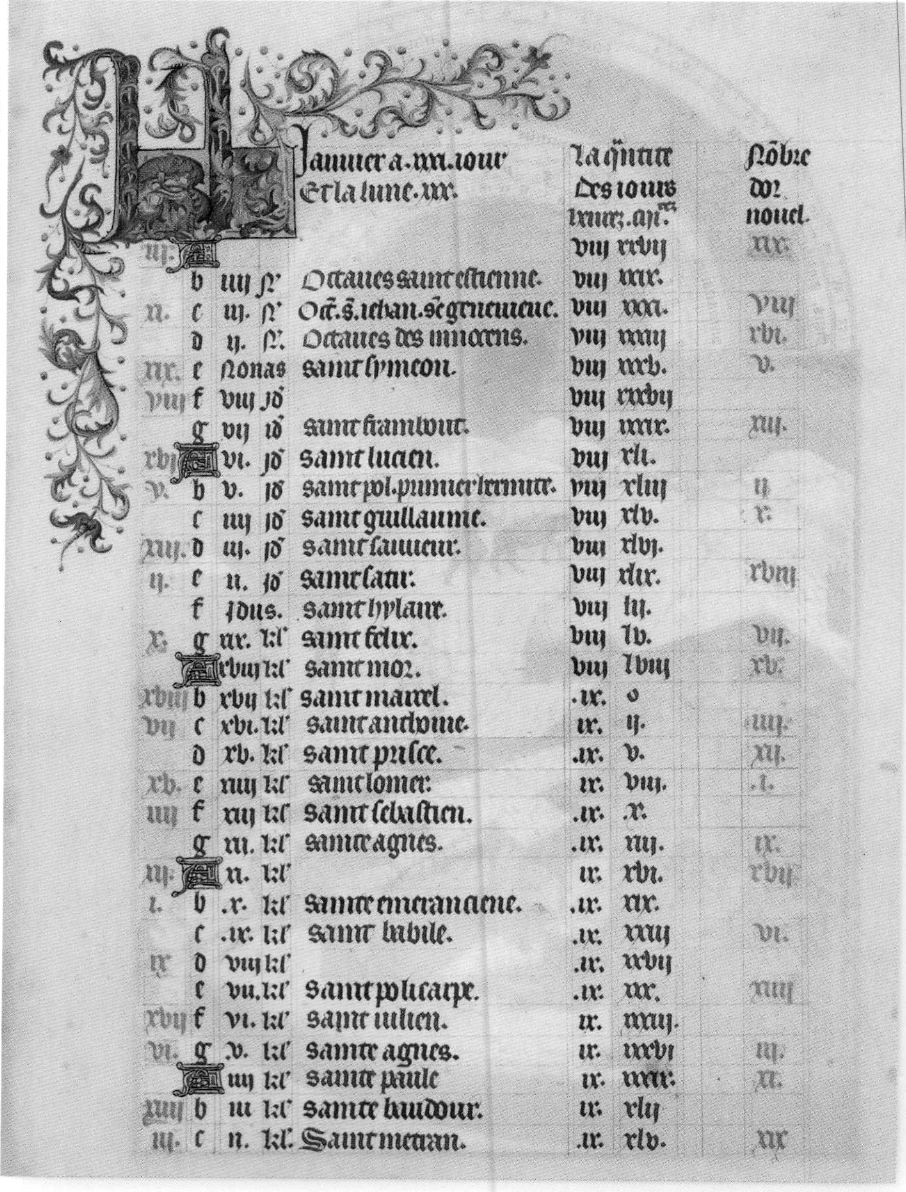

▲ **CALENDAR** *Les Très Riches Heures* opens with a liturgical calendar that lists key dates in the church year, month by month; the page above is for January. The feast days of saints were listed according to their date, with the more important ones written in red. Opposite each page is a painting representing the Labour of the Months (see pp.68–69).

IN CONTEXT

In the 15th century artists were typically commissioned by wealthy patrons, who would bear the cost of their labour and materials, which enabled the creation of lavish works of art that reflected the high status of their sponsor.

The Limbourg brothers, Paul, Jean, and Herman, were born into an artistic family in the Netherlands, and became innovative, highly gifted miniaturists. Their first commission came in 1402, when Phillipe, duc de Bourgogne asked them to illuminate a bible, now believed to be the Bible moralisée (held in the Bibliothéque Nationale, Paris). Bourgogne died in 1404, before the bible was finished. Shortly after the duke's death, the Limbourgs were engaged by his brother, Jean, duc de Berry. Under his patronage they produced their two most renowned works: their masterpiece, the *Belles Heures* (c.1405–09), noted for its realism and technical experimentation, and *Les Très Riches Heures*, which more closely followed the artistic convention of the time.

The Limbourgs died in 1416, probably during an outbreak of plague. It was only when the book was purchased in the mid-18th century (its whereabouts unknown since the 16th century) that the brothers' work came to light.

➤ **The Limbourg brothers** produced a series of extraordinary works in their lifetimes, including this scene of the Pentecost in *Les Très Riches Heures*.

➤ **ANATOMICAL MAN** The calendar concludes with a depiction of the 12 signs of the zodiac encircling front and back views of a nude youth. This illustration is often referred to as Anatomical Man because each zodiacal sign corresponds to a different part of his body, with the fish representing Pisces positioned at the feet, and continuing upwards to the ram, which represents Aries, at the head.

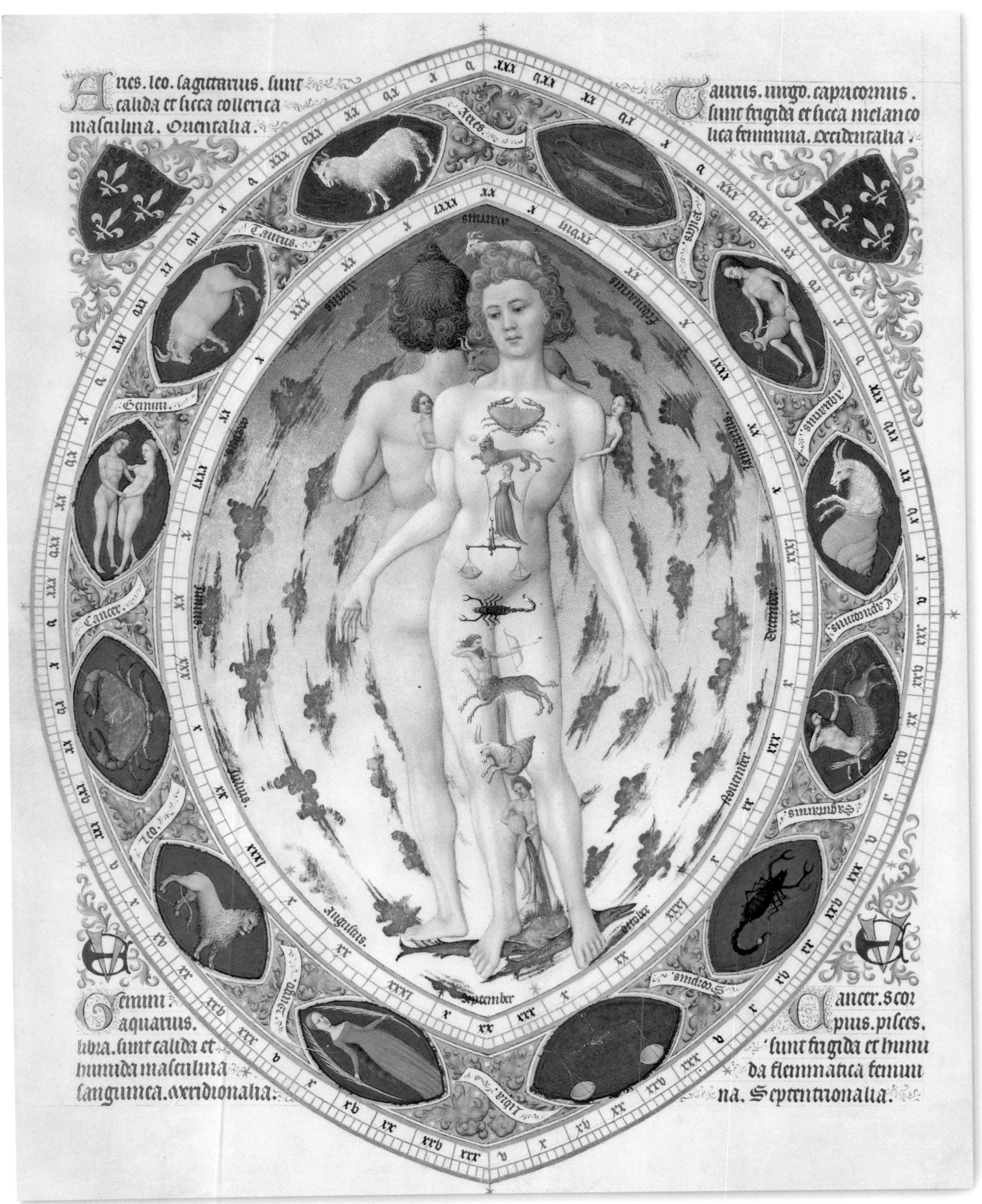
Aries. leo. sagittarius. sunt calida et sicca collerica masculina. Orientalia.
Taurus. virgo. capricornus. sunt frigida et sicca melancolica feminina. Occidentalia.
Gemini aquarius. libra. sunt calida et humida masculina sanguinea. Meridionalia.
Cancer. scorpius. pisces. sunt frigida et humida flemmatica feminina. Septentrionalia.
Aries.
Taurus.
Gemini.
Cancer.
Leo.
Libra.
Scorpius.
Sagittarius.
Capricornus.
Aquarius.
Pisces.

In detail

▲ **MARCH CALENDAR PAGE** In this beautifully rendered and carefully observed scene, peasants undertake the first agricultural tasks of the year – planting crops and pruning vines. The setting is the expansive fields below the Château de Lusignan, one of 17 lavish residences owned by Jean, duc de Berry. The ultramarine pigment used to create the luminous sky, which figures so prominently in the book, was ground from the lapis lazuli stone, imported into Europe from mines in Afghanistan.

▲ **SEPTEMBER CALENDAR PAGE** Discrepancies in artistic style and historical details suggest that the Limbourgs did not create all the calendar miniatures. This scene of a grape harvest at the foot of the Château de Saumur is believed to have been painted by two later artists. The figures are often attributed to The Master of the Shadows (possibly Dutch illuminator Barthélemy van Eyck), while the landscape is thought to be by an artist known as the "rustic painter".

◄ **ARTISTIC MASTERPIECE** *Les Très Riches Heures* is considered the most important illuminated manuscript of the 15th century, and a superlative example of the stylized International Gothic style. The level of detail in the book's illustrations suggests that the Limbourg brothers were given special access to the duke during its creation. The calendar painting for January shows a ritual exchange of New Year's gifts inside one of the duke's castles. The duke himself is seated at his table, wearing a vivid blue robe.

Les Très Riches Heures is important in the history of the book… [It is] a visual text that spans the divide between the reading culture of books and the viewing culture of visual art ”

DONNA BETH ELLARD, TRANSLITERACIES PROJECT, 2006

Directory: 1000–1449

THE BOOK OF HEALING
IBN SĪNĀ

MOROCCO (1027)

Also known as *The Cure* (or *Kitab al-Shifa* in Arabic) this is, not as its title suggests, a book about medicine, but an encyclopaedia of philosophy and science. The Islamic physician and philosopher Ibn Sīnā (also known by his Latin name, Avicenna) began writing it in 1014 and completed it in 1020. Ibn Sīnā (see pp.56–57) was one of the most famous and influential philosophers of the medieval Islamic world. In writing *The Book of Healing* he intended to "cure" or "heal" the ignorance of the soul, rather than the body. The work is divided into four parts examining logic, natural sciences, psychology, and metaphysics. Ibn Sīnā was influenced by Ancient Greek figures such as Aristotle and Ptolemy, as well as Persian thinkers. His views were contrary to contemporary established teachings and it is alleged that in 1160 the Baghdad rulers ordered the book to be burned. *The Book of Healing* was translated into Latin in the 12th century, and some of the existing Latin manuscripts predate surviving Arabic texts.

▼ HISTORIA REGUM BRITANNIAE
GEOFFREY OF MONMOUTH

ENGLAND (C.1136)

Originally titled *De gestis Britonum* (or *On the Deeds of the Britons*) this is a pseudo-history of the kings of England over the course of 2,000 years. Written as a series of 12 volumes between 1135 and 1139 by the English chronicler Geoffrey of Monmouth (c.1100–c.1155), the work claimed to trace a line from the first settlement of Britain by Brutus the Trojan, through the invasion by the Romans, to the arrival of the Anglo-Saxons in the 7th century. Although Monmouth presented it as an authentic historical account – even citing Archdeacon Walter of Oxford, Gildas, and Venerable Bede, Durham, as sources – it proved to be largely fictitious. The inaccuracy of the work was noted immediately by contemporary historians and it was roundly discredited – for example, Monmouth's version of events, such as Julius Caesar's invasion of Britain chronicled in volume four was easily invalidated as it had been well-documented at the time. Today its historical value is viewed as almost zero. Yet the *Historia Regum Britanniae* was very popular at the time and influenced many later chroniclers of history, and is seen as a valuable piece of medieval literature. Monmouth is credited with introducing the figure of King Arthur to the English canon. The second volume also includes the earliest known version of the story of King Lear (or "King Leir"), later picked up by the playwright William Shakespeare.

BRUT
LAYAMON

ENGLAND (C.1200–C.1220)

One of the most important English poems of the 12th century, *Brut* was written by the English priest Layamon. The poem narrates the legendary history of Britain in 16,095 lines of alliterative verse. Layamon's primary source was Robert Wace's Anglo-Norman poem *Roman de Brut*, itself an adaptation from Geoffrey of Monmouth's *Historia Regum Britanniae* (see left). Layamon's poem differs notably from its predecessor in its greatly extended section on King Arthur. *Brut* was written in Middle English at a time when French and Latin had almost completely superseded English as the literary language. *Brut* heavily influenced the development of Arthurian literature and helped enable the revival of English literature following the Norman Conquest of 1066.

Brutus the Trojan setting sail for Britain, from the first volume of Geoffrey of Monmouth's *Historia Regum Britanniae*.

DE LA CONQUÊTE DE CONSTANTINOPLE
GEOFFREY DE VILLEHARDOUIN

FRANCE (C.1209)

This book, known in English as *On the Conquest of Constantinople* is a first-hand account of the events of the Fourth Crusade (1202–04) written by the 13th century French crusader and knight Geoffrey de Villehardouin (c.1150–c.1213). It is the oldest surviving example of historical French prose, and tells the story of the battle for Constantinople (modern-day Istanbul), the capital of the Byzantine Empire, between the Christians of the West and the Christians of the East on 13 April 1204. Villehardouin wrote in the third person – a style that was unprecedented in French texts at the time. He gave vivid descriptions of the events, and followed these with personal views and religious reasons for the outcomes. The narrative used in *De la Conquête de Constantinople* influenced a series of histories and became a characteristic of medieval French literature. This work is one of the primary sources of the events that culminated in the fall of the city of Constantinople. Villehardouin supposedly gave an eyewitness account, however, scholars doubt the accuracy of certain details. The manuscript was not illustrated, but illuminations in the form of decorated initials, borders, and miniatures were added to later printed editions.

SUMMA THEOLOGICA
THOMAS AQUINAS

ITALY (WRITTEN 1265–1274)

An extensive theological compendium, *Summa theologica, or Summa*, is the greatest work by the Italian Dominican theologian Thomas Aquinas (c.1224–74), although he died before it was completed. One of the most important works of medieval theology and philosophy, *Summa* is a comprehensive summary of the teachings of the Catholic Church, and was intended as an instructional guide for students of theology. Among non-scholars it is perhaps most famous for its five arguments for the existence of God, known as the "five ways". It addresses many other fundamental questions of Christianity, such as Christ, the nature of man, and incarnation. Throughout the work Aquinus cites sources from many traditions – Islam, Judaism, and Paganism – as well as Christianity. *Summa* is an expanded version of one of Aquinas's earlier works, *Summa Contra Gentiles. Summa Theologica* was published in 1485, after it had been completed using material from Aquinus's extensive texts.

THE TRAVELS
IBN BATTUTA

MOROCCO (1355)

This book, also known as *Rihla* in Arabic, is regarded as one of the world's most famous travel books, and its author 14th-century Moroccan scholar Ibn Battuta (1304–c.1368), as the world's greatest medieval Muslim traveller. Ibn Battuta set out on his journey in 1325 and returned in 1354, 29 years later. During this time he travelled around 120,000 km (75,000 miles), from North Africa to Southeast Asia, over most of the lands of the Islamic world (Dar-al-Islam) as well as many other areas. On his return to Morocco, Ibn Battuta was asked by the Sultan to dictate an account of his travels. At the time *The Travels* was met with limited appreciation, and it was not until European scholars found the manuscript in the 19th century that it gained international acclaim. Ibn Battuta made no written notes, and although scholars have questioned parts of his narrative, overall he is regarded as a reliable source who offers a key insight into the cultural and social context of the Islamic world in the 14th-century.

➤ LE LIVRE DE LA CITÉ DES DAMES
CHRISTINE DE PISAN

FRANCE (1405)

Known in English as *The Book of the City of the Ladies*, this is the best-known work by French Renaissance writer Christine de Pisan (1364–c.1430) who argued for the rights of women in 15th-century society. *Le Livre de la Cité des Dames* was the first feminist text to be written by a woman in Western literature. In it Pisan created an allegorical world that she used to shed light on the role of women. Many copies of the book were printed with illuminations, in which de Pisan took a deep interest. In her lifetime she was famed both for her success as a writer, and her pursuit of the cause of women. Widely regarded as the first female author in Europe, Christine de Pisan was hugely popular and influential long after her death.

THE BOOK OF MARGERY KEMPE
MARGERY KEMPE

ENGLAND (C.1430)

In the early 1430s the English mystic Margery Kempe (c.1373–1440) dictated the story of her life to scribes (claiming illiteracy), and in doing so she is believed to have created the first "written" autobiography in the English language. The book was dictated entirely from memory and offers a fascinating window into the domestic, religious, and cultural aspects of 15th-century life from a female perspective. Kempe was an orthodox Catholic, and gave birth to 14 children, after which she negotiated a chaste marriage. Kempe went on many pilgrimages during her lifetime and claimed to converse directly with Jesus, Mary, and God. Excerpts from her spiritual autobiography appeared in print in 1501 and again in 1521. The manuscript itself was lost until the 1930s when the only complete copy was discovered in a private library. Her book has since been reprinted and translated into numerous editions.

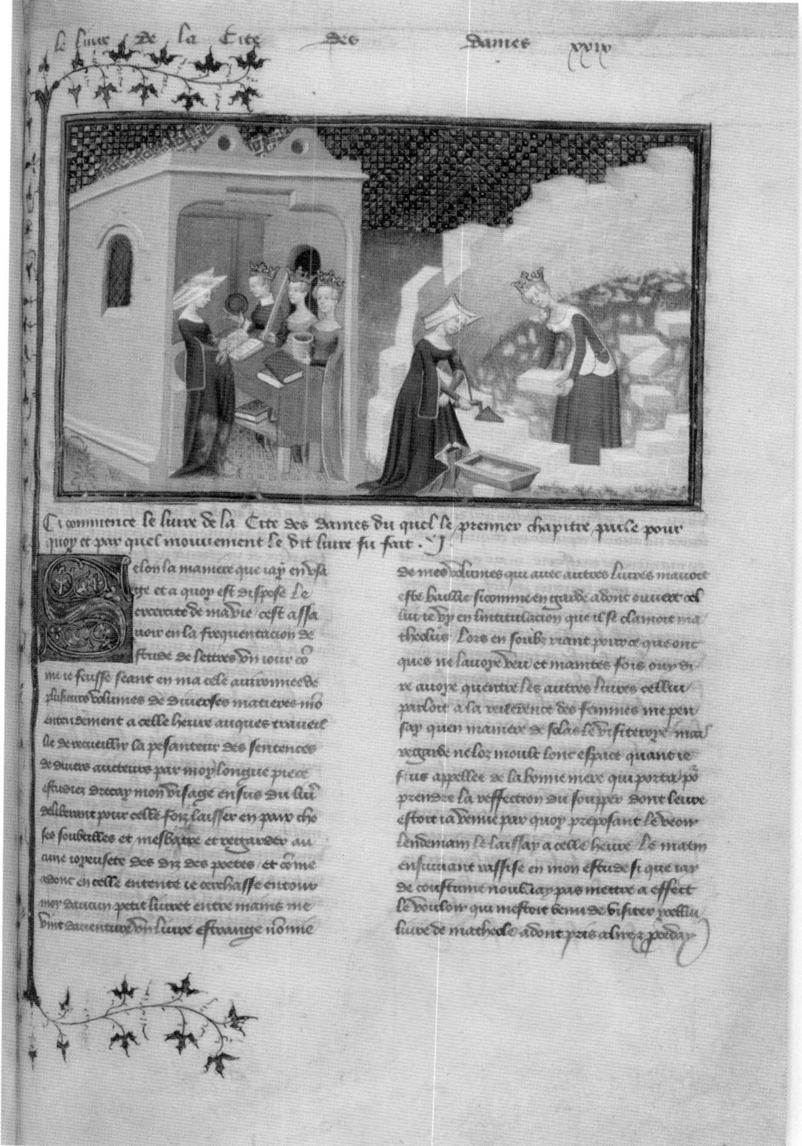

This detail from *Le Livre de la Cité des Dames*, shows de Pisan in her study (above left) and building the city (above right).

CHAPTER 3

1450 – 1649

- Gutenberg Bible
- Elementa Geometriae
- Nuremberg Chronicle
- Divine Comedy
- Hypnerotomachia Poliphili
- The Harmonice Musices Odhecaton
- The Codex Leicester
- Vier Bücher von menschlicher Proportion
- Il Principe
- Epitome
- Cosmographia
- Les Prophéties
- Aubin Codex
- The Discoverie of Witchcraft
- Don Quixote
- King James Bible
- Hortus Eystettensis
- Tutte l'opere d'architettura et prospetiva
- Mr. William Shakespeare's Comedies, Histories, & Tragedies
- Dialogo sopra i due massimi sistemi del mondo
- Bay Psalm Book

Gutenberg Bible

1455 ▪ VELLUM OR PAPER ▪ c.40 × 28.9 cm (16 × 11 in) ▪ 1,282 PAGES (VELLUM IN 3 VOLUMES) ▪ GERMANY

SCALE

JOHANN GUTENBERG

As the first significant book to be printed in Europe using mass-produced movable type, the Gutenberg Bible marked a transformation in the way that books were created. Before the 1450s all books were either copied out by hand or made using wooden blocks: they were owned by the wealthy, or the monasteries where most were scribed. Books were so rare that even the greatest works were seen by only a few people. In the mid 15th century Johann Gutenberg invented a mechanical printing press that revolutionized book production – for the first time in Europe, many copies of the same text could be printed speedily. By the end of the 15th century, millions of books were in circulation across the continent.

Gutenberg had adopted the concept of movable type first developed by the Chinese; and while he had "printed" pamphlets before, the Bible was his first book. He designed 300 different letters to include capitals and punctuation, and is likely to have used a crude sand-casting system in which metal alloy was poured into moulds. Each page of his bible used about 2,500 individual pieces of type. The letters were arranged side-by-side in a frame which could be used to print any number of copies of the same page. Gutenberg developed a special oil-based ink (scribes traditionally used water-based inks) that could be applied to type with leather pummels and then used to print on paper and vellum.

It is thought that the initial print run of the Gutenberg Bible comprised at least 180 copies: 145 on paper and the rest on vellum. The paper copies were printed on fine handmade paper imported from Italy – each page bore watermarks left by the paper mould of either an ox, a bull, or bunches of grapes. The Gutenberg Bible was a copy of the Latin Vulgate Bible, a version translated by Saint Jerome in the 4th century. It was printed after Constantinople fell to Turkish invaders in 1453, during a period when scholars with their Greek and Latin translations dispersed West.

➤ **TRADITIONAL STYLING** Gutenberg designed fonts now known as Textualis, or Textura, and Schwabacher, which are elegant and clear. The text, as shown here, is "justified" (has straight margins) – another of his innovations. Each page had two 42-line columns, hence the book's alternative name, the 42-line Bible. The initial letters or *rubrics* were originally printed in red ink, but this method was too time consuming, so Gutenberg left the spaces blank for scribes to draw them in by hand.

In detail

▲ **HAND-DECORATED PAGES** In order to appeal to people familiar with illuminated manuscripts, artists were commissioned to hand paint floral motifs, decorative initial letters, and lavish borders in the wide margins surrounding the text. The level of illumination differed from copy to copy, depending on how much the buyer was prepared to pay.

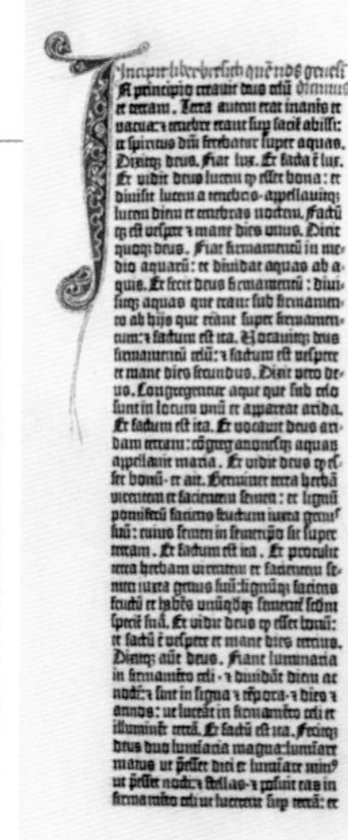

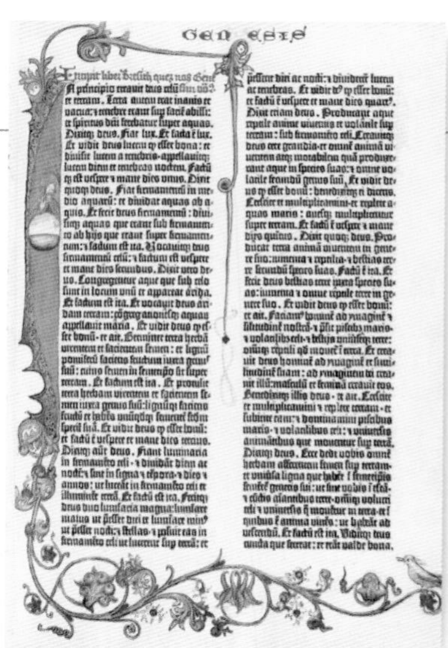

▲ **VELLUM VERSUS PAPER** Gutenberg developed a printing ink that could adhere to either vellum – prepared calfskin (above left) or paper (above right). He printed his new bible on both mediums. It is not known how many bibles were produced altogether, but 48 survive today – 36 printed on paper (in two volumes) and 12 printed on vellum (bound in three volumes as it is heavier).

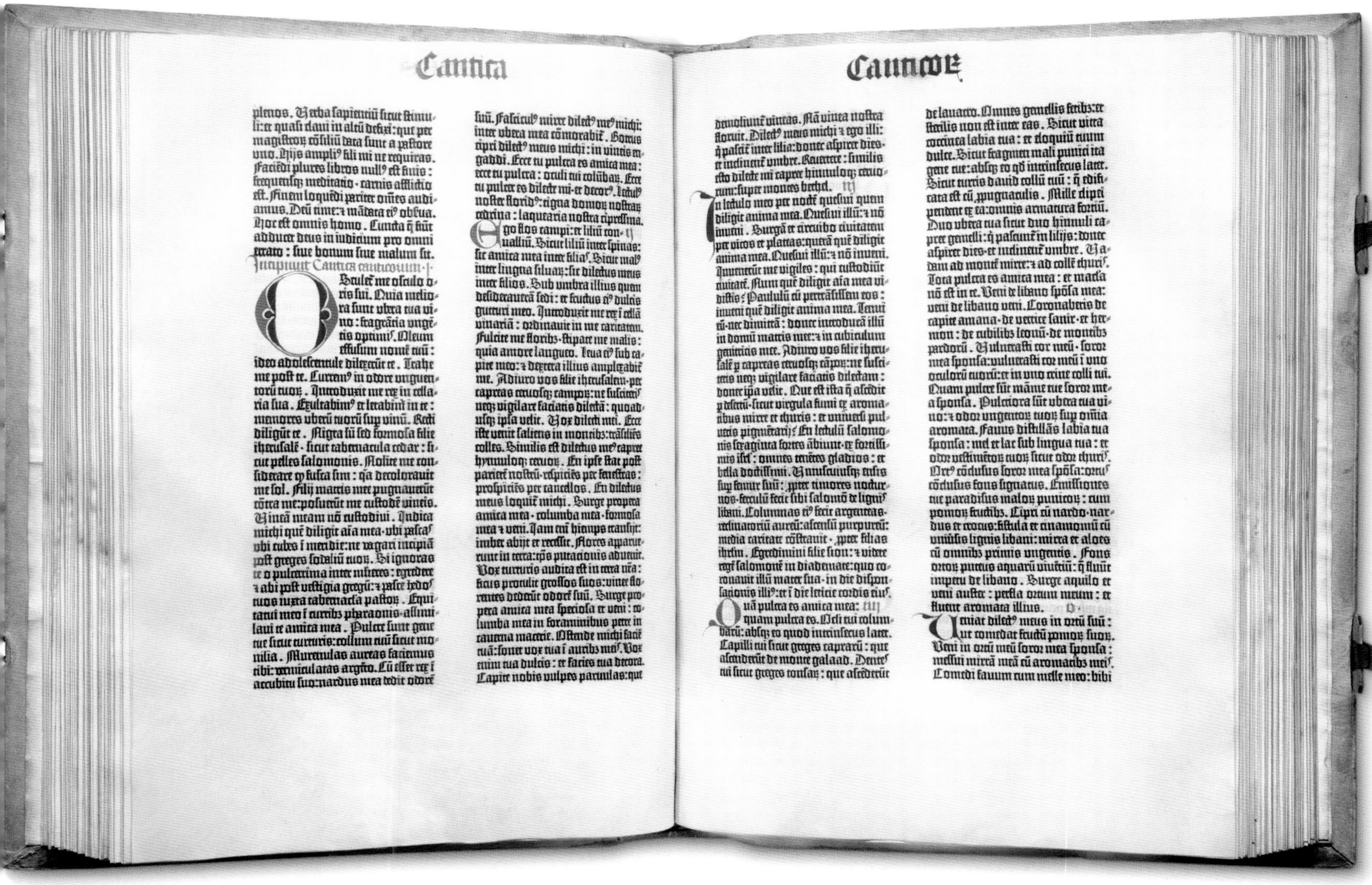

> The script was very neat and legible… your grace would be able to read it without effort, and indeed without glasses
>
> **FUTURE POPE PIUS II**, IN A LETTER TO CARDINAL CARVAJAL, MARCH 1455

IN CONTEXT

The invention of movable type and the printing press in 15th-century Europe had an enormous impact on society. Literacy was no longer the preserve of the elite, and the dissemination of knowledge through books led to ever-increasing numbers of educated people. Rulers were challenged by those who now understood national politics more thoroughly. The Church in particular was confronted by critics who opposed both parts of its teaching and its discipline. When the 16th-century German Augustinian friar and university lecturer Martin Luther (1483–1546) campaigned for Church reform, he was assisted by the accessibility of printing. In particular, Luther's translation of the Bible from Latin into German had a profound impact on modern German language.

▲ **By 1500** there were 1,000 Gutenberg printing presses operating across western Europe, rolling out more than 3,000 pages a day, and making books accessible to wider society.

Elementa Geometriae

1482 ■ PRINTED ■ 32 × 23.2 cm (12 × 9 in) ■ 276 PAGES ■ ITALY

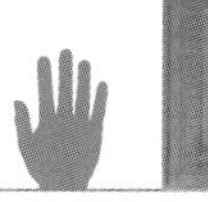

SCALE

EUCLID

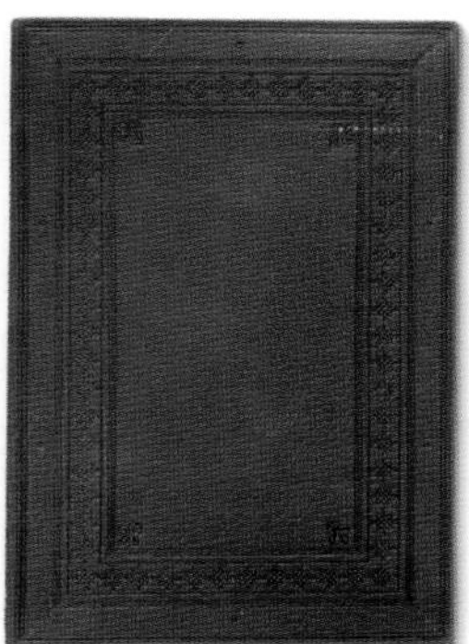

Euclid's *Elements of Geometry* is the most influential mathematical treatise ever published. It was compiled around 300 BCE in Alexandria, Egypt, which was newly under Greek rule and a burgeoning centre of learning. The strength of the work lies not in its originality – much of the material came from other sources – but in its achievement of presenting within a single text the striking advances that had been made in Greek mathematics over the previous three centuries. To a large extent the text focuses on geometry – this being the basis on which Greek mathematics developed – and Euclid himself is commonly referred to as the "father of geometry". However, this 13-volume work ranges across the entire mathematical world as it was known to the Greeks.

Its lasting significance lies in Euclid's treatment and organization of his varied source material: by logically arranging the theorems of other mathematicians he was able to show development from a set of propositions to results. Euclid's methods formed the bedrock of mathematical teaching in both the West and the Arab world for more than 2,000 years. *Elements* owes its survival to its translation from Greek to Arabic in about 800 CE. It was this Arabic text that was translated into Latin and disseminated across Christendom by an English monk in the early 12th century. Later, medieval translations from Greek to Latin were also undertaken.

The first printed edition (shown here) was *Elementa Geometriae*, which is a work of huge importance – it was the first mathematical textbook ever to be printed, and is also one of the first to feature geometric illustrations. As such, it represents a breakthrough in Renaissance printing.

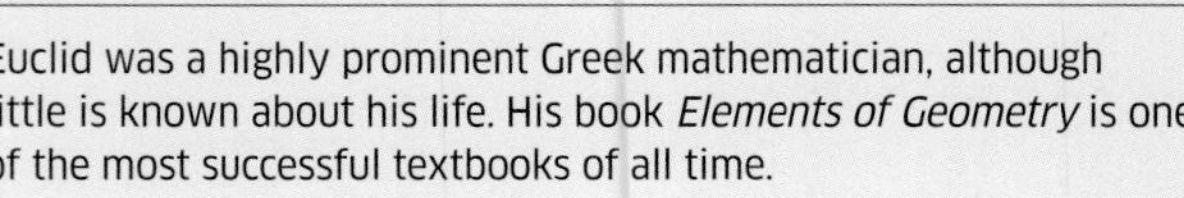

EUCLID

c.400–c.300 BCE

Euclid was a highly prominent Greek mathematician, although little is known about his life. His book *Elements of Geometry* is one of the most successful textbooks of all time.

Euclid was active in Alexandria at the time of Ptolemy I Soter (323–285 BCE), but the date, place, and exact circumstances of his birth and death are unknown. According to the Greek philosopher Proclus (c.410–485 CE), Euclid drew on previous work proposed by pupils of Plato – Eudoxus of Cnidus, Theaetus, and Philip of Opus – in order to compile *Elements*. Many other books are also ascribed to him, including *Optics*, *Data*, and *Phaenomena*.

In detail

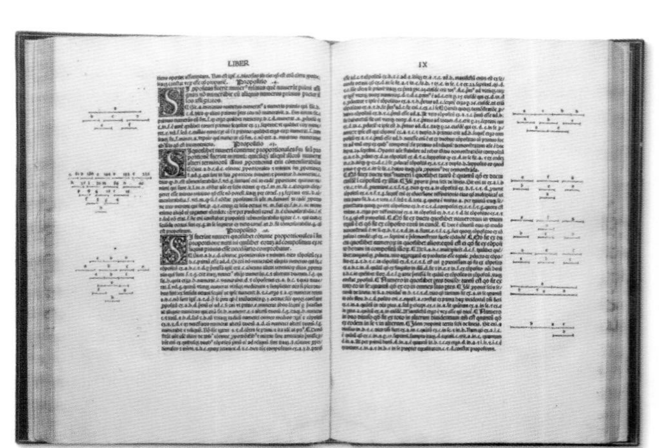

▲ **EXQUISITE DESIGN** *Elementa Geometriae* is a beautifully presented Latin translation of Euclid's text. The perfectly proportioned wide outer margins are interspersed with simple, carefully designed geometric diagrams that complement the central solid block of text.

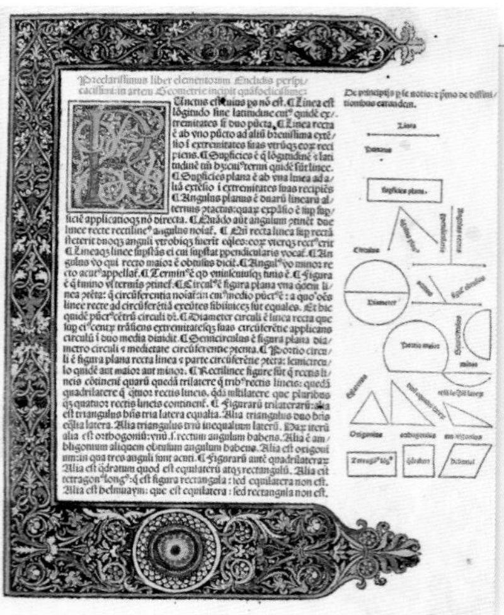

▲ **BOLD WOODCUT** The title page of the *Elementa* is enhanced by an elegant three-sided woodcut border. Most of the typography on the page is in black, with some text picked out in red.

▲ **DECORATIVE TYPE** The book is lavishly produced with intricately decorated small capitals at the start of every section or "proposition". Delicately drawn botanical forms curl around the type like intertwining vines.

▼ **GEOMETRY** The first printed edition of Euclid's book was published in Venice in 1482 by a German, Erhard Ratdolt, as *Elementa Geometriae*. The spread shown here is typical of the book's design – neat geometric illustrations, precisely wedded to the accompanying text.

Elements is one of the **most perfect monuments** of the Greek intellect

BERTRAND RUSSELL, *A HISTORY OF WESTERN PHILOSOPHY*, 1945

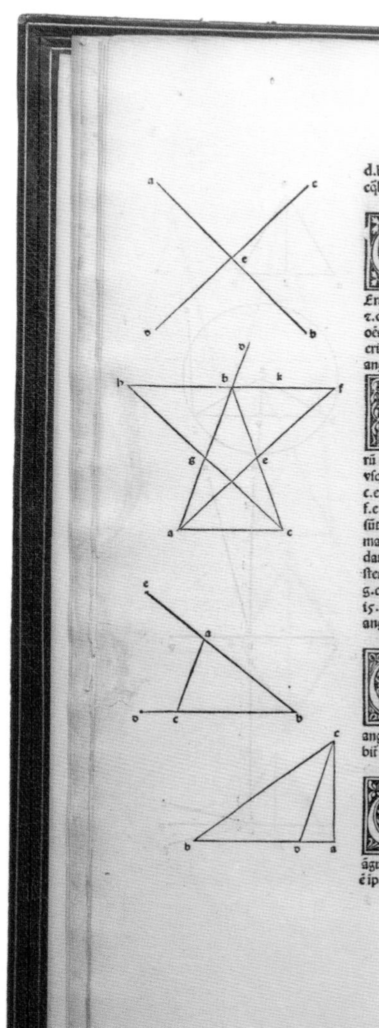

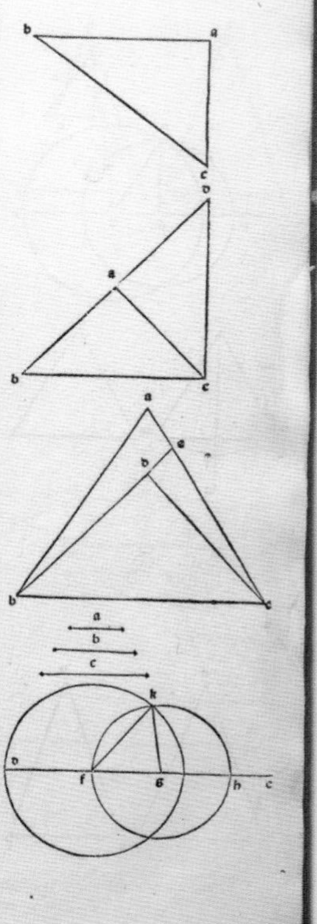

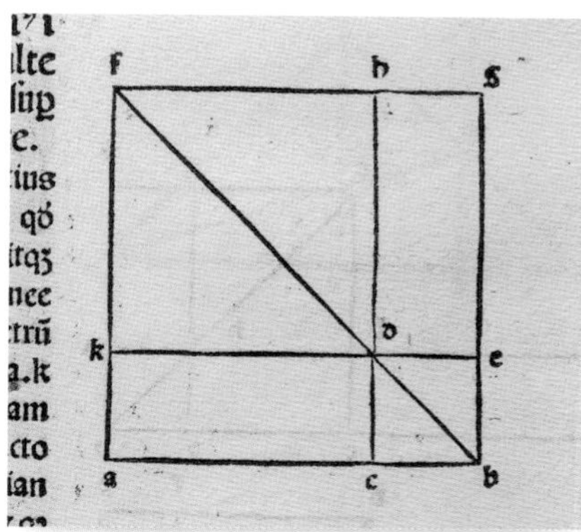

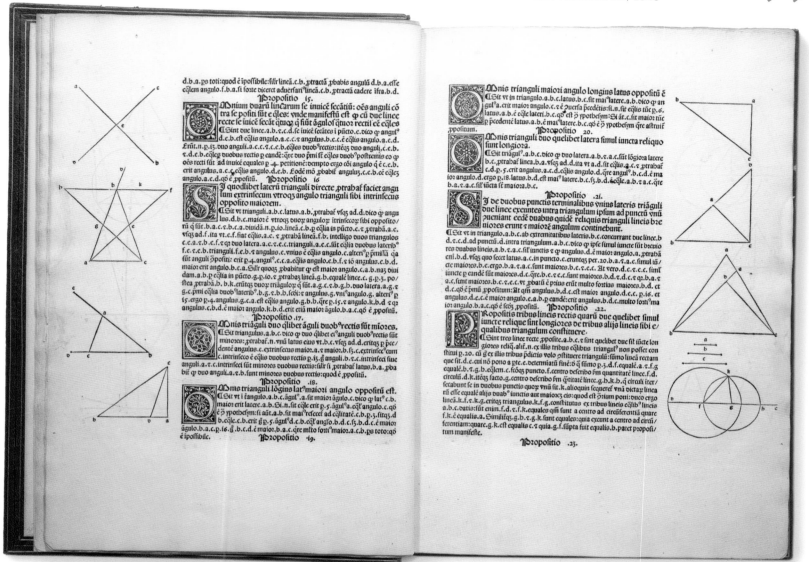

▲ **GEOMETRICAL DIAGRAMS** A key aspect of Ratdolt's edition is the inclusion of 420 precisely printed geometrical diagrams, yet it is debateable whether these were created from woodcuts or metalcuts. The simple line diagrams are integrated with the relevant text and are used to illustrate key points.

IN **CONTEXT**

It is generally believed that more than 1,000 different versions of Euclid's *Elements* have been published. Among the most innovative editions was an 1847 English publication produced by civil engineer Oliver Byrne. Byrne's edition presents Euclid's proofs in the form of pictures, using as little text as possible. He uses coloured blocks to explain the first six books of Euclid's theories of elementary plane geometry and the theory of proportions, although Byrne insisted that: "Care must be taken to show that colour has nothing to do with the lines, angles, or magnitudes, except merely to name them." The book's striking use of colour makes it a masterpiece of early graphic design.

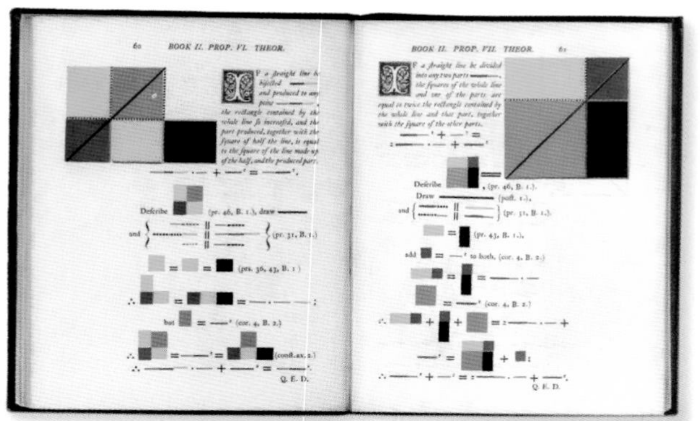

▲ **The vivid colours** of Byrne's edition of *Elements* were intended to help the reader understand by simplifying Euclid's complex concepts. Yet they also possess an abstract quality, and their crisply-printed colours and shapes seem to prefigure 20th-century graphics, such as the work of the Dutch abstract painter Piet Mondrian (1872–1944).

Nuremberg Chronicle

1493 ▪ PRINTED ▪ 45.3 × 31.7cm (18 × 12in) ▪ 326 PAGES (LATIN), 297 PAGES (GERMAN) ▪ GERMANY

SCALE

HARTMANN SCHEDEL

The *Book of Chronicles* or the *Nuremberg Chronicle*, as it is more popularly known, presents an encyclopedic world history from a biblical and classical perspective, and is one of the most impressive and technically advanced examples of 15th-century printing. The book is extensively illustrated with over 1,800 woodcuts created from 645 different woodblocks (many of the pictures used the same woodblock), which are hand-coloured in many copies. In addition to depictions of biblical and historical events, portraits, and family trees, the book includes views of nearly 100 different major cities throughout Europe and the Near East (many never recorded before), as well as a map of the world.

The *Nuremberg Chronicle* is named for the German city in which it was published, then one of the Roman Empire's most prosperous cities. It was commissioned by two merchants, Sebald Schreyer (1446–1520) and Sebastian Kammermeister (1446–1503), and the printing and binding were entrusted to the celebrated printer Anton Koberger (1440–1513). Published in two different languages in 1493, the Latin text written by Hartmann Schedel was issued in Nuremberg on 12 July, and the German translation appeared on 23 December. About 1,500 Latin copies were made and around 1,000 produced in German. Today the book is highly valued by collectors, with about 700 partial or entire copies held in institutes or private collections.

HARTMANN **SCHEDEL**

1440–1514

Hartmann Schedel was a humanist, physician, cartographer, and book collector, who is best known for his groundbreaking work on the *Nuremberg Chronicle*.

Hartmann Schedel studied liberal arts at the University of Leipzig, then medicine at the Italian University of Padua in 1463. Here he encountered the humanist ideals of the Renaissance, which was then at its peak. He lived in Nördlingen and Amberg, southern German towns, from 1470 to 1480, then returned to Nuremberg where he frequented humanist circles. Noting his eclectic knowledge, the merchant Sebald Schreyer and his son-in-law Sebastian Kammermeister, commissioned him to write the world chronicle. Schedel compiled material from ancient sources for the book, many from his own library, which grew to hold 370 manuscripts and more than 600 books – a vast quantity, as printing had been invented only 50 years earlier.

▼ **BIBLICAL VIEW** In creating his *Chronicle* Schedel drew on traditional Christian biblical understanding. In the early pages he presents the story of the world's creation. Adam and Eve, shown here, eat from the Tree of Knowledge in the Garden of Eden, from which they are expelled by an angel on God's orders. The tree is depicted as an apple tree – *malum* in Latin means both "apple" and "evil".

Etas prima mundi Folium VII

In detail

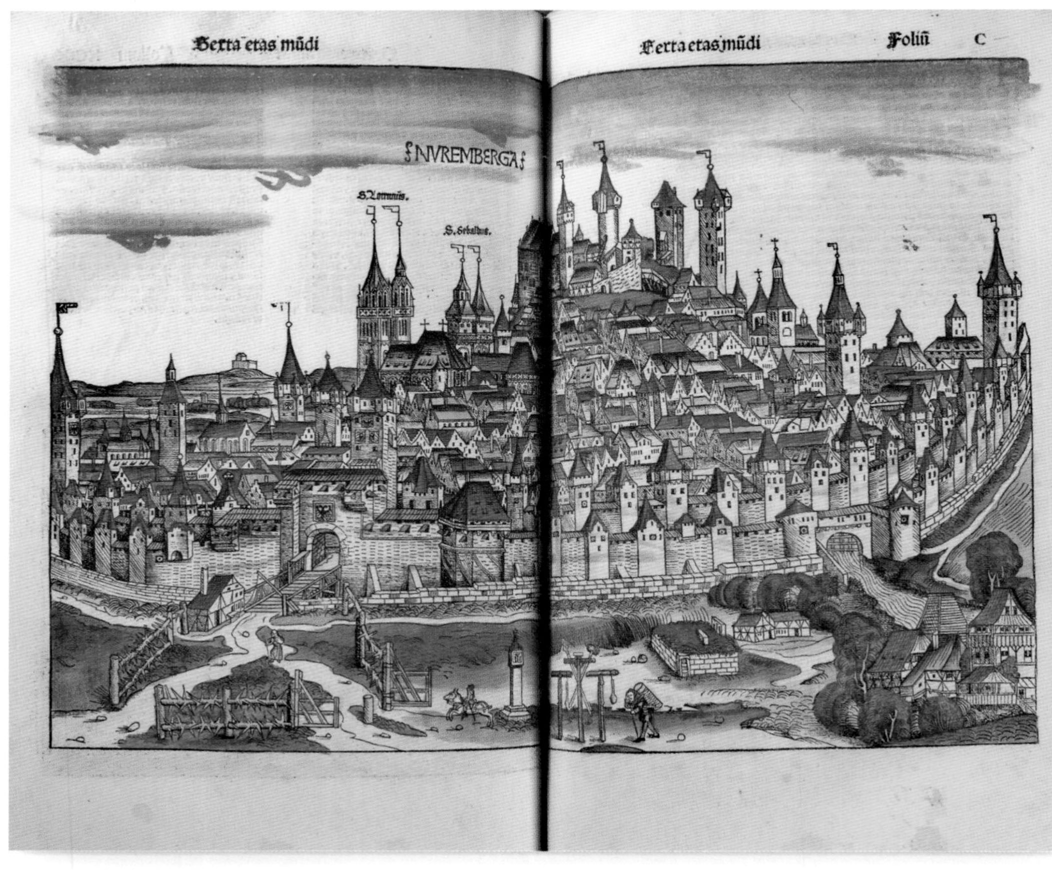

◀ **ACCURATE DEPICTIONS** This hand-coloured illustration of Nuremberg is one of around 30 of the city views in the book believed to be an accurate portrayal. Many of the drawings are used several times to represent different places, but this one appears only once. With a population of 45,000–50,000, Nuremberg was one of the most important cities in the Holy Roman Empire and the centre of Northern humanism.

▲ **REPEATED IMAGES** The city of Troy played an important part in Greek mythology, and Schedel recounted the story based on Homer's *Iliad*. Here the woodcut depicts Troy, but the identical image was also used for Ravenna, Pisa, Toulouse, and Tivoli.

IN CONTEXT

The *Nuremberg Chronicle* is highly significant in the history of print for its scope, its integration of text with lavish illustrations, and for its portrayal of the humanist movement, which had extended to northern Europe.

Humanism originated in Florence, Italy, as part of the Renaissance movement, which began around 1300. Italian scholars studied the writings and works of the Ancient Greeks and Romans, and wished to revive their cultural, literary, and moral philosophical traditions. Education, art, music, and science were key to this renewed way of thinking, and the invention of the printing press in around 1440 helped to record and disseminate these humanist ideals.

Humanism spread from Florence to the rest of Italy, then on to Spain, France, Germany, the Low Countries, and England, as well as eastern Europe. Schedel, who was exposed to humanist thought while studying in Italy, played a significant role in advancing the ideas of his humanist contemporaries, as he collected many of their thoughts in his *Chronicle*. His extensive library was the basis for his book – only a small percentage was his original work – and his most frequently referenced source was another humanist chronicle, *Supplementum Chronicarum*, by Jacob Philip Foresti of Bergamo. There is also evidence that Schedel did much to foment humanist thought by loaning the titles in his notable collection to other local scholars.

Schedel's outlook was shared by Sebald Schreyer, who commissioned the *Chronicle*. A businessman and patron of the arts, he was also a self-taught humanist.

▲ **Metal dyes** were gently hammered onto the pig-skin cover to provide the elegant designs in a technique called blind printing. Pages were stitched together using cotton at five points.

▲ **COMETS** The *Chronicle* features the first printed images of comets – 13 were depicted in the book, which cited appearances from 471–1472 CE. The comets are represented by only four varying woodblocks and are rotated according to the page layout.

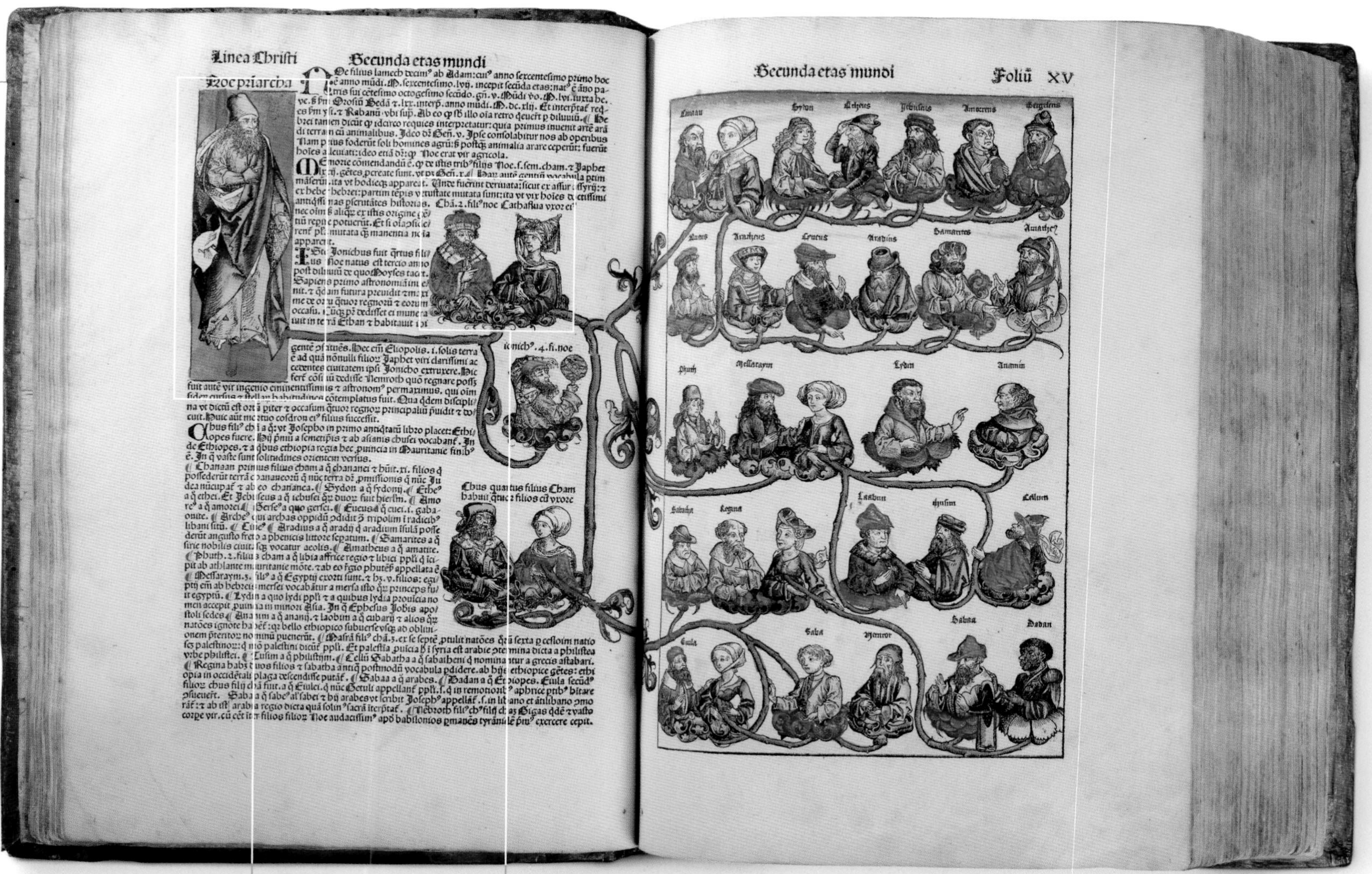

▲ **FAMILY TREE** The lineage of Jesus Christ, depicted in this family tree, is derived from St Matthew's Gospel. On the left page the biblical character of Noah opens the text, while on the right are the ancestors of Christ. Hundreds of historical figures were portrayed in the *Nuremberg Chronicle*, although many of these illustrations were reused, with the same figures appearing up to six times to represent different people.

◄ **NOAH'S DESCENDANTS** The first generational branch from Noah is to Ham, his second son, who is portrayed here along with his wife, Cathaflua. The *Chronicle* follows a medieval custom of beginning with the middle, rather than the eldest, child in detailing the order of offspring on a family tree.

◄ **THE PATRIARCH NOAH** The history of the *Chronicle* commences with the "First Age of the World" from Adam up until the Flood, detailing the building of the Ark by Noah and his family. The "Second Age of the World" traces events from after the Flood to Abraham's birth.

Visual tour

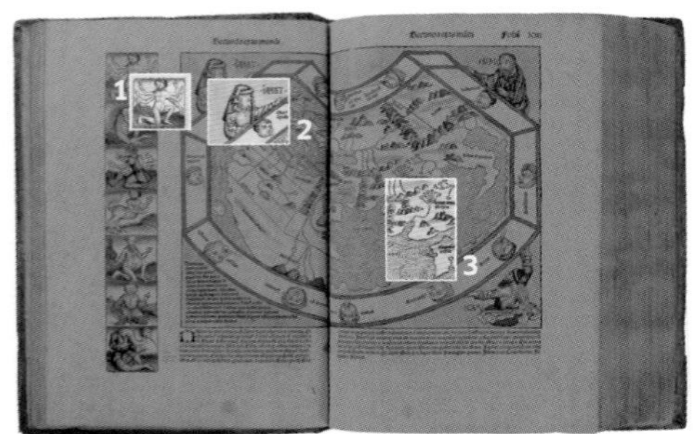

KEY

➤ **MAP OF THE WORLD** This woodcut map of the world is illustrated with Europe at its centre. Although the book appeared a year after Columbus had landed in the Americas, it does not reflect this discovery, but shows only Africa, Europe, and Asia. Twelve heads depict the directions of various winds, knowledge of which was important for sailing, while Noah's three sons (who repopulated the earth following the Flood) encircle the map.

1

▲ **SIX-HANDED FIGURE** The *Chronicle* records that "In the histories of Alexander the Great one reads of people in India who have six hands", as this detail shows. Numerous other unlikely peoples are also described and illustrated over several pages. These oddities are to be found in exotic lands, as the text notes: "In Ethiopia, toward the west, some have four eyes", while in Eripia, in Greece, there are "people with necks like those of cranes, and bills for mouths".

2

▲ **JAPHETH TAKES EUROPE** After the Flood, Noah's three sons supposedly shared out the then known world of Asia, Europe, and Africa. Noah's firstborn, Japheth, who holds the northwestern corner of the map, was given the continent of Europe.

3

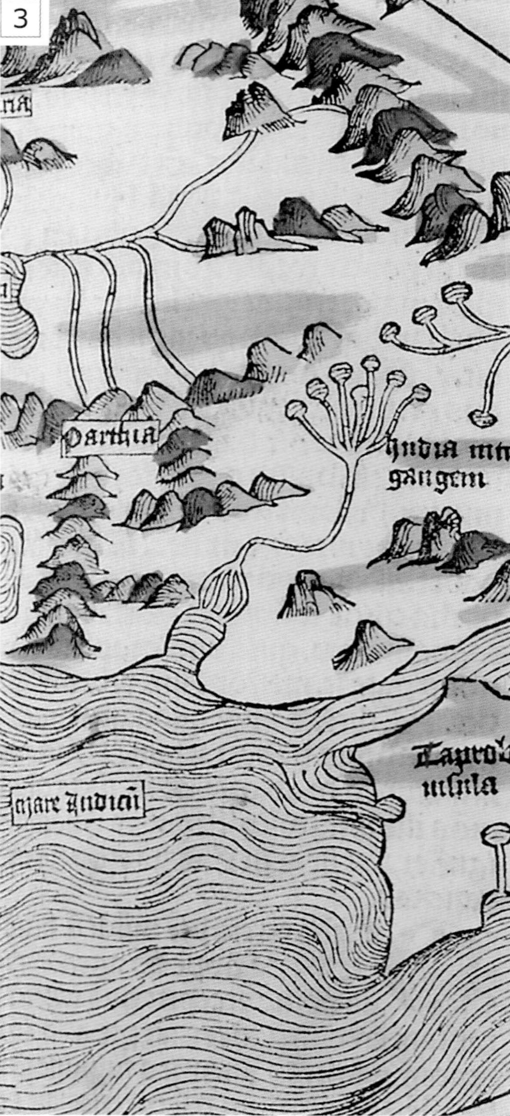

▲ **THE EAST** Compared to Europe, the map of Asia has far fewer annotations, with a huge swathe of northern and central Asia simply labelled Tartaria. Other, now obsolete, place names include Scythia – a region of central Eurasia; Media and Parthia – both part of modern-day Iran; and Serica – a northwest area of China, named perhaps for the silk it produced.

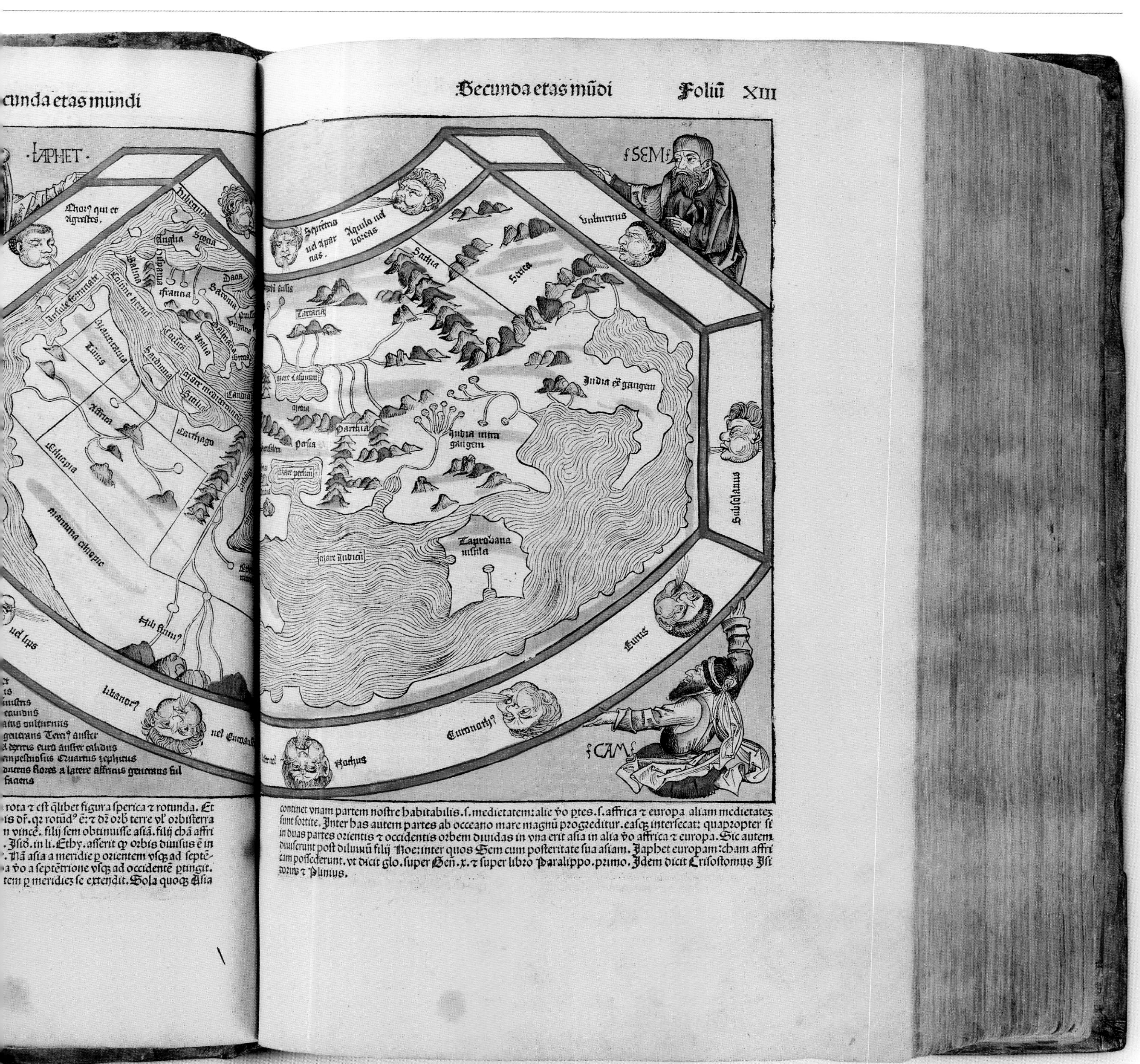

> Never before has your like been printed. A thousand hands will grasp you with eager desire
>
> **ANTON KOBERGER**, PRINTER OF THE *NUREMBERG CHRONICLE*

Divine Comedy

1321 (WRITTEN), 1497 (VERSION SHOWN) ▪ PRINTED WITH WOODCUT ILLUSTRATIONS ▪ 32 × 21.6 cm (12 × 8 in) ▪ 620 PAGES ▪ ITALY

SCALE

DANTE ALIGHIERI

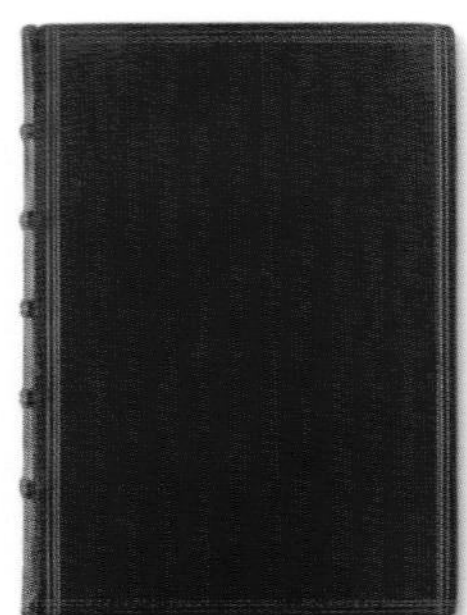

Dante's *Divine Comedy* is one of the greatest of all poetic works. Completed in 1320 while Dante was in exile from his native Florence and staying in Verona, it runs to over 14,000 lines, and tells the story of a poet's imaginative journey through the afterlife. Dante drew inspiration from a wide range of philosophies and ideas, including those of St Thomas Aquinas (1225–74), to capture the medieval world view.

The journey begins at nightfall in a supernatural forest, where the poet is met by the Roman poet Virgil, who has been sent by Dante's great love, Beatrice, to guide him. After an epic tour through the "Inferno" (Hell) and "Purgatory" to "Paradise", the poet eventually reaches "the Love that moves the sun and other stars".

The poem is structured around the number three, to reflect the holy Trinity of God, the Son, and Holy Ghost. There are three parts, each part containing 33 cantos or songs, and the verses are in *terza rima*, an ingenious interlocking rhyming scheme of three-line verses.

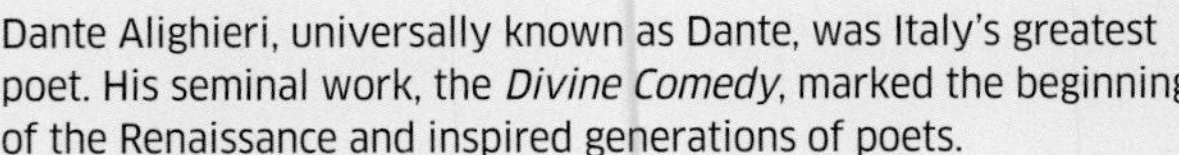

DANTE **ALIGHIERI**

1265–1321

Dante Alighieri, universally known as Dante, was Italy's greatest poet. His seminal work, the *Divine Comedy*, marked the beginning of the Renaissance and inspired generations of poets.

Born in Florence, Dante was betrothed aged 12 to Gemma Donati, but fell in (unrequited) love with a Florentine woman, Beatrice Portinari. Beatrice died in 1290, aged just 24, but would play a key role in the *Divine Comedy*. Dante included many other figures from his life, both friends and enemies. He became embroiled in the political battles dividing Florence between the Ghibellines (Holy Roman Empire) and Guelph (Pope) factions and was driven into exile around 1302. It was whilst in exile that he wrote his masterpiece.

Remarkably, Dante wrote the poem, not in Latin, despite his classical education, but in his native Tuscan language (close to modern Italian). He did it with such skill that it is regarded as the most beautiful poetry ever composed. It not only revolutionized the way poetry was written, but also led to the adoption of Tuscan as the language of Italy.

➤ **TEXTUAL ANALYSIS** The *Divine Comedy* was so layered with meaning that early print editions included lengthy explanatory texts. Here, a small section from "Inferno" is surrounded by a dense commentary by scholar Cristoforo Landino.

In detail

▲ **HIGH ART** Matteo da Parma's work, shown here, first featured in the 1491 edition. For the Benali edition (1481), the artist chosen to illustrate it was the celebrated Sandro Botticelli.

➤ **VENETIAN EDITION** This 1497 edition combines the most popular commentary from Landino with 99 wood engravings by Matteo da Parma. The poem had previously circulated in manuscript form and then in print from 1472. Typical of the drawings in this edition, Dante and Virgil are illustrated twice here to demonstrate the progression of their journey.

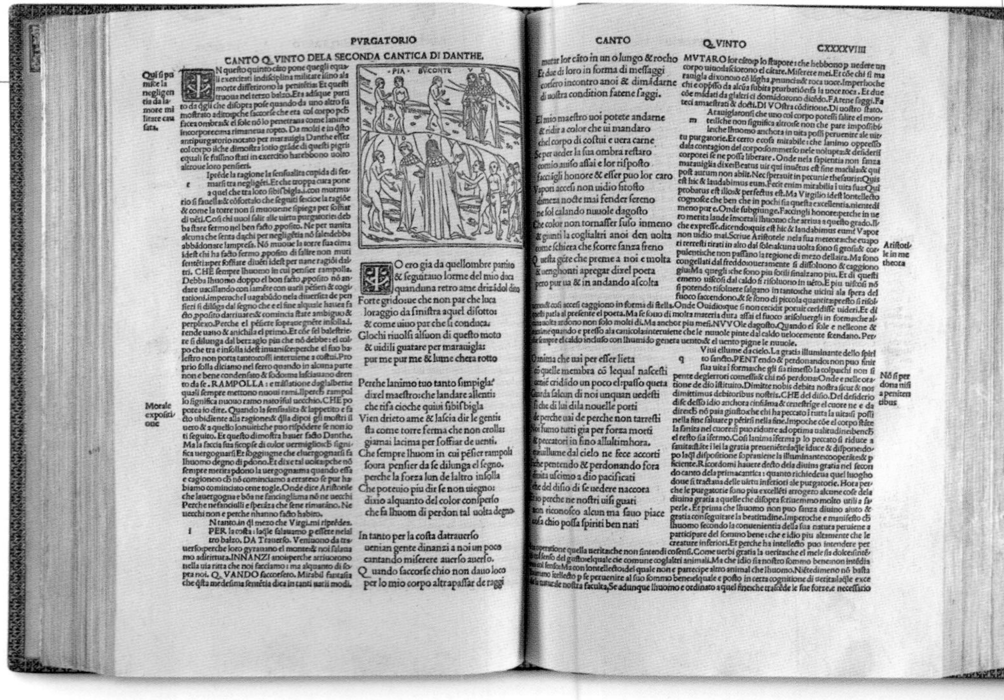

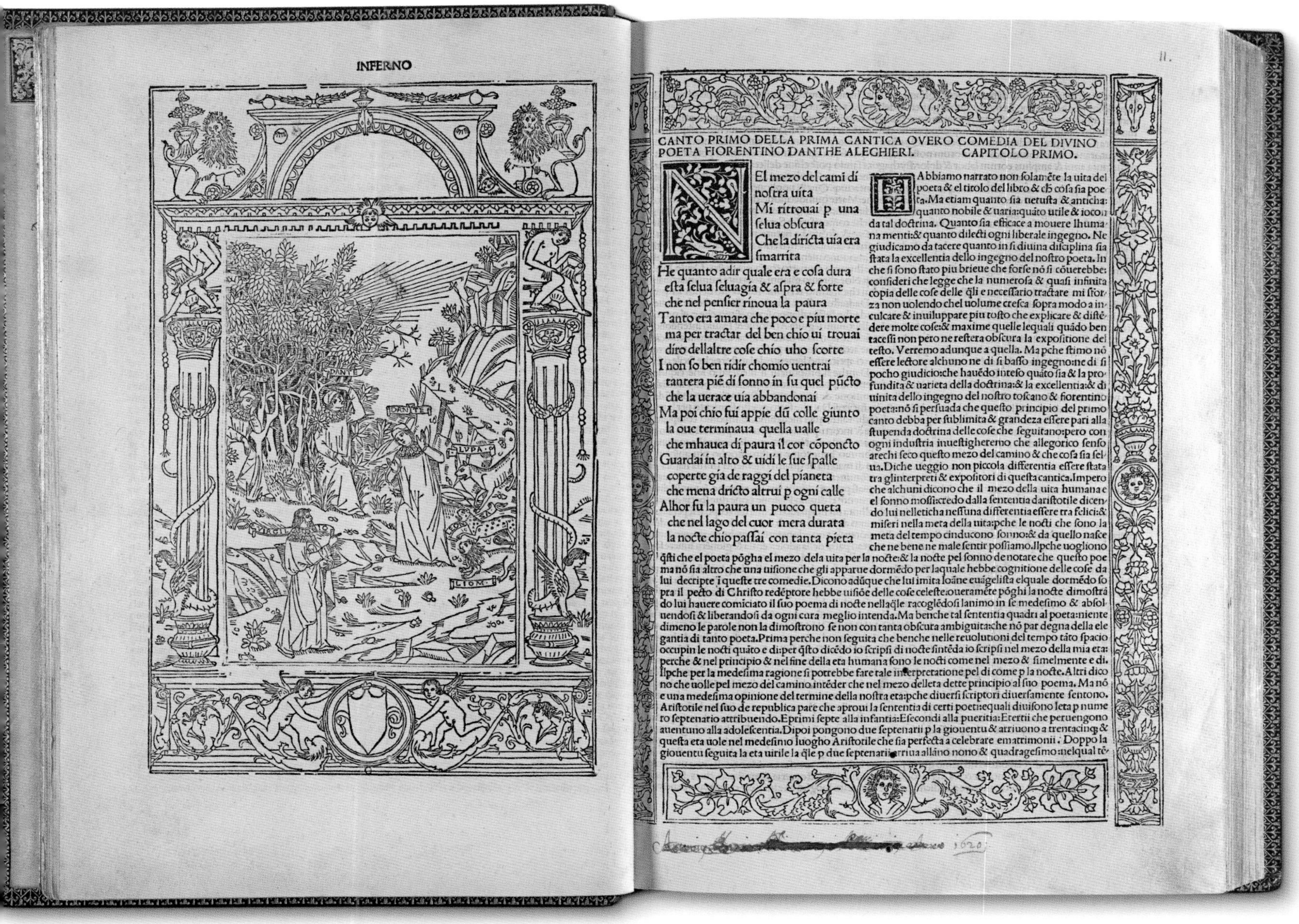

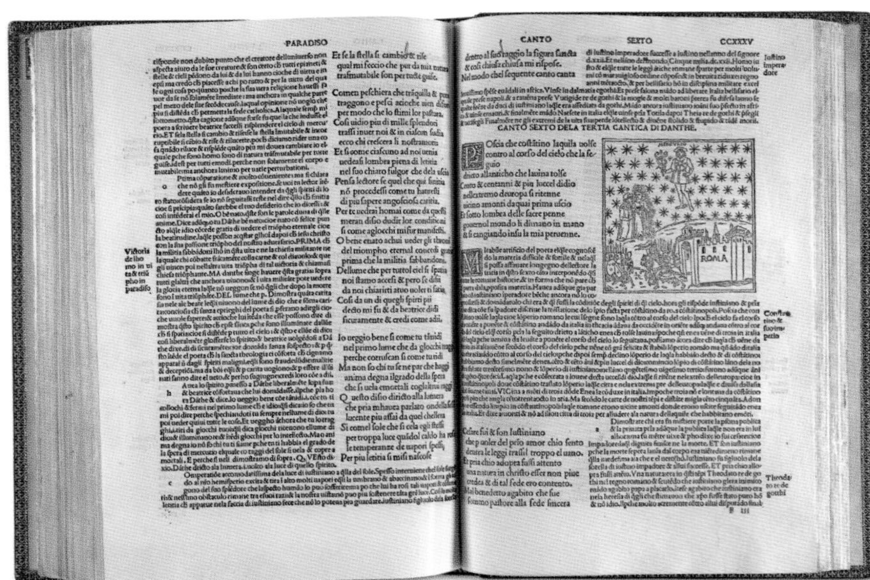

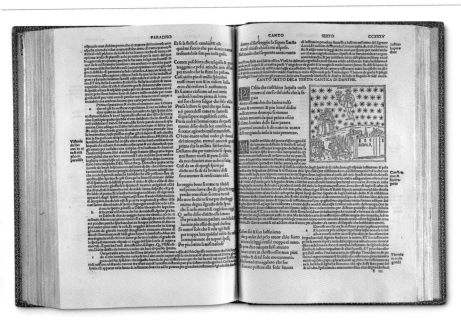

Abandon all hope, ye who enter here

DANTE, *DIVINE COMEDY*

◀ **ILLUSTRATIVE LINKS** The simple images accompanying each canto were intended to be easily understood by contemporary readers. This image comes from "Paradise", reflected in its inclusion of a spirit among stars. Such Venetian woodcuts, with their highly expressive characters, had a great influence on woodcut styles emerging in Western Europe over the next century.

Hypnerotomachia Poliphili

1499 ▪ PRINTED WITH WOODCUT ILLUSTRATIONS ▪ 32.7 × 22.2 cm (12 × 9 in) ▪ 468 PAGES ▪ ITALY

SCALE

AUTHOR UNKNOWN

Often cited as the most beautiful illustrated printed book of the Italian Renaissance, *Hypnerotomachia Poliphili* (or *The Dream of Poliphilus*) was the masterpiece of printer and publisher Aldus Manutius. Printed in Venice in 1499, it was remarkable for the elegance of its 172 woodcut illustrations, and for the visual integration of type and image. Throughout the volume there is an imaginative interplay between the function and position of text on the page – it flows freely around the illustrations and even forms shapes and patterns. The typeface was created by Manutius's typographer Francesco Griffo (1450–1518) who recut one of his existing fonts, Bembo – named after Cardinal Pietro Bembo (1470–1547) – creating larger and lighter upper case letters specifically for this book. Also notable is the treatment of double-page spreads, which Manutius often designed as a single entity rather than as separate pages, featuring paired images on both sides.

Manutius's printing house, which he founded in 1494, was called the Aldine Press. It was one of the most influential printing houses in Europe, renowned for its masterful innovations in type, illustration, and design. This volume, which is unique among Manutius's works for being the only illustrated book he ever printed, set a new standard for book design and typography.

The literary merit of *The Dream of Poliphilus* is debatable, however. Published anonymously, it is a story about a quest for lost love, written in a combination of Latin, a regional form of Italian, and a language of the author's own invention. It also featured some Greek and Hebrew, and the first Arabic words to appear in Western printing. It was consequently hard to understand, which in part contributed to the book's very poor sales.

➤ **DOUBLE PAGE SPREADS** This spread shows the innovative nature of Manutius's design. The sequential images across the pages give an impression of movement, suggesting progression within the story. The pair of illustrations at the top of both pages feature parts of the same procession, as if it were marching through the book.

In detail

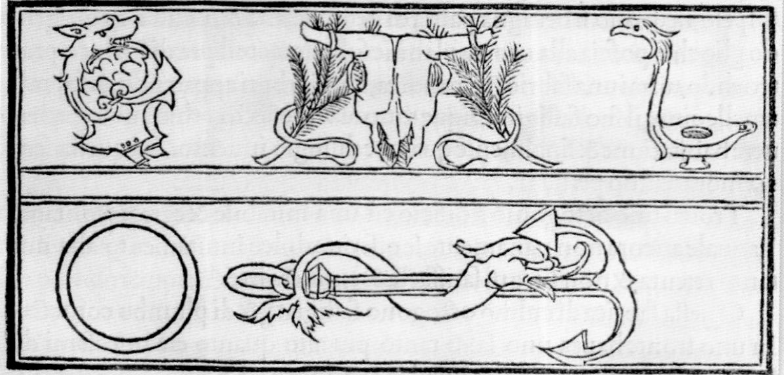

▲ **PRINTER'S MARK** The entwined dolphin and anchor became the emblem for the Aldine Press, with the dolphin symbolizing speed, and the anchor, stability. Manutius adapted the emblem from a coin he received from Cardinal Bembo bearing Emperor Titus on one side, and the dolphin and anchor on the other.

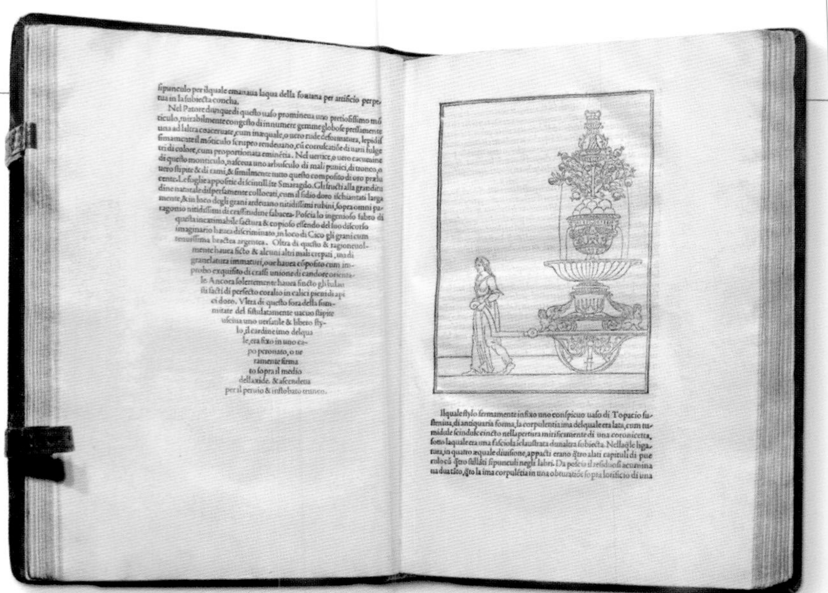

▲ **INNOVATIVE TYPE** The book shows an imaginative use of type to create shapes and patterns on the page. Forgoing traditional page layout, where the text extends to both margins, the text on the left-hand side of this double page has been typeset to form a goblet shape. At the time of publication the Bembo typeface, which is still in use today, was one of the most modern in appearance.

I.TAND.SOCERO.E.ET.M.SOCR.ANNVEN
B.SOLENNIHYMEN.NVPT.COPVLAMVR.
DOFATVMINFOEL.NOCTEPRI.CVM IM
RT.VOLVPTATISEX.L.FAC.EXTINGVERI
T.D.M.V.VOTA COGEREMVR REDD.HEV II
INACTV DOM.MARITALIS CORRVENSAI
AMEXTRE.CVMDVLCITVDINE LAETISS.
OMPLICATOS OBPRESSIT.FVNESTAS SO
OR.NEC NOVI QVID FECISS.PVTA. NON E
AT INFATIS TVM NOSTRA LONGIOR HO.
A.CARIPARENTES LVCTV NEC LACHRYMI
ISERA ACLARVATA NOSTRA DEFLEATIS
FVNERA NE REDDATIS INFOELICIORA
ATVOS NOSTROS DIVTVR
NIORES VIVITE ANNOS
OPTIME LECTOR
AC VIVE TVOS.

▲ **LATIN TEXT** This sample of Latin text is from an illustration of a mausoleum. Appropriately the text, all in capital letters, imitates the Latin inscribed by chisel on classical monuments, with rounded letters, such as "U", represented by a "V".

IN **CONTEXT**

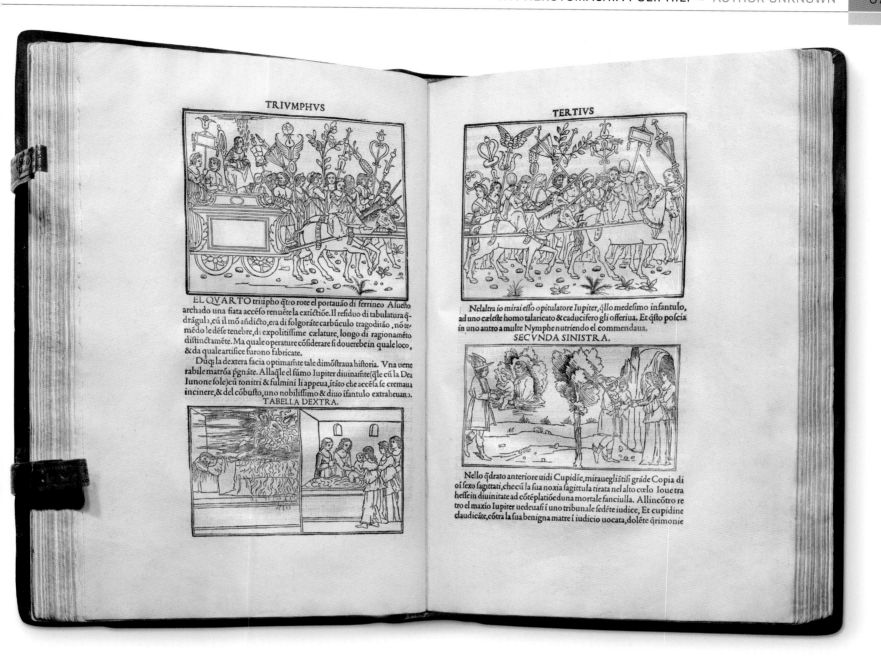

The Dream of Poliphilus was published anonymously and the author's identity has long been a matter of debate among scholars. However, most believe that it was written by a Dominican friar named Francesco Colonna (1433–1527). This theory is largely based on the ingenious Latin acrostic formed by the illustrated initial letters that begin each chapter of the book. Strung together, they spell out *Poliam Frater Franciscus Colonna peramavit*, which translates as "Brother Francesco Colonna loved Polia immensely". Colonna's name is mentioned only in the acrostic but, if he was indeed the author of the book he may have chosen to hide behind anonymity due to the erotic content of the story and his profession as a friar. Colonna was accused of immorality in 1516 and died in 1527, aged 94.

SOPRA.LAQVA
SVBTILMENTE
L A S
pato
som
fuso
sito
ti hc
strumosi iugi. Ma c
po altecia. Siluose d
ni,& di frondosi Es
lie,& di Opio,& de

► **This ornately decorated letter "L"** at the start of one of the 38 chapters forms part of the acrostic that suggests that Francesco Colonna was the author.

Harmonice Musices Odhecaton

1501 (FIRST PUBLISHED), 1504 (VERSION SHOWN) ▪ PRINTED ▪ 18 × 24 cm (7 × 10 in) ▪ 206 PAGES ▪ ITALY

SCALE

OTTAVIANO PETRUCCI

The publication of *Harmonice Musices Odhecaton* (*One Hundred Songs of Harmonic Music*) by the publisher Ottaviano Petrucci was a breakthrough in the circulation of music. It was the first book of "polyphonic" music – where several melodic lines combine to produce harmonies – to be printed using movable type. This enabled the printing of multiple copies, and for the first time polyphonic music could be distributed widely.

The publication of the collection of 96 secular songs for three, four, five, and six instruments had a dramatic effect. Suddenly musicians had a valuable but affordable resource. The book, edited by the Dominican friar Petrus Castellanus in Venice, was reprinted in 1503 and 1504. Early editions did not have words, suggesting it was initially for instruments, and only later editions were for voices too. A few songs were anonymous, but most were written by celebrated French-Flemish composers, such as Jacob Obrecht (1457–1505) and Loyset Compère (1445–1518). The emphasis was very much on these composers, and the book helped to ensure that their harmonic style came to dominate European music for the next 100 years.

Polyphony is now a common musical texture and one that is almost universal. But in the 15th century it was still a novelty, and a shock to ears used to plainchant – music in which all the voices sing an identical melody in unison. Indeed, some Church members regarded polyphony as the devil's music. Petrucci's book played a major part in gaining widespread acceptance for harmonies.

➤ **FOUR-PART HARMONY** The 1504 edition corrected errors from earlier editions. Here, four parts are printed over a spread, allowing a quartet to sing the prayer "Ave Maria" from one copy. Unlike modern notation, the notes are not split into bars. The Latin text above Petrucci's heart-shaped symbol threatens penalties for reprinting.

In detail

◄ **ELABORATE LETTER** Each song is introduced with an elaborate capital letter at the start of the first stave. In this example, the letter "U" introduces the song "Ung franc archier" ("A French archer") by the composer Compère. The letter is followed by a clef, a key signature, and a time signature, much as in modern notation. For clarity, a blank stave separates the voices.

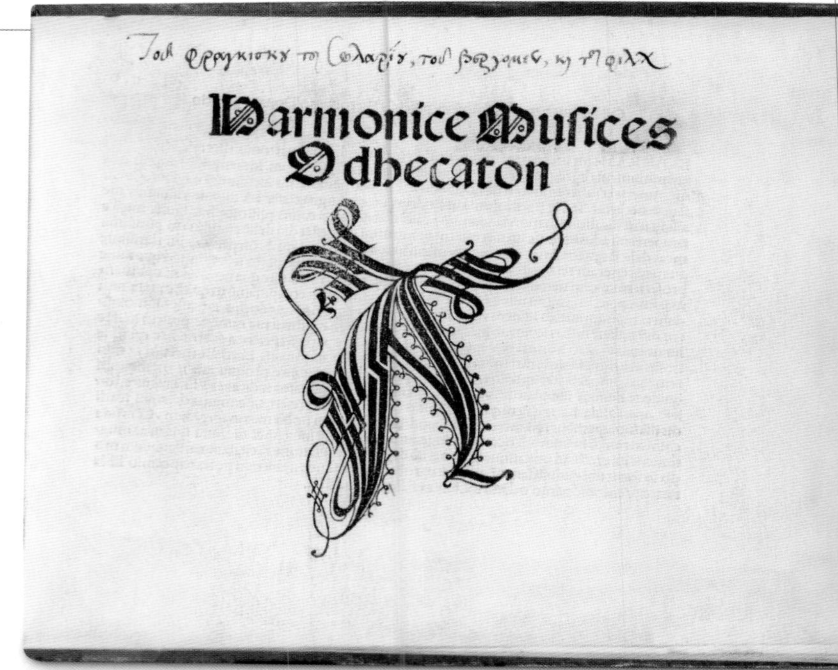

➤ **ODHECATON A** This is the title page to the first edition of Petrucci's polyphonic songs. The work contained many errors that were corrected in later editions. No complete volume of this edition survives today.

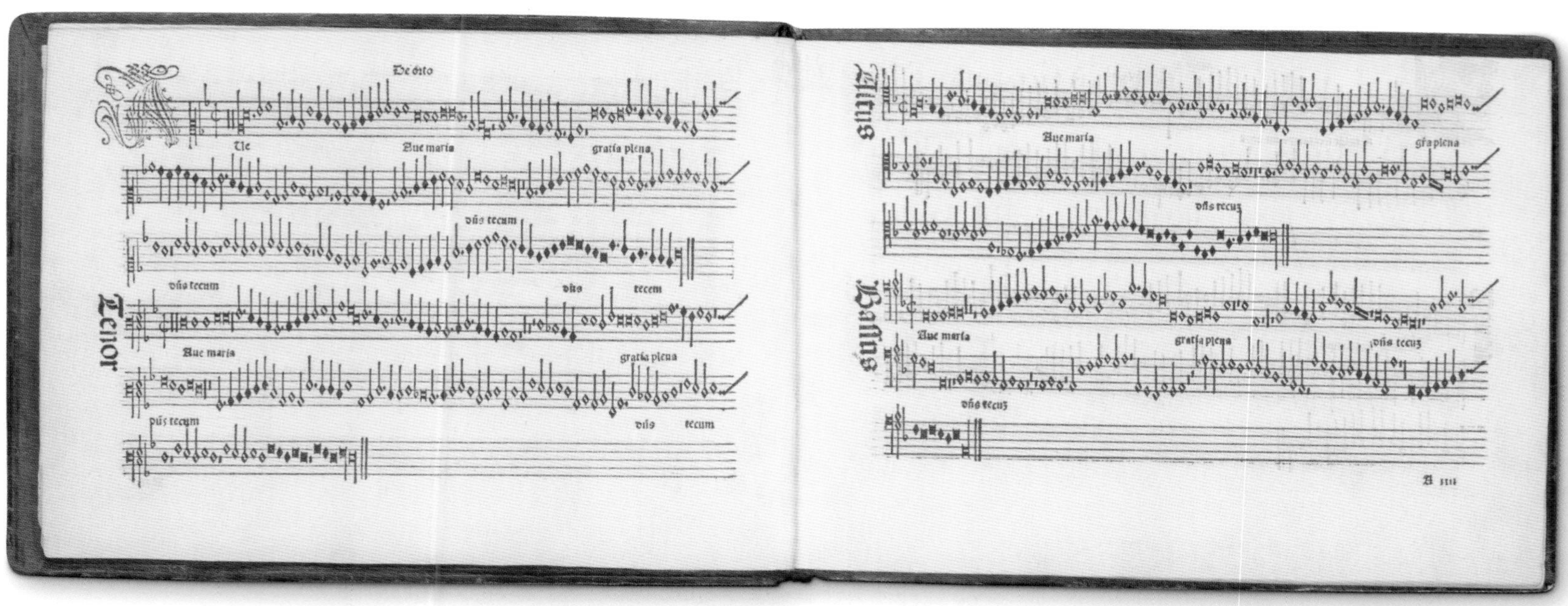

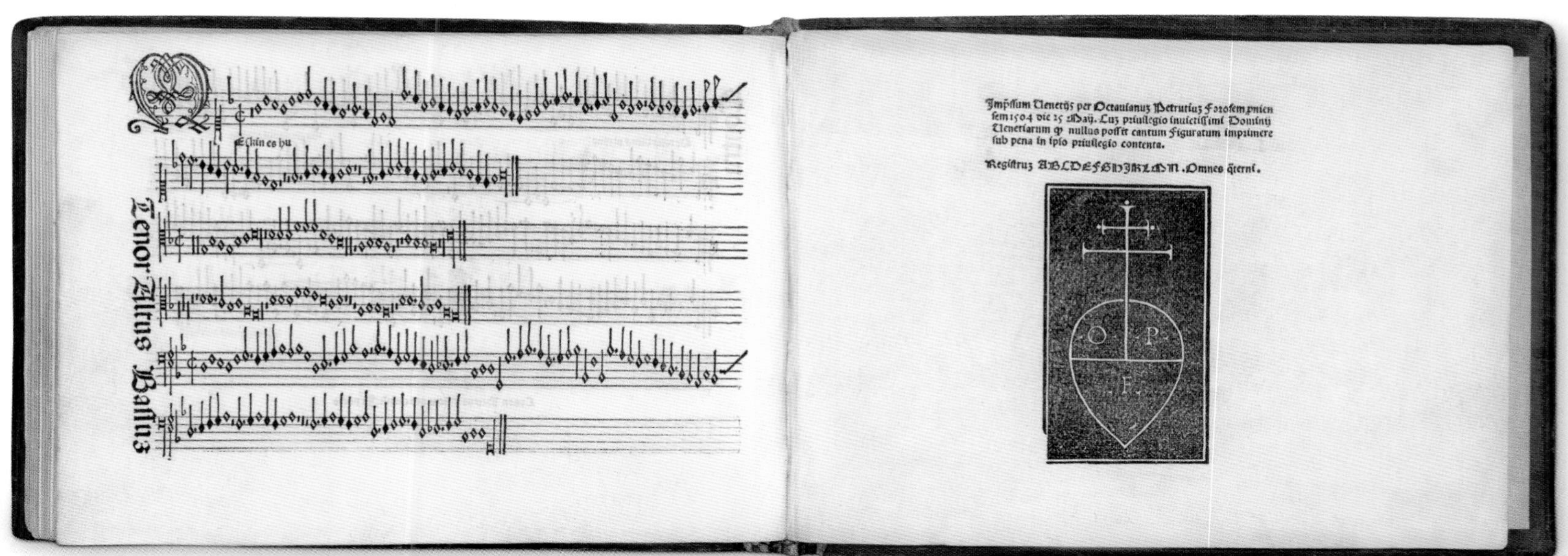

> To my longstanding friend the good Jerome; the best patron. This is the monument of your choice…

PETRUCCI'S DEDICATORY LETTER INTRODUCING *ODHECATON* TO GIROLAMO DONATO, A VENETIAN NOBLEMAN WHOSE BLESSING WOULD ENSURE THE BOOK WAS WIDELY ACCEPTED

OTTAVIANO **PETRUCCI**

1466–1539

Ottaviano Petrucci was an Italian printer and publisher. He was a pioneer in the publication of printed sheet music with movable type, and became famous for creating the first printed book of polyphonic music, the *Odhecaton*.

Born in Fossombrone, Italy, Petrucci lived there until 1490 when he went to live in Venice, a major printing centre. In 1498 it is likely that the Doges (magistrate) granted his request for the sole 20-year licence to print musical scores in the Venetian Republic. In 1501 Petrucci created the *Odhecaton*, modelling his work on the stave and notation system devised around the 11th century by Benedictine monk, Guido d'Arezzo. He left Venice at the outbreak of war in 1509 and returned to Fossombrone. As this town lay in the Papal States, he was granted a licence to print by Pope Leo X, but later had his right revoked after failing to make any keyboard music. During the battles of the papacy, Petrucci's printing equipment is thought to have been destroyed by papal troops in 1516 when the town was invaded. In 1536 he returned to Venice, where he printed Greek and Latin texts. The first major publisher of sheet music, Petrucci produced 16 books of masses, five of motets (polyphonic chorals), 11 of *frottole* (comic songs) and six books of lute music.

The Codex Leicester

1506–10 ▪ PEN AND INK ON PAPER ▪ 29 × 22 cm (11 × 9 in) ▪ 72 PAGES ▪ ITALY

SCALE

LEONARDO DA VINCI

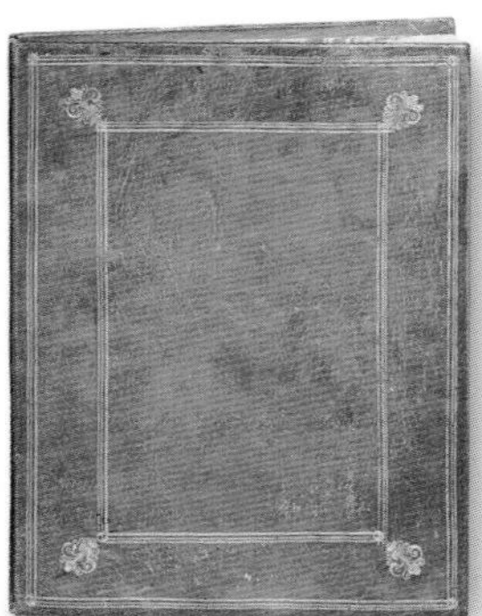

The *Codex Leicester* is a collection of scientific writings recorded in a notebook by the Italian polymath, Leonardo da Vinci. One of several notebooks compiled by da Vinci, the *Codex Leicester* is one of the most remarkable artefacts of the Renaissance. The *Codex* consists of 18 parchment sheets, each folded in two. The result is 72 pages of densely written text, with a series of over 300 ink-drawn illustrations, some hastily sketched in the page margins, others more obviously considered and detailed. The work highlights the interest that Leonardo took in the world around him, as well as his belief that it could only be explained by precise observation. As such, the *Codex* is a clear precursor to the scientific revolution of the 17th and 18th centuries.

Leonardo produced about 13,000 such pages, of which approximately half have survived in similar notebooks. Their subjects range from academic treatments of paintings, to studies of human anatomy, designs for flying and siege machines, and architecture. The principal subject matter of the *Codex Leicester* is water and its properties, but it also touches on a range of other topics. These include why the sky is blue, that mountains may once have been underwater, as well as subjects such as meteorology, cosmology, shells, fossils, and gravity.

The *Codex Leicester* takes its name from its acquisition in 1719 by an English nobleman, the Earl of Leicester. It is sometimes also known as the *Codex Hammer*, a reference to the American, Armand Hammer, who bought it in 1980 before selling it to Bill Gates for US$30.8m in 1994. Today it is not just the most expensive written work in the world, but the only one of Leonardo da Vinci's numerous notebooks to be kept in the United States.

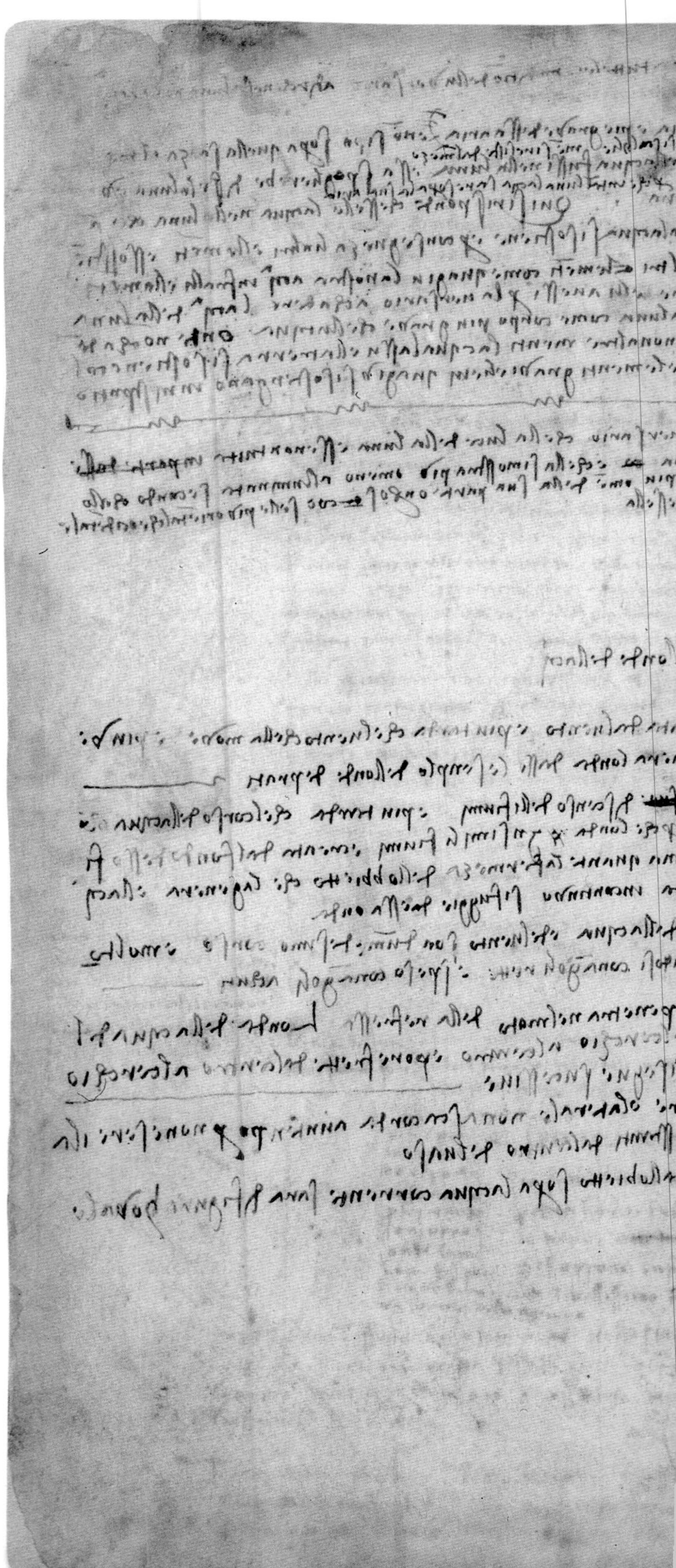

➤ **PRECISELY WRITTEN TEXT** Though littered with corrections and amendments, and jotted, marginal illustrations, Leonardo's neat handwriting, shown here, is typical of the *Codex*. The diagram on the bottom-right page illustrates the luminosity of the moon, with Leonardo showing, correctly, that the light of the moon is no more than a partial reflection of the light shone on it by the sun.

You will not laugh at me, Reader, if I make big jumps from one subject to another…

LEONARDO DA VINCI, THE *CODEX LEICESTER*

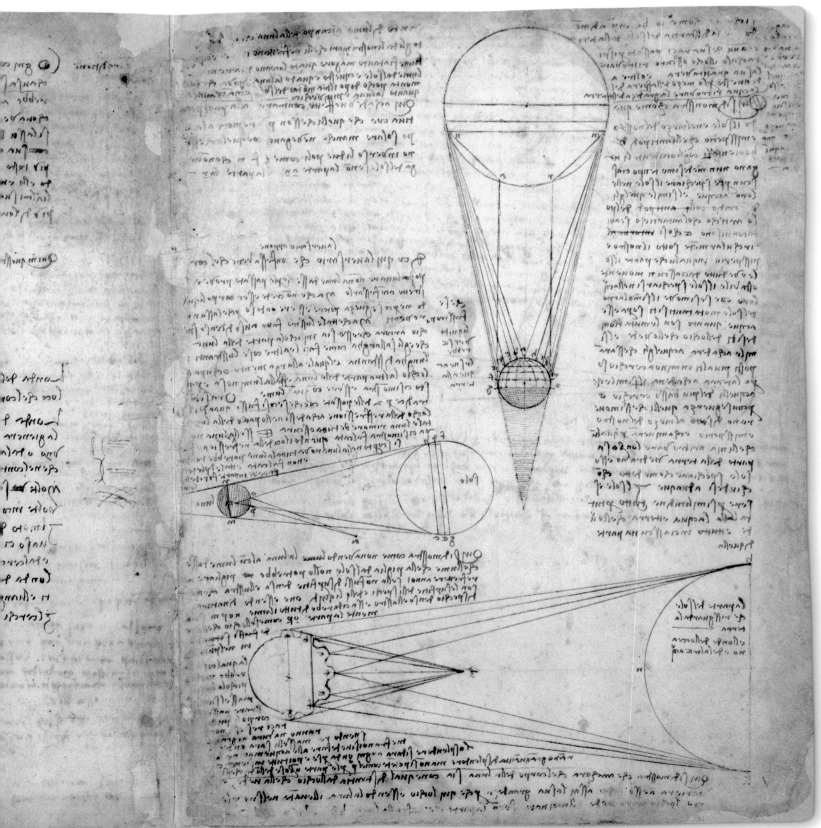

In detail

It's an inspiration that one person… kept pushing himself that he found knowledge itself to be the most beautiful thing

BILL GATES, CURRENT OWNER OF THE *CODEX LEICESTER*

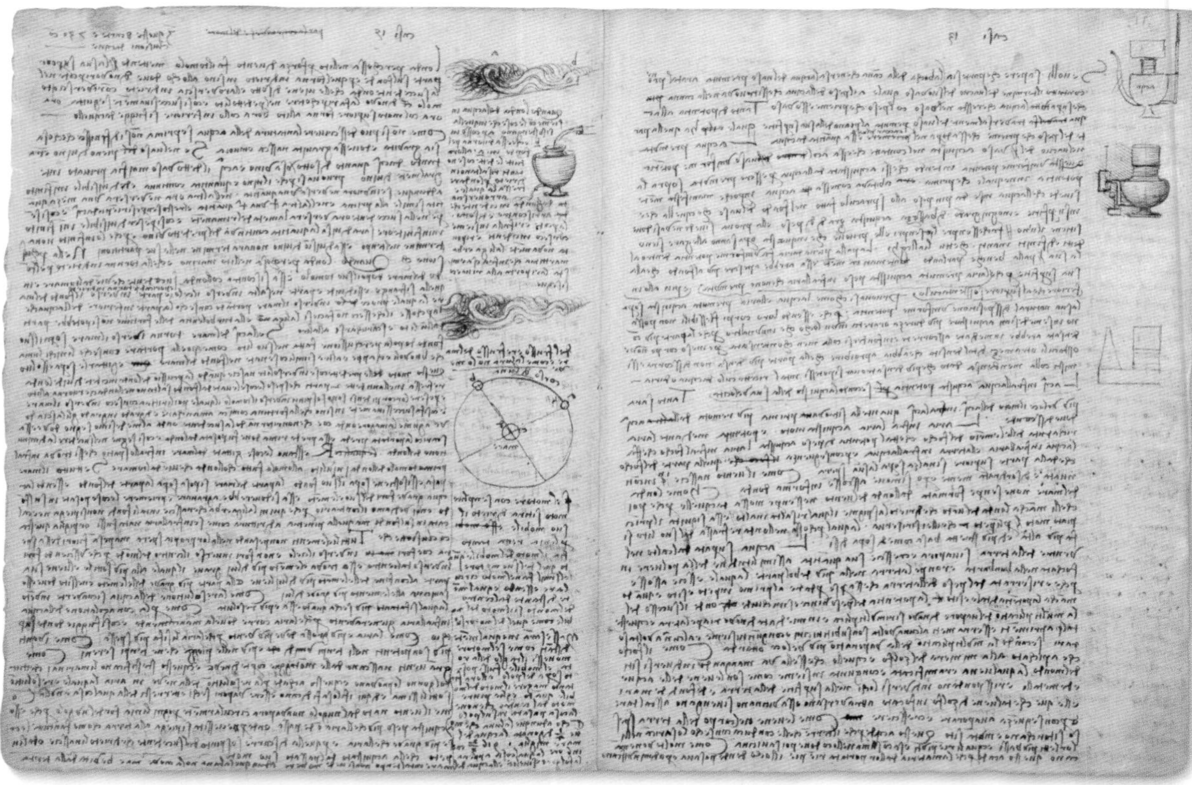

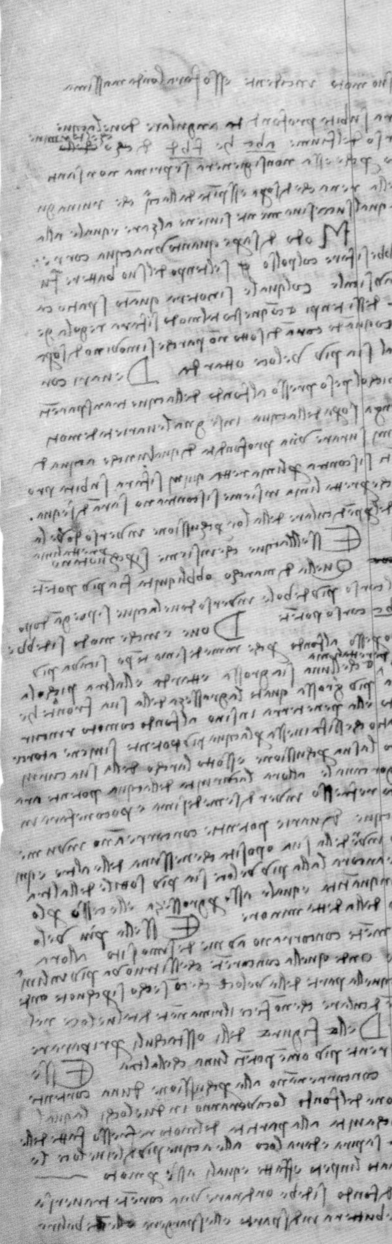

▲ **MIRROR WRITING** Leonardo composed the *Codex* in his characteristic mirror writing, where the text is written in reverse, and intended to be read from right to left. The reason for this is not known, as he only used the technique for his private works. It may have been an attempt to keep his work secret by making it harder to read.

▲ **MARGINAL ILLUSTRATIONS** Leonardo was interested in showing his ideas as much as he was in explaining them, and he frequently added sketches to the margins of his work. On this page he explores how water flows, and suggests experiments designed to study erosion. Among other things, his illustrations on this page consider the passage of water around different arrangements of obstructions.

LEONARDO **DA VINCI**

1452–1519

Italian polymath Leonardo da Vinci was one of the greatest creative minds in history. Best known as an artist and the painter of the *Mona Lisa*, he was also a talented sculptor, engineer, inventor, and scientist.

Born near the town of Vinci in Tuscany, Leonardo da Vinci was apprenticed aged 15 to the renowned Florentine artist, Andrea de Verrocchio, and qualified in 1478. He spent the next 17 years in Milan as a sculptor and artist, but also practised engineering and architecture. While in Milan he painted *The Last Supper*, a mural at the refectory of Monastery Santa Maria delle Grazie. After 1499, Leonardo returned to Florence where he painted his most famous portrait, the *Mona Lisa*. Although Leonardo is known primarily as an artist, the versatility of his brilliant mind is demonstrated in his collection of unpublished notebooks, including the *Codex Leicester*, which are filled with inventions and theories on a vast array of subjects, from anatomy to geology. As such Leonardo is regarded as being the finest example of the "Renaissance Man" – one with diverse talents and curiosity about multiple subjects. He died in France in the service of the French king, François I.

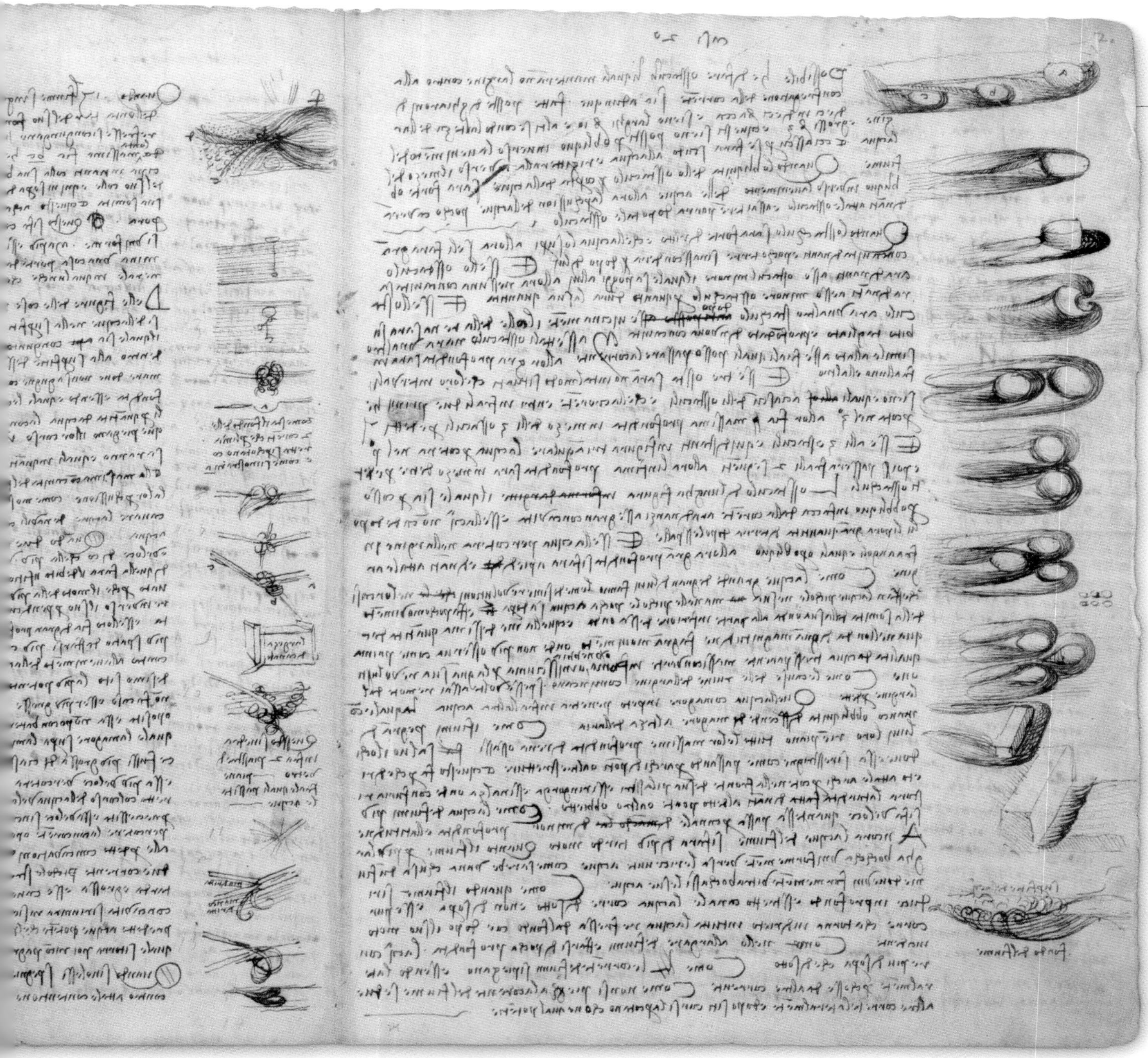

◄ **HAPHAZARD ENTRIES** The seemingly chaotic quality of the notebooks is exhibited in this unlikely juxtaposition of an aging man sitting on a rock (age was a recurring feature in Leonardo's work), with studies of water flowing, often violently, past obstacles. The capacity of water to erode even the most resistant objects was a subject that fascinated him.

► **SEESAW STUDY** Leonardo's hastily drawn image of two men on a seesaw was intended to show the impact of weight and distance on equilibrium. It also made a wider point: that Earth's hemispheres had unequal masses. Leonardo believed that the heavier hemisphere was sinking to the centre, causing rocks of the lighter hemisphere to rise up, forming mountains.

Vier Bücher von menschlicher Proportion

1528 ■ PRINTED WITH WOODCUT ILLUSTRATIONS ■ 29 × 20 cm (11 × 8 in) ■ 264 PAGES ■ GERMANY

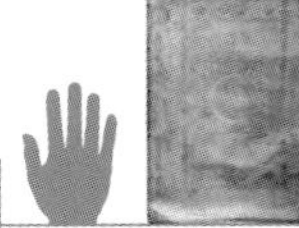

SCALE

ALBRECHT DÜRER

Translated as *Four Books on Human Proportion*, Albrecht Dürer's seminal work is an illustrated exploration of the human form through all the stages of life. It built on anatomical observations from antiquity, such as those of the 1st-century BCE Roman architect Marcus Vitruvius, and of Dürer's own contemporaries, such as Leonardo da Vinci. Unlike Vitruvius, who believed in an ideal set of human proportions, Dürer felt that the beauty of form was a relative quality. He created a system of anthropometry (the scientific study of measurements and proportions of the human body) that would enable artists to draw people of all shapes and sizes, as close to nature as possible.

There were woodcut illustrations on almost every page: around 136 full-length drawings of the human figure (men, women, and infants), as well as smaller proportional woodcuts detailing limbs, heads, hands, and feet, and four fold-out diagrams. To make the work accessible to a wider audience it was written in German, rather than Latin, using an ornate Gothic type in double columns.

Dürer's work existed only in manuscript form until his death in April 1528 – it was published posthumously by his wife and a friend, Willibald Pirckheimer, in October 1528 as four books. The first two cover anthropometry; the third considers variations, such as over- and underweight people, and irregular physical features; the fourth shows the human body in motion. The result was the first published work that attempted to harness the science of human anatomical proportions and apply it to aesthetics.

► **MEASURING STICK** Dürer devised a "canon of proportion" for portraying the idealized human form. Here the artist shows female models holding a measuring stick against which each section of the body could be measured and proportions gauged. In the book Dürer also pioneered the use of crosshatching in his wood engravings to represent shade and shadows.

In detail

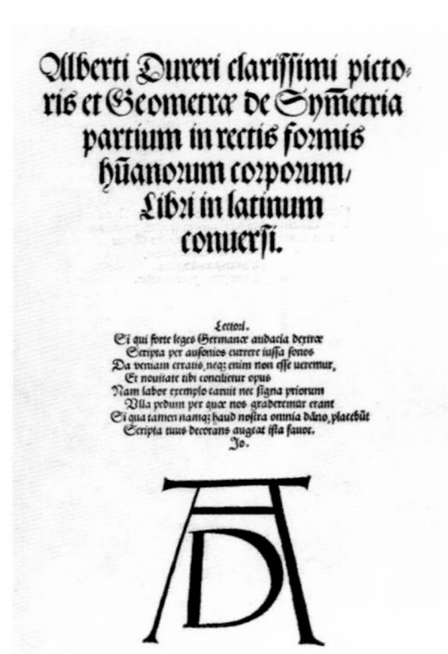

Alberti Dureri clarissimi picto-
ris et Geometrae de Symetria
partium in rectis formis
hūanorum corporum,
Libri in latinum
conversi.

Lectori.
Si qui forte leges Germanae audacia dextrae
Scripta per ausonios currere iussa sonos
Da veniam erratis, neq; enim non esse veremur,
Et novitate tibi concilietur opus
Nam labor exemplo caruit nec signa priorum
Ulla pedum per quae nos graderemur erant
Si qua tamen namq; haud nostra omnia dāno, placebūt
Scripta tuus decorans augeat ista favor.
Io.

▲ **TITLE PAGE** Albrecht Dürer's distinctive monogram, "AD", appears on the title page of the original publication.

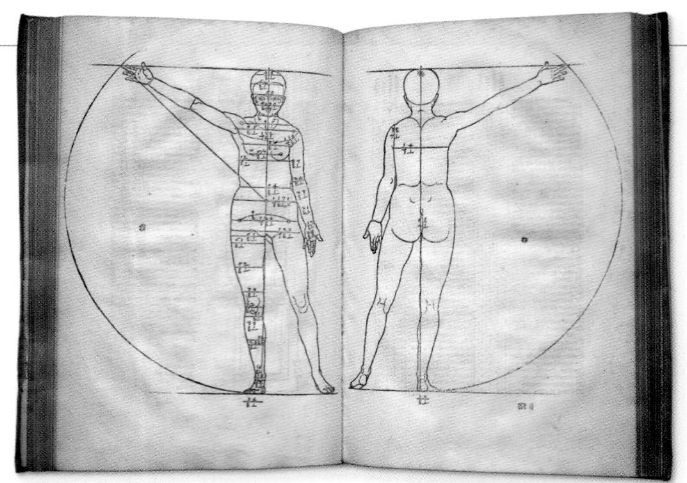

▲ **CIRCLES** Dürer not only illustrated the book, but wrote and designed it too. Some of his woodcuts follow Leonardo's approach to the study of anatomy, and depict figures within a circle with the navel indicated as the central point of the human adult. These diagrams show the measurements of the human form. Different parts of the body were described in more detail in charts on the following pages. Dürer's style of drawing was later adapted for use in books on medical anatomy.

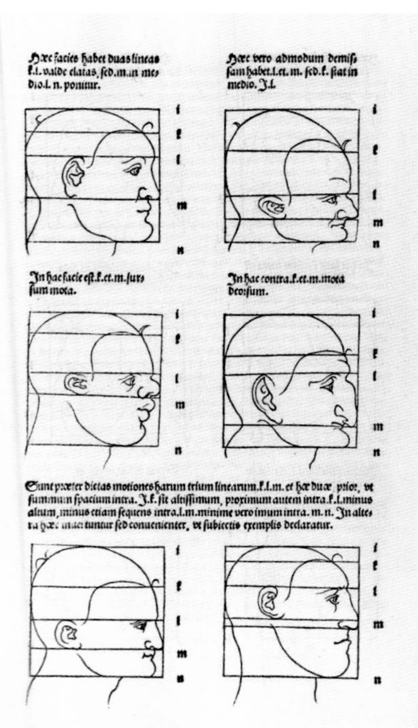

Haec facies habet duas lineas k.l. valde elatas, sed.m.n me-dio.l. n. ponitur.

Haec vero admodum demis-sam habet.l.et.m. sed.k. fiat in medio. J.l.

In hac facie est.k.et.m.sur-sum mota.

In hac contra.k.et.m.mota deorsum.

Sunt praeter dictas motiones harum trium linearum.k.l.m. et haec duae, prior, ut summum spacium intra. J.k. sit altissimum, proximum autem intra.k.l.minus altum, minus etiam sequens intra.l.m.minime vero imum intra. m. n. In alte-ra haec mactuntur sed convenienter, ut subiectis exemplis declaratur.

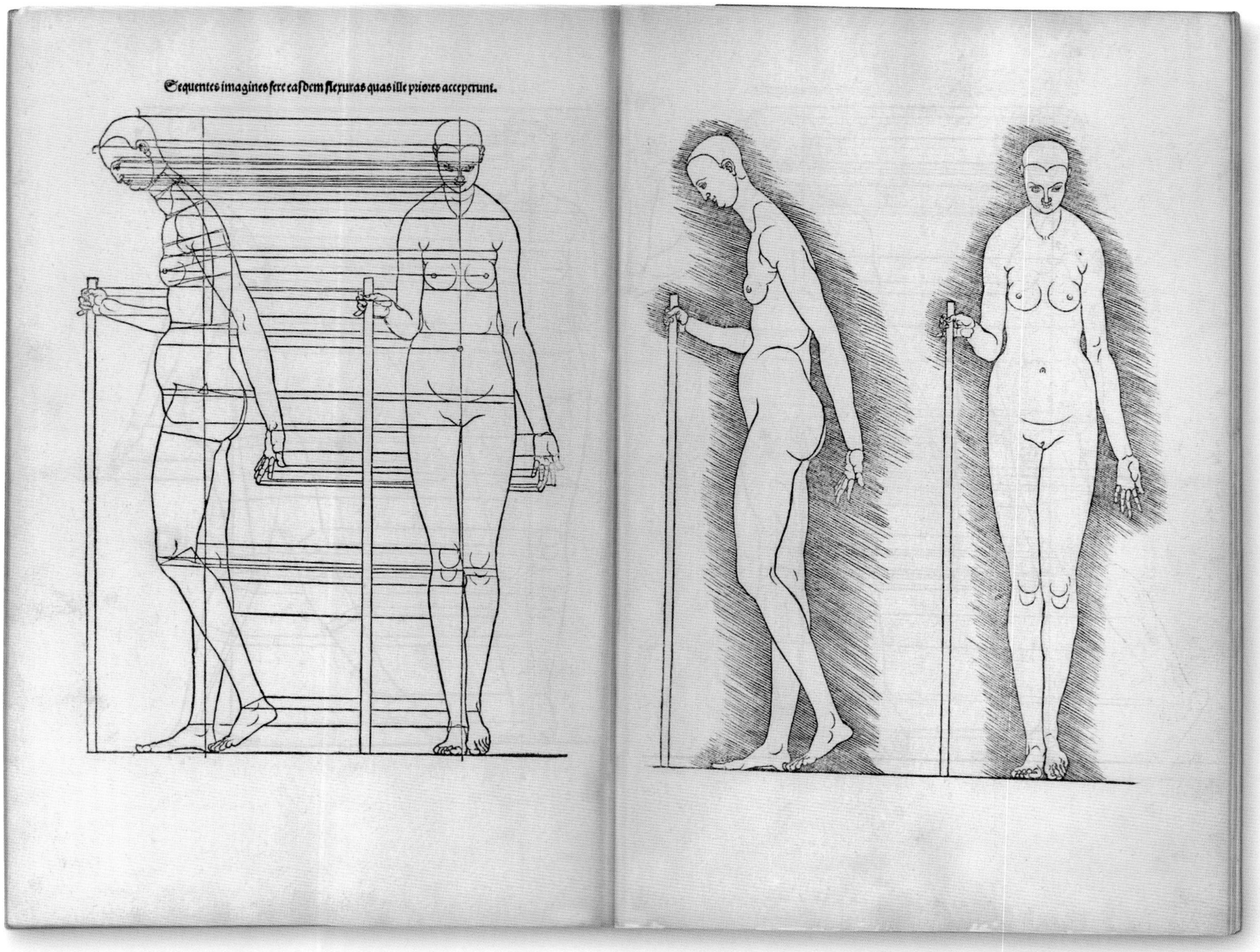

Sequentes imagines fere easdem flexuras quas ille priores acceperunt.

> I hold that the perfection of form and beauty is contained in the sum of all men

ALBRECHT DÜRER, *VIER BÜCHER VON MENSCHLICHER PROPORTION*

◄ **USING GRIDS** In the third book Dürer adjusts the "proper" proportions of the human form using mathematical rules and grids. This page focuses on the human head and shows the various proportional possibilities of facial features using a grid-box. These grids serve to demonstrate the unique structure of the human head, for example highlighting different nose lengths and shapes.

ALBRECHT **DÜRER**

1471–1528

Painter, printmaker, and mathematician, Albrecht Dürer is widely acknowledged as the greatest artist of the German Renaissance. Credited with some of the most sophisticated woodcuts ever produced, his graphic work had the greatest influence.

As a child Dürer showed prodigious artistic talent and was apprenticed at the age of 15 to the eminent painter and printmaker Michael Wolgemut. He furthered his studies between 1490 and 1494 when he travelled to Northern Europe and Alsace. Returning to Nuremberg in the summer of 1494 he married Agnes Frey before leaving to spend a year in northern Italy. During a second trip to Italy (1505–07) Dürer encountered the work of Leonardo da Vinci, among other artists, and deepened his knowledge of human anatomy and proportion, which he continued to study for the rest of his career. On his return to Nuremberg, he furthered his knowledge of geometry, mathematics, Latin, and humanist literature, although he still painted, becoming Court Painter to Emperor Maximilian in 1512. He died in Nuremberg on 6 April 1528 while still working on *Vier Bücher von menschlicher Proportion*. He left behind a huge body of work, from drawings and paintings to woodcuts and treatises.

Il Principe

1532 ▪ PRINTED ▪ 21 × 13.5 cm (8 × 5 in) ▪ 50 PAGES ▪ ITALY

SCALE

NICCOLÒ MACHIAVELLI

More than 500 years after it was conceived, *Il Principe* (*The Prince*) is still considered one of the most important treatises on political power. A handbook for politicians, it advises that rulers should be amoral in order to serve their own ambitions and overcome their enemies. It was written around 1515 and and published in 1532, five years after the death of the author, Niccolò Machiavelli. The book was so influential that the author's name spawned the word "Machiavellian", meaning unscrupulous and cunning.

Machiavelli, a foreign policy envoy for the regional state of Florence, wrote from experience. The main premise of his book, a relatively short text comprising 26 chapters, is that the well-being of the state is a priority, and that a ruler is justified in using any means to achieve that end – betraying others, manipulating human weakness – but being consistent no matter what the cost. The book was also intended as a blueprint for how Italy, weakened by internal fighting, could be restored to a strong position within Europe. In an attempt to ingratiate himself with the ruling Medici family, Machiavelli dedicated his book to the young prince Lorenzo de' Medici. A copy was given to the prince and handwritten copies were circulated privately. The book only acquired its title on publication nearly 20 years later. Considered shocking and immoral by critics – Pope Paul IV put it on the Vatican's Index of Forbidden Books in 1557 – it remains one of Western civilization's most influential texts. Its cynical chapters have inspired despots and tyrants, such as Hitler and Stalin, for over five centuries.

NICCOLÒ **MACHIAVELLI**

1469–1527

Credited with founding the science of modern politics, Niccolò Machiavelli changed the course of history with his theories on power, and the ruthlessness required of a leader.

Born during the height of the Renaissance in Florence, Machiavelli studied law, but became a diplomat working on behalf of his native city. This was a time of unrest in Italy, with its different regions fighting for dominance. In 1494 the ruling Medici family was expelled and the Republic was restored, during which time Machiavelli acted as an envoy in Italy and abroad. Machiavelli also worked for an enemy of the Medici family, and when they returned to power in 1513 Machiavelli was arrested and tortured on suspicion of conspiracy. He was released from prison soon after but confined to his family estate outside Florence, his political career over. Machiavelli wrote *Il Principe* at this time, as well as a play, *The Mandrake*. He died in poverty.

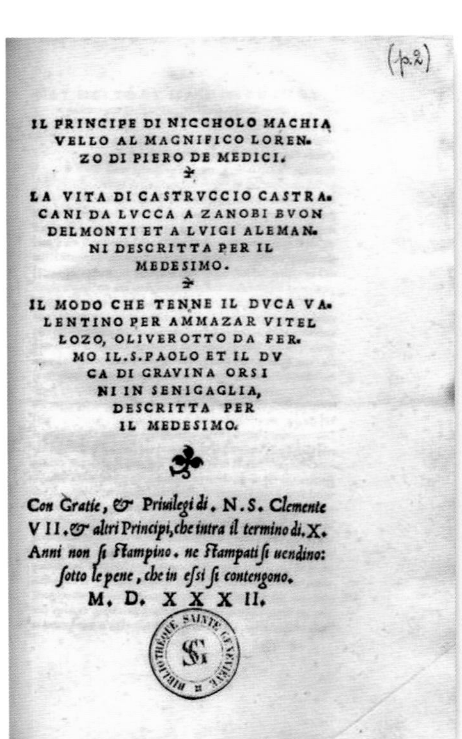

(p.2)

IL PRINCIPE DI NICCHOLO MACHIA VELLO AL MAGNIFICO LOREN. ZO DI PIERO DE MEDICI.

LA VITA DI CASTRVCCIO CASTRA. CANI DA LVCCA A ZANOBI BVON DELMONTI ET A LVIGI ALEMAN. NI DESCRITTA PER IL MEDESIMO.

IL MODO CHE TENNE IL DVCA VA. LENTINO PER AMMAZAR VITEL LOZO, OLIVEROTTO DA FER. MO IL.S.PAOLO ET IL DV CA DI GRAVINA ORSI NI IN SENIGAGLIA, DESCRITTA PER IL MEDESIMO.

Con Gratie, & Priuilegi di. N.S. Clemente VII.& altri Principi, che intra il termino di.X. Anni non ſi ſtampino. ne ſtampati ſi uendino: ſotto le pene, che in eſsi ſi contengono.

M. D. XXXII.

◀ **TITLE PAGE** The book's first edition bears a dedication to Lorenzo di Piero de' Medici, ruler of the city-state of Florence from 1513 to 1519. While Machiavelli hoped this inscription would win him favour with Medici, historians have found no evidence that the prince ever read the book.

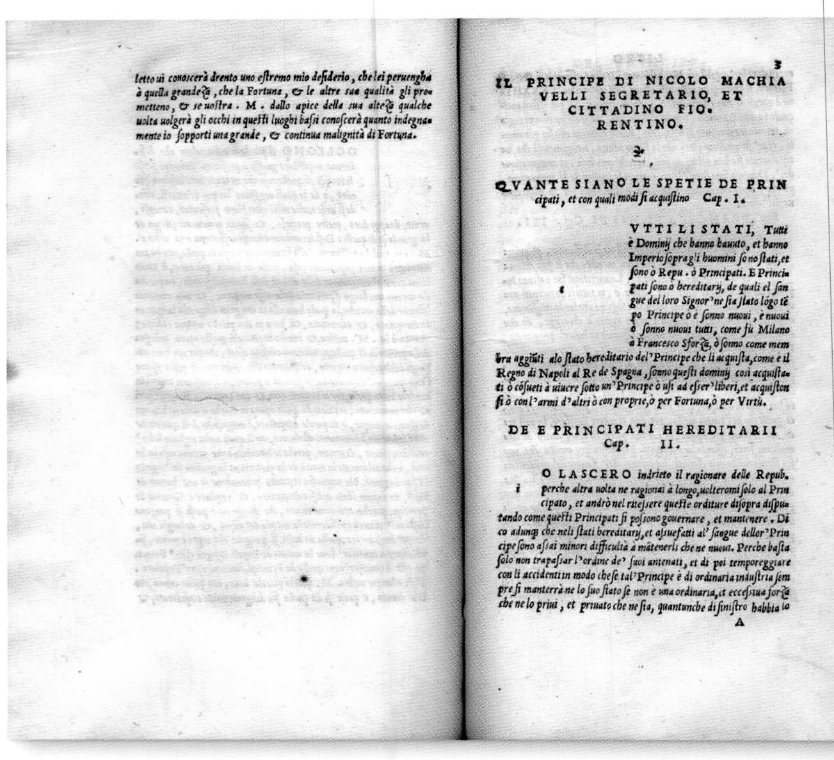

letto ui conoscerà drento uno eſtremo mio deſiderio, che lei peruengha à quella grandezza, che la Fortuna, & le altre sua qualità gli pro= metteno, & se uoſtra. M. dallo apice della sua altezza qualche uolta uolgerà gli occhi in queſti luoghi baſsi conoſcerà quanto indegna= mente io ſopporti una grande, & continua malignità di Fortuna.

3

IL PRINCIPE DI NICOLO MACHIA VELLI SEGRETARIO, ET CITTADINO FIO. RENTINO.

QVANTE SIANO LE SPETIE DE PRIN cipati, et con quali modi ſi acquiſtino Cap. I.

VTTI LI STATI, Tutti è Dominij che hanno hauuto, et hanno Imperio ſopra gli huomini ſono ſtati, et ſono ò Repu. ò Principati. E Princi= pati ſono ò hereditarij, de quali el ſan gue del loro Signor' ne ſia ſtato lógo tē po Principe ò è ſonno nuoui, è nuoui ò ſonno nuoui tutti, come ſu Milano à Francesco Sforza, ò ſonno come mem bra aggiūti alo ſtato hereditario del' Principe che li acquiſta, come è il Regno di Napoli al Re de Spagna, ſonno queſti dominij così acquiſta= ti ò cóſueti à uiuere ſotto un' Principe ò uſi ad eſser' liberi, et acquiſton ſi ò con l'armi d'altri ò con proprie, ò per Fortuna, ò per Virtù.

DE E PRINCIPATI HEREDITARII Cap. II.

O LASCERO indrieto il ragionare delle Repub. perche altra uolta ne ragionai à longo, uolteromi ſolo al Prin cipato, et andrò nel riteſsere queſte orditure diſopra diſpu= tando come queſti Principati ſi poſsono gouernare, et mantenere. Di co adunq; che neli ſtati hereditarij, et aſsuefatti al' ſangue dellor' Prin cipe ſono aſsai minori difficultà à mãtenerli che ne nuoui. Perche baſta ſolo non trapaſsar l'ordine de' ſuoi antenati, et di poi temporeggiare con li accidenti in modo che ſe tal' Principe è di ordinaria induſtria ſem pre ſi manterrà ne lo ſuo ſtato ſe non è una ordinaria, et eceſsiua forza che ne lo priui, et priuato che ne ſia, quantunche di ſiniſtro habbia lo

A

▶ **ITALIAN TYPESETTING** *Il Principe* is a fine example of 16th century Italian Renaissance printing, which was much more technically advanced than in Northern Europe. This edition is from the printing press of Antonio Blado de Asola in Rome, a renowned Italian printer.

LIBRO

ratione de l'armi, & la uariatione de li ordini. Et queste sono di quelle cose, che di nuouo ordinate, danno reputatione, & grandezza à uno Principe nuouo. Non si deue adunque lasciare passar' questa occasione, acciochè la Italia uegga doppò tanto tempo apparir un' suo redentore. Ne posso esprimere con quale amore ei fussi riceuuto in tutte quelle prouincie, che hanno patito per queste illuuioni esterne, con qual' sete di uendetta, con che ostinata fede con che pietà, con che lachrime. Quali porte se li serrerebbeno? Quali popoli li negarebbeno la obedientia? Quale inuidia se li opporrebbe? Quale Italiano li negarebbe l'ossequio? à ognun' puzza questo barbaro dominio. Pigli adunque la Illustre casa uostra questo assunto con quello animo, & con quelle speranze che si pigliono l'imprese iuste, accio che sotto la sua insegna, & questa patria ne sià nobilitata, è sotto i sua auspicij si uerifichi quello detto del' Petrarca.

Virtù contro al' furore
Prenderal' arme, & fia il combatter' corto,
Che l'anticho ualore
Nelli Italici cuor' non è ancor morto.

IL FINE DEL PRINCIPE.

36

LA VITA DI CASTRVCCIO CASTRACANI DA LVCCA DESCRITTA DA NICCOLO MACHIAVELLI ET MANDATA A ZANOBI BVONDELMONTI ET A LVIGI ALAMANNI SVOI AMICISSIMI.

PARE, ZANOBI ET LVIGI carissimi à quelli, che la considerano cosa marauigliosa, che tutti coloro, ò la maggior parte di essi che hanno in questo modo operato grandissime cose & intra gl'altri della loro eta siano stati eccellēti, habbiano hauuto il principio, & nascimento loro basso, & oscuro, ò uero dalla fortuna, fuora di ogni modo trauagliato. Perche tutti, ò ei sono stati esposti alle fiere, ò eglino hanno hauuto si uile padre che uergogniatisi di quello si sono fatti figliuoli di Gioue, ò di qualche altro Diò Quali sieno stati questi sendone à ciascuno noti molti, sarebbe cosa à replicare fastidiosa, & poco accetta à chi leggessi, perciò come superflua la posporremo. Credo bene che questo nasca che uolendo la fortuna dimostrare al' mondo di essere quella che faccia li huomini grandi, & non la Prudentia comincia à dimostrare le sue forze in tempo che la Prudentia non ci possa hauere alcuna parte, anzi da lei si habbia à riconoscere il tutto. Fu adunque Castruccio Castracani da Lucca, uno di quelli, il quale, secondo i tempi ne' quali uisse, & la Città donde nacque fece cose grandissime, & come li altri non hebbe più felice, ne più noto nascimento come nel' ragionare del' corso della sua uita s'intenderà la quale mi è parso ridurre alla memoria delli huomini, parendomi hauer' trouato in essa molte cose, & quanto alla Virtù, & quanto alla Fortuna di grandissimo essempio. Et mi e parso indirizarla à uoi come à quelli che più che altri huomini, che io conosca delle attioni uirtuose ui dilettate.

I ij

◄ **AN ELEGANT APPEARANCE** Although controversial, *Il Principe* was widely admired for technical reasons: firstly, for its accomplished use of Italian grammar, the rules for which had only just been formalized; and secondly, for the page design, which reflected the Renaissance ideals of harmony and symmetry. Text is mostly centred and justified, with tightly controlled spacing, while sections arranged in inverted pyramids draw the eye downwards. Wide margins were typical, to allow for the reader's notes.

> ... since love and fear can hardly exist together, if we must choose between them, it is far safer to be feared than to be loved
>
> **NICCOLÒ MACHIAVELLI**, *IL PRINCIPE*

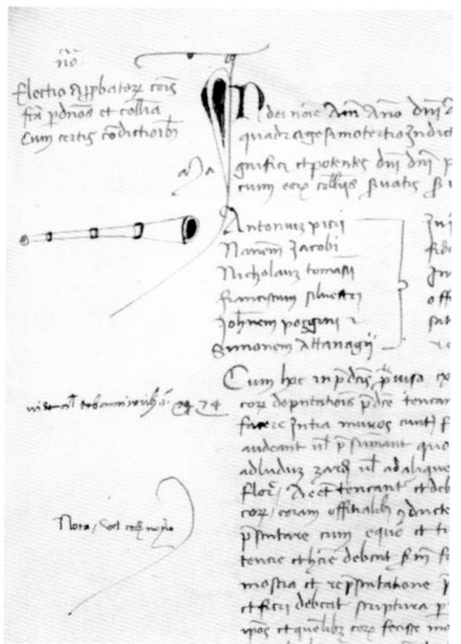

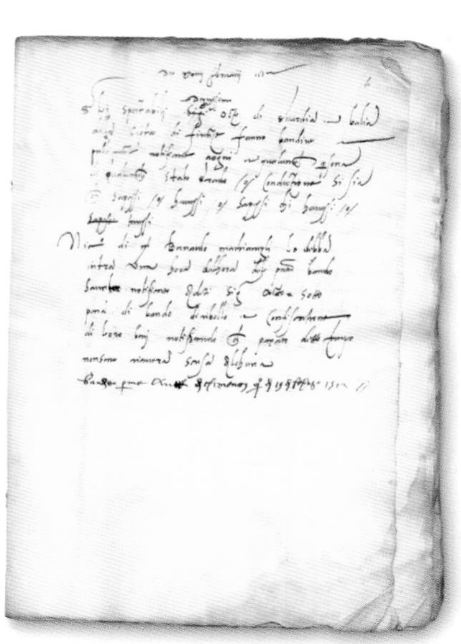

▲ **ARREST OF A TRAITOR** A proclamation read by the town crier of Florence in 1513 (recently found with a drawing of the trumpet the town crier used, left) declares the arrest of Niccolò Machiavelli on suspicion of plotting to overthrow the Medicis. He was later released, and shortly after began writing *Il Principe*.

IN **CONTEXT**

Il Principe provided the basis for some important principles adopted by the founding fathers of the United States. Leadership based on merit, not birthright, is enshrined in the Declaration of Independence, inspired by Machiavelli's idea that "he who obtains sovereignty by the assistance of the nobles maintains himself with more difficulty than he who comes to it by the aid of the people".

▲ **John Trumbull's** painting *Declaration of Independence*, shows the Founding Fathers, all of whom had read Machiavelli's ideas on power in *Il Principe*.

Epitome

1543 ■ PRINTED ON VELLUM AND PAPER ■ 55.8 × 37.4 cm (22 × 14 in) ■ 27 PAGES ■ SWITZERLAND

ANDREAS VESALIUS

Setting a new standard for anatomical illustration, the *Epitome* by Andreas Vesalius combined scientific accuracy with exquisite artistry in a way not seen before. It was a shortened version of his larger work *De humani corporis fabrica libri septem* (*On the Fabric of the Human Body in Seven Volumes*), a comprehensive investigation of the workings of the human body. Intended as a ready guide for medical students, the *Epitome* was printed in a large format that allowed the illustrations to be hung as wall charts, and had minimal text compared with the complex seven-volume version of 80,000 words.

Vesalius's masterful work is particularly remarkable for its innovative layout. The first half of the book shows the human body being gradually built up from its basic components. The skeleton is depicted first, then organs, muscles, and skin are added to it in layers, culminating in complete male and female nudes in the centre of the book. If the reader instead started at the centre of the book and worked towards the beginning, they could replicate the process of a dissection. The book also included pages to cut out and assemble into a 3D paper model.

Published in June 1543 this book was four years in the making. The illustrations are thought to have been commissioned by Vesalius from the Venice workshop of the artist Titian (1490–1576). When ready, Vesalius travelled to Basel in Switzerland, then the publishing centre of Europe, where he chose printer Johannes Oporinus to engrave and print the book. Oporinus was one of the best at his trade – meticulous and innovative. Most of the woodblocks he produced for the book were housed in the Bavarian State Library in Munich, Germany, but were destroyed during Allied bombing in 1944.

ANDREAS **VESALIUS**

1514–1564

Flemish physician and surgeon, Andreas Vesalius emerged as the most gifted anatomist of the Renaissance, reviving the practice of human dissection after it fell from favour during the Middle Ages.

Born in Brussels and educated in Paris, Vesalius studied medicine at the University of Padua, Italy. It was one of the few institutions that promoted human dissection, a technique that had all but disappeared after the fall of the Roman Empire as it was considered immoral under the codes of medieval Catholicism. Unlike most medical practitioners at the time, Vesalius advocated the use of dissection as the key to understanding how the body worked.

At the age of 23 he became Professor of Surgery at the University of Padua. He dissected cadavers in front of his students, and made new discoveries that contradicted and challenged existing theories about the human body, most notably those of the Greek physician, Galen of Peramum (129–c.216).

In 1543 Vesalius published his groundbreaking work, *De humani corporis fabrica libri septem*, which became the definitive volume on human anatomy. He was made physician to the Holy Roman Emperor, Charles V, and later to his son.

▲ **FRONTISPIECE** Considered one of the finest engravings of the 16th century, the frontispiece shows author and publisher Vesalius at the centre, surrounded by his students and fellow physicians, along with nobles and church dignitaries. Vesalius indicates his break with convention by demonstrating his knowledge of dissection on the cadaver next to him, rather than by lecturing from his chair.

these things **should be learnt,** not from pictures but from **careful dissection** and examination **of the actual objects**

ANDREAS VESALIUS, *DE HUMANI CORPORIS FABRICA LIBRI SEPTEM,* 1543

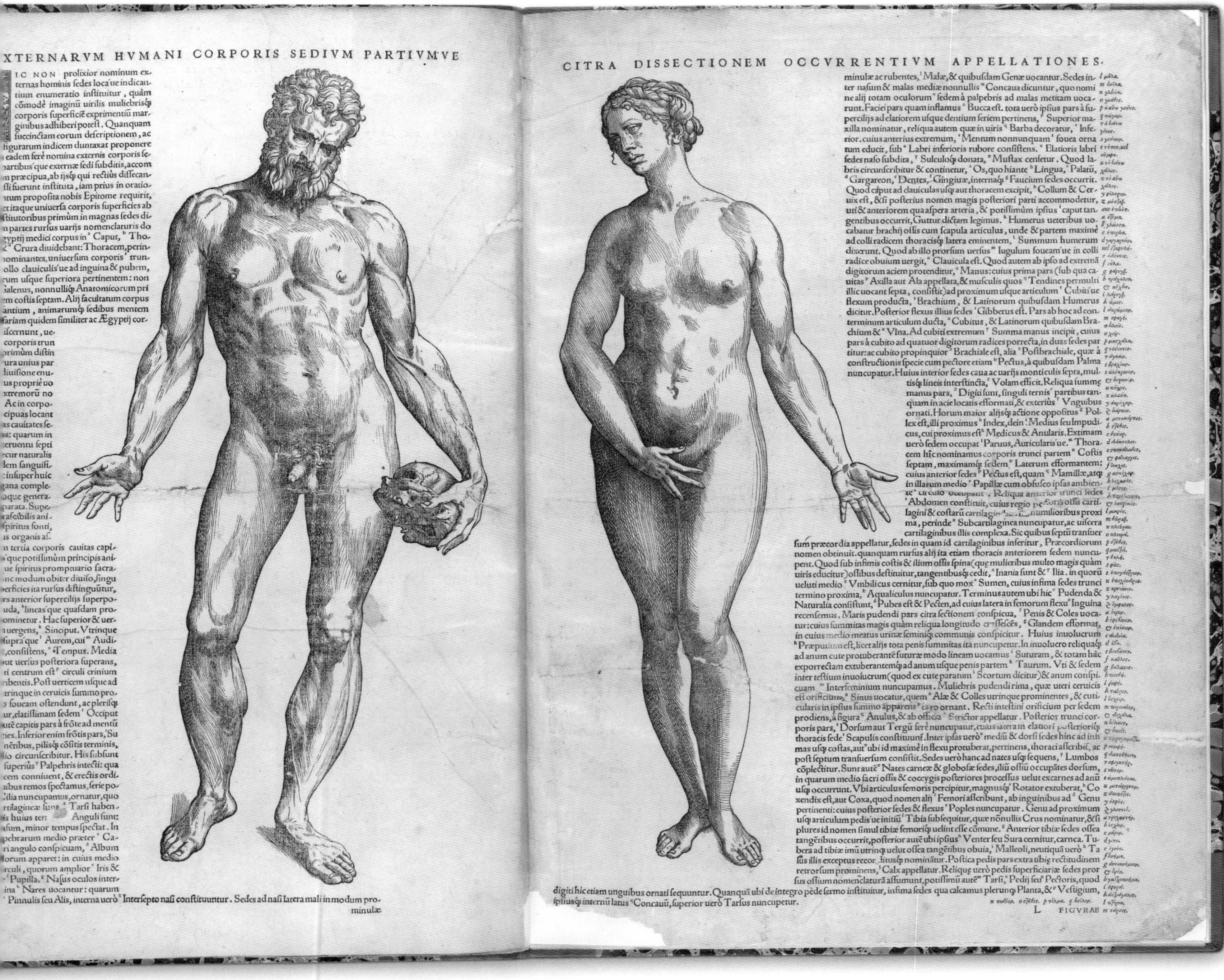

▲ **THE CENTREPIECE** At the centre of the book are male and female nude figures drawn in the style of classical Greek sculpture. The typesetting flows around them, creating an impression of balance and harmony. The male figure is depicted in a pose reminiscent of Hercules, with a full beard and sturdy muscular body, holding a skull in his left hand. His female counterpart is posed like a classical Venus, with her hair braided and pinned up, her eyes downcast, and her right hand positioned to maintain her modesty.

In detail

▼ **UPPERMOST MUSCLE LAYERS** Apart from the female figure of the centrepiece, all other dissected figures in the book are male. They are posed in an active fashion with the arms outstretched, the legs in a natural stance, and the head in varying positions. This figure shows the two uppermost layers of muscle in detail, revealing how they overlap and fit together.

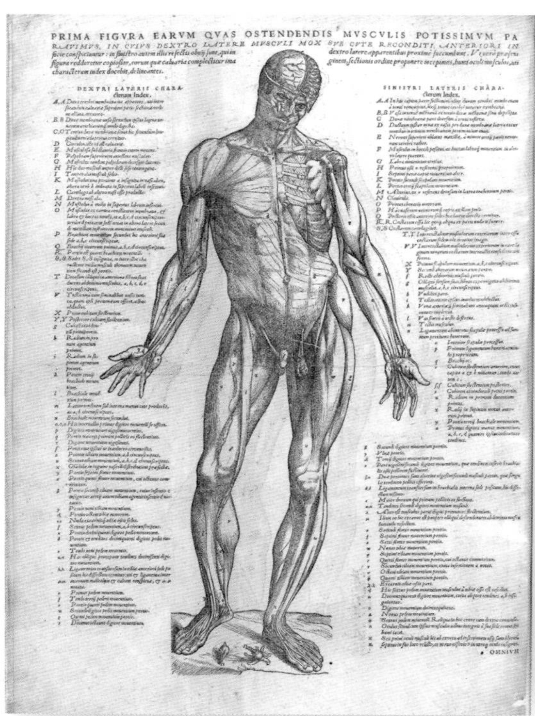

▼ **DIGESTIVE SYSTEM** Continuing on from the nude figures at the centre of the book, Vesalius provides meticulously detailed charts of the digestive system, with intricately drawn organs.

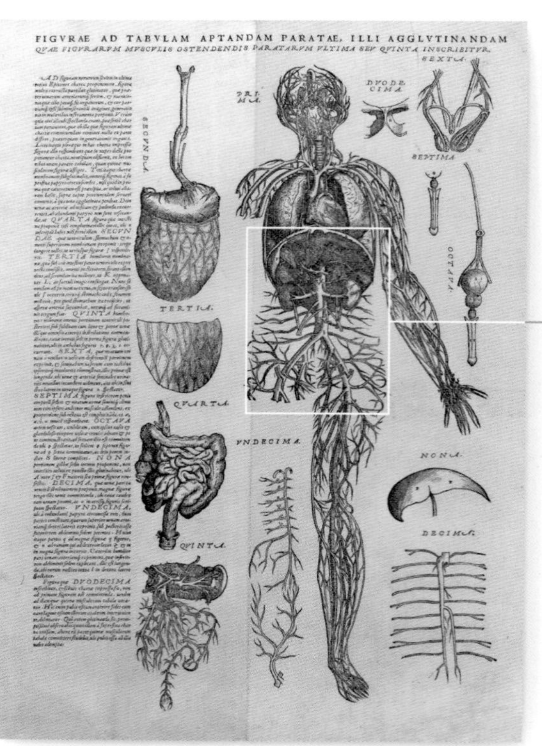

▼ **FURTHER DISSECTION** This figure shows the next stage of dissection. The upper (superficial) layers of muscle have been stripped away to reveal the deeper muscles beneath. An additional lower layer of muscle has been peeled away on the right-hand side of the figure to enable the reader to see deeper still into the body.

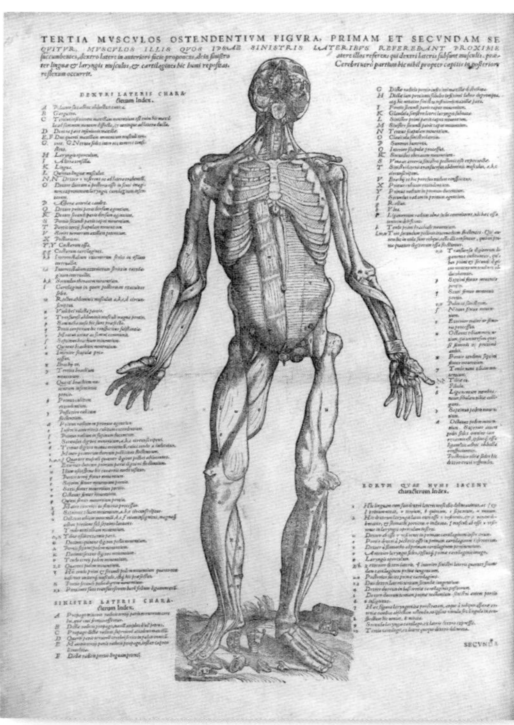

▼ **END OF SERIES** The final figure in the series (when reading from the centre to the front of the book) is a full skeleton. The ribcage is shown opened up and peeled back at one side to reveal its curved structure. In the skeleton's left hand is a skull, which has also been opened up. The skull is supported in a casual pose against the figure's hip.

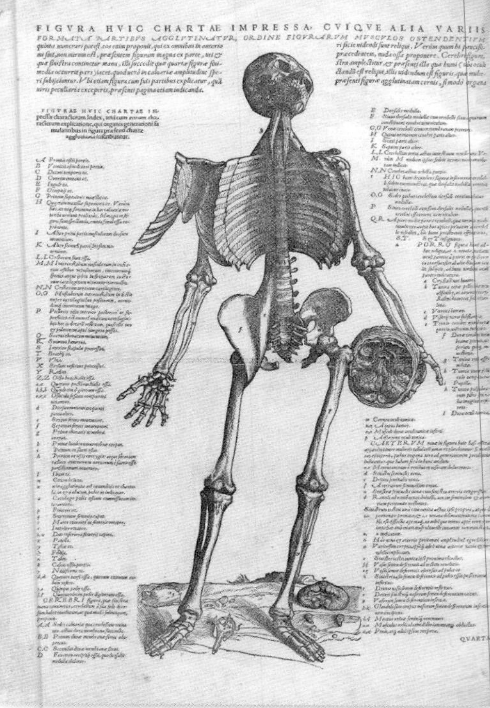

▲ **FINE DETAILS** Vesalius reveals the tightly packed tube of the small intestine within the surrounding loop of the large intestine.

◀ **CLEAR IDENTIFICATION** This section is carefully angled to reveal the structure and position of the kidneys, liver, and gallbladder inside the upper abdomen.

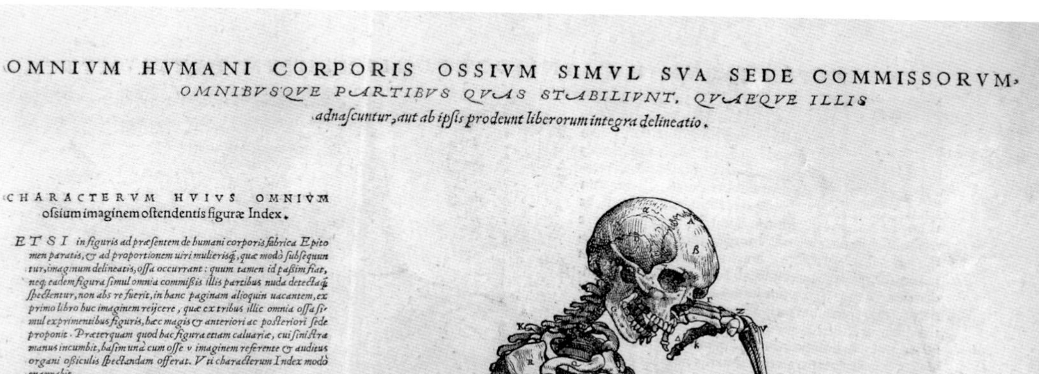

OMNIVM HVMANI CORPORIS OSSIVM SIMVL SVA SEDE COMMISSORVM, OMNIBVSQVE PARTIBVS QVAS STABILIVNT, QVAEQVE ILLIS adnascuntur, aut ab ipsis prodeunt liberorum integra delineatio.

CHARACTERVM HVIVS OMNIVM ossium imaginem ostendentis figuræ Index.

ETSI in figuris ad præsentem de humani corporis fabrica Epitomen paratis, & ad proportionem uiri mulierisq́, quæ modò subsequuntur, imaginum delineatis, ossa occurrant: quum tamen id paßim fiat, neq; eadem figura simul omnia commißis illis partibus nuda detectaq́ spectentur, non abs re fuerit, in hanc paginam alioquin uacantem, ex primo libro huc imaginem reijcere, quæ ex tribus illic omnia ossa simul exprimentibus figuris, hæc magis & anteriori ac posteriori sede proponit. Præterquam quod hac figura etiam caluariæ, cui sinistra manus incumbit, basim unà cum osse v imaginem referente & auditus organi oßiculis spectandam offerat. Vti characterum Index modò enarrabit.

A Suturarum capitis quæ transuersim feruntur anterior, coronalisq́ dicta.

B Sedes alterius transuersæ suturæ, quæ Λ imaginem proponit, & à cuius uertice alia ad coronalem, & rarò hinc ad nasi summum fertur, quam à recto ductu sagittalem nuncupamus.

D In temporibus obuia instar duarum squamarum quæ inuicem incumbunt, commissura, cui ab imagine nomen inditum est. Reliquis uerò caluariæ superiorisq́ maxillæ suturis, quæ nominibus proprijs destituuntur, nullus adhibitus est character.

α Alterum uerticis os.

β Frontis os nunquam geminum, nisi quum rarißimè à coronalis suturæ medio ad summum usque nasi sutura quæpiam pertingit. In huius basi in interna caluariæ amplitudine os spectatur, quod capitis octauum appello.

γ Occipitis os, in grandioribus natu similiter unum.

δ Dextri temporis os, cuius processus styli aut acus aut galli calcaris
ε. imagini comparatus, ε insignitur: is uerò qui uberis papillæ confer-
ζ. tur, ζ inscriptum ostendit.

η,κ Hæc caluariæ sedes ab imagine & duritia quam cum prærupta rupe similem gerit, nomen obtinet, quod permultis temporum duntaxat oßibus asscribitur.

E Os cuneo à dissectionis proceribus comparatum. Huius processus,
θ. quos alis aßimilamus, θ insigniuntur.

F Hæc caluariæ sedes duorum oßium efformata proceßibus, perinde ac si peculiare os esset, iugale os nominatur. Superioris autem maxillæ ossa mihi duodenario numero comprehensa, quũ nominibus careãt, hac exigua tabella characteribus non obruenda putaui.

G Inferior maxilla, similiter ac superior sedecim dentibus ut plurimum decorata.

H Os v imaginem exprimens, unitatisq́ nomine, & si pluribus constet oßiculis, donatum.

q,* E regione dicti oßis hic iuxta caluariæ basim duo occurrunt auditus organi oßicula, quorum alterum q insignitum molari denti duabus tantũ radicibus donato, aut incudi comparamus: alterum uerò * indicatum, malleo cuipiam, aut magna ex parte femoris oßi.

I,K,L,M,N His characteribus dorsi oßium seu uertebrarum notatur series, quarum septem ab I ad K pertinentes collum efformant. duodecim à K ad L numeratæ, thoracem. quinque ab L ad regionem M succedentes, lumbos. à regione M, quo oßis sacri in quinta musculorum tabula apparentis, sedes indicatur, ad N sacrum os sex extructum oßibus consistit, cui coccyx os subijcitur.

O Pectoris os pluribus conformatum ossibus.

P Mucronata cartilago, in quam pectoris os gladij modo exacuitur.

1,2,3,4,5,6,7,8,9,10,11,12 Numeri characteribus duodecim costæ indicantur, quarum septem superiores & uertebris & pectoris oßi articulantur, hinc ueræ nuncupatæ: inferiores autem quinque spuriæ dictæ, ad solas uertebras articulationem moliuntur.

Q Clauicula.

R Scapula, cuius superior processus, quem summum humerum dicimus,
λ,μ. λ insignitur. interior autem, qui anchoræ imagini confertur, μ.

S Brachij os, multis humerus appellatum.

T,V A T ad V sedes metitur, quam cubitum uocamus, duabus constructa oßibus, quorum longius inferiusq́, ac Y insignitum, cubitus priuatim & ulna appellantur. Huius posterior, iuxta illius cum bra-
ν. chij osse articulationẽ processus ν insignitur. Processus autem illius
ξ. acutus iuxta brachiale conspicuus, ξ inscribitur. Porrò superius in cu-
X. bito os, radius appellatum, X notatur.

Z Octo brachialis ossa, duplici ordine digesta.

Γ Quatuor postbrachialis ossa.

Δ Quindecim digitorum ossa.

Θ Hoc charactere sinistrum os eorum quæ sacri oßis lateribus committuntur obuium est: quod in tres sedes, perinde ac si tribus peculiaribus ossibus constitueretur, nomine diuidimus, quæ dextrum os
ο,π. characteribus notata refert. ο nanq; ilium os, π coxendicis, ρ pu-
ρ,ς. bis indicat, ς uerò cartilaginem pubis oßiũ coalitũ interuenientem.

Λ Femur, cuius exterior maiorq́; rotator τ indicatur, interiori &
τ. minori interim hic nusquam conspicuo.

Ξ Os scuti patellæq́ instar, genu articulo præpositum.

Π,Σ A Π ad Σ sedes metitur, quam tibiam nuncupamus, quæq́ duobus
Φ. constat ossibus, uno interiori & crassiori, ac tibia appellato, ac Φ in-
Ψ. signito: altero graciliori exteriorique, quod Ψ inscriptum fibulæ nomen obtinuit.

φ,χ Inferiorum appendicum ossium quæ tibiam constituunt processus, quos malleolos appellare consueuimus.

Ω Talus tibiæ subditus, calciq́ instratus.

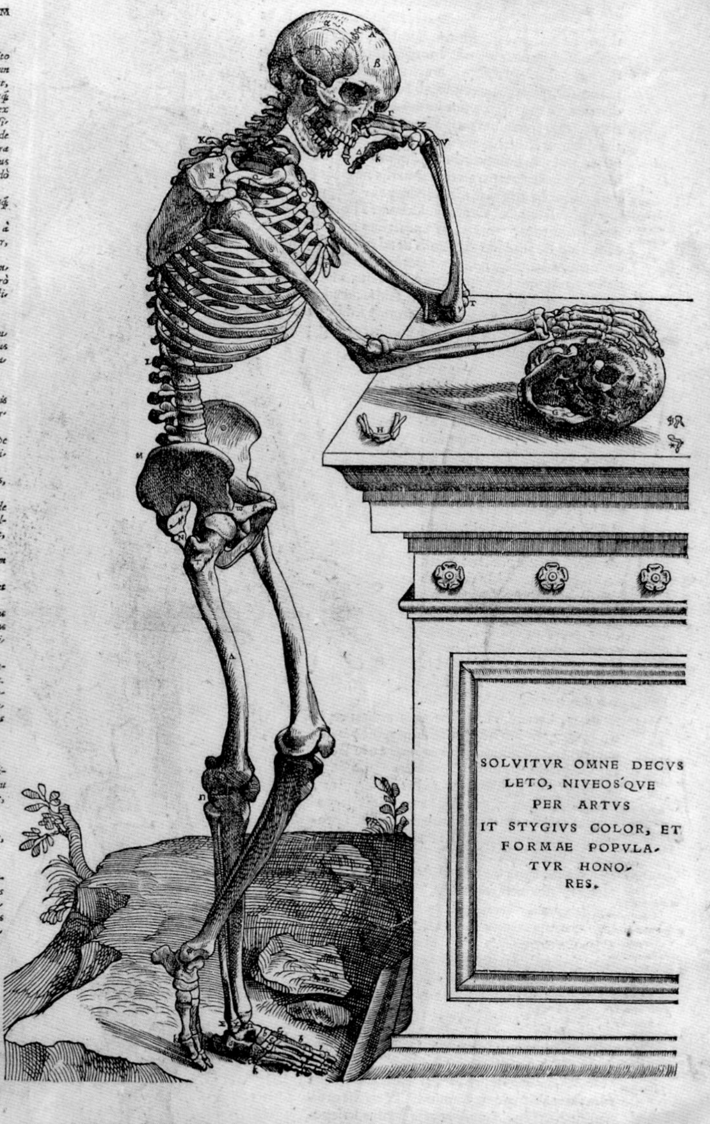

a Calcis os, tibiæ rectitudinem longè excedens.

b Os cymbæ imagini à dissectionum peritis comparatum.

c,c Quatuor tarsi ossa, quæ singulis characteribus d, e, f, & g in-
d,e, dicantur. ut sic interiora tria quæ nominibus carent, ab extimo,
f,g. quod g insignitur, & tesseræ & cubo confertur, distingui queat.

h Quinque ossa tarsum sequentia, pedionq́ constituenti

i Quatuordecim pedis digitorum ossa.

k Pluribus locis hac figura k occurrit, oßicula indicaturum quæ à sesami similitudine nomen inuenerunt.

K EXTERNA.

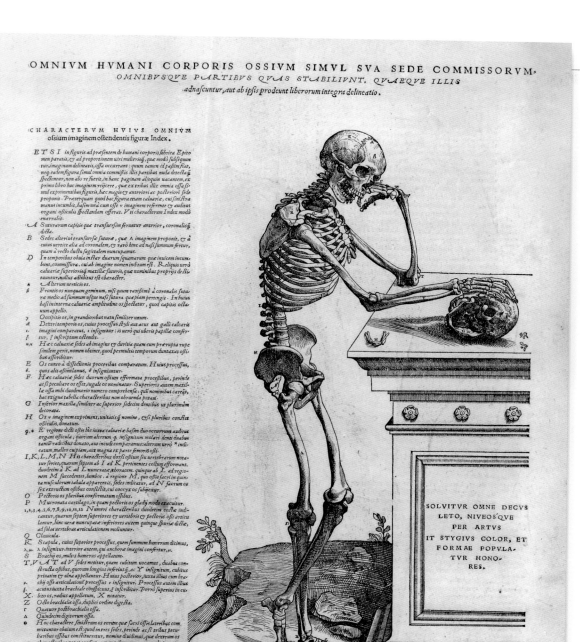

▲ **DETAIL FROM THE FRONTISPIECE** Vesalius believed that medicine had suffered because physicians had lost their practical knowledge of the body. The frontispiece, showing Vesalius holding a cadaver during a dissection, shows the hands-on approach he favoured for his research, and indicates that the images and information in the book are a direct result of the author's own observations.

◀ **NATURAL POSTURE** Striking a thoughtful pose beside a grave, this skeleton is apparently contemplating the certainty that all humans die. It is positioned in a natural way, which demonstrates how all of the bones fit together and work to make the body move. Vesalius was the first to depict a male skeleton with 24 ribs, countering the biblical view that God took a rib from Adam to make Eve, meaning men had one rib fewer than women.

I am **not accustomed** to saying anything with **certainty** after only **one or two** observations

ANDREAS VESALIUS

Cosmographia

1544 ▪ PRINTED WITH WOODCUT ILLUSTRATIONS ▪ 32 × 20 cm (12 × 8 in) ▪ 640 FOLIOS ▪ GERMANY

SCALE

SEBASTIAN MÜNSTER

One of the most popular releases of the 16th century was Sebastian Münster's *Cosmographia*, the first visual guide to the known world to be published in the German language. In the mid-1500s the spirit of the Renaissance was still strong in northern Europe, and prosperous Germany led the field of publishing, catering for a wealthy audience hungry for knowledge. The *Cosmographia* was based on a work written by the Greek mathematician Ptolemy (100–168 CE) in around 150 CE, but was updated with more recent material from travellers. Encyclopedic in its scope, the six-volume publication set the standard for geographic illustration. Maps are a key feature of the book. Münster, who is considered one of the finest cartographers of the age, drew detailed maps of the continents and major European cities, and collaborated with over 100 talented artists to fill *Cosmographia*'s pages with views of countryside, towns and villages, history, industry, and customs. In an age when information spread slowly and new discoveries about the world took decades or longer to establish, the book remained influential throughout the 16th century.

Cosmographia was widely cited by other mapmakers and scholars, and sections of the text were reprinted by publishers long after the book's initial publication. Although Münster died in 1550, his stepson Heinrich Petri took over the job of refining and republishing new editions. Around 40 different editions were published between 1544 and 1628, including translations into Latin, French, Italian, and Czech.

SEBASTIAN **MÜNSTER**

1488–1552

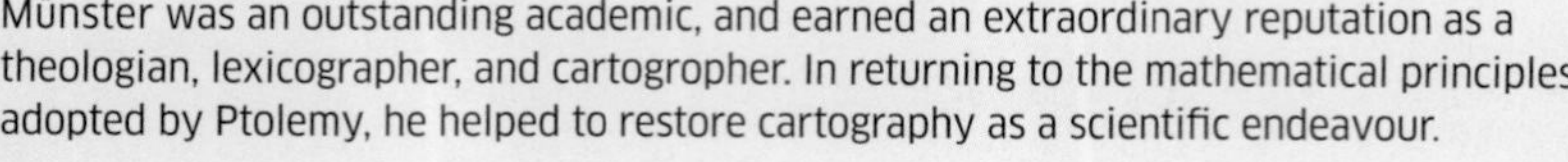

Münster was an outstanding academic, and earned an extraordinary reputation as a theologian, lexicographer, and cartogropher. In returning to the mathematical principles adopted by Ptolemy, he helped to restore cartography as a scientific endeavour.

Born in Nieder-Ingelheim on the Rhine River, Münster's education shaped how he would approach the job of mapmaking. After studying arts and theology at Heidelberg University, he immersed himself in mathematics and cartography under the tutelage of mathematician Johannes Stöffler. He first trained as a Franciscan monk, but then converted to Lutheranism in order to become a professor of Hebrew at the University of Basel, where he eventually settled in 1529.

Münster was the first cartographer to make separate maps of each continent, and to list the sources he had used to draw them. While earlier mapmakers, such as Ptolemy, had taken a more empirical view of the world, maps produced during the Middle Ages were based largely on religious beliefs. At a time when most of his peers were simply making copies of Ptolemy's antiquated maps, Münster made his as accurate as possible by incorporating the recent discoveries of European explorers. His most famous publications were his reworkings of Ptolemy's *Geographia* (1540), and his own work, *Cosmographia* (1544).

▼ **CITY VIEWS** *Cosmographia* showcased Münster's cartography skills and those of the artists whose cityscapes and country views filled its pages. Here the distinctive dome of the Mosque of Omar in Jerusalem takes centrestage, while other annotated features appear in the surrounding landscape, including Mount Zion in the top left-hand corner.

lem ciuitas sancta, olim metropol regni Iudaici, hodie uero colonia Turcæ.
1017
Jerusalem
Salomōs tēpel
Herod. haus
Pilatus haus
Die kot port
Ierícho.
braica uox bonum odorē. De hoc Plinius sic scribit: Omni
bus odoribus præfertur balsamum, uni terræ Iudææ conces
sum. Quondam in duobus tantū hortis, utroque regio, cre
uit. Malleolis seri dicitur, uincitur ut uitis, nec sine admini
culis se sustinet. Properat nasci, intra tertiū annum fructum
ferens. Folium proximū rutæ perpetua coma. Inciditur ui
tro, lapide, osseis'ue cultellis. Ferro lædi uitalia, odit. Inciden
tis manus libratur, ne quid ultra corticē uioler. Succus è pla
ga manat, quem opobalsamum uocāt, eximiæ suauitatis, sed
tenui gutta. Alexandro magno ibi res gerente, toto die æsti
uo unam concham impleri iustū erat. Præcipua gratia est la
chrymæ, secūda semini, tertia cortici, minima ligno. Cæterū
postq̄ Ro. princeps Titus destruxit Ierosolymā in ultionē
mortis Christi & Iudæos in perpetuū exilium adegit, balsa
mi quoq; herba & plantatio trāslata est in Aegyptū: de quo
& iuxta urbem Cairi nonnihil dicam. De rosis Hierichunti
Balsamum.
Rosa Iericho
YY 5 Iericho,

In detail

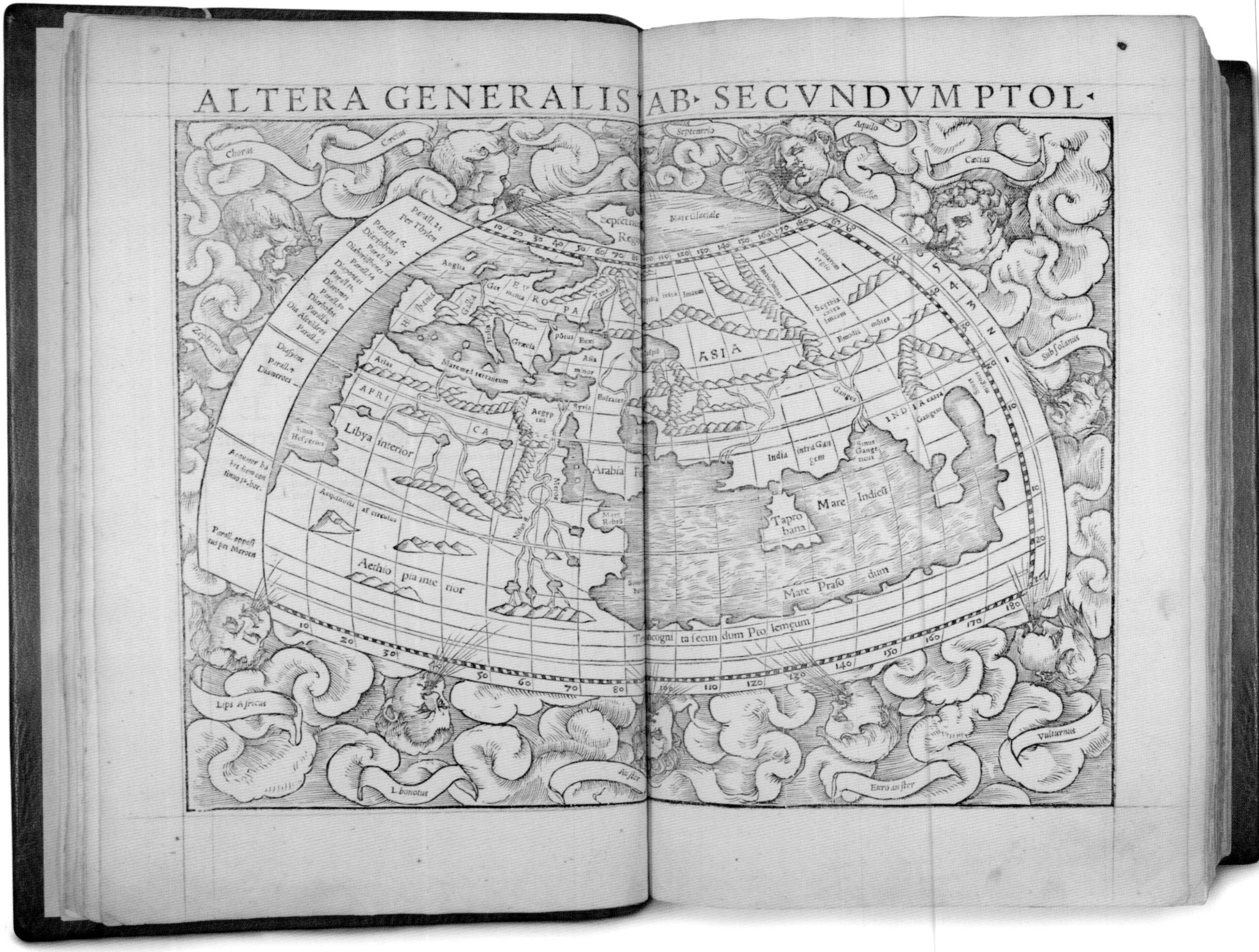

▲ **PTOLEMIC STYLE** Münster styled his world map after that of Ptolemy, who had produced the world's first atlas in the 2nd century CE. Here Africa is depicted as extending east from the equator to meet Asia, making a landlocked Indian Ocean. The continents are surrounded by the 12 ancient winds, which represent different points of the compass.

RELATED **TEXTS**

Before Münster the most influential mapmaker was Claudius Ptolemaeus (100–170 CE). Ptolemy, as he was better known, lived in Egypt but wrote in Greek, and is thought to have been of Greek heritage. A mathematician, astronomer, and geographer, Ptolemy established geography as a science, setting out the techniques required for accurate mapmaking. One of his chief innovations was in calculating the size of countries mathematically. It would take almost a millennium before Ptolemy's work became known in Europe, when Byzantine scholars copied and translated his maps. Sebastian Münster's *Geographica* was one of the most reliable versions of Ptolemy's work to be produced during the Renaissance.

▲ **Lines of longitude and latitude** on Ptolemy's map give an impression of the Earth's spherical surface.

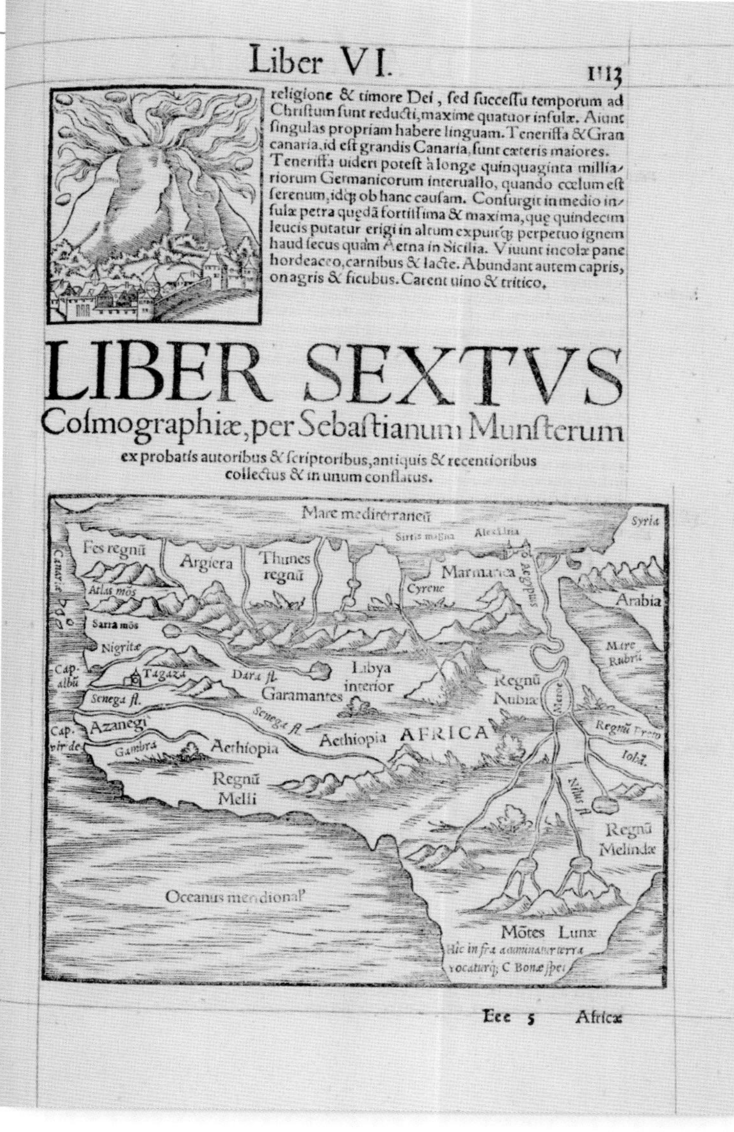
Liber VI. 1113

religione & timore Dei, ſed ſucceſſu temporum ad Chriſtum ſunt reducti, maxime quatuor inſulæ. Aiunt ſingulas propriam habere linguam. Teneriffa & Gran canaria, id eſt grandis Canaria, ſunt cæteris maiores. Teneriffa uideri poteſt à longe quinquaginta milliariorum Germanicorum interuallo, quando cœlum eſt ſerenum, idq; ob hanc cauſam. Conſurgit in medio inſulæ petra quędã fortiſſima & maxima, quę quindecim leucis putatur erigi in altum expuitq; perpetuo ignem haud ſecus quàm Aetna in Sicilia. Viuunt incolæ pane hordeaceo, carnibus & lacte. Abundant autem capris, onagris & ficubus. Carent uino & tritico.

LIBER SEXTVS

Coſmographiæ, per Sebaſtianum Munſterum ex probatis autoribus & ſcriptoribus, antiquis & recentioribus collectus & in unum conflatus.

Eee 5 Africæ

▲ **ACCURATE PRESENTATION** Using Ptolemy's mathematical approach to mapmaking, Münster was able to create the most accurate depictions of individual countries, as well as entire continents. In this image the outline of Africa is very close to that known today, as are many of the annotated features. These include the Nile and the Red Sea, and the countries: Syria, Tunisia, Algeria, and Libya.

Liber III. 47

Officina excoctionis, liquefactionis, conflationis & ſeparationis metallorum, Germanice Schmeltz hutte: ubi rota aqua impulſa mouet ſine ceſſatione folles ignem ſubinde excitantes. Conflator continuo excipit reſolutum metallum & à contuſis metallicis lapidibus ſeparatum, atq; in modulos transfundit.

De Alſatia eiuſque dominio.

Reges Franciæ olim ſub ſuo dominio habuerunt Alſatiam, habitaueruntq; in ea ducentos circiter annos. Fuit autem pars regni Auſtriaci, cuius ſuprà in Francia feci mentionem. Atq; hinc eſt, quod in quibuſdam hiſtorijs hæc regio uocatũ minor Francia. Antea uero fuit quingẽtis ferè annis ſub Rom. poteſtate, fuit̃.ꝗ Argentina gazophylacium eorũ, ubi colligebant cenſum, quem in Alſatia & alijs circumiacentibus terris leuabant. Sunt etiã qui uolunt anno domini 685. regẽ Frãciæ Hildericũ tradidiſſe Alſatiã affini ſuo duci Eticoni, qui reſidentiã & curiã ſuã habuit in ſuperiori Ehẽ- Minor Frãcia.

P heim

▲ **DETAILED ENGRAVING** An extensive section of Münster's book was devoted to mining and smelting, which had boomed in Central Europe in the early 1500s. Here the engraving shows the process of smelting metals, with a waterwheel powering the bellows that fired the furnace.

◄ **DOMESTIC SLANT** Münster focused large sections of the book on Germanic history and landscape. This graphic print depicts German Christians engaging in battle for King Otto I the Great against the Hungarians, who invaded Germany, south of the Danube, in 954 CE.

Visual tour

KEY

▼ **LAND AND SEA MONSTERS** This plate was derived from the *Carta marina*, a map made by Swedish scholar, Olaus Magnus, in 1539. The map's index of sea creatures captured the popular imagination, and Münster felt it essential to include a variant in his own book six years later.

> Wonders of the sea and rare animals, as they are found in the midnight lands in the sea and on the land
>
> **SEBASTIAN MÜNSTER**, *COSMOGRAPHIA*

➤ **CREATURES OF THE LAND** Depictions of land animals like the snakes being warded off here, included reindeers, bears, martens, and wolverines, which were all based on real animals. However, some of the descriptions were more fanciful, for example the entry for the wolverine notes that the "nature of people wearing this fur is often changed into this beast's nature".

▲ **SEA SERPENT** The book describes sea snakes measuring between 200 and 300 ft (60–91 m) long, which "twist around the ship, harm the sailors, and attempt to sink it, especially when it is calm". The real creature in question is likely to have been a giant squid, which has been the subject of folklore since ancient times.

▲ **FROM THE DEEP** Münster's collection of beasts from the midnight sea and lands, includes animals from countries such as Norway and Sweden. In this image, a galleon ditches its cargo in an attempt to outrun a sea creature spouting water from its blowhole, while one shipmate takes aim with his musket. Earlier written accounts of whale sightings had generated fascination about the existence of sea monsters.

◄ **CREATURE IDENTIFICATION** Each monster is labelled with a letter, linked to an index. The explanation for "N" read: "A gruesome beast, partly resembling a rhinoceros. Pointed at the nose and the back, eats large crabs called lobsters, is twelve feet long."

Les Prophéties

1555 ▪ PRINTED ▪ DIMENSIONS AND EXTENT UNKNOWN ▪ FRANCE

NOSTRADAMUS

French apothecary, physician, and astrologer Nostradamus published *Les Prophéties*, which translates as *The Prophecies*, in 1555. The book contained 353 four-line verses, or quatrains, that purported to forecast future events. These quatrains were arranged in groups of 100, or centuries. Further editions added more quatrains to bring the total to nine centuries with 942 verses. The book had a mixed reception when first published. Although very popular among the French nobility and royalty, who believed the prophecies to be genuine, others considered Nostradamus to be either mad or a charlatan. It was widely criticized by churchmen, who hinted that it was the work of the devil, although the prophecies were never actually condemned and Nostradamus never claimed they were spiritually inspired, but that they were based on "judicial astrology".

To make his predictions Nostradamus calculated the future positions of the planets and searched for similar planetary alignments in the past. Then, by borrowing freely from ancient historians such as Suetonius and Plutarch, and from earlier prophecies, he matched those past alignments to recorded events. In the belief that history repeats itself he created an overall picture of the future. Inevitably his predictions were full of major disasters such as plague, fire, wars, and floods.

MICHEL DE **NOSTREDAME**

1503–1566

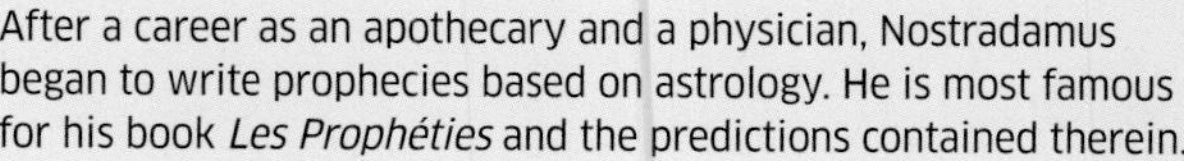

After a career as an apothecary and a physician, Nostradamus began to write prophecies based on astrology. He is most famous for his book *Les Prophéties* and the predictions contained therein.

Michel de Nostredame, better known by his Latinized name, Nostradamus, was born in Saint-Rémy de Provence, France. After an outbreak of plague forced him to curtail his studies for his baccalaureate at the University of Avignon, he spent time researching herbal remedies and became an apothecary. In the 1530s he started his medical practice, albeit with no medical degree, and gained a reputation for his innovative plague treatments. He began writing prophecies around 1547 and came to the notice of Catherine de Médicis, the French Queen, drawing up the horoscopes of her children. By the time of his death Nostradamus was the King's Counsellor and Physician-in-Ordinary.

Professional astrologers were highly critical of his methodology and accused him of incompetence and devoid of even basic astrological skills.

Perhaps to guard against criticism, or even charges of heresy, Nostradamus deliberately obscured the meaning of the prophecies by using codes, metaphors, and a mix of languages, such as Provençal, Ancient Greek, Latin, and Italian. The result is that the prophecies are so open to interpretation that almost anything can be read into them, yet enthusiasts claim they predict everything from the rise of Napoleon to, more recently, the election of Donald Trump as US president.

IN **CONTEXT**

Nostradamus started publishing almanacs in 1550, which included astrological predictions, weather forecasts, and tips for when to plant crops. Their success led to commissions for horoscopes from the wealthy, as well as prompting him to compose more complicated prophecies in poetic form, which he published as *Les Prophéties*.

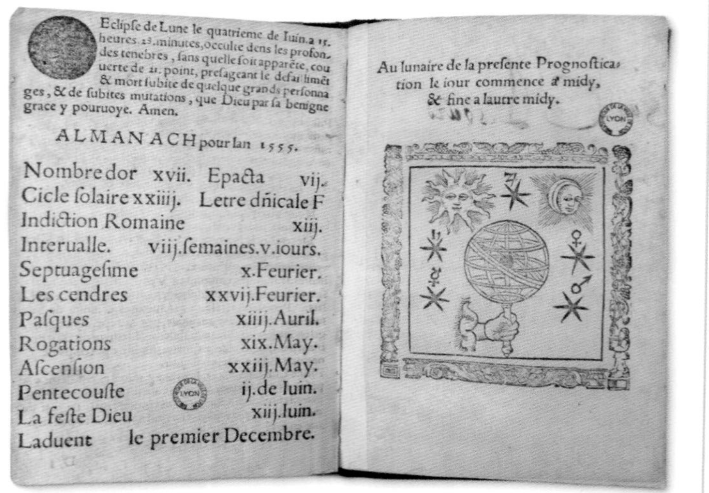

ALMANACH pour lan 1555.

Nombre dor xvii. Epacta vij.
Cicle solaire xxiiij. Letre dñicale F
Indiction Romaine xiij.
Interualle. viij.semaines.v.iours.
Septuagesime x.Feurier.
Les cendres xxvij.Feurier.
Pasques xiiij.Auril.
Rogations xix.May.
Ascension xxiij.May.
Pentecouste ij.de Iuin.
La feste Dieu xiij.Iuin.
Laduent le premier Decembre.

Au lunaire de la presente Prognostication le iour commence a midy, & fine a lautre midy.

➤ **Nostradamus incorporated** his visions into popular almanacs that were published yearly until his death. *Almanachs* were detailed predictions; *Prognostications* or *Presages*, were more generalized.

> I had **determined** to go as far as **declaring…** the future causes of the **"common advent"**
>
> **NOSTRADAMUS**, IN A LETTER TO HIS SON CESAR, MARCH 1555

LES VRAYES CENTURIES
ET PROPHETIES
De Maiſtre MICHEL NOSTRADAMUS.

CENTURIE PREMIERE.

1.

STANT aſſis, de nuict ſecret eſtude,
Seul, repoſé ſur la ſelle d'airain ?
Flambe exigue, ſortant de ſolitude
Fait proferer qui n'eſt à croire en vain.

2.

La verge en main miſe au milieu des branches,
De l'onde il moulle & le limbe & le pied,
Un peur & voix fremiſſent par les manches,
Splendeur divine, le devin pres s'aſſied.

3.

Quand la lictiere du tourbillon verſée
Et feront faces de leurs manteaux couverts :
La republique par gens nouveaux vexée,
Lors blancs & rouges jugeront à l'envers.

4.

Par l'univers ſera fait un Monarque,
Qu'en paix & vie ne ſera longuement,
Lors ſe perdra la piſcature barque,
Sera regie en plus grand detriment.

5.

Chaſſez ſeront ſans faire long combat,
Par le pays ſeront plus fort grevez :
Bourg & Cité auront plus grand debat
Carcas, Narbonne, auront cœurs eſprouvez.

6.

L'œil de Ravenne ſera deſtitué,
Quand à ſes pieds les aiſles failliront,

A Les

◄ **MEMORABLE VERSE** This page shows the start of the first century (100 quatrains) of *Les Prophéties*, in the original French, with its decorated initial letter "E". All but one of Nostradamus's prophecies rhymed in an ABAB pattern, known as alternate rhyme. The use of such simple verse made the prophecies particularly memorable, as intended, and gave them a resonance that made the reader inclined to believe that they were divine wisdom. The book brought Nostradamus fame and fortune. To date over 200 editions have been published worldwide, and it has rarely been out of print.

Aubin Codex

1576 ■ PAPER BOUND IN LEATHER ■ 15.5 × 13.4 cm (6 × 5 in) ■ 81 FOLIOS ■ MEXICO

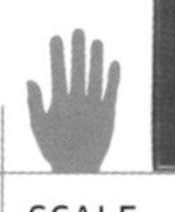

SCALE

VARIOUS AUTHORS

Few rare books document a moment in history as eloquently as the *Aubin Codex*, which was written and beautifully illustrated by indigenous Mexicans in the 16th century, but bound in the European style. The volume tells the history of the Mexican people, and records first-hand their experience with Spanish colonists, including their arrival and the subsequent death of locals by smallpox, a disease the Spanish brought with them. Manuscripts written by South American cultures prior to colonization were typically written on bark or hide, which was then folded up. The *Aubin Codex* differs in that it is written on paper made in Europe and bound in red leather. This native Mexican point of view, presented in the format of the Spanish conquistadors, marks a transition from an autonomous people to a colony in which European, Catholic ways would eventually become the norm.

Following in the style of pre-colonial documents, events are depicted visually. Full-page paintings introduce the main sections of the book, with smaller pictograms conveying dates and the identity of royal figures in the Aztec dynasty. The supporting text is penned in Nahuatl, the native language used for centuries by the people of Central and South America. Historians believe that several contributors wrote and illustrated the book, probably under the guidance of the Dominican missionary, Diego Durán (1537–88). Although Durán was initially credited as author, the codex takes its name from the French intellectual Joseph Marius Alexis Aubin (1802–91), who acquired the manuscript while living in Mexico between 1830 and 1840.

◄ **ONE OF A KIND** The *Aubin Codex* is unique; the only copy known to exist is the one held at the British Museum in London. Although most of the pages are filled with pictograms, dense text is used by the authors to describe more complex events, such as war.

> Here is the written history of the Mexica who came from the place of Aztlan

THE *AUBIN CODEX*

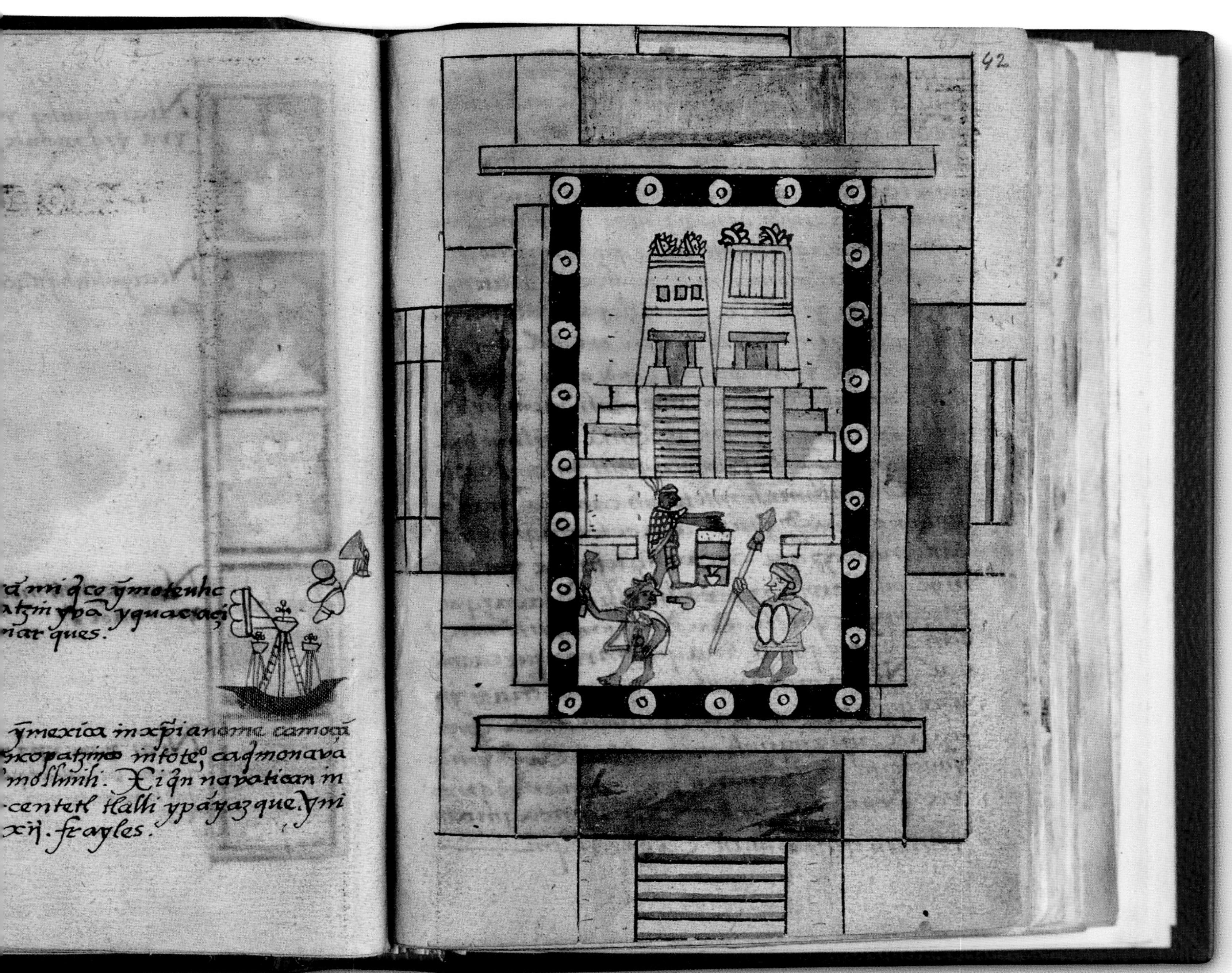

▲ **DEPICTING THE SPANISH CONQUEST** The column of blocks on the left-hand page show the date; the notes second from bottom refer to the arrival of Spanish ships. The full-page painting depicts an Aztec warrior and a Spaniard facing each other on the steps of the twin temples of Templo Mayor in the ancient city of Tenochtitlan.

In detail

➤ **RICH RED** One of the dominant colours of the *Aubin Codex* is a reddish-brown tint called annatto, which is used for the background of each small pictogram. Made from the seeds of the native achiote tree, *Bixa orellana*, the tint was common in Mexican manuscripts of the 16th century. Annatto was also a colourant in textiles, and is still used today as food colouring.

▼ **DOCUMENT OF EVENTS** The text and pictures on this page record significant events. The illustration of the Sun sits alongside an account of a solar eclipse, during which "all the stars appeared and Axayacatzin died". The figure in blue seated on the golden throne is Tizozicatzin, who took his place, becoming the seventh "tlàtoani", or ruler, the following year.

➤ **SYMBOLIC DISCS** An important aspect of the book is its listing of the monarchs who reigned during several Aztec dynasties. The blue discs beside each ruler denote the number of years each ruler was in power. On the left is Diego de Alvarado Huanitzin, who was the first emperor under the colonial government.

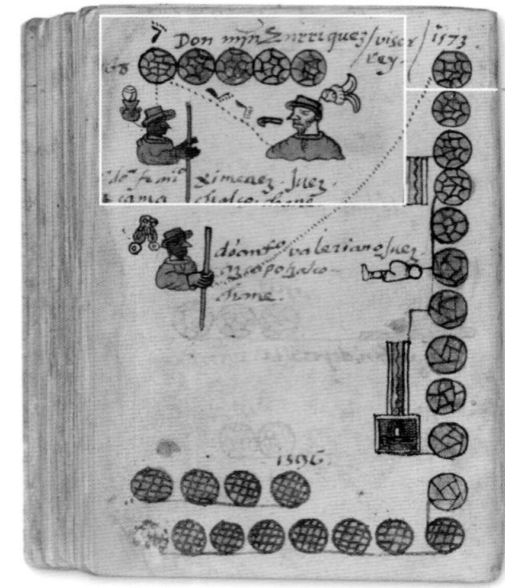

◄ **FULL-PAGE PAINTING** This illustration is used to introduce the story of how the Mexican people founded a new imperial capital, Tenochtitlan, in 1325. Built on an island in Lake Texcoco, it served as a base for the growing Aztec Empire. The event is represented by an eagle eating a snake on a prickly pear cactus – elements that are still found on the Mexican coat of arms.

▼ **ILLUSTRATIONS** The stylized paintings illustrate what is recorded in the text. Events depicted here, running from top to bottom down the right-hand side, are: the death of an Archbishop; the capture of black slaves; the digging of a boat canal; memorial prayers; the burial of a monk; the construction of a wooden church; and the arrival of some clerics.

1572. Años.

xJnomomi qli arçobispo don fray alonso de montofar axcan viernes. a vij. dias delmes demarço.

xJno analloque tiltique sancto domingo axcan Jueves a xvij. marco.

xJnomotatacac acallotli sant Joan

xJnotlatlatlauhtiloc ypapa omicovac atlā yoa otlamalloc axcā miercoles a ix. dias delmes de abril.

xJnomotocac totatzin fray p degā te axcā domingo a xx. de abril.

xJnomoqtz quauhteocalli ynipapa ye yx cuitilloq tlatoq inqnin tepeva lloc moros ymuhchnivalloq yepe valloq ynuhq mcalcatca yvan. ymuhqnchnuhq achtopa axivallo que ynacalcotlayecoque niman yeaxivalloypa tlayecoq catepan axivalloque ytlacxipanviaya yuan tla pancoenca omochiuh axcā viernes a xxv. dias delmes de Julio.

x Nicāvallaq ynqreticos deaqnos.

RELATED **TEXTS**

In the centuries before European colonization, the people of Central and South America cultivated a rich tradition of using art and hieroglyphics to record information, such as annual calendars, astronomical observations, and ritual practices. These documents, referred to as codices, or codex in the singular, consisted of leaves of bark cloth joined in an accordion format. The Dresden Codex is one of best examples and is also the oldest surviving Mayan manuscript. Little is known about the origin of this codex but it is dated to around 1200–50. After disappearing from the Americas, it resurfaced in Dresden, Germany, in 1739 when the director of the city's Royal Library bought it for the collection from a private owner in Vienna.

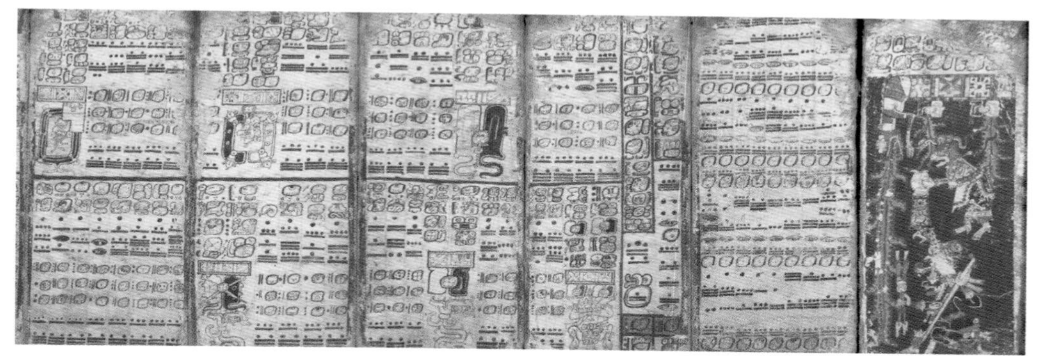

▲ **The *Dresden Codex*** consists of 39 leaves, painted on both sides. It measures 3.5 m (11 ft) when laid out flat.

The Discoverie of Witchcraft

1584 ▪ PRINTED WITH WOODCUT ILLUSTRATIONS ▪ 17.2 × 12.7 cm (7 × 5 in) ▪ 696 PAGES ▪ ENGLAND

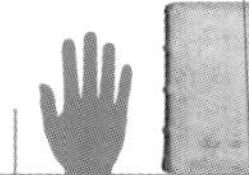
SCALE

REGINALD SCOT

Writing at a time when witchcraft was recognized as a crime, Reginald Scot published a highly controversial work in which he argued against its very existence, advocating that a belief in witches and magic was irrational and unchristian. Considered heretical when published, it can now be seen to be a radical and forward-thinking exposé. Scot blamed the Roman Catholic Church for fostering paranoia and fuelling the on-going witch-hunts, and he attributed psychological disorders to self-confessed "witches" or witnesses of witchcraft.

The volume was divided into 16 books, within which Scot outlined contemporary beliefs about witchcraft before systematically discrediting them. In the later chapters, he concerned himself with magic tricks, explaining the mechanics behind those most commonly performed at the time. This is believed to be the first written record in the history of conjuring.

The Discoverie of Witchcraft was vilified by James VI of Scotland, later James I of England, in his 1597 treatise *Daemonologie*. Copies of Scot's book are very rare – many were allegedly burned on the orders of James I on his accession to the throne in 1603 – yet it was widely read. It is even believed to have influenced Shakespeare's portrayal of the witches in *Macbeth*.

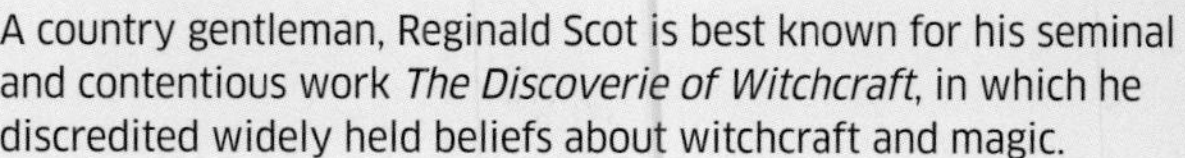

REGINALD **SCOT**

1538–1599

A country gentleman, Reginald Scot is best known for his seminal and contentious work *The Discoverie of Witchcraft*, in which he discredited widely held beliefs about witchcraft and magic.

Privately tutored, Scot entered Hart Hall College in Oxford at the age of 17, although there are no records of his graduation. He married twice and devoted himself to managing his family estate. He served a year as an MP and was a Justice of the Peace. Although a member of the Church of England, Scot was affiliated to a religious sect called the Family of Love, which taught that the devil's influence was psychological, not physical. This teaching fostered Scot's scepticism about witchcraft and led to him writing his book.

In detail

➤ **SEVERED HEAD** A popular trick among conjurors in the 16th century, and one that is still practised today, was to "sever" a person's head. In *The Discoverie of Witchcraft*, Scot unmasked the deception, showing in this woodcut how a second person was placed underneath a table in which a hole had been inserted. The "severed head", covered with flour and bull's blood, then protruded from the hole to the delight and amazement of the crowds.

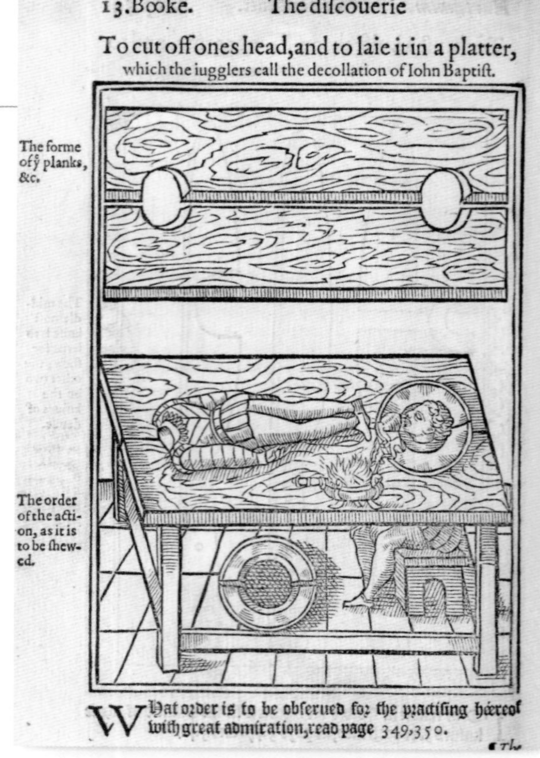

13.Booke. The diſcouerie

To cut off ones head, and to laie it in a platter, which the iugglers call the decollation of Iohn Baptiſt.

The forme of planks, &c.

The order of the action, as it is to be ſhewed.

What order is to be obſerued for the practiſing hereof with great admiration, read page 349, 350.

Here is no queſ[...]
theme (ſaith Hier[...]
dane) ſo difficult t[...]
nor ſo noble an [...]
to diſpute vpon, as
uels and ſpirits.
being confeſſed o[...]
of, the eternitie o[...]
is either affirmed
The heathen philo[...]
ſon hereof among
ſelues in this ſort.
that mainteine [...]
tuitie of the ſoule,
the ſoule died with the bodie; to what end ſhould men ta[...]

▲ **WOODCUT DECORATIONS** Large, embellished initial letters, such as this "T", entwined with flowers and foliage, featured at the start of every chapter. These, together with many other woodcuts (some purely decorative, others instructive) and the ornate Gothic script made the work attractive as well as insightful.

> But whatsoever is reported or conceived of such maner of witchcrafts, I dare avow to be false and fabulous…
>
> **REGINALD SCOT**, *THE DISCOVERIE OF WITCHCRAFT*

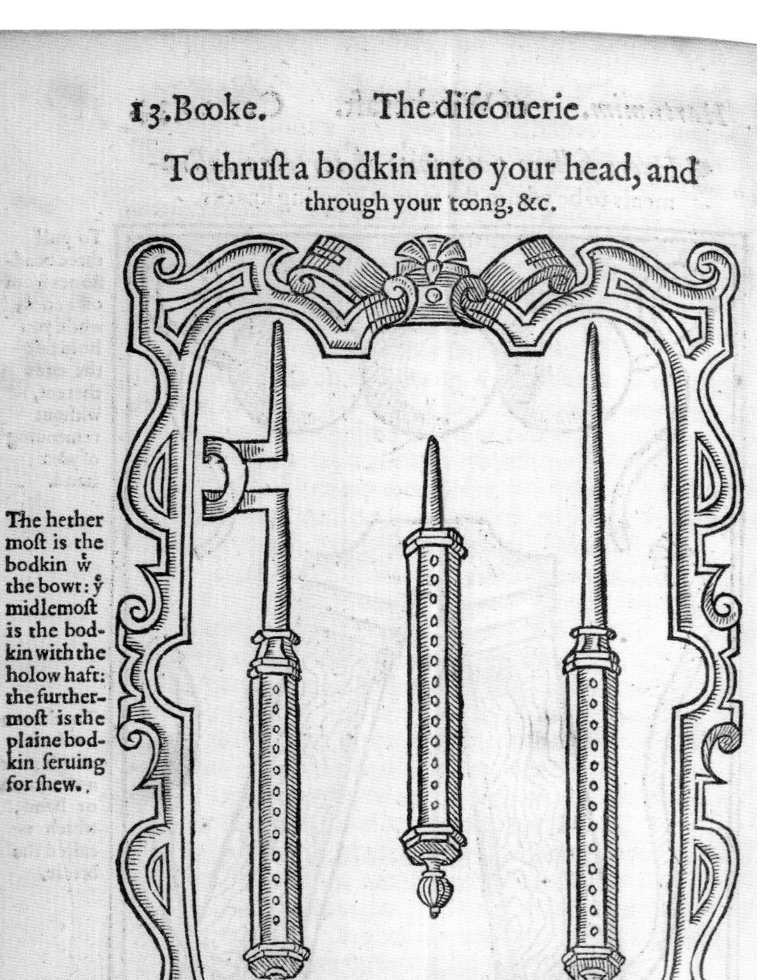

13.Booke. The diſcouerie

To thruſt a bodkin into your head, and through your toong, &c.

The hethermoſt is the bodkin wͤ the bowt: yͤ midlemoſt is the bodkin with the holow haft: the furthermoſt is the plaine bodkin ſeruing for ſhew.

To be inſtructed and taught in the right vſe and readie practiſe of theſe bodkins, read page 347.

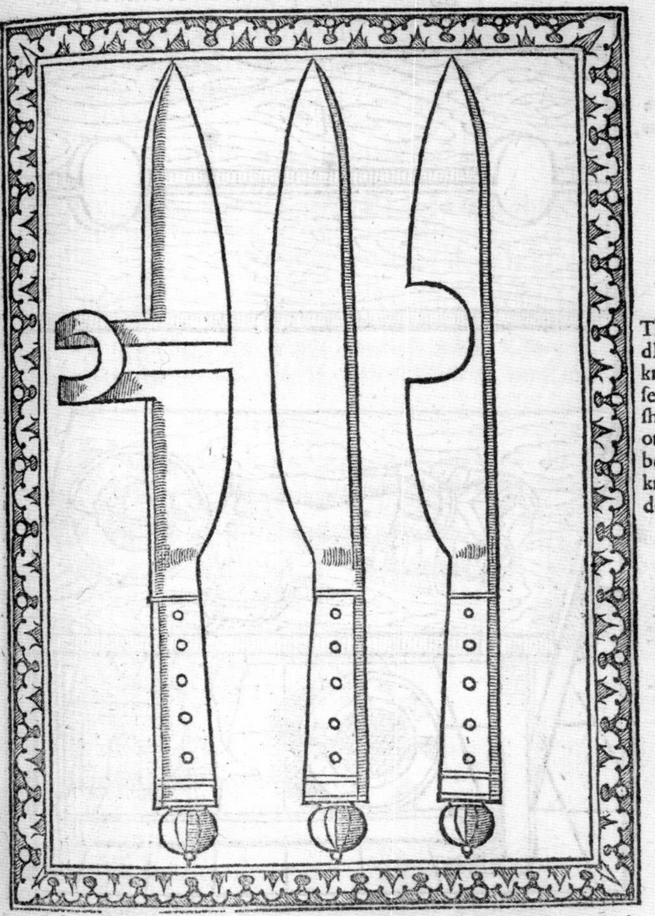

Hartumim. of Witchcraft. Cap.34.

To thruſt a knife through your arme, and to cut halfe your noſe aſunder, &c.

The middlemoſt knife is to ſerue for ſhew; the other two be the kniues of deuiſe.

To be readie in the vſe and perfect in the practiſe of theſe kniues here portraited, ſee page 347. and 348.

▲ **TRICKS UNMASKED** In spite of the law passed by Henry VIII (1491-1547) in 1542 that forbade conjuring as well as witchcraft, magic tricks were still widely performed. In his book Scot gave clear written instructions on how to dupe the onlooker with illusion and sleight of hand, and he also provided woodcut illustrations to make the tricks easier to understand. Here he shows how magicians could create the illusion of inflicting stab wounds by using "bodkins" (daggers) or knives with either retractable blades, or blades with portions removed or extensions added to wrap around the body part in question.

Don Quixote

1605 AND 1615 ▪ PRINTED ▪ 14.8 × 9.8 cm ($5^1/_2$ × $3^1/_2$ in) ▪ 668 AND 586 PAGES ▪ SPAIN

MIGUEL DE CERVANTES SAAVEDRA

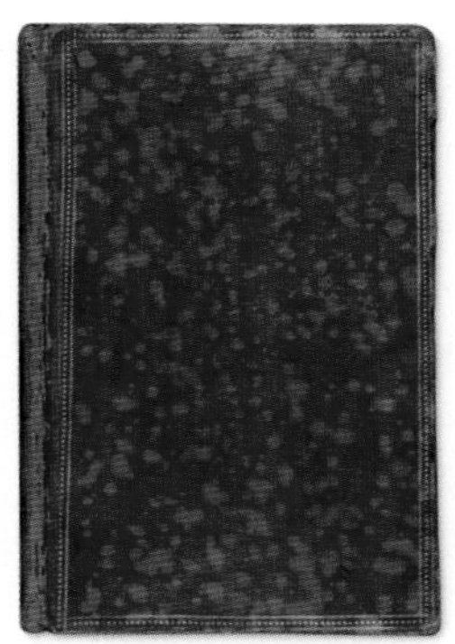

Published in two parts in 1605 and 1615, *Don Quixote* is often regarded as the first "modern" novel. Touching on themes of class, morality, and human rights, it combines humour, fantasy, and brutality, as well as social critique, in a way not seen before in other novels at the time.

Miguel de Cervantes Saavedra sold the rights to part one of the book to Madrid publisher Francisco de Robles, who, in the hope of greater profits, exported the majority of the first edition to the New World, but all were lost in a shipwreck. Despite this setback *Don Quixote* proved an instant success with the public, and it was soon translated into French, German, and Italian – the first English edition was published in 1620. Since that time it has been translated into more than 60 languages, in almost 3,000 editions.

Don Quixote is open to endless interpretations. Its subject is an elder, minor Spanish nobleman driven mad by endless readings of chivalric romances. Seeing himself as a knight errant, he travels through Spain on horseback hoping to right the wrongs of the world, accompanied by the peasant, Sancho Panza. Propelled on by an image of his imagined love, Dulcinea, the result is both comic and tragic – Don Quixote is humiliated, stripped of his dreams, and forced to admit that he has been pursuing an illusion.

The impact of *Don Quixote* on the development of the novel as an art form was profound. Without the model it provided, it is impossible to imagine the great outpouring of 19th- and 20th-century novel-writing from the likes of Dickens and Joyce, Flaubert and Hemingway.

MIGUEL **DE CERVANTES SAAVEDRA**

1547–1616

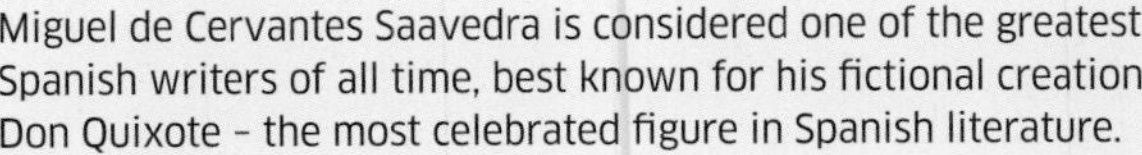

Miguel de Cervantes Saavedra is considered one of the greatest Spanish writers of all time, best known for his fictional creation, Don Quixote – the most celebrated figure in Spanish literature.

Cervantes was born near Madrid, although little is known of his early life. In 1569 he moved to Italy, and a year later enlisted in a Spanish infantry regiment near Naples. Cervantes fought at the great naval battle of Lepanto in 1571, where he lost the use of his left hand. Between 1575 and 1580 he was a prisoner of Algerian pirates, and held for ransom. He eventually returned to Spain but found only menial employment and unsuccessful literary endeavours, which left him impoverished and bitter. It was almost 25 years before Cervantes achieved success through publication of part one of his masterpiece, Don Quixote. He died in 1606, a year after part two was published.

In detail

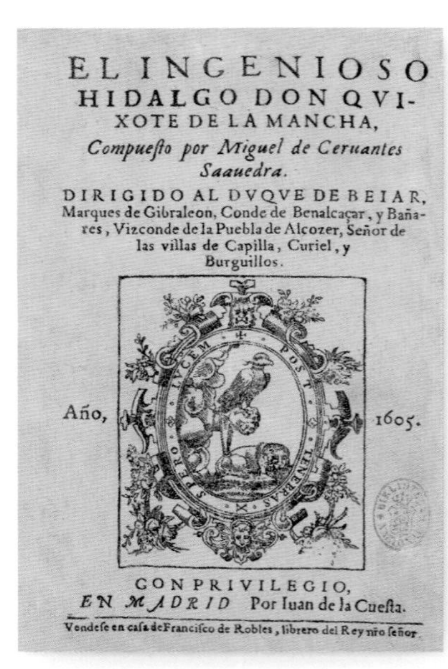

EL INGENIOSO
HIDALGO DON QVI-
XOTE DE LA MANCHA,
Compuesto por Miguel de Ceruantes Saauedra.
DIRIGIDO AL DVQVE DE BEIAR,
Marques de Gibraleon, Conde de Benalcaçar, y Bañares, Vizconde de la Puebla de Alcozer, Señor de las villas de Capilla, Curiel, y Burguillos.
Año, 1605.
CON PRIVILEGIO,
EN MADRID Por Iuan de la Cuesta.
Vendese en casa de Francisco de Robles, librero del Rey nro señor.

◂ **ORNAMENTAL LLUSTRATIONS** Although Don Quixote and Sancho Panza lend themselves well to illustration, the pair and their exploits were not depicted in early editions. Woodcut illustrations were reserved for ornamentation and the opening and closing pages, such as the elaborate crest on this title page from the first 1605 Madrid edition.

▸ **CONTENTS PAGE** The contents page, shown here, appears at the back of the book, and lists 54 chapters spread over four parts. In addition to the main story, the book also includes a prologue by Cervantes, explaining to the "idle reader" why he wrote the novel.

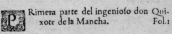

Quarta parte de don

Estos fueron los versos que se pudieron leer, los demas por estar carcomida la letra, se entregaron a vn Academico, para que por congeturas los declarasse. Tienese noticia que lo ha hecho, a costa de muchas vigilias, y mucho trabajo, y que tiene intencion de sacallos a luz, con esperança de la tercera salida de don Quixote.
(.?.)

Forsi altro cantera con miglior plectio.

FINIS.

TABLA DE LOS
Capitulos que contiene esta famosa Historia del valeroso cauallero don don Quixote de la Mancha.

Rimera parte del ingenioso don Quixote de la Mancha. Fol. 1

Capitulo primero, que trata de la condicion, y exercicio del famoso y valiente hidalgo don Quixote de la Mancha. 1
Capitulo segundo, que trata de la primera salida que de su tierra hizo el ingenioso don Quixote. 4
Capitulo tercero, donde se cuenta la graciosa manera que tuuo don Quixote en armarse cauallero. 7
Capitulo quarto, de lo que le sucedio a nuestro cauallero quando salio de la venta. 11
Capitulo quinto, donde se prosigue la narracion de la desgracia de nuestro cauallero. 15
Capitulo sexto, del donoso escrutinio que el cura y el barbero hizieron en la libreria de nuestro ingenioso hidalgo. 18
Capitulo septimo, de la segunda salida de nuestro buen cauallero. 22
** Capi-

Nunca ſereys de alguno reprochado,
Por home de obras viles, y ſoezes.
Seran vueſſas fazañas los joezes,
Pues tuertos desfaziendo aueys andado,
Siendo vegadas mil apaleado,
Por follones cautiuos, y rahezes.
Y ſi la vueſſa linda Dulzinea,
Deſſaguiſado contra vos comete,
Ni a vueſſas cuytas mueſtra buen talante.
En tal deſman vueſſo conorte ſea,
Que Sancho Pança fue mal alcaguete,
Necio el, dura ella, y vos no amante.

DIALAGO ENTRE BABIECA, y Rozinante.

SONETO.

B. Como eſtays Rozinante tan delgado?
R. Porque nunca ſe come, y ſe trabaja,
B. Pues que es de la ceuada, y de la paja?
R. No me dexa mi amo ni vn bocado.
B. Andà ſeñor que eſtays muy mal criado.
Pues vueſtra lengua de aſno al amo vltraja,
R. Aſno ſe es de la cuna a la mortaja,
Quereyslo ver, miraldo enamorado.
B. Es necedad amar? R. Nó es gran prudencia.
B. Metafiſico eſtays. R. Es que no como.
B. Quexaos del eſcudero. R. No es baſtante.
Como me he de quexar en mi dolencia,
Si el amo, y eſcudero, o mayordomo,
Son tan Rozines como Rozinante.

PRI-

Fol.1

PRIMERA PARTE DEL INGENIOSO hidalgo don Quixote de la Mancha.

Capitulo Primero. Que trata de la condicion, y exercicio del famoſo hidalgo don Quixote de la Mancha.

EN Vn lugar de la Mancha, de cuyo nombre no quiero acordarme, no ha mucho tiempo que viuia vn hidalgo de los de lança en aſtillero, adarga antigua, rozin flaco, y galgo corredor. Vna olla de algo mas vaca que carnero, ſalpicon las mas noches, duelos y quebrãtos los Sabados, lantejas los Viernes, algun palomino de añadidura los Domingos: conſumian las tres partes de ſu hazienda. El reſto della concluian, ſayo de velarte, calças de velludo para las fieſtas, con ſus pantuflos de

A lo

▲ **ILLUSTRATED INITIALS** The chivalric setting of *Don Quixote* is reflected by the decorated initial letters at the start of each chapter, which were a feature of many medieval documents of the period.

QVARTA PARTE DEL INGENIOSO hidalgo don Quixote de la Mancha.

Cap. XXVIII. Que trata de la nueua, y agradable auentura que al Cura, y Barbero ſucedio en la meſma Sierra.

FELICISSIMOS Y venturoſos fueron los tiempos, donde ſe echò al mundo el audaciſsimo cauallero don Quixote de la Mancha, pues por auer tenido tan honroſa determinacion, como fue el querer reſucitar, y boluer al mundo, la ya perdida, y casi muerta orden de la andante caualleria. Gozamos aora en eſta nueſtra edad neceſsitada, de alegres entretenimientos, no ſolo de la dulçura de ſu verdadera hiſtoria, ſino de los cuentos, y epiſodios della, que en parte, no ſon menos agradables, y artificioſos, y verdaderos, que la miſma hiſtoria: la qual proſiguiẽdo ſu raſtrillado, torcido, y aſpado hilo, cuenta, que aſsi como el Cura començo a preuenirſe para conſolar a Cardenio, lo

◄ **SECOND VOLUME** Despite being published 10 years after the first instalment, the second volume of *Don Quixote* bears a strong visual resemblance. In the chapter opener shown here, the illustrated initial letter and woodcut decorations are almost identical to those found in volume one.

IN CONTEXT

Such was the popularity of *Don Quixote* that there were soon calls for illustrated editions that would bring his adventures to life. The first of these appeared in a Dutch translation printed by Jacob Savery in 1657, and featured 24 engravings depicting some of the more dramatic scenes from the novel. Many other illustrated versions followed, with the main characters changing in appearance each time. This changed in the 1860s, when a French edition illustrated by renowned painter and engraver, Gustave Doré, captured the spirit and personality of *Don Quixote* and his fellow characters so well that their popular appearance was established.

► **Gustave Doré's 1863 illustration** depicts Don Quixote and his portly servant, Sancho Panza, setting out for another adventure.

King James Bible

1611 ■ PRINTED ■ 44.4 × 30.5 cm (17 × 12 in) ■ 2,367 PAGES ■ ENGLAND

SCALE

TRANSLATION COMMITTEE

There were five English versions of the bible in 1603 when James VI of Scotland became James I of England, but only two of them had been authorized by the Anglican Church. One was the Great Bible (1539), which was also authorized by King Henry VIII of England. The other, the Bishop's Bible (1568), translated during Elizabeth I's reign, was so obscurely written that few used it. The Geneva Bible (1560) proved much more popular, but was unauthorized and full of anti-royalist notes.

King James wanted to unite his fractured kingdom with a bible that was accurate, yet in plain language and without contentious footnotes. And so, in January 1604 he summoned bishops and scholars to Hampton Court Palace and commissioned a new bible. A translation committee of 50 scholars based in Oxford, Cambridge, and London was divided into six groups, each working on different parts of this bible using Hebrew, Aramaic, and Greek texts, as well as Tyndale's English version of 1525. Each person made a translation of their own, which was then tested by reading it out loud. The best were then sent forward to the overseeing committee. It is the commanding beauty of the resulting prose, repeated in churches across the world every Sunday, that has ensured the lasting influence of the King James Bible.

Finally published in 1611 by royal command for use in all Anglican church and cathedral services and Divine public services, the first edition of the King James Bible was printed by Robert Baker. Copies of this first edition were available unbound for 10 shillings, or leather bound for 12 shillings. The widest distributed book ever, today over 6 billion copies have been published, making it one of the world's most influential religious texts.

Prince, IAMES by the grace of God
King of Great Britaine, France and Ireland,
Defender of the Faith, &c.

THE TRANSLATORS OF *THE BIBLE*,
wish Grace, Mercie, and Peace, through IESVS
CHRIST *our* LORD.

Reat and manifold were the bleſsings (moſt dread Soueraigne) which Almighty GOD, the Father of all Mercies, beſtowed vpon vs the people of ENGLAND, when firſt he ſent your Maieſties Royall perſon to rule and raigne ouer vs. For whereas it was the expectation of many, who wiſhed not well vnto our SION, that vpon the ſetting of that bright *Occidentall Starre* Queene ELIZABETH of moſt happy memory, ſome thicke and palpable cloudes of darkeneſſe would ſo haue ouerſhadowed this land, that men ſhould haue bene in doubt which way they were to walke, and that it ſhould hardly be knowen, who was to direct the vnſetled State: the appearance of your MAIESTIE, as of the *Sunne* in his ſtrength

DEDICATION TO KING JAMES Every edition of the King James Bible included a dedication written by the translators. It was largely based on one included in the Geneva Bible of 1560 written by the humanist scholar Erasmus of Rotterdam. The dedication thanks the king, but is also a powerful political act, as it firmly linked the king with the authorization of the Bible. It was only in editions that were printed in the 20th century that publishers were permitted to drop the dedication.

CLEAR PRESENTATION Intended as a book to be read out in church, this bible has no colour. The text is presented in an old-fashioned Gothic "black letter" script that not only gives it weight and authority, but is also clear and easy to read. A simple Roman typeface is used to differentiate the summaries given at the head of each chapter.

> We desire that the Scripture may speake like it selfe that it may bee understood even of the very vulgar

PREFACE TO THE 1611 KING JAMES BIBLE

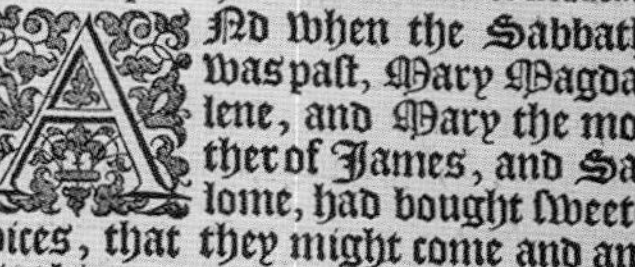

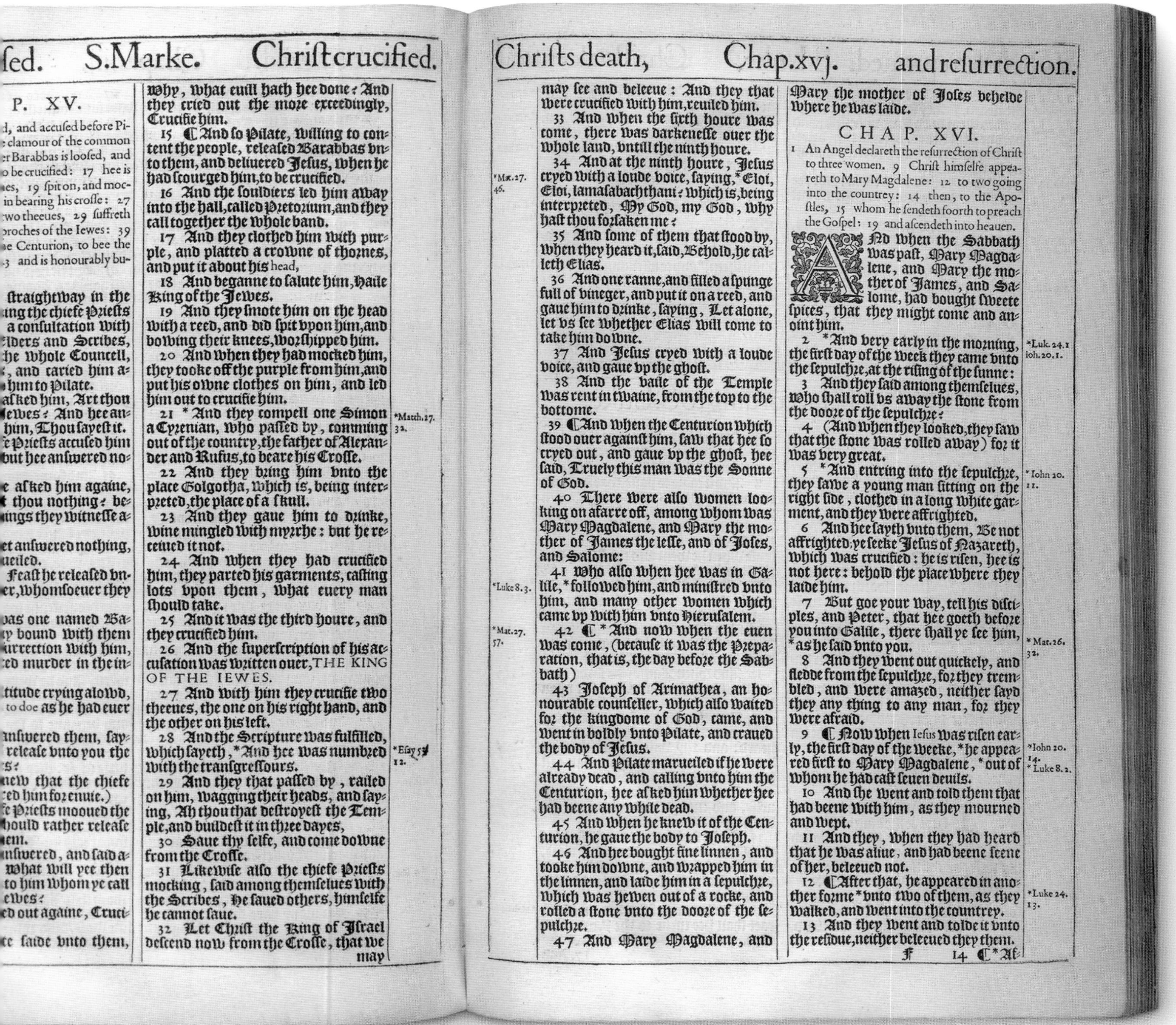

In detail

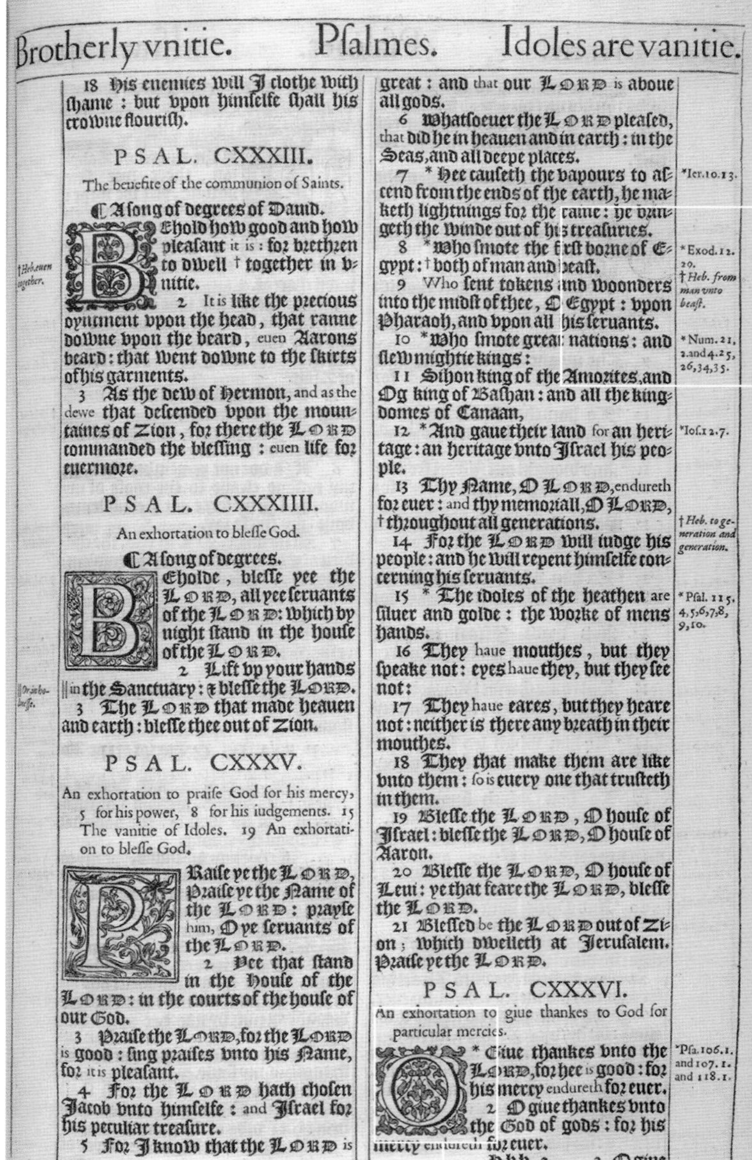

Brotherly vnitie. Pſalmes. Idoles are vanitie.

18 His enemies will I clothe with
ſhame : but vpon himſelfe ſhall his
crowne flouriſh.

PSAL. CXXXIII.

The benefite of the communion of Saints.

¶ A ſong of degrees of Dauid.

Behold how good and how
pleaſant it is : for brethren
to dwell † together in v-
nitie.
2 It is like the precious
oyntment vpon the head, that ranne
downe vpon the beard, euen Aarons
beard : that went downe to the ſkirts
of his garments.
3 As the dew of Hermon, and as the
dewe that deſcended vpon the moun-
taines of Zion, for there the LORD
commanded the bleſſing : euen life for
euermore.

† Heb. euen together.

PSAL. CXXXIIII.

An exhortation to bleſſe God.

¶ A ſong of degrees.

Beholde, bleſſe yee the
LORD, all yee ſeruants
of the LORD: which by
night ſtand in the houſe
of the LORD.
2 Lift vp your hands
‖ in the Sanctuary : & bleſſe the LORD.
3 The LORD that made heauen
and earth : bleſſe thee out of Zion.

‖ Or, in holineſſe.

PSAL. CXXXV.

An exhortation to praiſe God for his mercy, 5 for his power, 8 for his iudgements. 15 The vanitie of Idoles. 19 An exhortation to bleſſe God.

Praiſe ye the LORD,
Praiſe ye the Name of
the LORD : prayſe
him, O ye ſeruants of
the LORD.
2 Yee that ſtand
in the Houſe of the
LORD : in the courts of the houſe of
our God.
3 Praiſe the LORD, for the LORD
is good : ſing praiſes vnto his Name,
for it is pleaſant.
4 For the LORD hath choſen
Iacob vnto himſelfe : and Iſrael for
his peculiar treaſure.
5 For I know that the LORD is
great : and that our LORD is aboue
all gods.
6 Whatſoeuer the LORD pleaſed,
that did he in heauen and in earth : in the
Seas, and all deepe places.
7 * Hee cauſeth the vapours to aſ-
cend from the ends of the earth, he ma-
keth lightnings for the raine : he brin-
geth the winde out of his treaſuries.
8 * Who ſmote the firſt borne of E-
gypt : † both of man and beaſt.
9 Who ſent tokens and woonders
into the midſt of thee, O Egypt : vpon
Pharaoh, and vpon all his ſeruants.
10 * Who ſmote great nations : and
ſlew mightie kings :
11 Sihon king of the Amorites, and
Og king of Baſhan : and all the king-
domes of Canaan,
12 * And gaue their land for an heritage : an heritage vnto Iſrael his people.
13 Thy Name, O LORD, endureth
for euer : and thy memoriall, O LORD,
† throughout all generations.
14 For the LORD will iudge his
people : and he will repent himſelfe concerning his ſeruants.
15 * The idoles of the heathen are
ſiluer and golde : the worke of mens
hands.
16 They haue mouthes, but they
ſpeake not : eyes haue they, but they ſee
not :
17 They haue eares, but they heare
not : neither is there any breath in their
mouthes.
18 They that make them are like
vnto them : ſo is euery one that truſteth
in them.
19 Bleſſe the LORD, O houſe of
Iſrael : bleſſe the LORD, O houſe of
Aaron.
20 Bleſſe the LORD, O houſe of
Leui : ye that feare the LORD, bleſſe
the LORD.
21 Bleſſed be the LORD out of Zion ; which dwelleth at Ieruſalem.
Praiſe ye the LORD.

* Ier. 10. 13.
* Exod. 12. 29.
† Heb. from man vnto beaſt.
* Num. 21. 2. and 4. 25, 26, 34, 35.
* Ioſ. 12. 7.
† Heb. to generation and generation.
* Pſal. 115. 4, 5, 6, 7, 8, 9, 10.

PSAL. CXXXVI.

An exhortation to giue thankes to God for particular mercies.

O * Giue thankes vnto the
LORD, for hee is good : for
his mercy endureth for euer.
2 O giue thankes vnto
the God of gods : for his
mercy endureth for euer.

* Pſa. 106. 1. and 107. 1. and 118. 1.

Hhh 2 3 O giue

treaſuries.
ſt borne of E-
aſt.
d woonders
Egypt : vpon
is ſeruants.
nations : and
Amorites and

* Exod. 12. 29.
† Heb. from man vnto beaſt.
* Num. 21, 2. and 4. 25, 26, 34, 35.

◀ **THE PSALMS** A collection of 150 prayers and songs, the psalms were used by Hebrews to express their relationship with God. They are the most enduring part of the King James Bible. Even when modern bibles were introduced in the mid 20th century, churches continued with the King James versions of the psalms owing to their lyrical beauty.

▲ **MARGIN NOTES** The translators made a point of avoiding long notes and commentaries, so that readers could simply focus on the holy text. The only exceptions were when a word or phrase in the Greek or Hebrew original could not be translated easily. As shown above, a simple explanation of the alternative translation is then given in the margin.

▶ **DECORATIVE INITIAL LETTERS** The King James Bible was designed as a text to be read, not admired from a distance. Elegant in their simplicity, the initial capitals illustrated in simple black line at the beginning of each section, or, as here, at the start of each psalm, were there to help readers find their place easily.

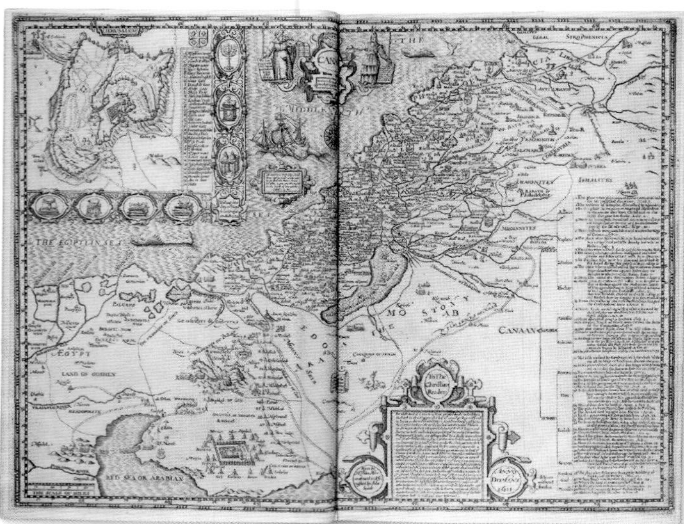

▲ **FOLD-OUT MAP OF THE HOLY LAND** One of the few illustrations in the King James Bible is this map of the Holy Land by John Speed. The map is there to inform readers of the locations in the bible stories, not simply to add decoration. Only about 200 copies of the first edition that include this map are known to survive.

▼ **FROM GOD TO CHRIST** At the beginning of the Bible is a 30-page genealogy that traces the ancestral path from God the Father (below), to Christ the Son (right). To overcome the fact that Jesus's father is not Joseph, but rather the Holy Spirit, the King James Bible uses a reading of St Luke's Gospel to follow the line back through his mother Mary, rather than Joseph, so Jesus can be traced to Adam and Eve.

▼ **COMPLETING THE GENEALOGY** This is the last page of the genealogy that links Christ to Adam and Eve. Altogether there are 1,750 names given including some well known biblical figures such as Jonah, Job, Lot, Abraham, Sarah, David, Solomon, Delilah, Goliath, and Moses. As with other illustrations, the genealogy "tree" is presented as a diagram in the style popular in the 17th century.

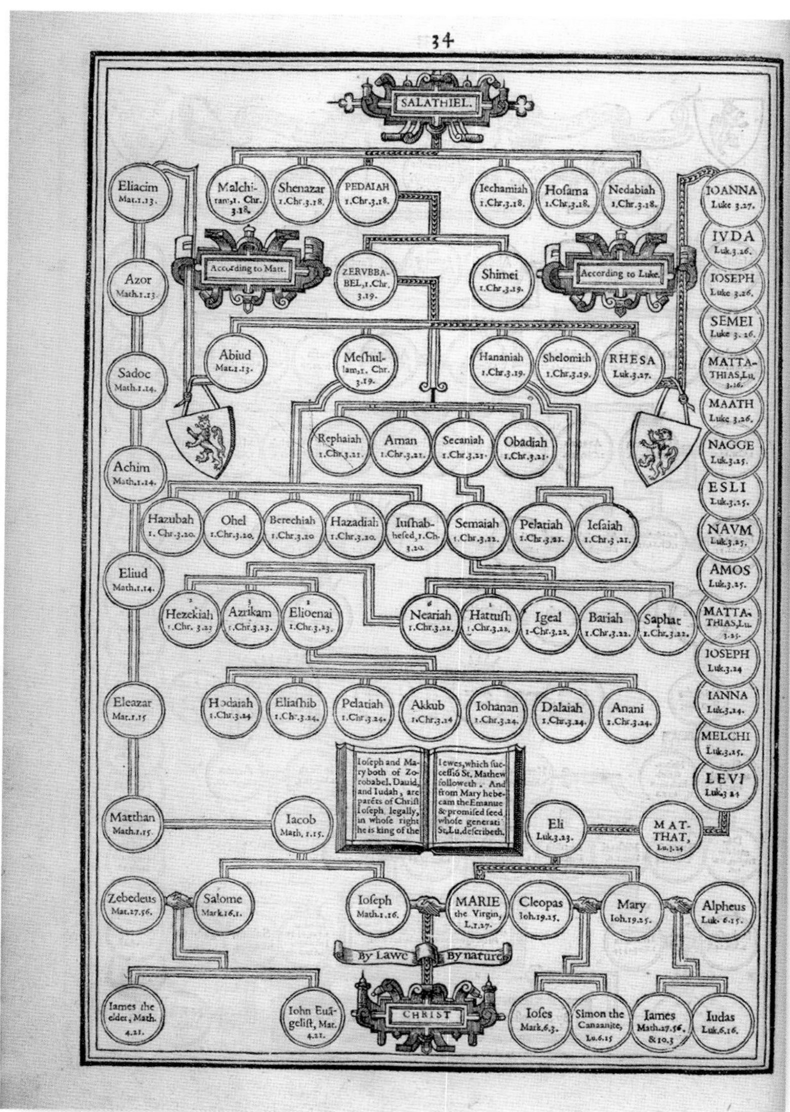

RELATED **TEXTS**

Central to the Protestant Reformation was the provision of bibles in the language of the people. In 1395 John Wycliffe produced the first translation of the Bible into English (based on a Latin script). William Tyndale followed in 1525, but his translation came from Greek and Hebrew. Both versions were banned by the Church, who considered the translation of the Bible into English blasphemous, but Tyndale's was the basis for the first "authorized" bible in English, Henry VIII's Great Bible of 1539. A group of Protestants published a new translation, the Geneva Bible, in 1560, but as this failed to reflect the theology of the Church, the Elizabethan church countered it with the official Bishop's Bible of 1568.

▶ **The Geneva Bible** was popular, but full of anti-royal margin notes. It was the bible that William Shakespeare chose to quote extensively from in many of his plays.

Hortus Eystettensis

1613 ▪ LETTERPRESS PRINTING FROM COPPER-ENGRAVED PLATES, HAND-COLOURED ▪ 57 × 46 cm (22 × 18 in) ▪ 367 ILLUSTRATED PLATES ▪ GERMANY

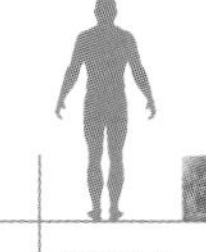
SCALE

BASILIUS BESLER

The finest illustrated botanical work of the early 17th century, *Hortus Eystettensis*, with its 367 beautifully illustrated plates, is a visual catalogue, or florilegium, of the gardens established by Prince Bishop Johann Konrad von Gemmingen (1561–1612) around his episcopal palace of Willibaldsburg at Eichstätt, near Nuremberg. Pleasure gardens were in vogue around 1600, and Johann Konrad was especially proud of his. In 1601 he commissioned the Nuremberg apothecary Basilius Besler to oversee publication of the *Hortus*. Artists worked to produce drawings of the most spectacular specimens in the prince's garden, which were then transferred onto copper plates by a team of 10 engravers. Previous florilegiums had tended to focus on medicinal and culinary herbs, using crude drawings that failed to enable a clear identification of each featured plant, and did not value the aesthetic qualities that the *Hortus* showcased.

The book was published in 1613 in two editions: one with black and white plates, with the text backing onto them; the other with separate text and illustration pages, allowing the botanical plates to be coloured by hand. The original budget was 3,000 florins, but the final cost of the work was estimated at 17,920 florins. Coloured copies excited huge demand, in part because the initial print run was just 300 copies – and the price soon rose to 500 florins per copy (at a time when the grandest house in Nuremberg cost 2,500 florins). Johann Konrad did not live to see the *Hortus* completed, having died in 1612, but its breadth and beauty stand testament to one of the age's greatest botanical patrons.

➤ **DETAILED DEPICTIONS** The detail in this page, which shows five species of hollyhock, depicts the *Hortus*'s botanical illustration at its finest. The plants would have been familiar to the apothecary, Besler, as they were commonly used in medicines for sore throats.

> Some while ago I have ordered sketches to be made of what had been observed in my own modest, narrow little garden
>
> **PRINCE BISHOP JOHANN KONRAD VON GEMMINGEN**, LETTER TO DUKE WILHELM V OF BAVARIA, 1 MAY 1611

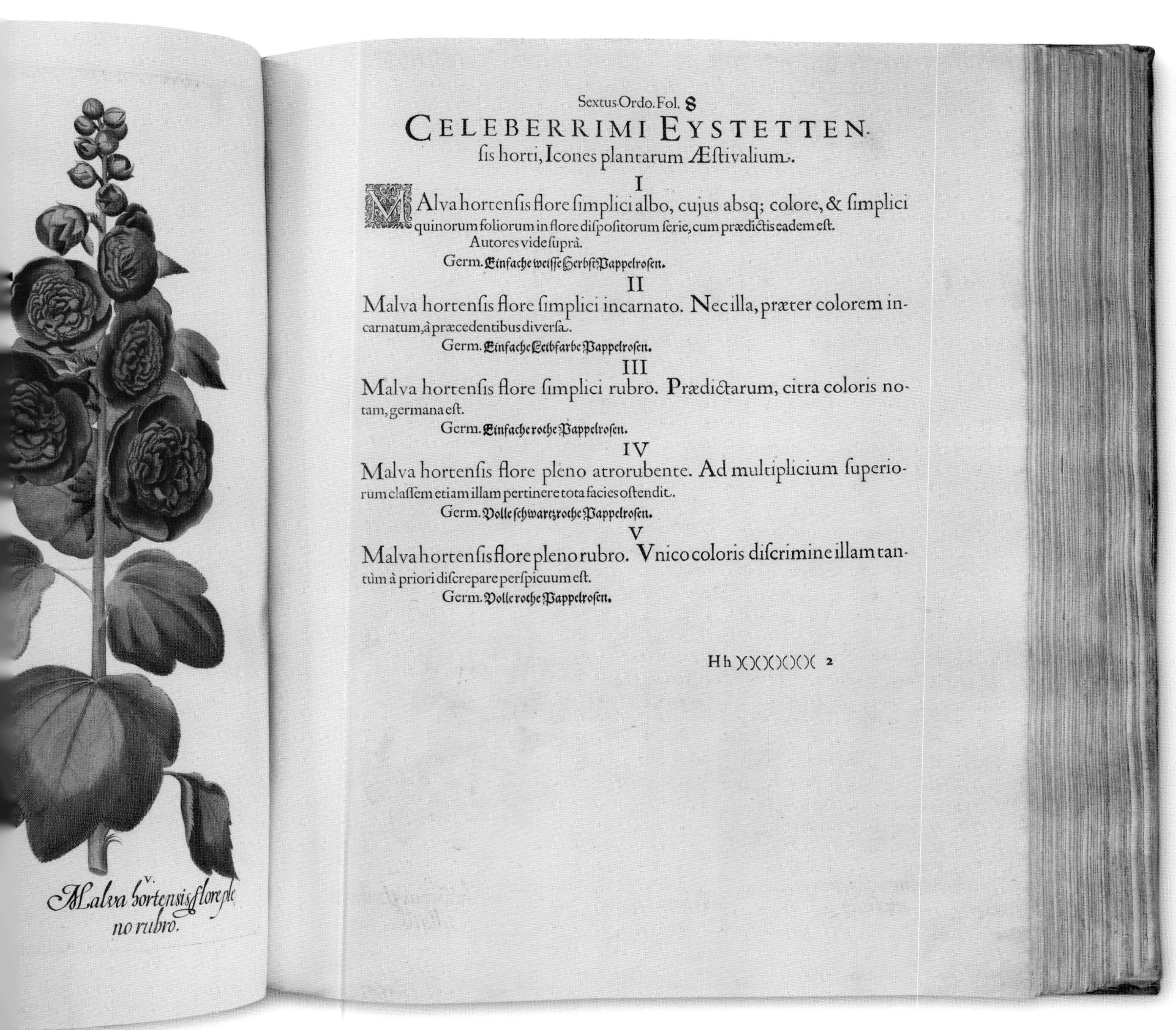

Sextus Ordo. Fol. 8

CELEBERRIMI EYSTETTENſis horti, Icones plantarum Æſtivalium.

I

MAlva hortenſis flore ſimplici albo, cujus absq; colore, & ſimplici quinorum foliorum in flore diſpoſitorum ſerie, cum prædictis eadem eſt.
Autores vide ſuprà.
Germ. Einfache weiſſe Herbſt Pappelroſen.

II

Malva hortenſis flore ſimplici incarnato. Nec illa, præter colorem incarnatum, à præcedentibus diverſa.
Germ. Einfache Leibfarbe Pappelroſen.

III

Malva hortenſis flore ſimplici rubro. Prædictarum, citra coloris notam, germana eſt.
Germ. Einfache rothe Pappelroſen.

IV

Malva hortenſis flore pleno atrorubente. Ad multiplicium ſuperiorum claſſem etiam illam pertinere tota facies oſtendit.
Germ. Volle ſchwartzrothe Pappelroſen.

V

Malva hortenſis flore pleno rubro. Vnico coloris diſcrimine illam tantùm à priori diſcrepare perſpicuum eſt.
Germ. Volle rothe Pappelroſen.

Hh)()()()()(2

In detail

HORTVS
EYSTETTENSIS
SIVE
M.DC.XIII
SALOMON
CYRVS

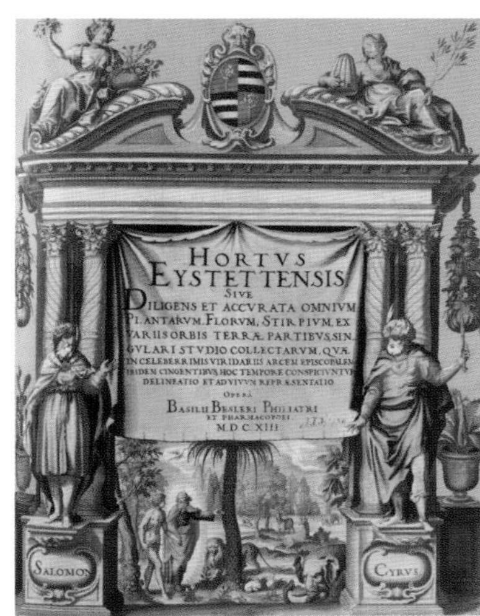

▲ **COAT OF ARMS** The title page of the *Hortus* shows the Prince Bishop's coat of arms mounted above an archway. Either side of it are figures representing Ceres, the Roman goddess of agriculture, and Flora, the Roman goddess of flowers. At the base of the arch stand King Solomon and King Cyrus of Persia, next to whom is a Mexican agave plant – one of the few plants in the book to come from the Americas.

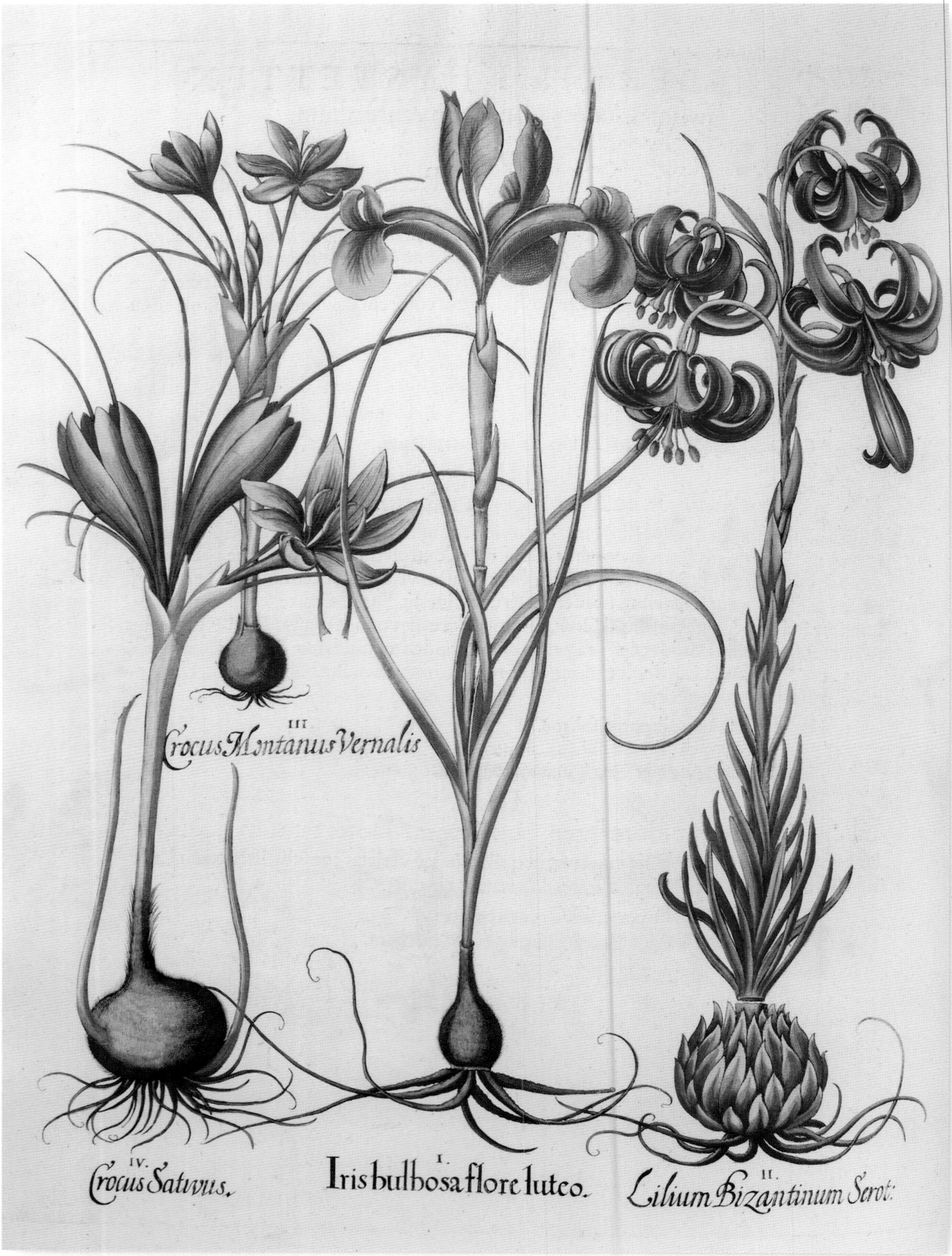

III
Crocus Montanus Vernalis
IV.
Crocus Sativus.
I.
Iris bulbosa flore luteo.
II.
Lilium Bizantinum Serot:

▲ **LIFE-SIZED IMAGES** The florilegium was printed on royal paper, the largest sheet size then available. This allowed the plants to be illustrated at almost life-size and at a level of intricacy that had rarely been possible before. Here (clockwise from top left), the Dutch Crocus, Spanish Crocus, Spanish Iris, and Scarlet Turk's Cap Lily are shown. In the convention of botanical illustration of the time, the roots are also included.

▼ **SOPHISTICATED COLOURING** The many shades of yellow used to show the contours of each petal indicate a high level of artistry and accuracy, as well as aesthetics.

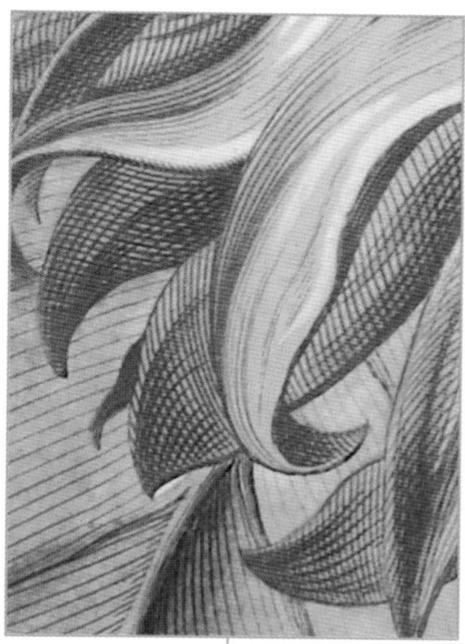

▼ **METICULOUS REPRESENTATION** The large scale of the book allowed for very fine work enabling depiction of minute plant features. Here a detail shows the individually painted disk florets, the tiny flowers at the sunflower's centre.

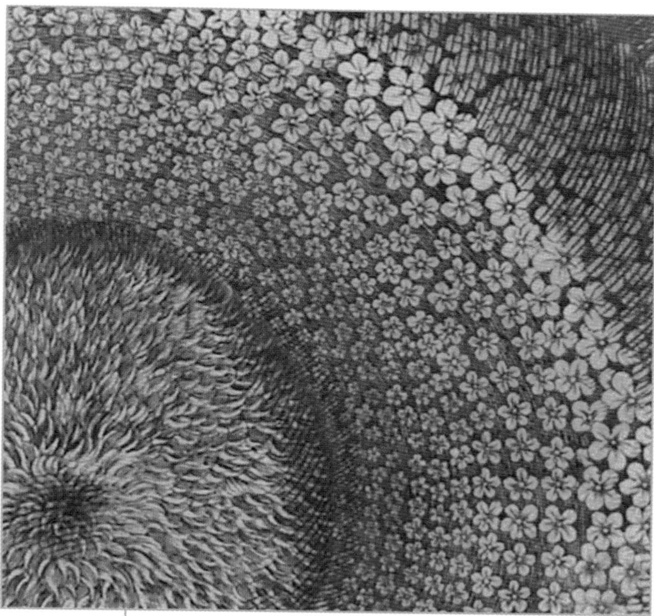

◄ **SEASONALITY** The *Hortus* was arranged broadly by season. It began with winter and finished with autumn. This sunflower appeared in the largest section of the book – summer plants.

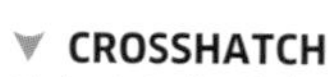

▼ **CROSSHATCH** This detail of the stalk shows fine hatching used as a tint, a method that was characteristic of the miniaturist's technique.

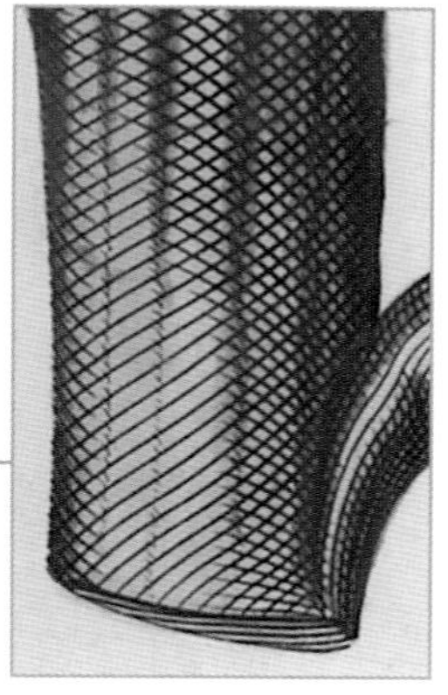

IN **CONTEXT**

Besler's *Hortus* drew on a strong tradition of botanical drawing that began with Conrad Gesner (1516–65) the Swiss botanist, and which included Joachim Camerarius the Younger (1534–98), who may have helped lay out the gardens at Willibaldsburg.

The *Hortus* marks the definitive transition from woodcut techniques to copper plates. Besler sent weekly shipments of flowers from Eichstätt to studios in Nuremberg, where they were sketched. These images were then finely etched onto copper printing plates by a team of 10 engravers, including Wilhelm Killian. Pages printed for the coloured edition were then hand coloured by expert illustrators, such as Georg Mack, who could take up to a year to complete a single copy of the book.

Just over half the 667 species portrayed in the *Hortus* were native to Germany. The remainder were imported from around the world: a third came from the Mediterranean, 10 per cent from Asia (notably tulips), and around five per cent from the Americas.

▲ **Coloured sketches** made for the *Hortus* by Nuremberg artist Sebastian Schedelare, including this opium poppy, are compiled in a book called Schedel's *Calendarium*.

Tutte l'opere d'architettura, et prospetiva

1537–75 (WRITTEN), 1619 (VERSION SHOWN) ■ PRINTED ■ 25.5 × 18.5 cm (10 × 7 in) ■ 243 PAGES ■ ITALY

SCALE

SEBASTIANO SERLIO

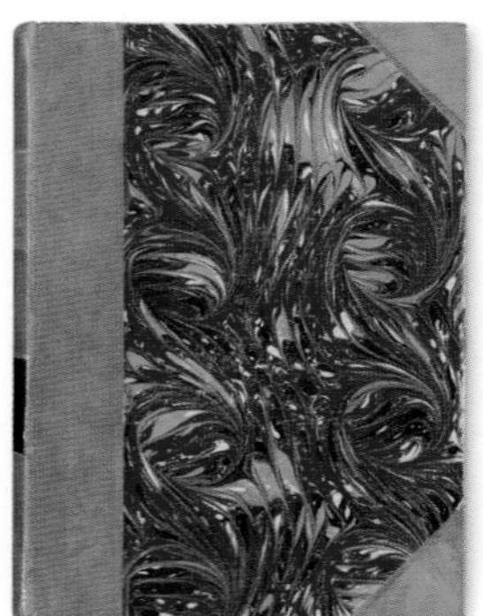

Published in seven volumes, *The Complete Works on Architecture and Perspective* was the most influential treatise on architecture produced in the Renaissance, and was widely studied in Europe after being translated from the original Italian. As an architect, Sebastiano Serlio's legacy is modest, but with his *L'Architettura* (as the work is often known) he created the first practical architectural handbook, and the most widely used edition is shown here.

Prior to *L'Architettura*, the principal tome on Renaissance architecture was the 1485 work *Dei re aedificatoria* (*Ten Books on Architecture*), by Florentine architect Leon Battista Alberti. Although authoritative, it was written in Latin, purely theoretical, and largely unillustrated. Serlio took a radically different approach: his books addressed the needs of architects, builders, and craftsmen by providing explanatory text alongside detailed drawings. Among the books' practical elements were models for copying and solutions for everyday design problems. The volumes did not appear in sequence – what became Books I and II were, respectively, the third and fourth to be published, but as a set they helped to cement the Renaissance belief in the primacy of Classical architecture.

SEBASTIANO **SERLIO**

1475–1554

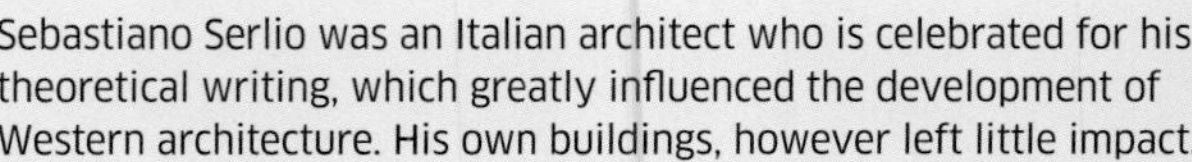

Sebastiano Serlio was an Italian architect who is celebrated for his theoretical writing, which greatly influenced the development of Western architecture. His own buildings, however left little impact.

Serlio was born in Bologna, Italy, where he trained as a perspective painter in his father's workshop. In 1514, he moved to Rome to study architecture; later, he practised there, and in Venice, although he devoted much of his time to *L'Architettura*. In 1541, Serlio's writing came to the attention of Francis I of France, who summoned him to become part of an Italian design team he had assembled to consult on the rebuilding of the royal residence at Fontainebleau, outside Paris. Through his work at Fontainebleau, and through the hugely informative volumes of his treatise, Serlio transmitted the principles of Classical architecture from Italy to France, and elsewhere in northern Europe.

In detail

➤ A LIFE'S WORK Each volume of *L'Architettura* was written and published gradually, while Serlio was practising as an architect in Italy and France; Books VI and VII were published after his death. Book I (1545), whose lavish title page is seen here, investigates the essentials of Classical architecture: above all, the rules of geometry and perspective. The perfect symmetry of the Classical columns, illustrated here, reflects the fascination with Ancient Greece and Rome that characterized the Renaissance period. Indeed, for the next 250 years, most significant European buildings were designed along Greco-Roman lines.

LIBRO PRIMO
D'ARCHITETTVRA
DI SEBASTIANO SERLIO
BOLOGNESE,
Nel quale con facile, & breue modo si tratta de' primi principij della Geometria.
Con nuoua aggiunta delle misure, che seruono a tutti gli ordini de' componimenti, che vi si contengono.

IN VICENZA,
Per Iacomo de' Franceschi.

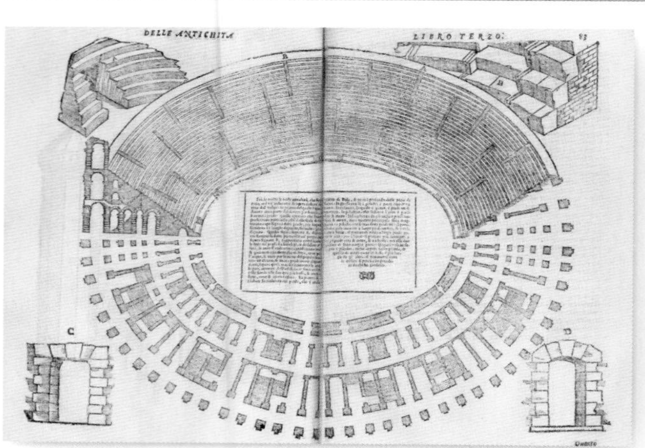

▲ ARCHITECTURAL PLAN Carefully rendered in fine detail, this plan of the 1st-century-CE arena in Verona, Italy, reflects Serlio's dedication to the Classical style. He derived his knowledge from two sources: the ruins of ancient buildings, and the treatise *On Architecture* (c.27 BCE) by Roman architect Vitruvius.

▼ **CLASSICAL MEETS CHRISTIAN** No subject exercised a greater hold on the imagination of Renaissance architects than churches. The goal was to find ways of adapting Classical precedents to Christian use. In reality, the ideal solution – the symmetrical "Greek cross" building in this illustration – proved impossible to reconcile with the practical needs of the Church.

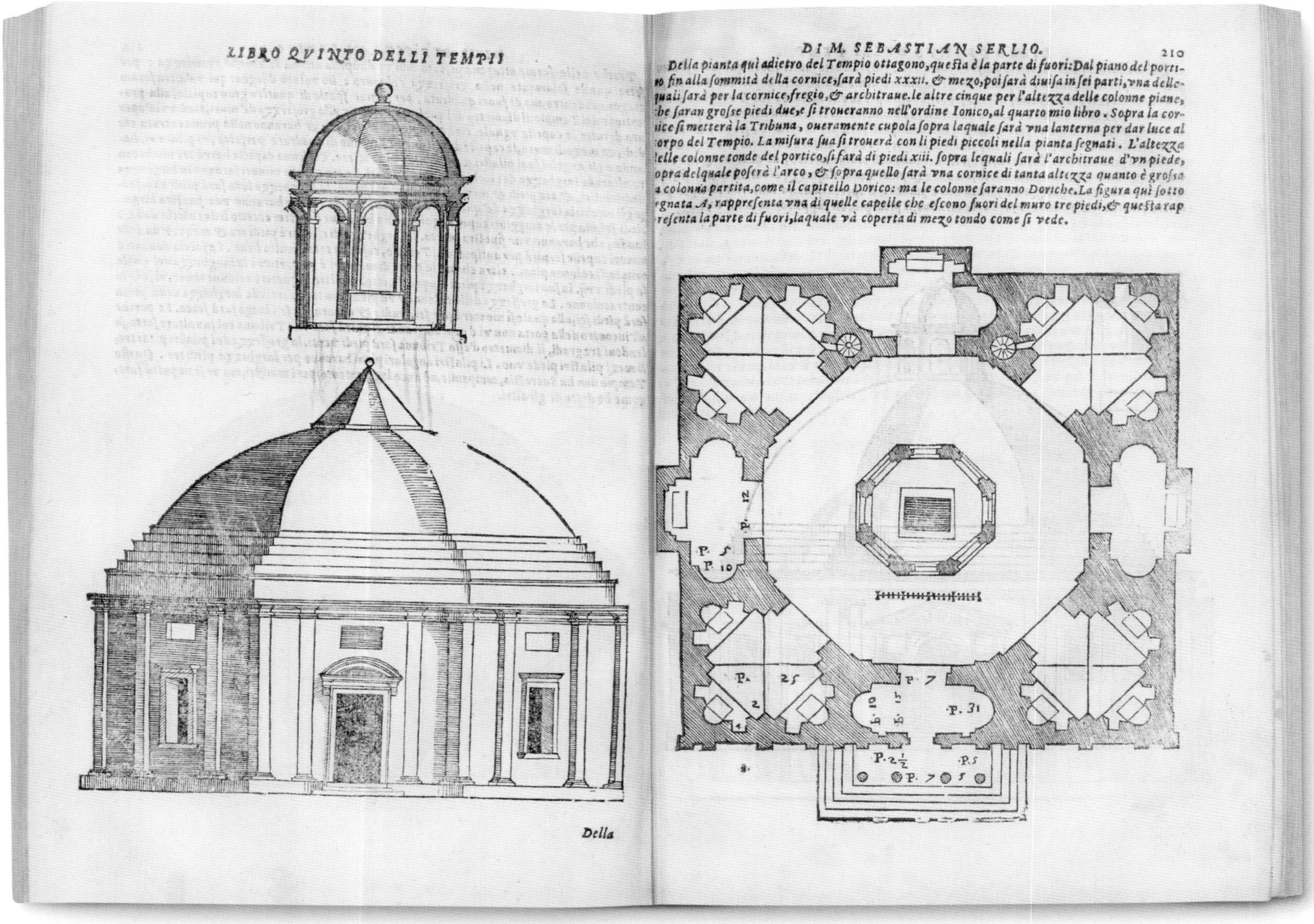

▲ **COMPOSITE COLUMNS** Serlio included illustrated examples of different types of Classical columns: Tuscan, Doric, Ionic, Corinthian, and Composite (shown here) – arranged in an order of increasing intricacy. Serlio had studied these in situ at ancient sites in Italy. *L'Architettura* was the first work to give a systematic guide to the main orders of Classical architecture, which are defined by their columns.

> ... much more can be learned from the figure than from the text since it is such a difficult thing to write about
>
> **SEBASTIANO SERLIO**

Mr. William Shakespeares Comedies, Histories, & Tragedies

1623 ■ PRINTED BY ISAAC JAGGARD AND EDWARD BLOUNT ■ 33 × 21 cm (13 × 8 in) ■ c.900 PAGES ■ COMPILED BY JOHN HEMINGE AND HENRY CONDELL ■ ENGLAND

SCALE

WILLIAM SHAKESPEARE

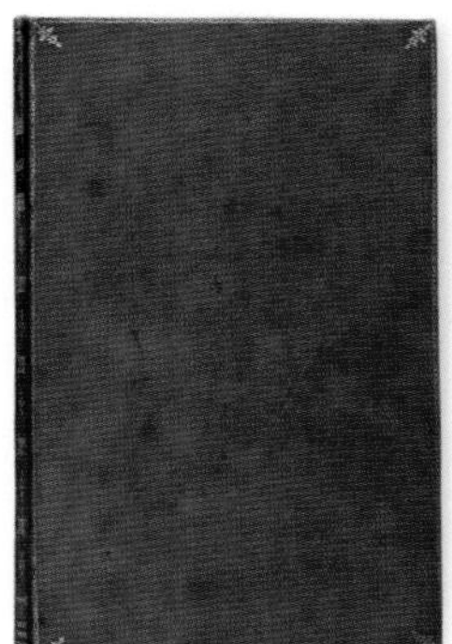

The *First Folio*, as it is also known, was the first authoritative publication of all but one of the 37 plays widely attributed to William Shakespeare. Its importance is absolute. When it appeared seven years after his death, only 17 of his plays had been published – most in rogue editions.

It is almost certain that without the *First Folio*, those plays which had not yet appeared in print, including *Macbeth* and *The Tempest*, would have been lost. In addition to being as definitive a collection of Shakespeare's plays as was possible, the *First Folio* marked a deliberate attempt to celebrate the impact of the playwright. Its format was as imposing as its goal which, according to his contemporary Ben Jonson, was to present Shakespeare "not of an age but for all time". The *First Folio* remains arguably the most important, and certainly the most sought-after, English-language book ever published. Approximately 750 copies are believed to have been printed; of these 235 survive, but only 40 are complete.

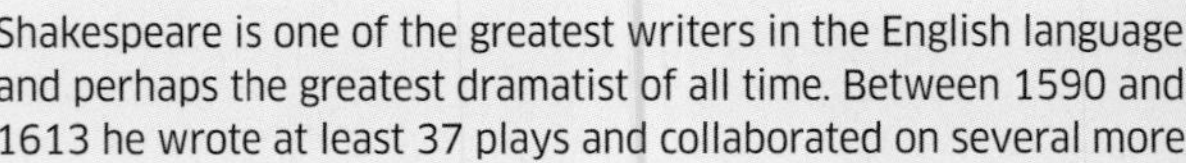

WILLIAM **SHAKESPEARE**

1564–1616

Shakespeare is one of the greatest writers in the English language and perhaps the greatest dramatist of all time. Between 1590 and 1613 he wrote at least 37 plays and collaborated on several more.

Little is known about Shakespeare's early life. In 1582, he married Anne Hathaway in Stratford-upon-Avon, and had three children with her. The first mention of his presence in London is 1592, by which time he was a successful playwright. He became a shareholder in the Lord Chamberlain's Men, a theatre company, which performed before Queen Elizabeth I (1533-1603). In 1599, the company moved to the Globe theatre in London. When the theatre was destroyed by fire in 1613, Shakespeare left the city and returned to Stratford-upon-Avon.

In detail

➤ **LATE ADDITION** Only 35 plays are listed in the table of contents, or Catalogue, of the *First Folio*. The 36th play, *Troilus and Cressida*, written in around 1602 and the last to be printed, was included only at the last minute, and was therefore not included on the contents page. The grouping of the plays into the three categories of Comedies, Histories, and Tragedies was first implemented in the *First Folio*, and the works are still defined in that way.

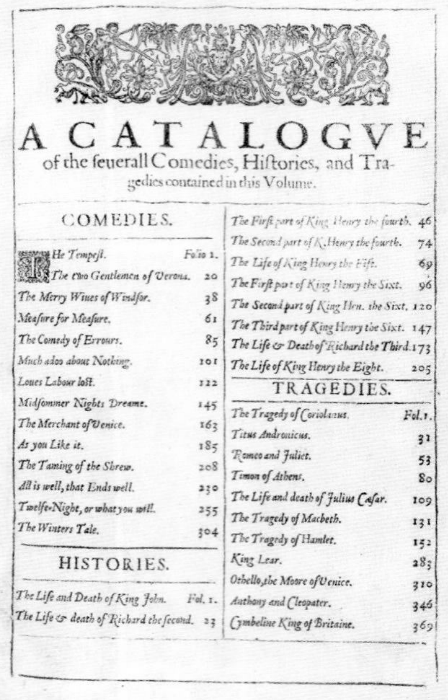

A CATALOGVE
of the seuerall Comedies, Histories, and Tragedies contained in this Volume.

COMEDIES.

THe Tempest.	Folio 1.
The two Gentlemen of Verona.	20
The Merry Wiues of Windsor.	38
Measure for Measure.	61
The Comedy of Errours.	85
Much adoo about Nothing.	101
Loues Labour lost.	122
Midsommer Nights Dreame.	145
The Merchant of Venice.	163
As you Like it.	185
The Taming of the Shrew.	208
All is well, that Ends well.	230
Twelfe-Night, or what you will.	255
The Winters Tale.	304

HISTORIES.

The Life and Death of King John.	Fol. 1.
The Life & death of Richard the second.	23
The First part of King Henry the fourth.	46
The Second part of K. Henry the fourth.	74
The Life of King Henry the Fift.	69
The First part of King Henry the Sixt.	96
The Second part of King Hen. the Sixt.	120
The Third part of King Henry the Sixt.	147
The Life & Death of Richard the Third.	173
The Life of King Henry the Eight.	205

TRAGEDIES.

The Tragedy of Coriolanus.	Fol. 1.
Titus Andronicus.	31
Romeo and Juliet.	53
Timon of Athens.	80
The Life and death of Julius Cæsar.	109
The Tragedy of Macbeth.	131
The Tragedy of Hamlet.	152
King Lear.	283
Othello, the Moore of Venice.	310
Anthony and Cleopater.	346
Cymbeline King of Britaine.	369

➤ **FIRST APPEARANCE** *The Tempest* is the first play to feature in the *First Folio*, although it is believed to be one of the last plays that Shakespeare ever wrote – at least, that he wrote alone – around 1610. It is listed on the Catalogue page under the heading of Comedies, even though there are elements of tragedy to the play.

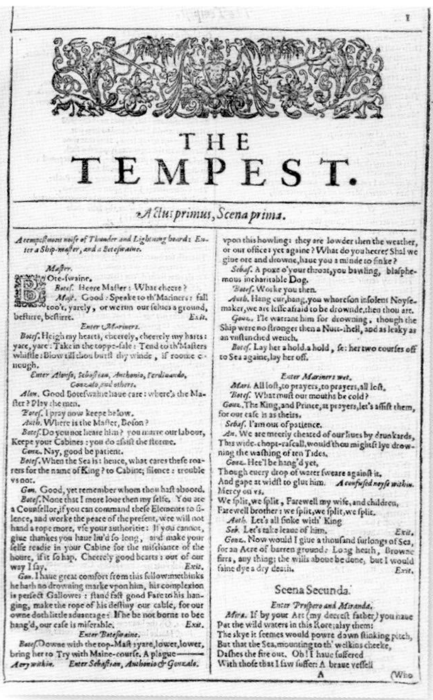

THE TEMPEST.

Actus primus, Scena prima.

Scena Secunda.

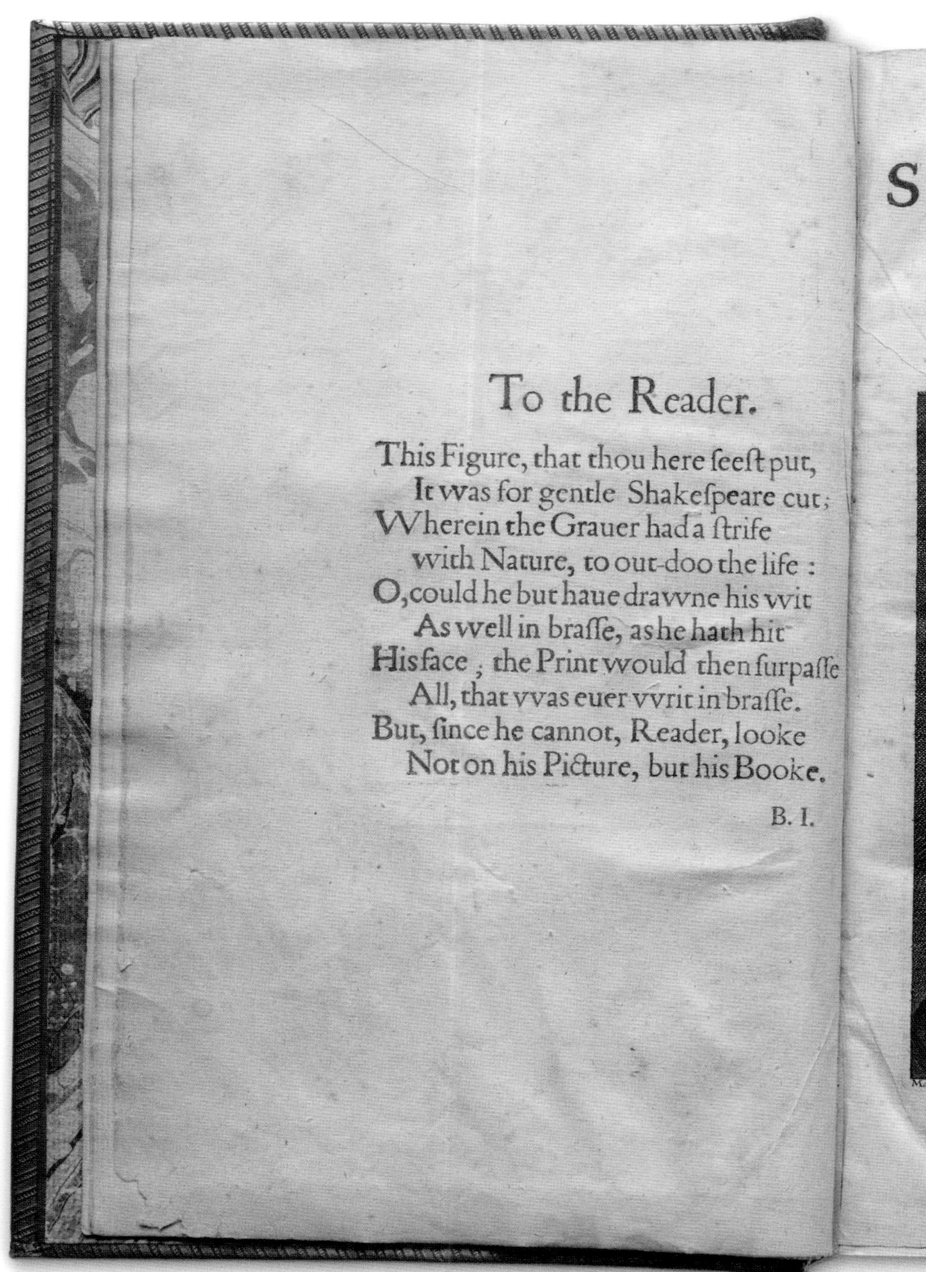

To the Reader.

This Figure, that thou here ſeeſt put,
It was for gentle Shakeſpeare cut;
Wherein the Grauer had a ſtrife
with Nature, to out-doo the life:
O, could he but haue drawne his wit
As well in braſſe, as he hath hit
His face; the Print would then ſurpaſſe
All, that vvas euer vvrit in braſſe.
But, ſince he cannot, Reader, looke
Not on his Picture, but his Booke.

B. I.

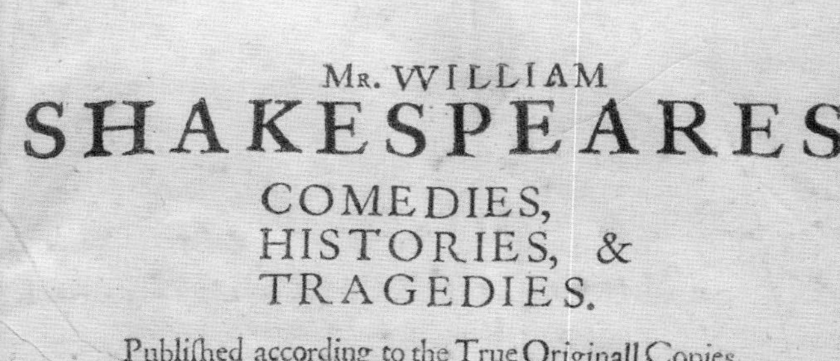

Mr. WILLIAM
SHAKESPEARES
COMEDIES,
HISTORIES, &
TRAGEDIES.

Publiſhed according to the True Originall Copies.

LONDON
Printed by Iſaac Iaggard, and Ed. Blount. 1623.

▲ **SHAKESPEARE'S LIKENESS** Martin Droeshout's engraving of Shakespeare on the title page is one of only two images of the playwright generally accepted as a true likeness. Although Droeshout did not know Shakespeare personally, the compilers of the *First Folio*, John Heminge and Henry Condell, did and it is unlikely they would have accepted an unfaithful representation.

IN **CONTEXT**

More than 400 years after Shakespeare's death, his plays have lost none of their appeal or relevance. They are studied and performed throughout the world, with new editions still being printed in English and in translation. One of the most ambitious editions to date is that of *Hamlet* by the German publisher Cranach-Presse. First published in German in 1928, then in English two years later, the margins feature original and translated extracts from two of Shakespeare's likely sources – a 12th-century Norse folk-tale and a 16th-century French story. Illustrating the edition are 80 striking woodcuts by Edward Gordon Craig.

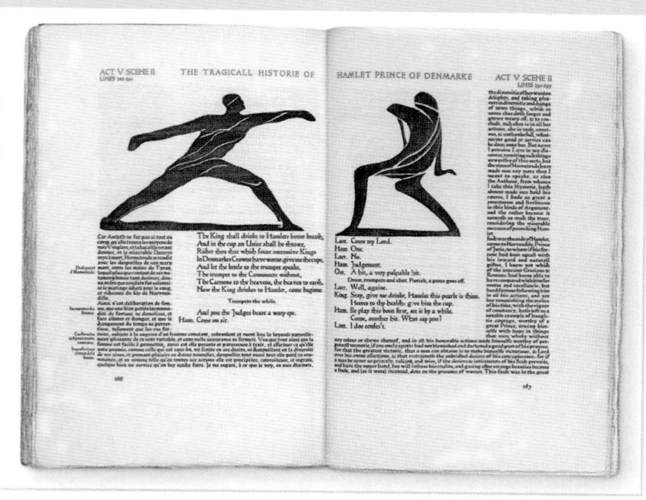

ACT V SCENE II   THE TRAGICALL HISTORIE OF   HAMLET PRINCE OF DENMARKE   ACT V SCENE II

➤ **Only 300 hand-printed copies** of Cranach-Presse's 1930 edition of *Hamlet* were produced, using hand-made paper and featuring bold imagery and elegant typefaces.

Dialogo sopra i due massimi sistemi del mondo

1632 ▪ PRINTED ▪ 21.9 × 15.5 cm (8 × 6 in) ▪ 458 PAGES ▪ ITALY

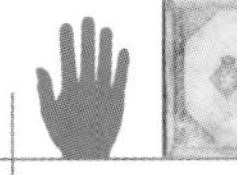

SCALE

GALILEO GALILEI

This is the book that changed people's view of the Universe. In *Dialogo sopra i due massimi sistemi del mondo* (*Dialogue Concerning the Two Chief World Systems*) the Italian mathematician Galileo Galilei (1564–1642) compared the Copernican view of the Universe (1541) which proposed that the Earth revolved around the Sun, with the traditional Ptolemaic view, which placed the Earth at the centre of the Universe.

Galileo's book, written in Italian rather than scholarly Latin, takes the form of an imaginary discussion, set over four days, between three fictitious characters. Salviati argues in favour of the Copernican view, Simplicio favours the Ptolemaic view, and Sagredo is the neutral foil, who is eventually won over by Salviati. Copernicus had already presented his theory, but Galileo based the *Dialogo* on his own observations. In discussing a number of viewpoints, the book poked fun at those who refused to accept the possibility that the Earth revolved around the Sun.

Galileo's findings set him on a collision course with the Catholic Church, which opposed Copernicus's theory. In 1633 Galileo was found to be "vehemently suspect of heresy". He was taken to Rome and forced to recant his views, then placed under house arrest. *Dialogo* was put on the Vatican's Index of Prohibited Books, remaining there until 1835. A modified version, *The Dialogue on the Tides,* was permitted by the Church in 1741.

◄ **FRONTISPIECE** Stefano della Bella's engravings feature Aristotle and Ptolemy in debate with Copernicus, and a dedication to Galileo's patron, the Grand Duke of Tuscany. The illustration reflects the imaginary discussion Galileo uses in the book to convey his theory.

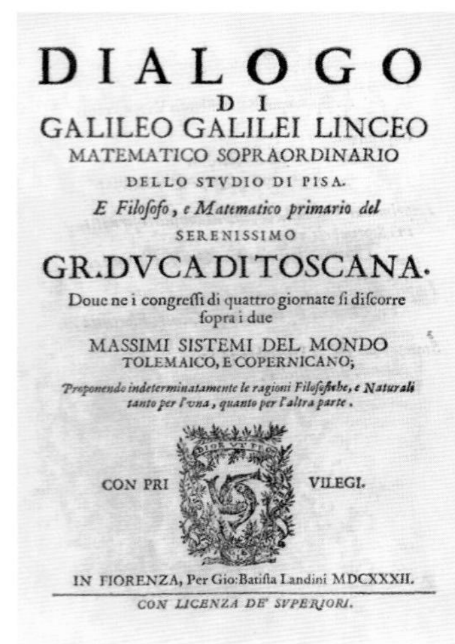

DIALOGO
DI
GALILEO GALILEI LINCEO
MATEMATICO SOPRAORDINARIO
DELLO STVDIO DI PISA.
E Filosofo, e Matematico primario del
SERENISSIMO
GR. DVCA DI TOSCANA.
Doue ne i congressi di quattro giornate si discorre sopra i due
MASSIMI SISTEMI DEL MONDO
TOLEMAICO, E COPERNICANO;
Proponendo indeterminatamente le ragioni Filosofiche, e Naturali tanto per l'vna, quanto per l'altra parte.

CON PRIVILEGI.

IN FIORENZA, Per Gio: Batista Landini MDCXXXII.

CON LICENZA DE' SVPERIORI.

► **MAPS OF PLANETS AND STARS** Galileo included 31 woodcuts and diagrams to illustrate how the Copernican theory works. This one, from the third day's discussion shows the orbit of Jupiter and Earth around the Sun.

◄ **FIRST EDITION TITLE PAGE** This bears another dedication to the Grand Duke, and describes Galileo as an extraordinary mathematician. *Dialogo* was printed in Florence by Giovanni Battista Landini; this page bears his family crest of three circling fish.

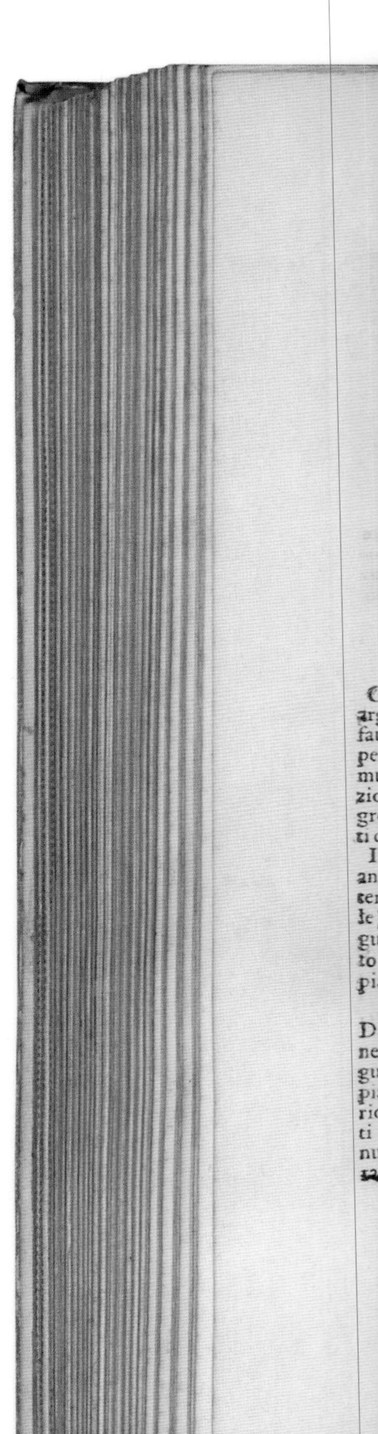

> I have written many direct and indirect arguments for the Copernican view, but until now I have not dared to publish them, alarmed by the fate of Copernicus himself

GALILEO, IN A LETTER TO KEPLER, 1597

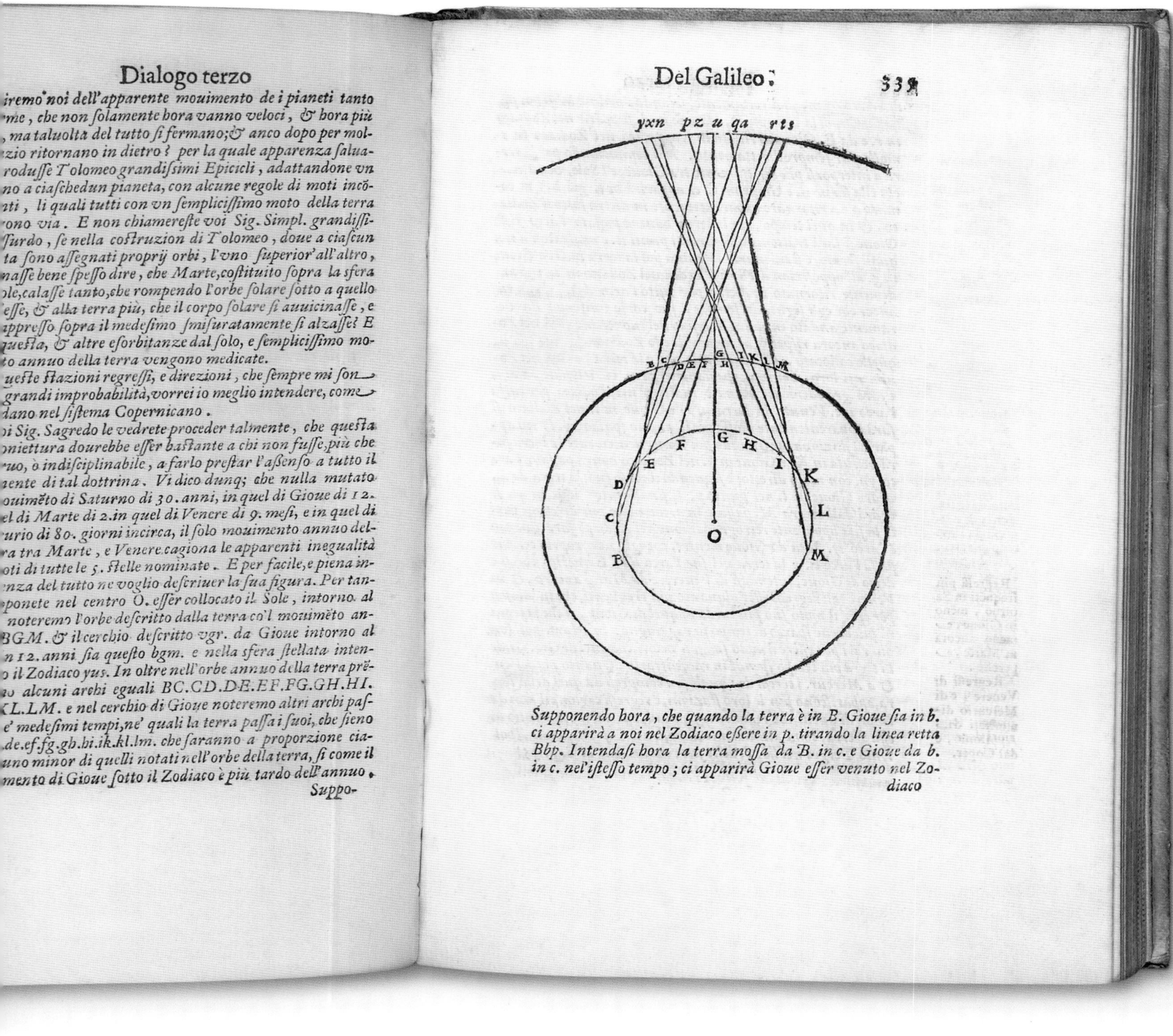

Dialogo terzo

iremo noi dell'apparente mouimento de i pianeti tanto
me, che non solamente hora vanno veloci, & hora più
, ma taluolta del tutto si fermano;& anco dopo per mol-
zio ritornano in dietro? per la quale apparenza salua-
rodusse Tolomeo grandissimi Epicicli, adattandone vn
no a ciaschedun pianeta, con alcune regole di moti incō-
nti, li quali tutti con vn semplicissimo moto della terra
ono via. E non chiamereste voi Sig. Simpl. grandissi-
surdo, se nella costruzion di Tolomeo, doue a ciascun
ta sono assegnati proprij orbi, l'vno superior all'altro,
nasse bene spesso dire, che Marte, costituito sopra la sfera
ole, calasse tanto, che rompendo l'orbe solare sotto a quello
esse, & alla terra più, che il corpo solare si auuicinasse, e
appresso sopra il medesimo smisuratamente si alzasse? E
questa, & altre esorbitanze dal solo, e semplicissimo moto annuo della terra vengono medicate.
ueste stazioni regressi, e direzioni, che sempre mi son
grandi improbabilità, vorrei io meglio intendere, come
dano nel sistema Copernicano.
i Sig. Sagredo le vedrete proceder talmente, che questa
niettura dourebbe esser bastante a chi non fusse, più che
uo, ò indisciplinabile, a farlo prestar l'assenso a tutto il
ente di tal dottrina. Vi dico dunq; che nulla mutato
ouimēto di Saturno di 30. anni, in quel di Gioue di 12.
el di Marte di 2. in quel di Venere di 9. mesi, e in quel di
urio di 80. giorni incirca, il solo mouimento annuo del-
ra tra Marte, e Venere cagiona le apparenti inegualità
oti di tutte le 5. stelle nominate. E per facile, e piena in-
nza del tutto ne voglio descriuer la sua figura. Per tan-
ponete nel centro O. esser collocato il Sole, intorno al
noteremo l'orbe descritto dalla terra co'l mouimēto an-
BGM. & il cerchio descritto vgr. da Gioue intorno al
n 12. anni sia questo bgm. e nella sfera stellata inten-
o il Zodiaco yus. In oltre nell'orbe annuo della terra prē-
o alcuni archi eguali BC.CD.DE.EF.FG.GH.HI.
KL.LM. e nel cerchio di Gioue noteremo altri archi pas-
e' medesimi tempi, ne' quali la terra passa i suoi, che sieno
de.ef.fg.gh.hi.ik.kl.lm. che saranno a proporzione cia-
uno minor di quelli notati nell'orbe della terra, sì come il
mento di Gioue sotto il Zodiaco è più tardo dell'annuo.
Suppo-

Del Galileo. 339

Supponendo hora, che quando la terra è in B. Gioue sia in b. ci apparirà a noi nel Zodiaco essere in p. tirando la linea retta Bbp. Intendasi hora la terra mossa da B. in c. e Gioue da b. in c. nel'istesso tempo; ci apparirà Gioue esser venuto nel Zodiaco

Bay Psalm Book

1640 ▪ PRINTED ▪ 17.4 × 10.4 cm (7 × 4 in) ▪ 153 PAGES ▪ USA

SCALE

RICHARD MATHER

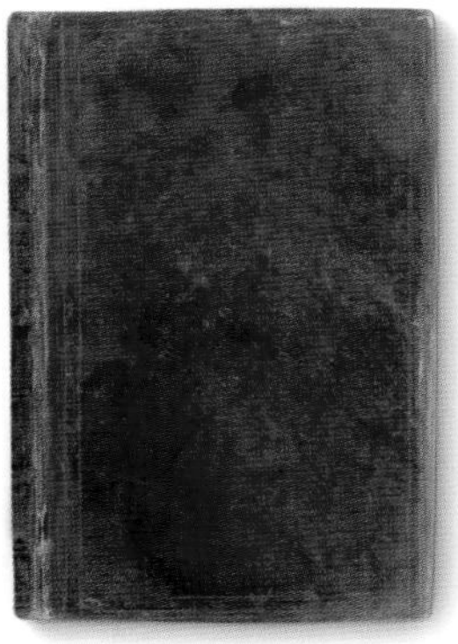

Commonly heralded as the first book to be printed in British North America, the *Bay Psalm Book* was a translation of the Book of Psalms. It was created for a group of Christian evangelical dissenters, who sailed from England to America in 1620, where they settled in Plymouth, Massachusetts. Facing persecution in England, the group, who are sometimes called the Pilgrim Fathers, sailed for the colonies in search of religious tolerance. There, they established a form of worship that placed particular emphasis on the *Book of Psalms*, which contains hymns of praise, and appears in the Hebrew Bible and Old Testament of the Christian Bible.

The settlers wanted a new translation of the *Book of Psalms* that was closer to the original Hebrew. And so they commissioned 30 translators to prepare the new version, and produced *The Whole Booke of Psalms*, now known as the *Bay Psalm Book*. The book was a metrical psalter, with verses rhythmically arranged for singing to familiar tunes. Although a revised version was published in 1761, taking contemporary language into account, the updated psalms lacked finesse and none are in use today. The *Bay Psalm Book* was the third text to be printed in British North America, 20 years after the settlers' arrival. The pressman was unskilled and, as a result, there are many errors throughout the book. Only 11 copies of the first edition are known to exist. In 2013, a rare copy of the 1640 *Bay Psalm Book* was sold by the British auction house, Sotheby's – for a staggering $14,165,000.

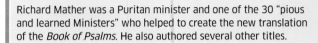

RICHARD **MATHER**

c.1596–1669

Richard Mather was a Puritan minister and one of the 30 "pious and learned Ministers" who helped to create the new translation of the *Book of Psalms*. He also authored several other titles.

Richard Mather was born in Lancashire and was ordained in the Anglican (Episcopalian in USA) Church. It was a tumultuous era in which several branches of Protestantism developed in England. Mather was suspended for non-conformity to liturgical regulations by the Archbishop of York in 1634. The next year he decided to emigrate and sailed with his wife, Katherine Holt, and four sons to the New World, settling in Dorchester, Massachusetts. Mather was a persuasive preacher and assisted the clergy who translated the Hebrew psalter as the *Bay Psalm Book*, taking responsibility for some of the largest sections. In the early years of New England Congregationalism, he wrote extensively on questions of discipline for the new community.

In detail

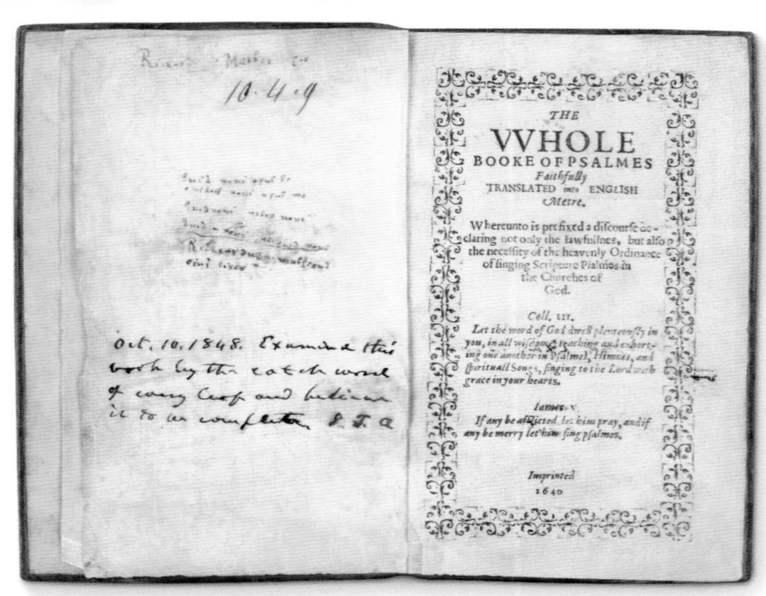

THE
VVHOLE
BOOKE OF PSALMES
Faithfully
TRANSLATED into ENGLISH
Metre.

Whereunto is prefixed a discourse declaring not only the lawfullnes, but also the necessity of the heavenly Ordinance of singing Scripture Psalmes in the Churches of God.

Coll. III.
Let the word of God dwell plenteously in you, in all wisdome, teaching and exhorting one another in Psalmes, Himnes, and spirituall Songs, singing to the Lord with grace in your hearts.

Iames v.
If any be afflicted, let him pray, and if any be merry let him sing psalmes.

Imprinted
1640

◄ **PRINTING ERRORS** The first edition was poorly printed, and contains numerous typographical errors. The type was uneven, punctuation mixed up, and words incorrectly broken over lines. More than 1,700 copies of the 298-page volume were printed in the first run in 1640, with a further 26 smaller print runs following.

► **RHYMING METRE** The psalms were written in a crude metre, particularly in the first edition, an example of which is shown here. The writers placed more importance on faithful translation of the text than poetic finesse.

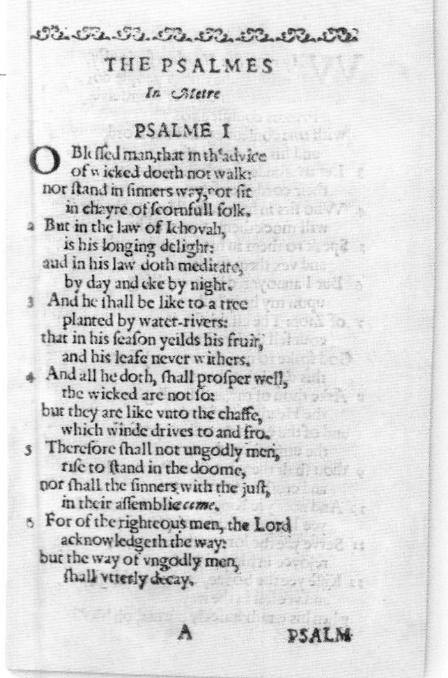

THE PSALMES
In Metre

PSALME I

O Blessed man, that in th'advice
of wicked doeth not walk:
nor stand in sinners way, nor sit
in chayre of scornfull folk,
2 But in the law of Iehovah,
is his longing delight:
and in his law doth meditate,
by day and eke by night.
3 And he shall be like to a tree
planted by water-rivers:
that in his season yeilds his fruit,
and his leafe never withers.
4 And all he doth, shall prosper well,
the wicked are not so:
but they are like vnto the chaffe,
which winde drives to and fro.
5 Therefore shall not ungodly men,
rise to stand in the doome,
nor shall the sinners with the just,
in their assemblie come.
6 For of the righteous men, the Lord
acknowledgeth the way:
but the way of vngodly men,
shall vtterly decay.

A PSALM

▼ **NUMBERED VERSE** Each psalm was numbered in accordance with the relevant Biblical verses. Without any accompanying musical notation, musicians had to choose a suitable tune to fit the metre.

PSALM xli.
mercifull unto mee;
heale thou my soule,because that I
have sinned against thee.
5 Those men that be mine enemies,
with evill mee defame:
when will the time come hee shall dye,
and perish shall his name?
6 And if he come to see *mee*, hee
speaks vanity: his heart
sin to it selfe heaps, when hee goes
forth hee doth it impart.
(2)
7 All that me hate,against mee they
together whisper still:
against me they imagin doe
to mee malicious ill.
8 T*hus doe they say* some ill disease,
unto him cleaveth sore:
and *seing now* he lyeth downe,
he shall rise up noe more.
9 Moreover my familiar freind,
on whom my trust I set,
his heele against mee lifted up,
who of my bread did eat.
10 But Lord me pitty, & mee rayse,
that I may them requite.
11 By this I know assuredly,
in mee thou dost delight:
For o're mee triumphs not my foe.
12 And mee, thou dost mee stay,
in mine integrity; & set'st
mee

PSALME xli, xlii.
mee thee before for aye.
13 Blest hath Iehovah Israels God
from everlasting *been*,
also unto everlasting:
Amen, yea and Amen.

THE
SECOND BOOKE.
PSALME 42
To the chief musician, Maschil, for the
Sonnes of Korah.
LIke as the Hart panting doth bray
after the water brooks,
even in such wise o God, my soule,
after thee panting looks.
2 For God, even for the living God,
my soule it thirsteth sore:
oh when shall I come & appeare,
the face of God before.
3 My teares have been unto mee meat,
by night also by day,
while all the day they unto mee
where is thy God doe say.
4 When as I doe in minde record
these things, then me upon
I doe my soule out poure, for I
with multitude had gone:
With them unto Gods house I went,
with voyce of joy & prayse:
I with

> ... We have a **printery here** and think to goe to worke with some **special things**...
>
> **HUGH PETER**, 10 DECEMBER 1638, ON THE ARRIVAL OF THE PRINTER IN CAMBRIDGE, MASSACHUSETTS

ON TECHNIQUE

The first printing press was brought to British North America by a minister named Joseph Glover, who in 1638 had sailed from England with his wife and five children, taking his second-hand printing press with him. When Glover died at sea, his widow employed one of his technician's, a near-illiterate locksmith, Stephen Daye, to assist her in setting up a business in Massachusetts. Among the first commissions was the newly translated *Bay Psalm Book*.

The early printing presses were made from wood and used ink and paper. The typeface was covered in an oil-based ink and placed in reverse. The wooden screw was turned to apply pressure to the page which absorbed the ink. When the page was printed, the pages were hung to dry.

▲ **The printing press** with its two trays of second-hand type, was shipped from England, along with ink and reams of paper.

Directory: 1450–1649

MORIAE ENCOMIUM
DESIDERIUS ERASMUS

HOLLAND (1511)

A satirical essay written in Latin, but known in English as In *Praise of Folly*, this is one of the best-known works of Desiderius Erasmus (1469–1536), the Dutch humanist scholar and leading intellectual of the 16th century. With subversive and ironic humour the narrator (a personification of Folly, who parades as a Goddess) celebrates life's pleasures, while criticizing corrupt theologians and clergymen, and the Catholic doctrine. Erasmus wrote the essay to amuse his friend Sir Thomas More (see right). It was extremely popular at the time, much to Erasmus's astonishment – 36 Latin editions were printed during his lifetime as well as French, German, and Czech translations. Pope Leo X and Cardinal Cisneros were said to have been amused by it. But 20 years after Erasmus's death, *Moriae Encomium* was put on the Vatican's Index of Forbidden Books and was not removed from it until 1930.

▼ DA COSTA HOURS
SIMON BENING

BELGIUM (1515)

A Book of Hours by the celebrated Flemish manuscript illuminator from Bruges Simon Bening (1483–1561), the *Da Costa Hours* was named after the Portuguese family who commissioned it and whose coat of arms appears in the book. The manuscript is richly illustrated, boasting 121 miniatures including colourful landscapes, highly detailed portraits, and 12 full-page calendars, the likes of which had not been seen since the *Trés Riches Heures* a century earlier (see pp.64–69). This is one of Bening's earliest manuscripts and its lavish illuminations demonstrate his exceptional talent: even when he used traditional templates he reinterpreted and embellished them to create truly original works. Bening, who learned the skill of illumination from his father, Alexander Bening, was painting at the height of the Ghent-Bruges School, an artistic movement of manuscript illumination that developed in Belgium, and his work was famous across Europe. Yet with the rise of the printing press, manuscript illumination had become a dying art, and on Bening's death the Ghent-Bruges School died with him.

A miniature from *Da Costa Hours* depicting the month of May.

UTOPIA
THOMAS MORE

ENGLAND (1516)

This work of fiction is the best-known book by the English statesman and lawyer Sir Thomas More (1478–1535). More describes a fictitious island located in the Atlantic ocean where humans live harmoniously in a society that advocates peace, religious tolerance, equality, shared ownership, and euthanasia. He named the Island "Utopia", from the Greek *ou-topos* meaning "nowhere". More's text is a strong criticism of European society immediately before the Reformation; yet as a devout Roman Catholic More's own views on tolerance sat in contrast to those outlined in the book. *Utopia* was extremely popular when it was published, establishing More as one of the leading humanists of the era. While More may not have intended his island to be viewed as an image of perfection, the word "utopia" has become a by-word for an idealized society or place. The utopia of More's fiction has largely been eclipsed by the literary genre that evolved from it – the Utopian novel.

DE REVOLUTIONIBUS ORBIUM COELESTIUM
NICOLAUS COPERNICUS

GERMANY (1543)

Translated as *On the Revolutions of Celestial Spheres*, this ground-breaking work by Polish astronomer Nicolaus Copernicus (1473–1543) was published in Nuremberg just before his death. It was the most important and controversial scientific publication of the 16th century. Copernicus proposed a "heliocentric system" of planetary motion that identified the sun as the centre of the universe around which all other planets, including Earth, revolved. This view challenged Ptolemy's accepted "geocentric system" (which placed Earth at the centre of the universe) and was met with controversy from philosophers, scientists, and theologians alike. Copernicus dedicated his book to Pope Paul III, but 70 years later the Vatican placed it on the Index of Forbidden Books, pending alterations – it was not fully condemned because Copernicus's theory meant that the Church could calculate the date of Easter Sunday accurately. *De Revolutionibus Orbium Coelestium* transformed the way that the solar system was viewed. It led to further studies by Galileo (see pp.130–31) and Sir Isaac Newton (see pp.142–43), and formed the basis of modern astronomy.

HISTORIA ANIMALIUM
CONRAD GESNER

SWITZERLAND (VOLUMES 1–4 1551–58; VOLUME 5 1587)

The *History of the Animals* (or *Historia Animalium*) was a comprehensive study of natural history by the Swiss naturalist scholar and doctor of medicine, Conrad Gesner (1516–65). It was published in Zurich, initially in four volumes, but a fifth volume was published posthumously in 1587. *Historia Animalium* was a complete compendium of all animals, including newly discovered species, detailing their place in folklore, mythology, art, and literature. Gesner's text drew on contemporary research as well as classical sources, such as that of the Ancient Greeks Aristotle and Pliny the Elder. This exhaustive work, which spanned over 4,500 pages, was remarkable for the vast quantity of images – around 1,000 woodcut illustrations, mostly by Lucas Schan from Strasbourg, feature in the book. *Historia Animalium* was very popular and became the most widely read of all Renaissance natural histories – an abridged version was published in 1563, and an English translation appeared in 1607. However, it was placed on the Vatican's Index of Forbidden Books as Pope Paul IV (1476–1559) felt that Gesner's views would be biased because he was a Protestant.

I QUATTRO LIBRI DELL'ARCHITETTURA

ANDREA PALLADIO

ITALY (1570)

Written by the Italian architect Andrea Palladio (1508–80) *I quattro libri dell'architettura* (or *The Four Books on Architecture*) has been heralded the most successful and influential treatise on the design and construction of buildings in the Renaissance, and Palladio as one of the most important figures in Western architecture. Palladio based his ideas on the purity and simplicity of the palaces and classical temples of the ancient world, and founded the movement that takes its name from him – Palladian architecture. First published in four volumes, the book was extensively illustrated with woodcuts after Palladio's own drawings. His classical style was immediately popular and was widely adopted by contemporary designers and builders across Europe. While Palladio was responsible for many outstanding buildings, mostly in the Republic of Venice, it is for this treatise that he is best known.

ESSAIS

MICHEL DE MONTAIGNE

FRANCE (1580)

French writer and philosopher Michel de Montaigne (1533–92) was one of the most significant figures of the late French Renaissance, and has been credited with establishing the "essay" as a new literary genre. All of his literary and philosophical works are contained within *Essais* (meaning *Attempts,* but known in English as *Essays),* a collection of 107 texts that he began writing in 1572. Montaigne covered a vast range of topics in *Essais* and demonstrated a new and modern way of writing and thinking that proved highly popular. Montaigne made many changes and additions to his work, but never deleted any pre-existing text as he wanted to create a record of the developments in his views over time. His work influenced a great many writers, philosophers, and theologians.

EXERCITATIO ANATOMICA DE MOTU CORDIS ET SANGUINIS IN ANIMALIBUS

WILLIAM HARVEY

GERMANY (1628)

The English physician to King James I, William Harvey (1578–1657) wrote this seminal work of physiology, in Latin, translating as *An Anatomical Study of the Motion of the Heart and Blood in Animals.* It was first published in Frankfurt at the annual book fair, and an English edition followed in 1653. This 72-page scientific paper, with 17 chapters, outlined Harvey's ground-breaking discovery that the blood circulates around the human body in a single system. At the time it was thought that blood did not flow, but was produced and absorbed by the body within two separate systems. Based on his experiments Harvey's calculations revealed that the volume of blood pumped by the heart was too great to be absorbed, suggesting that the blood circulated within a single closed system. Harvey's book provided a detailed description of the structure of the heart as well as the different blood vessels. His findings were met with scepticism, but by the time of his death the circulation of blood and was accepted theory. Harvey's work had a significant impact on the study of physiology, and eventually led to the possibility of blood transfusion.

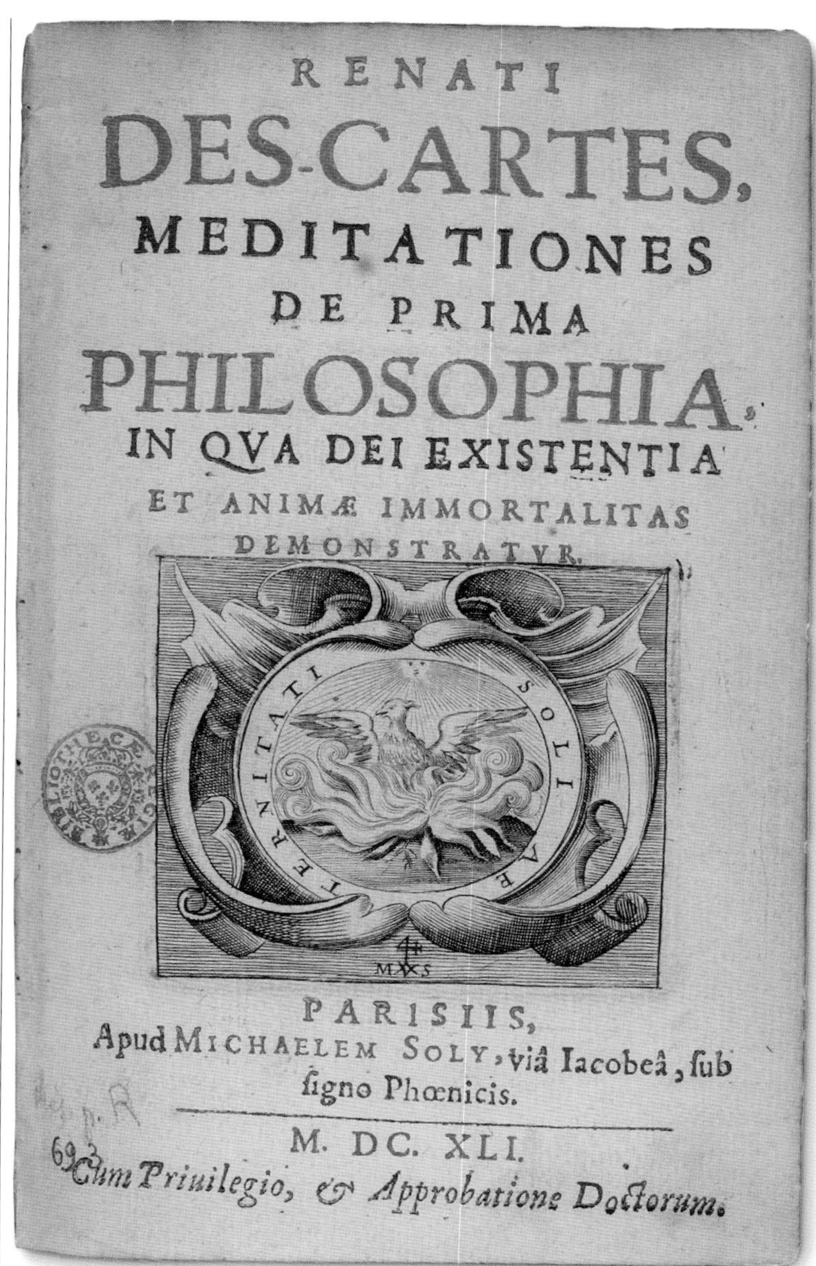
RENATI DES-CARTES, MEDITATIONES DE PRIMA PHILOSOPHIA, IN QVA DEI EXISTENTIA ET ANIMÆ IMMORTALITAS DEMONSTRATVR.

PARISIIS, Apud MICHAELEM SOLY, viâ Iacobeâ, sub signo Phœnicis.

M. DC. XLI.

Cum Priuilegio, & Approbatione Doctorum.

Title page from the first edition of René Decartes's *Meditationes de Prima Philosophia.*

▲ MEDITATIONES DE PRIMA PHILOSOPHIA

RENÉ DESCARTES

FRANCE (1641)

René Descartes's (1596–1650) book *Meditations on First Philosophy* subtitled *In which the existence of God and the immortality of the soul are demonstrated* was a ground-breaking philosophical text. First published in Latin, it was written at a time when scientific advances were threatening the teachings of the Church. *Meditationes de Prima Philosophia* attempted to bridge the gap between science and religion by offering a philosophical foundation for scientific theory. By doing this Descartes abandoned the accepted wisdom of Aristotelian philosophy, which lead to him being branded a revolutionary by many. The Vatican considered his views dangerous and placed the book on the Index of Forbidden Books in 1663. Descartes's most popular work, *Meditationes* is heralded as the foundation of modern Western philosophy, and Descartes as the "father of modern philosophy".

CHAPTER 4

1650 — 1899

- Micrographia
- Philosophiæ Naturalis Principia Mathematica
- Systema Naturae
- L' Encyclopédie… des Sciences, des Arts et des Métiers
- A Dictionary of the English Language
- Bucolica, Georgica et Aeneis
- Tristram Shandy
- Fables in Verse
- The Wealth of Nations
- Rights of Man
- Songs of Innocence and of Experience
- Birds of America
- Procedure for Writing Words, Music, and Plainsong in Dots
- Baedeker guidebooks
- The Pickwick Papers
- The Holy Land
- Photographs of British Algae: Cyanotype Impressions
- Uncle Tom's Cabin
- Leaves of Grass
- On the Origin of Species
- Alice's Adventures in Wonderland
- Das Kapital
- The Works of Geoffrey Chaucer Now Newly Imprinted
- Un Coup de Dés Jamais˚N' Abolira Le Hasard

Micrographia

1665 ▪ PRINTED ▪ 30.3 × 19.8 cm (12 × 7 in) ▪ 246 PAGES ▪ ENGLAND

SCALE

ROBERT HOOKE

Robert Hooke's pioneering work *Micrographia*, published in 1665, was the world's first book on microscopy (the examination of minute objects through a microscope). Hooke studied insects, microbes, and inanimate objects under a microscope and recorded his observations with intricate detail and accuracy. His scientific discoveries are brought to life in *Micrographia* by a magnificent series of illustrations, drawn with the aid of his friend Sir Christopher Wren (1632–1723). These spectacular copperplate engravings, some so large that they required fold-out pages, are arguably the book's most notable feature.

The book also records Hooke's discovery of the plant cell, which he identified while studying slices of cork. Prior to the invention of the microscope, scientists were unable to see such small details, and the discovery of plant cells paved the way for a new branch of scientific research. Other areas that Hooke touches on in the book include wave of light theory, and observations of distant planets.

Micrographia was a masterpiece of scientific observation, revealing a miniature world that had never been seen before, and its impact on the public was enormous. The great diarist, Samuel Pepys (1663–1703), is recorded as having stayed up most of the night marvelling at the extraordinary illustrations. It was the first publication released by the Royal Society – the national academy of science in England, founded in London in 1660 – and became a bestseller, giving scientists in the field a brilliantly illustrated introduction to the little-known world of microscopic observation.

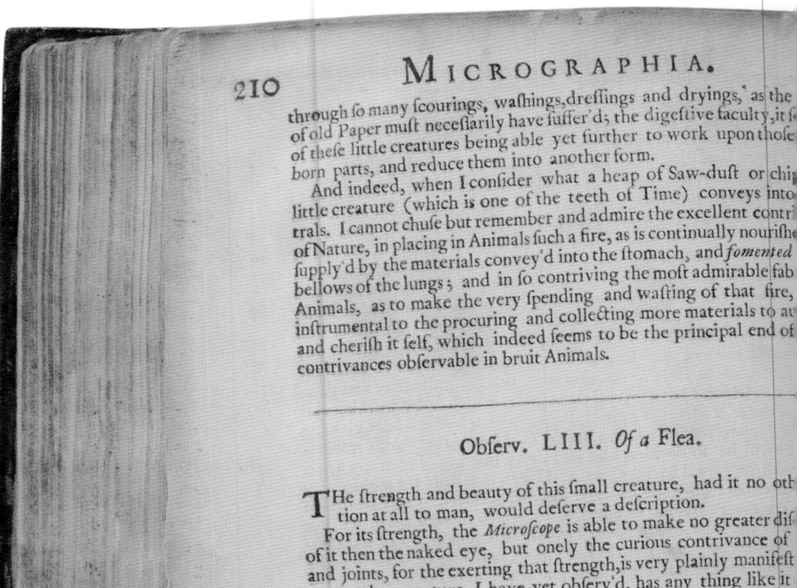

210 MICROGRAPHIA.

through ſo many ſcourings, waſhings, dreſſings and dryings,' as the
of old Paper muſt neceſſarily have ſuffer'd; the digeſtive faculty, it ſ
of theſe little creatures being able yet further to work upon thoſe
born parts, and reduce them into another form.
And indeed, when I conſider what a heap of Saw-duſt or chi
little creature (which is one of the teeth of Time) conveys into
trals. I cannot chuſe but remember and admire the excellent contri
of Nature, in placing in Animals ſuch a fire, as is continually nouriſh
ſupply'd by the materials convey'd into the ſtomach, and *fomented*
bellows of the lungs; and in ſo contriving the moſt admirable fab
Animals, as to make the very ſpending and waſting of that fire,
inſtrumental to the procuring and collecting more materials to au
and cheriſh it ſelf, which indeed ſeems to be the principal end of
contrivances obſervable in bruit Animals.

Obſerv. LIII. *Of a* Flea.

THe ſtrength and beauty of this ſmall creature, had it no oth
tion at all to man, would deſerve a deſcription.
For its ſtrength, the *Microſcope* is able to make no greater diſ
of it then the naked eye, but onely the curious contrivance of
and joints, for the exerting that ſtrength, is very plainly manifeſt
as no other creature, I have yet obſerv'd, has any thing like it
joints of it are ſo adapted, that he can, as 'twere, fold them ſhort o
in another, and ſuddenly ſtretch, or ſpring them out to their whol
that is, of the fore-leggs, the part A, of the 34. *Scheme*, lies w
and B within C, parallel to, or ſide by ſide each other; but
of the two next, lie quite contrary, that is, D without E, and
out F, but parallel alſo; but the parts of the hinder leggs, G,
bend one within another, like the parts of a double jointed R
like the foot, legg and thigh of a man; theſe ſix leggs he clitch
together, and when he leaps, ſprings them all out, and thereb
his whole ſtrength at once.
But, as for the beauty of it, the *Microſcope* manifeſts it to be
adorn'd with a curiouſly poliſh'd ſuit of *ſable* Armour, neatly
and beſet with multitudes of ſharp pinns, ſhap'd almoſt like Po
Quills, or bright conical Steel-bodkins; the head is on either
tify'd with a quick and round black eye K, behind each of
appears a ſmall cavity, L, in which he ſeems to move to and
tain thin film beſet with many ſmall tranſparent hairs, which pro
be his ears; in the forepart of his head, between the two fore
has two ſmall long jointed feelers, or rather ſmellers, M M, w
four joints, and are hairy, like thoſe of ſeveral other creatures
theſe, it has a ſmall *proboſcis*, or *probe*, NNO, that ſeems to c

ROBERT **HOOKE**

1635–1703

Robert Hooke was a scientist, architect, inventor, and natural philosopher – he made significant contributions to many scientific fields, and in 1660 discovered the law of elasticity, also known as Hooke's Law.

Hooke studied science at Christ Church, Oxford, before settling in London. He was a founding member of the Royal Society, the national academy of science, and became their Curator of Experiments in 1662. Two years later he was made Professor of Geometry at Gresham College in London. Hooke's scientific interests were varied. His investigation into elasticity led to his formulation of Hooke's Law, and he correctly identified fossils as having once been living creatures. He was fascinated by astronomy and helped construct telescopes. After the Great Fire of London in 1666 he was commissioned as Surveyor to the City of London to oversee rebuilding along with Sir Christopher Wren. Among the buildings under Hooke's care were the Royal Observatory at Greenwich and the Bethlehem Royal Hospital. He died a wealthy man, aged 67.

> By the help of microscopes, there is **nothing so small, as to escape our inquiry**; hence there is a **new visible world discovered** to the understanding
>
> **ROBERT HOOKE**, *MICROGRAPHIA*

▼ **INTIMATE DETAIL** Hooke's famous fold-out engraving of a flea is the largest illustration in the book, measuring 30 x 46 cm (12 x 18 in). While most readers were familiar with the minute creature, none had seen such a large-scale drawing, and so the result was both monstrous and spectacular. Through his magnification of this tiny insect Hooke illuminates the possibilities of the microscopic world – the ability to study in intimate detail the anatomy of any creature, no matter how small. At this time nobody knew that the minuscule parasite was largely responsible for the spread of many diseases in 17th century Britain, including the devasting Bubonic Plague.

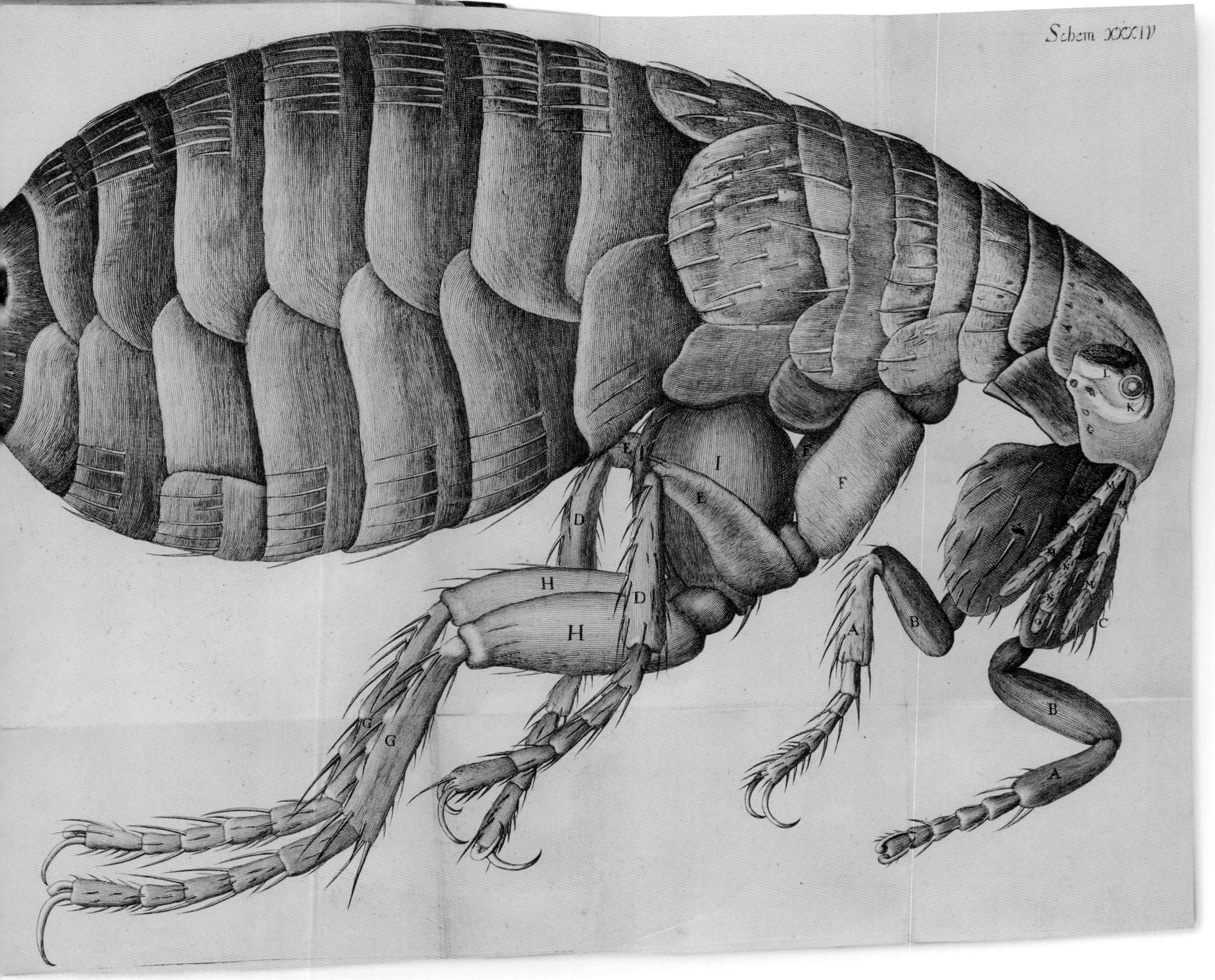

In detail

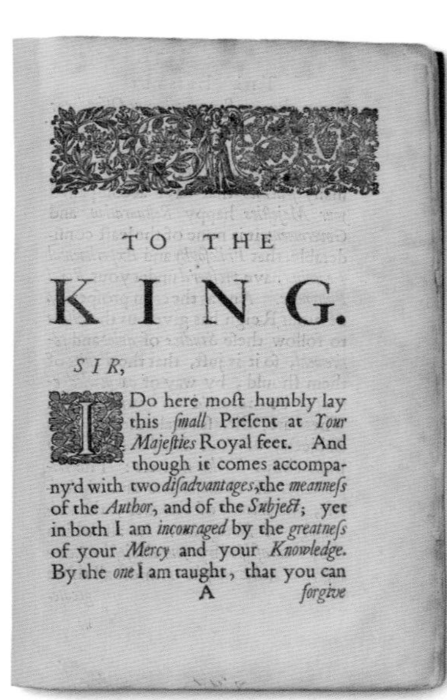

TO THE
KING.

SIR,

I Do here most humbly lay this *small* Present at *Your Majesties* Royal feet. And though it comes accompany'd with two *disadvantages*, the *meanness* of the *Author*, and of the *Subject*; yet in both I am *incouraged* by the *greatness* of your *Mercy* and your *Knowledge*. By the *one* I am taught, that you can

A *forgive*

▲ **ROYAL DEDICATION** Hooke dedicated *Micrographia* to the reigning monarch, Charles II (1630–1685) (as was the practice of the day). Having seen microscopic drawings of insects by Sir Christopher Wren, the king had approached the Royal Society asking for an illustrated book on microscopy. As Wren was busy, Hooke was given the job, and by dedicating his book to a royal patron, he increased the likelihood of financial assistance from other aristocrats.

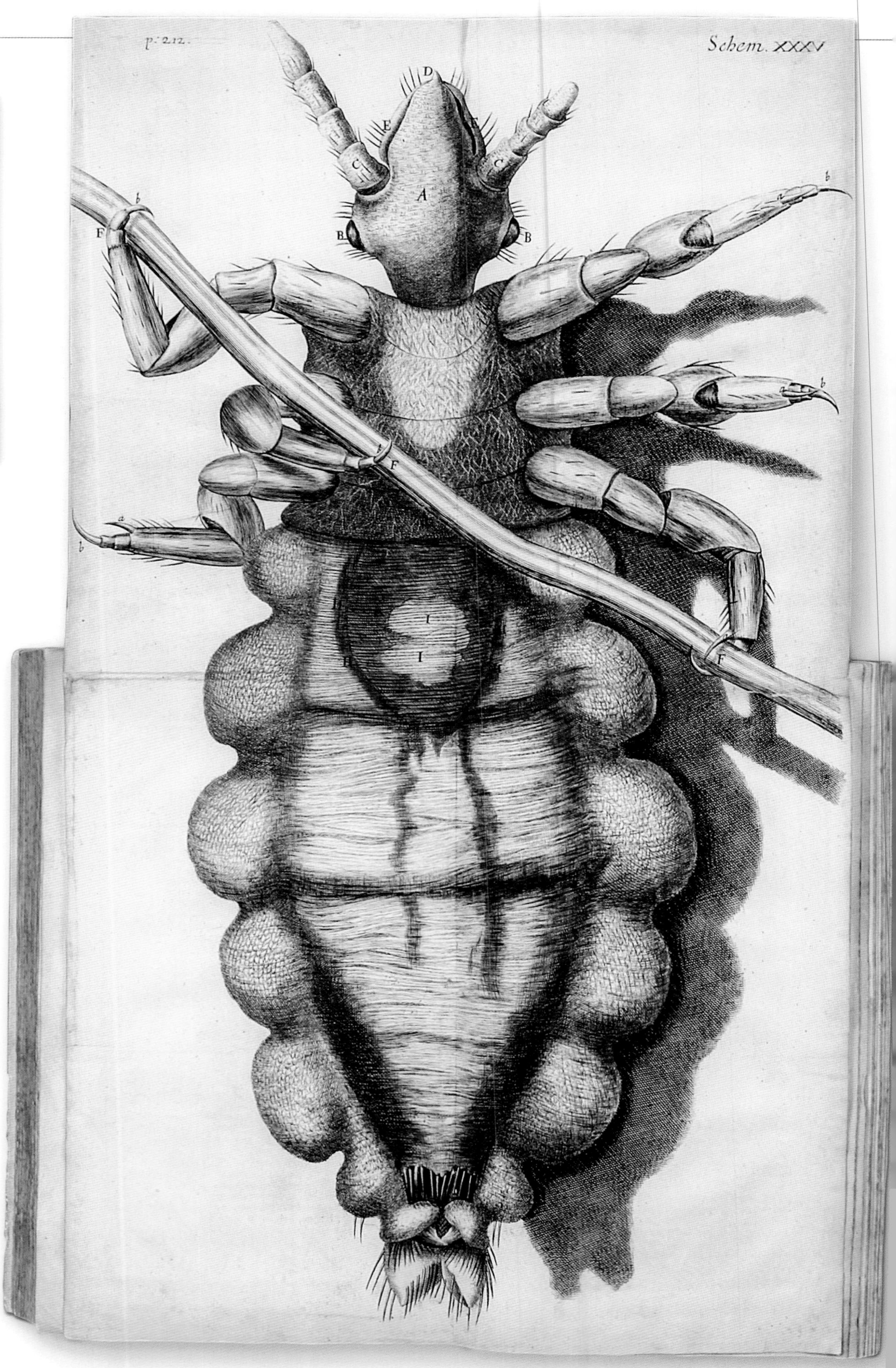

► **FOLD-OUT ILLUSTRATIONS** Hooke's portrait of a louse holding a human hair was a shocking revelation. The drawing folded out to four times the size of the book. Lice were a common feature of 17th century life, but never before had insects been represented in such fine detail.

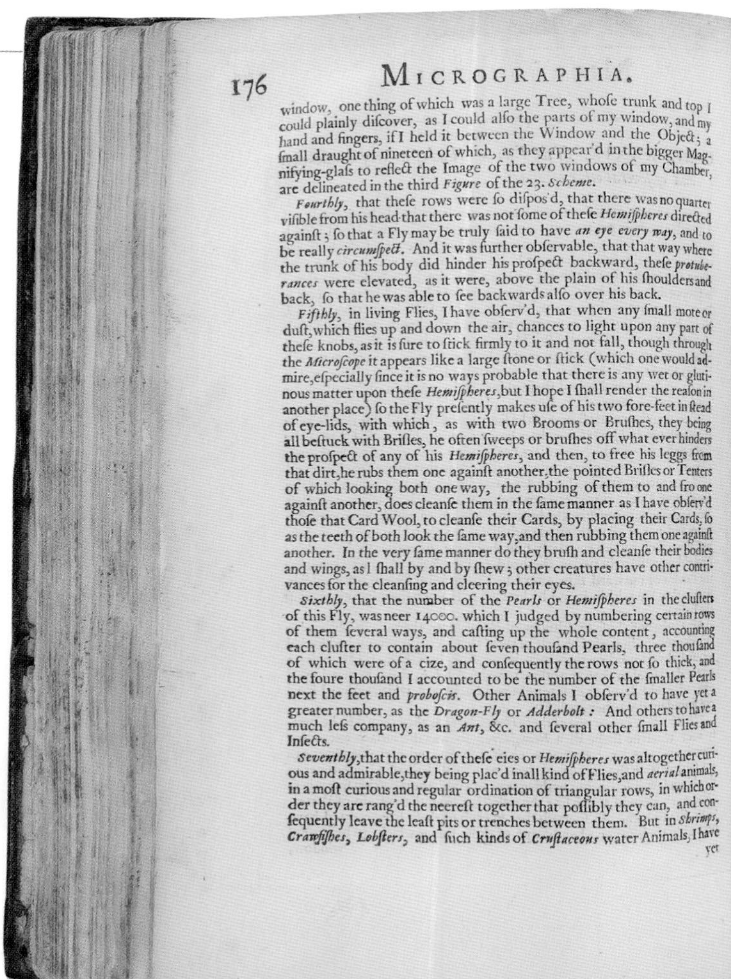

176 MICROGRAPHIA.

window, one thing of which was a large Tree, whoſe trunk and top I could plainly diſcover, as I could alſo the parts of my window, and my hand and fingers, if I held it between the Window and the Object; a ſmall draught of nineteen of which, as they appear'd in the bigger Magnifying-glaſs to reflect the Image of the two windows of my Chamber, are delineated in the third *Figure* of the 23. *Scheme*.

Fourthly, that theſe rows were ſo diſpos'd, that there was no quarter viſible from his head that there was not ſome of theſe *Hemiſpheres* directed againſt; ſo that a Fly may be truly ſaid to have *an eye every way*, and to be really *circumſpect*. And it was further obſervable, that that way where the trunk of his body did hinder his proſpect backward, theſe *protuberances* were elevated, as it were, above the plain of his ſhoulders and back, ſo that he was able to ſee backwards alſo over his back.

Fifthly, in living Flies, I have obſerv'd, that when any ſmall mote or duſt, which flies up and down the air, chances to light upon any part of theſe knobs, as it is ſure to ſtick firmly to it and not fall, though through the *Microſcope* it appears like a large ſtone or ſtick (which one would admire, eſpecially ſince it is no ways probable that there is any wet or glutinous matter upon theſe *Hemiſpheres*, but I hope I ſhall render the reaſon in another place) ſo the Fly preſently makes uſe of his two fore-feet in ſtead of eye-lids, with which, as with two Brooms or Bruſhes, they being all beſtuck with Briſles, he often ſweeps or bruſhes off what ever hinders the proſpect of any of his *Hemiſpheres*, and then, to free his leggs from that dirt, he rubs them one againſt another, the pointed Briſles or Tenters of which looking both one way, the rubbing of them to and fro one againſt another, does cleanſe them in the ſame manner as I have obſerv'd thoſe that Card Wool, to cleanſe their Cards, by placing their Cards, ſo as the teeth of both look the ſame way, and then rubbing them one againſt another. In the very ſame manner do they bruſh and cleanſe their bodies and wings, as I ſhall by and by ſhew; other creatures have other contrivances for the cleanſing and cleering their eyes.

Sixthly, that the number of the *Pearls* or *Hemiſpheres* in the cluſters of this Fly, was neer 14000. which I judged by numbering certain rows of them ſeveral ways, and caſting up the whole content, accounting each cluſter to contain about ſeven thouſand Pearls, three thouſand of which were of a cize, and conſequently the rows not ſo thick, and the foure thouſand I accounted to be the number of the ſmaller Pearls next the feet and *proboſcis*. Other Animals I obſerv'd to have yet a greater number, as the *Dragon-Fly* or *Adderbolt*: And others to have a much leſs company, as an *Ant*, &c. and ſeveral other ſmall Flies and Inſects.

Seventhly, that the order of theſe eies or *Hemiſpheres* was altogether curious and admirable, they being plac'd in all kind of Flies, and *aerial* animals, in a moſt curious and regular ordination of triangular rows, in which order they are rang'd the neereſt together that poſſibly they can, and conſequently leave the leaſt pits or trenches between them. But in *Shrimps*, *Crawfiſhes*, *Lobſters*, and ſuch kinds of *Cruſtaceous* water Animals, I have yet

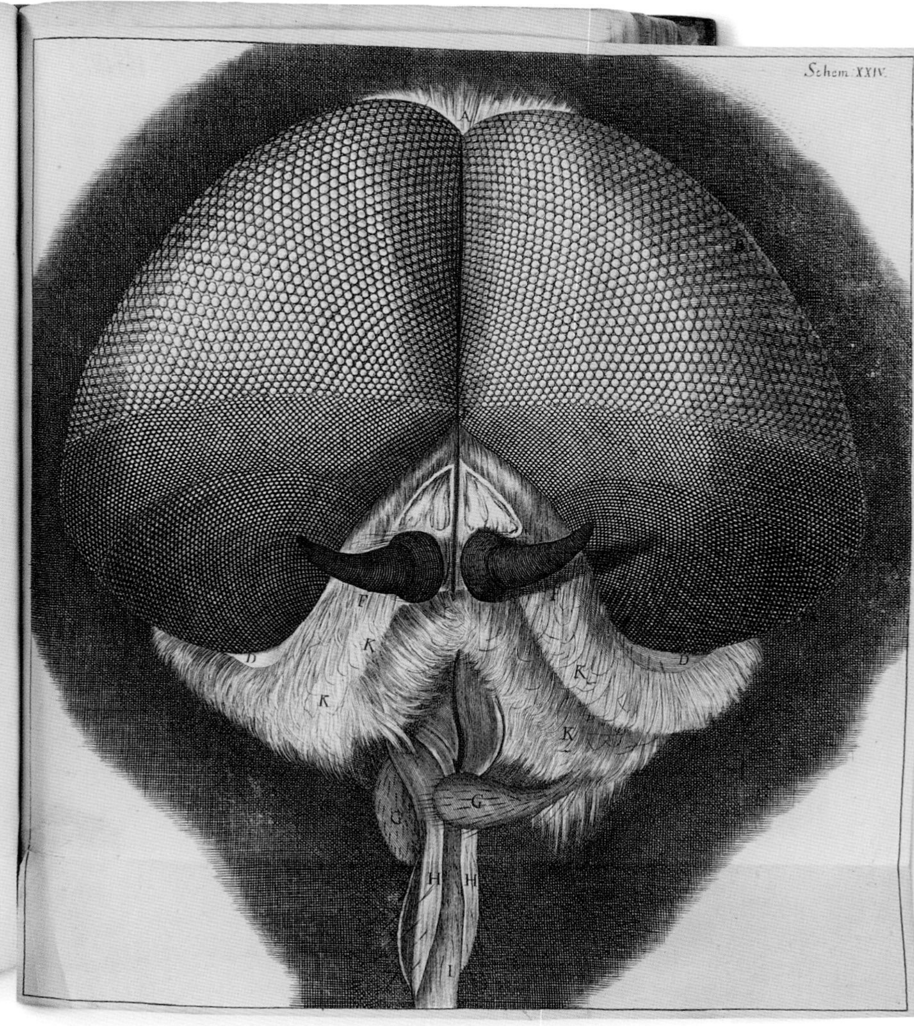

▲ **ACCURATE ETCHING** The illustrated head of a grey drone-fly shows the extraordinary precision of Hooke's observations. To achieve this level of accuracy Hooke employed an etching technique, whereby an illustration was scratched onto a copperplate through an acid-resistant coating. The plate was dipped in acid, which bit through the exposed metal until the image was etched onto the plate. It could then be transferred onto paper with ink.

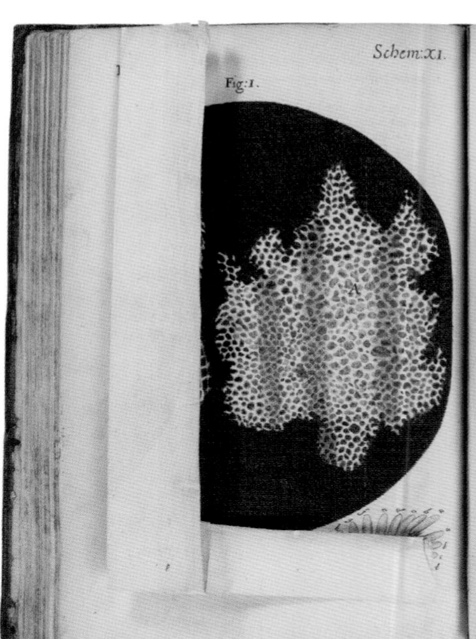

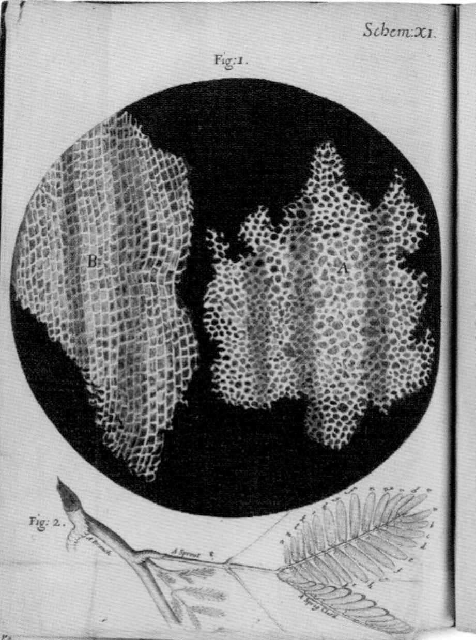

▲ **ADDING THE IMAGES** The insertion of the illustrations into each individual copy of the book was done manually. The copperplate engravings were first folded by hand and then glued onto the page. This time-consuming task increased the price of the volumes. In these prints Hooke illustrates his study into the properties of a *Mimosa pudica* leaf – a peculiar plant that appears "sensitive" to touch, as it shrinks back in response to stimuli.

Philosophiæ Naturalis Principia Mathematica

1687 ▪ PRINTED ▪ 24.2 × 20 cm (10 × 8 in) ▪ 506 PAGES ▪ ENGLAND

SCALE

SIR ISAAC NEWTON

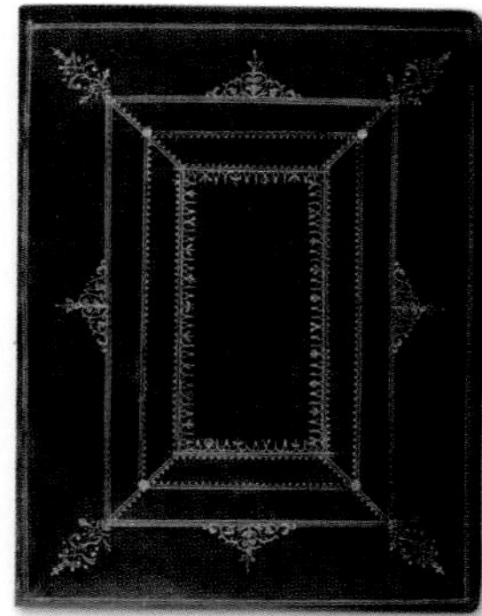

The publication of one of the most influential scientific works of all time, the *Philosophiae Naturalis Principia Mathematica*, or *Mathematical Principles of Natural Philosophy* by Sir Isaac Newton (1643–1727) arose in part from an academic dispute. A groundbreaking text that laid out in mathematical terms Newton's three laws of motion, as well as his theory of universal gravity, the book provided incontrovertible support for Copernicus's much-disputed world system (see p.134). The quarrel that sparked the book arose in 1684 between Robert Hooke (see p.138) and English astronomer Edmund Halley (1656–1742) over the nature of planetary orbits, for which Hooke offered a theory but no proof. Halley consulted his friend, the mathematician and physicist Isaac Newton, who claimed to have already solved the problem. Newton sent a short written document, *De motu corporum* (*On the motion of bodies*), to Halley three months later, but continued to work on the text, tailoring it to a general audience. However, when the first volume of the expanded work – the *Principia* – was presented to the Royal Society in 1686, Hooke claimed the ideas about what came to be called "gravity" were his. In response, Newton developed his third volume into a densely reasoned mathematical work. The publication was overseen by Halley, funded by the Royal Society, and took three years. The *Principia* was a scientific tour de force and, despite its small print run of 250–400 copies, it won Newton instant fame.

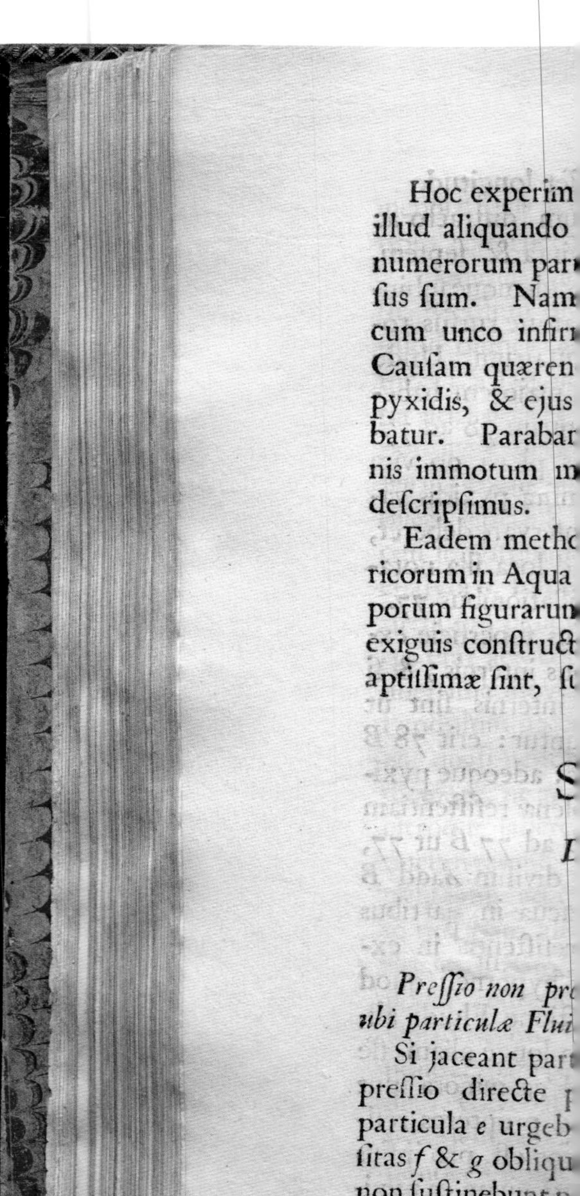

RELATED **TEXTS**

Ever since the German astronomer Johannes Kepler (1571–1630) had formulated laws explaining the motion of the planets in 1609, scholars had struggled to explain the force that shaped their orbits. French philosopher René Descartes (1596–1650) tried to provide a comprehensive explanation of the physical workings of the solar system, in his *Principia Philosophiæ* (*Principles of Philosophy*) of 1644. His idea that the motion of a body will remain stable – and in a straight line – unless altered by another force was adopted by Newton as his First Law of Motion. However, Newton criticized Descartes' theory that the planets were held in their orbits by bands of particles he called "vortices".

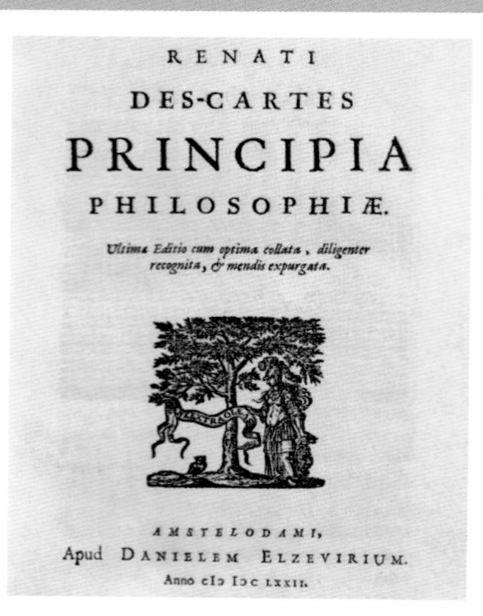

RENATI
DES-CARTES
PRINCIPIA
PHILOSOPHIÆ.

Ultima Editio cum optima collata, diligenter recognita, & mendis expurgata.

AMSTELODAMI,
Apud DANIELEM ELZEVIRIUM.
Anno clɔ Iɔc LXXII.

➤ **Descartes' *Principia Philosophiæ*** summarized knowledge about the universe, combining metaphysics, philosophy, physics, and mathematics.

> Newton has brushed aside all the difficulties together with the Cartesian vortices

CHRISTIAAN HUYGENS, NOTE MADE ON *PRINCIPIA*, 1688

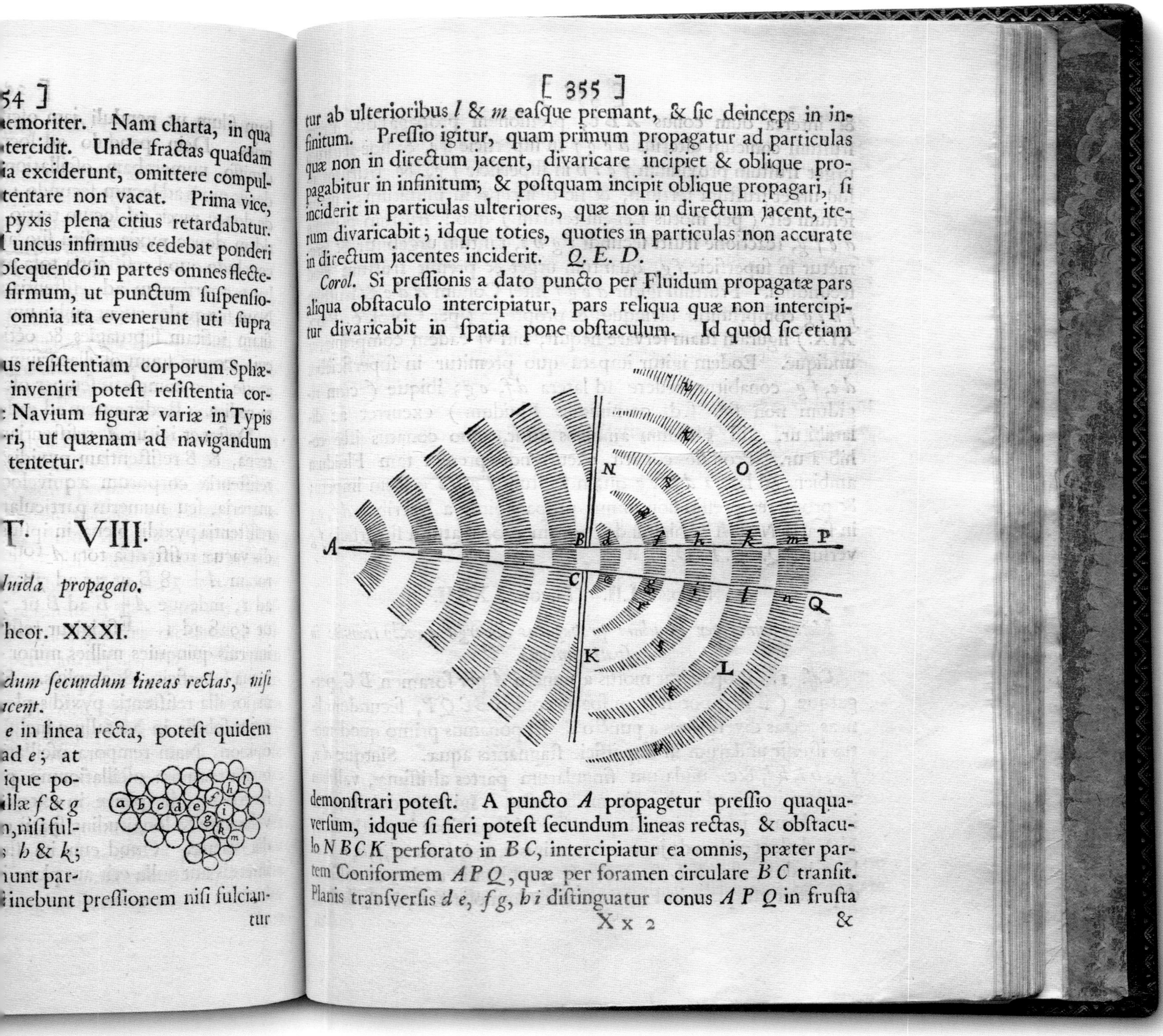

54]
emoriter. Nam charta, in qua
tercidit. Unde fractas quaſdam
ia exciderunt, omittere compul-
tentare non vacat. Prima vice,
pyxis plena citius retardabatur.
uncus infirmus cedebat ponderi
oſequendo in partes omnes flecte-
firmum, ut punctum ſuſpenſio-
omnia ita evenerunt uti ſupra
us reſiſtentiam corporum Sphæ-
inveniri poteſt reſiſtentia cor-
Navium figuræ variæ in Typis
ri, ut quænam ad navigandum
tentetur.

T. VIII.

luida propagato.

heor. XXXI.

dum ſecundum lineas rectas, niſi
acent.
e in linea recta, poteſt quidem
ad e; at
ique po-
llæ f & g
n, niſi ful-
h & k;
unt par-
inebunt preſſionem niſi fulcian-
tur

[355]

tur ab ulterioribus *l* & *m* eaſque premant, & ſic deinceps in infinitum. Preſſio igitur, quam primum propagatur ad particulas quæ non in directum jacent, divaricare incipiet & oblique propagabitur in infinitum; & poſtquam incipit oblique propagari, ſi inciderit in particulas ulteriores, quæ non in directum jacent, iterum divaricabit; idque toties, quoties in particulas non accurate in directum jacentes inciderit. *Q. E. D.*

Corol. Si preſſionis a dato puncto per Fluidum propagatæ pars aliqua obſtaculo intercipiatur, pars reliqua quæ non intercipitur divaricabit in ſpatia pone obſtaculum. Id quod ſic etiam

demonſtrari poteſt. A puncto *A* propagetur preſſio quaquaverſum, idque ſi fieri poteſt ſecundum lineas rectas, & obſtaculo *NBCK* perforato in *BC*, intercipiatur ea omnis, præter partem Coniformem *APQ*, quæ per foramen circulare *BC* tranſit. Planis tranſverſis *de*, *fg*, *hi* diſtinguatur conus *APQ* in fruſta &

Xx 2

▼ **DETAILED DIAGRAMS**
Newton's *Principia* is illustrated with diagrams that explain his mathematical reasoning. This page from Book II shows how force exerted will travel in a straight line unless diverted by particles placed at an oblique angle (left-hand page) or by a barrier (right-hand page).

Systema Naturae

1735 ▪ PRINTED ▪ DIMENSIONS UNKNOWN ▪ 11 PAGES ▪ NETHERLANDS

CAROLUS LINNAEUS

A large-format pamphlet of just 11 pages, *Systema Naturae* was written by Swedish botanist Carl Linnaeus under his Latinized name Carolus Linnaeus; in it Linnaeus introduced a scheme for the classification of living things. 13 editions of the work were printed in total, with the extent increasing each time, so that by the 12th edition (the last that Linnaeus oversaw himself) there were 2,400 pages. The system of classification proved so effective that it is still used by scientists today. At the time of the book's publication, many naturalists were attempting to classify life, but Linnaeus's hierarchical system prevailed because of its beautiful simplicity. He divided the natural world into three kingdoms – minerals, plants, and animals – then subdivided living things initially into class, then order, then genus, and, finally, species.

In the 1735 edition of *Systema Naturae*, Linnaeus argued that nearly all plants have sexual or reproductive organs, just like animals, and that these could be used to classify them through easy-to-learn structural differences. He divided all flowering plants into 23 classes according to the length and number of their stamens (the male reproductive organs, which produce pollen), then subdivided them into orders according to the number of pistils (the female organs, which produce the ovules).

He also gave each species a two-part (or binomial) Latin name, such as *Linnaea borealis* (twinflower), supposedly his favourite plant, the first part of the name referring to the genus to which the species belongs, the second part, the species name. In the 1735 edition of *Systema Naturae*, Linnaeus used this binomial only for plants, but in later editions he extended it to animals. During his life he named almost 8,000 plants, as well as many animals, and was also responsible for the scientific designation for humans: *Homo sapiens*.

CARL **LINNAEUS**

1707–1778

Carl Linnaeus was a Swedish botanist who devised the system that all scientists use today to label living things under a two-part Latin name. Considered the "Father of Taxonomy", he was also a pioneer in the study of ecology and the relationship between living things and their environments.

Born in Småland in southern Sweden, Carl Linnaeus was the son of a clergyman, a keen gardener who shared his botanical knowledge with his son. Linnaeus started training as a medical student in Uppsala, which included studying the use of plants, minerals, and animals in medicine, but finished his degree in the Netherlands. While there, he sketched out his system for classifying plants according to their sexual organs in his 1735 publication *Systema Naturae*. In 1738, back in Sweden, he first practised medicine, then became a botany professor at Uppsala Unversity in 1741, where he established a botanical garden to which his many students brought back specimens from around the world. Linnaeus published other books using his system of classification, including *Species Plantarum* (1753). When he was given a knighthood in 1757, he took the name Carl von Linné. He died in Uppsala in 1778 and is buried in the city's cathedral.

> ...objects are distinguished and known by classifying them methodically and giving them appropriate names... the foundation of our science

CAROLUS LINNAEUS, *SYSTEMA NATURAE*

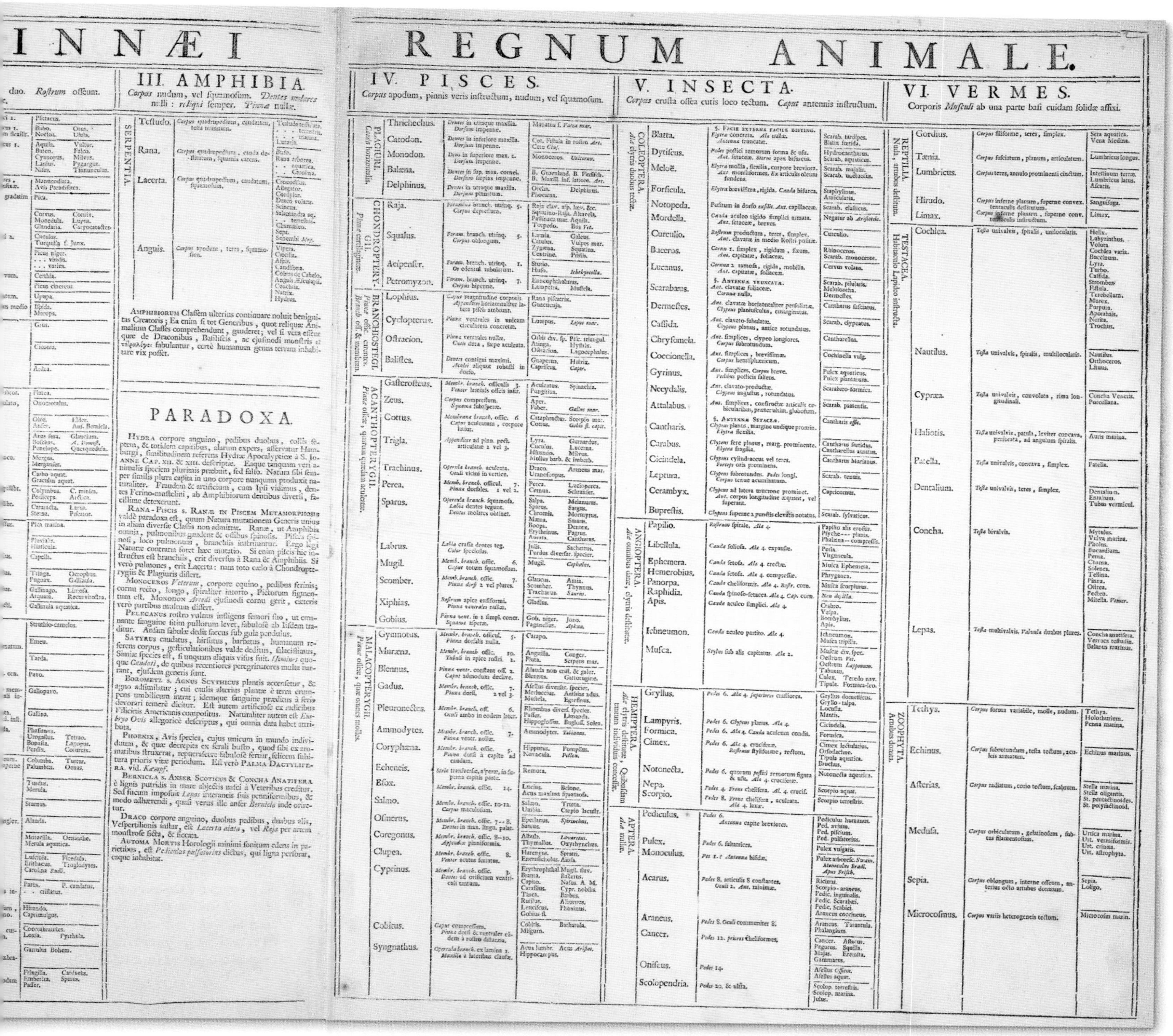

▲ **CLASSIFICATION CHART** In this large chart drawn by artist Georg Ehret, Linnaeus organizes the animal kingdom into six classes: quadrupeds, birds, amphibia (including reptiles), fish, insects, and worms. He also added the class Paradoxa, mysterious creatures that included unicorns and phoenixes. Classes are then further divided, for example quadrupeds into humanlike animals (such as primates) and Ferae (such as dogs, cats, and bears). In the 10th edition Linnaeus replaced the label Quadrupedia – a term that he adopted from Aristotle – with Mammalia.

L'Encyclopédie… des Sciences, des Arts et des Metiers

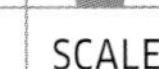
SCALE

1751–72 ▪ PRINTED ▪ 26.5 × 39.5 cm (10½ × 15½ in) ▪ 28 VOLUMES, 18,000 PAGES OF TEXT ▪ FRANCE

EDITED BY DENIS DIDEROT AND JEAN D'ALEMBERT

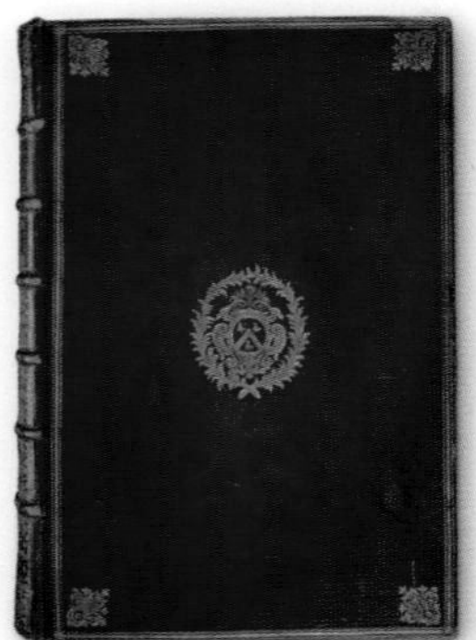

Few books have had such a profound influence on the world as *L'Encyclopédie, ou Dictionnaire raisonne des sciences, des arts et des metiers*. This huge work, translated as *Encyclopaedia, or a Classified Dictionary of the Sciences, Arts, and Trade*, provided the first complete summary of human knowledge, and aimed to guide people towards the Enlightenment idea that the future belonged to humanity and reason.

The *Encyclopédie* began simply as a French translation of the groundbreaking English work *Cyclopaedia*, written by Ephraim Chambers in 1728. Yet under the leadership of Denis Diderot and mathematical editor Jean d'Alembert (1717–83), it grew into a vast work in its own right that employed more than 150 writers, including some of the greatest thinkers of the age, such as Voltaire (1694–1778) and Jean-Jacques Rousseau (see p.211). In the *Encyclopédie* Diderot and d'Alembert aimed to bring together all that was known about the world, and they divided this information into three categories: Memory, Reason, and Imagination. No subject was too grand or too small and the work covered big ideas, such as absolute monarchy and intolerance, as well as everyday skills, like jam-making.

The *Encyclopédie*'s democratic message deliberately challenged the Jesuits of the Catholic Church, who jealously guarded knowledge, as well as the idea that any person had the right to rule over another. In an effort to avoid conflict with censors, criticism of the Church and State was often hidden within obscure articles. However, Louis XV (1710–74) placed a ban on the work in 1759, which resulted in contributors having to write in secret, and Diderot commissioning volumes of illustrations (which were exempt from the ban) to be printed. Diderot continued to oversee the work until 1772, by which time it had grown to 28 volumes, with over 72,000 articles and 3,000 illustrations.

DENIS **DIDEROT**

1713–1784

Denis Diderot was a French philosopher and one of the great writers of the 18th century. He dedicated his life to the *Encyclopédie*.

The son of a knifemaker, Diderot was raised a Jesuit and intended to become a priest. Instead he wrote plays and novels, such as *Jacques the Fatalist*, but he never made much money and his political views put him in conflict with the authorities. In 1749 he was sent to prison for his attack on religion in *Letter on the Blind*. His fame as a shaper of modern thought comes from his part in creating the *Encyclopédie*. Hearing of Diderot's poverty, Russian empress Catherine the Great brought him to St Petersburg in 1773 where the two conversed deeply. Diderot died in a luxury apartment in Paris provided by Catherine during his last illness.

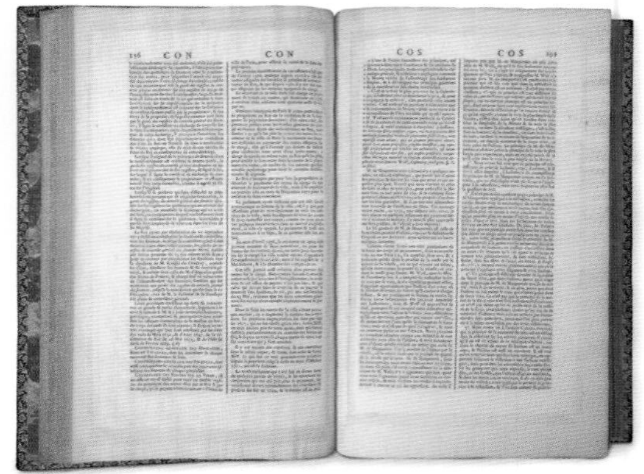

▲ **CENSORED WORK** American collector Douglas Gordon purchased this unique "18th volume" in 1933; he was interested in its censored article proofs, 46 of which were written by Diderot. It is thought to have belonged to *Encyclopédie* publisher André Le Breton.

> The goal of an encyclopaedia is to assemble all the knowledge scattered on the surface of the earth… so that… our descendants, by becoming more learned, may become more virtuous & happier
>
> **DENIS DIDEROT**, *ENCYCLOPÉDIE*

▼ **BRANCHES OF KNOWLEDGE** The *Encyclopédie* is divided into three main branches of knowledge: Memory, Reason, and Imagination. Memory covers history, while Reason focuses on philosophy, and Imagination, poetry. Reason is sub-divided into the physical sciences, mathematics, and logic, and then further divided to include medicine and surgery. The plate below shows a surgeon drilling into a patient's skull alongside a selection of surgical instruments.

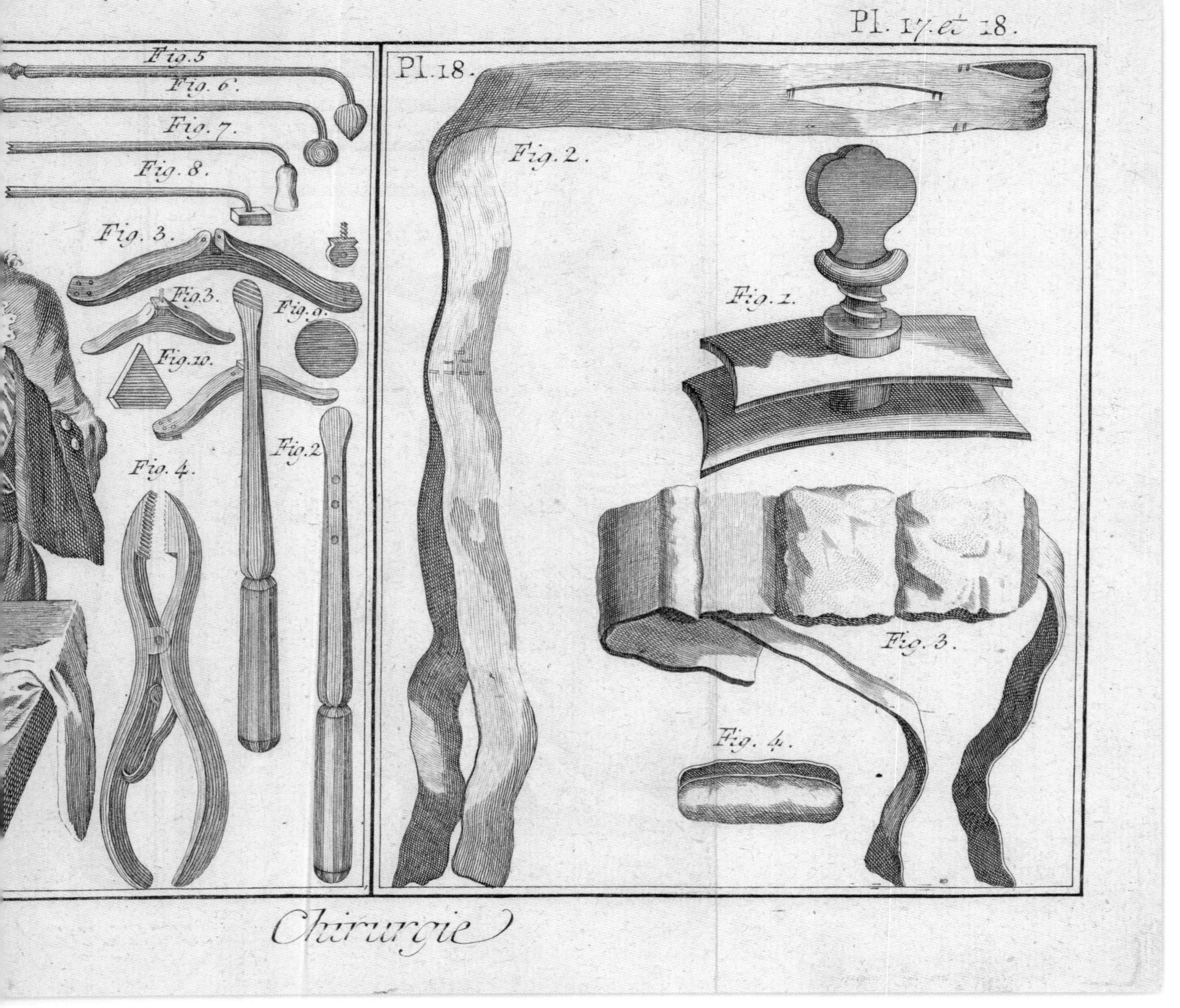

In detail

◀ **ENLIGHTENED ILLUSTRATION** The illustration for the *Encyclopédie*'s frontispiece was drawn by the French engraver Charles-Nicolas Cochin (1715–90) in 1764, and is a reflection of the way the book divides knowledge. It puts the figure of Truth at the centre of the book's vision, between Imagination and Reason, with illustrations of other figures such as Memory, Geometry, and Poetry underneath. The Enlightenment heralded the supremacy of Truth over superstition and prejudice, which is why it presented such a challenge to the Church. Significantly, this illustration shows Truth wearing a veil, receiving her light from Reason and Philosophy above, while Theology is merely one of her handmaidens. Diderot described it as "a very ingeniously composed piece".

▼ **TRADE DRAWINGS** The illustrations for this entry on fireworks, from the Memory section, are typical of the *Encyclopédie*. The upper half depicts a scene from an artist's workshop; the lower, catalogues tools of the trade. While the editors insisted that they visited workshops in order to present these trades realistically, this scene is clean and tranquil, unlike the chaotic reality of such a place.

▼ **ELABORATE ILLUSTRATIONS** The 11 volumes of plates were devised to provide readers with an expansion on the 17 volumes of text, and also offer them quick access to information. The plate below, from the Imagination section, uses a floorplan and a corresponding key to present the ideal system for organizing instruments in an orchestra. Summarizing the topic of music required the editors to include illustrations of musical notations in order to educate the reader.

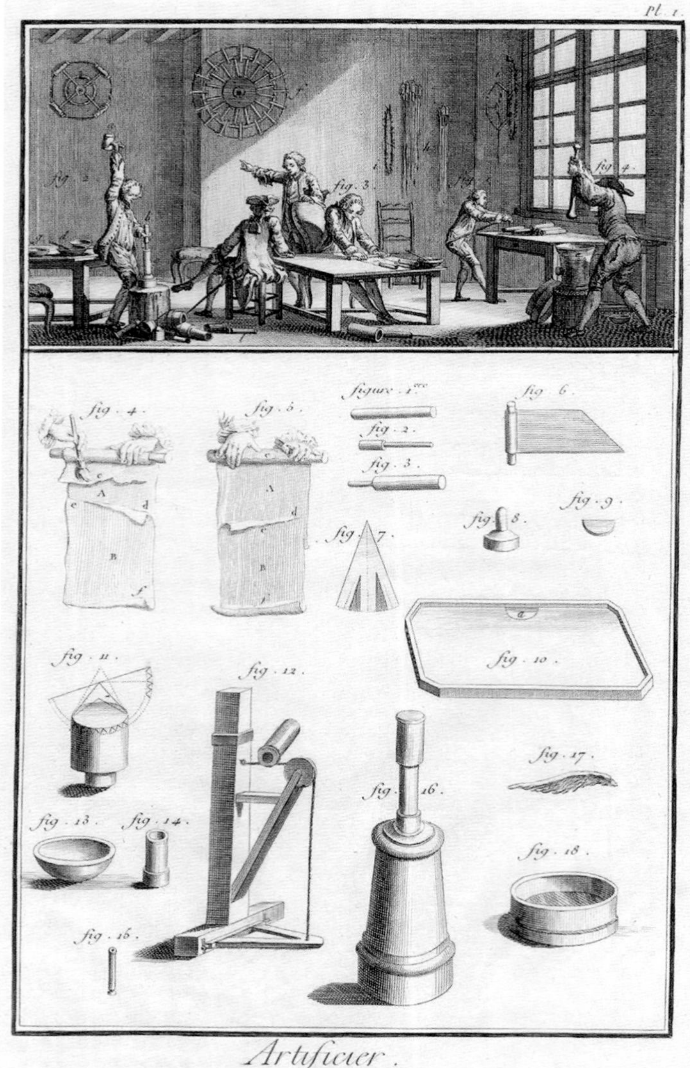

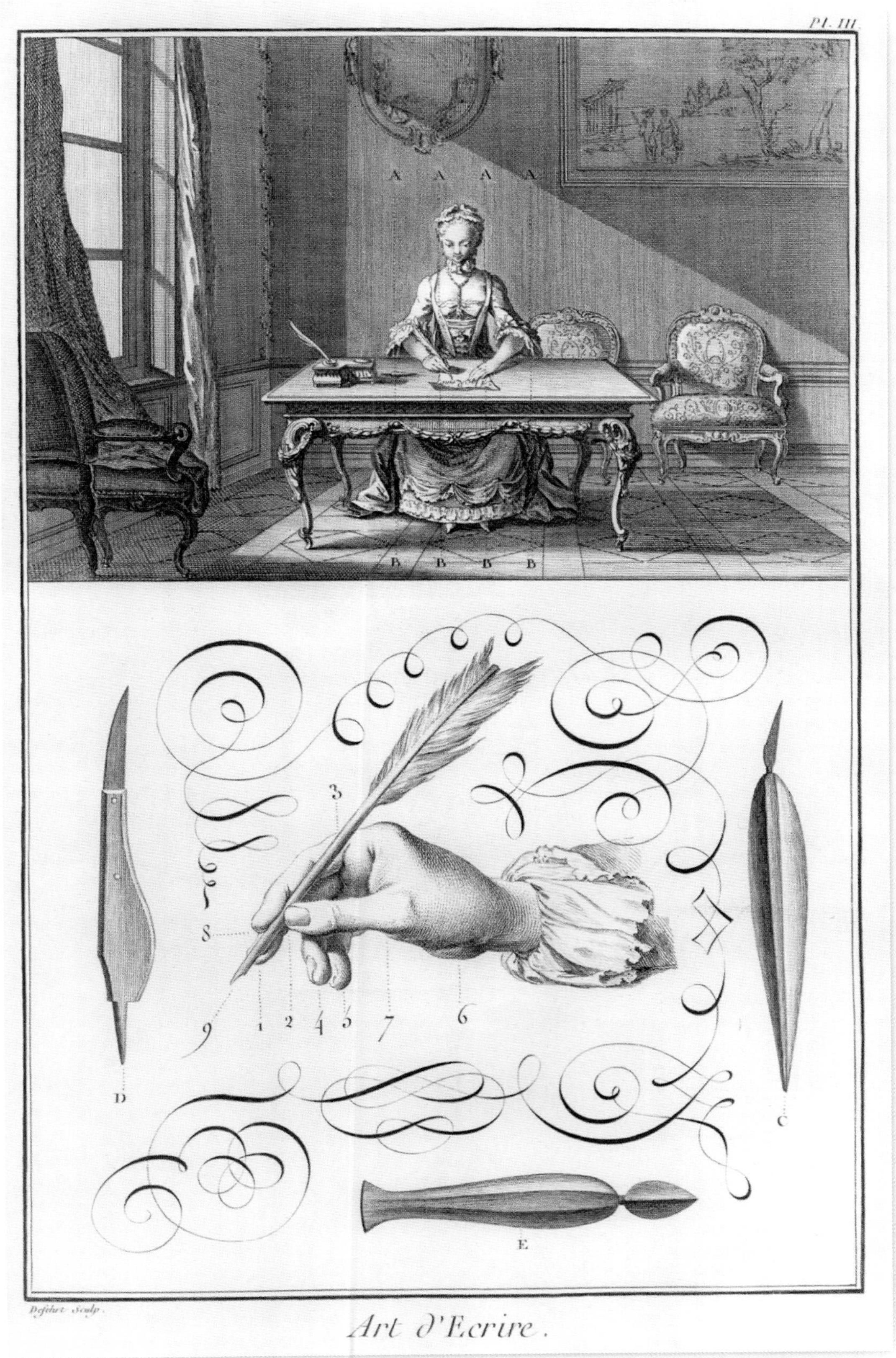

▲ **PLATE DESIGN** This plate from the Reason section follows the same template as the trade plates to depict "the position of young ladies to write". The designs of over 900 of the plates are credited to Louis-Jacques Goussier – who also wrote for the *Encyclopédie* – and most of the plates were drawn long after the articles were written.

RELATED **TEXTS**

The *Encyclopaedia Britannica* is often believed to be the world's oldest dictionary, yet it was actually launched 40 years after Ephraim Chambers' *Cyclopaedia*, which was published in 1728 and became the starting point for Diderot's *Encyclopédie*. When the first edition of *Britannica* was published in 1768, the *Encyclopédie* was still being worked on. However, whereas the *Cyclopaedia* did not last beyond Chambers's death in 1740 – except for a one-off relaunch in 1778 – *Britannica* is still going today, almost 250 years after its initial launch. As such it is the oldest English language encyclopaedia still in production.

Britannica was the brainchild of printer Colin Macfarquhar and engraver Andrew Bell, both residents of Edinburgh, Scotland – a city that played an important role in the Enlightenment. The first edition of the *Britannica* was produced in a series of thick weekly pamphlets, known as "numbers", for which customers paid a subscription fee. The numbers were then bound into three volumes: A–B, C–L, and M–Z. The text was edited by a young scholar called William Smellie, who drew on many of the great thinkers of the time for information. It was a huge success, prompting the need for a second edition as early as 1783.

Britannica continued to expand over the course of its 15 official editions, and by the end of the 19th century its stature had risen so far that it was seen by many as the ultimate authority on any subject. From 1933 *Britannica* adopted a policy of "continuous revision" by which every article was regularly updated. The last print edition in 2010 ran to a massive 32 volumes. Today it is only produced in digital form.

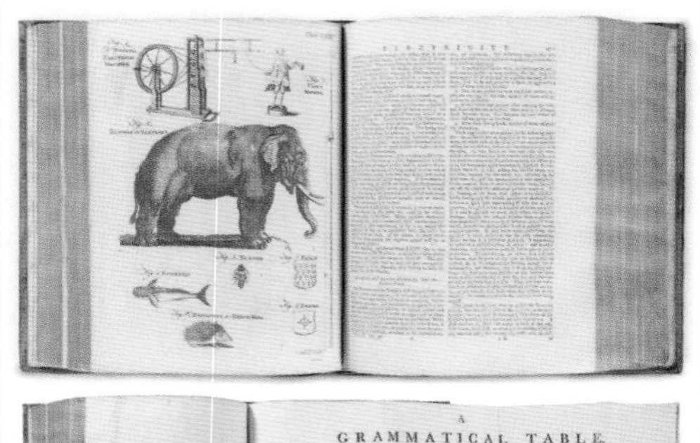

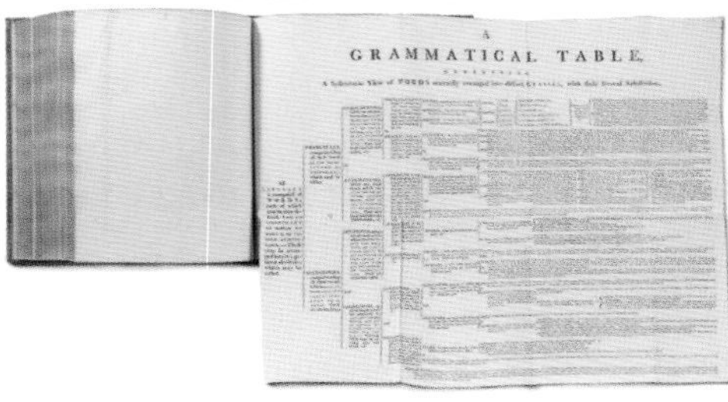

GRAMMATICAL TABLE

▲ **These pages** belong to an edition of *Britannica* from the late 1800s, a time when this encyclopaedia reached the height of its prestige with contributions from some of the greatest authorities in each field. It included articles on science written by James Clerk Maxwell and Thomas Huxley.

A Dictionary of the English Language

1755 ▪ PRINTED ▪ 43.2 × 30.5 cm (17 × 12 in) ▪ 2,300 PAGES ▪ UK

SCALE

SAMUEL JOHNSON

The publication in April 1755 of Samuel Johnson's *A Dictionary of the English Language* in two volumes marked the culmination of perhaps the most extraordinary endeavour in English literature. The book began as an initiative by a group of publishers and booksellers in London who wanted to produce a definitive English dictionary, with agreed standards of spelling and usage, to meet the demands of the increasingly literate population. In its aim to fix and understand language as precisely as the scientific discoveries of the period, this ambitious project chimed exactly with the demands of the Age of Enlightenment, or Age of Reason – to codify the rapidly expanding world of knowledge. The result remains an astonishing monument to its sole author, Johnson.

The *Dictionary* was a dazzling display of erudition, which set entirely new standards in lexicography. It determined how and why dictionaries should be ordered, explained the etymology of words, and provided precise definitions. Additionally, Johnson illustrated his definitions with a vast array of quotations – more than 114,000 in total. That these came primarily from writers whom Johnson most admired – including Shakespeare, Milton, Dryden, and Pope – reinforced the idea that literature, as Johnson put it, was England's "chief glory".

Although *A Dictionary of the English Language* was produced in only nine years, it was extraordinarily meticulous, comprehensive, and precise. It remained the single most authoritative English dictionary for over 170 years, supplanted only by the publication in 1928 of *The Oxford English Dictionary* in 10 volumes.

SAMUEL **JOHNSON**

1709–1784

Samuel Johnson (often referred to as Doctor Johnson) was an English writer and critic, who through his groundbreaking work on *A Dictionary of the English Language* became one of the greatest figures of 18th century literature.

Johnson came from humble beginnings. Born in Lichfield, a town in the Midlands, he was the son of impoverished booksellers and as a child was prone to illness. He was educated at grammar school before attending Oxford University in 1778, but had to leave early due to lack of funds. To support himself he worked as a journalist in London, and in his mid-20s married a woman 25 years his senior. His prospects seemed bleak, as he was often on the brink of financial ruin, but his talents were obvious: he had a remarkable capacity for work, coupled with an instinctive understanding of the power of words, his own and those of others. His growing literary reputation resulted in him being commissioned to write *A Dictionary of the English Language*, a challenge from which he emerged as the undisputed literary lion of London. Beyond the accomplishment of writing the book itself, Johnson's particular achievement was that he infused the work with such a rich sense of his own personality. Buried in Westminster Abbey in 1784, Johnson remains perhaps the most commanding figure of English literature.

◄ **WEIGHTY TOMES**
Published in two volumes, Johnson's *Dictionary* was as remarkable for its size as it was for its content. An impressive work of scholarship, it remains one of the most famous dictionaries in history.

▲ **ALPHABETICAL ARRANGEMENT**
This spread is taken from the original 1755 version of Johnson's *Dictionary*, with the content arranged in two columns per page. An abridged edition was published the following year, in which Johnson's abundant quotes were removed, and the contents laid out in three narrow columns. Every single definition in the *Dictionary* – all 42,773 of them – was written by Johnson himself, and the only help he employed was essentially secretarial – the copying and organizing of the definitions into alphabetical order.

Wherever I turned my view, there was perplexity to be disentangled, and confusion to be regulated

SAMUEL JOHNSON, PREFACE TO *A DICTIONARY OF THE ENGLISH LANGUAGE*, 1755

In detail

DICTIONARY

OF THE

ENGLISH LANGUAGE:

IN WHICH

The WORDS are deduced from their ORIGINALS,

AND

ILLUSTRATED in their DIFFERENT SIGNIFICATIONS

BY

EXAMPLES from the beſt WRITERS.

TO WHICH ARE PREFIXED,

A HISTORY of the LANGUAGE,

AND

AN ENGLISH GRAMMAR.

BY SAMUEL JOHNSON, A. M.

IN TWO VOLUMES.

VOL. I.

Cum tabulis animum cenſoris ſumet honeſti:
Audebit quæcunque parum ſplendoris habebunt,
Et ſine pondere erunt, et honore indigna ferentur.
Verba movere loco; quamvis invita recedant,
Et verſentur adhuc intra penetralia Veſtæ:
Obſcurata diu populo bonus eruet, atque
Proferet in lucem ſpecioſa vocabula rerum,
Quæ priſcis memorata Catonibus atque Cethegis,
Nunc ſitus informis premit et deſerta vetuſtas. HOR.

LONDON,
Printed by W. STRAHAN,
For J. and P. KNAPTON; T. and T. LONGMAN; C. HITCH and L. HAWES;
A. MILLAR; and R. and J. DODSLEY.
MDCCLV.

▲ **TITLE PAGE** Unlike the rest of the work, the title page of the *Dictionary* was printed in red and black ink. It includes a quotation in Latin from Horace's *Epistles*, in which the Roman poet addresses those who wish to write poetry. The *Dictionary* was printed on the finest-quality paper, at a cost of £1,600 – more than Johnson's own fee for writing the book.

LOVE. *n. ſ.* [from the verb.]

1. The paſſion between the ſexes.

Hearken to the birds *love*-learned ſong,
The dewie leaves among! *Spenſer.*

While idly I ſtood looking on,
I found th' effect of *love* in idleneſs. *Shakſp.*

My tales of *love* were wont to weary you;
I know you joy not in a *love* diſcourſe. *Shakſp.*

I look'd upon her with a ſoldier's eye,
That lik'd, but had a rougher taſk in hand
Than to drive liking to the name of *love*. *Shakſp.*

What need a vermil-tinctur'd lip for that,
Love-darting eyes, or treſſes like the morn? *Milt.*

Love quarrels oft in pleaſing concord end,
Not wedlock treachery, endang'ring life. *Milton.*

A *love* potion works more by the ſtrength of charm than nature. *Collier.*

You know y' are in my power by making *love*. *Dryden.*

Let mutual joys our mutual truſt combine,
And *love*, and *love*-born confidence be thine. *Pope.*

Cold is that breaſt which warm'd the world before,
And theſe *love*-darting eyes muſt roll no more. *Pope.*

2. Kindneſs; good-will; friendſhip.

What love, think'ſt thou, I ſue ſo much to get?
My *love* till death, my humble thanks, my prayers?
That *love* which virtue begs, and virtue grants. *Shakſpeare.*

God brought Daniel into favour and tender *love* with the prince. *Daniel.*

The one preach Chriſt of contention, but the other of *love*. *Philippians.*

By this ſhall all men know that ye are my diſciples, if ye have *love* one to another. *John.*

Unwearied have we ſpent the nights,
Till the Ledean ſtars, ſo fam'd for *love*,
Wonder'd at us from above. *Cowley.*

3. Courtſhip.

Demetrius
Made *love* to Nedar's daughter Helena,
And won her ſoul. *Shakſpeare.*

If you will marry, make your *loves* to me,
My lady is beſpoke. *Shakſpeare.*

The enquiry of truth, which is the *love*-making or wooing of it; the knowledge of truth, the preference of it; and the belief of truth, the enjoying of it, is the ſovereign good of human nature. *Bacon.*

4. Tenderneſs; parental care.

No religion that ever was, ſo fully repreſents the goodneſs of God, and his tender *love* to mankind, which is the moſt powerful argument to the love of God. *Tillotſon.*

5. Liking; inclination to: as, the *love* of one's country.

In youth, of patrimonial wealth poſſeſt,
The *love* of ſcience faintly warm'd his breaſt. *Fent.*

6. Object beloved.

Open the temple gates unto my *love*. *Spenſer.*

If that the world and love were young
And truth in every ſhepherd's tongue;
Theſe pretty pleaſures might we move,
To live with thee, and be thy *love*. *Shakſpeare.*

The baniſh'd never hopes his *love* to ſee. *Dryden.*

▲ **EXTENSIVE QUOTATIONS** The immense number of quotations – more than 114,000 – that Johnson included was in part due to his incredible memory, but more particularly as a result of his familiarity with an enormous range of literature. In compiling his *Dictionary*, it is claimed he read over 2,000 different books by more than 500 different authors.

OA'TMEAL. *n. ſ.* [*panicum.*] An herb. *Ainſworth.*

OATS. *n. ſ.* [aten, Sax.] A grain, which in England is generally given to horſes, but in Scotland ſupports the people.

It is of the graſs leaved tribe; the flowers have no petals, and are diſpoſed in a looſe panicle: the grain is eatable. The meal makes tolerable good bread. *Miller.*

The *oats* have eaten the horſes. *Shakſpeare.*

It is bare mechaniſm, no otherwiſe produced than the turning of a wild *oatbeard*, by the inſinuation of the particles of moiſture. *Locke.*

For your lean cattle, fodder them with barley ſtraw firſt, and the *oat* ſtraw laſt. *Mortimer.*

His horſe's allowance of *oats* and beans, was greater than the journey required. *Swift.*

OA'TTHISTLE. *n. ſ.* [*oat* and *thiſtle.*] An herb. *Ainſw.*

▲ **WRY DEFINITIONS** Whatever his claims to literary authority, Johnson took great pleasure in teasing the reader. For example, he mockingly defined a lexicographer, or compiler of dictionaries, as "a harmless drudge". Similarly, here, under the entry for "Oats", he asserts provocatively that the Scottish people eat oats, which in England are fed only to horses.

DEOPPILA'TION. *n. ſ.* [from *deoppilate.*] The act of clearing obſtructions; the removal of whatever obſtructs the vital paſſages.

Though the groſſer parts be excluded again, yet are the diſſoluble parts extracted, whereby it becomes effectual in *deoppilations.* *Brown.*

DEO'PPILATIVE. *adj.* [from *deoppilate.*] Deobſtruent.

A phyſician preſcribed him a *deoppilative* and purgative apozem. *Harvey.*

DEOSCULA'TION. *n. ſ.* [*deoſculatio*, Lat.] The act of kiſſing.

We have an enumeration of the ſeveral acts of worſhip required to be performed to images, viz. proceſſions, genuflections, thurifications, and *deoſculations.* *Stillingfleet.*

▲ **STRANGE OMISSIONS** A curiosity of Johnson's *Dictionary* is his omission of a number of commonplace words, such as "Banknote", "Blond", and "Port" (the drink, not the harbour). Many of the words he did choose to include were also obscure and unfamiliar to the average reader, such as "Deosculation", shown here, which Johnson defined as "The act of kissing".

RES RES RES

▲ **ABRIDGED EDITION** The prohibitive selling price of £4.10s for Johnson's original 1755 *Dictionary*, to say nothing of its daunting size, contributed to its poor sales – only around 6,000 copies sold over the course of 30 years. The abridged edition, a page from which is shown here, was priced at 10 shillings, and found a much readier and larger audience.

RELATED **TEXTS**

The first English dictionaries were published in the 13th century, and were originally used to provide definitions of French, Spanish, and Latin words. The first English-only dictionary, and also the first to be organized alphabetically, was *A Table Alphabeticall*, compiled by Robert Cawdrey in 1604, listing 2,543 words.

The 18th-century desire to organize knowledge was the prime motive behind the compilation and publication of Johnson's *Dictionary*. In 1807, American lexicographer Noah Webster (1758–1843) aimed to build a system of the American language and began composing *An American Dictionary of the English Language*. The first dictionary to include characteristically American words words such as "Chowder", it exceeds Johnson's dictionary with 70,000 entries, and led to Webster being considered the "Father of American Scholarship and Education".

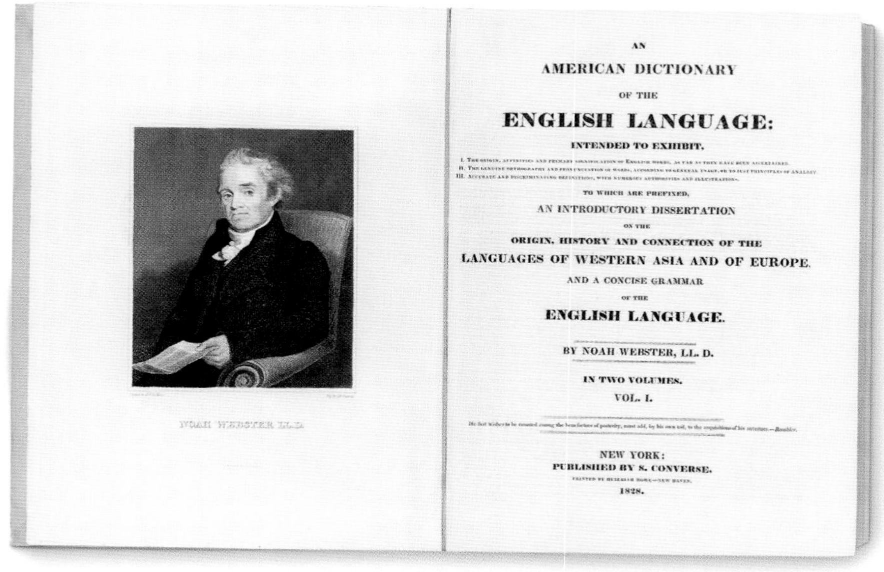

AN
AMERICAN DICTIONARY
OF THE
ENGLISH LANGUAGE:
INTENDED TO EXHIBIT,
TO WHICH ARE PREFIXED,
AN INTRODUCTORY DISSERTATION
ON THE
ORIGIN, HISTORY AND CONNECTION OF THE
LANGUAGES OF WESTERN ASIA AND OF EUROPE,
AND A CONCISE GRAMMAR
OF THE
ENGLISH LANGUAGE.
BY NOAH WEBSTER, LL. D.
IN TWO VOLUMES.
VOL. I.
NEW YORK:
PUBLISHED BY S. CONVERSE.
1828.

▲ **Webster worked** on his *Dictionary* for 22 years before it was published in 1828. In much the same way, 62 years of work were needed before *The Oxford English Dictionary* made its first appearance, in 10 volumes, in 1928.

Bucolica, Georgica et Aeneis

1757 ▪ PRINTED BY JOHN BASKERVILLE ▪ 30 × 23 cm (12 × 9 in) ▪ 432 PAGES ▪ UK

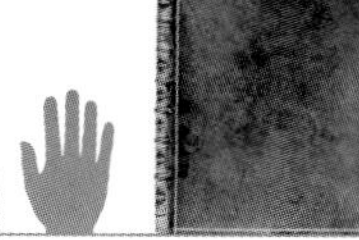
SCALE

VIRGIL

The first printing venture of typographer and printer John Baskerville was the publication of Virgil's *Bucolica, Georgica et Aeneis*, which was heralded as a masterpiece of typography and design. Available by subscription, the book was a huge success, in part due to its subject: the works of the Ancient Roman poet Virgil. One of the greatest poets in history, Virgil was rediscovered in the late 1600s when the poet John Dryden (1631–1700) translated his works from Latin into English.

John Baskerville was a groundbreaking publisher. He had studied calligraphy and stone-cutting before making his fortune in manufacturing, and he applied these skills to the design and typsetting of his project. Baskerville oversaw every aspect of production, both technical and creative. Rejecting existing typefaces, he developed a fine, elegant font, now known as Baskerville after its inventor. For the layout, he used wide margins and wide spacing between text, making it easy to read. He opted for James Whatman's wove paper, as its smooth surface allowed for a delicate rendering of his font. As Whatman was only able to supply enough paper for half the book, the remainder was printed on traditional laid paper; both paper types were also glazed.

VIRGIL

70–19 BCE

The man who would become the greatest poet of Ancient Rome, Publius Vergilius Maro, was born the son of a cattle farmer. His epic poems have been hugely influential on Western literature

Virgil's father had ambitions for his son, and planned an education that would lead to a legal career. The shy and thoughtful Virgil went to school in Cremona and Milan before arriving in Rome to study law, rhetoric, and philosophy. His real passion, however, was poetry. One of his fellow students, Octavian, would become the emperor, Augustus, and a devoted patron of the budding poet. Virgil's love of the Italian countryside influenced many of the epics he wrote, endearing him to the general public as well as the political elite. His most notable works include the *Eclogues*, or *Bucolics* (pastoral poems), the *Georgics* (about farming), and *Aeneis*, or *Aeneid*, the poet's last, unfinished piece, which told the story of Rome's foundation. After his death from fever, Virgil became a national hero and his works were taught in schools. His influence on other poets has been huge, and he has inspired many including Ovid, Dante, and Milton.

In detail

PUBLII VIRGILII

MARONIS

BUCOLICA,

GEORGICA,

ET

AENEIS.

BIRMINGHAMIAE:

Typis JOHANNIS BASKERVILLE.

MDCCLVII.

◄ **SIMPLE STYLE** In contrast with the typical title pages of books at the time, Baskerville's version was remarkably minimal. He cut the information to the book's title, author, publisher, date, and city of publication – a convention that is still used today.

P. VIRGILII MARONIS

AENEIDOS

LIBER SECUNDUS.

CONTICUERE omnes, intentique ora tenebant:
Inde toro pater Aeneas ſic orſus ab alto:
Infandum, Regina, jubes renovare dolorem;
Trojanas ut opes, et lamentabile regnum
Eruerint Danai: quæque ipſe miſerrima vidi,
Et quorum pars magna fui. quis talia fando,
Myrmidonum, Dolopumve, aut duri miles Ulyſſei,
Temperet a lacrymis? et jam nox humida cœlo
Præcipitat, ſuadentque cadentia ſidera ſomnos.
Sed, ſi tantus amor caſus cognoſcere noſtros,
Et breviter Trojæ ſupremum audire laborem;
Quanquam animus meminiſſe horret, luctuque refugit,
Incipiam. Fracti bello, fatiſque repulſi
Ductores Danaum, tot jam labentibus annis,
Inſtar montis equum, divina Palladis arte
Aedificant; ſectaque intexunt abiete coſtas.
Votum pro reditu ſimulant: ea fama vagatur.
Huc delecta virum ſortiti corpora furtim
Includunt cæco lateri; penituſque cavernas
Ingentes, uterumque armato milite complent.
Eſt in conſpectu Tenedos, notiſſima fama
Inſula, dives opum, Priami dum regna manebant:
Nunc tantum ſinus, et ſtatio maleſida carinis.

Huc

P. VIRGILII AENEIDOS LIB. II. 130

Huc ſe provecti deſerto in litore condunt.
Nos abiiſſe rati, et vento petiiſſe Mycenas.
Ergo omnis longo ſolvit ſe Teucria luctu:
Panduntur portæ. juvat ire, et Dorica caſtra,
Deſertoſque videre locos, lituſque relictum.
Hic Dolopum manus, hic ſævus tendebat Achilles:
Claſſibus hic locus: hic acies certare ſolebant.
Pars ſtupet innuptæ donum exitiale Minervæ,
Et molem mirantur equi: primuſque Thymœtes
Duci intra muros hortatur, et arce locari;
Sive dolo, ſeu jam Trojæ ſic fata ferebant.
At Capys, et quorum melior ſententia menti,
Aut pelago Danaum inſidias, ſuſpectaque dona
Præcipitare jubent, ſubjectiſque urere flammis:
Aut terebrare cavas uteri et tentare latebras.
Scinditur incertum ſtudia in contraria vulgus.
Primus ibi ante omnes, magna comitante caterva,
Laocoon ardens ſumma decurrit ab arce.
Et procul: O miſeri, quæ tanta inſania, cives?
Creditis avectos hoſtes? aut ulla putatis
Dona carere dolis Danaum? ſic notus Ulyſſes?
Aut hoc incluſi ligno occultantur Achivi;
Aut hæc in noſtros fabricata eſt machina muros,
Inſpectura domos, venturaque deſuper urbi;
Aut aliquis latet error: equo ne credite, Teucri.
Quidquid id eſt, timeo Danaos, et dona ferentes.
Sic fatus, validis ingentem viribus haſtam
In latus, inque feri curvam compagibus alvum
Contorſit. ſtetit illa tremens, uteroque recuſſo
Inſonuere cavæ gemitumque dedere cavernæ.
Et, ſi fata Deum, ſi mens non læve fuiſſet,

R 2 Impulerat

▲ **LANDMARK TYPEFACE** Baskerville's early interest in calligraphy, and the hours he spent practising lettering, influenced the typeface he created for his first book. The Baskerville font has sharp edges, rounded lines, and a spacious appearance. Existing printing presses did not do justice to his new font, so Baskerville modified his press so it would dry the ink as soon as it touched the paper. He also invented a richer, more lustrous black ink to provide a crisper finish.

242 *P. VIRGILII AENEIDOS* LIB. VI.

Scrupea, tuta lacu nigro, nemorumque tenebris:
Quam ſuper haud ullæ poterant impune volantes
Tendere iter pennis: talis ſeſe halitus atris
Faucibus effundens ſupera ad convexa ferebat:
Unde locum Graii dixerunt nomine Aornon.
Quatuor hic primum nigrantes terga juvencos
Conſtituit, frontique invergit vina ſacerdos:
Et ſummas carpens media inter cornua ſetas,
Ignibus imponit ſacris libamina prima,
Voce vocans Hecaten, cœloque Ereboque potentem.
Supponunt alii cultros, tepidumque cruorem
Suſcipiunt pateris. ipſe atri velleris agnam
Aeneas matri Eumenidum magnæque ſorori
Enſe ferit; ſterilemque tibi, Proſerpina, vaccam.
Tum Stygio Regi nocturnas inchoat aras:
Et ſolida imponit taurorum viſcera flammis,
Pingue ſuperque oleum fundens ardentibus extis.
Ecce autem, primi ſub lumina Solis et ortus,
Sub pedibus mugire ſolum, et juga cœpta moveri
Silvarum, viſæque canes ululare per umbram,
Adventante Dea. Procul, o, procul eſte profani,
Conclamat Vates, totoque abſiſtite luco:
Tuque invade viam, vaginaque eripe ferrum:
Nunc animis opus, Aenea, nunc pectore firmo.
Tantum effata, furens antro ſe immiſit aperto.
Ille ducem haud timidis vadentem paſſibus æquat.
Di, quibus imperium eſt animarum, umbræque ſilen-
Et Chaos, et Phlegethon, loca nocte ſilentia late; (tes,
Sit mihi fas audita loqui: ſit numine veſtro
Pandere res alta terra et caligine merſas.
Ibant obſcuri ſola ſub nocte per umbram,

Perque

▲ **INTRICATE ILLUSTRATION** One of several intricately detailed, engraved plates in Baskerville's edition of the collected works, this plate depicts the hero of Virgil's *Aeneis*. Here Aeneis wears armour and bears a shield given to him by his mother as he encounters the underworld. The inks used in the engraving process could be "burnished", or polished, on the plate to give the impression of light.

◀ **MAPPING ROUTES** A fold-out map of Italy and Greece inserted before the title page, set the scene for Virgil's *Aeneis*. It marks the journeys made by the hero, Aeneis, a Trojan warrior who travels to Italy, where he becomes the founding ancestor of Rome.

> It gives me great Satisfaction, to find that my Edition of Virgil has been so favourably received
>
> **JOHN BASKERVILLE**

Tristram Shandy

1759–67 ▪ PRINTED ▪ 16.4 × 10.4 cm (6 × 4 in) ▪ 1,404 PAGES ▪ UK

SCALE

LAURENCE STERNE

A comic masterpiece that gleefully overturned existing notions of how a novel should be written, structured, and even printed, *The Life and Opinions of Tristram Shandy, Gentleman* continues to this day to pose questions about the nature of fiction and of reading itself. Published in nine volumes over an eight-year period, the novel toys with the reader with its disjointed narrative, and playful typographical and visual quirks that pushed at the prevailing limits of print design. Laurence Sterne frequently substitutes "bad" words with dashes or asterisks, bringing attention to them while giving the appearance of showing discretion. Whole pages are also left blank, coloured black, or marbled, as he turns the familiar structure of a printed book on its head.

The novel is a fictional autobiography in which Shandy tells of his peculiar existence. Sterne dispenses with an orderly, linear plot, however, and narrative themes are dropped and resumed at random; chapters are skipped, only to crop up later, their absence commented on; and the pagination is muddled. Sterne/Shandy also make regular appeals to the reader, forcing them to take part in the story.

In volume one, Shandy realizes the difficulty in determining precisely *when* his life began. Thereafter he continually interrupts his narration with a stream of digressions that dwell on a diverse array of topics, and sweep back and forth in time. Stories-within-stories, and the expression of his own and other characters' opinions also serve to postpone the "action": by volume three, Shandy has still not been born. Details of his life are offered via the views and actions of his eccentric family, notably his father and war veteran uncle, Toby.

Tristram Shandy was a huge success when published. Today it is regarded as a forerunner of post-modern literature.

LAURENCE **STERNE**

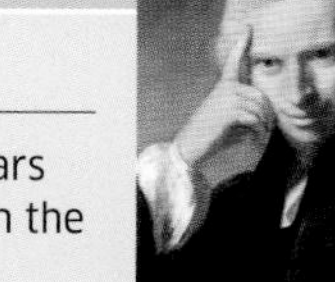

1713–1768

Laurence Sterne was an Irish-born novelist who, after 20 years as a rural parson, became a celebrated literary luminary with the publication of the first volume of *Tristram Shandy* in 1759.

Having spent his early childhood in Ireland, following his father (a soldier) to a succession of postings, in 1724 Sterne was sent to the northern English county of Yorkshire, to be educated. Later he was admitted to Cambridge University, graduating in 1737. The following year he was ordained in the Anglican church and became vicar of Sutton-on-the-Forest, near York. In 1741, he married Elizabeth Lumley, with whom he had a daughter, but the marriage was unhappy; she had a nervous breakdown and he was unfaithful.

Sterne's emergence as a major literary figure came abruptly in 1759 with the publication of *A Political Romance*, a satire of churchmen in York. The book sparked instant controversy and effectively ended his clerical career. That same year, the first two volumes of *Tristram Shandy* appeared, published at Sterne's expense. He became a celebrity throughout Europe and made a fortune, fulfilling a long-held ambition: "I wrote", he said, "not to be fed but to be famous". Ill-health (he had incurable tuberculosis) forced Sterne overseas in 1762, in search of a warmer climate. The trip provided material for his last novel, *A Sentimental Journey Through France and Italy* (1768), an unorthodox mix of travel memoir and fiction. He died one month after its publication.

▼ **BLACK PAGE** Perhaps the most famous (and notorious) of *Tristram Shandy*'s many typographical tricks is the black page that announces the death of a minor character, Parson Yorick, in volume one. The device is simultaneously shocking and unexpected. The novel, a literary form, is suddenly re-cast in abstract visual terms.

[74]

[75]

CHAP. XIII.

IT is ſo long ſince the reader of this rhapſodical work has been parted from the midwife, that it is high time to mention her again to him, merely to put him in mind that there is ſuch a body ſtill in the world, and whom, upon the beſt judgment I can form upon my own plan at preſent, --- I am going to introduce to him for good and all: But as freſh matter may be ſtarted, and much unexpected buſineſs fall out betwixt the reader and myſelf, which may require immediate diſpatch; ----- 'twas right to take care that the poor woman ſhould not be loſt in the mean time; ---becauſe when ſhe is wanted we can no way do without her.

I

What is all this story about?

ELIZABETH SHANDY, VOLUME NINE, *TRISTRAM SHANDY*

DEDICATION.

I beg your Lordſhip will forgive me, if, at the ſame time I dedicate this work to you, I join Lady SPENCER, in the liberty I take of inſcribing the ſtory of *Le Fever* in the ſixth volume to her name; for which I have no other motive, which my heart has informed me of, but that the ſtory is a humane one.

I am,
My Lord,
Your Lordſhip's
Moſt devoted,
And moſt humble Servant,

LAUR. STERNE.

L. Sterne

THE
LIFE and OPINIONS
OF
TRISTRAM SHANDY, Gent.

CHAP. I.

IF it had not been for thoſe two mettleſome tits, and that madcap of a poſtilion, who drove them from Stilton to Stamford, the thought had never entered my head. He flew like lightning——there was a ſlope of three miles and a half——we ſcarce touched the ground——the motion was moſt rapid —moſt impetuous—'twas communicat-

VOL. V. B ed

▲ **AUTHOR'S AUTOGRAPH** The novel's popularity led to the printing of pirate versions. In order to protect his commercial rights, Sterne autographed every copy of the first two editions of volume five, shown above, and the first editions of volumes seven and nine. In doing this, Sterne was able to guarantee the authenticity of almost 13,000 copies.

In detail

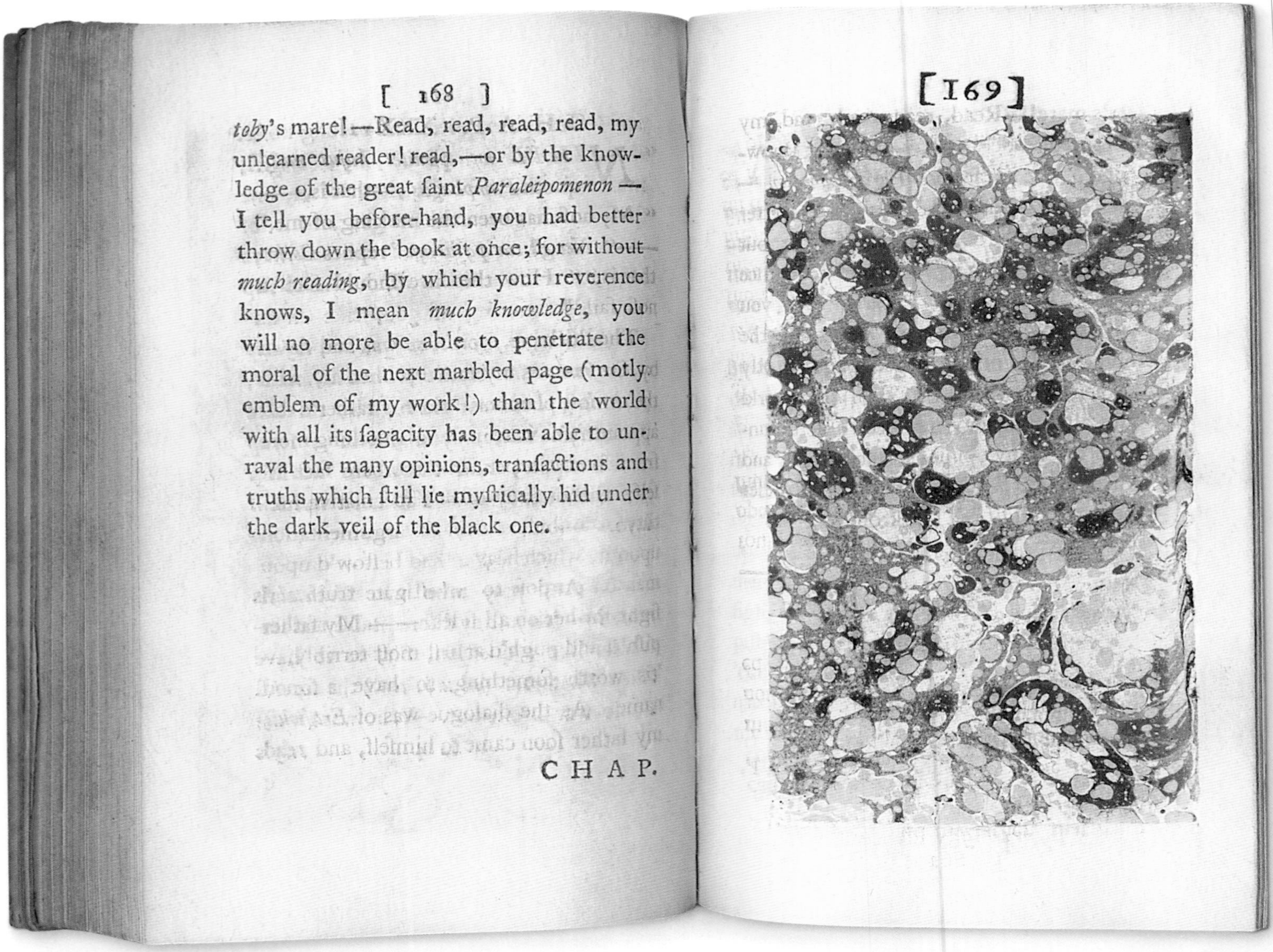

[168]

toby's mare!—Read, read, read, read, my unlearned reader! read,—or by the knowledge of the great ſaint *Paraleipomenon* — I tell you before-hand, you had better throw down the book at once; for without *much reading*, by which your reverence knows, I mean *much knowledge*, you will no more be able to penetrate the moral of the next marbled page (motly emblem of my work!) than the world with all its ſagacity has been able to unraval the many opinions, tranſactions and truths which ſtill lie myſtically hid under the dark veil of the black one.

CHAP.

[169]

▲ **UNIQUE MARBLING** Part-way through volume three (published with volume four in 1761) Sterne plays an especially elaborate and exotic visual game. Shandy claims that his "book of books" is utterly unique, and "describes" this using two marbled pages. In the novel's original publication each would have been made by hand, so no two would have been alike. The facing text challenges readers to say what the page is doing there.

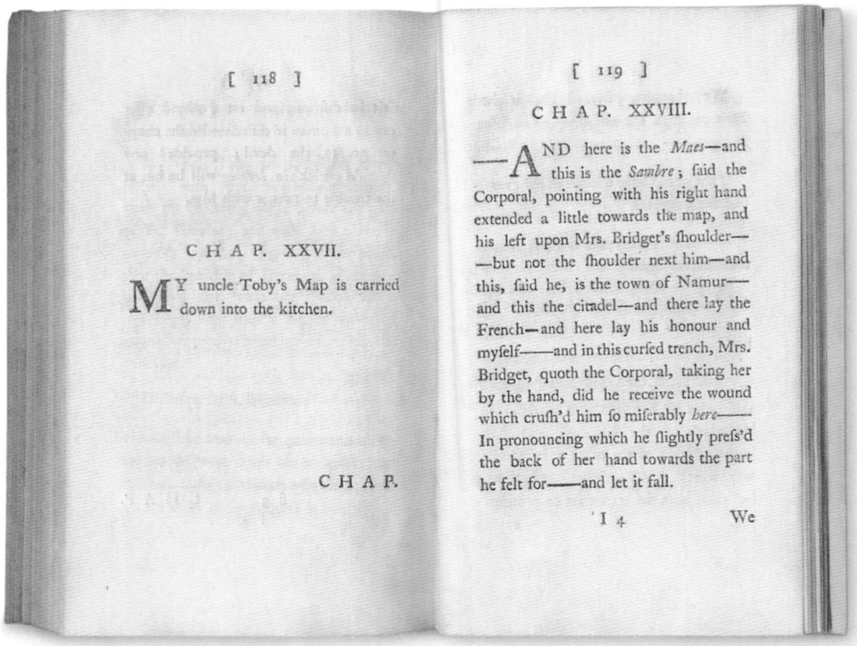

[118]

CHAP. XXVII.

MY uncle Toby's Map is carried down into the kitchen.

CHAP.

[119]

CHAP. XXVIII.

—AND here is the *Maes*—and this is the *Sambre*; ſaid the Corporal, pointing with his right hand extended a little towards the map, and his left upon Mrs. Bridget's ſhoulder——but not the ſhoulder next him—and this, ſaid he, is the town of Namur—and this the citadel—and there lay the French—and here lay his honour and myſelf——and in this curſed trench, Mrs. Bridget, quoth the Corporal, taking her by the hand, did he receive the wound which cruſh'd him ſo miſerably *here*——In pronouncing which he ſlightly preſs'd the back of her hand towards the part he felt for——and let it fall.

I 4 We

► **SHORTEST CHAPTER** Typical of the playfully disjointed structure of Sterne's novel is the way he swapped chapters between the different volumes. Shown here is chapter seven from volume eight, published as part of volume seven. It is the shortest chapter in the whole novel, consisting of a single, wonderfully inconsequential, 10-word sentence: "My uncle Toby's map is carried down into the kitchen."

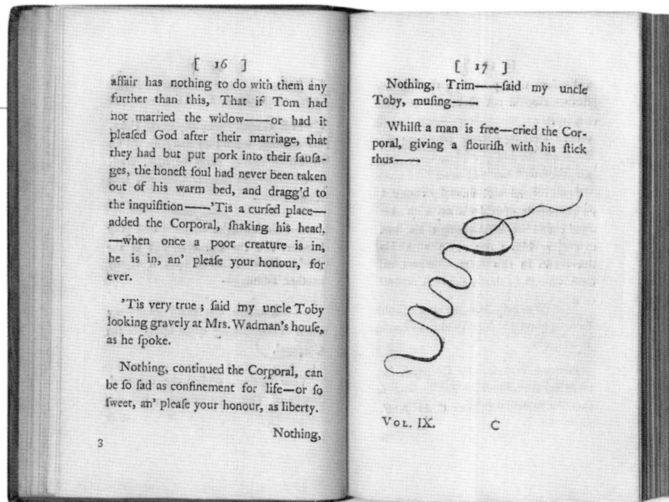

[16]

affair has nothing to do with them any further than this, That if Tom had not married the widow——or had it pleaſed God after their marriage, that they had but put pork into their ſauſages, the honeſt ſoul had never been taken out of his warm bed, and dragg'd to the inquiſition——'Tis a curſed place—added the Corporal, ſhaking his head, —when once a poor creature is in, he is in, an' pleaſe your honour, for ever.

'Tis very true; ſaid my uncle Toby looking gravely at Mrs. Wadman's houſe, as he ſpoke.

Nothing, continued the Corporal, can be ſo ſad as confinement for life—or ſo ſweet, an' pleaſe your honour, as liberty.

Nothing,

3

[17]

Nothing, Trim——ſaid my uncle Toby, muſing——

Whilſt a man is free—cried the Corporal, giving a flouriſh with his ſtick thus——

Vol. IX. C

◄ **VISUAL LANGUAGE** On occasion Sterne favours graphic elements over words to convey meaning – an innovation way ahead of its time. This serpentine squiggle represents Corporal Trim – Uncle Toby's loyal servant, a former soldier – waving his baton as he wordlessly comments on the ups and downs, and ins and outs, of marriage.

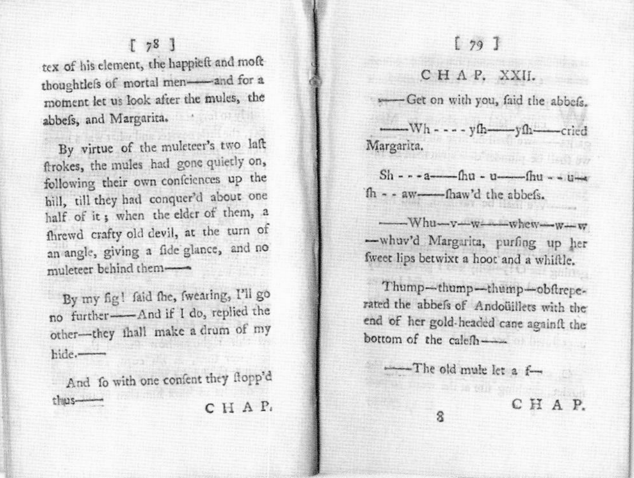

[78]

tex of his element, the happieſt and moſt thoughtleſs of mortal men——and for a moment let us look after the mules, the abbeſs, and Margarita.

By virtue of the muleteer's two laſt ſtrokes, the mules had gone quietly on, following their own conſciences up the hill, till they had conquer'd about one half of it; when the elder of them, a ſhrewd crafty old devil, at the turn of an angle, giving a ſide glance, and no muleteer behind them——

By my fig! ſaid ſhe, ſwearing, I'll go no further——And if I do, replied the other—they ſhall make a drum of my hide.——

And ſo with one conſent they ſtopp'd thus——

CHAP.

[79]

CHAP. XXII.

——Get on with you, ſaid the abbeſs.

——Wh - - - - yſh——yſh——cried Margarita.

Sh - - - a——ſhu - u——ſhu - - u——ſh - - aw——ſhaw'd the abbeſs.

——Whu—v—w——whew—w—w—whuv'd Margarita, purſing up her ſweet lips betwixt a hoot and a whiſtle.

Thump—thump—thump—obſtreperated the abbeſs of Andoüillets with the end of her gold-headed cane againſt the bottom of the caleſh——

——The old mule let a f—

8 CHAP.

▲ **RULE-BREAKING TEXT** Throughout the book, words are omitted, entire pages are filled with asterisks, or left blank, and odd footnotes appear. En – and em – rules of varying length are used to indicate a meaningful pause, or an impatient wait. The coded appearance of text serves to reinforce the elusive nature of the novel, which tells the reader very little about Shandy himself.

[152]

CHAP. XL.

I Am now beginning to get fairly into my work; and by the help of a vegitable diet, with a few of the cold ſeeds, I make no doubt but I ſhall be able to go on with my uncle *Toby*'s ſtory, and my own, in a tolerable ſtraight line. Now,

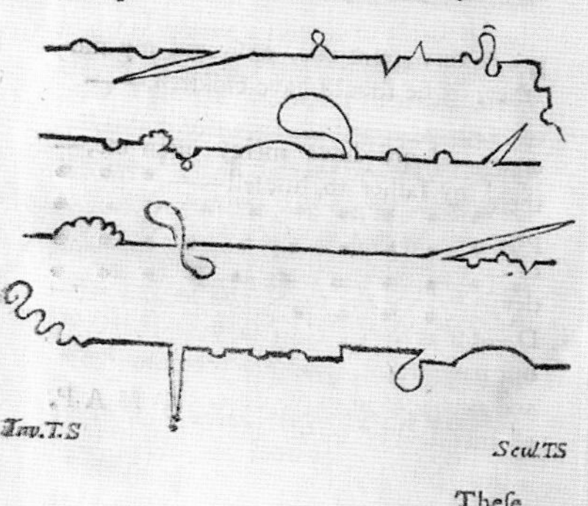

Theſe

[153]

Theſe were the four lines I moved in through my firſt, ſecond, third, and fourth volumes.——In the fifth volume I have been very good,——the preciſe line I have deſcribed in it being this:

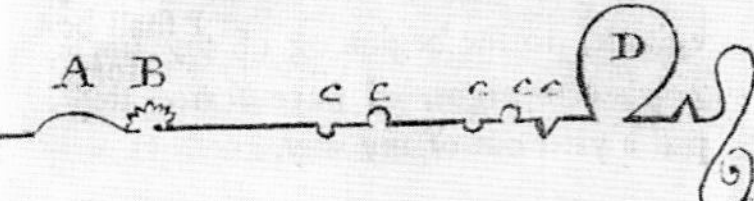

By which it appears, that except at the curve, marked A. where I took a trip to *Navarre*,—and the indented curve B. which is the ſhort airing when I was there with the Lady *Bauſſiere* and her page,—I have not taken the leaſt friſk of a digreſſion, till *John de la Caſſe*'s devils led me the round you ſee marked D.—for as for *c c c c c* they are nothing but parentheſes, and the common *ins* and *outs* incident to the lives of the greateſt miniſters of ſtate; and when compared

◄ **PLOT LINES** Here, Shandy draws attention to the haphazard nature of his storytelling, with graphic representations of the routes taken by his plot in the first five volumes of the book. There are occasional advances, followed by setbacks, diversions, and dead ends. It shows how the story, and Shandy's life, progress in anything other than a straight line.

IN **CONTEXT**

The inevitable question about *Tristram Shandy* is whether it is a virtuoso joke or a seriously intended contribution to the art of the novel. In mid-18th-century Europe the genre was growing in popularity and sophistication, but it was an artificial construct: the realism it boasted existed only within its pages. Perhaps Sterne's most obvious achievement as a writer was his recognition that any novel, however acute its insights, could never reflect the confusion of human existence, with all its arbitrariness and disorder.

His solution was to produce a work as chaotic, unresolved, and farcical as the world itself. It would become real precisely because of its lack of formal structure. *Tristram Shandy* has divided opinion ever since. Dr Johnson (see p.150), the revered English writer and critic, declared in 1776 that "nothing odd will do long", implying that the book was too idiosyncratic to be taken seriously. Later luminaries disagreed: the German philosopher Schopenhauer declared it one of the four greatest novels ever written. Largely decried in the 19th century as buffoonish and irrelevant, *Tristram Shandy* was rehabilitated in the 20th century and profoundly influenced writers including Virginia Woolf and James Joyce. It is, incontestably, an astonishingly original work.

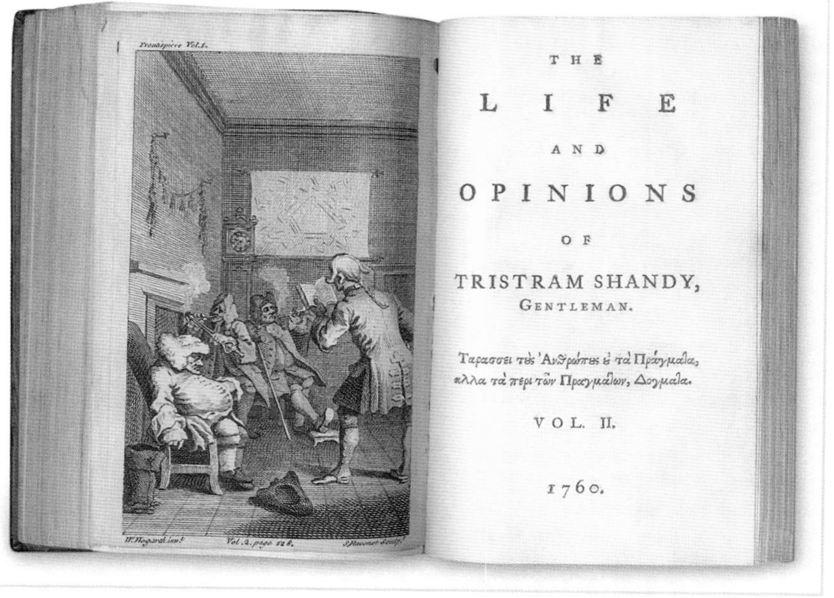

THE

LIFE

AND

OPINIONS

OF

TRISTRAM SHANDY,

GENTLEMAN.

Ταρασσει τὸς Ἀνθρώπες ὀυ τὰ Πράγματα, ἀλλα τὰ περὶ τῶν Πραγμάτων, Δογματα.

VOL. II.

1760.

► **Fittingly, Sterne chose** William Hogarth, the famous chronicler of English foibles and follies, to provide the first illustrations for *Tristram Shandy*, in 1760.

Fables in Verse

1765 ▪ PRINTED BY JOHN NEWBERY ▪ 10.6 × 7.2 cm (4 × 3 in) ▪ 144 PAGES ▪ UK

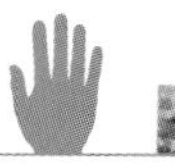

SCALE

AESOP

For more than 2,000 years, *Aesop's Fables* – a set of cautionary and moralistic tales – have been told, retold, and endlessly reinterpreted. Although there is no certainty that Aesop even existed, he is thought to have been a Greek-speaking slave in the Greco-Roman world, in the 5th or 6th century BCE. The fables, which number over 725, belong to the oral tradition and they highlight truths that are sometimes cruel, often amusing, but always pithy and exact. They use animal characters to represent human qualities, such as greed, deceit, strength, or perseverance – a device that has captured the imagination across cultures and ages. Many moral tales have been attributed to Aesop, even some arising long after his death.

In the context of antiquity, such stories served to develop the conscience of all individuals. A collection of *Aesop's Fables* was produced as early as 4th century BCE, in the form of a text for orators and public speakers by orator Demetrius of Phaleron (320–280 BCE). His text formed the basis for numerous other versions during the Middle Ages. In the Renaissance, the tales were taught in schools, and with the invention of printing in the 15th century were amongst the earliest works to be published. The first, produced in Germany, was called simply *Esopus*, appearing in around 1476. Within 25 years, over 150 editions were printed. The tales soon spread across the world, and now there is a translation in nearly every language.

Today *Aesop's Fables* are primarily viewed as children's stories, which in part could be attributed to John Newbery's 1765 edition (shown here). Newbery reworded the fables, only including those which he thought would appeal to his young audience. The book begins with the "Life of Aesop", some anecdotes, then 38 illustrated *Fables in Verse*, finishing with "The Conversation of Animals".

JOHN **NEWBERY**

1713–1767

The London-based printer John Newbery was one of the first people to publish children's books. He aimed to cater to the interests of the younger generation by creating literature that was both entertaining and informative.

Born in Berkshire in 1713, John Newbery's publishing career began in 1730 when he was hired by William Carnan of the *Reading Mercury*. He started publishing books in 1740 in Reading, before relocating to London where he expanded his business into children's writing. His first book for children, *A Little Pretty Pocket-Book*, appeared in 1744. Widely considered to be the first children's book, it contained poems and proverbs, and was bound in bright colours. *Fables in Verse* followed in 1765, and pupils often had to memorize the moralistic verses in school. His contribution to children's literature is commemorated in the US with the annual award, the Newbery Medal.

In detail

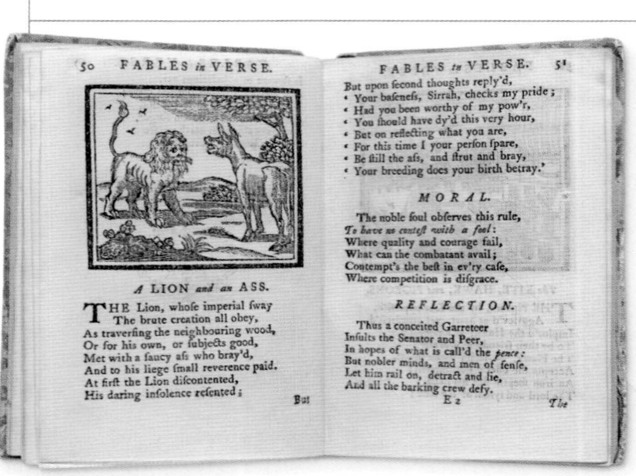

50 FABLES *in* VERSE.

A LION *and an* ASS.

THE Lion, whofe imperial fway
The brute creation all obey,
As traverfing the neighbouring wood,
Or for his own, or fubjects good,
Met with a faucy afs who bray'd,
And to his liege fmall reverence paid.
At firft the Lion difcontented,
His daring infolence refented;
But

FABLES *in* VERSE. 51

But upon fecond thoughts reply'd,
'Your bafenefs, Sirrah, checks my pride;
'Had you been worthy of my pow'r,
'You fhould have dy'd this very hour,
'But on reflecting what you are,
'For this time I your perfon fpare,
'Be ftill the afs, and ftrut and bray,
'Your breeding does your birth betray.'

MORAL.

The noble foul obferves this rule,
To have no conteft with a fool:
Where quality and courage fail,
What can the combatant avail;
Contempt's the beft in ev'ry cafe,
Where competition is difgrace.

REFLECTION.

Thus a conceited Garreteer
Infults the Senator and Peer,
In hopes of what is call'd the *pence*:
But nobler minds, and men of fenfe,
Let him rail on, detract and lie,
And all the barking crew defy.
E 2 The

◄ **INSTRUCTIVE TEXT** Newbery's introduction makes explicit that these stories were intended to instruct, with "such lesson in prudence and morality as may be of service to the riper years", as this layout, with its moral and reflection, shows.

► **TALKING ANIMALS** The book finishes with "The Conversation of Animals" – short, moralistic tales that draw on the parallels between the actions of humans and other animals.

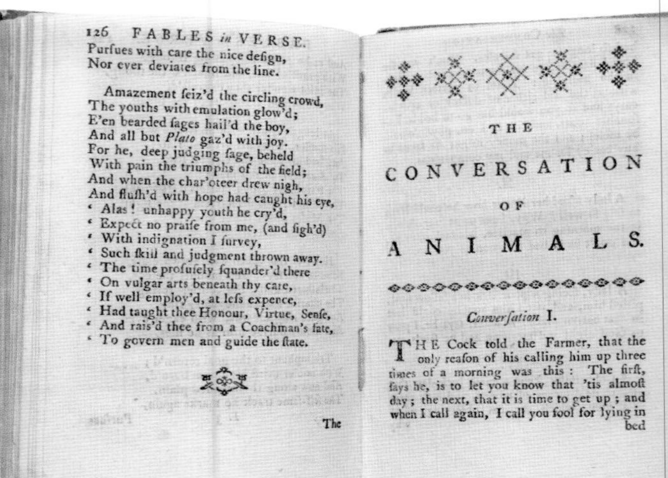

126 FABLES *in* VERSE.

Purfues with care the nice defign,
Nor ever deviates from the line.

Amazement feiz'd the circling crowd,
The youths with emulation glow'd;
E'en bearded fages hail'd the boy,
And all but *Plato* gaz'd with joy.
For he, deep judging fage, beheld
With pain the triumphs of the field;
And when the char'oteer drew nigh,
And flufh'd with hope had caught his eye,
'Alas! unhappy youth he cry'd,
'Expect no praife from me, (and figh'd)
'With indignation I furvey,
'Such fkill and judgment thrown away.
'The time profufely fquander'd there
'On vulgar arts beneath thy care,
'If well employ'd, at lefs expence,
'Had taught thee Honour, Virtue, Senfe,
'And rais'd thee from a Coachman's fate,
'To govern men and guide the ftate.
The

THE

CONVERSATION

OF

ANIMALS.

Conversation I.

THE Cock told the Farmer, that the only reafon of his calling him up three times of a morning was this: The firft, fays he, is to let you know that 'tis almoft day; the next, that it is time to get up; and when I call again, I call you fool for lying in bed

▼ **MORAL GUIDANCE** All 38 of the fables in Newbery's edition are illustrated with woodcuts, as seen in these pages that tell the familiar story of "The Ants and the Grasshopper". It is easy to see why this fable, with its talking insects, held appeal for children. Yet it is a classic allegory of industry versus indolence, and the cautionary tale advises the reader to prepare for the future.

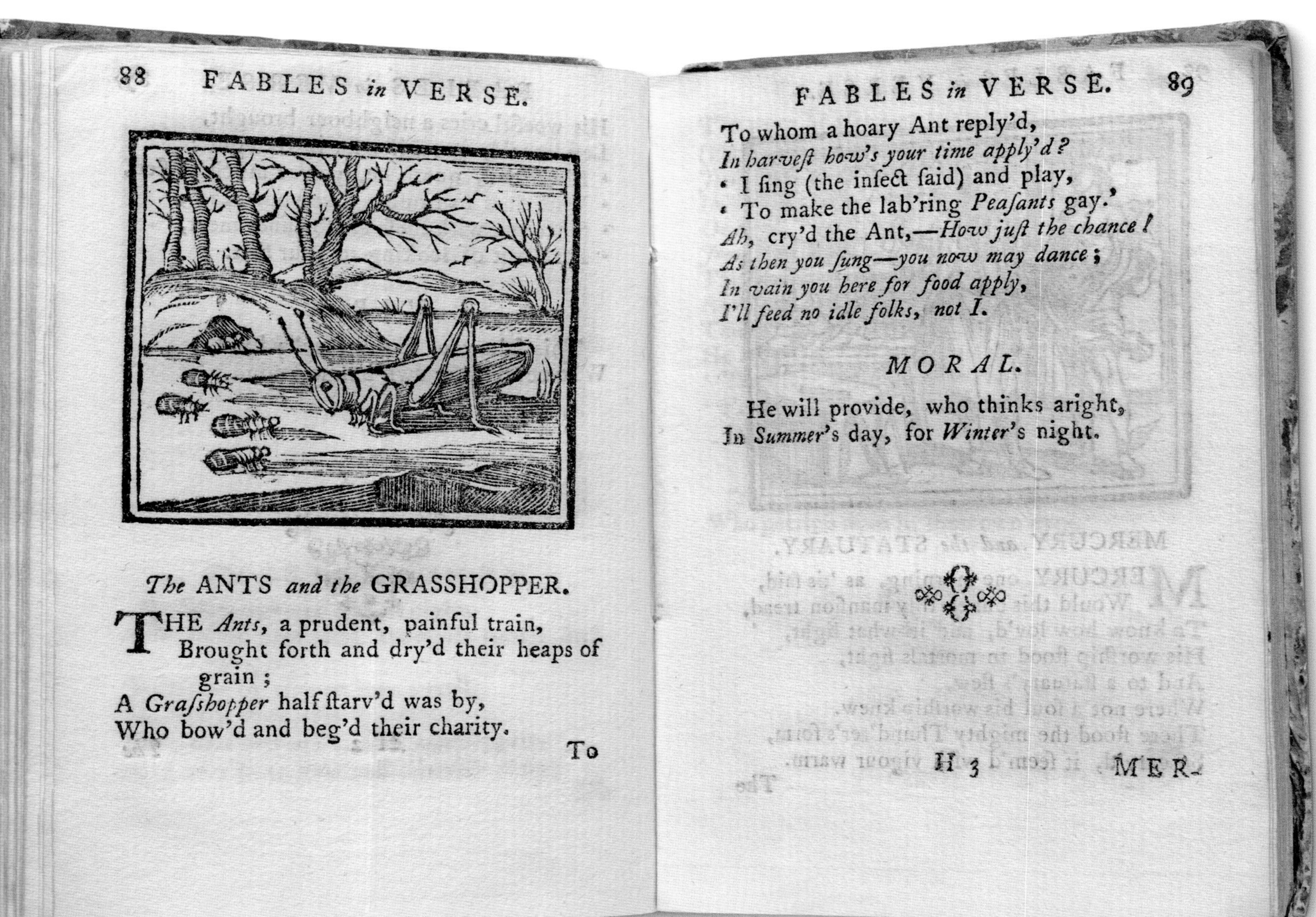

88 FABLES *in* VERSE.

The ANTS *and the* GRASSHOPPER.

THE *Ants*, a prudent, painful train,
Brought forth and dry'd their heaps of grain;
A *Graſshopper* half ſtarv'd was by,
Who bow'd and beg'd their charity.

To

FABLES *in* VERSE. 89

To whom a hoary Ant reply'd,
In harveſt how's your time apply'd?
• I ſing (the inſect ſaid) and play,
• To make the lab'ring *Peaſants* gay.'
Ah, cry'd the Ant,—*How juſt the chance!*
As then you ſung—you now may dance;
In vain you here for food apply,
I'll feed no idle folks, not I.

MORAL.

He will provide, who thinks aright,
In *Summer*'s day, for *Winter*'s night.

H 3 MER-

> Like those who dine well off the plainest dishes, he made use of humble incidents to teach great truths

APOLLONIUS OF TYANA, ON AESOP, 1ST CENTURY BCE

The Wealth of Nations

1776 ▪ PRINTED ▪ 28.3 × 22.5 cm (11 × 9 in) ▪ 1,097 PAGES ▪ UK

SCALE

ADAM SMITH

The publication in 1776 of *An Inquiry into the Nature and Causes of the Wealth of Nations*, also known simply as *The Wealth of Nations,* caused a sensation. In addition to being the first modern economic textbook, it had a revolutionary idea at its core: that the measure of any nation's wealth was not how much gold it held or land it possessed, but the product of the operation of unfettered free markets and free trade. Adam Smith argued that free markets weeded out the inefficient and simultaneously rewarded the enterprising. At the heart of this process was self-interest. By maximizing individual profits in a free market, the prosperity of the nation as a whole was increased.

The influence of Smith's work was huge. It effectively instigated the birth of the free-market economy. People had previously thought of trade as one person getting something at the expense of another, but Smith argued that both parties in a transaction could prosper. This concept forms the basis of modern economics and *The Wealth of Nations* became a classic text. Indeed, the ideas it outlines form the "Classical school" of economics.

ADAM **SMITH**

1723–1790

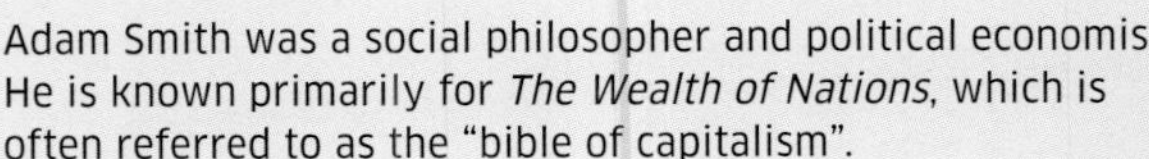

Adam Smith was a social philosopher and political economist. He is known primarily for *The Wealth of Nations*, which is often referred to as the "bible of capitalism".

Born in Scotland, Smith studied at Glasgow University and Oxford before he began teaching in Glasgow in 1751. In 1764, he became tutor to the 18-year-old Duke of Buccleuch. During a two-year Grand Tour of Europe with the duke, Smith met many of the continent's leading thinkers, chiefly in France. They included a group of economists, known as the physiocrats, who were concerned by the reckless expenditure of the French state. Smith was impressed by their proposals, but not by their dismissal of the potential of manufacturing and trade. *The Wealth of Nations* was Smith's magisterial response to what to him was this obvious shortcoming. A leading figure in the Scottish Enlightenment, he helped to make Edinburgh one of the most dynamic intellectual centres of Europe. Smith is widely considered to be the father of modern economics.

The timing of the publication of *The Wealth of Nations* in its two volumes was pertinent. Britain was poised on the brink of the Industrial Revolution, which would bring vast increases in trade and manufacturing. That Britain – and all subsequent capitalist societies – was able to prosper so dramatically, however, was very largely the result of the economic liberalism that Smith so compellingly advocated.

In detail

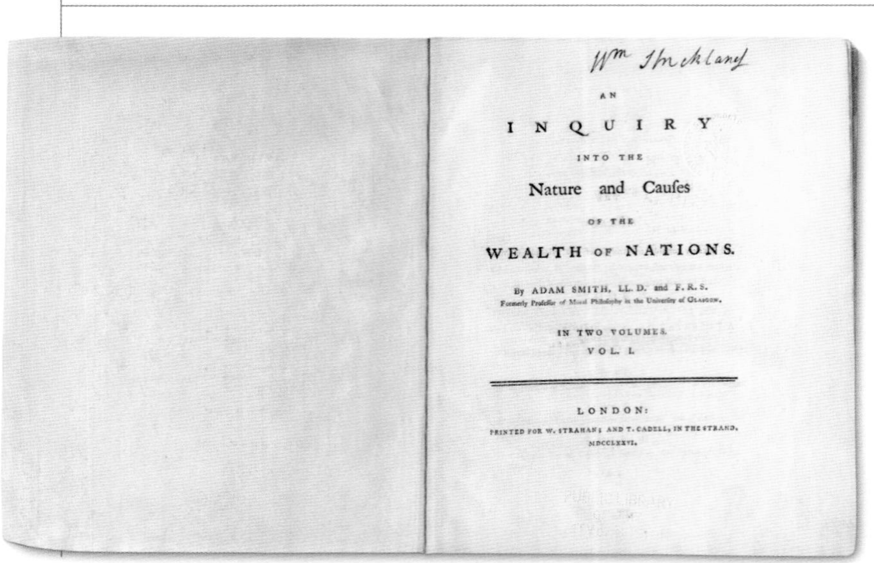

Wm Strickland

AN
INQUIRY
INTO THE
Nature and Causes
OF THE
WEALTH OF NATIONS.

By ADAM SMITH, LL.D. and F.R.S.
Formerly Professor of Moral Philosophy in the University of Glasgow.

IN TWO VOLUMES.
VOL. I.

LONDON:
PRINTED FOR W. STRAHAN; AND T. CADELL, IN THE STRAND.
MDCCLXXVI.

◄ **TITLE PAGE** This title page is from the London printing of the first edition, dated 1776. It lists Smith's credentials as a former professor of moral philosophy at Glasgow University in Scotland.

CONTENTS.

BOOK III.

Of the different Progreſs of Opulence in different Nations.

CHAP. I.
Of the natural Progreſs of Opulence – – Page 459

CHAP. II.
Of the Diſcouragement of Agriculture in the antient State of Europe after the Fall of the Roman Empire – 466

CHAP. III.
Of the Riſe and Progreſs of Cities and Towns, after the Fall of the Roman Empire – – – 480

CHAP. IV.
How the Commerce of the Towns contributed to the Improvement of the Country – – – 494

CONTENTS.

BOOK II.

Of the Nature, Accumulation, and Employment of Stock.

INTRODUCTION – – – – Page 317

CHAP. I.
Of the Diviſion of Stock – – – 330

CHAP. II.
Of Money conſidered as a particular Branch of the general Stock of the Society, or of the Expence of maintaining the National Capital – – – 341

CHAP. III.
Of the Accumulation of Capital, or of productive and unproductive Labour – – – 400

CHAP. IV.
Of Stock lent at Intereſt – – – 426

CHAP. V.
Of the different Employment of Capitals – – 437

▲ **EXTENDED CONTENTS** The first edition of the book was produced in two volumes of 510 pages and 587. These were subdivided into Books, which were split into Chapters, as shown on this contents page.

> The most important **substantive proposition in all of economics**
>
> **GEORGE STIGLER**, *US ECONOMIST*

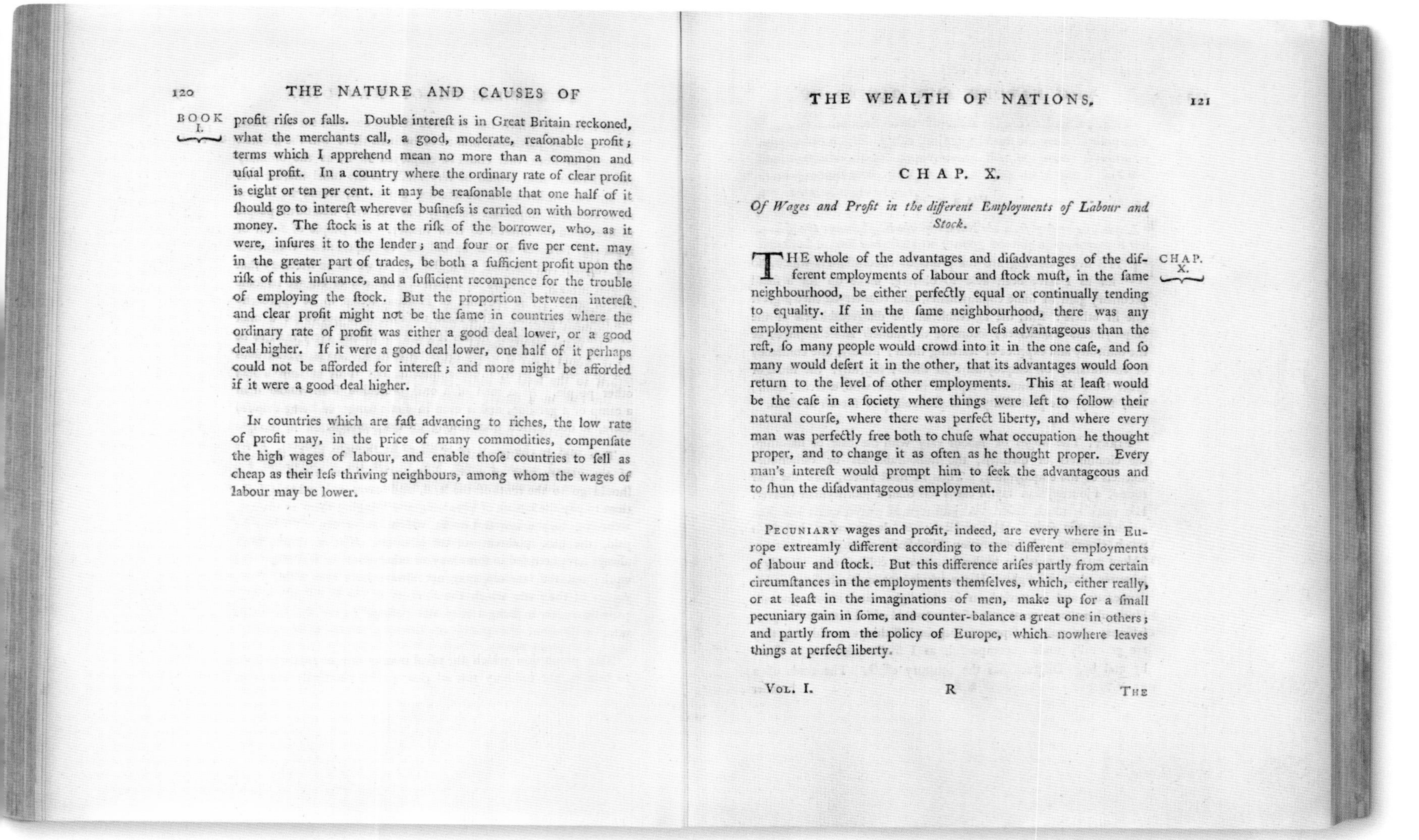

120 THE NATURE AND CAUSES OF

BOOK I. profit riſes or falls. Double intereſt is in Great Britain reckoned, what the merchants call, a good, moderate, reaſonable profit; terms which I apprehend mean no more than a common and uſual profit. In a country where the ordinary rate of clear profit is eight or ten per cent. it may be reaſonable that one half of it ſhould go to intereſt wherever buſineſs is carried on with borrowed money. The ſtock is at the riſk of the borrower, who, as it were, inſures it to the lender; and four or five per cent. may in the greater part of trades, be both a ſufficient profit upon the riſk of this inſurance, and a ſufficient recompence for the trouble of employing the ſtock. But the proportion between intereſt and clear profit might not be the ſame in countries where the ordinary rate of profit was either a good deal lower, or a good deal higher. If it were a good deal lower, one half of it perhaps could not be afforded for intereſt; and more might be afforded if it were a good deal higher.

IN countries which are faſt advancing to riches, the low rate of profit may, in the price of many commodities, compenſate the high wages of labour, and enable thoſe countries to ſell as cheap as their leſs thriving neighbours, among whom the wages of labour may be lower.

THE WEALTH OF NATIONS. 121

CHAP. X.

Of Wages and Profit in the different Employments of Labour and Stock.

THE whole of the advantages and diſadvantages of the different employments of labour and ſtock muſt, in the ſame neighbourhood, be either perfectly equal or continually tending to equality. If in the ſame neighbourhood, there was any employment either evidently more or leſs advantageous than the reſt, ſo many people would crowd into it in the one caſe, and ſo many would deſert it in the other, that its advantages would ſoon return to the level of other employments. This at leaſt would be the caſe in a ſociety where things were left to follow their natural courſe, where there was perfect liberty, and where every man was perfectly free both to chuſe what occupation he thought proper, and to change it as often as he thought proper. Every man's intereſt would prompt him to ſeek the advantageous and to ſhun the diſadvantageous employment. CHAP. X.

PECUNIARY wages and profit, indeed, are every where in Europe extreamly different according to the different employments of labour and ſtock. But this difference ariſes partly from certain circumſtances in the employments themſelves, which, either really, or at leaſt in the imaginations of men, make up for a ſmall pecuniary gain in ſome, and counter-balance a great one in others; and partly from the policy of Europe, which nowhere leaves things at perfect liberty.

VOL. I. R THE

▲ **CHAPTERS AND PARTS** Each Chapter of the Books was subdivided into smaller sections. For example, the right-hand page above shows Chapter 10, which begins with an introduction on the wages and profits available in different types of employment. The first section of the Chapter then focuses on the inequalities that arise from this.

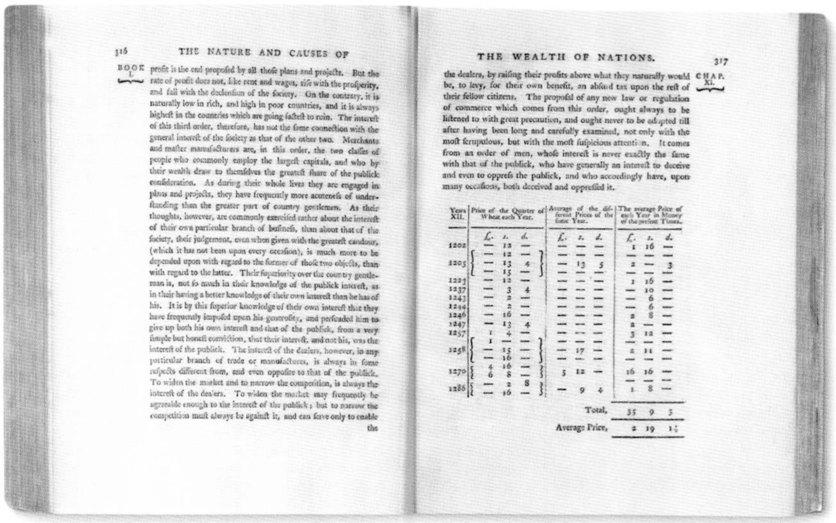

◄ **TABLES AND CHARTS** Smith's text is broken up in places by his inclusion of charts and calculations. These are used to clarify and demonstrate his arguments. The chart shown here compares annual prices of wheat.

Rights of Man

1791–92 ■ PRINTED ■ DIMENSIONS AND EXTENT UNKNOWN ■ UK

THOMAS PAINE

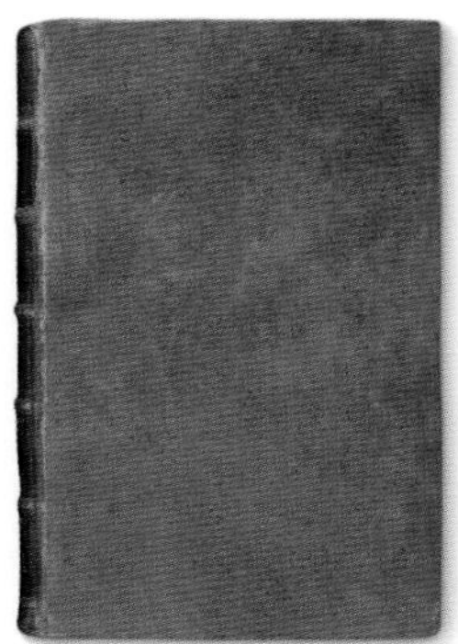

Two years after the outbreak of the French Revolution British-American political propagandist Thomas Paine wrote *Rights of Man*, a visionary two-part pamphlet whose publication caused a sensation. Paine posited the then radical view that governments have a responsibility to protect the natural and civil rights of their citizens, ensuring their freedom, security, and equal opportunity. And, that crucially, should a government fail to safeguard those rights, then the people would be justified in overthrowing it.

Rights of Man began as an historical account of the French Revolution, of which Paine was an avid supporter. But when Anglo-Irish statesman Edmund Burke denounced the uprising and defended the monarchy in a 1790 book, Paine hastily reworked his text. *Rights of Man* became an incendiary counter-argument to Burke's view. It lauded the Revolution's principles, railed against aristocratic privilege, and made a case for representative democratic republican government over hereditary monarchy. In 1792 came *Rights of Man Part II*, which proposed wide-ranging reforms. Paine called on England's government to introduce a system of social welfare to ease the economic hardship endured by the lower classes, and uphold their civil rights. His vision included free education, old-age pensions, and public works for the unemployed, all funded by a scaled income tax that would favour the poor.

Rights of Man was a publishing success, selling around 200,000 copies, and today it is regarded as a founding document of modern liberal democracy. But in its day it horrified the authorities. After *Part II* appeared, the work was banned. In December 1792, Paine – who had fled to France – was tried in absentia for advocating an end to monarchy in Britain, found guilty, and declared an outlaw.

THOMAS **PAINE**

1737–1809

From humble beginnings as a labourer in the shipyards of Norfolk, England, Thomas Paine rose to fame as writer whose visionary words shaped political events on both sides of the Atlantic.

Born into a working-class family, Paine had a basic formal education. At 13, he began working with his father, making stays: ropes used to stabilize the masts of sailing ships. From 1756 he tried several other occupations, with little success. In 1772 he was fired from his job as an exise tax collector after printing a political pamphlet arguing for better pay and conditions for workers.

In 1774 Paine met the great American statesman Benjamin Franklin, who suggested he begin a new life across the Atlantic. Paine landed in America just as the 13 colonies were debating whether to declare independence from Britain. He became assistant editor of Philadelphia's *Pennsylvania Magazine*, and began writing articles expressing his sense of injustice at the world. In 1776 he published *Common Sense* (see p.211), a pamphlet containing an impassioned but rational argument in favour of American independence. It sold 500,000 copies and helped garner support for a revolt from British rule. In 1787 Paine returned to England, where he wrote *Rights of Man*. His next work, *The Age of Reason* (1794) – an attack on organized religion, which he wrote in France – alienated many of his admirers. He spent his final years in the US, living in poverty.

RIGHTS OF MAN:

BEING AN

ANSWER TO MR. BURKE's ATTACK

ON THE

FRENCH REVOLUTION.

BY

THOMAS PAINE,

SECRETARY FOR FOREIGN AFFAIRS TO CONGRESS IN THE AMERICAN WAR, AND AUTHOR OF THE WORK INTITLED *COMMON SENSE.*

LONDON:

PRINTED FOR J. JOHNSON, ST PAUL's CHURCH-YARD.

MDCCXCI.

[110]

of the Rights of Man, as the baſis on which the new conſtitution was to be built, and which is here ſubjoined.

DECLARATION OF THE RIGHTS OF MAN AND OF CITIZENS,

BY THE NATIONAL ASSEMBLY OF FRANCE.

" The Repreſentatives of the people of FRANCE formed into a National Aſſembly, conſidering that ignorance, neglect, or contempt of human rights, are the ſole cauſes of public misfortunes and corruptions of government, have reſolved to ſet forth, in a ſolemn declaration, theſe natural, impreſcriptible, and unalienable rights: that this declaration being conſtantly preſent to the minds of the members of the body ſocial, they may be ever kept attentive to their rights and their duties: that the acts of the legiſlative and executive powers of government, being capable of being every moment compared with the end of political inſtitutions, may be more reſpected: and alſo, that the future claims of the citizens, being directed by ſimple and inconteſtible principles, may always tend to the maintenance of the conſtitution, and the general happineſs.

" For theſe reaſons, the NATIONAL ASSEMBLY doth recognize and declare, in the preſence of the Supreme Being, and with the hope of his bleſſing and favour, the following *ſacred* rights of men and of citizens:

' I. *Men*

[111]

' I. *Men are born and always continue free, and ' equal in reſpect of their rights. Civil diſtinctions, ' therefore, can be founded only on public utility.*

' II. *The end of all political aſſociations is the preſervation of the natural and impreſcriptible rights ' of man; and theſe rights are liberty, property, ' ſecurity, and reſiſtance of oppreſſion.*

' III. *The nation is eſſentially the ſource of all ſovereignty; nor can any* INDIVIDUAL, *or* ANY ' BODY OF MEN, *be entitled to any authority which ' is not expreſsly derived from it.*

' IV. Political Liberty conſiſts in the power of ' doing whatever does not injure another. The ' exerciſe of the natural rights of every man, has ' no other limits than thoſe which are neceſſary ' to ſecure to every *other* man the free exerciſe of ' the ſame rights; and theſe limits are determinable ' only by the law.

' V. The law ought to prohibit only actions ' hurtful to ſociety. What is not prohibited by ' the law, ſhould not be hindered; nor ſhould any ' one be compelled to that which the law does ' not require.

' VI. The law is an expreſſion of the will of ' the community. All citizens have a right to ' concur, either perſonally, or by their repreſentatives, in its formation. It ſhould be the ſame to ' all, whether it protects or puniſhes; and *all ' being equal in its ſight, are equally eligible to all ' honours, places, and employments, according to ' their different abilities, without any other diſtinction than that created by their virtues and talents.*

P 2 ' VII. No

▲ ***RIGHTS OF MAN PART I*** Paine developed an engagingly direct writing style that made his ideas accessible to people from all walks of life. The two parts of *Rights of Man* focused solely on the rights of men as declared above; it was up to his contemporary Mary Wollstonecraft (see p.212) to advocate equal rights for women in her *A Vindication of the Rights of Women* (1792).

◄ **COURTING CONTROVERSY** Paine clarifies his motivation for writing *Rights of Man* on the title page: the sub-deck plainly states, the work stands as a rebuke to those who criticized the French Revolution. In particular, his target was a conservative pamphlet *Reflections on the Revolution in France* written by the liberal Anglo-Irish politician Edmund Burke.

IN CONTEXT

The French Revolution (1787–99) shook the countries of Europe, with their long tradition of absolute monarchy and feudal privileges for the nobility and clergy. In particular, the 1792 abolition of royalty in France caused ructions in Britain, sparking intense debate among political commentators and dividing public opinion. Those who supported the Revolution argued for democratic change, while those against it countered that Britain's constitution protected citizens from disorder and the threat of military oppression.

One of the cornerstones of the Revolution was the Declaration of the Rights of Man and of the Citizen, a charter of 17 articles outlining the principles of human liberty. The most important of these was article 1, which stated that all men are born equal and free and entitled to such basic rights as holding private property and resisting oppression. In 1789 the declaration was adopted as the basis of the constitution of the new French Republic, although women of the time had no access to most of the rights it listed.

► **This engraving from 1792** portrays the events of the Revolution from a royalist perspective: mocking the movement's principles of liberty by showing commoners attacking the aristocracy.

Songs of Innocence and of Experience

1794 ▪ ENGRAVED AND HAND-PRINTED ▪ 18 × 12.4 cm (7 × 5 in) ▪ 54 PLATES ▪ UK

SCALE

WILLIAM BLAKE

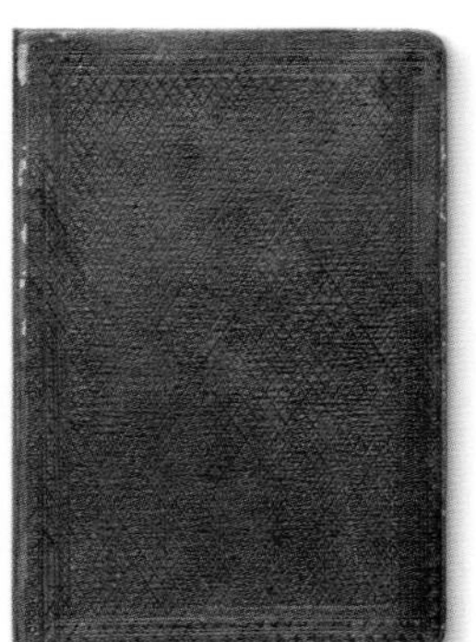

This richly illustrated collection of poems, William Blake's most famous work, is lauded for both its literary and artistic value. Originally published as two separate collections, Blake combined and published them as a set in 1794, aiming to juxtapose the innocence of childhood with the corruption that comes with adulthood. In his poems Blake saw an intimate link between text and illustration, believing that each added a layer of meaning to the other to create an integrated whole. To produce the collection he developed a new printing technique that combined text and image onto a single etching plate (see p.168). He engraved, hand-printed, and coloured every copy of the collection himself, making changes to the colour, text, or sequence of the poems that rendered each copy unique. Blake's process was laborious and costly, and only a limited number of copies were circulated during his lifetime. These were initially gifted to family and friends, before Blake decided to sell copies commercially.

The small, colourful format, evocative of a children's book, belied the sophistication of the work – the poems were critical and subversive, questioning society and the role of the Church. On publication they were poorly received and it was not until the early 20th century that Blake's achievement was recognized.

WILLIAM **BLAKE**

1757–1827

Painter and poet William Blake is considered one of Britain's foremost poets of the Romantic era, although his works went largely unrecognized until after his death.

Blake's early artistic skills led to an apprenticeship with a printmaker at age 12, and he qualified as an engraver aged 21. In 1779 he enrolled at the Royal Academy in London, where he developed his own distinctive style. He married Catherine Boucher in 1782, and published his first set of poems the following year. Although he was a committed Christian, Blake was strongly opposed to institutionalized religion and the controlling influence of the Church on society.

Blake claimed to have visions that inspired his work, and he considered the realm of the imagination to be as real and valid as the physical world. In this he was influenced by the teachings of the Swedish philosopher and mystic, Emanuel Swedenborg (1688–1772). Much of Blake's work was imbued by his view of the Church and his political radicalism, but it failed to find a willing audience at the time. Depressed by his lack of professional success, Blake retreated from society, although he continued working until the very end of his life. He died in 1827, leaving an illustrated manuscript of the *Book of Genesis* unfinished.

➤ **ARTISTIC DUALITY** The title page reflects the duality that runs through the work, summed up in the sub-title "Shewing the Two Contrary States of the Human Soul". Below it Blake depicts Adam and Eve cast out of Eden against a background of flames – the loss of innocence. Opposite, a pastoral scene shows a piper looking up at a naked boy flying freely above him.

42

The Tyger

Tyger Tyger, burning bright,
In the forests of the night:
What immortal hand or eye,
Could frame thy fearful symmetry?

In what distant deeps or skies
Burnt the fire of thine eyes!
On what wings dare he aspire?
What the hand, dare sieze the fire?

And what shoulder, & what art,
Could twist the sinews of thy heart?
And when thy heart began to beat,
What dread hand? & what dread feet?

What the hammer? what the chain,
In what furnace was thy brain?
What the anvil? what dread grasp,
Dare its deadly terrors clasp!

When the stars threw down their spears
And water'd heaven with their tears:
Did he smile his work to see?
Did he who made the Lamb make thee

Tyger Tyger burning bright
In the forests of the night:
What immortal hand or eye,
Dare frame thy fearful symmetry?

◄ **DARK EXPERIENCE** The dark artwork mirrors the hidden malevolence of "The Tyger", in this, perhaps the best-loved, poem from *Songs of Experience*. In the poem, Blake poses a series of questions that marvel at the subject's majesty. Few readers would have seen a real tiger but knew that it symbolized power and strength. The clue to the poet's intention comes in the last lines. Could a God who made the meek lamb also create the fierce tiger?

In detail

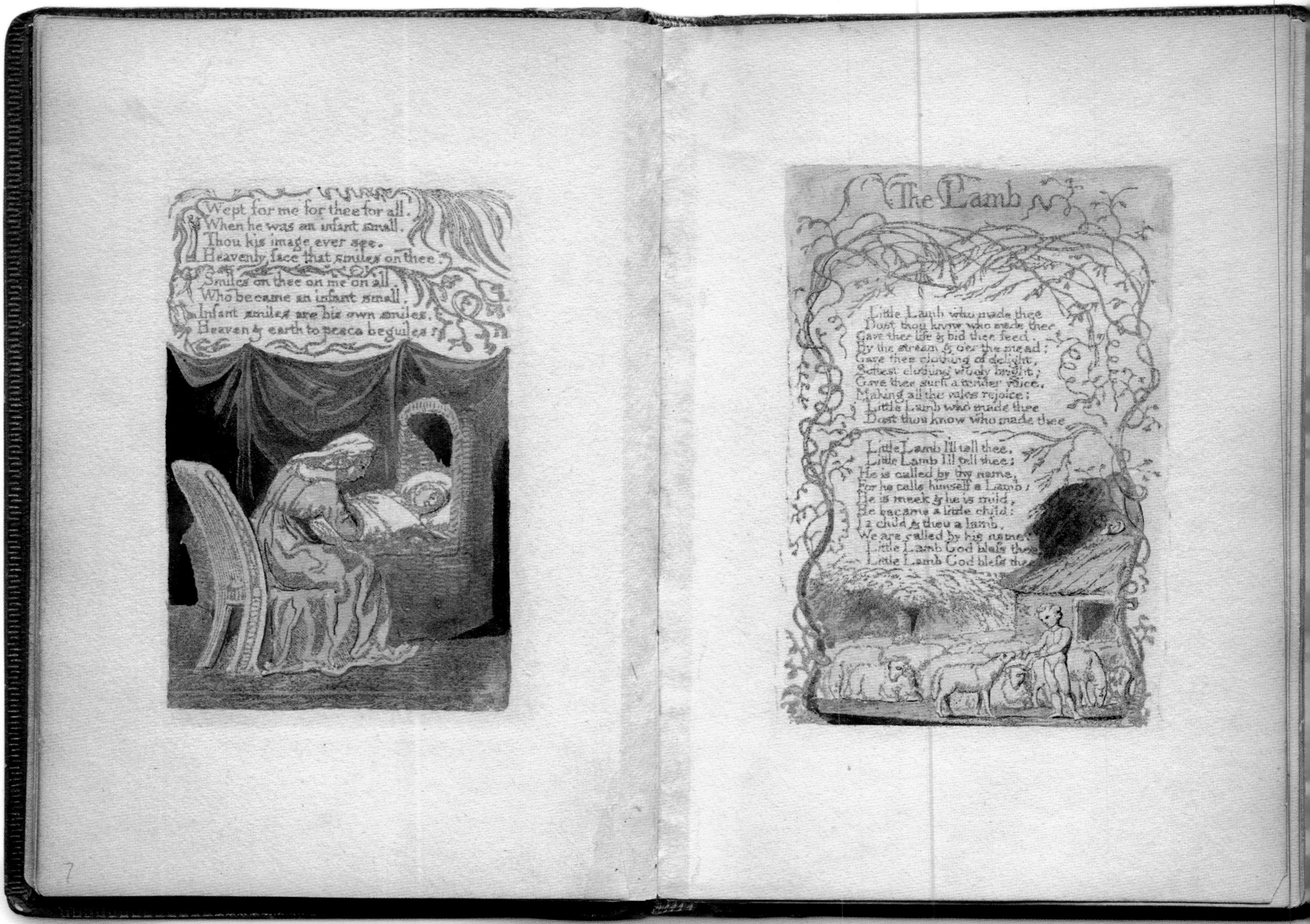

ON TECHNIQUE

From the 16th to the early 19th centuries illustrated books were printed by two presses. The first printed the text using raised lead plates, the second added the etchings in spaces left in and around the text. Blake's innovation was to print his pages in a single process. Writing and illustrating in reverse, he added his text and illustrations to copper printing plates using a special varnish, known as "stop-out" varnish. When the plates were then treated with acid, the varnish prevented the areas covered from being dissolved, leaving them raised. Ink could then be carefully applied to the plate in fine layers, before paper was rolled across the plate on a traditional rolling press.

▲ **In the press** shown here, one worker is preparing the print, another inks a copper plate, while a boy turns the handle on the rolling press.

▲ **TRANQUIL BEAUTY** Taken from *Songs of Innocence*, both text and illustrations for "A Cradle Song" and "The Lamb" exude gentleness. The first is a lullaby comparing a sleeping child to Jesus, and is illustrated with a mother gazing at her baby in its cot. In the second the child is described as a pure and gentle lamb, referring to Jesus, Lamb of God. The author asks the child if he knows who made him, before providing the answer: God. The ochre colours are bright and luminous to suggest the tranquil surroundings in which the child lives in the countryside.

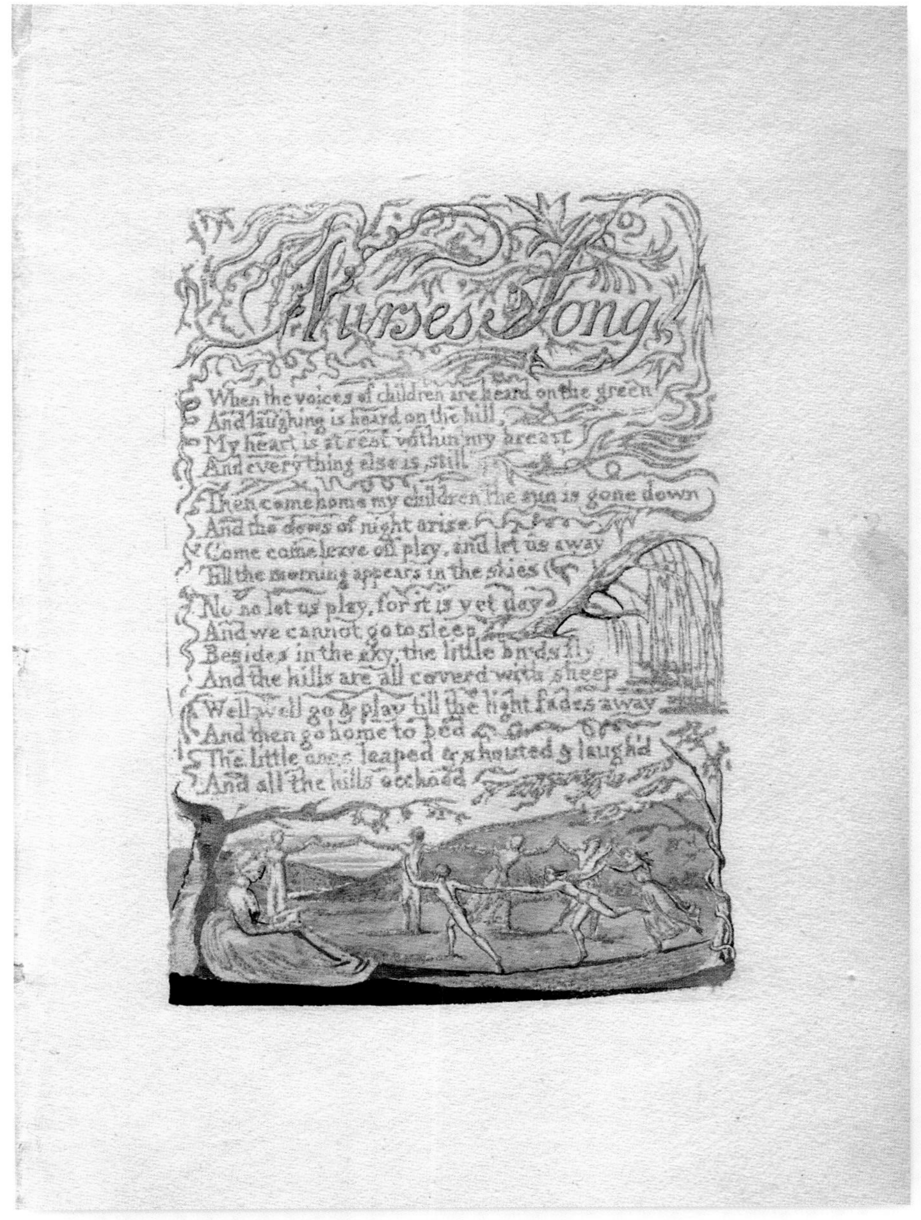

◄ **CONTRASTING PAIRS** Some of the poems in *Songs of Innocence* have counterparts in poems of the same name in *Experience*. For example, the "Nurse's Song" in *Innocence* (see left) joyfully tells children to "go and play till the light fades away", while the "Nurse's Song" in *Experience* (below) commands them to come home. The images reflect this, as children skipping in a ring contrast with a nurse combing a sulky boy's hair.

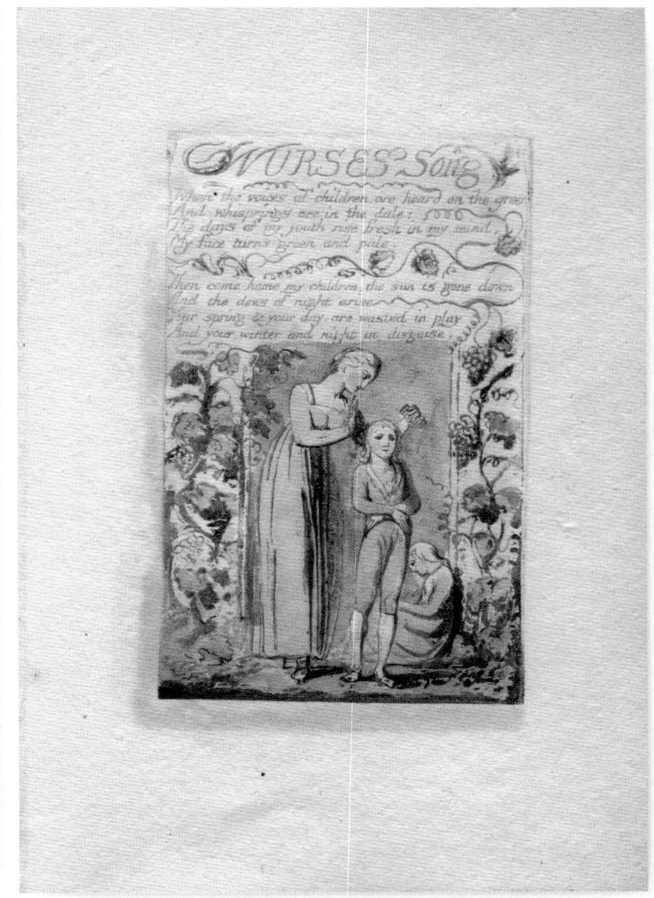

◄ **SCENE-SETTING FRONTISPIECE** In both collections, the frontispieces feature a pastural scene, complete with a flock of sheep, a male figure, and a winged cherub. Here, in the frontispiece for the *Experience* portion of the book, the two figures are holding hands, which represents the constraint of childhood freedoms, or perhaps childhood innocence as a burden to be endured.

► **INTIMATE LINK** In *Innocence* the text of the poem "Infant Joy" is closely enveloped by an illustration of a twining plant, suggesting the natural beauty of the subject – the bond between mother and child. The poem itself reads as a dialogue between a mother and her new baby, shown nestled within a flower, who announces him- or herself as happy: "Joy is my name".

▲ **GOD'S BLESSING** An angel is shown attending the mother and child in "Infant Joy", and all three figures are bathed in a golden glow, suggesting that the maternal bond is blessed by God.

Birds of America

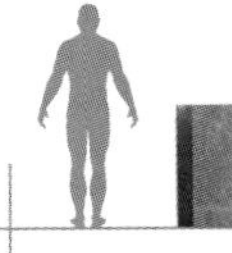

1827–38 ▪ PRINTED ▪ 99 × 66 cm (39 × 26 in) ▪ 435 LIFE-SIZE PRINTS ISSUED IN 87 PARTS ▪ USA

JOHN JAMES AUDUBON

John James Audubon's 19th century masterpiece is a hand-drawn, visual catalogue of the birds of North America, first published as a series of prints between 1827 and 1838. The book features 435 life-size prints of 497 bird species, each depicted in its natural habitat with exquisite detail and accuracy. Reaching approximately 1 m (3 ft) in height and comprising four separate volumes, *Birds of America* is the largest book ever produced. The original edition was printed using a complex combination of pastel and watercolour illustrations reproduced from hand-engraved plates. At the time of publication wildlife books typically had blank backgrounds, but Audubon included a detailed backdrop to each picture, giving the reader an idea of the habitats of the birds featured.

The book's great artistic value is equalled by its contribution to cultural and ornithological history. It identifies birds that were not known to inhabit America, and also provides a vital historical record since six of the birds featured are now thought to be extinct. In compiling his book Audubon discovered 25 new species of bird and 12 new subspecies. *Birds of America* took nearly 12 years to complete, and only 120 complete sets of the illustrations still exist.

▼ **THE BIGGEST BOOK** The original edition of *Birds of America* was printed on "double elephant" folios, sheets of handmade paper measuring 99 x 66 cm (39 x 26 in). The Carolina parrot, shown here feeding on a cockle-bur plant, is one of six species of bird drawn by Audubon that is now extinct.

> As I grew up I was **fervently desirous** of becoming **acquainted** with **Nature**
>
> **JOHN JAMES AUDUBON**

▼ **LIFE-SIZE DRAWINGS** Audubon's patrons received a tin box each month with hand-coloured engravings and etchings, including images of large, medium, and small birds. The great white heron, pictured here, is the largest species of heron and Audubon had to draw it with a bent neck in order to enable the life-size drawing.

In detail

▼ **SETTING A SCENE** All the birds shown in the book were killed; Audubon then examined the formation of feathers and measured the body and wingspan of the dead specimen. Before he began drawing, the birds were posed by pinning them to a wooden frame with wires – as shown with these gyrfalcons. This allowed Audubon to continue his precise and painstaking work for several days.

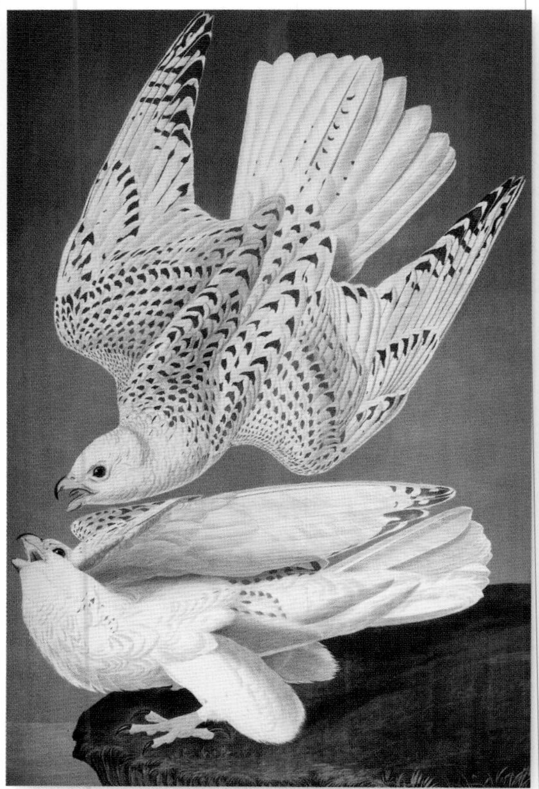

▲ **VIBRANT ILLUSTRATIONS** This print captures the elegance and majesty of the trumpeter swan, which Audubon praised in his accompanying text. The prints themselves were produced by London-based engraver Robert Havell Jr, and his father. Each was placed on a production line, colourists then applied different tints to specific parts of each print, using a variety of techniques.

◄ **PRINTING EFFECTS** The white lines and highlights on the swan's feathers emphasize the form of its wings, while areas of shadow add a three-dimensional effect. Added aquatint gives graded levels of greenish tone to the water, hinting at its transparency as well as providing a sense of undulating movement.

JOHN JAMES **AUDUBON**

1785–1851

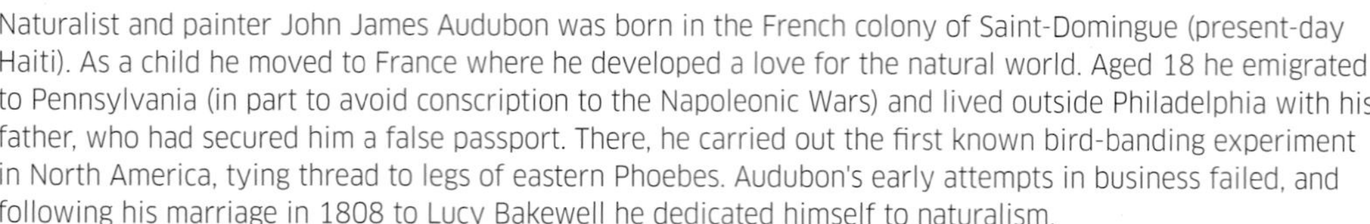

John James Audubon was an American naturalist, ornithologist, and artist. He is best known for his detailed paintings and illustrations of North American birds. This extensive and ambitious work, *Birds of America* was to occupy him for most of his life.

Naturalist and painter John James Audubon was born in the French colony of Saint-Domingue (present-day Haiti). As a child he moved to France where he developed a love for the natural world. Aged 18 he emigrated to Pennsylvania (in part to avoid conscription to the Napoleonic Wars) and lived outside Philadelphia with his father, who had secured him a false passport. There, he carried out the first known bird-banding experiment in North America, tying thread to legs of eastern Phoebes. Audubon's early attempts in business failed, and following his marriage in 1808 to Lucy Bakewell he dedicated himself to naturalism.

In 1820 Audubon embarked on his life's project: to draw all the birds of North America. He set off down the Mississippi with a gun and his drawing materials, travelling for months at a time in search of specimens, which he shot before drawing the birds in precise detail. The epic scale and complexity of the project made financing it difficult and in 1826, having failed to find sufficient funds in America, Audubon sailed to England to secure patronage for his half-finished book. He eventually found wealthy patrons from America, Great Britain, and France to finance his vastly ambitious *Birds of America* (these patrons included King George IV and President Andrew Jackson). Returning to America, Audubon moved with his family to New York in 1841, where he died on 27 January 1851.

▲ **NATURAL HABITATS** In an era before photography, Audubon's coloured prints, complete with their detailed backgrounds, gave the reader a rare and intimate view of birds in their own environments, such as the bald eagle depicted here with a fish carcass. Audubon employed up to 150 artists to paint these backgrounds; his assistant, Joseph Mason, painted 50 of them.

◄ **FITTING THE FRAME**
Drawing birds life-sized was problematic for species such as the American flamingo, as the bird reaches 1.5 m (5 ft) in height. In order to fit the flamingo within the frame of the page, Audubon shows the bird with its neck bent over and legs at an angle.

▼ **BACKGROUND DETAIL**
The flamingos perching in the background, including this bird in its characteristic one-legged pose with an outstretched neck, add a dramatic sense of movement to the engraving. Audubon painted the flamingos in a large group, indicating that they are social birds.

Procedure for Writing Words, Music and Plainsong in Dots

1829 ▪ EMBOSSED ON PAPER ▪ 28.5 × 22 cm (11 × 9 in) ▪ 32 PAGES ▪ FRANCE

SCALE

LOUIS BRAILLE

At the age of just 20, Louis Braille presented his *Procedure for Writing Words, Music and Plainsong in Dots*, and unveiled a means of reading and writing that would transform the lives of visually impaired people, like himself. Educated in Paris, he was taught to read (but not write) using Valentin Haüy's system of embossed lettering. In 1821 Braille became aware of Captain Charles Barbier's "night reading" code. A French Army officer, Barbier had invented a system in 1808 that allowed soldiers to communicate silently on the battlefield using a series of signals that could be "read" with fingertips. Braille was inspired to develop his own simplified version that would be easy to learn, and could also enable writing. He refined Barbier's system and invented his own code of "cells" or letters using a system of six raised "dots", so that each cell could be "read" with a fingertip. He grouped them in nine "decades", or characters, including letters, numbers, and punctuation. Braille published his work in 1829, with additional symbols for both mathematics and music. The book was printed with the alphabet embossed on both sides of each page, using a technique that involved wooden blocks being pressed into wet paper. The book introduced the braille system to the world, bringing literacy to generations of visually impaired people.

LOUIS **BRAILLE**

1809–1852

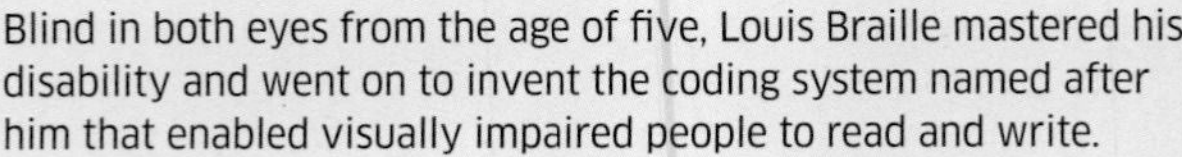

Blind in both eyes from the age of five, Louis Braille mastered his disability and went on to invent the coding system named after him that enabled visually impaired people to read and write.

Born in a small town outside Paris, Braille was educated at the local school until the age of 10 when he won a scholarship to the Royal Institution for Blind Youth, Paris. He learned to read using a form of embossed lettering, devised by the school's founder, Valentin Haüy. At the age of 19 Braille was appointed a teacher and musician at the institute. He died of consumption at the age of only 43, before his system achieved recognition, and is buried in the Pantheon in Paris. Today, Braille is a French national hero.

In detail

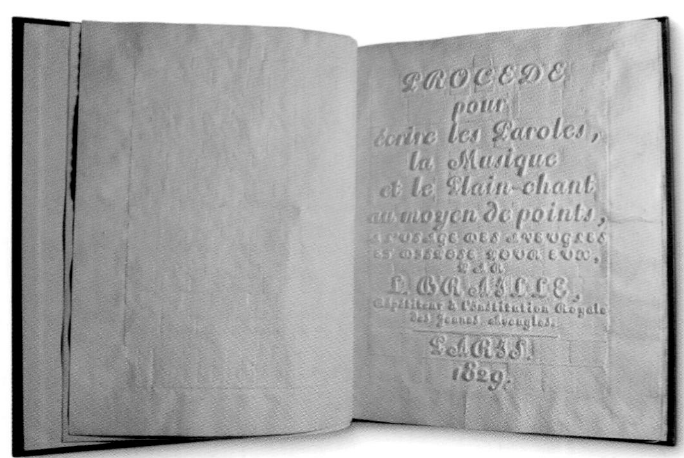

▲ **FIRST EDITION** The book had to be printed using Haüy's system of embossed letters to translate Braille's new "dot" system. The full French title, *Procédé pour Écrire les Paroles, la Musique et le Plain-chant au moyen de points*, is shown here using Haüy's letters.

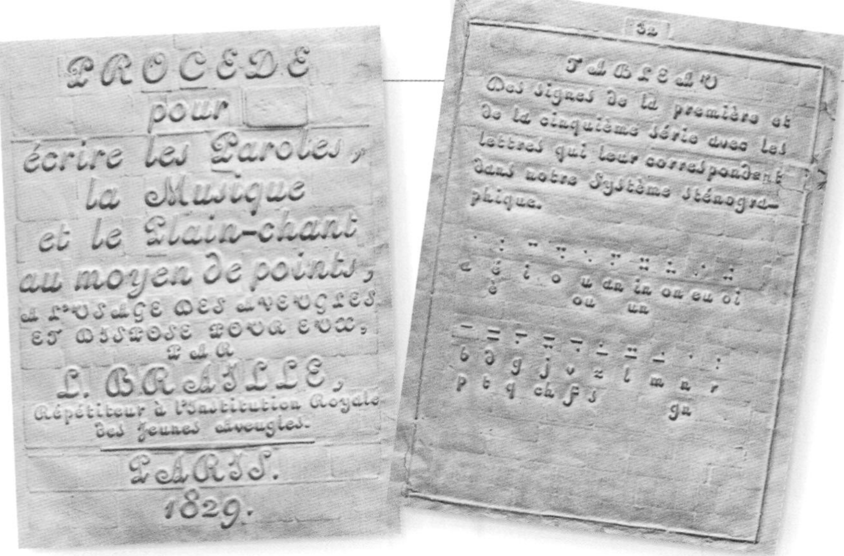

▲ **FIRST AND LAST PAGES** The title page (left) clearly shows the raised letters in the printing. On the last page of the book (right), Braille gives a table, or key, to the letters and the corresponding dots and dashes used in his new system. The dashes were dropped from the second edition printed in 1837.

> We (the blind) must be treated as **equals,** and **communication** is the **way** we can bring this about

LOUIS BRAILLE

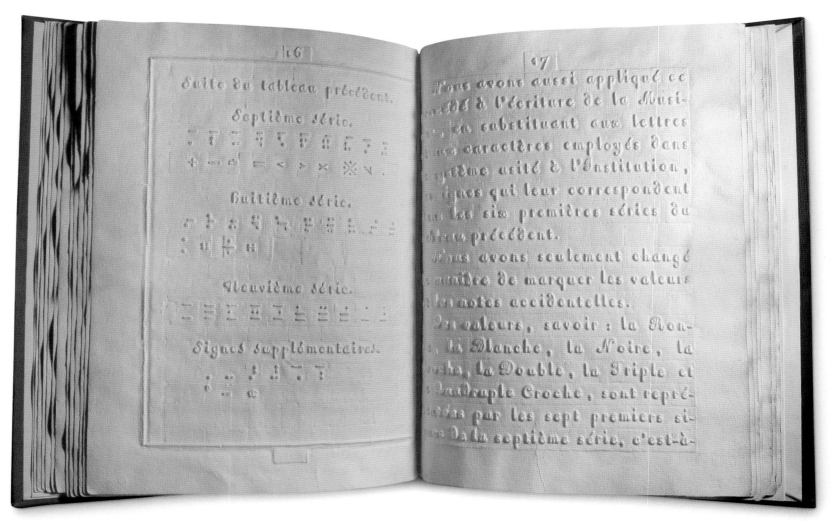

▲ **BRAILLE'S CHARACTERS EXPLAINED** The page above (numbered 16) presents the dot codes for Braille's seventh, eighth, and ninth decades, which relate to mathematics and music. On the opposite page Braille explains how they are used.

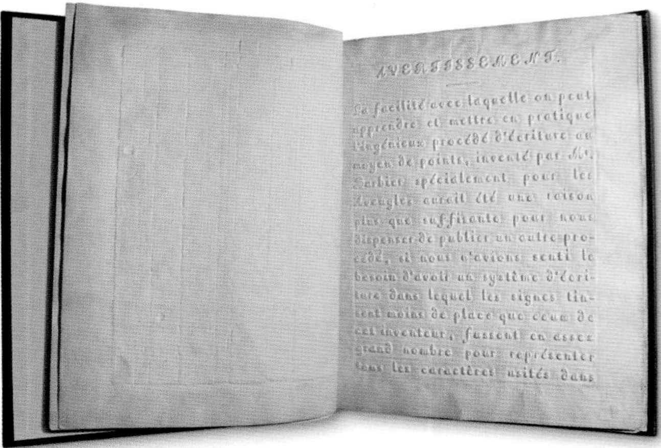

AVERTISSEMENT.

La facilité avec laquelle on peut apprendre et mettre en pratique l'ingénieux procédé d'écriture au moyen de points, inventé par M. Barbier spécialement pour les Aveugles aurait été une raison plus que suffisante pour nous dispenser de publier un autre procédé, si nous n'avions senti le besoin d'avoir un système d'écriture dans lequel les signes tinssent moins de place que ceux de cet inventeur, fussent en assez grand nombre pour représenter tous les caractères usités dans

▲ **CREDIT TO CAPTAIN BARBIER** In this preface to *Procédé pour Écrire*, Braille states that he developed his system from Barbier's work, but Barbier's 20 signs did not suffice for writing every word in the French language. Only six copies of this first edition have survived.

IN **CONTEXT**

In 1854, two years after Braille's death, France adopted his system of reading and writing for the visually impaired. In 1878 the World Congress for the Blind adopted braille as their official means of communication around the globe. The system has proved remarkably adaptable, with versions developed for Slavic languages, such as Russian and Polish, as well as the major Asian languages. Its simplicity also made the large-scale production of braille typewriters practical. However, recent developments in audio books and digital technology has resulted in a decline in its use.

▲ **Printers began to develop** braille presses in the 19th century. This one dates from the 1920s.

Baedeker guidebooks

FROM 1830s ▪ PRINTED ▪ EARLY EDITIONS 16 × 11.5 cm (6 × 4½ in) ▪ VARYING NUMBER OF PAGES ▪ GERMANY

SCALE

KARL BAEDEKER

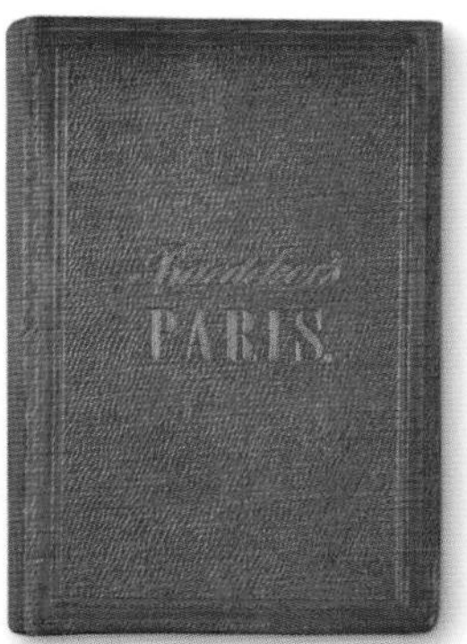

In its heyday, from the 1840s until 1914, the German publishing company Baedeker produced the world's most popular travel guidebooks – a genre it did not invent, but wholly transformed.

In 1835, while revising an 1828 tourist guide to the Rhine valley acquired from another publisher, Founder Karl Baedeker created the practical, user-friendly format for which the Baedeker guides became renowned. He added to the existing guide's coverage of the area's history and attractions, an innovative feature: advice on ways to get around and where to stay. The target reader of this book, and of the Baedeker guides that developed out of it, was a new kind of tourist: one who wanted to travel independently, rather than hire a tour guide.

From 1839, the Baedeker guidebook series grew rapidly; before his death in 1859, Karl personally produced a title for every major destination in Europe. Under the ownership of his three sons, the list expanded further, but the brand's hallmarks were maintained: scrupulously researched text, detailed listings, state-of-the art maps and plans, and a "star" system for rating sights, hotels, and restaurants. The Baedeker guides' success was driven by the advent of mass travel in late 19th-century Europe; for the newly wealthy middle-class, a trip overseas had become affordable and accessible due to the new railways and steamships. But the guides played a role in encouraging this tourism boom too, particularly after French and English editions were produced. By 1870, a Baedeker, with its distinctive red cover, had become synonym for "guidebook".

KARL **BAEDEKER**

1801–1859

Karl Baedeker was a German publisher and bookseller who, through his celebrated series of guidebooks, established the template for the modern travel guide.

Born into a family of booksellers and printers in Essen, Germany (then part of Prussia) Baedeker was the eldest of 10 children. He studied in Heidelberg in 1817 and then worked for various booksellers, before starting his own bookselling and publishing business in Koblenz in 1827. Having spotted the emerging market for authoritative travel guidebooks, he exploited it relentlessly. He insisted that Baedeker guides contained accurate information – much of which he researched himself – and also saw the importance of regularly updating existing titles. The last two decades of Baedeker's life were spent tirelessly writing, revising, and updating his guides, and travelling extensively. He died aged 58, and his sons, Ernst, Karl, and Fritz successively took over the business, and increased the Baedeker series range: by 1914 it covered much of the globe.

In detail

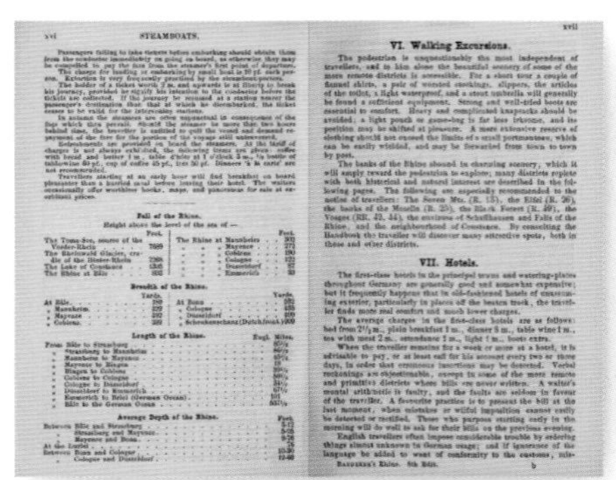
STEAMBOATS.

VI. Walking Excursions.

VII. Hotels.

▲ **METICULOUS DETAIL** The books held lots of information. This copy of *The Rhine from Rotterdam to Constance* (1882) shows a table with the river's fall, breadth, length, and depth.

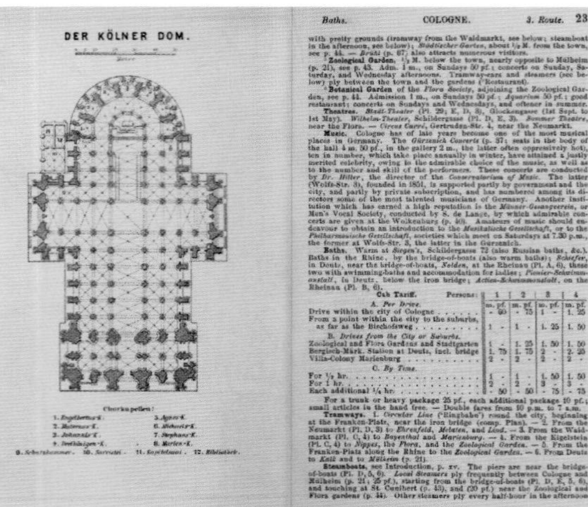
DER KÖLNER DOM.

COLOGNE. 3. Route. 23

▲ **FLOORPLANS OF KEY SIGHTS** The guidebooks were renowned for the breadth of their historical research: this plan is of Cologne cathedral, a sight which Baedeker remarks "justly excites the admiration of every beholder".

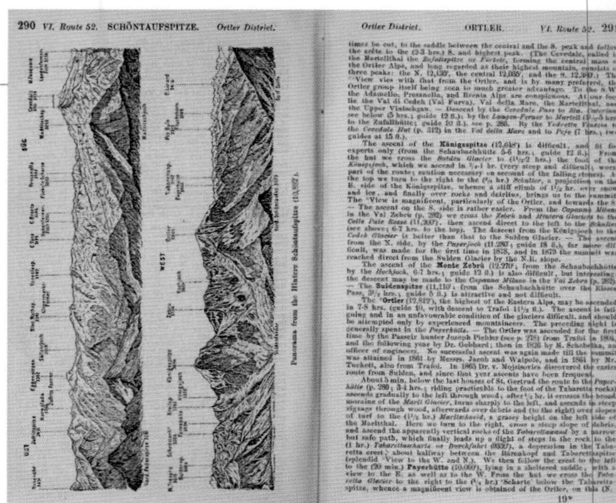
290 VI. Route 52. SCHÖNTAUFSPITZE. Ortler District.

Ortler District. ORTLER. VI. Route 52. 291

▲ **PANORAMA** Accurate and technically accomplished hand-drawn views, such as this one of the Eastern Alps, were a mainstay of the earlier guides produced in the era before photographic reproduction.

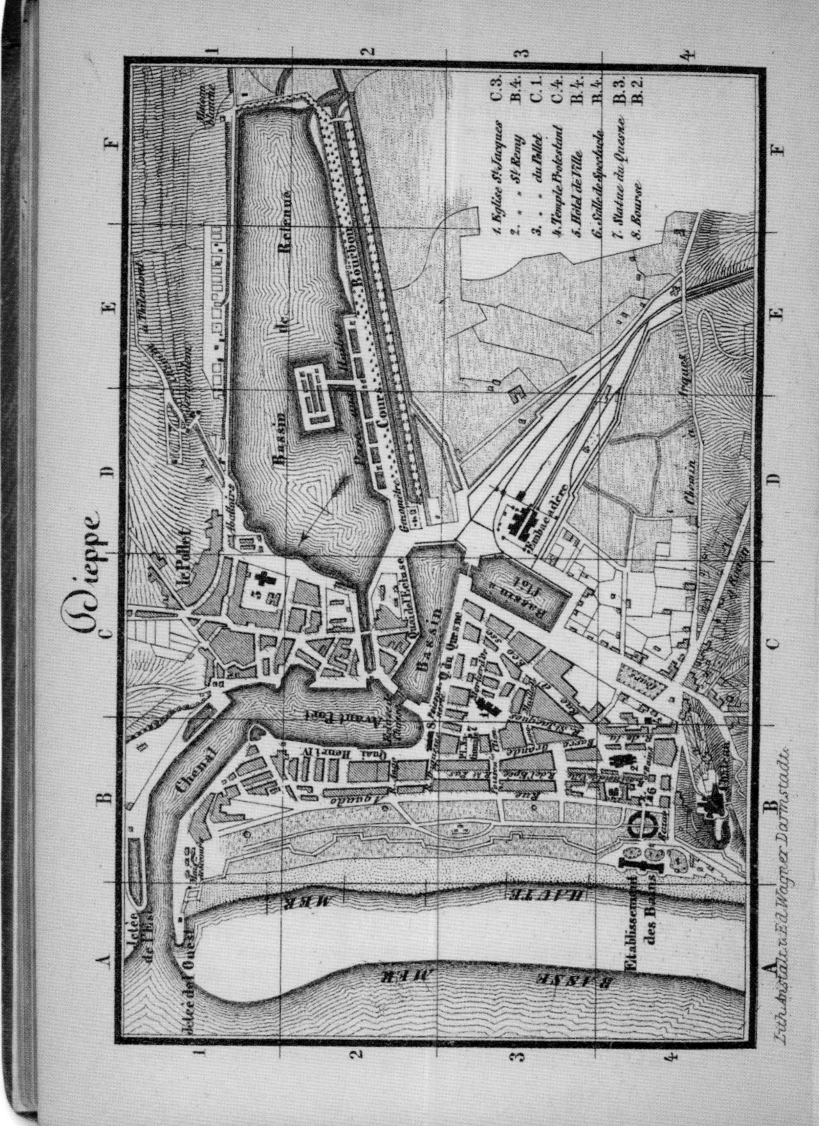

to Paris. DIEPPE. *41. Route.* 225

English fleet, then returning from an unsuccessful attack on Brest; an unequal contest which resulted in the total destruction of the town. The view from the summit, and especially from the lofty bridge, is very extensive, but beyond this the castle possesses nothing to attract visitors.

The church of **St. Jacques** (the patron saint of fishermen), in the *Place Nationale*, dates from the 14th and 15th centuries. The interior is, however, sadly disfigured. Near the church is the **Statue of Duquesne,** a celebrated admiral and native of Dieppe (d. 1687), who conquered the redoutable De Ruyter off the Sicilian coast in 1676. The Dutch hero soon after died of his wounds at Syracuse. Duquesne, who was a Calvinist, was interred in the church of Aubonne on the Lake of Geneva.

On market-days (Wednesdays and Saturdays) an opportunity is afforded to the stranger of observing some of the singular head-dresses of the Norman country-women.

The **Jetée de l'Ouest,** situated at the N.W. extremity of the town, forms an agreeable evening promenade, and with the opposite *Jetée de l'Est* constitutes the entrance to the harbour. Towards the S.E. the harbour terminates in the **Bassin de Retenue,** flanked by the *Cours Bourbon*, an avenue $^3/_4$ M. in length, affording a retired and sheltered walk.

This basin contains an extensive **Oyster Park,** formerly one of the principal sources from which Paris derived its supplies. The oysters are first brought from the inexhaustible beds of *Cancale* and *Granville* to *St. Vaast* near Cherbourg, whence they are afterwards removed to Dieppe. Here they are 'travaillées', or dieted, so as materially to improve their flavour and render them fit for exportation. It has been observed that the oyster, when in a natural state, frequently opens its shell to eject the sea-water from which it derives its nourishment and to take in a fresh supply. In the 'park' they open their shells less frequently, and after a treatment of a month it is found that they remain closed for ten or twelve days together, an interval which admits of their being transported in a perfectly fresh state to all parts of the continent. Since the completion of the railway from Paris to Cherbourg, the oyster-park of Dieppe has lost much of its importance, and the metropolis now derives its chief supplies from a more convenient source.

Contiguous to the oyster-park is a restaurant of humble pretensions, where the delicious bivalve (75 c. per dozen), fresh from its native element, may be enjoyed in the highest perfection.

Le Pollet, a suburb of Dieppe inhabited exclusively by sailors and fishermen, adjoins the Bassin de Retenue on the N. side. The population differs externally but little from that of Dieppe. It is, however, alleged that they are the descendants of an ancient Venetian colony, and it is certain that to this day they possess a primitive simplicity of character unknown among their neigh-

BÆDEKER. Paris. 3rd Edition. 15

▲ **CLEAR LAYOUTS** Baedeker guides were viewed as the most reliable of all tourist reference books, giving rise to the English verse: "Kings and governments may err – but never Mr. Baedeker." These pages – from *Paris and Northern France* (1867) – are typical of the well-planned context, which as well as descriptions of attractions, gave information on local customs, and hints on tipping and how best to conduct oneself.

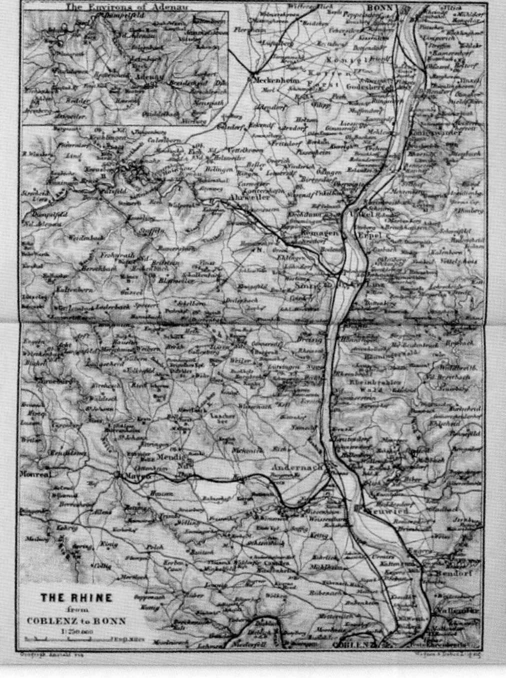

◄ **HIGH-QUALITY MAPS** The guides' maps and plans were as detailed and precise as those produced by cartographic companies. They were mostly coloured, and easy to read; the larger maps could be folded out.

> Its **principal** object is to keep the **traveller** at as great a distance as **possible** from the **unpleasant…** and… to assist him in **standing** on his own feet

KARL BAEDEKER, PREFACE TO *GERMANY*, 1858

The Pickwick Papers

1836–37 ▪ PRINTED ▪ 21.3 × 12.6 cm (8 × 5 in) ▪ 609 PAGES ▪ UK

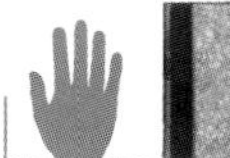
SCALE

CHARLES DICKENS

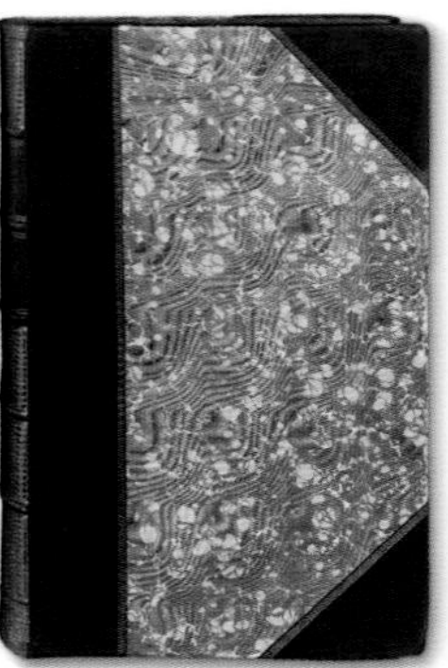

The Posthumous Papers *of the Pickwick Club*, commonly known as *The Pickwick Papers*, was Charles Dickens' first novel. Published in 19 monthly installments between April 1836 and November 1837, and as a two-volume book in 1837, it proved a phenomenal publishing success on a scale never seen before. While the first instalment sold just 500 copies, the final, double instalment sold 40,000 and established Dickens as an author. He would later go on to become one of the best-known and best-loved of all Victorian novelists.

The periodicals were not initially intended as a novel: Dickens was commissioned to write extended captions for a series of comic sporting scenes by an illustrator, Robert Seymour (1798–1836). However, Dickens proposed that the process be reversed, with Seymour's illustrations serving his text. After two instalments Seymour committed suicide, and the remainder of the story – with text taking a more central role – was illustrated by Habbot Knight Browne ("Phiz") (1815–82), who later illustrated 10 other books by Dickens.

The vivid and gleeful portrait of late Georgian England captivated the public: readers from all strata of society followed the escapades of the four members of the Pickwick Club. There was no plot to speak of – just a series of adventures by the friends, led by the ever-genial Samuel Pickwick, as they set out to explore England – but the work teemed with life and humour. Although Dickens still signed his work with his nom de plume, "Boz", the publication of *The Pickwick Papers* ensured his enduring fame, and opened up a 40-year-long career as a novelist and a literary sensation.

CHARLES **DICKENS**

1812–1870

Charles Dickens is one of the most famous and best-loved novelists in the English language. He created numerous fictional characters that have captivated generations of readers.

In 1824, Dickens's father was sent to a debtor's prison and the 12-year-old Charles was forced to work in a boot-blacking factory – an experience that haunted him his whole life. Dickens eventually began a career as a political journalist in 1832, and, having quickly made a name for himself, he was offered the chance to work on *The Pickwick Papers* alongside Robert Seymour. Published in 1836, it was the starting point of his life-long career as a novelist.

Dickens married Catherine Hogarth in 1836, and although they had ten children together, they separated in 1858 after he began an affair with actress, Ellen Turnan. In addition to writing novels and plays, Dickens edited periodicals and newspapers, and assisted several charities. A champion of the poor, he created armies of extraordinary characters and the vast tableaux that emerged played a crucial part in society's awakening social conscience. As a novelist and social commentator, Dickens became one of the age's most famous figures.

In detail

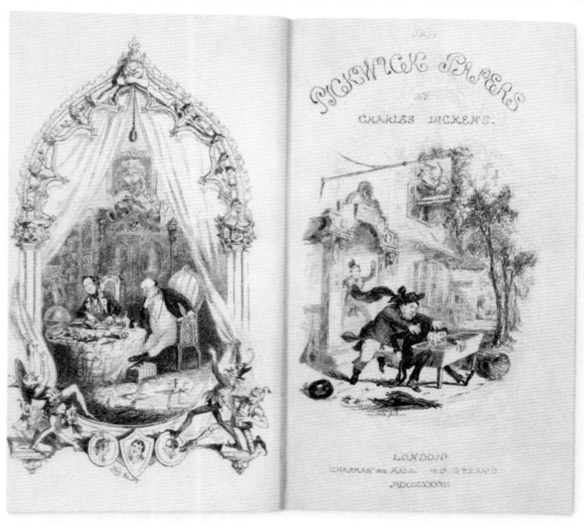

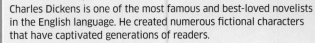

➤ **FRONTISPIECE AND TITLE PAGE** Following the death of the work's first illustrator, Seymour, other artists were trialled, such as Robert Buss, but Hablot K. Browne ("Phiz") was ultimately chosen, and his drawings are primarily used in the book. In his frontispiece, Sam Weller and Mr Pickwick review papers together. The title page shows Tony Weller "baptizing" the pastor, Mr Stiggins, in the horse trough.

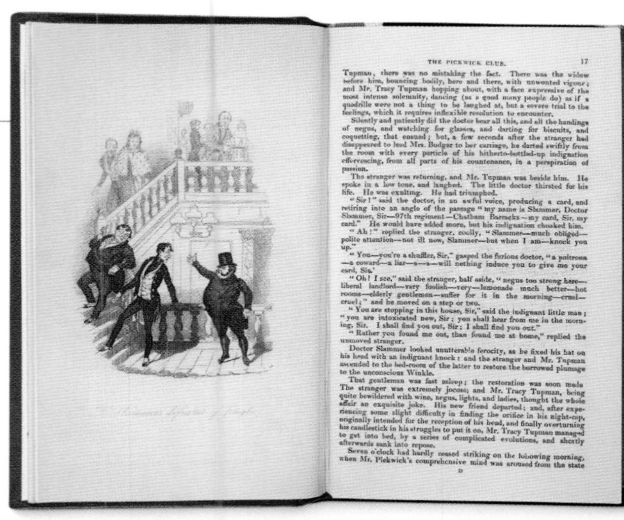

▲ **RIVALS IN LOVE** This is one of the few illustrations drawn by Robert Seymour shortly before he committed suicide. It depicts army surgeon, Dr Slammer, challenging Alfred Jingle to a duel after he seduced a wealthy widow that the doctor had been pursuing.

▼ **CHRISTMAS SPECIAL** To profit from the Christmas period, the publishers shrewdly issued a special edition, published on 31 December 1836, for which Dickens wrote a sentimental piece. This image by "Phiz", a steel engraving, shows detail and humour in the depiction of Mr Wardle's Christmas party in which partygoers kiss under the mistletoe. Phiz initially studied Seymour's style, before later coming into his own. His images often included allegorical references in the background.

296 POSTHUMOUS PAPERS OF

branch of misletoe instantaneously gave rise to a scene of general and most delightful struggling and confusion; in the midst of which Mr. Pickwick with a gallantry which would have done honour to a descendant of Lady Tollimglower herself, took the old lady by the hand, led her beneath the mystic branch, and saluted her in all courtesy and decorum. The old lady submitted to this piece of practical politeness with all the dignity which befitted so important and serious a solemnity, but the younger ladies not being so thoroughly imbued with a superstitious veneration of the custom, or imagining that the value of a salute is very much enhanced if it cost a little trouble to obtain it, screamed and struggled, and ran into corners, and threatened and remonstrated, and did every thing but leave the room, until some of the less adventurous gentlemen were on the point of desisting, when they all at once found it useless to resist any longer, and submitted to be kissed with a good grace. Mr. Winkle kissed the young lady with the black eyes, and Mr. Snodgrass kissed Emily; and Mr. Weller, not being particular about the form of being under the misletoe, kissed Emma and the other female servants, just as he caught them. As to the poor relations, they kissed everybody, not even excepting the plainer portion of the young-lady visiters, who, in their excessive confusion, ran right under the misletoe, directly it was hung up, without knowing it! Wardle stood with his back to the fire, surveying the whole scene, with the utmost satisfaction; and the fat boy took the opportunity of appropriating to his own use, and summarily devouring, a particularly fine mince-pie, that had been carefully put by, for somebody else.

Now the screaming had subsided, and faces were in a glow and curls in a tangle, and Mr. Pickwick, after kissing the old lady as before-mentioned, was standing under the misletoe, looking with a very pleased countenance on all that was passing around him, when the young lady with the black eyes, after a little whispering with the other young ladies, made a sudden dart forward, and, putting her arm round Mr. Pickwick's neck, saluted him affectionately on the left cheek; and before Mr. Pickwick distinctly knew what was the matter, he was surrounded by the whole body, and kissed by every one of them.

It was a pleasant thing to see Mr. Pickwick in the centre of the group, now pulled this way, and then that, and first kissed on the chin and then on the nose, and then on the spectacles, and to hear the peals of laughter which were raised on every side; but it was a still more pleasant thing to see Mr. Pickwick, blinded shortly afterwards with a silk-handkerchief, falling up against the wall, and scrambling into corners, and going through all the mysteries of blindman's buff, with the utmost relish for the game, until at last he caught one of the poor relations; and then had to evade the blind-man himself, which he did with a nimbleness and agility that elicited the admiration and applause of all beholders. The poor relations caught just the people whom they thought would like it; and when the game flagged, got caught themselves. When they were all tired of blind-man's buff, there was a great game at snap-dragon, and when fingers enough were burned with that, and all the raisins gone, they sat down by the huge fire of blazing

> If I were to live a hundred years, and write three novels in each. I should never be so proud of them, as I am of Pickwick.

CHARLES DICKENS, NOVEMBER 1836

IN CONTEXT

The Pickwick Papers had an instant and lasting impact on the 19th-century novel. Initially published monthly, each episode concluded with a cliffhanger, creating a sense of excitement and an ever-growing readership - as well as allowing publishers to spread the cost of publication. Each instalment was sold for a shilling, and wrapped in a green paper cover. Advertisements inside increased profit for the publishers, which today provide a fascinating window on Victorian Britain. The serial's monthly deadlines demanded a high degree of discipline, but Dickens rose to the challenge. He even wrote the last 10 episodes having already started his next acclaimed novel, *Oliver Twist*.

➤ **The original 1837 cover** of the serialized novel includes a description of the sporting themes initially proposed as its subject matter. "Boz" was Dickens's pen name.

The Holy Land

1842–49 ▪ LITHOGRAPHS ▪ 60 × 43 cm (24 × 17 in) ▪ 247 PLATES ▪ UK

SCALE

DAVID ROBERTS

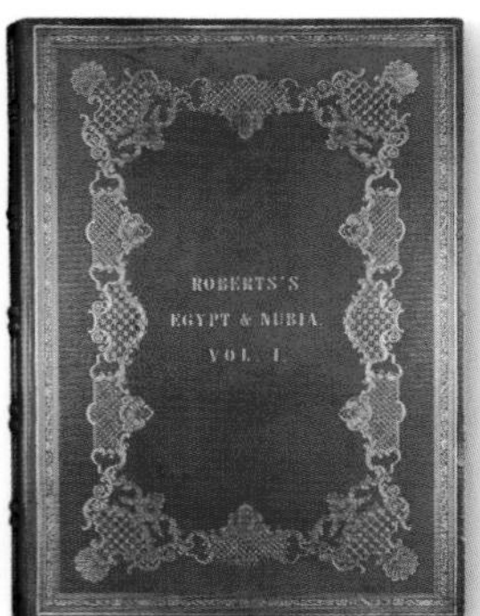

The publication, from 1842, of the first prints of David Roberts's magisterial *The Holy Land, Syria, Idumea, Egypt and Nubia* – its full title – was a publishing sensation. The impact was reinforced with the publication of further such images in a variety of lavish formats and titles. The immense success of the project reflected, not just a deepening European fascination with the perceived exotic allure of the Near East, but also a celebration of the exceptional technical sophistication of the prints themselves. The collaborative venture combined the efforts of David Roberts; Louis Haghe, a Belgian lithographer, who made the prints; and publisher, Francis Moon, who took a great financial risk in publishing the various volumes.

Roberts arrived in the Middle East in 1838 and spent 11 months sketching and painting a vast range of views: "enough material to serve me for the rest of my life". Haghe then reproduced these as lithographs. This intensely demanding form of printing sees the images recreated in reverse on stones, which were covered with ink, and turned into prints. The resulting black-and-white images were then hand-coloured, meaning that no two were identical. The book was one of the first great examples of mass-produced lithography, heralding the rise of mass media. It was also, for the Victorians, an inspiring vision of another world.

▲ **BINDING** Many of the first subscribers chose to have the plates bound.

▼ **AESTHETIC AND ACCURATE** Roberts had an inherent sense of the dramatic. His most famous image from *The Holy Land* shows the Sphinx and the Great temple complex at Giza, outside Cairo, during the arrival of the simoom (meaning "poison wind"), a hot desert wind which sweeps before it clouds of suffocating dust and sand. The huge sun adds to the sense of impending doom.

In detail

➤ **ROBERTS'S SKETCH** The spontaneous quality of Roberts's original drawings reflects his experience of painting large volumes of material: he produced over 272 watercolours of temples, monuments, and people for *The Holy Land*. This scene illustrates his bold style, which creates an accurate depiction of the landscape without the need for delicate detail. The orange hues reflect the heat of the atmosphere, while the light reflecting off the top of the buildings enhances this by emphasizing the sun's presence.

➤ **HAGHE'S LITHOGRAPH** When creating his lithographs, Haghe made exact copies of Roberts's original sketches and watercolours. However, he brought a visual delicacy to what was essentially a technical exercise through the process of lithography – which sharpens lines, and adds contrast to areas of light and shade – and matched and precisely complemented Roberts's work. In this view Haghe enhances the detail in the foreground, but still manages to capture the warmth found in Roberts's drawing.

DAVID **ROBERTS**

1796–1864

David Roberts was a prolific British painter and Royal Academician. He had some success with oil painting, but it was his scenes painted abroad that brought him renown.

Born in Scotland Roberts had no formal training as an artist, working instead as a painter of stage sets, initially in Scotland then in London. His obvious talent was such that from the 1820s he was able to establish himself as a landscape painter. A series of journeys to France and the Low Countries, and then to Spain and North Africa, cemented his reputation as a virtuoso painter of architecture. He had exceptional technical skill and a striking capacity for hard work, as well as an instinctive talent for conveying mood and drama in landscapes and buildings alike. *The Holy Land* was a triumph – Queen Victoria was the first subscriber to the prints: her copy is still in the Royal Collection. This success was repeated in a second three-volume work, *Egypt and Nubia*, published between 1846 and 1849. In 1859, he published a similarly sumptuous work on Italy: *Italy, Classical, Historical and Picturesque*.

◄ **ILLUSTRATED FRONTISPIECE** The frontispiece of Roberts's *Egypt and Nubia*, his follow-up to *The Holy Land*, shows travellers surveying the vast statues at grand entrance to the 13th-century BCE Great Temple of Aboo Simbel (Abu Simbel today), in Nubia, in the far south of Egypt. The text for the book was provided by antiquarian, William Brockedon.

➤ **RICH DECORATION** When Roberts visited the Isis temple complex on the Nile island of Philae, it was already among the most popular archeological sites in Egypt. Roberts's inclusion of Nubian tribesmen in his sketch emphasizes the monumental size of the columns of this temple's portico. He also captures the rich patterning of papyrus and lotus motifs.

In detail

➤ **MASTER OF THE ART** Haghe's ability to exploit lithographic techniques in order to produce dramatic highlights and shadows delighted Roberts. As he stated, "There can be only one opinion as to the masterly manner in which he executed his work". Figures bring touches of colour to a palette that is otherwise dominated by sand tones.

▲ **HIGH CONTRAST** In this detail of Haghe's untinted lithograph, expert shading can be seen, with deep black shadows at the rock's base and bright white highlights at its sunlit top. The figures added to the scene help give a sense of the scale of this colossal statue.

◄ **A FINE TOUCH** This detail from Haghe's untinted lithograph makes clear the exceptional delicacy and accuracy of Haghe's work, with flawless contouring of the statue's face and headdress.

IN **CONTEXT**

The success of Roberts's *The Holy Land* stemmed partly from the financial acuity of the publisher, Francis Moon, but was mainly due to the convergence of two developments in the Victorian world. The first was the burgeoning interest in the mysteries of what were, then, little-known lands. A series of French artists, notably Ingres (1780–1867) and Delacroix (1798–1863), were the first to exploit this. British artists, among which Roberts was a forerunner, soon followed suit, and demand for these compellingly rich images soared. The second development was that of lithography, which occurred at the end of 18th century, initially in Germany. The word comes from the ancient Greek *lithos* meaning "stone" and *graphein* meaning "write", since the image was drawn on a lithographic stone with a wax crayon. In this period, just before the widespread use of photography, it was the first time that such high quality reproductions were possible. In the hands of two such supreme technicians as Roberts and Haghe, the results were startling.

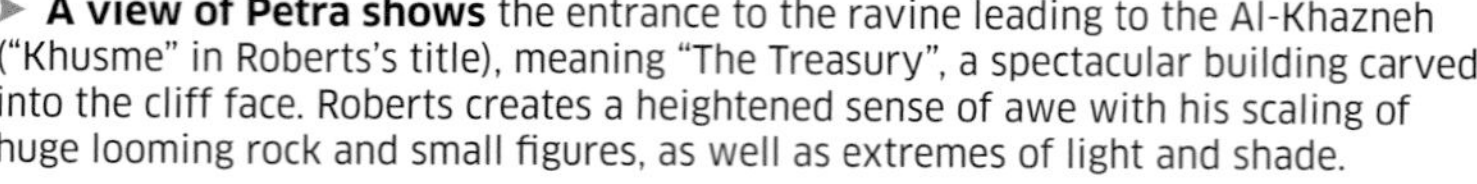

➤ **A view of Petra shows** the entrance to the ravine leading to the Al-Khazneh ("Khusme" in Roberts's title), meaning "The Treasury", a spectacular building carved into the cliff face. Roberts creates a heightened sense of awe with his scaling of huge looming rock and small figures, as well as extremes of light and shade.

▲ **ROMANTIC VISION** Roberts's compositions drew on a European landscape tradition of Romanticism, in which aspects of the natural world were often enhanced and dramatized to convey emotion. This view of Jerusalem, with Arabs in the foreground and the city looming beyond, captured the British public's imagination and led to wealthy Victorians buying Roberts's works in great quantities. Any such major set-piece image took Haghe a month of painstaking labour to complete the lithograph.

They [the prints] are **faithful** and **laborious** beyond any **outlines** from nature I have **ever seen**

JOHN RUSKIN, ON *THE HOLY LAND*

Photographs of British Algae: Cyanotype Impressions

1843–1853 ■ PHOTOGRAMS ■ 25.3 × 20 cm (10 × 8 in) ■ 411 SHEETS ■ UK

SCALE

ANNA ATKINS

Photography was just a few years old when botanist Anna Atkins created the first-ever book to be photographically illustrated and printed. *Photographs of British Algae: Cyanotype Impressions* was a collection of photographs, or rather photograms (shadow images), of seaweeds, and had no text to speak of, apart from the introductory pages and labels. The book was never published, but Atkins made a handful of copies, bound them by hand, and sent them out to friends in three volumes between 1843 and 1853.

Atkins's book was probably intended as a companion to William Harvey's *Manual of British Algae* (1841), which was not illustrated. Although it broke no new ground scientifically, her beautiful, blue-tinged images were an artistic triumph, which Atkins achieved using a cutting-edge photographic technique (see p.189).

It was just four years since Louis-Jacques-Mandé Daguerre (1787–1851) and William Fox Talbot (1800–77) had independently reported the first two successful photographic processes: the daguerreotype and the calotype. Fox Talbot was a family friend, from whom Atkins learned about calotypes, as was Sir John Herschel (1792–1871), who invented the cyanotype process just a year before Atkins produced her first volume.

There is no proof that Atkins ever took a photograph with a camera. Creating the cyanotype pictures in her book required an intricate scientific process and yet through her careful arrangement of the algae on the page she was able to blend this science with artistic presentation. With the exposure of algae-covered, light-sensitive paper to sunlight, ghostly silhouettes of the algae appeared against a background of rich blue. The result was wholly original, and Atkins's book is considered one of the most significant landmarks in the art of photography.

ANNA **ATKINS**

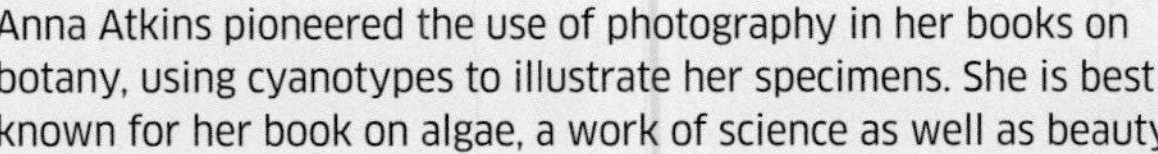

1799–1871

Anna Atkins pioneered the use of photography in her books on botany, using cyanotypes to illustrate her specimens. She is best known for her book on algae, a work of science as well as beauty.

An early female member of the Botanical Society of London, Anna Atkins was an English amateur botanist and a pioneer of scientific photography. Her mother died soon after she was born and she was brought up by her botanist father, John Children. He was a Fellow of the prestigious Royal Society, who encouraged his daughter's botanical interests and introduced her to many of the leading scientists of the time.

In 1825 she married John Pelly Atkins, who would later become Sheriff of Kent, and went to live in Halstead Place, Kent. The Atkins had no children, allowing Anna to devote time to her interest in botany. On learning about the cyanotype process, she realized that it could be used to produce accurate and highly detailed botanical images. She created her photographic book of algae, specifically seaweed, between 1843 and 1853, and went on to produce similar photographic books of flowers and ferns with her friend Anne Dixon, as well as some unillustrated books on botany.

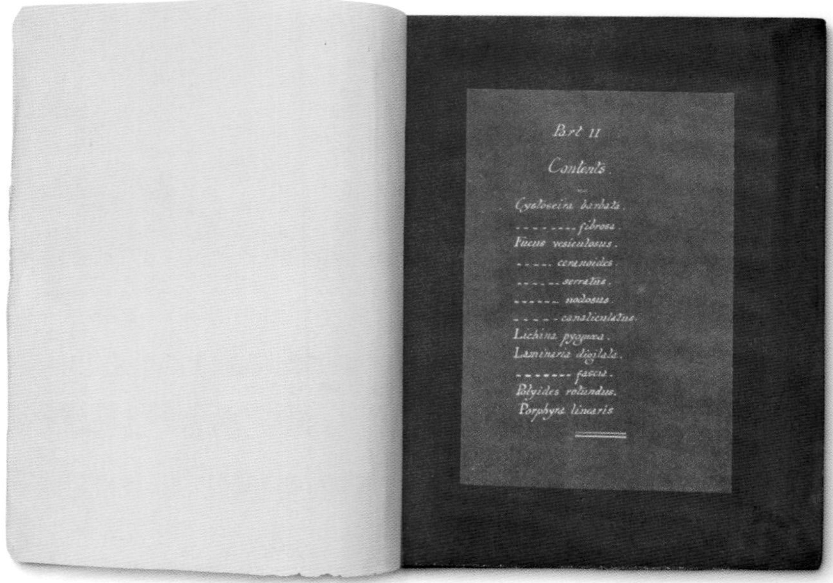
Part II
Contents.
Cystoseira barbata.
- - - - - - - - fibrosa.
Fucus vesiculosus.
- - - - - ceranoides.
- - - - - serratus.
- - - - - nodosus.
- - - - - canaliculatus.
Lichina pygmaea.
Laminaria digitata.
- - - - - - - fascia.
Polyides rotundus.
Porphyra linearis.

➤ **PIONEERING WORK** The first volume of *Photographs of British Algae* came out in October 1843 and so earned its place as the first book to be illustrated photographically, beating Fox Talbot's famous *The Pencil of Nature* by a year. Copies of Atkins's book are rare – there are known to be 13, although not all of them are complete. The cyanotype process was used to create both the seaweed illustrations as well as the text pages, such as this contents page.

> The difficulty of making accurate drawings of objects as minute as many of the Algae and Confervae, has induced me to avail myself of… Herschel's beautiful process of Cyanotype ”
>
> **ANNA ATKINS**, PREFACE TO *PHOTOGRAPHS OF BRITISH ALGAE*

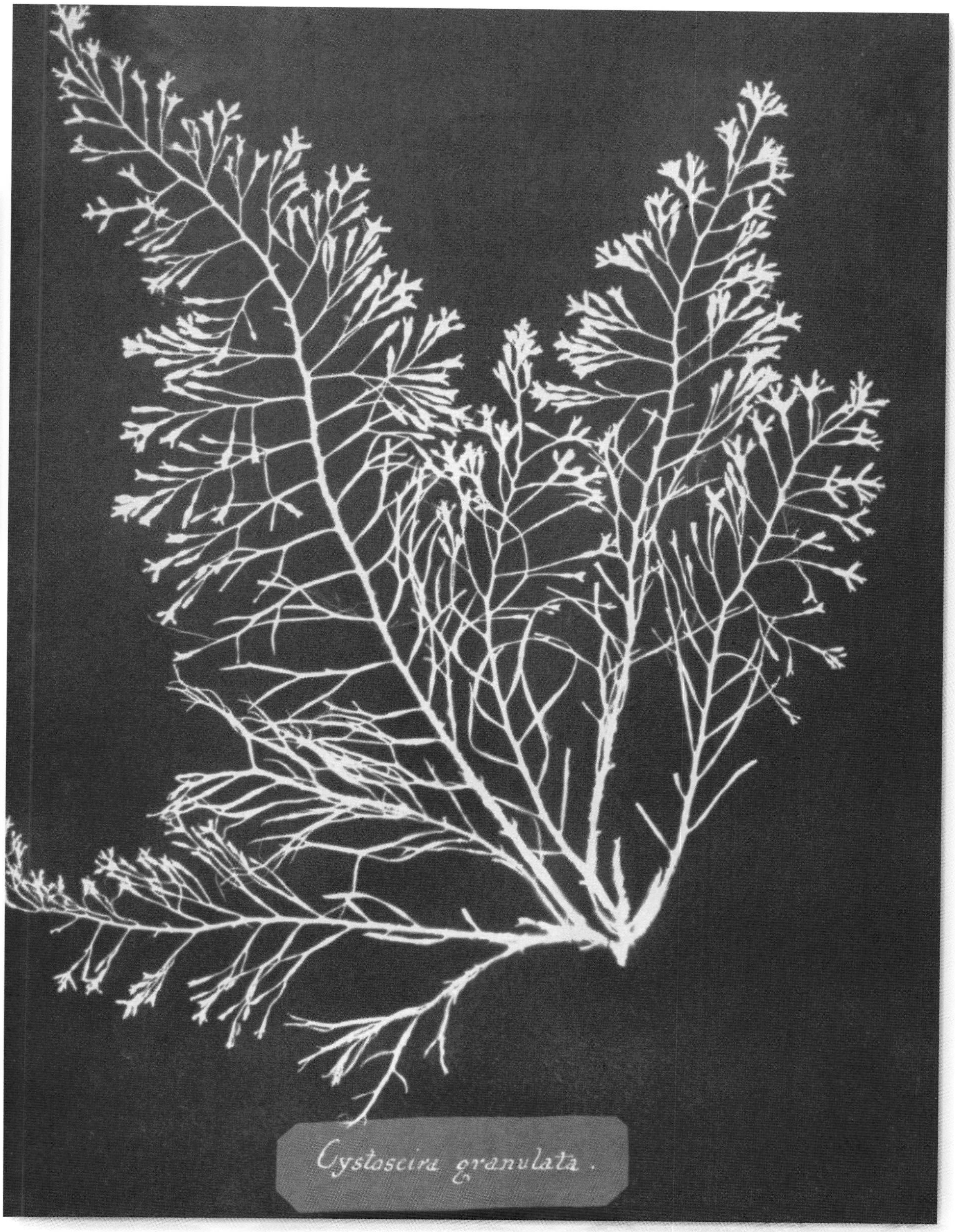

➤ **ARTISTRY** Throughout the book Atkins combined her detailed botanical knowledge with a rare artistic skill. One of the first images in the 1843 volume, beautifully presented on the page, is of the brown alga *Cystoseira granulata*.

Cystoseira granulata.

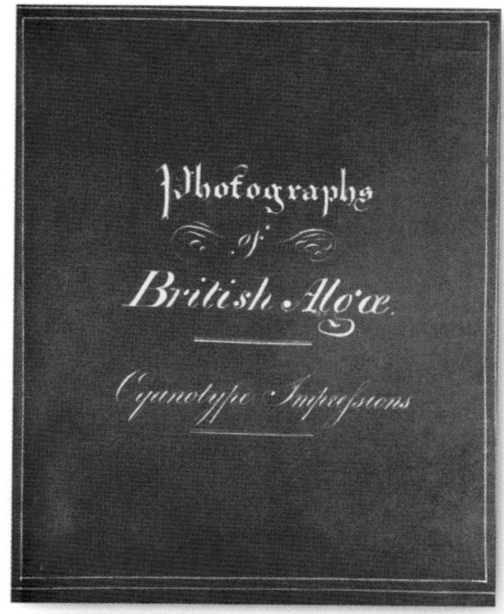

▲ **TITLE PAGE** Inscribed carefully in elegant, handwritten script, the title page was photographed using the cyanotype process. The subtitle, *Cyanotype Impressions*, indicates the artistic approach of the book.

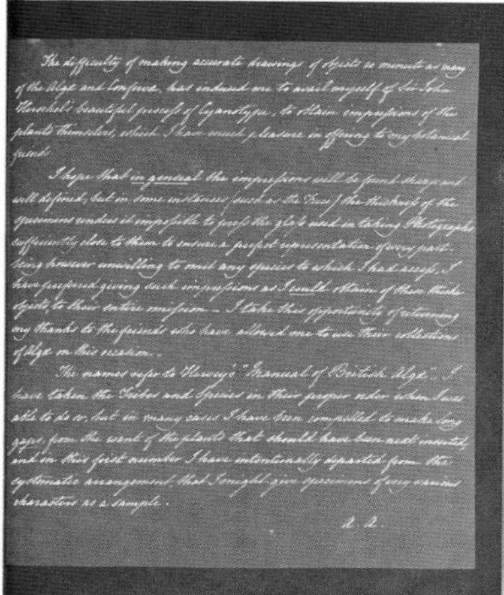

▲ **ARTISTIC INTEGRITY** In her introductory text, Atkins mentions why she chose to use the cyanotype process for her book and acknowledges her debt to Sir John Herschel for his invention.

In detail

◄ CAPTURING DETAIL
This cyanotype of the crimson seaweed *Delesseria sanguinea*, from the 1843 volume shows how quickly Atkins had mastered the new photographic process. Even modern photographers would find it a challenge to capture the subtle detailing so accurately.

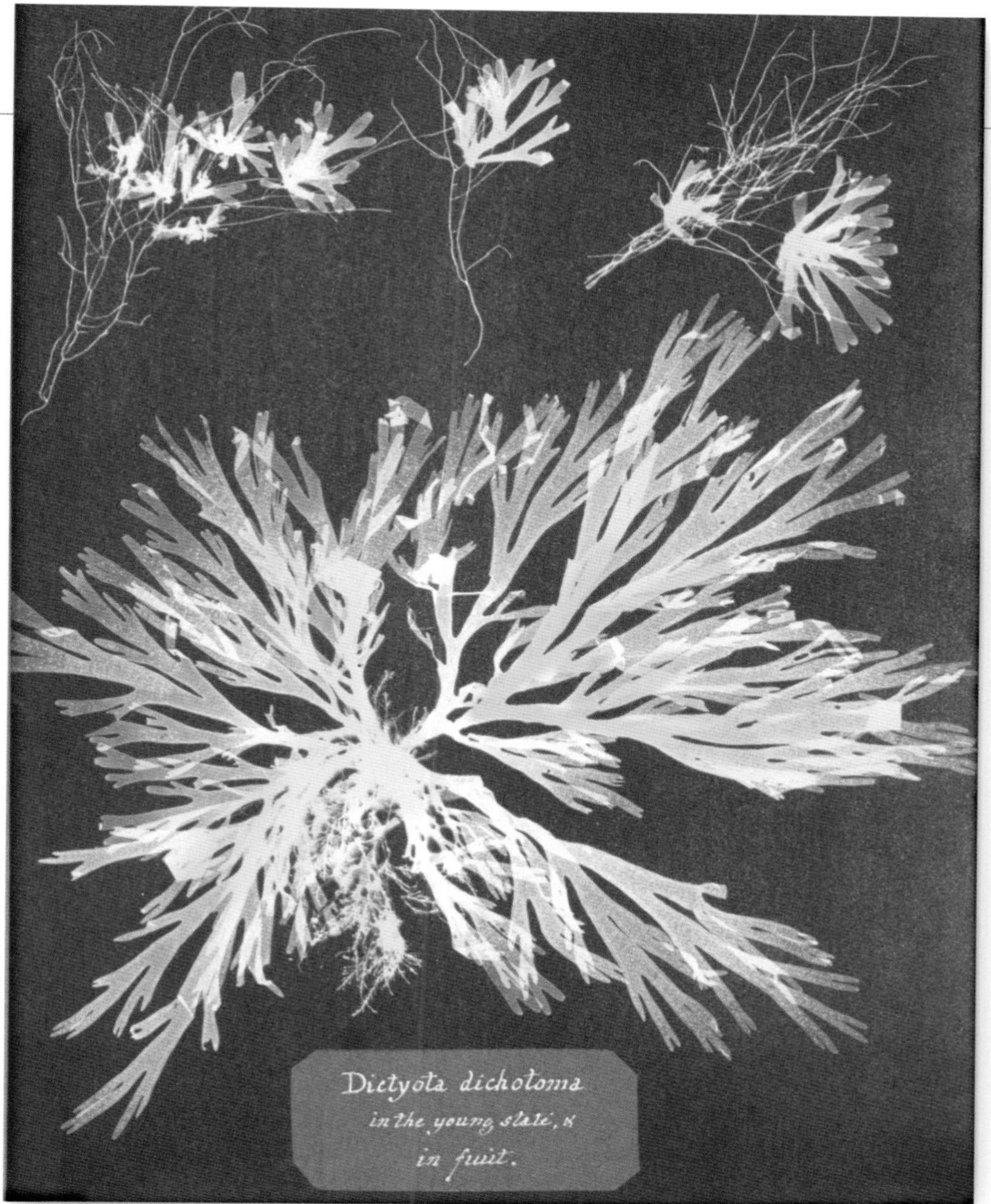

▲ **ARTISTIC APPROACH** This sample of the golden brown seaweed *Dictyota dichotoma* in its young state and in fruit, was probably made around 1861, eight years after Atkins's first cyanotype, and showcases her command of the photographic process.

ON TECHNIQUE

The cyanotype is a photographic process invented by the English scientist Sir John Herschel, and it does not require a camera. Paper is coated with a mix of ammonium citrate and potassium ferricyanide. To create the image, the object is simply laid on the cyanotype paper and exposed to sunlight. Washing the paper in water reveals a white silhouette on a deep blue background. Cyanotypes are so durable that they came to be the standard process for making copies of technical and architectural plans for everything from ships to cathedrals. The word "blueprint" comes from the blue of cyanotype plans.

▲ **The cyanotype process** was used to create portraits, such as this image taken by Herschel in 1836, titled "The Right Honourable Mrs. Leicester Stanhope".

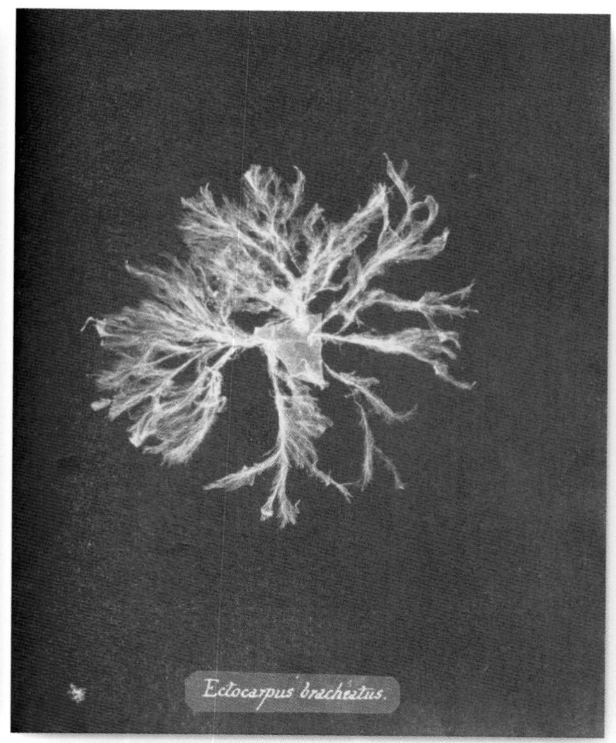

► **UPDATES** As Atkins issued new volumes she would often include updates and new plates to replace earlier images for which she had found better specimens. The first version of *Ectocarpus brachiatus* (right), for instance, was later replaced with a much more impressive specimen (far right).

Uncle Tom's Cabin

1852 AND 1853 ■ PRINTED ■ 19.2 × 12 cm (7 × 5 in) ■ 312 AND 322 PAGES ■ USA

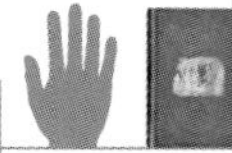
SCALE

HARRIET BEECHER STOWE

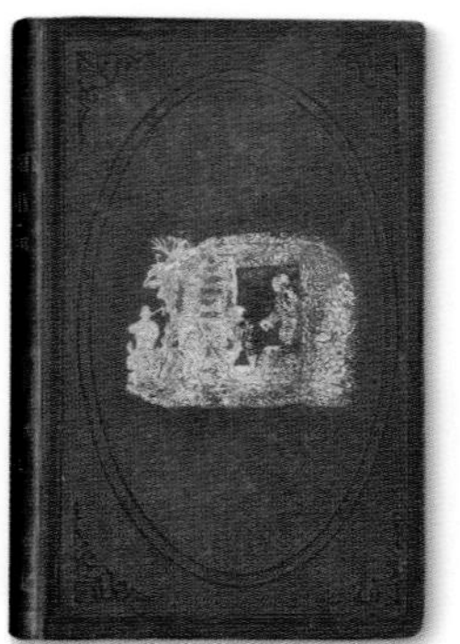

Carrying the subtitle, *Life Among the Lowly*, *Uncle Tom's Cabin* was originally serialized in 1851 by *The National Era* newspaper in Washington D.C. The story caused a sensation, and was published in book form a year later, featuring six engravings by Hammatt Billings. It sold 300,000 copies in the US and one million in the UK in its first year, and a second edition followed in 1853 with 117 illustrations. During the 19th century, only the Bible sold in greater numbers.

Beecher Stowe was a passionate abolitionist, and the theme throughout *Uncle Tom's Cabin* is the immorality of slavery – an issue that became the great fault line of 19th-century America. While the industrial North opposed slavery, the agricultural South defended it fiercely, as its economy was dependent on more than four million slaves. This conflict of opinion, possibly inflamed by *Uncle Tom's Cabin*, resulted in the American Civil War of 1861. The eventual Northern victory in 1865 freed the slaves, but the war cost an estimated 620,000 lives, and left the South in dire economic straits.

HARRIET **BEECHER STOWE**

1811–1896

American abolitionist and writer Harriet Beecher Stowe was an early champion of women's rights and campaigned against inequality her whole life.

Born in Connecticut, she was the daughter of a Calvinist preacher. After her own education she taught in a school set up by her sister, before they moved with their father to Cincinnati, Ohio in 1832. She continued teaching and in 1836 married a clergyman and passionate abolitionist, Calvin Ellis Stowe. During her time in Cincinnati, Beecher Stowe was exposed to the harsh reality of slavery, which she fiercely opposed, and started writing what would become *Uncle Tom's Cabin*. Its huge success was not matched by any of her later work – she wrote 30 books, including novels and memoirs. Her husband died in 1886 when her own health then declined – her final years were clouded by dementia.

Uncle Tom's Cabin can be seen as maudlin, and is often cloyingly sentimental. It has also been attacked for being patronizing, and almost racist, by a number of modern scholars due to the condescending descriptions of some of the black characters. Yet its success in championing the plight of slaves in the US and helping to bring an end to slavery there cannot be questioned. *Uncle Tom's Cabin* is a product of a social conscience outraged that slavery could exist at all in a country that had been conceived in liberty.

In detail

LITTLE EVA READING THE BIBLE TO UNCLE TOM IN THE ARBOR. Page 63

▲ **UNCLE TOM'S FAITH** Central to the book are the encounters between Eva, daughter of Tom's well-meaning second master, Augustine St Clare, and Tom himself. Though Eva is still a child, her faith crucially reinforces Tom's Christian beliefs. Her subsequent lingering death, illuminated for her by a vision of heaven, presages what amounts to Tom's martyrdom at the end of the book.

▲ **SLAVE OWNERSHIP** Plantation owners in the South counted slaves as their legal property, much like their horses or other domestic animals. Not only did these human beings have no rights, but they could be bought and sold at will, often at auctions. Tom, for example, is sold twice – the first time privately to St Clare after rescuing his daughter, then to Legree at auction, as shown here.

I did not write it. God wrote it. I merely did His dictation

HARRIET BEECHER STOWE, ON DESCRIBING THE WRITING OF *UNCLE TOM'S CABIN*

Eliza comes to tell Uncle Tom that he is sold, and that she is running away to save her child. Page 62.

▲ **FIRST IMAGE OF TOM** To encourage sales of the costly two-volume novel, its publisher, John P. Jewett, commissioned Charles Howland Hammatt Billings to produce six full-page illustrations. The first is shown here, and depicts Eliza, a slave, telling Tom that he is to be sold by his current owner, Arthur Shelby, to pay off his debts. Tom is bought by the cruel Simon Legree.

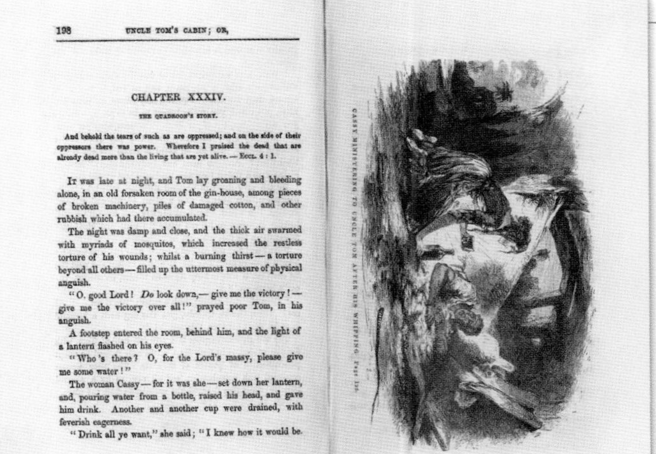

198 UNCLE TOM'S CABIN; OR,

CHAPTER XXXIV.

THE QUADROON'S STORY.

And behold the tears of such as are oppressed; and on the side of their oppressors there was power. Wherefore I praised the dead that are already dead more than the living that are yet alive. — Eccl. 4 : 1.

It was late at night, and Tom lay groaning and bleeding alone, in an old forsaken room of the gin-house, among pieces of broken machinery, piles of damaged cotton, and other rubbish which had there accumulated.

The night was damp and close, and the thick air swarmed with myriads of mosquitos, which increased the restless torture of his wounds; whilst a burning thirst — a torture beyond all others — filled up the uttermost measure of physical anguish.

"O, good Lord! *Do* look down, — give me the victory! — give me the victory over all!" prayed poor Tom, in his anguish.

A footstep entered the room, behind him, and the light of a lantern flashed on his eyes.

"Who 's there? O, for the Lord's massy, please give me some water!"

The woman Cassy — for it was she — set down her lantern, and, pouring water from a bottle, raised his head, and gave him drink. Another and another cup were drained, with feverish eagerness.

"Drink all ye want," she said; "I knew how it would be.

CASSY MINISTERING TO UNCLE TOM AFTER HIS WHIPPING.

▲ **MARTYRDOM OF TOM** The antisalvery movement was heavily influenced by the Christian Church, and it is Tom's devotion to the faith that ultimately leads to him being whipped to death by his owner, Legree. In this illustration, Tom is given water by fellow slave, Cassey, following the beating that later claims his life.

IN CONTEXT

The publication of *Uncle Tom's Cabin* unleashed a storm of criticism in the South. Beecher Stowe was attacked not only for never having visited a plantation, but also for fundamentally misunderstanding what many in the South saw as the "essentially benign nature of slavery": that blacks were like children, requiring the firm, but kindly hand of whites to guide them. In 1853, Beecher Stowe published an impassioned defence of *Uncle Tom's Cabin* that documented the sources of her information for the original book.

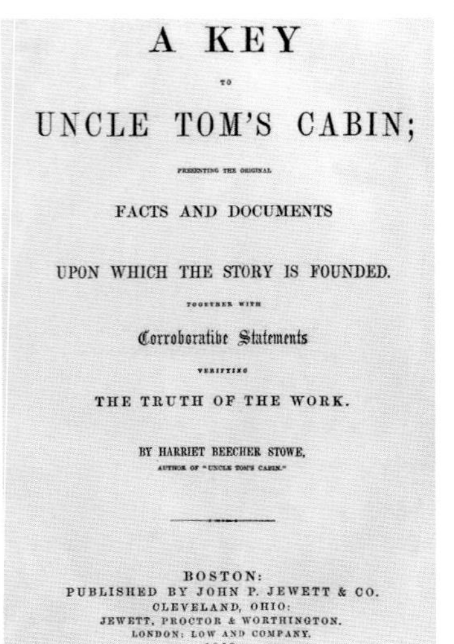

A KEY

TO

UNCLE TOM'S CABIN;

PRESENTING THE ORIGINAL

FACTS AND DOCUMENTS

UPON WHICH THE STORY IS FOUNDED.

TOGETHER WITH

Corroborative Statements

VERIFYING

THE TRUTH OF THE WORK.

BY HARRIET BEECHER STOWE,

AUTHOR OF "UNCLE TOM'S CABIN."

BOSTON:
PUBLISHED BY JOHN P. JEWETT & CO.
CLEVELAND, OHIO:
JEWETT, PROCTOR & WORTHINGTON.
LONDON: LOW AND COMPANY.
1853.

► **Hailed in the North**, Beecher Stowe's *A Key to Uncle Tom's Cabin* was loathed in the South – hostility between the regions was unremitting.

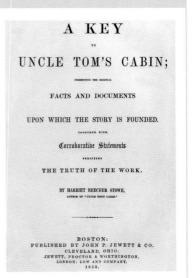

Leaves of Grass

1855 (FIRST EDITION) ▪ PRINTED ▪ 29 × 20.5 cm (11 × 8 in) ▪ 95 PAGES ▪ USA

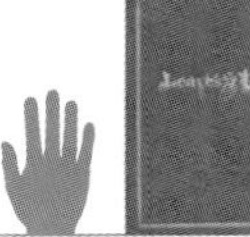

SCALE

WALT WHITMAN

The first edition of Walt Whitman's *Leaves of Grass,* a book of 12 poems, contained only 95 pages, yet it had a huge influence on the development of American literature. In the standard bibliographical reference work *Printing and the Mind of Man* it was referred to as "America's second Declaration of Independence: that of 1776 was political; that of 1855 intellectual". Aged 36, Whitman, was unknown to the literary world when *Leaves of Grass* was published, and not even named as the book's author (although he did identify himself in one of the poems). But his collection revolutionized not just American literature but literature across the English-speaking world. Whitman pioneered a completely new poetic voice that was wild, rapturous, concrete, sensuous, harsh, and unmistakably modern. It deliberately avoided any sort of tone or subject matter that might conventionally be thought poetic. Though infused with an extraordinary lyricism, Whitman's poetic forms similarly disregarded rhythm, metre, and rhyme.

In part the book celebrated America and ordinary Americans, and in World War II the US government gave each soldier a copy to remind them of the America that they were fighting for. More particularly though, the book celebrated Whitman himself and his astonishingly intense response to, and identification with, every aspect of the world. The initial reaction to the book varied from the baffled to the outraged. Only a handful of critics, most notably Ralph Waldo Emerson (1803–82), the pre-eminent American literary figure of the time, recognized that here was not just a new poetic vision but an indisputably great one.

Whitman devoted the rest of his life to expanding *Leaves of Grass*, adding poems – the book's final edition in 1881 contained 389 – and endlessly revising those already written. Single-handed and unheralded, Whitman recast every expectation of what poetry might mean.

WALT **WHITMAN**

1819–1892

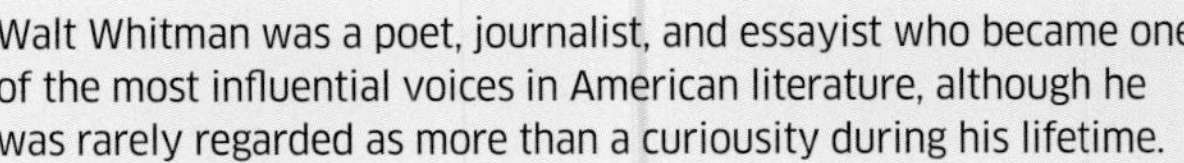
Walt Whitman was a poet, journalist, and essayist who became one of the most influential voices in American literature, although he was rarely regarded as more than a curiosity during his lifetime.

Whitman was born on Long Island, New York, and was one of eight children. His early life was impoverished and he undertook a variety of menial jobs, latterly as a printer and journalist. The publication of *Leaves of Grass*, financed by Whitman himself, represented a radical departure. Service as a medical orderly in the American Civil War imbued in him a shocked revulsion of the horror of war. His life thereafter was devoted to an endless reworking of *Leaves of Grass*.

In detail

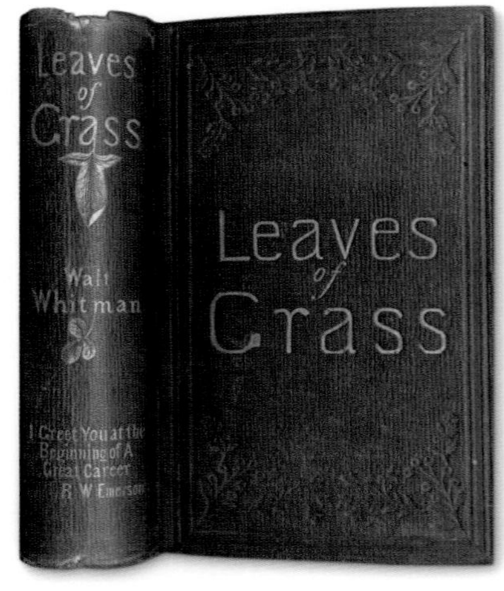

▲ **SECOND EDITION**

▲ **THIRD EDITION**

▲ **SIXTH EDITION**

◄ **CHANGING TIMES** There were six editions of *Leaves of Grass*, published in 1855, 1856, 1860–61, 1867, 1871–72, and 1881–82. The first two editions were bound in green to reflect the organic nature of Whitman's poetry. For the second edition Whitman designed the font used on the spine himself. The third edition, printed just before the American Civil War, is bound in red to represent looming bloodshed. The sixth edition, with its yellow cover, is suggestive of autumn, and reflects Whitman's belief that his life was drawing to an end.

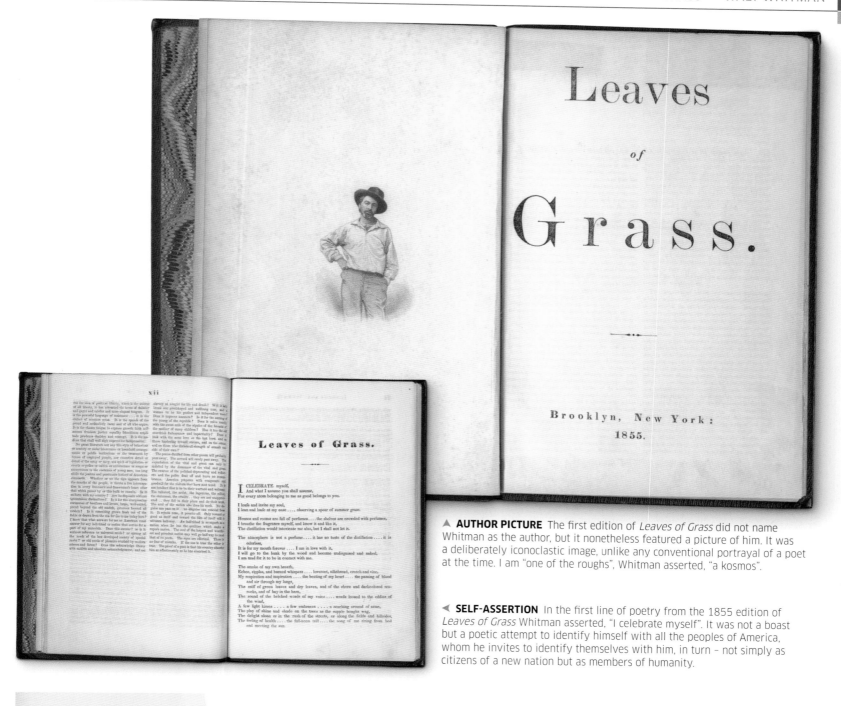

▲ **AUTHOR PICTURE** The first edition of *Leaves of Grass* did not name Whitman as the author, but it nonetheless featured a picture of him. It was a deliberately iconoclastic image, unlike any conventional portrayal of a poet at the time. I am "one of the roughs", Whitman asserted, "a kosmos".

◄ **SELF-ASSERTION** In the first line of poetry from the 1855 edition of *Leaves of Grass* Whitman asserted, "I celebrate myself". It was not a boast but a poetic attempt to identify himself with all the peoples of America, whom he invites to identify themselves with him, in turn – not simply as citizens of a new nation but as members of humanity.

◄ **INVOLVEMENT** With his background in printing, and his keen eye for detail, Whitman was always involved in the design and production of his books. He considered this project to be "The Great Construction of the New Bible", which is reflected in this contents page from the 1860 edition, where the poems are numbered and grouped, resembling divisions in the Bible.

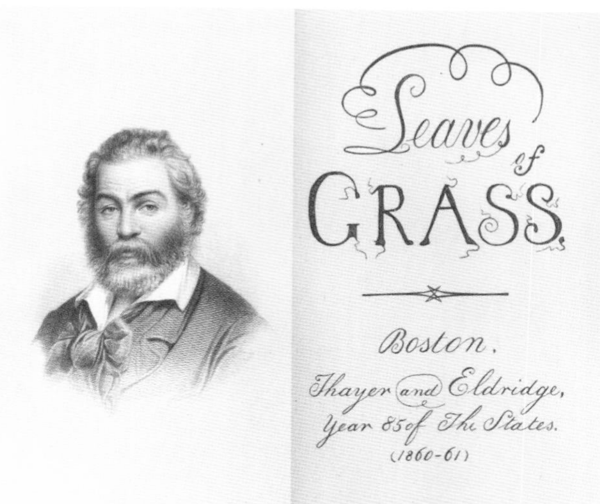

◄ **NEW IMAGE** For the frontispiece of the 1860 edition, Whitman dropped his American Everyman image (as above) and appeared in Byronic collar and cravat. The poet added a tail to the full-stop after the word "grass" in the title, which makes it look similar to a sperm – reflecting the book's themes of procreation and growth.

On the Origin of Species

1859 ▪ PRINTED ▪ DIMENSIONS UNKNOWN ▪ 502 PAGES ▪ UK

CHARLES DARWIN

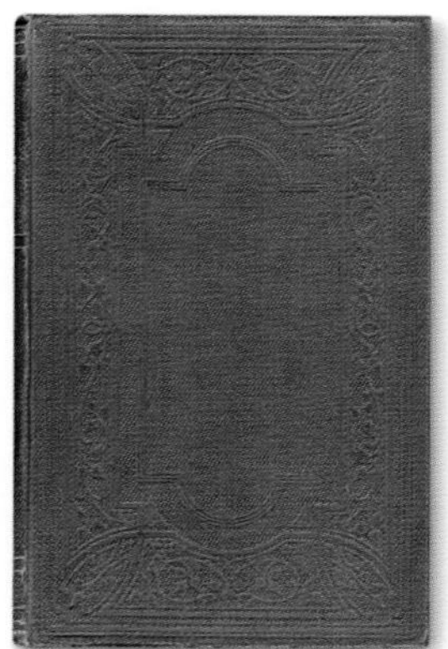

The publication of Charles Darwin's *On the Origin of Species* sent shock waves through pious Victorian society. His views on the theory of evolution were highly controversial, and contradicted what many believed at the time – that all life on earth had been created intact and was unchanging. In his book Darwin questioned this widely held belief, and suggested that evolution had occurred by a process called "natural selection" – a direct challenge to the Christian view of the divinely created world. As a Christian himself Darwin struggled with this idea, and in old age would come to describe himself as agnostic.

Darwin had first pursued a career in medicine, then in the Church, but in late 1831 he joined an expedition on the HMS *Beagle* as an unpaid geologist. The five years he spent on the ship led him to conclude that species were not fixed, as was popularly thought, but evolved over time through natural selection. Darwin laboured for more than 20 years formulating these ideas, and delayed publishing his theory as he "kept amassing information he could use to present a lengthy and well-reasoned argument". But in 1858 he was forced to publish an abstract of his work about evolution after receiving word that the anthropologist Alfred Russel Wallace had arrived at the same conclusion independently.

Darwin's book *On the Origin of Species by Means of Natural Selection, or the Preservation of Favoured Races in the Struggle for Life* was published in 1859 – the first run of 1,250 copies sold out immediately. A further 3,000 were printed, with additions and corrections, for January 1860. Six more editions came out in Darwin's lifetime.

While the concept of evolution in the animal kingdom gained in popularity, the idea that humans had also evolved was opposed by Christians (the book was hugely influential in the separation of the Church and science). During a debate in 1860, Darwin was as furiously denounced by the Bishop of Oxford, as he was passionately defended by biologist T.E. Huxley. Also present was *Beagle* captain, Robert Fitzroy, clutching a bible and appalled at his companion's betrayal.

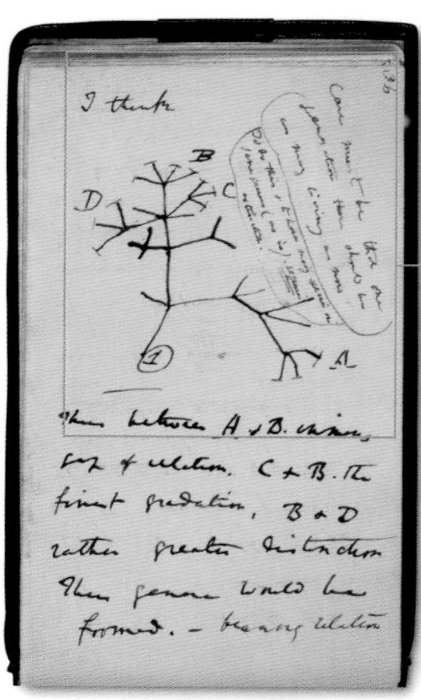

▲ **NOTEBOOK B** Darwin recorded his observations in a series of notebooks, labelled A to N. This is page 36 from book B and dates from July 1837.

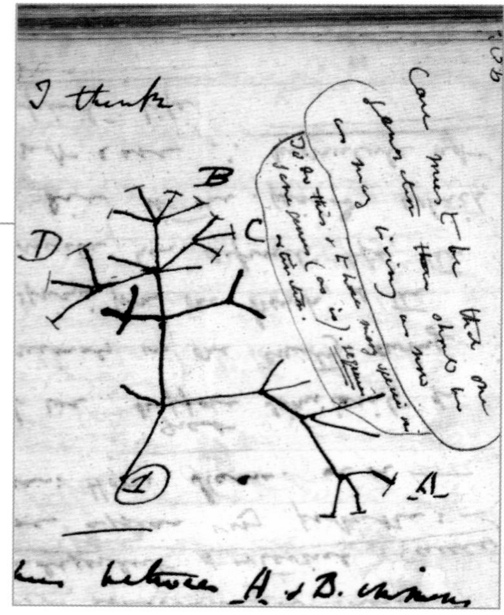

▲ **THE "EVOLUTIONARY TREE"** Darwin's notebooks contain sketches and diagrams, such as this version of his evolutionary tree, which describes his theory about the relationship between species in the same family, or genus.

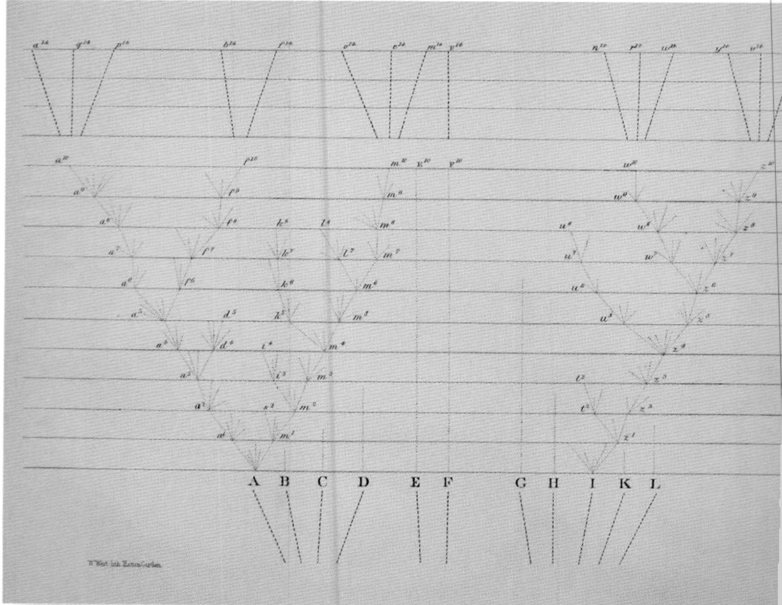

▲ **THE TREE OF LIFE** The only illustration in the first edition of *On the Origin of Species* was this fold-out lithograph by William West based on Darwin's earlier diagram (left). The species in it are labelled A to L along the base (and spaced irregularly to show how distinct they are from each other). The Roman numerals (I–XIV) represent thousands of generations.

"But with regard to the material world, we can at least go so far as this—we can perceive that events are brought about not by insulated interpositions of Divine power, exerted in each particular case, but by the establishment of general laws."

W. WHEWELL: *Bridgewater Treatise.*

"To conclude, therefore, let no man out of a weak conceit of sobriety, or an ill-applied moderation, think or maintain, that a man can search too far or be too well studied in the book of God's word, or in the book of God's works; divinity or philosophy; but rather let men endeavour an endless progress or proficience in both."

BACON: *Advancement of Learning.*

Down, Bromley, Kent,
October 1st, 1859.

ON

THE ORIGIN OF SPECIES

BY MEANS OF NATURAL SELECTION,

OR THE

PRESERVATION OF FAVOURED RACES IN THE STRUGGLE FOR LIFE.

BY CHARLES DARWIN, M.A.,

FELLOW OF THE ROYAL, GEOLOGICAL, LINNÆAN, ETC., SOCIETIES;
AUTHOR OF 'JOURNAL OF RESEARCHES DURING H. M. S. BEAGLE'S VOYAGE ROUND THE WORLD.'

LONDON:
JOHN MURRAY, ALBEMARLE STREET.
1859.

The right of Translation is reserved.

▲ **FIRST EDITION** Determined to publish ahead of Russel Wallace, Darwin completed his 155,000-word draft in April 1859 and was reading the printer's proofs by October. There was no time to commission engravings, which would also have made the book more expensive than the original price of 15 shillings, so the design is simple. On this left-hand page, from the first edition, there are quotes from the writings of philosophers William Whewell and Francis Bacon.

> One general law, leading to the advancement of all organic beings, namely, multiply, vary, let the strongest live and the weakest die ”
>
> **CHARLES DARWIN**, *ON THE ORIGIN OF SPECIES*

IN **CONTEXT**

In 1831 Darwin joined the crew of the HMS *Beagle* as a "gentleman naturalist" and set out on a voyage across the Atlantic. The ship explored the entire coastline of South America, then completed its circumnavigation via Tahiti, Australia, Mauritius, and the Cape of Good Hope. During the voyage Darwin kept a diary, filling up its 770 pages with detailed observations and notes. He meticulously collected fossils and other geological specimens, and drew up catalogues of bones, skins, and carcasses. HMS *Beagle* returned to England five years later in October 1836, and Darwin began formulating his ideas.

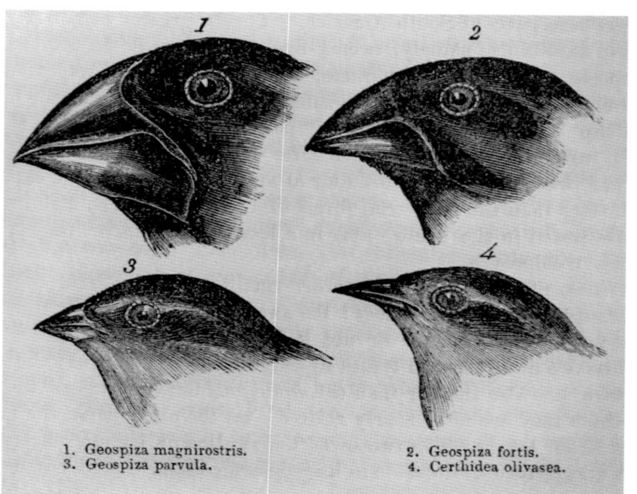

▲ **In September 1835** HMS *Beagle* visited the Galápagos Islands in the Pacific. Here Darwin discovered 13 different species of finches, all with different types of beak, which he realised had evolved independently to deal with the food available to the birds.

Alice's Adventures in Wonderland

1865 ▪ PRINTED ▪ 18.1 × 12.1 cm (7 × 5 in) ▪ 192 PAGES ▪ UK

SCALE

LEWIS CARROLL

Lewis Carroll's *Alice's Adventures in Wonderland* is one of the best-loved children's books ever created, and considered a cornerstone of the literary nonsense genre. In the first edition the fanciful story was perfectly matched by the exquisite pen and ink drawings of British illustrator John Tenniel. Countless illustrators have since tried their hands at portraying the Alice story, but none has yet come close to capturing the public's imagination or affection like the illustrations of the first edition.

Carroll originally made up his story about young Alice who falls down a rabbit hole, in the summer of 1862. He had befriended the daughters of the Dean of his Oxford College, and captivated the girls with his story while out with them on a boat trip. Alice Liddell was so enchanted that she begged Carroll to put the story down on paper. It took him over a year to write out the tale in his tiny, neat hand, and to illustrate it with 37 of his own sketches. Alice finally received the 90-page book in November 1864, dedicated to "a dear child, in memory of a summer day". This single, handwritten, personally illustrated manuscript, entitled "Alice's Adventures Under Ground", is now one of the British Library's greatest treasures. Friends who saw the manuscript urged him to publish it, and Carroll agreed, extending the story, adding jokes, and retitling it *Alice's Adventures in Wonderland*. He chose John Tenniel, a cartoonist for the magazine *Punch*, to illustrate it.

Tenniel was given precise instructions by Caroll and the author's own sketches to start from, but while the illustrations he created expertly capture Carroll's fantastic tale, they were uniquely his own style. Since its initial publication in 1865, *Alice's Adventures in Wonderland* has never been out of print and this perennial children's book remains popular to this day.

LEWIS **CARROLL**

1832–1898

Lewis Carroll was the pen-name for British mathematician and writer, Charles Lutwidge Dodgson, best-known for his *Alice* books.

The eldest of 11 children, Carroll was born in Cheshire but spent his teenage years in North Yorkshire – he often entertained his siblings by making up games and stories. He was a brilliant mathematician and became a lecturer in mathematics at Christ Church, Oxford, where he also wrote the children's books that made him famous: *Alice's Adventures in Wonderland* and its sequel *Through the Looking-Glass*, both of which display his love of wordplay and logic puzzles. Carroll was ordained as a church deacon in 1861 but he never became a priest. He was also an accomplished photographer. The huge popularity of the *Alice* books brought Carroll fame and wealth, although his later writings were less successful. He died of pneumonia in 1898.

32.

She sat for some while sorrowful and silent, but she was not long before she recovered. her spirits, and began talking to herself again as usual: "I do wish some of them had stayed a little longer! and I was getting to be such friends with them — really the Lory and I were almost like sisters! and so was that dear little Eaglet! And then the Duck and the Dodo! How nicely the Duck sang to us as we came along through the water: and if the Dodo hadn't known the way to that nice little cottage, I don't know when we should have got dry again —" and there is no knowing how long she might have prattled on in this way, if she had not suddenly caught the sound of pattering feet.

It was the white rabbit, trotting slowly back again, and looking anxiously about it as it went, as if it had lost something, and she heard it muttering to itself "the Marchioness! the Marchioness! oh my dear paws! oh my fur and whiskers! She'll have me executed, as sure as ferrets

18 33

are ferrets! Where can I have dropped them, I wonder?" Alice guessed in a moment that it was looking for the nosegay and the pair of white kid gloves, and she began hunting for them, but they were now nowhere to be seen — everything seemed to have changed since her swim in the pool, and her walk along the river-bank with its fringe of rushes and forget-me-nots, and the glass table and the little door had vanished.

Soon the rabbit noticed Alice, as she stood looking curiously about her, and at once said in a quick angry tone, "why, Mary Ann! what are you doing out here? Go home this moment, and look on my dressing-table for my gloves and nosegay, and fetch them here, as quick as you can run, do you hear?" and Alice was so much frightened that she ran off at once, without

◀ **A LABOUR OF LOVE** If it had not been for the persuasion of friends, Carroll's manuscript would have remained simply a private memento of a summer day with Alice and her sisters. Alice Liddell might have been the inspiration for Carroll's Alice, but with her short, dark, straight hair (see p.199), she was clearly not the model.

▶ **A COMPLETE VISION** Lewis Carroll's original manuscript is remarkable for how fully the story and images were realized. This page depicts the scene in which Alice plays the Queen at croquet, using hedgehogs as balls and a puzzled ostrich as a mallet. In the final published edition, Tenniel swaps the ostrich for a flamingo in his illustration, heightening the absurdity.

76

on their feet and hands, to make the arches.

The chief difficulty which Alice found at first was to manage her ostrich: she got its body tucked away, comfortably enough, under

her arm, with its legs hanging down, but generally, just as she had got its neck straightened out nicely, and was going to give a blow with its head, it would twist itself round, and look up into her face, with such a puzzled expression that she could not help bursting out laughing: and when she had got its head down, and was going to begin again, it was very confusing to find that the hedgehog had unrolled itself, and was in the act of crawling away: besides all this, there was generally a ridge or a furrow in her way, wherever she wanted to send the hedgehog to, and as the doubled-up soldiers were always getting up and walking off to other

> Why, sometimes I've believed as many as six impossible things before breakfast

THE QUEEN, *ALICE'S ADVENTURES IN WONDERLAND*

36

than she expected: before she had drunk half the bottle, she found her head pressing against the ceiling, and she stooped to save her neck from being broken, and hastily put down the bottle, saying to herself "that's quite enough — I hope I shan't grow any more — I wish I hadn't drunk so much!"

Alas! it was too late: she went on growing and growing, and very soon had to kneel down: in another minute there was not room even for this, and she tried the effect of lying down, with one elbow against the door, and the other arm curled round her head. Still she went on growing, and as a last resource she put one arm out of the window, and one foot up the chimney, and said to herself "now I can do no more — what will become of me?"

20 37.

▲ **INTERWOVEN NARRATIVE** Carroll's creative way of combining pictures and text can be seen to great effect in his "handmade copy". Here the illustration on the left shows the growing Alice, her form appearing to push against the text after drinking a magic potion. On the right she fills the whole page, her large head squeezed into the bottom corner, with her relatively small feet extending to the top.

In detail

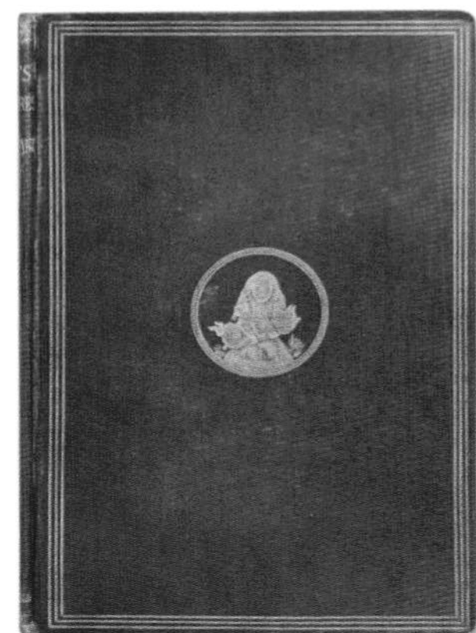

▲ **THE RED COVER** Conscious of his young readers, Carroll wanted his book to have a bright red cover rather than the green that his publishers, Macmillan, usually used. "Not the best, perhaps, artistically" he wrote to Macmillan, "but the most attractive to childish eyes".

26 49.

and her eyes immediately met those of a large blue caterpillar, which was sitting with its arms fold-ed, quietly smoking a long hookah, and taking not the least notice of her or of anything else.

For some time they looked at each other in silence: at last the caterpillar took the hookah out of its mouth, and languidly addressed her.

"Who are you?" said the caterpillar.

This was not an encouraging opening for a conversation: Alice replied rather shyly, "I — I hardly know, sir, just at present — at least I know who I was when I got up this morning, but I think I must have been changed several times since that."

"What do you mean by that?" said the caterpillar, "explain yourself!"

"I can't explain myself, I'm afraid, sir,"

▲ **ORIGINAL CHARACTERS** A popular character in the book is the caterpillar, which appears smoking a pipe on a mushroom. Carroll drew his own version of the caterpillar in his manuscript – a kind of optical illusion in which the folded length of the caterpillar forms the body of a seated mystic. In keeping with his strange appearance, the caterpillar's speech is obscure and he repeatedly asks Alice the existential question, "Who are you?", in a sleepy, languid tone.

CHAPTER V.

ADVICE FROM A CATERPILLAR.

THE Caterpillar and Alice looked at each other for some time in silence: at last the Caterpillar took the hookah out of its mouth, and addressed her in a languid, sleepy voice.

"Who are *you?*" said the Caterpillar.

▲ **TENNIEL'S INTERPRETATION** Tenniel drew his own version of Carroll's caterpillar, but an ambiguous one that toyed with visual interpretations: its head could be read as a man's face in profile, with protruding human nose and chin, or as the anatomically correct body of a caterpillar. The elongated, looping hose of the pipe adds to the overall sense of mystery. For many of the illustrations Tenniel received explicit instructions from Carroll, but his style, with its precise classical lines, is instantly recognizable.

▲ **HATTER'S TEA PARTY** As he prepared his manuscript for publication, Carroll elaborated on his story considerably, adding scenes such as "The Caucus Race", "Pig and Pepper", and, most famous of all, "A Mad Tea-Party" in which the Hatter and the March Hare bombard Alice with riddles.

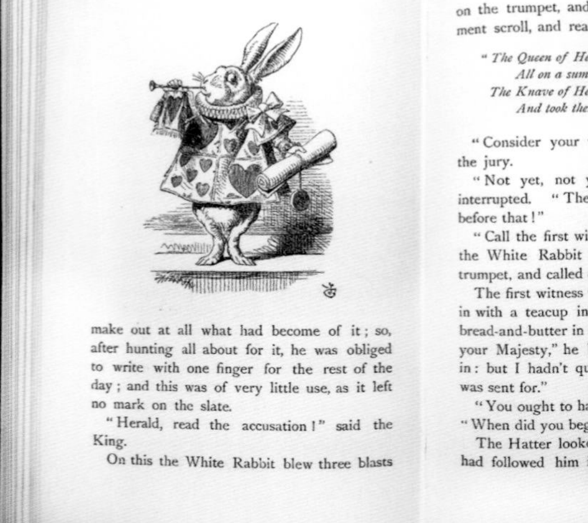

150 WHO STOLE

make out at all what had become of it; so, after hunting all about for it, he was obliged to write with one finger for the rest of the day; and this was of very little use, as it left no mark on the slate.

"Herald, read the accusation!" said the King.

On this the White Rabbit blew three blasts

THE TARTS? 151

on the trumpet, and then unrolled the parchment scroll, and read as follows:—

"The Queen of Hearts, she made some tarts,
All on a summer day:
The Knave of Hearts, he stole those tarts,
And took them quite away!"

"Consider your verdict," the King said to the jury.

"Not yet, not yet!" the Rabbit hastily interrupted. "There's a great deal to come before that!"

"Call the first witness," said the King; and the White Rabbit blew three blasts on the trumpet, and called out "First witness!"

The first witness was the Hatter. He came in with a teacup in one hand and a piece of bread-and-butter in the other. "I beg pardon, your Majesty," he began, "for bringing these in: but I hadn't quite finished my tea when I was sent for."

"You ought to have finished," said the King. "When did you begin?"

The Hatter looked at the March Hare, who had followed him into the court, arm-in-arm

◀ **LINE ENGRAVINGS** Tenniel traced his original ink drawings onto woodblocks using a hard pencil. The woodblocks were then engraved by the Brothers Dalziel and used to make the metal electrotypes, which captured the detail of Tenniel's illustrations – as seen here in this drawing of the anthromorphic White Rabbit.

▼ **TALE OF A TAIL** Carroll's wit shone through even in the book's inventive use of typography. The mouse's tale is a multiple pun. Besides being a tale about a tail, it is also typeset in the shape of a tail, and is a "tail rhyme" – a poem in which rhymed lines are followed by a shorter, unrhyming "tail" line.

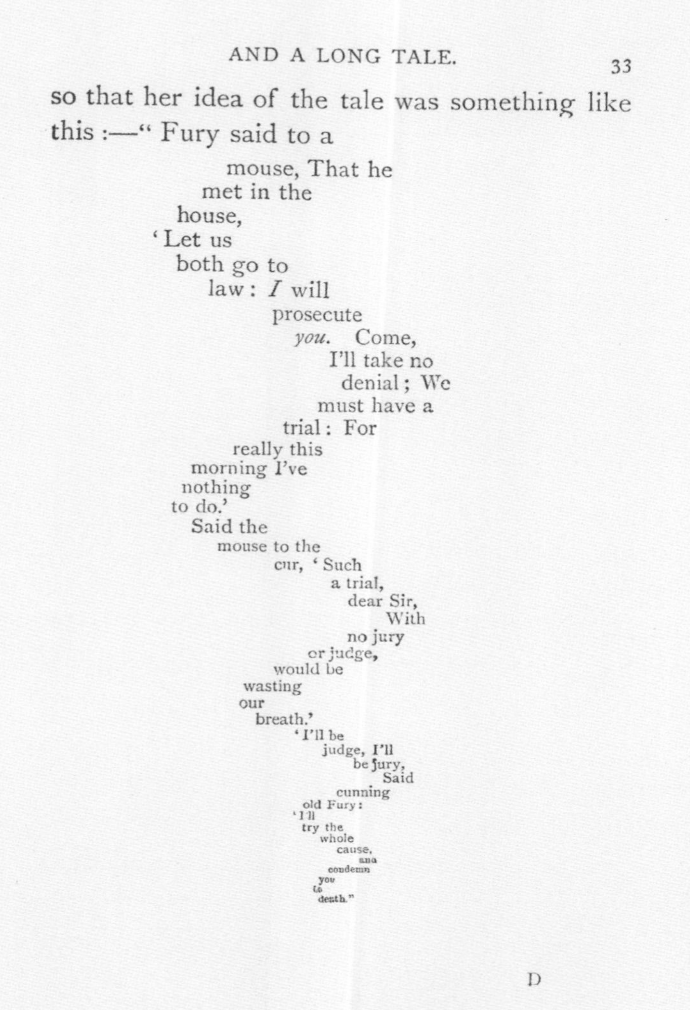

AND A LONG TALE. 33

so that her idea of the tale was something like this :—" Fury said to a
mouse, That he
met in the
house,
'Let us
both go to
law: *I* will
prosecute
you. Come,
I'll take no
denial; We
must have a
trial: For
really this
morning I've
nothing
to do.'
Said the
mouse to the
cur, 'Such
a trial,
dear Sir,
With
no jury
or judge,
would be
wasting
our
breath.'
'I'll be
judge, I'll
be jury,'
Said
cunning
old Fury:
'I'll
try the
whole
cause,
and
condemn
you
to
death."

D

82 PIG AND PEPPER

"But I don't want to go among mad people," Alice remarked.

"Oh, you can't help that," said the Cat: "we're all mad here. I'm mad. You're mad."

"How do you know I'm mad?" said Alice.

"You must be," said the Cat, "or you wouldn't have come here."

Alice didn't think that proved it at all; how-

▲ **EXTRA CHARACTERS** The Cheshire Cat, with its wide, mischievous grin, was added by Carroll when he expanded his initial story for its first publication with Tenniel's black and white illustrations.

And that reminds me. There's a little lesson I want to teach *you*, while we're looking at this picture of Alice and the Cat. Now don't be in a bad temper about it, my dear Child! It's a very *little* lesson indeed!

Do you see that Fox-Glove growing close to the tree? And do you know why it's called a *Fox*-Glove? Perhaps you

▲ **CHILDREN'S EDITION** In 1890 Lewis Carroll wrote a shortened version: *The Nursery "Alice"*, aimed at younger readers. It was, in Carroll's words, a book "to be cooed over, to be dogs'-eared". The publication was the first in which Alice appeared in colour.

> "How do you know I'm mad ?" said Alice. - "You must be" said the cat "or you wouldn't have come here."
>
> **ALICE AND THE CHESHIRE CAT**, *ALICE'S ADVENTURES IN WONDERLAND*

IN **CONTEXT**

Experts have long debated the relationship between the Alice of Carroll's book and Alice Liddell. Alice Liddell was born on 4 May, 1852, and was just 10 years old when Carroll took her and her sisters, Lorina and Edith, on the memorable boating trip on which he first invented his story. Carroll was fond of his young friend, taking several photographs of her, including a famous one of her dressed as a beggar girl. Carroll was naturally shy and awkward with a pronounced stutter, and he openly preferred the company of children. Sometime during 1863, Alice's mother stopped Carroll from seeing Alice and her sisters, following an argument that has since been the cause of much speculation. However, Alice's links with the book remained. Carroll dedicated both of his *Alice* books to her, and in *Through the Looking Glass* he included a poem, "A Boat Beneath A Sunny Sky", in which the first letter of each line combine to spell out her name in full. From the day *Alice's Adventures in Wonderland* was published in 1865 until she died in 1934, aged 82, Alice Liddell was known as "the real Alice". She kept her manuscript of "Alice's Adventures Under Ground" until she was forced to sell it in 1928 for money to pay death duties.

► **The dark, short-haired**, sharp-looking Alice Liddell appeared very different to the fair, long-haired Alice of Tenniel's illustrations.

Das Kapital

1867, 1885, AND 1894 ■ PRINTED ■ DIMENSIONS UNKNOWN ■ 2,846 PAGES (IN 3 VOLUMES) ■ GERMANY

KARL MARX

Vast, sprawling, and dense, Karl Marx's theoretical economic and political text *Das Kapital* provided the intellectual foundation of communism. Part history, part philosophy, but with economics at its core, it formed a blueprint of what Marx considered the destiny of humanity. Marx argued that capitalism, the economic system powering a newly industrialized world, was merely a phase in a continuing historical evolution, and therefore would inevitably be superseded.

The text's primary focus was the exploitation of the working classes (proletariat). Marx believed that as the proletariat became increasingly class conscious it would rise up, sweeping away its capitalist oppressors. Marx asserted that in this way, capitalism contained the seeds of its own downfall, and that a rational economic system, centrally planned in the interests of all, would develop in its place. Privilege and subjugation would play no part in the new system, its dominant creed being, "From each according to his ability, to each according to his needs" – a socialist utopia. This message struck a chord at a time of immense social and industrial change (see opposite) and *Das Kapital* came to be known as "the Bible of the working classes".

KARL **MARX**

1818–1883

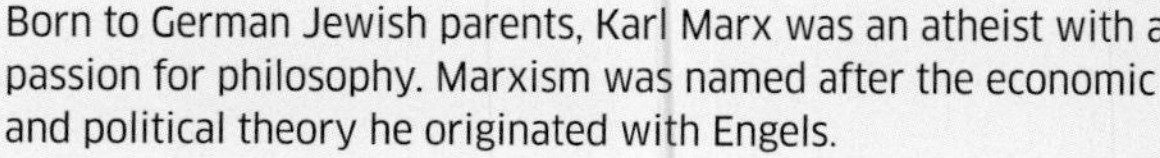

Born to German Jewish parents, Karl Marx was an atheist with a passion for philosophy. Marxism was named after the economic and political theory he originated with Engels.

Marx was a product of the political chaos that engulfed much of Europe after 1830. While at Berlin University for five years studying law and philosophy, he was introduced to the philosophy of the late Georg Hegel, who contended that humanity was destined to suffer from violent change. Marx used his talents as a journalist to criticize the political and cultural establishments of the time, but his writings caused him to be expelled by the French, German, and Belgian governments. In 1848, he co-wrote *The Communist Manifesto* with Friedrich Engels. In 1849, he moved to London, where he stayed for the rest of his life.

The book was published in three volumes. The first, written by Marx alone and published in 1867, was the only one of the three manuscripts to be completed while Marx was still alive. His lifelong friend and editor, Friedrich Engels (1820–95), compiled the remainder from Marx's notes and his own research. The second and third volumes were published in 1885 and 1894 respectively.

Marx's influence was far-reaching. The Russian Revolution (1917) and Chinese Revolution (1949) both claimed Marxism as their justification. By the mid 20th century, half the world lived in self-proclaimed Marxist states.

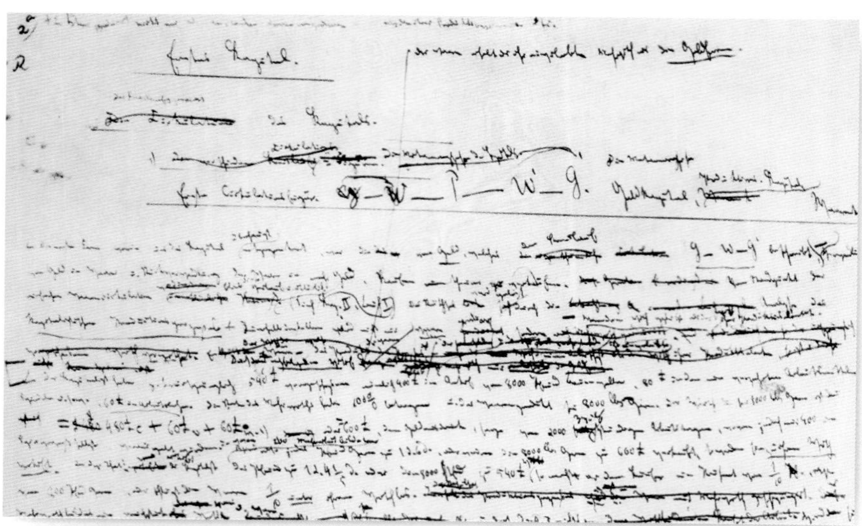

▲ **ORIGINAL NOTES** Marx made vast amounts of notes and amendments when preparing his book. By 1865 he had an indecipherable manuscript of around 1,200 pages. It took a year of editing to reach a final, clean copy that was ready to be published.

➤ **FIRST VOLUME** The first volume of *Das Kapital* highlights the inherent unfairness that Marx saw in the capitalist mode of production or *Der Produktionsprozess des Kapitals*, as stated in the title here.

Erstes Buch.

Der Produktionsprozess des Kapitals.

Erstes Kapitel.

Waare und Geld.

1) Die Waare.

Der Reichthum der Gesellschaften, in welchen kapitalistische Produktionsweise herrscht, erscheint als eine „ungeheure Waarensammlung"[1], die einzelne Waare als seine Elementarform. Unsere Untersuchung beginnt daher mit der Analyse der Waare.

Die Waare ist zunächst ein äusserer Gegenstand, ein Ding, das durch seine Eigenschaften menschliche Bedürfnisse irgend einer Art befriedigt. Die Natur dieser Bedürfnisse, ob sie z. B. dem Magen oder der Phantasie entspringen, ändert nichts an der Sache[2]). Es handelt sich hier auch nicht darum, wie die Sache das menschliche Bedürfniss befriedigt, ob unmittelbar als Lebensmittel, d. h. als Gegenstand des Genusses, oder auf einem Umweg, als Produktionsmittel.

Jedes nützliche Ding, wie Eisen, Papier u. s. w., ist unter doppeltem

[1]) Karl Marx: „Zur Kritik der Politischen Oekonomie. Berlin 1859", p. 4.

[2]) „Desire implies want; it is the appetite of the mind, and as natural as hunger to the body .... the greatest number (of things) have their value from supplying the wants of the mind." Nicholas Barbon: „A Discourse on coining the new money lighter, in answer to Mr. Locke's Considerations etc. London 1696", p. 2, 3.

I. 1

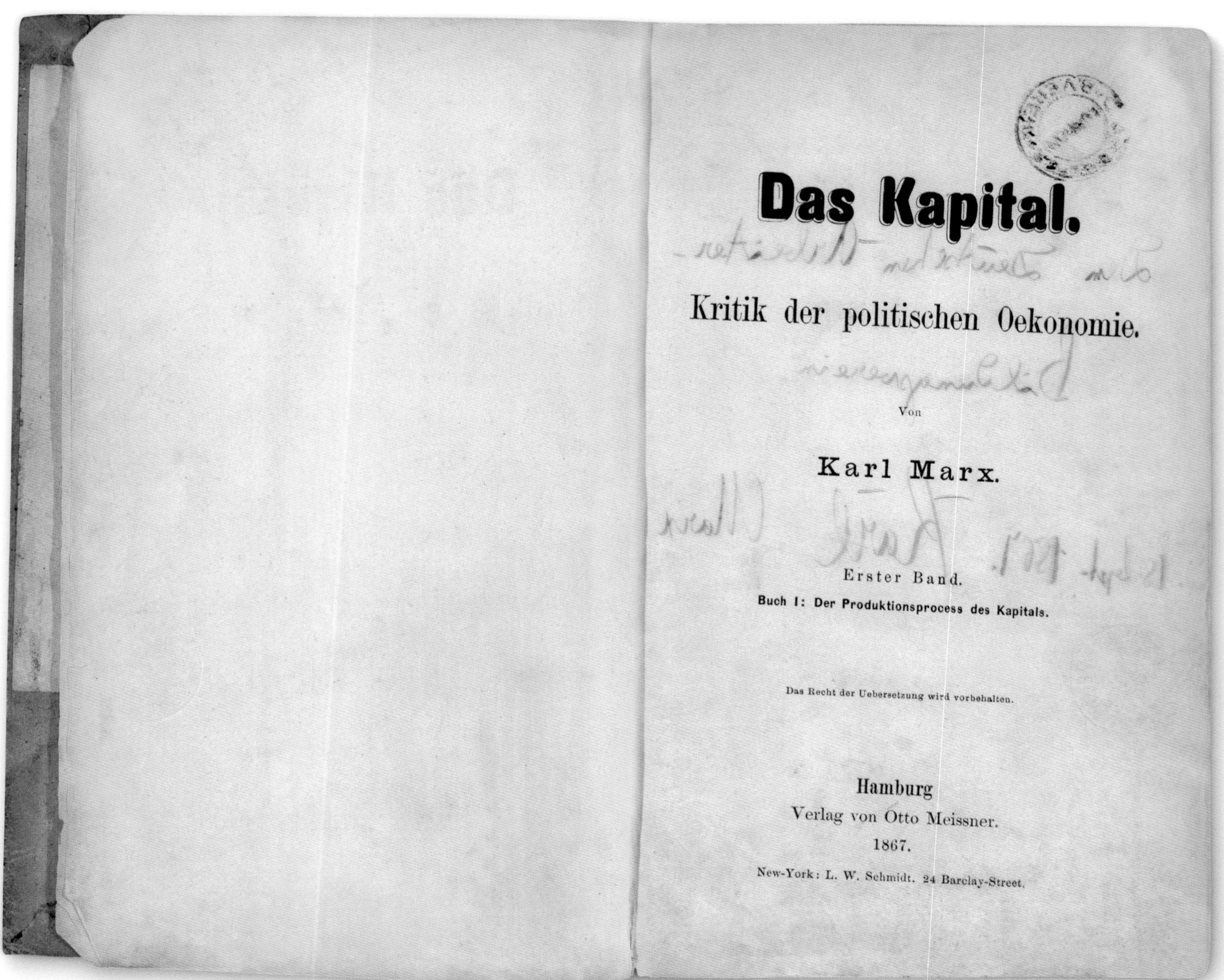

Das Kapital.

Kritik der politischen Oekonomie.

Von

Karl Marx.

Erster Band.

Buch I: Der Produktionsprocess des Kapitals.

Das Recht der Uebersetzung wird vorbehalten.

Hamburg

Verlag von Otto Meissner.

1867.

New-York: L. W. Schmidt. 24 Barclay-Street.

▲ **TITLE PAGE** As recorded on this page, *Das Kapital* was published in Hamburg, Germany, by publisher Otto Meissner, who had previously published Engels' work. Marx delivered the manuscript in 1866 and a small run of 1,000 copies was printed the following year.

> Money is the alienated essence of man's labour and life; and this alien essence dominates him as he worships it
>
> **KARL MARX**, *DAS KAPITAL*

IN **CONTEXT**

It was in the Reading Room of the then British Museum that Marx wrote the first volume of *Das Kapital*, at a time of huge social change. The Industrial Revolution had resulted in workers living in grinding poverty while their masters amassed great wealth. Marx believed it was inevitable that the workers would eventually overthrow their masters, whom he termed the "bourgeoisie". Many of Marx's revolutionary ideas had been published before *Das Kapital*, for example in his *The Communist Manifesto* (1848) (see p.212), which had little impact when published. However, Marx's works became a call to arms for revolutionaries in the 20th century, and within a hundred years of Marx's death, some of the world's most brutal dictators, including Stalin and Mao, ruled their populations in the name of Marxism.

КАПИТАЛЪ.

КРИТИКА ПОЛИТИЧЕСКОЙ ЭКОНОМІИ.

КАРЛА МАРКСА.

ТОМЪ ПЕРВЫЙ.

КНИГА I. ПРОЦЕССЪ ПРОИЗВОДСТВА КАПИТАЛА.

С.-ПЕТЕРБУРГЪ.

ИЗДАНІЕ Н. П. ПОЛЯКОВА.

➤ **This cover** is from the Russian edition of *Das Kapital* (1872). The censors considered it irrelevant, believing no capitalist exploitation occurred in Tsarist Russia.

The Works of Geoffrey Chaucer Now Newly Imprinted

1896 ▪ PRINTED BY KELMSCOTT PRESS ▪ 43.5 × 30.5 cm (17 × 12 in) ▪ 564 PAGES ▪ UK

SCALE

GEOFFREY CHAUCER

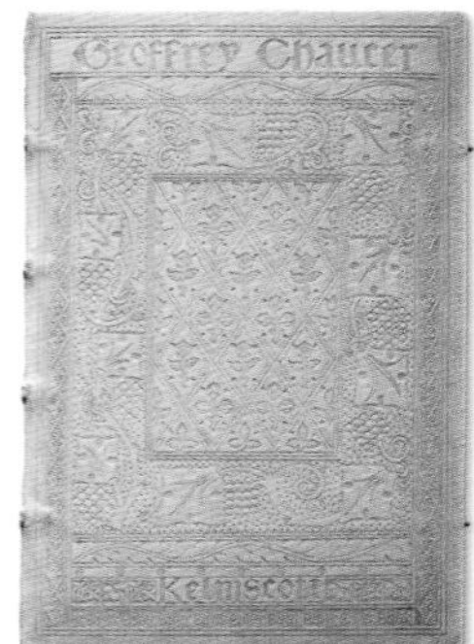

This exquisite edition of Geoffrey Chaucer's works is one of the most glorious examples of late Victorian printing, and the crowning achievement of the Kelmscott Press, which was founded by 19th-century designer William Morris. Known as the Kelmscott Chaucer and designed by Morris himself, it was a masterpiece of artistry, and exceptional for its lavish ornamentation and the quantity of its illustrations. The book features 87 woodcut illustrations, 14 different richly decorated borders, 18 individual frames, and 26 large ornamental initials. Edward Burne-Jones (1833–98), the British artist and lifelong friend of Morris, designed the woodcuts and worked closely with Morris throughout the project. Morris's own Troy typeface was used for the titles, while the main text was set in a smaller version of that type and printed in black and red. The book was printed on Batchelor handmade paper with a watermark also designed by Morris.

Morris, a former designer of luxurious fabrics and furniture, believed the quality of book printing had deteriorated with machine printing during the Industrial Age, and wanted to revive old crafts. The labour-intensive hand-printing method that Morris favoured resulted in the book taking four years to complete and being hugely expensive to produce. Morris printed (and pre-sold) just 425 copies of the book, as the production costs made it uneconomical to print any more.

The harmonious partnership of Morris and Burne-Jones meant that the level of illustration and decoration that lavished every single page set a new standard for book design: the Kelmscott Chaucer is still considered one of the most beautiful books ever published.

GEOFFREY **CHAUCER**

1343–1400

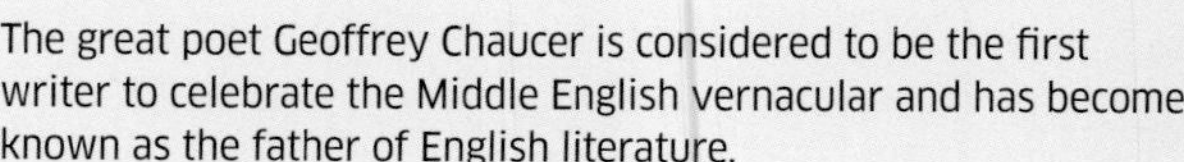

The great poet Geoffrey Chaucer is considered to be the first writer to celebrate the Middle English vernacular and has become known as the father of English literature.

It is thought that Chaucer was born in London, although the precise date and location of his birth is not known. His father was a vintner (wine merchant) based in London, who came from a line of merchants. Chaucer studied law at the Inner Temple, and then through his father's connections became a page to Elizabeth de Burgh, the Countess of Ulster. This was a kind of apprenticeship and it brought the young Chaucer into the circle of the court, and was the beginning of his successful career as a bureaucrat, courtier, and diplomat. Chaucer's best-known work is *The Canterbury Tales*, which he started writing around the 1380s, after moving to Kent. The collection of 24 stories paint a twisted picture of English society at the time. The book stands apart from the literature of the day, partly for its language – vernacular English, rather than French or Latin, which were commonly used for the written word – but also for the wide variety of the tales it contains, and the naturalism of its narrative and characters. His other works include the epic poem *Troilus and Criseyde*, *Parlement of Foules*, *Treatise on the Astrolabe*, as well as some translations.

▼ **DECORATIVE INITIALS** Several different versions of capital letters were designed to provide variety and interest throughout the text. Each elaborately decorated initial, printed using stiff, black, German ink, took up several lines of ordinary text.

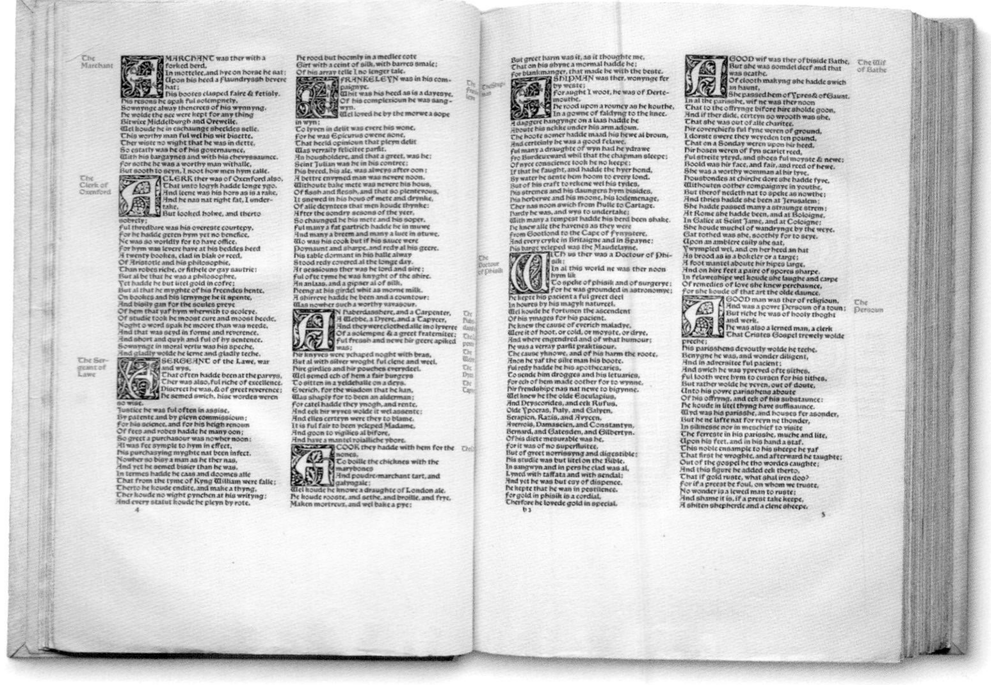

> If we live to finish it, it will be like a **pocket cathedral** – so **full of design** and I think Morris the **greatest master of ornament** in the world
>
> **EDWARD BURNE-JONES**, IN A LETTER TO CHARLES ELIOT NORTON, 1894

the works of Geoffrey Chaucer now newly imprinted

HERE BEGINNETH THE TALES OF CANTERBURY AND FIRST THE PROLOGUE THEREOF

WHAN THAT Aprille with his shoures soote
The droghte of March hath perced to the roote,
And bathed every veyne in swich licour,
Of which vertu engendred is the flour;
Whan Zephirus eek with his swete breeth
Inspired hath in every holt and heeth
The tendre croppes, and the yonge sonne
Hath in the Ram his halfe cours yronne,
And smale foweles maken melodye,
That slepen al the nyght with open eye,
So priketh hem nature in hir corages;
Thanne longen folk to goon on pilgrimages,
And palmeres for to seken straunge strondes,
To ferne halwes, kowthe in sondry londes;
And specially, from every shires ende
Of Engelond, to Caunterbury they wende,
The hooly blisful martir for to seke,
That hem hath holpen whan that they were seeke.

BIFIL that in that seson on a day,
In Southwerk at the Tabard as I lay,
Redy to wenden on my pilgrymage
To Caunterbury with ful devout corage,
At nyght were come into that hostelrye
Wel nyne and twenty in a compaignye,
Of sondry folk, by aventure yfalle
In felaweshipe, and pilgrimes were they alle,
That toward Caunterbury wolden ryde.

▲ **TITLE PAGE** With its elaborate borders, this spread reflects Morris's desire to revive the quality and elegance of 15th-century hand-printing. The Kelmscott Chaucer was printed on Bachelor handmade paper with a perch-shaped watermark, which Morris designed himself. The paper was made from linen rags; Morris refused to add wood pulp to his paper as it turned pages slightly brown; rag paper retained its brightness for longer.

In detail

▼ **TREATISE ON THE ASTROLABE** Leading on from the last page of *The Book of the Duchess* (left), which was Chaucer's first major poem, is his *Treatise on the Astrolabe*. This treatise is a significant example of early technical writing. The first page (right) has a richly decorated margin enclosing the text and illustration, which shows a man holding an astrolabe, next to a boy who clutches his robe while looking up at the sky. This reflects Chaucer's text, which is addressed to his son, "Lowis".

► **FLORAL MOTIF** Morris did not draw his flowers from real life, but copied them from photographs and pictures in books. Many English flora were included in the ornamentation.

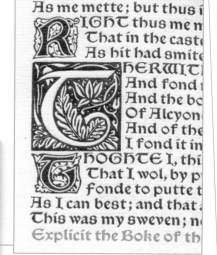

As me mette; but thus i
RIGHT thus me m
That in the cast
As hit had smit
HERWITH
And fond
And the bo
Of Alcyon
And of the
I fond it in
THOGHTE I, thi
That I wol, by p
fonde to putte t
As I can best; and that
This was my sweven; n
Explicit the Boke of th

▼ **FIRST WORD** Intricate decoration is used to highlight the first word of the paragraph, in this case "little". The letters are surrounded by coiling leaves, flowers, and berries.

RIKNE how manye degrees of almikanteras, in the meridional lyne, be fro the cercle equinoxial unto the senith; or elles fro the pool artik un/ to the north orisonte; & for so gret a latitude or for so smal a latitude is the table compouned. And for more declaracion, lo here thy figure.

22. To knowe in special the latitude of oure countray, I mene after the latitude of Oxen/ ford, and the heighte of oure pol. (Adcognoscendum specialiter latitudinem nostri regionis, scilicet latitudinem Oxonie, et altitudinem poli nostri.)

A Treatise on the Astrolabe

▲ **RUNNING HEAD** Aligned with the top of the column text on each page in the margin is a running head printed in red ink. It simply repeats the title of the text to help orientate the reader through the volume.

► **TYPOGRAPHY** Morris designed the typeface himself to suit the character of Chaucer's text. The text is set in double columns, printed largely in black ink interspersed with shorter paragraphs of red. The decorative capitals at the beginning of the paragraphs are six lines deep.

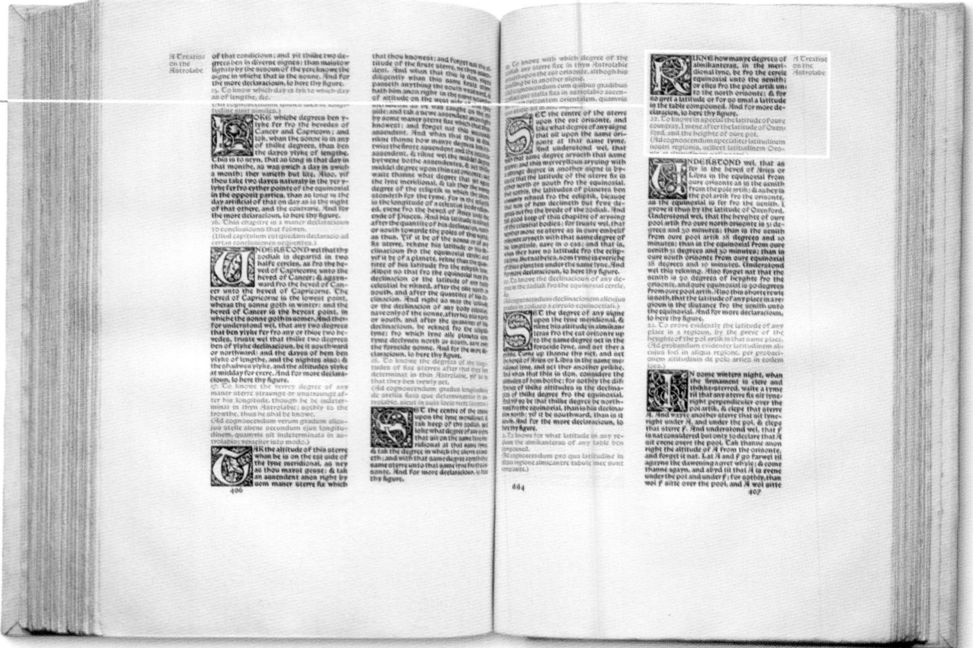

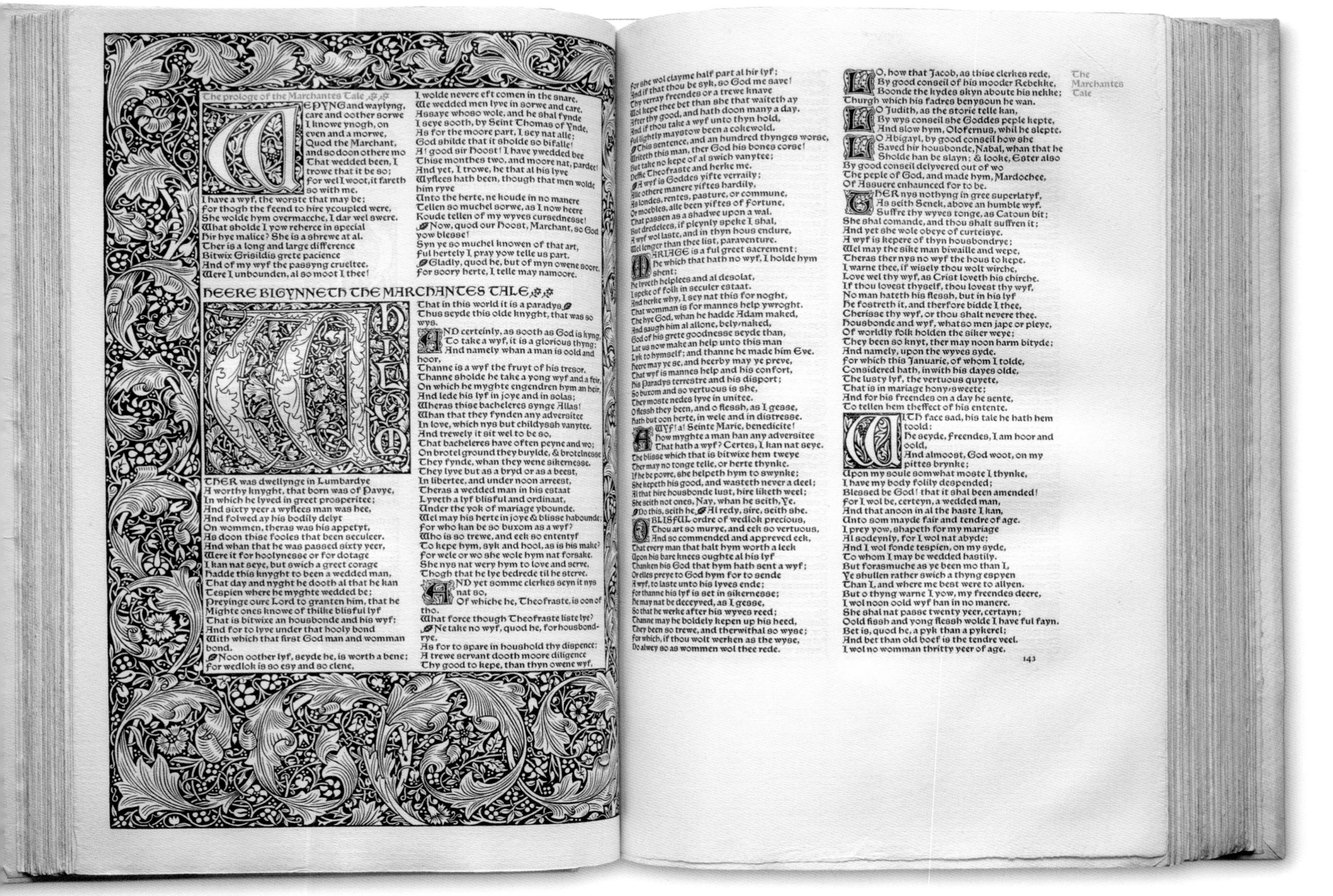

▲ **"THE MERCHANT'S TALE"**
One of Chaucer's *Canterbury Tales*, "The Merchant's Tale" is deeply satirical and – as with some of his other Tales – somewhat lewd by the standards of the time. Morris presents it inside a deep margin, beautifully decorated with the natural motifs of leaves and flowers that run throughout the volume. The first capital letter of the Tale, after the prologue, takes up the full width of one column and is 19 lines deep. Decorative capitals three lines deep and small capitals are used at the start of each paragraph. A small leaf motif is dropped into the text to indicate the start of a character's speech.

IN **CONTEXT**

The 15th-century printer William Caxton produced the first printed English edition of Chaucer, and this edition influenced Morris in his work at Kelmscott Press. Caxton had observed books printed using movable type during his travels in Europe, and learned the art of printing during his time in Cologne in the early 1470s. In 1476 he returned to London and set up the first printing press in Westminster. His early books included two editions of *The Canterbury Tales*, the second of which featured 26 woodcut illustrations. The illustrations, produced locally, were based on woodcuts that Caxton had seen in France. He used an elegant Burgundian type – the second edition had a smaller version of the script in order to fit more words on each page. It was this second illustrated edition that inspired Morris's Kelmscott Chaucer.

▲ **Mounted pilgrims** precede each tale in Caxton's second edition, decorating the pages and enlivening the text. The woodcuts were made by a local artist and some are used more than once.

In detail

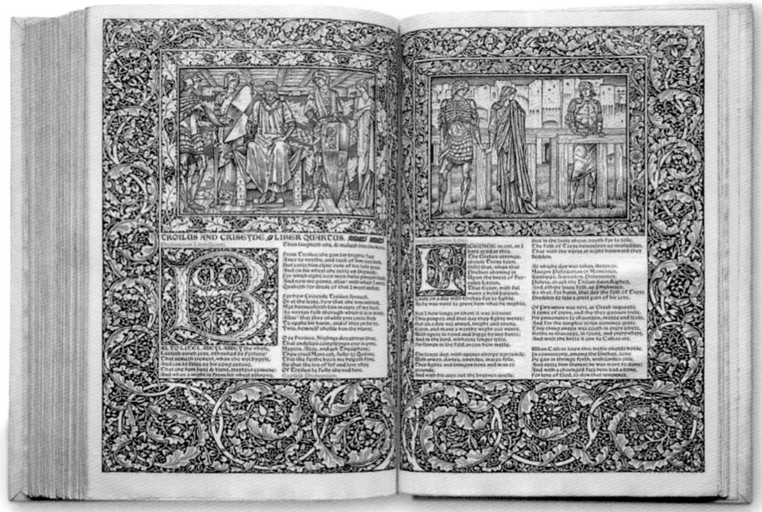

▲ **TROILUS AND CRISEYDE** Chaucer's epic poem was a tragic tale of love and betrayal set against the backdrop of the Trojan wars. These scenes are evocative of the pre-Raphaelite School to which Edward Burne-Jones was affiliated, and which enjoyed popularity in Victorian England.

ON **TECHNIQUE**

Turning his back on the increasing mechanization and industrialization of the age, William Morris prized the beauty and skill of true craftsmanship, and sought to use traditional techniques in the manufacture of all the books produced by Kelmscott Press. Just as he employed hand-printing inside his books, the outer covers were also crafted by hand. The Industrial Revolution threatened bookbinding and the elaborately decorated first editions of the Kelmscott Chaucer represent a direct reaction against the utilitarian approach that was becoming more commonplace at the time. The pigskin binding is set over oak boards and decorated with a pattern created by hand-stamping. This technique involved creating impressions with hand tools to form a background, while leaving the motifs of the design standing out in relief. The work was undertaken by the Doves Bindery in Hammersmith, London, then operated by TJ Cobden-Sanderson. Like Morris, Cobden-Sanderson was active in the Arts and Crafts Movement. In creating the Kelmscott Chaucer they undoubtedly achieved their aim of producing a book that was a work of art in itself rather than simply a useful object.

▲ **Four styles of binding** were made – the most luxurious of which was pigskin. Morris sent 48 of the first printed copies to the Doves Bindery for these editions to be specially bound in white pigskin with intricate decorative stamping, and finished with silver clasps on white pigskin straps.

▲ **BOLD DESIGNS** This decorative border is reminiscent of the hand-drawn medieval manuscripts that Morris hoped to emulate in his design of the Kelmscott Chaucer. Burne-Jones completed 87 pencil sketches in total, working long into the night to finish them. Artist Robert Catterson-Smith then used Indian ink and Chinese white to trace the drawings, in preparation for engraving the image onto woodblocks to create bold, black and white designs.

ER TERCIUS.

heried be thy might and thy goodnesse!

n hevene and helle, in erthe and salte see
s felt thy might, if that I wel descerne;
s man, brid, best, fish, herbe and grene tree
hee fele in tymes with vapour eterne.
od loveth, and to love wol nought werne;
nd in this world no lyves creature,
ithouten love, is worth, or may endure.

e Joves first to thilke effectes glade,
horugh which that thinges liven alle and be,
omeveden, and amorous him made
n mortal thing, and as yow list, ay ye
eve him in love ese or adversitee;
nd in a thousand formes doun him sente
or love in erthe, and whom yow liste, he
ente.

e fierse Mars apeysen of his ire,
nd, as yow list, ye maken hertes digne;
lgates, hem that ye wol sette afyre,
hey dreden shame, and vices they resigne;
e do hem corteys be, fresshe and benigne,
nd hye or lowe, after a wight entendeth;
he joyes that he hath, your might him
ndeth.

Ye holden regne and hous in unitee;
Ye soothfast cause of frendship been
also;
Ye knowe al thilke covered qualitee
Of thinges which that folk on wondren so,
Whan they can not construe how it may jo,
She loveth him, or why he loveth here;
As why this fish, and nought that, cometh
to were.

Ye folk a lawe han set in universe,
And this knowe I by hem that loveres be,
That whoso stryveth with yow hath the
werse:
Now, lady bright, for thy benignitee,
At reverence of hem that serven thee,
Whos clerk I am, so techeth me devyse
Som joye of that is felt in thy servyse.

Ye in my naked herte sentement
Inhelde, and do me shewe of thy swetnesse.
Caliope, thy vois be now present,
For now is nede; sestow not my destresse,
How I mot telle anon-right the gladnesse
Of Troilus, to Venus heryinge?
To which gladnes, who nede hath, God him
bringe!

Explicit prohemium Tercii Libri.

Incipit Liber Tercius.

LAY al this mene whyle
Troilus,
Recordinge his lessoun
in this manere:
Ma fey! thought he,
thus wole I seye and
thus;
Thus wole I pleyne un-
to my lady dere;
That word is good, and
this shal be my chere;
This nil I not foryeten in no wyse.
God leve him werken as he gan devyse.

And Lord, so that his herte gan to quappe,
Heringe hir come, and shorte for to syke!
And Pandarus, that ladde hir by the lappe,
Com ner, and gan in at the curtin pyke,
And seyde: God do bote on alle syke!
See, who is here yow comen to visyte;
Lo, here is she that is your deeth to wyte.

Therwith it semed as he wepte almost:
A ha, quod Troilus so rewfully,
Wher me be wo, O mighty God, thou wost!
Who is al there? I see nought trewely.
Sire, quod Criseyde, it is Pandare and I.

Un Coup de Dés

1897 (MAGAZINE), 1914 (BOOK) ▪ PRINTED ▪ 32 × 25 cm (12 × 10 in) ▪ 32 PAGES ▪ FRANCE

SCALE

STÉPHANE MALLARMÉ

Generally translated as *A Throw of the Dice Will Never Abolish Chance*, the poem *Un Coup de Dés*, more properly *Un Coup de Dés Jamais n'Abolira Le Hasard*, was written by the Symbolist poet Stéphane Mallarmé. It exemplifies the late 19th-century revolution in Western art that redefined every certainty of what art was – definitions established 400 years earlier during the Renaissance. The radical shift occurred almost exclusively in France, but its influence soon swept around the world.

No poet was more important in its development than Mallarmé. Rejecting realism and naturalism, he used dreams and symbols to explain the enduring mysteries of human existence, giving rise to a new sense of what poetry might mean. This "Symbolism", as it became known, for Mallarmé meant a new poetic language in which the sounds of spoken words played as key a role as their meanings. In addition, their exact placement around the page encouraged a non-linear reading that allowed ambiguity and an infinite series of interpretations. Mallarmé's approach would have an enduring influence on numerous 20th-century poets and thinkers – Eliot, Joyce, and Pound among them. For non-French readers, however, Mallarmé's poetry remains elusive, as its many-layered meanings are almost impossible to translate. It is perhaps as close to the abstraction of music as any poetry has ever been.

Un Coup de Dés was only partially published during Mallarmé's lifetime, but his exact intentions can be seen in the marked-up proofs shown here, which related to the precise layout of the text, its size, and font. Few of these instructions were acted on for the 1914 publication, but today many editions are more faithful to Mallarmé's vision.

STÉPHANE **MALLARMÉ**

1842–1898

Stéphane Mallarmé was a major French Symbolist poet who inspired many artistic movements, such as Surrealism and Cubism. A central figure among intellectuals in Paris, he was a pioneer of the Symbolist movement in poetry.

Born in Paris, Mallarmé knew sadness from an early age: his mother died when he was five, his sister ten years later, and his father shortly afterwards. He learned English in London before becoming a schoolteacher in France. Married in 1863, he had two children (although his son would die of respiratory disease in 1879). Mallarmé moved to Paris in 1871 and became known for hosting intellectual gatherings on Tuesdays, which attracted figures such as WB Yeats, Rainer Maria Rilke, and Paul Verlaine (the group were known as *les Mardistes*). While a schoolmaster Mallarmé also produced his disciplined, yet wholly new style of poetry, impacting hugely on the Symbolist movement.

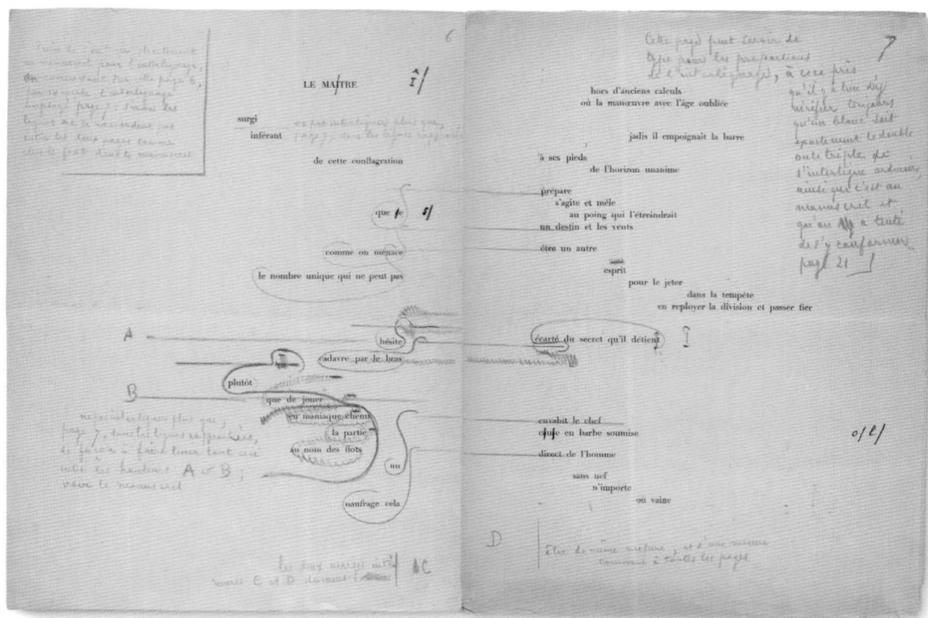

◀ **FORM OVER CONTENT** The startling, almost shocking novelty of *Un Coup de Dés* stemmed as much from the "indefinite regions" inhabited by its poetry, as from its page layout, over which Mallarmé took great pains, as these corrections in his own hand to an early proof make clear.

▶ **SHAPE AND SIZE** The copy of the poem Mallarmé gave the printers in May 1897 contained precise instructions as to the placement of text on the page, such as these seen here, as well as type styles and sizes. It was Mallarmé's intention that the work resemble a form of musical notation.

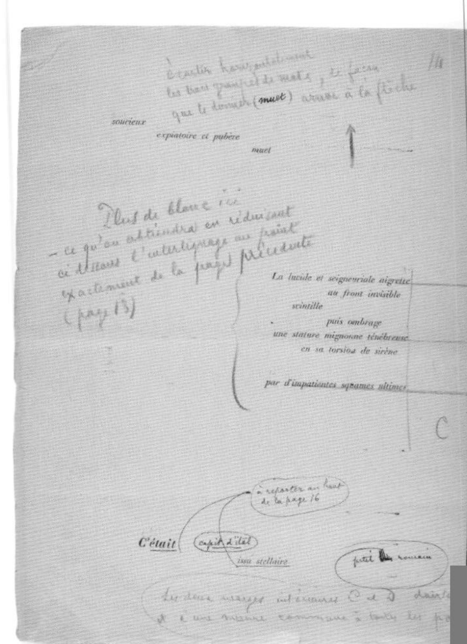

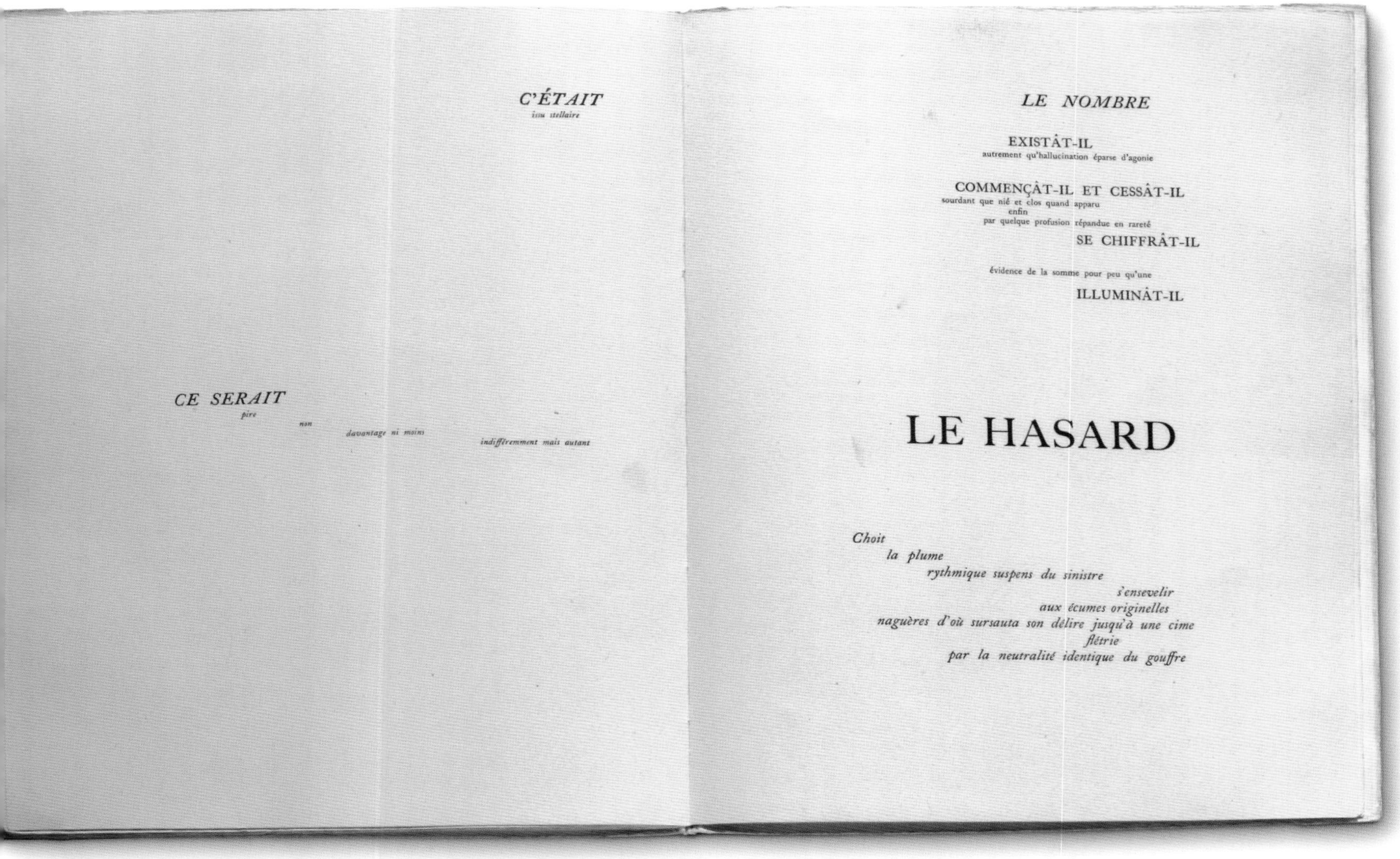

C'ÉTAIT
issu stellaire
CE SERAIT
pire
non
davantage ni moins
indifféremment mais autant
LE NOMBRE
EXISTÂT-IL
autrement qu'hallucination éparse d'agonie
COMMENÇÂT-IL ET CESSÂT-IL
sourdant que nié et clos quand apparu
enfin
par quelque profusion répandue en rareté
SE CHIFFRÂT-IL
évidence de la somme pour peu qu'une
ILLUMINÂT-IL
LE HASARD
Choit
la plume
rythmique suspens du sinistre
s'ensevelir
aux écumes originelles
naguères d'où sursauta son délire jusqu'à une cime
flétrie
par la neutralité identique du gouffre

▲ **FIRST EDITION** *Un Coup de Dés* did not appear in book form until 1914, but Mallarmé's plans had all but been ignored. He had not been happy with the way the poem was laid out in *Cosmopolis* magazine in 1897, and had hoped his next "luxury edition" would include lithographs by his friend Odilon Redon, and his exact typography.

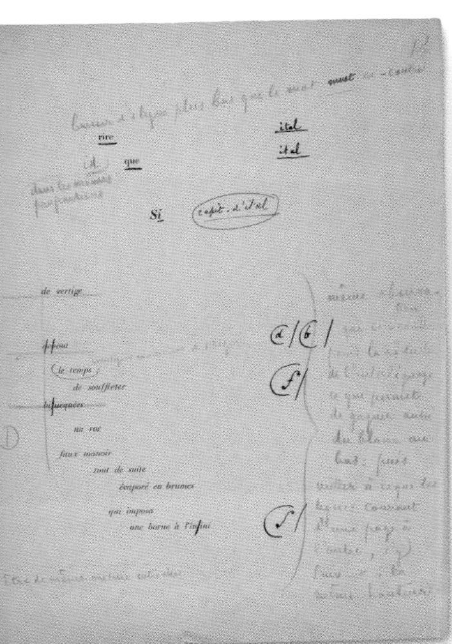

◄ **MUSICAL WORDS** One of Mallarmé's goals was to highlight that words are, in essence, no more than sounds, much like music. He surrounded these "sounds" with large areas of blank space or "surrounding silence" as he called it – much like a musical score.

C'ÉTAIT
le nombre
EXISTÂT-IL
COMMENÇÂT-IL ET CESSÂT-IL
SE CHIFFRÂT-IL
ILLUMINÂT-IL
ce serait
LE HASARD

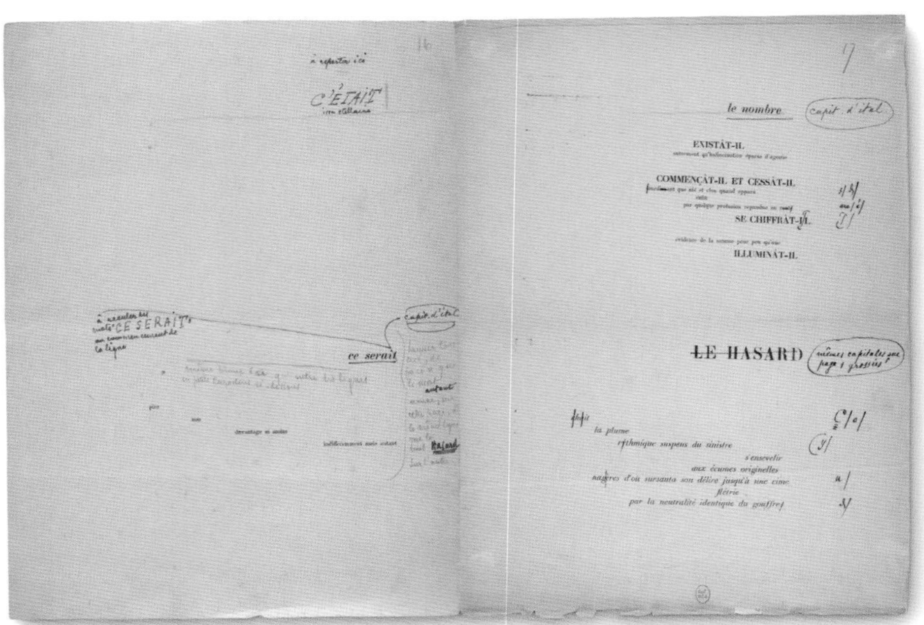

▲ **NEGATIVE SPACE** Mallarmé wanted the poem's 714 words to be laid out on 22 facing pages, the impact of their apparently artless placing lifted by the white spaces around them. The layout became a form of abstraction in itself – "he unwittingly invented modern space".

Directory: 1650–1899

ETHICA
BENEDICT DE SPINOZA

HOLLAND (1677)

This philosophical treatise is often acknowledged as the greatest work of Benedict de Spinoza (1632–77), one of the most important and radical philosophers of the early modern age. Published shortly after Spinoza's death, *Ethica*, or *Ethics*, was a bold work of metaphysical and ethical philosophy that questioned the traditionally accepted philosophical thought about the relationship between God, nature, and humanity. Rather than writing in ordinary prose, Spinoza presented his text in a "geometrical method" which takes the form of axioms (statements taken to be true as a basis for argument), definitions, propositions, and demonstrations. Through this complex structure Spinoza's treatise criticized the Catholic Church. As a direct result, all of Spinoza's works were placed on the Vatican's Index of Forbidden Books. The author George Eliot (1819–80) – nom de plume of Mary Anne Evans – published the first English translation in 1856.

TWO TREATISES OF GOVERNMENT
JOHN LOCKE

ENGLAND (1689)

This ground-breaking work by English political philosopher John Locke (1632–1704) was initially published anonymously. Presented in two parts, it is considered to be the foundation of modern political liberalism, and one of the most influential works in the history of political theory. The *First Treatise* argues against belief in the divine right of kings; the *Second Treatise* outlines a framework for civilized society, placing a moral imperative on government to enforce laws only for the public good. Written between 1679 and 1680, during a period of great political upheaval in England, Locke did not publish *Two Treatises of Government* until after the Glorious Revolution of 1688 when the Dutch Protestant William of Orange had invaded England and overthrown the Catholic James II of England (James VII of Scotland). Locke claimed his work provided justification for England's Glorious Revolution. The *Two Treatises of Government* is also credited with inspiring the European Enlightenment, and the US Constitution.

▼ SEFER EVRONOT
ELIEZER BEN YAAKOV BELLIN

GERMANY (1716–1757, SHOWN)

The *Sefer Evronot* (meaning *Book of Intercalations*) was a beautifully illustrated Hebrew manuscript intended as a handbook for the Jewish lunisolar calendar. According to this calendar the months are determined by the moon, while the year is determined by the sun – intervention from an expert in astronomy was therefore needed to ensure that the Jewish community could fulfil their religious duties on the correct days. The *Sefer Evronot* was compiled to aid these intercalations (insertion of days into a calendar) and it proved highly popular. First printed in 1614, with further editions up until the 19th century, by the fifth edition – printed

Illustrations representing Zodiac signs Leo, *above left*, and Virgo, *above right*, from a 1716 edition of *Sefer Evronot*.

in 1722, in Offenbach, Germany – diagrams and intricate multi-layered wheel charts, known as volvelles, with rotating parts were included.

DU CONTRAT SOCIAL; ÉMILE, OU DE L'ÉDUCATION; AND LES CONFESSIONS

JEAN-JACQUES ROUSSEAU

FRANCE (1762, 1782, AND 1789)

These are three of the most important works by the Swiss-born, French philosopher and writer Jean-Jacques Rousseau (1712–78). *Du Contrat Social* and *Émile, ou de l'éducation*, known respectively as *The Social Contract* and *Émile, or On Education* were published in 1762.

Du Contrat Social was a work of political philosophy seen as influential in the instigation of the French Revolution (1789–99). Rousseau claimed that society was the product of the collective will of its people, and that laws should only be binding if they were supported by that collective will. In saying this Rousseau challenged the traditional order of society.

Émile, ou de l'éducation was a pioneering treatise that explored the possibility of a system of learning where the pupil is taught in isolation, away from the corrupting influence of society and civilization. Part novel, part instructive and moralistic essay, *Émile* was radical in its call for a reform of teaching and child-rearing, and advocated that religious instruction should not begin until late adolescence. *Émile* was banned in Paris and Geneva, and was even publically burned when it was first published. Yet it was widely read and greatly influenced the reform of education in France after the French Revolution, as well as in other countries across Europe.

Both of these books outraged the French parliament to such a degree that Rousseau spent much of the latter part of his life in hiding in France and Switzerland. But after the French Revolution he was hailed in France as a national hero.

Les Confessions (or *The Confessions*) is an autobiographical work divided into two parts, each comprising six books, and covers the first 53 years of Rousseau's life. Volumes I–VI were completed by 1767 and published in 1782; volumes VII–XII were complete by 1770, but not published until 1789. A few autobiographical books already existed at this time, but all had a religious agenda. Rousseau's text was an exploration of his own personal experiences and feelings since childhood, exposing his darkest deeds, as well as his finest, to account for the personality of his adult self.

THE HISTORY OF THE DECLINE AND FALL OF THE ROMAN EMPIRE

EDWARD GIBBON

UK (VOLUME I,1776; VOLUMES II –III, 1781; IV – VI, 1788–89)

This historical work by the British historian and scholar Edward Gibbon (1737–94) traces the trajectory of Western civilization from the height of the Roman Empire to the fall of Byzantium. Gibbon used a dramatic and elegant literary style, and was notable for his extensive referencing of original source material – this technique became a model for subsequent writers of history.
The text claimed that there was a moral decline in the people of Rome, which Gibbon felt made the fall of the Empire inevitable – he cited the rise of Christianity as having instilled in the Roman people an apathy that allowed the barbarians to conquer them. Although the work was highly acclaimed, Gibbon was criticized for the scepticism he expressed towards the Christian Church.

COMMON SENSE

THOMAS PAINE

AMERICA (1776)

This incendiary pamphlet, published anonymously by English political activist Thomas Paine (1737–1809), was written as a wake-up call to the people of the 13 colonies of America's Eastern seaboard who were advocating independence from the British government. It is one of the most influential publications in US history and credited with transforming colonial unrest into the American Revolution (1765–83). Paine's prose was passionate and populist in tone,

Critik
der
Urtheilskraft
von
Immanuel Kant.

Neueste Auflage.

Frankfurt und Leipzig,
1794.

Title page from the first German edition of Kant's *Critique of Pure Reason*.

and his words united the people with their political leaders. *Common Sense* was the most widely read publication of the Revolution – around 500,000 copies of the pamphlet are thought to have been sold at the time.

▲ KRITIK DER REINEN VERNUNFT

IMMANUEL KANT

GERMANY (1781)

Written by German philosopher Immanuel Kant (1724–1804) and known in English as *Critique of Pure Reason*, this treatise on metaphysics is considered to be one of the most important in the history of philosophy. A dense and complex text, it was the product of 10 years of work. However, it proved so difficult to understand that Kant was obliged to write a more accessible companion two years later to ensure that it was not misinterpreted. Kant's text radically expands on two schools of thought that were central to the Enlightenment era: rationalism (which states that reason is the basis of knowledge) and empiricism (which states that knowledge can only come from experience). Kant's ground-breaking work on the theory of knowledge and ethics opened up an entirely new branch of philosophical thought. *Critique of Pure Reason* is sometimes referred to as Kant's *First Critique*, as he followed it with *Critique of Practical Reason* in 1788, and *Critique of Judgement* in 1790.

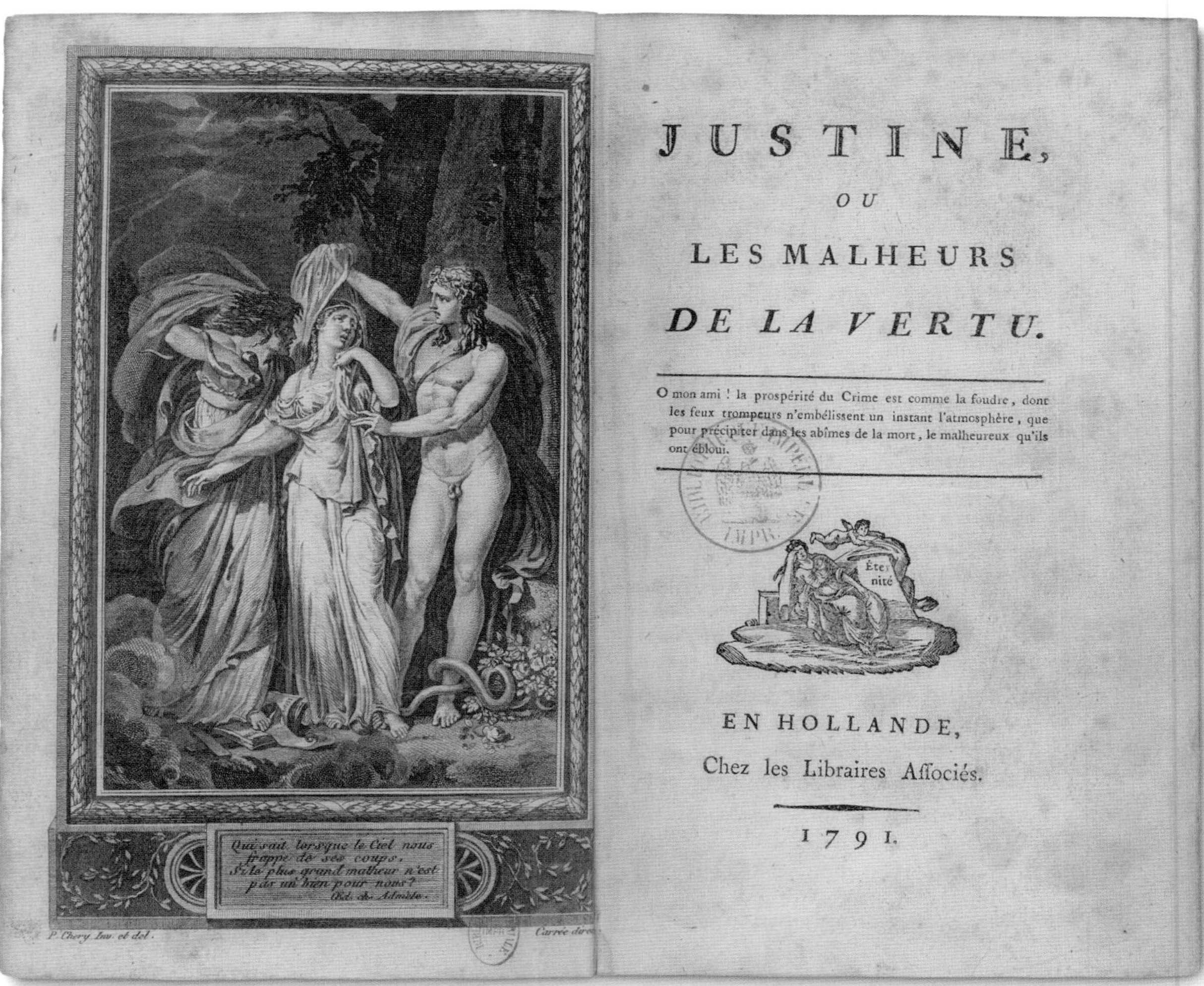

JUSTINE,

OU

LES MALHEURS

DE LA VERTU.

O mon ami ! la prospérité du Crime est comme la foudre, dont les feux trompeurs n'embélissent un instant l'atmosphère, que pour précipiter dans les abîmes de la mort, le malheureux qu'ils ont ébloui.

EN HOLLANDE,

Chez les Libraires Aſſociés.

1791.

The first edition of the Marquis de Sade's controversial novel *Justine, ou Les Malheurs de la Vertu.*

▲ JUSTINE, OU LES MALHEURS DE LA VERTU

MARQUIS DE SADE

FRANCE 1791

This disturbing novel (*Justine, or the Misfortunes of Virtue*, in English) is the best-known work by the infamous French aristocrat, the Marquis de Sade (1740–1814). *Justine* was written in 1787 as a novella while de Sade was imprisoned in the Bastille. It was reworked as a full novel after he was released and published anonymously. *Justine* encapsulates de Sade's amoral philosophy that goodness is evil and vice should be rewarded – as such the virtuous heroine suffers deeply for her goodness, and the novel resounds with the depravities, exploitation, and sexual violence for which de Sade is famed ("sadism" originates from de Sade's name). In 1801 Napoleon Bonaparte ordered de Sades's arrest due to the obscene nature of *Justine* and its sequel, *Juliette* – de Sade spent the rest of his life in prison.

A VINDICATION OF THE RIGHTS OF WOMAN

MARY WOLLSTONECRAFT

UK (1792)

This ground-breaking text by the English writer Mary Wollstonecraft (1759–97) advocated the need for political reform that would enable the formal education of women. One of the earliest expressions of feminist politics, Wollstonecraft's *A Vindication of the Rights of Woman* predated the actual use of the term "feminism". Many of Wollstonecraft's views proved to be prescient, for example her appeal for co-educational schooling, and her recognition of the importance of enabling women to earn money and be self-supporting. Despite its controversial and radical content Wollstonecraft's book was well-received at the time of publication and two editions were printed in the first year. However, the book fell out of favour when details of her unorthodox lifestyle were revealed after her untimely death at the age of only 38 (she had had several affairs and an illegitimate child, but pretended to be married). Her reputation blighted book sales and it was not reprinted until the mid-19th century.

PHÄNOMENOLOGIE DES GEISTES

G.W.F. HEGEL

GERMANY (1807)

German philosopher Georg Wilhelm Friedrich Hegel's (1770–1831) best-known work *Phenomenology of Mind* (or *Phenomenology of Spirit*) was published just after Napoleon Bonaparte (1769–1821) invaded Hegel's native Prussia. The earliest of his major works, *Phenomenology of Mind* proposed that humans share a collective consciousness which evolves according to a "dialogue". In this dialogue, an initial thesis (or idea) arises and is countered by an antithesis, the two are then reconciled in a synthesis. The pattern is continually repeated, building towards the attainment of "absolute truth". Although Hegel was an idealist like Immanuel Kant, his approach to human progress differed from Kant's philosophy. *Phenomenology of Mind* was a complex philosophical treatise exploring innovative concepts that proved highly influential both within the realm of philosophy, as well as in other fields, such as theology and political science.

BOOK OF MORMON

JOSEPH SMITH

USA (1830)

The *Book of Mormon* is the recognized holy scripture of the Latter Day Saint (LDS) movement, founded in New York in the 1830s by the American preacher Joseph Smith (1805–44). The text from the *Book of Mormon* is said to have derived from a set of golden plates inscribed with a script referred to as "reformed Egyptian". Smith claimed an angel presented him with the plates, and with divine assistance he translated the text into English. Smith's original manuscript was sealed within a stone wall until the 1880s by which time much of it had been destroyed – the remnants are now in the LDS archives. Smith reportedly returned the golden plates to the angel. Certainly, no trace of them has ever been found, nor has archaeological evidence of Egyptian scripts been discovered in the US. However, Mormonism became the name given to the religious tradition of the members of the LDS movement.

THE COMMUNIST MANIFESTO

FRIEDRICH ENGELS AND KARL MARX

UK (1848)

First published anonymously, this 23-page pamphlet was co-authored by the German philosophers and social activists Karl Marx (1818–83) and Friedrich Engels (1820–95), although in reality Marx was the principle writer. Claiming socialism would replace capitalism, the authors aimed to initiate social change across Europe by encouraging the workers (the proletariat) to rise up against the middle classes (the bourgeoisie).

The *Communist Manifesto* became the most influential and widely read political pamphlet in history, and was the foundation of Marxist philosophy. While it had no immediate political impact, the ideas in the manifesto persisted into the 20th century, and in 1917 – 23 years after the death of Karl Marx – the world's first successful communist revolution took place in Russia with Marxist theory at its core.

ON LIBERTY
JOHN STUART MILL

ENGLAND (1859)

This short essay written by the British philosopher and economist John Stuart Mill (1806–73) is one of the key texts of political liberalism. Mill believed passionately in the freedom of the individual, and in *On Liberty* he defended individuality against the strictures of society. He also promoted diversity and non-conformity in the book, claiming that it was the challenges presented to society by the non-conformists that prevented it from stagnating. Crucially, he argued for freedom of speech and emphasized that the expression of any individual should be free from state control. Mill's work was not without its critics, but *On Liberty* has been in print since its first publication.

THE INNOCENTS ABROAD
MARK TWAIN

USA (1869)

Also known as *The New Pilgrim's Progress*, this work began as a series of travel letters and developed into what became one of the bestselling travel books of all time. *The Innocents Abroad* chronicles a boat journey across Europe, Egypt, and the Holy Land made by the American author Samuel L. Clemens (1835–1910), writing under his better-known pseudonym, Mark Twain. Through his humorous and satirical narrative, Twain redefined the genre of travel writing by encouraging the reader to find their own experiences, rather than doing only what a guidebook has instructed them to do. *The Innocents Abroad* was sold on a subscription-only basis and was immediately popular, selling over 70,000 copies in its first year, and it became Twain's bestselling book during his lifetime.

➤ LE AVVENTURE DI PINOCCHIO
CARLO COLLODI

ITALY (1883)

Written by the Italian author Carlo Collodi (1826–90) *Le Avventure di Pinocchio* (known in English as *The Adventures of Pinocchio*) is a children's novel about an animated wooden puppet, which became one of the best-loved and most iconic stories of all time. *Le Avventure di Pinocchio* was published as an illustrated novel following the huge success of its serialization in a children's magazine between 1881 and 1882. The original tale explored dark themes of morality and the nature of good and evil, and it even resulted in Pinocchio being hanged for his misdeeds. However, Collodi changed the ending for the novel to make it more child-friendly. The novel has been translated into over 240 languages, and is considered an Italian national treasure. The character of Pinocchio became immortalized as a popular icon in Walt Disney's 1940 film.

ALSO SPRACH ZARATHUSTRA
FRIEDRICH NIETZSCHE

GERMANY (1883–92)

Written by the German philosopher who has influenced 20th-century thought more than any other – Friedrich Nietzsche (1844–1900) – *Also sprach Zarathustra: Ein Buch für Alle und Keinen*, is known in English as *Thus Spoke Zarathustra: A Book for All and None*. A philosophical novel, the book chronicles the travels and speeches of a fictitious character, Zarathustra, using Nietzsche's concepts of "Eternal Recurrence" (that all events will be repeated over and over again for all eternity) and the "Overman" (someone who has overcome himself fully and obeys no laws except the ones he gives himself). Marking the end of Nietzsche's mature period, *Thus Spoke Zarathustra* was written in four parts between 1883 and 1885. He wrote the first three in 10-day bursts, while battling serious ill health – they were all published individually from 1883, and only combined in one volume in 1887. Nietzsche originally intended the third book to be the last and gave it a dramatic climax, but subsequently decided to write another three – although in the end he composed only one. Written in 1885, the last section remained private until all four parts were combined in a single volume in 1892. *Thus Spoke Zarathustra* was first translated into English in 1896.

THE INTERPRETATION OF DREAMS
SIGMUND FREUD

AUSTRIA (1899)

Sigmund Freud (1856–1939) was an Austrian neurologist who founded a new branch of scientific theory known as psychoanalysis. It was in his book *The Interpretation of Dreams* that Freud first outlined his theory of the unconscious mind and the fundamental importance of dreams on the human psyche. Freud believed that all dreams, even nightmares, were a form of wish-fulfilment, and he was one of the first scientists to formally research this field by performing clinical trials as well analyses of his own dreams. Despite slow initial sales, Freud produced eight revised editions of *The Interpretation of Dreams* in his own lifetime. He also published an abridged version of the book in 1901 called *On Dreams*, which was aimed at readers discouraged by the 800-page original. *The Interpretation of Dreams* is arguably Freud's most significant and influential work. This book has had an enormous impact on the development of scientific research into mental health and is considered to be the foundation of all modern psychotherapy.

Pinocchio as depicted in the first edition, 1883, by the artist Enrico Mazzanti.

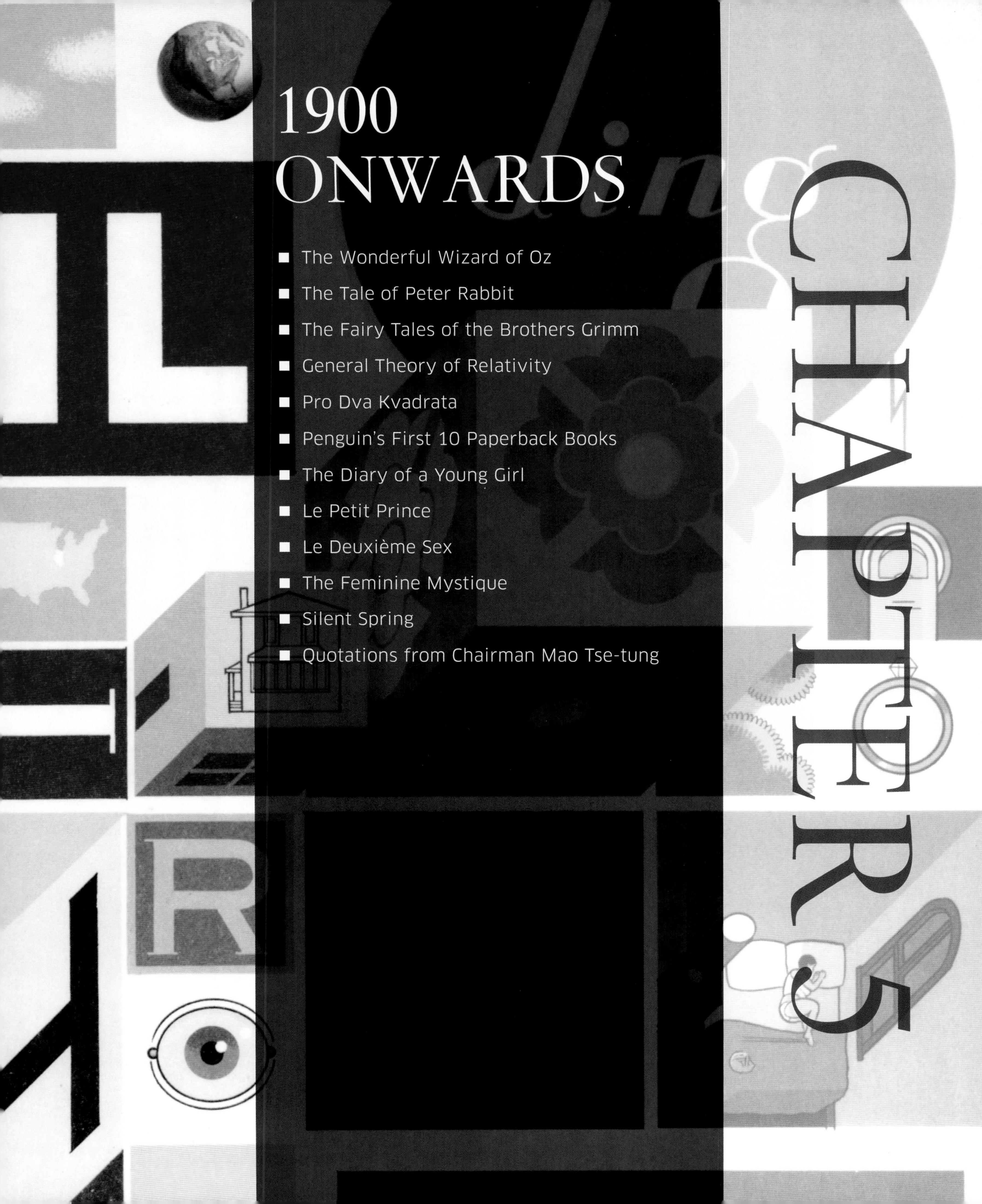

CHAPTER 5

1900 ONWARDS

- The Wonderful Wizard of Oz
- The Tale of Peter Rabbit
- The Fairy Tales of the Brothers Grimm
- General Theory of Relativity
- Pro Dva Kvadrata
- Penguin's First 10 Paperback Books
- The Diary of a Young Girl
- Le Petit Prince
- Le Deuxième Sex
- The Feminine Mystique
- Silent Spring
- Quotations from Chairman Mao Tse-tung

The Wonderful Wizard of Oz

1900 ▪ PRINTED ▪ 22 × 16.5 cm (9 × 6½ in) ▪ 259 PAGES ▪ USA

SCALE

L. FRANK BAUM

L. Frank Baum's tale of young Dorothy from Kansas, who is carried away by a cyclone to the magical Land of Oz, is considered to be the first American fairy tale. Unusually for fiction of the time *The Wonderful Wizard of Oz* was lavishly illustrated, with 24 colour plates as well as intricate colour pictures woven into the text. Baum believed the illustrations to be integral to the story and shared full copyright with the illustrator, W.W. Denslow. The publisher, George M. Hill Company, agreed to print all of the pictures in colour provided that Baum and Denslow paid the cost of including full-colour plates.

First published in a print run of 10,000 copies in September 1900, the book was produced as three separate component parts – text, colour plates, and case – which were then bound together. It was an instant success with press and public alike. The next print run of 15,000 copies, which followed just a month later, met with equal success. Within six months 90,000 copies had been sold and the book remained on the bestseller list for two years. To date it has been translated into over 50 languages and seen many adaptations, including a Broadway musical in 1902 (with the involvement of Baum and Denslow), three silent films, and the classic film from 1939, *The Wizard of Oz*, starring Judy Garland. Such was the demand for *Oz* stories that, after Baum's death, 21 sequels were written by children's author, Ruth Plumly Thompson.

In detail

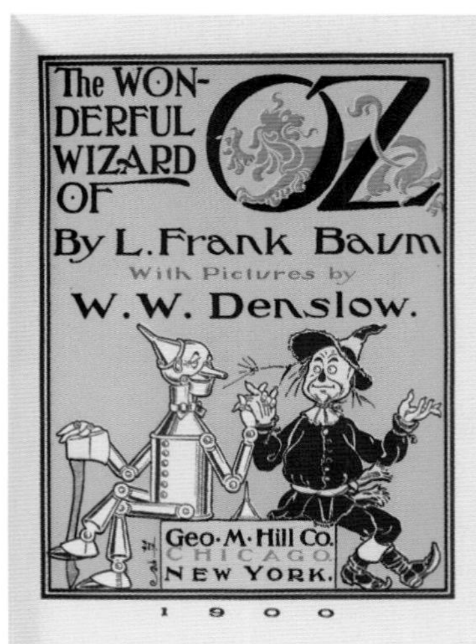
The WONDERFUL WIZARD OF OZ
By L.Frank Baum
With Pictures by
W.W. Denslow.
Geo. M. Hill Co.
CHICAGO
NEW YORK.
1900

◄ **DENSLOW'S ILLUSTRATIONS**
The title page shows Denslow's instantly recognizable artworks for the Tin Woodman and the Scarecrow. Despite the success of the book, the publisher, George M. Hill, went bankrupt in 1902. The next publisher, Bobbs-Merrill, gradually reduced the number of illustrations in future editions and shortened the title to *The Wizard of Oz*.

► **BACKDROP ARTWORK**
Many pages in the first edition had colour illustrations that wove their way in and around the text, creating a backdrop.

110 THE WONDERFUL WIZARD OF OZ.

and such small animals as mice have saved my life. How strange it all is! But, comrades, what shall we do now?"

"We must journey on until we find the road of yellow brick again," said Dorothy; "and then we can keep on to the Emerald City."

So, the Lion being fully refreshed, and feeling quite himself again, they all started upon the journey, greatly enjoying the walk through the soft, fresh grass; and it was not long before they reached the road of yellow brick and turned again toward the Emerald City where the great Oz dwelt.

The road was smooth and well paved, now, and the country about was beautiful; so that the travelers rejoiced in leaving the forest far behind, and with it the many dangers they had met in its gloomy shades.

THE WONDERFUL WIZARD OF OZ. 111

Once more they could see fences built beside the road; but these were painted green, and when they came to a small house, in which a farmer evidently lived, that also was painted green. They passed by several of these houses during the afternoon, and sometimes people came to the doors and looked at them as if they would like to ask questions; but no one came near them nor spoke to them because of the great Lion, of which they were much afraid. The people were all dressed in clothing of a lovely emerald green color and wore peaked hats like those of the Munchkins.

"This must be the Land of Oz," said Dorothy, "and we are surely getting near the Emerald City."

"Yes," answered the Scarecrow; "everything is green here, while in the country of the Munchkins blue was the favorite color. But the people do not seem to be as friendly as the Munchkins and I'm afraid we shall be unable to find a place to pass the night."

"I should like something to eat besides fruit," said the girl, "and I'm sure Toto is nearly starved. Let us stop at the next house and talk to the people."

So, when they came to a good sized farm house, Dorothy walked

WIZARD OF OZ.

ew, and he walked close to
en bark in return.
ne child asked of the Tin
of the forest?"
answer, "for I have never
t my father went there once,
aid it was a long journey
lthough nearer to the city
is beautiful. But I am not
l-can, and nothing can hurt
r upon your forehead the
, and that will protect you

anxiously; "what will pro-

selves, if he is in danger,"

ne from the forest a terrible
great Lion bounded into
nis paw he sent the Scare-
the edge of the road, and
lman with his sharp claws.
could make no impression
man fell over in the road

had an enemy to face, ran
he great beast had opened

"You ought to be ashamed of yourself!"

◄ **COLOUR CODING** Part of the novelty of the first edition was the importance of colour: each chapter was represented by a different colour that linked to the text. For example, the illustrations in Chapter 2, "The Council with the Munchkins", are predominantly blue, the Munchkins' favourite colour. Other colours used were green (for Chapter 11 "The Emerald City of Oz"), red, yellow, and grey.

LYMAN FRANK **BAUM**

1856–1919

L. Frank Baum pursued a few different careers before settling on writing. *The Wonderful Wizard of Oz*, which was published when he was 44, is one of the most famous works of children's literature.

Baum's lifelong passion was for the theatre, but it proved unreliable financially and he turned to journalism. He married Maud Gage in 1882 and had four sons, for whom he often made up bedtime stories. These stories formed part of his first book, *Mother Goose in Prose*, published in 1897. He first collaborated with the illustrator William Wallace Denslow (1856–1915) on a children's book of nonsense poetry called *Father Goose, His Book*. Published in 1899 it was a bestseller. After *The Wonderful Wizard of Oz* their collaborations were less successful and they parted company in 1902. Baum continued to enjoy success as a children's writer of fantasy novels, with 13 of his later books built around the Land of Oz. In the last nine years of his life he adapted works for cinema.

The Tale of Peter Rabbit

1901 (PRIVATE EDITION) 1902 (FIRST COMMERCIAL EDITION) ▪ PRINTED ▪ 15 × 12 cm (6 × 5 in) ▪ 98 PAGES ▪ UK

SCALE

BEATRIX POTTER

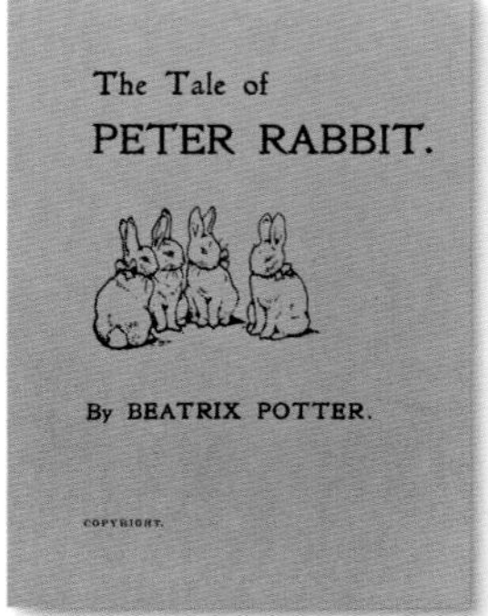

One of the best known of all children's books, Beatrix Potter's *The Tale of Peter Rabbit* is a charming story of a naughty little rabbit called Peter, accompanied by Potter's equally charming artworks. This story has sold over 40 million copies, and the character, Peter Rabbit, appears in five more of Potter's stories.

The first edition of the *Tale* (see left) was self-published. During the 1890s Potter sent a number of stories to the children of her former governess, Annie Moore, and at Moore's suggestion, she decided to seek a publisher. She chose the story of Peter Rabbit, recounted in an illustrated letter she had written in September, 1893 to Moore's five-year-old son, Noel, who was sick. "My dear Noel," she wrote, "I don't know what to write to you, so I shall tell you a story about four little rabbits whose names were – Flopsy, Mopsy, Cottontail and Peter." The story told of the escapades of Peter Rabbit who enters the vegetable garden of their neighbour, Mr McGregor and wreaks havoc. Potter later expanded the story and created a colour illustration and 41 line drawings – one for each page.

Potter believed children wanted a tiny book they could hold, but publishers at the time would only print in large formats. Adamant, she decided to self-publish, producing 250 copies in December 1901, which she presented as Christmas gifts to family and friends. They proved so popular that within two months she had 200 more printed. Publisher Frederick Warne and Co. reconsidered the book's small format, and published the work the following year in an edition with all full-colour illustrations. It was so successful that Potter went on to write 22 more stories.

BEATRIX **POTTER**

1866–1943

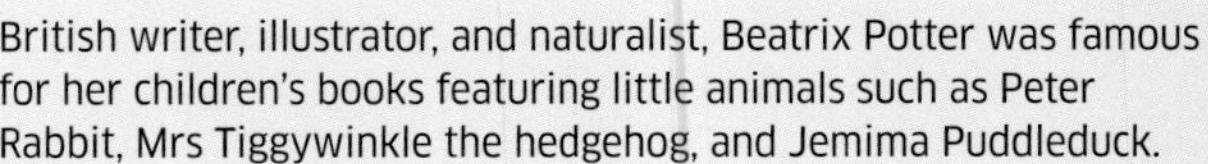

British writer, illustrator, and naturalist, Beatrix Potter was famous for her children's books featuring little animals such as Peter Rabbit, Mrs Tiggywinkle the hedgehog, and Jemima Puddleduck.

Beatrix Potter was born in London to a wealthy family. She was largely educated by governesses, but grew up with a love of nature, fostered by summer visits to Scotland and the Lake District. Women were discouraged from higher education in Victorian England, but Potter became an adept scientific illustrator at Kew Gardens, where she wrote a paper on fungi. She also illustrated children's stories and greeting cards, but her big success came with *The Tale of Peter Rabbit*. She fell in love with her editor, Norman Warne, despite her parents' disapproval, and was devastated by his death a month after their engagement. With the royalties from her publications and an inheritance, Potter bought a farm and moved to the Lake District in 1905, where she continued to write successful children's stories and married local solicitor William Heelis in 1913. At her death in 1943, Potter left sixteen farms and some 4,000 acres to the National Trust.

▼ **PET SKETCHES** Long before writing her Peter Rabbit story, Beatrix Potter repeatedly sketched her beloved pet rabbit, Peter Piper. Her drawings are scientifically accurate and show both her innate love of animals and her skill as an artist. Her rabbit characters developed naturally from these first studies.

She also had a little field in which she grew herbs and rabbit tobacco. ~~(Uncle Remus says that rabbit tobacco is what we call Lavender.)~~ She hung it up to dry in the kitchen, in bunches, which she sold for a penny a piece to her rabbit neighbours in the warren.

73

74

▲ **ORIGINAL MANUSCRIPT** This page from the original manuscript of Potter's *The Tale of Peter Rabbit*, complete with corrections, gives a wonderful insight into how she created the story – crafting the words and illustrations in tandem.

ONCE upon a time there were four little Rabbits, and their names were—
Flopsy,
Mopsy,
Cotton-tail,
and Peter.

▲ **FIRST EDITION** Beatrix Potter's creativity is evident in the inventive typesetting on the opening page of this self-published edition. Because of the expense, illustrations were limited to pen and ink drawings, with the exception of the colour title page that was produced with the recently introduced three-colour press.

> Thank goodness I was never sent to school; it would have rubbed off some of the originality
>
> **BEATRIX POTTER**

In detail

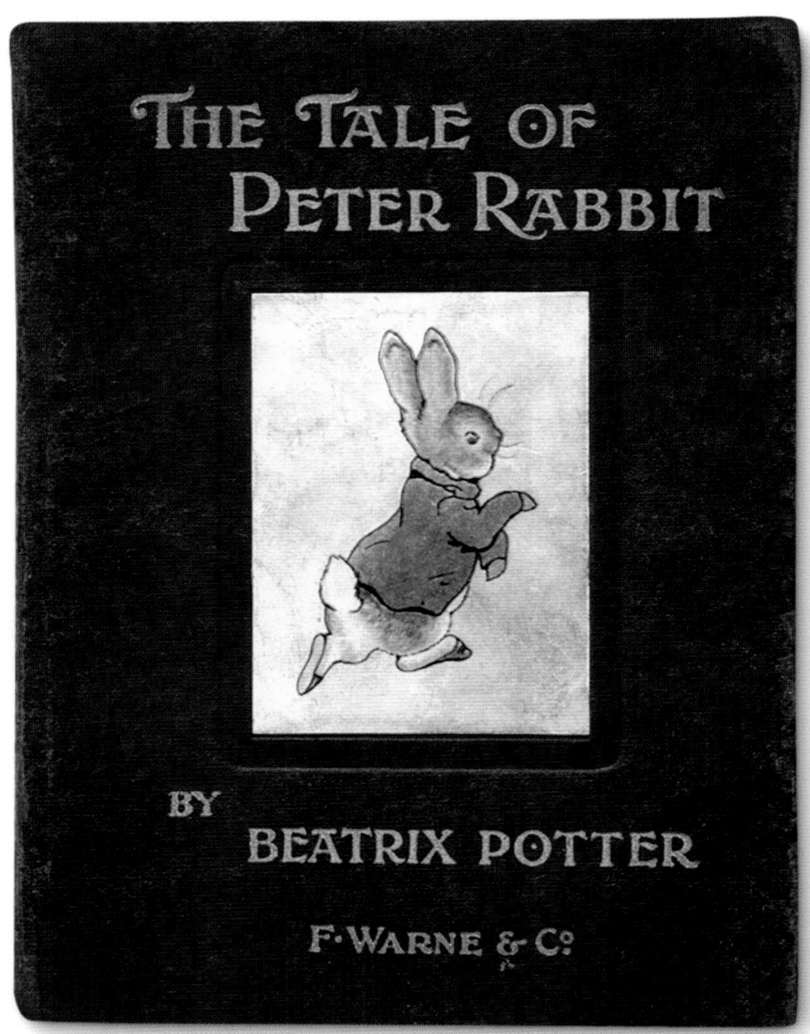

◄ **FIRST COMMERCIAL EDITION** Seeing the popularity of Potter's own edition, children's publisher Frederick Warne, who had first rejected Potter's proposal, agreed to print the "bunny book" commercially. They wanted colour illustrations, so Potter redid all of her drawings in watercolour in just a few months. In October 1902, 8,000 copies with coloured prints were published. Of these, 2,000 were bound in deluxe linen covers, with the remainder in paper boards, the latter shown here.

▼ **HIGH QUALITY** Potter's watercolour illustrations were pale and subtle. To render them accurately in the book, Frederick Warne had to use the latest "Hentschel three-colour" printing technique.

AND then, feeling rather sick, he went to look for some parsley.

22

23

THEN he tried to find his way straight across the garden, but he became more and more puzzled. Presently, he came to a pond where Mr. McGregor filled his water-cans. A white cat was staring at some gold-fish, she sat very, very still, but now and then the tip of her tail twitched as if it were alive. Peter thought it best to go away without speaking to her; he had heard about cats from his cousin, little Benjamin Bunny.

46

47

I AM sorry to say that Peter was not very well during the evening.

His mother put him to bed, and made some camomile tea; and she gave a dose of it to Peter!

'One table-spoonful to be taken at bed-time.'

56

57

▲ **FULL-PAGE IMAGES** In order to hold a young child's attention, Potter insisted that each spread have text on the left and a full-page image on the right. She also directed that the commercial editions have rounded edges, which could be held comfortably by children. Potter had initially resisted colour prints but was later convinced by the publishers to include them.

▲ **MORAL OF THE STORY** The combination of simple moral tales and delightful illustrations ensured Potter's popularity with generations of young children. *The Tale of Peter Rabbit* highlights the perils of disobeying one's parents: after his escapades Peter feels unwell and is put to bed. The books contributed enormously to literacy in Edwardian Britain and were widely read by children of all ages.

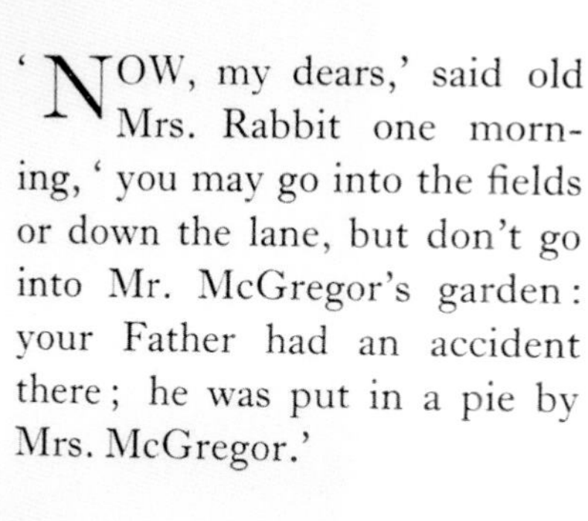
'NOW, my dears,' said old Mrs. Rabbit one morning, 'you may go into the fields or down the lane, but don't go into Mr. McGregor's garden: your Father had an accident there; he was put in a pie by Mrs. McGregor.'

10

11

◄ **HUMANLIKE ANIMALS**
Key to Potter's appeal was the way she combined rabbit behaviour with human traits. The rabbits eat parsley and get sick from lettuce, but also drink tea from cups. Blending fact and fantasy, all the little rabbits were drawn with the anatomical accuracy of a trained naturalist, yet stand upright like humans and are dressed in clothes.

IN **CONTEXT**

The success of *The Tale of Peter Rabbit* compelled Potter to compose a further 22 short stories for children. These were all published by Warne, earning both the publisher and author considerable royalties and profits through numerous reprints. However, Warne failed to register copyright in the US, allowing pirated copies to be printed from 1903 onwards, which constituted a considerable loss of earnings. The entrepreneurial Potter learned from the American experience: when she designed a cloth rabbit based on Peter she was careful to register it at the patent office, making it the first licensed literary character. Seeing the marketing potential of her creation she also approved the sale of tea sets, children's bowls, and slippers, and other novelties based on her animal characters. In 1904 she invented a Peter Rabbit board game, which finally went on sale, redesigned by Warne, in 1917. Potter was always deeply involved in product design and was determined that every bit of merchandise should remain faithful to her book characters. When Walt Disney offered to make an animated film version of Peter Rabbit, Potter turned him down, feeling "To enlarge… will show up all the imperfections". Today, merchandise remains popular, with many large toyshops devoting entire sections to Potter's characters.

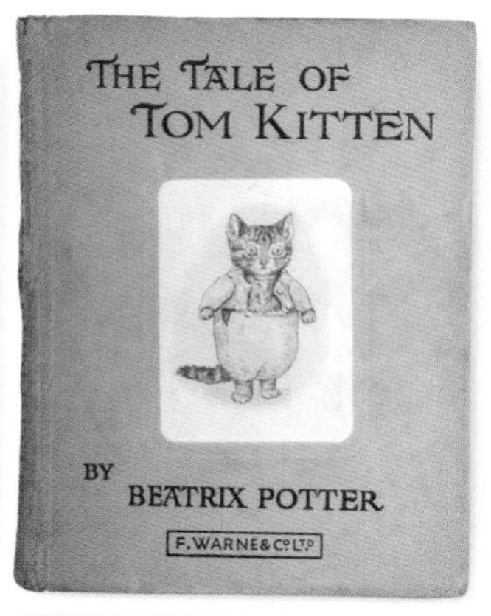

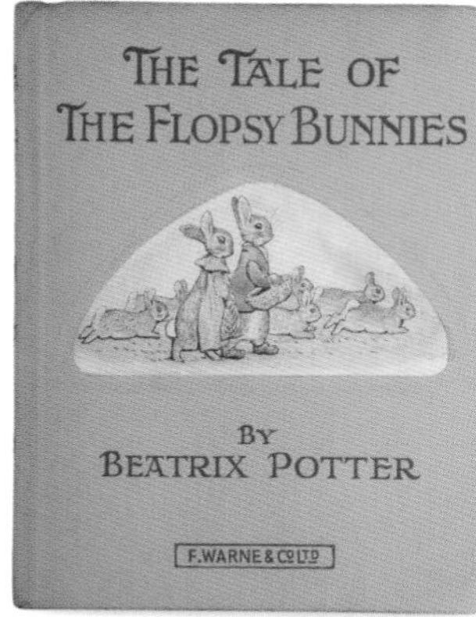

➤ **Beatrix Potter** followed up the huge success of *The Tale of Peter Rabbit* with five more books in which he features, although the other animals he meets are the focus, including *The Tale of the Flopsy Bunnies*, shown here.

The Fairy Tales of the Brothers Grimm

1909 ▪ PRINTED ▪ 20 × 26 cm (8 × 10 in) ▪ 325 PAGES ▪ UK

SCALE

JAKOB AND WILHELM GRIMM

Published in 1909, this collection of Grimm Brothers' fairy tales featuring exquisite illustrations by Arthur Rackham (1867–1939), was a visual treasure of the Edwardian era. The public's interest in fairy tales had been sparked in the early years of Queen Victoria's reign, and by the late 19th century they were entrenched in popular culture. At a time of great social change, brought about by industrialization and the mass migration of people from the countryside to the expanding cities, the tales provided simple escapism.

The market was saturated with fairy tale imagery at the time, yet none quite captured the spirit of the stories, or popular imagination, like the illustrations by Arthur Rackham. Expressive and intricate, 100 of his black and white line drawings first appeared in a 1900 edition of the tales, but the work was revised in 1909, with more detailed illustrations and forty subtly coloured new plates. Drawn using pen and India ink, Rackham's artworks were magical and macabre, and depicted the brutality and malevolence behind many of the tales with an innocent, rustic charm, and beauty.

The accompanying stories were translated by Mrs Edgar Lucas from the original German folk tales, compiled in 1812 by Jacob and Wilhelm Grimm, and the book was highly sought after. Rackham would later become one of the most celebrated British artists of the Edwardian era.

BROTHERS **GRIMM**

JAKOB GRIMM • 1785–1863
WILHELM GRIMM • 1786–1859

Jakob and Wilhelm Grimm were German academics and folklorists who succeeded in popularizing hundreds of classical fairytales, with which their names are now synonymous.

Although their surname is famously associated with fairy tales, Jakob and Wilhelm Grimm were not children's storybook writers. They were scholars and historians, whose passion for the folklore of the past inspired them to write down the tales that had been part of the oral heritage of Europe for many centuries. Born just a year apart, Jakob and Wilhelm were virtually inseparable as children. Even in adulthood they remained close, studying and working together on shared research projects. After studying law, they both became librarians, devoting their careers to documenting the origins of German language, literature, and culture.

The Grimms recorded European folk tales that had been passed down by word of mouth for centuries, publishing their results in 1812 as a collection of 156 stories entitled *Kinder-und Hausmärchen* (*Children's and Household Tales*). Over the next few years, they added more stories, publishing a second edition in 1815. They gradually edited and reworded the tales to make them suitable for children, since many of the originals were thought to contain too much sex and violence. They also often added moral messages and Christian references, and fleshed out some stories with more detail. The definitive version was published in 1857, two years before Wilhelm's death.

▲ **LITTLE RED CAP** The story of "Little Red Riding Hood" dates back to the 10th century, but one of the best-known versions is Grimms' "Little Red Cap". Rackham's use of colour draws the reader's eye towards Red Riding Hood, allowing the wolf's true identity to be partly obscured by the surrounding detail, so adding to the suspense.

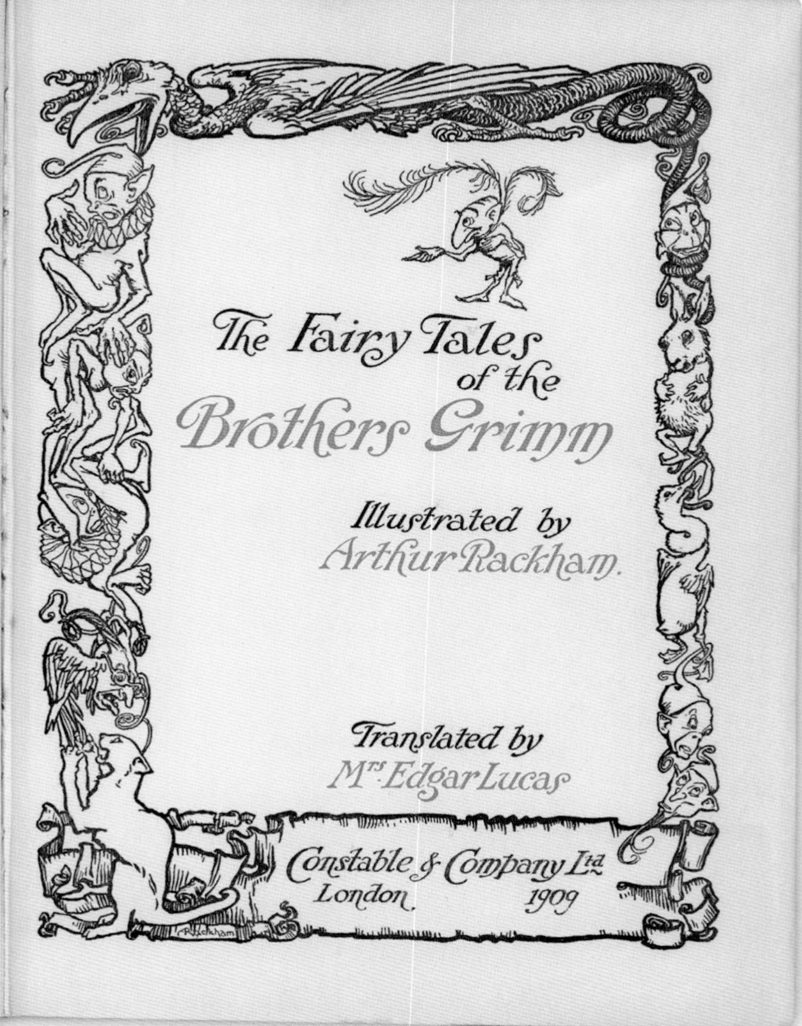

GRIMM'S FAIRY TALES

In the early morning, when she and Conrad went through the gateway, she said in passing—

'Alas! dear Falada, there thou hangest.'

And the Head answered—

'Alas! Queen's daughter, there thou gangest.
If thy mother knew thy fate,
Her heart would break with grief so great.'

Then they passed on out of the town, right into the fields, with the geese. When they reached the meadow, the Princess sat down on the grass and let down her hair. It shone like pure gold, and when little Conrad saw it, he was so delighted that he wanted to pluck some out; but she said—

'Blow, blow, little breeze,
And Conrad's hat seize.
Let him join in the chase
While away it is whirled,
Till my tresses are curled
And I rest in my place.'

Then a strong wind sprang up, which blew away Conrad's hat right over the fields, and he had to run after it. When he came back, she had finished combing her hair, and it was all put up again; so he could not get a single hair. This made him very sulky, and he would not say another word to her. And they tended the geese till evening, when they went home.

Next morning, when they passed under the gateway, the Princess said—

'Alas! dear Falada, there thou hangest.'

Falada answered:—

'Alas! Queen's daughter, there thou gangest.
If thy mother knew thy fate,
Her heart would break with grief so great.'

70

▲ **REVISED EDITION** A special feature of the 1909 edition was the "tipped-in" colour illustrations: the images were printed separately from the rest of the book on different paper, then glued in before the book was bound. Opposite the title page, shown here, is an illustration from "Briar Rose" now "Sleeping Beauty", in which the king jumps for joy on the occasion of the birth of his daughter. The twisting decoration on the wall and door above the characters alludes to the briars that eventually ensnare the castle while Sleeping Beauty sleeps.

◄ **SIGNATURE SCENE** Many of the tales, such as "The Water of Life", shown here, feature perilous forests. To convey a sense of forboding, Rackham illustrated them using extensive detailing and fine line work so that they appear dark and impenetrable. In the background to this image the outline of a trapped figure can be mistaken for the branch of a tree.

In detail

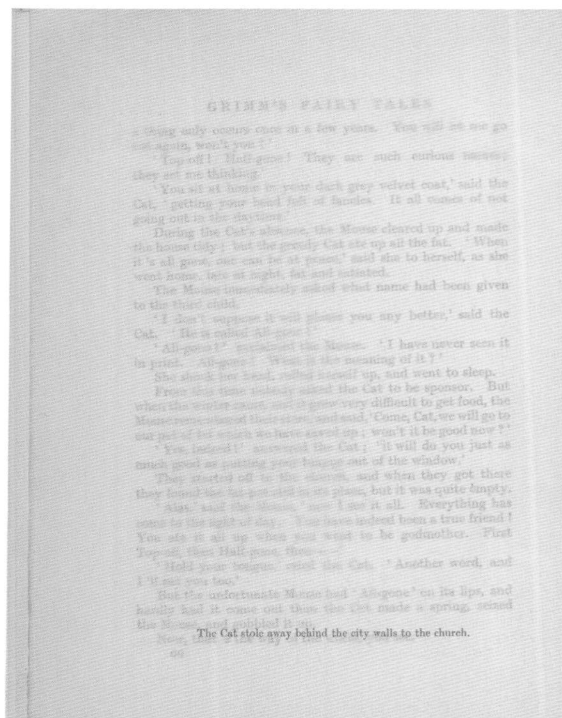

GRIMM'S FAIRY TALES

The Cat stole away behind the city walls to the church.

◄ **CONCEALED CHARACTERS** Many of the tales have a theme of deception, where characters are not what they seem. Rackham reflected this in his illustrations, by giving characters a physical appearance that often belied their true nature. In this illustration from "The Cat who Married the Mouse", the handsome-looking cat appears harmless, although the tale reveals the opposite.

▼ **LIGHT AND SHADOW** Rackham's illustrations often feature light and shadow to hint at the opposing forces of good and evil, as in the image below from "The Goose Girl". In this tale an innocent young girl, raised by a loving single mother, is sent out into the world to marry a stranger in the company of a chambermaid who deceives the girl, but is ultimately punished.

GRIMM'S FAIRY TALES

In the early morning, when she and Conrad went through the gateway, she said in passing—

'Alas! dear Falada, there thou hangest.'

And the Head answered—

'Alas! Queen's daughter, there thou gangest.
If thy mother knew thy fate,
Her heart would break with grief so great.'

Then they passed on out of the town, right into the fields, with the geese. When they reached the meadow, the Princess sat down on the grass and let down her hair. It shone like pure gold, and when little Conrad saw it, he was so delighted that he wanted to pluck some out; but she said—

'Blow, blow, little breeze,
And Conrad's hat seize.
Let him join in the chase
While away it is whirled,
Till my tresses are curled
And I rest in my place.'

Then a strong wind sprang up, which blew away Conrad's hat right over the fields, and he had to run after it. When he came back, she had finished combing her hair, and it was all put up again; so he could not get a single hair. This made him very sulky, and he would not say another word to her. And they tended the geese till evening, when they went home.

Next morning, when they passed under the gateway, the Princess said—

'Alas! dear Falada, there thou hangest.'

Falada answered :—

'Alas! Queen's daughter, there thou gangest.
If thy mother knew thy fate,
Her heart would break with grief so great.'

70

◄ **THREAT OF DANGER** Sex and violence lie at the heart of traditional fairy tales, but the Grimm Brothers edited the stories they had first published to make them more palatable to a young audience. Rackham's illustrations also tempered the frightening elements of the fairy tales, but conveyed just enough potential danger to be exciting. "Hansel and Gretel", shown here, is an example of an edited story: in the original story, the children's own mother sends them away to die, but in the later version it is their stepmother who plots to kill them.

> It is hardly too much to say that these tales rank next to the Bible in importance
>
> **W.H. AUDEN**, ON *GRIMM'S FAIRY TALES*

RELATED **TEXTS**

The fairy tales of the Grimm Brothers are predated by Charles Perrault's *Histoires ou contes du temps passé, avec des moralités: Contes de ma mère l'Oye* (*Stories or Tales of The Past with Morals: Tales of Mother Goose*), published in France in 1697. It consisted of eight stories, with titles that are instantly recognizable today, including "The Sleeping Beauty in the Wood", "Little Red Riding Hood", "Cinderella", and "Mother Goose". Perrault, a lawyer by trade, did not invent the tales – they were already well known as part of European folklore – but by writing them down in an engaging way, he established them as literature. He fleshed out the stories, adding complexity and details not in the original versions. Like the Grimm's first publication, the French volume was intended for an adult readership, with violent themes and sexual content, but, over the space of several years, the book was edited and repackaged for children. Little Red Riding Hood's wolf morphed from a sexual predator to simply a hungry beast, while Sleeping Beauty changed from a sexually active mother of two to a virgin. Perrault's book remained popular for decades, with several editions published in Paris, Amsterdam, and London between 1697 and 1800.

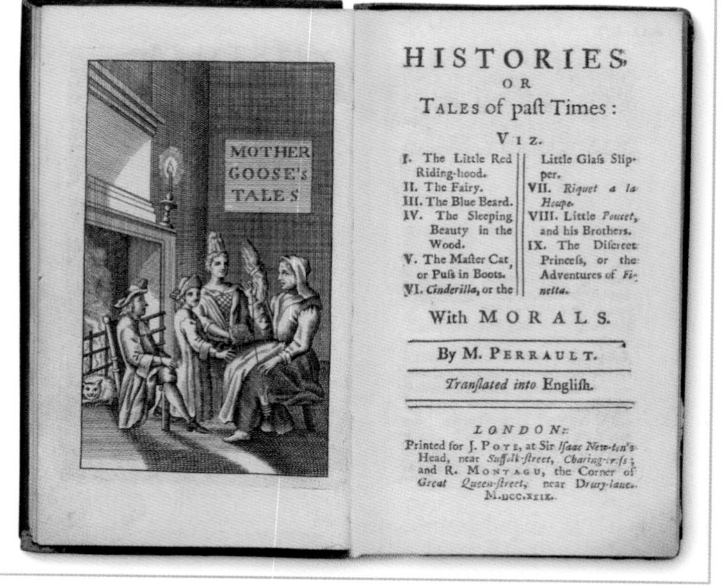

HISTORIES
OR
TALES of paſt Times:
VIZ.

I. The Little Red Riding-hood.
II. The Fairy.
III. The Blue Beard.
IV. The Sleeping Beauty in the Wood.
V. The Maſter Cat, or Puſs in Boots.
VI. *Cinderilla*, or the Little Glaſs Slipper.
VII. *Riquet a la Houpe.*
VIII. Little *Poucet*, and his Brothers.
IX. The Diſcreet Princeſs, or the Adventures of *Finetta*.

With MORALS.

By M. PERRAULT.

Tranſlated into Engliſh.

LONDON:
Printed for J. POTE, at Sir *Iſaac New-ton's* Head, near *Suffolk-ſtreet*, *Charing-croſs*; and R. MONTAGU, the Corner of *Great Queen-ſtreet*, near *Drury-lane*.
M.DCC.XXIX.

➤ **Robert Samber's** captivating translation for the English edition of 1729 helped to popularize the fairy tales in Britain.

General Theory of Relativity

1916 ■ PRINTED ■ 24.8 × 16.5 cm (10 × 6 in) ■ 69 PAGES ■ GERMANY

SCALE

ALBERT EINSTEIN

On 24 November 1915, in Berlin, the German-born physicist Albert Einstein presented a revolutionary mathematical physics paper on gravity. Painstakingly formulated over the previous decade, his General Theory of Relativity would have a seismic effect on the scientific world. Its ideas displaced one of the great pillars of physics – the law of universal gravitation put forward by English scientist Isaac Newton (1642–1727) in the 17th century – and forced physicists to re-assess their most fundamental beliefs about space, time, matter, and gravity.

Newton's landmark work *Principia* (see pp.142–43) had described the notion that any two objects exert a gravitational force of attraction on each other. Newton believed that gravity affects everything: causing an apple to fall from a tree and keeping the planets orbiting the Sun. Yet he was unable to explain where gravity comes from or the laws of physics that govern it. Einstein saw these theoretical difficulties as puzzles to probe, and he set about solving the mystery of how gravity works.

ALBERT **EINSTEIN**

1879–1955

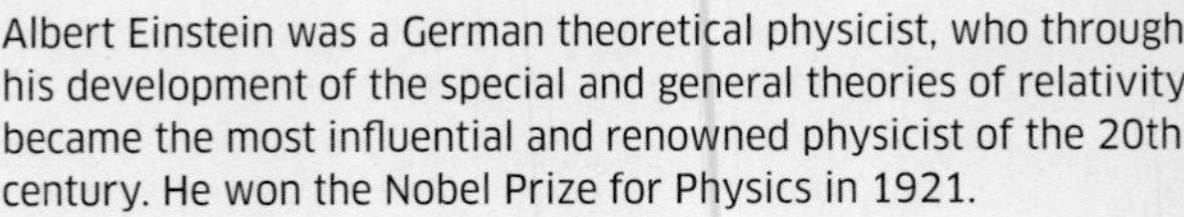

Albert Einstein was a German theoretical physicist, who through his development of the special and general theories of relativity became the most influential and renowned physicist of the 20th century. He won the Nobel Prize for Physics in 1921.

Born to Jewish parents in Ulm, Germany, as a child, Einstein's questioning mind led him to challenge existing ideas about science. After school he trained to be a physics and maths teacher, but he was unable to secure a teaching post, and instead worked as a clerk at the Swiss patent office for seven years from 1909. During this time he calculated the speed of light and published his Special Theory of Relativity, which featured the now famous equation $E=mc^2$.

Einstein quickly rose in the academic world, holding senior posts at famous institutions. In 1919 a key prediction of his 1916 General Theory of Relativity – that gravity should bend light – was proven correct, and Einstein became a world-renowned icon. With the rise of Nazism, and a specific threat to Einstein himself, in 1932 he emmigrated to the US where he spent the rest of his life.

In 1905 after conducting research while holding down a job as a clerk, Einstein published three remarkable papers that would alter the course of physics. One of these, the Special Theory of Relativity, showed that the laws of physics for space and time are the same when two objects are moving at a constant speed relative to each other. But there was a hitch – gravity did not fit within this theory because it involved acceleration.

And so Einstein spent the next 10 years working tirelessly on a larger, more explanatory vision that would account for acceleration in space and time. The result was the General Theory of Relativity, which posited that massive objects cause a distortion in space and time that is felt as gravity. It also explained why some things accelerate in reference to each other. Einstein said that gravity does not pull matter, as Newton thought – it pushes. He theorized that there is curved space around the Earth that pushes on the atmosphere and all the objects on the planet.

The consequences of the General Theory of Relativity have been profound. It unleashed new cosmological concepts, including black holes and the Big Bang, and underpins modern technology such as GPS and smart phones.

IN **CONTEXT**

In 1912 Albert Einstein penned a draft manuscript of the General Theory of Relativity. Although he tweaked and modified his calculations many times after this point, the handwritten manuscript remains a historic document that offers a glimpse into the brilliant physicist's mind.

In particular it reveals Einstein's rediscovered passion for mathematics in helping him realize his ideas. While producing the manuscript he wrote to fellow physicist Arnold Sommerfeld, saying, "I have gained great respect for mathematics, whose more subtle parts I considered until now, in my ignorance, as pure luxury." Today the manuscript is held in the Albert Einstein Archives at The Hebrew University of Jerusalem, Israel.

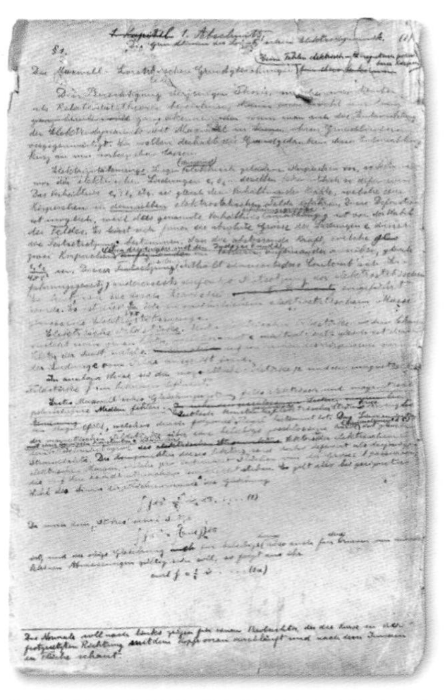

➤ **The 72 pages** of the 1912 manuscript show extensive reworking, revealing Einstein's thought processes more clearly than any other of his handwritten works.

> Put your hand on a stove for a minute, and it seems like an hour. Sit with that special girl for an hour, and it seems like a minute. That's relativity

ALBERT EINSTEIN, EXPLAINING HIS THEORY OF RELATIVITY

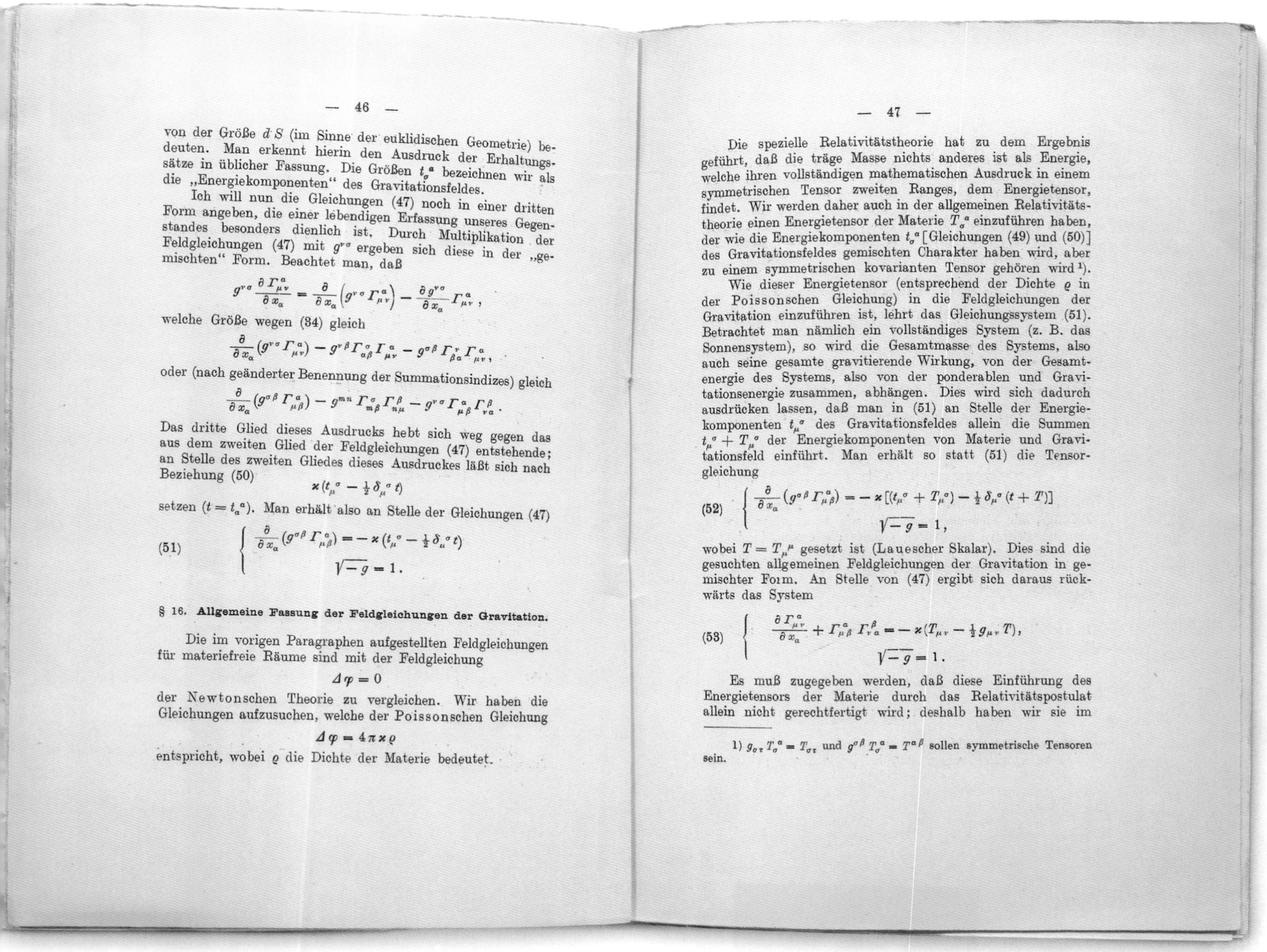

— 46 —

von der Größe dS (im Sinne der euklidischen Geometrie) bedeuten. Man erkennt hierin den Ausdruck der Erhaltungssätze in üblicher Fassung. Die Größen t_σ^{α} bezeichnen wir als die „Energiekomponenten" des Gravitationsfeldes.

Ich will nun die Gleichungen (47) noch in einer dritten Form angeben, die einer lebendigen Erfassung unseres Gegenstandes besonders dienlich ist. Durch Multiplikation der Feldgleichungen (47) mit $g^{\nu\sigma}$ ergeben sich diese in der „gemischten" Form. Beachtet man, daß

$$g^{\nu\sigma}\frac{\partial \Gamma^{\alpha}_{\mu\nu}}{\partial x_\alpha} = \frac{\partial}{\partial x_\alpha}\left(g^{\nu\sigma}\Gamma^{\alpha}_{\mu\nu}\right) - \frac{\partial g^{\nu\sigma}}{\partial x_\alpha}\Gamma^{\alpha}_{\mu\nu},$$

welche Größe wegen (34) gleich

$$\frac{\partial}{\partial x_\alpha}(g^{\nu\sigma}\Gamma^{\alpha}_{\mu\nu}) - g^{\nu\beta}\Gamma^{\sigma}_{\alpha\beta}\Gamma^{\alpha}_{\mu\nu} - g^{\sigma\beta}\Gamma^{\nu}_{\beta\alpha}\Gamma^{\alpha}_{\mu\nu},$$

oder (nach geänderter Benennung der Summationsindizes) gleich

$$\frac{\partial}{\partial x_\alpha}(g^{\sigma\beta}\Gamma^{\alpha}_{\mu\beta}) - g^{mn}\Gamma^{\sigma}_{m\beta}\Gamma^{\beta}_{n\mu} - g^{\nu\sigma}\Gamma^{\alpha}_{\mu\beta}\Gamma^{\beta}_{\nu\alpha}.$$

Das dritte Glied dieses Ausdrucks hebt sich weg gegen das aus dem zweiten Glied der Feldgleichungen (47) entstehende; an Stelle des zweiten Gliedes dieses Ausdruckes läßt sich nach Beziehung (50)

$$\varkappa(t_\mu^{\sigma} - \tfrac{1}{2}\delta_\mu^{\sigma} t)$$

setzen ($t = t_\alpha^{\alpha}$). Man erhält also an Stelle der Gleichungen (47)

$$\left\{\begin{aligned} &\frac{\partial}{\partial x_\alpha}(g^{\sigma\beta}\Gamma^{\alpha}_{\mu\beta}) = -\varkappa(t_\mu^{\sigma} - \tfrac{1}{2}\delta_\mu^{\sigma} t) \\ &\sqrt{-g} = 1. \end{aligned}\right. \tag{51}$$

§ 16. Allgemeine Fassung der Feldgleichungen der Gravitation.

Die im vorigen Paragraphen aufgestellten Feldgleichungen für materiefreie Räume sind mit der Feldgleichung

$$\Delta\varphi = 0$$

der Newtonschen Theorie zu vergleichen. Wir haben die Gleichungen aufzusuchen, welche der Poissonschen Gleichung

$$\Delta\varphi = 4\pi\varkappa\varrho$$

entspricht, wobei ϱ die Dichte der Materie bedeutet.

— 47 —

Die spezielle Relativitätstheorie hat zu dem Ergebnis geführt, daß die träge Masse nichts anderes ist als Energie, welche ihren vollständigen mathematischen Ausdruck in einem symmetrischen Tensor zweiten Ranges, dem Energietensor, findet. Wir werden daher auch in der allgemeinen Relativitätstheorie einen Energietensor der Materie T_σ^{α} einzuführen haben, der wie die Energiekomponenten t_σ^{α} [Gleichungen (49) und (50)] des Gravitationsfeldes gemischten Charakter haben wird, aber zu einem symmetrischen kovarianten Tensor gehören wird[1]).

Wie dieser Energietensor (entsprechend der Dichte ϱ in der Poissonschen Gleichung) in die Feldgleichungen der Gravitation einzuführen ist, lehrt das Gleichungssystem (51). Betrachtet man nämlich ein vollständiges System (z. B. das Sonnensystem), so wird die Gesamtmasse des Systems, also auch seine gesamte gravitierende Wirkung, von der Gesamtenergie des Systems, also von der ponderablen und Gravitationsenergie zusammen, abhängen. Dies wird sich dadurch ausdrücken lassen, daß man in (51) an Stelle der Energiekomponenten t_μ^{σ} des Gravitationsfeldes allein die Summen $t_\mu^{\sigma} + T_\mu^{\sigma}$ der Energiekomponenten von Materie und Gravitationsfeld einführt. Man erhält so statt (51) die Tensorgleichung

$$\left\{\begin{aligned} &\frac{\partial}{\partial x_\alpha}(g^{\sigma\beta}\Gamma^{\alpha}_{\mu\beta}) = -\varkappa[(t_\mu^{\sigma} + T_\mu^{\sigma}) - \tfrac{1}{2}\delta_\mu^{\sigma}(t + T)] \\ &\sqrt{-g} = 1, \end{aligned}\right. \tag{52}$$

wobei $T = T_\mu^{\mu}$ gesetzt ist (Lauescher Skalar). Dies sind die gesuchten allgemeinen Feldgleichungen der Gravitation in gemischter Form. An Stelle von (47) ergibt sich daraus rückwärts das System

$$\left\{\begin{aligned} &\frac{\partial \Gamma^{\alpha}_{\mu\nu}}{\partial x_\alpha} + \Gamma^{\alpha}_{\mu\beta}\Gamma^{\beta}_{\nu\alpha} = -\varkappa(T_{\mu\nu} - \tfrac{1}{2}g_{\mu\nu}T), \\ &\sqrt{-g} = 1. \end{aligned}\right. \tag{53}$$

Es muß zugegeben werden, daß diese Einführung des Energietensors der Materie durch das Relativitätspostulat allein nicht gerechtfertigt wird; deshalb haben wir sie im

1) $g_{\sigma\tau}T_\sigma^{\alpha} = T_{\sigma\tau}$ und $g^{\sigma\beta}T_\sigma^{\alpha} = T^{\alpha\beta}$ sollen symmetrische Tensoren sein.

▲ **A TOWERING ACHIEVEMENT** Einstein first announced his General Theory of Relativity late in 1915, as part of a series of lectures before the Prussian Academy of Science. The final paper was published by the scientific journal *Annalen der Physik* in March 1916 and consisted of a set of mathematical equations. The field equations of gravitation displayed here show, among other things, that space and time are part of one continuum – called space-time – and that gravity is not a force, as Newton described it, but the effect of objects bending space-time.

Pro Dva Kvadrata

1922 ▪ NEWSPRINT ▪ 29 × 22.5 cm (11 × 9 in) ▪ 24 PAGES ▪ RUSSIA

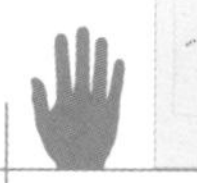

SCALE

EL LISSITZKY

Translated as *About Two Squares*, *Pro Dva Kvadrata* is a masterpiece of Suprematist book illustration: the almost stark simplicity of its six main plates encapsulates a revolution in art and typography, an appeal to social revolution, and a simple children's fable. The book's author and designer, El Lissitzky, was working at a time of enormous political upheaval in his home country of Russia, which culminated in the Revolution of 1917 and the first communist government led by Vladimir Lenin (1870–1924). The Revolution also unleashed huge creative energy. Lissitzky, who had been rejected by Russia's conservative art schools, became Professor of Architecture at Vitebsk in 1919. Here the radical artist Kasimir Malevich introduced Lissitzky to the theory of Suprematism, which rejected artistic attempts to imitate naturalistic shapes, and favoured instead strong, distinct, geometric designs.

Many Russian artists of the era supported the Revolution and turned their talents to promoting the social justice they believed it would bring. Lissitzky drew propaganda posters for the Communist Party and designed their first flag. He also began a series of projects called PROUNS (Projects for the Affirmation of the New) with which he hoped to move Suprematism from a two-dimensional stage to a three-dimensional one through his architectural expertise. *Pro Dva Kvadrata*, printed by letterpress in red and black, was part of this effort. Outwardly a children's tale, it depicts the adventures of the red square (communist ideals) as it overcomes the black square (convention), to create a better world. The typography, sparse but bold, is closely linked to the illustrations, breaking the bounds of conventional book design and setting new standards for what an illustrated book could be.

EL LISSITZKY

1890–1941

Lazar ("El") Lissitzky was a leading proponent of the Suprematist movement, championing the purity of simple artistic forms and integrating them with the revolutionary ideals of the Soviet Union.

Artist, architect, typographer, and designer, El Lissitzky grew up in provincial Russia, but studied architecture in Germany, where he was influenced by the clean, uncluttered lines of Walter Gropius's work. Returning to Russia during World War I, Lissitzky found few major architectural commissions and turned to book illustration. In 1919 he became professor of architecture in his home town of Vitebsk. Two years later he went to Berlin as an artistic emissary for the USSR, where he was exposed to the new avant-garde and Dadaism, before returning to Moscow in 1926. In the late 1920s he experimented with photomontage and continued to illustrate and design books. Crippled by tuberculosis and a political atmosphere in the Soviet Union that became ever more stifling under Joseph Stalin, his later work concentrated on designing exhibition pavilions for the USSR and propaganda posters. He completed the last of these posters, *Make More Tanks*, to help in the war effort against Nazi Germany, shortly before his death in Moscow in December 1941.

In detail

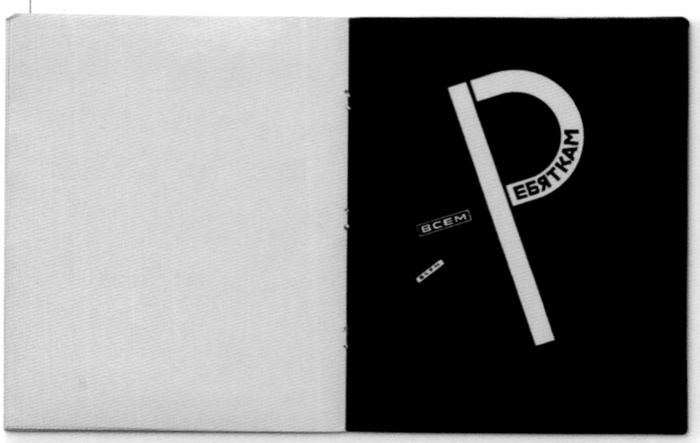

◄ **DEDICATION PAGE** With striking white typography on a black background, Lissitzky dedicates his book "To all, all children". The large, slanting capital Cyrillic "P" forms the first letter of "Children".

► **CHAOS** The distinct words "black" and "alarming", also slanting, contrast with the jumble of blocks and angular objects that float disturbingly in mid-air, without any sense of perspective or logic.

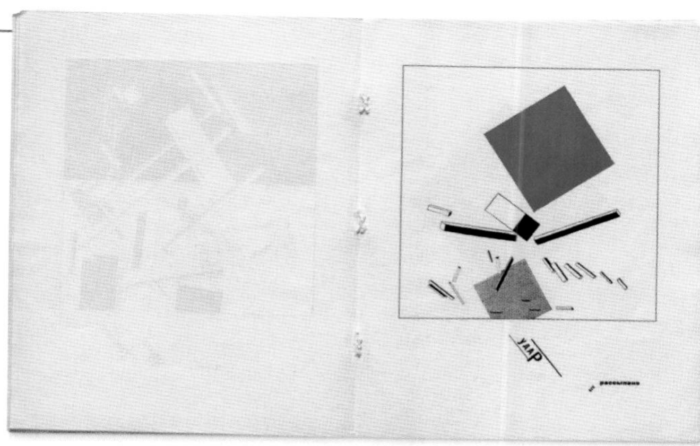

◄ **ORDER** Even though a corner of the red square has crashed down onto the objects below, scattering them, a sense of order seems to have been achieved with the items grouped together by shape and size. Beneath the image sit the words "crash", set slanted, and "scattered", set straight.

▼ **INTRODUCTION** In this plate Lissitzky shows the red square of communism rising pointedly beneath the black square of convention, as if pushing it aside. The bold, stark graphics, and the simple sans serif type below are typical of the book and the Suprematist movement's disdain for unnecessary ornamentation.

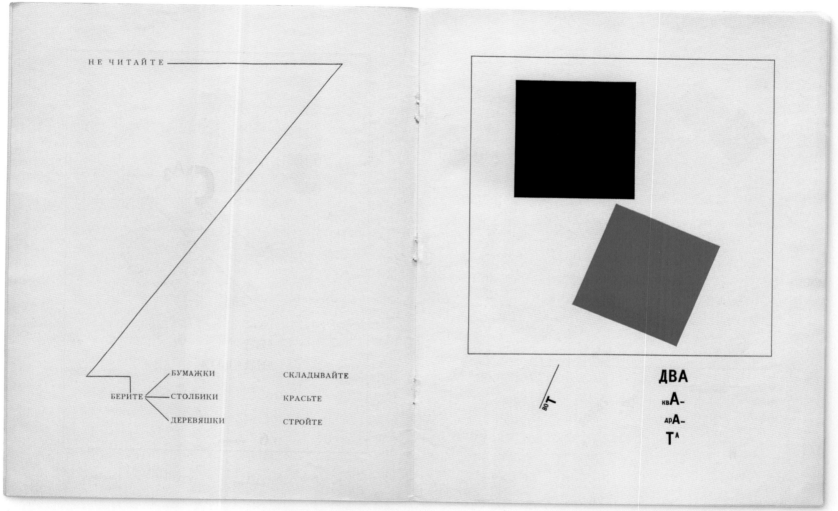

НЕ ЧИТАЙТЕ

БЕРИТЕ БУМАЖКИ СТОЛБИКИ ДЕРЕВЯШКИ

СКЛАДЫВАЙТЕ КРАСЬТЕ СТРОЙТЕ

ВОТ

ДВА
квА-
арА-
ТА

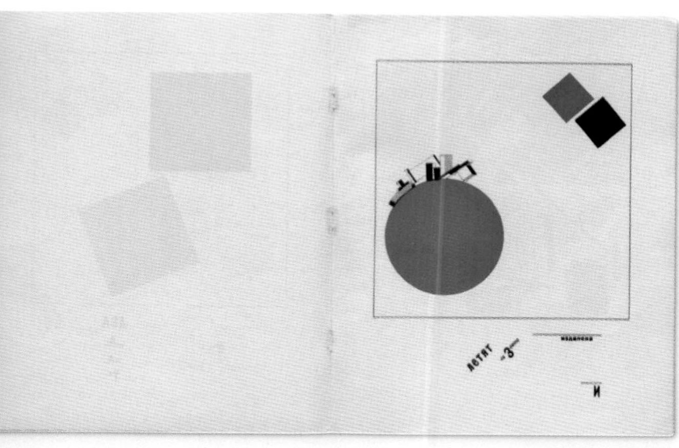

◄ **ON COURSE** One of the tenets of Suprematism was to take a work to the extreme of abstraction, while still being recognized as art. In this plate the image is both abstract and artistic, yet still conveys a political message – the Soviet red square is ahead of the old order black one in the race to Earth.

> We are faced with a book form in which representation is primary and the alphabet secondary

EL LISSITZKY, *OUR BOOK*, 1926

Penguin's first 10 paperback books

1935 ▪ PRINTED ▪ 18 × 11 cm (7 × 4½ in) ▪ VARIOUS EXTENTS ▪ UK

SCALE

VARIOUS AUTHORS

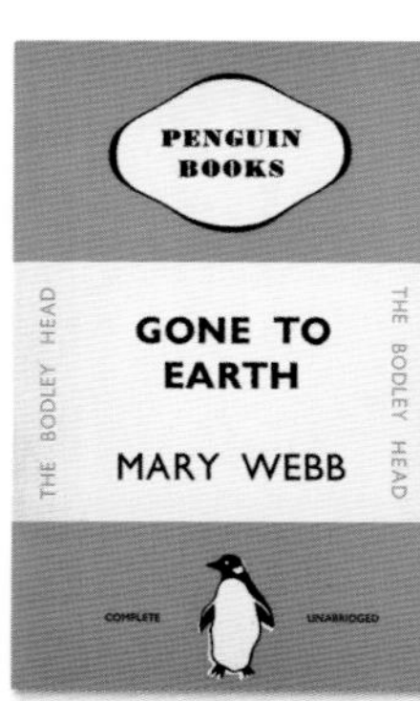

The publication of 10 Penguin books on 30 July 1935 changed the course of publishing across the globe. Paperback versions of 10 popular books (already published as hardbacks) were put on sale for the very low price of 6d. Their appeal was instant – they were cheap, yet high-quality, and had bold, colourful covers. The Penguin list featured writers as celebrated as Ernest Hemingway (1899–1961), Agatha Christie (1890–1976), and Compton Mackenzie (1883–1972). It was precisely because other publishers were convinced that the venture was doomed to failure that they allowed the creator of the list, Allen Lane, to pick up the rights to these books for almost nothing.

More significantly, the books were packaged with simple, elegant, clear, obviously modern covers. This was not just serious publishing made accessible to almost anyone: it was the first, perhaps the most lasting, demonstration of the power of design-led branding in the book world.

Lane's idea for the graphic cover design was not quite as original as it appeared. It was the German publisher, Albatross, which, in 1932, first recognized the potency of bold colours, simple typefaces, and low prices in creating a new market. But it was Lane who had the crucial insight that quality, in every sense, was the key to mass-market success. The story of Penguin remains an enduring lesson in how culture can be popularized without cheapening it.

ALLEN LANE

1902–1970

Allen Lane set up Penguin Books in 1936 after leaving Bodley Head. His cheap, boldly-coloured paperbacks revolutionized publishing, and brought high-quality literature to the mass market.

In 1919, Lane joined the London publishing house Bodley Head, founded by his uncle John Lane. He initially fell out with his board of directors over the publication of James Joyce's controversial *Ulysses*, and they were equally sceptical of his launch of the first Penguins as an imprint. Vindication followed when Woolworths placed an order for 63,000 books. In January 1936 he launched Penguin as a separate company. Lane had conceived the idea of cheap, high-quality books that could be sold from vending machines in 1934, after finding himself at Exeter station with nothing to read. By March 1936, over one million Penguin paperbacks had been sold. Lane built brilliantly and relentlessly on this initial success. In 1937, he formed the educational list, Pelican, with *The Pelican History of Art* becoming one of the great successes of post-War publishing. Puffin, a children's list, was established in 1940, with Penguin Classics following in 1945. Courtesy of Penguin, the likes of Evelyn Waugh, Aldous Huxley, E.M. Forster, and P.G. Wodehouse found new readers as the Penguin paperback became an intrinsic part of British cultural life.

IN CONTEXT

In 1935, 21-year-old Edward Young, an office junior at Bodley Head, was commissioned by Lane to create the new logo and a cover design for the fledgling Penguin list. He would later say: "It was time to get rid of the idea that the only people who wanted cheap editions belonged to a lower order of intelligence and that therefore cheap editions must have gaudy and sensational covers." After World War II, Penguin would set higher standards still. The books that followed were in obvious contrast to the "yellow-backs" and their US equivalent, Dime novels, expected of popular publishing.

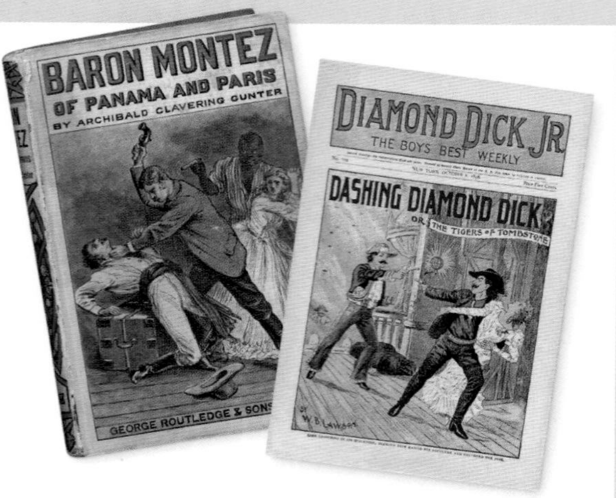

▲ **Mass market fiction** on both sides of the Atlantic had no pretensions to literary merit. Sold as entertaining reading, yellow-backs and Dime novels were popular reads.

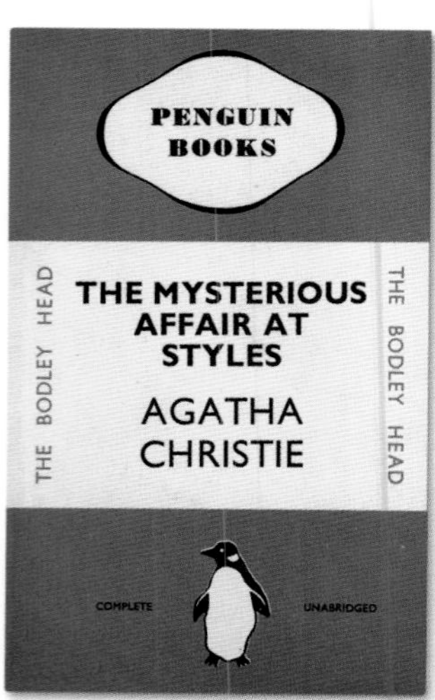

▲ **PURE DESIGN** The early Penguins were almost monastic in their purity: two bands of colour at the top and at the foot, with a white central panel containing the book's title and the author's name.

[Lane created] an institution of national and international importance, like *The Times* or the BBC

J.E. MORPURGO, *ALLEN LANE, KING PENGUIN* (1979)

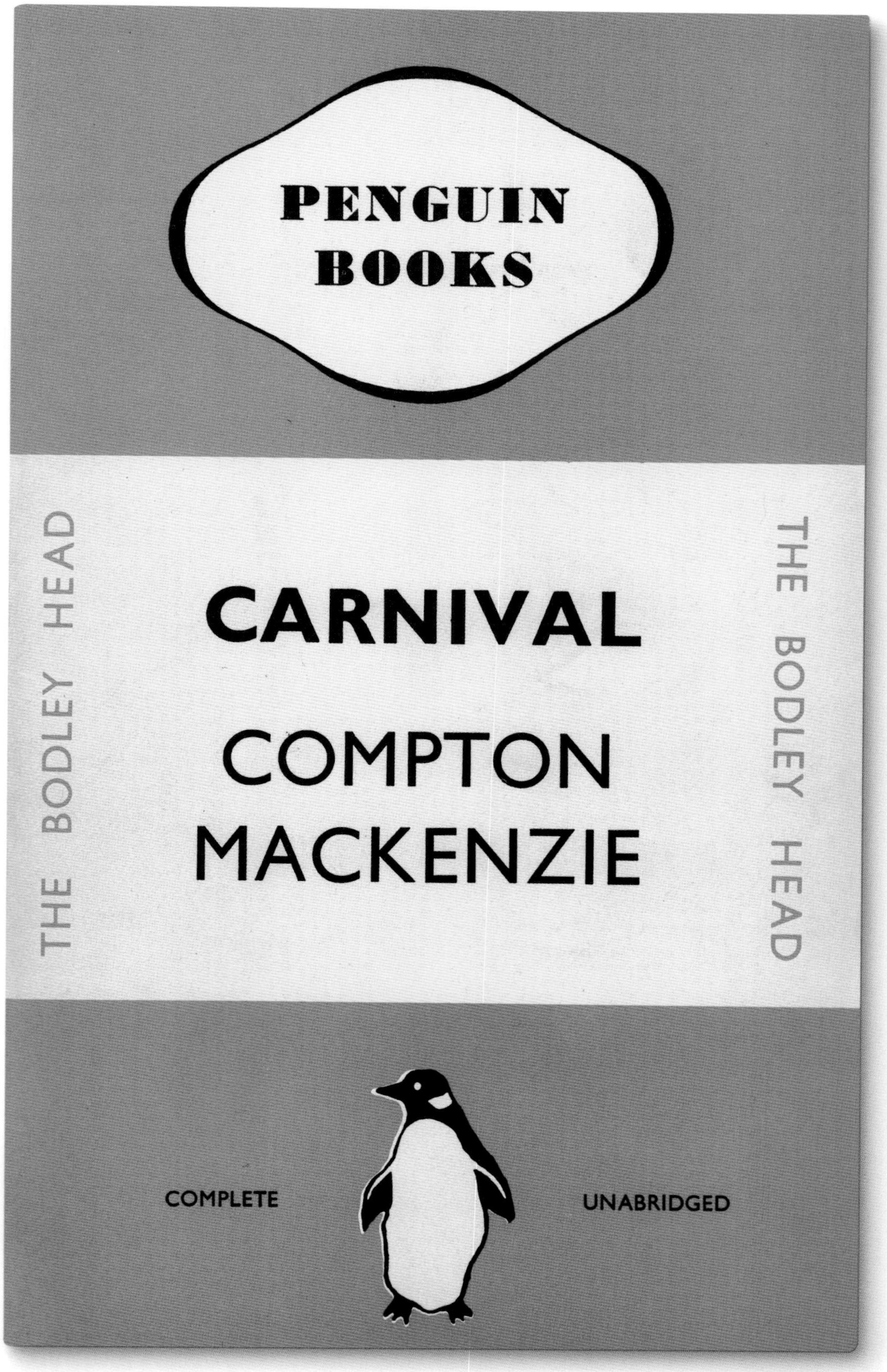

PENGUIN BOOKS

THE BODLEY HEAD

CARNIVAL

COMPTON MACKENZIE

THE BODLEY HEAD

COMPLETE UNABRIDGED

▲ **COLOUR CODING** Penguin books were colour-coded, with the template strictly adhered to: orange and white for fiction; green and white for crime fiction; and blue and white for biography.

The Diary of a Young Girl

1942–44 ▪ AUTOGRAPH BOOK, EXERCISE BOOKS, AND LOOSE-LEAF PAGES ▪ THE NETHERLANDS

ANNE FRANK

In 1947 a Jewish man named Otto Frank published the diary of his 13-year-old daughter. Anne had died of typhus two years previously in Bergen-Belsen, a concentration camp in Germany. Her diary records the two-year period that she and her family (along with four others) spent in hiding in a secret annex above her father's office during the Nazi occupation of Amsterdam. Anne's account became one of the most poignant and widely read books about the Second World War, and Anne became one of the most renowned victims of the Holocaust. Historians also value the work, seeing it as an integral example of Jewish persecution.

Anne Frank's writing filled three books (one autograph book and two school exercise books), as well as 215 loose sheets of paper. She began the diary in July 1942 to record her years in hiding, but decided to revise her work after hearing a radio bulletin in March 1944 calling for diaries and letters to be preserved for posterity. Anne then rewrote her diary on separate pages with a view to publication, adding context and omitting passages of less general interest. She had intended to publish it after the war as *Het Achterhuis* (*The Secret Annex*), but in August 1944 Nazi soldiers raided the annex, and Anne, her family, and the other occupants were deported to Westerbork concentration camp. Anne's diary was found by two of her father's office workers, who secured it until Otto Frank – the only survivor from the annex – returned after the war. He then had the diary published in Anne's memory.

➤ **DEAR KITTY** In a few of her original diary entries, Anne wrote her thoughts in the form of letters addressed to various imaginary friends – the letters on the left-hand page of the diary opposite are written to "Jet" and "Marianne". During her rewriting phase, Anne standardized her diary entries, addressing them all to "Dear Kitty". Whether Kitty was a real person or not is unknown.

In detail

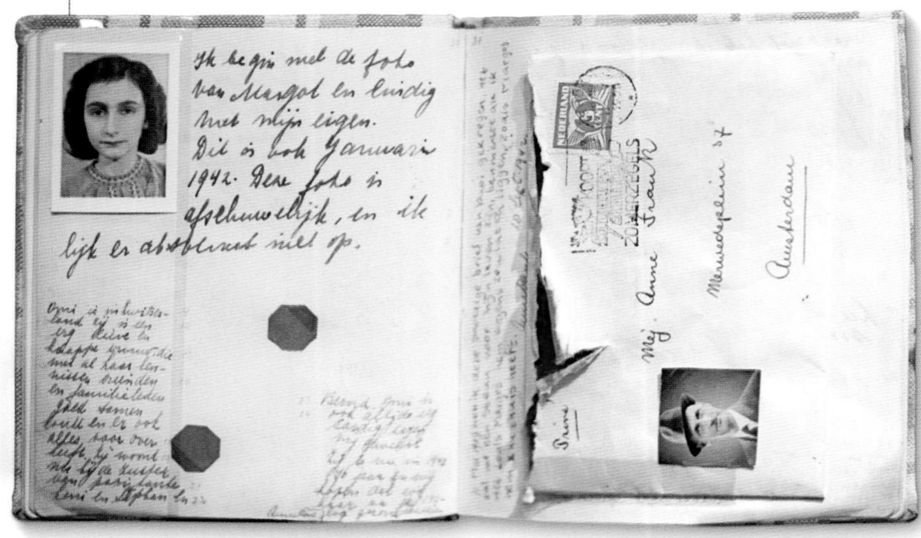

◀ **WISDOM IN YOUTH** Although only 13, Anne showed extraordinary maturity. In addition to keeping a record of daily life in the annex, Anne's entries often revealed deep thoughts and introspection as she contemplated the plight of the Jews and the fate that might await her family. She also expressed her ambition to become a writer and composed several short stories.

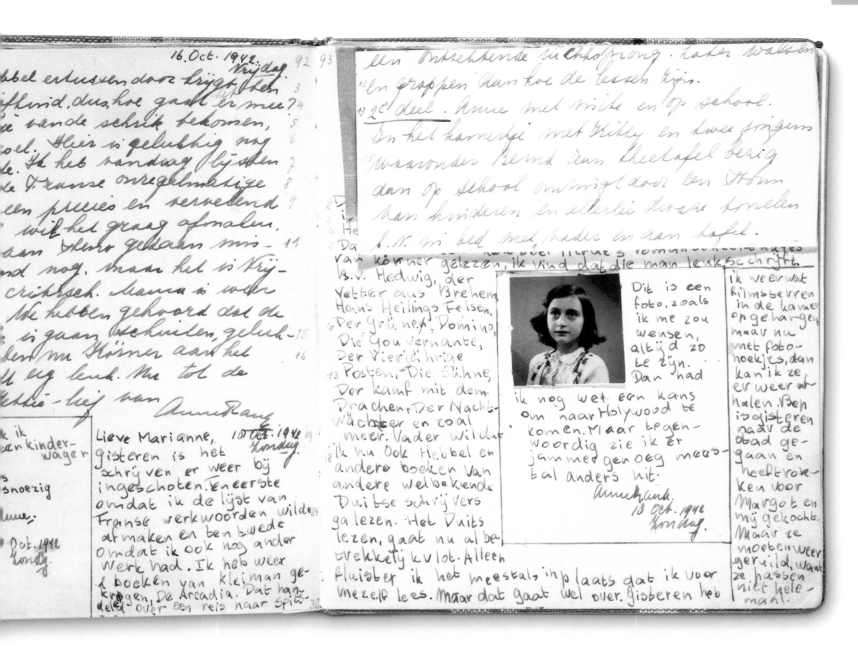

◀ **REMEMBERING BRIGHTER DAYS** As she coped with the close confinement in the attic Anne recalled happier times, pasting photos of friends and family holidays in her diary. The snapshots here, from 1939 and 1940 show Anne and family enjoying trips to the seaside. Anne notes that the photo at the top is the only one of her grandmother.

IN **CONTEXT**

On reading the salvaged remains of Anne's diary, Otto Frank discovered a side to his daughter that he had not been aware of. He was impressed and surprised by her depth of feeling and maturity, and decided to honour Anne's repeated wish to publish her diary. In selecting text for publication Otto realized that some sections of the diary were missing, and so he had to combine entries from her original text with those of her subsequent rewrites. He also made his own edits, removing Anne's references to her budding sexuality as well as unkind comments she had made about her mother.

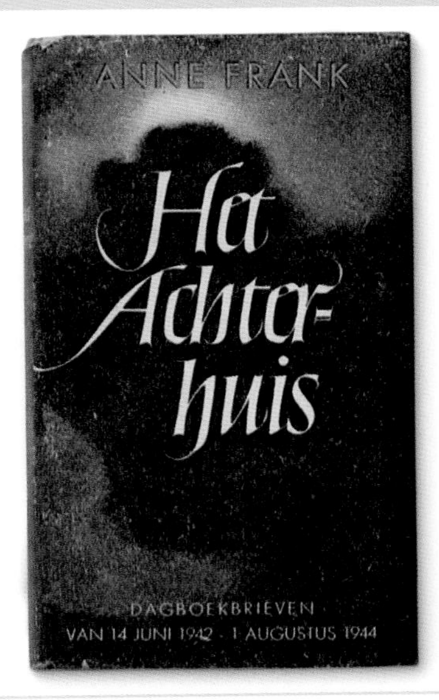

► **Anne's diary** was published on 25 June 1947 as *Het Achterhuis*. It has since been translated into 60 languages.

Le Petit Prince

1943 ▪ PRINTED ▪ 23 × 16 cm (9 × 6 in) ▪ 93 PAGES ▪ USA

ANTOINE DE SAINT-EXUPÉRY

SCALE

A rare example of a children's book that has equally captured the hearts of adults, *Le Petit Prince* remains an international bestseller more than 70 years after its debut. First published in 1943 in both French and English, it has since been translated into over 250 languages and dialects, and is estimated to have been read by 400 million people worldwide. It is the tale of a lonely boy prince who comes to Earth from another planet in search of friendship and understanding. The story is a parable that warns against narrowmindedness and teaches the importance of exploration in order to grow spiritually. It has also been interpreted as a fable about the isolation and bewilderment of war.

Much of the appeal of *Le Petit Prince* lies in Antoine de Saint-Exupéry's watercolour illustrations, which feature throughout the book. They recreate specific scenes, and are also used by the narrator to test characters he meets, and to rediscover his childhood. Saint-Exupéry's original handwritten manuscript includes several watercolours that did not appear in the first edition. The draft manuscript – the only complete handwritten copy known to exist – is held at the Morgan Library & Museum in Manhattan.

ANTOINE **DE SAINT-EXUPÉRY**

1900–1944

Antoine de Saint-Exupéry was a French writer, aviator, and aristocrat. Although best remembered for his novella, *Le Petit Prince*, he also wrote several award-winning novels based on his experiences as a mail pilot and service in the French air force.

Antoine de Saint-Exupéry grew up in a castle in France and enjoyed a carefree childhood. He was privileged to experience his first aeroplane flight at the age of 12, which had a lasting impact on him. In April 1921 he trained as a pilot as part of his compulsory French military service. Later, while working as a mail pilot in North Africa, he wrote his first novel *Courrier Sud* (*Southern Mail*), published in 1929 – the first of several books based on his flying exploits. When World War II broke out, Saint-Exupéry flew for the French air force, until the German occupation of France compelled him to flee to the US with his wife Consuelo Gómez Carillo in 1939. He settled in New York City, where he wrote and published *Le Petit Prince*, but thoughts of the war in Europe were on his mind, and in 1943 he enlisted with the Free French forces. He was declared missing in action while on a reconnaissance mission over France in July 1944.

In detail

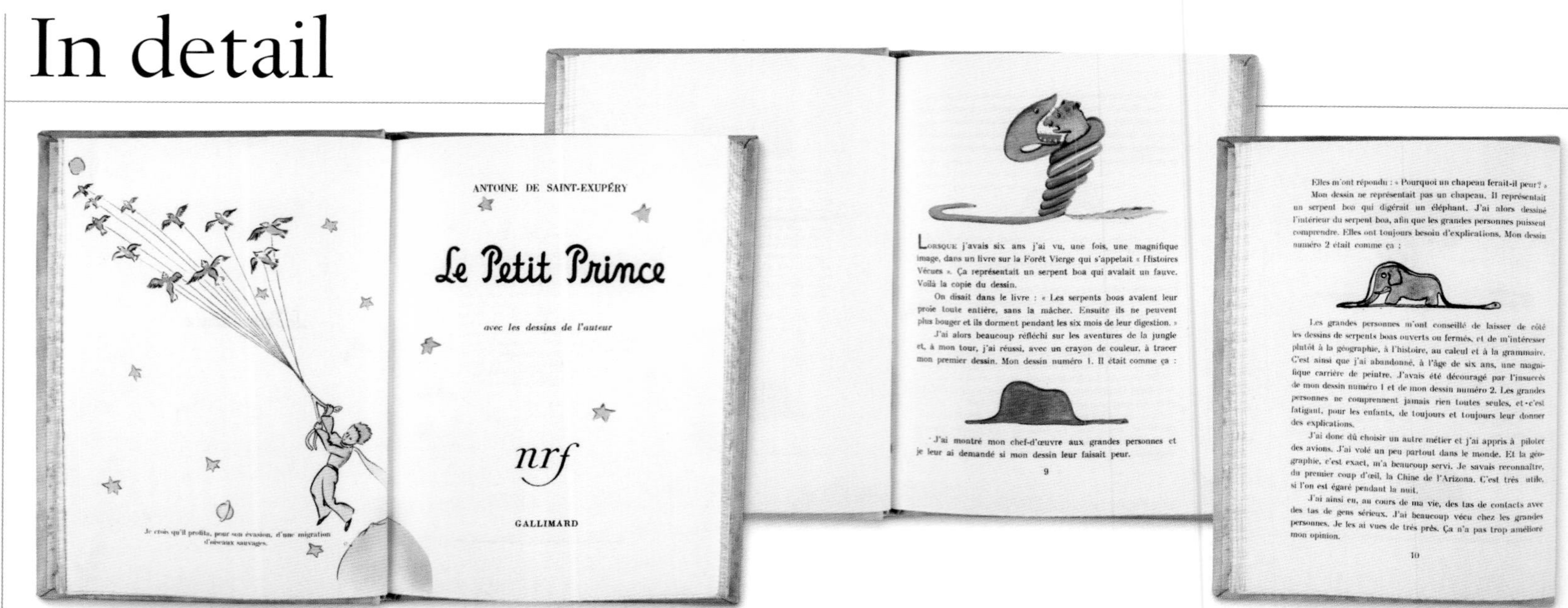

Je crois qu'il profita, pour son évasion, d'une migration d'oiseaux sauvages.

ANTOINE DE SAINT-EXUPÉRY

Le Petit Prince

avec les dessins de l'auteur

nrf

GALLIMARD

Lorsque j'avais six ans j'ai vu, une fois, une magnifique image, dans un livre sur la Forêt Vierge qui s'appelait « Histoires Vécues ». Ça représentait un serpent boa qui avalait un fauve. Voilà la copie du dessin.

On disait dans le livre : « Les serpents boas avalent leur proie toute entière, sans la mâcher. Ensuite ils ne peuvent plus bouger et ils dorment pendant les six mois de leur digestion. »

J'ai alors beaucoup réfléchi sur les aventures de la jungle et, à mon tour, j'ai réussi, avec un crayon de couleur, à tracer mon premier dessin. Mon dessin numéro 1. Il était comme ça :

J'ai montré mon chef-d'œuvre aux grandes personnes et je leur ai demandé si mon dessin leur faisait peur.

9

Elles m'ont répondu : « Pourquoi un chapeau ferait-il peur ? »

Mon dessin ne représentait pas un chapeau. Il représentait un serpent boa qui digérait un éléphant. J'ai alors dessiné l'intérieur du serpent boa, afin que les grandes personnes puissent comprendre. Elles ont toujours besoin d'explications. Mon dessin numéro 2 était comme ça :

Les grandes personnes m'ont conseillé de laisser de côté les dessins de serpents boas ouverts ou fermés, et de m'intéresser plutôt à la géographie, à l'histoire, au calcul et à la grammaire. C'est ainsi que j'ai abandonné, à l'âge de six ans, une magnifique carrière de peintre. J'avais été découragé par l'insuccès de mon dessin numéro 1 et de mon dessin numéro 2. Les grandes personnes ne comprennent jamais rien toutes seules, et c'est fatigant, pour les enfants, de toujours et toujours leur donner des explications.

J'ai donc dû choisir un autre métier et j'ai appris à piloter des avions. J'ai volé un peu partout dans le monde. Et la géographie, c'est exact, m'a beaucoup servi. Je savais reconnaître, du premier coup d'œil, la Chine de l'Arizona. C'est très utile, si l'on est égaré pendant la nuit.

J'ai ainsi eu, au cours de ma vie, des tas de contacts avec des tas de gens sérieux. J'ai beaucoup vécu chez les grandes personnes. Je les ai vues de très près. Ça n'a pas trop amélioré mon opinion.

10

▲ **SKY OF STARS** Images of stars, appearing here on the title page, are repeated throughout the book. The narrator, a pilot, relies on stars for navigation, while the little prince lives among them. Stars symbolize the vastness of the universe, as well as the pilot's loneliness.

▲ **A CHILD'S VIEWPOINT** Saint-Exupéry immediately engages the reader with the illustrations. Here, what grown-ups only recognized as a hat, is shown to be a boa constrictor that has eaten an elephant. The different ways in which adults and children see the world is a recurring theme.

All grown-ups were once children… but only few of them remember it

ANTOINE DE SAINT-EXUPÉRY, *LE PETIT PRINCE*

reviendras me dire adieu, et je te ferai cadeau d'un secret.

Le petit prince s'en fut revoir les roses :

— Vous n'êtes pas du tout semblables à ma rose, vous n'êtes rien encore, leur dit-il. Personne ne vous a apprivoisées et vous n'avez apprivoisé personne. Vous êtes comme était mon renard. Ce n'était qu'un renard semblable à cent mille autres. Mais j'en ai fait mon ami, et il est maintenant unique au monde.

Et les roses étaient bien gênées.

— Vous êtes belles, mais vous êtes vides, leur dit-il encore. On ne peut pas mourir pour vous. Bien sûr, ma rose à moi, un passant ordinaire croirait qu'elle vous ressemble. Mais à elle seule elle est plus importante que vous toutes, puisque c'est elle que j'ai arrosée. Puisque c'est elle que j'ai mise sous globe. Puisque c'est elle que j'ai abritée par le paravent. Puisque c'est elle dont j'ai tué les chenilles (sauf les deux ou trois pour les papillons). Puisque c'est elle que j'ai écoutée se plaindre, ou se vanter, ou même quelquefois se taire. Puisque c'est ma rose.

Et il revint vers le renard :

— Adieu, dit-il...

— Adieu, dit le renard. Voici mon secret. Il est très simple : on ne voit bien qu'avec le cœur. L'essentiel est invisible pour les yeux.

— L'essentiel est invisible pour les yeux, répéta le petit prince, afin de se souvenir.

— C'est le temps que tu as perdu pour ta rose qui fait ta rose si importante.

— C'est le temps que j'ai perdu pour ma rose... fit le petit prince, afin de se souvenir.

72

Et, couché dans l'herbe, il pleura.

▲ **THE INVISIBLE ESSENTIAL** Saint-Exupéry laboured over one of the most important phrases in the book, "*l'essentiel est invisible pour les yeux*" ("what is essential is invisible to the eye"), reworking it up to 15 times. Such reflections on human nature are frequent in the book, here suggesting that what one feels is most important.

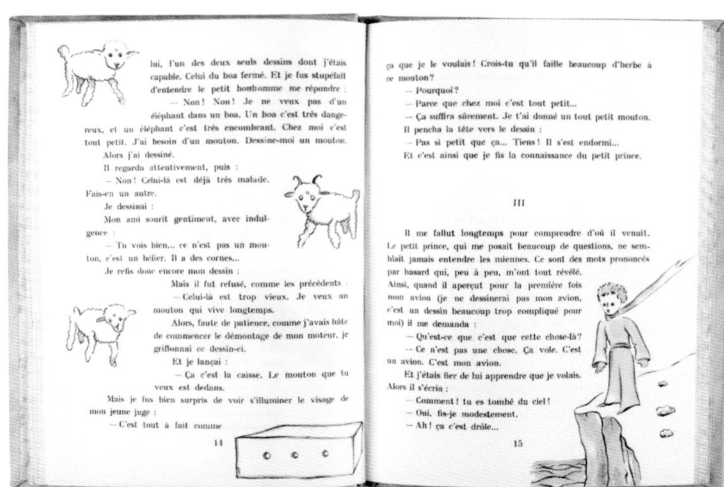

lui, l'un des deux seuls dessins dont j'étais capable. Celui du boa fermé. Et je fus stupéfait d'entendre le petit bonhomme me répondre :

— Non ! Non ! Je ne veux pas d'un éléphant dans un boa. Un boa c'est très dangereux, et un éléphant c'est très encombrant. Chez moi c'est tout petit. J'ai besoin d'un mouton. Dessine-moi un mouton.

Alors j'ai dessiné.

Il regarda attentivement, puis :

— Non ! Celui-là est déjà très malade. Fais-en un autre.

Je dessinai :

Mon ami sourit gentiment, avec indulgence :

— Tu vois bien... ce n'est pas un mouton, c'est un bélier. Il a des cornes...

Je refis donc encore mon dessin :

Mais il fut refusé, comme les précédents :

— Celui-là est trop vieux. Je veux un mouton qui vive longtemps.

Alors, faute de patience, comme j'avais hâte de commencer le démontage de mon moteur, je griffonnai ce dessin-ci.

Et je lançai :

— Ça c'est la caisse. Le mouton que tu veux est dedans.

Mais je fus bien surpris de voir s'illuminer le visage de mon jeune juge :

— C'est tout à fait comme

14

ça que je le voulais ! Crois-tu qu'il faille beaucoup d'herbe à ce mouton ?

— Pourquoi ?

— Parce que chez moi c'est tout petit...

— Ça suffira sûrement. Je t'ai donné un tout petit mouton.

Il pencha la tête vers le dessin :

— Pas si petit que ça... Tiens ! Il s'est endormi...

Et c'est ainsi que je fis la connaissance du petit prince.

III

Il me fallut longtemps pour comprendre d'où il venait. Le petit prince, qui me posait beaucoup de questions, ne semblait jamais entendre les miennes. Ce sont des mots prononcés par hasard qui, peu à peu, m'ont tout révélé. Ainsi, quand il aperçut pour la première fois mon avion (je ne dessinerai pas mon avion, c'est un dessin beaucoup trop compliqué pour moi) il me demanda :

— Qu'est-ce que c'est que cette chose-là ?

— Ce n'est pas une chose. Ça vole. C'est un avion. C'est mon avion.

Et j'étais fier de lui apprendre que je volais. Alors il s'écria :

— Comment ! tu es tombé du ciel !

— Oui, fis-je modestement.

— Ah ! ça c'est drôle...

15

▲ **SHEEP IN A BOX** Black and white illustrations, drawn by the narrator, help to establish his relationship with the prince. Here, the prince requests a sheep drawing, but is dissatisfied with the result. The sketch of a box for the animal, however, pleases the prince, as it allows him to imagine the sheep.

IN CONTEXT

Le Petit Prince's themes of loss, loneliness, and a longing for home, were close to author's heart, as he wrote it while living in exile in the US during World War II. The narrator's plane crash in the desert was also inspired by real events: Saint-Exupéry's own plane came down in the Sahara desert in 1935, where he and his navigator were stranded for four days, coming close to death. *Le Petit Prince* was published in April 1943, but was initially not available to buy in France (the Vichy government of German-occupied France had banned the works of Sainte-Exupéry after he fled the country). The book was not published in France until the country was liberated in 1944, but went on to be elected the greatest book of the 20th century in France.

▲ **Saint-Exupéry**, shown here in 1929, used his experiences as a pilot to inform many of his books.

Le Deuxième Sexe

1949 ▪ PRINTED ▪ 20.5 × 14 cm (8 × 5 1/2 in) ▪ 978 PAGES ▪ FRANCE

SCALE

SIMONE DE BEAUVOIR

The Second Sex (*Le Deuxième Sexe*) is considered one of the founding texts for the feminist movement. It proposes that women are not born with feminine qualities but learn to take them on; furthermore, it outlines how women are conditioned from birth to fit a stereotype, which prevents them from ever being free. De Beauvoir maintained that three steps were necessary for women to challenge the set path laid out for them by society: they must work, develop their intellect, and strive for economic equality. Published in France in 1949, the book did not fully make an impact until the English edition, heavily cut, was published in the US in 1953, causing widespread controversy.

SIMONE **DE BEAUVOIR**

1908–1986

Born in Paris, Simone de Beauvoir was a philosopher, writer, and committed socialist. She remains best known for her impact on the women's movement and her feminist treatise *Le Deuxième Sexe*.

At the age of 14 de Beauvoir rejected the existence of God and decided never to marry, devoting herself to the idea of life as a philosopher and teacher. She studied philosophy at the Sorbonne, Paris, and taught the subject. With fellow philosopher Jean-Paul Sartre, who would become her partner and lifelong friend, she was one of the leading figures in the French existentialist movement in the mid-20th century. She wrote varied works, including the novel *Les Mandarins*. *Le Deuxième Sexe* became essential reading for feminists in the 1960s, inspiring Betty Friedan and Germaine Greer among others.

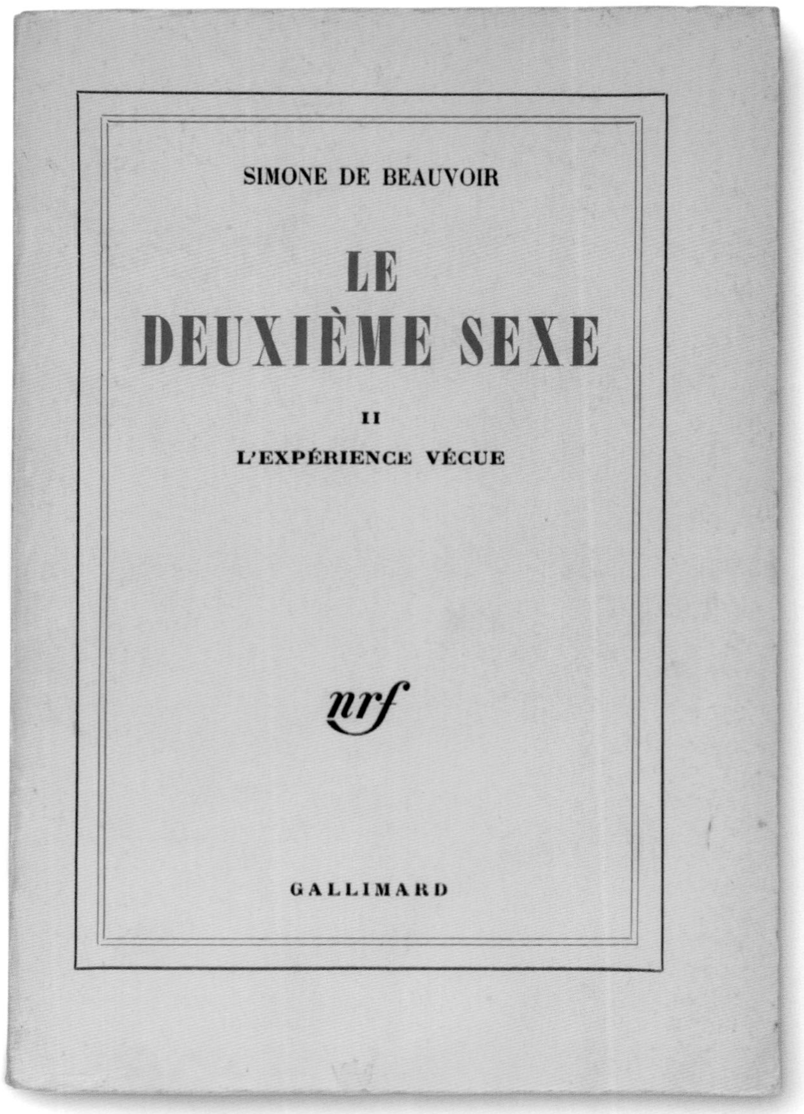

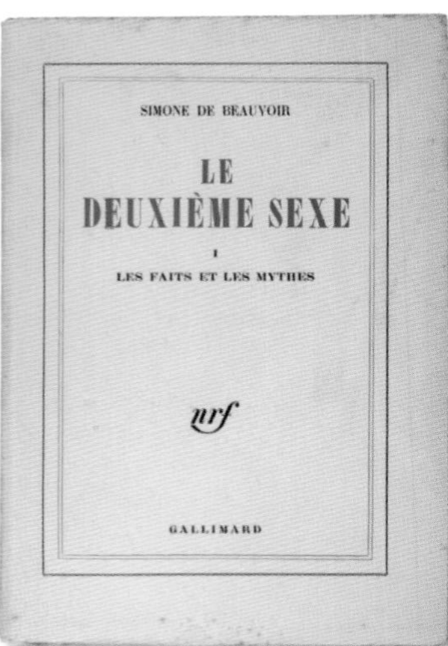

◄ **TWO PARTS** Conceived in two parts, *Le Deuxième Sexe* was written as a history of women in which the author presents men as oppressors, and women as the "other", the second sex. The first part, entitled "Facts and Myths", explores the events and cultural forces that forced women to be subordinate to men.

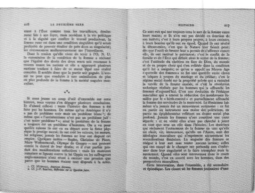

◄ **CREATED HISTORY** The "History" section in Volume 1 covers the historical suppression of women by men. Here, de Beauvoir concludes that men – as the creators of values and ideologies – have composed women's history, but that the majority of women have adapted to their subordinate status rather than acted against it.

◄ **LIFE JOURNEY** "One is not born, but rather becomes, a woman," de Beauvoir famously wrote. The second half of her book, "Lived Experience", attempts to describe in detail how this happens. The author takes a personal view of a woman's journey from birth to old age, to explain how she learns to take on feminine qualities.

The Feminine Mystique

1963 ■ PRINTED ■ 21 × 15 cm (8 × 6 in) ■ 416 PAGES ■ USA

SCALE

BETTY FRIEDAN

Betty Friedan's book about women's dissatisfaction with their roles in society triggered a chain of events in the US that eventually changed the balance of power between the sexes, both culturally and politically. Friedan wrote that women in the 1950s suffered under the expectation that they should be perfect housewives and mothers, projecting an image of idealized femininity, which the author dubbed "the feminine mystique". With its discussion of women who had gone against this image, the book made a powerful contribution to a new wave of feminism that resulted in legislation for equal pay and the formation of numerous women's groups to champion the rights of women.

BETTY **FRIEDAN**

1921–2006

Acknowledged as one of the most influential women of the 20th century, Betty Friedan (born Bettye Naomi Goldstein) championed the right of women to break free from stifling traditional roles.

The feminist pioneer Betty Friedan graduated with a degree in psychology from the University of California. In 1947 she moved to New York City where she worked as a reporter before marrying Carl Friedan and having three children. Frustrated at being a stay-at-home mum, and with the lack of workplace options for mothers, she began to research how other women felt. The book that resulted, *The Feminine Mystique*, raised awareness about women's discontent and is credited with sparking "second-wave feminism", which spanned the 1960s to the late 1980s (the "first wave" being the fight for suffrage in the early 1900s).

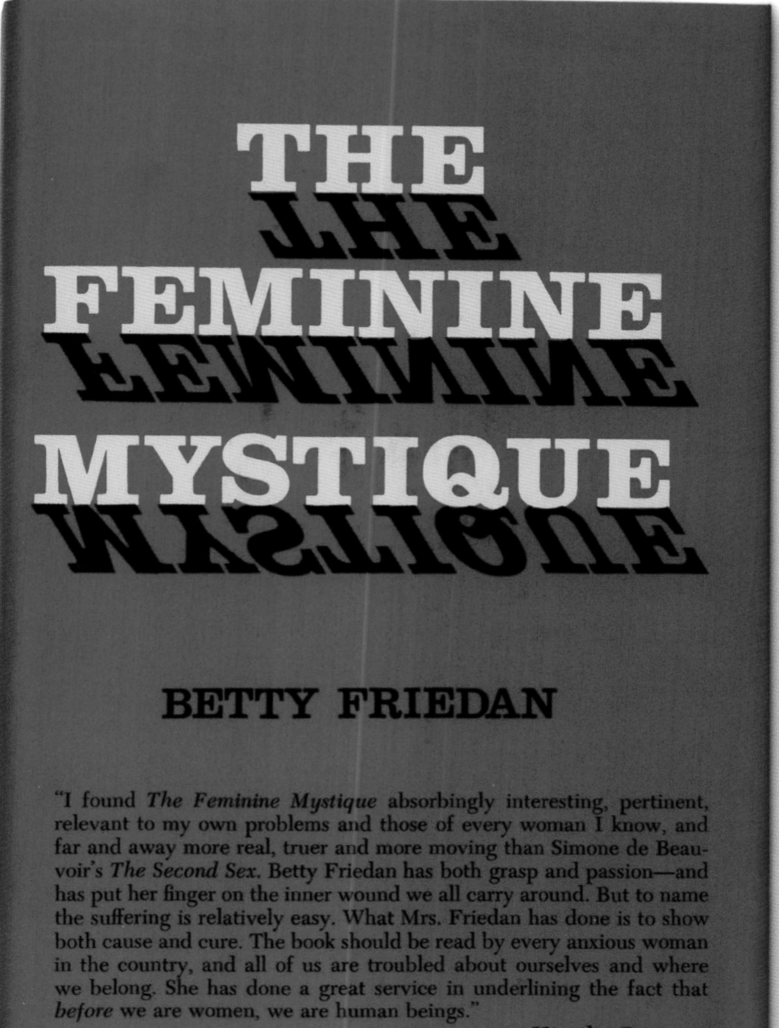

14

A NEW LIFE PLAN FOR WOMEN

"Easy enough to say," the woman inside the housewife's trap remarks, "but what can I do, alone in the house, with the children yelling and the laundry to sort and no grandmother to babysit?" It is easier to live through someone else than to become complete yourself. The freedom to lead and plan your own life is frightening if you have never faced it before. It is frightening when a woman finally realizes that there is no answer to the question "who am I" except the voice inside herself. She may spend years on the analyst's couch, working out her "adjustment to the feminine role," her blocks to "fulfillment as a wife and mother." And still the voice inside her may say, "That's not it." Even the best psychoanalyst can only give her the courage to listen to her own voice. When society asks so little of women, every woman has to listen to her own inner voice to find her identity in this changing world. She must create, out of her own needs and abilities, a new life plan, fitting in the love and children and home that have defined femininity in the past with the work toward a greater purpose that shapes the future.

To face the problem is not to solve it. But once a woman faces it, as women are doing today all over America without much help from the experts, once she asks herself "What do I want to do?" she begins to find her own answers. Once she begins to see through the delusions of the feminine mystique—and realizes

338

A NEW LIFE PLAN FOR WOMEN 339

that neither her husband nor her children, nor the things in her house, nor sex, nor being like all the other women, can give her a self—she often finds the solution much easier than she anticipated.

Of the many women I talked to in the suburbs and cities, some were just beginning to face the problem, others were well on their way to solving it, and for still others it was no longer a problem. In the stillness of an April afternoon with all her children in school, a woman told me:

I put all my energies into the children, carting them around, worrying about them, teaching them things. Suddenly, there was this terrible feeling of emptiness. All that volunteer work I'd taken on—Scouts, PTA, the League, just didn't seem worth doing all of a sudden. As a girl, I wanted to be an actress. It was too late to go back to that. I stayed in the house all day, cleaning things I hadn't cleaned in years. I spent a lot of time just crying. My husband and I talked about its being an American woman's problem, how you give up a career for the children, and then you reach a point where you can't go back. I felt so envious of the few women I know who had a definite skill and kept working at it. My dream of being an actress wasn't real—I didn't work at it. Did I have to throw my whole self into the children? I've spent my whole life just immersed in other people, and never even knew what kind of a person I was myself. Now I think even having another baby wouldn't solve that emptiness long. You can't go back—you have to go on. There must be some real way I can go on myself.

This woman was just beginning her search for identity. Another woman had made it to the other side, and could look back now and see the problem clearly. Her home was colorful, casual, but technically she was no longer "just a housewife." She was paid for her work as a professional painter. She told me that when she stopped conforming to the conventional picture of femininity she finally began to *enjoy* being a woman. She said:

I used to work so hard to maintain this beautiful picture of myself as a wife and mother. I had all of my children by natural childbirth. I breastfed them all. I got mad once at an older woman at a party when I said childbirth is the most important thing in life, the basic animal, and she said, "Don't you want to be more than an animal?"

▲ **ALTERNATIVE LIFE** In the final chapter Friedan proposes an alternative way of life for women, in which they can combine the traditional role of homemaker with meaningful work. She gives examples of women who have successfully managed motherhood and a career, but she also acknowledges the challenges that come with juggling both.

◄ **FEMININE REFLECTIONS** The cover's bold design, with the reflected title, plays with the idea that Friedan believed that women were frustrated because they felt pressured to present an idealized exterior to society. In reality they were harbouring unfulfilled desires, which Friedan called "the problem that has no name".

Silent Spring

1962 ▪ PRINTED ▪ 22 × 15 cm (9 × 6 in) ▪ 368 PAGES ▪ USA

RACHEL CARSON

SCALE

One of the most powerful natural history books ever written, Rachel Carson's *Silent Spring* was the spark that ignited the environmental movement. The book's detailed exposure of the damage done by agricultural pesticides – in particular DDT, one of the strongest ever developed – was the wake-up call that alerted people to the perils of pollution by chemicals.

In 1958, Carson, a best-selling author of nature books, was prompted to investigate the use of pesticides when a friend wrote to her about how DDT was killing birds in nearby Cape Cod. The pesticide was first employed in World War II to control insects that caused malaria, but by the 1950s it was used extensively on farm crops.

As Carson worked on her book, she communicated with many scientists and built up a compelling case against DDT. She showed how it entered the food chain and accumulated in the fatty tissues of animals, including humans, causing genetic damage and diseases such as cancer. Birds were suffering too – especially the bald eagle, the US's national symbol – as DDT thinned the shells of their eggs.

RACHEL **CARSON**

1907–1964

Rachel Carson was an American marine biologist and natural history writer whose seminal book *Silent Spring* brought the dangers of pesticides to public attention.

Born on a farm in Pennsylvania, Carson grew up among animals and wrote stories about them. She trained as a marine biologist, then worked for the US Department of Fisheries. In 1951 she wrote *The Sea Around Us*, a poetic introduction to marine life, which became a best-seller and established her reputation as a writer. In the late 1950s she turned her attention to conservation and the perils of pesticides, revealed in *Silent Spring* in 1962. She died two years later at her home in Maryland.

Carson's great achievement with *Silent Spring* was to make her findings accessible and compelling to a general readership. She instilled a sense of urgency and fear in the wider public, which forced social and political change. *Silent Spring* led to an eventual ban on the use of DDT, and to the establishment of the Environmental Protection Agency in the US.

► **RIVERS OF DEATH** In one of the key chapters, Carson explains the effects of DDT on salmon as it leaks into rivers. She describes how poisons can be passed up the food chain to reach human consumers.

In detail

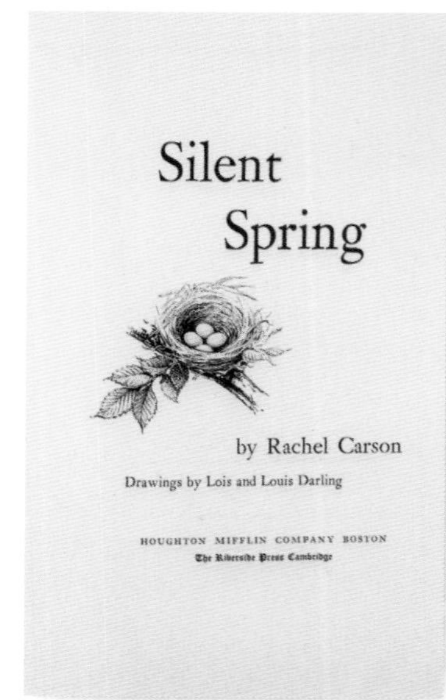

Silent

Spring

by Rachel Carson

Drawings by Lois and Louis Darling

HOUGHTON MIFFLIN COMPANY BOSTON

The Riverside Press Cambridge

◄ **LOUD AND CLEAR** The title *Silent Spring* originates from the description of a scenario in which all spring songbirds were killed by DDT. It became a metaphor for the way humans could destroy the environment.

► **UNIQUE COMBINATION** Making the argument more accessible, Carson's powerful and poetic language was beautifully complemented by the exquisite drawings of American illustrators Lois and Louis Darling.

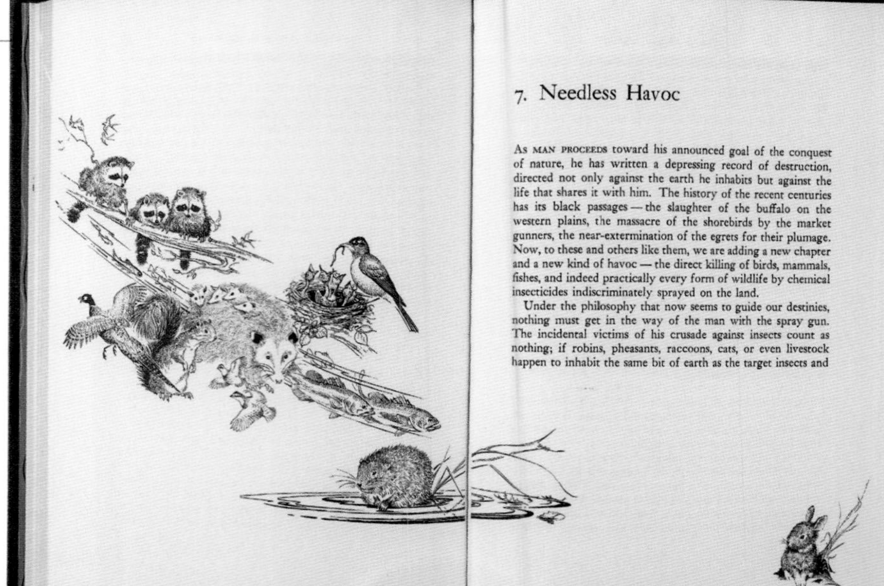

7. Needless Havoc

AS MAN PROCEEDS toward his announced goal of the conquest of nature, he has written a depressing record of destruction, directed not only against the earth he inhabits but against the life that shares it with him. The history of the recent centuries has its black passages — the slaughter of the buffalo on the western plains, the massacre of the shorebirds by the market gunners, the near-extermination of the egrets for their plumage. Now, to these and others like them, we are adding a new chapter and a new kind of havoc — the direct killing of birds, mammals, fishes, and indeed practically every form of wildlife by chemical insecticides indiscriminately sprayed on the land.

Under the philosophy that now seems to guide our destinies, nothing must get in the way of the man with the spray gun. The incidental victims of his crusade against insects count as nothing; if robins, pheasants, raccoons, cats, or even livestock happen to inhabit the same bit of earth as the target insects and

9. Rivers of Death

FROM THE GREEN DEPTHS of the offshore Atlantic many paths lead back to the coast. They are paths followed by fish; although unseen and intangible, they are linked with the outflow of waters from the coastal rivers. For thousands upon thousands of years the salmon have known and followed these threads of fresh water that lead them back to the rivers, each returning to the tributary in which it spent the first months or years of life. So, in the summer and fall of 1953, the salmon of the river called Miramichi on the coast of New Brunswick moved in from their feeding grounds in the far Atlantic and ascended their native river. In the upper reaches of the Miramichi, in streams that

> Only [in] the present century has one species – man – acquired significant power to alter the nature of the world
>
> **RACHEL CARSON**, *SILENT SPRING*

IN **CONTEXT**

After the publication of *Silent Spring*, chemical companies rushed to defend the use of DDT. They argued that many people would die of malaria without it. But Carson's argument swayed President John F. Kennedy to order an investigation, which then vindicated her research. The use of DDT came under close scrutiny by government officials, and in 1972 it was banned in the US as a crop spray; other countries followed, including the UK in 1984. In 2001 the Stockholm Convention introduced a worldwide ban for the agricultural use of DDT; its use has been so drastically curtailed, and today its sole legal use is to control malaria-carrying mosquitoes.

▲ **The widespread spraying** of crops with synthetic chemicals to combat insects that caused disease or attacked crops became commonplace in the 1950s.

Quotations from Chairman Mao Tse-tung

1964 ▪ PRINTED ▪ 15 × 10 cm (6 × 4 in) ▪ 250 PAGES ▪ CHINA

SCALE

MAO TSE-TUNG

Vying with the Bible as the bestselling book of all time, *Quotations from Chairman Mao Tse-tung* is a collection of sayings from the former Chinese Communist leader. It is estimated that more than five billion copies have been printed in 52 languages, with 800–900 million copies sold worldwide. Aside from its status as a publishing phenomenon, the book was a vital political tool, unifying the people of China during the country's transition to a strict form of Communism in the mid to late 1960s.

Running to 88,000 words, the collection of quotations was conceived by Mao and his Defence Minister, Lin Biao, as an inspirational guide for members of the Red Army. Communist Party officials saw its potential in helping to change popular opinion and vowed to distribute a copy to every citizen – in 1966 new printing houses were built to realize this aim. The book was taught in schools and studied in the workplace, and it was also obligatory to memorize passages to show allegiance to the Party.

IN CONTEXT

In May 1966 the ruling Communist Party in Beijing, led by Mao Tse-tung, launched a programme of measures aimed at purging the country of what it saw as capitalist pro-bourgeois elements. This movement became known as the Cultural Revolution. Lasting a decade, it resulted in strict social and political control at every level of society, enforced by a militant student army called the Red Guards.

▲ **Every member** of the Red Guard was given their own "Little Red Book". In time, all citizens were expected to carry a copy.

Outside China, Mao's collection of quotations was dubbed the "Little Red Book", an allusion to its red cover. It caught the imagination of diverse political groups, such as the African-American Black Panthers in the 1960s and 1970s, and Peru's Shining Path guerrillas in the 1980s.

▲ **POCKET SIZE** The book, scaled to fit the breast pocket of an army uniform, was first published with either paper covers, as here, for individual soldiers, or harder-wearing vinyl covers for sharing.

▲ **RED STAR** The five-pointed red star is a well-known symbol of revolutionary communism. Widely used during Mao's time in power, it is shown here centred on the title page of the book, drawing attention to his socialist outlook.

▲ **LINKS WITH HISTORY** "The people, and the people alone, are the motive force in the making of world history," declared Mao in his book, which he modeled on the published sayings of Confucius (see p.50). The inclusion of calligraphy opposite Mao's portrait creates a link between him and the great philosophical traditions of China's past. Mao's aphorisms were gathered from several decades of his political career and embraced varied subjects, such as socialism, communism, youth, and the importance of frugality.

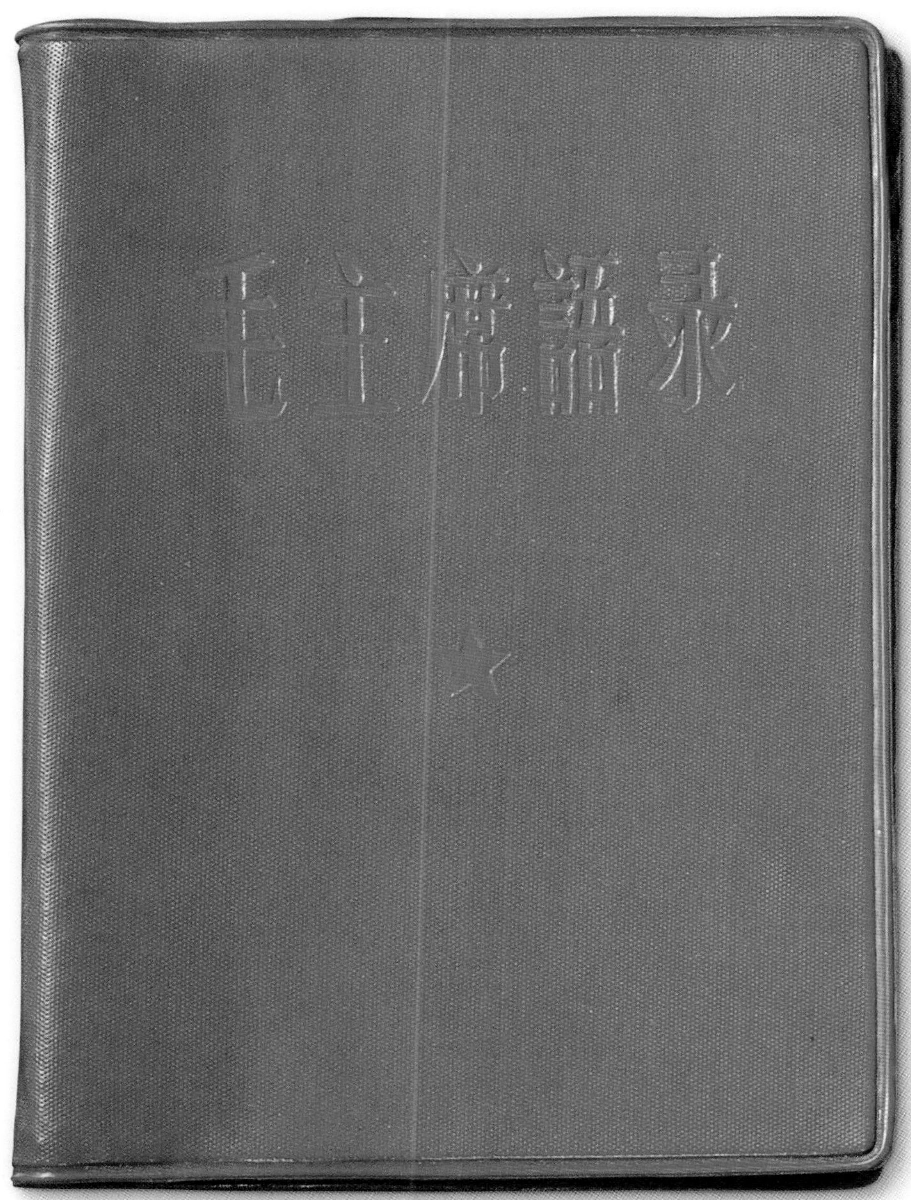

> A revolution is not a dinner party, or writing an essay, or painting a picture, or doing embroidery… A revolution is an insurrection, an act of violence by which one class overthrows another

MAO TSE-TUNG, *QUOTATIONS FROM CHAIRMAN MAO TSE-TUNG*

◄ **COMMUNIST ICON** The book's red cover became an icon of Communist China. Red was not only the colour of good luck in China, but also of communism, representing the blood spilled by workers in their revolutionary struggle, and it was associated with China's ethnic Han majority. Until the Chinese Revolution of 1911–12, China had been ruled for over two centuries by the minority Manchu, represented by the colour yellow, so the use of red had powerful connotations for the 1.2 billion mainland Han Chinese. After Mao took control of China in 1949 the national flag was changed from yellow to red, and the song "The East is Red" was popularized as part of the effort to cement Mao's image as China's saviour.

目　录

▲ **REVISED EDITIONS** The book was revised a few times before the final volume was published in May 1965. The 1964 original, shown here, had 250 pages, divided into 30 chapters, with 200 quotations on 23 different topics. After feedback from Communist Party officials and members of the People's Liberation Army, it was extended by 20 pages, with 33 chapters and 427 quotations.

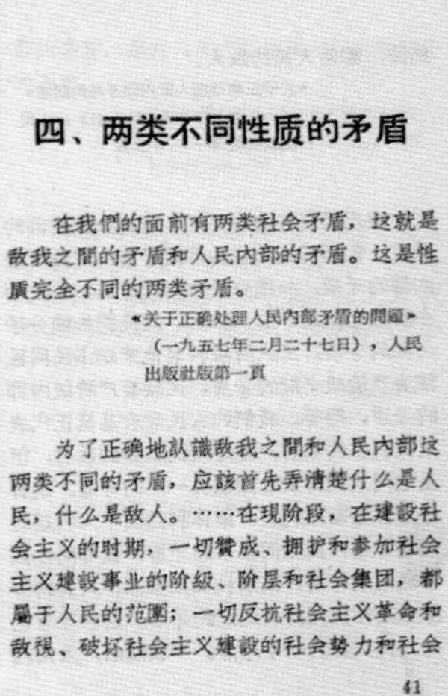

四、两类不同性质的矛盾

在我們的面前有两类社会矛盾，这就是敌我之間的矛盾和人民内部的矛盾。这是性质完全不同的两类矛盾。

«关于正确处理人民内部矛盾的問題»（一九五七年二月二十七日），人民出版社版第一頁

为了正确地认識敌我之間和人民内部这两类不同的矛盾，应該首先弄清楚什么是人民，什么是敌人。……在现阶段，在建設社会主义的时期，一切贊成、拥护和参加社会主义建設事业的阶級、阶层和社会集团，都属于人民的范围；一切反抗社会主义革命和敌視、破坏社会主义建設的社会势力和社会

41

▲ **ACCESSIBLE TEXT** The book distilled Mao's dictates on politics, culture, and society into short sayings using everyday language so that it was easily understood.

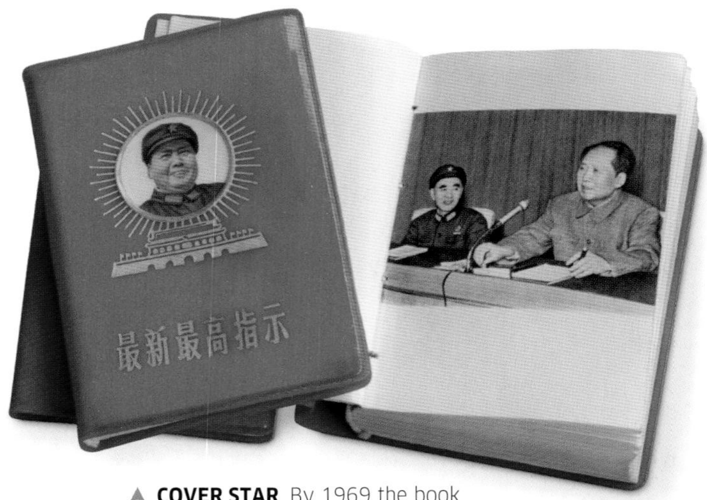

▲ **COVER STAR** By 1969 the book featured a portrait of Mao on the cover, as well as a photograph of him inside with his second-in-command, Lin Biao. Mao had been in power since 1949, but it was Lin who was instrumental in building the cult of Mao in the 1960s. "Every lesson in political education must use the works of Chairman Mao as an ideological guide", he decreed in 1961.

Directory: 1900 onwards

MARRIED LOVE
MARIE STOPES

UK (1918)

Written for married couples by British scientist and activist Marie Stopes (1880–1958), this book, sometimes called *Love in Marriage*, was the first to openly discuss birth control, and promote equality between men and women as sexual partners. *Married Love* revolutionized contemporary views on contraception and marital sex. It was condemned by the Church – in particular the Roman Catholic Church – medical establishments, and the press, and was banned in the US until 1931. Yet the book was instantly popular and its first print run of 2,000 copies sold out within two weeks; by 1919 it was in its sixth revised, updated, and expanded edition. Marie Stopes became an overnight sensation among young women, and *Married Love* the platform to launch her campaign for women's right to birth control. In 1921 she opened a family planning clinic in London, the first in the country.

WIRTSCHAFT UND GESELLSCHAFT
MAX WEBER

GERMANY (1922)

Known in English as *Economics and Society*, this is important work of German sociologist, philosopher, and political economist Max Weber (1864–1920). *Economics and Society* is a collection of theoretical and empirical essays that set out Weber's theories and views on topics such as social philosophy, economics, politics, world religion, and sociology. Weber died before finalizing the texts, so his wife (a feminist and author in her own right), edited and prepared the essays for publication. *Economics and Society* was not translated into English until 1968. It is now widely acknowledged to be one of the most influential sociological texts ever written.

MEIN KAMPF
ADOLF HITLER

GERMANY (VOLUME I, 1925; VOLUME II, 1927)

Translating as "My Struggle", *Mein Kampf* was written by Nazi leader Adolf Hitler (1889–1945) while he was imprisoned following the failed Munich Putsch of 1923. *Mein Kampf* was one of the most contentious and inflammatory books ever written, and came to encapsulate the doctrine of the Nazi Party. Part political manifesto, part autobiography, it outlined Hitler's racist ideology – his glorification of the Aryan "master" race and his vilification of Jews and Communists - as well as his desire for vengeance against France for Germany's defeat in World War I, and his plans for establishing power in a new Germany. Although poorly written and stretching to 1,000 pages, *Mein Kampf* became a bestseller and had sold 5.2 million copies by 1939, rising to 12.5 million by 1945. After World War II copyright was awarded to the state of Bavaria, which banned its publication. This copyright ownership expired on 1 January 2016.

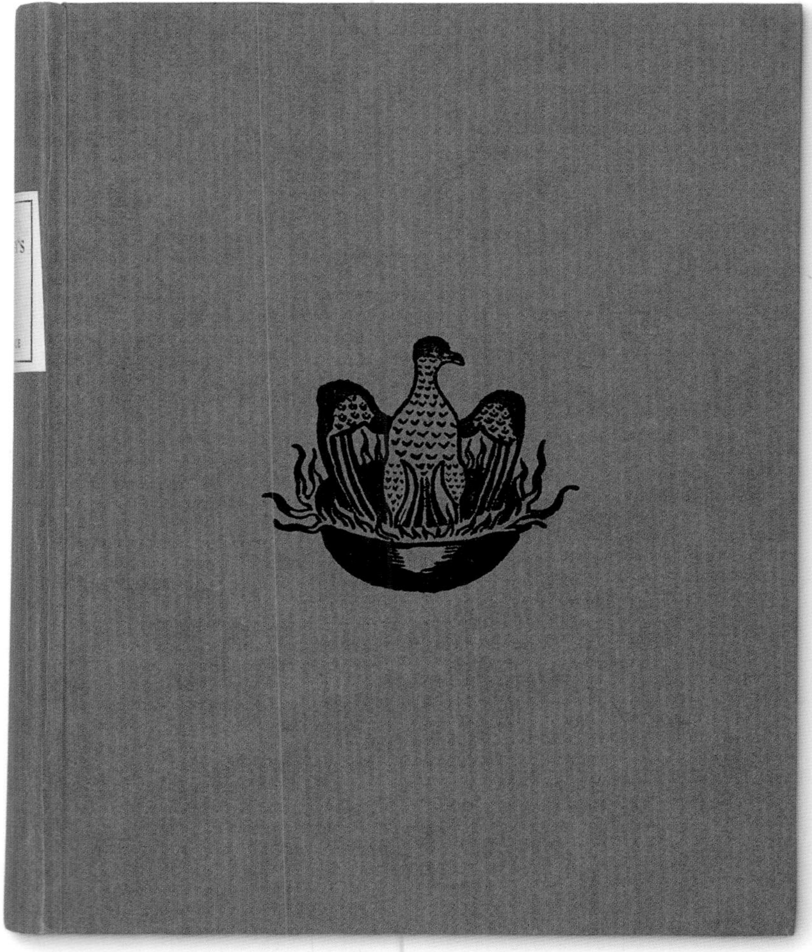

First edition of *Lady Chatterley's Lover*, published by Tipografia Giutina, Italy.

➤ LADY CHATTERLEY'S LOVER
D.H. LAWRENCE

ITALY (1928)

Perhaps the 20th century's most notorious piece of fiction, and certainly the one for which D.H. Lawrence (1885–1930) was best known, *Lady Chatterley's Lover* was a landmark novel that broke the contemporary boundaries of moral and sexual taboos. First published privately in Florence, Italy, this story of an affair between an upper-class, titled woman and her husband's gamekeeper was immediately banned in Britain and the US for its explicit sexual content and its repeated use of offensive four-letter words. In 1960 Penguin Books published an uncensored edition and was prosecuted under the Obscene Publications Act 1959. The trial that followed eventually ruled in favour of Penguin Books, citing the literary merit of *Lady Chatterley's Lover*. The book quickly became a bestseller and has since been adapted for film, television, and the theatre. The publicity during the trial and the momentous ruling paved the way for increased liberalism in publishing and heralded the start of a sexual revolution in books in the decades that followed.

A SAND COUNTY ALMANAC
ALDO LEOPOLD

USA (1949)

Written by US scientist, ecologist, and environmentalist Aldo Leopold (1887–1948), *A Sand County Almanac* has been named as one of the most significant environmental works of the 20th century, along with Rachel Carson's *Silent Spring* (see pp.238–39). Leopold was a champion of biodiversity and ecology, and a founder of the science of wildlife management. *A Sand County Almanac* takes the form of a collection of essays in which Leopold called for preservation of ecosystems, and argued for a responsible, ethical relationship between humans and the land they live in. His writing is notable for its simple directness. Published shortly after his death by his son Luna, *A Sand County Almanac* was Leopold's most important book. It was a landmark publication for the developing US environmental movement and encouraged widespread interest in ecology as a science. This remarkable text has been translated into 12 languages.

THE STORY OF ART
E.H. GOMBRICH

UK (1950)

This illustrated narrative history, which traces the origins of art from ancient to modern times, was the masterwork of Austrian-born art historian and scholar Ernst Gombrich (1909–2001). Since its first publication *The Story of Art* has maintained its position as the world's bestselling art book. Divided into 27 chapters, each covering a specific period of art history, it is renowned for its clear and accessible narrative and features hundreds of full-colour reproductions of pieces of art. The book has been updated regularly and translated into at least 30 languages. The 16th edition was published in 2007.

NOTES OF A NATIVE SON
JAMES BALDWIN

USA (1955)

American novelist, playwright, poet, and essayist James Baldwin (1924–87) was in his 20s when he wrote the 10 essays collectively published as *Notes of a Native Son*. The essays had all been published previously in magazines, such as *Harpers*, and together established him as one of the leading and most insightful writers of Black America. Part autobiography and part political commentary on the racial climate in the US and Europe at the early stages of the Civil Rights Movement, *Notes of a Native Son* became a classic text of the black autobiographical genre. In his essays Baldwin attempted to empathize with the white population, while at the same time vilifying the treatment of all black people. As a result *Notes of a Native Son* ignited fierce criticism as well as critical acclaim.

➤ ON THE ROAD
JACK KEROUAC

USA (1957)

Lauded as one of the most significant novels of the 20th century, *On the Road* by American writer Jack Kerouac (1922–69) describes a group of friends on road trips across the US set against a heady backdrop of jazz, sex, and drugs. In this iconic blend of fiction and autobiography, Kerouac began the Beat literary movement and captured the spirit of the idealistic youth searching for freedom. Kerouac wrote the first draft of *On the Road* in a three-week, amphetamine and caffeine-fueled stint, in which he fed taped-together sheets of tracing paper into a typewriter and typed using single-spaced text (and no margins or paragraph breaks) until he completed the novel; the resulting "scroll" was 37 m (120 ft) long. Kerouac subjected the text to many rewrites until 1957 when the book was published. It was an overnight sensation; its literary and cultural influence was enormous and *On the Road* – heralded as the bible of the Beat generation – has been studied ever since.

LA GUERRA DE GUERRILLAS
ERNESTO "CHE" GUEVARA

CUBA (1961)

Written by the Marxist revolutionary Che Guevara (1928–67) *La Guerra de Guerrillas* (or *Guerrilla Warfare*) was intended to inspire revolutionary movements across Latin America. Drawing on his experiences and success in the Cuban Revolution, Guevara's book outlined his tactical philosophy for guerrilla warfare, emphasizing it as a tool against totalitarian regimes where legal and political tactics had failed. In his quest to bring communism to Latin America and alleviate the grinding poverty he had witnessed there as a young man, Che Guevara created a text that became the guidebook for leftwing insurgents around the world.

THE MAKING OF THE ENGLISH WORKING CLASS
EDWARD PALMER THOMPSON

UK (1963)

In his 900-page volume *The Making of the English Working Class*, left-wing historian Edward Palmer Thompson (1924–93) presented a revolutionary new look at British social history. Thompson's book looks at the origins of working class society as it grew following the Industrial Revolution. The book concentrates especially on its formative years from 1780 to 1832, and was the first systematic examination of the working class ever undertaken. Thompson drew on a wide range of source material, but much of it was unorthodox as official historical documents included very little from working class people themselves, due to widespread illiteracy. Instead Thompson gained much of his information from material enshrined in popular culture, such as songs and ballads, stories, and even sports. Thompson made an effort to recreate the life experience of the working classes, and by doing so he gave a voice to a people who were typically viewed as an anonymous mass. *The Making of the English Working Class* is one of the most significant works of history in the post-World War II period.

PHOENIX
OSAMU TEZUKA

JAPAN (1967–88)

Created by the Japanese artist, cartoonist, animator, and film producer, Osamu Tezuka (1928–89), *Phoenix* comprises a series of manga tales. A major part of the Japanese publishing industry, manga are comics that conform to a style first developed in the 19th century and are read by people of all ages. *Phoenix* features 12 stories based on reincarnation. Each one is set in a different era, but they are all linked by the appearance of the mythical bird. Tezuka's work was highly visual and experimental, and his subject matter ranged from love to science fiction. After many attempts at publication, *Phoenix* was serialized in the Japanese magazine *COM*. Tezuka considered this to be his most important work, but he died before completing it.

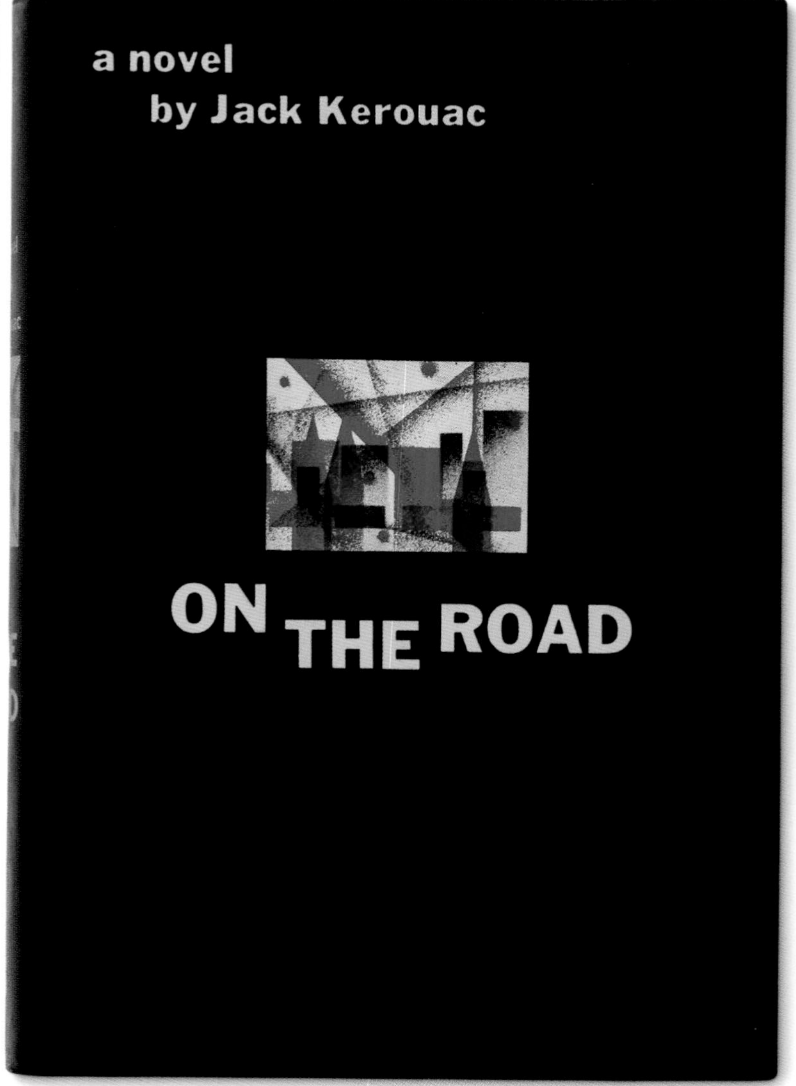

Cover of a US first edition of Jack Kerouac's *On the Road*.

THE FEMALE EUNUCH
GERMAINE GREER

AUSTRALIA AND UK (1970)

The publication of *The Female Eunuch* launched the Australian writer and feminist Germaine Greer (b.1939) as one of the leading voices in second-wave feminism. Following writers such as Simone de Beauvoir (see p.236) and Betty Friedan (see p.237), Greer challenged the role of women in society at a time when they could not get a mortgage, or even buy a car, unless their husband or father countersigned the documents. Greer argued that the accepted repression of women castrated them emotionally, sexually, and intellectually. The book, notable for its iconic and shocking cover featuring a hanging female torso, promoted lively debate around the world and was both acclaimed and criticized by many. *The Female Eunuch* was an immediate bestseller and by early 1971 even the second printing had almost sold out.

WAYS OF SEEING
JOHN BERGER

UK (1972)

This pioneering book by British writer, artist, and art critic John Berger (1926–2017) was written alongside a BBC television series of the same name that featured four 30-minute programmes on the nature of art. An introduction to the study of images, *Ways of Seeing* comprises seven essays, four of which have words and images, and three of which use only images. The book aimed to change the way people perceive and respond to art.

SURVEILLER ET PUNIR
MICHEL FOUCAULT

FRANCE (1975)

A history of the prison system in Western Europe, known in English as *Discipline and Punish: The Birth of the Prison*, this book was written by the French historian and philosopher Michel Foucault (1926–84). In it Foucault examined how the penal system developed from castle dungeons, brutal gaols, and the 18th-century focus on corporal or capital punishment, to the modern “softer” form of discipline, or correction, through incarceration. Foucault argued that the various reforms implemented over time had been made to enable a more effective means of control, rather than to improve prisoner welfare.

Cover of the first edition of Lovelock’s *Gaia: A new look at life on Earth.*

ORIENTALISM
EDWARD SAID

USA (1978)

This ground-breaking book by the Palestinian-American academic Edward Said (1935–2003) is one of the most influential academic texts of the 20th century. Said argued that the academic field of “Orientalism” (the Western study of the Orient, or societies and peoples who inhabit Asia, North Africa, and the Middle East) is the product of a biased, imperialist ideology that created false cultural stereotypes of the East (in particular of the Islamic world) in order to support and re-affirm Western superiority and colonial policy. *Orientalism*, the work Said was best-known for, redefined the way that academics understood colonialism. It has had a lasting influence on the development of literary theory and cultural criticism in the field of Middle Eastern studies, and has become a foundation text in the study of Post-colonialism.

GAIA
JAMES LOVELOCK

UK (1979)

Subtitled “*a New Look at Life on Earth*”, this popular science book by the English chemist James Lovelock (b.1919) outlined his “Gaia” hypothesis to a lay readership. First proposed in scientific journals in 1972, Lovelock’s theory suggested that living and non-living organisms on Earth form part of an integrated, self-regulating system that maintains ideal conditions for life to flourish. While it was initially met with scepticism, the Gaia principle is now acknowledged as accepted scientific theory. Lovelock made various predictions on the basis of his proposal, many of which have proved correct, including global warming. *Gaia* was written at the start of the environmentalist movement, and Lovelock has since produced several more texts on his hypothesis including: *The Revenge of Gaia: Why the Earth is Fighting Back and How We Can Still Save Humanity*, which was published in 2007.

MANUFACTURING CONSENT
NOAM CHOMSKY AND EDWARD S. HERMAN

USA (1988)

In this book the US theoretical linguist Noam Chomsky (b.1928) and US economist Edward S. Herman (b.1925) delivered a searing attack on the mainstream media. In *Manufacturing Consent*, Chomsky and Herman examined evidence suggesting that the mainstream (corporate-owned) media work to support the financial interests and political prejudices of the companies that own them, and of the advertisers who financially support them. Referred to by Chomsky as the “propaganda model of communication”, this unprecedented critique of the media undermined the Western concept of a free press.

A BRIEF HISTORY OF TIME
STEPHEN HAWKING

UK (1988)

A landmark work by the British physicist Stephen Hawking (b.1942), *A Brief History of Time: From Big Bang to Black Holes* was targeted at a non-scientific readership. In it, Hawking used nontechnical terms to explain the structure, origin, and development of the universe, and what he proposed as its eventual fate. In doing so he addressed some of the most baffling questions concerning space and time, including the Big bang theory, the expanding universe, quantum theory, and general relativity, as well as his own radical theories on black holes. Hawking's greatest achievement was to render such complex subject matter so accessible to a lay readership. More than 10 million copies of *A Brief History of Time* were sold within 20 years, and it has been translated into 40 languages. In 2005 a shorter version – *A Briefer History of Time* – was published in collaboration with US popular science writer Leonard Mlodinow (b.1954).

HARRY POTTER AND THE PHILOSOPHER'S STONE

J.K. ROWLING

UK (1997)

The first in a series of novels that became a publishing phenomenon, this book launched the writing career of Joanne (J.K.) Rowling (b.1965). The series chronicles the passage from childhood to adulthood of a young wizard and his friends at Hogwart's School of Witchcraft and Wizardry. *The Philosopher's Stone* was followed by *The Chamber of Secrets* (1998), *The Prisoner of Azkaban* (1999), *The Goblet of Fire* (2000), *The Order of the Phoenix* (2003), *The Half-Blood Prince* (2005), and *The Deathly Hallows* (2007), which became the fastest-selling book in history with 11 million copies sold in the first 24 hours. The Harry Potter books were simultaneously published in children's editions and adult editions (the latter with more sophisticated covers). The series has been translated into more than 65 languages, including Latin and Ancient Greek. Publication dates have even been timed to coincide with school holidays so as not to cause truancy in children desperate to read the books as soon as they appear.

Front cover of Chris Ware's *Building Stories* box set.

➤ BUILDING STORIES

CHRIS WARE

USA (2012)

This uniquely crafted graphic "novel" was created by the US artist Chris Ware (b.1967). It is presented as a boxed set comprising 14 separate printed elements, including pamphlets, newspapers, comic strips, and posters, which together graphically depict the lives of three groups of inhabitants of a three-storey Chicago apartment block (mainly from the women's standpoint), and that of a bee – the only male character in the book. Each of the 14 elements can be read in any order, or even independently, but they combine to create a rich multi-layered story of loss and loneliness. Ware is heralded as one of the leading practitioners in this experimental genre – the book has won many prizes.

THE DRINKABLE BOOK

WATERISLIFE IN PARTNERSHIP WITH DR THERESA DANKOVICH

USA

This 3D-printed water sanitation manual is the brainchild of US scientist Dr Theresa Dankovich, and is being developed in conjunction with the non-profit organization WATERisLIFE. Part information guide, part water filter, this book has the potential to bring clean water to millions. The pages are impregnated with bacteria-killing nanoparticles of silver, and have hygiene and sanitation information printed on them. Each page can filter around 100 litres (22 gal) of water, so a single book could provide a clean water supply to one person for four years.

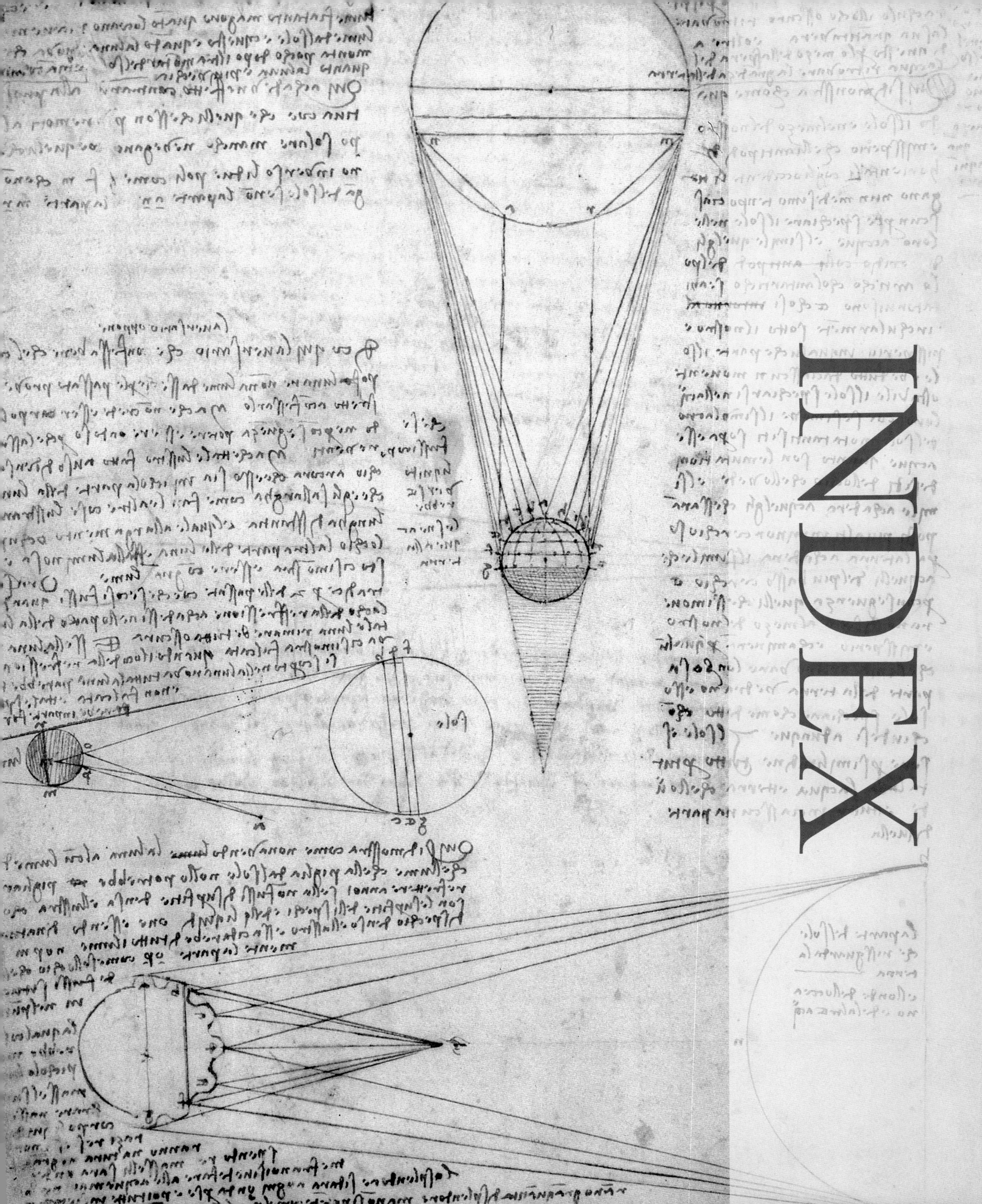

INDEX

Index

Page numbers in **bold** refer to main entries.

C

D

E

Q

R

S

Acknowledgments

Dorling Kindersley would like to thank the following people for their assistance with this book:.

Jay Walker founder of **The Walker Library** for access to his collection

Angela Coppola at Coppola Studios for photography; Ali Collins, Chauney Dunford, Cressida Tuson, Janashree Singha and Sugandha Agrawal for editorial assistance; Ray Bryant and Rohit Bhardwaj for design assistance; Tom Morse for creative technical support; Steve Crozier for retouching; Joanna Micklem for proofreading; Helen Peters for compiling the index; Roland Smithies at Luped for picture research; Nishwan Rasool for picture research assistance; Syed Mohammad Farhan, Ashok Kumar, Sachin Singh, Neeraj Bhatia, Satish Gaur and Sachin Gupta for Hires and DTP assistance; Angela Coppola at Coppola Studios for photography.

The publisher would specially like to thank the following people for their help in providing DK with images:
John Warnock (rarebookroom.org); Dr Chris Mullen (for providing images of his first edition volumes of *Tristram Shandy*).

The publisher would like to thank the following for their kind permission to reproduce their photographs:

(Key: a-above; b-below/bottom; c-centre; f-far; l-left; r-right; t-top)

1 Library of Congress, Washington, D.C.: Music Division (c). **The Metropolitan Museum of Art, New York:** Purchase, Lila Acheson Wallace Gift, 2004 (cl). **PENGUIN and the Penguin logo are trademarks of Penguin Books Ltd:** (cr). **2 Herzog August Bibliothek Wolfenbüttel::** Cod. Guelf. 105 Noviss. 2°. **3 Herzog August Bibliothek Wolfenbüttel::** Cod. Guelf. 105 Noviss. 2°. **4-5 akg-images**. **6-7 Alamy:** The Natural History Museum (b). **The Trustees of the British Museum:** (t). **RMN:** RMN-Grand Palais (domaine de Chantilly) / René-Gabriel Ojéda (c). **8 The Trustees of the British Museum:** (bl). **Harvard Art Museums:** Unknown Artist, Ink, opaque watercolour and gold on paper; 18 x 14.7cm / Arthur M. Sackler Museum, The Stuart Cary Welch Collection, Gift of Edith I. Welch in memory of George Bickford, 2009.202.37 (br). **9 Alamy:** www.BibleLandPictures.com (tr). **The Metropolitan Museum of Art, New York:** Purchase, Lila Acheson Wallace Gift, 2004 (bl). **Courtesy Of The Board Of Trinity College, Dublin:** (br). **10 Bridgeman Images:** British Library, London, UK (bl, br). **11 Library of Congress, Washington, D.C.:** Music Division (br). **Octavo Corp.:** Stanford Library (tr). **12 Octavo Corp.:** Stanford Library (br). **13 Dr Chris Mullen, The Visual Telling of Stories:** (bl). **The Stapleton Collection:** (br). **The Master and Fellows of Trinity College, Cambridge:** (tr). **14 Octavo Corp.:** Warnock Library (br). **15 PENGUIN and the Penguin logo are trademarks of Penguin Books Ltd:** (tr). **Photo Scala, Florence:** The Museum of Modern Art, New York (bl). **16-17 Courtesy Of The Board Of Trinity College, Dublin**. **18-19 Getty Images:** DEA / S. Nannini. **18 Bridgeman Images:** Louvre, Paris, France (bl). **20-21 The Trustees of the British Museum**. **22-23 The Trustees of the British Museum**. **24 Alamy:** Granger Historical Picture Archive (cr). **FOTOE:** Yin Nan (bl). **National Library of China:** (br). **25 Bibliothèque nationale de France, Paris:** (t). **Gottfried Wilhelm Leibniz Bibliothek:** (bl). **26 Special Collection, University of California Riverside:** Vlasta Radan. **27 Alamy:** Universal Art Archive (cr). **AlexHe34:** https://creativecommons.org/licenses/by-sa/3.0/legalcode (br). **Special Collection, University of California Riverside:** Vlasta Radan (cl, bl, bc). **28-29 Harvard Art Museums:** Unknown Artist, Ink, opaque watercolour and gold on paper; 18 x 14.7cm / Arthur M. Sackler Museum, The Stuart Cary Welch Collection, Gift of Edith I. Welch in memory of George Bickford, 2009.202.37. **29 National Gallery Of Australia, Canberra:** Balinese People, The Adiparwa, first book of the Mahabharata palm-leaf manuscript (lontar) mid-late 19th century, palm leaf, ink, cord, Chinese coin, 4.5 x 53 cm, Purchased 1994 (br). **30 Alamy:** www.BibleLandPictures.com (bl). **Zev Radovan / www.BibleLandPictures.com:** (tl). **30-31 The Israel Museum, Jerusalem, by Ardon Bar-Hama:** Shrine of the Book. **31 The Israel Museum, Jerusalem, by Ardon Bar-Hama:** Shrine of the Book (bl). **32 The Israel Museum, Jerusalem, by Ardon Bar-Hama:** Shrine of the Book (t, b). **33 Alamy:** Uber Bilder (br). **The Israel Museum, Jerusalem, by Ardon Bar-Hama:** Shrine of the Book (t, bl). **34 Alamy:** AF Fotografie. **34-35 akg-images:** Interfoto (b). **35 akg-images:** Interfoto (tl, tc, tr). **36 akg-images:** Interfoto (tc, cl). **Alamy:** Interfoto (tr). **36-37 akg-images:** Interfoto (b). **37 akg-images:** Interfoto / picturedesk.com / ÖNB (tl, tr). **National Library of Sweden:** (br). **38 akg-images:** Pictures From History (bl). **38-39 Courtesy Of The Board Of Trinity College, Dublin:** (b). **39-br Courtesy Of The Board Of Trinity College, Dublin**. **40-41 Courtesy Of The Board Of Trinity College, Dublin**. **42 Bridgeman Images:** The Board of Trinity College Dublin (tr). **Getty Images:** Print Collector (cr, br). **Courtesy Of The Board Of Trinity College, Dublin:** (l). **43 akg-images:** (bl). **Bridgeman Images:** British Library Board. All Rights Reserved (bc, br). **Courtesy Of The Board Of Trinity College, Dublin:** (tl, tr). **44-45 The Metropolitan Museum of Art, New York:** Purchase, Lila Acheson Wallace Gift, 2004. **46 Bridgeman Images:** British Library, London, UK (l, r). **46-47 Bridgeman Images:** British Library, London, UK (t, b). **48 Exeter Cathedral Library and Archives**. **49 Alamy:** Universal Art Archive (br). **Exeter Cathedral Library and Archives:** (t). **50 Bridgeman Images:** Lovers, from the 'Science of Erotics', 'the Kama-Sutra', Himachal Pradesh, Pahari School, Indian School / Victoria & Albert Museum, London, UK (bl). **51 The Metropolitan Museum of Art, New York:** Gift of Richard Ettinghausen, 1975 (tr). **52-53 RMN:** RMN-Grand Palais (domaine de Chantilly) / René-Gabriel Ojéda. **54 Mary Evans Picture Library:** J. Bedmar / Iberfoto (cr). **New York Public Library:** Spencer Collection (bl, br). **55 Alamy:** Uber Bilder (br). **New York Public Library:** Spencer Collection (t, c, bl). **56 Alamy:** AF Fotografie (cr). **McGill University:** Reproduced by permission of the Osler Library of the History of Medicine (cl, fcr, bc, bl). **57 Bridgeman Images:** Bibliotheque Nationale, Paris, France / Archives Charmet (br). **McGill University:** Reproduced by permission of the Osler Library of the History of Medicine (t). **58 The National Archives of the UK:** (cl, bl, bc, br). **59 The National Archives of the UK:** (tl, b). **60 akg-images:** (cb). **Herzog August Bibliothek Wolfenbüttel::** Cod. Guelf. 105 Noviss. 2° (br). **61 Mary Evans Picture Library:** Hubertus Kanus. **62 Herzog August Bibliothek Wolfenbüttel:** Cod. Guelf. 105 Noviss. 2° (tl, tc, bl). **62-63 Herzog August Bibliothek Wolfenbüttel:** Cod. Guelf. 105 Noviss. 2°. **64 RMN:** RMN-Grand Palais (domaine de Chantilly) / René-Gabriel Ojéda (cl, cr, bl). **65 RMN:** RMN-Grand Palais (domaine de Chantilly) / René-Gabriel Ojéda. **66 RMN:** RMN-Grand Palais (domaine de Chantilly) / René-Gabriel Ojéda (tl, tr, bc). **67 RMN:** RMN-Grand Palais (domaine de Chantilly) / René-Gabriel Ojéda. **68 RMN:** RMN-Grand Palais (domaine de Chantilly) / René-Gabriel Ojéda. **69 RMN:** RMN-Grand Palais (domaine de Chantilly) / René-Gabriel Ojéda (l, r). **70 Bridgeman Images:** Bibliotheque Nationale, Paris (b). **71 Bridgeman Images:** British Library, London, UK (br). **74 Bridgeman Images:** British Library, London, UK (bl). **British Library Board:** (bc, br). **Octavo Corp.:** Library of Congress (cl). **75 AF Fotografie:** (br). **Octavo Corp.:** Library of Congress (t, t); Library of Congress (t, t). **Octavo Corp.:** Library of Congress (t, t); Library of Congress (t, t). **76 Alamy:** AF Fotografie (cr). **Octavo Corp.:** The Bancroft Library, University of California, Berkeley (cl, bl, br). **Science Photo Library:** Royal Astronomical Society (bc). **77 AF Fotografie:** Private Collection (br). **Octavo Corp.:** The Bancroft Library, University of California, Berkeley (t, bl). **78 Alamy:** Uber Bilder (bc). **80 AF Fotografie:** Private Collection (tr). **The Trustees of the British Museum:** (bc). **84 Getty Images:** Stock Montage (cr). **Octavo Corp.:** Stanford Library (cl, bl, br). **85 Octavo Corp.:** Stanford Library. **86 AF Fotografie:** (bl). **Octavo Corp.:** Library of Congress, Rare Book and Special Coll. Div. (cl, br). **87 AF Fotografie:** (bl, br). **Octavo Corp.:** Library of Congress, Rare Book and Special Coll. Div. (t). **88 Library of Congress, Washington, D.C.:** Music Division (br, cl, bl). **89 Library of Congress, Washington, D.C.:** Music Division (c, t, cr). **90 Getty Images:** Seth Joel (tl). **90-91 Bridgeman Images:** Boltin Picture Library. **92 Bridgeman Images:** Boltin Picture Library (cl). **Getty Images:** Bettmann (cb). **92-93 Bridgeman Images:** Boltin Picture Library. **93 Getty Images:** Seth Joel (br). **Mary Evans Picture Library:** J. Bedmar / Iberfoto (bl). **94 AF Fotografie:** Private Collection (bl, br). **Octavo Corp.:** The Warnock Library (cl, bc). **95 AF Fotografie:** Private Collection (t). **Alamy:** Universal Art Archive (bl). **96 Bibliothèque Sainte-Geneviève Livres, Paris:** (bl, br). **Getty Images:** De Agostini Picture Library (cr). **97 Alamy:** Universal Art Archive (br). **Bibliothèque Sainte-Geneviève Livres, Paris:** (t). **The State Archives of Florence:** Reproduced with the authorization of the Ministero Beni e Att. Culturali (bl, bc). **98-99 Wellcome Images http://creativecommons.org/licenses/by/4.0/**. **98 ETH-Bibliothek Zürich:** BPU Neuchâtel (tl). **U.S. National Library of Medicine, History of Medicine Division:** (cb). **100 Wellcome Images http://creativecommons.org/licenses/by/4.0/:** (tl, tc, tr). **102 Alamy:** Vintage Archives (cb). **ETH-Bibliothek Zürich:** Rar 9162 q, http://dx.doi.org/10.3931/e-rara-14459 (tl). **102-103 Bridgeman Images:** The

University of St. Andrews, Scotland, UK. **104 Alamy:** Universal Art Archive (bc). **Bridgeman Images:** The University of St. Andrews, Scotland, UK (t). **105 Bridgeman Images:** The University of St. Andrews, Scotland, UK (tl, tr, b). **106 Bridgeman Images:** The University of St. Andrews, Scotland, UK (c). **107 Bridgeman Images:** The University of St. Andrews, Scotland, UK (tc, tr, c, bc). **108 Alamy:** Vintage Archives (tr). **Bibliothèque Municipale de Lyon, France:** (bc). **109 Getty Images:** Fototeca Storica Nazionale. (l). **110 The Trustees of the British Museum:** (cl, bl). **110-111 The Trustees of the British Museum**. **112 The Trustees of the British Museum:** (cl, tr, bl). **113 The Trustees of the British Museum:** (tl, cr). **SLUB Dresden:** Mscr. Dresd.R.310 (br). **114 AF Fotografie:** Private Collection (tl, bc, br). **North Carolina Museum of Art, Raleigh,:** Gift of Mr. and Mrs. James MacLamroc, GL.67.13.3 (cr). **115 Bridgeman Images:** British Library Board. **116 Biblioteca Nacional de España:** CERV / 118 (bl). **ETH-Bibliothek Zürich:** Rar 7063, http://dx.doi.org/10.3931/e-rara-28464 (cl). **Getty Images:** Bettmann (cr). **117 Alamy:** Penrodas Collection (br). **Biblioteca Nacional de España:** CERV / 118 (bl). **118 The Ohio State University Libraries:** (cl). **Penrodas Collection:** (bl). **119 The Ohio State University Libraries**. **120 The Ohio State University Libraries:** (tl, bl, br). **121 The Ohio State University Libraries:** (tl, tr). **125 RBG Kew:** (br). **126 Alamy:** Universal Art Archive (cr). **ETH-Bibliothek Zürich:** Rar 460, http://dx.doi.org/10.3931/e-rara-370 (cl). **© J. Paul Getty Trust. Getty Research Institute, Los Angeles (NA2515):** (bl, br). **127 © J. Paul Getty Trust. Getty Research Institute, Los Angeles (NA2515):** (t, bl). **128 AF Fotografie:** Private Collection (br). **Alamy:** Universal Art Archive (cr). **British Library Board:** (bl). **Octavo Corp.:** Folger Shakespeare Library (cl). **129 Alamy:** The British Library Board / Universal Art Archive (b). **Octavo Corp.:** Folger Shakespeare Library (t). **130 Alamy:** Universal Art Archive (cl, bl, bc). **131 Alamy:** Universal Art Archive. **132 AF Fotografie:** Private Collection (cr). **John Carter Brown Library at Brown University:** (cl, br). **133 Alamy:** North Wind Picture Archives (br). **John Carter Brown Library at Brown University:** (t). **134 Photo Scala, Florence:** The Morgan Library & Museum / Art Resource, NY (bl). **135 Bibliothèque nationale de France, Paris:** (tr). **136-137 Alamy:** The Natural History Museum. **140 AF Fotografie:** Private Collection (r). **142-143 Octavo Corp.:** Stanford Library. **142 National Central Library of Rome**. **Octavo Corp.:** Stanford Library (cl). **144 Alamy:** The Natural History Museum (cb). **Image from the Bidioversity Heritage Library:** Digitized by Missouri Botanical Garden (cl). **144-145 Image from the Biodiversity Heritage Library:** Digitized by Missouri Botanical Garden. **146 Getty Images:** Heritage Images (bl). **University of Virginia:** Albert and Shirley Small Special Collections Library (cl, bc). **146-147 Getty Images:** Science & Society Picture Library. **148 Alamy:** Universal Art Archive (tl, bl). **Getty Images:** DEA PICTURE LIBRARY (br). **149 Alamy:** Universal Art Archive (l). **150 Getty Images:** Rischgitz (cb). **152 AF Fotografie:** Private Collection (l, r). **153 AF Fotografie:** Private Collection (tl, tr, bl, br). **154 AF Fotografie:** Private Collection (bl, br). **Getty Images:** Design Pics (cr). **Le Scriptorium d'Albi, France:** (cl). **155 AF Fotografie:** Private Collection (t, bl). **156 Alamy:** ILN (cr). **Dr Chris Mullen, The Visual Telling of Stories:** (cl). **Dr Chris Mullen, The Visual Telling of Stories:** (br). **158 Dr Chris Mullen, The Visual Telling of Stories:** (t, br). **159 Dr Chris Mullen, The Visual Telling of Stories:** (tl, tr, cl, br). **160-161 Octavo Corp.:** Bodleian Library, University of Oxford. **160 Octavo Corp.:** Bodleian Library, University of Oxford (cl, bl, br). **161 Octavo Corp.:** Bodleian Library, University of Oxford (c). **162 Boston Public Library:** Rare Books Department (cl, bl, br). **Getty Images:** Hulton Archive (cr). **163 Boston Public Library:** Rare Books Department. **164 Alamy:** Universal Art Archive (cl, cb, br). **165 AF Fotografie:** Private Collection (br). **Alamy:** Universal Art Archive (t). **166 AF Fotografie:** Private Collection (cr). **Octavo Corp.:** Library of Congress, Rare Book and Special Coll. Div. (br, cl). **167 British Library Board**. **168 Getty Images:** De Agostini Picture Library (b). **Octavo Corp.:** Library of Congress, Rare Book and Special Coll. Div. (t). **169 Octavo Corp.:** Library of Congress, Rare Book and Special Coll. Div.. **170-171 Alamy:** The Natural History Museum. **170 Bridgeman Images:** Christie's Images (cl). **172 Alamy:** Chronicle (cb); The Natural History Museum (tl, cl). **174 Bridgeman Images:** Musee Valentin Hauy, Paris, France / Archives Charmet (bc, br). **Courtesy of Perkins School for the Blind Archives:** (bl). **Getty Images:** Universal History Archive (cr). **175 Bridgeman Images:** PVDE (br). **Courtesy of Perkins School for the Blind Archives:** (t, bl). **176 Harold B. Lee Library, Brigham Young University:** (br). **The Stapleton Collection:** (cl). **University of California Libraries:** (bl, bc). **177 Penrodas Collection:** (bl). **The Stapleton Collection:** (t). **178 The Stapleton Collection:** (br, bl, cr). **179 AF Fotografie:** Private Collection (br). **The Stapleton Collection:** (t). **180-181 Darnley Fine Art / darnleyfineart.com**. **180 Donald A Heald Rare Books:** (cl). **The Stapleton Collection:** (tr). **182 AF Fotografie:** Private Collection (bc). **Alamy:** AF Fotografie (cb). **Andrew Clayton-Payne:** (tc). **Library of Congress, Washington, D.C.:** 3g04054u (c). **183 Getty Images:** De Agostini Picture Library. **184 AF Fotografie:** Private Collection (tc, c, cl). **Darnley Fine Art / darnleyfineart.com:** (bc). **184-185 The Stapleton Collection**. **186 Alamy:** Universal Art Archive (cr). **New York Public Library:** Spencer Collection (br, cl). **187 New York Public Library:** Spencer Collection. **188 New York Public Library:** Spencer Collection. **189 Harry Ransom Center, The University of Texas at Austin:** (cr). **New York Public Library:** Spencer Collection (tl, bl, br). **190 AF Fotografie:** Private Collection (bl, br, cl). **Getty Images:** Heritage Images (cr). **191 AF Fotografie:** Private Collection (t, bl, br). **192 Alamy:** Universal Art Archive (cr). **Special Collections of Drew University Library:** (cl, bl, bc, br). **193 AF Fotografie:** Private Collection (bc, br). **Library of Congress, Washington, D.C.:** 03023679 (cl, t, bl). **194 Image from the Biodiversity Heritage Library:** Digitized by Smithsonian Libraries (br, cl). **The Darwin Archive, Cambridge University Library:** (bl, bc). **195 Image from the Biodiversity Heritage Library:** Digitized by Smithsonian Libraries (t). **Penrodas Collection:** (br). **196 Alamy:** Private Collection (cra); Universal Art Archive (bl, br). **197 Alamy:** Universal Art Archive. **198 Alamy:** Universal Art Archive (tl, tc). **199 AF Fotografie:** Private Collection (tr). **Alamy:** AF Fotografie (bc, br). **200 Alamy:** Everett Collection Historical (bl). **The Stapleton Collection:** (cr). **The Master and Fellows of Trinity College, Cambridge:** (cl, br). **201 AF Fotografie:** Private Collection (br). **The Master and Fellows of Trinity College, Cambridge:** (t). **202 Alamy:** Classic Image (cr). **Octavo Corp.:** Bridwell Library, Southern Methodist University (cl, br). **203 Octavo Corp.:** Bridwell Library, Southern Methodist University (c). **204 Octavo Corp.:** Bridwell Library, Southern Methodist University. **205 Bridgeman Images:** British Library Board (br). **Octavo Corp.:** Bridwell Library, Southern Methodist University (t). **206-207 Octavo Corp.:** Bridwell Library, Southern Methodist University. **208 Alamy:** AF Fotografie (cr). **Bibliothèque nationale de France, Paris:** département Réserve des livres rares, RESFOL-NFY-130 (bl, br). **Getty Images:** Mondadori Portfolio (cl). **209 Bibliothèque nationale de France, Paris:** département Réserve des livres rares, RESFOL-NFY-130 (br). **Getty Images:** Mondadori Portfolio (t). **210 Alamy:** Granger Historical Picture Archive (bl, bc). **211 Bridgeman Images:** De Agostini Picture Library / G. De Vecchi (tr). **212 Bibliothèque nationale de France, Paris:** (tl, tc). **213 Penrodas Collection**. **214-215 Roland Smithies / luped.com:** © 2012 BUILDING STORIES by Chris Ware published by Jonathan Cape. All rights reserved.. **217 Library of Congress, Washington, D.C.:** 3c03205u (br). **218 AF Fotografie:** Private Collection (cl). **Courtesy Frederick Warne & Co.:** National Trust (cr); Victoria and Albert Museum (bl, br). **219 AF Fotografie:** Private Collection (bl). **Courtesy Frederick Warne & Co.:** (t). **220 Courtesy Frederick Warne & Co.:** (tl). **222 SLUB / Deutsche Fotothek:** (cb). **The Stapleton Collection:** Private Collection (cl, br). **223 The Stapleton Collection:** Private Collection (t, bl). **224 The Stapleton Collection:** Private Collection (b). **225 President and Fellows of Harvard College:** Houghton Library (br). **The Stapleton Collection:** Private Collection (tl). **226 akg-images:** (bc). **Getty Images:** Culture Club (cr). **Octavo Corp.:** Warnock Library (cl). **227 Octavo Corp.:** Warnock Library (c). **228 Alamy:** Penrodas Collection (cr). **Photo Scala, Florence:** The Museum of Modern Art, New York (bl, br, cl). **229 Photo Scala, Florence:** The Museum of Modern Art, New York (tl, c, bl). **230 AF Fotografie:** (bc). **Getty Images:** Hulton Deutsch (cr). **Science & Society Picture Library:** National Railway Museum (bl). **230-231 PENGUIN and the Penguin logo are trademarks of Penguin Books Ltd**. **232-233 Getty Images:** Anne Frank Fonds Basel (b, t). **232 Alamy:** Heritage Image Partnership Ltd (tl). **Rex Shutterstock:** (bl). **233 AF Fotografie:** Private Collection (br). **234 Alamy:** A. T. Willett (cl). **Getty Images:** Keystone-France (cr). **235 Getty Images:** Roger Viollet (br). **236 ©** 1943 LE DEUXIEME SEXE by Simone de Beauvoir published by Éditions Gallimard. All rights reserved. **Getty Images:** Hulton Deutsch (cr). **237** From THE FEMININE MYSTIQUE by Betty Friedan. Copyright © 1983, 1974, 1973, 1963 by Betty Friedan. Used by permission of W.W. Norton & Company, Inc. **237 Alamy:** Universal Art Archive (tr). **238 Getty Images:** Stock Montage (cr). **238-239** Photographs and quotations from SILENT SPRING by Rachel Carson: Copyright © 1962 by Rachel L. Carson, renewed 1990 by Roger Christie. Used by permission of Frances Collin, Trustee and Houghton Mifflin Harcourt Publishing Company. All rights reserved. **239 Science Photo Library:** CDC (br). **240 AF Fotografie:** Private Collection (bc). **Getty Images:** Rolls Press / Popperfoto (cr). **New York Public Library:** General Research Division (br, bl). **241 Alamy:** CharlineX China Collection (br). **Courtesy of the Thomas Fisher Rare Book Library, University of Toronto:** (t). **New York Public Library:** General Research Division (bc, bl, fbl). **242 Bridgeman Images:** Private Collection / Christie's Images (tr). **243 AF Fotografie:** Private Collection (br). **244 AF Fotografie:** © 1979 GAIA: A NEW LOOK AT LIFE ON EARTH by James E. Lovelock. Used by permission of Oxford University Press. (bl). **245 Roland Smithies / luped.com:** © 2012 BUILDING STORIES by Chris Ware. Used by permission of Jonathan Cape.. **246-247 Bridgeman Images:** Boltin Picture Library

All other images © Dorling Kindersley

For further information see:
www.dkimages.com